N RICHARD GORDON RICHAR
DON RICHARD GORDON RIC
N RICHARD GORDON RICHARD GORDON RICHAR
DON RICHARD GORDON RICHARD GORDON RICH
N RICHARD GORDON RICHARD GORDON RICHAR
DON RICHARD GORDON RICHARD GORDON RICH
N RICHARD GORDON RICHARD GORDON RICHAR
DON RICHARD GORDON RICHARD GORDON RICH
N RICHARD GORDON RICHARD GORDON RICHAR
DON RICHARD GORDON RICHARD GORDON RICH
N RICHARD GORDON RICHARD GORDON RICHAR
DON RICHARD GORDON RICHARD GORDON RICH
N RICHARD GORDON RICHARD GORDON RICHAR
DON RICHARD GORDON RICHARD GORDON RICH
N RICHARD GORDON RICHARD GORDON RICHAR
DON RICHARD GORDON RICHARD GORDON RICH
N RICHARD GORDON RICHARD GORDON RICHAR
DON RICHARD GORDON RICHARD GORDON RICH
N RICHARD GORDON RICHARD GORDON RICHAR
DON RICHARD GORDON RICHARD GORDON RICH
N RICHARD GORDON RICHARD GORDON RICHAR
DON RICHARD GORDON RICHARD GORDON RICH
N RICHARD GORDON RICHARD GORDON RICHAR
DON RICHARD GORDON RICHARD GORDON RICH
N RICHARD GORDON RICHARD GORDON RICHAR
DON RICHARD GORDON RICHARD GORDON RICH
N RICHARD GORDON RICHARD GORDON RICHAR
DON RICHARD GORDON RICHARD GORDON RICH
N RICHARD GORDON RICHARD GORDON RICHAR
DON RICHARD GORDON RICHARD GORDON RICH
N RICHARD GORDON RICHARD GORDON RICHAR
DON RICHARD GORDON RICHARD GORDON RICH
N RICHARD GORDON RICHARD GORDON RICHAR
DON RICHARD GORDON RICHARD GORDON RICH
N RICHARD GORDON RICHARD GORDON RICHAR
DON RICHARD GORDON RICHARD GORDON RICH
N RICHARD GORDON RICHARD GORDON RICHAR
DON RICHARD GORDON RICHARD GORDON RICH
N RICHARD GORDON RICHARD GORDON RICHAR
DON RICHARD GORDON RICHARD GORDON RICH

Richard Gordon

Richard Gordon

Doctor in the House

Doctor at Sea

Doctor at Large

Doctor in Love

Doctor in Clover

The Facemaker

The Medical Witness

Heinemann/Octopus

Doctor in the House first published in Great Britain in 1952 by
Michael Joseph Limited
Doctor at Sea first published in Great Britain in 1953 by
Michael Joseph Limited
Doctor at Large first published in Great Britain in 1955 by
Michael Joseph Limited
Doctor in Love first published in Great Britain in 1957 by
Michael Joseph Limited
Doctor in Clover first published in Great Britain in 1960 by
Michael Joseph Limited
The Facemaker first published in Great Britain in 1967 by
William Heinemann Limited
The Medical Witness first published in Great Britain in 1971 by
William Heinemann Limited

This edition first published in 1979
jointly by

William Heinemann Limited
15–16 Queen Street
London W1

Martin Secker & Warburg Limited
54 Poland Street
London W1

and
Octopus Books Limited
59 Grosvenor Street
London W1

ISBN 0 905712 35 8

Printed in the United States
by R. R. Donnelley and Sons Company,

Contents

Richard Gordon

Doctor in the House

Doctor in the House

To Jo

Note: St Swithin's Hospital does not exist; neither do its staff, students, or patients.

Chapter One

The large and completely unused set of surgical instruments that my father kept in his consulting-room held for the old gentleman the melancholy fascination of a hopefully gathered layette to an ageing childless wife. For twenty years he had not troubled to exercise the self-deception that he might one day come to use them. They lay in the slots of their metal trays, fitting in with each other like the pieces of a Chinese puzzle. There was a sharp-toothed circular trephine for boring holes in the skull; bone forceps like a pair of shiny pliers; a broad hacksaw for amputations; scissors with long, sharp blades; probes, trocars, and bistouries; and a row of scalpels as impotent as a line of ceremonial swords.

The instruments were in a heavy black wooden box with his name in copperplate script on its tarnished metal label. He had stowed it away some years ago at the bottom of a tall cupboard in the corner, where it had become silted over with old medical journals, out-of-date diaries, and bright advertisements from the big drug firms that he had slung in there from time to time with the vague belief that he might want to refer to them one day. Occasionally, rummaging his way through the dusty papers, he would uncover the box and light up in himself a momentary glow of frustration: he had once been convinced he was going to be a great surgeon, and the instruments were an expensive gift from his admiring mother the day he qualified as a doctor.

My grandparents were, unhappily, the only ones to share his confidence in his professional destination. The first step in becoming a surgeon of even mediocre ability is the acquisition of the Fellowship of the Royal College, an examination he sat regularly twice a year for six years before he faced up to the truth that his ability was not a powerful enough propellant for his ambition. His history after that was the not disagreeable one of a good many other unsuccessful young surgeons: he married and went into general practice in the provinces.

When he saw the brass plate being screwed in to his new doorpost he recognized it as the coffin-lid of his surgical aspirations. For a few months he was bitter at his abandonment of specialization, but his resentment was rapidly smoothed down by the heavy planes of domesticity, busy practice, and the momentous trivia of provincial social life. He became a prosperous, and even fairly efficient, general practitioner, and reflected on his dead ambitions only when he came across his case of instruments or thought seriously about the education of his son.

Like most doctors' children, I had from my earliest schooldays come to look upon a medical qualification like a hereditary title. Graduation seemed a future occurrence over which I had no control; indeed, neither my parents nor myself contemplated my earning a living by any other means. My father sometimes wondered timidly if I might fulfil his own surgical hopes, but experience had made him guarded in predicting his son's postgraduate attainments. I had certainly not demonstrated in adolescence any aptitude for my already settled career. Up to the age of six I had a habit of pulling to pieces birds and small mammals ingeniously trapped in the garden, and this was thought by my parents indicative of a natural inclination towards the biological sciences. The practice of medicine was to me no more than a succession of mysterious people coming twice a day through the front door, and the faint tang of antiseptic which had been in my nostrils as long as I could remember, like the scent of the sea to a fisherman's son.

Once my father stood me up on his leather examination couch, on which the most respected bodies in the district had lain in their forbidding nakedness, and showed me the framed photograph that hung above it. It was the rugby team at his old hospital, the year he had managed to scrape into the side owing to a fortunate attack of diphtheria in the regular wing threequarter.

'Which one's you, Daddy?' I asked, running my forefinger along the double row of solemn young men in shorts.

He indicated a thin fellow at the end of the back row.

'Good old St Swithin's!' he muttered sadly. 'You'll be there one day, my lad. And mind you get in the first fifteen like your father did.'

His love for his old hospital, like one's affection for the youthful homestead, increased steadily with the length of time he had been shot of it. As a medical student, he had felt a surge of allegiance to the place only for an hour or so a week on the football field; now it represented a glowing period in his life when he was single, irresponsible, and bouncing with ambition. I grew into the impression that St Swithin's combined the medical efficiency of the Mayo Clinic with the teaching of Hippocrates and the recreational facilities of the Wembley Stadium. For most of my schooldays the place was an ill-defined but agreeable and definite destination, like Heaven, and it was not until I found myself on the point of going there that I troubled to crystallize my thoughts about it.

St Swithin's was, in fact, an undistinguished general hospital which spread its grey, insanitary-looking walls across a grimy section of North London. It was not even one of the oldest hospitals in the Metropolis, and as age is esteemed in England as the first of the virtues, this alone imbued the staff and students with a faint sense of inferiority. St Swithin's did not possess the proud antiquity of St Bartholomew's, which for several centuries looked on to the crisp green of Smithfield and the sweet waters of the Fleet tumbling unconfinedly into the Thames; nor was it as ancient as St Thomas's over the River, which was already old when Shakespeare came to the Globe. Its origins were obscure, but there was a tradition that it was founded to deal with the outbreak of syphilis that rolled over Europe after the discovery of America, whence it had been imported by Columbus's sailors (so setting a persistent maritime habit). St Swithin's had, however, been in existence sufficiently long for Londoners to accept it as one of the settled institutions of their city that seemed completely reliable, like Westminster Bridge or St Paul's. It now attended only to the pale inhabitants of the streets crammed against its walls, to whom it had been for three or four generations simply 'The Hospital', a place you went into and either got better or died according to your luck.

I had not seen St Swithin's until the morning I was interviewed by the Dean of the Medical School. The Dean had replied to my father's explanatory letter with the assurance that the school was always glad to see the sons of former Swithin's men, but he added that he was nevertheless obliged by the Governors to inspect each candidate and allot places solely on the strength of the aptitude they showed for the practice of medicine. As the course of study was fixed by law for a time not less than six years, this struck me as a task comparable in difficulty with determining the sex of day-old chicks. For a week I was coached earnestly by my father on every question the Dean could possibly ask; then I put on my best suit and went up to London.

St Swithin's was heavily disappointing. It was like the time I was taken to the Zoo to see my first elephant: it was distinctive enough, but not nearly so large, clean, and dignified as I had imagined.

I walked gingerly inside the forecourt, which was separated from the main road by a long line of heavy iron railings and a gatehouse. The court contained a few plane trees and a patch of pale grass in the centre, and a pair of large black statues representing St Swithin's most renowned sons. On the right of the gate as you went in was Lord Larrymore, the famous Victorian physician who maintained for some years that he had almost discovered the cause of tuberculosis but was cruelly forestalled by Robert Koch in Germany. On the left you saw Sir Benjamin Bone, Larrymore's celebrated surgical contemporary, who was nearly appointed to the Queen's household but was dropped at the last minute because Her Majesty objected to the expensive, but distracting, aroma of cigars and brandy exuded all day from his person.

When St Swithin's began to find its feet as a teaching hospital at the beginning of the century the staff were as aware of their lack of presentable antecedents as a newly rich family. These two gentlemen had therefore undergone a process of medical canonization and were invested with professional abilities and intellectual qualities certainly not indicated by their true histories. Shortly after they had been elected to the staff a quarrel broke out between them, and for thirty years afterwards they refused to speak to each other. Communication was necessary on professional matters, and this was conducted by short notes in the third person carried from one to the other by a hospital porter specially employed for the purpose. In the later part of his life Sir Benjamin refused to utter the name of his colleague at all, and gave no indication that he was conscious of the other's existence until he saw on New Year's Day that Larrymore had been given a barony and immediately died of apoplexy.

The two doctors now stared in placid, set annoyance at each other across the court, and were disturbed only by an occasional painting-up from the students and the indiscriminate droppings of the London pigeons. What they originally quarrelled about had long ago been forgotten, but it was probably too trivial to be of interest.

My attention wandered from replicas of St Swithin's staff to their living counterparts. The personnel of the hospital seemed to be in a state of constant transition across the courtyard. The consultant physicians and surgeons could easily be picked out, for they always moved from one spot to another in public as if they were in a desperate hurry. This gave the impression that their services were urgently needed in many places at once, and was good for their professional reputations. The junior practitioners had quickly picked up the habit from their superiors. The housemen strode importantly across the courtyard, their short white coats flying behind them, their stethoscopes trailing from their necks, wearing the look of grave preoccupation seen only in the faces of very fresh doctors. This drab, hurrying band of physicians was sprinkled with nurses in long mauve dresses and starched white caps that turned up at the back like the tails of white doves. They tripped smartly from one block to another and to the Nurses' Home in the rear. Of the people in the court they were the only ones genuinely in a hurry, for they had so little time to themselves they devoured their lives with a perpetual rush to get on and go off duty.

The bulk of the pedestrians in the courtyard was made up of almost equally important-looking and hasty people whom I was unable to identify. Apart from the doctors and nurses, a hospital has to employ men and women from a good many other occupations to run it. There must be chefs to prepare the food and dieticians to tell them what to cook; girls to work the X-ray machines and wardmaids to scrub the floors; physiotherapists to prevent the patients' muscles melting away in bed, and occupational therapists to stop their minds being similarly affected by showing them how to make mats, rugs, stuffed horses, and other unexciting articles while they are imprisoned in the wards. There must be liftmen and laundrymaids, porters and padres, stokers and statisticians; and as all these people must be paid and controlled there had to be a large number of clerks, typists, and secretaries to do so. The staff at St Swithin's had come to outnumber the patients by four to one and now seemed to be expanding naturally, like a water-lily covering a small pond.

There were patients, too, in the courtyard. A couple of them lay on each side of the statues in their beds, tucked up firmly in red blankets and sucking convalescence from the dirty London air. A few more hobbled about on their sticks, tossed helplessly in the strong cross-currents of hospital activity; one or two fortunate ones had found quiet alcoves and stayed there, like trout backing under the bank of a rocky stream. And, as I watched, there passed through the whole lot a cheery-looking man jauntily propelling a six-foot barrow with a stiff canvas cover towards a small door in one corner labelled 'Mortuary'.

I asked for the office of the Dean, Dr Lionel Loftus, F.R.C.P. A porter showed me into a small bare waiting-room decorated only by framed black-and-white pictures of past deans, which ran along the walls like a row of dirty tiles. As there were no chairs I sat on the edge of the dark polished table and swung my legs. The surroundings, and a week of my father's coaching, had made me depressed and nervous. My mind was filled with the awkward questions that Dr Loftus was even then contemplating asking me, and I found to my surprise I could give no satisfactory replies to any of them. I wondered what I should say if he simply asked me why I wanted to be a doctor. The answer was, I suppose, that neither my parents nor myself had the originality to think of anything else, but this didn't seem a suggestion likely to help me into the medical school.

This disheartening introspection was interrupted by the waiting-room door opening. An old man stood on the threshold, looking at me silently. He wore a heavy black jacket buttoned high in the chest, narrow trousers, and a two-inch collar. In his hand he held a pair of gold-rimmed pince-nez, which were attached to his right lapel by a thick black silk ribbon. He was so thin, so old, so pale, and so slow he could have taken his place in the nearby post-mortem room without attracting attention.

He clipped his glasses on to his nose with a slow, shaky movement and inspected me more carefully. I leapt to my feet and faced him.

'Gordon?' croaked the old man from the doorway. 'Mr Richard Gordon?'

'Yes, sir. That is correct, sir,' I replied with great respect.

'So you have come for entrance to St Swithin's?' the old man asked slowly.

'Yes, sir, I have.'

He nodded, but without enthusiasm.

'Your father is a Swithin's man, I believe?'

'Oh yes, sir.'

'I am not the Dean,' he explained. 'I am the medical school Secretary. I was Secretary here long before you were born, my boy. Before your father, probably. I remember well enough when the Dean himself came up to be admitted.' He removed his glasses and pointed them at me. 'I've seen thousands of students pass through the school. Some of 'em have turned out good, and some of 'em bad–it's just like your own children.'

I nodded heartily, as I was anxious to please everyone.

'Now, young feller,' he went on more briskly, 'I've got some questions to ask you.'

I folded my hands submissively and braced myself mentally.

'Have you been to a public school?' he asked.

'Yes.'

'Do you play rugby football or association?'

'Rugby.'

'Do you think you can afford to pay the fees?'

'Yes.'

He grunted, and without a word withdrew. Left alone, I diverted my apprehensive mind by running my eye carefully over the line of black-and-white deans, studying each one in turn. After ten minutes or so the old man returned and led me in to see the living holder of the office.

Dr Loftus was a short, fat, genial man with wispy white hair like pulled-out cotton wool. He was sitting at an old-fashioned roll-topped desk that was stacked untidily with folders, copies of medical journals, letters, and reference books. On top of these he had thrown a Homburg hat, a pair of yellow gloves, and his stethoscope. He was obviously in a hurry.

'Sorry to keep you waiting, old man,' he said cheerily. 'I was held up at a post-mortem. Have a seat.'

I sat down on a hard leather chair beside the desk.

'Now,' the Dean began. 'Have you been to a public school?'

'Yes.'

'Your people can afford the fees and that sort of thing?'

'I believe so.'

'You play rugby, I suppose?'

'Yes, sir.'

The Dean began to look interested.

'What position?' he asked.

'Wing threequarter.'

He drew a pad of paper towards him and pencilled fifteen dots on it in rugby formation.

'Threequarter . . .' he murmured to himself. 'How old are you?' he asked sharply.

'Almost eighteen, sir.'

'Umm. First fifteen at school?'

'Oh, yes, sir.'

The Dean traced lines through his dots, crossed others out, and rustled through a sheaf of typewritten papers beside him. He jerked back in his chair and inspected me closely all over.

'You're rather thin, aren't you,' he announced. 'I suppose you've got the speed?'

'I've got cups for the hundred,' I told him eagerly.

'Well, you may shape well. Lucky you're a three. The hospital's full of forwards,' he added in disgust.

He frowned at his paper pad for a few seconds. His face suddenly lightened, and I saw he had come to a decision: my hands gripped the arms of the chair as I waited to receive it. Rising, he shook me briskly by the hand and told me he had pleasure in admitting me to St Swithin's.

I wondered for some time afterwards how he had been able to discover from these questions that I had the attributes of a successful doctor, but I later found out that even this brief interview was superfluous, as the Dean always took the advice of his old secretary and told applicants this man disliked the look of that there were no vacancies.

Chapter Two

The medical school of St Swithin's hospital was an offshoot of the main buildings and had its own entrance on the main road. It was a tall, gloomy structure that held three floors of laboratories, an anatomical dissection room, a lecture theatre that was clothed in perpetual dusk, and the smelliest lavatories in the district.

The school had been built by the richest brewer in London, who was happily knocked over by a hansom outside the hospital gates one slippery winter's morning in 1875. He was restored to health and normal locomotion in the wards, and to show his gratitude he purchased his peerage the following year by founding the school. The place was now far too old, dark, and small for the requirements of the students, but as the hospital could see little prospect of the accident being repeated it was impossible to tear it down.

At the beginning of October thirty new students collected there for a lecture of welcome and introduction by the Dean. Carrying a new and shiny loose-leaf folder under my arm, I walked up the stone steps for the first time and into the dingy, small entrance hall. The brewer's name was carved in stone over the doorway to indicate the hospital's enduring gratitude, and was reflected in green and gold across the face of the King George public house opposite. Below his chiselled title were the serpents entwined round the winged staff, the doctors' universal trademark, and below that Hippocrates' discouraging aphorism 'The Art is Long'.

The hall, which was painted in yellow and green, contained a small kiosk bearing the word 'Enquiries' in which a porter had firmly shut himself by pulling down the glass window, turning his back on it, and reading the *Daily Mirror* with undistractable attention. There was a short row of clothes-hooks as heavy as an orchard in August, and a long notice board thickly covered by overlapping sheets of paper.

I glanced at the board as I passed, feeling some faint obligation to do so. The notices were an untidy jumble of typewritten official instructions about lectures, examinations, and so forth, and scraps of paper torn from notebooks scrawled with students' writing. These indicated the pathetic undercurrents of medical school life as much as the agony column of *The Times* reflects those below the existence of the middle class. The first to catch my eye was in green ink, and said angrily 'Will the *gentleman* (underlined four times heavily) who took my umbrella from the physiology lab last Thursday bring it back? How can I afford a new one?' Next to it was a faded invitation for two students to make up a party to dissect an abdomen in Edinburgh during the vacation, adding temptingly, 'Digs and abdomen fixed up. Good pubs'. There were lists of textbooks for sale, triumphantly set up by men who had passed their examinations and therefore had no necessity to learn anything else; several small earnest printed appeals for support of the local Student Christian Association; and a number of unfulfilled wants, from a disarticulated foot to a cheap motor-bike.

A hand on the wall pointed upwards 'To the Lecture Theatre'. The way was by a thin iron spiral staircase that ended in darkness. I mounted it, and found myself against a dull brown door attached to a spring that creaked violently as it opened.

The door led to the back of a steep tier of narrow wooden benches rising from the lecturer's desk like a football stand. Behind the desk were three large blackboards screwed to the walls, which were otherwise panelled with stained perpendicular planks. The roof was lost in a criss-cross of thin iron girders through which half a dozen electric globes were suspended to supplement the thin light that filtered through the windows under the eaves.

I sat down shyly at the extreme end of the last row of benches. Most of the new students had already arrived, and had scattered themselves here and there in the tier of seats. A few seemed to know one another and were conversing softly among themselves. The rest were isolated and silent and looked blankly at the blackboards ahead of them, like a congregation in church waiting for the service.

We were as variegated as a bunch of conscripts. Most of the students were my own age, but in the row immediately below me a middle-aged bald-headed man was scribbling some private notes with a pencil in an exercise book; every now and then he jumped, looked round him anxiously, and fidgeted like a schoolgirl. The only other occupant of my row was a pale youth with untidy ginger hair who appeared to be about fifteen, and was reading *The Origin of Species* with alarming concentration.

The clock on the wall above the lecturer's desk reached twenty past ten: the Dean was late again. We later found that this was a common occurrence as he emphasized his complete superiority over the students in his appointments by being scrupulously unpunctual. I was still staring expectantly at the blackboards when the door behind me groaned and another student entered.

'I say, do you mind if I squeeze in?' the newcomer asked. 'I hate being far from the exit.'

I shifted along the hard bench hastily. The new man seemed so much at ease in his surroundings it appeared he was senior to the rest of the waiting class. He was certainly more distinctive in his appearance. He was a tall, good-looking young man with thick black hair and a small moustache. He wore a long brown hacking jacket, narrow corduroy trousers, a green shirt, and a yellow silk square instead of a tie. He set down on the floor beside him a polished black walking-stick, and taking a monocle from his breast pocket surveyed his companions through it with blatant disgust.

'Good God,' he said.

He then opened a copy of *The Times* and began reading it.

The abashed silence in the room was maintained for another ten minutes, broken only by my new neighbour noisily turning over the pages. At ten thirty, half an hour late, a small door behind the desk opened and the Dean bounced in. He was all smiles and geniality. He stood for a moment and beamed at the class like a bishop inspecting his confirmation candidates.

The Dean was not only late but in a tearing hurry. He briefly welcomed us to St Swithin's, made a few remarks about its history and traditions, rapidly ran through the ethics of the medical profession, and explained that in future we would be bound by professional secrecy, and forbidden to make love to our patients' wives, do abortions, or walk on the grass in the hospital courtyard. He flung a few final remarks of encouragement at his listeners and shot off. His address had lasted seventeen minutes, and the only acknowledgement that the student next to me had made of his presence was folding his paper twice over and reading it under cover of the man in front.

'Oh, he's finished, has he?' said the man with the paper, as the scuffling of students getting to their feet disturbed him. He peered at the clock through his monocle. 'H'm,' he remarked. 'He's cut three minutes off his best time so far. Did he leave out that bit about the hospital traditions?'

'No,' I told him. 'He seemed to have quite a lot to say about them.'

The student raised his free eyebrow. 'Did he now? Then he's speeding up his delivery. Next year I bet the old boy gets it down to fifteen minutes dead.'

I was very afraid of this superior and critical young man, but I could not help asking a question.

'You've heard the lecture before?' I said hesitantly. 'I mean, you haven't just arrived in the hospital like the rest of us?'

'This makes the fourth time I've heard old Lofty say his little piece,' he replied, smiling faintly. 'Wouldn't have come today, except that I got the dates mixed. I was expecting an anatomy lecture.'

The rest of the class was filing past us through the door and clattering down the iron stairs. We rose and joined the end of the line.

'You must be a very senior student,' I said respectfully.

'Not a bit of it, old boy.' My companion absently flicked a crumpled piece of paper to one side with his stick. 'I'm not a minute senior to you and the end of the year will probably find me back here again.'

'But surely,' I said from behind him as we descended the stairs, 'if you have four years' study to your credit . . .'

He laughed.

'Ah, the ingenuousness of youth! Four years' study, or at least four years' spasmodic attendance at the medical school, is of no significance. Exams, my dear old boy, exams,' he explained forcibly. 'You'll find they control your progress through hospital like the signals on a railway line–you can't go on to the next section if they're against you. I've come down in my anatomy four times now,' he added cheerfully.

I condoled with him over this quadruple misfortune.

'Don't sympathize, old boy. I appreciate it, but it's wasted. All my failures were achieved with careful forethought. As a matter of fact, it's much more difficult to fail an examination skilfully than to pass the damn thing. To give that impression of once again just having been unfortunate in the choice of questions, you know. . . . Come along and have a beer. The King George will be open.'

We crossed the road and the experienced examinee thrust open the door of the saloon bar with his cane. I had meanwhile decided the medical course was a far more complicated affair than I had imagined.

The King George was one of those dark, cosy, poky little pubs that, like brewers' drays and paralytic drunks, seem to be disappearing from the London drinking scene. The small saloon bar was heavy with dark wood and thick mirrors splashed with gilt *fleurs de lis*. The dingy white ceiling was gathered into plaster rosettes, the lamps sprouted out of the walls on curly metal stems, and in the corner a pale palm drooped over a large brass pot.

The influence of the hospital on the King George was noticeable immediately. Between the mirrors the walls were covered with framed photographs of past rugby and cricket teams, from which there stared down defiantly several hundred young gentlemen who were now respectable and ageing practitioners all over the country. Above the bar, in a glass vase like a stuffed pike, was the rugby ball with which the fifteen had once won the hospitals' cup for the third year running. Next to it there hung a large, old-fashioned brass fireman's helmet. Behind the beer taps a fat old man in an apron, waistcoat, and grey trilby hat stared gloomily across the empty bar.

'Good morning, Padre,' my guide called cheerily.

The old man gave a smile of welcome and stretched his hand over the counter.

'Good morning, sir!' he exclaimed. 'Well! This is a treat to see you here again! Back for the new session is it, sir?'

'Every autumn, Padre, I return faithfully to my studies. Allow me to introduce a new student–what's your name, old boy?'

'Gordon–Richard Gordon.'

'Mr Gordon, Padre. My name's Grimsdyke, by the way,' he explained.

The landlord shook hands heartily.

'And very pleased to meet you, sir!' he said warmly. 'I expect we'll be seeing some more of you in the next five or six years, eh? What's it to be, gentlemen?'

'Bitter for me,' said Grimsdyke, settling himself on a wooden stool. 'Will you take the same?'

I nodded.

'I should explain,' Grimsdyke continued, as the landlord filled the glasses, 'that this gentleman behind the bar is really called Albert something or other, I believe. . . .'

'Mullins, sir.'

'Mullins, yes. But no one in Swithin's would have the faintest idea who you were talking about. For the memory of living man he has been known as the Padre . . . how many years have you been dishing out the booze here, Padre?'

'Thirty-five, sir, just on.'

'There you are! He remembers the present senior physicians when they were students themselves–and a pretty rowdy crowd, by all accounts. There was the incident of Loftus introducing a carthorse into the Matron's bedroom . . .'

The Padre chuckled loudly.

'That was a real night, sir! Nothing like it happens any more, worse luck.'

'Well look at the beer you sell now,' said Grimsdyke reproachfully. 'Anyhow,' he went on to me, 'this pub is now as indispensable a part of the hospital as the main operating theatre.'

'But why the Padre?' I asked cautiously.

'Oh, it's a custom by the housemen. One can say in front of patients "I'm popping out to Chapel at six this evening" without causing alarm, whereas a poor view might be taken by the old dears if they got the idea their doctors drank. Besides, the old boy has a not unclerical function. He's a sort of father confessor, Dutch uncle, and Dr Barnardo to the boys sometimes–you'll find out about it before you've been here much longer.'

I nodded acknowledgement for the information. For a minute we drank our beer in silence.

'There's just another thing,' I began.

'Speak on, my dear old boy. I am always too glad to give what help I can to new students. After all, I have been one myself now five times.'

I pointed silently at the shiny brass helmet.

'Ah, yes, the sacred helm of St Swithin's, by God! Feared and coveted in every medical school in London. You must learn about that before you go any further. How it got there, no one knows. It's been the property of the rugger club for longer than even the Padre can remember, so I suppose one of the boys must have lifted it on a Saturday night years ago. Anyway, it has now become a totem, a fetish, a fiery cross. For the big matches against Guy's or Mary's and so on the helmet is laid on the touchline for luck and inspiration. Afterwards it is filled with beer and emptied by all members of the team in turn.'

'It would hold a lot of beer,' I observed nervously.

'It does. However, on the occasion of qualification, engagement, birthday, marriage, or death of rich relatives, the thing is taken down and the man stood a helmet of beer by his friends. Are you engaged or married?' he asked suddenly.

'Good Lord, no!' I said. I was shocked. 'I've only just left school.'

'Well . . . anyhow, it's quite a point with me at the moment. But to return to our helmet. Often the gentlemen of lesser institutions attempt to steal it–we had quite a tussle with a gang of roughs from Bart's last season. Once last year some fellows from Tommy's got it as far as the River, but we won it back from them on Westminster Bridge. By jove, that was an evening!' He smiled at the memory. 'One of the chaps got a fractured mandible. Will you have another beer?'

I shook my head.

'No thanks. I don't drink much, you know. Hardly at all, in fact. Only if I've been out for a long walk or something and I'm thirsty.'

I saw Grimsdyke wince.

'Of course, one must remember . . .' he began. 'You will find that in a little while at St Swithin's you will learn enough bad habits to make life bearable. However, there is time enough for that. Padre,' he called. 'The other half for me, if you please.'

'Could you tell me . . . ?' I began, feeling I had better collect all the information I could from my companion while he was talkative.

'Yes?'

'Why–why do you fail your examinations on purpose?'

Grimsdyke looked inscrutable.

'That is a little secret of my own,' he said darkly. 'Maybe I'll let you into it one day, old boy.'

I learnt about Grimsdyke's little secret earlier than he expected. It was common knowledge in the medical school and seeped down into the first-year students within a few weeks of their arrival.

Grimsdyke's reluctance to pass examinations was wholly the fault of his grandmother, a well-to-do old lady who had passed the long-drawn-out twilight of her life in Bournemouth. As she had nothing else to occupy her she developed a wide selection of complaints, which were soothed away, all in good time, by the expensive attentions of her charming physicians. Her regard for the medical profession mounted with each indisposition, and was tempered only with the regret that she had not a single medical gentleman in her own family. The only person who could have rectified the omission was young Grimsdyke, and she conceived the idea while he was still at school of enticing him into the profession by offering to pay his expenses for the course. Unfortunately, the grandmother shortly afterwards developed a malady beyond the abilities of her doctors and was carried away; but her will contained a clause bequeathing a thousand a year to the young man during the time that he was a medical student.

Grimsdyke did not immediately realize the full significance of this, and had begun his first year's study at St Swithin's before it dawned on him that he had an excellent opportunity to spend the rest of his life in London on a comfortable allowance without the tedium of doing any work. He therefore took great pains always to fail his examinations. He came to the hospital once or twice a week, paid his fees promptly, and behaved himself, which was sufficient for St Swithin's. He had a flat in Knightsbridge, an old two-seater car (known as The Ulcer, because it was always breaking down), a large number of friends, and plenty of spare time. 'I sometimes think,' he would admit to his cronies, 'I have discovered the secret of graceful living.'

About the time that I joined the medical school Grimsdyke's spacious days became limited. He had fallen in love with a girl and proposed to her, but she was a shrewd young woman and not only discovered the secret of his existence but refused to accept him unless he altered it.

'An embryo doctor, yes,' Grimsdyke would explain sadly, 'but a chronic hanger-on in a medical school, no. I was obliged to go out and buy some books. The power of women, my dear old boy. It is for them that men climb mountains, fight wars, go to work, and such unpleasant things.'

She must have had the personality of a Barbary slave-master, for he thenceforward applied himself to his studies as enthusiastically as anyone else in the hospital.

Chapter Three

As there was no classes arranged for the day of the Dean's lecture I had the afternoon to myself. I slipped off quietly from the King George shortly after a bunch of senior students burst in and started a noisy drinking session with Grimsdyke. The light-hearted way in which my new companions slipped down pints of beer alarmed me. I drank very little, for I had recently left school and was under the impression that more than two glasses of beer ruined your rugger and led to equally serious moral degeneration.

'So you are going in for–um–medicine?' my house-master had said to me during my final term.

'Yes, sir.'

'A very–er–esteemed profession, Gordon, as you should know. Unfortunately, I find the means of entry to it seems to have a bad influence on boys of even the highest character. No doubt the effect of dealing daily with the–um–fundamental things in life, as it were, is some excuse. Yet I must warn you to exercise continual restraint.'

'Oh yes, sir, I will, of course, sir.'

'I expect you will soon become as bad as the rest,' he sighed. His small opinion of medical students sprang largely from the days when he had been reading theology at Cambridge and, on his attempt to break up a noisy party of medicals in the adjoining rooms late one night, he had been forcibly administered an enema of Guinness's stout.

I had lunch alone at the A.B.C. and went down to a medical bookshop in Bloomsbury to buy some textbooks. I had to get a copy of *Gray's Anatomy*, the medical student's Bible, as unquestionable an authority on anatomy as Hansard on a parliamentary debate. When I saw the book my heart sank under its weight. I flicked over the two thousand foolscap pages of detailed anatomical description split up by beautiful bold drawings of yellow nerves, bright red arteries, and blue veins twining their way between dissected brown muscles that opened like the petals of an unfolding flower. I wondered how anyone could ever come to learn all the tiny facts packed between its covers as thickly as the grains in a sack of wheat. I also bought a set of volumes giving directions for dissection of the body, a thick tome on physiology full of graphs and pictures of vivisected rabbits, and a book of Sir William Osler's addresses to medical sudents.

'Is there anything else, sir?' the assistant asked politely.

'Yes,' I said. 'A skeleton. Do you happen to have a skeleton?'

'I'm sorry, sir, but we're out of skeletons at the moment. The demand on them is particularly heavy at this time of the year.'

I spent the rest of the afternoon hunting a skeleton for use in the evenings with the anatomical textbooks. I found one in a shop off Wigmore Street and took it back to my digs. Most landladies had become accustomed to a skull to be dusted on the mantelpiece and a jumble of dried bones in the corner, but students moving into lodgings that had previously sheltered such inoffensive young men as law or divinity pupils were sometimes turned out on the grounds that their equipment precipitated in the good lady a daily attack of the creeps.

For the first two years of their course medical students are not allowed within striking distance of a living patient. They learn the fundamentals of their art harmlessly on dead ones. The morning after the Dean's lecture the new class was ordered to gather in the anatomical dissecting room to begin the term's work.

The dissecting room was a high, narrow apartment on the ground floor of the medical school that exhaled a strong smell of phenol and formaldehyde. A row of tall frosted glass windows filled one wall, and the fluorescent lights that hung in strips from the ceiling gave the students themselves a dead, cyanotic look. The wall opposite the windows supported a length of blackboard covered with drawings of anatomical details in coloured chalks. In one corner was a stand of pickled specimens, like the bottles on a grocer's shelves, and in the other a pair of assembled skeletons grinned at each other, suspended from gallows like the minatory remains of highwaymen. Down the room were a dozen high, narrow, glass-topped tables in two rows. And on the tables, in different stages of separation, were six or seven dissected men and women.

I looked at the bodies for the first time curiously. They were more like mummies than recently dead humans. All were the corpses of old people, and the preserving process to which they had been subjected had wrinkled them beyond that of ageing. Four untouched subjects lay naked and ready for the new class, but at the other tables the senior students were already at work. Some of the groups had advanced so far that the part they were dissecting was unidentifiable to an unknowing onlooker like myself; and here and there a withered, contracted hand stuck out in silent supplication from a tight group of busy dissectors.

We stood nervously just inside the door waiting for instructions from the Professor of Anatomy. Each of us wore a newly starched white coat and carried a little canvas roll containing a pair of forceps, a freshly sharpened scalpel, and a small wire probe stuck into a pen-handle. The others, to impress their superiority on the newcomers, disregarded us completely.

The Professor had the reputation of an academic Captain Bligh. He was one of the country's most learned anatomists, and his views on the evolution of the hyoid bone in the throat were quoted to medical students in dissecting rooms from San Francisco to Sydney. His learned distinction was unappreciated by his students, however, all of whom were terrified of him.

He had several little unnerving peculiarities. For some reason the sight of a student walking into the medical school with his hands in his pockets enraged him. His private room was next to the main entrance, so it was convenient for him to shoot out and seize by the shoulders any man he saw through the window sauntering into the building in this way. He would shake him and abuse him thoroughly for some minutes before stepping back into his room to watch for the next one. This habit was thought unpleasant by the students, but nothing could be done about it because the Professor, who controlled the examinations, held the power of justice at all levels in the anatomy school.

The Professor appeared suddenly in the dissecting room through his private entrance. The hum of conversation at the tables immediately ceased and was replaced by serious, silent activity.

He stood for some moments looking at his new class narrowly. The sight apparently did not please him. He grunted, and drawing a sheet of paper from the pocket of his white coat called a roll of our names in a voice rough with disgust. He was a tall thin man, shaped like a bullet. His bald head rose to a pointed crown and his body sloped outwards gently to his tiny feet far below. He wore a mangy ginger beard.

He put the list of names back in his pocket.

'Now listen to me, you fellows,' he began sternly. 'You've got to *work* in this department, d'you understand? I'm not going to put up with any slacking for a moment. Anatomy's tough–you can't learn it unless you put your backs into it. Any laziness here, and . . .' He jerked his thumb over his shoulder. 'Out! See?'

We nodded nervously, like a squad of recruits listening to their first drill sergeant.

'And I don't want to see any of you men slopping round with your hands in your pockets. It's all right for errand boys and pimps, but you're supposed to be medical students. The attitude is not only unanatomical but gives you osteoarthritis of the shoulder girdle in your middle age. No wonder you all grow up into a hunchbacked crowd of deformities! I know I'm ugly, but I can stand up straight, which is more than some of you people. Do you follow me?'

We assented briskly.

'Right. Well, get on with some work. The list of parts for dissection is up on the board at the end there.'

With a final glare he disappeared through his door.

I had been allotted a leg for my first term's work. We dissected in pairs, two men to each part. My partner was a student called Benskin–a large, sandy-haired man who wore under his white coat a green check shirt and a red tie with little yellow dogs on it.

'What ho,' said Benskin.

'Good morning,' I replied politely.

'Are you conversant with the mysteries of anatomical dissection?' he asked.

'No. Not at all.'

'Nor I.'

We looked at each other silently for a few seconds.

'Perhaps we had better read the instructions in the dissecting manual,' I suggested.

We sat down on a pair of high wooden stools and propped the book against the dead thigh on the table in front of us. After turning over several preliminary pages we reached a drawing of a plump leg with bold red lines over it.

'That seems to be our skin incision,' I said, pointing to one of the lines. 'Will you start, or shall I?'

Benskin waved a large hand generously.

'Go ahead,' he said.

I drew a breath, and lightly touched the greasy rough skin. With my new scalpel I made a long sweeping incision.

'I think I've cut the wrong thing,' I said, glancing at the book.

'It doesn't look quite like the picture,' Benskin admitted. 'Perhaps we ought to raise some help.'

There were a pair of demonstrators in the dissecting room–young doctors passing grey years in the anatomy department for small wages in the hope of being appointed to the surgical staff of St Swithin's in middle age. They flitted from one group of students to another like bees in a herbaceous border, pollinating each pair with knowledge. Both of them were far away from our table.

At that moment I caught sight of Grimsdyke, in a shining starched coat, strolling between the dissectors like an Englishman in a Suez bazaar. He waved languidly to me.

'How are you progressing?' he asked, crossing to our table. 'Good God, is that as far as you've got?'

'It's very difficult,' I explained. 'You see, we don't quite know how to start. Could you give us a bit of a hand?'

'But certainly, my dear old boy,' Grimsdyke said, picking up a scalpel. 'I have now dissected four legs and consider I have something of a flair for the knife. This is the gluteus maximus muscle.'

Grimsdyke slit his way rapidly through the muscles and in half an hour did our work for the week.

The routine of lectures and dissection passed the time agreeably. After a few weeks I began to distinguish more sharply the personalities of my fellow students, as an eye gradually sees the objects in a darkened room. My dissecting partner, Tony Benskin, was a cheery young man whose mental horizon was bounded by rugby football and beer drinking and clouded over only with a chronic scarcity of cash. Dissecting the fellow to our leg was the ginger-haired youth I had noticed at the Dean's lecture reading Darwin. He turned out to be a quiet and disturbingly brilliant Welshman called Evans, who started the course under the impetus of a senior scholarship. Evans dissected away conscientiously and efficiently from the start–which was fortunate, as his own companion rarely put in an appearance in the anatomy room at all. He was a handsome fellow named John Bottle, whose interests in life were ballroom dancing and the dogs.He spent most of his afternoons in the palais and his evenings at Harringay or the White City. The middle-aged man with the notebook I soon discovered to be an ex-bank clerk called Sprogget, who was left a little money after twenty years' looking at a ledger and immediately fulfilled an almost forgotten ambition of taking up medicine. Sprogget was unfortunate in being partnered by the most objectionable student in the class–a man named Harris, whom Grimsdyke named immediately the Keen Student. Harris knew everything. His greased black hair, parted precisely in the middle, and his thick-rimmed spectacles popped frequently between a pair of dissectors.

'You know, old man,' he would volunteer, 'you're not doing that bit according to the book. You ought to have exposed the nerve before you cut away the tendons. Hope you don't mind my mentioning it, but I thought it might save you a bit of trouble with the Prof later. I say, you've made a mess of the brachial artery, haven't you?'

He was incorrigible. He sat at the front of the lectures and asked grave questions to which he already knew the answers. He ate a lunch of sandwiches in the locker room of the anatomy department, reading a textbook; and his conversation was limited strictly to anatomy. He regarded the barracking to which he was inevitably subjected as another instance of persecution of the intellectuals.

Grimsdyke was a useful acquaintance, for his four years' start put him on familiar terms with the senior students. One afternoon shortly after my arrival he hailed me as I was walking out of the medical school doorway.

'I say, old lad,' he called. 'Come and meet Mike Kelly. He's secretary of the rugger club.'

There was a broad young man with a red face standing beside him. He wore an old tweed jacket with leather on the elbows and a brilliant yellow pullover.

'How do you do,' I said respectfully. Kelly was not only rugby secretary but two years senior to myself.

'Pleased to meet you,' said Kelly, crushing my hand. 'You play a bit, do you?'

'A bit. Threequarter.'

'Jolly good. The hospital's going to be short of good threes in a year or so. First fifteen at school, I take it?'

'Yes.'

'Which school?'

I told him.

'Oh,' said Kelly with disappointment. 'Well, there's no reason why they shouldn't turn out a decent player once in a while. We'll give you a run with the extra B fifteen on Saturday and see how you make out. Grimsdyke here's the captain. He'll fix you up.'

'The extra B is a bit of a joke,' Grimsdyke said as Kelly strode off. 'Actually, we are more of a social side than anything. Our boast is that we can take on any team at any game. Last summer we played a dance band at cricket, and I've arranged a shove-ha'penny match with the police for next month. I'll meet you here at lunchtime on Saturday and give you and that fat chap–what's his name . . . ?'

'Benskin.'

'Benskin, that's right. I'll give you both a lift to the ground in my car. Don't worry about shirts and things.'

The St Swithin's ground was in a North London suburb, and the extra B was the only one of the half-dozen teams run by the hospital that was playing at home that week-end. The game was not brilliant and St Swithin's ended up with a narrow win.

'Well done,' said Grimsdyke, as I was changing. 'You and that Benskin fellow shaped pretty well. You must both be horribly healthy. With any luck you might make the third fifteen before the season's out.'

'Thank you very much.'

'Now get a move on. It's after five and we don't want to waste time.'

'What's the hurry?' I asked.

Grimsdyke looked at me with amazement.

'Why, they open at five-thirty! We'll just make the King George, if we step on it.'

'Thank you,' I said. 'But I think I ought to go back to my digs. . . .'

'On Saturday night! Good Lord, old boy, that's not done at all! Hurry up and put your trousers on.'

Afraid of social errors in this new way of living, I obeyed. We arrived outside the King George as the Padre was opening the doors. Both teams pushed into the small saloon bar while a line of glass tankards clinked temptingly on the counter. Everyone was in a good humour, pleasantly tired and bathed. We were laughing and joking and clapping each other on the shoulder.

'Here you are,' Grimsdyke said, pushing a pint into my hand. 'There'll be a five-bob kitty.'

I handed over two half-crowns, thinking it was a great deal to spend on beer in one evening.

'Drink up!' Grimsdyke said a few minutes later. 'I'm, just getting another round.'

Not wishing to appear unusual, I emptied the glass. A fresh one was immediately put into my fingers, but I timidly held it untouched for a while.

'You're slow,' said Benskin jovially, bumping into me. 'There's bags more left in the kitty.'

I took a quick gulp. I suddenly made the discovery that beer tasted most agreeable. The men round me were downing it with impunity, so why shouldn't I? I swallowed a large draught with a flourish.

With the third pint a strange sensation swept over me. I felt terribly pleased with myself. Damn it! I thought. I can drink with the best of them! Someone started on the piano and Benskin began to sing. I didn't know any of the words, but I joined in the choruses with the rest.

'Your drink, Mr Gordon,' said the Padre, handing me another tankard.

I downed the fourth glass eagerly. But I felt the party had become confused. The faces and lights blurred into one another and the voices inexplicably came sometimes from far away, sometimes right in my ear. Snatches of song floated into my brain like weed on a sluggish sea.

'*Caviare comes from the virgin sturgeon*,' Benskin chanted.

'Virgin sturgeon, very fine fish.
Virgin sturgeon needs no urgin',
That's why caviare's a very rare dish.'

I wedged myself against the bar for support. Someone next to me was telling a funny story to two men and their laughter sounded far off and eerie, like the three witches.

'That pair of red plush breeches
That pair of red plush breeches'

came from the piano corner.

'That pair of red plush bre-e-e-ches
That kept John Thomas warm.'

'Are you feeling all right?' a voice said in my ear.

I mumbled something.

'What's that, old man?'

'Bit sick,' I confessed briefly.

'Hold on a moment. I'll take you back to your digs. Where's he live, Benskin? Help me to get him in the car someone. Oh, and bring something along in case he vomits.'

The next morning Grimsdyke came round to my lodgings.

'How is it?' he asked cheerily.

'I feel awfully ill.'

'Simply a case of hangover vulgaris, old boy. I assure you the prognosis is excellent. Here's half a grain of codeine.'

'What happened to me?' I asked.

Grimsdyke grinned.

'Let's say you've been blooded,' he said.

Chapter Four

Even medical students must have somewhere to live. The problem of finding suitable accommodation is difficult because they are always disinclined to spend on mere food and shelter money that would do equally well for beer and tobacco. And they are not, as a rule, popular lodgers. They always sit up late, they come in drunk on Saturdays, and they have queer things in bottles in their bedrooms. On the other hand, there are a small number of landladies who think it a privilege to entertain a prospective doctor under their roof. The connexion with the profession raises their social standing in the street, and the young gentlemen can always be consulted over the dinner table on the strictly private illnesses to which landladies seem distressingly liable.

I started off in lodgings in Finchley, which were clean, fairly cheap, and comfortable. The landlady had a daughter, a tall, blank-faced brunette of nineteen, an usherette at the local Odeon. One evening after I had been there about six weeks she tapped at my bedroom door.

'Are you in bed?' she asked anxiously.

'No,' I called through the door. 'I'm studying. What is it?'

'It's me foot,' she said. 'I think I've sprained it or something. Will you have a look at it for me?'

'In the kitchen,' I replied guardedly. 'Take your stocking off and I'll be down in a minute.'

The following week she developed a pain in the calf, and the one after stiffness of the knee. When she knocked on the door and complained of a bad hip I gave notice.

I moved into a top-floor room of a lodging-house near Paddington Station. Its residents represented so many nationalities the directions for working its tricky and uncertain lavatories had to be set up in four different languages, as in the Continental expresses. There was another medical student there, a man from St Mary's, who kept tropical fish in a tank in his bedroom and practised Yoga.

As I had to take all my meals out I saw little of the other lodgers except when they passed on the stairs and said 'Excuse me' in bad English. In the room next to mine was a stout young blonde, but she lived very quietly and never disturbed anyone. One morning she was found strangled in Hyde Park, and after that I thought I ought to move again.

For the following twelve months I lived in a succession of boarding-houses. They were all the same. They had a curly hat-stand in the hall, a red stair-carpet worn grey in the middle, and a suspicious landlady. By the time I reached the end of the anatomy course I was tired of the smell of floor-polish, damp umbrellas, and frying; when I was offered a share in a flat in Bayswater I was so delighted I packed up and moved without even waiting to work out the week's rent.

The share was awarded to me through the good offices of Tony Benskin, who lived there with four other students. There was John Bottle, the man who liked dancing and dogs; Mike Kelly, now Captain of the first fifteen; and a .outh known about the hospital as Moronic Maurice, who had surprised the teaching staff and himself by finally passing his qualifying exams, and had gone off to practise the art, to the publicly expressed horror of the Dean, as house-surgeon to a small hospital in the country.

These four were really sub-tenants. The flat was leased by a final-year student, a pleasant fellow called Archie Broome, who had lived there during most of his time at St Swithin's and took his friends as lodgers to help out with the rent.

'We're pretty free and easy there,' he explained to me in the King George. 'I hope you're not terribly particular about the time you have your meals or go to bed and that sort of thing?'

As I had found unpunctuality for meals was taken by landladies as a personal outrage and sitting up to midnight regarded as sinful, I told my prospective landlord warmly I didn't give a damn for such formalities.

'That's good,' Archie said. 'We usually kick in together for the groceries and beer and so forth, if that's all right with you. Here's the key, and you can move in when you like.'

I shifted the following afternoon. The flat was in a large, old, grimy block just by the Park, up a dark flight of stairs. I dropped my suitcases on the landing outside the door and fumbled for the key. While I was doing so the door opened.

Standing in the hallway was one of the most beautiful women I had ever seen. She was a tall blonde with a figure like a model in a dress-shop window. She wore slacks and a sweater, which sharply defined her slight curves. Taking her cigarette out with a long graceful hand, she said with great friendliness, 'Hello, Richard. Come on in and make yourself at home.'

'I'm afraid . . .' I began. 'I mean, I was looking for a fellow called Broome, you know. . . .'

'That's right,' she said. She had a slight, attractive, and unplaceable accent. 'The boys are all at the hospital at the moment, but just come in anyway. Would you like a cup of tea? My name's Vera.'

'How do you do,' I said politely. I picked up my cases and entered hesitantly. After conditioning myself to living with four coarse men, being greeted by a delicate girl was puzzling.

'This is the sitting-room,' Vera continued. 'How about the tea?'

'No thanks. Very kind of you, but I've had some.'

'That's good, because I've got to go and change anyway. If you do want anything the kitchen's through there, just look round as you please.'

The girl slipped through a door leading off the hall, leaving me in the centre of the sitting-room feeling like a participant in the opening scene of a bedroom farce. I had learnt since being at St Swithin's that the best way to treat anything unusual was to ignore it, so I directed attention towards my new home.

The furniture in the sitting-room had an original touch which reflected the profession of the occupants. Like Axel Munthe's room in the Hôtel de l'Avenir, there were books everywhere. A row of them stood along the mantelpiece, from which the names of distinguished consultants could stare at the students in gold lettering from red and black bindings, rebuking their loose activities like a row of church elders. In the window an uneven line of thick volumes ran along the ledge like battlements. There were books on the floor, dropped carelessly behind chairs, or lost between pieces of furniture and the wall. They were scattered over the table like litter on a beach, mixed up with jam-pots, pieces of bread, tobacco, newspapers, and beer bottles. There was Price's famous *Medicine*, four inches thick, with two thousand pages that told you about everything from measles to leprosy, from sore throat to heart failure (it was also useful for propping open windows in summer and supporting a reading lamp); there were books on diabetes, appendicitis, bacteria, and bones; books full of photographs of skin diseases, rashes, or broken limbs; heavy dull books on pathology from Scotland, with no more than a bare picture or two of a growth or an ulcer to interrupt their closely-packed print; books on obstetrics with line drawings of nonchalant babies being recovered from disquieting predicaments; and scattered among them all like their young were the thin little brown volumes of the Students Aid series–an invaluable collection of synopses that students fall back on, like compressed emergency rations, when faced with imminent defeat by the examiners. All this knowledge–all this work, experience and advice from so many experts–all the medical instruction in the world was concentrated into a few square feet. It was ours for the taking, if only we had ever sat down and started reading.

A microscope stood in the corner, conveniently tilted to take the eye, with an open window box of glass slides beside it. The articulated bones of a hand lay on the table, mixed up with everything else. From the top of a cupboard in one corner a skull grinned down and provided a stand for a green hat with white cord round it that Benskin was sometimes moved to wear.

As well as this academic litter the room contained pieces of sports kit–rugger boots, woollen socks, a couple of cricket bats, and a dartboard on a splintered plywood backing. The occupants' leisure activities were also represented by a collection of signs, notices, and minor pieces of civic decoration that had from time to time been immorally carried off as trophies. It was a bad habit of St Swithin's rugby team when playing away from home to pick up souvenirs of their visit before leaving, and in the course of seasons these had grown to a sizeable collection. There was a thirty-miles-limit sign in the corner and an orange beacon next to the skull on the cupboard. From a hook in the wall hung a policeman's helmet with the badge of the Cornwall Constabulary that had been carried off in a burst of vandalism at the end of a successful tour of the West Country. Below it a framed notice declared that the passing of betting slips was illegal, and on the opposite wall a board announcing the opening and closing times of the park. I discovered a little later that the bathroom door bore a metal notice saying 'Nurses Only', and inside, at the appropriate place, was a small printed request not to use the adjacent apparatus while the train was standing at a station.

My inspection was interrupted by the reappearance of Vera. She was in her stockinged feet and wore only a skirt and a brassière which she was holding on with her hands.

'Richard, please do my bra up for me,' she asked. 'This damn fastener's gone wrong.'

She turned her slender shoulders.

'Thanks so much,' she said casually. She strolled back into her room and shut the door. I shrugged my shoulders and decided the only thing was to wait until the male members of the household arrived and guardedly discover Vera's precise function.

Vera, it turned out, was Archie's mistress. She was an Austrian girl, with an ensnaring personality and the ability to conduct herself towards her four sub-tenants with such graceful, impartial sisterliness that none of us would have thought of making advances towards her more than we could have contemplated committing incest. Besides, she did all the cooking and most of the little feminine odd jobs about the flat. This was appreciated as highly as her decorative qualities, for our own abilities in the kitchen did not go beyond baked beans and we were able to mend socks only by running a surgical purse-string suture round the hole and pulling it tight. Floor-scrubbing, fire-making, and the coarser domestic tasks were done by the men on a rough rota; but it was Vera who thought of buying a new shade for the lamp, ordering the coal, or telling one of us it was time to change his collar or have his hair cut.

Vera unfortunately had a bad habit of periodically upsetting the smooth running of the place by having sudden fierce quarrels with Archie which always ended by her packing up and leaving. Where she went to in these absences none of us knew. She had no relatives and no money, and Archie was so horrified at his own suspicion of how she maintained herself while she was away that he never dared to ask her outright. The flat would become untidy and unscrubbed. The boiler would go out for lack of coal, and the five of us would nightly sit down to a progressively repellent supper of orange-coloured beans. In a week or so she would re-appear, as beautiful, as graceful, as sisterly as ever, throw herself into an orgy of reconciliation with Archie, and continue her household duties as if nothing had happened.

I floated contentedly into the drift of life in the flat. My companions treated the time-table of domestic life with contempt. They took meals when they were hungry, and if they felt like it sat up all night. Archie lived with Vera in a bed-sitting room, and as they were an uninhibited couple this afforded them sufficient privacy. His guests had the run of the rest of the place. We all shared the bathroom and, as we had to put shillings in the geyser, quite often the bath water as well. It was in connexion with the bathroom that Vera became her most sisterly. She would walk in and start cleaning her teeth unruffled by a hairy male in the bath attempting to retain his modesty with the loofah. Although we were all far too gentlemanly knowingly to intrude while she was in the bath herself she was never worried by anyone bursting in. 'After all,' she would say flatteringly, 'you are all doctors.'

I felt I was living the true liberal life and developing my intellect, which were excuses for not settling down to the more concrete problems set by my textbooks. The thought of the anatomy exam nevertheless hung over me uncomfortably, like the prospect of the eventual bill to a guest enjoying himself at a good hotel. One evening we discovered with a shock that the contest was only a month away, which gave Benskin and myself no alternative to cramming. We opened our textbooks and drew a deep breath of knowledge, which we hoped we could hold until the examination was over. It was the worst time we could have chosen to start work. Mike Kelly had decided to learn the clarinet, Archie's landlord was trying to raise the rent, and Vera had disappeared again. On this occasion she never returned, and by the time the exam was held I was as miserable as her lover.

Chapter Five

When I heard I had passed the anatomy examination I felt like a man who had received an unexpected legacy. I had cut down my work preparing for the test by refusing to study at all topics that had been asked in the past few papers, in the belief that examiners, like lightning, never strike twice in the same place. I scraped into the pass list in company with Tony Benskin, John Bottle, Sprogget, Evans, and Harris. Grimsdyke also succeeded, and confessed himself amazed how near he must have come on previous occasions to the disaster of getting through.

I was elated: now I was released from the dull tyranny of the study of the dead in the dissecting room to the investigation of the dying in the hospital wards. I could start to perform like a real doctor; I could buy myself a stethoscope.

I strolled into a surgical instrument-maker's in Devonshire Street to select one, like a boy buying his first pipe. With the grave and critical air of a consultant cardiologist, I chose an impressive instrument with thick rubber tubes, a chest-piece as big as a jam-pot cover, and a few gadgets I could twiddle while delivering my professional opinions.

The choice was an important one, because in hospital a stethoscope is as undisputable a sign of seniority as long trousers in a prep. school. It was not thought good taste to exhibit the instrument too blatantly, but a discreet length of tubing poking out of the coat, like a well-set pocket handkerchief, explained to your colleagues you had quitted the anatomy rooms for ever. With a bit of luck you might even be taken by the public for a real doctor. To the layman the stethoscope is the doctor's magic wand; if he sees a man with one round his neck he assumes he is a physician as readily as he takes a fellow in a clerical collar for a parson. These are a pair of conditioned reflexes that have from time to time been used for extracting small sums of money from well-meaning citizens by sufficiently respectable-looking confidence tricksters.

The next morning I walked proudly through the gates of St Swithin's itself instead of going into the narrow door of the medical school. My first call was the students' lobby, to find which consultant I was appointed to.

Teaching of the clinical subjects–medicine, surgery, gynaecology, and midwifery–is carried on by a watered-down continuation of the old apprenticeship system. The year is divided into three-monthly terms, each of which the student spends attached to a different consultant. The doctor is the Chief, who usually takes on six or seven pupils known collectively as his firm, and dignified in the physician's wards with the title of medical clerks.

Each of the clerks is given four or five beds to look after. He is obliged to examine the patients admitted to them, write their notes, and scrape up an account of the case on the consultant's weekly list. Teaching is done at the bedside either by the Chief himself, his junior consultant, the registrar, or the houseman, and the students are expected to educate themselves in the intervals by nosing round the ward for instructive signs and symptoms and doing the unending medical odd jobs.

I began clinical work on a medical firm under the instruction of Dr Malcolm Maxworth, M.D., F.R.C.P. Dr Maxworth was one of the hospital's oldest physicians and had charge of male and female wards–Patience and Virtue. As he appeared only once a week the new students had to start by attending a small class given by the houseman on examination of the patient. We had at the time no more idea of the correct method for this than water-divining, and a Boy Scout with a first-aid certificate would have been more use in the wards than any of us.

The wards of St Swithin's, which were contained in two large red-brick blocks, were dull, hostile galleries made up of a succession of irritating corners in which the nurses' dusters flapped for ever in defiance. They were repeatedly being redecorated in an attempt to give them an air of modernity and cheerfulness, but the original design of the corridor-like rooms made fresh paint as ineffective as make-up on a crone. There was always a plan on foot to pull them down and rebuild, but the execution of this seemed to meet with baffling postponements. Meanwhile the staff took pride that they trod the same boards in the exercise of their art as their professional forebears, and the nurses spent a great deal of time they should have given to the patients sweeping the floors.

I walked across the court and up the dark stone stairs to Virtue ward. Tony Benskin, Grimsdyke, and Evans were already standing outside the heavy glass doors, dangling their stethoscopes and trying not to appear a little in awe of their surroundings, like Oxford freshmen or new prisoners at Dartmoor. We greeted each other in low, church tones.

The houseman came jumping down the stairs three at a time. We stiffened ourselves, like sentries coming to attention. He shot straight past and through the ward door, without appearing to notice us. A moment later his head popped out again.

'Are you relatives waiting to see someone?' he asked. He caught sight of our proud stethoscopes. 'Oh, you're the new clerks, I suppose. Damn it! I'm far too busy to show you anything.'

He scratched his curly head. He was a pleasant-looking fellow, about three years older than ourselves.

'Look,' he went on cheerfully. 'Get a sheet of instructions from Sister Virtue and see how you get on examining a few patients. I've got a lumbar puncture and a couple of aspirations to do, but I'll give you a hand when I can.'

He disappeared again. The small glow of self-importance over our promotion was dimmed. Glancing nervously at one another we went through the doors into the ward.

The houseman had already disappeared behind some screens round a bed at the far end. One or two nurses were busy attending to the patients. The four of us stood by the door for ten minutes. No one took the slightest notice.

From a small door on one side of the ward the Sister appeared. She immediately bore down on our quartet.

'Get out!' she hissed savagely.

I had never seen a Sister close to before. This unexpected proximity had the effect of being in a rowing-boat under the bows of the *Queen Mary*.

Sister Virtue was a fine body of a woman. She was about six feet tall, her figure was as burly as a policeman's, and she advanced on her adversaries with two belligerent breasts. Even her broad bottom as she passed looked as formidable as the stern of a battleship. Her dress was speckless blue and her apron as crisp as a piece of paper. She had a face like the side of a quarry and wore a fine grey moustache.

My immediate impulse was to turn and run screaming down the stairs. Indeed, all of us jumped back anxiously, as if afraid she might bite. But we stood our ground.

'We're the new clerks,' I mumbled in a dry voice.

She looked at us as if we were four unpleasant objects some patient had just brought up.

'I won't have any nonsense here,' she said abruptly. 'None at all.'

We nodded our heads briskly, indicating that nonsense of any sort was not contemplated.

'You're not to come in the ward after twelve o'clock, in the afternoons, or after six in the evening. Understand?'

Her eyes cauterized each of us in turn.

'And you're not to interfere with the nurses.'

Grimsdyke raised an eyebrow.

'Don't be cheeky!' she snapped.

She turned quickly to her desk and came back with some foolscap sheets of typewritten notes.

'Take these,' she commanded.

We selected a sheet each. They were headed 'Instructions on Case-Taking for Students'.

'You may look at patients number five, eight, twelve, and twenty,' Sister Virtue went on sternly. 'You will replace the bedclothes neatly. You will always ask the staff nurse for a chaperon before examining any female patient below the head and neck. Kindly remember that I do not like students in my ward at all, but we are forced to put up with you.'

Her welcome finished, she spun round and sailed off to give a probationer hell for not dusting the window-ledges the correct way.

We silently crept through the doors and leant against the wall of the corridor outside to read the instruction papers. Grimsdyke was the only one to speak.

'I wonder if she goes to lunch on a broomstick?' he said.

I turned my thoughts to the typewritten paper. 'A careful history must be taken before the patient is examined,' I read. There followed a list of things to ask. It started off easily enough–'Name. Address. Age. Marital state. Occupation. For how long? Does he like it?' It continued with a detailed interrogation on the efficiency with which the patient performed every noticeable physiological function from coughing to coitus.

I turned the page over. The other side was headed 'Examination'. I read half-way down, but I was burning to try my luck on a real patient. I stuffed the paper in my pocket, like a child tossing aside the instructions for working a new complicated toy. I carefully put my nose inside the door and was relieved to find Sister had returned to her lair. I thought she was probably digesting someone.

Timidly I walked down the rows of beds to patient number twelve.

'Look where you're going!' a female voice said angrily in my ear.

I spun round. Behind me was a cross-looking nurse. She was young and not bad-looking, and she wore the bows and blue belt of a qualified staff-nurse.

'Can't you see that floor has just been polished?' she demanded.

'I'm sorry,' I mumbled. She tossed her head and stalked off with a swish of starched apron.

Number twelve was a stout young blonde browning at the roots–a frequent condition in female wards. She was sitting up in bed in a green woollen jacket reading a book by Peter Cheyney.

'Good morning,' I said humbly, expecting she as well would attack me.

She immediately slipped a piece of paper in her book, set it down on her bedside locker, threw off her bed-jacket, and dropped the top of her nightdress off her shoulders to reveal a large and not unpleasant bosom. Then she smiled.

'Good morning,' she said. She was obviously used to the routine.

I felt a little at a loss. I had never been in such circumstances before, anywhere.

'Er–do you mind if I examine you?' I asked diffidently.

'Go ahead,' she said invitingly, giving me a bigger smile.

'Thanks awfully.'

The experience was so unusual I couldn't think of anything to say. I groped for remembrance of the instructions, but the sheets in my mind's eye were as blank as the patient's counterpane. I felt like an after-dinner speaker who had risen to his feet and found he'd forgotten his notes. Then an idea rescued me unexpectedly–I would take her pulse. Seizing one wrist, I felt for the throbbing radial artery while I gazed with unseeing concentration at the face of my wrist-watch. I felt I had held her arm for five minutes or more, wondering what to do next. And all the time her gently heaving breasts kept tugging at my eyes. They fascinated me, not with any sexual appeal but alarmingly, as if they were a couple of dangerous snakes. I noticed they had fine drops of sweat on them near the nipples.

A thought exploded in my mind.

'I must fetch a nurse!' I exclaimed. I dropped her wrist as if she had smallpox. 'A chaperone, you know.'

She giggled.

'Oh, go on with you!' she said playfully.

I backed away quickly. A nurse undecorated with belts or bows was dusting a locker on the other side of the ward. She looked hearteningly junior.

'I wonder if you would kindly chaperone me with a patient for a few minutes?' I asked urgently.

'No!' she said. She paused in her dusting to glance at me. I must have looked so miserable a little pity glowed in her heart. 'Ask the junior probationer,' she suggested brusquely. 'It's her job. She's in the sluice-room cleaning the bedpans.'

I thanked her humbly and went to look for my help-meet. She was a worried-looking girl of about eighteen who was busy polishing a pile of metal bedpans as if they were the family silver.

'Will you please be my chaperone?' I asked meekly.

She pushed a lock of straw-coloured hair out of her eyes wearily.

'I suppose so,' she said. 'If I have to.'

We went back into the ward together and gathered some screens round the stout blonde's bed. The probationer stood opposite me with a look of contempt on her face for my inexpert manipulations while I examined the blonde's tongue, her eyes, and her teeth. I stuck my stethoscope warily here and there on her chest, though the noises were as uninformative to my ears as the sound of sea on a distant shore.

Taking the earpieces out I said 'Good!' as if I had completed my diagnosis.

'Aren't you going to examine my tummy?' asked the blonde with disappointment. 'All the doctors examine my tummy. It's my tummy what's wrong.'

'Tomorrow,' I said firmly. 'I have to go and operate.'

How could I tell her in front of the nurse I had not yet learned as far as the tummy?

Inspection, palpation, percussion, auscultation–the unalterable, ever-applicable tetrad. They were drummed into us like drill to recruits. Whatever part of the patient you examine, whatever disease you suspect, the four motions must be gone through in that order. You look first, then feel; when you have felt, you may tap, but not before; and last of all comes the stethoscope.

I began to learn how to look at a patient so that even the fingernails might shine with a dozen diagnoses. They taught us to feel lumps, livers, and spleens; how to percuss correctly and to understand the evasive murmurs transmitted through a stethoscope. Diagnosis is simple observation and applied logic–detection, in fact. A matter of searching for clues, igniting a suspicion and knowing where to look for proof. Conan Doyle modelled Sherlock Holmes on a physician, and the reverse holds perfectly well.

Dr Maxworth took his firm round the ward every Wednesday morning. He was a thin, desiccated little man who had never been known to appear in public dressed in anything but black coat and striped trousers. He was not really interested in students at all. For most of the round he forgot we were crowding in his footsteps, and would suddenly recall our presence by throwing a few half-audible scraps of instruction over his shoulder. He was a specialist in neurology, the diseases of the nervous system. This is the purest and most academic branch of medicine and requires for its practice a mind capable of playing three games of chess simultaneously while filling in a couple of stiff crossword puzzles between the moves. As almost all the nervous diseases we saw in the ward appeared to be fatal, it seemed to me a pretty barren speciality. But Maxworth drew exquisite pleasure from it. He was not primarily concerned with treating his patients and making them better, but if he scored a diagnosis before the proof of the post-mortem he was delighted. He was, his houseman said, a fairly typical physician.

I began to see how the ward was managed by Sister, whom I avoided like a pile of radium. Every bodily occurrence that could be measured–the pulse, the amount of urine, the quantity of vomit, the number of baths–was carefully entered against the patient's name in the treatment book, which reduced the twenty or so humans in the ward to a daily row of figures in her aggressive handwriting.

There were two functions of the physiology which Sister thought proceeded wholly in her interest. One was temperature. The temperature charts shone neatly from the foot of the beds, and each showed a precise horizontal zigzag of different amplitude. Sister wrote the dots and dashes on them herself every morning and evening. The temperatures were taken by the junior nurses, who used four or five thermometers. In spite of inaccuracies due to a different instrument being used daily on each patient and the varying impatience of the nurse to whip the glass spicule away, the figures were looked upon as indispensable. Any errors occurring through mercurial or human failings were not of great importance, however, because Sister always substituted figures of her own if the ones returned by the patient did not fit with her notion of what the temperature in the case ought to be.

The other particular concern of the Sister was the patient's bowels. A nurse was sent round the ward every evening with a special book to ask how many times each inmate had performed during the past twenty-four hours. 'How many for the book?' she would inquire with charming coyness. The patients caught the spirit of the thing, and those returning fair scores to the nurse did so with a proud ring in their voices but anyone making a duck confessed with shame and cowered under the bedclothes.

The number of occasions was written in a separate square at the foot of the temperature chart. A nought was regarded by Sister as unpleasant, and more than two blank days she took as a personal insult. Treatment was simple. One nought was allowed to pass without punishment, but two automatically meant cascara, three castor oil, and four the supreme penalty of an enema.

We rapidly became accustomed to our position of inferiority to everyone on the ward staff. Like all apprentices, the students were used as cheap labour by their superiors. We did all the medical chores–urine-testing, gruel meals in patients with duodenal ulcers, blood samples, and a few simple investigations. For the first few weeks everything seemed easy. It was only at the end of the three-month appointment that there crept up on me an uneasy certainty that I did not yet even know enough to realize how ignorant I was.

Chapter Six

The impact of surgery on the student is likely to be more dramatic than the first gentle touch of medicine. Although surgeons have now abandoned such playful habits as hurling a freshly amputated leg at a newcomer in the theatre, the warm, humid atmosphere, the sight of blood spilt with apparent carelessness, and the first view of human intestines laid out like a string of new sausages sometimes induce in a student a fit of the vapours–a misfortune which draws from his unaffected companions the meagre sympathy afforded a seasick midshipman.

Nevertheless, I started the surgical course with a feeling of superiority over my predecessors of ten or fifteen years ago. As I went to the pictures fairly regularly I was already as familiar with the inside of an operating theatre as with my father's consulting room. From a seat in the local cinema not only myself but most other people in the country had achieved a thorough and painless knowledge of what went on behind the doors marked 'Sterile'. I was ready for it all: the crisp white gowns; the cool, unhurried efficiency; the tense concentrated silence broken only by the click of instruments, a curt word of command from the surgeon, or a snapped-out demand for a fresh ligature by the theatre sister. I prepared myself to face the solemnity of an operation, with the attention of everyone in the room focused on the unconscious patient like the strong beam of the operating spotlight.

I was attached to Sir Lancelot Spratt for my surgical teaching. My official title was Sir Lancelot's dresser, which meant not that I had to help him into his white operating trousers in the surgeon's changing-room, but that I was supposed to be responsible for the daily dressings of three or four patients in the ward. The name had a pleasing dignity about it and suggested the student really did something useful in the hospital instead, as it was always impressed on him by the nurses and houseman, of getting in everyone's way like a playful kitten.

The appointment to Sir Lancelot's firm was something of an honour, as he was the Senior Surgeon of the hospital and one of its best-known figures. He was a tall, bony, red-faced man with a bald head round which a ring of white fluffy hair hung like clouds at a mountain top. He was always perfectly shaved and manicured and wore suits cut with considerably more skill than many of his own incisions. He was on the point of retiring from the surgical battlefield on which he had won and lost (with equal profit) so many spectacular actions, and he was always referred to by his colleagues in after-dinner speeches and the like as 'a surgeon of the grand old school'. In private they gave him the less charming but equivalent epithet of 'that bloody old butcher'. His students were fortunate in witnessing operations in his theatre of an extent and originality never seen elsewhere. Nothing was too big for him to cut out, once he had formed an impression it was exercising some indefinite malign influence on the patient, and no viscus would remain for longer than a week *in situ*.

Sir Lancelot represented a generation of colourful, energetic surgeons that, like fulminating cases of scarlet fever, are rarely seen in hospital wards today. He inherited the professional aggression of Liston, Paget, Percival Pott, and Moynihan, for he was trained in the days when the surgeon's slickness was the only hope of the patient's recovery, the days before complicated anaesthetics, penicillin, blood-transfusion, and the other paraphernalia of modern surgery had watered down the operator's skill and threatened to submerge him completely.

Sir Lancelot had made a fortune, chiefly from the distressing complaints of old gentlemen, and was charging two hundred guineas for an appendectomy while Aneurin Bevan was still thumping a local tub in Ebbw Vale. His real success started in the twenties, when he earned his knighthood by performing a small but essential operation on a cabinet minister that allowed him to take his seat in the House with greater ease. The minister was delighted, and recommended him in every drawing-room of importance in London. Just at that time Sir Lancelot got it into his head that rheumatism could be cured by the removal from the body of all organs not strictly necessary for the continuance of life. As most people over the age of fifty have rheumatism and it is impossible to make it much better or much worse with any form of treatment his practice increased tenfold overnight.

The rheumatism rage lasted long enough for him to buy a house in Harley Street, a country home on the Thames, a cottage in Sussex, a small sailing yacht, and a new Rolls, in which he was still wafted round between the four of them and the hospital. By then he was ready to operate on anything–he was, he told his dressers with pride, one of the last of the general surgeons. He claimed to be capable of removing a stomach or a pair of tonsils with equal success, or to be able to cut off a leg or a lung.

Every Tuesday and Thursday afternoon he operated in his own theatre on the top floor. The list for the session was pinned up outside like a music-hall bill–the best cases were always at the top for Sir Lancelot to operate on himself, and the programme degenerated into a string of such minor surgical chores as the repair of hernias and the removal of varicose veins, to be done by his assistants when he had gone off to his club for a glass of sherry before dinner.

On the first Tuesday after my appointment to the firm I walked up the stairs to the theatre–students were not allowed to use the hospital lift–and went into the dressers' changing room. A row of jackets and ties hung under a notice in letters three inches high: DO NOT LEAVE ANYTHING IN YOUR POCKETS. Everyone entering the theatre had to wear sterile clothing, which was packed away in three metal bins opened by foot pedals. Using a pair of long sterile forceps I took an oblong cap from one, a mask from another, and a rolled white gown from the third. Unfortunately there was no indication of the size of these coverings, and the gown fell round my feet like a bridal dress while the cap perched on my head like a cherry on a dish of ice-cream. I pushed open the theatre door and stepped inside reverently, like a tourist entering a cathedral. Standing by the door, my hands clasped tightly behind me, all I wanted was completely to escape notice. I felt that even my breathing, which sounded in my ears like the bellows of a church organ, would disturb the sterile, noiseless efficiency of the place. I was also a little uncertain of my reactions to cut flesh and wanted to keep as far away from the scene of activity as possible.

'You, boy!'

Sir Lancelot's head popped above the caps of his attendants. All I could see of him was a single brown, bushy strip that separated the top of his mask and the edge of his cap, through which there glared two unfriendly eyes like a hungry tiger inspecting a native through the undergrowth.

'Come over here,' he shouted. 'How often have I got to tell you young fellers you can't learn surgery from the door-post?'

The operating table was in the centre of the bare, tiled room, directly under the wide lamp that hung like a huge inverted saucer from the ceiling. It was completely invisible, as about twenty figures in white gowns were packed round it like tube passengers in the rush-hour. These were mostly students. The operating team was made up of Sir Lancelot himself, who was a head higher than anyone else in the room; his theatre Sister, masked and with all her hair carefully tucked into a sterile white turban, standing on a little platform beside him; his senior houseman, Mr Stubbins, and his registrar, Mr Crate, assisting him from the opposite side; and his anaesthetist, sitting on a small metal piano stool beside a chromium-plated barrow of apparatus at the head of the table, reading the *Daily Telegraph*. On the outskirts of this scrum two nurses in sterile clothes dashed round anxiously, dishing out hot sterilized instruments from small metal bowls like waiters serving spaghetti. A theatre porter, also gowned and masked, leant reflectively on a sort of towel rail used for counting the swabs, and another strode in with a fresh cylinder of oxygen on his shoulder. The only indication that there was a patient present at all was a pair of feet in thick, coarse-knitted bed-socks that stuck pathetically from one end of the audience.

As soon as Sir Lancelot spoke, the group round the table opened as if he were Aladdin at the mouth of his cave. I walked unhappily into the centre. My companions closed tightly behind me, and I found myself wedged against the table opposite Sir Lancelot with a man who played in the second row of the hospital forwards immediately behind me. Escape was therefore out of the question, on physical as well as moral grounds.

The operation was on the point of starting. The patient was still invisible, as the body was covered with sterile towels except for a clean-shaved strip of lower abdomen on the right-hand side of which the operating light was focused diagnostically. I couldn't even see if it was a young man or a woman.

Having forced me into a ringside seat, Sir Lancelot then appeared to dismiss me from his mind. He paused to adjust the cuff of the rubber glove that stretched over his bony hand. Stubbins and Crate were waiting with gauze dabs, and the theatre sister was threading needles with catgut as unconcernedly as if she was going to darn her stockings.

'Stubbins,' said Sir Lancelot chattily, making a three-inch incision over the appendix, 'remind me to look into Fortnum's on my way home, there's a good lad. My missus'll give me hell if I forget her dried ginger again. I suppose it was all right for me to start?' he asked the anaesthetist.

The *Daily Telegraph* rustled slightly in assent.

I was surprised. Dried ginger in an operating theatre? Shopping lists disturbing the sanctity of surgery? And the *Daily Telegraph*?

'I've got a damn funny story to tell you lads,' went on Sir Lancelot affably, deepening his incision. 'Make you all laugh. Happened to me last week. An old lady turned up in my rooms in Harley Street . . . Sister!' he exclaimed in a tone of sudden annoyance, 'do you expect me to operate with a jam-spreader? This knife's a disgrace.'

He threw it on the floor. Without looking at him she handed him another.

'That's better,' Sir Lancelot growled. Then, in his previous tone, as though he were two people making conversation, he went on: 'Where was I? Oh yes, the old lady. Well, she said she'd come to see me on the advice of Lord–Lord Someoneorother, I can't remember these damn titles–whom I'd operated on last year. She said she was convinced she'd got gallstones.

'Now look here, Stubbins, can't you and Crate keep out of each other's way? Your job is to use that gauze swab sensibly, not wave it around like a Salvation Army banner. How the devil do you think I can operate properly if everything's wallowing in blood? Why am I always cursed with assistants who have a couple of left hands? And I want a clip, Sister. Hurry up, woman, I can't wait all night!'

Sir Lancelot had cut through the abdominal wall while he was talking, like a child impatient to see inside a Christmas parcel.

'Well,' he went on, all affability again, seemingly conducting the operation with the concentration of a gossipy woman knitting a pair of socks, 'I said to this old lady, "Gallstones, eh? Now, my dear, what makes you think you've got gallstones?" And I've never seen anyone look so embarrassed in my life!'

He returned to the operation.

'What's this structure, gentlemen?'

A reply came from under a student's mask on the edge of the crowd.

'Quite correct, whoever you are,' said Sir Lancelot, but without any congratulation in his voice. 'Glad to see you fellers remember a little fundamental anatomy from your two years in the rooms . . . so I wondered what was up. After all, patients don't get embarrassed over gallstones. It's only piles and things like that, and even then it's never the old ladies who are coy but the tough young men. Remember that bit of advice, gentlemen. . . . Come on, Stubbins, wake up! You're as useless as an udder on a bull.'

He produced the appendix from the wound like a bird pulling a worm from the ground, and laid it and the attached intestine on a little square of gauze.

'Then the old lady said to me, "As a matter of fact, Sir Lancelot, I've been passing them all month. . . ." Don't lean on the patient, Stubbins! If I'm not tired you shouldn't be, and I can give you forty or fifty years, my lad.

'So now we come to the interesting part of the story. She showed me a little box, like those things you send out pieces of wedding cake in. . . . Sister! What in the name of God are you threading your needles with? This isn't catgut, it's rope. What's that, woman?' He leant the red ear that stuck out below his cap towards her. 'Speak up, don't mutter to yourself. I'm not being rude, damn you! I'm never rude in the theatre. All right, tell your Matron, but give us a decent ligature. That's more like it. Swab, man, swab. Stubbins, did I ever tell you about the Matron when she was a junior theatre nurse? She had a terrible crush on a fellow house-surgeon of mine–chap called Bungo Ross, used to drink like a fish and a devil for the women. Became a respected G.P. in Bognor or somewhere. Died last year. I wrote a damn good obituary for him in the *British Medical Journal*. I'm tying off the appendicular artery, gentlemen. See? What's that, Stubbins? Oh, the old lady. Cherry stones.'

He tossed the appendix into a small enamel bowl held for him by Stubbins.

'Looks a bit blue this end, George,' he said in the direction of the anaesthetist. 'All right, I suppose?' The anaesthetist was at the time in the corner of the theatre talking earnestly to one of the nurses who had been serving out the instruments. Theatre kit is unfair to nurses; it makes them look like white bundles. But one could tell from the rough shape of this one, from the little black-stockinged ankles below her gown and the two wide eyes above her mask, that the parcel would be worth the unwrapping. The anaesthetist jumped back to his trolley and began to twiddle the knobs on it. Sister, who was already in a wild temper, injected the nurse with a glance like a syringeful of strychnine.

'Forceps, Sister!' bellowed Sir Lancelot. She handed him a pair which he looked at closely, snapping them together in front of his mask. For some reason they displeased him, so he threw them over the heads of the crowd at the opposite wall. This caused no surprise to anyone, and seemed to be one of his usual habits. She calmly handed him another pair.

'Swabs correct, Sister, before I close? Good. Terribly important that, gentlemen. Once you've left a swab inside a patient you're finished for life. Courts, damages, newspapers, and all that sort of thing. It's the only disaster in surgery the blasted public thinks it knows anything about. Cut their throats when they're under the anaesthetic, yes, but leave anything inside and you're in the *News of the World* in no time. Shove in the skin stitches, Stubbins. What's the next case? Tea? Excellent. Operating always makes me thirsty.'

Chapter Seven

During the following three months I learnt a little about surgery and a lot about surgeons. I learnt more than I wanted about Sir Lancelot.

In the theatre he was God. Everything in the routine for operating sessions was arranged to suit his convenience. A white linen suit, freshly starched, was carefully warmed by the junior nurse before being laid out in his changing-room in the morning. A Thermos pitcher of iced water labelled 'Sir Lancelot Spratt ONLY' was set on a silver tray nearby. He had his own masks, his own scrubbing brush, and his own soap. When he crossed the theatre floor from the scrub-up basins to the table the onlookers scattered before him like unarmed infantry in front of a tank. If anyone got in his way he simply kicked them out of it. He rarely asked for an instrument but expected the Sister to guess which one to place in his waiting hand. If she made a mistake, he calmly dropped the wrong instrument on to the floor. Should she do no better at her second attempt he repeated his little trick. Once he silently reduced a whole trayful of instruments to an unsterile heap at his feet, and the Sister had hysterics.

Sir Lancelot had a personality like an avalanche and a downright bedside manner that suited equally well a duchess's bedroom or the hospital out-patient department. He radiated confidence like a lighthouse through a storm. His suggestions on the removal of his patients' organs never met with their objection. The more he did to them, the greater the complications that resulted from his interference, the larger the number of supplementary operations he had to perform to retrieve his errors, the more they thanked him: there was never one but died grateful.

His teaching in the ward, like his surgery in the theatre, was full-blooded. He had a long string of aphorisms and surgical anecdotes, none of which was original or strictly accurate, but they stuck in the minds of his students long after the watery lectures of his colleagues had evaporated.

His round was held every Tuesday morning at ten o'clock, and had the same effect on the ward as an admiral's inspection of a small warship.

The preparations for his visit began about five in the morning. The night nurses started the long business of sprucing up the ward to its best pitch of speckless sterility, and when Sister and her day staff arrived at seven the energy given to preparing the long room so that nothing in the slightest way offensive should fall on the great man's eye was increased tenfold. Every article in it was scrubbed and polished thoroughly–the floor, the medicine cupboards, the windows, the instruments, the patients' faces. The bedside lockers, which usually carried a friendly jumble of newspapers, soap, jam, football coupons, and barley-water, were stripped clean and their contents buried out of sight. Even the flowers looked sterile.

The tension and activity in the ward rose together, like the temperature and pulse in a fever. At nine the senior house-surgeon, in a fresh white jacket, looked in for a worried, whispered conversation with Sister to be certain everything commanded on the Chief's last visit had been done. He didn't glance at the patients. That morning they were part of the ward furniture, or at most instruments by which the medical staff could demonstrate their abilities to Sir Lancelot.

There was one point, however, on which the patients could not be argued away from their humanity. At nine-fifteen bedpans were issued all round. The acquisition of one of these at such an hour (seven and five were the official times for their use) was usually a business comparable with catching the eye of a waiter in a busy restaurant. At nine-fifteen on Tuesdays, however, they were forced upon the patients. The nurses tripped briskly out of the sluice-room, each carrying a couple under a cloth. This was because Sister thought a request for one of these articles while Sir Lancelot was in the ward unreasonable to the highest degree–indeed, almost indecent.

The bedpans were whipped away a quarter of an hour before the Chief was due. There followed an energetic final ten minutes occupied by a process known as 'tidying' the patients. They could obviously not be allowed to disturb the general symmetry of the scene by lolling about in bed anyhow, like a squad of soldiers falling in with their hands in their pockets. They had to be fitted in to the ward neatly and unobtrusively. The technique was simple. A pair of nurses descended on the patient. First he was shot into the sitting position, and retained there by one nurse while the other smoothed and squared up his pillows (the open ends of the pillow-cases always to face away from the door). He was then dropped gently on his back, so as not ruffle the smooth surface unnecessarily with his head. The bedclothes were seized at the top by the two young women and pulled taut between them like a tug-of-war; they next applied the tension upwards from the patient's feet, which brought the top edge of the bedclothes level with the patient's nostrils. In one quick motion, without releasing the tension to which the blankets were submitted, they tucked them in firmly all round. This made it impossible for the occupant of the bed to perform any muscular movement whatever, except very shallow breathing.

The ward by ten was silent, orderly, and odourless. Sister and the nurses had changed into fresh white aprons and each of them felt like Moses immediately on his arrival at the top of the mountain. Meanwhile another focus of consternation had formed not far away.

It was the tradition of St Swithin's that the Chief should be greeted in the courtyard and lead his firm to the ward. Surgeons were met in front of the statue of Sir Benjamin Bone and physicians before that of Lord Larrymore. This form of reception resulted in everyone becoming cold in winter, hot in summer, and wet all the year round, and as it had apparently been going on for three or four hundred years this seemed an excellent reason for refusing to alter it.

We gathered for our first ward-round under the cold eye of Sir Benjamin. The differences that divided the firm, which were emphasized on Tuesday mornings, had already become obvious. The students stood in a little subdued group behind the statue. We wore our suits, with stethoscopes coiling out of our pockets and foolscap notebooks under our arms. We chatted quietly between ourselves, but would not have contemplated exchanging words with the two house-surgeons, who stood apart murmuring to each other with expressions of intense seriousness on their faces.

The third section of the party consisted only of Crate, the registrar. He was allowed to wear a long white coat like the Chief, but as he had no companion to talk to and was unable to converse with his housemen or students at such a solemn moment he had to content himself with looking at the sky in a reflective and earnest way, as if he were turning over in his mind the niceties of surgery or trying to forecast the weather.

At ten the Rolls drew into the courtyard and stopped opposite our group. Crate opened the door and wished Sir Lancelot good morning. The car was driven to its parking-place by the chauffeur and the Chief disappeared with his registrar towards the staff common room to leave his hat and put on his white coat. When they reappeared the rest of the party followed them to the wards.

Once Sir Lancelot burst through the ward door more people arranged themselves in his wake. Indeed, it was impossible for a man of his importance to walk about St Swithin's at all without a procession immediately forming up behind him.

First, of course, was Sir Lancelot, the therapeutic thunderbolt. A pace behind came the registrar, and behind him the two house-surgeons, the senior one leading. After the two housemen was Sister, her long cap trailing behind her like a wind-stocking on an aerodrome. She was followed by her senior staff nurse, who carried a trayful of highly-polished instruments with which the patients could be tapped, scratched, and tickled in the aid of making a diagnosis. Sir Lancelot never used any of them and probably did not know how to, but they were produced every Tuesday nevertheless, like a ceremonial mace. Behind the staff nurse was a junior nurse bearing a thick board covered with a pad of paper, to which a pencil was attached with a piece of string. The board was marked sternly 'SIR LANCELOT SPRATT'S DRAWING PAPER'. On this he would sometimes sketch points of anatomy–not often, about once every six months, but the board had to be flashed to his hand if he asked for it. In the rear of the junior nurse, in the winter months a probationer carried a hot-water bottle in a small red blanket for Sir Lancelot to warm his hands before applying them to exposed flesh.

At the end of the party, behind even the hot-water bottle, were the students: an un-uniformed, disorderly bunch of stragglers.

The Chief spent two hours examining the candidates for the afternoon's operating list, with whom he illustrated to us the principles of surgery. Sometimes he passed all morning on one case, if the patient contained a lump of sufficient interest to him; on the other Tuesdays he would whip round the whole ward, diagnosing like a machine-gun. Sitting was forbidden, and towards lunchtime the students shifted heavily from one foot to the other. Sir Lancelot thought any young man incapable of standing on his own feet for a couple of hours as another disagreeable product of modern life, like socialism.

On our first ward round we were pushed easily into place by the precision with which the rest of the troupe fell in. Sir Lancelot strode across the ward, drew up sharply, and looked over the patients in the two rows of beds, sniffing the air like a dog picking up a scent. He thundered over to the bedside of a small, nervous man in the corner. The firm immediately rearranged itself, like a smart platoon at drill. The Chief towered on the right of the patient's head; Sister stood opposite, her nurses squeezed behind her; the students surrounded the foot and sides of the bed like a screen; and the registrar and housemen stood beyond them, at a distance indicating that they were no longer in need of any instruction in surgery.

Sir Lancelot pulled back the bedclothes like a conjurer revealing a successful trick.

'You just lie still, old fellow,' he boomed cheerfully at the patient. 'Don't you take any notice of what I'm going to say to these young doctors. You won't understand a word of what we're talking about, anyway. Take his pyjamas off, Sister. Now you, my boy,' he continued, gripping me tightly by the arm as I was nearest, 'take a look at that abdomen.'

I stretched out a hand to feel the patient gingerly in the region of the umbilicus. I noticed his skin was covered with goose-pimples and twitched here and there nervously.

'Take your dirty little hand away!' said Sir Lancelot savagely, flicking it off the surface of the abdomen like a fly. He paused solemnly, and continued in a heavy tone, wagging his finger: 'The first rule of surgery, gentlemen–eyes first and most, hands next and least, tongue not at all. Look first and don't chatter. An excellent rule for you to remember all your lives. Now look, boy, look.'

I gazed at the abdomen for a whole minute but it appeared no different from any that might be seen on Brighton beach. When I thought I had inspected it long enough to satisfy the Chief, who rose uncomfortably above me, I diffidently stretched out my arm and prodded about with my finger in search of a lump.

'*Doucemong, doucemong*,' Sir Lancelot began again. 'Gently, boy–you're not making bread. Remember'–his finger came up again warningly–'a successful surgeon must have the eye of a hawk, the heart of a lion, and the hand of a lady.'

'And the commercial morals of a Levantine usurer,' murmured Grimsdyke under his breath.

With a glow of relief, I finally discovered the lump. It was about the size of an orange and tucked under the edge of the ribs. We lined up and felt it one after the other, while Sir Lancelot looked on closely and corrected anyone going about it the wrong way. Then he pulled a red grease-pencil from the top pocket of his coat and handed it to me.

'Where are we going to make the incision?' he asked. By now the patient was forgotten; it was the lump we were after. Sir Lancelot had an upsetting habit of treating the owners of lumps as if they were already rendered unconscious by the anaesthetic.

I drew a modest line over the lesion.

'Keyhole surgery!' said SirLancelot with contempt. 'Damnable! Give me the pencil!' He snatched it away. 'This, gentlemen, will be our incision.'

He drew a broad, decisive, red sweep from the patient's ribs to below his umbilicus.

'We will open the patient like *that*. Then we can have a good look inside. It's no good rummaging round an abdomen if you can't get your hand in comfortably. What do we do then? Right–take a better look at the lump we've been feeling. Do you think it's going to be easy to remove?' he asked me, gripping my arm again.

'No, sir.'

'Correct–it's going to be most difficult. And dangerous. There are at least a dozen ways in which we can make a slight error–even though we are experienced surgeons–and kill the patient like that!' He snapped his fingers frighteningly.

'Now!' He tapped the abdomen with his pencil as if knocking for admission. 'When we have cut through the skin what is the next structure we shall meet? Come on, you fellers. You've done your anatomy more recently than I have . . . what's that? Yes, subcutaneous fat. Then, gentlemen, we first encounter the surgeon's worst enemy.' He glared at us all in turn. 'What?' he demanded in general. There was no reply. 'Blood!' he thundered.

At that point the patient restored his personality to the notice of his doctors by vomiting.

Surgery was Sir Lancelot's life and St Swithin's was his home. He had given more of his time for nothing to the hospital than he ever used to make his fortune. He was president or vice-president of almost every students' club and supported the rugby team from the touchline in winter with the same roar he used on ignorant dressers in the theatre. During the war he slept every night at the hospital in the bombing, and operated on casualties in an improvised theatre in the basement as long as they came in. A team of students lived in as well and he used to play cards with them or share a pint of beer, actions which at first caused as much dismay as if he had arrived to operate in his underpants. One night St Swithin's was hit while he was operating. The theatre rocked, the lights went out, and part of the ceiling fell in. But Sir Lancelot simply swore and went on–bombs to him were just another irritation in surgery, like fumbling assistants and blunt knives, and he treated them all the same way.

The only time Sir Lancelot became at all subdued was when he talked of his retirement. It hung over him all the time I was on his firm. The prospect of losing his two days a week at St Swithin's depressed him, though he was cheered by remembering that the hospital would immediately acknowledge him as an emeritus consultant and perhaps call him in for cases of supreme difficulty. His connexion with St Swithin's would therefore not be completely broken; he could go on meeting the students at their clubs, and as for surgery he could continue that in private.

One day, shortly after I left his firm, he disappeared. He said good-bye to no one. He left his work to his assistant and wrote a note to the Chairman of the Governors simply stating he would not be in again. The hospital radiologist explained it later with an X-ray film. Sir Lancelot had a cancer in his stomach and had gone off to his cottage in Sussex to die. He refused to have an operation.

Chapter Eight

The Nurses' Home at St Swithin's was known, with a fair degree of accuracy, as the Virgins' Retreat. Virginity and nursing certainly seem to go together, and the Matron of St Swithin's put her Ursulian duties first. Her regulations for the nurses' conduct suggested she was convinced they went through their waking and sleeping life at the hospital in unremitting danger of rape. It is true that a student or two occasionally entertained sinful thoughts towards one of her charges; like any other bunch of young men they were romantic souls, and the fact that young ladies took off their clothes for them in the wards did not deter them from trying for the same result in their lodgings. But, taking the nurses as a whole, their Matron's book of rules was nothing more than a blatant piece of flattery.

Intercourse between the nurses and students had to be but social to attract the Matron's displeasure. If a nurse was seen talking to a student in the hospital, apart from a brief necessary exchange of medical matters in the ward, she was dismissed unquestioned. For her to meet a student in her off-duty time–to go to the pictures or a concert, for instance–was automatically reckoned, if discovered, as the equivalent of a week-end in Brighton. And if a nurse was found in the students' quarters or a man of any sort discovered in the Nurses' Home it was an event apparently unmeasurable in terms of human horror.

In order to reduce the possibility of these alarming situations overtaking the nurse the opportunities she could present for them were heavily reduced. All first-year nurses had to be in by ten every night. The senior girls were allowed out once a week until eleven, and staff nurses were permitted in comparison a life of uninhibited lechery by being able to claim two weekly passes until twelve.

Nurses, when in hospital, were authoritatively stripped of their sexual characteristics as far as was possible without operative interference. Make-up of any sort was looked upon by the ward sisters as the prerogative of women of the streets, and hair was supposed to be tightly tucked inside a starched uniform cap designed to be worn just over the eyebrows. The nurse's figure was de-contoured beneath uniform made out of a material similar to sailcloth, and the skirt was raised only far enough from the floor to let the poor girl walk without breaking her neck.

These regulations were naturally broken, as efficiently and as subtly as the lock on a medieval chastity belt. There were plenty of quiet corners about the hospital where a date could be arranged between student and nurse, and the couple had the whole of London to meet in. A thin, skilful brush with a lipstick could bring even from Sister Virtue nothing worse than suspicion and powder was almost invisible. As the cap had to be folded out of a linen square, with a little practice a girl could reduce it sufficiently in size so that it stuck attractively on the back of her head. As for the uniform, a nurse with any feelings of femininity in her veins immediately took her new outfit to a dressmaker to be shortened.

Shyness and the restrictions surrounding the nurses' social contacts kept me clear of my helpmeets in the ward, apart from the small amount of professional chat I dared to exchange with them. At the same time, the nurses took very little notice of me. With the senior students it was different: for them was the favour of a quick smile behind Sister's back, or a giggle in the sluice-room when no one was in earshot. The house-surgeons, who were doctors and therefore safe matrimonial investments, got cups of coffee when Sister was off duty and had their socks mended; and the registrar could quicken wildly any heart behind a starched apron bodice with a brief smile.

During my stay on Sir Lancelot's firm I began to gain a little confidence in myself in defiance of my surroundings. There was one nurse on the ward who seemed different from the rest. She was a slight little probationer downtrodden by the ward staff as heavily as I, which immediately spun a fine strand of sympathy between us. I felt sorry for her; and I thought, when I was being competently reduced to nothingness by Sister for using Sir Lancelot's special soap at the wash basin, that she was silently commiserating with me.

She was a snub-nosed brunette with grey eyes and a small mouth which she kept firmly closed in the ward. Her experience of St Swithin's was even less than mine, for she had arrived at the hospital only a fortnight previously. It was axiomatic that any nurse who could stand the first six weeks would last the whole course and I was interested to watch her lips growing tighter and tighter as this critical period wore on, while she was discovering it was far less important to save a patient's life than to drop a plate of pudding, and to break a thermometer was a feminine crime just short of persistent shoplifting.

By glances, shy smiles, and putting myself in proximity to her in the ward as much as I dared, I managed to indicate my interest. One morning I was in the sluice-room half-heartedly performing the routine chemical tests on my patients' excreta when she came in and resignedly began to clean out the sink. Sister had sent her there obviously not knowing of my presence; the door shut us off from the ward; we were alone; so I took a chance.

'I say,' I said.

She looked up from the sink.

'I say,' I repeated, 'number six looks much better today, doesn't he? The Chief did a good job on him all right. You should have seen the way he got hold of the splenic artery when a clip came off! I've never seen so much blood in my life.'

'Please!' she said, holding her stomach. 'You're making me feel sick.'

'Oh, I'm awfully sorry,' I apologized quickly. 'I just thought you'd be interested.'

'I'm not,' she said. 'The sight of blood makes me sick. In fact, the whole damn place makes me sick. I thought I was going to put my cool hands on the fevered brows of grateful young men, and all I do is clean the floors and give out bedpans to bad-tempered old daddies who smell.'

'If you don't like it,' I suggested, shocked by her confession, 'why did you take it up at all? Why don't you leave?'

'The hell I won't! My mother was a nurse and she's been ramming it down my throat for nineteen years. If she could take it I damn well can!'

'Would you like to come out to the pictures?' I asked. I thought it best to cut out her complaints and reach my object without further skirmishing. Our privacy might be broken at any moment.

'You bet!' she said without hesitation. 'Anything to get out of this place! I'm off at six. Meet me in the tube station. I must get back to the ward or the old woman will tear me to bits.'

Feeling demurely pleased with myself, I went down to the King George to tell someone about this swift conquest. I found Tony Benskin and Grimsdyke sitting at the bar, energetically talking about racing with the Padre.

'I've just dated up that little pro on the ward,' I told them nonchalantly. 'I'm taking her out tonight.'

Benskin was horrified. He had an obsession that he might one day be trapped into matrimony by a nurse and walked round the hospital as warily as a winning punter passing the men with the three-card trick.

'It's the thin end of the wedge, my boy!' he exclaimed. 'You watch your step, or you'll end up as aisle-fodder before you know where you are. They're vixens, the lot of them.'

'And good luck to them,' Grimsdyke added emphatically. 'After all, that's what they come to the hospital for–to find a husband. They wouldn't admit it, but it's buried in the subconscious of all of them somewhere.'

'I thought nursing was supposed to be a vocation and a calling,' I said defensively.

'No more than our own job, my dear old boy. Why have we all taken up medicine? I've got a good reason, that I'm paid to do it. You've got a doctor as a father and a leaning towards medicine in your case is simply a hereditary defect. Tony here took it up because he couldn't think of anything better that would allow him to play rugger three times a week. How many of our colleagues entered the noble profession through motives of humanity?' Grimsdyke screwed his monocle hard in his eye. 'Damn few, I bet. Humanitarian feelings draw more young fellows annually into the London Fire Brigade. It's the same with the girls–nursing offers one of the few remaining respectable excuses to leave home. Let them marry the chaps, I say. They're strong, healthy girls who know how to cook. To my mind the most important function of the St Swithin's nursing school is that it provides competent wives to help in general practice anywhere in the world.'

'Three beers please, Padre,' I said, interrupting him. 'Don't you think Grimsdyke's being unfair?'

'You've got to watch your step, sir, you can take it from me,' he said sombrely. 'I've seen more of you young gentlemen caught into marriage when you haven't a ha'penny to your name than I'd like to think about. Children soon, too, sir. Houses, gas bills, vacuum cleaners, and all the other little trappings of matrimony. It's an expensive hobby, take my word, sir, for young fellers before they're settled in practice.'

'Damn it,' I said, 'I've only asked the girl to the pictures. If I don't like her I won't see her again.'

'Easier said than done, sir. Ask Mr Grimsdyke about that young lady last Christmas.'

Grimsdyke laughed. 'Ah, yes, Padre! I've still got it on me, I think.' He pulled out his wallet and rummaged through the papers it contained. 'Most tiresome woman–tried everything to get rid of her for a fortnight. Then I received that one morning, handed to me by a hospital porter, if you please.'

He gave me a note in angry feminine handwriting. '*If you do not send an answer to this by midday,*' it said curtly, '*I shall hurl myself off the roof of the Nurses' Home.*'

'What on earth did you say?' I asked, horrified.

'What could I say?' Grimsdyke demanded. 'Except "No reply".'

'Did she throw herself off?'

'I really don't know,' he said, replacing the letter. 'I never troubled to find out.'

I met my little nurse at six. We passed an innocuous evening and arranged a rendezvous for the next week. But the appointment was never kept. The following day she was transferred to Sister Virtue's ward, where she cracked up. One afternoon she threw a pink blancmange at Sister and went out and got a job as a bus conductress.

This incident temporarily cooled my enthusiasm for nurses. After a few weeks I attempted to kindle an affection for a fat blonde in the out-patient department, but after we had spent a few evenings together she began to drift away from me, almost imperceptibly at first, like a big ship leaving dock. It was then that I started to worry about myself. Was it that I had no attraction for women? I never enjoyed success with my consorts while my friends apparently had no difficulty in committing fornication with theirs. I slunk into the library and looked up the psychology books: horror overcame me as I turned the pages. In my first few weeks in the wards I had been convinced that I was suffering from such complaints as tuberculosis, rheumatic heart, cancer of the throat, and pernicious anaemia, all of which successfully cleared up in a few days, but now I faced the terrible possibility of harbouring a mother fixation, oral eroticism, and a subnormal libido. I mentioned these fears to my friends that evening after supper.

'The trouble with you, my lad,' said John Bottle, without taking his eye from the microscope he was studying, 'is that you are suffering from that well-recognized clinical condition *orchitis amorosa acuta*, or lover's nuts.'

'Well,' I said sadly, 'I would willingly surrender my virginity if I could find someone to cooperate with me in the matter.'

'Can't you wait for a week?' Kelly asked testily. 'My path. exam is too near to let me go out for a night.'

His objection to my making an immediate start in my love life reflected the most serious menace to harmony in the flat.

We all agreed that it was important we should be able to ask our girl-friends to our home, and with the privacy without which the invitation would be pointless. As accommodation was limited it was equally important that the other three should not be obliged to tramp the streets angrily during the entire evening, or go to bed. Archie and Vera had been no problem because they kept to their own room, but some arrangement had to be made among the rest of us. We decided that each should have one evening a fortnight in which the sitting-room was to be his. A code was arranged: if the girl was brought in and presented to the others it required her host only to mention that it looked like rain for his friends to rise and troop out into the night like a well-drilled squad of infantry. (If he remarked that the weather was turning warmer they did an equally important service by sticking by him.) Then it was up to the man himself. But he had not the entire evening to fritter away in light amours. As the pubs shut at eleven he knew he could only count on the period until then as his own. His comrades would heartlessly return, considering they had left him time enough for a brisk seduction. If he failed to achieve his object in the time, that was his look-out. This probably had bad effects on our psychology, but it made us very persuasive.

'What about the girl from the out-patient department you were taking out?' Tony Benskin asked.

I shrugged my shoulders. 'No good.'

'Won't play?' John Bottle asked with interest. 'I thought as much . . . you want to take my tip and lay off the probationers. Altogether too young and unappreciative. They can still remember the games mistress said it would ruin their hockey.'

Mike Kelly was sitting in an armchair by the fire, frowning into a yellow-covered book on fevers. He carefully put his finger on his place before speaking.

'You might try the theatre sister from number six,' he suggested faintly.

'Oh, she's no use,' John said with authority. 'Registrars only in that department. She's the sort of girl who'd hardly look at a houseman, let alone a poor bloody student.'

'There's that little blonde staff nurse just come on Loftus's ward,' Mike continued helpfully. 'She looks as if she'd be worth making advances to.'

'Hopeless!' John said. 'She suffers badly from tinnitus–ringing in the ears, and they're wedding bells.'

'How about Rigor Mortis?' Tony suggested, suddenly looked pleased with himself.

'Old Rigor . . . that's more like it!' John agreed. 'She's always ready for a tumble with anybody.'

'The nursery slopes for our friend,' remarked Mike warmly.

'Rigor Mortis?' I asked dubiously.

'Oh, that's not her real name of course,' Tony explained. 'It's Ada something or other. Haven't you come across her?'

'I don't think so.'

'She's not a great beauty,' he went on, 'so perhaps that's why you haven't noticed her. But she has the kindest heart imaginable. She's the staff nurse on Loftus's male ward. I knew her well, old man. I'll introduce you. The more I think of it the more certain I am that she's what you need. She expects the minimum of entertainment and it is hardly necessary to do more than hold her hand and look plaintive. Capital! You shall meet her tomorrow.'

Tony took me to meet Rigor Mortis the following afternoon, when the ward sister was off duty. I immediately agreed that she wasn't much to look at. She had dull black hair which she pushed into her starched cap like the stuffing in a cushion, a chin like a boxer's, and eyebrows that met in the middle.

She was about six feet tall and had a bosom as shapeless as a plate of scrambled eggs. But all these blemishes melted before my eyes, which were fired with Benskin's firm recommendation that she had a kind heart.

After a minute's cheery conversation Tony explained that I had been bursting to make her acquaintance for some months. He asked her if she was doing anything on her next night off; all I had to do was mumble an invitation to the pictures, which she briskly accepted. I arranged to meet her outside Swan and Edgar's at six and we parted.

'There you are, old man,' Tony said as we left the ward. 'Meet her at six, whip her into a flick, take her back to the flat for a drink–that'll be about nine-thirty. You'll have two solid hours to do your stuff.'

I arranged for the seduction with considerable care. I stayed away from the afternoon lecture and spent the time cleaning up the sitting-room, putting the books away, straightening the cover on the divan, and arranging the reading light so the glow fell romantically in the corner. I set out a new packet of cigarettes and invested in half a bottle of gin. There were two glasses in the kitchen that happened to be the same pattern, and these I carefully washed, dried, and placed on the mantelpiece. It was only five, so I sat down and read the evening paper. I was nervous and worried, as though I was going to the dentist. I began to wish I hadn't introduced the idea at all. But I could no longer back out. I must be victorious by eleven or sink in the opinions of my friends. I took a nip of the gin and set out.

For a few minutes I hoped she wouldn't turn up, but she lumbered out of the Underground right enough. She looked a little better in civilian clothes, but I still thought her as unattractive as an old sofa. I suggested the New Gallery, and she agreed. She seemed fairly friendly, but I soon discovered that she was disinclined to take the initiative in conversation. If I spoke she replied; if I remained silent she appeared to be concentrating heavily on thoughts of her own. I had therefore to keep up a run of inane patter, every sentence on a different subject, until the film released us into merciful mutual silence.

About half-way through the picture I abruptly recalled the object of my expedition. Should I give just the faintest hint of what was to come, I wondered, and hold her hand? It would be the herald's call to the approaching tussle. Would she rebuff this forwardness so early, for I had hardly known her an hour? I gave a sly glance through the darkness and seized her rough palm. She gripped mine without thinking, without an indication that her mind was distracted a hairsbreadth from the screen.

The two of us stood outside in Regent Street. I asked casually if she would care to come home for a drink, and meet the boys. She assented with the same air as she accepted my hand in the cinema. We went to Oxford Circus tube station and I bought a couple of tickets. I held her arm as we walked down the road to the flat and up the steps. The stairs . . . opening the door . . . my surprise that no one was there. She sat down on the divan without a word, and I lit the gas-fire. She took a drink in an off-hand way. We sat in the glow of the gas and the dim light of my romantic bulb.

I finished a cigarette and gave her another drink. Surely, I thought, this would have some effect? She had two or three more, but sat looking absently at the fire, dully returning a sentence for each one of mine, unanimated, unresponsive, unworried.

I nervously looked at my watch and saw with alarm that it was past ten-thirty. I had to get a move on. I felt like a man going out to start an old car on a cold morning.

I held her hand tighter. She didn't object. I drew closer. She moved neither away nor nearer. I put my arm round her and started stroking her off-side ear. She remained passive, like a cow with its mind on other things.

The seconds ticked away from my wrist, faster and faster. At least, I thought, I have gone this far without rebuff. I kissed her on the cheek. She still sat pleasantly there, saying nothing. Carefully setting down my glass, I stroked her blouse firmly. I might just as well have been brushing her coat. I threw myself at her and she rolled back on the divan like a skittle. With great energy I continued her erotic stimulation. Any moment now, I thought excitedly, and the object of the evening would be achieved. She lay wholly unconcerned. Suddenly she moved. With one hand she picked up the evening paper I had left on the divan. She read the headlines.

'Oh look!' she exclaimed with sympathy, 'there's been an awful train crash at Chelmsford. Seventeen killed!'

'So you had no luck?' Tony asked at midnight.

'None. None at all.'

'That's tough. Cheer up . . . other fish, you know.'

I decided to do my fishing in future in more turbulent waters, even if I had no catch.

Chapter Nine

In order to teach the students midwifery St Swithin's supervised the reproductive activities of the few thousand people who lived in the overcrowded area surrounding the hospital. In return, they cooperated by refusing to water down the demands of Nature with the less pressing requests of the Family Planning Association.

The midwifery course is of more value to the student than a piece of instruction on delivering babies. It takes him out of the hospital, where everything is clean and convenient and rolled up on sterile trollies, to the environment he will be working in when he goes into practice–a place of dirty floors, bed-bugs, no hot water, and lights in the most inconvenient places; somewhere without nurses but with bands of inquisitive children and morbid relatives; a world of broken stairs, unfindable addresses, and cups of tea in the kitchen afterwards.

It was fortunate that I was plunged into the practice of midwifery shortly after my unfruitful love life, for it is a subject which usually produces a sharp reactionary attack of misogyny in its students. Tony Benskin, Grimsdyke, and myself started 'on the district' together. We had to live in the hospital while we were midwifery clerks, in rooms the size of isolation cubicles on the top floor of the resident doctors' quarters. My predecessor, a tall, fair-haired, romantic-looking man called Lamont, had been so moved by his experiences he was on the point of breaking off his engagement.

'The frightful women!' he said heatedly, as he tried to cram a pile of textbooks into his case. 'I can't understand that anyone would ever want to sleep with them. That someone obviously has done so in the near past is quite beyond me.'

'How many babies have you had?' I asked.

'Forty-nine. That includes a couple of Caesars. I'd have made a half-century if I hadn't missed a B.B.A.'

'B.B.A.?'

'Born before arrival. Terrible disgrace for the midder clerk, of course. I reckoned I'd have time for my lunch first, and when I got there the blasted thing was in the bed. However, mother and child did well, so I suppose no real harm was done. Don't try and open the window, it's stuck. I'm going out to get drunk. Best of luck.'

Picking up his bag he left, the latest penitent for the sin of Adam.

I sat on the bed, feeling depressed. It was an unusually raw afternoon in November and the sky hung over the roof-tops in an unbroken dirty grey sheet. There was no fire in the room and the pipes emitted flatulent noises but no heat. The only decoration was a large black-and-white map of the district on which some former student had helpfully added the pubs in red ink. I looked out of the window and saw a few flakes of snow–ominous, like the first spots of a smallpox rash. I wished women would go away and bud, like the flowers.

The three of us reported to the senior resident obstetrical officer, a worried-looking young man whom we found in the ante-natal clinic. This clinic was part of the St Swithin's service. Every Thursday afternoon the mothers came and sat on the benches outside the clinic door, looking like rows of over-ripe poppy-heads. The obstetrical officer was absently running his hands over an abdomen like the dome of St Paul's to find which way up the baby was.

'You the new clerks?' he asked, without interest.

We each nodded modestly.

'Well, make sure you're always within call. When you go out on a case a midwife will be sent separately by the local maternity service, so you've got nothing to worry about. Don't forget to carry two pennies in your pocket.'

'To phone, of course,' he said when I asked why. 'If you get into trouble dash for the nearest box and call me, and I'll come out in a police car. Don't wait till it's too late, either.'

He dismissed us and bent over to listen to the foetal heart rate with a stethoscope shaped like a small flower-vase.

Our next call was on the Extern Sister, who controlled all the midwifery students. I found her a most interesting woman. She was so ugly she could never have had much expectation of fulfilling her normal biological function; now she had been overtaken by the sad menopause and was left no chance of doing so at all. As she had not been offered the opportunity of bearing children she had thrown herself into midwifery like a novice into religion. She knew more about it than the obstetrical officer. She could talk only about mothers and babies and thought of everyone solely as a reproductive element. In her room was a gold medal she had won in her examinations, which she proudly displayed in a small glass-covered frame between two prints of Peter Scott's ducks. She talked of the anatomy involved in the birth of a baby as other women described their favourite shopping street. She had, however, the unfortunate trick of awarding the parts of the birth canal to the listener.

'When your cervix is fully dilated,' she told us gravely, 'you must decide whether to apply your forceps to your baby. You must feel to see if your head or your breech is presenting.'

'Supposing it's your shoulder or your left ear?' asked Benskin.

'Then you put your hand in your uterus and rotate your child,' she replied without hesitation.

She gave us a rough idea of delivering babies and demonstrated the two instrument bags we had to take on our cases. They were long leather affairs, like the luggage of a dressy cricketer, containing sufficient material to restore the biggest disaster it was likely a student could pull down on himself. There were bottles of antiseptic, ether and chloroform, needles and catgut in tins of Lysol, a pair of obstetrical forceps, a peculiar folding canvas arrangement for holding up the mother's legs, enamel bowls, rubber gloves, and a number of unidentifiable packages.

'You must check your bags before you go to your mother,' Sister said.

We chalked our room-numbers on the board in the hall and went out for a drink in the King George. The snow was falling thickly, swirling round the lamp-posts and clinging to the hospital walls, giving the old building a more sinister appearance than ever.

'What a night to start stork-chasing!' Grimsdyke exclaimed.

'What happens when we get out there?' I asked.

'Getting nervous, old boy?'

'I am a bit. I haven't seen a baby born before. I might faint or something.'

'There's nothing to worry about,' Benskin told me cheerfully. 'I was talking to one of the chaps we're relieving. The midwife always gets there first and tells you what to do under her breath. They're a good crowd. They let the patient think you're the doctor, which is good for the morale of both of you.'

We went back to the hospital for dinner. Afterwards Benskin asked the duty porter if everything was still quiet.

'Not a thing, sir,' he replied. 'It's a bad sign, all right. After it's been as quiet as this for a bit they start popping out like rabbits from their warrens.'

We sat in Grimsdyke's room and played poker for matches for a couple of hours. It was difficult to concentrate on the game. Every time the phone bell rang in the distance we jumped up nervously together. Grimsdyke suggested bed at ten, predicting we would be roused as soon as we dropped off to sleep. We cut for who should be on first call: I lost.

It was four when the porter woke me up. He cheerily pulled off the bedclothes and handed me a slip of paper with an address scribbled on it in pencil.

'You'd better hurry, sir,' he said. 'They sounded proper worried over the phone.'

I rolled out of bed and dressed with the enthusiasm of a prisoner on his execution morning. The night outside was as thick and white as a rice pudding. After a glance through the curtains I pulled a green-and-yellow hooped rugby jersey over my shirt and a dirty cricket sweater over that. I tucked the ends of my trousers into football stockings, wrapped a long woollen scarf round my neck and hid the lot under a duffle coat. I looked as if I was going to take the middle watch on an Arctic fishing vessel.

The reason for this conscientious protection against the weather was the form of transport allotted to the students to reach their cases. It was obviously impossible to provide such inconsequential people with a car and we were nearly all too poor to own one ourselves. On the other hand, if the students had been forced to walk to their patients the race would have gone to the storks. A compromise had therefore been effected some ten years ago and the young obstetricians had the loan of the midwifery bicycle.

This vehicle had unfortunately not worn well in the service of the obstetrical department. It had originally been equipped with such necessaries as brakes, mudguards, lights, and rubber blocks on the pedals, but, as human beings sadly lose their hair, teeth, and firm subcutaneous fat in the degeneration of age, the machine had similarly been reduced to its bare comfortless bones. The saddle had the trick of slipping unexpectedly and throwing the rider either backwards or forwards, it was impossible to anticipate which. The only way to stop the machine was by falling off. It was the most dangerous complication of midwifery in the practice of the hospital.

I searched for the address on the map. It was on the other side of the district, a short, narrow, coy street hiding between a brewery and a good yard. It seemed as remote as Peru.

I waddled down to the out-patient hall to collect the instrument bags. The place was cold and deserted; the porter who had called me was yawning in the corner over the telephone, and the two night nurses huddled in their cloaks round their tiny electric fire, sewing their way through a stack of gauze dressings. They took no notice of the globular figure coming down the stairs: an insignificant midwifery clerk wasn't worth dropping a stitch for. For the houseman, or, if they were lucky, one of the registrars come to open an emergency appendix–to them they would give a cup of coffee and a flutter of the eyelids. But what good were the junior students?

The bicycle was kept in a small shed in the hospital courtyard, and had for its stablemate the long trolley used for moving unlucky patients to the mortuary. I saw that the first problem of the case was balancing myself and my equipment on the machine. As well as the two leather bags I had a couple of drums the size of biscuit barrels containing the sterilized dressings. There was a piece of thick string attached to the bicycle, which I felt was probably part of its structure, but I removed it and suspended the two drums round my neck like a yoke. Carefully mounting the machine, I clung to the bags and the handlebars with both hands and pedalled uncertainly towards the front gate. The snowflakes fell upon me eagerly, like a crowd of mosquitoes, leaping for my face, the back of my neck, and my ankles.

The few yards across the courtyard were far enough to indicate the back tyre was flat and the direction of the front wheel had no constant relationship to the way the handlebars were pointing. I crunched to a stop by the closed iron gates and waited for the porter to leave his cosy cabin and let me out.

'You all right, sir?' he asked with anxiety.

'Fine,' I said. 'I love it like this. It makes me feel like a real doctor.'

'Well,' he said dubiously, 'good luck, sir.'

'Thank you.'

The porter turned the key in the lock and pulled one of the gates open against the resisting snow.

'Your back light isn't working, sir,' he shouted.

I called back I thought it didn't matter and pedalled away into the thick night feeling like Captain Oates. I had gone about twenty yards when the chain came off.

After replacing the chain I managed to wobble along the main road leading away from the hospital in the direction of the brewery. The buildings looked as hostile as polar ice-cliffs. Everything appeared so different from the kindly daytime, which gave life to the cold, dead streets with the brisk circulation of traffic. Fortunately my thorough knowledge of the local public houses provided a few finger-posts, and I might have done tolerably well as a flying angel of mercy if the front wheel hadn't dropped off.

I fell into the snow in the gutter and wished I had gone in for law. As I got to my feet I reflected that the piece of string might have been something important to do with the attachment of the front wheel; but now the lesion was inoperable. Picking up my luggage, I left the machine to be covered by the snow like a dead husky and trudged on. By now I was fighting mad. I told myself I would damn well deliver that baby. If it dared to precipitate itself into the world ungraciously without waiting for me I decided I would strangle it.

I turned off the main road towards the brewery, but after a few hundred yards I had to admit I was lost. Even the pubs were unfamiliar. I now offered no resistance to my environment and submissively felt the moisture seeping through my shoes. I leant against a sheltering doorpost, preparing to meet death in as gentlemanly a way as possible.

At that moment a police car, forced like myself into the snow, stopped in front of me. The driver swung his light on my load and on myself, and had no alternative than to decide I was a suspicious character. He asked for my identity card.

'Quick!' I said dramatically. 'I am going to a woman in childbirth.'

'Swithin's?' asked the policeman.

'Yes. It may be too late. I am the doctor.'

'Hop in the back!'

There is nothing that delights policemen more than being thrown into a midwifery case. There is a chance they might have to assist in the performance, which means a picture in the evening papers and congratulatory beer in the local. The constable who walked into St Swithin's one afternoon with an infant born on the lower deck of a trolley bus looked as pleased as if he were the father.

The warm police car took me to the address, and the crew abandoned me with reluctance. It was a tall, dead-looking tenement for ever saturated with the smells of brewing and shunting. I banged on the knocker and waited.

A thin female child of about five opened the door.

'I'm the doctor,' I announced.

The arrival of the obstetrician in such a briskly multiplying area caused no more stir than the visit of the milkman.

'Upstairs, mate,' she said and scuttled away into the darkness like a rat.

The house breathed the sweet stench of bed-bugs; inside it was dark, wet, and rotting. I fumbled my way to the stairs and creaked upwards. On the second floor a door opened a foot, a face peered through, and as the shaft of light caught me it was slammed shut. It was on the fifth and top floor that the accouchement seemed to be taking place, as there was noise and light coming from under one of the doors. I pushed it open and lumbered in.

'Don't worry!' I said. 'I have come.'

I took a look round the room. It wasn't small, but a lot was going on in it. In the centre, three or four children were fighting on the pockmarked linoleum for possession of their plaything, a piece of boxwood with a nail through it. A fat woman was unconcernedly making a cup of tea on a gas-ring in one corner, and in the other a girl of about seventeen with long yellow hair was reading last Sunday's *News of the World*. A cat, sympathetic to the excited atmosphere, leapt hysterically among the children. Behind the door was a bed beside which was grandma–who always appears on these occasions, irrespective of the social standing of the participants. Grandma was giving encouragement tempered with warning to the mother, a thin, pale, fragile woman on the bed, and it was obvious that the affair had advanced alarmingly. A tightly-packed fire roared in the grate and above the mantelpiece Field-Marshal Montgomery, of all people, looked at the scene quizzically.

'Her time is near, Doctor,' said grandma with satisfaction.

'You have no need to worry any longer, missus,' I said brightly.

I dropped the kit on the floor and removed my duffle coat, which wept dirty streams on to the lino. The first step was to get elbow room and clear out the non-playing members of the team.

'Who are you?' I asked the woman making tea.

'From next door,' she replied. 'I thought she'd like a cup of tea, poor thing.'

'I want some hot water,' I said sternly. 'Lots of hot water. Fill basins with it. Or anything you like. Now you all go off and make me some hot water. Take the children as well. Isn't it past their bedtime?'

'They sleep in 'ere, Doctor,' said grandma.

'Oh. Well–they can give you a hand. And take the cat with you. Come on–all of you. Lots of water, now.'

They left unwillingly, in disappointment. They liked their entertainment to be fundamental.

'Now, mother,' I started, when we were alone. A thought struck me–hard, in the pit of the stomach. The midwife–the cool, practised, confident midwife. Where was she? Tonight–this memorable night to the two of us in the room–what had happened to her? Snowbound, of course. I felt like an actor who had forgotten his lines and finds the prompter has gone out for a drink.

'Mother,' I said earnestly. 'How many children have you?'

'Five, Doctor,' she groaned.

Well, that was something. At least one of us knew a bit about it.

She began a frightening increase in activity.

'I think it's coming, Doctor!' she gasped, between pains. I grasped her hand vigorously.

'You'll be right as rain in a minute,' I said, as confidently as possible. 'Leave it to me.'

'I feel sick,' she cried miserably.

'So do I,' I said.

I wondered what on earth I was going to do.

There was, however, one standby that I had thoughtfully taken the trouble to carry. I turned into the corner furthest away from the mother and looked as if I was waiting confidently for the precise time to intervene. Out of my hip pocket I drew a small but valuable volume in a limp red cover–*The Student's Friend in Obstetrical Difficulties.* It was written by a hard-headed obstetrician on the staff of a Scottish hospital who was under no illusions about what the students would find difficult. It started off with 'The Normal Delivery'. The text was written without argument, directly, in short numbered paragraphs, like a cookery book. I glanced at the first page.

'Sterility,' it said. 'The student must try to achieve sterile surroundings for the delivery, and scrub-up himself as for a surgical operation. Newspapers may be used if sterile towels are unobtainable, as they are often bacteria-free.'

Newspaper, that was it! There was a pile of them in the corner, and I scattered the sheets over the floor and the bed. This was a common practice in the district, and if he knew how many babies were born yearly straight on to the *Daily Herald* Mr Percy Cudlip would be most surprised.

There was a knock on the door, and grandma passed through an enamel bowl of boiling water.

'Is it come yet, Doctor?' she asked.

'Almost,' I told her. 'I shall need lots more water.'

I put the bowl down on the table, took some soap and a brush from the bag, and started scrubbing.

'Oh, Doctor, Doctor . . . !' cried the mother.

'Don't get alarmed,' I said airily.

'It's coming, Doctor!'

I scrubbed furiously. The mother groaned. Grandma shouted through the door she had more hot water. I shouted back at her to keep out. The cat, which had not been removed as ordered, jumped in the middle of the newspaper and started tearing at it with its claws.

Suddenly I became aware of a new note in the mother's cries–a higher, wailing, muffled squeal. I dropped the soap and tore back the bedclothes.

The baby was washed and tucked up in one of the drawers from the wardrobe, which did a turn of duty as a cot about once a year. The mother was delighted and said she had never had such a comfortable delivery. The spectators were readmitted, and cooed over the infant. There were cups of tea all round. I had the best one, with sugar in it. I felt the name of the medical profession never stood higher.

'Do you do a lot of babies, Doctor?' asked the mother.

'Hundreds,' I said. 'Every day.'

'What's your name, Doctor, if you don't mind?' she said.

I told her.

'I'll call 'im after you. I always call them after the doctor or the nurse, according.'

I beamed and bowed graciously. I was genuinely proud of the child. It was my first baby, born through my own skill and care. I had already forgotten in the flattering atmosphere that my single manoeuvre in effecting the delivery was pulling back the eiderdown.

Packing the instruments up, I climbed into my soggy duffle coat and, all smiles, withdrew. At the front door I found to my contentment that the snow had stopped and the roads shone attractively in the lamplight. I began to whistle as I walked away. At that moment the midwife turned the corner on her bicycle.

'Sorry, old chap,' she said, as she drew up. 'I was snowed under. Have you been in?'

'In! It's all over.'

'Did you have any trouble?' she asked dubiously.

'Trouble!' I said with contempt. 'Not a bit of it! It went splendidly.'

'I suppose you remembered to remove the afterbirth?'

'Of course.'

'Well, I might as well go home then. How much did it weigh?'

'Nine pounds on the kitchen scales.'

'You students are terrible liars.'

I walked back to the hospital over the slush as if it were a thick pile carpet. The time was getting on. A hot bath, I thought, then a good breakfast . . . and a day's work already behind me. I glowed in anticipation as I suddenly became aware that I was extremely hungry.

At the hospital gate the porter jumped up from his seat.

''Urry up, sir,' he said, 'and you'll just make it.'

'What's all this?' I asked with alarm.

'Another case, sir. Been waiting two hours. The other gentlemen are out already.'

'But what about my breakfast?'

'Sorry, sir. Not allowed to go to meals if there's a case. Orders of the Dean.'

'Oh, hell!' I said. I took the grubby slip of paper bearing another address. 'So this is midwifery,' I added gloomily.

'That's right, sir,' said the porter cheerfully. 'It gets 'em all down in the end.'

Chapter Ten

Everyone working in hospital is so preoccupied with the day-to-day rush of minor crises that the approach of Christmas through the long, dark bronchitic weeks of midwinter comes as a surprise. The holiday cuts brightly into hospital routine, like an unexpected ray of sunlight in an Inner Circle tunnel. At St Swithin's there was, however, one prodromal sign of the approaching season–a brisk increase in attendance at the children's department.

Every year at Christmas the Governors gave a tea-party in the main hall of the hospital for a thousand or so of the local boys and girls. They were men not used to stinting their hospitality, and provided richly for the tastes of their guests. It was the sort of affair that could be adequately described only by Ernest Hemingway, Negley Farson, or some other writer with a gift of extracting a forceful attractiveness from descriptions of active animals feeding in large numbers.

The children began to collect outside the locked doors of the out-patient department soon after midday; by three the front of the hospital looked like an Odeon on Saturday morning. At four sharp the doors were opened by the porters and the mob were funnelled into the building–scratching, fighting, shouting, and screaming, their incidental distractions from the fists and elbows of their neighbours overwhelmed with the urgent common desire to get at the food. They rushed through the entrance lobby, stormed the broad, wooden-floored hall, and expended their momentum in a pile of sticky, white-glazed buns.

The buns were the foundation of the party, but there was a great deal more besides–a high Christmas cake flaming with candles, churns of strawberry ice-cream, jellies the colours of traffic lights, oranges with a tenacious aroma, and sweet tea in long enamelled jugs. The non-edible attractions included paper chains, crackers, funny hats, a tree ten feet high, and Father Christmas. It was the duty of the children's house-physician to play this part. The gown, whiskers, sack, and toys were provided by the Governors; all the doctor had to do was allow himself to be lowered in a fire-escape apparatus from the roof into the tight mob of children screaming below. This obligation he discharged with the feelings of a nervous martyr being dropped into the bear-pit.

It was inevitable that he should breathe heavily on his little patients a strong smell of mixed liquors, which never missed their sharp, experienced noses and gave rise to delighted comments:

'Coo! 'E's bin boozing!'

'Smells like Dad on Saturday!'

'Give us a train, Mister!'

All this the house-physician had to endure with a set smile of determined benevolence.

The party was controlled, where possible, by the out-patient sister and a reinforced staff of nurses. Their starched caps and aprons melted in the afternoon with the ice-cream as they attempted to impose the principle of fair shares on a community demonstrating a vigorous capitalist spirit of grabbing what they could. The energy of the children diminished only if they had to retire to a corner to be sick; but the hospitality of St Swithin's was unlimited, and it usually happened that several of the little guests were later asked to stay the night.

The reason that the annual tea-party afforded as sure an indication that Christmas was approaching as a polite postman lay in the rules for admission to the jamboree. The Governors had decided many years ago that as it was impossible to entertain every child in the district invitations should be sent only to those who had attended the hospital in the months of November and December. As all the children within several miles knew of the party and were perfectly familiar with the qualifications for entry the increase in juvenile morbidity after October 31st was always alarming. This had recently led an ingenuous new house-physician in the department to sit down and prepare for publication in the *Lancet* a scientific paper on the startling increase in stomach-ache and growing pains among London school children in the last quarter of the year.

The goings-on at Christmas-time were conducted with the excuse that the staff was obliged to entertain the patients, just as adults take themselves off to circuses and pantomimes on the pretext of amusing the children. The wards were decorated, the out-patient hall spanned with streamers, and on Christmas Day even the operating theatres were festooned. The hospital presented the grotesque appearance of a warship during Navy Week, when the guns and other sinister implements aboard are covered with happy bunting. Relatives, friends, visiting staff, old graduates, and students overran the place; it was an enormous family party.

I had dutifully returned home the first Christmas I was in the hospital, but for the second I decided to stay and join in the fun. I was then coming to the end of my second session of medical clerking, this time as a protégé of the Dean, Dr Loftus, on Prudence ward.

A week before Christmas Eve the ward sister distributed sheets of coloured crêpe paper round the patients and set them cutting frilly shades for the bedlamps, paper chains, cut-outs for sticking on the windows, and the other paraphernalia of Christmas. Sister Prudence was different from the majority of her colleagues at St Swithin's. She was a fat, kindly, jovial woman with an inefficiently concealed affection for Guinness' stout. She never had a bitter word for the students, whom she regarded as pleasantly irresponsible imbeciles, and she treated the nurses as normally fallible human beings. Above all, she had the superb recommendation of hating Sister Virtue's guts.

'I'm so worried about number twelve,' she said to me quietly one afternoon. I followed her glance to a wizened, sallow old man lying flat on his back cutting out a red paper doll with no enthusiasm. 'I do hope he won't die before Christmas,' she continued. 'It would be such a pity for him to miss it all!'

On Christmas Eve the students and nurses tacked up the paper chains and fixed the Christmas tree in front of the sanitary-looking door of the sluice-room. Sister beamed at the volunteers, as she was by then certain her ward would be more richly decorated than Sister Virtue's. It was a vivid jungle in paper. Red and yellow streamers hung in shallow loops across the forbidding ceiling and the dark woodwork of the walls was covered refreshingly with coloured stars, circles, and rosettes, like a dull winter flower-bed in springtime. The severely functional lights over the beds were softened by paper lanterns, which emitted so little light, however, that they transformed even a simple manoeuvre like giving an injection into an uncomfortable and dangerous operation. The black iron bedrails were garlanded with crimson crêpe, the long table down the middle of the ward was banked with synthetic snow, and blatantly unsterile holly flourished unrebuked in every corner. Most important of all, a twig of mistletoe hung over the doorway. By hospital custom, to avoid interruption in the daily working of the ward the sprig was not put into use until Christmas morning; before then the nurses and the students took a new and keen appraisal of each other with sidelong glances, each deciding whom they would find themselves next to when the sport opened. As for Sister Prudence, she would have taken it as a personal insult not to be embraced by everyone from Dr Loftus down to the most junior student. 'I *do* like Christmas!' she said enthusiastically. 'It's the only time an old body like me ever gets kissed!'

The students had a more exacting task at Christmas than simply decorating the ward. It was a tradition at St Swithin's that each firm produced, and presented in one of the main wards, a short theatrical entertainment. This was in accordance with the established English custom of dropping the national mantle of self-consciousness at Christmas-time and revealing the horrible likeness of the charade underneath. No one at St Swithin's would have shirked acting in, or witnessing, the Christmas shows any more than they would have contemplated refusing to operate on an acute appendix. They were part of the hospital history, and it was handed down that Sir Benjamin Bone himself when a student contributed a fine baritone to the Christmas entertainment while the young Larrymore accompanied him on a violin, deliberately out of key.

The dramatic construction of these performances was as rigidly conventional as classical Greek drama or provincial pantomime. There were certain things that had to be included, or the audience was left wondering and cheated. It was essential at one point for a large student to appear dressed as a nurse, with two pairs of rugger socks as falsies. There had to be a song containing broad references to the little professional and personal idiosyncrasies of the consultant staff–oddities that they had previously been under the impression passed unnoticed. Equally important were unsubtle jests about bedpans and similar pieces of hospital furniture. One scene had to represent a patient suffering under the attentions of a scrum of doctors and students, and there was always a burst of jolly community singing at the end.

The players had their conventions as well. No troupe would have contemplated for a moment taking the boards sober, and the most important member of the cast was the supernumerary who wheeled round the firkin of beer on a stretcher. It was also essential to carry a spare actor or two in the company, as on most occasions some of the active performers were overcome before the last scenes and had to be carried to the wings.

Two days before Christmas Grimsdyke took the initiative by ordering our firm to assemble in the King George at opening time that evening. They were seven of us: Grimsdyke and Tony Benskin, John Bottle, the middle-aged student Sprogget, Evans, the brilliant Welshman, the keen student

Harris, and myself. We collected round the piano in a corner of the bar.

'Now, look here, you fellows,' Grimsdyke began with authority. 'We must scratch up a bit of talent between us. Time's getting short. We've only got a day and a half to write, produce, and rehearse what will be the most magnificent of performances that ever hit St Swithin's. Can any of you chaps play the piano?'

'I can play a bit,' I said. 'But mostly hymns.'

'That doesn't matter. Those hymn tunes can be turned into anything you like with a bit of ingenuity. That's one thing settled at any rate. What sort of piece shall we do? A panto, or a sort of pierrot show?'

'I think I ought to tell you,' said Harris aggressively, 'that I am considered pretty hot stuff at singing Little Polly Perkins from Paddington Green. I gave it at the church concert at home last year and it made quite a sensation.'

'Please!' said Grimsdyke. 'Can anyone else do anything? You can conjure, can't you, Tony?'

'One does the odd trick,' Benskin admitted modestly. 'Nothing spectacular like sawing a nurse in half, though–just rabbits out of hats and suchlike.'

'It'll amuse the kids, so we'll put you in. You can also dress up as a nurse somewhere in the show. John, you'd better take the romantic lead. What can you do, Sproggett?'

'Me? Oh, well, I don't do anything . . . that is, well, you know . . .' He gave an embarrassed giggle. 'I do child imitations.'

'Good for you. Child imitations it shall be. Evans, my dear old boy, you shall be general understudy, stage manager, wardrobe mistress, and ale carrier. You haven't got one of those lilting Welsh voices, I suppose?'

'My voice is only any good when diluted with forty thousand others at Twickenham.'

'Oh well, Harris will have to sing, I suppose. It's unavoidable. That seems to have settled the casting difficulties.'

'What about you? What are you going to do?' I asked him.

'I shall write, produce, and compère the piece, as well as reciting a short poem of my own composition in honour of St Swithin's. I think it should go over very well. I suppose nobody has any objections to that?'

We shook our heads submissively.

'Good. Now what we want is a title. It must be short, snappy, brilliantly funny, and with a medical flavour the patients can understand. Any suggestions?'

The seven of us thought for a few minutes in silence.

'How about "Laughing Gas"?' I suggested.

Grimsdyke shook his head. 'Too trite.'

'"Babes in the Ward"?' said Benskin eagerly. 'Or "The Ninety-niners"?'

'They were both used last year.'

'I've got it!' Harris jumped up from behind the piano. '"Enema for the Skylark"! How's that?'

'Horrible.'

We thought again. Grimsdyke suddenly snapped his fingers. 'Just the thing!' he announced. 'The very thing! What's wrong with "Jest Trouble"?'

His cast looked at him blankly.

'"Jest trouble", you see,' he explained. 'Pun on "Chest Trouble". All the patients know what that means. Get it? Exactly the right touch, I think. Now let's get on and write a script.'

The production was born with–in relation to its small size and immaturity–intense labour pains. As the cast had to continue their routine hospital work the producer found it difficult to assemble them on one spot at the same time; and when they did arrive, each one insisted on rewriting the script as he went along. I drooped over the piano trying hard to transform the melody of 'Onward Christian Soldiers' into a suitable accompaniment for a cautionary duet Benskin and Grimsdyke insisted on singing, beginning:

'If the ill that troubles you is a tendency to lues,
And you're positive your Wasserman is too.'

And ending:

'My poor little baby, he's deaf and he's dumb,
My poor little baby's insane:
He's nasty big blisters all over his tum,
What a shame, what a shame, what a shame!'

When the King George closed we moved to the deserted students' common room; when we were hoarse and exhausted we flopped to sleep on the springless sofas. We rehearsed grimly all the next day. Late on Christmas Eve Grimsdyke rubbed his hands and announced: 'This would bring a smile to the lips of a chronic melancholic.'

Chapter Eleven

The patients saw plenty of Christmas Day. They were woken up by the night nurses at five a.m. as usual, given a bowl of cold water, and wished a Merry Christmas. After breakfast the nurses took off their uniform caps and put on funny hats, and shifted into hidden side-wards any patients who seemed likely to spoil the fun by inconsiderately passing away. Sister Virtue was particularly successful in the role of Valkyrie: her long experience of diseases and doctors enabled her to spot a declining case several days before the medical staff. She had only to fix her glare on an apparently convalescent patient and give her bleak opinion that 'He won't *do*, sir,' and the houseman confidently made arrangements for the post-mortem.

When I arrived on the ward in the middle of the morning I found a wonderful end-of-term spirit abroad. People were allowed to do things they felt forbidden even to contemplate at any other time in the year. Smoking was permitted all day, not only in the regulation hour after meals, the radio was turned on before noon, and, as if this wasn't enough, the patients were issued with a bottle of beer apiece.

Sister was visiting each of the beds distributing presents from the tree, and two up-patients, dressing-gowned old gentlemen with a brace of alarming blood pressures, were dancing the highland fling in nurses' caps and aprons. Three or four of the students were steadfastly pursuing nurses with sprigs of mistletoe: the chase was not exacting.

As I entered the ward a giggling nurse ran out of the sluice-room followed by Tony Benskin, who had a look of intense eagerness on his face.

'That's enough, Mr Benskin!' she cried. 'You've had enough!'

Benskin pulled up as he caught sight of me.

'I thought you said you were coming early to test urine,' I remarked.

'One meets one's friends,' he explained simply. 'One must be social. After all, it's Christmas. Come in the sluice-room. I've got a bottle.'

I followed him in.

'And I thought you were scared of nurses.'

'Delightful creatures,' said Benskin, beaming. 'So refreshingly sex-starved.'

I noticed the gin bottle he had invited me to.

'Good God, Tony,' I said. 'Have you got through all that so early in the day?'

'It's Christmas, old boy.'

'Tony, you're sloshed already.'

'What of it? There's plenty more gin in the instrument cupboard. Grimsdyke hid it there yesterday. After all, it's Christmas. Have a drink.'

'All right. I suppose it's my party as much as yours.'

The gin in the instrument cupboard was finished by midday, when Dr Lionel Loftus appeared with his wife, and his two ugly daughters that were produced every Christmas-time like the decorations but without success. He got a hilarious reception.

'Here's the old Dean!' cried Benskin, leaping up on a bed. 'Three cheers for the Dean, boys! Three cheers for old Lofty! Three cheers for the jolly old Dean!'

The Dean stood, all smiles, in the doorway, while three cheers were given and the ward broke into 'For He's a Jolly Good Fellow'. He kissed Sister under the mistletoe, presented his housemen with a bottle of sherry, and shook hands with the patients. His own part in the programme was fairly simple: all he had to do was put on a chef's hat and carve the turkey in the middle of the ward. He was not good at carving and the last patients had a cold meal, which was the disadvantage of eating Christmas dinner on the medical side of the hospital. The surgeons were naturally more skilful, and Sir Lancelot Spratt had been known to slit a bird to ribbons in a couple of minutes.

During dinner Grimsdyke appeared. I was sitting on a bed with my arm round a nurse. Both of us were blowing squeakers.

'Hello, old boy,' Grimsdyke said in a worried tone. 'Merry Christmas and all that sort of thing. How are you feeling?'

'Fine; have a drink.'

'All the boys are pretty high, I suppose?'

'Of course. Benskin's as stiff as a plank.'

'Oh God! I hope he'll be all right to go on this afternoon.'

I put my squeaker down contritely.

'I'd clean forgotten about that! Perhaps we'd better go and see how he is.'

'Where's he got to?' Grimsdyke asked nervously.

The nurse told him. 'I saw him going into the sluice-room. He said he felt tired and wanted a rest.'

Benskin was resting when we found him. He was lying on the stone floor with his head against the base of the sink.

'Wake up! Wake up!' Grimsdyke commanded, with an anxious note in his voice. 'The show, man! We're due to start in half an hour!'

Benskin grunted.

'Oh Lord!' Grimsdyke said in despair. 'We'll never get him on the stage. . . . Tony! Benskin! Pull yourself together!'

Benskin opened his eyes fleetingly.

'Merry Christmas,' he muttered.

'Why not try an ice-pack on his head?' I suggested. 'Or an intravenous injection of vitamin C? It's supposed to oxidize the alcohol.'

'We'll try throwing water over him. It might be some use. Give me that measuring glass.'

We poured a pint of cold water over the ineffective actor; he lay dripping like a cherub on a fountain, but equally inactive.

'Let's hold him by the arms and legs and shake him,' I said.

'Do you think it would do any good?'

'It may do. Shock therapy is sometimes effective.'

Grimsdyke held Benskin's arms, and I took his feet. He was a heavy man, and we strained as we lifted him.

'Ready?' Grimsdyke asked. 'Right–one, two, three, shake.'

We were still shaking when the sluice-room door opened and Sister Prudence walked in.

'Hello!' she said. 'What's up?'

'Mr Benskin fainted,' Grimsdyke said quickly. 'I think the excitement was too much for him.'

Sister Prudence shot a diagnostic look at the patient. Her professional training enabled her to act swiftly and decisively when faced with an emergency.

'Nurse!' she called, starting to roll up her sleeves. 'Run down to the accident department and bring up the suicide box. Take your jacket off, Mr Grimsdyke. You can help me with the stomach pump.'

Benskin's stomach was washed out with bicarbonate solution, which was always kept handy to frustrate local suicides. He was given a cup of black coffee and a benzedrine tablet. By that time he maintained that he was ready to face his audience.

'It will be a pallid performance,' he admitted thickly. 'But at least I shall be on my feet.'

The show was due to open in Fortitude ward, on the male surgical side.

'Always test on men's surgical,' Grimsdyke said. 'Surgical patients are either well or dead. They don't hang about in the miserable twilight like medical ones. Besides, half the medical patients have got gastric ulcers, and who can feel jolly on Christmas Day after a poached egg and a glass of milk?'

Our troupe arrived made-up and in the costume of white flannels and shirts with green bow ties that Grimsdyke had ordered. The stage was improvised on the floor at one end of the ward out of the screens otherwise used to hide patients from their companions. Grimsdyke, who succeeded in looking smart in his flannels, worried his way round his indifferent actors like the headmistress at a kindergarten play.

'Are we ready to start?' he asked anxiously. 'Where's the piano?'

'It looks as if we've lost it somewhere,' I told him.

'It doesn't matter about the bloody piano,' John Bottle cut in. 'We've lost the beer as well.'

Grimsdyke and Bottle disappeared to find these two essential articles of stage furniture, while Harris muttered the words of Polly Perkins over to himself repeatedly, Sprogget stood in the corner with a look of painful concentration on his face talking like a three-year-old girl, and I rubbed red grease-paint into Benskin's white cheeks.

'What are you feeling like now?' I asked him.

'I often wondered what it was like to be dead,' he said. 'Now I know. Still, the show must go on. One cannot disappoint one's public.'

The piano, the actors, and the beer were collected on the same spot; the audience, who had been waiting uncomfortably on the floor, on the edge of beds, or leaning against the wall began a burst of impatient clapping.

'For God's sake!' said Grimsdyke frantically. 'Let's get going. Are you ready, Richard? What the hell are you doing underneath the piano?'

'I seem to have lost the music for the opening chorus,' I explained.

'Play any damn thing you like. Play the closing chorus. Play God Save the King.'

'I'll vamp.'

The screen representing the proscenium curtain was pushed aside, and the only presentation of Jest Trouble took the boards.

The performance was not a great success. It happened that Mr Hubert Cambridge, the surgeon in charge of Fortitude ward, had a desire to remove two hundred stomachs during the year and had approached Christmas in a flurry of gastrectomies. As the patients had not a whole stomach between them and each had suffered a high abdominal incision that made even breathing painful they were not a responsive and easy-laughing audience. The nurses, students, and doctors who made up the bulk of the house were already unsympathetic to the actors because of the long wait for the curtain to be pulled aside when they could have spent longer over their dinner. Only the cast, who (with the exception of Benskin) had been going strongly at the beer, thought themselves devilishly funny.

The opening chorus successfully defied the audience to make out a word of it, then Grimsdyke told a joke about a student and two nurses that extracted a languid round of clapping. The next item was Benskin's conjuring act. He appeared in a black cape and a tall magician's hat, and scored instant applause when, during his preliminary patter, John Bottle was seized with the idea of setting a match to its peak over the top of the backcloth. The hat blazed away for some seconds before Benskin realized what had happened and angrily put it out in a bowl of goldfish.

His proudest trick was pouring water from one jug to another and changing its colour in the transference; but his aim was not good that afternoon and at his first attempt most of the liquid slopped on to the ward floor.

'Nurse!' came an easily audible hiss from the back. It was Sister Fortitude. 'Go and clear up the mess that young man's making!'

A nurse with a mop picked her way through the audience and started swabbing round the performer's feet while he pretended that he, out of everybody else in the room, did not notice her. After that he angrily produced a string of flags out of a top hat and left the stage in a huff.

The rest of the performance was received by the audience with good-natured apathy. Harris made his appearance to sing Little Polly Perkins in a Harry Tate moustache, standing in front of Bottle, Sprogget, and Benskin, who joined in the choruses. Towards the end of the third verse a roar of laughter swept the audience. Harris felt the glow of success in his heart, and sang on lustily. When the laughter rose to a second peak a few seconds later he hesitated and glanced behind him. The cause of his reception was obvious at once. Benskin, finally overcome, had been suffering a sharp attack of hiccoughs before being sick in the corner of the stage. At that moment the lights fused, and no one thought it worth finishing the performance.

At Christmas-time came the few hours of every year that the official barrier between students and nurses was gingerly raised: there was a dance in the nurses' dining-hall which the young men were allowed to attend.

The dance disorganized life in the Virgins' Retreat for some weeks before the French chalk went down on the floor. Each nurse's escort was discussed in detail that would have been justified only if the young lady expected to remain in his arms for the rest of her life. Dresses were cleaned, repaired, and borrowed, and the probationers wept in front of their mirrors at the devastation already done to their figures by the carbohydrates in the hospital diet and the muscular exercise of nursing. On the evening of the dance the girls flew off duty eagerly, bathed, powdered, dressed, and scented themselves, and went down to meet their men under the marble eye of Florence Nightingale in the hall.

As I had no particular attachments in the hospital at the time I approached a gawky nurse on the ward called Footte and asked, with a smirk, if she would be my consort. She gave her gracious acceptance. Shortly afterwards I met Benskin in the courtyard.

'Are you going to the nurses' hop?' I asked him. 'I've just let myself in for taking the junior staff on Prudence.'

'You bet I am, old boy! Having recovered from the excesses of Christmas Day I shall be taking old Rigor Mortis along. It's the biggest party of the year.'

I was surprised.

'Is it? I thought it was a strictly teetotal affair.'

'And so it is. You don't imagine the Matron would allow liquor to befoul the chaste floors of the Virgins' Retreat, do you? It's as dry as a bishop's birthday. This has the effect of making everybody get a big enough glow on beforehand to last them the night, and results in some interesting spectacles.'

On the evening of the dance Benskin and I spent an hour of determined drinking with the Padre before crossing over to the Nurses' Home to meet our partners. Benskin immediately suggested a few scoops. 'Bad form to arrive too early, you know,' he explained to the girls. 'People think you want to hog all the sausage rolls.' The four of us went back to the King George, which was now full of young men and young women in evening dress taking prophylaxis against a dull evening. We settled ourselves at a corner of the bar. After some time Miss Footte started looking mistily at me and stroking the back of my neck; I noticed that even Rigor Mortis, who had an apparent amnesia about the incident in the flat, was becoming mildly animated.

The first time I looked at my watch it was after ten.

'It's getting on,' I said. 'Hadn't we better go?'

'Perhaps we'd better. Where's the Padre?' Benskin leaned over the bar counter. 'Padre! I say, how about a little this-and-that for the hip?' He handed a silver flask across the bar. 'There's a long way to go yet.'

'Certainly, sir! How about you, Mr Gordon? If I might advise you, sir, from my experience . . .'

'I'll have a bottle of gin,' I said. 'Can you put it on the slate until the New Year?'

'Of course, Mr Gordon. You get your allowance quarterly, don't you? Anything you like, sir.'

Arm in arm, all four, we went singing to the Nurses' Home.

The gaunt dining-hall was dripping with paper chains, and a five-piece band was stuck up on a tinsel-ringed dais in one corner. There was a Christmas tree, a running buffet on trestles, streamers, paper hats, Chinese lanterns, and all the standardized trappings of respectable jollity. On a stage at one end, opposite the band, there sat throughout the evening the Matron, in full uniform. Next to her, also uniformed, were the three sister tutors. Behind them were five or six of the senior sisters in a row, and the lot were separated by sandwiches and sausage rolls on small tables. They were a jury that was constantly forming unspoken verdicts. Very little escaped them. If a girl danced with too many men or too few it was remembered until the end of her training, and if she turned up in an off-the-shoulder gown she might as well have had 'Hussy' tattooed across her clavicles.

There was an interval between dances when we arrived. We pushed our way up to the buffet.

'Look at that!' Benskin said in disgust, pointing to a row of glass jugs. 'Lemonade!'

He reached across the table and picked up a half-full pitcher.

'I think we might stiffen this a little,' he continued, with a shifty glance over his shoulder towards the stage. 'Hold the jug, old boy, while I get my flask out.'

He tipped his flask of whisky into the drink and I added half my bottle of gin.

'That should be more like it,' Benskin said with satisfaction, stirring the mixture with a jelly spoon. 'Guaranteed to bring the roses to the cheeks. One sip, and never a dull moment afterwards.'

He was still stirring when Mike Kelly appeared at the table with one of the operating theatre nurses.

'Mind if we join the party, Tony?' he asked. 'I've got some rum in my pocket.'

'Put it in, old boy!' Benskin invited him. 'Nothing like a lemonade cocktail to get the party going. That's right, pour the lot in. You didn't have much left, anyway.'

'The best part of half a bottle!' Kelly said indignantly. 'It's all I've got, too.'

'Fear nothing,' Benskin said, stirring rapidly. 'I know of secret caches. Now! Let us taste the devil's brew.'

He poured a little in six glasses and we sipped it with some foreboding.

'It's strong,' Benskin admitted, gulping. 'Odd sort of taste. I suppose that rum was all right, Mike? You hadn't been palmed off with a bottle of hooch, had you?'

'Of course it was all right. I got it off the Padre.'

'Oh well, it must be the lemonade. Cheers, everyone.'

We had almost finished the jug when Harris pushed his way into the group.

'You dirty dogs!' he exclaimed angrily. 'You've pinched my blasted jug of lemonade! I had half a bottle of sherry and some crème de menthe in that, too!'

I did not remember much about the dance. Isolated incidents came back to me in flashes the next day, like fragments of a dream. I recalled two gentlemen doing the old-fashioned waltz with their partners, catching the tails of their coats together, and covering the floor with broken glass and the best part of two bottles of gin; other gentlemen overcome with the heat and having to be assisted to the fresh air; nurse Footte laughing so loudly in my arms I noticed her uvula waggling in the back of her throat, and my thinking how horrible it was. All the students were drunk, and the Matron, being unaware of such things, beamed and thought she was giving these high-spirited young men a great evening. The next morning, however, she democratically joined in cleaning the hall herself and was horrified to find a hundred and thirty empty spirit bottles tucked away in the potted palms, behind the curtains, in the seats of the sofas, and on top of the framed portraits of her predecessors in office.

The nurses' dance marked the end of the Christmas holiday at St Swithin's. Everyone knew that the next morning the operating theatres would start work again, new patients would be admitted, lectures would begin, and the students would troop round the bare and gloomy wards with their Chiefs. But that night it was still Christmas, and the hospital was alive with marauding students who leaped on the night nurses while they made cocoa in the ward kitchens. And they, dear girls, screamed softly (so as not to wake the patients) before surrendering themselves to their students' arms. After all, there had to be some compensations for being a nurse.

Chapter Twelve

In the New Year I began work in the out-patient department. It was my first contact with the hard routine of the general practitioner's surgery. In the wards the patients are scrubbed, combed, and undressed, and presented to the doctors in crisp sheets; but in out-patients' they came straight off the streets and examination is complicated by clothes, embarrassment, and sometimes the advisability of the medical attendant keeping his distance.

The department was the busiest part of the hospital. It was centred round a wide, high, green-painted hall decorated only by coloured Ministry of Health posters warning the populace against the dangers of spitting, refusing to have their babies inoculated, cooking greens in too much water, and indiscriminate love-making. There led off from the hall, on all sides, the assortment of clinics that it had been found necessary to establish to treat the wide variety of illnesses carried in through the doors every day. There were the big medical and surgical rooms, the gynaecological department and the ante-natal clinic, the ear, nose, and throat clinic, the fracture clinic, and a dozen others. The V.D. department was approached through discreet and unmarked entrances from the street; in one corner the infertility clinic and the birth control clinic stood next to one another; and at the other end of the hall were the shady confessionals of the psychiatrists.

On one side was a long counter, behind which four or five girls in white smocks sorted the case notes from their filing cabinets and passed them across to the patients with the carefully cultivated air of distaste mixed with suspicion employed by Customs men handing back passports. There were telephones in the middle of the hall for emergency calls, and, outside every clinic door, rows of wooden benches that looked as inviting to sit on as a line of tank-traps.

The department was run chiefly by the hospital porters. These were an invaluable body of men, without whom the work of the hospital would immediately have come to a standstill. They were experts at such common tasks beyond the ability of the doctors as directing patients to the correct departments, holding down drunks, putting on strait-jackets, dealing tactfully with the police, getting rid of unwanted relatives, and finding cups of tea at impossible hours. They stood, in their red and blue livery, inspecting with experienced Cockney shrewdness the humanity that daily passed in large numbers under their noses.

As soon as a patient entered the building he came up against a porter – a fat one sitting on a stool behind a high desk, like a sergeant in the charge-room of a police station.

'What's up, chum?' the porter demanded.

The patient would begin to mumble out his leading symptoms, but he would be cut short with 'Surgical, you', or 'Throat department', or the name of the appropriate clinic. The porters were the best diagnosticians in the hospital. They unerringly divided the cases into medical and surgical so that the patients arrived in front of the correct specialist. If a porter had made a mistake and consigned, for instance, a case of bronchitis to the surgical side, the complications that would have arisen and the disaster that might have overtaken the patient were beyond speculation.

After passing the porter the patient visited the counter to collect his case notes. St Swithin's kept faithful records of its visitors, and several residents of the district had been neatly represented by a green folder containing the obstetrical notes of his birth, an account of the removal of his tonsils, the surgical description of the repair of his hernias, a record of his mounting blood pressure, and details of the post-mortem following the final complaint that carried him off. Clutching his folder in one hand, he took his place at the end of the queue seated outside the door of his clinic. The queue shifted up the wooden seat as each patient was called inside by the stern-faced nurse at the door: the movement was slow and spasmodic, like the stirrings of a sleepy snake.

For the first half-hour the patient amused himself by reading carefully through his folder of confidential notes, comparing in his mind what the doctors had written about him with what they told him to his face. After a while this became boring, so he read the morning paper. When he had exhausted the paper, he passed the remainder of the time in clinical discussion with his neighbours. This was the most attractive part of the visit, and a pleasure he had been storing up for himself.

Discussion of one's illness with neighbours on the bench was done with pride: the patients wore their symptoms like a row of campaign medals.

'Wot you in for, cock?' he began to the man next to him.

''Art trouble,' was the reply, delivered with gloomy zest.

'Anyfink else?'

'That's enough, ain't it?' replied the neighbour sharply. ''Ow about you?'

'The doctor says I am a walking pathological museum.' The patient rolled the syllables off his tongue deliberately.

'Go on!'

'I've got diabetes mellitus, 'emeroids, normocytic anaemia, chronic bronchitis and emphysema, 'ammer toe, cholecystitis, and an over-active thyroid.'

'That's a packet, all right,' his neighbour admitted grudgingly.

'And I 'eard 'im say I've got a positive Wasserman, too!' he added in triumph.

''Ave you 'ad any operations?' inquired a thin woman on the other side of him in a voice rich with misery.

'Not to date, touch wood, I 'aven't.'

The woman gave a loud sigh.

'I wish as I could say the same,' she remarked, shaking her head sadly.

''Ow many 'ave you 'ad, missus?' asked the patient, anxious over his own record.

'Fifteen,' she told him, in tones of exquisite martyrdom.

'Coo! I'm glad I 'aven't got your complaint.'

'That's the trouble. They don't know wot's wrong with me. The last time they took out my colon. The doctor said it was the worst they'd ever 'ad in the 'ospital. Took them four and a 'arf hours, it did. Then they 'ad to leave some of it behind. I'm lucky to be 'ere now, if you ask me.'

'Must have been a bad do,' the patient said, respectful of such exuberant pathology.

'Bad do! I was left to die four times!'

''Oo's your doctor, missus?'

'Mr Cambridge. Wot a lovely man! 'E's got such soft 'ands.'

I soon discovered another peculiarity of out-patient work. In the wards the patients are all ill: in out-patients' they are nearly all healthy. Men and women with organic disease formed a small fraction of the hundreds who came past the fat porter at the door every day. Most of them complained of vague aches and pains that they had been trotting up to the surgeries of their own doctors for several months, and they, poor men, had got rid of them temporarily by handing them a note to St Swithin's. This was an example of an established medical practice known as snag-shifting, which went on just as actively in St Swithin's itself.

The most usual condition in out-paients' was headache, which was slightly more common than troubles of the poor feet, giddy spells, the rheumatics, and insomnia ('Not a wink for forty years, Doctor'). Most of the symptoms were manifestly incompatible with life if they had existed, but every patient had to be investigated in case something sinister lay beneath. This provided an excellent opportunity for snag-shifting. A persistent patient with headaches could, with a few strokes of the pen, be transferred to the eye department. It simply needed the houseman to scribble 'Headaches. Any eye signs?' on the notes and the patient moved to another queue outside another doctor's door. After the eye department had found nothing and were tired of the fellow appearing in front of them week after week they sent him to the throat clinic. The throat surgeons usually operated on all their patients and would probably remove his tonsils or the inside of his sinuses; when he continued to attend with his headaches afterwards, they would pack him off to the general surgeons with the suggestion his complaint was the result of sepsis lurking in his gall-bladder, kidney, or some other organ comfortably outside their province. The surgeons might operate or not, according to the length of their waiting-list at the time; whatever happened, after a few more visits to out-patients' he would find himself having all his teeth out in the dental section, who packed him off afterwards to the physiotherapy department in case the headaches–which continued–were due to disfunction of the neck muscles. From the physiotherapy department the patient went as a last resort to the psychiatrists, and as they were then unable to transfer him to anyone he probably continued to visit them and talk about his headaches once a week for the remainder of his life.

While I was working in out-patients' the hospital authorities installed a bar for tea and buns in the hall to break the tedium of the long wait. The regular patients were delighted, and showed their appreciation by spending as many of their afternoons as they could enjoying a medical tea-party with their fellow sufferers.

'Times have changed,' one of the old porters said gloomily, looking at the girl distributing cups of tea from the new counter. 'None of this 'ere nonsense in the old days. Mollycoddling, I call it.'

He wistfully described the routine of forty years ago. The patients had to be inside the building and seated at the benches by eight o'clock every morning. Then the doors were locked and anyone coming late had no alternative than to wait until the next day. The consultant arrived at nine, and strode to his room accompanied by a senior porter. When the doctor had settled himself in his chair the porter went to the door and shouted: 'Nah then! All them with coughs, stand up!' A handful of patients came to their feet and shuffled into the room. When they had been seen the porter returned and commanded: 'Stomach pains, diarrhoea, and flatulence!' The possessors of these alimentary disorders filed before the doctor while the porter marshalled the chronic cases who had come simply for a new bottle of medicine. The patients found the system convenient, and it was abolished only when the senior physician left for Harley Street after a remarkably heavy morning treating chest symptoms and found a stall outside the hospital from which was being sold 'Genuine St Swithin's Cough Mixture'. This was bought off the patients for twopence and retailed to the public by the stallkeeper at sixpence a bottle.

We each spent two days a week in the accident room, where I began to feel I was at least learning a little medicine by discovering how to put a bandage on without dropping it on the floor, to sew up cuts, to remove foreign bodies from eyes, and to apply a kaolin poultice. A pair of us were obliged to sleep once a week in a couple of bunks in a small room by the accident entrance, to attend the minor injuries that trickled in unendingly during the night. This system was nearly the end of Tony Benskin. In his wanderings round the sleeping hospital he had met, and taken a fancy to, one of the night nurses, and turned himself into a red-eyed wreck all day by sitting most of the night in her company.

The conditions in a ward at night are admittedly lightly aphrodisiac. The nurse sits alone at one end of the long room, which melts away on each side into shadows and is illuminated only by a single red-shaded lamp on the desk in front of her. The soft warm light makes her as desirable as a ripe peach. There is not much room at the desk, so the student and nurse sit close together. To avoid disturbing the patients they must whisper, which turns every remark into an intimacy. They are the only two awake in a sleeping world and they draw together with a tingling sense of isolation.

The nurse mixes the student a milk drink from the patients' night rations. It is surprising what can occur in such conditions over a couple of cups of

Horlicks. Their knees touch under the desk; their hands brush together in a determined accident; their fingers entwine and they sweat into one another's palms until the night sister is due on her rounds. The student pours soft endearments over the girl like treacle on a pudding, though his technique is sometimes ruined by his being interrupted in a delicate submission to her charms by a rough voice from the nearest bed demanding 'Can I 'ave the bedpan please, nurse?'

Benskin's romance might have ended harmlessly if it had not been for a lapse on the last night of our appointment. We were on duty together, and to celebrate the end of the session we persuaded the casualty nurse to do our work and spent the evening in the King George. At closing time Benskin rushed to see his night nurse, while I flopped into bed.

Just after three I was shaken awake. Automatically I reached for my trousers, thinking it was the porter demanding my attendance in the accident room: but it was Benskin. He was in a pitiful state.

'Old man!' he said urgently. 'You've got to help me! Something terrible's happened!'

I tried to concentrate on the disaster.

'What's up?' I asked sleepily.

'You know that girl up in the ward–Molly. Remember, the one I've been popping up to see?'

'Umm.'

'Well–listen, old man, don't go to sleep for God's sake! Tonight I nipped up to see her as usual, and I was brimming over a bit with the old joys of spring and so forth owing to being full of beer . . .'

'Disgusting.'

'. . . and Christ Almighty, before I knew where I was I'd proposed to the bloody woman!'

I tried to clear sleep and alcohol out of my eyes, like soapsuds.

'Did she accept?' I asked, yawning.

'Accept! She said "Yes, please," as far as I remember. Don't you realize what's happened? Can't you see the gravity of the situation?'

'Perhaps she'll have forgotten by the morning,' I suggested hopefully.

'Not on your life! You know what these women are–at night nurses' breakfast it'll be a case of "Guess what, girls! Tony Benskin proposed to me at last and we're going to be married in May!" Oh God, oh God?' He clasped his head. 'It'll be all round the hospital by nine o'clock.'

'I gather you're not keen on the idea of marrying her?'

'Me! Married! Can you see it?' he exclaimed.

I nodded my head understandingly and propped myself up on an elbow.

'This needs some thought.'

'How right you are!'

'Surely there must be something you can do . . . can't you go back and explain it was all in fun?'

Benskin gave a contemptuous laugh.

'You go,' he said.

'I see your point. It's tricky. Let's think in silence.'

After about twenty minutes I had an idea. I criticized it to myself carefully and it seemed sound.

'I think I've got the answer,' I said, and explained it to him.

He leapt to his feet, shook me warmly by the hand, and hurried back to the ward.

The solution was a simple one. I sent Benskin round to propose to every night nurse in the hospital.

Chapter Thirteen

The clock on the lecture-room wall crept towards ten past four: the Professor of Pathology had overrun his time again.

It was a gloomy, overcast afternoon at the beginning of April. The lights were reflected from the brown varnish on the walls in dull yellow pools. The windows just below the ceiling were, as usual, shut tight, and the air was narcotic. The students packing the tiers of uncomfortable benches were sleepy, annoyed at being kept late, and waiting for their tea.

The Professor was unconscious of the passage of time, the atmosphere in the room, or the necessity for food and drink. He was a thin little white-haired man with large spectacles who was standing behind his desk talking enthusiastically about a little-known variety of louse. Lice were the Professor's life. For thirty years they had filled his thoughts during the day and spilled into his dreams at night. He had, at points during that time, married and raised five children, but he was only faintly aware of these occurrences. The foreground of his mind was filled by lice. He spent his time in his own small laboratory on the top floor of the hospital wholly occupied in studying their habits. He rarely came near his students. He left the teaching to his assistants and considered he had done his share by occasionally wandering round the students' laboratory, which he did with the bemused air of a man whose wife has invited a lot of people he doesn't know to a party. He insisted, however, on giving to each class a series of lectures on his speciality. He was the greatest authority on lice in the world, and when he lectured to other pathologists in Melbourne, Chicago, Oslo, or Bombay, men would eagerly cross half a continent to hear him. But the students of his own hospital, who had only the effort of shifting themselves out of the sofas in the common room, came ungracefully and ungratefully, and found it all rather boring.

As the lecturer droned on, describing the disproportionately complicated sexual habits of an obscure species of louse, the students glanced sullenly at the clock, shuffled their feet, yawned, folded up their notebooks, put away their pens, and lolled in their seats. Some of the class started chatting to their neighbours or lit their pipes and read the evening paper as comfortably as if they were sitting in their own lodgings. From the back row came a subdued stamping of feet on the wooden floor–the students' only means of retaliation on their lecturers. But the Professor had by now forgotten the presence of his audience and if we had all marched out into the fresh air or set the lecture theatre on fire he would have noticed it only dimly.

I was sitting at the back with Tony Benskin and Sprogget. Benskin always took a place as far back as he could, for some lecturers had the unpleasant habit of asking questions of students who were dreamily inspecting the ceiling and at a distance it was possible to give the impression of overpowering concentration even if asleep. It was also convenient for making an exit unobtrusively when the lecturer became insupportably boring. Attendance at lectures was compulsory at St Swithin's, and a board was passed round the benches for each student to record his presence by signing it. This led to everyone in the medical school rapidly becoming competent in forgery, so that the absence of a friend could easily be rectified. This unselfish practice diminished after the Dean counted the students at his own lecture and found not only that thirty-odd men were represented by ninety signatures but that some of the absentees had in their enthusiasm forgetfully signed the board in different places four times.

The Professor had left me behind some time ago. I was cleaning my nails, letting my thoughts wander pleasantly to the comfortable drone of the lecturer's voice. Unfortunately, in their wanderings they stumbled across a topic I wished they could have avoided.

'I say, Tony,' I asked softly. 'I suppose you couldn't lend me three or four quid, could you?'

Benskin laughed–so loudly that men in the three rows in front of him turned round.

'I thought not,' I said. 'All the same, it's damned difficult. Now we've started the path. course I've got to have my microscope back. While we were in the wards it was perfectly all right for it to lodge in Goldstein's window, but if I don't get it soon I shan't be able to do the practical classes at all.'

'I sympathize,' Benskin said. 'Have no doubts about that. My own instrument is at present locked in the coffers of Mr Goldstein's rival down the road, and I see no prospect of recovering it from the clutches of said gentleman at all. The old money-bags are empty. For weeks now I've had to wait outside the bank until the manager goes to lunch before cashing a cheque.'

My microscope was an easy way of raising ready money; I could pawn it without inconvenience when broke and reclaim it the moment my allowance came in. But I had recently piled up so many other commitments that this simple system had broken down. My tastes had altered expensively since I first arrived at St Swithin's, though my allowance had stayed much the same. Then I smoked a little, drank hardly at all, and never went out with girls; now I did all three together.

'The funny thing is, old man,' said Benskin when the Professor had exhausted the educational qualities of lice, 'that I was just thinking of putting the leeches on you for a quid or so. The cost of living is extremely high with me at the moment. I suppose there really is no possiblity of a small loan?'

'None at all.'

'I must raise a little crinkly from somewhere. Surely one of the students has a couple of bob he can jingle in his pocket?'

'You can try Grimsdyke,' I suggested. 'He usually has a bit left over for his friends.'

Benskin frowned. 'Not since he got married, old boy. The little woman takes a dim view of the stuff being diverted from the housekeeping to the pockets of old soaks. No, there's nothing for it–it's a case of bashing the old dishes again.'

All of us had recurrent bouts of insolvency, and each had his favourite way of raising enough money to pay his debts. Dishwashing by the night was the most popular way of earning small sums, as it did not interfere with classes, it could be taken up with notice, and the big hotels and restaurants in

London paid comparatively well for a few hours spent in the still-room. Baby-sitting was Sprogget's speciality, and John Bottle occasionally brought home a few pounds from the Tote or by winning the waltz competition at an Oxford Street palais. But Benskin sometimes overspent himself so much that more settled employment had to be found. One afternoon during a time when he was suffering a severe attack of poverty he appeared in the students' common room in his best blue serge suit, with his shoes brightly polished, his hair neat, a white handkerchief smartly in his pocket, and a plain peaked cap in his hand.

'What on earth are you doing?' Grimsdyke asked. 'Playing bus conductors?'

Benskin beamed at him.

'Not a bit, old boy. I've got a job for a couple of weeks. A damn smart move on my part it was.'

'A job? What sort of job? More dishwashing, I suppose?'

'Private chauffeur,' Benskin told him proudly. 'In a Rolls, too. I'll tell you what happened. I was up at out-patients' this morning when a fellow came in with the most horrible gastric ulcer I've seen. He had to leave off work at once, of course, and when he told me his job was chauffeur to an old bird with bags of oof who makes jam or something I saw ways of relieving the old exchequer. Do you follow me? I nipped smartly round to the old boy's house in Hampstead and told him the bad news in person–very impressively, too. I then explained the situation in a few words, and offered humble self to fill the gap in his household.

'It so happened that the old chum and his missus are due to start a fortnight's holiday touring Scotland tomorrow, which would have been squashed by the chauffeur's ulcers if I hadn't presented myself as a worthy alternative. I got all this from the patient of course, but I didn't let on and gave the impression that I could tear myself away from my valuable studies just so the old folk wouldn't miss their nice restful holiday. He seemed a decent old cove and was very upset about his old chauffeur, but he has no more idea of driving a car himself than working a railway engine. So my offer was gratefully accepted.'

'Have you got a licence?' I asked him.

'Of course,' he replied in a hurt tone. 'For almost a month now.'

Benskin disappeared the following morning. After four days he reappeared in the hospital. He had lost his cap, his best suit was torn and covered with oil, one of his shoes was ripped, and he was still broke.

'Well?' I said.

'One meets snags,' Benskin replied in a subdued voice. 'All was well to begin with. The old jam merchant was a great believer in the quiet life, and we trundled gently out of Town to Doncaster. They put me up in the servants' quarters of the local hostelry, where I met a hell of a nice little piece among the chambermaids–however, that will do for later. The next day I drove in an exemplary fashion to Newcastle, by which time I could see that the old couple had invested plenty of confidence in Benskin, whom they looked upon as a clean and careful driver.'

'What happened after Newcastle?' Grimsdyke asked resignedly.

'That's where the rot set in. I'd driven all that bloody way without a drink, as I left London flat broke. At Newcastle I touched the old boy for a quid, and when we stopped for lunch at some old-world boozer on the road I sneaked round the back and downed a few scoops. This would have been all right, but the old chum decided he wanted a stroll to look at the local countryside and left me among the lackeys in the servants' hall or whatever it is. I met a most amusing type there–an Irish porter who had started off life studying divinity at Trinity. We had a lot to talk about–bobbing back scoops all the time, of course. I set off with my customers about four o'clock, but regret to say I only made about a hundred yards. After that I piled the crate up in a ditch. I didn't hurt myself, luckily, but now the old couple are languishing in the local cottage hospital with a fractured femur apiece.'

He added that he did not see much chance of the engagement being renewed.

To retrieve my microscope I washed dishes with Tony Benskin in a West End hotel for a couple of nights and sold some of my textbooks. I was then content to return to academic life, but Benskin was aflame to increase his savings by trying his hand at another trade.

'Do you see that notice?' he asked eagerly as we left the staff entrance of the hotel in the early morning. '"Extra waiters wanted. Apply Head Waiter." That's an idea, isn't it?'

'No,' I said. 'I'm going to spend a few nights in bed. Besides, I don't know anything about waiting. And neither do you.'

Benskin lightly brushed these objections aside.

'There's nothing to it, old man. Anyone can dish up a bit of fish. It's money for nothing, if you ask me. And the tips! Think of the tips. At a swep-up joint like this the customers don't slip threepenny bits under the plate when they swig down the remains of their brandy and wipe the caviare off their lips. I've been waited on quite long enough to grasp the technique–if you want a fat tip it's only a matter of handing out the soup with a look of haughty distaste on your face.'

'You think you could look haughty, do you?'

'One is a gentleman,' Benskin replied stiffly. 'I'm going to stay behind and have a word with this head waiter chap.'

'I'm going home to bed. We've got to appear at a lecture in five hours' time.'

'All right. See you later.'

I was dropping off to sleep when Benskin got back to Bayswater. He was jubilant.

'A push-over, old boy!' he said. 'I saw the head waiter–a nasty piece of work he was, too. However, he took one look at me and said to himself "Benskin's the man! He'll raise the tone in the dining-room all right."'

'So you got the job?'

'Starting tonight. I'll just have time to nip away from the hospital, get my evening clothes out, and appear as the Jeeves of the chafing dish.'

'I suppose they know at the hotel that you have had no experience of waiting at all?'

'Well, no, not exactly. I saw no reason for putting obstacles in my own way, so I gave the impression I had dished it out at some of the larger doss-houses around Town, with summer sessions on the coast. They seem pretty hard-up for fish-flingers at the moment, as they took me at my word.'

'Well,' I said, turning over. 'Don't forget to wear a black tie.'

When I reached the flat after work that evening Benskin was in a high state of excitement.

'Must get the old soup and fish out,' he said, hauling his battered tin trunk from the top of the wardrobe. 'I pinched a bottle of ether from the theatre this afternoon to get the stains out.'

Benskin's tail suit had been bought for him by his father when he was sixteen. Since then he had greatly increased in size in all directions. We all worked hard to straighten out the creases with John Bottle's travelling iron, while Benskin rubbed hard at the lapels to remove the grease.

'I must have been a dirty little devil at table,' he reflected.

'Some moths have been having a go at it down here,' I said, pointing to the trousers.

'That doesn't matter,' Benskin replied testily. 'I'm only the bloody waiter, anyway.'

He put the clothes on. By lowering the braces as far as he dared the trousers could be made to cover the upper part of his ankles; the braces themselves, which were red and yellow, only remained invisible behind the lapels of the coat when he remembered not to breathe too deeply. The sleeves came as far as the mid-forearm, and the top buttons of the trousers had to be reinforced with safety-pins. But it was the shirt that presented an apparently insoluble difficulty. It was tight, and the buttonholes were worn; even the shallowest of respirations caused the studs to pop out and expose a broad strip of hairy, pink, sweaty chest.

'Quite enough to put the people off their meal,' John Bottle remarked.

We tried using bigger studs and brass paper-fasteners, but, if Benskin wished to continue to breathe, the shirt was unwearable. Even strips of sticking-plaster inside the stiff front were not strong enough to withstand the pressure of his inhalations. For half an hour we worked hard at the infuriating gap while the shirt-front became limp under our fingers.

'For God's sake!' Benskin exclaimed angrily. 'Isn't there anything we can do about it? Look at the time! If I'm not there in twenty minutes I've had it. Surely one of you fellows has got a stiff shirt to lend me?'

'What! Your size?' Bottle asked.

'Why the devil didn't I think of buying a dickey!'

I had an idea.

'Let us apply the first principles of surgery,' I said.

'What the hell are you getting at now?'

'Supposing you have tension on a surgical incision. What do you do? Why, make a counter-incision, of course, in a site where it doesn't matter. Take your jacket off, Tony.'

A quick rip with the scissors up the length of the shirt-back from the tail to the collar and Benskin was once again the perfect English gentleman. He left the flat in high spirits, convinced that he would make enough in the evening to keep him in drinks for a fortnight. Unhappily he was no better at serving hot soup than at driving a car and was dismissed by the furious maître d'hôtel between the fish and the entrée.

Chapter Fourteen

'B.I.D.,' I said. 'Brought in dead. What an epitaph!'

I was standing in the cold, bright post-mortem room on the top floor of the hospital. It was a large room with a glass roof, tiles round the walls, three heavy porcelain tables, and one side made up of a bank of numbered metal drawers like the front of a large filing cabinet. The unfortunate patients were brought by the cheery-looking fellow on his trolley to a special lift, taken to the roof, and packed away neatly in the refrigerated drawers. Each corpse bore a label giving the name, religion, and diagnosis, but the man on the table in front of me had only the three letters on his tab. He had been picked up in the street by the police a few hours before and brought futilely to the accident room.

I pulled the heavy rubber gloves tight and began my incision with the big post-mortem knife. I never liked doing post-mortems. They made me feel sick. However, under the medical school regulations I was required to perform three of them, so I had to get on with it.

Every morning at twelve the physicians and surgeons came up to the room to see their unsuccessful cases demonstrated by the heartless pathologist. Often they had been right in life, and had the satisfaction of feeling with their fingers the lesion they had built up in their imagination from examination of the body surface, deduction, and studying the black and grey shadows on X-ray films. Occasionally they were humbled.

'So there *was* a tumour of the cerebellum after all!' I once heard Dr Malcolm Maxworth exclaim, going red in the face. 'Damn it, damn it, damn it!'

Maxworth was not angry on the dead patient's behalf: it was simply that in the daily contest between his mind and the tricks of the body the body had for once won a game.

Our afternoons were spent wandering round the dusty pathology museum inspecting the grotesque specimens in the big glass jars of spirit. They had everything in the St Swithin's museum, from two-headed babies to tattoo marks. Each specimen was neatly labelled and numbered, and a clinical history of the case was set out on a card attached to the bottle. 'How much better than a tombstone!' Grimsdyke said as he read the last dramatic illness of John O'Hara in 1927 and held the remains of his ruptured aneurism in his hand. 'I suppose everyone wants to be remembered somehow. What could be better than giving a bit of yourself to the pathologists? Nobody knows or cares where this fellow's grave is, but his memory is kept fresh in here almost daily. A whopping aneurism! I bet it caused a panic in the ward when it burst.'

Twice a week during the three-month pathology course we had classes in forensic medicine. This was a subject that fascinated me, because I was a conscientious reader of detective stories and took delight in the realization that I too now knew how to distinguish human blood from animal's, compare bullet wounds, and differentiate murder from suicide. The lecturer was a portly, genial man whose picture appeared fairly regularly in the Sunday papers inspecting the scene of all the more attractive crimes. We learnt from him the favourite ways of committing suicide, abortion, homicide, and rape: the lecture on the last subject, which was illustrated with lantern slides, was the only one I can remember when I couldn't find a seat.

After the pathology course we began a round of the special departments, spending a few weeks in each. I was sent to learn a little about eyes and then to the throat surgeons, where I learned how to look into ears, up noses, and down throats. The E.N.T. clinic was busy from early morning until long after the others had finished at night, for the London atmosphere silted up patients' sinuses and roughened their lungs. 'That stuff's really irrespirable,' said the surgeon, flinging his arm in the direction of the window. 'Thank God I live in the country.' He was a big, brusque, overworked man who had nevertheless extracted a fortune from the respiratory damage caused by London air. He was supposed to be the fastest remover of tonsils and adenoids in the country, which he did every Thursday afternoon in out-patients', passing the anaesthetized children through his hands with the efficiency of a Chicago pig-killer.

After the throat department I was glad to sink into the restful atmosphere of the skin clinic. This was run by two very old and very gentlemanly specialists who conversed with each other, the students, the nurses, and the patients in whispers. They were both formally dressed in expensive suits, and each arrived at the hospital with a Rolls and a chauffeur. I had not expected such opulence and satisfied tranquillity from dermatologists, but on reflection it struck me that diseases of the skin were the most agreeable of all to specialize in. They are quiet, undramatic affairs which never get you up in the middle of the night nor interrupt your meals. The patients never die, but on the other hand they never seem to get better. A private patient, once diagnosed, is therefore a regular source of income to his doctor for the rest of his long life.

I still lived in the flat in Bayswater with Benskin and Bottle. Archie Broom and Mike Kelly had qualified and left, and we had been joined by Sprogget and Evans.

One evening after supper Bottle leant back in his chair and said, 'What shall we do tonight? Could you take a flick, anyone?'

'There's nothing on much,' said Tony in a bored voice. 'We might pop out for a pint a bit later.'

'I've got a novel to finish,' Evans said. 'It's got to go back to the library by the sixteenth. What's the date today, John?'

Bottle picked up the calendar from the mantelpiece. 'The fourteenth,' he said. He frowned. 'I say, do you chaps realize it is exactly five weeks today to our finals?'

'What!' Benskin jumped up in his chair. 'It can't be. They're not till the end of October.'

'Well, this is the middle of September.'

'Good God!' said Sprogget nervously. 'We shall have to start doing some work.'

Bottle put the calendar back.

'I'm afraid you're right. I've hardly looked at a book since we came out of the anatomy rooms. We've had a bloody good holiday, and now we've got to pay for it.'

Benskin, who believed in making his unpleasant decisions swiftly, immediately picked up a copy of Price's *Practice of Medicine* from the bookshelf and wiped the dust off the cover with his sleeve.

'At least that settles our evening for us,' he said. 'From now on it's a case of burning the old midnight oil. Good Heavens! Is there all this on tuberculosis?'

Our evenings afterwards were swiftly blown away in a gale of industry. We collected up our dusty books from the floor, the chairs, and the back of the cupboards, and left them in heaps, open, on the table. As soon as we returned from our work in the hospital we started reading. We ate bread and cheese when we felt like it and took caffeine and benzedrine tablets to keep awake. We worked past midnight, sometimes until four in the morning, cramming three years' study into thirty-five nights.

Each of us developed a favourite attitude for concentration. I found I could learn best sitting on a hard chair with my elbows on the table; Benskin was apparently able to absorb knowledge comfortably only if he removed his collar, tie, shoes, belt, and socks and stuck his large pink feet on the mantelpiece. Bottle preferred to take his textbook and sit alone in the lavatory, and Sprogget would pace nervously up and down the narrow hallway repeating under his breath the signs and symptoms of innumerable diseases and giggling grotesquely when he couldn't remember them. Only Evans passed the pre-examination stage in tranquillity. His mind was so efficient he found it necessary to do no more than loll in an armchair and read gently through his textbooks as though they were the Sunday papers.

For an hour or so we would work without speaking, filling the room with tobacco smoke. But it was a thin, taut silence, like the skin of an inflated balloon. Benskin was usually the first to break it.

'What the hell's the dose of digitalis?' he asked angrily one night.

'Six grains eight-hourly for three doses, followed by three grains three times a day for two days, and half that dose four times daily for two days,' I replied brightly.

'I'm sure that's not right,' he said. 'It's somewhere round two grains a day.'

'Of course it's right!' I barked at him. 'I've only just learnt it.'

'Richard's right,' said Evans quietly from his chair.

'All right, all right! Don't fly off about it. I haven't got as far as digitalis yet, anyway.'

Sprogget's head appeared at the door.

'Is a presystolic murmur at the apex diagnostic of mitral stenosis?' he asked anxiously.

'Yes,' Evans said.

'Oh damn! I didn't think it was.' He looked as if he was going to burst into tears. 'I'm bound to fail, I know I am!' he exclaimed.

'You'll be all right,' Benskin told him gruffly. 'It's nervous types like me who'll come down. Do you get cyanosis in pneumonia?'

We took one night a week off: on Saturday we all went out and got drunk. The rest of the time we were irritable with each other, uncommunicative, and jumpy. Benskin's usual sunny good humour seemed to have left him for ever. He scowled at his companions, complained about everything in the flat, and developed the symptoms of a gastric ulcer.

The grim period of study and Benskin's bad temper were relieved by only one incident before the examination. One Sunday night the famous helmet disappeared from the King George. No one knew who had taken it and no one had seen it go: it had simply vanished from its hook some time during the evening. The theft made Benskin furious, particularly as he had reason to suspect the students from Bart's, whom St Swithin's had beaten soundly earlier on in the year in the inter-hospitals' rugby cup. The next night he took himself off to Smithfield and climbed over the venerable walls of that ancient institution. He didn't find the helmet, but he put his foot through a window and was asked to leave by a porter. His foray came to the ears of the Dean of St Swithin's, who called him to his office, abused him soundly for ten minutes, and fined him three guineas. The Dean could not appreciate at all Benskin's plea that the loss of the helmet justified such strong action. Whether this had any connexion with an event that occurred shortly afterwards and established itself for ever in the hospital tradition with the title of the Dean's Tea Party was never known. Benskin was suspected, and there was a rumour that he had been spotted coming out of a small printer's in the City: but there was never any proof.

A few days after his interview with Benskin the Dean entered his office to find his personal secretary rummaging through his desk.

'Hello!' he said. 'Lost something?'

'Not exactly, sir,' she said, giving him a worried look. 'I was just wondering why I hadn't seen the invitations.'

'Invitations? What invitations?'

'To your At Home tomorrow,' she replied simply. 'The phone's been ringing all morning. The Deans of all the other hospitals in London have been through to say that the notice is a little short but they will be glad to come for cocktails in the library. There have been some people from the Medical Research Council, too, and a professor from Birmingham.' She looked at a pencilled list in her hand. 'About thirty have accepted so far, and there looks like a good many more have arrived by the second post.'

The Dean hurled his hat on the floor.

'It's an outrage!' he shouted in fury. 'It's a disgrace! It's a . . . ! By God, these bloody students! By God, I'll punish them for this! You just wait and see!' He poked a quivering finger at her so forcefully she leapt back with a little squeal.

'You mean–it's a hoax?' she asked timidly.

'Of course it's a hoax! It's these damn hooligans we've been giving the best years of our lives trying to educate! Send me the School Secretary! And the Professor of Medicine! Get me the Head Porter! Ring up all those people and tell them the thing's a damnable practical joke!'

'What, all of them?'

'Of course, woman! You don't think I'm going to be made a fool of by my own students, do you? Get on to them at once!'

At that moment the phone rang again. She picked it up.

'Hello . . .' she said. 'Yes, he's here now. Certainly. One moment please.'

She turned to the Dean. 'The Lord Mayor's Secretary,' she exclaimed. 'He says the Lord Mayor would be delighted.'

The Dean fell into his armchair like a knocked-out boxer.

'Very well,' he groaned. 'Very well, I know when I'm beaten. Get me those catering people, whats-is-names, instead.'

The party was a great success. Although the Dean entered the library black with anger he found himself in the middle of so many of his distinguished contemporaries that he mellowed rapidly. Didn't the leading heart specialist in the country grip him by the arm and tell him how much he appreciated his latest paper? Didn't the Lord Mayor himself hint of a donation towards the new library, and, more important, ask for an appointment in Harley Street? Besides, he had quickly seen to it that the expenses would be borne by the Governors. He said a genial good-bye to his last guests as they climbed into their cars in the courtyard. Suddenly he saw Benskin, with his hands in his pockets, grinning at him from the shadow of Lord Larrymore's statue. The Dean's face twisted malignantly.

'Do you know anything about this, damn you?' he demanded.

'Me, sir?' Benskin asked innocently. 'Not at all, sir. I think it may have been someone from Bart's.'

Chapter Fifteen

To a medical student the final examinations are something like death: an unpleasant inevitability to be faced sooner or later, one's state after which is determined by the care spent in preparing for the event.

The examinations of the United Hospitals Committee are held twice a year in a large dingy building near Harley Street. It shares a hidden Marylebone square with two pubs, a sooty caged garden, an antique shop, and the offices of a society for retrieving fallen women. During most of the year the square is a quiet and unsought thoroughfare, its traffic made up by patrons of the pubs, reclaimed women, and an unhappy looking man in sandals who since 1931 has passed through at nine each morning carrying a red banner saying 'REPENT FOR YE DIE TOMORROW'. Every six months this orderly quiet is broken up like a road under a pneumatic drill. Three or four hundred students arrive from every hospital in London and from every medical school in the United Kingdom. Any country that accepts a British qualification is represented. There are brown, bespectacled Indians, invariably swotting until the last minute from Sir Leatherby Tidy's fat and invaluable *Synopsis of Medicine*; jet-black gentlemen from West Africa standing in nervous groups and testing their new fountain-pens; fat, coffee-coloured Egyptians discussing earnestly in their own language fine points of erudite medicine; hearty Australians, New Zealanders, and South Africans showing no more anxiety than if they were waiting for a pub to open; the whole diluted thoroughly by a mob of pale, fairly indifferent, untidy-looking British students conversing in accents from the Welsh valleys to Stirlingshire.

An examination is nothing more than an investigation of a man's knowledge, conducted in a way that the authorities have found to be the most fair and convenient to both sides. But the medical student cannot see it in this light. Examinations touch off his fighting spirit; they are a straight contest between himself and the examiners, conducted on well-established rules for both, and he goes at them like a prize-fighter.

There is rarely any frank cheating in medical examinations, but the candidates spend almost as much time over the technical details of the contest as they do learning general medicine from their textbooks. We found the papers set for the past ten years in the hospital library, and the five of us carefully went through the questions.

'It's no good wasting time on pneumonia, infant diarrhoea, or appendicitis,' Benskin said. 'They were asked last time. I shouldn't think it's worth learning about T.B. either, it's come up twice in the past three years.'

We all agreed that it was unnecessary to equip ourselves with any knowledge of the most frequent serious illnesses we would come across in practice.

'I tell you what we *ought* to look up,' said Evans. 'Torulosis.'

'Never heard of it,' Benskin said.

'It's pretty rare. But I see that old Macready-Jones is examining this time, and it's his speciality. He has written a lot of stuff about it in the *B.M.J.* and the *Lancet*. He might quite easily pop a question in.'

'All right,' I said. 'I'll look it up in the library tomorrow.'

My chances of meeting a case of torulosis after qualification were remote, and I wouldn't have recognized it if I had. But to be well informed about torulosis in the next fortnight might make the difference between passing and failure.

Benskin discovered that Malcolm Maxworth was the St Swithin's representative on the Examining Committee and thenceforward we attended all his ward rounds, standing at the front and gazing at him like impressionable music enthusiasts at the solo violinist. The slightest hint he was believed to have dropped was passed round, magnified, and acted upon. Meanwhile, we despondently ticked the days off the calendar, swotted up the spot questions, and ran a final breathless spring down the well-trodden paths of medicine, snatching handfuls of knowledge from the sides where we could.

The examination is split into three sections, each one of which must be passed on its own. First there are the written papers, then *viva voce* examinations, and finally the clinical, when the student is presented with a patient and required to turn in a competent diagnosis in half an hour.

On the morning the examination began the five of us left the Bayswater flat early, took a bus along Oxford Street, and walked towards the examination building in a silent, sickly row. I always found the papers the most disturbing part of the contest. They begin at nine o'clock, an hour when I am never at my best, and the sight of other candidates *en masse* is most depressing. They all look so intelligent. They wear spectacles and use heavy fountain-pens whose barrels reflect their own mental capacity; once inside they write steadily and sternly, as though they were preparing leaders for the next week's *Lancet*; and the women students present such an aspect of concentration and industry it seems useless for men to continue the examination at all.

I went with a hundred other students into one of three large, square halls used for the examination. The polished wooden floor was covered with rows of desks set at a distance apart that made one's neighbour's writing completely indecipherable if he had not, as was usually the case, already done so himself. Each desk was furnished with a card stamped with a black examination number, a clean square of pink blotting-paper, and a pen apparently bought second-hand from the Post Office. The place smelt of floor-polish and freshly-sharpened pencils.

A single invigilator sat in his gown and hood on a raised platform to keep an eye open for flagrant cheating. He was helped by two or three uniformed porters who stood by the doors and looked dispassionately down at the poor victims, like the policemen that flank the dock at the Old Bailey. The students scraped into their chairs, shot a hostile glance at the clock, and turned apprehensively to the buff question paper already laid out on each desk.

The first paper was on general medicine. The upper half of the sheet was taken up with instructions in bold print telling the candidate to write on one side of the paper only, answer all the questions, and to refrain from cribbing at peril of being thrown out. I brought my eyes painfully to the four questions beneath. At a glance I saw they were all short and pungent.

Give an account of the signs, symptoms, and treatment of heart failure was the first. 'Hell of a lot in that!' I thought. I read the second and cursed. *Discuss the changes in the treatment of pneumonia since 1930*. I felt the examiners had played a dirty trick by asking the same disease two papers in succession. The next simply demanded *How would you investigate an outbreak of typhoid fever?* and the last was a request for an essay on worms which I felt I could bluff my way through.

Three hours were allowed for the paper. About half-way through the anonymous examinees began to differentiate themselves. Some of them strode up for an extra answer book, with an awkward expression of self-consciousness and superiority in their faces. Others rose to their feet, handed in their papers, and left. Whether these people were so brilliant they were able to complete the examination in an hour and a half or whether this was the time required for them to set down unhurriedly their entire knowledge of medicine was never apparent from the nonchalant air with which they left the room. The invigilator tapped his bell half an hour before time; the last question was rushed through, then the porters began tearing papers away from gentlemen dissatisfied with the period allowed for them to express themselves and hoping by an incomplete sentence to give the examiners the impression of frustrated brilliance.

I walked down the stairs feeling as if I had just finished an eight-round fight. I reached desperately for my packet of cigarettes. The other candidates jostled round, chattering like children just out of school. In the square outside the first person I recognized was Grimsdyke.

'How did you get on?' I asked.

'So-so,' he replied. 'However, I am not worried. They never read the papers, anyway. I'm perfectly certain of that. Haven't you heard how they mark the tripos at Cambridge, my dear old boy? The night before the results come out the old don totters back from hall and chucks the lot down his staircase. The ones that stick on the top flight are given firsts, most of them end up on the landing and get seconds, thirds go to the lower flight, and any reaching the ground floor are failed. This system has been working admirably for years without arousing any comment. I heard all about it from a senior wrangler.'

Benskin's broad figure appeared among the crowd in the doorway. He was grinning widely and waved cheerily at us.

'You look pretty pleased with yourself,' I said.

'I am, old boy. Today I tried out Benskin's infallible system for passing exams, and it worked beautifully. What number are you?'

'Three hundred and six.'

'I'm a hundred and ten. All I had to do was walk into the room labelled "Two to Three Hundred", wander round a bit while people got settled, and tell the invigilator chap they hadn't given me a place. He apologized at first, then he looked at my card and turfed me out pretty sharply to find the right room. I was pretty humble, of course, and murmured a lot of stuff about my nerves–however, in my wandering round the desks I'd taken damn good care to read all the questions. Now, if you look up the regulations you'll see candidates are admitted up to twenty minutes after the start of the examination, so I had plenty of time to dodge down to the lavatory and look it all up before presenting myself, breathless and distraught, at the correct room. Pretty smart, eh?'

'I hope they can't read your writing,' I said bitterly.

The oral examination was held a week after the papers. I got a white card, like an invitation to a cocktail party, requesting my presence at the examination building by eleven-thirty. I got up late, shaved with a new blade, and carefully brushed my suit. Should I wear a hospital tie? It was a tricky point. Examiners were well known for harbouring an allergy towards certain hospitals, and although my neckwear might convince them I was not from St Mary's, for instance, or Guy's, my interrogators were quite as likely to be opposed to men from St Swithin's.

I put on a quiet nondescript tie and a white stiff collar. The dressing-up was important, for the candidate was expected to look like a doctor even if he gave no indication of ever becoming one; one fellow who had once unhappily appeared in his usual outfit of sports coat and flannels was turned over to a porter by the outraged examiner with instructions to 'Show this gentleman to the nearest golf-course.'

It is the physical contact with the examiners that makes oral examinations so unpopular with the students. The written answers have a certain remoteness about them, and mistakes and omissions, like those of life, can be made without the threat of immediate punishment. But the viva is judgement day. A false answer, an inadequate account of oneself, and the god's brow threatens like an imminent thunderstorm. If the candidate loses his nerve in front of this terrible displeasure he is finished: confusion breeds confusion and he will come to the end of his interrogation struggling like a cow in a bog. This sort of mental attitude had already led to the disgrace of Harris, who had been reduced to a state just short of speechlessness by a terrible succession of *faux pas*. The examiner finally decided to try the poor fellow with something simple and handed him a breast-bone that had been partly worn away with the life-long pressure of an enlarged artery underneath. 'Now, my boy,' said the examiner. 'What do you think caused that hollow?' All he wanted for a reply was the single word 'Pressure', but Harris looked at the specimen in blank silence. With a sigh, the kindly examiner removed his pince-nez and indicated the two indentations they left on each side of his nose. 'Well,' he continued helpfully, 'what do you think caused that?' Something clicked in Harris's panicky brain. The depressed nasal bridge . . . a picture flashed up that he had seen so often in the opening pages of his surgery book. 'Congenital syphilis, sir,' he replied without hesitation.

I was shown to a tiny waiting-room furnished with hard chairs, a wooden table, and windows that wouldn't open, like the condemned cell. There were six candidates from other hospitals waiting to go in with me, all of them in their best clothes. They illustrated the types fairly commonly seen in viva waiting-rooms. There was the Nonchalant, lolling back on the rear legs of his chair with his feet on the table, showing the bright yellow socks under his blue trouser-legs. He was reading the sporting page of the *Express* with undeceptive thoroughness. Next to him, a man of the Frankly Worried class sat on the edge of his chair tearing little bits off his invitation card and jumping irritatingly every time the door opened. There was the Crammer, fondling the pages of his battered textbook in a desperate farewell embrace, and his opposite, the Old Stager, who treated the whole thing with the familiarity of a photographer at a wedding. He had obviously failed the examination so often he looked upon the viva simply as another engagement to be fitted into his day. He stood looking out of the window and yawning, only cheering up when he saw the porter, with whom he was now on the same warm terms as an undergraduate and his college servant.

'How are you getting on this time, sir?' the porter asked him cheerily.

'Not so dusty, William, not so dusty at all. The second question in the paper was the same one they asked four years ago. What are they like in there?'

'Pretty mild, this morning, sir. I'm just taking them their coffee.'

'Excellent! Put plenty of sugar in it. A low blood-sugar is conducive to bad temper.'

'I will, sir. Best of luck.'

'Thank you, William.'

The other occupant of the room was a woman. A trim little piece, I noticed, probably from the Royal Free. She sat pertly on her chair with her hands folded on her lap. Women students–the attractive ones, not those who are feminine only through inescapable anatomical arrangements–are under a disadvantage in oral examinations. The male examiners are so afraid of being prejudiced favourably by their sex they usually adopt towards them an undeserved sternness. But this girl had given care to her preparations for the examination. Her suit was neat but not smart; her hair tidy but not striking; she wore enough make-up to look attractive, and she was obviously practising, with some effort, a look of admiring submission to the male sex. I felt sure she would get through.

I sat alone in the corner and fingered my tie. They always made the candidates arrive too early, and the coffee would delay them further. There was nothing to do except wait patiently and think about something well removed from the unpleasant quarter of an hour ahead, such as rugby or the lady student's legs. Suddenly the door was flung open and a wild-eyed youth strode in.

'It's not too bad!' he exclaimed breathlessly to the nonchalant fellow. The two apparently came from the same hospital.

'I had Sir Rollo Doggert and Stanley Smith,' he said with a touch of pride. This brought a nod of appreciation from all of us, as they were known as two of the toughest examiners in London.

'Doggert started off by asking me the signs and symptoms of pink disease,' he continued. 'Luckily I knew that as I had happened to look it up last night . . .'

'Pink disease!' cried the worried man. 'My God, I forgot about that!'

'So I saw at once the way to handle him was to talk man-to-man, you know–none of this servile business, he much prefers to be stood up to I reeled off pink disease and he said very good, my lad, very good.'

'Did he ask you anything else?' his friend said anxiously.

'Oh yes. He said, supposing I was out golfing with a diabetic who collapsed at the third tee, what would I do? Well, I said . . .'

The visitor gave a description of his examination in detail, like the man who comes out of the dentist's surgery and insists on telling the occupants of the waiting-room his experiences on the excuse that none of the frightful things that can happen really hurt.

The raconteur was stopped short by the porter. He marshalled us into line outside the heavy door of the examination room. There was a faint ting of a bell inside. The door opened and he admitted us one at a time, directing each to a different table.

Chapter Sixteen

'You go to table four,' the porter told me.

The room was the one we had written the papers in, but it was now empty except for a double row of baize-covered tables separated by screens. At each of these sat two examiners and a student who carried on a low earnest conversation with them, like a confessional.

I stood before table four. I didn't recognize the examiners. One was a burly, elderly man like a retired prize-fighter who smoked a pipe and was writing busily with a pencil in a notebook; the other was invisible, as he was occupied in reading the morning's *Times*.

'Good morning, sir,' I said.

Neither of them took any notice. After a minute the burly fellow looked up from his writing and silently indicated the chair in front of him. I sat down. He growled.

'I beg your pardon, sir?' I said politely.

'I said you're number 306,' he said testily. 'That's correct, I suppose?'

'Yes, sir.'

'Well, why didn't you say so? How would you treat a case of tetanus?'

My heart leapt hopefully. This was something I knew, as there had recently been a case in St Swithin's. I started off confidently, reeling out the lines of treatment and feeling much better.

The examiner suddenly cut me short.

'All right, all right,' he said impatiently, 'you seem to know that. A girl of twenty comes to you complaining of gaining weight. What do you do?'

This was the sort of question I disliked. There were so many things one could do my thoughts jostled into each other like a rugger scrum and became confused and unidentifiable.

'I–I would ask if she was pregnant,' I said.

'Good God, man! Do you go about asking all the girls you know if they're pregnant? What hospital d'you come from?'

'St Swithin's, sir,' I said, as though admitting an illegitimate parentage.

'I should have thought so! Now try again.'

I rallied my thoughts and stumbled through the answer. The examiner sat looking past me at the opposite wall, acknowledging my presence only by grunting at intervals.

The bell rang and I moved into the adjoining chair, facing *The Times*. The newspaper rustled and was set down, revealing a mild, youngish-looking man in large spectacles with a perpetual look of faint surprise on his face. He looked at me as if he was surprised to see me there, and every answer I made was received with the same expression. I found this most disheartening.

The examiner pushed across the green baize a small sealed glass pot from a pathology museum, in which a piece of meat like the remains of a Sunday joint floated in spirit.

'What's that?' he asked.

I picked up the bottle and examined it carefully. By now I knew the technique for pathological specimens of this kind. The first thing to do was turn them upside down, as their identity was often to be found on a label on the bottom. If one was still flummoxed one might sneeze or let it drop from nervous fingers to smash on the floor.

I upturned it and was disappointed to find the label had prudently been removed. Unfortunately there was so much sediment in the jar that it behaved like one of those little globes containing an Eiffel Tower that on reversal cover the model with a thick snowstorm. I could therefore not even see the specimen when I turned it back again.

'Liver,' I tried.

'What!' exclaimed the surprised man. The other examiner, who had returned to his writing, slammed down his pencil in disgust and glared at me.

'I mean lung,' I corrected.

'That's better. What's wrong with it?'

I could get no help from the specimen, which was still tossing in swirling white particles, so I took another guess.

'Pneumonia. Stage of white hepatization.'

The surprised man nodded. 'How do you test diphtheria serum?' he demanded.

'You inject it into a guinea-pig, sir.'

'Yes, but you've got to have an animal of a standard weight, haven't you?'

'Oh yes . . . a hundred kilogrammes.'

The two men collapsed into roars of laughter.

'It would be as big as a policeman, you fool!' shouted the first examiner.

'Oh, I'm so sorry,' I stammered miserably. 'I mean a hundred milligrammes.'

The laughter was renewed. One or two of the examiners at nearby tables looked up with interest. The other candidates felt like prisoners in the condemned block when they hear the bolt go in the execution shed.

'You could hardly see it then, boy,' said the surprised man, wiping his eyes. 'The creature weighs a hundred grammes. However, we will leave the subject. How would you treat a case of simple sore throat?'

'I would give a course of sulphonamide, sir.'

'Yes, that's right.'

'I disagree with you, Charles,' the other interrupted forcibly. 'It's like taking a hammer at a nut. I have an excellent gargle I have been prescribing for years which does very well.'

'Oh, I don't know,' said the surprised fellow warmly. 'One must make use of these drugs. I've always had excellent results with sulphonamides.'

'Did you read that paper by McHugh in the *Clinical Record* last winter?' demanded the first examiner, banging the table again.

'Certainly I read it, George. And the correspondence which followed. Nevertheless, I feel it is still open to doubt—'

'I really cannot agree with you—'

They continued arguing briskly, and were still doing so when a second tinkle of the bell allowed me to slide out and rush miserably into the street.

The days after the viva were black ones. It was like having a severe accident. For the first few hours I was numbed, unable to realize what had hit me. Then I began to wonder if I would ever make a recovery and win through. One or two of my friends heartened me by describing equally depressing experiences that had overtaken them previously and still allowed them to pass. I began to hope. Little shreds of success collected together and weaved themselves into a triumphal garland. After all, I thought, I got the bottle right, and I knew about tetanus . . . then I forgot about it in my anxiety over the last section of the examination, the clinical.

The clinical is probably the most chancy of the three parts. The student may be allotted a straightforward case with sounds in the chest that come through his stethoscope like the noise of an iron foundry; or he may get something devilish tricky.

The cases for clinical examinations were collected from the out-patient departments of hospitals all over London, and were in the class referred to by physicians informally as 'old chronics'. They have their lesions healed as far as possible; now they walked round in fairly good health but with a collection of clicks, whistles, or rumbles inside them set up by the irreversible process of their diseases. These are just the sort of things examiners like presenting to students. A case of vague ill-health or an indefinite lump are too arguable, but a good hearty slapping in the chest gives a right to fail a man forthright if he misses it.

For this service the patients were given seven-and-six and free tea and buns. But most of them would happily have performed with a strictly amateur status and provided their own sandwiches. The six-monthly visits to the examination were their principal outings of the year. They attended their own hospitals monthly to show off the signs they proudly possessed to a single doctor and discuss their ailment with fellow-patients on the benches outside, but in the exam they were inspected by hundreds of doctors–or as good as–and chatted to the élite of fellow sufferers. It is much the same as winning an international rugby cap.

I arrived at the examination building in plenty of time, to find out what I could of the cases from men who had already been examined. I knew Benskin had been in early and looked for him in the hall to ask what there was upstairs.

'There's an asthma in a red scarf, old boy,' he said helpfully. 'And an old man with emphysema just behind the door as you go in–if you get him be sure to examine his abdomen, he's got a couple of hernias thrown in.'

I made a mental note of it.

'Then there's a little girl with a patent ductus–you can't miss her, she's the only child in the room. Oh, and a woman with burnt-out tabes. He'll ask you what treatment you'd give her, and he expects the answer "None".'

I nodded, thanked him, and made my way to the examination room.

My first impression of the clinical examination was of a doctor's surgery gone into mass-production. Patients were scattered across the room on couches, beds, and wheel-chairs, the men divided from the women by screens across the centre. They were in all stages of undress and examination. Circulating busily between them were a dozen or so nurses, examiners in white coats, and unhappy students dangling their stethoscopes behind them like the tails of whipped puppies.

I was directed to a pleasant, tubby little examiner.

'Hello, my lad,' he began genially. 'Where are you from? Swithin's, eh? When are you chaps going to win the rugger cup? Go and amuse yourself with that nice young lady in the corner and I'll be back in twenty minutes.'

She was indeed a nice young lady. A redhead with a figure out of *Esquire*.

'Good morning,' I said with a professional smile.

'Good morning,' she returned brightly.

'Would you mind telling me your name?' I asked politely.

'Certainly. Molly Ditton, I'm unmarried, aged twenty-two, and my work is shorthand-typing, which I have been doing for four years. I live in Ilford and have never been abroad.'

My heart glowed: she knew the form.

'How long have you been coming up here?' I asked. 'You seem to know all the answers.'

She laughed.

'Oh, years and years. I bet I know more about myself than you do.'

Just the thing! There is a golden rule for clinical examinations–ask the patient. They attend the examination for so many years and hear themselves discussed so often with the candidates they have the medical terms off pat. All I had to do was play my cards correctly. I talked to her about Ilford, and the wonderful advantages of living there; of shorthand-typing and its effects on the fingernails; of her boy friends and her prospects of matrimony (this produced a few giggles); of the weather and where she went for her holidays.

'By the way,' I said with careful casualness, 'what's wrong with you?'

'Oh, I've mitral stenosis due to rheumatic fever, but I'm perfectly well compensated and I've a favourable prognosis. There's a presystolic murmur at the apex, but the aortic area is clear and there are no creps at the bases. By the way, my thyroid is slightly enlarged, they like you to notice that. I'm not fibrillating and I'm having no treatment.'

'Thank you very much,' I said.

The tubby man was delighted when I passed on to him the patient's accurate diagnosis as my own.

'Capital, capital!' he beamed. 'Spotted the thyroid, too . . . glad some of you young fellers use your powers of observation. Been telling my own students for years–observe, observe, observe. They never do, though. Right you are, my lad. Now just take this ophthalmoscope and tell me what you can see in that old woman's eye.'

My heart, which had been soaring like a swallow, took a sharp dive to earth. The examiner handed me the little black instrument with lenses for looking into the eye. I had often seen it used in the wards but I never seemed to find time to learn how to employ it myself. There was a knack to it, which I did not possess; and I knew plainly enough that the defect was sufficient to fail me out of hand. I imagined the examiner's sunny friendliness turning into a storm of irritation; my hand shook as I took the instrument. Slowly I placed it closely between my eye and the patient. All I could see was something that looked like a dirty tank in an aquarium with a large, dim fish in it. The time had come for quick thinking. Looking intently through the instrument I let out a long whistle of amazement.

'Yes, it is a big retinal detachment, isn't it?' the examiner said happily, taking away the ophthalmoscope and patting me on the back. I saw myself marked over the pass number, and with a grateful smile at the redhead tripped downstairs in elation.

In the hall I met Benskin again. He was looking profoundly miserable. 'What's up?' I asked anxiously.

Benskin shook his head and explained in a choked voice what had happened. While I was examining medical cases he had been questioned in practical midwifery. One of the tests for prospective obstetricians was provided by a life-size papier mâché model of half the female trunk, into which a straw-stuffed baby was slipped through a trapdoor. The candidate was then provided with a pair of obstetrical forceps and required to deliver it *per via naturalis.* This was demanded of Benskin. He solemnly applied the two blades to the head, taking care to put the correct one on first. He locked the handle, took it in the approved grip, and gave a strong pull. Nothing happened. He pulled harder, but the straw foetus refused to be born. He felt sweat on his brow and his mouth went dry; he saw his chances of passing fading like a spent match. He gave a desperate heave. His feet slipped on the polished floor and over his head flew mother, baby, forceps and all.

The examiner looked at him lying on the floor for a second in silence. Then he picked up one blade of the forceps and handed it to him.

'Now hit the father with that,' he said sourly, 'and you'll have killed the whole bloody family.'

Chapter Seventeen

'One doesn't fail exams,' said Grimsdyke firmly. 'One comes down, one muffs, one is ploughed, plucked, or pipped. These infer a misfortune that is not one's own fault. To speak of failing is bad taste. It's the same idea as talking about passing away and going above instead of plain dying.'

We were sitting with Benskin in the King George. It was immediately after opening time in the morning and we were alone in the bar. We sat on stools, resting our elbows on the counter and our heads on our hands. All three of us looked pitifully dejected. The examination results were to be published at noon.

'It's the heartless way they do it,' I said. 'Picking you out one at a time in front of everybody. I wish they'd show a little decent discretion about the business. I'd much prefer it if they sent you a letter. You can at least slink away and open it in the lavatory or somewhere.'

'In Tibet, I believe,' Grimsdyke went on, 'they simply execute the unsuccessful candidates on the spot.'

'Well, they probably welcome it.'

'They failed Harris pretty decently,' Benskin said reverently, as though speaking of the dead. 'He's so sure he'll have to take it again in six months he's not even bothering to hear the results. When he floundered badly in his viva the old boy simply looked dreamily out of the window and said, "Young man, how mysterious and wonderful is Nature! Now we see the leaf turning gold on the branch and falling to the ground. The flowers and plants have lost their summer beauty and withered, and the earth looks dead beyond hope of resurrection. But in the month of April the spring will come, the trees will burst into green flames, the shoots will leap up through the black soil, and petals will cover the bare flowerbeds. And you and I, my boy, will be here to see it, won't we?"'

'I think that was very bad form,' said Grimsdyke.

The Padre put three small glasses in front of us.

'Whisky?' Grimsdyke said. 'I thought we ordered beer.'

'If you will permit me, Mr Grimsdyke, I would like to suggest, on the basis of my experience, something a little more nourishing. I know what a difficult time this is for you young gentlemen. Will you please accept these with the compliments of the house?'

'Here I say, Padre . . . !'

He held up his hand.

'Not a bit of it, sir. The money I have been obliged to take off you in our long acquaintance more than justifies it. Here's jolly good luck, gentlemen!'

'Bottoms up,' said Benskin.

'I'm sure I've failed, all the same,' I said, putting my glass down. 'How could I get through after that terrible viva?'

Benskin snorted.

'It's all very well for you to talk. What about my midwifery clinical? That came under the heading of ugly incidents.'

'You never know, my dear old boy,' Grimsdyke said hopefully. 'You may have done brilliantly in the papers.'

'Let's not talk about it,' I said. 'Let's discuss rugger instead.'

At noon we arrived in the examination building. The same number of candidates were there, but they were a subdued, muttering crowd, like the supporters of a home team who had just been beaten in a cup tie.

We pushed our way into the large hall on the ground floor. It was packed full with anxious students. On the side of the hall facing us was the foot of a marble staircase. To the left of the staircase was a plain, open door, over which had been recently pinned a large black and white card saying 'EXIT'. To the right was a clock, which stood at a few minutes before twelve.

We had heard exactly what would happen. At midday precisely the Secretary of the Committee would descend the stairs and take his place, flanked by two uniformed porters, on the lowermost step. Under his arm would be a thick, leather-covered book containing the results. One of the porters would carry a list of the candidates' numbers and call them out, one after the other. The candidate would step up closely to the Secretary, who would say simply 'Pass' or 'Failed'. Successful men would go upstairs to receive the congratulations and handshakes of the examiners and failures would slink miserably out of the exit to seek the opiate of oblivion.

'One thing, it's quick,' Benskin muttered nervously.

'Like the drop,' said Grimsdyke.

One minute to twelve. The room had suddenly come to a frightening, unexpected silence and stillness, like an unexploded bomb. A clock tinged twelve in the distance. My palms were as wet as sponges. Someone coughed, and I expected the windows to rattle. With slow scraping feet that could be heard before they appeared the Secretary and porters came solemnly down the stairs.

They took up their positions; the leather book was opened. The elder porter raised his voice.

'Number two hundred and nine,' he began. 'Number thirty-seven. Number one hundred and fifty.'

The tension in the room broke as the students shuffled to the front and lined up before the staircase. The numbers were not called in order, and the candidates strained to hear their own over the low rumble of conversation and scraping of feet that rose from the assembly.

'Number one hundred and sixty-one,' continued the porter. 'Number three hundred and two. Number three hundred and six.'

Grimsdyke punched me hard in the ribs.

'Go on,' he hissed. 'It's you!'

I jumped and struggled my way to the front of the restless crowd. My pulse shot high in my ears. My face was burning hot and I felt my stomach had been suddenly plucked from my body.

I lined up in the short queue by the stairs. My mind was empty and numb. I stared at the red neck of the man in front of me, with its rim of blue collar above his coat, and studied it with foolish intensity. Suddenly I found myself on top of the Secretary.

'Number three oh six?' the Secretary whispered, without looking up from the book. 'R. Gordon?'

'Yes,' I croaked.

The world stood still. The traffic stopped, the plants ceased growing, men were paralysed, the clouds hung in the air, the winds dropped, the tides disappeared, the sun halted in the sky.

'Pass,' the man muttered.

Blindly, like a man just hit by blackjack, I stumbled upstairs.

The bar of the King George was full. I crashed through the door like a hot wind.

'I've passed!' I screamed.

The bar rose in turmoil. I couldn't see any of it. It was a pink jumble of faces, a numb sensation of handshakes, a dim perception of backslapping.

'Congratulations, sir!' shouted the Padre, thrusting his hand through the mob. 'Congratulations, Doctor! Here you are, sir. A quart tankard, sir. With my every best wish.'

Someone pushed the deep pewter mug into my hands.

'Down the hatch!'

'One gulp, old man!'

I was too breathless to drink. I wanted to laugh, cry, dance, and run all at the same time.

'I can't believe it!' I exclaimed. 'It isn't true! The first thing I knew I was shaking hands with the old boys and signing my diploma.'

'How about the other two gentlemen?' the Padre called.

'Oh Lord!' I felt suddenly guilty. 'I'd quite forgotten to wait for them!'

At that moment the door flew open. There entered Benskin and Grimsdyke wearing each other's jackets, attempting to pull in with them a violently neighing carthorse.

'I think it's all right,' the Padre said.

The party went on until closing time. Every student in the school seemed to be inside the tiny bar. I emptied and re-emptied my tankard. Everyone was shouting and singing, leaning on each other, jostling their neighbours, slapping their friends on the back. The angry owner of the horse had been asked inside and was now singing 'The Lily of Laguna' to a cooperative audience. The room filled tighter as the news of more successes was brought in, like victories to a triumphant headquarters.

'Bottle's through,' I heard Evans bawling over the hubbub. 'So's Sprogget.'

'How about you?' I shouted back.

Evans delightedly stuck his thumb in the air.

I suddenly found myself jammed between Benskin and Grimsdyke.

'Hooray!' shouted Benskin, ruffling my hair.

'It's bloody funny!' Grimsdyke shouted. 'Bloody funny!'

'What is?' I bawled at him.

'We're three bloody doctors,' he hollered.

We burst into roars of laughter.

My feelings in the next few days were those of a private unexpectedly promoted to general overnight. In a minute or two I had been transformed from an unearning and potentially dishonest ragamuffin to a respectable and solvent member of a learned profession. Now banks would trust me with their money, hire firms with their cars, and mothers with their daughters. I could sign prescriptions, death certificates, and orders for extra milk, and no one could contradict me. It was wonderful.

As soon as the exam results were out the Chiefs made appointments to the resident staff of St Swithin's. I became house-physician to Dr Malcolm Maxworth, and had to begin work the next week. I saw from the list that Evans had been awarded the plum position of house-surgeon to the Professor, and Grimsdyke became a junior obstetrical officer. Sprogget had not bothered to apply for a job at St Swithin's and Benskin was not given one. The Dean had vetoed the appointment.

I packed up and left the Bayswater flat. The landlord had been wanting to get rid of us for some time and took the opportunity of taking possession himself. We had a row about damages, but Sprogget settled it by threatening officially to report the plumbing to the local Medical Officer of Health unless the estimate was reduced considerably.

In the hospital I was given a small, bleak room with an iron bedstead, a desk, a chair, and a telephone. But I unpacked with delight–I was living there free of charge, and at last, at the age of twenty-three, I was earning some money.

There was a letter waiting for me, addressed ostentatiously to Dr Gordon in Benskin's handwriting. I opened it.

'Dear old boy,' it began. 'I expect you will be surprised to hear that I have got married. As a matter of fact, I have for a long time been bloody keen on Molly (the nurse I proposed to that night), and we decided to do the old ring stuff as soon as I got through. I didn't say anything to you coarse fellows, because you have such warped ideas on such things. I have a job waiting for me in general practice at home, and we are now having the old honeymoon in Cornwall. Let me warn you against the swank of calling yourself doctor, old lad. I signed myself in the visitors' book as Dr Benskin, and we had only just got into bed when the porter came banging on the door shouting at me that the cook had scalded herself. The marriage was consummated, but only just. Your old chum, Tony.'

'I'm damned!' I said. 'The old stoat!'

I was still staring at the letter when the phone rang. It was Sister Virtue, whom I now had to work with as a colleague. Her tone was only a little less severe than the one she used on students–to her, new housemen were hardly less reprehensible.

'Dr Gordon,' she rasped. 'When are you going to appear in the ward? I have a stack of notes for you to sign and three new patients have been admitted. You can't expect the nursing staff to run the hospital on their own.'

I looked at my watch. It was six in the evening. I had to tell the Padre about Benskin.

'Half past six, Sister,' I said. 'I've only just arrived. Will that be all right?'

'Not a minute later,' she snapped, discontinuing the conversation.

I walked across to the King George with Benskin's letter.

'I knew it all along, sir, if I may say so,' the Padre said calmly. 'It's always the same with the ones that run a mile if they see a nurse and talk big about staying single. I've seen it a good many times now, sir. And you watch out, Dr Gordon–I bet you're next.'

'Well, I don't know about that, Padre. There's no one on the cards at the moment.'

'Ah yes, sir, but wait till you've been about the hospital a bit as a doctor instead of a student. Why, the nurses are all over you. You get proper spoilt, you lads do.'

'I must confess noting a certain sweet cooperation among the girls I hadn't found before. Perhaps you're right. Anyway, I'll watch my step.'

I took a few sips of my beer.

'It's quiet in here, Padre, tonight.'

'Early in the evening yet, sir.'

'I know . . . but it seems oppressively quiet, if you know what I mean. I suppose it's because there's been so much fun and games going on the last few days. It's . . . well, lonely. This qualification business is all very well, but it soon wears off. For about three days the world is at your feet, then you realize it's the beginning, not the end. You've got to fight a damn sight harder than you did in your exams to do your job decently and make a living.'

'That's right, sir. They all say the same. You've got to face it, them carefree student days is over for good. Life is hard, sir. It's bad enough for a publican, but a damn sight worse for a doctor.'

'Well, let's not get miserable about it,' I said. 'Still, these last few days I've begun to wish I'd got a bit more out of my education.'

'Come off it, sir,' said the Padre genially. 'You've made a lot of friends, which mark my words you'll hang on to till your dying day. And that's valuable, sir. A lot of people can get an education, but not many of 'em can collect as sound a bunch of good friends as you young gentlemen do. Wherever you go, sir, no matter how many years to come, you'll still remember Mr Benskin and the rest and the good times you've had in these four walls.'

'You know, Padre,' I said, 'that's exactly what I think myself. I was just too frightened to say so.'

The door opened. A porter stood there.

'Dr Gordon,' he said. 'I've been looking for you all over. Wanted at once in the ward, sir. Emergency just come in.'

I looked at the half-full glass of beer. I picked it up, hesitated, and left it.

'All right,' I said, pulling my stethoscope out of my pocket. 'I'm coming.'

Times have changed, I thought as I walked over to the hospital. I suddenly realized that from now on it was always going to be like this.

Richard Gordon

Doctor at Sea

Doctor at Sea

To the Merchant Navy–
They have a lot to put up with

Note: The *Lotus* and her crew are as fictitious as the *Flying Dutchman* and her insubstantial company

Chapter One

It would be unfair to describe the *Lotus* as an unlucky ship. It was just that she was accident prone, like a big, awkward schoolgirl.

Even her period of gestation in the shipyard was full of mishaps. She was laid down in Wallsend in 1929, and had advanced to the shape of a huge picked chicken when the depression blew down bitterly on Tyneside. For the next four years she rusted untouched behind locked gates, and when they started work again her design was changed on the drawing-board from a North Atlantic ship to a Far East trader. Shortly afterwards the company ordering her went bankrupt and she was bought on the stocks by another, who began to turn her into a whaler. They too rapidly slid into insolvency and abandoned her to a fourth, the Fathom Steamship Company of St Mary Axe. It was this concern that succeeded in launching her, after she had been through as many fruitless changes in construction as a human embryo.

At her launch she holed and almost sank a small tug, and on her maiden voyage as a cargo-passenger ship she lost a propeller during a gale in the Australian Bight. At the beginning of the war she came home from New Zealand, painted grey, and was one of the first vessels to reveal to the Admiralty the effectiveness of the magnetic mine. She lost most of her bows in the Thames Estuary, but stayed afloat long enough to be dragged into dock for repairs. After several months she set off again to join a convoy, and had her stern blown away by a bomb twenty-five minutes after leaving port.

The stern was patched up, and she managed to pass the rest of the hostilities without getting herself involved in any dangerous action, apart from shooting down an American Mustang in error with her Oerlikons in 1945. At the end of the war she refitted and returned to peaceful trading, disturbed only by an explosion in the engine-room in the Caribbean and the cook going abruptly insane one insupportably hot afternoon in the Red Sea and passing among his shipmates with the meat hatchet.

Much of the damage from both these accidents was repaired, but the repeated structural changes had induced in the *Lotus* a premature senility, a state of chronic invalidism. She was too cold in the higher latitudes, too hot in the Tropics, and she groaned pitifully in bad weather. But the Fathom Steamship Company unmercifully sent her anywhere in the world where she could find the shareholders a profit. She carried lead and lemons, boiler-tubes and barley, copra and cows. She took steel from Baltimore to Brisbane, wool from Auckland to Archangel, coal from Swansea to Singapore. She was one of the world's shopping baskets.

There was enough room on board for thirty passengers, though she rarely carried more than a dozen and often none at all. They were people going to unusual places, or too poor to afford a big ship, or experienced travellers who cringed before the bonhomie of the boat-deck and the deadly gin-and-sin routine of a sophisticated liner. The Company was indifferent to them: passengers earned little more than complaints, but freight meant money.

In the opinion of the crew, one of the severest disasters to overtake the *Lotus* since the war was her Commander, Captain Vincent Hogg, who was officially required to act at various times once his ship was at sea as the sole representative on board of the Fathom Steamship Company, the King, and God; for all three of them he substituted himself with impartial grandeur. His officers accepted him as farmers tolerate a prolonged drought, giving daily prayers for Divine removal of the affliction. The weight of her personality fell most heavily on the Mate, Mr Hornbeam, who had passed his Master's examination twenty years before and was waiting for a command with the pitiful patience of an impoverished expectant relative. Promotion in the Company was simply a matter of dead men's shoes. He had in a drawer in his cabin an alphabetical list of the Fathom Line's Captains, with their exact ages and notes on their partiality for drink, loose women, and other items reputed to shorten life, but all of them retained irritatingly good health. He enjoyed the unstinted sympathy of the Chief Engineer, Mr McDougall, who hated the Captain like a red-hot bearing; and the Captain disliked the Chief Engineer like fog round the Goodwins. McDougall looked upon the ship as a shell for the transportation of his engines, and complained daily when the navigational position from the bridge was some miles astern of the one he calculated from his revolutions. Indeed, according to the Chief Engineer, the machinery and boilers of the *Lotus* should have arrived in any port several days in advance of the rest of the vessel.

There were two other Mates, a gang of engineers, a wireless operator and–as the *Lotus* carried more than ninety-nine souls when she was full–a doctor.

The doctor was by order of the Ministry of Transport, the uncompromising power who prescribes on every item of a sailor's life from the number of lifeboats to be available in emergency to the number of times he shall have eggs for his breakfast. Ninety-eight souls can sail the seas until they are carried away with obscure nautical illness, like the shipmates of the Ancient Mariner: their health is preserved with a bottle of black draught, the *Ship Captain's Medical Guide*, and a scalpel also used for sharpening the chart-room pencil. The Second Mate or the Chief Steward holds the keys of the drug chest and practises daily, after breakfast. All pains below the umbilicus are treated with strong purgative, all disturbances above with Ministry cough mixture, and lesions on the remainder of the body with turpentine liniment. Obviously there occur from time to time more alarming complaints, and these are submitted to surgery under wireless instructions by the Captain on the saloon table, after the patient and the surgeon have taken sufficient brandy to instil in each other confidence that both will survive the operation.

But one more soul on board brings to all the benefits of medical science–or as much of it as the doctor can remember, because ship surgeons are notoriously forgetful of these things. The sea induces an attitude of pleasant detachment towards problems that strain thought ashore, including those of the diagnosis and prognosis of disease, and the doctor has few professional obligations to distract him from his pastimes or enrich him with experience. For these reasons the companies naturally dislike the expense of carrying him–but then, the Fathom Steamship Company would have objected to the expense of lifeboats.

When I met the *Lotus* she was lying in Liverpool, due to sail with a cargo of machinery and motor-cars to Santos, in Brazil. It had then been raining on Merseyside for four days. The damp November wind channelled itself down the river, broke against the waterfront buildings, and ran up the cold streets behind. The birds on the Liver building, that are unfairly supposed by Liverpool seafarers to flap their wings when passed by a woman of untarnished virtue, wept ceaselessly on to the bleak pierhead. The Birkenhead ferry forced its way miserably across the choppy harbour, the landing-stage looked as forlorn as a bandstand in midwinter, and even the stonework of the St George's Hall appeared in danger of showing through its crust of soot.

It was about eight in the evening, the hour when the shipowners are fed in the Adelphi. As they glumly finished their Martinis in the little American bar they calculated among themselves the rain's cost in delayed cargo working. Outside in Lime Street the adolescent tarts already clung hopefully to their damp doorways. The dripping buses took home the last pale shipping clerks, the overhead railway rattled along its grotesque track, and the dock police steamed themselves warm in front of the stoves in their cabins. The *Lotus* herself lay lifeless at her quay with tarpaulins tented over her hatches, creaking gently at her mooring ropes like an old bed in a bad dream.

I stood in the rain on the quayside reading a large sheet of printed instructions for resuscitating the apparently drowned. This was the only information of any sort available to passers-by. The wharf was deserted. The cranes huddled together in a row, a few railway trucks crouched between their legs; the warehouses were shut, locked, and abandoned even by the cats; the *Lotus*, lit with a few dim lights, looked as uninviting as a shut pub.

I was a young doctor with a bad diploma passing through the difficult stage of professional adolescence when you discover the medical schools teach as little about medicine as the public schools do about life. My knowledge of seafaring was based only on *Treasure Island*, pictures in the windows of Cook's, and a walking-on part I had been allowed to play in a students' production of *The Middle Watch*. I was nevertheless a recognized sailor. I had in my pocket a new seaman's identity card with my fingerprints on it, a document that made me the professional descendant of Drake and Cabot, subject to and protected by a batch of Parliamentary Acts, the target of missionaries' good intentions and girls' bad ones, and entitled, if I felt like it and there was enough room, to doss down in the Sailors' Home.

The first problem presented by nautical life was how to get aboard the ship. A slippery gangway reached up from the wharf to the *Lotus*'s afterdeck, but there was no one to welcome me at the top. After a few damp minutes I climbed the gangway nervously and looked around me. I was on a dirty iron deck littered with pieces of timber, scraps of rope, and coils of wire, like the junk room in a ship chandler's. A heavy wooden door led into the upper works, and as the rain was coming down my neck persistently I opened it and stepped inside.

Hostile darkness surrounded me; I smelt the faint bitter-almonds tang of cyanide. Uneasy tales of the sea blew through my mind, like a sudden cold draught in an old house. It occurred to me that the *Lotus*, like the *Marie Celeste*, had been freshly abandoned by her terrified crew, or was manned with lost souls from the *Flying Dutchman*. I shivered.

A light, an oil lantern, sprung into mid air in front of me. A voice behind it snapped:

''Op it!'

I jumped back, hitting the door with my head.

'Get the 'ell out of it, Charlie,' the voice continued, coming nearer.

'I–I'm a member of the crew,' I managed to say.

The light advanced on me. Behind it two eyes stared with concentrated suspicion.

'The new doctor,' I explained humbly.

The voice at once took on a friendly inflection.

'Sorry Doc! I thought you was trying to pinch something.'

'No . . . I just came aboard. There didn't seem to be anyone about. I hope it was all right?'

'Sure, it's all right. Liberty Hall, this hooker. Make yourself at home. Spit on the deck and call the cat a bastard.'

'Thank you.'

'Glad you've come, Doc,' he continued affably. 'I've got a bit of a cold like.' He sneezed to add point to the remark. 'Could you give us something for it?'

'Yes, certainly . . . But wouldn't a bit later do? I'm extremely wet. I'd like to find my cabin and so forth.'

'Sure, Doc. Follow me. I'll take you to see the Mate.'

He walked off, the lamp swinging high in his hand. I stepped timidly behind him, along narrow alleyways, round sharp corners, up unidentifiable ladders.

'Sorry there ain't many lights,' he apologized over his shoulder. 'But the engineers has got the jennies stripped tonight.'

'Oh, really?'

That sounded more alarming than ever.

He came to a cabin door and opened it.

'The new Doctor,' he announced, as if he had just materialized me out of a hat.

There were three men in the cabin–the Mate, Archer the Second, and Trail the Third. Hornbeam was sitting in the only chair with his reefer unbuttoned and his stockinged feet on the washbasin. It was a small cabin, designed like a crossword puzzle, and the visitors had to adapt themselves to the interlocking pieces. Archer, who was a tall, pale man with an expression like a curate just beginning to have doubts, had wedged himself between the bunk and the bookcase above it with his legs dangling on to the deck, like a human question mark. Trail, squatting between the locker and the desk, was a fat youth going through a florid attack of *acne vulgaris*.

'Talk of the devil!' Hornbeam said immediately.

'We wondered when you were going to turn up,' Archer said. 'Have a bottle of beer.'

'Move over, Second, and let the Doctor park his fanny,' Hornbeam said. He introduced himself and the others. 'Give us another bottle, Third. Do you mind drinking out of a tooth-glass?'

'No, not at all.'

The welcome was cordial enough, but it disturbed me. It is a habit among seafarers to accept every newcomer on terms of intimacy, but I was a fairly new doctor and stood on my professional dignity like a girl with her first pair of high heels.

'I hope I'm not butting in,' I said stiffly.

'Not a bit of it! Throw your coat on the hook there. We were only having a quick peg.'

I climbed up on the bunk next to Archer without enthusiasm. It seemed as comfortable as trying to drink on a bus in the rush hour.

'You just passed out of medical school?' Archer asked.

'Certainly not! I've been in practice for . . . some years.'

'Oh, sorry. Been to sea before?'

'I'm afraid not.'

'You'll soon pick up the routine. I hope you're hot stuff on the diseases sailors get.'

This brought a roar of laughter from the other two.

'We doctors have to be "hot stuff" on very many things,' I said.

I gave a superior smile. Since I qualified I had fed on professional respect and I found the conversation irritating.

'By George, we find some queer doctors at sea,' Trail said, handing me a glass of beer. 'Don't we, Mr Hornbeam? Usually they're getting away from their wives or the police, or both sometimes. Or else it's drink. That's the commonest. Sometimes it's drugs, though.'

'I drink very little.'

Trail took no notice. 'I remember old Doc Parsons I sailed with when I was doing my time,' he went on cheerfully. 'He was a real scream. As tight as a tick from morning to night. We reckoned he got through a couple of bottles of gin a day, easy. Started before breakfast, every morning. Said the world was so bloody awful he couldn't face it at the best of times, but especially with his last night's hangover. Then one day in the Red Sea the Mate ripped his arm open, and old Parsons said he'd operate. Laugh! The lot of us went down to the hospital to watch. I was doubled up. He'd been at the bottle extra strong and he was as blind as a bat. Kept dropping the knife on the deck and falling over the table. In the end the Mate clocked him one and got the Chief Steward to do it.'

Archer leant forward.

'Do you remember old Doc Hamilton in the *Mariesta*?' he asked.

The other two began to laugh again.

'He was a real queer 'un,' he explained to me. 'Started on the grog before we sailed–had to be carried up the gangway. By the time we reached Gib. the Old Man stopped his tap–no more booze, you understand. So he went down to the dispensary and drank all the surgical spirit. When he finished that he scrounged meths from the engineers. They tumbled to it, of course, and wouldn't let him have any more. In the end he drank the acid from the wireless batteries.'

'The police came for him when we got home,' Hornbeam added. 'I don't know what it was for. Something about abortions, I think.'

'I remember we buried an old doctor off Teneriffe,' Archer said thoughtfully. 'He hanged himself. He did it with his belt,' he continued in my direction.

I began to understand that the medical profession was not held in the highest esteem at sea.

'I assure you I shall not commit any of those things,' I said.

'The voyage hasn't started yet,' Archer observed. 'Why, look what happened to old Doc Flowerday.'

'Yes, that was a shame,' Trail said, nodding his head sadly. 'He was as mad as you make 'em. But I was sorry about it, for one.'

Hornbeam agreed.

'He was a nice old boy. You heard all about it, I suppose, Doc?'

'No, I haven't. Why? Should I?'

He suddenly looked uncomfortable.

'I thought they might have told you something about it in the office,' he said vaguely. 'He was the last doctor before you.'

He sighed gently into his beer.

'It was a pity,' he continued. 'In a way.'

I shifted myself nervously on the bunk.

'What was a pity?'

Hornbeam drained his glass.

'His . . . well, his end, as you might say.'

They sat in silence for a while. The reference to Dr Flowerday had saddened them, and no one seemed to wish to reopen the conversation. I sat and anxiously speculated on his possible fate, for which I had now a good number of workable theories.

Chapter Two

I went to bed that night feeling like my first day at school when someone pinched my tuck-box. But in the morning the rain had stopped and the sun threw a bloodshot early glance on Merseyside. The ship had come to life overnight. She rattled with the noise of steam winches loading cargo, and the ghosts of the evening were replaced by persons who shouted, coughed, and used bad language on each other with comforting humanity.

I had breakfast in the saloon with Hornbeam and the Mates. Their conversation was as mysterious to me as the chat at the hospital lunch-table would have been to them: it was about 'tween decks and stowage, dunnage and ullage, tank tops and cofferdams. The only fact I could grasp was that the *Lotus*'s sailing date was as unpredictable as Judgement Day.

After breakfast I went to my cabin, sat on the narrow strip of settee, and opened the first page of *War and Peace*. This I had bought in three volumes from a bookseller's near Euston Station before catching the train for Liverpool. I thought the voyage would allow me to achieve a ten-years' ambition of finishing the thing; besides, I was determined to make use of the time I was obliged to spend inactively at sea improving my mind. And its long, restful paragraphs might begin to soothe my headaches.

A fortnight ago I had been an assistant in general practice–the medical equivalent of the poor curate, the unbriefed barrister, the new subaltern–living in an atmosphere of Dettol and damp overcoats and dispensing the loot of the National Health Service like a maniacal Lady Bountiful. My principal had a bedside manner and two stock remedies with which he had built up a local reputation of infallibility, and we divided the work between us. He saw the private patients, who diminished in number each Budget day, and took the morning surgery; I had the night calls and the evening clinic. As my clinic came conveniently after work, school, and high tea, it was popular with everyone who wanted a certificate, new teeth, hair, or spectacles, or simply to pass the time. The patients brought their troubles and left them on my doorstep like unwanted babies. They wedged themselves into the uncomfortable and unhygienic-looking sofas in our waiting-room, mirthlessly turning the pages of *Punch*, and glancing shiftily at their neighbours wondering what they had got and if it was catching. There were so many of them they could idle the drab hours of their evening away contentedly. It was cheaper than the pub, and more interesting.

For this I was paid the same wages as an engine-driver; in ten or fifteen years, however, if I behaved myself, I would become a partner and take a share in the spoils. But my life at the time was illuminated with a more pressing excitement: I was going to be married.

Marriage is as much of an obligation for a young doctor as celibacy for a Roman Catholic priest. A medical bachelor is unpopular with the patients, except for visits to eligible daughters, and as even these are now obtainable on the National Health he is a frank financial liability to the practice. My principal had no intention of losing his patients through marital hesitation on the part of his young assistant, and after he had made this as plain as possible he asked his wife to apply a woman's practical mind to the problem and set about finding me a bride.

She procured the daughter of a town councillor. She was a girl called Wendy, a blonde, but of the arid sort, like the stubble in a wheatfield after a hot harvest. Her position in local society made it impossible for me to escape: once the town saw what my principal's wife was up to, Wendy and I were mated as firmly as two rats put in the same cage in the biological laboratory.

We became engaged. The wedding approached with the speed of an early winter.

I suppose, looking back on it, there was good reason for my subconscious to slip into disorder, like a wrecked gear-box in an overdriven car. Wendy was a nice girl. She was well educated, and could talk about things like trigonometry and economics. But she had her defects. Her voice was as dull and authoritative as a Salvation Army drum, she walked like an overloaded wheel-barrow, and she had a figure like a stook of corn. I began to suffer an attack of *terror celebans*, or bachelor's panic.

More robust personalities than mine would have stood up to it: it is a common premarital complaint. But I did not. I developed headaches. I immediately diagnosed a cerebral tumour and hurried to London to see a brain specialist, savouring everything on the way with exquisite farewell tenderness, even the fish served for lunch by British Railways.

The brain specialist listened to me for five minutes and packed me off to a psychiatrist. The psychiatrist was an important and busy man and I arrived at the end of the day, but he let me talk for a quarter of an hour while he signed a few letters and looked for his car key.

'A long holiday,' he said sternly, putting on his overcoat.

'Why don't you take a ship? You won't have any work to do. I did it when I was your age. Signed on a cattle boat going to Murmansk. Half the deckhands were washed overboard one night and I had to turn-to with the rest of them to work the ship. Great fun.'

'I don't think I'd be much good as a deckhand.'

'Anyway, you've got to have a holiday. Put on your best suit and walk down Leadenhall Street. You never know your luck.'

'All right, sir,' I said doubtfully. 'If you advise.'

Thus my honour was saved by modern psychiatry.

The next afternoon I tramped Leadenhall Street, trying to get a berth out of every big shipping office and, by mistake, a branch of Barclay's Bank. It was one of those unfriendly November days when dawn and dusk meet each other in a dim conspiracy over the lunch-table. The rain drizzled on to the grimy pavements, soaking through my mackintosh and the seams of my shoes, and my depression deepened with the twilight. It looked as if the sea had rejected me.

When the offices began to close and the important shipping men were already hurrying westwards I walked up the creaking stairs of the Fathom Line building, prepared to sail with Captain Bligh if necessary. There I was introduced to a Mr Cozens, a little bald man crouched in a high leather chair. He was suspiciously pleased to see me.

'Our *Lotus*, Doctor,' he said, 'is in need of a surgeon. We should be delighted to have you. Forty pounds a month, no need for uniform, just the Company's regulation cap. Can you leave for Santos on Monday?'

But a seafaring friend had once warned me to treat a new ship like a prospective bride and discover her exact age and precise tonnage before committing myself. And I was touchy on such points.

Cozens rapidly sketched for me a description of the *Lotus*. 'She isn't a *big* ship,' he concluded. 'Nor a *fast* ship, exactly.' He smiled like a house agent. 'But she's a very *nice* ship.'

I wondered what to do. I was being asked to sail in a ship I had never seen, to a place I had never heard of, in the employ of a business I knew nothing about. I looked anxiously through the dark window running with comforting English rain. The wisest course was obviously to go back to Wendy and settle for a fortnight in Sidmouth instead.

'Very well,' I said. 'I accept.'

'Excellent!' said Mr Cozens, with relief. 'I'm sure you'll find yourself well suited, Doctor. She's a very nice ship indeed. Quite a lady.'

I nodded. 'Where do I go now?'

'There are a few formalities to be gone through I'm afraid, Doctor. Regulations and such things, you understand. First of all, I must supply you with a letter of appointment. If you'll just wait one minute I'll get one of the girls to type it.'

Running away to sea has become more elaborate since the unhedged days when the errant son slipped down to the docks at nightfall, mated up with a bos'n at a wharfside tavern, and sailed with an Indiaman on the dawn tide. Now there are forms to be filled in, documents to be issued, permits to be warily exchanged for a string of personal data. The next day I was sent down to the Merchant Navy Office, an establishment which was a cross between a railway booking-hall and the charge-room of a police station on a Saturday night. There I poked my letter of appointment nervously through a small window at a clerk, who glanced through it with the unconcealed disgust of a post office employee reading one's private thoughts in a telegram.

'Got your lifeboat ticket?' he asked gloomily, his steel nib arrested in mid-air.

'My what?' I saw for a second the picture of myself shivering on a sinking deck, refused permission to enter the lifeboat because I had not purchased my ticket at the proper counter. 'Where do I buy it?' I asked wildly.

The man looked at me with pity. 'They sends us some mugs these days,' he observed wearily. 'Lifeboat ticket,' he repeated, mouthing the words as if addressing a deaf idiot. 'Ministry certificate. Savvy?'

'No,' I admitted. 'I haven't.'

'Got any distinguishing marks?' he asked, giving me a chance to redeem myself. 'Or blemishes? Tattoos?'

'No. None at all. As far as I know.'

He nodded and gave me a chit entitling me to a free photograph at a shop across the street. I queued between a tall negro in a jacket that half covered his thighs and a man in a strong-smelling roll-necked sweater who picked his teeth with a safety-pin. When my turn came I had to face the camera holding my number in a wooden frame under my chin, and I felt the next step would be in handcuffs.

Now, sitting in my cabin with *War and Peace*, my Company's Regulation Cap hanging from a hook above me, I saw that Mr Cozens was wrong. The *Lotus* wasn't a nice ship at all. She was a floating warehouse, with some accommodation for humans stuck on top like a watchman's attic. All the cabins were small, and mine was like a railway compartment quarter-filled with large pipes. I wondered where they went to, and later discovered I was situated immediately below the Captain's lavatory.

My appraisal of the *Lotus* was interrupted by a knock on the jalousie door. It was Easter, the Doctor's steward. He was a little globular man, who felt his position was not that of a mere servant but of a slightly professional gentleman. As an indication of his superiority to his messmates a throat torch and a thermometer poked out of the top pocket of his jacket, and he frequently talked to me about 'We of the medical fraternity'. He was always ready to give advice to his companions on problems of a medical or social nature that they felt disinclined to pour into the ears of the Doctor, and had an annoying habit of counselling them, for the good of their health, to hurl into the sea the bottles of physic just handed to them by their medical attendant.

'Good morning, Doctor,' he said. 'I have a message from Father.'

'Father?'

'The Captain.'

'Oh.'

'He said he wants a bottle of his usual stomach mixture, pronto.'

'His usual stomach mixture?' I took off my spectacles and frowned. 'How do I know what that is? Has he got a prescription, or anything?'

'Dr Flowerday used to make him up a bottle special.'

'I see.'

The problem grew in importance the more I thought of it.

'The Captain suffers from his stomach quite frequently, does he?'

'Ho, yes, sir. Something chronic.'

'Hm.'

'When he has one of his spasms he gets a cob on, worse than usual. Life ain't worth living for all hands. The only stuff what squares up his innards is the special mixture he got from Dr Flowerday. Makes him bring up the wind, Doctor. Or belch, as we say in the medical profession.'

'Quite. You don't know what's in this medicine, I suppose?'

'Not the foggiest, Doctor.'

'Well, can't you remember? You were with Dr Flowerday some time, weren't you?'

'Several voyages, Doctor. And he was very satisfied, if I may make so bold.'

It occurred to me that this might be the point to clear up the Flowerday mystery for good.

'Tell me, Easter,' I said sharply, 'what exactly happened to Dr Flowerday?'

He scratched his nose with a sad gesture.

'If you wouldn't mind, sir,' he replied with dignity, 'I'd rather not talk about it.'

I got up. It was useless sounding Easter on the fate of my predecessor or on his balm for the Captain's gastric disorders.

Down aft there was a cabin with a notice stencilled above the door saying CERTIFIED HOSPITAL. It was a fairly large apartment which smelt like an underground cell that hadn't been used for some time. There were four cots in it, in a couple of tiers. One bulkhead was taken up with a large locker labelled in red POISONS, one door of which was lying adrift of its hinges on the deck.

Inside the locker were half a dozen rows of square, squat bottles containing the supply of medicines for the ship. These – like the Doctor – were prescribed by the Ministry of Transport. Unfortunately the Ministry, in the manner of the elderly, elegant physicians who come monthly out of retirement to grace the meetings of the Royal Society of Medicine, holds trustingly to the old-established remedies and the comely prescriptions of earlier decades. There were drugs in the cupboard that I had seen only in out-of-date books on pharmacology. I picked up a bottle: *Amylum.* What on earth did one do with amylum? There was a pound of Dover's powder and a drum of castor oil big enough to move the bowels of the earth. At the back I found an empty gin bottle, some Worcester sauce, a tennis racket with broken strings, a dirty pair of black uniform socks, two eggs, a copy of the *Brisbane Telegraph*, and a notice saying NON FUMARE.

I dropped these through the porthole, taking care with the eggs. Below the shelves of bottles was another compartment. I looked into it. It held a heavy mahogany case labelled INSTRUMENT CHEST, which contained the left component of a pair of obstetrical forceps, a saw, a bottle-opener, and a bunch of tooth-picks; but there were five gross of grey cardboard eyeshades, over seven apiece for all hands.

I saw that prescribing was going to be more difficult than in general practice, where I scribbled a prescription on my pad and the patient took it to the chemist, who deciphered my writing and slickly made up the medicine. We had been obliged to attend a course of lectures on pharmacy and dispensing in medical school, but these were always held on a Saturday morning, when most of the students were already on their way to the rugger field. For this reason there was an informal roster among the class to forge the signatures of their companions on the attendance sheet, before slipping softly away themselves when the lecturer turned to clarify some obscure pharmacological point on the blackboard. As I had attended the greater number of my pharmacy lectures by proxy in this way, I now felt like a new wife in her first kitchen.

I picked up one or two bottles hopefully, and I was delighted to find that my predecessor, Dr Flowerday, had his pharmacy lectures on Saturday mornings also. On the back of each bottle was a small label bearing in shaky handwriting guidance such as 'Good for diarrhoea', or 'This mixed with Tinct. Ipecac. seems all right for colds', or 'Apparently inert'. There was also a sheet of cardboard on which Dr Flowerday had written in Portuguese, Spanish, French, and Hindustani translations of three questions which he seemed to find adequate for investigating his patients: 'Have you a cough?' 'Where is the pain?' and 'Have you been with any dirty women recently?'

I found an old pair of pharmacist's scales and a glass graduated in drachms, and started to make up the Captain's medicine. The first one turned into a pink putty, and was abandoned (it later came in useful for minor infections of the crew's feet). The second tasted strongly of peppermint but seemed adequate. I corked it and carried it up to the Captain's cabin.

I had not met Captain Hogg before. He had been ashore the previous night and he never came down for breakfast. When I had asked Hornbeam about him he replied unconvincingly, 'He has his good points.'

'What are they?' Trail asked gloomily.

I inquired what form Captain Hogg's malignity took.

'Oh, he thinks the sun shines out of his bottom,' Trail said. 'They all get like that. It's living alone too much that does it. They ought to be made to carry their wives with them to keep them under control.'

'The Old Man isn't married,' Hornbeam told him.

'Neither was his father,' Trail said.

I knocked on the cabin door.

'Enter!'

I went in.

Captain Hogg was of a curious shape. He was like a huge pear. From the sharp top of his bald head he came out gradually until the region of the umbilicus, from which point he spread abruptly in all directions. He was sitting in an armchair in his shirt-sleeves, his face obscured by the book he was reading. It was a periodical called *True Horrors*, on the front of which a vivid blonde, with an alarming bosom was struggling unsuccessfully with a gorilla, a man in a black mask, and her underclothes.

The book didn't move. I stood just inside the door, holding the medicine bottle in front of me like a talisman. He spoke:

'Well?'

I rubbed my right shoe slowly up my left calf.

'Doctor, sir,' I said.

The magazine came down. For a moment we stared at each other with interest. I thought he looked as friendly as a firing-squad.

'Ah!' he said.

I proffered the bottle.

'Your stomach mixture, sir.'

Either my prescribing or Dr Flowerday's directions were at fault; perhaps the ship's drugs had degenerated with time. Some unplanned reaction occurred within the bottle. With a sharp pop the cork flew into the air.

'You may find this a little strong,' I said, picking up the cork quickly. 'I recommend taking it well diluted.'

He took the bottle silently and stood it on the desk beside him.

'Your cap,' he said. 'You have a cap?'

'Yes, sir. Company's regulation pattern.'

'Why aren't you wearing it?'

'I'm sorry sir, I—'

'The cap is worn on all official visits to the Captain. If I were asking you up here for a peg, that would be different. But I'm not. It's a matter of etiquette. There's no tramp ship stuff about this vessel. This is my ship, you understand, Doctor? *My* ship. If we get that straight we shall rub along splendidly together.'

'Yes, sir.'

I was a medical student again, before the Dean for filling the senior surgeon's rubber operating boots with iced water.

'Good. You haven't been to sea before?'

'No, sir.'

'You'll find the routine fairly simple, as far as you're concerned. You take your surgery at nine every morning, and at ten you bring me up a list of the sick on board and what's wrong with 'em. There's none of this damn medical secrecy nonsense at sea. I want to know all about them. I have to carry the can in the end. Understand?'

'Yes, sir.'

'Good. Then at eleven o'clock we inspect the ship–you wear your cap again. Dinner is at twelve-thirty and supper at six. Do you play cribbage?'

'No, sir.'

He looked disappointed.

'Pity. The last Doctor played a good hand. Passes the tedium of the evenings at sea.' He indicated the magazine. 'I'm a great reading man myself, but I like a game of crib now and then.'

On a sudden thought he leant over and rummaged in the desk.

'I've got a book on it here. Read that through, then we might be able to have a few games.'

'Thank you, sir.'

He hesitated a moment, staring at the square toes of his shoes.

'Did you know Dr Flowerday?' he asked.

'No, sir.'

'He was the last Doctor. Very good man. We all liked him very much. Unfortunately, he didn't know when to stop. I shouldn't like to see you go the same way. The Company might think there was something wrong with my ship.'

My mouth went dry.

'What–er, what happened to him, sir?'

Captain Hogg glanced at me, then returned to inspecting his toes.

'Of course, a man's entitled to think what he likes,' he said forcefully. 'I'm a respecter of anyone's opinions. But there are limits, Doctor. Limits.'

'Yes, sir.'

'You've never thought you were somebody else, for instance? Have you, Doctor?'

'No, sir. I–I can't recall doing so.'

'Well, there you are. It happens sometimes at sea. I've seen some of the best of fellows get taken that way. I remember when I first went Mate, the Third thought he was Cleopatra. Very awkward it was for all hands.'

'I can see it would be, sir.'

'But Dr Flowerday had a weakness. I tell you in strict confidence, Doctor.'

'Of course, sir.'

It appeared that my predecessor, after having drunk two bottles of gin a day for several years in the service of the *Lotus*, got religion shortly after leaving Singapore, and extinguished himself one night in the Indian Ocean through the mistaken impression that he had the rightful ability to walk upon the water.

Chapter Three

The *Lotus* sailed, to the surprise of her crew, three days later. We spent the time tethered to the quay, loading heavy packing-cases from railway trucks. It was an interesting performance. The cases were raised to the level of the ship's deck, drawn horizontally inwards, and lowered into the holds. This was done with the derricks and steam winches, each set manned by a gang of Liverpool dockers, who went about their work with the leisurely decorum of the House of Lords considering an unimportant Bill on a hot afternoon.

There was a docker at each winch, and the rest of them worked either down the hold or on the quay. Each gang was controlled by a man in a long overcoat and a bowler hat, who directed their activities with the economy of gesture of an experienced bidder at an auction. The twitch of a little finger, an inclination of the head, the drop of an eyelid, and four tons of crated machinery went spinning through the air and down the hatch as cleanly as a holed-out golf ball.

The stowage of the cargo was supervised by the Mates, under the directions of Archer. He had his bunk covered with cargo manifests, bills of lading, and plans of the ship with the different merchandise coloured in with crayon.

'The Second gets the thin end of it,' he said. 'He's always cargo officer. Too much work in it for me.'

'But it looks fairly simple. Don't you just go on putting the stuff in until the ship's full?'

'Haven't you ever packed a case for a holiday? The things you want first always seem to be at the bottom. If that happened in the ship there'd be trouble. You can't tip everything out.'

'I see what you mean.'

'Besides, there's the trim of the ship to think about. There's more in cargo than meets the eye.'

He looked at his plan. 'Nos. 1 and 4 are full, but there's plenty of room in 2 and 3. We'll be here a week yet, you can bet on that.'

But orders, based on some deep calculation in the Fathom Line offices, came for us to sail. Twenty-four hours later, in the morning, the *Lotus* left.

An air of excitement spread through the ship before sailing, as everyone began to go about their jobs more briskly. I was greatly stimulated by the promising departure, for I had become thoroughly used to living alongside the wharf in the past few days and occasionally doubted that we would ever sail at all. The dockers who had made free with our decks were turned down the gangway, leaving behind them a litter of newspapers, cigarette packets, and matches trampled into the rusty steel. The wide hatches were covered with heavy slabs of wood, and square tarpaulins lashed over them. At the head of the gangway the quartermaster fixed a blackboard announcing confidently THE S.S. LOTUS WILL SAIL AT 10 O'CLOCK FOR SANTOS NO SHORE

LEAVE, and a thin black stream of smoke shot powerfully upwards from the funnel. Our bleak masts were enlivened with flags: the red ensign trailed over our stern, the Company's house-flag–a red F topped by an anchor on a white square–was hoisted at the mainmast, and from the foremast the blue-and-white P announced our intentions to the waterside.

'That at least is a flag I recognize,' I said to Trail. 'The Blue Peter.'

'Yes, we'll soon be on our way, Doc. It's a bloody nuisance. I was just getting a nice little piece lined up last night. It's always the same.'

'I shall be glad to get to sea, I must say. I've seen enough of Liverpool.'

'You'll get your bellyful of sea all right, don't you worry. Shouldn't get too excited, though. They may change their minds and send us into Cardiff when we get out in the Irish Sea. Not a bad place, Cardiff, though I prefer Middlesbrough myself. The pubs are better.'

Shortly afterwards Trail reappeared on deck with his cap on, looking very determined and ten years older.

'Got to do the testing,' he explained brusquely. 'Tugs'll be here any minute now.'

I heard him ring the bridge telegraphs and sound the whistle, which blew a long silent plume of steam into the air for some seconds before it struck its note. The customs officers gave us a final suspicious look and made for the shore, their threatening bags of rummage tools over their shoulders. Men in yellow raincoats and misshapen trilbys hurried aboard with desperate last letters addressed to Captain Hogg, and rushed away again anxiously looking at their watches. A Mr Swithinbank, a pale youth with steel spectacles from the Liverpool office, came breathlessly down the deck after me, with a paper in his hand.

'Here's the Bill of Health, Doctor,' he said. 'Cripes! For a moment I thought I'd lost you! You can't sail without it.

'Thank you very much,' I said, taking the document reverently.

'Are you all right?' he asked quickly, making for the gangway. 'Medical stores O.K.? Too late now, anyway. Have a good voyage. Cheery-bye!'

'Good-bye,' I shouted after him helplessly. 'We seem a bit short of sulphonamides.'

'Bring us a ham from Brazil if you remember it,' he called over his shoulder. 'Don't forget the poor starving English.'

He hurried away between the railway waggons and lorries on the quay. It was almost ten. Two sailors, who had somehow managed to drink themselves to a standstill at that hour, staggered up the gangway and collapsed on the deck.

'Take 'em below,' Hornbeam shouted to the Bos'n, with the air of a man handling a familiar situation. 'They'll be logged tomorrow morning. Has Smiley turned up yet?'

'No sign, Mr Hornbeam.'

'I dunno,' Hornbeam said resignedly. 'If you docked a ship in Hell you'd still get deserters. Get my watch turned-to, Bos'n. I'm going to stations.'

'Aye aye, sir.'

Two tugs nuzzled under our bow and stern, their skippers standing impassively at the wheel in their oilskins like waiting taxi-drivers. The pilot came aboard–an alarmingly unnautical figure in a tweed overcoat and bowler hat, carrying an umbrella and a black Gladstone bag. I watched Trail knock on the Captain's door, salute, and announce 'Tugs alongside and pilot aboard, sir.' He stepped aside as Captain Hogg appeared, resplendent in gold braid, and mounted solemnly to the bridge. The gangway came up, the two tugs plucked the ship away from the quay, and the ropes fell into the water with long splashes. The *Lotus* became suddenly changed into an entity, a being in her own right, instead of a rusty appendage of a dirty Liverpool wharf.

I leant over the rail with Easter, watching the steadily widening gap of water between us and the shore. I had never been on a moving ship before, apart from a brief passage from Margate to Southend in a paddle steamer, and I felt excited and apprehensive. I found the belief that we should now all be transported by the *Lotus* from Liverpool to the Tropics too outlandish to take seriously.

'Well, we're off,' was all I could think to say.

'Yes, sir. In an hour or so we'll be well out in the River.'

'You know, Easter, to me it seems almost impossible for this little ship to take us all the way to South America.'

'Sometimes, sir,' he answered gloomily, 'I think it's a bloody miracle she moves at all.'

We shook with a gentle ague as the engines picked up speed, slipped down the channel of thick Mersey water, passed the tolling buoys and the Bar light, out into the Irish Sea; in the afternoon a sharp sea-wind blew down the deck and the Welsh mountains were huddling on the horizon. I pranced delightedly round the ship, which was now musical with the wind, looking at everything like a schoolboy in the Science Museum.

I had a letter in my pocket from Wendy, which I purposely kept unopened until we were under way. It was a short prim note, wishing me a good voyage, hoping my headaches were better, and mentioning that I was not to think of ourselves as betrothed any longer. It appeared she had become enamoured of the son of the local draper. I tore the letter up and scattered it over the side: the pieces spread on the sea and were left behind. I laughed. I felt a cad, a devilish cad. But now, surely, I was allowed to be: I was a sailor. A wife in every port for me! I thought. Watch out, my girls, watch out! A rollicking sailor lad, indeed! With a snatch of sea-shanty on my lips I went below for a cup of tea, aware that I was perhaps not quite myself.

My elation lasted less than a day. The next morning I was sick.

The *Lotus* creaked and groaned her way through the water like an old lady in a bargain sale. She climbed to the top of a wave, paused for breath, shook herself, and slid helplessly into the trough of the next. I lay on my bunk and watched the sprightly horizon jumping round the porthole, trying to think about eminently terrestrial objects, such as the Albert Hall.

Easter put his head round the door. In his hands he had a cup of tea and a small roseless watering-can, of the type preserved for the conveyance of tepid water in English country hotels.

'Good morning, Doctor,' he said briefly. 'Will you be in for breakfast?'

I rolled my head on the pillow.

'Not feeling too good, Doctor?'

'I think I am going to die.'

He nodded, gravely assessing the clinical findings.

'Throwing up much?' he asked pleasantly.

'Everything.'

'If I may take the liberty, a good meal is what you want. Plate of fried eggs and bacon and you'll be right as rain. Works like a charm. Hold it a moment,

Doctor, I'll fetch a bowl.'

I held the bowl like a mother with a newborn infant.

'Feeling better now you've got all that up?' he asked solicitously.

'A bit.'

A thought struck him.

'Wouldn't like a bit of cold beef and a few pickles, would you? They'd do just as well.'

'No, no, no! I don't want anything. Nothing at all. I just want to be left alone.'

'Very good, Doctor. Just as you say. Perhaps you might feel like a bit of lunch?'

'I doubt it very much.'

He left me in ecstatic solitude. I lay rigidly on the bunk, concentrating on the words stencilled, by order of the Ministry of Transport, immediately above me: CERTIFIED TO ACCOMMODATE ONE SEAMAN. Seaman, indeed! All I wanted to see was a tree.

It was essential to keep my mind fixed on something beyond the clouds of nausea spiralling round me, so I started to count the rivets in the deckhead. I had reached ninety-eight when Hornbeam came in. He was smoking a pipe.

'Hello, Doc! I hear you're off colour. What's the trouble?'

'I'm seasick.'

He looked surprised.

'Yes, I suppose she is pitching a bit,' he admitted, glancing through the porthole. 'Do you mind if I use one of your matches?'

He blew mouthfuls of smoke into the cabin.

'Better out than in,' he said, as I put the bowl down again.

'I suppose so.'

'You know what, Doc? I'm going to give you a genuine cure for seasickness. I can't often treat a doctor, but this is just the thing. Do you want to try it?'

'What is it?'

'A pint of sea-water. It's an old sailor's cure. When I was an apprentice it was the only thing that stopped me on my first voyage. If we were sick we got kicked down the bridge ladder and given a pint glass just out of the sea-bucket by the Mate. Shall I get you some?'

I raised my hand.

'I think I'd rather not have anything at all at the moment, thank you.'

'As you like, Doc. I'm only making a suggestion. Have you tried covering one eye?'

'It wasn't much good.'

'No, I don't believe it is. Damn! Can I have another match? My pipe's gone out again.'

'Would you mind lighting it outside? It's a bit–a bit strong at the moment.'

'Oh, sorry! I didn't think of that.'

I called weakly after him at the door.

'How long is this likely to go on for?'

He calculated for a few seconds.

'Not very long. I should say we'd be in pretty calm water in five or six days.'

'Five or six days!'

I groaned.

I lay and tried to analyse my condition, like the dying surgeon, John Hunter. It was, of course, a ridiculously simple malady when one looked at it with scientific detachment. The endolymph in my semicircular canals was stimulating the endings of my cochlear nerve, which transmitted influences to the brain and initiated the reflex arc of vomiting. It should be easy for a little will-power to inhibit the reflex. After all, the brain was the master . . . I exercised the will-power.

'Morning!' Trail said from the doorway. 'When you've got your head out of that bowl I'll tell you a sure-fire cure for seasickness.'

I fell back on the pillow. I had given up. When the angel of death arrived I would shake him cordially by the hand.

Trail came over to the bunk. He put his hands in his trouser pockets and pulled out two bottles of stout.

'Guinness,' he said proudly. 'Drink these and you'll be fine by lunch-time. Works like magic.'

'Oh God!' I said. 'Oh God, oh God!'

Trail looked puzzled.

'What's the matter? Don't you like stout? Here, take it easy! That one nearly went over my uniform.'

He left me wondering submissively how long it would be before Easter came back and started talking about lunch. And it was bound to be Irish stew.

After three days the sea and I achieved a compromise. The sun came out, the wind dropped and lost its malice, the water was tidied up like a room after a wild party. For myself, I learned to lean against the sway of the ship, and I felt well enough to risk lunch in the saloon.

It was my first meal at sea. I sat with the Captain, the Chief Engineer, Hornbeam and Archer, and the Chief Steward, a thin little mouse-faced man called Whimble. As soon as the bell rang we converged on the dining saloon with the briskness of seaside boarders: Captain Hogg disliked anyone to be late.

I was on the Captain's right hand, the Mate on his left. The Chief Engineer faced the Captain, and the other two sat themselves between.

'Ah, Doctor!' Captain Hogg said, jovially enough. 'Decided to join us at last, have you?'

'Yes, sir.'

He unfolded his napkin and tucked it under his chin with deliberation.

'Seasickness,' he said slowly, 'is entirely mental. You imagine it.'

I shrugged my shoulders.

'Well,' I said, in my professional tone, 'there are more complicated reasons than that. I admit there may be a psychological element. But there is obviously some fault with the balancing apparatus in the ears, and probably with the gastric nerves.'

The Captain broke a roll.

'No.' He said it decisively. 'It is entirely mental.'

He started drinking soup loudly.

No one spoke until he had finished.

'Mr McDougall,' he said, slipping half a roll into his mouth, 'have you got that book you were going to lend me at supper last night?'

The Chief looked up. He was a thin, wrinkled Scot with a face dominated by a thick strip of sandy eyebrow, from which his eyes looked out like a couple of Highland gamekeepers inspecting poachers through the undergrowth.

'Aye,' he said. 'You mean *The Squeaker*?'

The Captain nodded.

'That's it. I like a bit of Peter Cheyney.'

'But surely,' I said immediately. '*The Squeaker* was by Edgar Wallace? It was written over twenty years ago.'

'No,' the Captain said. 'It was Peter Cheyney.'

'You know, sir, I'm perfectly . . .'

'Peter Cheyney,' he said, with the emphasis of a full stop. He then fell upon a plate of mutton chops, which disappeared into his mouth like a rush-hour crowd going down an escalator.

We continued eating in silence.

Captain Hogg finished his chops and brought his knife and fork together with a flourish.

'Mr Whimble,' he said.

'Sir!'

The Chief Steward jumped, and choked over a chop bone.

'I have, I suppose, tasted worse chops than these. In a fifth-rate café on the Mexican coast possibly. Why don't you throw the cook over the side? If he'd served filth like this to the Captain when I was an apprentice the fellow would have had his bottom kicked round the deck.'

'I'm sorry, Captain,' Whimble mumbled. 'I'll see to it.'

'I should think so. You never get cooking like you used to. All they think about these days are vitamins and calories, and such stuff. What good's that to a man? Fad, that's all it is. You don't need vitamins or calories,' he said with disgust. 'Eh, Doctor?'

'Well, they are really two quite different factors. And vitamins are terribly important.'

'Bosh! I'm not a doctor–I don't pretend to be. But if you get a good bellyful of meat and spuds every day you'll be all right.'

'You must have vitamins,' I insisted, but feebly.

'Vitamins are bosh, Doctor. Bosh!'

I began to see that opinions were forbidden, even professional ones. Our mealtimes were going to be rollicking.

Chapter Four

The next morning after breakfast I went to my cabin, wedged myself on the settee, and again opened *War and Peace* at page one. I had not felt well enough to start the book since we sailed, but now I looked forward to a leisurely stroll through its pages during the rest of the voyage. I had almost reached the end of the first paragraph when a conversation started in the alleyway outside my cabin door.

The door was on a hook for ventilation, so I was able to overhear it clearly. There were two speakers, who used the adenoidal grunts with which the citizens of Liverpool communicate with each other.

'Ullo,' said one. 'Whatcher doin', la'?'

'Come to see ——ing quack.'

'Ar. What's ——ing trouble, la'?'

'Dunno. Reckon I must've picked up a ——ing dose, or something.'

'Where, in Liverpeule?'

''Sright. Nice bit of skirt she was too.'

'You can never tell, la'.'

'——ing right there.'

A short silence.

'What's quack like?'

'Oh, he's a young ——er.'

'Reckon he's much good?'

'——ing medical student, most likely.'

'If we was homeward bound reckon I'd wait and see a proper doctor,' the sufferer said. I opened the door. 'Good morning, Doc,' he added brightly. 'Can you see us a second, in private like?'

'Go down to the hospital,' I said coldly. 'I'll be along in a few minutes.'

'Very good, Doctor.'

When I arrived at the hospital I found that Easter had diagnosed and prescribed for the condition with an efficiency founded on wide experience of it.

'Take these, chum,' he said, handing over a bottle of sulphathiazole tablets, 'and in a couple of days you'll be feeling like a box of birds, as they say in New Zealand.'

The patient stuffed the bottle in his waistband and jauntily walked out.

'Don't you think I ought to give him a short lecture?' I suggested.

Easter seemed to find this amusing.

'We all has our thoughtless moments, Doctor, don't we? Take a card,' he said, abruptly drawing a pack from his pocket. 'Any one. Don't let me see it.'

I took one automatically.

'Right,' he said. 'I will now shuffle them, see? No deception. You could have taken any card in the pack. Let me concentrate.' He screwed up his fat face in a spasm of thought. 'Four of diamonds,' he said.

'That is perfectly correct. Though I hardly think we should be doing this sort of thing when we are supposed to be treating patients.'

Easter slipped the cards back into the top pocket of his jacket with a subdued air of triumph.

'Dr Flowerday always liked me to show him a few tricks. Used to have him in fits, sometimes. Didn't half get narked when he couldn't find how they was done.'

'And how was that one done, if I may ask?'

'Them's all four of diamonds, actual,' Easter said carelessly, tapping his pocket.

'You seem to be quite a specialist in this sort of thing.'

'For three years ashore I was Pin Hung, the Famous Chinese Magician. Round the halls. Mostly the North–Barrow, Carlisle, Sunderland. Grimsby was my favourite. Always hit the jackpot in Grimsby. I've a book of cuttings down below . . .'

'All right. Later on in the voyage, possibly.'

He flicked three cards from his sleeve and manipulated them on the top of a tin of bandages.

'Now then, Doctor. Try your luck. Bet you a dollar that you can't spot the lady.'

'Easter,' I said with interest, 'how is it that you have come to land up in your present position? A man of your peculiar talents would be far more at home on the racecourse than in a ship's hospital.'

'That's the trouble, Doctor. I worked the race trains for years. But I got fed up with it. You can get put inside too many times.'

I stared at him.

'Do you mean–are you trying to say that you have been in prison?'

I was alarmed. In shore practice this was not a condition usually found in one's colleagues.

'Ho, yes,' he replied, with the air of a man admitting he knew Brighton or Scarborough fairly well. 'Didn't like it much, though. Too bloody cold in winter.'

'So you came to sea instead?'

'That's right, Doctor. Used to be on the Western Ocean run for donkeys' years in the big passenger boats. When I was a lad that is, and could run about a bit more. So I came back to it. Signed on as a steward. It's a good life, and you gets your grub regular. I took this job on when a mate of mine jumped ship in Sydney and I helped out in the surgery homeward bound. I like it better than waiting in the saloon. More dignified. And Dr Flowerday used to let me dispose of surplus equipment and stores on the coast, if I could. Penicillin and such like, that ain't got long to go before it's U.S. That be all right with you, Doctor? Dr Flowerday and I used to have an understanding about the proceeds.'

'I think we shall have to consider that later.'

'Very good, Doctor. There's one of the crew sick in his cabin.'

'Then why the devil didn't you tell me before? Instead of fooling around with all these damn card tricks?'

'There ain't no hurry, Doctor. It's only Chippy. The Carpenter.'

'What's the matter with him?'

'He's having one of his turns.'

I was suspicious. A diagnosis of the turns, to which over half of the middle-aged population of the country seems liable, can represent any condition from attacks of flatulence to full-blown epileptic fits.

'We'd better go and see him at once.'

'Very good, Doctor.'

I followed Easter aft, to the crew's accommodation in the poop. We went up an iron ladder to a door with CARPENTER AND LAMPTRIMMER stencilled over it. It was a bleak little cabin, with green-painted steel bulkheads and a couple of metal bunks one above the other. The only decoration was a photograph of an oblong tombstone with 'Mother's Grave' written underneath it.

On the top bunk was the patient, huddled under a grey ship's blanket. I gave him a shake. A head poked out at me, and I recognized the man with the lamp I had met at the top of the gangway. He needed a shave, there was dried saliva at the corners of his mouth, and his eyes looked like a couple of cherries on a blancmange.

'Aghurrr!' he said.

'Now what's the trouble, my man? I started briskly.

He disregarded me. His eyes were on something else in the cabin, behind me. He pointed shakily to the corner.

'Get away you bastards!' he yelled.

I jumped.

'Now don't get excited . . .' I said nervously.

He crouched into a corner of the bunk, pulling the blanket tightly round him.

'Get away!' he screamed. 'Get away from me!'

He brushed something from the bunk rail.

'What is it?' I asked. 'What's the trouble?'

The man started muttering, so that I had to lean closely over him to hear.

'It's them dogs,' he said. 'Bloody great Alsatians. Bloody great green ones. Look! Five of the bastards!'

I turned sharply round to Easter.

'This man has got D.T.s,' I announced.

'Ho, yes,' Easter said casually, not shifting from the doorway. 'Been having them for years. Long as I can remember, anyway.'

'But we must do something about it! I hope you realize this is a serious condition? You seem to treat it very lightly.'

'He always gets 'em about this part of the trip. He'll be as right as rain for weeks now. Been on the booze since we sailed. Says it makes him sad leaving Liverpool.'

The patient rattled the bunk.

'Get your paws orf of my face!' he yelled.

'If I might make so bold, Doctor,' Easter said, still leaning on the door, 'I would say this was an occasion for the medical comforts.'

'Medical comforts? What on earth are you talking about?'

'Bottle of brandy,' he explained. 'It's issued buckshee, like, for the hospital. You can get another from the Chief Steward if you indent for it.'

'But I haven't seen anything of this brandy.'

'I usually keeps it in my cabin, Doctor. Dr Flowerday and I had an understanding about it.'

'Is there any left?'

'Almost half, Doctor,' he said proudly. 'Dr Flowerday used to give him a glassful and talk to him, gentle like, as if he was a baby. Worked like a charm. Shall I fetch the bottle?'

'Here they come again!' the patient shouted.

'Perhaps you'd better,' I said.

I gave him a tumbler of brandy and explained that the five green Alasatians were not really present, like a nurse soothing a night-scared child. After a couple of glasses and half an hour's persuasion I had reduced the intruders to three in number, and to terriers of normal colour. I felt entitled to be satisfied with this. I left the patient sleeping in his bunk with the empty glass in his hand and went back to my cabin.

'Seen many cases like him ashore?' Easter asked with interest, collecting the remains of the brandy.

'No. I have not. There seems a great difference, Easter, between the practice of medicine on shore and at sea.'

'Funny you should say that. Same thing always struck me about the doctors.'

Chapter Five

It is remarkable what spiritual contentment can be obtained from washing your own socks. I soaped a pair in the basin and hung them to dry on a line Easter had stretched across my cabin. I glowed with a modest sense of achievement. This was the first time I had been obliged to do any washing, which I had previously looked upon as an esoteric feminine function comparable with giving birth.

The crew of the *Lotus* did their own laundering–even Captain Hogg, who appeared in the early afternoon on the strip of deck round his cabin with a bundle of white uniforms under his arm and a basket of clothes-pegs. The other officers hung their shirts over their bunks and smartened them afterwards in the bathroom with the Third Mate's travelling iron. Down aft, the crew set aside Sunday afternoon for the laundry, when it was usual to see large firemen and deckhands dressed only in underpants and tattoos scrubbing their singlets with bar soap in the fire-buckets. The clothes were then strung thickly round the winches and ventilators and flapped round the stern of the ship like some fantastic signal.

Drying was simple, for we had reached the Tropics and the ship's company was in white uniforms. I had only to fix a white cover on my Company's regulation cap, but the officers appeared unexpectedly one morning in white shorts and shirts like a crop of snowdrops. The other hands were less affected by the order. Easter changed his blue serge jacket for a white one, but the rest were permitted the informality of uniform usual in the Merchant Service and did no more than roll their dungaree trousers half-way up their calves and remove their shirts.

'We should have been in whites two days ago,' Hornbeam grumbled. 'It's the Old Man's fault.'

'Why? What's he done now?'

'The old bastard sunbathes every afternoon and keeps us in blues until his knees are brown.'

I felt I was becoming quite a sailor. I let my days pass uncaringly, carried away in the drift of the sea routine. In a ship everybody seems constantly to be getting up or going to bed. The watch changes every fourth hour, which brings one of the mates, warm from his bunk, to the bridge, and sends a couple of engineers scuttling down the complicated ladders into the engine-room and stokehold. As well as the officers, two A.B.s go on the bridge to take turns at the wheel, and a gang of greasers and firemen troop below. All this movement is set off by the ship's bell on the bridge, which rings through each watch an arithmetical progression of half-hourly strokes.

Members of the ship's company who had no watches to keep–people like Whimble, Easter, and myself–all arranged their days round the after-dinner siesta. In the afternoon the whole ship died. All hands, apart from those essential for the running of the vessel, tottered away from the saloon table and, encouraged by a weighty meal and the noon session of gin, crashed gratefully into their bunks. This was a habit I found condemnable, but irresistible. In medical school and practice the afternoon had been my busiest time, and I was determined to pass the hours between one and four studying *War and Peace*. At first I never drank before the meal and avoided the cook's suet roll, of which Captain Hogg must have eaten several fathoms every voyage. But–whether I was the subject of mass-suggestion or sea air contains some subtle narcotic–I was unconscious before I got the taste of the ship's cheese out of my mouth, and I stayed asleep until Easter shook me at four with a cup of tea and a small piece of confectionery known in the Merchant Service as a tabnab. This habit I regarded nervously as the first indication of moral degeneration.

At five-thirty every evening my bath was run by Boswell, the bath steward. Boswell, like Easter, had seen better days, and the courtly manners he had learned in big P. & O.s and Cunarders had not deserted him. Whatever the temperature, he wore a shining white jacket, a stiff wing collar, and a black bow tie. He would arrive at my cabin door at half-past five precisely, a clean blue-and-white towel folded over his arm, and announce 'Your bath awaits, Doctor', as if it were an important delegation. He followed me to the officers' bathroom, which smelled like a seaside cave at low tide, spread the towel over the chair, and mixed the water with his skinny hand. He dipped in a foot-long thermometer with a little metal bucket at the end, anxiously inspecting the temperature, and made a careful adjustment to the taps (later I found the thermometer had not worked for several years). He then poured some fresh hot water from a large shining copper can into a small bowl for the feet, and laid on the white wooden rack across the bath my flannel, a long-handled scrubbing brush, a loofah, and a bar of sea-water soap.

'Would there be anything else you require, sir?' he asked every evening. I found it difficult to complicate such a simple act as taking a bath any further, and he would bow deeply and retire backwards through the steam. I knew he did so with disappointment, for a bath suggested to him as many variations as soup to a French chef. Every few days he would press me to take a few spoonfuls of mustard in it, or some washing soda, or a tumbler of rosewater. 'Might I recommend a little Sloan's?' he asked once. 'I used to put it in regularly for one doctor I looked after in the Cunard. Very good for the joints, I believe.'

Boswell's manners were unfortunately not sufficient to overcome the discomforts of the *Lotus*'s bathroom. There were no portholes or ventilators, so water collected on the deckhead as efficienly as in the main condenser in the engine-room, and thence fell thickly in rusty brown drops. The deck was covered with some crumbling material that left potholes to trip the bather and make him catch his head or his shins against sharp projecting pieces of steel. The bath itself was shaped like a coffin, and was furnished with a pair of fearsome taps that gave between them hot and cold sea water and a disproportionate amount of steam. There was an alternative –the fresh-water shower outside Hornbeam's cabin, but owing to some subtle mechanical fault many feet below in the engine-room this emitted only ice-cold water or superheated steam, and after escaping a third-degree burn I decided to stick to the safe tepid waters under Boswell's supervision.

Boswell did not stop at baths: far greater was his pride in the officers' lavatories. These were not much more efficient than the bath, and in rough weather became alarmingly unreliable. But to Boswell they were a porcelain monument to his own calling. He spent the morning cleaning and polishing them, and on our arrival for inspection would bow low and flush each as we passed with the jaunty pride of the satisfied artist.

'There's more in lavatories than meets the eye, sir,' he explained to me one day, with a sigh. 'You've got to *understand* lavatories to do this job.' I gathered from Easter that as he contentedly did his morning task Boswell dreamed of his retirement in charge of a small underground nest of them at one of the quieter corners of Liverpool.

My professional duties were not exacting. I saw a couple of patients in the morning, perhaps half a dozen at five. The most common trouble was the constipation, doctor. This I first treated with pharmacopoeial doses of the usual remedies, but I soon found it was necessary to multiply the amount by three for most of the patients and by five for the Bos'n and firemen. There were boils and warts, a few burns from the engine-room, and several vague illnesses whose leading symptom was a disinclination to work. We had a few more cases resulting from careless choice of friends during our last nights in Liverpool. The approach to the medical attendant by sufferers from this embarrassing condition varied from the shifty request–with a sidelong glance at Easter–to ''Ave a word wiv you a minute, Doctor,' to the full-blooded storming of the surgery by the experienced invalid with his 'Say, Doc, can you fix this for us by Friday?'

At eleven we inspected the ship. Hornbeam, Whimble, McDougall, and myself gathered outside the saloon door and saluted when Captain Hogg's boots appeared on the companionway from his cabin. This homage he returned with the grace of a publican handing back a counterfeit half-crown.

We lined up behind him and set off touring the decks, each of us trying to look as disagreeable as possible. We filed in and out of Boswell's lavatories with dignity, and zealously searched for dust under the coconut matting. The progress was broken only when Captain Hogg's eye was jarred by something that gave him displeasure, when he would turn his fury not only on the man responsible but on his parents as well. At first I shivered at the onslaught: then I grew to appreciate the range and power of the Captain's imagination and the felicity with which he turned his sentences, until I listened to him with fascination. As for the victims, they shrugged their shoulders and took no notice. Raving Captains were just like storms at sea: you had to put up with them until they blew themselves out, and not become unreasonably excited.

After inspection the Captain went on the bridge to supervise the daily ceremony of finding the noon position of the ship. I went up there only once, because Captain Hogg looked on visitors like a sour landowner spotting picnickers on his front lawn. It was a shady, restful place, lined with dark wood and brass, like an old-fashioned saloon bar. The sea was surprisingly far below, and the only sound was the irregular loud clicking of the gyro repeater, like the ticking of an arrhythmic clock. Abaft the bridge was the chartroom, where rulers, set-squares, and neatly sharpened pencils were arranged like a tidy school desk, and the chronometers nestled under thick glass like a pair of premature infants in an incubator. Hornbeam once offered me his sextant and let me work out our position, but I disgusted him by putting the *Lotus* within a few miles of Cleveland, Ohio.

I spent most of my time chatting to the officers off watch, leaning on the rail, playing quoits, or nosing round the deck. I was beginning to learn what everything was called. Ships have a distinct anatomy of their own, and our daily rounds were as confusing to me as my first demonstration in the dissecting room. I recognized fairly early on the difference between port and starboard, fore and aft, and a binnacle and a barnacle; but I was still uncertain where to find such obscure pieces of marine furnishing as the jumper stays, the monkey island, and the shrouds.

The tenth morning of the voyage I sat down resolutely in my cabin and took *War and Peace* from the locker. Somehow I had not yet found time to pass the first page. I opened it, smoothed down the paper, and began again the first paragraph. Hornbeam rattled the jalousie door and came in.

'Morning, Doc! Everything bearing an even strain?'

'Good morning, Chief,' I said. 'I think so, thanks very much.'

'Good.'

Picking up the first volume of *War and Peace* he neatly squashed a cockroach that was scuttling across the bulkhead.

'These damn roaches,' he said. 'Come out in families once it turns hot. Had any in bed with you?'

'No, not yet.'

He pulled a tobacco tin from his pocket.

'Would you like the makings?' he asked, offering it.

'No, thank you. I'm afraid it's a nautical knack I haven't picked up.'

'It's easy enough. Can't stand tailor-mades.'

He neatly rolled a cigarette between his fingers and thumbs. Whenever I tried the same manoeuvre I squeezed the tobacco out like the cream from an éclair.

'Wish you'd have a look at the Sparks, Doc,' Hornbeam continued affably.

'Why, what's the trouble?'

'I just saw him shake hands with a lifeboat.'

'Ah, yes. I was rather afraid something like that might happen.'

Our Wireless Operator was probably the luckiest man on the ship. He was one of those blithe people who live in a world of their own. He had been at sea for forty years, crouched over a telegraph key with the staccato song of Morse in his ears. This seemed to have induced psychological changes in him. For the rest of us, our universe was bounded by the steel and wooden limits of the *Lotus*–but not the Sparks. He passed his day in the company of soft-skinned maidens and amiable philosophers, with whom he could often be seen laughing, conversing, and singing while he walked round the deck or sat in the corner of his cabin. Sometimes he did a coy little dance with some of his companions, or played a simple game; and occasionally they would have a restrained tiff, which always ended happily in the way just observed by the Mate. The Sparks was by far the happiest person under Captain Hogg's command.

'I suppose he's quite harmless?' I asked. 'I mean, he doesn't send out dangerous messages or anything?'

'Oh, he's not in that stage yet.' Hornbeam assured me tolerantly. 'I've seen a good many worse than him. The Morse gets 'em in the end. I just thought you ought to know. I saw him kissing a ventilator yesterday,' he added darkly.

'We are all entitled to our little aberrations, I suppose.'

'You're right there, Doc. Life at sea wouldn't be possible without a bit of give and take. Old Sparks is all right. Just a bit dippy. Like some of these tanker types.'

'Tanker types?'

He nodded, lighting the cigarette and filling the cabin with smoke.

'Men in tankers. It's a dog's life. They run to places like the Persian Gulf and they can unload in a couple of days. That means the boys don't get much of a run ashore when they're home. Besides, you can't live on top of a few thousand tons of petrol all your life without getting a bit queer. Of course, they get the money . . . But is it worth it? Friend of mine went mate in a tanker to make a bit and ended up by cutting his throat. Made a hell of a mess in the chartroom, so they told me.'

From Hornbeam's conversation I gathered that suicide at sea had a panache not seen ashore.

'I think I'll stick to dry cargo,' I said. 'That seems dangerous enough for doctors.'

'Are you coming to the Third's do tonight?' Hornbeam asked. 'That's the reason I looked in.'

'I didn't know he was having one.'

'It's his birthday–twenty-first–and he's having a few beers. You're invited.'

'I don't drink much, you know.'

'Oh, don't be scared, Doc. None of us drinks while we're at sea. I'll say you're coming.'

The party was after supper, in the Third Mate's cabin. As I was anxious not to appear at all anti-social I was the first to arrive.

I had not been in his cabin before. It was smaller than mine, with just enough room for a man to stand between the bunk and the strip of settee on the opposite bulk-head. There was a porthole over the settee and a forced-draught vent in the deckhead that stabbed a narrow stream of cold air across the bunk. Opposite the door was a small desk covered with bottles of gin. The rest of the cabin was covered with girls.

They were everywhere–in frames over the bunk, pasted to the bulkhead, suspended from the pipes crossing the deckhead. There were plain photographs of ordinary girls, shadowy nudes from *Men Only*, taut scissor-legged girls in impossible brassieres from *Esquire*, a few bright beer advertisements from Australia of surprised but unresisting girls with their skirts caught in mangles, car doors, stiles, and dog leads, girls with no clothes playing on the beach, girls with all their clothes caught in a highly selective gale, even pictures of Chinese girls covered from neck to ankle.

'Come in, Doc!' the Third said. 'Have a peg.'

He pushed a glass into my hand and half-filled it with gin in one motion.

'Happy birthday,' I said faintly. 'You seem to have an eye for art.'

'Got to brighten the old cart up a bit. Here's to you.'

He pointed above the bunk to the photograph of a sharp-chinned young lady trying earnestly to look like Dorothy Lamour.

'That's a nice bit of crumpet. Met her in Hull last voyage. She's an intelligent bit, mind you,' he added seriously. 'Works in Boots' library.'

He indicated her rival next to her.

'Now there's a girl for you. Came across her in Adelaide. Last time we were there her brother came and socked me on the nose. She still writes to me, though.'

'I hope he didn't hurt you.'

'He did a bit. He's one of the wharfies. That one's from St John. But this Sheila here's the best of the bunch. Lives in Durban. Father's got pots of cash.'

'You seem to scatter your affections pretty widely.'

'They all love sailors. When a girl knows a fellow's going half-way round the world in a week's time she takes the brakes off a bit. Have a seat on the bunk.'

I sat down and rested my head uncomfortably on the paper bosom of a blonde.

The other guests arrived together. There was Hornbeam, the crazy Sparks, Whimble, the Second Steward, and the Chief, Second, Third, and Fourth Engineers. Archer was absent, keeping Hornbeam's watch on the bridge. The ten of us crammed ourselves into the tiny cabin. Hornbeam had his elbow in my face and his shoes on the Chief Engineer's knees. Whimble wedged himself behind the door and stuck his feet against the end of the bunk. The host struggled between everyone's legs, handing out drinks. I felt that something would shortly give way and project the lot of us into the sea.

The Third's health was drunk by all hands.

'Have another, Doc,' he said.

'No, really . . .'

'Come off it! It's only five bob a bottle.' He half-filled my tumbler again. 'How do you like the sea?' he asked.

'It is a very interesting form of existence.'

'Of course, you realize this is only part of it,' Hornbeam explained. 'It varies a good bit. As you know, British ships are in three classes.'

'Tankers . . .?'

'No. First of all there's the P. & O. Then there's the Merchant Navy, which is the set-up we're in. After that there's the Old Grey Funnel line.'

'Also known as the Royal Navy,' McDougall explained. 'It was nationalized years ago.'

'The P. & O. must not be confused with ordinary hookers,' Hornbeam continued. 'It's a sort of–well, a floating Horse Guards, if you get me. They hate to be called Merchantmen. If you make a noise drinking your soup . . .'

'They wear swords and spurs,' Trail said.

'I don't believe it.'

'Well, they ought to. Oh, very posh, very posh. Good shower of bastards on the whole, though. Have some more gin.'

'Not for . . . Oh, all right, as you've poured it out. It tastes better than the stuff you get ashore.'

'Everything does. By the way, you know the Second Engineer, Doc? Mr Macpherson.'

'Pleased to meet you.'

'Mr McPhail the Third and Mr Macintosh the Fourth.'

'What, are you all Scots in the engine-room?'

'We've a Taffy and a couple of Geordies,' Macpherson said. 'Had to have them in to do the dirty work.'

'You know what they say,' McDougall added proudly. 'If you open the engine-room hatch of any British ship and shout "Jock" someone'll be bound to come up.'

McPhail started singing 'I belong to Glasgow,' but petered out for lack of support.

'Coming ashore with us in Santos, Doc?' Hornbeam asked.

'Certainly. I intend to take advantage of the voyage to broaden my education.'

'Santos will broaden it all right. Plenty of nice girls there.'

'I'm sure I should be pleased if you'd introduce me to them.'

This remark started everyone laughing.

'You don't need any introductions. It's keeping them away that's the trouble.'

'Well, I shall not be interested in meeting any of that sort.'

'Oh, you'll have to come with us to Madame Mimi's,' Hornbeam said reproachfully. 'It would be like going to London and missing the Houses of Parliament.'

'Are you suggesting,' I said coldly, 'that I should visit a brothel?'

'Where the hell else do you think there is to go in Santos?' Trail said testily. 'Anyway, Madame Mimi's is as respectable as the Liverpool Museum.'

'I wouldn't put that past suspicion,' Hornbeam said.

Trail cut the conversation short by pouring out gin all round and beginning a complicated story about two sailors losing their way in Lime Street station.

After an hour everyone was pretty cheerful.

'Don't make such a row,' Trail said. 'Father'll hear.'

'To hell with Father,' I heard myself say.

'Spoken like a sailor, Doc!' Hornbeam slapped me on the chest. 'Good old Doc! Best one I've ever sailed with.'

'I say, really . . .'

'You're the only one that's sane!'

This brought a round of applause.

'You're all mad at sea,' I said defiantly. 'The lot of you.'

The company immediately indicated their disbelief with the usual word.

'You are,' I said. 'Or you wouldn't be here.'

'Have some more gin,' Trail said.

'Thank you.' I swallowed another mouthful. 'As I was saying. I have made a diagnosis. From careful–not to say exacting–study of you in the past ten days I conclude that you're all suffering from the death wish.'

'What the hell's that?' McDougall asked angrily.

I held up a hand.

'Silence. As a disciple of Hippocrates I demand respect and silence. The death wish. When you are born all you want to do is die.'

This again filled the cabin with derision.

'Shut up, you blokes. Let the poor blighter speak,' Trail said.

I continued. 'That is what the psychologists say. Some people hang themselves. Others go into monasteries and . . . and things. Some climb mountains and live in caves. Others write poetry. Look at English poetry,' I demanded hotly of Hornbeam. 'Look at it! Redolent with the death wish!' I screwed up my eyes and struck an attitude of recitation.

'. . . for many a time
I have been half in love with easeful Death,'

I declaimed stumblingly.

'Call'd him soft names in many a musèd rhyme,
To take into the air my quiet . . .'

I slipped off the bunk, but Hornbeam caught me.

'Death wish to the eyebrows, the lot of you! You withdraw–to sea. To sea! That's what it is!'

'You're full of prune-juice, Doc,' someone said.

'I will not have insults,' I cried. 'If you would care to defend yourself like a gentleman, I shall take you up on it. You have the death wish, by God! You've all got it. So had Nelson. I've got it as well.'

I fell over McDougall's feet and no one bothered to pick me up.

Chapter Six

The next morning I was suffering from a sharp attack of the death wish. But my performance had raised me surprisingly in the eyes of my shipmates. My earnest years as a medical student, my dignified excursion into practice, my prim approach to seafaring had built a scaffold underneath me: the Third Mate's gin had slipped the bolt.

My companions were relieved to find that I was not only sane but human: for my part, I began to realize that the sea, which washes away terrestrial affectations and inhibitions, had a great deal to recommend it. Sailors are of the few remaining people who make their way in companies across the unsignposted face of the world with the help of the sun and the stars, and spend most of their lives lying at the unhindered fancy of the weather. Their sense of values in human and elemental behaviour is therefore unblunted; they look on their existence as a long uproarious joke relieved by not unentertaining interludes of necessary tragedy. I thought them the last of the Elizabethans.

I believe there is no process so restful as moving at bicycle pace through the sunshine of the South Atlantic. We were steaming at ten knots, which meant we should be about three weeks reaching Santos. The metallic fragment of England in which we all existed–except the Wireless Operator–creaked easily onwards with a faint haze of smoke rolling from the funnel, scattering the nimble flying fish with her bow. Even crossing the Line caused no more disturbance than my having to stand drinks all round. The hot sun welded the days together so that they became indistinguishable. It was impossible to tell whether it was Tuesday or Thursday, and it didn't matter.

Only twice a week were we reminded of the calendar–Friday and Sunday. At four-thirty on Friday afternoons we had boat drill. Captain Hogg stood on the bridge and pulled the cord of the whistle, which sent us scurrying up the ladders in our blue-and-orange life-jackets to the boat-deck. I was in boat number four, in charge of the Third Mate, who ticked our names off with a roll-call. I was alarmed to find that among my companions in an emergency would be the Carpenter with a tendency to D.T.s and a pleasant-faced greaser who, I heard from Easter, had just returned from a ten-year stretch for armed robbery.

'Swing out!' Captain Hogg shouted through the loud hailer.

The canvas covers were stripped off the boats, and three men set to the handle of each davit to lean it out from the ship's side. When this had been done to Captain Hogg's satisfaction the boats were swung in again and everyone dispersed.

'Board of Trade sports,' Trail said with disgust. 'Waste of time.'

'Why do we do it then?' I asked.

'Oh, it has to go in the log-book. There'd be hell in Liverpool if we didn't. Some skippers cook the log, but not this baby. Anything to give him a chance of bawling through a loud hailer.'

Sunday was recognizable, as it was the only occasion when we flew the flag at sea. From eight to midday the red ensign waved from the gaff on the mainmast, to convince the Almighty that we had not forgotten him–for there was no one else but ourselves to see it. The appearance of the flag that symbolized the Sabbath was greeted warmly by all hands, not through reverence but because, under Ministry of Transport regulations, we all got an extra half-day's pay.

Sunday was also marked by the ceremony of full inspection. This was ordered by Captain Hogg's copy of *Instructions for Masters*, the manual through which the Fathom Steamship Company directed and advised their commanders, which contained in its yellow pages regulations designed to right such nautical disasters as mutiny, epidemics of smallpox, lost anchor, and imminent shipwreck. At eleven o'clock the four of us fell in behind the Captain, who indicated the exceptional occasion by carrying a torch and a walking-stick. On the poop the ship's company was lined up ready for us–deckhands under the charge of the Bos'n on the port side, firemen and greasers to starboard, and catering staff, in fresh white jackets, standing nervously athwartships. Captain Hogg passed down the ranks scowling into each face like a vengeful but short-sighted victim at an identification parade, then we marched in and out of the little green-painted crews' cabins that each smelt of feet and hair oil. They had been cleaned and tidied so that nothing in the slightest degree disturbing could fall into the Captain's visual fields. The decks were scrubbed, the blankets folded ostentatiously, and the owners' possessions–varying from a guitar to a caged canary–were set in unnaturally tidy piles. Captain Hogg shone his torch beneath the bunks, inspected the undersurfaces of tables and chairs, and thrust the crook of his walking-stick into every inviting orifice. Usually his rummaging produced nothing more than a cloud of dust and an empty beer-tin, but occasionally he would drag out a saloon plate, a silver coffee-pot, a mildewed loaf, a pair of underpants, or the crumpled photograph of an inconstant girl friend.

'Mr Hornbeam!' he would shout, waving the find under the Mate's nose. 'What's the meaning of this? Eh? We'll find the chronometers in here next!'

The last call was in hospital. Sunday was the only occasion when it was inspected, and Easter spent the morning polishing the brasswork and tipping all the small moveable objects and surgical debris into a large white bin labelled 'Sterile Dressings'. As we arrived he stood smartly to attention beside the door, hiding a large black patch on the bulkhead.

'All correct, Doctor?' the Captain growled every Sunday.

'Yes, sir. All correct.'

He fixed Easter with his eye.

'Any complaints?'

'I am very happy, Captain,' Easter replied unctuously.

'All right. Pipe down, Bos'n.'

The crew were scattered to their Sunday indolence and we went up to the

Captain's cabin, where we stood in a line in front of him, our caps under our arms, and he emphasized the points that had incurred his disapproval. Then we all sat down and had a gin.

There were no religious observances on board the *Lotus*–an omission that was deplored only by Easter. This surprised me. 'I didn't know you were a church-goer,' I told him.

'Ho, yes, Doctor. I likes a nice service of a Sunday. Breaks the monotony a bit. Not much good in an old tub like this, but in the big passenger boats I used to sing hymns at the back. I've got a bit of a voice,' he added modestly.

'I'm very pleased to hear it.'

'Used to take the plate round as well. Real nice job that is. Must be the sea air what makes them generous. You see them old skinflints what wouldn't give a tanner to a blind baby at home sticking in quids and suchlike. Made quite a bit out of that in my time.'

'You mean you actually helped yourself from the collection?'

'Sort of commission, as you might say,' he explained amiably. 'Nothing much, mind you. No one knows what there is in the kitty, but you've got to be pretty nifty slipping it out before the Purser spots you. Charity begins at home, don't it, Doctor?'

My clinical practice continued its easy routine, and was centred round preservation of the health of the Captain's stomach. I had never known an organ to produce such widespread clinical effects. If it functioned painlessly life was tolerable, even at mealtimes; but the first twinges of dyspepsia immediately communicated themselves to everyone on board. Fortunately I was able to denature my mixture of its explosive properties, and it combated spiritually with the Captain's diet. My morning visit to him with the sick-list gave me an opportunity to see how the battle was going by judging the state of the old gentleman's temper–a matter of importance on the ship beyond the belief of any landsman. If he was in a good mood he took the chit without question, and sometimes even demonstrated extreme geniality by offering me a gin (he saw nothing unusual in drinking after breakfast). If my mixture was not up to strength, or if he had eaten too many platefuls of Madras curry the night before, he would seize the paper and scowl at it like a Tudor monarch affirming a list of executions.

'What's wrong with that man?' he would demand, stabbing the sheet with his blunt finger. 'McKlusky, J., Ordinary Seaman. Why's he off duty? What's this–P.U.O.?'

'Pyrexia of unknown origin, sir,' I explained timidly. 'He had a temperature.'

'Well, why has he?'

'I'm afraid I don't know, sir.'

'Why don't you? You're the Doctor, aren't you? What the devil do you think would happen to us all if I didn't know a lighthouse when I saw one? Eh? What have you got to say to that?'

He slammed the paper down on his desk. I said nothing to it.

'Now, look here, Doctor,' he went on. 'I'm not in your line, and I don't pretend to be. But I can tell you what's wrong with this man–he's constipated. I haven't been to sea for forty years for nothing. Give the bastard a double dose of black draught and kick him back on duty. If he still shirks I'll put him in the log-book. That's an order!'

'Yes, sir.'

This put me in a state of professional agitation. But Captain Hogg would have agitated the whole General Medical Council.

The Captain was at his most terrifying when conducting the ceremony of placing an offender's name in the log-book. This was the only disciplinary action left in his hands: flogging at the mainmast, keel-hauling, and hanging from the yardarm at sunset have been abolished by Parliament, and Captain Hogg made it plain that he thought the world all the worse for it.

One night shortly after we reached the Tropics I was pulled from my bunk by Hornbeam to see a couple of firemen who had been fighting in the foc's'le. Both of them were drunk. They were in the hospital, blood-spattered and muttering surly threats at each other, separated by Easter with the heavy pestle from the drug locker.

'Now keep quiet for the doctor,' he said cheerfully, 'or I'll bash your ruddy brains in with this. These two have filled each other in something proper,' he added to me as a clinical explanation.

During the two hours needed to sew them up I gathered that the pair of them, Kelly and Crosby, came from the opposite sides of a Liverpool street; and a feud had smouldered between them since they first threw stones at each other from the shelter of their mothers' skirts. Too late they had found themselves both aboard the *Lotus*, and had been living in grudging amicability since we sailed. But that evening Kelly had been unable to repress any longer his opinion that Crosby's mother was not only a harlot, but the oldest and most ugly in all Liverpool, and Crosby cracked the end of a bottle and went for him.

The next morning at ten I was summoned to the Captain's cabin, which had the ceremonially grim air of a Portsmouth court-martial. Sitting at the desk was Captain Hogg, an expression on his face of uninhibited malevolence. Set before him were his gold-braided cap, *Instructions for Masters*, the log-book open at the correct page, a sheet of yellow blotting-paper, and a large silver ink-pot with a pen in it, so that everything was at hand for making the damning entry. Hornbeam was in a chair beside the Captain, looking seriously at his own feet. The Bos'n and the Donkeyman were positioned on each side of the door, and I was ordered curtly to the corner. In the middle of the circle were the two delinquents, twisting their caps in their hands and throwing nervous glances round the cabin from the gaps in their bandages.

'Right,' Captain Hogg began briskly. 'Now we are all assembled we can begin. First of all I want to make something perfectly plain to you two. You are going to get a completely fair hearing this morning. Understand? You are quite at liberty to put questions to me or any other of the officers. You may call any witness you like in your defence. As far as I'm concerned a man is innocent until he's proved guilty, whether it's murder or pinching a ha'penny stamp. You'll never find me giving a man a bad character till it's proved. I'm a fair captain, I am. Get me?'

The two firemen nodded hesitantly.

'Very well. Now, tell me your version of the affair.'

He folded his arms judicially.

The feud that had burned so brightly a few hours before was now outshone by the peril that faced the two opponents. They had composed a story during breakfast, which was begun by Kelly in the tone of bitter repentance that had occasionally swayed sympathetic members of a magistrate's bench.

'Well, sir, it was like this 'ere, sir. Me and me mate was 'avin' a cupper tea . . .'

'You bloody liar!' Captain Hogg shouted. 'You were rotten drunk, both of you bastards! Oh, yes, you were! Don't answer me back or I'll kick you round the deck. You were drunk in the foc's'le and you started fighting like the pair of goddam cut-throats you are. My God, you're a crowd of loafers up forrard! You oughtn't to be at sea, you ought to be in jail, the lot of you! Stand up straight when I'm talking to you, blast you!' He thrust a finger under Kelly's nose. 'You turn my ship into a Liverpool rough-house and you come up here with some cock-and-bull story you think I'm going to swallow. What do you take me for, eh? I was at sea when you were playing marbles in the filth of a Liverpool gutter. Mr. Hornbeam!'

'Sir?'

'You found these men fighting?'

Hornbeam nodded.

'Doctor!'

'Sir?'

'Did you or did you not find these men were drunk?'

'Well, sir, the scientific tests . . .'

'There you are! The Doctor agrees with me! You were soused, the pair of you!' He banged the desk with his fist, making the pen leap out of the ink-pot. 'Do you know what I'd like to do to you?' he demanded. 'I'd like to give you every holystone on board and make you scrub the boatdeck till the plates showed through. Then I'd put you in irons in the chain-locker and keep you on bread and water till we got back to Liverpool. That's the sort of treatment scum like you need! I'd like to put you in an open boat here and now, and get rid of the pair of you for good. Do you understand, you couple of lazy sons of bitches?'

But fortunately the Captain's justice was obligatorily tempered with mercy. 'Fined five shillings,' he muttered. 'Good morning.'

It was fortunate that Captain Hogg was, through reason of his being a captain, confined most of the day to his own quarters. He passed his time sitting in an armchair reading magazines similar to the one hiding his face on the first occasion I met him. In the corner of his cabin was a pile three feet high of these periodicals, from all parts of the English-speaking world. He consumed them earnestly and steadily, like a man with plenty of time looking up a train in Bradshaw. 'There's one thing I do like,' he announced at dinner one day, a forkful of beef and vegetables at his mouth, 'and that's a good book.'

For the rest of the voyage I bowed to his opinions like a Victorian schoolboy and took the greatest pains possible to avoid him.

The Leader of the Opposition in the *Lotus* was the Chief Engineer, McDougall. He alone of the engineers had unresented entry into the saloon and our company: the mates looked upon them instinctively as intruders, a relic of the days when thin funnels first poked their way through the proud canvas. The engineers lived away from the rest of us in tiny hot cabins clustered amidships, and ate in a pokey messroom ventilated by the oily breath of the engines. We saw them only when they leant over the rail in their black and sweaty boiler suits, or lay on their backs dissembling one of the pieces of ugly machinery that sprung from the *Lotus*'s deck.

McDougall had a noisy cabin by the engine-room hatchway, in which he received visitors with a half-tumbler of neat whisky (he maintained that gin was a drink fit only for harlots). His surroundings were as untidy as a nursery. Scraps of steel and paint-pots littered the deck, the bunk sagged under pieces of dismantled machinery, and the bulkheads supported charts, graphs, a row of sombre engineering books, and an incongruous nude leaving her bath on a boilermakers' calendar. Scattered everywhere, like thistledown blown by a breeze, were scraps of half-used cotton waste.

'Where would ye all be without my engines?' he demanded. 'Do ye know what you've got to thank us for? Everything from the propeller revolutions to your shaving water and the ice in your gin.'

He thought of his engines, as Boswell did of his lavatories, as living beings possessed of souls.

'Ye'll be no damn good as an engineer till you make friends with your engines,' he told me. 'Talk to 'em, that's what you've got to do. Give 'em hell if they play you up. It pays in the end, lad. Many a time I've had a row with me mates or the wife, and it's been a comfort to know I've got a real pal down below. If ye cut my veins, Doc, ye'll find fuel oil there, not blood.'

McDougall believed that the best engineers came from Scotland, the best Scots from Glasgow, and the only effect of modern innovations like oil furnaces, engine-room ventilation, and refrigerators was a glaring deterioration in the standard of young men coming to sea. When he showed me round his engine-room he exhibited the reverence of an old dean in his cathedral. We stood on the quivering control platform in the centre of the *Lotus*'s clamorous viscera and he waved his arm proudly and shouted. 'This is where we do a man's job, Doc.'

I nodded, looking nervously at the pipes straining with the pressure of superheated steam.

'That's the main steam gauge,' McDougall explained, pointing to a dial on the panel in front of us.

'What's the red line for?' I shouted back.

'That? Och, that's the safety mark.'

'But, I say, isn't the needle well past it?'

'That doesn't matter, lad. We've got to get the old tub moving somehow.'

He took me down greasy ladders, along a narrow cat-walk between pieces of spinning machinery, through the boiler-room where Turnbull, the Geordie Seventh Engineer, sweated eight hours of his twenty-four watching the oil fires. We crouched along the tunnel that carried the propeller shaft to the stern, and stood at the end in a little triangular humid space where the thick revolving metal pierced the plates and disappeared into the sea.

'There ye are, Doc. All us lads and all that machinery to keep this turning. If it wasn't for us that old windbag on the bridge would be out of a job.'

'He doesn't seem to be very appreciative, Chief.'

'Och, we've got better than him conducting the trams in Glasgow,' McDougall said with disgust. 'You watch, Doc. I'll run him off this ship before he's much older. You wait and see.'

McDougall's threat was wholly serious. He had in a locked drawer in his cabin a foolscap book labelled shamelessly HOGG, in which he entered immediately every derogatory fact he discovered about the Captain. When he was particularly annoyed he took the book out and read it, underlining in red ink wherever he thought a passage was not sufficiently condemnatory standing on its own. This book he sent to the Marine Superintendent of the Fathom Line by registered post every time the ship returned to Britain, but its effect was largely cancelled by a similar volume about McDougall put in the Superintendent's hands by the Captain. The two passed their lives in a running fight on oil consumption, engine revolutions, and repair bills, and the daily ceremony by which McDougall handed Captain Hogg a chit on his speed and fuel supplies was always conducted in bitter silence. About once a week the Captain became too much for him, and the Chief Engineer then shut himself in his cabin, took out a fresh bottle of whisky, and determinedly threw the cap through the porthole.

As the ship's company became used to me they paid me the compliment of sharing their troubles with me. I soon discovered all of them were hypochondriacs. In small ships where they had no doctor they worried in case they caught anything; in bigger ships, where there was a doctor living down the alleyway, they brought along their symptoms like bruised children running to their mother. The Second Mate was the severest sufferer from hypochondriasis. The locker in his cabin was a therapeutic bar: he had five different brands of antiseptic, all the popular stomach powders, lotions for rubbing under the arms and between the toes, drops for sticking in his eyes or up his nose, gargles and liniments, hair-food and skin-balm, and a frightening collection of purgatives.

I found him gargling lustily in his cabin one afternoon.

'Hello, Second,' I said. 'What's up? Got a cold?'

He spat guiltily into the basin, as though I had caught him at some wickedness.

'No,' he explained. 'I always gargle three times a day. I was reading an article in *Happy Health* that said that every cubic inch of air is loaded with millions of microbes.'

'Well, so's every inch of your throat.'

'Listen, Doc,' he went on, sounding worried. 'There's something I've been wanting to ask you for a long time. Where could I get my blood cholesterol measured?'

'Your what!'

'Yes, you see there was an article in–either the *Reader's Digest* or one of the Sunday papers at home–that said some doctors in California had discovered if your blood cholesterol was above 245 milligrams per cent you were bound to get arteriosclerosis. I've all the symptoms. I . . .'

'You're far more likely to fall down a hatch and break your neck.'

'Do you think so?' he asked eagerly. 'Still, it's got me worried. I'm sure I've got an intervertebral disk as well. There's a pain I get round here in my back every time I sit down.'

'Rubbish! You're healthier than I am.'

He looked dolefully at his medicine chest for a few moments. 'Of course,' he continued, 'what I really need is a woman.'

'I'm inclined to agree with you,' I said.

I sat down reflectively on his bunk. I had become aware in the past few days of feeling–not blatantly sex-starved but unquestionably peckish. I put it down to the sea air. My life ashore had passed undisturbed except for Wendy and occasional vague thoughts that it would be nice to take a girl to the pictures. But now I began to think even the girls in the Third Mate's cabin were delightful. Wendy herself became frighteningly glamourized as my mind's eye behaved like a magazine photographer's lens, and substituted curves for angularity and an inviting expression for the usual one that indicated she thought her nose was running.

'Now, if this was a real passenger ship,' the Second continued, 'everything would be squared up by now. Have you been in one?'

'This is my first ship.'

'I forgot. I was Third in one for a bit. It was like a floating Ball of Kirriemuir. I don't know what it is. As soon as these females get aboard a ship they're all after you. Not a moment's peace. Then there's dances and race meetings and all the fun and games. Not to mention the moonlight and the phosphorescence on the water. I haven't seen any phosphorescence yet. But they fall for it, every time. The places they get to! We found one couple on the steering engine. I used to go under the lifeboats.'

'What about the Captain?'

'He was at it like everyone else. He jacked himself up a nice bit of snicket first day out of Southampton. What a trip that was!'

'I take it you're not married,' I said.

'I've been married. Got hitched during the war when I was a Third. It didn't work out. We've split it up now.' He took a cigarette out of the tin thoughtfully. 'It's no good being married at sea. Oh, yes, every leave's a honeymoon, I know what they say. But long voyages and young wives don't mix. You leave the allotment of your pay and if you don't get a letter at every port you wonder what's up. Anyhow, I reckon you can't ask a girl to sit by the fireside for six months, or a year, or two years maybe. It isn't fair. It isn't human.'

'What about you?' I asked.

'Oh, I always hold you're entitled to count yourself as single at sea,' he said.

Our reflections were interrupted by the engine-room telegraph ringing faintly on the bridge above.

'What's that?' I asked. 'I thought they tested them at noon.'

'I expect she's stopped,' Archer said calmly.

'Stopped! But isn't that important?'

'She often stops. It's the first time she's done it this trip. Something's blown up down below, I suppose. Come on deck. From now on it's usually pretty funny.'

We stepped on to the sunny deck, just below the wing of the bridge. The *Lotus* had stopped sure enough. She wallowed in the swell like a dead whale.

'Now watch,' the Second said.

Captain Hogg appeared on the bridge. He had been disturbed in his siesta, and was dressed only in a tartan dressing-gown. He looked like Macbeth the day the wood moved.

'Mr McDougall!' he shouted. 'Mr McDougall!'

He banged the rail with his fist.

'Quartermaster! Present my compliments to the Chief Engineer and ask him to come to the bridge!'

'Aye aye, sir.'

Captain Hogg clasped his hands behind him and strode fiercely across the deck. After five minutes McDougall appeared. He was in a boiler-suit and held in his hand a scrap of cotton waste, material that appears as indispensable to engineers as stethoscopes to doctors. They glared across the bridge, playing havoc with each other's blood pressure.

'The ship's stopped,' Captain Hogg announced.

'Aye,' said McDougall. 'I know.'

'Well . . . why the devil has she stopped?'

McDougall lit his pipe.

'You tell me, Cap'n, and then we'll both know.'

'Damn it, Mr McDougall! Can't you keep the ship going between ports?'

'Not this ship.'

'When I first came to sea engineers took their orders from the bridge. Their job was to raise steam and keep it.'

'When I first came to sea Cap'ns behaved like gentlemen.'

'I will not be spoken to like that!'

'I will speak to ye how I like.'

'I'll have you put in the log-book, Mr McDougall!'

'I'll report ye to the Company, Cap'n.'

'I will not be obstructed by a pigheaded Scot!'

'An' I will not be told my job by an ignorant Sassenach!'

'Damn you, sir!'

'And damn you, too!'

At that moment the argument was annulled by the telegraph ringing again and the *Lotus* slowly getting under way.

'It's always like that,' the Second said.' 'You know how it is. Oil and water won't mix.'

Chapter Seven

The voyage extended. The ship ran deeply into the Tropics and Captain Hogg started work on his Master's Letter from Santos. We stayed fairly peaceful until the afternoon he threw the Chief Steward down the bridge ladder.

Whimble was the most introverted and anxious member of the *Lotus*'s company; and he had a strict rule on board–he never drank. When he came to my cabin early in the voyage and I recalled that the social formulae of my new life demanded I offered him a peg, he grasped his abdomen with a sign of horror.

'Not a drop, Doctor!' he declared. 'Never touch a dram of it!'

'What, not at all?' Finding a teetotaller in the *Lotus* was like running into a sober Scot on Burns night.

'Not for twenty years! It's my liver, Doctor.' He warily indicated the region of his umbilicus. 'I had a real bad turn in Cardiff. Five operations and left to die three times. I need say no more to you, need I, Doctor?'

'No, no more at all.'

'So I said to myself, "Walter," I said, "be a man! Not another drink you're going to have till your dying day!" And not a drop's soiled my lips since. Will-power, Doctor, that's what it is. I used to do Pelmanism a bit when I was younger.'

When I passed this information to Hornbeam, illuminated with admiration, he pushed his cap back on his head and roared with laughter.

'He's right in a way, Doc,' he said. 'You'll never see him with a glass in his hand. He keeps it in his locker, mostly. Or his hot-water can, or under the bunk. He gets a bottle a day easy–buckshee, of course. Pinches it from the bond-room and fiddles the bar accounts so it's poor beggars like you and me that have to pay for it in the end.'

'He cooks the books, does he?' I said in surprise. 'I'd have thought he was too timid to be dishonest.'

'Don't you believe it. There isn't a chief steward afloat who wouldn't flog the funnel if he thought he could get away with it.'

I observed Whimble fairly closely after that. Once Hornbeam had given me the diagnosis it was simple to pick out the symptoms. In the early morning, when he did his round of the galley and the stores, he was a pale and nervous man who flattened himself against the bulkhead when he glimpsed Captain Hogg's threatening silhouette at the other end of the alleyway. At nine he paid his daily visit to the little bond-room below the water-line, and came up with the ship's supply of liquor. After that he went to his cabin to clean his teeth. He reappeared slightly flushed, and took his place in the inspection procession with confidence. Then he cleaned his teeth again. He found it necessary to clean his teeth before dinner, at teatime, and on several occasions during the evening. By ten at night, when he prepared the Captain's sandwiches in the pantry, his spectacles were awry and he sang snatches of bawdy songs as he slapped on the mustard with a flourish. The end of his day was marked shortly afterwards by the flash of a bottle sailing out of his porthole, and the light splash as it hit the water and joined the others that marked, at neatly regular intervals, the progress of the Chief Steward round the world.

To restore this and other profitable discrepancies, Whimble was forced to spend several hours a day sitting in his tiny office with the store-books and a ready-reckoner, biting his pen and working out worried sums on a scrap of paper.

'Father's very hard, very hard!' he explained to me one day. 'Always chasing me up over the catering. And the Company looks at every grain of rice they give you. What d'you think they'd do if I was a pound of butter out at the end of the voyage?' He indicated the sea with his thumb. 'It would be "Out, Walter, me boy," and no mistake. I don't know how I make ends meet sometimes, really I don't.'

His problem was not so much making ends meet but arranging them to do so with a worthwhile overlap. The drawers under his bunk were filled with tins of ham, peaches, lard, tongue, and pineapple, which were ready to be slipped over the side to a furtive rowing-boat our first night in port. Tins of cigarettes were stacked behind his books in the office, and two or three bottles of whisky were locked in the glass locker with the ostentatious label FOR ENTERTAINMENT OF CUSTOMS. 'If you're wanting any medical stores on the coast, Doc,' he confided in me when I dressed a cut on his hand one evening, 'let me have the list and we'll split the comish fifty-fifty.'

'Very kind of you, I'm sure.'

'Of course, there won't be much in it. There isn't much of anything in this hooker. In a big passenger job that's different. The Purser gets his comish on everything down to the bell-boy's tips. Why, the barman in one of those makes more than the Old Man.' He looked gratefully at his fresh bandage. 'If you want a few bottles of Scotch to flog the other end it might be arranged,' he added generously. 'I can get it ashore for you. Trust Walter. Never touch a drop of it myself, mind you.'

Whimble had justification enough for secret drinking at our expense in the Captain's table manners alone. Captain Hogg made a point of complaining at least once a meal about the menu or cooking. 'Beef!' he would exclaim, contemptuously spitting out a half-chewed morsel as big as a golf ball. 'Flea-ridden cow, more likely! Where the devil did you dig this up from, Mr Whimble?'

'Fresh on board this trip, sir. Saw it loaded with my own eyes, if I may respectfully say so, sir.'

'I don't believe you, Mr Whimble. You've had this in the freezer since last voyage, or I'm a Dutchman. What do you say, eh, Doctor?'

As there was no point in disagreeing with the Captain about anything I nodded sympathetically.

When he was especially enraged with a dish Captain Hogg would lift his plate shoulder high, bellow 'Steward!' and demand, 'Throw that muck over the side and bring us a decent piece of bread and cheese.' This he would eat glaring at Whimble, in a silence broken only by the rhythmical snapping of his jaws. On other occasions he would suddenly be overcome with longings, like a pregnant woman. 'Mr Whimble,' he would demand in the middle of a plate of liver and bacon, 'why don't we ever have any avocado pears?' Or, 'Steward! Are there any pikelets on board?'

After the meagre nourishment of my student's lodgings and the G.P.'s table the portions served in the *Lotus*'s saloon looked heavy with the threat of dyspepsia; but the sea air and the prospect of sleeping all afternoon soon led to my eating as much as anyone else, apart from Captain Hogg. The menu was conservative, like a good commercial hotel's, and ran mostly to joints and puddings. All of them were prepared with care by the First Cook, a large, soft-eyed, likeable man, who sweated among his spitting roasts in the galley whistling and basting the meat with the delight of an esteemed craftsman.

'A contented cook, Doc,' he said, 'and you gets a contented crew.' He whistled a few bars. 'Nice leg of pork cold for supper. Fond of crackling?'

'I'm glad you're contented,' I told him. 'Most of the cooks I meet ashore seem to have duodenal ulcers.'

He wiped his hands on his trousers and felt in his hip pocket.

'That's why I'm contented,' he said. He flourished a photograph of a thin simpering young woman in an off-the-shoulder dance frock. 'Sweetest little girl in the world. That's the wife.'

'You're a very lucky man.'

'Yes, Doc, I reckon I am. One of the luckiest of the lot. How'd you like a bit of dressed crab as well?' he added, glowing with bonhomie. 'I could always open a tin.'

But already, three thousand miles away, disaster was being prepared for the *Lotus*'s cooking. The next afternoon Easter came to my cabin and said, 'Beg pardon, Doctor, but the Cook reckons he wants to do himself in.'

'What! You mean commit suicide?'

'That's right, Doctor. He's been on the booze since dinner, and the lads spotted him rigging up a bit of rope in his cabin.'

'Good Heavens man! Haven't you done something about it?'

'Ho, it's all right now,' Easter said calmly. 'The Bos'n slugged him and he's out cold. He'll be tame enough when he comes to. It's always the same. They never string themselves up in the end.'

'But what's the trouble?' I asked. It seemed barely credible. 'He struck me as a happy enough sort of fellow.'

'Sheilas,' Easter said with contempt. 'Drive a man to it some of them, don't they, Doctor? His wife's vamoosed with a bus-driver. Just got a cable from his pal to say so.'

'That's a bit of tough luck. He seemed to be pretty fond of her.'

'It ain't the first time it's happened by a long chalk. Cor, I've seen these bits waving good-bye to their husbands at the docks, then going home to collect the allotment, a quid a week regular, and ending up with black babies and suchlike. There ain't no depths, Doctor, what women won't stoop to. And the worse they treat the blokes the more they seem to like 'em. Mugs, ain't we?'

'Well, I think you'd better keep an eye on the Cook,' I told him. 'Perhaps I should have a chat with him–psychology, you know. I hope he won't let it interfere with his cooking.'

The next morning was Sunday. The Cook was back at work–but a sad, lonely, tuneless man. He pottered miserably round the galley, pausing every now and then to break into unexpected tears over the carrots or the boiling duff. Suddenly he would cry out startlingly, 'Rosie! Rosie! I love you!', then he would fall silent and look grimly along the edge of his carving-knife, under the terrified glance of the galley-boy who crouched over the potato-bucket.

The Sunday dinner, nevertheless, appeared on the saloon table. Rosie could not have chosen a worse day for her defection, for the menu was the longest of the week: there was always Scotch broth, boiled turbot, steak-and-kidney pie, beef, carrots, boiled and roast potatoes, and plum duff, all of which the Captain consumed steadily and usually without complaint. But that day the Cook's grief had intruded into the meal. The soup was cold, and Captain Hogg flung his spoon into the plate after the first mouthful with the command: 'Steward! Chuck this dishwater into the scupper!' The turbot was underdone, and it was barely touched by anyone. Only the steak-and-kidney pie seemed up to the usual standard. 'Give us a big helping,' the Captain growled. 'If the rest's as filthy as the soup it won't be worth eating. Call yourself a Chief Steward, Mr Whimble? You're not fit to be in charge of an ice-cream barrow.'

He began eating his pie in silence. We were all a little bad tempered, for Sunday dinner was pleasantly anticipated and we had prepared ourselves with extra morning gin. I watched the Captain sorting out the portions of kidney and felt thankful for the sake of our digestions that peace had fallen on the table.

Captain Hogg suddenly jumped to his feet. He held his napkin to his mouth and his face was the colour of the port light.

'Look!' he hissed. 'Look at that!'

His finger quivered in the direction of his food. Whimble nervously stretched across the table and removed from a pile of pie-crust a dental plate with three teeth attached to it.

'Oh, dear!' Whimble said.

'Is it yours?' the Captain thundered.

'Oh, no, sir! I've never seen it before, sir.'

Captain Hogg thrust his napkin forward.

'Put it in that!' he commanded. The teeth, in a pool of gravy, were wrapped up. 'I am taking this up to my cabin and stowing it in the safe. I am then showing it to the general manager the minute we arrive in Liverpool. By God, I'll see you pay for this, Mr Whimble!'

Shaking his fist he left the saloon, pausing to shout an order for cold ham and pickles in his cabin. We sat in silence, the pie going cold in front of us. Whimble tried to take a drink of water, but he was shaking so much he spilled it over the cloth.

'I don't think I want any more,' Hornbeam said, pushing his plate away. 'Whose are they, Doc? Yours?'

'They're probably the Cook's. He's been a bit forgetful this morning.'

'Har!' Whimble croaked. 'The Cook!' He jumped from the table, eager to pass on his castigation. The gentle, easy-going Cook, who filched tins of ham and corned beef through Whimble's good graces, was the only person on board whom he could bully. Pausing only to clean his teeth on the way, he confidently made for the galley.

But it was a changed Cook whom he found sitting on the potato locker with a gin-bottle, crooning to himself. He saw the accident in a different light. Before Whimble could say anything he was gripped by the shirt, a chopping-knife pointed at his throat, and the Cook demanded 'Give me my bloody teeth back!'

Whimble broke away with a shout that brought us all from the saloon. We found him running down the deck chased by the Cook, who had his knife in his hand and was wearing a frightening toothless snarl.

'Murder!' Whimble shouted.

The Cook was not steady on his feet, fell over a stay, and burst into tears. But Whimble had no time to see this. His only thoughts were of self-protection, and he decided the unpleasantness represented by Captain Hogg was less than that embodied in the Cook. He jumped up the ladder leading to the bridge and hammered on the door of the Captain's cabin.

'Help!' he cried. 'Save me!'

The door was flung open.

'What the blazes is the matter with you?'

'Look,' said Whimble, pointing behind him.

'Are you mad!'

'The Cook's after me with a knife!' he whimpered, calming at the sight of Captain Hogg. 'He wants his teeth back.'

'Teeth! Teeth! Did you say teeth? Get off my bridge!'

'He'll murder me!'

'Get off my bridge, damn you!'

'Give me the Cook's teeth first!'

Captain Hogg picked Whimble up by his shirt collar and gave him a push. He uttered a little squeal as he lost his balance at the top of the ladder and came sliding down feet first. At that moment the steward was mounting it with the Captain's tray of ham and pickles.

'There goes our supper,' Hornbeam said gloomily. After that no one thought it worth while finishing the meal.

Chapter Eight

The next morning my professional tranquillity was split like an old sail in a storm.

I had settled down in my cabin after breakfast to read *War and Peace*, with which I first killed three or four cockroaches, when Easter came in. He showed me a new card trick and described the occasion when he was steward on a Greek tramp and had won from the skipper, an incorrigible but luckless gambler, as a final stake one night in the Mediterranean the exclusive services of his stout but agreeable wife until Gibraltar.

'There's something, Doctor,' Easter went on. 'One of the crew took queer in the night.'

'What's wrong with him?'

'Vomiting and suchlike. Shall I chase him up here?'

'I think we'd better pay a domiciliary visit.'

The patient was a young deckhand. He was lying on his bunk, holding his abdomen and groaning.

'Good morning,' I said briskly, taking his pulse. 'What's the trouble?'

'Aw, cripes! I got the bellyache something horrid.'

'Just let me have a look at the – er, stomach.'

He stretched himself on his back. I reached out a hand and felt the right-hand quadrant of his abdomen. Immediately I felt as if I had eaten a bunch of safety-pins and they had all opened inside at once.

I dragged Easter outside the door and shut it.

'Easter,' I said hoarsely. 'This man has acute appendicitis.'

'Cor!'

'This is urgent. How far are we out of Santos?'

'About two days, the Mate reckons.'

'Well, we must make land before then and put the poor chap in hospital. I'll go up and see the Captain.'

Captain Hogg had just got out of his bath. He stood in his slippers with a towel round him, looking at me like Bligh offering Christian the cheese. I could appreciate that it was one of his gastric mornings.

'Well?'

'Er – good morning, sir.'

'Good morning!'

'Could you do twice the speed you are, sir?'

'What!'

He jumped so violently he shook drops of water from his chest on to the carpet.

'I mean – you see, sir, one of the crew has developed acute appendicitis. He will have to be operated on as soon as possible. I understand from the engineers that it is possible for the vessel to make a few more knots, and I thought . . .'

Captain Hogg sat down on the edge of his desk. He gave a sharp tug to his left ear, as though pulling the pin out of a Mills bomb.

'For every knot above the cruising speed of my ship,' he began quietly, 'the bill for fuel oil practically doubles itself. What do you think the Company would have to say? Eh?' He banged the desk. 'Operate, Doctor, operate!' he shouted. 'What do you think I pay you for?'

'Yes, sir,' I said.

I recognized at once that the Captain's advice on therapy had obvious drawbacks. In the first place, I had a meagre idea of how to remove an appendix. A medical qualification is like a marriage licence – it gives you official permission to go ahead, but it doesn't guarantee you know enough to tackle all the difficulties after the honeymoon. I had diligently attended the operating theatre in my hospital, but there were always so many students present whenever the surgeons removed an appendix that all I usually saw of the operation were the boils on the neck of the man in front of me.

The second difficulty was equipment. Although appendices have reportedly been removed by second mates with bent spoons and a bos'n's knife, I felt that my academic inhibitions made it impossible for me to operate skilfully with the products of an ironmonger's shop. Thirdly, there was professional assistance. Easter was an admirable character for whom I had a sincere admiration as a man of the world, but when it came to dabbling in clinical medicine he was as dangerous as an unlabelled bottle of strychnine.

I called him into my cabin.

'Easter,' I said earnestly, 'have you seen a case of acute appendicitis before?'

'Ho, yes, Doctor. Every time I eats pickles I'm reminded of it.'

'Pickles?'

'That's right, Doctor. I was on the Western Ocean run at the time. The old Doc was scared to operate, so he puts the patient in the ship's hospital and tells me to keep him on a light diet, see. That night I goes along and asks if there's anything he wants, like, before I turn in, and the patient says to me "Yes," he says, "I should like just a few pickles." "Pickles!" I says. "You can't have no pickles! Don't be balmy! The doctor would have me over the side if I was to give you pickles. We of the medical fraternity don't reckon pickles is a light diet. Not for 'arf a minute we don't," I says.'

'Well the next morning I brings him 'is breakfast – two poached eggs done special – and when I goes to shake him – Cor! He was cold to the touch. Them pickles was his last wish, Doctor, and I refused him. Sad, ain't it?'

'Quite so, Easter,' I said. 'Let's have a little less of your reminiscences and a little more action. We must operate on this man before sundown. Do you realize what that means? We must strip the hospital, scrub it out with antiseptic, rig up some lights and an operating table, and find some instruments from somewhere. Savvy?'

'Very good, Doctor. We of the fraternity always rises to the occasion, as they say.'

'Well, start rising.'

He hesitated.

'If I might be so bold, Doctor . . .'

'Yes?'

'Perhaps it might make things go a little easier if you and me was to have a bit of the medical comforts to start with.'

I clapped him gratefully on the shoulder.

'Capital idea, Easter. Reach down the bottle from my locker.'

Rumours of my intended surgical assault spread through the ship faster than the news of a landfall. It was not only a pleasurable interruption to the tedium of the voyage but it had the attributes of mystery and originality as well. The crew hadn't had such fun since a boiler blew up off Panama.

I shut myself in my cabin and opened the text-book of surgery I had prudently included in my packing. Turning over the pages to appendicitis, I ran my finger down the print. I started to read the section headed 'operation'. 'The incision is made at McBurney's point,' it said. Oh God! What was McBurney's point? It sounded like a mountain in California.

There was a rap on the jalousie.

'Come in!'

I unlatched the door. It was the Chief Engineer.

'I heard about this wee party you're having, Doc,' he said affably. 'I reckoned you'd be needing some lights so's you can get a good squint at the innards. I can rig up a cargo cluster for you, if you're willing.'

'Thanks very much.'

He gave a grin.

'Of course, you won't mind me turning up to see the fun, Doc, will you? I reckon I ought to be there in case the lights go on the blink. You never can tell with these cargo clusters.'

'That'll be all right, Chief.'

'Thanks, Doc. Give us a shout when you want to stand-by.'

I opened the book again, and had read far enough to learn that the appendix may be in any of six positions when Hornbeam put his head round the door. He laughed loudly.

'Hello, Doc! Making you do a bit of work for a change?'

'That's what I'm here for,' I said casually.

'Reading it all up in the old almanac, I see,' he said genially.

I shut the heavy book with a bang and dropped it behind the bunk.

'One must refresh one's memory,' I said. 'Even Lord Lister had to do that sometimes.'

'What I came down for, Doc,' he went on, 'was to offer you a bit of a hand. I remember seeing one of these done in the war when I was trooping. Thought you might like me to hold the blood-bucket or something.'

I considered.

'All right,' I said. 'I'd be pleased to have someone with common sense around. You won't faint, will you?'

'What after all these years at sea? I'll come along later.'

I was still looking for my place in the surgery book when I saw Sparks in the doorway. He brushed aside a couple of imaginary companions and grinned at me.

'Yes?' I asked uninvitingly.

'I hear you're going to carve'em up, Doc.'

'I am intending to operate, certainly.'

'Wouldn't mind if I watched, would you? I'm a bit of a photographer, and I'd like a few pictures to show the kids.' His grin widened. 'Makes a change from seagulls.'

'I don't think there'll be enough room for me and the patient if you come too.'

'Would you like to send a message to his mother?' he asked.

'No I would not.'

'Haven't got a spot of gin handy, have you?'

'Not now. Later. I'm very busy.'

'All right, Doc. Have a good time.'

He went off, singing with his friends. But there had now collected outside the door a bunch of deckhands, led by the Bos'n with his cap respectfully in his hands.

'What the hell do you want?' I asked crossly.

'Sorry to disturb you, Doctor, only seeing as we're all pals of Erb's, we was thinking you'd let us come in, see, to 'ave a dekko. 'E says its all right wiv 'im, as long as we behaves decent.'

'Go away,' I said. 'Go away at once. All of you. Who do you think I am? A music-hall turn? I shall report you all to the Mate.'

I slammed the door and returned to the intricacies of appendectomy.

I found Easter in the hospital. He had dismantled the cabin furnishings and was on his knees scrubbing the deck, stripped to the waist.

'How's it going?' I asked.

'It's bloody 'ot.'

'What's the temperature?'

He got up and inspected the thermometer in the corner.

'Hundred and six,' he said.

'Can't you put the forced draught on?'

'Blows soot in.'

'Oh, all right. We'll have to put up with it I suppose. How have you got on with the operating table?'

He had a wooden trestle table along one bulkhead, which he set up proudly. It left just enough room on either side for the pair of us.

'I got it off Chippy,' he said. 'He uses it for mixing the paints on.'

'It's better than nothing. If you scrub it hard enough it'll be reasonably sterile.'

As I spoke, two large, rusty drops fell from a pipe crossing the deckhead on the spot where the operation wound would be.

'Damnation! Can't you do anything to stop that?'

Easter shook his head.

'Been like it for years. It's a job for the shore engineers, that is.'

'Well, you'll have to fix up some sort of screen. Have we got any dressings and gloves, and so forth?'

'There was some in the locker. Seem to have been there since the war.'

'Get them sterilized in the galley. How about instruments? What have you found?'

Easter pulled two handfuls of metal objects from his trouser pockets.

'I've been on the scrounge,' he explained. 'I thought these would come in handy, like.'

I looked at his booty, which he spread on the table. There was a pair of pliers, two saloon forks, a packet of darning needles labelled 'A Sailor's Friend', some paper-clips, a stiletto, a potato knife, a pair of tweezers, a surgical scalpel, and a uterine curette.

'You'd better sterilize the lot,' I said gloomily. 'Except the pliers. Shouldn't there be a set of surgical instruments on board?'

'They seem to have disappeared, Doctor.'

'You mean you flogged them?' He scratched his nose guiltily. 'There's nothing for it but to use what we've got,' I told him crossly. 'I damn well hope you get an appendix, too!'

I went out on deck. I needed some fresh air. The day was already becoming too much for me.

Outside the hospital I found Chippy. He was sitting on the deck with a hatch cover – a thick piece of wood about six feet by two used in rows to cover the hatches. He was polishing it carefully with emery paper.

'Hello, Chips,' I said. 'Getting everything shipshape for Santos?'

He looked up at me gloomily.

'He'll slide off this lovely,' he said.

'Who will?'

'Why – 'im down there.' He pointed aft with his thumb. 'The poor bloke what's for the knife. Slide off it like a wet fish, he will,' he added with relish.

I was perplexed.

'What's he want to slide off a hatch cover for?' I asked.

'Why, when they buries 'im, of course.' He gave it another rub. 'Lot of work I've put in on this 'ere 'atch cover.'

'Now, look here, Chippy. What gives you the idea my patient's going to die?'

'Oh, they always does. I've seen five appendicitises at sea. 'Ad their time, every one of 'em. Over the wall they went on a 'atch cover.'

I stamped off in disgust. I felt I had been professionally insulted. I climbed the bridge ladder angrily to report the Carpenter's pessimism to one of the Mates. There I found the Second moodily sorting out flags.

'What ho, Doc,' he said. 'When's the carve-up?'

'In about an hour.'

'Think that ensign'll do?'

'Do? What for?'

'Why, in case – in case of accidents. To cover the body.'

'There isn't going to be any body, damn you!'

'Well, Father told us to take precautions. Means a lot of work for all hands, Doc. It'll be a shame if they're all disappointed now.'

I admit that they do give one an excellent funeral at sea. The properties are traditionally adapted from the ship's gear and the routine is prescribed as firmly as that for entering and leaving port. As soon as the body is available it is turned over to the bos'n, who sews it up in canvas with half a dozen firebars from the galley. For this he receives a bottle of whisky. Meanwhile, the carpenter has been polishing and attaching rope handles to a hatch cover, and the quartermasters have been pressing their best uniforms. The ceremony is held at sunset or sunrise on the same day, because ships spend most of their time in tropical waters and the performance might be marred by the corpse if it became aggressively high. The vessel stops, a rail is taken away from the side, and the ship's officers, including the abashed Doctor, line up with the Captain. Caps are removed, and at the appropriate moment the body is marched to the rails on the hatch cover by the quartermasters – who receive a bottle of whisky between them for their services – and smartly tipped overboard. The Mate, who has charge of all deck stores including flags, at the same time edges himself down to the rail and grabs the ensign – which costs the Company money – before it slips into the sea with its bundle. The ship then starts again and everybody goes off for an obituary peg.

'I should hate to spoil your fun,' I said coldly, 'but this patient is going to walk off the ship in Liverpool.'

I returned into the hospital, where Easter was boiling the instruments over a Primus stove.

'Everyone thinks there's going to be a funeral,' I said. 'I never heard such nonsense.'

'Ho, yes,' Easter remarked calmly. 'That's why I couldn't fit a screen under that there pipe as you said. Bos'n says he's got to keep all his spare canvas for the shroud.'

'But it's monstrous!'

Easter chuckled over the steaming instruments.

'Cor, I've seen some funny funerals at sea! Remember one we had in the Indian Ocean. Chinaman it was. Got knifed. Blimey, we pushed him overboard all right, but he wouldn't sink. Bobbed about like a buoy. The Old Man wasn't 'arf flummoxed. In the end we had to leave him to it. Couldn't pull him out again, could we? Probably still bobbing about somewhere, if the sharks ain't got him.'

'I'm going to see the patient,' I said sternly. 'Get everything ready in an hour's time.'

The patient was sitting in his cabin eating fish and chips and drinking a bottle of beer.

'What the devil's this!' I shouted. 'I thought I told you to have nothing by mouth?'

'Oh, sorry, Doc,' he said awkwardly. 'But seeing I was feeling so much better like, I thought I could do with a bit of grub.'

'Better, man! How dare you say you're better! That's for me to decide. You only think you're better. You've got an acute appendix inside you.'

He pulled a fish bone out of his mouth repentantly.

'There's just one thing, Doc,' he said respectfully. 'Do people often get this appendix taken out twice.'

'Twice? What do you mean?'

'Well, I had it taken out the first time in Birkenhead when I was six . . .'

I sprang at him and pulled up his shirt. A faint, white two-inch scar. I started to laugh.

'Not operating, Doctor? Why?' Captain Hogg demanded.

'I've charmed it away, sir,' I explained. 'A trick I learnt in infancy from a gypsy.'

Chapter Nine

We arrived at Santos in the early afternoon. As we slowed down to approach the river mouth between the deep green hills the shore heat hit us like the blast from the engine-room hatchway.

'It'll be nice and cosy alongside,' Easter said gloomily.

We sailed up the greasy river between the rows of ships tied thickly along each bank, the ensign of the United States of Brazil flying in courtesy from our foremast. Hornbeam went to his station forrard, and Archer took the Lamptrimmer and his gang of deckhands aft. The tugs came up, the mooring ropes flew out, and we were pushed into place as neatly as a well-parked car. The gangway rattled down and a section of the rail was pulled away: we had arrived.

But we were still flying the yellow Q flag, indicating we were in quarantine. A troop of stout Brazilian customs and health officials immediately tramped aboard, headed by an important-looking man in a white suit whom I took to be the Doctor.

I saluted.

'Boa dia, senhor,' I said in carefully incubated Portuguese.

He held out his hand.

'Afternoon, old boy,' he replied. 'How's tricks?'

'Very well, thank you.'

'Nothing infectious?'

'No.'

'Haul down the yellow peril, then. Can you let me have a few hundred English cigarettes?'

Once the quarantine flag was down people came aboard like Navy week visitors on a bank holiday. There were policemen, stevedores, money-changers, ship chandlers, water purveyors, fruit sellers, harbourmasters, launderers – and the agents. The agents were the men in charge of the Fathom Line's business in Santos, and could get any commodity at short notice from five thousand tons of oil to a new bell for the ship's cat. They were a pair of tall genial Englishmen with minds like efficiently arranged shopping lists.

'Hello, Doc,' one said. 'Want any medical stores?'

'Chief Steward's got the list.'

'Good. You've taken over from Flowerday, have you? He was a rum bird. Coming to have a peg?'

'Not just now.'

'Fair enough. By the way, there's some mail for you somewhere.'

I had forgotten that the agents look after the ship's mail. I went out on deck and found most of it had been distributed. All over the ship men were leaning on uncomfortable steel corners reading their letters. I passed the Carpenter, who had several closely-written sheets in his hand and kept saying 'No! It can't be! It can't be!' to himself. I hoped it was nothing serious.

'Coo!' one man shouted. 'I've 'ad a baby!'

'I've 'ad six,' his companion said morosely, not looking up. This nonplussed the new father.

'Wot, all at once?' he asked.

I ran into Whimble.

'Letter for you, Doc,' he said. 'I gave it to Easter.'

I suddenly felt excited. I had forgotten England and home in the past three weeks as efficiently as a patient with amnesia. My past seemed a disconnected existence. All at once I felt a letter would be like a familiar face in a big crowd.

I saw Easter leaning on the rail and hurried towards him. I wondered who it was from. Wendy, perhaps? Telling me she was crying over my picture and reading Conrad? From my principal, genially wishing me a good voyage? Or my parents, asking where I'd put the keys of the garage? From old classmates envious of my double release? I didn't care. It was a letter, a letter. Whoever sent it proved the most important thing in the world – I was not forgotten.

I took the envelope from Easter. I couldn't recognize the handwriting. I tried to open it with dignity, but excitedly tore the flap. It said: '*The—— Laundry. Dear Sir, If you do not collect your washing within seven days of this date it will be sold to defray charges.*'

I tossed it into the dock. I leant on the rail and looked at the unfamiliar colours, the dirty yellow sheds, the strange un-English mountains in the background with the white road wriggling up them to São Paulo, the dusky lounging men and slim graceful women on the wharfside, the signs in Portuguese, the odd open tramcar behind, the surprising uniforms of the police, the glare of the unaccustomed sun . . . I realized tardily I was on another side of the world.

After conditioning myself to the exclusive company of my shipmates for three weeks I found the rush of locals on board unsettling. The silence of the sea passage was broken by the noise of the winches, and the bare decks became littered with hatch covers, wires, tarpaulins, pieces of dropped cargo, and resting Brazilians. The Brazilians have a great capacity for rest. When they have nothing to do for a few minutes they see no point in continuing to support the burden of keeping awake and fling themselves into the nearest piece of shade. Whether they are lying on a stone wharf, the top of a couple of packing-cases, or some pieces of scrap metal does not appear to detract from the enjoyment.

The cargo came out by the exact reverse of the technique that put it in at Liverpool. As I had nothing else to do I joined Easter, who was watching crates of machinery being drawn out of number five hatch with the pleasantly indolent air of a Londoner observing road excavations.

'Hope you've locked your cabin, Doctor,' he said. 'And screwed up the port. These boys would pinch the soles off your shoes if you wasn't careful.'

I pointed towards the policemen on the gangway.

'But don't they keep an eye on it?'

'What, them vigilantes? Them's the worst of the lot.'

As the winches paused I heard feminine giggles and zestful screams coming from the crew's quarters in the poop. A plump dark girl with a basket of washing under her arm appeared on the deck, struggling formally with a large sailor.

'That's Maria,' Easter explained. 'She does your laundry for you. Three blokes got something off her last trip.'

'What!'

'Wouldn't mind having a go at her myself,' he continued solemnly. 'They don't seem to think much of things like that out here. All the girls is tenderhearted. I reckon it's the climate.'

'It all seems very unhygienic to me, to say the least.'

'Mind you, some of 'em's real smashers. Ho, I've had some fun here, I have. You going ashore tonight, Doctor?'

'I might stretch my legs. Though I fear I shall do nothing more exciting than go to the pictures.'

'Ah, you can get some queer pictures out here too,' Easter went on. 'Pal of mine went ashore one night to have his pleasure, as you might say, and the next day he went off with a crowd of the lads to one of them odd picture houses. Blimey, he was the big feature. Didn't 'arf get his leg pulled about it.'

'I think I will go and see Mr Hornbeam,' I said. Santos sounded a place that would have provided Easter with extensive reminiscences.

Hornbeam's cabin was as full as a compartment in a suburban train in the rush-hour. There were the agents, the chief stevedores, the customs, the immigration officers, and a few unidentifiable officials. Hornbeam was sitting with his white shirt undone to the waist, looking pleased with himself. His table was filled with bottles of gin, whisky, and beer, and half a dozen open tins of Players. Everyone was helping themselves.

'Come in, Doc!' he called. 'Have a peg. This is our Doctor, gentlemen.'

'How do you do,' I said, taking a glass.

'It's always open house in the Mate's cabin in port,' Hornbeam explained, pouring himself another gin. 'Everyone wants the poor bloody Mate. Now what about this trouble in number three?' he said to the head stevedore. 'Can you get another gang on there tonight?'

'Tomorrow morning, Mister Mate. Tonight, no good.'

'We'll have to put up with it, I suppose.'

He took a sheaf of papers from a ragged Brazilian who appeared in the doorway.

'Cargo plans? All right. Have a peg, chum. Coming ashore tonight, Doc?' he added to me.

'I thought of it. Are you?'

'Certainly I am. Never been ashore in Santos yet. Tonight I am. We'll collect here about midnight . . .'

'Midnight?'

'There's no point in going anywhere before eleven in this part of the world. Nothing livens up before twelve.'

'If that's the case I think I'd better turn in for a bit.'

'That's the idea, Doc. You're in the land of the siesta now, don't forget. God, it's hot, isn't it?'

I screwed the closely-meshed wire-netting in the port-hole to keep the flies out and went to sleep. The Second woke me up about nine.

'Coming ashore?' he asked. 'We're going up to the Mate's cabin. They sting you for drinks in Brazil so we reckoned we'd get a glow on us before we went off.'

I sat up and rubbed the sweat off me with a sheet.

'I'll be up when I've had a shower. The Mate's coming with us, isn't he?'

Archer laughed.

'I wouldn't know about that. I've never seen him get ashore anywhere yet.'

When I reached the Mate's cabin I saw at once that he had not been taking a siesta himself. His visitors had gone and the bottles were empty. He sat behind a jumble of dirty glasses and cigarette-ends, humming absently to himself.

''Lo, Doc,' he said languidly. 'Fetch a bottle out of the locker there. I'm coming ashore with you young lads tonight. Keep you out of trouble, eh? Muy bien. Cheerio.'

Archer and Trail were in the cabin, dressed in their shore-going rig. The scattered places in which they bought their clothes and their over-compensation for wearing uniform most of their lives gave them a startling appearance. Trail was particularly arresting. He wore a pair of green cotton trousers he had bought in Rio, a yellow shirt from Calcutta, the sort of sports coat that is, fortunately, popular only on the Australian beaches, suede shoes from Ceylon, and a tie with a luminous girl on it from New York.

We all sat down and drank determinedly.

'Have to drink beer ashore,' Trail said. 'A gin costs about twelve bob. I got some cruzeiros for you, Doc.' He handed me a bundle of dirty notes. 'That's the sub you put in for. How about you, Mr Hornbeam?'

'Got some in the kitty,' he said thickly.

He pulled a tin out of his locker and spilt the contents on the table. There was currency from all over the world – Australian florins, South African sixpences, nickels and quarters, escudos and francs, Canadian dollars, Japanese yen, New Zealand pounds, rupees, pesos, pesetas and guilders, a few marks, and a couple of Pitcairn Island postage stamps.

'Always like to have a bit of ready cash,' he explained, rummaging through the pile. 'No cruzeiros, though. What's this?' He held up a coin and squinted at it. 'Springbok ha'penny. No good. I'll take the dollars ashore and flog 'em. Don't you blokes go without me,' he added threateningly. 'I'll get a cob on if you don't wait. Where are we bound for, anyway? Have another peg.'

The Third drew a small book from his pocket and turned over to the letter S.

'Santos . . .' he said, 'Oh, that's fixed. We'll take the Doc to the Whores' Ball.'

'The what did you say?' I asked.

'The Whores' Ball. Funniest thing this side of the Line. It doesn't start till midnight. We'll look into the Ritz Bar first.'

'I want to see the Bidu Bar,' Archer added. 'I met a hot bit of blonde in there last time.'

'You game, Doc?'

By this time my critical faculties were mildly blunted with gin.

'Game? Of course I'm game. I'm a sailor, aren't I?'

'That's the spirit!' Trail said. 'Down the hatch, lads, and let's get moving. It's after eleven.'

'What about the Mate?' I asked. I turned to look at him. He was lying with his head in a pool of currency, asleep.

'It's always the same with the Mate,' Archer explained. 'He never makes it. Hasn't been ashore for years. It's best to leave him there until he wakes up. Now for the bright lights!' Trail put down his glass. 'Come on, Doc!'

Singing softly we filed down the gangway and, slightly intoxicated, for the first time in my life I put foot on foreign soil.

Chapter Ten

There are few attractive cities in Brazil, and Santos is not one of them. In the centre is a fairly pleasant square with gardens in it, a new post office, and the Town Hall. It would pass for a little bastion of bourgeoisie in the South of France on a hot day. But the waterfront caters, efficiently, for different tastes. It is a tall line of buildings on a cobbled street that looks like the slums in Glasgow draped with neon.

The Third led us jauntily towards a lighted doorway with RITZ BAR—DRINKS AND GIRLS shining over it.

'Here we go lads!' he said. 'If our mothers could see us now!'

The three of us piled inside and took a table by the door. It was a long room, brightly lit, with a bar down one side, a small dance floor, and a band. The walls were lined with foreign flags and signs such as WELCOMES TO OUR BRITISH FRIENDS, HAVE A SWELL TIME BABY, and WE TAKE POUNDS AND DOLLARS. The room was full, but not with Brazilians. There seemed to be sailors there from every country with a seaboard. There were stiff blond Swedes and Norwegians, a crowd of drunk Greeks in the corner, some Dutchmen, a pack of Frenchmen arguing with Spaniards, blank-faced masticating Americans, and a good many small dark-eyed dangerous-looking men of unplaceable nationality. By the door, stroking his long moustache, stood a nervous Brazilian policeman.

'I say!' I exclaimed. I stared at the place like a child brought up to Town to see the lights. 'It looks a bit tough, doesn't it?'

'The Santos waterfront is the toughest in the world,' Archer said lightly. 'That's why we're sitting near the door. If anything starts don't wait to see what it's all about, but hop it. They have a habit of arresting everyone in sight down here. Ever been in jail?'

'Not yet.'

'This isn't the place to start. I got pinched two years ago for being drunk. They let me go next morning, luckily. Had to rub shoulders with some pretty queer birds. None of this single cell and bath business you get in Britain.'

A Brazilian girl, dark and rounded, in a black dress and a decorative lace apron came upon us.

'Três cerveja,' Trail said.

'Sure, baby.'

She strolled off, giving us the benefit of her hips.

'She brings the beer,' Trail explained. 'If you like you can dance with her. Look over there.'

There were about twenty of the girl's colleagues in the room, all similarly dressed. I watched one at the table next to ours being asked for a dance by an American, who used the technique of slapping her on the bottom and grabbing her arms as she passed. The girl smiled acquiescence, and they took the floor.

The band played only sambas and rumbas. The polite versions of these dances produced in London restaurants have the same relationship to Santos sambas as vintage Burgundy to raw applejack. Similarly with the dancing. The Brazilian girls, though languid in daytime, come to life like flashing electric signs at nightfall. Not only do they dance lustily, but they do so without any inhibitions whatever. If any couple in London were seen performing in the manner accepted as normally sociable in Brazil, they would be immediately asked to leave.

The girl brought our beers and opened them. Trail handed her a hundred-cruzeiro note and pinched her bottom. She grinned at him. I wondered what would have happened if he had tried the same technique in a Lyons' teashop.

'Don't reckon we'll stay here long,' Trail said. 'It's getting on. How do you like Brazilian beer?'

'It tastes like soapy water to me.'

'It carries a kick in it somewhere. Finish it up, we've got to look in at the Bidu.'

'Saw a chap get killed outside there last trip,' Archer said to me.

The Bidu Bar was exactly the same as the Ritz except that the signs round the walls were in Portuguese and the girls were fatter.

We didn't stay long. We had a couple more beers and left. Trail rubbed his hands. 'And now,' he said, 'for the Whores' Ball.'

The function to which Trail was so attracted was held on the top floor of an old building on one of the side streets. We could hear the music, the inescapable samba, blaring down the street from the open windows before we turned the corner. The way in was through a narrow door with TAXI DANCING painted over the top of it and up a long, narrow, unbroken flight of stairs. At the foot of the stairs was a ticket office, inside which a fat man in his vest was barred up like the crown jewels.

We paid, and mounted the staircase. At the top were two solemn policemen, who immediately advanced on us. Archer's remarks about the carelessness of the police in arresting people flashed into my mind. I jumped nervously and began to walk backwards down the stairs.

'Don't be alarmed,' Archer said. 'In England you leave your hat and coat, don't you?'

By that time a policeman had grabbed hold of me, pulled aside my arms, and searched me for weapons. I caught sight of a table behind him that explained Archer's remarks. On it was neatly arranged a collection of revolvers, knives, blackjacks, knuckle-dusters, and razors.

'The Brazilian likes going around with a bit of cutlery in his belt,' Trail explained. 'Makes him feel big. Unfortunately he tends to be a bit on the excited side. These cops sometimes miss a knife or two, so we'd better keep near the windows. Don't mind a jump, do you?'

We went inside. Three girls immediately came up to us and told us they loved us. Trail waved them aside. 'We came to hear the music,' he told them affably.

We strode across the floor and sat down. It was bigger than the American Bar and had more space for dancing. The walls were bare of any decoration and the floor was rough boards polished only by the customers' feet. There were tables scattered round the floor, and girls scattered round the tables. The atmosphere was like a laundry with a breakdown in the ventilating system.

At one end was the band–on the platform six feet above the floor and surrounded by barbed wire.

'What's the barricade for?' I asked.

'If they dislike the music here they don't hide their feelings,' Trail explained.

'What about all these girls? What do they do?'

'If you pay fifty cruzeiros you'll find out.'

'Oh, I see. Let's have some beer.'

We sat and drank and watched the dancing. It was the sort that Trail described as 'the bumps and grinds'. I looked nervously at men sitting at the other tables, with an expectant sensation between my shoulder-blades. When they saw a girl they fancied they grabbed her and joined the jactitating couples on the floor. After the dance they either went off with her, dragged her back to their own tables, or left her, according to the strength of their inclination. I saw a party of our Liverpool greasers in the corner, their shirts unbuttoned and outside their trousers, throwing Merseyside witticisms at their neighbours. Everyone seemed to be having a good time.

A warm brunette descended on my knee.

'Hallo darling!' she said. 'You come wit' me?'

'No!'

She laughed and ruffled my hair.

'You dance wit' me, no?'

'Go on, Doc,' Archer called. 'Give the girls a treat.'

'But I can't dance.'

'Come on, darling,' said the girl. She snatched hold of me and pulled me out of my chair. Then she clapped me to her bosom like a belladonna plaster and pushed me on the dance floor.

We jostled with the rest of the dancers. It was like being lashed to an upholstered pneumatic drill. I struggled round in her clammy embrace, trying to keep my feet, wriggling out of other men's way, and reflecting that I was a long way from home.

When the music stopped I disengaged myself and looked for our table. By this time the Third was talking earnestly to a thin, brown girl who had taken my chair.

'Thirty cruzeiros,' he said forcefully. 'Trinta. See?' He held up three fingers.

She shook her head. 'No!' she insisted. 'Cincoenta. Fifty, fifty, fifty!'

'Oh hell,' the Third said. 'Let's get out of here.'

We trooped down the stairs. 'Where now?' Archer asked when we were in the street.

'Madame Mimi's,' Trail said with finality. 'it's the only place where you can get a decent bottle of beer in town.'

'I think I'm going back to the ship,' I said.

'Come on, Doc! You don't have to sample the goods. Besides you'd get knifed walking back alone. Where is it, Second? Somewhere near the Rua Bittencourt, I think . . .'

He led us along threatening unlighted streets, where the pedestrians shuffled guiltily in the shadows like large rats.

'I think this is the number,' he said, stopping by the heavy door of an unlighted house. 'You fellows stay here and I'll go and see.'

He jumped up the steps and rang the bell. After a minute or so I saw him jab it again. The door opened. An old woman with her hair tied in a handkerchief stood against the inside light.

'Boa noite, senhora,' Trail began. He held a conversation in Portuguese with her, and I saw that he spoke the language rapidly and with great force, but unintelligibly. After he had delivered a string of sentences embellished heavily with gestures she held up a finger and disappeared to fetch help. A tall man in a dressing-gown came back with her. After a few words he pushed the Third abruptly down the steps, delivered a few hostile sentences, and slammed the door.

'Wrong place,' Trail explained, picking himself up. 'That seems to be the dentist's. It must be the house on the other corner.'

At the next door we were received with pleasure and shown immediately into the parlour.

Madame Mimi's was a sedate establishment. The parlour was furnished in the austere, grubby style popular with the Continental middle-class; it was a large apartment with big shuttered windows, containing several small tables and a larger one in the corner where Madame sat with three or four of her charges. On a dark broken sideboard down one side were two unlighted candelabra, a sickly-looking plant, and a radio. Round the walls were pictures of the saints. Business was poor, and the room was quiet and inactive. One felt one had called on the vicar's daughters for tea.

Madame immediately recognized my companions and greeted them warmly.

'Ah, hello my little boys! Back so soon, eh? How goes it in cold England?'

She embraced the two of them. She was a big, over-powdered woman in a black dress, with a figure like a thawing snowman.

'Not so dusty,' Archer said. 'Meet one of our shipmates.'

We embraced.

'Madame is a wonderful character,' Trail explained. 'Hails from France originally. She built up her own team here like a football manager.'

'Now, boys,' Madame said. 'You would like some beer, no?'

'Lay it on, Madame,' Archer said, sitting down and slapping his knee. 'Lay on everything.'

Madame clapped her hands.

'Is that little girl Dina still here?' Trail asked.

Our hostess shrugged her shoulders powerfully.

'She is gone. She married a gentleman from São Paulo.'

'Well, he hasn't done badly,' Trail observed. 'Let's have a look at the latest talent.'

Madame's assistant brought the tall green beer bottles and glasses, and three girls came over to sit with us. They were pretty girls–slim, dainty, smiling, glowing with cooperation.

'Americano?' asked the one next to me eagerly.

'No. Ingles.'

'Cigarette?' she asked, as winsomely as a schoolgirl appealing for pocket money. I gave her one, which she put carefully in her handbag. She began to stroke the back of my neck. I clasped my hands in front of me and stared defensively at the opposite wall.

'I lof you,' she said.

We sat like that for some time. Meanwhile, Trail and Archer had their girls on their knees and were conducting a conversation in a mixture of English, Portuguese, and giggles.

'You come with me?' the girl asked, playfully pulling a hair from my neck.

'No,' I said. 'I–I não gostar, or whatever it is. Nothing doing. Go and talk to my amigos . . .'

I looked round and saw Trail and Archer disappearing up the stairs leading to the operational portion of the building.

'Hey!' I called, jumping up. 'Don't you fellows leave me!'

'It's all right, Doc. We won't be long.' Trail called over his shoulder. 'Finish the beer for us.'

I sat gloomily down and bit my lip, feeling like a warning to young men. The girl, discouraged, got up and left me. I took my handkerchief out and wiped my forehead.

But Madame, ever solicitous, assumed immediately that my companion had for some reason not pleased me. She directed a large grinning blonde to take her place.

'No, no! I said in alarm. 'No! Please . . . go away, there's a good girl.'

'Não?'

'No. Sorry and all that.'

I looked uncomfortably round me. I wanted to get out. But I didn't know the way back to the ship, and I was scared to walk out of the place on my own. I took a gulp of beer and sat biting my thumbnail.

I was hardly aware that another had joined me. She sat quietly beside me without speaking. I looked up. She was sitting demurely with her hands clasped in her lap, as pathetic as a wallflower at a village dance.

'Hop it! Vamos! Pronto!' I told her.

'Please . . . please!' she said.

'My dear young lady, I have no intention . . .'

Two tears rolled compellingly down her thin cheeks.

'Please come,' she urged softly. 'No one come with me this week. If you no come I get fired.'

I licked my lips. This was the sort of dilemma even Big White Carstairs would have had difficulty sorting out.

She laid a hand on my arm, as softly as an alighting butterfly.

'Please come,' she whispered.

I coughed, and ran my finger round my collar. My conscience strained to suppress my sense of gallantry. Just then two large tears followed the first.

'How much?' I heard. It was me.

'Hun'red Cruzeiro.'

'Oh . . . ah . . . very well then . . .'

I pulled the note from my pocket. Seizing it, she pulled me by the hand towards the staircase of sin.

We went into a bare room that contained only a bed, a basin, and several more pictures of the saints. She locked the door. I stood and scratched my left ear.

Deftly, as though peeling a banana, she stripped off her clothes. She jumped on the bed and gave me an inviting smile. Suddenly she held her right side and groaned.

'Hello,' I said, immediately interested. 'What's the trouble?'

She bit her lip for a moment, then said, 'Nada . . . nada.'

'Have you got a pain? Er–dor?'

She nodded.

'Where?'

She pointed under her right ribs.

'That's curious,' I said. 'Just let me have a look a minute, will you? By jove, this is unusual . . . Deep breath, now.'

After five minutes' careful examination of her abdomen I concluded that the young lady was suffering from inflammation of the gall-bladder.

'Look here,' I said, 'you ought to go to hospital.'

She smiled up at me from the pillow.

'Hospital . . . operaçao, or whatever it is.'

I indicated with signs.

'Oh, não,' she said.

'Oh, yes,' I said firmly. 'Here'–I took a pencil and paper from my pocket and wrote on it–'you take that to the chemist–farmacêutico–and they'll give you something to make it better. Then you must go to hospital, see? O.K.?'

She took the prescription and grinned.

'Very well,' I said automatically, 'call me if you have any severe pain during the night. Good evening.'

I let myself out. Trail and Archer were waiting downstairs.

'Come on, you dirty old man,' Trail said, grabbing my arm. 'Time to get back to the ship.'

It occurred to me that was the only consultation I had ever paid for.

Chapter Eleven

The next morning I woke, sweating and penitent, in my unventilated cabin. Jumbled harbour sounds replaced our usual noiseless morning at sea, and the steam winches were already working in frantic bursts on the deck outside. There were footsteps and shouting all over the ship, and when I turned over for my watch I saw an unknown, half-naked Brazilian picking his teeth and solemnly inspecting me from the open cabin door. As I shaved I reflected sharply on the change in my recreations in the last four weeks.

At breakfast I found Archer and Trail as unruffled as if they had spent the evening in a suburban cinema.

'I hear you had a bit of a lash-up last night,' Hornbeam said. 'Have a good time in Mimi's?'

'One must see how the other half lives,' I murmured.

'She was a nice little piece you got hold of,' Trail said, in a complimentary tone. 'Wouldn't have minded her myself.'

Hornbeam, who had an unphysiological resilience to alcohol, nodded as he ate his way with relish through a dish of bacon, chops, eggs, and liver.

'Sorry I couldn't come with you blokes,' he said cheerfully. 'I reckon I was tired. The quartermaster put me in my bunk about three.'

'This is not much of a place, anyway,' Trail said. 'Not a patch on B.A.'

'They've cleaned up B.A. a lot now,' Archer added, with disappointment. 'Do you remember Underneath the Arches, Mr Hornbeam? A string of them running down behind a sort of colonnade affair from the Boca practically to the Plaza de Majo. They had a purity campaign down there after the war.'

'They needed it,' Hornbeam said, reaching for the tomato sauce. 'Any more bacon going, steward? I get peckish in port.'

'What are you doing today, Doc?' Archer asked. 'Going ashore?'

'I was thinking of it.'

'What, going back for an encore?' Trail said.

'No, I assure you I was only thinking of a haircut.'

'You're right there, Doc,' Hornbeam said. 'You look like an old rope fender.'

My hair had last been cut in the wintery twilight of a London afternoon, more than a month ago: now it overhung my newly sunburned ears, and its length reflected our distance from home. But I was reluctant to step ashore alone, for the only Portuguese I was confident of saying was 'Good morning,' and I was not in the position to refuse a shampoo, singeing, scalp massage, hot towels, and any unusual luxuries that might be provided by Brazilian barber's shops. I explained this to Easter during surgery, and he immediately relieved my difficulties.

'I should be very glad to oblige, Doctor,' he said with dignity. 'If requested.'

'You cut hair, too, do you?'

'Done quite a few hair-cutting jobs ashore. Worked six months steady at it once, helping out a pal what had a little barber's shop in Doncaster. He ran a book really, but the shop kept the coppers away. Got pinched last year, so I heard.'

'Very well, Easter. You may try your skills on me.'

He set up his saloon on the strip of deck outside my cabin. He first spread out several sheets of the *Liverpool Echo*, then brought from his quarters a camp stool and a length of cloth striped like a butcher's apron. He tied the cloth tightly round my neck and drew a pair of scissors and a comb from his hip pocket.

'How do you like it?' he demanded.

'Oh, sort of short round the back.'

'Wouldn't like a crew cut, would you? Suit your sort of head, if I may be so bold, Doctor.'

'No thank you.'

He began snipping round the nape of the neck.

'Bit of fun and games about noon,' he continued. 'The *Violet*'s coming in astern of us where that Royal Mail boat was yesterday.'

'The *Violet*? What's she?'

'Another one of the Fathom hookers. Does the run from the River Plate to Pernambuco and New York. Captain Beamish in command. Cor! He ain't 'arf a queer 'un. Needs his head examined, I reckon.'

'That's what they're cleaning up the wheelhouse for, is it?'

'Ho yes, got to have her looking posh when we has company. Sorry, Doctor, was that your ear?'

'If I get a septic wound from this,' I said sternly, 'I shall order your kit to be burned as a sanitary measure.'

He blew hard through the comb and bit deeply into my hair with it.

'I likes hair-cutting,' he continued, unruffled. 'Bit of an art, like knocking up a sculpture. You never know how it's going to turn out when you start.'

I sat in the sunshine, unresisting, while my hair fell in small bundles across the *Liverpool Echo*. The increasing warmth and Easter's conversation behind the regular sharp snip of his scissors encouraged a pleasant feeling of euphoria. I was looking forrard, towards the mouth of the river; the long quay, with the tall German cranes grouped eagerly round open hatchways, was lined with ships as far as I could see. In the water on our port side a clean, grey-and-white, neat Swedish tanker was being turned slowly by a pair of tugs, like a birch log between two water-rats. Immediately ahead of us the Stars and Stripes dropped over the stern of the *Omar C. Ingersoll* of Baltimore, a cargo ship the same size as the *Lotus*, designed with the American combination of stark lines and grotesque mysterious appendages. Just below me, on the foredeck, a dozen Brazilians clutched a swaying crate labelled AUSTIN that hovered from the sling over No. 2 hatch.

'I reckon you was right not to trust the barbers ashore,' Easter said. 'They ain't up to much, and they'll rook you as soon as look at you. Not as bad as the ones in Port Said, though–for a dollar they'll give you a shampoo and introduce you to their sister.' He wiped the comb on the leg of his trousers thoughtfully. 'Mind you,' he went on, 'you can have some fun in Port Said if you're up to the tricks. Very rude in places, it is, very rude.' He swept away the cloth and stood back proudly. 'Lovely,' he said. 'Care for me to read your bumps while I'm at it? Used to be Phreno the Bump Man at fairs for a bit.'

'That will be enough, thank you. How much do I owe you?'

'Fifty Woods, Doctor, seeing it's you.'

I went to my cabin to fetch the cigarettes, and found I looked like a caricature of a Prussian general; I suspected that Easter had learned the elements of barbering while serving one of his terms in jail. The advent of the *Violet* seemed to justify the Company's Regulation Cap, so I fitted a new white cover and stepped back on deck with Easter's art hidden underneath.

By now there was an atmosphere of serious preparation on board. Captain Hogg was shouting at a pair of deckhands painting the large red F on the funnel, Hornbeam was supervising the desperate removal of a potful of black paint just spilled over the white bridge, and the Bos'n was trying to rig a line of electric bulbs along the gangway without disturbing the fat policeman who slept in a deckchair by the rail. As noon approached, the crew began leaning over the port rail and Captain Hogg climbed on the monkey island over the wheelhouse and impatiently trained his glasses towards the bow. I went to the boatdeck and squeezed between two davits, trying to catch the familiar Fathom Line houseflag moving slowly through the forest of strange masts.

'Mind you don't fall in,' Hornbeam said, coming up the ladder. 'A mouthful of this water would kill you. Any sign of her yet?'

'Can't see anything from here.'

'The Old Man and Beamish are great pals,' he told me contentedly. 'They'd ram each other's ships if they thought they could get away with it. Not that I have any time for Beamish,' he added. 'In fact, I'm not certain I wouldn't rather sail with the one we've got.'

This struck me as severely damning to Captain Beamish.

'What's the matter with him?'

'Thinks he's one of the big ship boys–you know, everything frightfully pukka, wipe your feet at the top of the gangway, kiss me hand and call me Charlie. They say he was a cadet in the P. & O., but got chucked out. I can't say I blame them.'

'But surely,' I said despairingly, 'there must be some good captains in the world?'

'There's one or two. Old Morris on the *Daisy* isn't bad. He did me a good turn once in Belfast when I got mixed up with the cops. But as soon as they get their fourth ring most of 'em get bloody-minded. You wait and see–I'll go the same way.'

We stood chatting between the lifeboats for a while, until Captain Hogg bellowed from above us: 'Ahoy there, Mr Trail! Stand by to dip ensign!'

'There she is,' Hornbeam said, pointing down the river, 'See?'

'What, that?'

His account of Captain Beamish made me imagine his ship as equally superior; but the *Violet*, as she swung round the bend in the river, turned out to be a vessel smaller than the *Lotus*, narrow, as angular as a piano, with patches on her plates and two tall, mournful ventilators drooping over her bridge. She was high in the water, with a wide streak of red showing at the bottom of her rusty hull, and the tips of her propeller blades cut the surface below her overhanging stern.

'Makes us look like the *Queen Lizzie*, doesn't it?' Hornbeam said as she drew nearer. 'Watch for the fun when we start saluting.'

It was clear that Captain Hogg was going to pay his respects grudgingly. He stood on top of the wheelhouse glaring across the water to the *Violet*, and on the wing of the *Violet*'s bridge a thin, tall figure in a shining white uniform glared back at him. As the mainmasts of the two ships drew level Captain Hogg shouted 'Lower away!' and the *Violet*'s ensign fluttered down a foot in curt acknowledgement. The two Captains scowled at each other as they passed, and no one in either crew would have been surprised if they had stuck out their tongues.

'The brotherhood of the sea,' Hornbeam said. 'I bet Father's just waiting for her to foul our ropes as she comes alongside.'

Captain Beamish nevertheless arrived for lunch on board the *Lotus* as soon as his gangway was down. He turned out to be a thin, brown, wrinkled man with a face like a tortoise. He compensated for his own shabby ship by turning himself out sprucely; his long neck stretched from the high, starched collar of his uniform, two rows of glossy medal ribbons shone on his bosom, his trousers were unsullied with sitting, and his feet stood in white buckskin shoes. He sat down at the table, placed a monocle in his right eye, and crumbled a roll in his bony hand with an expression on his face as if he expected it to release an unpleasant smell.

Captain Hogg was coldly polite, and introduced us all. 'This is my chief Officer, Mr Hornbeam . . . my Doctor . . . my Chief Engineer . . . my Chief Steward.' Captain Beamish received these presentations in silence. Before we had finished the soup it appeared that he was a man sparing of words, for the only conversation he permitted himself was to interrupt his host's remarks every few minutes with the expression ''Strordinary!'

When we reached the treacle roll he cut into Captain Hogg's description of how he once docked in Liverpool without tugs, by glaring at me and snapping, 'Doctor!'

'Sir?'

'Which hospital d'y' come from?'

'St Swithin's, sir.'

''Strordinary! Must know Dr Jenkins.'

'Jenkins? No, I'm afraid I don't, sir.'

'Jenkins was a very well-known man in the Line.'

I shook my head solemnly, without making any comment. I had gathered that doctors became well known in seafaring life only through the originality with which they left it.

'You look very young, Doctor,' he continued. 'Fully qualified, I suppose?'

'Of course I am!' I said angrily.

''Strordinary. Looks very young indeed,' he added in a slightly softer voice to Captain Hogg, who immediately began looking at me with suspicion.

'Lost my damned Bos'n this trip,' Captain Beamish went on. 'Blast him.'

'What was up?' Captain Hogg asked, piling the last fragments of suet roll on to his spoon.

'Had to put him over the wall off Pernam. Dead, y'know.'

'Go on! What of?'

''Strordinary thing altogether. Meant to ask your Doctor. Had a turn of the shakes and died before sunset.'

'Very likely smallpox,' I said firmly. 'Your ship will have to be fumigated for three weeks and all hands isolated in the fever hospital. The one in Santos is extremely unpleasant, but they will probably take you up to São Paulo as you're certain to get it anyway.'

I sat and sulked over the cheese-dish.

'Bad about the Bos'n,' Captain Beamish said. 'Don't get his type any more. Respectful. Knew my ways. I may not be in command of a big ship, but I'll have her run decently. Eh, Captain?'

Captain Hogg had his mouth full of cheese, but he nodded violently enough to spill pieces on to the tablecloth.

'Don't know what things are coming to. The Third wore the same uniform three days running last week. D'y'know what happened yesterday? Steward brought me a glass of water without a tray. Communism, that's what it is.'

Captain Beamish then said nothing else for the rest of the meal.

The *Violet*'s officers came aboard before supper and noisily packed themselves into Hornbeam's cabin. I found it startling to see the familiar Fathom Line uniforms and badges with different faces over them. They sat and drank gin, enjoying the fragmentary friendship of the sea that had been established by a few hours or a day or two in a dozen years at ports all over the world.

'Here's our Doc,' Hornbeam said, as I squeezed through the door. 'Meet Mr Molony, Chief Officer from that old barge down aft.'

'Hello, Doc,' he said, shaking hands. 'Enjoying the sea?'

'I am rather, thank you.'

'How did you get on with our Old Man at dinner?'

'I must say he was pretty rude.'

Molony laughed loudly, while Hornbeam filled up his glass.

'He takes some getting used to. Do you know what?' he asked Hornbeam. 'He chased me up for eating peas off a knife the other day. Can you imagine it? Now, there's bugling, too. We signed on a Yankee galley-boy in New York who brought a trumpet with him, so we get bugle calls to meals. Anyone would think we were a ruddy battleship.'

'All skippers are the same,' Hornbeam said wearily. 'Do you remember old Jack Andrews in the *Buttercup*? What happened to him?'

'Didn't you hear? He got put ashore in Cape Town last year.'

They began to talk earnestly of men and ships I had never heard of, and their conversation took on an odd parochialism extending across the face of the earth.

As the *Violet* was due to sail again at midnight our guests left early. I leant on the rail and watched her float slowly into the river, her portholes drawing yellow streaks across the greasy water. She blew three hoots of farewell to us and followed her tug towards the sea. Captain Hogg stood outside his cabin staring after her, and no doubt Captain Beamish was on the bridge glaring astern at us. I wondered if I should meet any more Fathom Line captains, and if they would be any less unnerving.

A man in a pair of khaki trousers and a loose orange shirt was waiting in my cabin. He grinned as I came in.

'Hi'ya, Doc,' he said. 'I'm off the *Omar C. Ingersoll*. Pleased to meet ya.'

We shook hands.

'I guess I shouldn't have bust in, but your Chief Mate said it was O.K.'

'Perfectly all right,' I said. 'What can I do for you?'

'I just want a bottle of aspirin. We're right out, and we ain't carrying a medic. I don't want to put you to no bother, though.'

'No trouble at all, my good man,' I said. 'I'll fetch you some from the hospital.'

'That's mighty swell of you, Doc,' he said, grinning at me again. 'Mighty swell.'

In return for the bottle of aspirins he presented me with two hundred Chesterfields, *The Case of the Luckless Legs*, three bars of chocolate, *Life*, and a photograph of the *Omar C. Ingersoll*. At the gangway he slapped me on the back and said, 'Come aboard and have a cup of coffee sometime, Doc. Just go up the gangway and ask for me.'

'Very kind of you,' I said. 'And you are . . . the Bos'n? Er, Mate, possibly . . .?'

'Aw, hell no, Doc! I'm the Captain. So long!'

I went to my bunk reflecting that the feudal system at least had the advantage of leaving you in no doubt whom you were talking to.

Chapter Twelve

We spent a week in Santos, all baking in our cabins like a big dish of *escargots*. Our next port was to be Buenos Aires, to load grain and hides for home.

'Shan't be sorry to get away,' said Trail the morning we sailed. 'Stinking place, this. Fancy living here!'

'When are we off?'

'About midday. They've finished cargo in all hatches except No. 5. It's hot, isn't it? I'll be liked a fried egg when I come off the bridge.'

We left the city of tolerance behind us and turned south towards the River Plate.

Our voyage down the coast was enlivened by Christmas, which fell upon us half-way between Santos and Montevideo. The festival is celebrated most warmly by Englishmen when away from their own country, just as London Scots afford the fiercest welcome to the New Year. As I had now a fair insight into the behaviour of the *Lotus* and her crew I expected the day would pass with a flourish.

On Christmas morning Easter awoke me with my tea at seven.

'Good morning, Doctor. And a Merry Christmas to you Doctor, with my best respects.'

'Thank you, Easter. And the same to you.'

'Bloody 'ot again, ain't it?'

'What's on the thermometer?'

He looked at it closely.

'Hundred and two. Won't be nearly so chilly by midday, neither.'

'It seems very strange to me to have Christmas in this climate.'

'Cor,' Easter continued, 'I remember one Christmas we had in the Timor Sea. I was in a Yankee ship then–one of them all-metal jobs inside. She was hot enough to melt a bos'n's heart. Early on Christmas morning the Chief Engineer goes and dies, see . . .'

'Really, Easter . . .'

'. . . so I reckons we got to chuck the poor bastard over the wall pronto, because in that heat you wouldn't be able to get near him after dinner-time, let alone dress him up in a canvas suit. I tells the Mate–nasty bit of work he was–but he won't have none of it. You know what these Yanks are. Crazy for embalming. "He's got to be embalmed," he says, "then we'll pop him in the galley freezer and he can have a decent burial in the soil of God's Own Country. Besides," he says, "we ain't going to have no funerals on Christmas Day." "Yes," I says, "but who's going to do the embalming?" "You are," he says, "there's instructions in the Pharmacist's Mate's Handbook, and you can get on with it. If you do him nice I'll give you a bottle of Scotch, and if you makes a pig's bottom of him I'll kick you round the deck."

'What could I do? I tells the Skipper, but he gets a cob on and says it's orders. So I reckon instead of arguing it's best to get on with it while he's still pretty fresh. The Butcher and me goes in there and gets to work, me promising the Butch half of the Scotch–used to be in the meat works at Chicago, the Butch, and reckoned something like that was right up his alley.

'Oh, we made a lovely job of him,' Easter continued with pride. 'It would have brought tears to his mother's eyes. When we'd finished the Butch and I gets the hospital stretcher to carry him down to the freezer, while the Skipper and all hands gathers round the cabin door to have a dekko. I goes in first holding one end of the stretcher, the Butch holding the other, and the Mate comes in after us to see what sort of a job we've made of him. Well, I dunno. Either we'd made the poor bloke so lifelike, or it was that hot, or he was starting to pong a bit, but the Mate gets inside and passes out like a light. So what could we do? The Butch and I puts him on the stretcher and carries him on deck for some air. When the Skipper sees us coming out with the Mate lying there instead of the corpse he takes one look and bloody well faints as well. Cor, what a lash-up! Stiffs all over the deck. Wasn't 'arf a funny Christmas, that wasn't.'

'Thank you, Easter,' I said. 'You have cheered my Christmas morn.'

'The Bos'n's got toothache,' he added.

'Has he? How badly?'

'Something cruel, he reckons.'

'Send him to the hospital. I'll be along in half an hour.'

The Bos'n was a big man with a complexion like an old football and a face as threatening as a battleship's gun-turret. I found him sitting in the hospital chair, holding his jaw and moaning.

'Merry Christmas,' I said.

I shone a torch in his mouth and announced 'It'll have to come out.'

'O.K., Doc,' he said, squaring his shoulders. 'I can take it.'

We had fortunately found a pair of dental forceps on board, and I hoped they would fit the tooth. I had never extracted one before, but from the ranks of dentists I had seen in action in the hospital out-patient department it looked pretty simple. One simply pulled hard, as though extracting a nail from a plank, and the tooth appeared in a flurry of saliva and blood.

'Easter,' I said. 'What have we in the way of anaesthetics?'

'If I may be so bold, sir, and especially seeing it's Christmas, how about the medical comforts?'

'Capital idea. Are there any left?'

'I took the liberty of telling the Chief Steward last night that you was wanting some special for the season.'

'Very well. Go and fetch them, Easter.'

The three of us sat in a circle and purposefully drank brandy.

'Have another glass,' I told the Bos'n. 'After all, you're the patient.'

He said the pain was beginning to wear off.

'Nevertheless,' I said firmly, 'we must proceed with the operation. I don't want you messing up my Christmas Day with toothache. Open wide,' I commanded. I applied the forceps. 'Is that the one?'

He nodded vigorously.

I gripped the forceps hard and pulled. It was like trying to crack a fresh Brazil nut. I gave another tug. The Bos'n grunted and screwed his eyes up.

'This may hurt a little,' I remembered to say.

I threw all my weight against the tooth. Sweat was running down my face and into my eyes and I was breathing like a middle-aged wrestler.

'It's no good!' I grunted. 'I'm just not tough enough. Easter, apply counter-pressure to his shoulders, will you? That's right. Now–one, two, three, together heave!'

The patient slipped down the chair.

'Oh Lord!' I said.

'If I might suggest,' Easter said. 'Dr Flowerday used to find it very useful to put his knee in the bloke's chest.'

'Like that?'

'That's right, Doctor. Now shove your elbows against his shoulders.'

There was a crash, and the patient landed on the deck with me on top of him.

'Hold on, Doctor!' Easter shouted. 'It's coming!'

I set my jaw and threw myself into a final effort; but the tooth was as firm as a rivet in a ship's plate. I was about to roll off the patient in exhaustion when he decided it was time to intervene himself. Two large, powerful hands came up and enveloped mine. The Bos'n gave a sharp heave and the tooth came out like a pip from an orange.

He stood up, spat a mouthful of blood in the sink and looked at me anxiously.

'Are you all right, Doctor?' he asked. 'Didn't hurt you, did I?'

'No, I think I'm all right,' I panted.

'Gawd, that's better! Merry Christmas, Doctor.'

The Bos'n walked contentedly aft, and I went to join my shipmates. There was an air of geniality on board, fostered not only by the season but by the fact that Christmas was technically Sunday and therefore everyone had another half-day's pay.

After midday the officers were invited to Captain Hogg's cabin for drinks. Everyone came–even the Chief Engineer, who allowed his aversion for both the Captain and the foolish Sassenach custom of celebrating on December 25th to be overcome by his satisfaction of getting a free drink out of his enemy.

The Captain had already been setting himself in the mood for Christmas, and welcomed us with guarded geniality. We were all cleanly dressed and sober, except the Wireless Operator, who had already been having a party in his cabin with his own friends.

'Good morning, gentlemen, good morning!' Captain Hogg said, giving us a cold smile. 'Compliments of the season, gentlemen, on behalf of myself and the Company.'

'It was Christmas Day in the workhouse . . .' the Sparks began. Hornbeam clapped a hand over his mouth.

'Help me with the drinks, Mr Whimble, will you? That's right. Pink gins all round, I suppose? Help yourselves to iced water, gentlemen. Here's to a Merry Christmas.'

'Same to you, sir!' everyone said, respectfully raising their glasses.

'. . . the Master called down the halls,' the Sparks continued. 'Did you like your Christmas dinner? And the inmates answered . . .'

Hornbeam shut him up again.

'I propose,' Captain Hogg said, glancing sternly round the company, 'on this solemn day in our year to make a short speech.'

There were murmurs of assent all round: he had as much risk of objection as Hitler ever had.

'This is *my* ship,' Captain Hogg went on. 'My ship. She is in my care, and so are the lives of all of you in her.' He took a swallow of gin. 'My ambition,' he continued, 'is to have a happy ship. Do you understand? That means that every damn one of you's got to knuckle under. This ship–my ship'–he waved his glass expansively–'is a floating village. We have our butcher, our baker, and our lamptrimmer. We have our own storekeeper–even our own doctor.' This brought a roar of laughter and a round of applause. 'But I'–he hit his chest–'I am the squire of the village. Get that straight. Give me another gin, Mr Whimble.'

'On this occasion,' he resumed, 'I look upon you all with a fatherly eye. All of you. I am proud of you. You are the best crew I've ever sailed with. You are–'

He stopped. He glared out of the porthole. His face twisted alarmingly. The *Lotus* had stopped.

'Mr McDougall,' he hissed, 'the ship's stopped.'

McDougall didn't move.

'Aye,' he said.

'What is it?' Captain Hogg asked heavily. 'Are you celebrating Christmas so much down below that you have let the boilers go out?'

McDougall carefully drained his gin.

'We no celebrate these cissy festivals in my department. We save it up for Hogmanay.'

'So! You come up here and take my liquor–'

'And listen to an old windbag like you—'

'How dare you sir! I have never been insulted like that in all my years at sea!'

'All your years! I was on watch below when you were flying yellow at the mizzen.'

Captain Hogg shook a fist at him.

'I was in sail, sir!'

'You ought to have stayed there. You'd make a good barge skipper.'

'We didn't need engineers in those days,' Captain Hogg shouted.

'And in ten years' time we won't need captains.'

'Damn you, sir! I won't be talked to like this! I'll have you logged. I will. I mean it. I—'

'It was Christmas Day in the workhouse—' the Sparks began.

'Aw, go to hell!' McDougall said.

'Please, please!' cried Whimble.

'I've had enough of this, Mr McDougall—!'

'And I've had more than enough—!'

'Steady the Buffs!' said Hornbeam jovially.

At that moment the Second Steward arrived and announced that dinner was served.

The saloon was decorated with dusty streamers that were produced every year, like the dinner menu, irrespective of the latitude in which the *Lotus* found herself. The English are the greatest colonizing race in the world, but they show a reluctance to part with their native habits in climates that render them highly unsuitable or even unhealthy. Wherever two Englishmen are together at Christmas the accustomed dinner must be eaten, in its full carbohydrate glory. The weather demanded a little salad and an ice cream, but we sat down and dutifully faced the full gastronomic trappings of the season–roast turkey, sausages, cold pork, roast beef, boiled cabbage, roast potatoes, mince pies, and Christmas pudding.

'We've got a nice veal and ham pie on as well, if you want any,' Whimble whispered in my ear as we went in.

All the officers off watch were crammed round the saloon table. Captain Hogg sat at the head, with McDougall opposite him. The *Lotus* shivered and started again, and they glared at each other over the tomato soup. Free whisky was given to all hands, and Whimble handed each officer a paper hat, with a plea not to crush it as they would have to make do for the following year.

I was cutting my first slice of turkey when Hornbeam, who was next to me, gave a nudge.

'Your man seems to want you,' he said.

Easter was standing sheepishly in the doorway.

I excused myself to Captain Hogg and went over to him.

'What is it?' I asked.

'Having a nice dinner, Doctor?'

'Well, if that's all you came to say . . .'

'There's been trouble in the poop.'

'Trouble? What sort of trouble?'

'Couple of the lads been fighting.'

'Oh, all right. Who are they?'

'Two of the stewards, Myrtle and Mavis.'

'Who did you say?'

Easter grinned. 'You'll find out,' he said.

Two tall, silky-haired young men who cleaned the cabins were sitting in the hospital. They were both covered in blood, and one was in tears.

'What the devil's been going on?' I asked the other.

His lip quivered and he, too, began to weep.

'Another little problem of the sea,' Easter remarked tolerantly. 'Them blokes as is a bit late making up their minds whether they're men or women.'

'Oh lord!' I said. 'What were they fighting about?'

'I didn't do it!' the first one cried. 'I swear on my honour I didn't!'

'Oh, yes you did!' the other shouted. 'You give it back at once, you mean thing!'

'How can I give it back if I haven't got it?'

'Yes you have! You've been trying to sneak it all the voyage!'

'I haven't got that beastly lipstick! It isn't my colour, anyway.'

They started pulling each other's hair.

'They're a bit queer,' Easter explained helpfully.

'Well, do something about them, man! Pour water on them! Get the Mate, and I'll have them logged.'

Easter hit one over the head with an arm-splint.

'Turn it up,' he said genially. 'It's Christmas.'

I put dressings on the unfortunate couple and went back to dinner. By that time everything had been eaten and Captain Hogg was on his feet again, making another speech.

'. . . I have said before,' he told the company, leaning on the table, 'and I say it again–I am proud of my crew. The crew of *my* ship. I shall put in my report to the Company that you are the best crew–'

His face clouded over. He snarled. The *Lotus* had stopped again.

Chapter Thirteen

The rest of the day passed unalarmingly. We were nearing the busy coast of Uruguay, where the River Plate shipping first turns north to Europe and the States. That night I stood on the hot deck in my pyjamas and watched the quiet sea swishing unhurriedly past the *Lotus*'s side. Another ship approached us, two broken rows of lights in the darkness, her green starboard light shining into ours. An Aldis light flashed from her bridge, calling us up. I watched the Third Mate reply. I supposed we only wished each other a Merry Christmas and exchanged the usual courtesy queries about name and destination, but it made me realize for the first time that the *Lotus* was not the only ship on the sea: all over the world there were tiny floating communities, with the same sort of people doing the same sort of things as we did–keeping parallel watches, eating similar meals, listening to the identical strokes of another ship's bell. There were other doctors, other mates, other captains, each ship struggling with its own apparently paramount problems, I yawned, as Captain Hogg shrank into comforting perspective.

When I went to turn in I found Hornbeam in my cabin.

'Hello, Doc. Just dropped in for a final peg, seeing it's Christmas night. Do you mind?'

'Not a bit. Help yourself to the Scotch.'

'Thanks.'

He put his feet up on the desk.

'Father made a fine showing today,' he said.

'Where is he now?'

'Sleeping it off. I just went up to see if the Third Mate's sober. You've never seen any of us go on watch sloshed, have you?'

'No, never.'

'It doesn't matter about the Old Man. Some of 'em kill a bottle a day and still keep their jobs.' He stretched. 'I wish this one would drop dead,' he said amiably.

'You'd get promotion, you mean?'

He nodded.

'I'm next on the list. Trouble is, all the other skippers in the Company are as healthy as apprentices. They'll have to give me a command soon,' he added, sadly. 'I'm getting too old and fat to go running up and down hatch ladders.'

'You'll get one soon enough.'

'I don't know. All I want is a command–it doesn't matter if the ship sinks as soon as we get out of port. As long as I can call myself Captain. That's what I've been at sea for all these years–all the way up, apprentice, third, second, mate. That's what keeps us sane, most of us. Waiting for a ship of our own.

Then I'm going to chuck the sea and raise chickens.'

'I bet you won't.'

'It's a mug's game. When you've been at it a couple of years they've got you where they want you. There's nothing for you ashore–what good's a master's ticket in the Labour Exchange? The sea's a positive bitch. You can't run away from her if you want to.'

'I suppose you're right there.'

'You staying at sea, Doc?'

'Me? Oh, no. I'm going back to general practice in the provinces, I suppose.' I saw the grey streets, the grey skies, the grey complexions of the patients; wet winter mornings and acrid summer ones; frightened faces on the doorstep at three in the morning; four o'clock parties with conversation like the weak over-sweetened tea; hedging respectability, the eternal narrowness of the persistent provincial.

'Perhaps,' I added.

'Well,' Hornbeam said. 'The only thing to do with life is to live it, you know. Shall we have a last one?' I passed him the bottle. 'We'll be in B.A. tomorrow,' he added more cheerfully. 'You can have some fun there.'

'Everything's on the top line here since they had the purity campaign,' the Third said. 'Now it's as clean as Blackpool. Pity.'

We were lying off the big, white, flat city of Buenos Aires, lines of tall, angular buildings running down to the clean waterfront.

'It's pretty nice here in the New Port,' the Third went on.

'Where do we go?' I asked.

'Down by the meat works.'

Two hours later the *Lotus* was coaxed through the narrow entrance of the South Dock, and tied up not far from the big grey refrigerating plant.

'Smells like a farm, don't it?' Easter remarked, as we were drawing alongside. 'Don't 'arf get a lot of flies down here. Thick as coppers on a racecourse, they are.'

'So this is where the beef comes from?'

'That's it. They walk in one end and half an hour later they slides out in a tin. Smart, these boys are.'

Our reception was the same as in Santos, except that everyone spoke Spanish. The same functionaries hurried aboard, made for the Mate's cabin, and drank the Mate's gin, from which the business of the ship seemed inseparable. But Hornbeam was determined, for once, to go ashore.

'I've only had a couple all day,' he said proudly to me. 'Look at the bottle for yourself. I'm going to take you lads on a treat tonight. See you about ten.'

'I'll hold you to that.'

'Word of honour, Doc.'

Hornbeam kept his promise. When Trail, Archer, and myself met him in his cabin he was glowing but not extinguished.

'Just a quick one before we leave,' he said, unclipping the cap of another gin bottle. 'It's all on me tonight, boys. I've got plenty of pesos.'

'Where did you land them from?' Archer asked.

Hornbeam winked.

'The Mate's got to have a few perks,' he explained. 'Small present from the stevedores for giving them the pleasure of our custom. Also a token from the chandlers for the honour of providing us with deck stores. Strictly against Company regs., of course. Oh, I've got about'–he pulled some notes from his pocket–'about a thousand pesos.'

'That's forty quid,' Trail said reverently.

'Nothing but the best tonight!' Hornbeam continued. 'Drink up, and we'll hit the town.'

'This is the Boca,' Hornbeam explained, as we walked over the railway tracks towards the gawky German gantry bridge. 'One of the toughest spots in South America. A bos'n I sailed with once got beaten up about here. Left him only his shoes. He was a big chap, too.'

'I wish they wouldn't put ships in such insalubrious districts,' I said. 'It's like living in the slums.'

'They reckon the slums are good enough for sailors, I suppose.'

To reach the town we climbed into a small boat and were rowed across the slimy river towards the Boca's main street.

'Hard work finding a taxi in B.A. these days,' Trail said. 'We'd better climb in a colectivo.'

'A quick one in old Mother Whitehead's first,' Archer insisted. 'After all, it's known to every Liverpool fireman since steam came in.'

We had a couple of drinks described guardedly as Special Cocktails, and ate bits of chopped meat, nuts, mussels, cheese, and olives from the small plates the citizens of Buenos Aires expect to be handed with their drinks.

'On me,' Hornbeam said firmly, pulling out a fifty peso note. 'Now let's go down town and have a steak.'

We went to the broad, bright Avenida Corrientes, the Broadway of B.A. In one of the grill rooms we sat down and ate steaks three inches thick.

'Nothing like nourishment,' Hornbeam observed. 'I'm going to have another of these. How about you, Doc?'

I shook my head, as my mouth was too full to speak.

'You'll want it in a few weeks' time when you're treating yourself to a nice spaghetti on toast. How about a bottle of Argentine wine? It's not bad. All on me, you blokes.'

We rose uneasily from the table when Hornbeam paid the bill. By now his already generous feelings towards the evening were accentuated by heavy feeding.

'I'm going to show you boys the town,' he said handsomely. 'Everything's my treat. Where shall we go to?'

'How about El Nidito?' Archer suggested. 'Or L'Atelier?'

'There's a joint I used to know round the corner,' Hornbeam said, scratching his forehead. 'Little redhead in there plays the guitar.'

He was delighted to find the bar was still there, though, reasonably enough, the redhead wasn't. It was a small, dim place with a band playing sambas in the corner and a tall girl caressing a microphone not much thinner than herself.

'Lovely grub!' Hornbeam said with relish. 'What's it to be? Scotch?'

There was no Scotch but they gave us the locally distilled whisky, which tasted like an old-fashioned carminative mixture. Trail got into earnest conversation with the girl behind the bar, who came from Lytham St Annes, and I sat wondering what the whisky was doing to my gastric lining.

'I've had this place,' Hornbeam said impatiently after a few minutes. 'Let's move on.'

'But we've only just arrived.'

'It's too quiet. Come on, blokes. It's my party, so I can take it anywhere.'

We went to a good many bars. They all offered the same–darkness, sambas, local whisky, and a girl behind the bar who came from some spot comparable to Lytham.

'It's half-past one,' I said to Archer later. 'Doesn't anyone go to sleep in B.A.?'

'Things are only beginning. They go on like this all night.'

'They must be a tougher race than we are. Apart from the hours, they seem to put up with their own whisky.'

Hornbeam was seized with a final inspiration.

'Let's go to the Saratoga, boys,' he announced.

'That's a posh do,' Trail told him dubiously. 'It's an expensive joint, particularly at this hour of the night.'

'Only the best is good enough for us,' Hornbeam insisted. 'Saratoga next stop. I want to see the dancing girls.'

We found a cab and drove down the street to the Saratoga. It was a class above the bars and night clubs we had been to–a small silk-lined place with two bands, a tiny dance floor, and a stage. Hornbeam strode in and demanded a table at the front.

'This is more like it!' he said contentedly. 'I'm fed up with slumming.'

He ordered some champagne.

I looked around me and saw it was certainly more fortunate in its clientele than the other places we had visited. The tone was marred only by our party in which Hornbeam was now leaning back in his chair, clapping his hands, and demanding 'Bring on the fat women!'

There aren't any here, are there?' I asked Archer.

'You wait, Doc,' he said. 'Three blokes can't sit down alone anywhere south of Panama without something turning up.'

He was right. A good-looking blonde in a white evening gown sat on the chair beside me.

'You buy me a t'rink, no?' she said.

The waiter had already appeared and brought her a thimbleful of red liquid in a liqueur glass. He also brought a green counter, which he handed to her. This she placed in her handbag.

'I'd better put you wise,' Archer said across the table. 'Out here you buy the coloured water and she gets the commission. If you can last out till four you go home with her buckshee.'

'I don't think I can last out the next ten minutes.'

The girl swallowed her glassful swiftly, like a bad medicine.

'You buy me another t'rink, no?'

The waiter gave her a second glass, and another counter.

'This is going to work out expensive,' I said.

'All on me, Doc,' Hornbeam said grandly. 'Tell her to send her friends over.'

Two more girls appeared and started drinking with the frightening rapidity of their companion. However, we all became very friendly, and Hornbeam ordered some more champagne.

When Trail fell asleep on the table I said, 'Hadn't we better get the bill, Chief? I could do with some sleep myself.'

'Mozo!' Hornbeam demanded. 'Bill, pronto!'

It was given to him immediately, neatly folded on a plate. He scowled at the figures, and began counting notes from his pocket.

'You buy me anot'er t'rink, no?' said the blonde.

'No. The bar's down.'

She got up and walked away.

'Say, Doc,' Hornbeam called. 'Can you lend me five hundred pesos?'

'What!'

'I seem to be a bit short.' Hornbeam spread his notes on the table. He had been carried away by his generosity into a ditch of insolvency.

We searched in our pockets, waking Trail up to join in.

'Ninety-eight pesos,' Archer said. 'That's all we can muster.'

Hornbeam looked shiftily over his shoulder. The waiter, with that second sight which waiters have, was aware that some hitch had arisen and threw dark glances at us. Visions of Argentine prisons shimmered before my eyes: I was sure the Buenos Aires police would arrest with the alacrity of their comrades in Santos.

'This is serious,' I said. 'Hasn't anyone got any money at all?'

We searched our pockets again.

'Not a centavo,' Trail said. 'I've got a couple of bob though.'

'Someone will have to go back to the ship and raise the wind,' Archer said. 'That's all there is for it. The others will sit here and pretend they're enjoying themselves. We'll toss for who goes.'

We tossed a twenty-centavo piece. I lost.

'Better take the ninety-eight pesos and see if you can get a cab,' Hornbeam said. 'Make it snappy. Ten pound notes will cover it at black-market rates.'

I stood outside in the hot dry air, already feeling the apprehending hand on my shoulder. I saw an empty cab on the other side of the street and leapt towards it.

'Dock Sul,' I said.

But the driver could take me only as far as the rowing boat. I had to cross the river and walk alone across the railway tracks to the ship. I strode breathlessly along the middle of the road, looking behind me more than in front. A cat leapt across my path from shadow to shadow and I yelped. I ran through the dock gates and up the gangway.

The *Lotus* was dead. The quartermaster was in a chair by the gangway, asleep. Everyone not ashore was in their bunks, wallowing in the deep unhindered unconsciousness of watch-keepers in port.

I thought my best chance was represented by the Chief Engineer. He was lying with his mouth open on top of his bunk.

'Chief!' I called softly. I shook him. 'Chief!'

He stopped snoring and grunted.

'Chief! Wake up!'

He opened his eyes.

'Stop the feed pumps and stand-by all engineers,' he said.

'No Chief! It's the Doc. Can you lend me some money?'

'Money? What for, man? At this hour of night.'

'I'll explain later. But I must have it now. In a hurry.'

'Wait till I put my teeth in, lad.'

He gave me five pound notes. The rest I collected by rousing Whimble, the Second Steward, three or four of the engineers, and Easter.

I ran back to the ferry, crumpling the notes in my hands. I had to walk half a mile up the long road to the City before I found a taxi. When I jumped out I found my expedition had taken the best part of an hour, and the Saratoga was rising to a final burst of activity before closing for the night. I looked in nervously, wondering if my companions had already been extracted by the police, or had generously been allowed to wash dishes in the basement.

Neither of these misfortunes had occurred to them. In my absence they had all drawn a second wind and were enjoying themselves hugely. They had three new girls and another bottle of champagne.

'I've got the money,' I said breathlessly, falling into a chair.

'Ah, there's the old Doc!' Hornbeam said with surprise. 'Where did you come from?'

'I went to get some money to pay the bill,' I said angrily. 'Don't you remember?'

'That's right,' Archer agreed. 'Good old Doc. Mozo! Bill!'

Another bill was presented. Before they read the figures I knew what was coming.

'That ten quid means five hundred pesos,' Hornbeam said solemnly. 'Then there's this here – have you got any left, Doc?'

I threw him a few peso notes.

'Umm,' he said. 'Looks as if we need about five hundred pesos.'

'Well,' Trail said brightly. 'The Doc had better go gack for some more.'

I banged the table.

'No!' I said. 'No, I damn well won't! I don't care if we all go to jail, but I'm not going back to the ship!'

The manager, who had been hovering in the distance like a well-preened vulture, put his head into our group.

'Anything wrong, gentlemen?' he asked.

'Yes,' I said. 'We can't pay the bill.'

I folded my arms and prepared to be arrested with the dignity of an Englishman.

'Unfortunate,' said the manager.

'Bloody unfortunate,' Hornbeam said.

'How much are you gentlemen short? Five hundred pesos, I see. You are seafaring gentlemen, are you not?'

'Don't we look like it?' I said.

'A not uncommon predicament. Always seafaring gentlemen. A nice watch you have,' he said to Trail. 'Must be worth at least a hundred pesos.'

'It cost me twenty quid in Durban,' Trail said hotly. I stopped him.

'Hand it over,' I said.

He sulkily unstrapped his watch.

'You other gentlemen have equally valuable time-pieces,' the manager continued.

'Your turn,' Trail said, brightening a little.

Hornbeam, Archer, and I surrendered ours.

'I think,' the manager continued, 'a Parker 51 would settle it.'

I gave him the pen from my pocket.

'Now get the hell out of here, you bums,' he said, 'or I'll get the cops on you.'

We stood, a forlorn quartet, on the pavement.

'Oh well,' said Hornbeam. 'You know what I told you the other night. The only thing to do with life is to live it. Now let's start walking back to the ship.'

Chapter Fourteen

If you must be broke, there are many conveniences in being broke as a seafarer on ship's articles. The necessities of life, such as food, shelter, cigarettes, and gin, continue to be supplied regularly, either free or on account until the end of the voyage; and the state arouses among one's companions a lively sympathy expressed on land only on occasions of severe illness or other bitter natural misfortune. When the story of our visit to the Saratoga spread round the ship the next morning we were chivvied with offers of help from all hands.

'Had a bit of a night of it, I hear, Doctor,' Easter said jovially.

'I'm afraid so.'

'I don't hold with that there Saratoga,' he continued reflectively. 'Mind you, they has some very posh tarts there, very posh. But they don't 'arf burn up the rhino. Is it worth it? I ask you. Now, me and Chippy goes ashore quiet like, and has a few beers in old Ma Whitehead's. If we feels like indulging, as you might say, we goes round the back to a little place what Chippy reckons he was first taken to by his father when he was sailing as a deckboy. Mind, they ain't no great beauties in there. In fact, Chippy reckons they're the same ones what his father knew. But they come economic like, and that's something these days, ain't it, Doctor?'

'Thank you, Easter. I appreciate your little lecture on thrift.'

'We lives and learns, Doctor. How about a small contribution, if you've run yourself short?' He pulled a bundle of peso notes from his jacket pocket.

'Definitely no!' I held up my hand. 'I insist on suffering justly for my indiscretions. Besides, I am already in debt to you. If you lent me any more you might not have enough left for your own modest pleasures, such as you have just described.'

'That's all right, Doctor. I just flogged some of that there penicillin what was expired. Dr Flowerday and I used to split it fifty-fifty, but I don't mind taking forty-sixty to oblige. Barmy on penicillin, these Argentinos, I got rid of them there pills we didn't know what they was – them green ones in the back of the locker. Told 'em they was good for virility and charged a peso each. They go in for that sort of stuff a lot down here.'

'It is very kind of you, Easter, but – for reasons which I should be ashamed to confess – I much prefer you to keep the proceeds to yourself.'

'As you say, Doctor. Tip me the wink if you wants anything flogging. Wouldn't like a few tins of beef, would you? I scrounged some when a case bust going into No. 1 hold.'

'No thank you. But I appreciate your generosity. Just get me another pitcher of iced water from the galley.'

I put on my cap and went on deck. It was almost noon. The sun, as coarse and uninhibited as everything else in the region, shone savagely on the white planks and brown steel of the decks; but the river, the ships, and the quay were as peaceful as an English village on a high summer afternoon. The purring electric cranes were still and stood at untidy angles along the wharf with crates of merchandise at their feet, abandoned by the dockers for the midday break. Some of the stevedores lay asleep in the shade that was sharply cut out here and there by corners and eaves; others languidly masticated their lunch inside the doors of the airless sheds. From somewhere downstream came the subdued hoot of a small ship's whistle, and the regular soft thumping of some essential pump. The steers mooed spasmodically in the unseen corrals behind the meat works, and the flies, unaffected by the general languor, buzzed in thick irritating squadrons everywhere.

I leaned on the hot rail and looked at the grey walls of the Frigorífico Anglo, which was temporarily inactive for lunch. I began to understand the disadvantages of my abrupt poverty: we should be in Buenos Aires for at least a fortnight, and the Frigorífico, though of superb interest as a commercial and technical undertaking and with appreciable merit as an example of functional design, would soon become oppressive as the largest segment of my daily horizon. I hadn't even the bus fare to the City.

While I was examining these bleak thoughts Trail came and leaned next to me. We discussed our condition in a few words.

'There's not much to be done here if you're broke,' he observed. 'We could rustle up enough to go to the pictures, I suppose.'

'I can do that in London.'

'That's true. They've got some nice parks, so they tell me.'

We had adjusted ourselves to a dull stay in one of the world's gayest capitals when a bright ray of entertainment abruptly shone into our lives from an unexpected source. I was lying on my bunk after dinner, reading the first paragraph of *War and Peace* with the drowsy inattentive righteousness of a good churchgoer sitting through a summer sermon, when Easter pulled aside the curtain across the doorway.

'Father's compliments,' he said. 'And will you come to his cabin, pronto.'

'Oh, lord! What's eating the old boy now?'

'Search me, Doctor. He's getting the Mate up there, and the Hunk.'

'Hunk?'

'Chief Steward, Mr Whimble.'

'Very well.' I rolled off the bunk and took my cap from the hook over the desk. 'I hope it isn't his stomach again.'

Hornbeam and Whimble were already sitting on the settee in the Captain's cabin. McDougall was in one of the armchairs. On either side of the desk sat Captain Hogg and Mr Montmorency, the Fathom Line's manager in Buenos Aires. All of them were smoking cigars and drinking liqueurs.

'Ah, Doctor, come in!' Mr Montmorency called, as I pushed the door curtain away. He got up and seized me by the hand. 'Have a seat. Move over there, Mr Whimble. Cigar? Real Havana. Won't find them in England, eh? Benedictine, Curaçao, or brandy? Some Kummel, perhaps? Or a flash of the old starboard light?'

'Benedictine will do nicely,' I said. I sat down between Whimble and Hornbeam, while Mr Montmorency lit my cigar. He was a lean, brown man with a brisk black moustache, dressed in a crisp linen suit. He was an office-wallah, and therefore formally despised; but he was secretly respected as an important and dangerous man in the lives of everyone who depended on the Fathom Line for their pay. Beneath the sunburnt hearty crust was a sharp brain eager to send damning cables to St Mary Axe, where a few words of code could hold up a man's promotion for ten years or tip him back into the uncertain currents of the shipping pool. Even Captain Hogg was affable to Mr Montmorency.

'Right, gentlemen,' Mr Montmorency went on forcefully. 'I have asked you up here today for a particular reason, apart from having the pleasure of meeting you. Captain Hogg assures me, I am glad to say, that he thinks highly of your services under his command.'

'A very happy ship,' Captain Hogg declared. He swallowed half a tumbler of Benedictine and glared at the rest of us in defiance of contradiction.

'I am sure it is, Captain. Now, gentlemen, I am going to talk to you on a most serious topic. It is British Prestige.' He took on his smartest Chamber of Commerce manner. 'It is hardly necessary for me to trace the course of events in this bustling sub-continent since the cessation of hostilities – hostilities, gentlemen, in which the Company we represent suffered as grievously as any – but you will, I am sure, all appreciate that the interest of our Motherland in its affairs has increased rather than diminished, though in the face of severe, and sometimes to us inexplicable, opposition. Some more Benedictine, Captain?'

'Thank you, Mr Montmorency.'

'Pass the bottle round, gentlemen. As I was saying. The tail of the British lion has been severely put out of joint . . .'

He went on about the Old Red Duster, Free Trade, the Socialists, Nationalization, Hard Times, the necessity to pull together, put our shoulders to the wheel, steer a straight course, and not rock the boat. All of us were hazily wondering where the speech was leading him and uneasily contemplating our own guilty consciences. I nervously calculated the turnover in Easter's dockside pharmaceutical dealings. Hornbeam thought anxiously about his stevedores' presents, and Whimble was wondering how to account for the ham and two cases of tinned pears that had somehow vanished between Santos and the River Plate. But, if these skeletons were visible to the penetrating eye of Mr Montmorency, he was not going to mention it. I suddenly realized he was saying '. . . there will, of course, be a running buffet and the best we can do in the way of drinks. It will give the British colony here a bit of an outing, reassure the local businessmen, send up the prestige of the Line, and, in a small way, that of the Old Country. Besides, gentlemen, it will fittingly usher in the New Year. Any comments?'

McDougall, who had fallen asleep, woke up at the words 'New Year' and blew his nose loudly.

'A very generous offer,' Captain Hogg growled. 'On behalf of my officers and crew, I should like to express my gratitude to the management.'

'Thank you, Captain. Now, gentlemen, you are the senior officers. You know my plans, and I expect you to make it a success. This dance on shipboard must be remembered in Buenos Aires as one of the events of the season.'

A dance on shipboard . . . I saw at once Tissot's painting – matchwood decks, fragile rails, graceful bright brasswork; summery officers with downy whiskers, in gold and blue and white; clean sailors, contented bandsmen, delicate ladies in sprays of frills; frail parasols pirouetting beneath a canopy of the majestic ensigns of half a dozen now forgotten empires . . . Into this they were going to turn the *Lotus*, tied up by a meat works.

The news of the New Year's Eve Dance fell upon the ship's company like a heavy breaker on the beach, overwhelming the minor ripples already set up by our misfortunes in the Saratoga the previous night. Reactions to the party differed sharply. Easter was frankly disgusted.

'I ask you!' he said, coming into my cabin and tossing an armful of my clean laundry peevishly on the bunk. 'What a lash-up! Fags, fairy-lights, and ladies' lavatories! Cor! I dunno what they think this hooker is. The *Queen Mary* isn't in it.'

'Surely, Easter, after your experience on the transatlantic boats you would welcome a touch of the atmosphere of a large liner?'

'What, on this old tramp? First-class smoke-room now, that's different. All the nobs in there getting stinko, not noticing you rook 'em on the measure. And slipping you a quid or two to show 'em the way to some young bit's cabin – discreet like. What are we going to get on this old tub? Crowd of shore-wallahs looking for free booze, that's what. Fat lot of good that is!'

'You may be able to interest some of them in the three-card trick.'

He brightened a little. 'I might that, Doctor. But there ain't no flies on them round these parts.'

Trail was ecstatic. 'Have you seen this, Doc?' he called to me the next day, waving a sheet of typewritten paper. 'List of guests. Take a dekko. Don't bother with this lot, Ambassador, Bishop, and so on, asked but not able to come . . . Look here – Mister and Missus *and daughter*. Here again – *and daughters*. All the way down – *Miss, Miss, Miss*. Lovely grub! The ship'll be like a bloody harem by eight bells!'

'I don't think you ought to get over-excited, Three-o. The Misses are probably elderly ladies, pillars of the Mission, and the daughters will most likely be still in short frocks. In any event, you can be sure they'll be kept under strict supervision by their watchful parents on a ship like this.'

'Steady on, Doc! There's bound to be some nice bits of crumpet among them. I think I know this one down here, anyway. Used to work in the Company's offices on Corrientes.' He rubbed his hands. 'It's going to be a Happy New Year, and no mistake.'

Hornbeam was less enthusiastic. 'More work for the bloody Mate,' he said. 'Half the bunting's gone mouldy and the Bos'n flogged the canvas awnings in the Canaries last trip. How the hell can I get the boatdeck holystoned and painted in three days? I bet we're short of Scotch homeward bound on the strength of it, too.'

A state of despair settled on Whimble. The greater part of the preparation fell to him, and he was expected to account for everything issued from his stores from a crate of Scotch to a jar of Maraschino cherries. Tablecloths, fruit bowls, glasses, and silver came from half-forgotten straw nests in dusty crates stowed under hundredweights of flour, rice, tinned vegetables, and a case of Gordon's gin he had lost three voyages ago and had been anxiously cooking the bar books to replace ever since.

'Oh dear, oh dear,' he said, coming out of the storeroom with his shirt stuck to his chest with sweat. 'Balloons they want now! Did you ever hear of it? I don't know what the office will say when we get home!'

The balloons were a whim of Captain Hogg's; he had taken an enthusiastic and forceful interest in the dance, and spent most of the day pacing up and down the boatdeck rearranging the deck furnishings and decorations.

'Mr Whimble!' he shouted frequently. 'Mr Whimble! Where the devil are you? I think the buffet would be better on the port side. Not so many flies. Get it changed over. What's happened to Mr Hornbeam? Bos'n, take down number three awning and rig it abaft the funnel so the holes won't show. Mr Trail, are you supposed to be in charge of lifeboats?'

'Yes, sir.'

'You aren't fit to sail a toy boat on a paddling pool. Get those ropes stowed properly.'

'Aye aye, sir.'

'Doctor!'

'Sir?'

'Flies, Doctor. The bluebottles from the meat works. They are a sanitary problem, are they not?'

'Yes, sir. Included in the syllabus for the examination in Public Health.'

'You are responsible for them. I don't want a damn fly on my ship by tomorrow night. Understand?'

'It's rather a tall order, sir.'

'That's your look out. Get some insect killer from Mr Hornbeam. I don't care how you go about it, but there aren't to be any flies.'

'Very good, sir.'

I could find only enough insecticide for one spray-gun, and this I gave to Easter with instructions to pump it vigorously round the Captain every time he stepped on to the deck. This seemed to satisfy him. He left me alone until the evening before the party, when he called a conference of officers in his cabin.

'This is going to be a damn good party,' he began sternly. 'The office expects everyone to enjoy themselves, and it's bloody well up to you to see they do. Get me? Now listen to this.' He picked up a sheet of paper from the desk. 'These are the Master's orders for tomorrow night. One: uniform. Clean number tens, with correct epaulettes and white shoes. Collars to be correctly buttoned up.' He glared at McDougall, who came to supper comfortably in carpet slippers, with the high collar of his jacket wide enough apart to allow the dragon tattooed on his chest to peep coyly over his second brass button. 'Doctor, you will wear white ducks, white shirt, black tie.'

'And Company's Regulation Cap, sir?'

'If necessary. Two: Guests are to be met at the head of the gangway by Master and senior officers. See the quartermaster's in uniform and sober, Mr Hornbeam.'

'Aye aye, sir.'

'Three: No ladies are on any account to be entertained in officers' cabins, or elsewhere than on the portions of the boatdeck assigned for that purpose.'

'There goes Trail's evening,' I whispered to Hornbeam.

'Four: All alcoholic liquors on board to be placed under seal at noon tomorrow and no such liquors to be served to any member of the ship's company before the arrival of guests at ten o'clock tomorrow night. Five: All shore leave stopped from noon tomorrow. Six: All members of ship's company to remain decent and sober throughout tomorrow night. My ship is on show, gentlemen. Understand?'

We murmured acceptance of the terms.

'The music will be provided by a band from one of the English clubs,' Captain Hogg continued. 'Get the Sparks to jack up the amplifying system in case we have to play records, Mr Hornbeam. Have you been through the ship's record library, Mr Whimble?'

'They seem to be sort of operas and stuff, sir.'

'Capital! I like a bit of opera. Right, gentlemen. Oh, Doctor, I've put that man of yours in charge of the bar.'

'Who? Easter?'

'Yes. Strikes me as a reliable honest sort of fellow.'

I swallowed. I felt any opinion of mine would spoil the contentment of both of them.

'Very well. Conference dismissed.'

As we went down the companionway together I said to McDougall, 'The prohibition order's going to delay you chaps getting Hogmanay away to a good start.'

He dropped a red eyelid over a crafty eye.

'It'ud take more than yon pipsqueak to stand in a Scot's way on Hogmanay, lad. Come along to my cabin when you've finished yer tea tomorrow. We'll find you a dram or two from somewhere.'

Chapter Fifteen

I was called from my shower at eight the next evening to put half a dozen stitches in the forehead of a fireman who had fallen down the stokehold ladder. For this reason I was the only officer who arrived on deck to greet the guests sober. Captain Hogg's orders had been punctiliously obeyed, except for the one impounding the ship's supply of liquor; since tea-time Whimble had been poking his head in his locker like a nervous ostrich in a perilous desert, in the Chief Engineer's cabin Scots accents rawed under the sting of neat whisky, Hornbeam and the Mates poured gin from the water-bottles above their basins, and Captain Hogg himself had been entertaining Mr Montmorency and his sleek Argentine wife.

The boatdeck of the *Lotus* looked surprisingly attractive. Fairy-lights shone on the fresh white chalk spread over the scrubbed deck, ensigns and signal flags lined the rails and obliterated the stark Frigorífico, and on the long tables garnished with blazing Argentine flowers, glass and linen fell pleasingly and promisingly on the eye. The band–three Argentines with piano, guitar, and drums–was seriously tuning up behind the ensign of the Commonwealth of Australia. At the head of the gangway, which was enlivened with bunting and a string of bulbs, a quartermaster stood nervously in white matelot's rig; stewards in shining jackets stood with silver trays and serviettes between the fresh-painted ventilators; behind the bar was Easter, with an expression of disarming honesty on his face that suggested a bishop going through the Dover customs with two bottles of brandy in his gyp.

Besides the quartermaster the ship's officers–in clean white number tens, white shoes, correct epaulettes, collar fully buttoned up–stood greeting the guests with great charm and affability. To me it seemed that the decorum of my shipmates had a certain brittleness about it, a nervous over-emphasis. This was noticeable in the way the Chief Engineer tenaciously kissed the hands of the ladies; the hesitation with which Whimble brought a match to a guest's cigarette; Hornbeam's roar of laughter; Trail, open-mouthed, mentally stripping every woman under forty stepping off the gangway; and the abandon with which Captain Hogg was pinching Mrs Montmorency's bottom.

I felt a tug at my elbow. It was Easter leaning across the bar, holding out a long glass of brownish fluid.

'Best respects, Doctor,' he said hoarsely. 'This is the stuff I'm making up for me and my mates.'

'What is it?'

'Little cocktail I invented on the Western run. I calls it "Fire Alarm".'

'Thank you, Easter. I fancy I have some leeway to make up.'

The guests seemed to be shippers and senior Fathom Line employees who knew each other and Mr Montmorency well, and were therefore relieved of the cumbrance of social chatter while getting down to the free drinks and lobster patties. As I was not in uniform no one bothered to talk to me, and I was content to stay in the shade of a ventilator by the bar, smoke the ship's cigarettes, drink Fire Alarms, and leave the entertaining to my companions.

'Ché, un cigarillo por favor.'

A slim brunette with incandescent eyes and teeth stood in front of me.

'I beg your pardon?'

'Oh, don't you speak Spanish? I only want a cigarette.'

I handed her one from my own tin.

'Thanks. You work in the meat-works too, do you?'

I was hurt. The *Lotus* may have been a rusting old-fashioned tramp, but that night I was proud of her.

'Not a bit. I'm one of the officers.'

'What of this old tub? You look too respectable. Why aren't you dressed up?'

'I am the doctor,' I explained stiffly.

Her eyes instantly shone brighter. 'Well, what do you know? I get the most crippling pain in my back.'

I saw at once that I had committed a social error. During my spell as a general practitioner I had learned that members of the public meeting a doctor socially believe they can entertain him only by briskly trotting out an account of their illnesses. When introduced to the bank manager they do not immediately start talking about their overdrafts, and on shaking hands with the local J.P. they are not compelled to discuss the number of times they have been summonsed. But they firmly hold the idea that the doctor can be diverted for half-hours at a time by details of their symptoms, or even those of faraway relatives and dead acquaintances.

'It sort of catches me round here,' she continued, twining her arm behind her and pushing her sharp bosom forward. 'Whenever I twist round suddenly–Ouch! See what I mean? I've been to doctors all over the world–London, Paris, New York, here in B.A. They never did me a bit of good, though. I still had my pain. Sometimes I woke up in the night and screamed.'

'Very distressing for you, I'm sure.'

'Oh, I began to lose faith in doctors. You don't mind my saying so, do you?'

'Not a bit. Have a Fire Alarm.'

'What is it?'

'It's a drink. Very good for backache.'

She giggled. 'Well, then I went to an osteopath in Wimpole Street–he was sweet. He told me I had a displaced spine. What do you think? He slipped it back again, like shutting a door. There!'

'I think that . . .'

'I only used to get it after that when it rained. Why do you think that was? And then I was playing tennis out at the Hurlingham Club last month, when Bingo! I . . .'

'May I introduce you to our Third Officer?' I interrupted. 'You will find him very charming.'

For the past few seconds Trail had been staring at my companion with his mouth open. He jumped at my remark so much he spilt his drink on the deck; then he stepped forward with the expression of a hungry deckhand going in for his Sunday dinner.

'Mr Trail,' I said, 'Miss . . .?'

'Ella Robinson.'

'Mr Trail is our most popular officer,' I whispered to her. 'The Captain thinks highly of him. But if I may speak as a shipmate, he is a little shy and needs encouragement. Enjoying the dance, Three-o?'

'Have another drink,' Trail said thickly.

'I think he's cute,' Miss Robinson decided, flashing him a swift glance of appraisal. I had been treating his spots since we left Santos, and in his clean white jacket and painstakingly Brylcreemed hair he looked as presentable as an Ian Hay subby.

'Har!' Trail said. 'How about a dance?'

'Mmm! I've never danced with a sailor before! Be a sweetie and hold my glass, Doctor.'

Grinning weakly, Trail drew her on to the chalked square of deck and began dancing with the spirit that nightly won him hearts in Reese's dance hall in Liverpool. I contentedly took another Fire Alarm from Easter and leant back on my ventilator. After the night at the Saratoga anyone so pressingly feminine as Miss Robinson was too much for me.

When the music stopped the couple came back to my corner of the deck. Both of them were flushed and breathless.

'You're a swell dancer,' Miss Robinson said to Trail, giving him a hot glance of admiration.

'Am I really?' he asked eagerly. 'Go on!'

'Yes, I mean it. Not like most Englishmen out here. When I dance with you I sure know I'm dancing.'

'Have another Fire Alarm,' I said, signalling to Easter.

'Do you dance, Doctor?' she asked.

'Definitely no. I come from a family with very strong views on the subject.'

'How amusing! Do you know, my pain's coming back. Look!' She turned round. 'Run your hand down my spine. That's right–just there! Ooo! Exquisitely painful! What do you think I ought to do about it?'

'I should go and see a doctor.'

She laughed playfully. 'Gee, you're funny! You're the nicest doctor I've ever met.'

'Thank you. Down the hatch, now.'

We drank our Fire Alarms, and the band began to play again.

'Let's dance,' she said to Trail.

'Not for a minute,' he said. 'Let me show you the steering gear.'

'What on earth should I want to see the steering gear for?'

'It looks most attractive in the moonlight,' I added encouragingly. 'Not many people are privileged to see it. Only Mr Trail and the Captain have the key.'

'C'mon,' Trail said. He gave her a look that would have terrified the heart out of any girl in England and stode off purposefully with her, hand in hand, towards the steel nooks and shadows of the stern. I moved to the rail, leant over the strip of dirty, oil-coated water between the *Lotus* and the quay, and exchanged glances with the two sour Argentine policemen standing at the foot of the gangway. The night was hot, and the awnings prevented ventilation. Shortly the ship's officers unhooked their high collars and wiped their foreheads with coloured handkerchiefs, and sweat began to run down the faces of the guests.

No one bothered me, so I sipped my way through my drink and thought guiltily about England. I was interrupted by 'A hundred pipers an' a'' from the corner where the band had been playing. It was almost eleven-thirty and the engine-room had by then taken over the party for themselves. The engineers were lolling round the piano with an air of genial possessiveness towards everything they could see, and McDougall was stripped to the waist, his dragon, hearts, and sailing ship glistening among the grey tufts of hair that sprouted from his thorax and shoulders like bracken on a Highland hillside. Singing with him was Captain Hogg, drunk to the point of harmlessness, and the Montmorencys. The music was provided by Easter, who was playing the piano in the style of Chico Marx.

With a flourish Easter finished his piece, rose to his feet, and announced solemnly, 'Ladies and Gentlemen, for my next number tonight I shall give you my rendering of the famous old English ballad "The Lily of Laguna". Jolly good luck to you, gentlemen, jolly good luck!' He sat down heavily and began the tune, to which most of the audience sang the words of 'Annie Laurie'. McDougall then shouted it was midnight by ship's time as the clocks were to be advanced half an hour, and broke into Auld Lang Syne. This was taken up by the company, and I was swept into a chain of crossed hands. McDougall sang with his eyes tightly shut, swaying between a pair of other Scots; suddenly he stopped, shouted 'Kiss all the lasses!' and dived towards Mrs Montmorency. He grasped her in his moist naked arms and kissed her hotly until he was elbowed out of the way by Macpherson, McPhail, and Macintosh. These were followed by Captain Hogg, Easter, Whimble, one of the Argentine policemen from the dock, the Quartermaster, Hornbeam, and myself. Then everyone sang Auld Lang Syne all over again.

At the end of the verse Captain Hogg shouted 'Eight bells! Quartermaster, ring eight bells! Midnight, ship's time!' Mrs Montmorency instantly threw her arms open, and was kissed by McDougall, Macpherson, Captain Hogg, McDougall again, myself, Easter, Hornbeam, McDougall once again, Macpherson, McPhail, and McDougall. She appeared to enjoy these unstinted tributes thoroughly, though Mr Montmorency, who stood fidgeting beside her, was moved during her fourth embrace with McDougall, to murmur nervously, 'Steady on Maria! I say, steady on, old girl!' We sang Auld Lang Syne and kissed Maria Montmorency several times, as a member of the circle recalled that it was midnight in Greenwich, Glasgow, Greenock, or some other point of overwhelming importance to himself. Finally her husband grabbed her by the arm and led her to the gangway while everyone cheered and Easter played 'Sons of the Brave'.

The engineers and Hornbeam then decided to visit the Taxi-Dance on the other side of the dock.

'Come on, Doc,' Hornbeam urged. 'It's only over the ferry. We can get there in ten minutes.'

'I thought you hadn't any money?'

'I flogged some whisky to the policeman. It's a cheap joint–the girls will darn your socks as well for twenty pesos.'

I shook my head. 'No thanks. I've got into enough trouble in B.A. already. Besides, I'm tired. I'm turning in.'

I left my shipmates, who were already on the gangway with bottles sticking out of the pockets of their white ducks. I was tired and muzzy. Easter's Fire Alarms had an effect like anaesthetic ether, producing a disturbing numbness and incoordination of the extremities; all I wanted was to lie on my bunk, turn on the forced draught, and sink on to the soft foam that overlies the dark cool liquor of unconsciousness. Yawning, I unhooked my cabin jalousie, pushed the curtain aside, and turned on the light. On the deck was Trail, asleep; two half-empty whisky bottles and some broken glasses were on the desk; lying on my bunk, her skirt round her waist and snoring heavily, was Ella.

I began with an attempt to resuscitate Trail by throwing the remains of my drinking water over him. From this it was apparent that he was in a state of deep surgical anaesthesia, and I could have cut a leg off without his noticing it. While I was shaking him and slapping his face I heard a deep groan from the bunk, and noticed that Ella was wearily moving her arm. I dropped Trail and began flicking her face with the end of a towel. She shook her head and muttered something.

'Ella! Ella!' I called. 'Wake up! Come on–for God's sake, woman! What's that?'

I bent my ear close to her.

'Wanna be sick,' she said.

'Oh, lord!' I lay the towel over her, poised my empty hot-water can on her bosom, and hurried down to the hospital to fine some sal volatile.

When I came back she was sitting on the edge of the bunk, her head held heavily in her hands, her long black hair scattered uncaringly over her shoulders and forehead, her eyes closed, and her face white. She looked like a patient at the end of a long operation.

'Here! Ella! Drink this,' I said cheerfully.

She pushed me away clumsily.

'Don't wan' another drink.'

'This isn't drink–it's medicine. Make you feel better, see? Jolly good stuff. Look! I'm having some myself.'

'Wanna go home.'

'Yes, I know. But drink this first. It's something special.'

'For Chrissake take me home. For Chrissake.'

'Oh, all right then. Where do you live?'

There was a pause. She slowly shook her head.

'Dunno.'

I looked hopefully at Trail, but he seemed unlikely to take part in any conversation before noon the following day.

'Ella,' I said gently. 'Think please. Where do you live? Haven't you got a phone number?'

'Wanna go to bed.' She started to roll back on my bunk, but I caught her.

'No, you can't go to sleep,' I told her firmly. 'There'll be hell to pay if I don't get you out of my cabin and off this ship. Now try and remember where you live. The street will do.'

I spotted her handbag wedged down the side of the bunk, opened it, and found one of her visiting cards. It bore an address in the Palermo district, which I thought was somewhere on the other side of Buenos Aires.

'All right,' I said, slipping my arm under her shoulders. 'We're going for a walk.'

The gangway quartermaster gave me a grin.

'Lovely grub, eh, Doctor?' he said. He winked and smacked his lips, in case I had missed the point of his remark.

'Benson,' I said sternly. 'I need about two hundred pesos. I should be obliged if you would lend it to me, if you have it. I see no prospect of repaying you until we return home, but if you refuse I shall give you hell should you happen to fall sick on the voyage back. Thank you.'

We stumbled down the gangway together, Ella grasping my collar and groaning. After picking our way over the railway lines and bollards on the quay we reached the little office of the dock police by the gate. I gave the policeman ten pesos and asked him to call a taxi; twenty minutes later we were bumping along the dirty road beside the Frigorífico, Ella already asleep and snoring on my shoulder.

The cab stopped outside a tall block of flats several miles from the ship. I gave Ella a shake, and she woke up with a start.

'You're home,' I said. 'End of the line.'

'Oh God, I feel horrible.'

'So do I.'

'Take me in . . . Please!'

'Can't you make it yourself?'

She shook her head.

'Oh, all right then.'

I helped her out of the cab, making signs to the driver to wait. We went into a small hall, which contained a staircase and an automatic lift. As I opened the lift doors Ella leant heavily on my shoulder and burst into tears.

She told me, through sobs, she lived in number seventeen, on the third floor; the key was in her handbag. I took her up to her own door and opened it. At that moment her knees gave way. She began to slide slowly down the doorpost.

'The room opposite,' she muttered. 'For God's sake help me in.'

I supported her across the hallway and into the room opposite the flat door. I turned on the light with my free hand, and found I was in her bedroom.

'Put your arm round my neck,' I commanded. She obeyed, and I lifted her up, laying her on the bed heavily.

'All right,' I said. 'You can unclasp my neck now.'

I heard a noise behind me and turned. Standing in the doorway was a tall, stern, greying gentleman with a stiff moustache and a military eye, dressed in a yellow silk dressing-gown. Behind him was a timid, sandy, becrackered woman in a faded housecoat.

'I've a damn good mind to horsewhip you,' the grey gentleman said decisively.

'Now look here, I say . . .' I began.

'I might tell you I consider you an unmitigated cad. I've no idea what your upbringing is, but I don't imagine it's very savoury. If I were a few years younger I'd give you a good hiding with my bare fists. A young puppy like you needs teaching a good lesson.'

'Be careful, Charles,' the woman said nervously. 'You know what you did to the Rolleston boy.'

Charles twitched his muscles under his dressing-gown. Ella seemed to have a Bulldog Drummond for a father.

'I should never have let her go on that damn ship,' he said bitterly. 'I believed at least the officers would be gentlemen. I was mistaken.'

'Mind your temper, Charles,' the woman added timidly, covering her eyes with her hands.

'Now, look here,' I said angrily. 'I assure you I have had nothing to do with your daughter . . .'

Charles snorted. 'Pray, how do you explain that lipstick all over your shirt? A disgusting exhibition! By God, I'm not at all certain I shan't horsewhip you after all . . .'

'Charles, Charles!'

'You have got quite the wrong end of the stick . . .'

Charles by now had time to look at me carefully and find I was much smaller than he was. He advanced, going red in the face.

'Put them up, you young hound!' he growled.

There was nothing for it. I threw one of Ella's pillows at him, sidestepped quickly, and dashed for the door. I shot into the lift, leaped for the taxi like a survivor grasping for a lifeboat, and drove back to the ship, looking nervously through the back window at every turn for cars bearing greying gentlemen in silk dressing-gowns, who were anxious to relieve the strangling monotony of Buenos Aires social life by avenging the honour of their daughters. And when I got back I found Trail had recovered sufficiently to climb into my bunk.

Chapter Sixteen

I spent the rest of our time in Buenos Aires walking the broad, criss-crossed, sun-drenched streets looking for a cheap watch. I kept out of the bars, and if I thought a woman looked at me I jumped.

The momentum that had carried us headlong into the pleasures of South America had expended itself by the end of the dance; afterwards our lives settled into the unexciting routine of a ship in port. Every morning I read carefully through the English *Buenos Aires Standard*, had a cup of tea with Hornbeam, and strolled round the active decks; in the afternoon I filled my cabin with the last squirts of our D.D.T. spray and slept soundly until tea, in defiance of the rattling winch just beyond my head. Now and then I picked up *War and Peace*, but the freezing plains of Russia seemed so fantastic I killed a few cockroaches with it and finally put the books away for the voyage home.

In the evening, when the sun had gone down and a breeze sometimes blew off the River Plate to refresh our decks, we sat in Hornbeam's cabin with a case of tinned beer playing sober games of bridge or liar-dice. I felt that I had been living alongside the wharf in Buenos Aires for a lifetime, and I sometimes stared at the familiar angles of my cabin in disbelief that they had ever been softened with the shadows of an English winter's day. When I told the others this one evening Hornbeam said: 'You'd get used to living in Hell, Doc, if we sailed there. All these places are the same, anyway.' He lay on his bunk half-naked, fanning himself with a copy of the *Shipping World*. 'They're hot and sweaty, and full of blokes ready to cut your throat for tuppence. It's the same out East and on the African coast. There's no more romance at sea than there is round Aldgate tube station.'

'When are we leaving for home?' I asked.

He shrugged his shoulders. 'I couldn't say. Maybe a week, maybe two. It depends how the cargo goes in. Once you're in port the wharfies have got you, whether it's in Cardiff or Calcutta. I heard from the agent today the boys might be cooking up a strike. That would fix us, right enough.'

'I wouldn't mind a pint of old English wallop out of the barrel just now,' Archer said seriously. 'Or a bit of backchat with a Liverpool barmaid. You can have too much of these high-pressure floozies out here.'

We sat looking miserably into our beer glasses, all suddenly homesick.

'I reckon I ought to have married and settled down,' Hornbeam continued. 'I nearly did once. I'm still engaged to her, if it comes to that. She's in Sydney. Sends me letters and sweets and things. I see her about once every two years.'

'I should have stuck to selling refrigerators,' Archer said to me. 'I did it for a bit after the war, but I had to give it up. Your money doesn't go anywhere ashore these days.'

'You fellows don't know how well off you are in the Merchant Navy,' I told him.

'The Merchant Navy!' Hornbeam said, folding his hands on his bare stomach reflectively. 'It's a queer institution. A cross between Fred Karno's army and a crowd of blokes trying to do a job of work.'

'There's no security at sea,' Archer added gloomily.

'Maybe it's better than sitting on your fanny in an office till you drop dead,' Hornbeam said. 'Pictures every Saturday night and Margate for a fortnight in summer. Drive me up the pole, that would.'

'Margate's all right,' Trail remarked, joining the conversation. 'I knew a girl who lived there once. Her father ran a shooting-alley in Dreamland.'

Chapter Seventeen

It was a fortnight before we sailed. A quiver of excitement ran through the ship with the fresh vibrations of the engines. The deckhands ambled about their work singing–not sea-shanties, because they heard those only occasionally, on the pictures, but anything they knew from 'She'll Be Coming Round the Mountain', to 'Rock of Ages'.

'All hands seem to be pretty happy,' I observed to Easter as a man sauntered past chanting 'Every turn of the screw brings me nearer to you'.

'Well, we're going home, Doctor!'

'But we've only been away a couple of months.'

'Still, it's always like this, whether you've been away two years or a fortnight. You gets a bit slap-happy when you leaves your final port.'

'I think I can understand it. For most of them I suppose it's only an attic in Liverpool or a dirty old house in the East End.'

'Still, it's home, sir.'

'You're right. Where do you live, Easter?'

'Down in Cheltenham.'

'Do you indeed?'

'I lives with the old lady,' he continued. 'She keeps a sweetshop down there. Getting a bit past it now, though. Well over seventy.'

The idea of Easter having a mother was disturbing. I thought of him vaguely as climbing out of the sea on the heels of Venus.

'Are you coming back next trip, Easter?'

'I suppose so,' he replied. 'I've tried it ashore. Done all sorts of jobs. Apart from the halls and the races, I've worked in pubs, laundries, hotels, fish-and-chip shops. Even done a bit of navvying. Sometimes I gets settled into something steady, but . . . well, you know how it is. I goes round to the public library and has a look at Lloyd's List on a Saturday afternoon, and I'm finished. I think how nice it would be getting away somewhere instead of standing in a queue in the rain.'

'I'm afraid I see your point, Easter. But perhaps you'll get married?'

'What, at my time of life? And after what I've seen of women? Cor! I've had 'em all, I have–black, white, brown, and yellow. They're all the same underneath.'

'Do you read Kipling, Easter?' I asked with interest.

'Kipling? He's dead now, ain't he?'

'He doesn't seem to be dead at sea.'

'No, I don't read much, Doctor. No time for books. Takes you all your life to keep going these days, don't it?'

We detached ourselves from the meat works and steamed slowly down the long buoyed channel along the shallow River Plate towards Montevideo and the Atlantic. From there we had a straight run home, broken only at the Canary Islands for oil. The sea was calm and the sky unbroken. Off Montevideo we left the last persevering seagull behind us and were again alone, ourselves and the sea.

'About another three weeks,' Hornbeam said, 'and you'll be having a pint at the Carradoc.'

'I hope it turns out cheaper than the last drink I had with you.'

He laughed.

'Remind me to get you a new pen, Doc. Anyhow, we ought to have a pretty quiet voyage till we reach the Bay.'

And so we did. Two days out Captain Hogg became more morose than usual, then took to keeping to himself. For a few days he came down to meals, which he consumed without passing a word or giving any indication that he sensed our presence at the table at all. As no one else dared to speak this meant that lunch and supper were eaten in a silence that amplified such noises as chewing a stick of celery to the volume of a Tropical thunderstorm. After that he took his meals in his cabin, and appeared only occasionally on the deck. He would stand outside his door for a few minutes, scratch his head, blow his nose, and disappear for the day. Everyone was delighted.

'The Old Man's got a proper cob on about something,' Hornbeam said. 'Never pokes his nose on the bridge. When I go to his cabin he just grunts and says he's left the running of the ship to me. Suits me fine. Life's nice and quiet, isn't it?'

'Yes, it's wonderful. I wonder how long it'll last?'

It lasted until the night of the shipwreck.

When we were two days away from the Canaries the weather broke suddenly, within a few hours. The sun was intercepted by heavy English-looking clouds, and a cold wind came down from the north and threw handfuls of rain across our decks. I lay in my bunk, rocking contentedly and confidently in the swing of the ocean. It was shortly after midnight, and I was suspended in the pleasant arcade between sleep and wakefulness, enjoying the best of both. Then the alarm bells rang.

I sat up and switched on the light. Seven short rings, meaning 'Boat Stations'. Someone on the bridge had obviously leant on the alarm button. I was wondering what to do when the whistle blew 'Abandon Ship'.

'Christ!' I said. I jumped from my bunk like a sprinter off the mark. I fell over the hot-water can, picked myself up, and threw open the cabin door. Trail lived opposite me, and had just come off watch. He was looking disturbed.

'What's up?' I asked anxiously.

'It's abandon ship.'

'I know! But why?'

'Search me, Doc. She was all right when I came off the bridge. We'd better get up top.'

I hitched up my pyjama trousers and started for the companionway.

'Your life-jacket, you fool!' Trail shouted at me.

'Oh Lord! I forgot.'

I ran back to my cabin, pulled on my life-jacket, and started tying it. It occurred to me I should make an attempt to save some of my possessions, so I picked up my empty sponge-bag and stuffed one or two handy articles into it. I later discovered I had preserved from the deep a shoehorn, two empty cigarette tins, a roll of film, and a copy of *Teach Yourself Spanish*. Grabbing a tin of morphine from the locker, I hurried towards the boatdeck.

The crew of the *Lotus* had boat drill at four-thirty every Friday afternoon, as prescribed by the Ministry of Transport, and this was always carried out efficiently, with calmness, and in an atmosphere of polite cooperation. There are, however, certain factors that complicate boat drill in earnest which are not operative during its harmless rehearsals. In the first place, it is usually night-time, there is a cold wind blowing, and it is raining. A strong sea is running, which makes it difficult to swing the boats out without smashing them. Everyone has been woken up from a deep sleep and is bad tempered. The Bos'n has forgotten where he put the handle to one of the davits. The Third has lost the roll-call. All hands are perplexed and naturally worried about saving themselves as well as giving wholehearted enthusiasm to preserving their shipmates. Also, all the lights are out.

I slipped over the wet deck, now alive with hurrying sailors, and found my way to the huddle of men round my own boat. They were cutting away the strings holding the canvas cover, under the directions of the Third.

'My God, what a lash-up!' the Third said. 'All right, Bos'n. Stand-by to swing.'

'Swing out all boats!' Captain Hogg's voice came through the loud hailer.

'Swing out!' the Third repeated.

Three men swung on each davit handle with an energy usually shown at sea only when arriving in port ten minutes before the pubs shut.

'Swing out, there!' Captain Hogg repeated. 'The ship is going down!'

A rocket flew into the air and exploded into gently falling coloured stars.

'Get a move on, you men!' he shouted.

'Come on, come on!' Trail ordered impatiently. 'Stand-by the falls, there!'

'Excuse my interrupting,' I said. 'But if we're sinking we don't seem to have much of a list on.'

'Cut it out, Doc! Right, lower away there! Steady forrard!'

Hornbeam, in his life-jacket and underpants, came breathlessly over to us.

'What's up?' I asked.

'Search me. The Old Man started it. I went up to the bridge and he kicked me off.'

Suddenly the deck lights snapped on. We all paused and looked at one another.

'Right!' came from the loud hailer. 'That was the poorest exhibition I've seen in all my years at sea. That was boat drill, see? As it should be done. None of this Friday afternoon tea-party stuff. You're the most inefficient crew I've ever had the misfortune to sail with. Swing 'em in again and dismiss.'

To a chorus of groans and ingenious profanity the boats were swung in and made fast.

I went below to change my clothes and pour myself a drink. I was still towelling myself when Trail came in.

'What the hell does Father think he's up to?' he demanded, throwing his wet life-jacket on my bunk.

'I suppose he's allowed to hold boat drill at night if he wants to.'

'He's allowed to, all right. He's allowed to do anything. He can marry you, bury you, put you in irons, or hang you from the yardarm. That doesn't mean to say he can do it every night.'

'What do the crew think of it?'

'They're complaining to their Union.'

'I wish I could complain to mine.'

Trail pulled his wet jacket off and sat down. 'I wonder what made the Old Man do it?' he asked more calmly. 'It's the first time we've seen him for a week.'

'Probably didn't want us to forget him.'

'That's likely. It's finished with now, anyway. It was bloodly cold up there on deck. You're going to have about twenty pneumonia cases tomorrow.'

'Care for a peg before we turn in?'

'Thanks, I'll have a quick one.'

I was handing him the whisky bottle when the whistle blew for the second time.

The scene on the boatdeck was repeated, but it was played at a much more leisurely pace. The crew showed no enthusiasm at all for the exercise.

'Come on!' Trail ordered. 'It's got to be done, so you'd better get it over with.'

'Put your backs in it!' the loud hailer roared. 'Call yourselves sailors? Get a move on with number four, Mr Trail!'

'For God's sake, lads,' Trail said. 'Keep the Old Man happy.'

Slowly our boat swung out, rocking in the wind, tugging at the arms of the swearing crew.

After twenty minutes on the cold, wet deck, Captain Hogg gave the order to swing in again. The boats were brought back to their blocks, lashed down, and covered with their canvas sheets.

Hornbeam, who had found time to put on his uniform, came back to us.

'All squared up, Third?' he asked anxiously.

'Aye aye, Mr Hornbeam.'

'All right. You lot can dismiss.'

The voice came from the loud hailer.

'Right! Now repeat the exercise!'

Hornbeam spun round.

'No!' he shouted towards the bridge. 'We won't!'

The wind and sea were making a fair noise, but these were obliterated by the silence that fell upon everyone on deck. I held my breath. The bridge was in darkness, but I imagined clearly the explosive figure standing there.

The loud hailer was still for a few seconds.

'This is mutiny!' it roared.

Hornbeam shrugged his shoulders.

'Dismiss, all hands,' he said. 'Disregard all further alarm signals.'

'Mr Hornbeam, I'll put you in irons!'

Hornbeam took no notice.

'You'll pay for this, by God!'

'You see everything's lashed down, Third,' Hornbeam continued calmly. 'I'm going on the bridge.'

He made towards the ladder.

'You come up here and I'll kick your teeth in!'

He reached the end of the ladder. A heavy fire-bucket fell on the deck, just missing his head. I got hold of him and pulled him away.

'Look here,' I said. 'Don't be a fool. Let me go up and see him. After all, I'm more or less out of this. I can explain it's bad for the crew on medical grounds, or something. He's got nothing against me. I can be an intermediary.'

'Nothing doing, Doc. This is my pidgin.'

'No, it isn't. I don't want to spend the rest of the night putting stitches in your scalp. I'm sure he won't chuck anything at me.'

'All right, Doc,' he said. 'But watch your step.'

Setting my teeth, I climbed up the ladder to the bridge. At first I thought the wheelhouse was empty. Then I caught sight of the Captain, standing by the terrified quartermaster who was steering. He looked like a fat malignant ape.

'Who's that?' he growled.

'Doctor, sir,' I began. 'I came on behalf of the Mate . . .'

'Get off my bridge!'

'I wondered if I might explain that on purely medical grounds . . .'

'Get out!'

'In my professional opinion,' I continued resolutely.

'Get out!' he screamed. 'Or I'll bash your bloody brains in!'

He seized from the bulkhead some heavy instrument. It was, I suppose, a marlin spike or some similar appliance that skippers are traditionally expected to take to beat in the brains of their crew. I did not wait to find out. I scrambled down the ladder and fell hard on to the deck. I hurt my arm and ripped my pyjamas; but already I had forgotten the incident. A new and more terrifying thought took possession of me: Captain Hogg was undoubtedly clinically insane.

Chapter Eighteen

'Delusions of grandeur,' I read aloud, 'occur frequently in this condition.'

It was the next morning. Hornbeam and Trail were sitting in my cabin while I read aloud from a text-book of medicine. The weather had calmed down and the storm that blew through the ship the night before had abated with it. Immediately after turning me off the bridge Captain Hogg had abruptly gone to his cabin, locked the door, and turned in. He appeared in the morning without making any reference to the night's excitement, and was even faintly friendly towards everyone on board. He gave the impression that he imagined the activity on the boatdeck was part of a particularly enjoyable dream.

'You see,' I explained to the others, 'delusions of grandeur. I ought to have spotted it before. Still, it's difficult in a ship's captain. No one notices if they have them.'

'What's wrong with him, Doc?' Hornbeam asked with interest.

'G.P.I.–general paralysis of the insane, undoubtedly. It's a late stage of syphilis. Listen to this: "The patient is usually a man in his middle fifties who suddenly becomes subject to attacks of bad temper, fits of sulking, and lack of judgement. These may alternate with periods of violent excitement. The condition is usually first noticed by members of the sufferer's family circle rather than the physician." Doesn't that fit in? The old boy picked it up thirty years ago on the Brazilian coast and now we're getting the benefit of it.'

Hornbeam rolled a cigarette thoughtfully.

'It's a serious business, Doc, if you're right.'

'I'm pretty certain I am.'

'Is there any sort of test you can do to make sure?' Trail asked.

'I couldn't give you a definite opinion without examining him.' I ran my eye down the page of the book. '"The patient has the sensation of walking on cotton-wool,"' I read out. 'Stabbing pains in the legs at night . . . loss of knee-jerks . . . loss of pain sensation in the tendo Achilles . . . pupils do not react to light . . . There's a good many signs, you see.'

'Yes, but do you suppose he's going to let you barge into his cabin and examine him?' Hornbeam asked. 'Have you thought about that?'

'You raise a difficulty in diagnosis, certainly,' I admitted. 'I don't feel he would be a highly cooperative patient. Particularly after last night.'

'Well, we'll have to let him go on being balmy, then.'

I shut the book and took my spectacles off.

'I have an idea,' I announced. 'I remember the way I was once told to examine children.'

'Children! This one's some baby!'

'It's the principle of the thing that matters. They taught us in hospital to deal with unwilling children by distracting their attention and examining what you wanted while they weren't looking. See what I'm getting at? The knee-jerks, for instance. I shall engage him in conversation and drop a book or a bottle of something on his patella, pretending it's an accident. Oh yes, I think that's the answer,' I said, warming to the idea. 'I'll build up a diagnosis in a couple of days and send in a report to the Company.'

'Mind he doesn't bite you,' Trail said.

I had a chance to try my new technique of fragmented diagnosis at dinner. Captain Hogg appeared for the first time since his retirement, and seemed in capital spirits. He sat down next to me at the head of the table, tucked his serviette in with a flourish, and fell upon the roast mutton.

'Good mutton, this, Mr Whimble,' he said through a mouthful of potatoes. 'Don't get much like it these days. Where did you buy it?'

'London, sir.'

'It's kept well. By the way, Mr Hornbeam. Get the hatch covers off number three by tonight, if the weather holds. We may be filling that twenty feet in Teneriffe.'

'Very good, sir.'

'I'm pleased to find the weather's cleared, sir,' I said brightly. 'This fresh breeze makes you feel you're walking on cotton-wool.'

He said nothing.

'Do *you* ever feel you are walking on cotton-wool, sir?' I asked.

'No,' he said. 'I don't.'

He swallowed another mouthful of greens and mutton. I was keenly disappointed.

'The weather ought to hold,' he said. 'The glass is going up.'

'I had an aunt,' I remarked. 'Every time the glass went up she had stabbing pains in her legs.'

'Did she?'

'Do *you* get stabbing pains in your legs, sir?'

'What the devil are you talking about, Doctor?'

'Oh, nothing of importance, sir.'

I miserably fiddled with a piece of roast potato. It seemed that my means of eliciting the patient's symptoms was not going to meet with clinical success. I decided I would go ahead and examine for the physical signs. I dropped my serviette on the deck. As I bent down to pick it up I pinched Captain Hogg hard behind the ankle.

'Ouch!' he said.

'I'm dreadfully sorry, sir . . .'

'What the hell are you playing at?'

'I thought . . . I thought it was the Mate's foot.'

'Well, what difference does that make?'

'We were having a little game.'

'I don't like games,' Captain Hogg said. 'Not in *my* ship.'

'Very good, sir.'

I jabbed moodily at my treacle sponge for the rest of the meal, despair freezing my heart.

'Find anything out?' Hornbeam said in my cabin afterwards.

'Not much. Couldn't you see?'

'Yes, you were making a bit of a mess of it. Supposing he's not potty at all, but just acting his own sweet self?'

'I'm *sure* he's insane,' I said heatedly. 'Certain of it. If they put him in the final examinations every student would get through. He's a classic case. The only trouble is I can't get near enough to prove it.'

'We'll have to be pretty certain before we say anything to the Company, Doc. I always believe in clearing my own yardarm.'

I banged the desk with my fist.

'Damn it! Here's this man–certifiably insane–with every one of us at his mercy. Why, any time he might break out again like last night! Supposing he goes and puts us aground at the Canaries? Or rams the *Queen Mary* or something off Bishop Rock? He's capable of absolutely anything. What would we do then?'

Hornbeam scratched his cheek with the lip of his pipe.

'It's a teaser, Doc. We'll have to think out some other scheme.' He looked at his watch. 'I must go and tell the Bos'n to take the covers off number three. If I think of anything, I'll let you know. Meantime, I'll keep a sharp watch on Father myself.'

'Thanks. I'll try and work something out. See you for a peg before supper.'

I passed the rest of the day sorting ingenious schemes for diagnosis in my mind. Nothing seemed workable. I thought of confessing frankly to the port doctor in Teneriffe that we had a madman loose on board and asking him to send for a couple of assistants and a straitjacket; but I felt that the port doctor, who was used to ship's captains, might find Captain Hogg not in the least abnormal. I wished sincerely that he would foam at the mouth or do something equally spectacular when we got in.

When Easter brought my tea I admitted my difficulties to him.

'I think the Captain is insane,' I told him.

'Ho, yes,' he said. 'He's as mad as a fiddler's bitch.'

'You've noticed it too, have you?'

'Dr Flowerday always reckoned he was.'

'Did he do anything about it?'

'Used to slip the cook half a dollar to lace his tea with a Mickey when he was real bad.'

'I hadn't thought of that. It might do in an emergency.'

'Wasn't much cop, as it happened. He chucked the tea at the steward usually.'

'We must think of some way, Easter, to settle this once and for all,' I said firmly. 'I am prepared to give you ten bob–a quid–if you can think of some legal means of getting the Captain off this ship at the first possible moment.'

Easter scratched his head.

'Very kind of you, Doctor, I'm sure. Can't think of anything offhand, like.'

'Well try, man, try. If I can't think of . . .'

I was cut short by a crash outside my cabin, a loud scream, confused shouting, the clatter of running feet.

'What the hell's happened now?' I exclaimed.

My door flew open. Hornbeam was outside. He was grinning like a toothpaste advertisement.

'Quick, Doc!' he said. 'Father's fallen twenty feet down number three hatch!'

I ran on to the deck. There was a crowd round the edge of the hatch, hurriedly letting down a rope-ladder. I pushed my way through and climbed over the coaming. In a few seconds I found Captain Hogg had solved all our problems for us by fracturing his right femur in three places.

Easter and I strung up Captain Hogg in splints on his bunk. He was a heavy man, and still not a remarkably cooperative patient. It took us a couple of hours, and we were sweating when we had finished.

'I'll have that Bos'n logged,' he muttered, as we arranged the pillows under his head. 'Leaving the covers loose like that . . . I'll have the Mate logged, too.'

'Now keep quiet,' I commanded. 'I forbid you to talk or move.'

'I will talk as much as I damn well like.'

'I give the orders now. I'm the doctor.'

'Well, I'm the Captain.'

'Easter,' I said. 'Just tighten up that splint a bit more, will you?'

'Ouch!' said Captain Hogg.

'Now,' I continued. 'If you will just stay quiet for a moment I can complete my examination. If you don't I shall have to consider putting you on a milk diet. Tinned milk, naturally.'

I pulled out my torch and shone it in his eyes.

'Ah, yes,' I said, in my most menacing professional tone. 'As I thought. Just take this down, Easter. Pupils do not react to light . . . loss of sensation to pinprick over the nose . . . abdominal reflexes absent . . . A classic picture! We will have to put you ashore tomorrow in the Canaries, of course.'

'You will not. I am not leaving my own ship for you or anybody.'

'Damn it, man! Use your sense. This leg has to be set properly. I can't do it here. It needs X-rays and so forth. You will have to go into hospital with it. I hear they have some excellent surgeons in Teneriffe.'

'I will not go, Doctor.'

'If we cable the Company and they say so, you'll have to go.'

'There is no reason why you should cable them. I am still fit to keep my command.'

'It's a bit late to think of that now. The message has already gone.'

'Gone!' He jerked his head from the pillow. 'No messages are allowed to leave the ship without my permission.'

'Really, you are a most difficult patient,' I said gently. 'I will leave Easter to read to you. You will find plenty of literature in the corner, Easter.'

'What, these here?' Easter asked, picking up one of the Captain's library. 'Cor! Looks like a bit of all right, eh?' He settled himself comfortably by the sick-bed. 'Right, sir,' he began. 'I will start with "I was a White Slave. True Confessions of a French Girl Kidnapped from a Convent and Sent to the Infamous Kasbah of Algiers". Cor,' he added to the Captain, 'I know Algiers all right. Funny thing happened to me last time I was there. I'd gone ashore with the Cook, see, and we was looking for a bit of fun, as you might say . . .'

I left them, feeling I had inflicted on Captain Hogg sufficient misfortune for the evening.

Hornbeam was sitting in his cabin writing up the logbook.

'Hello, Doc,' he said cheerfully. 'How's the patient, God rot his soul?'

'As well as can be expected, I'm afraid.'

'I'm just putting it in the log. You'll have to sign down here.'

'When will we get to Teneriffe?' I asked.

'About midday. We should be tied up alongside by one.'

'We've got to put Father ashore, you know. I can't treat a fracture properly at sea. The trouble is he won't shift. He says he won't go without instructions from the Company.'

Hornbeam tossed a cable across to me.

'Sparky just brought that down,' he said. 'Take a look at it.'

I unfolded the paper. It was from the Fathom Line head office.

TO CHIEF OFFICER SS. LOTUS. PLACE CAPTAIN ASHORE TENERIFFE IF DOCTOR SO ADVISES AND BRING VESSEL HOME UNDER YOUR COMMAND STOP PREPARE TAKE COMMAND IMMEDIATELY ON ARRIVAL UK SS PRIMROSE OWING RESIGNATION CAPTAIN BARSETT.

'Well, Doc,' he said smiling. 'Do you advise?'

'Do I advise! Yes, sir! Yes, indeed!' I grabbed his hand. 'Yes, Captain Hornbeam!'

Chapter Nineteen

The next day we arrived off the rocky, volcanic Canaries, sailed under the lee of the islands, and shortly after noon slipped into the tidy, clean harbour of Teneriffe. Archer and Trail took the bow and stern, tugs flying smoky red-and-yellow Spanish flags turned us round to face the sea, and we tied to the jetty between a smart Blue Star boat outward bound for Rio and a disconnected-looking craft flying the flag of Panama which had cows on the deck.

At first Captain Hogg refused to be moved. We showed him the cablegram but he accused us of forgery. So I filled him up with morphine and sent him to sleep.

He was carried out on the shoulders of the sailors, like Nelson's bier, arranged in a derrick sling, and unloaded by the steam winches between two bales of cowhide.

'You'll find the full history in the letter,' I said, handing the case report to the smiling, handsome Spanish doctor with the ambulance. 'The British Consul's fixed everything else up.'

The doctor shook hands, the ambulance doors swung shut, and Captain Vincent Hogg drove out of my life.

'Get rid of him all right?' Easter asked, as I reached the top of the gangway.

'It seems so. I don't think he'll have much chance to throw his weight about in a Spanish hospital. Especially after that letter I sent with him.'

'Wouldn't mind going ashore here for a spell myself,' Easter said meditatively. 'I've had some fun here, I have. I remember when I was on the South Africa run, the barber and me went . . .'

'All right. Easter. Later will do.'

'They got some lovely girls here,' Easter continued. 'Prettiest in the world, I reckon. Look at that one down there. See? They got the same as our girls at home, but they carry it around better.' He pointed to a slim, dark girl, stepping along the quay with a grace that is unhappily forgotten on cold

English parks and pavements.

'Ho, they got some smashing bits here!' Easter said enthusiastically. 'Mind you, you've got to be careful. Do you want a tablecloth?'

'A tablecloth? What should I want a tablecloth for?'

'This is the place to buy them.' He pointed over the side, where the wide pipes ran towards the ship in a pool of black fuel oil. An informal market had been set up on the quay, offering thick brocaded tablecloths, scarves with vivid bullfights on them, canaries in cages, metal ornaments, and dolls four feet high.

'Them dolls is all right,' Easter advised me. 'I used buy a lot of them at one time.'

'I'm pleased to hear you think of the children, Easter.'

'Ho, crikey no! I used to buy 'em here and flog 'em in Pernambuco. Good business, that was. Canaries, too. Make a good few bob on canaries, you could. Unless the little bastards went and died on you. Or you got gyped. Some of 'em's sparrows fed on quinine.'

'Well, I ought to buy a few presents, I suppose. But I haven't got much in the way of money.'

'They takes all kinds of junk here. Old clothes–a pair o' boots, worn out, if you've got 'em. Fags mostly. Get anything for a few hundred Woods.'

I exchange five hundred ship's Woodbines for two scarves, a small bracelet, and a decorated picture of General Franco. I supposed I had better make a return with some of the assets of a seafarer.

We stayed eight hours in Teneriffe; then we set off under Hornbeam's command, our next stop England.

The removal of Captain Hogg from the ship had the effect of dissolving a chronic state of anxiety. All hands walked about cheerfully, did their work amiably, and set to it with twice the effort.

'Got to have her looking nice for home now,' the Bos'n said, looking critically at the gang he had set painting the upper works. 'We can't let Mr Hornbeam down, can we?'

Hornbeam slipped easily into his new rank. He took over the Captain's cabin and his seat at table. Our meal-times now were lively with conversation, with the result that everyone ate more contentedly and the cases of dyspepsia among the officers dropped sharply. Even Archer began reluctantly to feel better, and admitted he hadn't taken any stomach powder for a week.

Our only excitement was a message to Hornbeam changing our destination from Liverpool to London because of a threatening dock strike. The order caused disapproval among the Liverpudlians in the crew, but this was charmed away quickly by Easter's account of the fun he had had at various times in London.

'Smashing place, London,' he claimed. 'You wait till you see West Ham.'

The sea became rougher, the weather became colder; spray came once again over the *Lotus*'s bows. The broken water took on the green-grey tint of European coasts, and the ship began to groan and stagger in the January waves. But now I was unaffected by the sea, and stood on deck innocuously watching the foc's'le head rise and dip with the swell and the tops of the masts trace wide irregular circles against the sky. All round us were signs that we were coming nearer to our own country. Boxes and cartons were lying in everyone's cabins, the ship's time became synonymous with that of Greenwich, three pounds Channel money was advanced to all hands, the

Light Programme assailed us diminished, and the weather remained persistently foul.

One evening Easter put his head round my door and said cheerfully 'Want to see the Ushant light, Doctor? Just coming up on the starboard bow.'

Together we stood in the shelter of the storm door leading on to the deck. I followed his finger towards the flashes.

'Well, there's old Europe again,' Easter said. 'Ain't a bad old continent, all things considered. We turns the corner here. The next mark's the Casquettes, then for Beachy. Blimey, I've seen folks in tears looking at that there light! When they've been gone for a long time, that is.'

'Yes, I expect everyone will start being excited from now on.'

'Ho, they'll have the channels tomorrow, you mark my word.'

'The channels?'

'Ah, there's a complaint what even you don't know, Doctor. All hands goes a bit balmy, like. You wait till tomorrow.'

Easter was right. The channels is a clinical entity that has not found its way into the medical text-books, but is as noticeable as scarlet fever. The next morning the crew were prancing round the decks like highly-strung lambs in springtime. Everyone had a bright word for their mates, a salute for the Captain, and even a few sirs left over for me. Work was done with a lighthearted air that drew scowls of disapproval from the Bos'n, who had been up the Channel so many times that he had developed an immunity to the complaint. Easter repeated his most successful card tricks and thought it a great joke to tell me falsely the hospital was three feet in water. I forgave him readily, for I too was walking the deck murmuring to myself, 'Every turn of the screw brings me nearer to you'. To whom? I wondered. It didn't matter. I could settle that when we arrived.

Beachy Head–white, shining in a brief ray of sunshine turned on like an effective spotlight on a darkened stage. I looked at it with mixed feelings of affection and disapproval that the voyager's first sight of England should be Eastbourne.

We came closer to the land, making for the pilot boat off Dungeness. The Atlantic rollers had flattened themselves in the narrow waters, but the sea was high enough to throw the pilot's launch about unenviably. He came round to the lee side and had two shots at grasping the Jacob's ladder. Trail and the Bos'n dangled from the foredeck; the third time he caught a rung as the launch dropped away from his feet. He climbed aboard, his black oilskins running with water, shook himself like a dog, gave me a cheerful 'Nice morning!', and climbed up to the bridge. The red and white pilot's flag broke over the wheelhouse, and the *Lotus* proceeded under the arrangement invariably stated in the log-book as 'Master's orders, Pilot's advice'.

The channel was busy that day. We passed, or were passed by, a representation of Lloyd's List. There were tankers making for Thameshaven, so low in the water they disappeared to the bridge between the waves; rickety tramps setting out fearlessly for voyages longer than ours; little coasters bound for a rough passage round Land's End; sodden fishing boats; cargo ships of all sizes and states of repair, British, Norwegian, Swedish, and Dutch; one of the ubiquitous City boats with a black and salmon funnel, homeward bound fully loaded from the Australian wool sales; even a couple of warships. They were a pair of corvettes steaming jauntily down Channel in line astern. The meeting led to a burst of activity at the foot of the mainmast as the deckboy afforded the King's vessels their salute by dipping our ensign. The correct form was for us to dip, watch for the white ensign fluttering down in reply, and follow its return to the masthead. Unfortunately, the wind caught our rain-soaked flag and twisted it in the rigging, so that we passed the fleet apparently in mourning. But the intention was there, and the Navy would be the first to understand.

A big white P. & O. passed us, outward bound for India and Australia and the sunshine that appeared to me to have vanished for ever.

'Be away for the best part of four months, that lot,' Easter remarked. 'All be taking their last look at old England.'

'As long as that?'

'They gets them dock strikes something horrid out Aussie way. It's a lovely life being a wharfie in Sydney or Melbourne–you draws your money and puts your feet up most of the day. Like being a lord. Or–if I may be so bold–ship's doctor.'

'Yes, I suppose you're right,' I admitted sadly. 'Except the dockers get paid more. I suppose they're all pretty excited on board–first night at sea, and so on.'

'Ho, yes. I've seen it often enough on the big passenger boats. All the blokes giving the girls the once-over in the dining saloon. Cor, I've seen them sweet little things with their eyes still wet with tears from saying good-bye to their husbands and sweethearts carrying on something shocking. Hardly out of the River we wasn't, neither.'

The red lamps were shining on the tops of the high radar masts when we crept close to Dover inside the Goodwins. The lights of Ramsgate and Margate passed off our port side, then we cut across to the Nore, where we were to anchor and await the tide. Someone gave me the morning paper that the pilot had brought aboard. I opened it and read the front page with the careless baffled interest of a holidaymaker inspecting the social column in the village weekly. We had been more or less newsless for three months, but the happenings that used to shake my breakfast table no longer aroused my concern. A paragraph near the foot of the page caught my eye; it was headed 'MAYOR REBUKES DANCERS', and went on: 'The Mayor of ——, Alderman ——, yesterday refused an application for an extension to midnight at a cycling club dance. He said he was highly disturbed at complaints of immoral behaviour that had followed the dance last year. "The place for young men and women at midnight," he told the secretary, "is in their own homes asleep."'

I knew I was back in England.

Chapter Twenty

The next morning we steamed into the Thames. The country raised a faint glow of sunshine to welcome us, but the effort was too taxing and the atmosphere soon relapsed into its habitual rain.

We passed the long finger of Southend Pier, which appears a far more dignified structure when seen in reverse, signalled our name, and passed down the channel towards Tilbury. The wet, orderly fields of England on the narrowing banks, with a demure English train jogging through them towards London, had the appearance of a winter's garden after the turbulent unfenced vegetation of the South American coast. Off Tilbury landing-stage we anchored for the Port of London doctor to board us. He was a large, friendly man in a naval battledress and a duffle-coat.

'Have a good voyage, old man?' he asked, running his fingers down the pages of my log-book.

'Pretty good, thanks.'

'Going again?'

'Oh, no. I don't think so, anyway.'

'Back to the N.H.S., eh?'

'That's it. If I can remember any of my medicine.'

He laughed. 'You can still sign your name, can't you? All right, free pratique granted.'

We continued down the River, and I was seized with a spasm of nostalgia by catching sight of an L.P.T.B. bus.

In Gallions Reach the tugs set about us and turned us towards the locks of the Royal Albert Dock.

'Is that all the room we've got?' I asked Easter, as we headed for the narrow entrance. As I always had difficulty parking a car in a busy street I was filled with admiration for the mates and tugmasters every time the *Lotus* came into port.

'There's bags of room,' Easter said. 'They gets them big New Zealand boats through here easy enough. Look at all them bright lads we've got to help us.'

I saw a chilly knot of longshoremen waiting to receive our ropes as we came into the lock: sad, damp Englishmen, their coat collars up to their sodden caps.

'That one there's been on the job for years,' Easter said. 'We calls him Knuckle 'Arry.'

He pointed to a depressed-looking man with a long moustache standing still and holding a rope fender over the end of the jetty.

'That's an odd name. What's his knuckles got to do with it?'

'The knuckle's what he's standing on. Now you wait.'

As the *Lotus* drew near the stonework the pilot shouted from the bridge: 'Keep her off the knuckle, 'Arry!' The man touched his cap, and solemnly manipulated his fender to save our paint. He then resumed his immobility in the thick rain.

We passed the knuckle, the locks, the entrance to the dock; the tugs dragged us slowly down to our waiting berth; more men in caps and old overcoats secured our ropes to the quay; the ensign came down from the gaff and was rehoisted, in compliance with custom, on the stern jack-staff.

'Lower away gangway!' Hornbeam shouted from the bridge.

The *Lotus* leant contentedly against the dock and, after three months all but five days, we were home.

There was a wonderful end-of-term spirit aboard. Everyone was packing up and behaving with the recklessness of men for whom there are no longer any consequences.

We were paying-off, the morning after our arrival. Mr Cozens and his colleagues came aboard and treated us with cordial superiority, and we looked on them with good-humoured contempt. Cozens himself questioned me closely about the exit of Captain Hogg.

'Very good, Doctor,' he said. 'I think you did entirely the correct thing. Our *Sunflower* is due at Teneriffe in three weeks' time and she will bring him home. We have your successor for next trip–a Dr Gallyman. Do you know him?'

'I'm sorry, I don't.'

Cozens sighed. 'I'm afraid he is a little on the old side,' he said. 'Retired from practice some years ago. I believe there was some trouble with the medical authorities, too . . . Still we must hope for the best. It's so difficult getting doctors for these ships just now.'

Apart from the office staff, the ship filled with taxi-drivers, luggage carters, laundrymen, dry cleaners, marine tailors, and haircutters, all of them pressing their services on the ship's company before it dispersed. I shut the door of my cabin, looked despairingly at the empty cases and my curiously augmented possessions, and wondered how I was going to pack. I started with the volumes of *War and Peace*. I hadn't got beyond the first page, but I had killed one hundred and thirty-two cockroaches with them. I was hesitantly fitting them into a case when Easter came in.

'Letter for you, Doctor.'

It was only the second one I had received since leaving Liverpool. It too was from the laundry.

> Dear Sir (*it said*), Further to ours of November 28th. I have to inform you that your laundry has been sold to defray expenses of the wash. The sum received was 6*s*. 3*d*., which is 2*s*. 9*d*. less than your account. We would appreciate your settling this deficit at your earliest convenience.

Sadly I put the letter into my pocket.

'Getting the loot packed, Doctor?' Easter asked.

'I only wish I could.'

'The Customs is pretty hot down here,' he went on. 'Not like some ports I could mention. Get away with murder, you used to. So long as you bought your tickets for the police ball.'

'What police ball?'

'I remember once the old arm of the law putting his head round our cabin door and saying, "I'm sure as you gentlemen would like to come to the police ball." Well, I knew the ropes, see, so I says, "Not 'arf we wouldn't. We've been thinking about it all voyage." So he hands over tickets at a dollar a time–but you mustn't take 'em, like. I looks at mine and says, "Ho, constable, I regrets but what I have a previous engagement." So he collects all the tickets back and flogs 'em again in the next cabin. Mind you, he keeps the five bob.'

'Well, I hardly think it worth while my making the investment. Apart from the junk I got at Teneriffe I've only some corned beef and a pair of nylons.'

'That's the ticket, Doctor! Girls round our way will do anything for a tin of corned beef. Show 'em the nylons as well, and cor! they're all over you.'

'I assure you these are destined for middle-aged relatives.'

'Used to do pretty well out of nylons during the war. Some of the blokes on the Western Ocean made a fortune flogging 'em in Southampton. The places they thinks of to hide 'em! Down the chain locket in the fo'c'sle's usual. One of the lads put a dummy pipe across the deckhead and filled it with nylons and fags. Lovely job he made of it. Painted it up just like it was real. But the Customs boys copped him. Oh, they're very fly, they are. I'll get you an empty beer-case from the Chief Steward.'

'Thank you, Easter.'

I sat wearily among the disheartening jumble. Well, this was the end of the trip. What had I got from it? Some corned beef, some nylons, a cure for headaches, two stones in weight, and a deep sunburn. But much more than that, surely I had found for the first time that the world isn't divided simply into two classes–doctors and patients. Three months at sea had taught me more than six years in a medical school. I had learned to give and take toleration, to grapple with grotesque predicaments, to appreciate there is some goodness behind everybody, that life isn't really so serious, and that doctors aren't such bloody important people after all.

The Customs man–young and keen–came in and rummaged my cabin. He did so like an old-fashioned physician searching for a diagnosis with an irritating air of professional detachment.

'Where did you get these from?' he asked, holding up my best pair of pyjamas.

'Swan and Edgars.'

'Umm. Have you any spirits?'

'Bottle of whisky.'

'Opened?'

'Certainly.'

'Umm. Have you a watch?'

'No.'

'What, not one at all?'

'I lost it one night in B.A.'

He looked at me narrowly.

'Watch your step, Doctor,' he said, leaving me alone.

I managed to throw my packing together before paying-off started in the saloon. It was more a ceremony than a business transaction. We were theoretically not entitled to any pay until the end of the voyage, though we could draw foreign currency at the pleasure of the Captain. Our wages were set out in a long narrow sheet, with additions for leave and Sundays at sea and deductions for advances, Channel money, bar bill, stores account, and anything else the Chief Steward thought he could add without protest.

The pay was distributed by the Fathom Line officials, under the eye of the Shipping Master. They sat at the big table behind exciting piles of five-pound notes, looking like the tote about to pay off on the favourite. Also on the table were the ship's articles and a pile of discharge books–the sailor's personal record–signed by the Captain with a comment on conduct like a school report.

The crew lined up eagerly, all in their best clothes. I had difficulty in placing the clean, modest-looking men in smart blue and grey suits as the half-naked roughs who strode round the decks with paint pots in the Tropics. The Carpenter was particularly baffling: he wore a dark herringbone tweed, a hard white two-inch collar, and an artificial rosebud in his buttonhole, giving the appearance of a moderately liberal-minded clergyman on holiday at Sandown.

Nothing gives such a pleasant feeling of false prosperity as paying-off a ship. By the time my wages had been reduced by deductions I had less than a month's salary in general practice, but I stuffed the notes into my pocket and felt like Lord Nuffield. Then I signed off the book of ship's articles opposite the space where I had signed on them three months ago. My contract with the Commander of the *Lotus* was broken: I was quit of my obligations to him to obey his lawful commands, to work the ship in emergency, to abstain from bringing my own liquor on board, and to check myself from using foul language in his presence. For his part, he had no longer to trouble about feeding me at the required standards, avoiding carrying me into Arctic or Antarctic latitudes, and returning me to my own country within a period of eighteen months. I was free–out of work, but free.

I said good-bye to as many of the crew as I could find; sailors' farewells are brief and shallow, for they make up half their lives. Easter shook hands heartily and impressed on me solemnly the importance of speed whenever I should come to do the three-card trick. Almost everyone left the ship–to go on leave, to quit her for good, or to be in Canning Town by the time the pubs opened. The rain prevented cargo being worked, and the *Lotus* was not only empty of people but silent, as miserable as a school when the children have gone home.

My taxi was coming later, so I went up to the deck to look round the docks. The sheds and the cranes did something odd to the *Lotus*'s proportions: at sea, when she was alone and stood unhindered from the water, she achieved a touch of dignity. Now that she lay in relation to other pieces of wood and steel she shrank and became ridiculous. The long boatdeck I used to walk was hardly the size of four railway waggons, and the enchanted spot where I sunbathed and watched the flying fish in the afternoon was nothing but a sooty piece of wet planking. Standing in the rain I saw clearly, but with regret, that the land is ever master of the sea.

I saw Hornbeam, in his blue raincoat, striding alone up and down the few feet of shelter below the bridge.

'Hello, Doc,' he said as I went up to him. 'You off now?'

'In a few minutes. I'm only waiting for my taxi.'

'Oh well, I'm sorry to see you go. We haven't had a bad voyage on the whole. We've made a bit of fun for ourselves.'

'We certainly have.'

We walked for a minute or two in silence.

'What are you going to do now, Doc?' he asked.

'I've no idea. Find a practice somewhere, I suppose.'

'Do you reckon you'll go back to sea again?'

'Some day I will. I'm making sure of that.'

'You might, at that.'

'How about you?' I said. 'Going on leave?'

'No leave for me, Doc. I'm off to Liverpool tonight to join the *Primrose*. She's sailing tomorrow for New Zealand.'

'Of course, I was forgetting. You know, to me our arrival is the end of an isolated adventure. But I suppose to you and everyone else it's just another stop in port.'

'That's it, Doc. Always on the move. It's a mug's life, isn't it? Still, someone's got to do it.'

My taxi came then. I waved to him from the dock, and watched him as I drove away. He was walking up and down the deck again in the rain, an incongruous and lonely figure.

The first person I went to see in London was the psychiatrist.

'Hello!' he said. 'When are you going away?'

Richard Gordon

Doctor at Large

Doctor at Large

All characters, institutions, and incidents are fictitious

Chapter One

Qualifying as a doctor is an experience as exciting for a young man as first falling in love, and for a while produces much the same addling effects.

Before my own new diploma had uncurled from its cardboard wrapper I was prancing through the streets hoping every pretty girl in sight would be seized with a fit of fainting, and longing at each crossroads for a serious accident. I scattered prescriptions like snowflakes, and squandered my now precious opinion on relatives, friends, and even people not looking very well who happened to sit opposite me in railway trains. I frequently started conversations with, 'Speaking as a medical man–' and an appeal for a doctor in a theatre would have brought me from my seat like a kangaroo.

After six years as a suppressed medical student this sudden importance was intoxicating, and was refreshed every morning with thick envelopes pouring through a letter-box which had previously breakfasted only on slim bills and orange packets from the football pools. The drug manufacturers pressed me with free samples, diaries the size of hymn-books, and sufficient blotters to soak up the Serpentine; shops in Wigmore Street offered to sell me clinical equipment from brass door-plates to X-ray machines; societies opposed to vivisection, smoking, meat-eating, blood sports, socialism, and birth control jostled on the breakfast table for my support; the bank that a week ago echoed my footsteps like a police court begged to advance me money, safeguard my valuables, and execute my will; even the British Medical Association officially recognized my existence by sending a free sixteen-page booklet on *Ethics and Members of the Medical Profession*, advising me henceforward to live a pure and moral life and not associate with unqualified midwives.

Unfortunately, both young doctors and young lovers soon descend from their rosy clouds on to the spiky realities of life. At the age of twenty-four I had to look for my first job, like a prospective office boy out of school. The quest was a serious one, for today even those students whose most thoughtful work in the lecture-room is carving their names on the benches are determined to become specialists. There seems no point in being anything else, when it is common knowledge in medical schools that general practitioners under the National Health Service are all seedy men signing forms in insanitary surgeries until they drop dead at forty through overwork.

Long before qualifying I had decided to become a surgeon. I had rather fancied myself cutting up the dogfish, frogs, and rabbits in the first-year zoology class, and thought the principle was probably the same further up the evolutionary tree; once I had passed my finals the only problem seemed to be finding the smoothest channel for pouring my surgical energies upon the public. My own hospital, St Swithin's, did not foster its sons beyond inviting them to the annual reunion dinner, at two guineas a head exclusive of wines; but I remembered that outside the medical school office hung a secretive notice in faded copper-plate behind speckled glass saying *Newly Qualified Men Should Consult the Secretary, Who Will Advise Them on Their Careers*. Few graduates obeyed the invitation, for the office was established in the students' eyes as a magistrate's court, which could give summary punishment for minor offences and refer promising cases to the more powerful majesty of the Dean next door. The secretary himself was a shrivelled old man with pince-nez on a thick black ribbon, who must have been the last person in London to wear elastic-sided boots, and he sat surrounded by piles of dusty official papers growing slowly from the floor like stalagmites. He suggested that I become a medical officer in the Regular Army. This advice was depressing, because I knew that he was an old-fashioned man who suggested the Army only to graduates he thought unfit to attend ordinary human beings.

Although I had won no distinctions, scholarships, or prizes at St Swithin's I boldly asked the secretary to enter me for one of the house surgeon's jobs, for these were well known among the students to be distributed in the same sporting spirit that enlivened the rest of the medical school. They were awarded by the hospital consultants sitting in committee, and represented their last chance of getting their own back on students they disliked. Youths who had sat on the front bench at lectures and asked intelligent questions to which they already knew the answers were turned down; so were earnest young men in open necks and sandals who passed round the *New Statesman* and held intense little meetings in corners of the common room on *The Conscience of the Doctor in a Capitalist Society*. Another advantage to an applicant like myself was the consultants' habit of always voting against the favourites of colleagues they disliked. A surgeon with the overwhelming personality of Sir Lancelot Spratt had condemned several dozen promising physicians to start their careers in provincial hospitals because the Professor of Medicine had once refused to let him park his Rolls in the shade of the medical laboratory.

'I fear you are letting your recent qualification unbalance you somewhat,' the secretary told me. 'There are over eighty-three thousand practitioners on the British *Register*. So you have added less than one eighty-third thousandth to the medical strength of the country. If not the Army, how about the Colonial Service?'

But St Swithin's showed extravagant confidence in its educational ability, and the next afternoon I was appointed Junior Casualty House Surgeon to the Professor of Surgery.

'They won't allow you to go cutting up real live people for a bit,' said my landlady with satisfaction, while I was excitedly doing my packing. 'They used to let the learners do the poor people who couldn't afford to pay, but the Government's gone and stopped all that with the National Health Service.'

'I am perfectly entitled to go cutting up whoever I like now I'm qualified,' I told her with dignity. 'Naturally, one starts in a small way, like in everything else. Bumps, ganglions, and cysts, you know–you work your way up through varicose veins and hernias, but after your first appendix it's more or less plain sailing.'

She sniffed. 'I certainly wouldn't want you to go cutting up anyone belonging to *me*.'

'I must ask you to remember, please, that I happen to be a doctor now, not a medical student.'

'Well, there's twelve and six to pay, Doctor, for the breakages.'

The casualty job was admittedly one of the lowliest in the hospital, coming ahead in academic status only to an obscure appointment known as 'Skins and VD'. It was performed in the casualty-room, which was really nothing more than a dressing-station in the battle between London's drivers and pedestrians, and its clinical responsibilities could have been undertaken by any confident member of St John Ambulance Brigade. These thoughts did not occur to me as I crossed the hospital quadrangle the next day to start work. The subaltern joining his first regiment sees only his promotion to colonel, the new clerk plans his managerial reorganization, and even the freshly-ordained clergyman probably spares a thought for the suitability of his calves for gaiters. At the time, the end of my career was clearer to me than the beginning. I saw myself already rising through the profession to become a consultant surgeon at St Swithin's itself, collecting on the way honours, fellowships, and degrees like a magnet in a box of iron filings.

'I say!' someone called across the courtyard, as I strode in my new stiff white coat towards the casualty entrance. 'I say, old man! Half a jiff!'

I turned, and recognized the first obstacle in my professional path. It was Bingham, the other Junior Casualty House Surgeon. He was a pale youth with thick spectacles and bushy hair, who still looked seventeen and always had boils. As a student he was never a front-bench squatter, but he had once won the Dean's Prize in applied anatomy and thereafter always walked through the students' quarters with the *Lancet* sticking from his pocket like a flag and a couple of large books under his arm. Every lunch hour he carried these books to the library, where he ate his cheese sandwiches and removed from the reference volumes dust which he transferred during the afternoon to the instructive abdomens of patients in the wards. Every Saturday when the library closed he moved to the surgical pathology museum, where patients' organs were stored away in thick glass jars on shelves like left luggage, and carried his books round the galleries instead. Bingham seemed to absorb a good deal of knowledge from the armpit.

'I'm jolly pleased you got the other cas. job, old chap,' he said, grabbing my sleeve. 'I wondered who it'd go to. Could have been deuced tricky. Suppose they'd given it to some awful stinker. See what I mean? But we'll get along top-hole together, won't we?'

'Yes, we're pretty well bound to, I suppose.'

'I say,' he went on enthusiastically. 'This is a lark, isn't it?'

'What's a lark?'

'Being qualified and all that. I mean, now we can get on with things properly. I've got a couple of septic fingers, a lipoma, and four circs. lined up for minor ops. already.' He rubbed his hands, as if contemplating a good dinner. 'The Prof. stuck his nose in and said I was pretty quick off the mark. By the way, old chap, he asked why you weren't there.'

'But why should I have been there?' I asked in surprise. 'The job only starts today, surely?'

'Yes, but from midnight last night or something, old chap. Technical point. Didn't you know? The last H.S. has cleared off, anyway. I told the Prof. you were really quite a reliable sort of fellow, and even if you were a bit prone to nip off for long weekends you'd be back in a few days. I said I'd willingly cope with the extra work in the meantime.'

I looked at Bingham coldly. 'And what, may I ask, did the Professor say to all that?'

'Nothing, old chap. He just sort of snorted and went off.'

'I see.'

This was a bad start. Before I could seriously begin my career I would have to win promotion to senior house surgeon and work in the wards themselves under the Professor of Surgery. The appointment would be made after we had finished three months' work in casualty–and only one of us could be chosen. The reject would be turned out in his medical infancy to wail on some other hospital's doorstep.

'I say, old chap,' Bingham continued as we walked along. 'You simply must nip up to the ward after supper and have a dekko at some wizard pancreatic cysts. There's a wonderful perf. up there too–pretty sick, you know, but I think he'll last till we've had a squint at him.' Bingham had the true surgeon's mentality, for it never occurred to him that interesting signs and symptoms were attached to human beings. 'There's a kid with a smashing ductus, too. Murmur as loud as a bus. Could hardly take my bally stethoscope away.'

'I thought casualty house surgeons weren't supposed to go into the wards?'

'Not really, old chap, but I told the Prof. I was working for Fellowship already and he said I could nose round as much as I liked. I expect it'll be all right for you to come too, as long as you're with me.'

I began to hate Bingham before we first crossed the threshold of our common work-place.

The casualty-room at St Swithin's was not likely to fire in any young man the inspiration to be a second Louis Pasteur or Astley Cooper. It was a long, tiled, semi-basement place, lit by small windows high in the walls, smelling strongly of carbolic and always crowded, like a public lavatory at a busy crossroads. As St Swithin's had to find money to buy all the latest antibiotics and isotopes, it saw no point in spending it on a department where the therapeutic technique had hardly changed since its patients were brought on shutters from beneath the wheels of hansom cabs. Everything in casualty was old: there were old horsehair examination couches, sagging screens of old sacking, dull old instruments, battered old dressing drums, and steamy old sterilizers. Even the porter was past retiring age, and all the nurses seemed to be old ladies.

As we entered, the rows of old wooden benches were already filled with people–one-quarter men, and a quarter each women, children, and policemen. There were policemen everywhere, as thick as tom-cats in a fish market. They stood in the corners holding their helmets, they hid behind the screens with open notebooks, they drank pints of free tea solemnly round the sterilizer, they peered across stretchers and requested eternal 'particulars.' Policemen are inseparable from casualty surgery, and it was well known at St Swithin's that anyone falling over in the district and not getting up damn quickly was immediately seized by the police and enthusiastically borne into the casualty-room.

I sat down at an old desk in one end of the room, which held a large brass ink-pot and a pile of different coloured forms. My job was simple. I handed one of these forms to any patient who I felt was beyond my own professional ability and thankfully disposed of him for ever into some inner department of the hospital. As my only post-graduate guidance from St Swithin's was a leaflet on what to do in case of fire and another describing the most fruitful way of asking relatives for a post-mortem, I was at first worried about matching the correct form to the case. Fortunately, the old porter had long ago accepted the responsibility of running casualty himself, and tactfully brought me the right document to sign after selecting it with the infallible diagnostic instinct of a St Swithin's employee.

The casualty-room never emptied before evening, and for a week I was too busy even to notice Bingham. We met professionally only once a day, at the noon interlude in the clinical rough-and-tumble known as 'minor ops'. This was for surgery too lowly for the main operating theatres, and was performed by Bingham and myself in an undignified theatre made by a partitioned corner of the casualty-room, containing a galvanized-iron operating table, an Edwardian dental-chair decorated with gilt *fleurs de lys*, and a small anaesthetic apparatus on which some former house surgeon had written *Property of the Gas, Fight, and Choke Company*. Although we made our incisions with scalpels that would have been hurled to the floor in the main theatre, and probably had been, it was minor ops. that made the casualty job tolerable: as newly-qualified prospective surgeons, both of us had the same enthusiasm for the knife as the Committee of Public Safety for the guillotine.

I shortly became aware that Bingham always had far more cases waiting on the benches outside minor ops. than I did. As we took alternative patients coming through the casualty-door I envied his luck, until I discovered that he had the habit of stopping people he saw in the street with promising boils, warts, moles or cysts, handing them his card, and telling them to come to the casualty-room of St Swithin's at midday and ask specifically for himself. This brought him a brisk practice of taxi drivers, railway porters, bus conductors, tea-shop waitresses, newsvendors, and roadmenders, and he not only removed the lump and others found by a more searching examination than was possible in public, but usually pulled out their ingrowing toe-nails and extracted their bad teeth as well.

This unsporting approach to surgery so annoyed me that one morning when Bingham was out of the casualty-room I felt justified in harvesting some of his crop myself. I was half-way through removing under local anaesthetic an interesting sebaceous cyst on the nose of an Underground ticket collector, when Bingham burst into the theatre.

'I say!' he started, his white coat flapping furiously. 'That cyst's bally well mine!'

I looked at him over my mask. 'Oh, is it?' I said in surprise. 'I thought you'd gone to lunch.'

'Lunch! Have you ever known me to go to lunch during minor ops.? Of course I wasn't at lunch, you chump. I was having a dekko at a p.-m.–jolly interesting ruptured kidney–and having a chat about it with the Prof., if you must know.'

'Well, there's plenty more,' I said, picking up the cyst in a pair of forceps. 'I'll be finished in five minutes.'

'That isn't the bally point,' he went on crossly. 'The fact is, old chap, I particularly wanted to do that cyst. I've been looking forward to it all morning. And I might add it's pretty unethical to pinch another chap's patients, old chap.'

'It's also pretty unethical for a chap to go round the streets of London touting for custom.'

He blushed. For a few seconds he said nothing. 'I don't think I like your tone, old chap,' he muttered.

'And I don't ruddy well care if you don't.'

The patient, now alarmed that his medical advisers were about to come to blows over his body, reminded them of their obligations with a noise through the sterile towels like the neigh of a dying horse.

'I'll report you to the Prof.,' Bingham hissed, and swept out.

He revenged himself immediately by directing all the 'old chronics' to my desk. These patients were a human sludge in the machinery of St Swithin's, of which it could never rid itself. They appeared regularly with notes as large as the score of a symphony, on which the words 'Rep. Mist.' were scrawled in the writing of twenty successive house surgeons. These abbreviations entitled them to another bottle of medicine, the original purpose of which was generally forgotten and the original prescriber probably dead.

The old chronics that morning seemed unending as they shifted slowly up the benches towards me. By two o'clock there were still a dozen left; I hadn't had my lunch, and I was in a bad temper. Then I noticed a patient queue-jumping.

He was a shifty-looking, elderly man dressed in a shabby black coat and striped trousers. He had sneaked down the room and sat himself on the edge of the foremost bench. He held the finger of one hand in a bloodstained handkerchief, and he still wore his black Homburg hat. I knew his type well: we often saw head clerks and managers from surrounding offices who carried their self-importance on to the equalizing benches of the casualty-room, and we were encouraged by the Professor to stop it.

'One minute, missus,' I told a fat woman with some obscure but ancient condition of the feet. 'Now look here, daddy,' I began sharply, crossing to the interloper. 'What's the meaning of this?'

He looked up at me in alarm.

'Yes, I saw you,' I went on sternly. 'Thought you were being clever, didn't you? Sneaking up the side like that. You ought to be ashamed of yourself. You won't bleed to death with that little cut, and there's plenty of people in the room more seriously injured than you. Where's your treatment card, anyway?'

'Card? I–I'm very sorry, but–what card?'

'Can't you read, daddy?' I asked in despair. 'There's a notice the size of Marble Arch inside the door. It says all patients must ask the clerk for a treatment card. So hop off and get one.'

'I'm sorry, I didn't think—'

'Run along, daddy,' I said waving him away. I returned to the lady's feet, feeling in a better temper already. Medical pomposity is an invigorating draught to a young doctor.

Within a few minutes the man had returned with his card. Now he started hovering round the back of my chair. For a while I pretended to ignore him, then I turned round and demanded angrily, 'What the devil's the matter with you now, daddy? Why can't you go to the end of the queue like everyone else?'

'Yes, but you see, I *am* in rather a hurry—'

'So is everybody else. So am I, if it comes to that. Now get back to the last bench.'

'Perhaps I should explain—'

'I'm not in the slightest interested. If you don't jump to it I'll get you shifted by one of the policemen.'

His mouth opened in horror. I congratulated myself–I had judged my man shrewdly. A fellow of his type would be frightened by such an indignity.

'Really, I must say, Doctor, it's a most—'

'Now stop arguing. You can't chuck your weight around as usual in here. And for God's sake, daddy, *take your blasted hat off!*'

'What on earth's going on here?'

I spun round, and found the Professor looking down at me. I had hardly spoken to him before, because he was far too occupied with the higher problems of academic surgery to worry about the poultices and fingerstalls of the casualty-room. He was a chilly, scientific man with a gravelly voice and a long nose and chin like Mr Punch. He had only once been known to laugh, the day Sir Lancelot Spratt arrived at the hospital in a brand-new plum-coloured Rolls and was rammed by an ambulance in the courtyard in front of all his students.

'This patient, sir—' I began.

'Are you in some sort of trouble, Charles?' the Professor asked.

'Yes, I am. This young man here has been behaving extremely rudely.'

The Professor looked at me as if I were one of the rats in his laboratory developing an interesting disease.

'Perhaps I had better introduce my friend, Mr Justice Hopcroft,' he said slowly. 'He unfortunately happened to cut his hand while we were lunching at my club. I have been collecting some instruments to suture it.'

I stared at him in silence. I felt the casualty-room was revolving round me at high speed.

'What did you say your name was? It's slipped my mind since making the appointment.'

'Gordon, sir,' I croaked.

'Gordon, eh?' The Professor grunted and nodded his head several times, shaking it well into his memory.

'What name?' demanded Mr Justice Hopcroft, staring hard into my face.

I repeated it.

He grunted too. 'Gordon. Yes, Gordon. I'll remember that.'

As they disappeared into minor ops. it not only seemed likely that I wouldn't retain my job, but that my first brush with the law would land me in Dartmoor for life.

Chapter Two

For the next few weeks I read with equal anxiety the opinions that the Professor expressed in his case-notes on my diagnoses and those that Mr Justice Hopcroft expressed in court on the characters of his convicted criminals. Bingham now smirked every time he spoke to me, and had become intolerable. He was a bad case of the seasonal disease that struck the medical school known as 'Diplomatosis', which was characterized by delusions of grandeur and loss of memory for recent events. He had thrown away his ignominious short student's jacket, and appeared everywhere in a long white coat which he reluctantly removed only for meals; his stethoscope, which he had never carried secretly, now sprouted from his head proudly as the horns of a rutting deer; he hurried round the hospital with jerky, urgent strides, which implied that consultations of the gravest aspect waited round every corner; he addressed patients, relatives, and junior probationers like a Victorian practitioner breaking bad news; and the responsibilities of qualification left him too preoccupied to recognize the faces of fellow-students who had been less fortunate with the examiners.

I thought Bingham's most irritating performance was in the lift. As well as the wide lifts for stretchers, St Swithin's provided for the staff a small creaking cage that usually had a worn notice on the gate saying OUT OF ORDER, which was traditionally forbidden the students. Bingham now used this lift even to descend between adjoining floors; he was particularly careful to summon it when walking along the corridor with a crowd of students, and would wait for them to arrive breathless upstairs. 'Jolly convenient, the old lift,' he said to me one morning. 'Can't understand how we used to manage without it.'

I was not left much time to brood on him, for either the drivers and pedestrians of London were becoming more careless or I was becoming less efficient: the patients in the casualty-room never thinned until supper-time, and I often had to go without my lunch as well.

'I say, old chap,' he began late one evening, as the benches were at last clearing. 'How about buzzing up to the ward and having a quiz round some cases? There's an absolutely top-hole pyelonephrosis and a retroperitoneal abscess side by side–bet you half a dollar you can't spot which is which.'

'No thanks,' I said. 'As a matter of fact, I'm fed up at looking at suffering humanity for a bit. I'm going out for a pint.'

'Forgive me for saying so, old man, but it's hardly the way to get through the Fellowship, is it?'

'I don't care a monkey's damn for the bloody Fellowship at the moment. My feet hurt, I've got a headache, I want my supper, and I'm thirsty.'

'Yes, cas. is a bit of a bind. I'll be glad to get out of it next month and start proper surgery in the wards.'

I looked him in the eye. 'I will remind you that the post of senior house surgeon will go to only one of us.'

He smirked 'Of course, old man. I was sort of forgetting for a minute. Best man win, and all that, eh?'

'Exactly, Bingham.'

Another fortnight went by, and I began to hope that the Hopcroft affair might be forgotten by a busy man carrying the responsibilities of a surgical Chair. Then one afternoon the Professor appeared in casualty. He stood before my desk, looking at me with the same stare of scientific interest and holding in his hand a patient's treatment card.

'Did you write this?' he asked.

I looked at it. It was directed to the Surgical Registrar, a genial young specialist with whom I had played rugger and drunk beer, and who disliked Bingham almost as much as he did the Fellowship examiners. The card asked for his opinion on a suspected orthopaedic case, but in the stress of casualty I had scribbled only three words:

Please X-ray. Fracture?

Now I remembered with alarm that the registrar had the afternoon off to visit the Royal Society of Medicine, and the Professor was taking over his work.

'Yes, sir,' I admitted.

'Have,' he snapped. 'Isn't.'

He turned on his heel and disappeared.

Bingham said eagerly a few days later, 'The Prof. was talking about you this morning, old man.'

'Oh, yes.'

'I'd nipped into the theatre to have a dekko at him doing an adrenalectomy, and he asked if I knew what school you went to. I told him I couldn't say off-hand. Then he made a most surprising remark, old chap–he thought it was probably one of those progressive ones, where the kids learn all about self-expression and bash the teachers over the head with rulers but are never taught to read or write. I suppose you didn't really go to a place like that, did you?'

'As a matter of fact I did. We never learnt to read, write, do arithmetic, play cricket, or swap marbles, but at least we were brought up not to go around kissing the backsides of people we wanted to get jobs from.'

Bingham stiffened. 'I might say that's an extremely offensive remark, old chap.'

'I might say that I meant it to be. Old chap.'

My ambition to be a surgeon now burned low. But it was not extinguished until the week before my casualty job was to end.

Bingham and I lived on the top floor of the Resident Medical Staff Quarters at St Swithin's, a tall, gloomy building containing a couple of dozen bleak bed-sitters and a dining-room enlivened by a battered piano and a picture of Sir William Osler gazing at us chidingly down his sad moustaches. On the table was a collecting-box in which anyone talking shop at supper had to drop half a crown; this was labelled FUND FOR THE BLIND, and underneath in smaller letters *And What a Blind!* Every six months, when half the house surgeons left, this box was broached. As the Professor's retiring house surgeon had also passed his Fellowhip, found a new job, and become engaged on the same day, he asked me to take his night duty for him. I was delighted, because it showed I was capable of accepting higher surgical responsibilities. Also, it made Bingham furious.

There was usually a trickle of emergency cases entering St Swithin's during the night, but that evening I was disappointed to find that the admission-room inside the gate was quiet. About midnight I went to sleep, leaving Hamilton Bailey's *Emergency Surgery* beside my bed and my trousers hopefully receptive on the chair. I dreamed that I was in casualty, operating with a soup spoon on Bingham's double hernias without an anaesthetic, and I woke with a start to the porter's knock.

'What is it?' In a second I was scrambling out of bed, switching on the light, and jumping into my shoes. 'What's the time?'

''Arf past three. Case of intermittent abdominal pain. Getting worse over the last three days. Mostly subumbilical.'

'Really? Does the patient look very ill?'

'Nah. Came in a taxi.'

I immediately felt sorry: it looked as though I would not have the chance of assisting at an emergency operation. The porter stood picking his teeth while I pulled a sweater over my pyjamas. 'Gall-stone colic I reckon it is,' he said.

I made my way downstairs, through the cold, empty, black halls of the out-patients' department. It was a bitter night outside, with sleet falling heavily and freezing immediately on the pavement. There was no one in sight except a porter sweeping in the distance in the thin light of a lonely bulb. I suddenly felt that I was the only doctor in the world.

I found the patient sitting under a blanket on an examination couch. He was a thin, neat-looking man in a blue suit and a white collar, with a small moustache, carefully-brushed hair, and horn-rimmed spectacles. He looked worried, but unfortunately not like an immediate candidate for the operating table.

'Well now, what's the matter?' I began, as briskly as possible.

'I'm extremely sorry to have troubled you, Doctor. Extremely sorry indeed.' He spoke quietly, with a faint Cockney accent. 'I have took you away from your no doubt well-earned repose. I apologize, Doctor, and ask your forgiveness for that which I have done.'

'That's quite all right. It's what I'm here for.'

'I said to myself as I came in, "The doctor is now, no doubt, reclining in the arms of Morpheus. He is sleeping the sleep of—"'

'What's the matter with you, please?' I interrupted.

He suddenly clutched his abdomen with both hands and groaned.

'Abdominal pain?' I said, flicking the pages of my surgical text-book through my mind. 'Colicky, no doubt? Any relation to food?'

He relaxed, looked round, and whispered, 'Are we alone, Doctor?'

'Alone? I assure you, professional confidences will not be divulged.'

'You're the Professor's house surgeon, ain't you, Doctor?' I nodded. 'Well, Doctor, it's like this here. The Professor operated on me six months ago–partial gastrectomy, up in Faith Ward. All was well, Doctor, until three days ago. Then I began to have pains.' He groaned as another spasm caught him. 'Something shocking, Doctor. Tonight, after a bite of supper, I coughed and found something hard in my throat.' He glanced over his shoulder again and whispered, 'It was a nut, Doctor.'

'You mean you'd been eating nuts?'

'No, no, Doctor. I mean a metal nut. Then five minutes later I produced a screw. And after that two more nuts and a bit of spring. I've been bringing up bits of old iron all night, Doctor. So I thought I'd better come along here.'

'But dash it, man! That's almost impossible. Are you sure?'

'Look Doctor,' he said proudly. From his pocket he pulled a screwed-up piece of the *Evening News*, which held several bright nuts and bolts and a small coiled spring. We looked at them solemnly. Our eyes lifted and met. I licked my lips.

'They *could* have come from a surgical retractor,' I murmured.

He nodded. 'That's what I thought, Doctor,' he went on in a low voice. 'I know, see. Used to be in the R.A.M.C. Come to think of it, after my operation I heard a sort of rumour something might be missing.'

'Let me have a look at your stomach,' I said.

There was a gastrectomy scar, about six months old.

'Umm,' I said. I scratched my head. I looked up and down the room. There was no one in sight. Even Bingham would have been welcome.

'This might be serious,' I suggested.

'That's why I came in, Doctor,' he continued calmly. 'Mind, I'm not one of them people that makes trouble with law courts and that. But if anything happened. . . Well, I've got a lot of relatives, Doctor.'

'Quite,' I covered him with the blanket and began to walk round the couch slowly. The hospital rules were clear: all serious cases at night were to be referred immediately to a consultant. And if the Professor had somehow managed to leave a spring-loaded retractor inside an abdomen, he certainly would want to know of it before anyone else.

'I think we'll hang on for a bit,' I said. 'By eight o'clock I can get your notes from the registry and organize proper X-rays—'

He grabbed his stomach violently. 'Something else, Doctor,' he cried. 'Coming up!'

The Professor had a Wimbledon number, and after ringing a long time the telephone was answered by a cross female voice.

'Yes?'

'Could I speak to the Professor, please?'

'Who's there?'

'St Swithin's.'

'Oh dear, oh dear! Don't you ever leave the poor man in peace? Ar-thur!'

When the Professor reached the telephone, which seemed to be several minutes' walk from his bed, I began, 'I'm terribly sorry to bother you, sir. This is the house surgeon—'

'Rogers?'

'Er–no, not Rogers, sir. Gordon.'

I heard him draw his breath. 'Where's Rogers?'

'He's out for the night, sir.' I felt this was truthful, as I had seen him carried to bed. I steadfastly gave the Professor a brief clinical history of the case.

'It's perfectly possible, I suppose,' he admitted. I could tell that he was worried. 'I can't remember the case offhand, but six months ago I certainly had a new theatre sister . . . You're sure it's bits of a retractor?'

'Oh, definitely, sir.'

There was a pause.

'Very well,' he decided grudgingly. 'I'll drive in. The Lord only knows how I'll manage it this weather. Admit him to Faith, and get the theatre ready for an emergency laparotomy.'

'Yes, sir.'

'And–er, Gordon.'

'Sir?'

'It was quite right of you to phone me.'

'Thank you, sir!' I said in delight.

But he had already rung off.

I spent the next half hour organizing the operation. I woke the theatre sister and her staff, brought the night sisters and porters from their suppers, and ordered the night nurses on Faith Ward to prepare a bed with hot-water bottles and electric blankets. Then I went back to the patient, who was now lying quietly on the couch.

'Don't worry, old man,' I said heartily, slapping him on the shoulder. 'Everything's under control.' I glanced at my watch. 'The Professor will be here any moment, and he'll fix you up in no time.'

'Thank you, Doctor,' he said, with a sigh of gratitude. He took my hand touchingly. 'I'm real pleased with the way you've looked after me, Doctor.'

'Oh, it's nothing. Just part of the service.'

'No, honest I am, Doctor. Real pleased. Mind you, I've got a soft spot for doctors. Especially young doctors trying to get on in the world like you.'

'That's very kind of you.'

'As a matter of fact, Doctor,' he said more cheerfully, 'I'd like to meet you again when all this is over. Socially, you know.'

'Perhaps we will,' I said with an indulgent smile. 'Who knows?'

'I'd like you to come and stay with me for a weekend. I've got quite a nice little place in the country. Down by the river. It's an old castle I picked up cheap. There's a bit of shooting and fishing if you care for it. Private golf links, of course. So bring your clubs along, Doctor, if you play.'

'I don't think I quite—'

'Tell you what I'll do. I'll send the Rolls for you on the Friday afternoon. The chauffeur can pick you up here. You can't miss it, it's solid gold all the way through, even the piston-rings. Just looking at me now, Doctor,' he said proudly, 'you wouldn't think I owned the Bank of England, would you?'

I met Bingham in the lift.

'Hello, old chap.' He grinned. 'Sorry you didn't get the senior H.S. job and all that.'

'Yes, I'm sorry, too.'

'You had hard cheese rather, old chap, didn't you? About the loony, I mean. You ought to have had him X-rayed before calling the Prof. Or asked "patient's occupation" as your first question. I'd have done.'

'I suppose I ought.'

'Now you're going to look for a job in the provinces, aren't you? There's some jolly good hospitals outside London, so they tell me. Not up to St Swithin's standards, of course, but you might do pretty well in time. Do you want me to say goodbye to the Prof. for you? I don't suppose you'll want to see him again, will you–after that.'

'It happens I've just been to him. For my testimonial.'

'Any time I can be of help to you, old chap, just let me know.'

'Thanks.'

We reached the ground floor, and I got out.

'I'm going to the basement,' Bingham explained. 'Going to have a dekko at some slides in the lab. Now I'm senior H.S. I thought I'd better run over my path. and bact.' I slammed the gates. 'Don't expect I'll see you before you go, old chap. Got to give a talk to the new cas. H.S.–they don't seem to know a thing, you know, these chaps who've just qualified. Toodle pip!'

He pressed the button. The lift moved six inches and stopped. Bingham pressed all the other buttons in turn. Nothing happened. He rattled the gate. It wouldn't open.

'I say, old chap,' he called after me anxiously, 'I'm stuck in the lift.'

'So I see, Bingham.'

'Absolutely bally well stuck.' He gave a nervous laugh and rattled the lattice again. Several nurses, porters, and patients had gathered round to watch. Passengers were often stuck in the St Swithin's lift, which provided a regular diversion to the otherwise monotonous aspect of the corridors.

'I say, old chap.' His voice wavered. 'Get me out, will you?'

'But I don't think I know how.' Some of the nurses began to titter. 'Do you mean I ought to send for the fire brigade, or something?'

'No, dash it, old man. This is beyond a joke.' He rattled the gate loudly, terrified that his dignity was slipping away from him. 'Be a sport, old chap,' he implored. 'Get some help. You can't leave a pal like this, can you?'

'Oh, all right,' I said testily. I supposed even Bingham had human rights. 'Wait a minute.'

'Thanks, old chap. I knew you'd do the decent.'

As I strolled away as slowly as possible to fetch a porter, I noticed a loaded food trolley moving down the corridor with the patients' lunch. An idea struck me. When I returned to the lift I was pleased to see the crowd had doubled and Bingham was rattling the bars again.

'Ah, there you are, old chap!' he said with relief. 'You've been pretty nippy, I must–here! What's the idea?'

I slowly peeled half a bunch of bananas and poked them one after another through the bars. This simple pantomime delighted the audience, which had now been joined by a party of convalescents from the children's wards and blocked the corridor. Bingham himself became mildly maniacal.

'I won't forget this!' he spat at me. 'I won't bally well forget it! You wait and see!'

I left him still in the lift and walked straight out of the hospital, for the first time in my qualified career feeling reasonably contented.

On the bus I opened the Professor's testimonial. It was short:

To Whom It May Concern

Dr Gordon has been my Casualty House Surgeon for the past three months, in which time he has performed his duties entirely to his satisfaction.

Chapter Three

I began to open the *British Medical Journal* as the Chinese open their newspapers, from the back: the last twenty pages are filled with advertisements for jobs, and I suddenly found myself less concerned over the progress of medical science as a whole than the next source of my own bread and butter.

There were plenty of hospitals advertising for house surgeons in the provinces, so I bought a book of stamps and wrote a dozen elegantly-phrased applications. As I would receive free third-class tickets to attend the interviews I felt that at least I would see something of the country at the National Health Service's expense.

I soon found that I was not a success at interviews. First of all, the waiting-rooms upset me. Before an oral examination, a group of students enjoy the deep, sad comradeship of a bunch of prisoners awaiting the firing squad, but when a job is being decided the atmosphere in the ante-room is more like a lifeboat with the food and water running low. Although none of the candidates could have wanted work more urgently than myself, I always reached the empty chair at the foot of the committee table with subconscious feelings of guilt. This made me always say the wrong things, find difficulty in knowing what to do with my hands, fiddle with my tie, break pencils in two, and tear the sheet of pink blotting-paper into little bits.

I went through several interviews, though now they are as indistinguishable in my mind as different visits to the dentist's. They were all held in hospital board-rooms, containing a fireplace crammed with coal, three portraits of men in frock-coats suffering from obesity and hypertension, the hospital reports since 1840 bound in red leather, a bust of Hippocrates in the corner, and black panels of donations recording in gold leaf how ennobled local manufacturers cast their bread upon waters with reliable tides. In the middle of the room was a mahogany table that looked strong enough to support a tank, round which sat a dozen of the most intimidating people I had seen in my life.

It was important to decide on entering the room which of the committee were doctors and which were lay governors, in order to tune the pitch of each reply correctly–there was no point in giving a clinical examination answer to a wholesale draper in his best suit. At one of my earlier interviews I was asked solemnly by a man in a clerical collar. 'What would you do, Doctor, if you were operating alone at midnight and suddenly produced an unstoppable haemorrhage?'

Feeling sure of myself, I replied, 'Pray to God for guidance, sir.'

A small man on my right stirred. 'Don't you think, young fellow,' he said quietly, 'you might ring up a consultant surgeon before calling on the advice of an unqualified practitioner?'

I didn't get the job.

Some of the committees wanted to know if I played cricket, others if I played the piano; some if I were married, or if I were moral; one chairman asked my politics, another the names of my clubs. Whatever answers I gave never seemed to be the right ones: there was always a sharp silence, a slight 'Oh!' from somewhere, and the chairman was thanking me very much and saying they would let me know in due course. My saddest discovery of all was that an education at St Swithin's did not automatically waft you to the head of the profession on the sweeping bows of your colleages. We had been brought up to assume the same relationship to the graduates of other hospitals as Sherlock Holmes to Watson, and it was a shock to find someone who had never heard of the place.

'What's your hospital, lad?' demanded one florid, fat surgeon, who held the degree of a northern medical school never mentioned in our wards.

'St Swithin's, sir.'

'Ee, lad, you'll live it down,' he said, and everyone roared with laughter.

This was too much, even at an interview. 'I might say, sir,' I declared indignantly, 'that I am extremely proud of the fact. At least, they say you can always tell a St Swithin's man.'

'Aye, lad, and you can't tell him anything.'

I didn't get that job either.

After a disheartening month of cold train journeys I began to feel worried. I no longer faced the problem of finding a befitting start to my surgical career, but of keeping myself alive and fed. I had four pounds ten in the bank, one suit, a bag of golf clubs, a roll of minor surgical instruments, and a small plaster bust of Lord Lister. I lived in a furnished room in Muswell Hill, the weather was wet and icy, all my shoes needed repairing, I always seemed hungry, and my depressing circumstances made me want to drink twice as much as usual. My microscope had been sacrificed long ago, and my skeleton lay in a pawnbroker's near St Swithin's, whose cellars must have resembled the catacombs after a plague year.

The only objects of value left were my text-books. I looked at them, packing my landlady's cheap bookcase with their plump smooth backs and rich gold lettering, like a hungry tramp eyeing a flock of geese. For a week I resisted temptation. Then I decided that there were two or three volumes on subjects like public health and biochemistry that a rising surgeon could do without. Later I unashamedly took the lot, one after the other, to the second-hand medical bookshop in Gower Street, saying at every meal a grace to its provider. Whitby and Britton's *Disorders of the Blood* gave only bacon and eggs and coffee in a teashop; but Price's *Text-book of the Practice of Medicine* was much more nutritious, and ran to tomato soup, steak and chips, a pint of beer, and apple tart. I saved up *Gray's Anatomy* for my birthday, and when I at last carried *The Encyclopaedia of Surgical Practice* downstairs I booked a table at Scott's.

Soon I had nothing left but a few *Students' Aid* handbooks, *What to do in Cases of Poisoning*, and *A Table of Food Values*, which together would hardly have risen to tea and sandwiches. I therefore set out to my next interview, at a large hospital in Northumberland, determined to win the job. I stood in the waiting-room staring out of the window, trying to forget the other candidates; I marched into the committee room, clasped my hands under the table, and answered all the questions like an efficient policeman in court. This time I had the whole length of the table to myself with the committee in a line opposite, which somehow increased my confidence. I felt I was doing well, particularly when the tall surgeon in the corner who had been asking most of the questions nodded after investigating my career at St Swithin's, and said, 'That seems all very satisfactory. And you really mean to go in for surgery, do you?'

'Most certainly, sir,' I answered promptly. 'However much personal hardship it means at first, that's always been my ambition.'

'Excellent. That's the spirit I like to see in my house surgeons. Don't you agree, gentlemen?'

A heartening volley of grunts came across the table.

'Very well,' the surgeon said. 'Now Dr Bryce-Derry, our Chairman, will ask you a few routine questions.'

The Chairman, who sat immediately opposite me, was a pleasant-looking, youngish man in a tweed suit, a check shirt, and a homespun tie.

'Now, Dr Gordon,' he started with a smile. 'You're certain you really want to work in our hospital?'

'Yes, sir.'

His smile vanished. His lips tightened.

'You have been qualified a little over three months, I believe?'

'Yes, sir.'

He paused. He glared at me.

'You are a member of the Medical Defence Union, I take it?' he went on slowly.

'Oh, definitely, sir.'

I felt bewildered. There was suddenly an odd atmosphere in the room. All the committee members were either looking at the ceiling or staring hard on to their squares of blotting-paper. Nobody spoke.

'And of the B.M.A.?' the Chairman continued, now scowling.

'Y-yes, sir.'

This sudden malevolence was impossible to explain. I felt awkward and nervous, and wanted fresh air. I pulled out my handkerchief to wipe my forehead, and pushed back my chair. Then I saw opposite me under the table the edge of a tweed skirt, thick fish-net stockings, and a pair of sensible brogues.

'I–I'm terribly sorry, my dear sir–I mean madam–I–I–Oh, God!' I jumped up and ran for the door.

I didn't get that job, either.

In the train to London I pulled the latest medical journal from my overcoat pocket and sadly turned again to the advertisements, which were conveniently arranged alphabetically under specialities from Anaesthetics to Venereology. It seemed time to try my luck at a different branch of medicine. Bacteriology meant regular hours and no talkative patients, but there was always the risk of catching something like smallpox or plague. Tuberculosis offered work in pleasant country surroundings with plenty of fresh butter and eggs, but the drowsy routine of a sanatorium often drugs the doctors as well as the patients. Orthopaedics needed the instincts of a carpenter, and pathology the instincts of Burke and Hare. Radiology sent you to work in unhealthy, dark, dripping grottoes underground, and paediatrics meant children being sick over your trousers.

I looked gloomily through the window at the English industrial landscape thirstily soaking up an afternoon's rain, and tried to review my years at St Swithin's to find another subject for which I had shown some aptitude. But my education was represented in my memory only by a series of smells–there was the acrid smell of the first-year chemistry class, the soft smell of Canada balsam used for mounting zoology slides, the mixed stink of phenol and formaldehyde in the anatomy room, the rich aromatic breath of the biochemistry laboratory, the smell of floor-polish in the wards and ether in the operating theatre, and the smell in the post-mortem room like a badly-kept butcher's shop. I sighed, and reluctantly turned back the pages: there was nothing left but general practice.

Under *Practices (Executive Councils)* was printed *For vacancies (except those in Scotland) apply on Form EC16A, obtainable from the Executive Council. . . .* The first breath of bureaucracy! It had such a depressing effect that I turned to the less formal advertisements tucked among prospectuses for private lunatic asylums and offers of used cars and second-hand R.A.M.C. uniforms in the back. One on the cover itself struck me:

EMINENTLY SUITABLE FOR RECENTLY
QUALIFIED PRACTITIONER

1. Medical Officer in luxury liner on world cruise. America, South Seas, West Indies, Australia, Japan, India. Leaving almost immediately. All found and salary £2,000 per annum (in U.S. dollars).

2. Personal Medical Officer required by South African millionaire travelling widely Africa, America, Asia. Salary by arrangement, but money no object for suitable man. Apply at once.

3. General Practice. Suitable partner required for quiet practice in Wye Valley. Free sixteenth-century house, fully modernized, free fuel and food, free car and chauffeur, three months' holiday a year.

Many Other Similar Posts

Apply to
WILSON, WILLOWICK AND WELLBELOVED
Medical Agency

The address was not far from St Swithin's.

The next morning was foggy, my rent fell due, and I was developing a cold, but even from Muswell Hill the agency shone brightly with hope. I made for it directly after breakfast. I had never seen the office, but I found it at the top of a bare, sagging staircase between a hospital for chronic diseases and a pub.

On the door was a notice saying WALK IN. Inside was a small room lined with varnished planks, containing two plain wooden benches facing each other and fixed to the wall, like seats in a French railway compartment. Opposite was a door with a cracked, frosted-glass panel saying PRINCIPAL; there was a window curtained with London grime, and on the floor the small, upturned face of a circular electric fire gave a wan greeting. Sitting on one bench was a pale, thoughtful man about my age reading *The Journal of Neurology, Neurosurgery, and Psychiatry*, and on the other an old, untidy, dirty-looking fellow with an insanitary moustache and a crumpled trilby was staring at the floor and muttering.

I sat next to the young man. None of us spoke. I waited until both of them had entered and left the inner room, then I went in myself.

The office was smaller than the waiting-room, and contained a high, narrow desk at which a benevolent-looking old man with gold-rimmed glasses and side-whiskers was sitting on a stool. He was wearing a wing collar, a cravat, and an old frock-coat. A light in a pale green shade hung from the ceiling to the level of his nose.

'Mr Wilson, Mr Willowick, or Mr Wellbeloved?' I asked cheerfully. The sensation of applying for a job as a customer rather than a supplicant was unreasonably stimulating.

'Alas, Doctor, I am neither.' He smiled good-heartedly. He put down his pen and clasped his arthritic fingers. 'And what can I do for you?'

'I came about your advertisement. I'd like the millionaire one if it's still going, but if not I'll take the cruise liner instead. I can pack up and go any time. I'm perfectly free.'

'Alas, again, Doctor,' he said, still smiling kindly, 'but those vacancies are already filled.'

'But the advert. only came out yesterday!'

'The rush was very great. . . . However, I have many equally attractive posts to offer. You wish to go abroad, Doctor?'

'I wouldn't mind. As long as it's sunny.'

'Then I have just the very place. The Acropolos Oil Company–a Greek concern, but most respectable–require a doctor in Iraq. Most interesting. The first tour of duty is five years. I have the contract here—'

'I don't think I want so much sunshine as that.'

'Are you a man of faith, Doctor? You look it, to my eyes. A medical missionary is needed in Siam. The remuneration is admittedly not high, but–' he sighed–'one gains one's reward in Heaven.'

'I should prefer to gain my reward here.' I was beginning to feel disappointed. 'I suppose you haven't any ordinary practices? I'm working for my F.R.C.S., you know, and taking up surgery and all that. I thought I'd better get a bit of G.P. experience first.'

'Of course, Doctor.' He picked up another bundle of papers. 'I thought that you wished to leave the country for some reason or another. . . . Of course we have many practices. I wouldn't like to say how many bright young men like yourself I've set on their way. It's a sort of hobby, really. This'–he indicated the office–'is not my true habitat. Oh, dear me, no! You'd be surprised if you knew what it was. I have many interests. But once'–he became sad–'the life of one I hold very dear to me was saved by the skill of a young doctor. Now it is my only pleasure in life, helping such young men along their difficult path.' He looked as if he were about to burst into tears, and I was beginning to feel it was my lucky day. 'Some might call me eccentric, but–' He smiled faintly, and dabbed beneath his spectacles with a handkerchief. 'Forgive an old man's ramblings. I am always touched at the sight of a doctor at the threshold of his career.'

He became more business-like and continued, 'Here's just the thing for you. Semi-rural in the Midlands–the Dukeries, you know. *Loçum tenens.* I know the doctor personally. A most excellent gentleman and a fine clinician, a fine clinician. You will learn a great deal from him. And the remuneration, Doctor! All found and ten guineas a week. Not to be sneezed at, eh?'

I hesitated.

'It'll be gone by lunch-time, I guarantee.'

'Semi-rural, you said?'

'More than semi.'

'All right. I'll take it.'

'You're very wise, I think. Now I expect you'd like some money?' He chuckled. 'Forgive me, Doctor, forgive me! An old man's privilege. I know with young doctors things are often a little–strained. You'll need your books. And some equipment. Eh?' He drew an old leather wallet from his pocket, took out a packet of white notes, and laid them on the desk. 'A hundred pounds would perhaps be of use to you?'

'But–but you mean as a gift?' I said in amazement. 'It's ridiculous! I couldn't take it.'

'Well, let us call it a loan, then? Yes, a loan. I understand your embarrassment perfectly, Doctor—'

'I haven't a scrap of security—'

'That doesn't worry me in the least. Not in the least. Just to make you feel it's no more than a business transaction perhaps you'll sign here—'

I signed.

'There's a little interest, to make it less personal,' he admitted. 'Fifteen per cent per annum, payable quarterly. Now perhaps you'll favour me with a signature on this too, Doctor—'

'What is it?'

'Just the usual form about the practice. I take a small commission to pay for overheads. So expensive these days.' He blotted both my signatures. 'That'll be thirty-three and a third per cent of your salary for the first year. After twelve months you won't have to pay me a cent. Not a cent. Good morning, Doctor. Here's the address of your practice. Go as soon as you can, won't you? The train service is very good. Don't lose touch with me, now. That would never do. Send me a postcard. Goodbye, Doctor. Goodbye. Next, please.'

Chapter Four

I descended the stairs feeling as though I had nodded to a friend at an auction and found myself the purchaser of a large suite of Chippendale furniture. At the bottom I bumped absently into someone coming through the door.

'Sorry,' I mumbled.

A violent blow on the back sent me staggering.

'Richard, you old bastard.'

'Grimsdyke!'

We shook hands delightedly. Although we were close companions in medical school, I hadn't seen him since the afternoon he failed his finals.

'What the devil are you doing in this den of thieves?' he demanded at once.

'Looking for work.'

'God help you! Is Father Bloodsucker up aloft?'

I looked puzzled.

'Old Pycraft–the vile criminal in a frock-coat and brass glasses.'

I nodded.

'Damn! Sure it wasn't old Berry? Tall thin character, bald as a pillar-box?'

'No, it's Pycraft all right.'

He frowned. 'I thought it was Berry's day. He's almost human, sometimes. But Pycraft–Oh, hell! We must go and have a drink.'

'In case there's any danger of this developing into an all-day session,' I said as we stepped out, 'I must warn you that I've just been given a job to go to.'

'What, by those people? Then you'll need a drink. Come on, they're open.'

The lights of the pub next door sent a warm yellow welcome through the fog. The bar was old-fashioned and cheerful, with a sprightly young fire leaping in the grate and the landlord screened away behind an arrangement of mahogany and frosted glass that afforded a cosiness contemptible to modern pub architects.

After several minutes' conversational back-slapping, Grimsdyke ordered the drinks and asked through the barrier. 'Have you the morning paper–*Times* or *Telegraph*? Thanks.'

He searched for the City page and read closely through it, moving his lips.

'Forgive me, Richard,' he said, glancing up. 'I was all right at the close of yesterday's business, but I'm a bit worried about Cunard and Vickers. However, they're holding their own. Pretty satisfactory all round, I'd say. My brokers are the smartest chaps in the City, but I like to keep an eye on my investments. Ah, the beer!' He folded the paper and poked it back, 'To the happier days of our youth!'

'And our future prosperity!'

After the first draught I lowered my glass and looked at him in puzzlement. As a student he had more money than the rest of his companions together, and had presented a smart and fashionable contrast to the remainder of the medical school. Now he was wearing a torn mackintosh over a baggy Donegal tweed suit, and a frayed yellow-and-green check waistcoat with brass buttons. His shoes were worn, his collar curled, his cuffs were grubby; one of his gayest bow-ties flew from his neck in jaunty defiance of the rest of his outfit. There was a moment of embarrassment as he noticed my look, then he put down his drink and announced, 'I'm qualified.'

'Qualified? Congratulations, my dear fellow! But–but how? There hasn't been an exam. since the one you failed.'

He laughed. 'Not in London, certainly. But I take a broad view of the whole subject of examinations. I am now entitled to put after my name the proud letters "P.C.A.M." I am a Preceptor of the College of Apothecaries of Mayo. Ever heard of it?'

'I can't say I have.'

'You're far from the only one. You know I never saw eye to eye with the examiners here. I take an intellectual view of medicine, old lad, and let's face it–medicine isn't an intellectual subject. Any fool with a good memory and a sharp ear for squeaks and rumbles can become a doctor.'

'True,' I admitted sadly.

'I heard about the Mayo College from a bloke I met in a pub in Fleet Street. Apparently this useful institution is still allowed to award diplomas that put you on the *British Medical Register*, and no one's tumbled to it. It's like not paying any income tax in Jersey, and all that. I booked a ticket to Mayo and arrived a couple of days later. It was early in the morning, so I walked up and down the street looking for this College, but all I could find was a door with a bloody great brass knocker on it, which I knocked. Inside was an old hag scrubbing the floor. "Have you come to be made a doctor?" she said. "I have," I told her. "Upstairs," she said, and went on scrubbing.

'Upstairs was a sitting-room with a nice fire and a young fellow sitting reading the *Irish Independent* over his breakfast. When I acquainted him with the nature of my business he said he'd be delighted to accommodate me, and if I'd come back after the weekend I could have the examination. I told him that was ridiculous–I had many pressing engagements in London on Monday morning. He said he was sorry, but he was off playing golf in the country and there was nothing he could do about it. Eventually he said, "Well, the examination consists only of a *viva voce*, and seeing that there's only one candidate we can just as well hold it in the taxi. Hand me my golf clubs, Mr Grimsdyke, and we'll be off."

'In the back of the cab he started. "Now tell me something about urea?" I asked, "You mean that chemical substance, or are you referring to my lug-hole?" He said, "Well, we won't go into it further. How would you treat an old woman of eighty who went crazy one Sunday afternoon and fell down and broke both legs?" I thought a good bit, and said, "I would bring about the unfortunate creature's timely demise with the soothing juices of the poppy." He agreed, "I think that's about right. I'm anti-clerical myself." He asked me a few more questions walking down the platform, then took his clubs and said I'd passed and the examination fee was fifty guineas. It happened I had fifty-odd quid on me, so he stuffed them in his mackintosh pocket and wrote out the receipt on a bit of newspaper. As the train left he yelled out of the window that my diploma would follow, and sure enough it did. Damn great thing with a seal on like the Magna Carta. I hear the Government's got wind of the place now, and they're going to shut it down. Shall we have the other half? Your turn.'

When I had ordered the drinks, Grimsdyke continued, 'That was the beginning of my troubles. You remember my grandmother's bequest–a thousand a year during my training to be a doctor? That stopped on the nail, of course. In short, my financial affairs were unprepared for the sudden disaster of my passing, as I had already got through the next three or four years' allowance on tick. A certain amount of retrenchment was necessary. Visits to the pop-shop. The car's gone, and so have the golf clubs. Even some of the suiting. Hence the appearance of having dropped off a hay-cart. Damn unpleasant.'

'But why on earth,' I demanded, 'did you ever bloody well qualify at all? You could have gone on failing and stayed a medical student the rest of your life. At a thousand a year, that's what I'd have done.'

'Pride, old lad,' he explained, looking into his glass sadly. 'Do you know why I failed my finals in London? I was doing damn well in the clinical. It was one of those days when golf-balls look the size of footballs and the greens as big as Piccadilly Circus–you know. The physical signs were sprouting out of my patient like broccoli. I found he'd got effusion at his left base, and I spotted he was fibrillating. I even heard his diastolic murmur, a thing I'd never been able to accomplish all my years in the medical school. Gave me quite a start. I trotted all this out to the examiner, feeling pretty pleased with myself. He kept nodding and saying, "Quite so, Exactly. Excellent", and I saw myself bowing out in a lofty sort of way to the applause of the assembled company. Then he asked, "Anything else?" And I said, "Impossible, sir!" And do you know,' said Grimsdyke savagely, banging his glass on the bar, 'the bloody patient had a glass eye. And the old fornicator failed me.'

'That really is hard luck,' I said sympathetically.

'Particularly as I'd been out the night before with Nicky Nosworth from Guys, who's had a glass eye for years. In fact, he showed me the bloodshot one he's got for the morning after, and the one he upsets everyone with when he gets bottled, with crossed Union Jacks instead of a pupil.'

We drank in silence for a few moments, contemplating this tragedy.

'All you fellows had got through,' Grimsdyke continued. 'So I thought, "To hell with the cash! I can damn well be a doctor too!" and look where it's got me.'

'There's always your investments.'

'Ah, yes,' he sighed. 'My investments.'

'Have you got a job?'

'I'm a sort of chronic *locum tenens*. Life really got difficult when I fell into the hands of the crooks next door. You must have been pretty hard put to it, ending up with those financial fiends?'

'I was. The cash was running pretty low. I had to get work somewhere, and I was lured by their advertisements.'

He nodded. 'How much is the job paying?'

'Ten guineas a week.'

'You ought to have stuck out for sixteen, at least. I suppose you've never been in practice before?'

I shook my head.

'Then watch out. It's not the doctors who are the trouble–it's their wives. Remember that, old lad, if nothing else. By the way, can you lend me some money? My investments take practically every penny these days.'

'Of course! My small resources are at your disposal.'

'I suppose Wilson, Willowick, and Wellbeloved pressed a hundred quid on you? A tenner will do me. Here's my card, though I hope you won't have to remind me. I may be poor, but I'm still honest. Thanks, old lad. Do you want any tips for the market? No? Then your very good health.'

Before going to my practice I had two essential purchases to make.

I went to a ready-made tailor's in Oxford Street and gingerly walked through the chromium halls looking at the dummies, which demonstrated that the suits fitted all right if you were in the grip of *rigor mortis*. I was sneaking towards the door when a salesman sprang at me from a thicket of Shaftesbury Avenue tweed, and within a minute was helping me off with my clothes in a cubicle.

'I want something for–er, business. Pretty dark and dignified, you know.'

'But you don't want to look like an undertaker's clerk, sir, do you?'

'No, I certainly don't want to look like an undertaker's clerk.'

'How about this, sir?' he said, briskly producing a suit with the air of a *maître d'hôtel* offering something exceptionally choice from the kitchen. It was a blue tweed, with a pronounced herring-bone, a mauve check overlay, and a faint red stripe. 'Wears like tin plate, sir. Just feel. Lovely bit of cloth. Magnificent quality. You won't be seeing anything like this again, sir.'

The suit certainly looked good value; but the pink lights and rosy mirrors in the shop would have sold out a stock of sackcloth and ashes.

'The sleeves are a bit long,' I said dubiously.

'They'll work up in no time, sir. Never fear.'

'All right, I'll take it.'

'I'm sure you'll be very satisfied, sir,' he said, immediately wrapping it up. He winked. 'You'll be cutting quite a dash with this at the Palais on Saturday nights, eh, sir?'

My next necessity was a car. A G.P. without a car is as useless as a postman without legs, but I had less than seventy pounds left with which to buy one. I looked wistfully in the manufacturers' showrooms in Piccadilly, where brand-new cars were displayed as carefully as the cigarette-cases in the jewellers next door, but even the second-hand ones in Euston Road garages were beyond my means. I finally arrived at a bomb-site in Camden Town where a line of cars with prices whitewashed on their windscreens stood under a banner saying HONEST PERCY PICK.

'Lovely job, this one,' said Percy Pick, kicking a tyre affectionately. He managed his business without moving his hands from his pockets, his hat from his head, or his cigarette from his mouth. 'Good for another fifty thou., easy.'

'The price is a bit steep for me, I'm afraid.'

He snorted. 'Garn! Don't expect me to give it away, do yer? I'll come down to a 'undred.'

I shook my head.

'How about this?' He slapped a bonnet in a row of cars waiting pathetically to be bought like puppies in a dogs' home. 'Only one owner.'

'He must have died a very old man.'

'How about a mo'bike if you're so broke?'

'How much is that one over there?' In the corner of the site was a large, black, heavy, hearse-like car which looked as immobile as a chicken-coop. Percy Pick seemed surprised to see it.

'You can have it for fifty,' he said quickly.

'Does it go?'

'Go? Of course it goes. All my cars go.'

'Very well,' I said. 'Let's see.'

The next morning I set off to my practice, wearing my new suit and driving my new car, reflecting that I had already learnt much of the sordid world outside the over-protective walls of St Swithin's.

Chapter Five

The journey north was exciting, for neither the car–which I had christened 'Haemorrhagic Hilda'–nor I had been on the road for some time. Hilda was originally an expensive limousine, but now she was constructed of so many spare parts that I thought of her fondly as the bastard of some noble line. Her vertical windscreen, which opened horizontally across the middle, was colourful with rainbows and bright with stars; there was worm in the dashboard, where all the dials pointed to zero except the engine temperature, which was stuck at boiling; her furnishings had been replaced by a former owner, and now consisted of a pair of bucket seats from an old baby Austin perched on a fruit-box in front, and an ordinary small domestic horse-hair sofa in the back. Behind the sofa were pieces of sacking, some old gnawed bones, a yo-yo, and scraps of newspaper prophesying the fall of Ramsay MacDonald's government. The front windows would not open, and the back windows would not shut. Birds had nested under the roof, and mice under the floorboards.

The mechanical part of Haemorrhagic Hilda aroused my clinician's interest rather than my alarm. The engine produced more rales, sibili, and rhonchi than a ward of asthmatics, and the steering gear, which had a wheel fit for a London bus, was afflicted with a severe type of *locomotor ataxia*. The only pleasant surprise was the horn. This was a long silver trumpet creeping from the windscreen to coil comfortably over the bonnet and front mudguard, which in squeezing the rubber bulb sounded like feeding-time in the seal pool. Hilda's other surprisingly good point was her brakes, which I shortly had a chance of demonstrating.

Outside Stony Stratford a police car waved me to the roadside.

'You the owner of this vehicle?' the policeman demanded, taking my licence.

'And proud of it,' I said cheerfully.

'I suppose you know there are regulations concerning the roadworthiness of motor vehicles?' he said in the tone used by Customs officers asking you to open the other suitcase. 'Is the vehicle equipped with an efficient braking system?'

'Brakes? Absolutely wonderful, officer. She can pull up on a postage stamp.'

'I am going to test the truth of your statement. Proceed along the highway at a reasonable speed. I will follow, and when I blow my horn apply your brakes.'

'Right-ho,' I said bravely.

I swung the engine, wondering what was going to happen: if the police decided to hound Hilda off the road, I would not only arrive late but lose the greater part of my working capital as well.

After I had travelled a few hundred yards my thoughts were interrupted by the urgent blast of a horn behind me. As I drove the brake-pedal into the floorboards I realized that it was not the policeman but a Bentley sweeping past our procession at eighty. There was a crash behind, and my windscreen fell on to the bonnet. As Haemorrhagic Hilda had been built in the same spirit as the Pyramids, she suffered only another dent in the rear mudguard; but the police car lay with its wheels turned out like flat feet, bleeding oil and water on to the roadway.

'You'll hear more about this,' the policeman kept muttering, as I dressed the small cut on his nose. I gave him a lift to the next telephone box, and continued my journey in an unreasonably cheerful frame of mind.

I began to move down the psychological slope towards depression as I entered the district where I was to work. It was a small English industrial town, which like many others stood as a monument to its own Victorian prosperity. There were long solid rows of grimy houses, factories walled like prisons, and chapels looking like pubs or pubs looking like chapels on every corner. There was a Town Hall ringed by stout old gentlemen petrified as they rose to address the Board, the station was a smoky shrine to the Railway Age, the football ground was a mausoleum of past champions, and the streets had not yet echoed the death rattle of their trams. Only the main thoroughfare had been changed, and consisted of cinemas, multiple chemists, tailors, and cheap chain-stores, looking exactly like anywhere else in the country.

Shortly it began to rain, though from the soggy ground and the depressed aspect of the pedestrians it appeared to have been raining there continuously for several years. I became gloomier as I searched for my address on the other side of the town, and finally drove into a long road of gently dilapidating Victorian villas behind caged gardens of small trees shivering in their seasonal nakedness. On the last door-post I spotted a brass plate.

The front door was opened by a cheerful-looking young blonde in overalls, holding a broom.

'Is Dr Hockett in?' I asked, politely raising my hat. 'I'm Dr Gordon.'

'Well, fancy that, now! I said to the Doctor this morning, I said, "I'm sure he ain't coming!"' She grinned. 'Silly, ain't I?'

'I was delayed on the road. I had to give medical attention in an accident.'

'The Doctor ain't in yet, but give us your bags, and I'll show you up to your room.'

As she climbed the dark stairs with my two suitcases, the maid called over her shoulder, 'You ain't 'arf young.'

'Well, I'm–I'm not exactly in the cradle, you know,' I said, wondering whether to feel flattered.

'Garn! I bet you ain't any older than what I am. The Doctor's had some real old fogeys, I can tell you. Old Dr Christmas was the last one–Cripes! He must have been ninety. Real old dodderer. Then there was Dr O'Higgins and Dr O'Rourke and Dr O'Toole–grandpas, they were. And before them there was Dr Solomons and Dr Azzis and Dr Wu—'

I was alarmed. 'There's been quite a number of assistants here?'

''Undreds and 'undreds of 'em.'

'Oh.'

'Here's your room,' she said brightly, opening a door at the top of the last flight of stairs. It was a bedroom the size of a cell, and furnished as sparsely. She dropped the cases and flicked briefly at the enamel washbasin with her duster. 'Bit chilly this weather, but it's comfy enough in summer.'

'Home from home, I assure you,' I murmured, looking round.

'You can get a nice fug up if you keep the window shut. Dr Wu, now–he used to burn incense and things. You won't be doing that, will you?'

'Not very much.'

'The light's switched off at the main at eleven, you pays your own laundry, it's extra if you've got a wireless, and you can have a bath on Saturday mornings,' she went on cheerfully. 'That's the Doctor's orders. He likes to keep an eye on the housekeeping.'

'I should ruddy well think he does!' This seemed too much to tolerate, even as a junior *locum*. 'Far be it for me to judge a man in advance,' I told her, 'but I must say he seems a bit of a mean old devil.'

'He can be a bit stingy sometimes, that's straight. Likes to look after the pennies.'

I sat down on a bed as unresilient as a park bench, and contemplated the discouraging start to my career as a general practitioner. The blonde continued to grin at me from the doorway, and I wondered if she was waiting for a tip; but as I felt in my pocket she went on, 'I must say, it is nice to see someone from London Town again. How's the old place getting along?'

'About the same I suppose. I thought you weren't a local girl,' I added.

'Not me! I ain't one of them provincials. 'Ow did you guess?'

I hesitated. 'You have a sort of sophisticated air about you.'

'Go on with you! I suppose you don't know the old "Bag o' Nails" in Ludgate Circus, do you? I used to be behind the bar there for a bit.'

'What, old Harry Bennett's pub? I know it very well. Often went there with a lot of chaps from Bart's.'

Her face took a tender look. 'Dear old Harry Bennett! After all these years! Funny you should know it, ain't it? We'll have a good old pijaw about it as soon as you're settled in. It'll be just as good as a holiday for me.'

'Have you been out here long?'

'Near on four years. I've got an old mum, you know–' A door slammed. 'The Doctor!' she gasped. 'Cheery-bye,' she whispered. 'I'll say you'll be down in a minute.'

I found Dr Hockett in the gloomy living-room, where the table was laid for high tea. He was standing in a green tweed overcoat in front of the gas fire, which was unlit. He was a tall, stooping man of about fifty, with a thin lined face and a thick grey moustache. His hands were clasped behind him and his gaze was fixed on his toes; his only movement as I entered was turning his eyes sharply up and glaring at me beneath his eyebrows, which hung across his face like tuft of steel wool.

'Good afternoon, sir,' I said politely.

'Good afternoon, Doctor. I had expected you a little earlier.' He spoke in a soft monotone, as though saying his prayers. Taking one hand from behind his back he shook mine flaccidly and replaced it. 'Remarkably warm for the time of year, isn't it?'

'Well, it strikes a little chilly up here after London.'

'No, I don't think it does,' he went on. 'I always wear wool next to the skin, Doctor. That is much more hygienic than filling the house with the fumes of combustible gases. If that is your car outside, you will have to leave it in the open overnight. There is only room in the garage for mine, and as it is no more than a few years old I don't intend to expose the coachwork. I often do my nearer visits on bicycle–it is much more healthy to take exercise in the open air. You might like to follow my example, though as you're paying your own petrol bills it's entirely up to you. We could make an arrangement by which you had part use of the bicycle, and I would make the appropriate deduction from your salary.'

As I said nothing he continued muttering, 'You've not been in general practice before, I believe? No, I thought not. The work here is hard, but the experience will be sufficient reward in itself.'

The door opened, and the blonde maid entered with a tray containing a large brown enamel teapot, a loaf of bread, a packet of margarine, and a small tin of sardines, half-empty.

'It is much healthier for the alimentary tract not to be overloaded with a heavy meal at night,' Dr Hockett continued, still looking at his feet. 'I never take further food after this hour, but if you wish to buy yourself some biscuits or suchlike for later consumption, of course I have no objection. Shall we sit down?'

He took off his overcoat and sat at the head of the table. Seeing a third place, and suddenly remembering Grimsdyke's warning, I broke the silence by asking, 'Are you married, sir?'

He gave me another glance under his eyebrows.

'I didn't quite catch your remark, Doctor,' he muttered. 'I thought you said, "Are you married?"' As the blonde took the third chair he went on, 'Pour the doctor his tea first, my dear. Possibly he likes it weaker than we do. Will you take a sardine, Doctor? I see there are one and one-third each. What, nothing at all? Perhaps after the excitement of your journey you are not very hungry? Well, it is best in the circumstances not to overwork the metabolism.'

Chapter Six

The shock of finding the Cockney blonde was Hockett's wife did not lead to my losing much nourishment. Nothing followed the bread and sardines, Hockett maintaining that margarine was biochemically the superior of butter, and weak tea had a low caffeine content which prevented eventual nervous, alimentary, and moral degeneration. The wife, whose name I gathered was Jasmine, said little because she ate steadily through a pile of bread and margarine; but while Hockett was carefully mopping up the sardine oil with his bread I was horrified to see her wink at me.

As we rose from the table Hockett was struck by an afterthought. 'You *didn't* take sugar, did you, Doctor?' he muttered.

'It's all right, I can do without it at a pinch.'

'I'm so glad, Doctor. Extremely unhealthy, sugar. Pure carbohydrate. Surplus carbohydrate in the diet leads to obesity, and then what? We all know that obesity is a cause of arteriosclerosis, arteriosclerosis causes heart failure, and heart failure is fatal. Taking sugar in the tea is suicidal, Doctor.'

'I want the fire on,' Jasmine declared.

'Do you, my dear? But it's extremely warm. I find it warm enough, anyway. So does Dr Gordon. You feel warm, don't you, Doctor? A remarkably mild winter we're having.'

'I'm frozen to the marrow, I am,' Jasmine said. She clutched herself and shivered dramatically.

'Very well, my dear,' he said with an air of solemn generosity, as though reading her his will. 'You shall have the fire. Doctor, do you happen to have a match on you?'

This conversation had taken place in the dark, as the daylight had been fading swiftly during the meal and neither of them had thought of turning on the light.

'Very restful, the twilight,' Hockett continued, stumbling over the furniture as he groped for the switch through the blackness. 'Extremely valuable for restoring the sensitivity of the retina. We suffer from far too much light.'

He lit the fire, carefully turned it half down, sat in a chair beside it, and began reading the *Daily Express* steadily from the headlines to the printer's name at the foot of the last sheet.

'You may smoke, if you wish, Doctor,' he said, looking up. 'We ourselves do not—'

'Liable to give fatal disease of the lung, you mean?'

'Exactly. If you wish for something to read, there are some books on the table behind you. They were left in the waiting-room by patients, but I expect they are perfectly readable.'

I started on *Pears' Cyclopaedia*. When I became tired of reading this, I stared for a while at a stuffed duck in a glass case opposite. Once I had seen enough of the duck, I took another dip into *Pears*. Jasmine sat between us knitting, and every time I looked at her she winked. Thus the evening passed.

At nine o'clock Jasmine yawned and said, 'I'm off to get a bit of kip.'

'Very wise of you, my dear. Early to bed and early to rise is a perfectly sound motto physiologically.'

'Good night one and all,' she said cheerfully, gathering her knitting. 'Sleep tight, Dr Gordon.'

As soon as she had left the room Dr Hockett turned the fire out.

'Sweltering in here, Doctor, isn't it? Now that my wife has retired we can have a talk on professional matters. I don't like to discuss such things in front of her. First of all, your duties. You will see the National Health patients twice a day at the surgery in Football Ground Road, and take all the night calls. I see the rest and the private patients, such as they are, in my consulting-room here. I don't go out at night.' He gave me another look under his eyebrows. 'I don't like leaving Jasmine alone. She is still very young.'

'Quite understandable.'

There was a pause.

'A very attractive woman, Jasmine,' he added.

'Most attractive, sir,' I agreed politely. As he continued to stare at me in silence, I shifted in my chair and added, 'I mean, in a sort of utterly platonic way, and all that, you know.'

After gazing at me for several more seconds he suddenly produced a key on a string from his waistcoat pocket. 'This is the duplicate key of the drug cupboard in my surgery next door. There are only two keys in the house. Please see that the cupboard is always locked. I do not think it wise for Jasmine to have access to it.' He handed me the key and went on, 'Jasmine is in many ways somewhat childish. As we are to work closely together, Doctor, I think it best for me to confide in you now. It may come as a shock to you to hear that Jasmine was my daily maid before becoming my wife.'

'No! Really?'

'I had practised abroad for many years. Out East. I never married. Marriage somehow seemed always beyond my means. However, when I settled here–I nevertheless love Jasmine very deeply, Doctor,' he continued, staring hard. 'I would not like to see anyone harm a hair of her head.'

'That's the spirit,' I said brightly. I was now feeling badly in need of a drink. 'After all, you're her husband and all that, aren't you?'

'Yes, Doctor,' he murmured. 'I *am* her husband.'

He then rose, switched out the light, and suggested we went to bed.

Breakfast the next morning was tea and porridge. Dr Hockett didn't believe in overloading the gastric absorption so early in the day.

The meal was begun in silence, because Hockett was attending to his morning mail. The general practitioner's daily postbag is filled with advertisements from the pharmaceutical firms and boxes of free samples, which are passed by most of their recipients directly into the waste-paper basket. But Hockett carefully opened each one, smoothing out the envelopes for future use and reading the shiny pages of advertisements from the coloured slogans at the top to the formulae in small type at the bottom.

'Surely, sir, you don't believe in all that rubbish?' I asked. I felt I had been bullied long enough in the house, and I had slept sufficiently badly to have the courage of a bad temper. 'At St Swithin's we were taught to chuck advertisements away unopened.'

'On the contrary, Doctor, I find I derive a great deal of medical information from them. One of the difficulties of a general practitioner is keeping up with the latest work. And all the medical journals are so infernally expensive.'

'But look at the muck they send in free samples! No G.P. in his right mind would prescribe it. This, for instance–' I picked up a large bottle of green liquid labelled DR FARRER'S FAMOUS FEMALE FERTILITY FOOD.

'Careful, Doctor! Don't drop it. As a matter of fact I keep all the samples. I have several hundred in the cupboard in my consulting-room. My private patients seem glad enough of them.'

'You charge for them, I suppose, sir?' I asked coldly.

'Naturally,' he replied without hesitation. 'Patients do not appreciate what they do not pay for. That is surely recognized as one of the evils of the National Health Service? Now I really think you should be getting along, Doctor–your surgery is well over a mile away, and it is bad for the practice to arrive late.'

I drove Haemorrhagic Hilda through the rain towards Football Ground Road, trying to suppress my feelings. If I were to be a G.P. I was going to be a damn good one, despite Hockett, Jasmine, a bed as uncomfortable as the rack in the Tower, and the effects of incipient frostbite and starvation. This determination wavered when I saw the surgery itself: it was a shop-front with the glass painted bright green and DR HOCKETT'S SURGERY written across it in red, like the window of a four-ale bar.

There was already a queue of patients on the pavement as I unlocked the door. Inside I found a single room filled with parish-hall chairs, with a partitioned cubby-hole for the doctor in the corner. This cubby-hole was largely filled with filing cabinets, though there was an old examination couch, a small stained desk, a basin, a Bunsen burner, and an oil stove, which I immediately lit. I washed my hands, took out my fountain-pen, put my head round the cubby-hole door, and said, 'First patient, please.'

A fat mother accompanied by a fat adolescent schoolgirl rose from the first line of chairs, and advanced on me with the expression of purposeful dislike used by women when demanding to see the manager.

'*Adiposa familians*,' I said brightly, as they entered.

'What's that?' the mother asked sharply.

'A Latin expression. Medical terminology. You wouldn't understand it.' I waved them towards the two chairs jammed beside the desk, placed my finger-tips together, and began, 'Now, what's the trouble?'

'Where's the doctor?' the mother asked.

'I am the doctor.'

'No, the real doctor.'

'I assure you I am a perfectly real doctor,' I said calmly. 'Surely you don't want me to produce my diploma?'

'You're Hockett's new boy, are you?'

'I am Dr Hockett's most recent assistant, certainly.'

She assessed me for some seconds.

'Well, I can't say I like the idea much of you meddling with our Eva,' she declared. Eva was meanwhile staring at me malevolently, saying nothing, and picking her nose.

'Either you want me as your daughter's medical attendant or you don't,' I said emphatically. 'If you don't, you can take your National Health card elsewhere. I assure you I shall have no regrets about it whatever.'

'It's the chest,' she said, nodding towards the girl.

'What's wrong with the chest?'

'Cough, cough, cough all night long she does. Why, I never get a wink of sleep, I don't sometimes,' she added indignantly.

'And how long have you had this cough, Eva?' I asked, with my best professional smile.

She made no reply.

'Very well,' I said, picking up my stethoscope. 'I'd better start by examining her, I suppose. Off with your things, now.'

'What, you mean take all her clothes off her chest?' the mother asked in horror.

'I mean take all her clothes off her chest. Otherwise I shall not be able to make a diagnosis, we won't be able to start treatment, Eva will get worse, and you won't get any sleep.'

Eva said nothing as her mother peeled away several layers of cardigans, blouses, and vests. At last her chest was exposed. I laid my stethoscope over the heart, winked at her pleasantly, and said with a smile, 'Big breaths.'

A look of interest at last illuminated the child's face. She glanced at me and grinned. 'Yeth,' she said proudly, 'and I'm only thixteen.'

The morning passed quickly. The patients came steadily to my cubby-hole, though every time I began to think of lunch and peeped outside there seemed to be as many waiting as ever. I was relieved to find that my work was reduced through most of them not needing a full diagnosis and treatment, but only a 'Sustificate, Doctor'. I signed several dozen of these, certifying that people were in a state to stop work, start work, go to the seaside, stay away from court, have a baby, draw their pension, drink free milk, and live apart from their relatives. I gained confidence with every signature, and was beginning to feel I had a flair for general practice when I came against the case of the cheerful old lady.

'Hallo, Doctor,' she began. 'And how are you this fine morning?'

'I'm extremely well,' I said, delighted to have a pleasant patient. 'I hope we'll find that you are too.'

'I'm not so dusty. Especially considering. Do you know how old I am, Doctor?'

'Not a day over fifty, I'll be bound.'

'Go on with you, Doctor!' She looked coy. 'I'm seventy next birthday, that's a fact.'

'You certainly don't look it,' I told her briskly, feeling it was time to start the professional part of the interview. 'And what's the trouble?'

'Trouble?' She looked startled, as if I had asked her whether she wanted lean or streaky. 'There ain't no trouble, Doctor.'

'Then why–forgive me if I ought to know–have you come to the doctor's?'

'To get another bottle of me medicine, of course.'

'Ah, I see.' I put my finger-tips together again. 'And what sort of medicine is this?'

'The red medicine, Doctor. *You* know.'

'I mean, what do you take it for?'

'The wind,' she answered at once.

'You suffer from the–er, wind?'

'Oh, no, Doctor!' She was now humouring the teasing of a precocious child. 'Haven't had the wind for years, I haven't.'

'And how long have you had the medicine?'

'Oh–let me see–I first 'ad it the year we went to the Isle of Wight–no, it couldn't be that year, because our Ernie was alive then. It must have been the year after. Except it couldn't have been, because we had our Geoff with us, and he's been under the sod a good fifteen—'

'Quite,' I interrupted. I saw before me as clearly as the eyesight chart hanging from the wall the Ministry of Health circular on extravagant prescribing. 'Well, I'm afraid you can't have any more medicine. You're as sound as a bell, really, and you don't need it. Take a walk in the park every day instead. Good morning to you.'

At first she didn't believe me. Then she said in a sad faint childish voice, 'But I must 'ave me medicine, Doctor.'

'You really don't need it.'

'But I always 'ave me medicine, Doctor–always. Three times a day regular after meals–' Then she suddenly burst into tears.

'Now please control yourself,' I said anxiously. I began to wish I had taken the Hospital Secretary's advice and chosen the Army. 'It's nothing to do with me. It's simply a Ministry regulation. If it was up to me you could have a dozen bottles of medicine a day. But we doctors have to cut it down.'

'I want me medicine!' she cried.

'Dash it! Do you wish to unbalance the Budget and ruin the country? Please be reasonable.'

Suddenly her grief became anger. Beating the desk with her umbrella she shouted, 'I want me medicine! I know me rights! I've paid me National 'Ealth like everyone else!'

'I will not stand for this,' I said, wondering if there was anything in the Hippocratic Oath against losing your temper. 'Kindly leave the surgery.'

'You thief! You robber! That's what you are! Taking all them shillings every week from poor folk like me what can't afford it! I know what 'appens to them insurance stamps! I know! Lining the pockets of the doctors, that's what! I want me medicine!'

She left the cubby-hole, but repeated her demand to the patients who had been listening intently outside, inciting them to riot. I held my head in my hands. For five years at St Swithin's I had probably ruined my health through overwork and deprived my parents of the last comforts of their declining years–for this. It would have been easier to face if I had eaten a nourishing breakfast.

'Sit down,' I said dully, hearing another patient enter. 'Name, age, and occupation?'

'Wilkins. Twenty-one. Trades union organizer.' A youth in a tight blue suit sat down, still wearing his hat. 'But I ain't a patient. At least, not at the minute.' He spoke softly and slowly, as though demanding my money and valuables in an alley on a dark night. 'You've upset my mother you 'ave.'

'If that lady outside is your mother, I'd be obliged if you'd kindly take her home.'

'Under the Regulations for the Conduct and Control of the National Health Service,' he continued, staring at the ceiling, 'a patient what receives inefficient service from a doctor can state a case before the local Executive Council, who, if they shall decide the facts proved, shall deduct an appropriate fine from the doctor's remuneration.'

I lost my temper.

'Get out!'

'Take it easy, Doc., take it easy,' he continued in the same tone. 'I'm not saying nothing against you–I'm only quoting regulations, see? It just happens that I know 'em.'

'And I suppose you go round making a damn good thing out of it?'

Picking his front teeth with a matchstick, he continued, 'I'd be careful what I was saying, if I was you, Doc. There's a law of libel in the land, don't forget. As a matter of fact, I've had five cases against doctors. Won every one. All fined. I'm worth near a thousand quid a year to the Executive Council, I'd say.'

'Now look here, Mr Watkins—'

'Wilkins.'

'I don't care who the bloody hell you are or what you intend to do, but if you don't get out of here at once I'll kick your ruddy coccyx so hard—'

'Violence won't get you nowhere,' he said imperturbably. 'I could lay a complaint before the General Medical Council in that case. That you was guilty of infamous conduct in a professional respect.' He rose. 'Don't forget the name, Doc., Wilkins. You'll be hearing more from me.'

Chapter Seven

When I got home Jasmine was laying the table for our midday dinner.

'Hello,' she said brightly. 'You look like you're a bear with a sore head, and no mistake.'

'At the moment I'd make a pack of bears with sore heads look like a basket of puppies. Where's Dr Hockett, Jasmine?'

'The Doctor ain't in yet. He had to go out to the Vicar.' She laughed. 'That's the first time what you've called me Jasmine.'

I threw myself into a chair and picked up my *Pears' Cyclopaedia*. After a while she went on, 'Didn't 'arf give you a start, didn't it? Yesterday at tea.' She giggled. 'Didn't know I was married to the Doctor, did you?'

'If you must drag the incident up again, Mrs Hockett, I will tell you that I didn't. And it did give me a start. Quite put me off my sardine.'

She laid out the last of the plates. 'I'm not blaming you,' she said amiably. 'Fancy me being the wife of a doctor! Phew! I can't get over it yet, sometimes.' As I said nothing, she came nearer my chair. 'Of course, he only married me to save the wages. Or mostly, I suppose. He's a mean old devil, like you said. Still, I acted for the best.'

'My dear Mrs Hockett—'

'Call me Jasmine, ducks.'

'I really cannot give opinions on your strictly domestic affairs. I have had an exhausting–in fact, excruciating–morning, and quite enough trouble for today, thank you.'

'Do us a favour, duckie,' she said.

'No.'

'Yes, go on. Be a sport.' She came near enough to stand over me. 'The Doctor's given you the key of the drug cupboard, ain't he?'

'No.'

'Yes he has–he always gives it to the assistant.'

'And what of it?'

'Be a gent and give us the lend of it a minute.'

'I certainly will not.' I turned to my *Cyclopaedia* again with finality.

'Oh, go on! I'll give it back. Dr Azziz let me have it.'

'Well, Dr Gordon won't.'

'Fetch us a bit of nembutal from the cupboard, then. I love nembutal.' She rubbed her stomach and rolled her eyes. 'Lovely grub, it is. Sends you to sleep and makes you forget what a bloody old miser the Doctor is.'

'That hardly seems the way for a woman to talk about her husband.'

Suddenly she made a grab for my waistcoat pocket. 'Come on! Give it over!'

'For God's sake, woman—!'

'Ooo! Let go! You're hurting!' she cried pleasurably.

'Damnation! Can't you control yourself?'

We struggled over the chair and fell on to the floor. Jasmine was a sturdy girl and obviously experienced in parlour fighting. I had managed to push her from above me with difficulty, when Dr Hockett came in.

I scrambled up. My collar had flown from its stud, my face was red, I was sweating and breathless. Hockett stood in his overcoat in the doorway with his hands behind him, staring at me in the usual way.

'We–er–I had lost something on the floor,' I explained.

He nodded.

'Jasmine–Mrs Hockett, that is–was helping me find it.'

There was a long silence, while Jasmine smoothed down her clothes.

'Time for dinner,' Hockett said quietly. 'My dear, it is surely not necessary to have the fire on at this hour of the morning? It is really remarkably warm for the time of year.'

None of us spoke during the meal, which was sausage and mash. When Jasmine had cleared away the dishes and left, Hockett said in his usual voice, 'Surprising the numbers of doctors who have sinned, isn't it?'

'Sinned?' I looked at him uncomfortably. 'You mean–er, sexually?'

'I mean who have committed murder.'

'Oh, yes?' I said faintly. 'I suppose it is.'

'There was Crippen–Palmer the Poisoner–Neil Cream in London. And many more. Do you remember the Ruxton case? He cut them up in the bath.'

'I suppose it's–sort of tempting to have all the stuff around. To go murdering people with.'

'Exactly.'

'Ah, well!' I said. I stood up, clutching the table for support. 'I must be getting along.'

'Many murderers are never detected, Doctor,' Hockett observed.

I ran to my room and wedged the bed behind the door.

The evening nevertheless passed the same way as the one before. Dr Hockett sat beside the faint-hearted fire and read the *Express*; Jasmine knitted, and winked every time she caught my eye; I looked at the duck and read my *Cyclopaedia*.

We went to bed at ten, parting as amiably as any trio which has shared for supper the same cod fillet. I heard Dr Hockett turn the electricity off at the main. I felt for my torch beside me, and went to sleep.

The telephone rang at one-thirty. As it was my job to take all night calls I automatically climbed out of bed, crept downstairs, and answered it.

'Fifteen Canal Place,' a man's voice said immediately. 'And hurry up.' The line went dead.

I pulled on my clothes, started up Haemorrhagic Hilda, looked for Canal Place on my new map, and bounced over the deserted tram-lines into the night. After losing myself three or four times I found the address at the far end of a long, narrow, twisting street too cramped for Hilda to pass. I walked the rest of the way, and as it was raining again I knocked on the door with my new suit soaked through to the pyjamas underneath.

'You've taken your time, I must say,' said the man who opened the door.

I shone my torch in his face. 'Wilkins!'

'The very same.'

'If this is some sort of joke—' I began angrily.

'Joke? I don't play jokes, Doc. Some people say I ain't got a sense of humour. It's mother.'

'What's wrong with her?'

'She's dying.'

'She is, is she? Well, we'll see.'

I found Mrs Wilkins in bed upstairs, suffering from the wind.

'She wants to go into 'ospital,' Mr Wilkins announced in a threatening voice.

'No doubt she does. So do half the population of the country. She needs a large glass of hot water, that's all.'

'She wants to go into 'ospital,' Mr Wilkins insisted.

'Good night,' I snapped, picking up my stethoscope.

''Ere!' He grabbed my lapel. 'You 'eard what I said–she ought to be in 'ospital.'

Mrs Wilkins belched loudly. 'I'm dying!' she cried.

'Now look here. I don't want to threaten you with bodily violence twice in a day, Mr Wilkins, but if you don't take your hands off me this instant—'

He stared at me, tight-lipped. 'All right. Have it your own way. I'm going to the Executive Council in the morning.'

'Go to the bloody Town Council tonight, if you want to.'

'And I'm going to the General Medical Council, too. You mark my words,' he shouted after me as I made for the street. 'Infamous conduct–professional respect!'

The words followed me as I ran through the rain, while his mother recovered sufficiently to stick her head out of the window and swear in a way that would certainly have been inadvisable for a dying woman.

By the time I left the car outside Dr Hockett's house I was trembling with indignation. This was really too much. I had been treated worse than a man come to fix the drains. Already composing an outraged letter to the B.M.A., I opened the front door and flashed my torch along the hall. I found Jasmine standing at the bottom of the stairs in her nightie.

'Good God!'

She giggled. 'Hello, duckie. The Doctor's out. He had to go to the Vicar.'

'Get back to bed at once!'

'Go on! You sound like my old dad.' She came towards me. 'I'll go to bed,' she whispered, 'if you come too.'

I dropped the torch in fright. 'Have you gone insane, woman? Are you crazy? What do you think I am? He'll be back in a second.'

'No he won't, ducks. He's only just gone.' She grabbed me in the darkness. 'Come on! Now's our chance–don't you want a bit of fun?' Then she started kissing me, in the spirit of a boxer limbering up on the punching bag.

I managed to push her away and said desperately, 'Let me go! Let me go! Haven't I got enough to worry about as it is? Damn it–if you'll only leave me alone and go back to bed I'll–I'll give you some nembutal.'

She hesitated. 'You really will?'

'Yes, I really will,' I wiped my face with my handkerchief. 'In fact,' I went on breathlessly, 'I wish I could give you the whole ruddy bottle. But only if you'll go to bed at once and stay there like a good girl. Thus preventing both of us being cut up in the bath by tomorrow morning.'

She thought for a moment, weighing up the alternative delights of me and nembutal.

'O.K.,' she decided. 'It's a deal.'

'Run along then. I'll get it from the surgery and bring it up.'

As she disappeared upstairs I opened the drug cupboard and nervously flashed my torch inside. It was filled with several hundred small bottles of samples, which rattled like Haemorrhagic Hilda going downhill as they began to tumble on to the floor all around me. I grabbed the nembutal bottle, pushed the others back, locked the cupboard, and made for the stairs.

On the landing I hesitated. Jasmine had gone back to her room. Her door was shut. Was I in honour bound to keep my side of the bargain? Perhaps I could sneak back to bed and barricade the door. She might come after me, but Hockett would be back before she could make much more trouble. . . . I heard a creak inside the room: she was impatiently getting out of bed. Her bare footsteps crossed the floor. I grabbed the door-handle and pulled.

''Ere!' she called. 'What's the big idea?'

'The idea is that you stay inside, my good woman.'

'Oh, is it—'

Together we pulled at the handle, one on each side of the door. As I had the nembutal bottle in one hand, I had to struggle to keep it closed. I didn't hear the front door shut, and as Hockett had returned to the house silently on his bicycle the first I knew of it was finding myself standing in the light of his torch.

'Lord Almighty!' I cried. Immediately it struck me how the situation would appear to him. 'It's all right,' I said urgently. 'Your wife couldn't sleep. I was just going to fix her up with some of this.'

I waved the bottle in my hand. Then I saw it wasn't nembutal, but Dr Farrer's Famous Female Fertility Foods.

Chapter Eight

'Back so soon, Doctor?' asked Mr Pycraft.

'Yes. Dr Hockett and I had a difference of opinion about a difficult case.'

'You did, did you, Doctor?' Pycraft looked different from our last interview. He seemed twenty years younger, his sugary benevolence had hardened like the icing on a cheap wedding-cake, his side-whiskers had receded, his spectacles had enlarged, his clothes were cleaner, and his hands were cured of their arthritis. 'Well, now. Surely you won't let a little thing like that come between you and your career? We have gone to great trouble providing you with a start, in a magnificent practice—'

'Magnificent practice! The only thing magnificent about it is old Hockett's minginess. Why don't you give it to one of your medical missionaries? It would suit a chap who could live on a handful of rice a week and take the temptations of women in his stride.'

'I hardly find it a cause for levity, Doctor.'

'If you'd been working there for thirty-six hours like I have, you'd find it even less. I want another practice please, and damn quick.'

'But, Doctor–' He picked up a steel pen and slowly tapped his cheeks with it. 'I'm afraid we have no more on our books just at the moment. It's a bad time for inexperienced young men like yourself. Your only course is to return to Dr Hockett immediately, apologize, and continue your career.'

I banged his desk. 'I'd rather work tearing up the bloody road!'

'As you well might, Doctor,' he said calmly. 'Under the agreement you signed with Wilson, Willowick, and Wellbeloved–which I have in the safe there–you agreed to pay us thirty-three and one-third per cent of your salary monthly for twelve months, or the equivalent amount should you through any reason leave your post beforehand. That comes to fourteen pounds *per mensem*, which incidentally is payable in advance. We should like the first instalment now, Doctor, and if the rest is not forthcoming I assure you we shall have no hesitation in taking out a summons. Then there is the interest on the loan, of course. The publicity, Doctor–most undesirable, don't you agree? Especially at the very beginning of a career. The General Medical Council take an extremely grave view—'

'Oh, go to hell!' I said. I strode from the office, slammed the door, and clattered down the stairs.

I stood in the street for a minute, breathing hard and wondering what the recent floods of adrenalin were doing in my arteries. Then I dived into the pub for a drink.

Over a pint, I assessed my position in the medical profession. I had a diploma, a car, a new suit shrunk in the service of Mrs Wilkins, no spare cash, a debt of a hundred pounds, and the legal obligation to pay one hundred and sixty-eight pounds in the next twelve months to Wilson,

Willowick, and Wellbeloved. I wanted a job and money – and unless I was prepared to make Haemorrhagic Hilda my home I wanted them at once. I was gloomily turning over these problems when I thought of Grimsdyke: although I gravely doubted that he could pay back my ten pounds, it would be pleasant to look at someone who owed money to me.

The address on his card was in Ladbroke Grove, and I drew up Haemorrhagic Hilda a little later that morning before a row of tall frowsy houses by the gasworks. Grimsdyke's apartments were in the basement. I rang a bell beside a blistered brown door under the area stairs, which after several minutes was gingerly opened.

'Yes?' said a woman's voice.

'I'd like to see Dr Grimsdyke, please.'

'He's gone away.'

'I'm a particular friend of his. Tell him it's Dr Gordon, and I've just had a row with Wilson, Willowick, and Wellbeloved.'

'Just a minute.'

She shut the door, and returned a few seconds later to let me in. I saw that she was about nineteen, dressed in a dirty pink satin housecoat, and wore a rather vacant look. Inside the door was a small hall full of rubbish, and beyond that a large room with a window just below the ceiling. This contained a bed, a gas-stove, a washstand, and a table covered with dirty plates and empty Guinness bottles. Grimsdyke was in his pyjamas, with his hair dangling over his face.

'I thought you'd gone up north, old lad,' he said in surprise.

'So I had. Now I'm back again.'

'Forgive this squalor – ' He waved a hand round the room. 'Fact is, I took these rooms – there's a lot more at the back – to oblige some friends, rather messy people—'

'I wondered if you could let me have my ten quid back?'

Grimsdyke sat on the edge of the bed suddenly. 'Surely you can't have spent the other ninety? In two days? That's certainly some going! You must have had a hell of a good time.'

'I bought a car.'

'What, that ruddy great thing that's blocking out the daylight? I thought the coal had arrived. A bit on the posh side, isn't it?'

'I felt a big car would be a good investment – to impress the patients.'

He nodded. 'It's the only way the blasted public chooses its doctors. Did I tell you about a pal of mine called Rushleigh? Good scout, he qualified right at the end of the war, when you couldn't get cars for love, money, or blackmail. Unless you were a doctor, of course. So he filled in the forms, and got a nice new little family bus for about three hundred quid. He'd happened to pal up with a Free French bloke who'd been in the orthopaedic wards, and when this fellow went home with a couple of bone grafts Rushleigh got an invitation to stay at his place down at Nice, buckshee. So he set off in his car, but he'd only got as far as Rouen when it conked out. You know what cars were like after the war. He went to a French garage, where they mumbled a bit about spare parts and so forth, and told him it would take at least a month to get anything to patch it up. However, the British being considered good chaps in France at the time, they sportingly offered to lend him a very old aristocratic English car they had in the back, which hadn't been used for seven years and then only for funerals.

'Rushleigh proceeded towards the sunny south, feeling he was driving a greenhouse. But he got there all right, and a month later showed up at Rouen. This put the garage in a bit of a fix, because there were apparently no spare parts anywhere. So they suggested to Rushleigh they did a straight swap. They could fix up his little family bus some time or other, and such vehicles sold like *gâteaux chauds*. Hot cakes, old lad.'

I sat down on the bed myself and asked, 'Did he agree?'

'You bet he did. He'd quite taken to the old hearse. One of the garage bloke's brothers was in the Customs and Rushleigh wasn't averse to a spot of fiddling, so off he went. When he was safely back in England he thought he'd send the thing up to the makers in Derbyshire somewhere and have her done up. A few days later he got a letter from the managing director asking him to come at once and enclosing first-class ticket with cheque for incidental expenses and loss of valuable time. Rushleigh went up there preparing to be led away by the police, but instead he was given a ruddy great lunch and asked what he'd sell the old conservatory for. Apparently this firm had a museum of all its old crocks, and the one he'd picked up in Rouen was the only model of its type ever made, for some millionaire or other in Cannes in 1927. Fortified by the directors' brandy, Rushleigh said he didn't see the point of selling, because where would he get another car to continue his life-saving work? "My dear sir," said the managing director, "if you prefer, we should be delighted to give you one of our brand-new Golden Sprites instead." Rushleigh now drives round his practice in one of these, and the old devil's worth an easy five thousand a year.'

'How about my tenner?' I said.

'Would you like a cup of tea? Virginia will make some.'

Virginia was standing with one foot on the table painting her toe-nails.

'No, thanks. I've just had a pint of beer.'

'Is it as late as that? I must be getting a move on. I've a good many appointments in the City. So if you'll excuse me—'

'At the moment I face bankruptcy, disgrace, and starvation,' I said. 'If you've got any of that ten quid left, I'd regard it as an act of charity if you'd let me have it. I owe Lord knows how much to that agency—'

'I can't exactly give you the cash, old lad, because I haven't got it. The market's been very sluggish of late. But I will tell you what I'll do – Would you like a job?'

'As long as it isn't like the one I got from Wilson and Willowick.'

'This is *bona fide* and real McCoy. Have you heard of Dr Erasmus Potter-Phipps?'

I shook my head.

'He's about the most posh G.P. in England – high class stuff, you know, none of this bob on the bottle and sawdust on the waiting-room floor.'

'Where's he hang out?'

'Park Lane, of course.'

'What's his wife like?'

'He isn't married.'

I felt encouraged for the first time since driving out of range of Dr Hockett in the middle of the night. 'The only fishy thing that strikes me is – I mean, I've the highest regard for your friendship and integrity, but why haven't you grabbed it yourself?'

'Long-term planning. I'll tell you in confidence – don't breathe it to a soul, particularly anyone in the district – I'm leaving for the country. Big opening. I shall settle down scratching pigs with walking-sticks—'

'Is Miss Virginia coming too?' She had taken no more notice of me and was leaning on the table among the plates plucking her eyebrows.

'No. She's psychologically unsuited for the country. I've found that out – I've been psychoanalysing her for the last few weeks. That's why she's here. You can't psychoanalyse anyone competently if you're not with them day and night. Jung and Adler, and all that. She's got a jolly interesting little ego.'

'I'm sure she has.'

Grimsdyke got up and felt in his jacket pocket. 'Here's the address. Give me half an hour and I'll speak to him on the blower first.'

'But how about references? A G.P. like that wouldn't take an assistant out of the blue.'

'Leave it to me,' he said confidently. 'It's all part of the Grimsdyke service.'

Chapter Nine

Dr Potter-Phipps practised in Park Lane from the first floor of a large modern block of flats, though the only indication of this was a small silver plate with his name on the door, as discreet as the single hat in a Bond Street milliner's window. Downstairs I was saluted by the doorman, bowed to by the porter, and grinned at by the lift boy; upstairs, the door was opened by a butler. Dr Potter-Phipps himself, who sat in a consulting-room like a film producer's office, was a slim, good-looking, fair-haired, middle-aged man wearing a grey suit with narrow trousers, a red carnation in his button-hole, a fawn waistcoat, a white stiff collar, and an Old Etonian tie.

'A frightful tragedy, dear boy,' he said languidly, offering me a gold cigarette-case. 'My partner's perforated his duodenal ulcer, poor fellow. Operated on by old Sir James last night. He'll be away a good three months. It's so terribly difficult to get a suitable man to replace him. This is a rather special practice you understand.' He held his cigarette with his finger-tips and waved it airily. 'We have rather special patients. To some people the National Health Service did not come quite as the crowning gift of parliamentary democracy. They still like manners with their medicine.'

'I'd certainly be pleased to meet some of them, sir,' I said feelingly.

'Of course, you've been out of the country a good time,' he went on. 'You must have found that Himalayan expedition quite fascinating. Grimsdyke told me about it when he rang up. I met him at the races last week-end, and rather hoped he could help us when this disaster occurred. A remarkable young man.'

'Oh, remarkable.'

'I must be getting old, dear boy, but I find most young doctors today are terribly dull. And they *will* treat their patients like guinea-pigs. It must be the result of this frightful slave-driving in medical schools these days. When I was at St George's, medicine was still acquired slowly, like any other gentlemanly accomplishment. But someone with the Alpine temperament like yourself would be eminently suitable. Did you meet old Charrington in the Himalayas?'

'Charrington? No, I don't think I did.'

'Really?' He looked surprised. 'But he's always shinning up mountains and things.'

'Big place, of course, the Himalayas.'

'Oh, of course.'

I had decided to stand up, draw a deep breath, make a confession, and go directly to the agency to throw myself at the mercy of Mr Pycraft. Then Dr Potter-Phipps went on–'Consider yourself engaged.'

'What–just like that?'

'Just like that, dear boy. I'm rather conceited that I can judge my fellow men.' He sighed. 'I wish I could do the same with horses. So much more profitable. By the way, if you want any salary ask the secretary next door. In my family,' he continued pleasantly, 'we never discuss money. It's thought rather vulgar. And forgive me–but perhaps you've something a little more formal to wear?'

I looked down at my new suit.

'I suppose you picked it up in Tibet or somewhere?' he suggested charitably. 'Here's the name of my tailor. Ask him to make you something quickly and charge it to the practice. It's a chastening thought, but good clothes are more important to the G.P. than a good stethoscope. You needn't worry about a car–we run three Rolls—'

'Three?'

'We have an extra one for the electrocardiograph. Do you know how to use it?'

'Oh, yes, sir,' I said eagerly, glad at last to be able to tell the truth. 'At St Swithin's they taught on the heart most thoroughly.'

'I'm glad. Terribly glad. I'm a little hazy about all those beastly dials and wires and things myself, but I must say once you've connected them up to the patient and pulled a few switches it makes them feel very much better. We got it second-hand from a doctor who went abroad, and I thought it worth using. I take it to almost every case. After all, even in neuralgia and appendicitis it's useful to know what the heart's up to, isn't it? And *two* cars arriving at the patient's door makes so much difference. When can you start? Tomorrow?'

That afternoon I again found myself in a tailor's but this time it was a dark, dusty, devout little shop in Savile Row, where the assistants moved with a funeral tread, everyone spoke in whispers, and the customers were measured in cubicles of dark carved wood like choir-stalls.

'What sort of suit did you have in mind, sir?' asked the old man who was pulling a tape-measure shakily round my middle.

'What's the well-dressed doctor about town wearing these days?'

'You can't go wrong with the black jacket and striped trousers, sir,' he said solemnly. 'A lot of the younger gentlemen in the medical profession are favouring ordinary lounge suits these days, sir. One surgical gentleman I couldn't care to mention even goes so far as'–he dropped his eyes–'tweed, sir.'

'Very well. Black jacket and striped trousers it is.'

'I *am* glad, sir,' he said. 'I really am. Just like old times, sir.'

I took a bed-sitting-room in Bayswater, and arrived for work in Park Lane the next morning. As I was still wearing my Oxford Street suit even Dr Potter-Phipps' good manners did not prevent a pained look crossing his face when I appeared, as though I were suffering from some exuberant skin disease. 'Perhaps, dear boy,' he suggested, 'you should stay in the background for a while. Get to know the practice. Would you like to wear a white coat? So easy to get one's clothes messy doing clinical tests with strange apparatus.'

For a week I spent my time in the small laboratory converted from a bathroom, performing medical-student pathology at five guineas a go. Then my black jacket and striped trousers arrived, and I was allowed to try my hand at Park Lane medicine. I started at the top: my first patient was a Duke.

During the morning Potter-Phipps hurried into the laboratory, where I was preparing blood samples. For the first time I saw him looking worried.

'A terrible thing has happened, dear boy,' he announced. I prepared to hear that someone had dropped dead in the waiting-room. 'It's my morning to visit old Skye and Lewis, and now this damn film actress has gone and got laryngitis. Which one shall I go to?'

He paced the floor, trying to solve this grave therapeutic problem.

'Couldn't one wait?' I asked.

'Dear boy,' he said patiently. 'In this sort of practice no one waits.'

After some minutes he decided, 'I'll take the actress. The newspapers will be there by now. Yes, definitely the actress. I can bring the electrocardiograph, too–it's important to see that the heart will stand the strain in such a nervous creature. You do the Duke. And pray, dear boy'–he laid a hand on my sleeve–'remember constantly that for all practical purposes, you and I, at any rate, are not living in an egalitarian society.'

'I shall not fail you, sir,' I said stoutly.

'Good fellow!' He made for the door.

'What's wrong with the Duke?' I called after him.

'Just give him his usual treatment,' he replied over his shoulder, and disappeared.

I drove to the Duke of Skye and Lewis in our number two Rolls, feeling as if I were again going to an examination. One outstanding problem worried me: what *was* the Duke's usual treatment? Apart from the electrocardiograph, our practice did not own much medical equipment, and I had with me only a stethoscope, a throat torch, a gadget for measuring the gap in sparking plugs, a short plastic ruler advertising a cough mixture, a silver-plated presentation bottle-opener, and a small brush for cleaning my lighter, with which to effect my ministrations.

The car stopped outside a door in Eaton Square. As I got out I said to the chauffeur, 'You must have taken Dr Potter-Phipps here a good few times. I don't suppose you know what the blue-blooded old boy's usual treatment is, do you?'

He shrugged his shoulders. 'Sorry, Doctor. There was a duke what lived round the corner, I remember, and he had varicose veins. There was another with prostate trouble up the road–but come to think of it, he was an earl.'

The door was opened by a young maid.

'The doctor,' I said, suddenly feeling that I was delivering the groceries.

'This way.' I followed her, tugging at the edge of my new jacket for support. Could I conceivably ask this girl what the usual treatment was? Then it struck me that I should have to start referring to my patient in a more regular manner. This was my second difficulty in the case. Although I had secretly bought the silver-covered book invaluable to young Englishmen wanting to get on–*Titles and Forms of Address: A Guide to Their Correct Use*–I had found the paragraphs more difficult to memorize than my anatomy and physiology. I summoned the pages urgently to mind, but in the perverted way that I could always remember in examinations the full structural formula of anhydrohydroxyprogesterone and forget all the signs of pneumonia, I now recalled only that the wives of the younger sons of earls share their husbands' titles and honorific initials never appear on visiting-cards.

'His Grace will see you in a minute,' said the maid.

His Grace! That was it. But did I call him 'Your Grace?' Or was that only for the Archbishops of Canterbury and York?

The Duke of Skye and Lewis was a fat red-faced man with a large moustache, lying on his bed in a yellow silk dressing-gown.

'Morning, Doctor,' he said amiably. 'I had a call to say Potter-Phipps couldn't come. Pity. Busy this time of the year, I shouldn't wonder?'

'Yes, er, your–your–sir.'

'Have a seat. You're not rushed for a minute, are you? Potter-Phipps said you knew everything about my case, but I like to have a chat with my doctor. I don't like being pulled about by someone I don't know. It's almost indecent. Doctoring's a man-to-man business, whatever you cook up these days in test-tubes. Do you play golf?'

We argued about mashie shots for ten minutes, then the Duke said with a sigh of resignation, 'Well, Doctor, I suppose it's time for you to give me the usual treatment?'

'Of course. The usual treatment.' I stood up and rubbed my hands slowly together. 'And how,' I asked craftily, 'is the usual complaint?'

'About the same.'

'I see.'

I nodded sagely. There was a pause.

'Let's get on with it, Doctor,' the Duke continued, setting himself on the bed, a brave man about to face an ordeal. 'The sooner it's started, the sooner it's finished.'

What the devil could it be? Manipulation of the vertebrae? Syphonage of the sinuses? Something internal with irrigation? Hypnosis?

'Come along, Doctor.' The Duke was becoming impatient. 'Potter-Phipps does it in a jiffy, with his bare hands.'

I blurted out, now desperate, 'Perhaps you will forgive me for asking, sir—'

'Oh, the new ones? They're in the box on the chimneypiece.'

I shot a glance hopefully towards the fireplace, but met only an unhelpful ormolu clock and some statuettes. 'Of course, sir, new ones—'

'They need new ones this time, and no mistake,' the Duke went on, waggling his feet. Suddenly I saw–I had been summoned to change his corn-plasters.

At the end of the operation the Duke said, 'I suppose you'll be expecting the same sort of outrageous fee as old Potter-Phipps?'

'I really couldn't say,' I told him, smiling with relief. 'I never discuss the money side of it.'

'Neither do I,' he agreed. 'In my family it's thought rather vulgar.'

Chapter Ten

Dr Potter-Phipps ran his practice as efficiently as a motor-car factory. Every morning at eight, three men in green overalls arrived with vacuum cleaners; at eight-fifteen a man dressed as a postilion called with the day's supply of clean towels; at eight-twenty a page-boy brought the waiting-room papers and magazines; at eight-thirty a girl looking like Lady Macbeth with pernicious anaemia came from a West End florist's to change the flowers; at eight-forty a fat man in a frock-coat and bowler entered with Dr Potter-Phipps' freshly-pressed suits; at eight-fifty the chauffeurs, the butler, the secretary, and the nurse appeared, and at nine sharp we were open for business.

The nurse was needed only to show patients from the waiting-room to the consulting-room, and was dressed in a white uniform so crisp and sparkling that she always appeared to have been just unwrapped from cellophane. She was also one of the prettiest girls I had ever met, which had spurred me to start a cosy conversation of hospital reminiscences during my first morning's work.

'I haven't actually been a nurse in *hospital*, darling,' she told me. 'Of course, I looked after my poor sister when she was poorly, but I'm not what you'd call an *invalid's* nurse. Razzy's such a sweet, he gave me the job because he said I looked the part. I played a nurse once, in *Men in White*. Did you see it?'

I said no.

'After all, darling, it's not as if anyone we saw here was *ill*. We just don't have those sort of patients, do we, darling?'

She was right: most of our practice consisted of old gentlemen wondering if they could take out more life insurance, young gentlemen wondering if they'd caught unfortunate diseases, and young women wondering if they were pregnant. Anyone seriously ill was immediately sent north of Oxford Street to the consultants who kept in most successfully with Razzy. It was St Swithin's casualty-room again, first class; but even Dr Hockett's practice would have been bearable with three Rolls-Royces.

Everyone seemed to like Razzy, and I soon became as fond of him as the rest of his employees. He was a shrewd clinician who had the supreme medical gift of always knowing whether a patient was really ill or not; he was an equally shrewd business man, whose polite patter about money always made people give him more and accept less. The only faintly shady part of the practice was our electrocardiograph, an instrument for taking electrical records of the heart, which represented the conflict between Razzy the doctor and Razzy the financier: he knew that as a diagnostic aid it was almost useless, but he hated not seeing a return on his capital. It was an old model, as untidy as an experimental television set, but every time he set out on a professional visit the electrocardiograph followed in its Rolls. The only occasion I saw Razzy looking worried after the case of the Duke's corn plasters was the morning he returned from an urgent call to a newspaper owner, who had suffered a stroke in the bathroom.

'A near thing, dear boy,' he told me, as he came through the door shaking his head. 'A damn near thing.'

'What, did you pull him through?'

'Oh, no, the old boy's dead. But I only got the electrocardiograph there in the nick of time.'

Our most constant, and most profitable, patients in the practice were several dozen neurotic women, all of whom were in love with Razzy. He had long, soothing telephone conversations with them frequently during the day, and they often appeared dramatically at the front door in the evening, dressed up like an advertisement for Cartier's.

'Yes, of course, they're in love with me, dear boy,' he stated one day. 'Speaking quite objectively, it's the only thing that keeps most of them from suicide. What else would you expect me to do?'

'But surely, Razzy,' I protested, 'don't you sometimes find it rather awkward?'

'Not in the least, dear boy. I don't have to be in love with *them*.'

My spell in Razzy's practice was delightful; I soon forgot Dr Hockett, Jasmine, and the Wilkins family, and even managed to shift Wilson, Willowick, and Wellbeloved from the front of my mind. Although I was never allowed to treat the aristocracy again, he let me try my hand at a few actors and an M.P. or two, until I had worked my way so deeply into the practice that a reminder of my impermanence came as a shock.

'I'm seeing my partner tomorrow,' Razzy said one Saturday morning, when I had been with him over two months. 'He's coming along famously. Absolutely famously. We'll have him back in another few weeks.'

'I'm glad,' I lied.

'And I expect you're simply itching to get back to the Himalayas again, aren't you, dear boy?'

'Well, not itching exactly—'

'I'm so pleased you came to help us out. You've done terribly well, you know. All my old dears think the world of you. The wife of that Coal Board fellow told me yesterday you were a pet.'

'I'll certainly be sorry to leave. I've even thought of having a go at a practice somewhere round here myself.'

For a second Razzy's eyes narrowed. 'I wouldn't advise it, dear boy. I really wouldn't. It's quite a dog's life really. The struggle to get started–terrible! And the competition. Most frightful. You'd be far better off in the Himalayas.'

There were no patients waiting, so we stood for a while looking silently out of the window. It was a brilliant spring day, the buds on the trees in Hyde Park were straining like hatching chicks, the passers-by were stepping along jauntily without their overcoats, and even the Park Lane traffic smelt warmly exciting.

'Spring, dear boy,' said Razzy with a contented sigh, as if hearing that a millionaire had fallen a couple of floors down our lift-shaft. He stayed watching the people hurrying away for their week-ends. 'Do you know, dear boy, I haven't had an afternoon off since I met that fellow Grimsdyke at the races? That's the sort of practice we're in. Always on tap. It's what they pay for I suppose.' After a pause he added, 'I know it's your free afternoon, but I wondered if you'd care to do a little fort-holding?'

'More than delighted, Razzy. Honestly.'

'Bless you, dear boy. Then I'm off to Sunningdale. I'll dine out and turn up about midnight in case there are any messages. Everyone will be out of town on a week-end like this, anyway.'

After lunch he changed into flannels, rang up a well-known film actress and persuaded her to keep him company, picked up his clubs, and set off for the links in the number one Rolls. Alone in the flat, I slipped off my shoes and sprawled on the soft curtained couch used for examining patients in the consulting room. Beside me I arranged a pile of the *New Yorker* and *Life*, *Recent Advances in Surgery*, a reprint of *The Citadel*, a box of chocolates I'd found in the secretary's desk, and the bottle of *Cordon Bleu* brandy kept in the medicine cupboard. I hoped that Razzy had an enjoyable day off, but I saw no reason for working on a Saturday afternoon myself in discomfort.

Before he had been away half an hour the door-bell rang. I jumped up, pulled on my shoes, swiftly pushed my comforts under the couch, and opened the door. On the mat was a tall, amiable-looking man with a droopy white moustache, who wore a tweed suit and carried a heavy dispatch-case embossed with the Royal cypher in gold.

'Good afternoon,' he said pleasantly. 'I have an appointment with Dr Potter-Phipps.'

I looked puzzled.

'My private secretary arranged it earlier in the week. I'm afraid Saturday afternoon is my only free time at present. I hope it is not unduly inconvenient for the doctor?'

'I'm terribly sorry, but there's been a mistake,' I said, letting him in. 'Doctor Potter-Phipps is away at the moment. I'm his assistant. Just a minute, and I'll look at the book.'

'Thank you. My name is Beecham. It seemed simpler to call here than to ask him to visit me.' He smiled. 'And no doubt more economical.'

'But I'm afraid the appointment was made for *next* Saturday.'

'Oh, dear! How infuriating. This is not the first time such a mistake has occurred. And next Saturday I shall be in Edinburgh.' He assessed me. 'Perhaps I could have a consultation with you instead, Doctor? I did rather want to be off to the country this lovely afternoon.'

'I should be very pleased,' I told him, with a brief bow. 'Kindly come into the consulting-room.'

'You will be wanting my medical history first, no doubt,' he went on, as he sat down. 'I have it specially tabulated in my mind. Age, sixty-one. Married. Occupation, cabinet minister. Usual childhood complaints. I'm not going too fast?'

'Did you say "cabinet minister?"' That was flying high, even for us.

'I am the Minister of Inland Development,' he added modestly, as though referring to a favourable golf handicap. I suddenly remembered seeing his photograph in the papers a week ago, snipping a tape and giving the country another bridge. He seemed a pleasant old boy, but as I had never even seen a cabinet minister before I wondered how to address him. I decided to play for safety, and treat him roughly like a duke.

'Of course, sir,' I said. 'I'm–I'm terribly sorry not to have recognized you at once. Please forgive me. Now perhaps you'd be so kind as to allow me to ask you a few questions?'

He folded his arms. 'Of course, Doctor. Do exactly what you wish. I place myself entirely in your hands. As I was saying to the Minister of Health yesterday, what on earth's the use of seeing a doctor if you don't follow his advice, disregarding entirely your own opinion of the complaint? He said your own opinion of the doctor was possibly more important.' My patient smiled. 'Of course, he was only joking. He has quite a wit.'

'Oh, quite. Now what's the trouble, sir?'

As the Minister seemed to be suffering from pains connected with the spinal column, I pointed to the examination couch and told him to take his clothes off.

'*All* my clothes, Doctor?'

'Yes, please. I want a good look at you.'

'Anything you say, of course.'

I had just drawn the curtains round him as he started unbuttoning his waistcoat, when the bell rang again.

'Just a minute,' I said.

On the doormat I found an attractive, tall, dark woman with a mink cape slipping off her shoulders, who clutched at her throat and cried, 'Oh, God! Oh, God! I'm going to die!'

All I could think of saying was, 'Here I say, steady on!' She pushed past me, threw herself on the waiting-room couch, and burst into tears.

I quickly shut off the Minister of Inland Development in the consulting-room.

'If I can possibly help you, dear lady,' I said anxiously, 'I certainly will. But if you could perhaps control yourself a little—'

'Razzy!' she cried. 'Razzy, darling! Where is he?'

'Dr Erasmus Potter-Phipps happens to have taken the afternoon off. He's playing golf.'

'He's with another woman,' she sobbed. 'Janet said he'd asked that bitch Helen.'

'Well, dash it, only golf,' I murmured. I began to feel I was not showing the mastery of the situation expected from the medical attendant. During my two months in Park Lane I had learned more about handling difficult people than in five years at St Swithin's, where most of the patients treated the doctors with the same frightened respect they gave the police; but the dynamic women in Dr Potter-Phipps' unilateral love-life were beyond me.

The girl moaned, covered her face with her hands, and cried, 'What shall I do? What shall I do? I want to die, that's all. To die–to die–'

As I was deciding what to try next, she suddenly looked up as if she had never seen me before.

'Who are you?' she asked.

'I'm Dr Potter-Phipps' assistant,' I said politely. 'Can I help you?'

'*No one* can help me!' Her face was pale, her eye-shadow was streaked down her cheeks, her hat was awry with emotion. Suddenly she threw aside her arms and began to scream.

My visitor had at least no disease of the respiratory system. There was nothing of the wronged woman's sobs about her: when she screamed, she took a deep breath, braced her larynx, and let fly like the knocking-off whistle in a shipyard.

'Please, please!' I shouted. 'Can't you compose yourself?'

She immediately drew another breath and started again, now pummelling her forehead with her fists, and hammering her heels on the floor.

By now I was less worried about her clinical condition–she was obviously well filled with the life force–than about my reputation. The most solemn piece of clinical advice we had received in St Swithin's was never to treat a female patient unless a nurse was present; and any minute now the door would probably be broken down by the porters, the police, or the fire brigade, all thirsting to play St George.

'Damnation!' I cried. 'Stop it!'

She settled herself in a higher key, and continued. Here was a major clinical problem: the gynaecological instruction at St Swithin's was excellent, but had included no advice on the way to treat hysterical women single-handed. Fortunately, I remembered from reading novels that the traditional remedy was a sharp slap across the face, and overcoming the inhibitions of an English public school education I crouched down and caught her a smart smack on the left cheekbone. Instead of this quelling her, she immediately countered with a powerful left uppercut which knocked me off my balance, and started picking up all the movable pieces of furniture in the waiting-room and throwing them at me.

I managed to struggle to my feet from a pile of broken china and glass, torn magazines, and telephone directories, just in time to prevent her concussing me with the standard-lamp.

'What the devil do you think you're up to?' I demanded angrily. I gripped her arms. 'Are you trying to kill me or something?'

'You struck a woman!' Through her redistribution of energy she had thankfully stopped screaming. 'You cad!'

'Of course I did! For your own good, you idiotic female. Why, you're as hysterical as a cat stuck in a chimney-pot!'

She looked at me closely, narrowing her eyes. 'I hate you!' she hissed. Then she fell into my arms and collapsed into humble tears.

After some minutes of patting her on the back and murmuring consolation I said, 'Don't you think you ought to go home and lie down? If you like I'll give you a prescription for a sedative. Have a good sleep–you'll feel ever so much better.'

She blew her nose miserably. 'I'll stay here until Razzy comes back.'

'But Dr Potter-Phipps may be away all night. I mean, he might have to go to a case somewhere after his golf,' I said quickly. 'I'd go home now if I were you.'

Still clutching me, she asked pathetically, 'Take me home. Please take me. I couldn't face it. Not alone.'

'Really, that's asking rather a lot, you know.'

'Please! It's not far.'

I hesitated. 'Oh, all right, then.' I had to get rid of her somehow. 'If you promise to behave yourself on the way.'

She nodded her head. 'I promise,' she said, like a penitent schoolgirl.

I left the flat, and helped her down the stairs to the street. I called a taxi and we got in together.

'Who is there to look after you?' I asked.

She shook her head.

'Haven't you any relatives or friends you could get hold of?'

'I hate them all.'

I turned and stared at the beautiful blue and gold afternoon outside and wished I had been Dr Potter-Phipps' caddie.

The girl lived at the far end of Curzon Street, and we drove along in silence. Suddenly she announced more cheerfully. 'You know, I've been a bloody fool.'

I swung round, and found her carefully doing her make-up.

'I must say you've been acting a little oddly, even for this part of the world.'

She smiled for the first time. 'I *am* a silly thing, aren't I? Fancy getting all worked up like that. I suppose I did have rather a lot to drink at lunch time. That always sends me off the rails a bit. Didn't you think I was crazy?'

'It did cross my mind to send for the strong-arm squad, I admit.'

'I'm so glad you didn't. And such a heavenly day, too!' She closed her compact with a snap. 'Here we are. Won't you come in for a minute and have a drink? I should think you need one.'

'I really don't think I should—'

'Come on! I'll ring the exchange and have your calls put through to my number. Razzy often does.'

I wavered. Being alone with female patients was bad enough; going to their flats afterwards for drinks would certainly raise every eyebrow on the General Medical Council. Still, it was spring. . . .

'Just a quick one, then,' I said.

'My name's Kitty,' she told me, opening the door. 'I've only got a very tiny flat, but make yourself at home. Razzy does.'

The flat would have taken my Bayswater room a dozen times, and was furnished with a amiable extravagance that must have taken Razzy's fancy. Kitty immediately threw open the window, took a deep breath, and trilled, 'Spring, spring, spring! Isn't it lovely? Don't you adore the spring? With the primroses and the cowslips and the bluebells and things? I swore I'd have a window-box this year. What'll you have to drink, darling.'

'I've started on brandy this afternoon already, I'm afraid. So I suppose I'd better go on, if you've got any.'

'Sure, my pet. Brandy it is. The place is stiff with it.'

She brought from the cupboard two tumblers, and a bottle with a plain label bearing only a crown and the date 1904.

'Here, steady on,' I called, as she half-filled both glasses. 'I'm sure that stuff's supposed to be drunk by the thimbleful.'

'Here's to life,' she said, taking a large drink. 'That's better!' Then she sat on the sofa beside me. 'Tell me about yourself.'

'There's not much to tell.' I licked my lips, savouring the brandy. 'I'm Dr Potter-Phipps' temporary assistant, that's all.'

'You're very young to be a doctor.'

'As a matter of fact–and it must prove something, because I wouldn't tell it to everybody–I haven't been a doctor very long.'

'I could tell you hadn't much practical experience the moment I fell into your arms in your flat.'

'Oh, dear! And I thougxt I was being such a commanding figure.'

She laughed.

'By the way,' I said modestly. 'I'm sorry I clocked you one.'

'And I'm sorry I clocked you one, too, Doctor darling.'

We both laughed and had some more brandy. After a while, everything seemed to become very cosy.

'It must be wonderful being a doctor,' she said dreamily. 'Curing people who are stricken.'

'There isn't all that much curing in it. And fortunately most of the people arriving on our doormat aren't very stricken.'

'But it's lovely to have someone to sympathize with you and hold your hand and tell you you're wonderful, even if you're not really ill. That's where Razzy's so marvellous. Have you noticed his eyes?' She threw back her head. 'Hypnotic! Cruelly hypnotic.'

'I'm afraid I can't reach those heights, but I can certainly sympathize with you and–' I held her hand–'tell you you're wonderful.'

'You're sweet,' she said, getting up. 'I'm going to change.'

I helped myself to another half-tumbler of her brandy, which had the effect of producing a pleasant conscious detachment from the world, like addiction to morphia. I recognized cheerfully that I was getting myself into a dangerous situation. My conduct was certainly becoming infamous in a professional respect, for Kitty's entering our waiting-room and smashing the furniture on my head placed us henceforward in a professional relationship. What should I do about it? I felt in my wallet for the B.M.A. booklet on *Ethics*, and turning over the pages found a great deal of sound advice on the size of doctor's door-plates, fee-splitting, and association with the clergy, but nothing on the tantalizing frontier between professional and social obligations where I was now dancing. A faint, fresh breeze rustled the curtains and a bird started singing on the window-ledge. And what the hell! I thought. It's spring. I put the book away and drank some more brandy.

Kitty came back wearing a négligé.

'How's it going?' she asked cheerfully.

'I'm responding to treatment. Have some more of your brandy. Liquor should be quaffed, not sipped.'

'Here's to life, Doctor darling.'

'Here's to you, patient pet.'

We drank with linked arms. With a sigh, she stretched herself on the sofa. She held out her arms and smiled.

'Doctor darling,' she murmured invitingly.

I licked my lips. There was a terrible risk making love to a patient. . . . But, damn it! Alone with a beautiful woman. Wasn't it worth it? Was I a man or a mouse? Anyway, I couldn't possibly disappoint her. . . .

'Come to me,' she breathed.

How lovely she looked! But how much more lovely she would look lying there without any clothes on at all. . . .

I jumped up. 'Get me a taxi!' I shouted. 'Quick!' And what, I wondered, would I now say to the Minister of Inland Development.

Chapter Eleven

When I dashed into the flat I found a note neatly pinned to the examination couch:

> Dear Doctor
>
> I fear that some dire emergency has called you away. I fully realize the trials of a doctor's life, and that some poor soul is in a worse state than me. However, lying on your couch seems to have relieved the discomfort, and as I am so

anxious to get away this afternoon I will go round the corner to an osteopath recommended by the Minister of Works. With thanks for your attention.

Yrs,
George Beecham

I had lost Razzy a patient, but my personal honour, and probably my professional life, were saved by the politician. I hoped he would become Prime Minister, and since that afternoon I have always read his speeches in the newspapers.

I did not tell Razzy the full story until the day that I was leaving the practice.

'Really?' he said mildly. 'Poor Kitty! I wonder what on earth you did to her psychology, bolting like that. I really must go round and see her soon.'

'And another thing,' I said gazing at the carpet, 'there aren't any Himalayas. As far as I'm concerned, I mean. I wasn't going to let on about it, but–well, you've been so good to me, Razzy, I hadn't the heart not to confess I've worked here under false pretences.'

'But I'm glad, dear boy. Terribly glad. Frightfully uncomfortable it must be, in all that snow and ice. So what other plans have you?'

'I thought I'd stay on in London for a bit and work for my Fellowship. Thanks to you, I've got a few quid in the bank to pay the rent, and I might be able to make a little by standing-in for doctors at week-ends. You see', I told him solemnly, 'I'm still determined to become a surgeon.'

'And good luck to you, dear boy,' he added indulgently, as though I were a schoolboy saying I wanted to be an engine-driver. 'I've always found surgery fascinating. Completely fascinating. Let me know if there's ever anything I can do for you. Would you like a bonus? The secretary will fix it up–you know I loathe discussing money.'

We shook hands, and I stepped from out of the glossy picture of fashionable medicine for ever.

I now had saved enough to pay off my hundred-pound debt to Wilson, Willowick, and Wellbeloved, and to maintain a modest medical-student standard of living until the Primary Fellowship examination of the Royal College of Surgeons in six weeks' time. I kept my room in Bayswater, took copies of *Gray's Anatomy* and Starling's *Physiology* from Lewis's medical lending library, borrowed a box of bones from a friend at St Swithin's, and continued my surgical career.

The Fellowship, like all British post-graduate examinations, is run on the Grand National principle, except that the highest fence is placed immediately in front of the tapes. Before you can enter for the Final exam you have first to pass the Primary in anatomy and physiology, subjects which are learnt in the second year of medical school and forgotten in the fourth. I had now to reopen the pages I had sweated over on coffee-drenched nights five years ago, unpleasantly aware that such traditional *aides-memoire* for the student as:

The lingual nerve
Took a swerve
Around the Hyoglossus–
'Well I'm mucked!'
Said Wharton's duct,
'The blighter's double-crossed us!'

were inadequate for the Fellowship examiners, who wanted to know the exact seventy-four relations of the lingual nerve and what it did in the monkey, dog, and rabbit as well.

I worked at my books fairly happily, for three months in Razzy's practice had given me the feeling of being a man of the world who could deal with dukes, manage cabinet ministers, and chum along with beautiful women, and could therefore confidently approach such prosaic individuals as the Fellowship examiners. This was my first mistake.

My second mistake was arriving for the examination in my black jacket and striped trousers. I had learnt in my first year as a medical student that the correct wear for facing examiners was a well-pressed, neatly-darned, threadbare old suit, which invited them to take a kindly attitude of superiority; appearing in a Savile Row outfit was like arriving at the Bankruptcy Court in a Rolls. But this did not occur to me as I made my way through the crowd of candidates in Queen Square.

Before the war the Fellowship was a private affair, in which a few dozen young men were treated to an afternoon's intellectual chat with the examiners and the proceedings were said to be interrupted for tea. Since the National Health Service the examination has been run on mass-production lines, but the traditional politeness of the examiners is steadfastly maintained. They politely made no comment on my Harley Street appearance, beyond smiling a little more heartily than usual in greeting; they brushed aside my ignorance of the precise location of the middle meningeal artery as unimportant among friends; they accepted my inability to identify the pathological specimens in glass jars as understandable between surgical gentlemen. The last examiner politely handed me a pickled brain and said, 'That sir, was removed post-mortem from a man of seventy. What do you find of interest in it?'

After a while I admitted, 'I see only the usual senile changes, sir.'

'They are not unusual, these changes, you mean, sir?'

'Oh, no, sir! After all, the patient *was* senile.'

'Alas,' he said gently. 'And I shall be seventy-six myself next birthday. Thank you, sir, for reminding me that I am rapidly getting past it all. Good day to you, sir.'

Politely, they thanked me; politely they bowed me out; just as politely they failed me.

Because I had been over-confident this depressed me more deeply than ploughing any of my student examinations. Once more I began opening my *British Medical Journal* from the back, but I was so dispirited that all I could bring myself to read in the rest of the pages was the obituaries. These are prepared on the first-, second-, or third-class funeral principle, overworked G.P.s succumbing in early life getting small print at the end, consultants larger type well-spaced out, and leaders of the profession whom everyone has thought dead long ago appearing with a photograph taken when they were twenty-four. All that could be said about the majority of dead doctors seemed to be that they were kind to their patients, popular with their colleagues, and liked walking in Ireland; at the most they had a disease named after them. I began to get deeply miserable about the futility of my profession, and wondered if I should have gone into the Church instead.

I found a part-time job helping a doctor in Brixton, and decided that if I gave up smoking I could afford to work for the next Primary Fellowship examination three months later. After a week I began to suspect he was doing abortions on the side, and I thought I'd better leave. My money was running out again, and I saw my Muswell Hill days returning: it was a moment of gathering depression. Then late one evening I had a telephone call from Grimsdyke.

'Where the devil have you got to, old lad?' he said crossly, as I leant on the coin-box in the hall and heard every door on the landing creak ajar. 'I've been trying to get you all over the place. Have you become a ruddy hermit, or something?'

'I've been working for my Primary.'

'Bit of a perversion this lovely weather, isn't it? I take it that now you've left Park Lane you're not in paid employment? Good. Then perhaps you could help me out. I've got an uncle who practises in the depths of the country–you know, simple rural GP., beloved by all, full of homespun philosophy and never washes his hands–whose partner's off for his month's holiday. When I qualified I said I'd help him out, but unfortunately I have a pressing professional engagement elsewhere. Would you fill the breach?

'I thought you *were* a country G.P.'

'On a different sort of level. Can't explain now. How about it?'

I hesitated. I wondered if it was wholly fair to judge Grimsdyke's relations by himself.

'Say you will, old lad,' he pressed. 'You can take your books and whistle through the work. It's as peaceful as a museum down there, but there's a nice pub next door and a pretty little bit in the post office if you feel like relaxation as well.'

'Tell me–is this uncle of yours married?'

Grimsdyke laughed. 'A widower. One daughter, permanently settled in Australia. How about it?'

I glanced round the dirty, stuffy hall of my lodgings, with the greasy green-baize board that would grow a crop of bills by next Friday morning.

'Well—'

'That's the spirit! I'll send you directions and a map. Can you start on Monday? The old boy's name is Farquharson. He's a funny old stick, but he thinks absolutely the world of me.'

After my first disastrous foray into general practice the prospect of playing the country G.P. for a month was alarming; also, I was a true Londoner who always felt uneasy beyond the friendly grin of the L.P.T.B. bus stops, or in the company of cows, sheep, cart-horses, goats, pigs, and other animals unknown in Leicester Square. But my confidence increased the next Monday afternoon as I drove Haemorrhagic Hilda deeper into the countryside, which wore a look of ripe and gentle peacefulness rarely captured outside brewers' advertisements. The village itself lay far from the main road, at the end of a winding lane in which a herd of cows, responding to the cow-attracting substance with which all cars are seemingly secretly coated by the manufacturers, licked Hilda over at their leisure. My new home consisted of a few houses, a couple of shops, the church, the vicarage, and the Four Horseshoes. In the middle was a triangular green on which a horse stared at me in offended surprise; across the green was Dr Farquharson's house, shaggy with creeper, its brass plate shining like a new penny in the sun, its front garden brilliant with flowers among which bees and wasps buzzed as contentedly as the people lunching off expenses in the Savoy Grill.

As Dr Farquharson was still on his rounds I was shown into the empty consulting-room by his housekeeper. This was a small, dark apartment tucked into the back of the house, containing a dirty sink, an old-fashioned sterilizer heated with a spirit lamp like a coffee machine, and an examination couch covered with white American cloth that looked as uninviting to lie upon naked as a fishmonger's slab. In one corner was a bookcase untidily filled with medical textbooks, mostly by Scottish authors and all out of date; in another stood a dusty pile of old copies of the *B.M.J.* and *Lancet*. I shook my head sadly. Looking round, I could see no haemoglobinometer, no erythrocyte-sedimentation-rate apparatus, no sphygmomanometer, no microscope, no ophthalmoscope, no centrifuge, no auroscope, no patella hammer, no spatulae, no speculae, no proteinometer, no pipettes. . . . It seemed to me impossible for anyone to practise medicine in the room at all.

Dr Farquharson turned out to be a tall, bony Scot with thick white hair, gold-rimmed spectacles, and big nobbly hands. He was dressed in a pair of patched tweed trousers, a black alpaca jacket, a striped shirt, a wing collar, and a spotted bow tie.

'Afternoon, Gordon,' he said dryly, as though we had parted just an hour ago. 'So you've come to help out an old fogy in the depths of the country, have you? How's that rascal of a nephew of mine?'

'He seems very well, sir.'

'How the Good Lord ever let him qualify I don't know. He hasn't half a brain in his head, and the rest of his cerebral space is filled up with a mixture of laziness and lubricity. Let's have a cup of tea.'

Tea was served under a mulberry tree in the garden by the housekeeper, whom Farquharson introduced as 'Mrs Bloxage, who's painstakingly kept my feet dry and my socks darned since my poor wife succumbed to *phthisis desperata* eighteen years ago.' We had raspberries and cream, tomato and cress sandwiches, brown bread and honey, buttered toast and home-made strawberry jam, scones and shortbread, and three kinds of cake. 'One of the few advantages for an out-of-date old man like me practising medicine in the back of beyond,' Farquharson continued, helping himself to more cream, 'is that the patients still bring you a little something out of the goodness of their hearts. They're simple souls, and haven't tumbled to it that the doctor's now a Civil Servant, like the Sanitary Engineer. What do you think of these raspberries?'

'Delicious, sir.'

'Aren't they? Old Mrs Crockett's varicose ulcer produces them year after year.'

When he had finished eating, Farquharson lit his pipe, pressed down the burning tobacco with a metal tongue spatula from his top pocket, and went on, 'The work's pretty easy round here, I suppose. There's hardly enough for two, especially this time of the year. But I'm glad enough to have someone to yarn to–I'm a bit of an old bore, you know. I was out in West Africa a good deal of my life. I settled down here because I totted up the ages on the gravestones across the way, and averaged out that this village has the lowest death rate in the country. I find plenty to interest myself in the natural history of the countryside–which includes the inhabitants. And in a couple of years the Government's going to chuck me out as too old and incompetent for anything except sitting on my backside and drawing my pension. God knows what I'll do then. But I'm rusty all right. Can't understand half the words in the *Lancet* these days.' He slapped me on the knee. 'You can put me right on all that, my lad. I suppose you know about these drugs they're bringing out like editions of the evening papers? You must give me a lecture on 'em some time. I'm just an old fogy of a country G.P.' He pulled a large gold watch from his pocket. 'I'm off to see a couple of patients before surgery. Settle in, and I'll see you for supper.'

Supper was cold salmon (the squire's gall-stones), cream cheese (the postmistress's backache), and to celebrate my arrival a glass of port (the vicar's hernia). Farquharson chatted entertainingly enough about West Africa, neatly comparing his native and his present patients, but I realized that he was as out of place in modern medicine as a jar of leeches. There were clearly several points on which I should be putting him right.

Within a week I discovered that medicine in the country is wholly different from medicine practised anywhere else. In the first place, most of the patients suffer from diseases totally unknown to medical science. At St Swithin's I examined my patients confident that their condition could be found somewhere between the green morocco covers of French's *Index of Diagnosis*; but in the country I puzzled over the significance of symptoms like horseshoes pressing on the head, larks in the stomach, and ferrets running up and down the spine at night. Even Dr Farquharson's former diagnoses were obscured by the patient's helpfully remembering the name, it taking me some time to recognize, for instance, that the woman complaining her child had been attacked by the infant tiger meant that he was suffering from impetigo.

Secondly, the visit of the medical attendant in most households provided less relief for the sufferer than entertainment for the rest of the family. The cry of 'Coo! it's the Doctor!' brought children running from their corners as powerfully as the smell of baking cakes. Arriving in the sickroom, I found it difficult to place the finger-tips together and demand with dignity, 'And how about the bowels?' when half a dozen small boys and girls were staring at me as though I were the hanging scene in a Punch-and-Judy show. When I insisted on having them shooed away they continued the enjoyment by taking turns to peer round the door, and my careful assessment of the pitch of a percussion note was often ruined by the awestruck whisper passing down the corridor, 'He's punching poor mummy all over the chest.'

In houses where there were no children, the patients reflected the more leisurely life of the country by using their attack of gastritis or summer flu to give the doctor a résumé of their life story and their opinions on their relatives. A brisk 'Good morning! And what can I do for you?' as I approached the bedside generally brought a contemplative folding of hands across the abdomen, a faraway look, a deep sigh, and the reply, 'Well, Doctor, in the 1914–18 war I was standing in a trench at Vimy . . .' or, 'I haven't been the same, Doctor, since that night me 'usband joined the Buffaloes. . . .'

When I mentioned these discoveries to Farquharson after supper one evening, he said, 'Oh, folk need to unburden themselves a bit. They don't like boring their friends, and their relatives won't listen to 'em any more. They're scared of the parson, so the doctor's the only one left they can pour their hearts out to.' He began to scrape out the bowl of his pipe with a scalpel he kept on the mantelpiece. 'I've got old-fashioned ideas, but that seems to me part of the doctor's job. That's something they never took into account when they got up this Health Service. Bloody silly, isn't it? Ask any G.P., and he'll tell you half his job is sympathizing with people, and that's ten times as difficult as treating 'em. Did you use the thermometer?'

'I couldn't–there's only one in the surgery, and it's broken.'

'It's broken all right. If I can't tell when a patient's feverish, I'm not much of a doctor. But shove it under their tongue, lad, and you've shut 'em up as long as you like. Or you can stick your stethoscope in your ears–it's not much good for anything else round here, because half of 'em think they'll drop dead if they take their vests off. Or you can take their pulse and scowl at 'em while you wonder what the devil's the matter. *That* shuts 'em up good and proper. You don't even need a watch. I couldn't afford a watch when I qualified, so I used to stare at my cupped hand instead, and nobody found out for eighteen months.

'As for the audience, always give 'em something to do. The public loves to see the vomit coming up or the baby coming down, but they love it even better playing the nurse. Get them to boil water–pots of it. When there aren't any saucepans left you can always start them tearing up the best sheets for bandages.' He lit his pipe, and went on reflectively, 'Never start off by asking a patient, "What are you complaining of?" They'll say, "I'll have you know I'm not the complaining type, not like some I could mention", and start some rigmarole about their sister-in-law who's been living with them since Christmas. Don't try "What's wrong with you?" because they like scoring one over the doctor and they'll reply, "I thought that was what you were here to find out." That starts the consulation on the wrong foot. And never ask, "What brought you here?" because ten to one they'll tell you the tram or the ambulance. Always listen to a patient's story, however long it is and however much you want your dinner. Usually they've come about something quite different, and they're too embarrassed or too scared to bring it out. And always give 'em a bottle of medicine, even if you and the whole Pharmaceutical Society know it's useless–even a straw's a comfort to a drowning man. Never tell them they're an "interesting case". Patients have got enough sense to know the only interesting cases are the ones we don't know anything about.

'You can diagnose half your patients as soon as you step through their front door, with a bit of practice. Brass gongs on the wall and tiger skins on the floor mean high blood-pressure. Box of chocolates on the piano and pekinese on the mat–that's obesity. Bills on the dresser and cigarette ash on the parlour carpet look like a duodenal ulcer upstairs. I've found aspidistras and antimacassars generally go with constipation. It's common sense. If you keep your eyes open you won't need the curate's legs sticking from under the bed to spot a case of female frustration. And never be squeamish asking about insanity in the relatives. I always start off, "How many in the asylum?" and you'd be surprised at the answers I get, even in the best families. But I'm rambling,' he said apologetically. 'You talk for a change. Seen any good cases today?'

There was an unusual psychiatric one. A farmer came in complaining that he experienced a strong sexual sensation every time he blew his nose.'

Farquharson stared at his burning tobacco. 'Well, now, that is interesting. What did you say?'

'Nothing much. I'm not well up in psychiatry. What would you have done?'

'I should have told him' said Farquharson without hesitation, 'that some people get all the luck.'

For the first time it occurred to me that Dr Farquharson knew much more medicine than I did.

Chapter Twelve

During my month in the practice I gained six pounds in weight, took on a deep sunburn, and learned more practical physic from Farquharson than I had gained from the whole staff of St Swithin's. The remaining gaps in my education were completed by the village constable, who was the fattest policeman outside pantomime, and seemed to have the single duty of supervising the nightly closing of the Four Horseshoes from the inside. After a pint or two he would unbutton his tunic and solemnly recount the medico-legal history of the countryside. 'It was but a year ago, as I recall,' he would begin with the air of a surgeon discussing a grave case with a colleague, 'that we had an indecency down at Smith's farm.' He frowned as he took some more beer. 'I can't remember off-hand whether it was a *gross* indecency, or just an ordinary one. But you'd be surprised what goes on round 'ere, Doctor. Why, we gets at least an indecent exposure once a week.' He continued to describe some of his recent cases in the odd anatomical terms used only by the police force. 'Mind you, it's hard work, Doctor,' he added proudly. 'You've got to be sure of your facts. It was only at the last Assizes there was an 'ell of a row because we had a case concerning a mare, and the barrister got hold of the idea it was one with a gold chain round his neck what we meant.'

A few days before I was due to leave, Grimsdyke paid a visit.

It was clear at once that he had enjoyed a change of fortune. He roared up in a bright sports car, he wore a new tweed coat and a clean waistcoat, his shoes shone, his face was plumper and better shaved, his hair was tidy, and he had a brand-new monocle with a fine sparkle to it. He carried a pair of yellow gloves, and a bulldog puppy leapt at his heels. He looked like the young squire after a good day at the races.

Although Farquharson began by asking him how the devil he had got qualified and when was he going to start a decent job of work, Grimsdyke still seemed to imagine himself the favourite nephew. Only when his uncle's conversation had been reduced to a string of grunts he suggested the pair of us went out to the Four Horseshoes.

'The market seems to be doing well of late,' I observed, as we entered the bar.

'The market?' Oh, yes, yes, of course. It's buoyant. By the way, I believe there's a few bob I owe you. Care for it now? Don't mind taking fivers, do you, it's all I've got? Cigarette–I suppose you like these black Russian things? Now let's have a drink. What can I get you?'

'A pint of bitter.'

'Beer? Nonsense! We'll have champagne! This is an occasion–the beginning of a great medical partnership. You know, Banting and Best, Florey and Fleming, Orth and Pettenkofer, and all that. I'll explain in a minute. Landlord! Your best vintage!'

The effect was lessened by the landlord of the Four Horseshoes having only a beer licence, so we had some Special Christmas Brew instead.

'Now what is all this,' I began firmly, wondering what trouble Grimsdyke was concocting for me and determined to stay clear of it.

'Have you had a go at the Primary yet?' he interrupted.

'Yes. The examiners were very undiscerning.'

'If you must wear a hair-shirt,' he said chidingly, 'you deserve to be tickled. Didn't you find out where they printed the examination papers? Some of these printer chaps'll do anything for a few quid.'

'I thought I'd better fail honestly, at least.'

'Quite right. I've been a great believer in professional honesty myself since old Moronic Maurice told me how he got through his surgical finals. At about the eighth shot, I might add. You know, those cases they got up for the exam–all the old chronics, the harvest of every out-patients' department in London. Maurice spent a couple of months nosing around the teaching hospitals until he was pretty confident he'd seen all the old familiar faces. Of course, he sneaked a bloody good look at their notes to see what was wrong. He went into the exam room knowing he'd already examined and diagnosed every case in the place, which he said gave him a wonderful feeling of confidence.'

'There's nothing very honest about that.'

'But wait a minute. The examiner grabbed him by the sleeve, and to his horror started dragging Moronic Maurice towards the one patient in the place he didn't recognize. Maurice realized it was the moment for honesty. "Sir," he said solemnly, "I feel I must inform you that I have already had an opportunity to examine this particular case in the hospital." "Very truthful of you, my lad", the old boy said. "Come and have a look at one of these over here instead." So he got through.'

'Quite. Now if you'll explain what new villainy you're up to—'

'By the way, I forgot to mention we're both out of debt to that trio of sabre-toothed tigers, Wilson, Willowick, and Wellbeloved.'

'Both?'

'I strode in there the other day to fling their filthy lucre in their faces. It was such a pleasant experience I flung a bit more for you, too. Here are the IOUs. We might have a pretty little ceremony burning them in the Piccadilly Bar, don't you think?'

'Look here,' I said in alarm. 'You're not doing anything dishonest, are you? I mean, false certificates and abortions and things?'

Grimsdyke looked pained. 'Have you ever known me try anything underhand outside the examination hall? No, old lad, it's simple. I'll let you into the secret. Through family influence, I've got myself a good job. Personal doctor to old Lady Howkins–you know, widow of the bloke that grabbed half Johannesburg and has been digging up useful little bits of gold ever since. She lives in a ruddy great house near Gloucester. She's as mean as a tax collector in the usual way, but she's pretty lavish with the cash to yours truly—'

'You mean you're a sort of clinical gigolo?'

Grimsdyke slapped down his glass in annoyance. 'Damn it, I pay your bloody debts—'

'I'm sorry. But you must admit it looks fishy on the face of it. Even you wouldn't admit you're a second Lord Horder.'

'Look, Lady Howkins is ninety-four, and to my mind as crazy as a coot. But fortunately, like my grandmother, she's crazy about doctors. All I do is recite to her the miracles of modern medicine, some of which I know and some of which I mug up in the *Reader's Digest*, and she thinks it's wonderful. She's fascinated by technical stuff. She knows more about things like isotopes and gastroscopes than I do. And she's bound to kick the bucket any day now.'

'And you'll be out of a job.'

'Yes, and no. I have it on good authority she's left me a terrific packet in her will. Think of it, old lad! Thousands of quids in the kitty, tax-free just like the football pools! And that's where you come in. I thought we might go off for a nose round the Bahamas or somehwere, and set up a little clinic for tired newspaper owners, film stars, and so forth. You'd do the medicine, with your Park Lane touch, and I'd fix the business side–you must admit, even though I may not know an appendix from an adenoid, I've a sharp eye for juggling the cash. What do you say?'

'Say? Damn it, this is a bit startling—'

'Think it over. Coming to the hospital dinner next month?'

I nodded.

'We'll discuss it again then. Don't think you're going to use ill-gotten gains, old lad, because they're not. I dance attendance like any other G.P., and call in specialists to the old dear as needed. If it wasn't for me she might be shared by dozens of Harley Street sharks. Lots of people leave money to their doctors, anyway. Must be damn brave,' he added reflectively. 'Have another?'

I shook my head. 'I've got to see some patients. One thing I've learned in general practice, if you smell faintly of alcohol just once, the word goes round by next morning that the doctor's a drunkard.'

'Have one of these,' Grimsdyke said, producing a tube of tablets. 'Chlorophyll removes all unpleasant odours. Fools patients and policemen alike.'

'Don't delude yourself. The goats round here eat it all day, and you should have a sniff at them.'

The St Swithin's reunion dinner was held every year in the Moorish Room of a huge banquet factory off Piccadilly Circus, and was anticipated by most of the guests as eagerly as Christmas in an orphanage. The majority of St Swithin's graduates were hardworking G.P.s scattered across the country, who faced ruin by being seen in the local pub or having more than two small ones in the golf club; the reunion dinner was their only chance to shed their inhibitions and splash for a while in the delightful anonymity of London.

I had arranged to meet Grimsdyke in the Piccadilly Bar before the dinner, which was five weeks later. He arrived in a new dinner-jacket with a red carnation in the buttonhole, smoking a cigar and looking jubilant.

'Well, old lad?' he demanded at once. 'Have you decided?'

'I've thought the matter over very carefully,' I told him. 'I must admit I'm a bit scared of the scheme, but my present system of casual employment is precarious, and I see no future for myself anywhere in England as a surgeon. So I'll come with you.'

'Capital!'

'The only snag seems to be that this patient of yours might quite easily live to be a hundred, and by that time will certainly have found out that you are simply an unprincipled—'

'But haven't you heard, old lad? Haven't you heard? The old dear snuffed it last week. Frightful pity of course, but who wants to live longer than ninety-four? And look at this–' He pulled a long letter from his pocket, typed on solicitor's paper. 'It came this morning–ten thousand quid! Ten thousand! Think of it! All for yours truly. Don't bother to read it all now, it's full of legal stuff. Shove it in your pocket. What an evening we're going to have! Barman! Champagne–the best in the house!'

We arrived in high spirits at the dinner, and found the Byzantine anteroom full of prosperous-looking middle-aged gentlemen in dinner-jackets, all drinking like pirates. The function always followed a strict ritual, and at eight o'clock the Dean himself climbed on a table and announced that dinner was served. This was a signal for the middle-aged gentlemen to cry 'Limerick! Limerick!' until the Dean coughed, and obliged tradition by reciting in his lecture-room voice:

'Ah–There was an old man of Manchuria
Who had the most painful dysuria.
The unfortunate chap
Had not only got clap
But haematoporphyrinuria.'

This brought the house down.

Grimsdyke and myself, with our old friends Tony Benskin and Taffy Evans, sat round the foot of one table with Mr Hubert Cambridge, who was one of the most popular of St Swithin's surgeons through being entertainingly eccentric. While the waiter with the chronic sinusitis was serving the chemical soup, Grimsdyke insisted on ordering champagne for all five of us.

'But, my dear boy, can you afford it?' Mr Cambridge asked. 'I assure you that pale ale is good enough for me.'

'Sir,' Grimsdyke said solemnly, 'it is a token of our appreciation of your tuition at St Swithin's. Within an hour the champagne will be carbon dioxide and water–but your teaching will remain with us all our lives.'

'And the Dean says the standard of our students is dropping!' he said, rubbing his hands. 'Tell me, what are the names of your excellent young men?'

After the soup came the mummified turbot, wearing its funeral wreath of shrivelled shrimps; next, the poor arthritic chicken, the devitaminized cabbage, the vulcanized potatoes; then the deliquescent ice and the strange compost on toast. Afterwards, we faced with British composure the stern British discipline which emphasizes that life is not all feasting and gaiety–the speeches. They were always long at the St Swithin's dinner, because the speakers were in the habit of lecturing for a full hour at a time to their students without fear of interruption. First the Dean told us what jolly good chaps St Swithin's men were; then the visiting medical Lord told us what a jolly good chap the Dean was; then the Senior Surgeon told us what jolly good chaps everyone was. After that we were released into the Gothic Smoking Room to sing the old student songs, while the Dean played the piano and the visiting Lord conducted with a loaf of French bread. We sang about the unfortunate adventures of The Baker's Boy Who to the Chandler's Went, The Honest Woman and the Rogue, The Man Who went

Fishing With Line and Rod, and of the wildly psychopathic evening in Kerriemuir. It was difficult to see anyone in the room ever gripping their lapels and declaring, 'No starchy foods, no alcohol, and no smoking–the human body's not a machine, y'know.' But all of them would be saying it tomorrow morning, sterner than ever.

In the excitement of the evening I had almost forgotten that I was committed to an alarming medico-commercial adventure. I was paying the waiter for a round of drinks when Grimsdyke's letter fell from my pocket. Concentrating, I began to read it in the light of one of the Tudor wall-lanterns.

Grimsdyke had just reached the top note in the St Swithin's version of 'She Was Poor But She Was Honest,' when I drew him carefully to one side.

'Are you sure you've read this letter through?' I asked.

'Of course I've read it,' he said crossly. 'Every word. All that guff about my being a dedicated young physician and all that.'

I nodded. 'Perhaps you'd better look at the last line again.'

'Last line? What are you up to, old lad? Some sort of joke?' He took the letter. 'It looks absolutely straightforward to me–"In recognition of your devoted service bequeaths to you the sum of ten thousand pounds–"' His voice trailed off. Like a man uttering his last words while suffering death in the garrotte he finished the sentence: '". . . for you to donate in its entirety within six months to the hospital performing medical research you consider the most rewarding."'

The letter fell to the floor.

'Hard luck, Grim,' I said sorrowfully. I summoned a waiter. 'You'd better swallow the rest of that tube of chlorophyll.'

Chapter Thirteen

The reunion dinner nevertheless ended in a gust of ill wind that blew Grimsdyke and myself a little good. Long after we had sadly staggered back to our lodgings, Mike Kelly, a heavy young man who had captained the first fifteen for several years and was now Mr Hubert Cambridge's house surgeon, found himself standing on the empty pavement in his dinner-jacket with only tenpence in his pocket. He resigned himself to walking back to the hospital, deciding to go by way of Covent Garden because he had heard that the pubs opened in the early hours to slake the thirsts of the busy fruiterers. Unfortunately, alcohol always had a confusing effect on Mike Kelly, and after trying to buy a drink in St Peter's Hospital for Stone and Stricture under the impression that it was the Strand Palace Hotel, he demonstrated his belief that the Royal Opera House was a gentlemen's convenience. When a policeman shouted at him unnecessarily, ''Ere! What do you think you're doing?' Mike Kelly made what he thought at the time to be the smartest remark of his life. Beaming at the constable he announced benignly, 'Officer, I am picking bloody gooseberries.'

Mike was then taken to nearby Bow Street and charged with being drunk and disorderly. As his head began to clear in the sobering surroundings, he remembered the only fact that had ever struck him as useful in his forensic medicine lectures: if you are charged with being drunk, you can choose your own doctor to come and examine you. 'Disorderly, yes,' he said sternly to the sergeant. 'Drunk, definitely no. I bet my blood-alcohol isn't even point one per cent. I demand my own doctor at once.'

'All right by us. It'll save the police surgeon getting out of bed. And who is your doctor?'

'Doctor–' Mike Kelly drew himself to add dignity to his words–'John Harcourt Bottle, Master of Arts at the University of Cambridge, Licentiate of the Royal College of Physicians of London, member of the Royal College of Surgeons—'

'All right, all right. Where's he to be found?'

'Ring the Resident Medical Staff Quarters at St Swithin's Hospital. Ask for', continued Mike, deflating slightly, 'the Assistant Junior Resident Anaesthetist.'

John Bottle, who had been continuing the party with the other residents in his room on the top floor of the Staff Quarters, expressed himself indignant over the telephone that the police should have submitted a member of the medical profession to such shame. He spoke at some length, giving the sergeant his opinion on his conduct, demanding an immediate apology, hinting at substantial compensation, and threatening to write to his M.P. He then declared that he would summon a taxi and appear immediately to put this regrettable matter of rights. The result of his intervention was not one doctor being charged with being drunk and disorderly in Bow Street that night, but two.

This was too much, even for St Swithin's, whose staff and governors showed remarkable tolerance towards purple paint on the statues, cart-horses in the quadrangle, and cami-knickers flying from the flag-staff on the morning of the Lord Mayor's visit. To avoid disproportionate damage to their careers the Staff Committee sent Kelly and Bottle on unpaid leave for the rest of their appointment, leaving two gaps on the resident staff until the next batch of students qualified in three months' time. As Mike Kelly had brought himself to his confused state by sympathizing with Grimsdyke at the dinner, he suggested his misfortune might at least be turned to the gain of his friends. Grimsdyke and I hurried to St Swithin's to see Mr Cambridge, and introduced ourselves as the charming young gentlemen who had been so appreciative of his teaching the night before. The next day I had become his temporary senior house surgeon and Grimsdyke was assistant junior resident to the hospital's anaesthetics department.

'I'm only a ruddy stuffist,' Grimsdyke complained. 'But by George! we're lucky to get paid work at all in our present state. It's hard luck on old Mike, though.'

I too was sorry for our former classmates, but I was overwhelmingly delighted to be back in St Swithin's. The disappointment of my earlier departure was wiped out. I was at last a senior house surgeon, if not an official one; there were hopes of resuscitating my moribund surgical career; and it would be a delicious affront to Bingham.

I returned to the Staff Quarters, the tall, cold, sooty building between the hospital laundry and the mortuary that had been used as the ear, nose, and throat wards until condemned by the Governors as unfit for the housing of patients. Mike Kelly's room was next to the one allotted Bingham, who was hurrying down the corridor in his white coat as I struggled in with my luggage.

He pulled up short. We had not met since the incident in the lift. He seemed uncertain what to say. He looked more boyish, more untidy, more pimply than ever, and his stethoscope seemed to have increased in size until it entwined his neck like a rubbery vine.

'Hello, Bingham,' I said.

He swallowed. 'Hello, old chap. Heard you were coming back.'

'Look here,' I said, dropping my suitcase and holding out my hand. 'I'm sorry about that business of the bananas in the lift. It was damn bad manners on my part, but I was a bit upset at the time. About not getting the job, you know. Not that I'm saying you didn't deserve the promotion. But we've got to live next door to each other for a bit, so can't we forget the whole thing?'

'Of course, old chap,' Bingham said awkwardly. There was a short silence. 'I'm–er, sorry if I hogged all the cases in cas., and all that.'

'You deserved them, too.'

We shook. 'If you want any tips about the work, old chap,' Bingham went on, 'I can put you right. Only if you ask, of course,' he added quickly. 'The Prof.'s been jolly decent, and letting me try quite a bit off my own bat. I've done a couple of hernias and some piles already, and there's a nice excision of warts on the list for me tomorrow. Must buzz off now, old chap, there's a query tib. and fib. just come into cas. See you at supper.'

I went to my room feeling like the head girl at St Agatha's making it up with the lacrosse skipper.

My job as a senior house surgeon in St Swithin's was looking after the day-to-day needs of the patients in the wards, assisting in the operating theatre, and acting as a clinical valet to Mr Cambridge. This was my most difficult duty, because Mr Cambridge, though an excellent surgeon who had plucked more stomachs than anyone else in the hemisphere, was alarmingly absent-minded. His professional memory was excellent: he never forgot a stomach. Socially, he couldn't remember the day of the week, whether he had come out in his overcoat, what he was supposed to be doing in the afternoon, and if he had already had lunch. As a young surgeon he had arrived at St Swithin's from his lodgings one winter's morning to operate as usual, and was aware as he scrubbed up of a strange loneliness about the place. Not only was the surgeon's room silent, but peeping into the theatre itself he found it deserted, with the table under a dust-sheet. At first he thought he was in the wrong operating block, but there was his name on his locker, as plain as ever. Next, he wondered if it might be Sunday; but he was certain it was Wednesday, because he paid his landlady every Tuesday and he remembered that he had forgotten to give her the cheque yesterday. It then occurred to him that he had noticed a strangeness about the streets while driving to the hospital. Was there a sudden general strike, perhaps, sweeping up the doctors and nurses as it hurricaned upon them? He padded down the corridor in his operating clothes, white rubber boots, and surgical mask, to seek information. At the ward door he stopped short. It was most extraordinary. There appeared to be some sort of riot inside, with nurses and patients dancing round the beds. Clearly, revolution had broken out in St Swithin's. 'Why, hello, Mr. Cambridge!' called the Sister from the door. 'Merry Christmas!'

My first morning on duty I waited in the quadrangle for Mr Cambridge's arrival, according to hospital tradition standing beneath the statue to its famous former surgeon, Sir Benjamin Bone.

'The Chief's getting late,' I said to the Registrar, a tall, thin, serious, but pleasant young man called Hatrick, who already had his F.R.C.S.

'There's nothing much you can do about it,' he said gloomily. 'The last time the old boy didn't turn up I found he'd gone on an American lecture tour.

We were due to begin operating at nine, but it was almost half-past when Mr Cambridge came cheerily through the main gates on foot.

'Ah, good morning, my dear Mr Er–er, and my dear Mr Ah–ah,' he greeted us. He could never remember the names of his assistants, and I was thankful that he had managed to recall mine twelve hours after the reunion dinner. 'Sorry I'm late. Got my notes?' I handed him three or four envelopes, addressed in his own barely legible handwriting. Whenever he thought of anything he ought to remember the next day, he wrote it on a card and immediately posted it to himself at St Swithin's. 'Let's see, we operate this morning, don't we?' he continued, as we marched towards the surgical block. 'There's a most interesting gastrocolic fistula I'd like you to inspect Mr Er–And of course you too, Mr Ah–'

There followed one of the most painful mornings since I qualified. As a medical student I had occasionally been ordered to scrub-up, dress in a sterile gown, and join the surgeon's assistants, but once at the operating table I only played dummy in the surgical quartet. Occasionally I would be given a retractor and told, 'Hang on to that, boy!' but usually I was edged away as the surgeon became more interested in the operation and spent most of the time watching nothing more illuminating than the buckle on the back of his braces. But as a house surgeon I was a necessary member of the surgical team, responsible for cutting the stitches, clipping off the bleeding points, and fixing the dressings. Conscious of this, I pulled on my rubber gloves with unusual determination, and split them from thumb to cuff.

'Nurse!' The sister's voice rang across the theatre. 'Another pair of gloves for Mr Gordon!'

A small nurse, muffled in her theatre clothes, darted across the floor and drew a white glove packet from the sterile drum with a pair of long forceps.

'Thank you,' I mumbled. I was now so flustered that I forgot to powder my damp hands with the small gauze bag of talc, and could hardly force them inside the rubber at all. I seemed to have two fingers jammed in the thumb space, while the end of the glove danced about like seaweed in a strong tide.

'A case of multipollices, isn't it?' murmured the small nurse.

This increased my agitation, and I pulled the glove in two.

'Nurse!' cried the theatre Sister, more loudly. '*Another* pair of gloves for Mr Gordon.'

I pulled on the third pair intact, though there was a small empty space like the teat of a baby's bottle at the end of each finger. I anxiously made towards the table, pushing aside a surgical trolley in my way.

'That trolley is *unsterile*,' declared the theatre Sister, louder than ever. 'Nurse! A complete change of clothes for Mr Gordon!'

When I reached the patient the operation was almost over. Mr Cambridge merely murmured, 'Hello, Mr Er–ah–Will you take the second retractor from Mr Ah–er–?' I determined to do my best and recover from the bad start, but I cut the stitches the wrong length, let the retractors slip, jammed my fingers in the handles of artery clips, and dropped several small instruments on the floor. Mr Cambridge seemed to take no notice. I decided that he was not only the politest surgeon in the hospital, but one of the cleverest in allowing for the assistance of fumbling house surgeons when planning his operating technique.

My only consolation that morning was watching Grimsdyke out of the corner of my eye. He was having a worse time than I was. When I had asked him at breakfast how he felt about giving anaesthetics he had replied lightly, 'Doing dopes? There's nothing to it. It's all done by machines these days–none of the old rag-and-bottle business any more. Just like driving a car. You twiddle a knob here, twiddle a knob there, and you're away.'

'Possibly–but supposing you make the mixture too rich?

'Too much choke, you mean? He started to laugh, but said, 'Sorry, old lad. Didn't mean it at breakfast. Anyway, it's perfectly simple to a chap with a mechanical mind like myself.'

'I suppose you've read up all the stages of anaesthesia, and so on?'

'Old lad, as far as I'm concerned there are only three stages of anaesthesia–awake, asleep, and dead.'

It was now clear that Grimsdyke knew nothing about the administration of anaesthesia whatever. He was sitting at the head of the table beside a large chromium-plated trolley thick with dials, and though only his eye and forehead were showing I had never seen him looking so worried since one of the pretty girls in the X-ray Department thought she was in the family way. Every now and then he hopefully turned a coloured tap, or buried under the sterile towels to look up Macintosh's *Essentials of Anaesthesia*, which he had propped against the unconscious patient's nose. Grimsdyke had come to the theatre confident that he would be expected only to assist the consultant anaesthetist, a cheerful fat man with the best stock of rude stories in London: but the consultant had the habit of returning to the surgeon's room and solving *The Times* crossword as soon as the patient was on the table, leaving his assistant at the controls.

Unlike most of the surgeons at St Swithin's, Mr Cambridge was considerate and polite to his anaesthetist. He made no remark about the grunts coming from beneath Grimsdyke's fingers, and an unexpected paroxysm of coughing from the patient left him unperturbed. Towards the end of the operation I was alarmed to feel something stir beneath the sterile towels. I glanced at Grimsdyke, but he had now given up the struggle and was leaning on the trolley with his eyes shut. To my horror the patient's arm came slowly into the air. 'Mr Anaesthetist,' said Mr Cambridge quietly, 'if the patient can keep awake during the operation, don't you think you might, too?'

When operating on other people's stomachs Mr Cambridge disregarded his own. As gastrectomy followed gastrectomy my fumbling became worse and I began to long for the release of lunch. After the fourth case the theatre Sister announced firmly as she handed me the dressing, 'We are stopping for an hour now, sir. It's two o'clock.'

'Two o'clock? Already? How the morning flies, Sister.'

'And there is a detective to see you.'

'Ah, yes. Which one this time?'

'Sergeant Flannagan.'

'Flannagan? Can't say I recall the name. What's he like?'

'Big and red-faced, sir,' said Hatrick.

'I know him very well. I'll be out directly. Just clean up the incision, will you Mr Ah–er–'

Mr Cambridge was well known to the Metropolitan Police because he was continually losing his car. As soon as he felt his feet as a surgeon he had bought the customary Bentley, but he either forgot where he had parked it, wondered if he had come out in it at all, or threw open the garage doors in the morning and found it wasn't there.

'This time I'm certain it's been stolen,' he explained to the policeman in the surgeon's room, as Hatrick, Grimsdyke, and I began tucking in to our cold congealed mutton stew. 'I came in by tube this morning, and I didn't have it out yesterday–I don't think so, anyway. But the day before, Sergeant Um–um, I distinctly remember I had it parked outside my rooms in Harley Street. When I came out I'm absolutely certain it was gone.'

The sergeant coughed. 'But why didn't you inform the police at the time, sir?'

'Well, you see, when I saw it had gone I was certain I hadn't brought it with me. You follow?'

'Quite,' said the sergeant.

Mr Cambridge disappeared after lunch to remove stomachs in another part of London, leaving Hatrick and myself to finish the list. As the consultant anaesthetist accompanied the surgeon, Hatrick pointedly told Grimsdyke that he would do the remaining minor operations under local. Grimsdyke took this as a slight, murmured something about, 'Any bloody fool with a sharp knife can be a surgeon,' and left the operating theatre in a huff. As the students had drifted away with the loss of their main attraction, and a milder staff nurse was substituted for the theatre Sister, the pair of us operated peacefully until nightfall. After the morning's exhibition I was then certain that I would never become a surgeon; but under Hatrick's gentle tuition I began to gain confidence.

'Always steady the blade of the scissors with your finger when you cut,' he murmured as I fumbled round the incision. 'Tuck them into the palm of your hand when you're not using them. Take the artery forceps with the *tips* of your fingers, so, then you won't get stuck. Tie a surgical knot like *this*, and you'll only have to use one hand. Never worry about cutaneous bleeding–it always stops. And use the *handle* of your scalpel if in doubt–it does less damage.'

When we returned to the surgeons' room as the last case was wheeled away, we found Sergeant Flannagan waiting.

'Mr Cambridge has left the hospital,' I told him. 'Is there any message?'

'Yes. There is. We've found his car.'

'Oh, really? And where was it in the end?'

'Locked in his ruddy garage at home.'

Chapter Fourteen

Mr Cambridge had charge of two wards at St Swithin's–Fortitude for men and Constancy for women–where my duties, though less exciting than in the operating theatre, were of more value to the hospital. Mr Cambridge himself skipped round the beds every Tuesday morning, his bedside manner consisting largely of poking a patient hard in the tummy and saying cheerfully, 'You'll be much better with it out.' Hatrick tidied up all the surgical odd jobs, and I was left in charge of the more domestic side of hospitalization. The patients were less concerned with the feats of surgery performed upon them under anaesthesia than the discovery that they were unable to sleep, their bowels wouldn't work, the fish for supper was cold, and there was a draught all day from the window opposite, all faults that I was expected to rectify. As I was obliged to make my rounds twice daily the patients saw far more of me than the other members of the surgical firm, and sometimes embarrassed me by imagining that I was the brilliant young doctor in charge. 'Which surgeon are you under?' I overheard one of them being asked in the X-ray Department downstairs.

'Dr Gordon.'

'I mean, who's the head surgeon in your ward?'

'Why, Dr Gordon,' said the patient in amazement. 'You know–the young feller.'

'Is there any *other* doctor?'

The patient thought for a time. 'There's another youngish chap called Hatrick what Dr Gordon gets to help him sometimes—'

'Yes, yes, yes! But who else?'

The patient tried to remember. 'No one else except an old man Dr Gordon asks in every so often out of the kindness of his heart. But he's past it, I reckon,' he added confidentially.

As the Professor's wards were immediately below mine in the surgical block, I saw a good deal of Bingham. We treated each other with aggressive politeness: Bingham markedly avoided the lift when we went downstairs together, and I pointedly asked his advice, as the senior surgeon by six months, about my difficult cases. Whenever our professional interests conflicted, we drenched each other in courtesy.

'Hello, old chap,' he said, coming to the duty operating theatre one evening. 'Just finished a case?'

'Well, er, no. Actually, I was just going to scrub up for a stitch abscess from the ward. But if you want the theatre first—'

'Not a bit, old chap, not a bit,' he said quickly. 'We *are* on duty tonight, I admit, and we do have priority in the theatre and all that, but I wouldn't dream of standing in your way. It's only a F.B. in the pop. foss., and that can wait.'

'No no, my dear Bingham! After all, I'm a septic case, so you should come first.'

'Well, that's terribly d. of you, old chap, but really–I know,' he announced, his eyes lighting up at the gentlemanly solution to this impasse, 'you shall have our centrifuge all tomorrow afternoon.'

'Really, I couldn't—'

'Yes, old chap. Absolutely insist.'

'That's awfully kind of you, Bingham.'

'Don't mench, old chap.'

A month passed like a fine April day. Then a strange feeling of depression began to creep over me. At first it puzzled me; my career was progressing splendidly, but I had the vague feeling of something missing from my life. I wondered if I were developing some dark psychological complaint, and mentioned this to Grimsdyke one evening over a pint of beer in the King George pub opposite.

'I don't know what it is exactly,' I told him. 'It's a sort of–well, unsatisfied feeling. Lord knows why. I love the work, I really feel I'm learning a bit of surgery at last, it's fun living in the hospital with the boys, and I haven't seen Bingham for two days. What more could I want? Do you think I ought to take an interest in art or music or something?'

Grimsdyke laughed. 'You don't want music, old lad, you want women. Or one woman at least.'

I was surprised. 'Do you really think so?'

'Absolutely certain. Can't miss the diagnosis. We're not run-around students any more, however much we try and pretend we are on Saturday nights. We're worthy citizens, God help us. "It is a truth universally acknowledged, that a single man in possession of a good fortune, must be in want of a wife." Jane Austen.'

'A wife!' I cried in horror.

'Well, I wouldn't go as far as that,' he added, finishing his beer. 'But you get the idea.'

I thought carefully about Grimsdyke's diagnosis, and decided that he was right. Fortunately, the treatment would be simple. Since returning to St Swithin's as a doctor, I had sensed a different relationship between myself and the hundreds of young women that the place was obliged to employ. Apart from the nurses, there were the buxom dieticians, the cheerful girls in X-ray, the neat secretaries, the occupational therapists in sandals and folk-weave belts, the laboratory assistants, the speech therapists, the child-guidance workers, and the statuesque physiotherapists in the massage department who were known as the 'slap-and-tickle honeys'. As students, these ladies had treated us like well-brought-up Wrens dealing with fresh ratings; but now that we were qualified and therefore pressingly marriageable the iron hand was eased a little from the velvet glove.

The sister of Mr Cambridge's female ward had resigned shortly before I arrived, leaving the patients in charge of the staff nurse until the matron could make another promotion. This was Nurse Plumtree, a pale, thin, dark, snub-nosed girl, passably pretty except for her hair, which appeared to be attended by a gardener in a spare second while occupied with the hedge-clippers. From my first entrance to the ward Nurse Plumtree clearly looked upon me as her own property. This was correct hospital etiquette, for the staff nurse was always allowed first bite at the new houseman; but Nurse Plumtree, perhaps because she was in supreme authority over the others, took pains to make this obvious. I preferred her second-in-command, a bright, red-headed, freckled Scots girl, to whom I chatted if Nurse Plumtree was out of the ward; when she returned she would cross directly to us with an extra briskness in her step, look her professional sister squarely in the eye, and order her to check the laundry. One afternoon, Nurse Plumtree came back from lunch to find the pair of us giggling over a joke in the sluice-room, and afterwards rarely took any time off at all. She insisted that this was through her devotion to duty; but it was clear to everyone else that it was through her devotion to me.

'Have you any socks that need mending?' she asked one morning. 'If you'll bring them up I'll darn them for you. I've nothing else to do in the evenings. I never go out.'

We were sitting alone in the Sister's private sitting-room, a small apartment fierce with yellow chintz and brassware next to the ward. Every day I was invited there for a cup of milky coffee served timidly by the junior probationer, while Nurse Plumtree took a tin of her own chocolate biscuits from the bureau, put her feet up on the rushwork stool, and lit a cigarette. 'In fact,' she went on, 'I've got an evening off tomorrow. From five o'clock. I don't know what on earth to do with it.'

'Really? Well, er–perhaps something may turn up,' I said warily. 'Who knows?'

She sipped her coffee sorrowfully.

The morning after my talk with Grimsdyke she threw into her conversation, 'I've got a half-day on Wednesday. Starting at twelve o'clock. And I'm due for a late pass till midnight. But I don't expect I shall take them. there just doesn't seem anything to do.'

I already knew this, having sneaked a glance at the nurses' off-duty book kept with the insurance certificates on her desk. I had made up my mind. Nurse Plumtree was presentable and pleasant; besides, there was not the faintest chance of being snubbed.

I coughed.

'If you're really without plans, perhaps you'd like to come to the pictures, or something?'

For an instant her eyes widened. 'I'm not sure if I can really leave the ward. Nurse Macpherson isn't very experienced.'

'Of course not.'

'As well as being a lot too familiar with the patients—'

'So I've noticed.'

'And anyway, she's far too interested in one of the students for the good of her work.'

'Really? Do try and come. I'll see you at six,' I said, rising. 'Outside the dental department.'

Chapter Fifteen

My romance with Nurse Plumtree caused no more surprise in the hospital than the annual blooming of the geraniums outside the Secretary's office in summer. My colleagues grinned more widely the more I asked them to stand-in for me during the evenings, and Nurse Macpherson once winked at me over a ward screen; but to most people at St Swithin's we were simply another staff nurse and houseman obeying the local laws of biology.

Like many other young couples with no money in London, we sat at the back in the Festival Hall and the Empress Hall, we dined at Lyons, and we drank in the cosy saloon bars of tucked-away pubs, of which my medical education had left me with a more precise knowledge than of human anatomy. Often Nurse Plumtree paid for herself and sometimes she paid for us both. She was an easy girl to entertain, because she was fond of long silences during which she would stare at the opposite wall as if recalling the faces of friends long dead; and her conversation, when it came, was almost wholly about the hospital. As my few former girl friends had all been nurses this failure to throw off the cap and apron did not discourage me, and I consoled myself that another companion might have talked only about ponies or Proust; but after a few weeks I found myself irresistibly wishing that she would stop telling me exactly what was happening to number twenty-two's blood chlorides, and the bright retort she had made to Nurse Macpherson when informed that the ward's allocation of liquid paraffin had been used up in a week.

There was another more disheartening impediment in my relationship with Nurse Plumtree. I confessed this late one evening to Grimsdyke, when he came into my room to scrounge cigarettes.

'How's the sex life?' he asked cheerfully. 'Feeling more contented?'

'Well–yes and no.'

'What? You mean the course of true love hasn't run smooth?'

'Too smoothly, if anything,' I told him. 'You know how it is with nurses–we go to a flick or a concert or something, then I rush her back to the hospital before her late pass expires, we have a quick neck among half the medical school outside the mortuary gate, then I push her into the Nurses' Home on the stroke of eleven. If I kept her out another minute her good name would be ruined for ever, so it seems.'

'Frustrating.'

'You don't have to read Freud and Kinsey to know it doesn't do a chap much good. But what's the alternative? Apart from holding hands in Hyde Park?'

'How about a little intramural love life?'

'In St Swithin's, where they separate the sexes like a Victorian swimming-bath?'

'There's always the fire-escape.'

'Ah, the fire-escape!' This ugly zigzag up the wall of the Residents' Quarters was a monument to the victory of the insurance company's prudence over that of the matron. By climbing the darkened floors of the empty out-patients' block at night, crossing the roof of the physiotherapy department, and dodging past the night porter's mess-room, we could smuggle a nurse into our forbidden corridors. This risky adventure was rarely suggested, for the nurse, if discovered, was regarded by the Matron to be fit for nothing more but the Chamber of Horrors.

'There's nothing to it, old lad,' Grimsdyke went on, as I looked at him dubiously. 'Wait for a dark night, lay in a bottle of courting sherry, have a decent shave, and you're all set for a cosy evening. So much warmer than Hyde Park, too.'

At our next meeting I mentioned the fire-escape to Nurse Plumtree. As I expected, she looked sad, sniffed, and said, 'Oh, Richard!'

Feeling I should provide some excuse, I went on quickly, 'But I mean, I thought we could just have a cup of coffee, and I could show you my microscope slides of gastric ulcers that I've been telling you about. I mean, it would be quite–well, you know, all right—'

'Oh, Richard! It would spoil everything.'

'What, you mean just looking at my slides? They're most interesting, and of course I have to borrow a microscope from one of the other residents, so I can't very well show them to you elsewhere. But of course, if you don't want to–'

She sighed deeply, and looked away. I felt that Grimsdyke would have managed the invitation much better! I had tempted her only with the pathological equivalent of etchings. There was another of her silences, then we talked about the best way of treating post-operative thrombosis.

Our affair jogged along for several weeks. There was no alternative, for she now simply told me when she was next off duty and assumed that I would be waiting to take her out. It was a relationship with many concrete advantages, for Nurse Plumtree was a tender-hearted girl whose motherly instincts were not wholly absorbed by her profession. From our first outing she had mended my shirts, lent me books, and provided currant cake with the morning coffee; now she bought me ties and bars of chocolate, pressed on me handfuls of vitamins from the medicine cupboard, knitted me a muffler, and made me wear braces instead of an old rugger club tie for keeping up my trousers, which she pressed proudly every Sunday with her iron in the Nurses' Home. My friends thought I had not looked so tidy or so well fed for a long time.

Two events disturbed the placid current of this romance. The first was Nurse Macpherson's transference to night duty.

In the printed charge handed to him by the hospital Secretary on his appointment, each senior house surgeon at St Swithin's was enjoined 'to visit your wards at least once nightly before retiring, to take the report from the senior night nurse and attend to the needs of the patients, at whatever hour that might be'. This night round was the most conscientiously performed of all the house surgeons' duties, for night nurses, who have to sleep all day and work alone all night, are lonely souls who suffer from a deficiency of masculine companionship. For this reason the most untidy and unromantic houseman is confident of a welcome in the darkened ward, even if he has just been thrown out of the King George and arrives, like my predecessor, wearing the head porter's hat and riding a bicycle. Besides, all nurses are good cooks and without the ward sister counting the rations over their shoulders gladly provide peckish housemen with bacon and eggs at midnight.

My night rounds had so far been dull, because the nurse on Fortitude was a newly-promoted girl who breathlessly read me the ward report with one timid eye on the door for the visit of the surgical night sister; on Constancy, the night nurse was a thin, spectacled woman with a faint moustache, who in the half-light reminded me of Groucho Marx. One night I came up the empty corridor after seeing Nurse Plumtree into the Nurses' Home as usual, and found Nurse Macpherson frying bacon and eggs and smoking a cigarette in the small kitchen next to the ward.

'What on earth are you doing here?' I asked in surprise.

'Why, hallo, there! For three months I'm to be Queen of the Night, tra-la! Didn't Plumtree tell you?'

I shook my head.

'How about some eggs and bacon? Or would you prefer'–she opened a box on the diet trolley–'some egg custard and puréed spinach?'

'As a matter of fact I could do with a bite. As usual, they gave us a rotten supper in the Residency. You know, that brawn stuff the patients won't eat.'

She nodded. 'How well I do! It would pass unnoticed in a pathology exam with "Draw, Label, and Identify this Tissue" stuck on it. There's a bottle of beer in the comfort cupboard,' she went on, breaking a couple more eggs. 'Help yourself and pour me a glass.'

'Aren't you worried about the night sister?' I asked, hesitating.

'What, old Muggsy Munson? She's got her feet up in the Sister's room with a nice cup of tea reading the *Washerwoman's Weekly*, I'll bet. She comes round as regularly as the hands of a clock.'

I sat down at the ward table, wondering why a nurse smoking in uniform always presented such a curiously abandoned appearance. Then I remembered that I had just kissed my girl-friend good night. 'How are the patients, Nurse?' I asked, trying to re-establish our professional relationship.

'Please, *please*, don't talk about them out of the ward, I beg.' She forked bacon from the pan. 'I cannot talk shop with my meals. The Nurses' Home is ghastly–it's mastoids with the mince, mumps with the macaroni, membranes with the mash. That's one of the things I've got against Plumtree–' She bit her lip. 'I shouldn't have said that, I suppose?'

'Not said it?' I tried to sound as indifferent as possible. 'Why?'

'Well–everyone knows that you and Plumtree–I mean, she's a very good sort at heart.'

'She certainly strikes me as being a decent sort of girl, I must say.'

'Oh, yes, very nice. Such a pity about her acne.'

'Acne?' I recalled that Nurse Plumtree's face was occasionally marred by a small square of sticking-plaster.

'Yes, all over her back. But of course–' She giggled. 'You wouldn't know about that, would you? But she's a nice placid person.'

'I happen to dislike chattering women,' I said, a little stiffly.

'She's no chatterbox. Why, sometimes she sits for hours and hours without saying anything, just looking into the middle distance.'

'I find her quite an interesting companion, anyway,' I insisted.

'So do we in the Home, these days. The things she tells us about you! My, my! I want to blush sometimes. Did you really go as far as that on the Inner Circle the other night?'

'Good God, did she tell you *that?*'

'That's only half of it. How many eggs'

I ate my bacon and eggs in silence. I was disillusioned. I had thought Nurse Plumtree above the common feminine habit of describing an evening out in the spirit of a boastful Grenadier in a pub after Waterloo.

When I met her the following evening I was more careful in my conversation and behaviour. This did not seem to disturb her, but as we came home I had to admit that her silences seemed longer and longer, and now extended from Piccadilly Circus to Russell Square on the Tube; and as she turned to allow me to kiss her good night I was sure I saw incipient acne all over her cheeks.

'I suppose you know Macpherson's on nights?' she said.

I murmured that I had noticed her while dashing through the ward on my night round.

'I'm asking the office to get her moved,' Nurse Plumtree went on. 'She's incompetent. Do you know that this morning she gave the high-protein diets to the low-proteins? And she mixed up the extra vitamins with the salt-deficients?'

'Oh, really? It doesn't seem to have done them much harm, anyway?'

She twisted the top button of my overcoat. 'Richard, I've got an evening tomorrow. Will you come to dinner at home?'

'Home?' I was startled. I had never thought of Nurse Plumtree having any home except the one provided by St Swithin's.

'It's only down in Mitcham. Mummy and Daddy would love to see you.' I hesitated. 'Please, Richard.'

I thought quickly. Dining with the parents would certainly be a trial. I could see it–gruff father, who I believed was a retired colonel, and sharp-eyed mother, both suspicious of my intentions towards their daughter. Still, Nurse Plumtree had been a kind companion to me, and I owed her some repayment–besides, I was running short of money, and it would mean a free meal.

'All right,' I said. 'I'll meet you at the usual place at six, if I can get away.'

The clock struck then, and she disappeared through the closing doors of the Nurses' Home.

'How's Plumtree?' Nurse Macpherson asked cheerfully, as I arrived in the ward kitchen two minutes later.

'Oh, all right.' I sat on the edge of the table, lit a cigarette and swung my legs.

'You don't sound very enthusiastic about it, I must say.'

'Oh, don't I?'

She put down a bowl of eggs she was beating and went on, 'Be a darling and lend me a cigarette. I left mine in the Home.'

She came across to me as I pulled a packet from my jacket pocket. When I lit her cigarette with the end of mine she gripped my hand tightly and said, 'You know what's wrong with Plumtree, don't you? She's undersexed.'

For a moment I looked at her. Nurse Plumtree was pale and dark, Nurse Macpherson red-headed and freckled. Nurse Plumtree always looked faintly ill, and Nurse Macpherson always buoyantly healthy, with a stride recalling a moor on a frosty morning and arms suggesting the tennis racket and the hockey stick. Nurse Plumtree was introverted and Nurse Macpherson extroverted, and if one was undersexed then the other was certainly oversexed. Before I realized what I was doing, I had kissed her.

'Ummm,' she said, nestling into my arms. 'Not quite the Nightingale spirit, but give me more.'

'What about the ward?' I gasped.

'The pro's looking after it.'

I kissed her again.

'But the night sister?'

'Not due for hours. Besides, I've got my cap on. That's the important thing. If they found a nurse stark naked with her cap on, it would still be respectable.'

It was late as I walked slowly up the stairs of the Residents' Quarters. I felt smugly sheikish. I now had two girl friends: one for companionship and comfort during the day, and one for excitement at night. As long as I could keep them reasonably separated and do without too much sleep, I was in for an interesting time.

Chapter Sixteen

The second disturbance to my romance with Nurse Plumtree was the dinner at home.

'Mummy and Daddy are very sweet really,' she said as I drove Haemorrhagic Hilda down to Mitcham.

'I'm sure they are.'

'Forgive daddy if he's a little crotchety sometimes. He's been rather like that since he retired from the Army. And Mummy's arthritis sometimes upsets her in weather like this. But I'm sure you'll like them very much. Just be yourself,' she advised me.

The Plumtrees lived in a small house called 'Blenheim' that stood in a neat garden containing a row of yews shaped into horses' heads, with a miniature brass cannon by the steps and a notice on the door saying CIVIL DEFENCE–CHIEF WARDEN. She rang the bell, which had the effect of a bomb going off in a zoo. Immediately there was an outburst of barking, caterwauling and human shouting from inside, and I waited nervously on the mat wondering if it was a pair of lions who were scratching hungrily for me inside the door.

'I do love animals so,' Nurse Plumtree said.

The door burst open, and two Great Danes sprang at me, put their paws on my shoulders and began licking my face.

'Alexander! Montgomery!' cried someone inside. 'Mind what you're doing to the doctor.'

'Don't worry,' said Nurse Plumtree calmly. 'They're only puppies.'

The dogs were pulled off, I staggered through the hall, and found myself in a sitting-room decorated with long photographs of regimental groups, a pair of crossed swords, a tiger-skin rug, and several ceremonial helmets under glass domes like forced rhubarb. the room seemed to be filled with human beings and animals. There were dogs in the corners, cats on the cushions, birds in the windows, and a tank of fish over the fireplace; scattered among them were a thin, stopping man with a white moustache, a fat dark woman in a purple dress, and a young man and a girl who both looked strongly like Nurse Plumtree.

'My dear, dear, Doctor,' said the Colonel, advancing with outstretched hand. 'How very pleased we are to see you! Edna has told us so much about you. May I introduce Edna's mother?'

As I shook hands she said warmly, 'Edna's told me so much about you, too.'

The young man held out his hand and said, 'Hel-lo. Name's Ian. I'm at the BBC. Sweet of you to come, old thing. This is Joan. We're Edna's brother and sister, and we've heard so much about you it isn't true.'

Joan said, 'Smashing you could come. Always hearing about you.'

I began to feel annoyed. I had expected the evening to be a quiet dinner, and it had been turned into a gathering of the clan.

'Naughty, Cromwell,' Joan said, picking up a wire-haired terrier which had sprung from the hearthrug to start biting my ankles. 'Naughty, naughty Cromwell! Did oo want to eat the Doctor, then?' She buried her nose in the struggling dog's neck. 'Don't you think he's got a lovely face?'

'He's getting married tomorrow,' Ian explained. 'Which makes him rather excited.'

'Now let's have a cocktail, Doctor,' said the Colonel, rubbing his hands. He smiled at me. 'Or I'd better call you Richard, hadn't I?'

'If you like, sir, of course.'

For some reason this made everyone roar with laughter.

Before long I could not help mellowing in the warmth of my reception. I had come prepared for suspicious tolerance at best, and now Edna Plumtree's father was treating me like the man bringing the winnings from Littlewoods. Even conversation at dinner was easier than I had feared, because the Plumtree family, like many others, believed that the only way to make a doctor feel at home was to narrate their ailments since childhood in a richness of clinical detail more suitable for the operating table than the dining table. First Colonel Plumtree described the pelvic wound he had suffered at Dunkirk, starting with a short sketch of the military situation leading up to it and finishing with an account of the croquet lawn of his convalescent hospital in Torquay. Mrs Plumtree took up the surgical saga by relating all the events occurring both outside and inside her from the moment of entering hospital for a cholecystectomy. Joan Plumtree was bursting to begin the story of the carbuncle she had as a child which had to be squeezed of pus every morning, when Ian put his head in his hands and groaned, '*Not* your beastly boils again, Joan darling, *please!*'

They all looked at him in surprise.

'But Richard's a doctor,' Joan said.

'I know,' Ian shakily reached for his glass. 'But I'm not. It makes me go all over and over inside. If you don't stop I'll throw up, really I will!'

The family stared at the brother like passengers on a business-man's train watching a parson come aboard in the middle of a good story.

'I can't even stand *talking* about blood,' Ian went on to me. 'It's one of my things. I've got all sorts of things. I've got a thing about heights, and a thing about being trapped in the Underground and it filling up with water and everyone being drowned, and a thing about suffocating when I'm asleep. In fact, I'm all things. It all started when I had a nasty experience in a beastly prep school in Broadstairs–' He went on to give a full history of his neurosis, and those of several of his friends in Broadcasting House.

For most of the meal Nurse Plumtree had remained silent. But as the sweet arrived the family ran out of clinical material, and kept the conversation going by asking her to repeat once more the story of the morning she put Mr Cambridge in his place, or the day she settled the Matron's hash in front of the whole hospital. It was soon clear that Colonel and Mrs Plumtree believed their daughter dominated the nursing staff at St Swithin's, in the same fond way that the parents of the spottiest fourth-form dunce imagine their child is the school's sparking-plug. I noticed that they afforded me similar status in the surgical department, and began asking my opinion on medical matters of the day. So far nothing had been expected of me beyond sympathetic 'Umms' and 'Really's' at long intervals, but the Colonel had provided a good bottle of Burgundy and I was feeling in the mood to let myself expand a little. After addressing them for some time like the President of the Royal College of Surgeons, I ended by giving a stitch-by-stitch description of removing a kidney, which brought Ian's face into his hands again but left me confident that I had been an overwhelming success with the rest of the family.

'Well,' said Colonel Plumtree as I finished, 'that was most interesting, Richard. Absolutely fascinating. And now, I expect the ladies would like to retire.'

The three women left us, followed by Ian, who murmured that he wanted to lie down. Colonel Plumtree brought a decanter of port from the sideboard and said genially, 'This is a drop I've been saving. It's from the old Regiment. I think you'll like it, my boy.'

'That's very good of you, sir. But I hope you haven't decanted it specially for me?'

'Not a bit, Richard, not a bit. Special occasion, special port, eh? Cigar?'

'Thank you, sir.'

Feeling that a medical qualification was worth the hard work if it could occasion such handsome treatment in a staff nurse's home, I lit my cigar and settled myself at the head of the table close to the Colonel.

'You haven't known Edna long really, have you?' he asked.

'No, not very long. I only started on her ward a few months ago.'

'That doesn't seem to matter,' he said and roared with laughter.

To be polite I laughed, too.

'Tell me something about your career,' he went on. 'By all accounts you're a rather brilliant young man.'

'Oh, not really, you know,' I said, feeling flattered. 'There's nothing much to tell. I got qualified, did a spell in general practice, and now I'm at St Swithin's again. My ambition is to be a surgeon, of course.'

'Capital!'

He poured me some more port.

'If you'll forgive a more personal question,' Colonel Plumtree continued. 'About–ah, how much are you making at the moment?'

'I don't mind telling you at all.' I enjoyed giving inside information about the National Health Service. 'All we poor housemen get is about three hundred a year, when they've knocked off the board and lodging. But, of course, it soon goes up. In another four years or so I should be well inside the four-figure bracket.'

He nodded thoughtfully over his cigar. 'That's pretty reasonable, on the whole.'

'Not too bad at all, I'd say.'

'But you'll probably find yourself a bit short of cash at the moment, eh? After all, you've got to pay for the ring.'

'The ring?'

What on earth was he talking about? I had said nothing about amateur boxing? The circus, perhaps? Opera? Or bookmakers?

He nudged me. 'Her mother insisted on diamonds,' he chuckled.

The room spun round. The port boiled in my mouth. The cigar shot from my fingers like a torpedo.

'Steady on, old chap, steady on!' The Colonel patted me heartily on the back. 'Something go down the wrong way?'

It was almost a minute before I managed to speak. 'The port–perhaps a little strong—'

'Of course, my boy. Mustn't have you choke to death just now, eh? Ha, ha! Come along in and join the family.'

I followed father into the sitting-room, looking like Ian having one of his things.

The rest of the evening passed in a sickly blur, as though I were recovering from a bad anaesthetic. Joan said she hoped we'd be jolly good pals, and Ian thought I'd like to meet his interesting chum Lionel at the BBC. Father showed us his photographs from the war, and mother kept pressing my hand, murmuring 'I'm so glad,' and bursting into tears. As soon as I dared I pleaded a headache, lack of sleep, and early duty. There were disappointed cries, and I bought my freedom with false pledges of returning for Sunday tea to meet the aunts and dining next week at Daddy's club.

We drove away in silence. 'Poor Richard,' said Edna, wrapping my muffler tenderly round me. 'Daddy's Regimental port *is* rather strong. But don't worry–you made an awfully good impression on the family. It really was time they knew about *us*, wasn't it?'

Chapter Seventeen

I burst into Grimsdyke's room as soon as I reached the hospital.

'Good God, what's the matter?' he asked in alarm. He jumped from his bed, where he was lying in his crimson silk dressing-gown. 'Been frightened by the ghost of a blighted patient, or something?'

'A drink!' I fell into his armchair. 'At once!'

'Coming up right away. You look so bloody awful you make me want one, too.'

He threw aside the novel he was reading and brought a bottle of gin from the commode thoughtfully provided by St Swithin's. After we had both drunk deeply from his tooth-glasses he screwed his monocle into his eye and said, 'Now tell the doctor all.'

I gave him the story of my tragic evening, and he roared with laughter.

'I can't see anything funny in it,' I said crossly. 'Damn it all, I treat this girl with perfectly normal good manners and affability, and what happens? Before I know what's happening I'm surrounded by her bloody family patting me on the back and saying how nice it will be to have grandchildren. What the devil can she have been telling them all this time? She must think like a story in a woman's magazine.'

'I'll admit you're in a bit of a fix,' Grimsdyke said cheerfully.

'Bit of a fix! I know that without your help. The question is, what the hell can I do about it?'

Grimsdyke took a long drink. 'I should think the easiest way out is to go ahead and marry the girl.'

'Marry her? Marry her? Are you mad too, man? Apart from anything else, have you seen her family? I wouldn't share the same railway carriage with that bunch, let alone marry into them.'

'Have another drink,' Grimsdyke said.

'Thanks. I will.'

'Let's suppose you did marry Nurse Plumtree,' he continued in a reflective tone, lying down again. 'The worst part's over of course–being inspected by the family. Think yourself lucky. Many fellows have gone down to the old folks bursting with love, and found themselves kicked into the rhododendrons before the fruit and coffee came round. You were a great success.'

I grunted.

'Then, as Father observed, you'd need a ring. Terribly expensive, engagement rings. The thing the best man loses in church is a brassy job worth a couple of quid, but the one you choose together in Mappin and Webb's is a sort of down payment on delivery of goods. You'll have to put it in *The Times* of course – you pay for that too–which will load your post for weeks afterwards with advertisements for photographers, florists, and contraceptives. All your bachelor chums will slap you on the back and tell you what a lucky chap you are, clearly implying what lucky chaps *they* are. They stand you drinks, I admit, but you don't get much chance for drinking because you spend all your spare time sitting on the edge of the sofa in her front parlour discussing the wedding. By now you may have decided that you don't want to marry the girl after all—'

'Must you go on?' I demanded. 'This isn't a bit funny.'

'. . . but that won't do you the slightest good because once you've set the terrible machinery of marriage in motion you stand as much chance as a crate of eggs under a pile-driver. You'll soon discover that marriage is nothing to do with the fusion of two souls, but an excuse for women to buy lots of expensive clothes. The bride is decked out to ride in triumph round the social circus, to the delight of her relations, the relief of her married friends, and the gratifying jealousy of those still single. You, of course, will be the horse. But I anticipate rather, because for several months you'll be forced to listen politely to exhaustive discussions about whether the bridesmaids should wear Juliet caps and if the bride can go to the altar in her usual undies. Incidentally the bridesmaids themselves–whom you'll later have to reward handsomely–will apparently be recruited from a home for female morons, while your own best man will be as socially acceptable to the bride, mother, and steering committee of aunts as Jack the Ripper. Your last loophole of escape is meanwhile blocked by a landslide of saucepans, teaspoons, egg-cups, gravy-ladles, toasting forks, and hand-embroidered tea-cosies, for all of which you will have to write a letter extending over at least one page beginning, "Dear Uncle Augustus and Aunt Beatrice. Thank you a thousand times for your delightful contribution to our new little home."'

Grimsdyke took another drink, and staring at the ceiling continued: 'Brightly dawns your wedding day. You have a terrible hangover as you climb into the outfit you've hired from Moss Bross and you still can't find your collar when the best man arrives to collect you. He generally tries to cheer you up with a few funny jokes. The last thing you want to do in the world is get married, but before you know what's happening you're in church with your eyes on the level of the clergyman's boots. The reception afterwards will be upstairs in a tea-shop, there won't be nearly enough to drink and everyone will make speeches–some of the uncles twice–several of the aunts will be in tears, and only the waiters will at all be mellowed by alcohol. Then the "going-away"–frightfully pagan and primitive really, old shoes and tin cans on the back of the car in the middle of the High Street on a Saturday afternoon. This brings me to the honeymoon. There you are, arriving at St Ives in a snowstorm in your best clothes, trying to pretend you've been married for years and feeling that everyone is looking at you as though you were performing one of those *expositions* in the back streets of Marseille. However, I will skip all that. I next see you and Edna Plumtree-that-was strolling from your villa on a Sunday morning with the pram and two–possibly three?–walking along beside–'

I smashed his glass on the floor and walked out.

The next morning was my most miserable since the final examinations. The newspapers seemed concerned only with actions for breach of promise, judges' remarks about broken homes, and advertisements for cheap wedding rings. I could hardly eat any breakfast and hurried across the quadrangle to the surgical block feeling that every nurse in the hospital was pointing her finger at me and giggling. As I scrambled into my operating trousers I wondered if Nurse Plumtree had already spread the news around the Nurses' Home or was waiting for the Matron's blessing and a ring.

In the operating theatre it was one of those mornings. The sister was in a bad temper, the catgut broke, the artery forceps slipped, the transfusion needles came adrift, the scissors were blunt, the swabs were lost. My own assistance was so clumsy that even mild Mr Cambridge was moved to murmur, 'My dear Mr Er–er, couldn't you do something more helpful to the patient than gaze at his umbilicus?'

Hatrick screwed up his eyes as he grinned and said through his mask, 'He must be in love, sir.'

I almost wept into the wound.

As I grasped my retractor through the long surgical morning I glanced at Grimsdyke, who was sitting smugly at my right elbow, and wondered if he was perhaps right. Should I give in and marry Nurse Plumtree? After all, I was past the facile flirtations of a penniless medical student, and almost every morning *The Times* proclaimed the virtuous love of one of my classmates. Nurse Plumtree would at least never be a nagger or a gossip, she was a tolerably good cook, and genuinely anxious to look after me. As the years rolled by I might be able to tolerate her brother and sister, while thankfully her parents could not live for ever.

Lunch was later, colder, and soggier than usual. Afterwards I made an excuse about discussing the next anaesthetic and managed to have a word with Grimsdyke alone.

'Sorry I was rather unsympathetic last night,' he said cheerfully in the anaesthetic room, gripping the chin of a freshly-unconscious patient. 'But your cosy little evening *chez* Plumtree sounded so bloody funny I couldn't spoil the joke.'

'I think I may take your advice after all,' I announced.

'What? Marry the woman? But you're not even in love with her, are you?'

I shrugged my shoulders, and started fiddling with an ampoule of pentothal. 'What's love?' I said. 'It merely means that a certain system of genes in my chromosomes is about to be placed in relationship to an arrangement of genes in hers. To this biological end certain endocrine cells in her and myself pour out secretions that produce our secondary sex characteristics, such as the full bosom and rounded hips of Nurse Plumtree and the deep voice and hair on the chest of myself. I don't see that there's any more to it—'

'What disgusting nonsense! Anyway, you can't possibly marry a nurse. They make your life a horror of purgatives.'

'Then what the devil *am* I to do?' I asked him anxiously. 'So far you've been as useless as a letter-box on a tombstone.'

'The answer's simple, old lad. Have a bash at another woman. Hadn't you thought of it before?'

They wheeled the patient into the theatre then, but I finished the operating list in a happier frame of mind. In the emotional stress of the last two days I had forgotten Nurse Macpherson, and it cheered me to think that I could choose the primrose path to escape.

Chapter Eighteen

I saw little of Nurse Plumtree that day, for the operating list ended in a string of hernias, varicose veins, lipomas, biopsies, and cystoscopies that kept Hatrick and myself in the theatre until eight at night. I threw a white coat over my blood-smudged theatre clothes and hurried down to the wards, which on operating evenings resembled the French lines after Agincourt. Outside Constancy I was surprised to run into Nurse Plumtree in her cloak.

'I've got a strep throat,' she said gazing at me sadly. 'I've got to go off duty.'

'Oh, hard luck.' I tried not to sound delighted. 'At least, it's nothing serious. I'll go round the ward with Nurse Summers instead. I couldn't have met you tonight anyway, not after that colossal list.'

'Don't give too much responsibility to that Nurse Macpherson,' she warned me. 'She's quite unreliable. Only this morning she mixed up the castor oils with the blanket baths. And don't stay up too late writing your notes. Promise?'

I nodded vigorously.

'I must go off to the path. lab. for a swab.' she ended softly. 'Good night, Richard, dear.'

'Good night. Hope you get better in no time, and all that.'

I went into the ward praying that her throat swab would reveal as sturdy a penicillin-resistant streptococcus as the bacteriologists had seen. It was a selfish thought, but at present complete isolation was the ideal state for Nurse Plumtree.

It was late before I left the ward with an armful of patients' notes to complete in my room. I ate my cold supper alone in the gloomy dining-room, found a bottle of beer in Grimsdyke's commode, and settled down at my small desk to reduce Mr Cambridge's surgical bravura to black and white. After midnight I wrote for the last time, 'Haemostasis secured and abdomen closed in layers,' collected the folders, and began to think constructively about Nurse Macpherson. As I walked across the quadrangle to the entrance of the surgical block, I prepared my plan. I would get her cosily into the corner of the ward kitchen, kiss her against the bread-cutting machine, and ask her out next Friday. She would accept delightedly, and the news would seep into the innermost cell of the nurses' isolation block by breakfast. I felt this was hardly the behaviour of a gentleman, but consoled myself by remembering that desperate ills need desperate remedies.

I was glad to find her in the ward kitchen as usual, alone.

'My, my, you're late!' she greeted me. 'Today's victims are all doing splendidly, and old Muggsy's sent up a couple of extras to help me cope. Hungry?'

'Phew!' I waved the air in front of my face. 'Have you been fumigating the mattresses or something?'

'Oh, that must be Jimmy Bingham's tobacco. How many eggs?'

I stiffened. Now I recognized unmistakably the foul breath of Bingham's pipe, which he lit with the air of a clumsy father on Guy Fawkes Night after every meal.

'Bingham has been up here, has he?'

'Been up! He's eaten me out of house and home.'

My eyes caught the plate on the table, polished clean except for a rim of egg and a few forlorn rinds of bacon.

'And what was he doing in my ward?' I demanded.

She laughed. 'Oh, Jimmy comes up every night after you've gone–didn't you know? I was in the Professor's ward before I was sent here on days. We got to know each other pretty well.'

'Oh. I see.'

I had not allowed for a rival in my calculations and I felt outraged that this complication should take the form of Bingham. Deciding quickly that no sane woman could award him greater sex-appeal than a fourth-form schoolboy, I continued my plan.

'Here! What's the idea?' she demanded, as I wedged her into a corner.

'I only wanted to kiss you.'

'Oh, you did, did you? Well you can get that out of your mind to start with.'

'But you let me yesterday,' I said in surprise.

'Well I won't today.'

'Come out on Friday.'

'No.'

'Why?'

'Because I'm going out with Jimmy Bingham. Now if you'd like the ward report, Mr Gordon, you may have it.'

I drew in my breath.

'Thank you, Nurse Macpherson. I should.'

I rose the next morning a bitter man. Not only had Bingham condemned me to a lifetime of living with Nurse Plumtree, but his rivalry for the favours of Nurse Macpherson had the familiar psychological effect of making her wildly desirable. It also brought to an end the professional honeymoon that Bingham and I had enjoyed since my return to the hospital. My toleration was already stretched thin, because of his unendearing social habits. There was only one bathroom on our floor, where he came to shave every morning while I was taking my bath. On my first day in the Staff Quarters he had greeted me heartily with, 'Good morning, old chap. While there's life there's soap, eh?' which was passably funny as a before-breakfast pleasantry, but when he repeated it the next morning, the morning after that, and every morning for the following weeks, I was ready to slit his throat with his own razor.

At meals, Bingham made a point of sitting next to me to emphasize our new chumminess, and though he was too careful about money to let slip a technicality and incur a fine he found it difficult to keep his thoughts away from his work while eating. 'Perirenal fat, hylum, medulla, and pelvis,' he murmured during supper one evening.

'Look out,' I whispered. 'If the Senior Resident hears you, you'll be down half a crown.'

'But I'm not talking shop, old chap,' he said, wide-eyed. 'See this–' He stuck his fork into the middle of his steak-and-kidney pie. 'Nicest piece of dissected kidney I've seen for a long time. Young too–look at those lobulations.'

Shortly afterwards I pointedly offered him the bananas, and I was glad to find he took the rest of his meals on the other side of the table.

I wondered at first if I was hypersensitive, but Bingham had already established his unpopularity with the rest of the Residency by taking all the magazines up to his bedroom, reading the *Lancet* at breakfast, and being unable to glance through a paper without leaving it fit only for wrapping chips. Although he glared furiously at anyone who talked in the common-room while he was listening to the Third Programme, he was unable to afford similar respect to his companions' ideas of evening entertainment. The brewer who had given the new surgical wing to the hospital had admirably topped off his donation with a supply of free beer to the resident doctors, so we never found ourselves short of an excuse for a party. These generally brought Bingham down in his dressing-gown, complaining, 'I say, let a chap sleep, won't you?' until one noisy evening he wrote to the hospital Secretary saying that he would be obliged for a room elsewhere as his colleagues were apparently tearing up the common-room immediately below. The Secretary hurried round the next morning to find the room looking as though it had been charged by a rhinoceros, locked the door, pocketed the key, and angrily strode off to find the Dean. We had an hour of dangerous climbing round the fire-escape and hard work with pails and brushes, but when the Secretary indignantly threw open the door the Dean found the room as neat as a barracks, with an aspidistra drooping from a brass pot on the piano and an open Bible on the table. But this did nothing to increase Bingham's likeability.

The crisis came the morning after my frustration by Nurse Macpherson, when I strode into the ward after breakfast and found five strange faces in the beds.

'Where did those patients come from?' I demanded from Nurse Summers in astonishment. 'They weren't here last night.'

'They're Mr Bingham's.'

'Bingham's? But damn it, they were my only empty beds! I've got five gastrectomies coming in this morning. What right has he got to put his patients in my beds?'

'They were the duty firm last night. They're allowed to board out patients if they're swamped with emergencies.'

'What's wrong with them, anyway?'

She picked up the diagnosis board from the Sister's desk. 'They're all in for observation.'

'Observation!'

After examining all five, I concluded that one was suffering from severe constipation and the rest had nothing wrong with them at all.

'Bingham!' I called, as I spotted him in the corridor, 'what the devil do you mean by cluttering up my ward with your cases?'

He stiffened. 'I've a perfect right to, old chap.'

'Perfect right my foot! There's nothing wrong with any of them. I bet you only admitted tham because you couldn't decide if they had acute abdomens. You were scared stiff of chucking them into the street.'

'That is a very unprofessional remark,' Bingham hissed. He stepped into the lift and slammed the gates. Unfortunately, this time it worked.

'It's so damnably irritating,' I told Grimsdyke in his room that evening. 'Here's this blasted Bingham, who's a walking disgrace to the medical profession, and here's this first-rate girl squandering her precious nights off duty at his feet. I can't believe it.'

'No accounting for the taste of women, old lad.' He stretched himself thoughtfully on his bed. 'Frightful gargoyles and crooks they fall for sometimes. You've only got to look through the wedding photos in the *Tatler*.'

'But this–this Caliban, Bingham. What on earth can she see in him?'

Grimsdyke screwed his monocle into his eye and stared at the ceiling. 'Let us not lose sight of the object of the treatment. You wish to purge yourself of the hookworm Plumtree. Right? You intend to administer Macpherson for this purpose. But why not try some other anthelmintic? The hospital's full of nurses ready to quiver at a houseman's smile.'

I was silent for a second. 'As a matter of fact, I'm rather fond of Nan Macpherson.'

'Balderdash! Simple psychology–you wish to assert your superiority over Bingham by nabbing his mate. It's happening to chaps all the time.'

'You don't understand. She's a terrific girl, really. Tremendous vitality and good looks, with a wonderful sense of humour.'

'Delusions, delusions, delusions.' Grimsdyke murmured, putting his finger-tips together.

'Anyway, what do you know about psychology? All your patients are asleep.'

'If you don't believe me, try the experiment in reverse. Dangle Plumtree in front of Macpherson. Make her think she's wrecking the home. I guarantee she'll act like a thirsty cat with a saucer of milk.'

Although I had no faith in Grimsdyke's ability as a psychiatrist, I decided to take his advice because he was a more experienced man of the world than myself. Unfortunately the next day was Friday, and Nurse Macpherson was placed beyond reach by her official three nights off duty. She had clearly hinted to Bingham of my rejection in his favour, because he met me in the quadrangle at lunch-time with a broad grin, slapped me on the back, and said, 'By the way, old chap. Do you think you'll need me for anything tomorrow night? I mean, to give you a hand with a drip for a perf. or something?'

'Why should I?' I asked coldly. 'I never have done.'

'No, but just in case. I mean to say, Duckworth's H.S. is standing in for me. I'm going out,' he added, as though announcing he was about to swim the Channel.

'I hope you enjoy yourself.'

He giggled. 'I shall, old chap. Don't go out much you know, but this is something special.' He slapped his thigh, grinned again, and winked. 'Eh, old chap?'

'If you make your intentions as obvious to Nurse Macpherson as you do to me,' I said sourly, 'you won't get her out of the Nurses' Home. Good afternoon.'

I strode angrily into the nearest doorway, feeling sick.

My determination to win Nurse Macpherson was fanned by Bingham's grinning at me, rubbing his hands, and declaring, 'Lovely life, eh?' every time I met him the next day. Meanwhile, I was glad to hear from the Junior Pathology Demonstrator that Nurse Plumtree was richly infected with *streptococcus pyogenes*, and would be off duty for at least a week. I sent her a letter of sympathy and a bunch of flowers, and patiently waited for the return of her rival.

The campaign was easier than I had expected. I apologized for my behaviour at our last meeting, and explained that her overwhelming attraction had swept me away from Nurse Plumtree, where my thoughts must henceforward dutifully repose. I murmured that, of course, Nurse Plumtree was a delightful girl, but if only Nurse Macpherson had been the staff nurse instead. . . . I passed on all the remarks that Nurse Plumtree had made about her, and prepared to sit in the ward kitchen every night and wait.

That was on Monday. By Wednesday she had agreed to come out to dinner on her night off–as long as I breathed not a word to Bingham–and by Friday she was inviting me to help her look for lost tea-cloths in the small, dark, cosy linen cupboard behind the ward. On Sunday I decided that I was in love with her; and on Monday more exciting ideas began to take shape in my mind.

'You know, I've been getting on damn well with Nan Macpherson, thanks to your advice,' I said to Grimsdyke. 'Do you think that–I mean, what would you say the chances were of her–well, being as cooperative on a grander scale, as it were?'

'Pretty good, I should think,' he replied thoughtfully. 'She has what the nurses call "a reputation". Though that might merely mean she paints her toe-nails red and uses mascara.'

'Do you think I dare ask?'

'Why not? At the worst, she can only kick your teeth in.'

After a brief and breathless spell in the linen cupboard that night, I began, 'Nan, about next week. Instead of just dinner, how about–' I swallowed. I had dismissed the fire-escape as impracticable, because of Bingham. 'How about nipping out to the country somewhere, you know, and, well, you know?'

There was a surprised pause. 'Doctor, Doctor!' she said playfully. 'Is that an indecent proposal?'

'It's a pretty decent one, as far as I can see,' I said brightly. 'I'm sorry, I didn't mean to be funny about it. But if you'd feel inclined—'

'You'll have to go. Night sister'll be here in a minute.'

'But about next week—?'

'I'll see,' she said, laying her finger on my lips.

'I promise I wouldn't tell a soul. Especially Bingham. He hasn't done the same sort of thing, has he?' I asked, with sudden horror.

She laughed. 'Jimmy isn't out of the mistletoe stage.'

'Do say yes,' I implored. 'I can't stand suspense.'

'You must *go*, Richard! Night sister's due any second.'

'I won't go till you tell me.'

'Oh, well–I suppose I was going to buy a new toothbrush anyway.'

'Nan, darling! How wonderful—'

'Shhh! And remember–not a soul.'

'How could you think I'd breathe a word?'

I immediately woke up Grimsdyke.

'Can you imagine it, Grim?' I said excitedly. 'What luck! She's agreed. We're nipping off for a dirty week-end. Or a night, anyway,' I corrected myself.

'You've woken me up to tell me this disgusting piece of news—'

'I want your advice. You see, I haven't had any experience of–of this sort of thing. Where do we go, for instance? Brighton? What do we sign in the visitors book–Smith or Jones? Supposing they ask for our marriage licence or something—'

'There's a sort of country hotel called The Judge's Arms, on the way north, which is very romantic I've heard. You could try that. Now for God's sake let me get some sleep.'

'The Judge's Arms. Thanks a million times, old fellow.'

'I suppose you're going to these lengths to unload Miss Plumtree?' he asked sleepily, turning over.

'Good Lord! I'd completely forgotten about her.'

'I don't like it,' Grimsdyke muttered, dropping off. 'I don't like it a bit.'

For the next few days Bingham and I both slapped each other on the back like brothers. What the psychology was behind it I didn't dare to work out.

Chapter Nineteen

The stubborn streptococcus in Nurse Plumtree's throat refused to budge. She soon felt well again, but as no nurse could be let loose to spray penicillin-resistant organisms over the patients, second opinions were summoned. The senior ear, nose, and throat surgeon recommended that he remove her tonsils, excise her nasal septum, scrape out her sinuses, and extract all her teeth; the Professor of Bacteriology, a simpler-minded man, advised a week's holiday. This was thought to be the most convenient course for everybody, and the next day she left the hospital for Mitcham with an armful of home-building magazines.

'We'll announce it when I get back,' she declared as I saw her off. 'So far, I haven't told a soul–except my best friends, of course. It'll be nice to have the date fixed for the wedding, won't it? Now don't forget–no late nights while I'm away.'

A couple of afternoons later, in a state of devilish excitement, I started Haemorrhagic Hilda and drove from the hospital car park to pick up Nurse Macpherson.

Our plans had been laid the night before, over a cup of Ovaltine. I had left my junior house surgeon on duty for me, asking Mr Cambridge for permission to spend the night away from the hospital; she had told Bingham that duty to her parents demanded a visit. To allay suspicion, I arranged to meet her outside the Zoo.

She was waiting with her attaché-case by the main gates.

'Hello, hello, hello!' I called, drawing up and unhooking the loop of string that restrained the near-side door. 'What a cad I am! Fancy keeping a girl waiting on an occasion like this.'

I noticed that she was staring at me in amazement. 'What's the matter?' I asked in alarm. 'Is my suit all right? It's my second best.'

'My God! Am I supposed to travel in *that?*'

I remembered that she hadn't seen Haemorrhagic Hilda before. 'It's a remarkably good motor car,' I told her stoutly. 'As reliable as a London bus and with a lot of charm about it. You wait till we get going.'

'Oh, it's charming all right. Like one of Emett's railway engines. How do I get aboard–do you let down a pair of steps?'

I helped her into the car, and she settled in the Windsor chair I had lashed specially to the floorboards beside me. I felt nettled. I was proud of Haemorrhagic Hilda, and even if she looked as startling on the road as George Stevenson's *Rocket*, such mockery hurt. But refusing to allow the start of a great adventure to be marred by the petty pride of ownership, I called cheerfully, 'Hang on!' and performed the rapid manipulation of the choke, ignition, throttle, brake, gear-lever, and hand petrol pump necessary to put Haemorrhagic Hilda in motion. 'Off we go to the wide open spaces!'

'By the way,' she said lighting a cigarette. 'I've got to go to Oxford Street first.'

'Oxford Street! But that's miles out of our way. What on earth do you want to go there for?'

'I simply must do my shopping. I've got to get a length of curtain material for my room–I can't stand the hospital stuff any longer–and a birthday present for Cissy Jenkins, and some kirbigrips and some linen buttons for my uniform and a tea-pot and some soap.'

'But couldn't you do it another time? I mean to say–Apart from anything else, I'd like to get there in daylight. The headlamps aren't terribly efficient.'

'What other time? You seem to forget I'm a working girl, my dear young man.'

'Oh, sorry. No offence, of course.'

She left me for an hour and a quarter in Oxford Street, though the time passed quickly enough because I spent it driving through side-streets looking for somewhere to park and anxiously peering out for policemen, as though I were about to hold up a bank. She rejoined me with a Christmas Eve load of parcels, which she threw on to the sofa in the back, and said, 'Phew! What a bloody tussle! Drive on, James.'

'Are you sure you've got everything?' I asked stiffly.

'Except some cigarettes. But that doesn't matter. I can smoke yours.'

My spirits had dropped badly since leaving St Swithin's, and now it occurred to me that I had never seen Nurse Macpherson out of uniform before. Indeed, I had never seen her in daylight at all for several weeks. She was unfortunately one of those nurses who are flattered by the starched severity of their dress, and she had chosen for our escapade an odd knitted outfit that recalled the woollen suits worn at one period by Mr Bernard Shaw. Her face, too, suffered away from the night-club dimness of a sleeping ward. Her make-up was careless, the freckles that had enchanted me across the Night Report Book now reminded me of a dozen skin diseases, and I reflected that she must have begun her nursing training comparatively late, because she was clearly several years older than I was.

My mood was darkened further by the weather, which had turned from a lunch-time of brittle blue sky and sharp-edged sun to an afternoon in which the clouds and the twilight were already conspiring to make me confess Hilda's deficient headlights. On top of this, I was getting a sore throat. Nurse Plumtree's streptococcus, breathed into our farewell kiss, was already breeding generations of grandchildren across the mucous membrane of my pharynx. I had left the hospital with a half-perceived tickling in the back of my throat, and now I felt like a fire-eater after a bad performance.

Fortunately, Nurse Macpherson became more romantic as we left the outskirts of London, and began stroking my arm against the steering-wheel while murmuring that she felt deliciously abandoned. She even managed a few flattering words about Hilda, expressing surprise that the car had managed to travel so far without stopping or coming off the road. This was encouraging, but I was too busy to listen attentively through contending with the traffic on the Great North Road, which that afternnon was composed only of cars driven by men late for important interviews, bicycles propelled by blind imbeciles, and lorries carrying boilers for ocean liners. But we progressed without breakdown or accident, and when darkness fell I was delighted to find that the headlights shone more brightly than before, sometimes both of them at once. By the time The Judge's Arms appeared in front of us I began to feel more cheerful and more appreciative of the unusual treat in store for me.

'Here we are, Nan,' I said, as I pulled up at the front door.

She peered through the cracked window. 'Are you sure? It looks like a municipal lunatic asylum to me.'

'It's very romantic inside. And–according to a friend of mine who ought to know–they're very broad-minded.'

My heart was beginning to beat more quickly. 'Sure you've got the ring on the right finger?' I asked nervously.

'Of course I have. Put these parcels in your case, will you? I can't possibly get them in mine.'

We got out of the car.

When I had asked Grimsdyke more about The Judge's Arms he had murmured that it was 'a coaching inn in the best English tradition'. It was in the English inn-keeping tradition, right enough, but the most widespread rather than the best. The walls of the hall sprouted thickly the heads of deer, otters, badgers, foxes, ferrets, stoats, and weasels, among the glazed bodies of pike, salmon, trout, perch, and bream in generous glass coffins; in the corner a pair of rigid snipe huddled beneath a glass dome, and over the stairs was impaled the horned skull of a buffalo. The place was so dark, empty, and musty that it immediately reminded me of a corner in the Natural History Museum in Cromwell Road.

On one side of the hall was a door with a cracked frosted-glass panel embossed with the words 'Coffee Room' in curly letters; opposite was a similar door marked 'Lounge'. In the corner, carefully hidden by a spiky palm leaning in a large brass pot, was a hatch with a panel inviting 'Inquiries'. In front of the hatch was a ledge bearing a small brass hand-bell, secured to the wall by a length of chain.

'Cosy place,' murmured Nurse Macpherson.

'It's bound to be rather quiet,' I said, feeling I ought to defend the hotel as well as Haemorrhagic Hilda. 'We're in the country, you know.'

She made no reply, so I set down our cases, picked up the bell, and gave a timid tinkle. She began to make up her face, and I read a large notice in a black frame explaining that it was your own fault if anyone walked off with your valuables. As no one appeared, I rang the bell again.

Not a sound came from the hotel.

'I suppose they haven't all been scared away?' said Nurse Macpherson, snapping her compact closed. 'You know, like the *Marie Celeste*?'

'It's just a sleepy part of the world,' I told her testily, for my throat was beginning to hurt badly. 'We're not in Piccadilly Circus, you know.'

'I can see it now,' she went on, gazing at the sooty ceiling where it was gathered round the root of the tarnished chandelier. 'We shall find every room empty, meals half-eaten on the tables, baths filled, beds turned down, fires burning in the grates. Some awful thing came through the front door, perhaps from Mars. Everyone has fled except for one corpse in the garden, with its features twisted into an expression of spine-chilling terror. What a wonderful story for the newspapers! We'll phone the *Daily Express*, and in no time there'll be reporters and photographers and those tedious little men from television saying, "Now, Doctor, will you explain how you happened to be here with a trained nurse—"'

'Please be quiet for a minute. I'm doing my best.'

I rang the bell again, as though vending muffins. With the other hand I rapped the frosted glass, and Nurse Macpherson tapped a large and greasy gong with her foot.

'Yes?'

The coffee-room door had opened. Through it poked the head of an old man, in no collar and a railway-porter's waistcoat.

'We want a room.'

'I'll fetch Mrs Digby,' he said, disappearing.

We waited in silence for some minutes. I was beginning to wonder whether it would be less trouble to bundle Nurse Macpherson into Haemorrhagic Hilda and turn her out at the Nurses' Home, when the glass suddenly shot up beside me.

'Yes?'

I turned to meet one of the most disagreeable-looking women I had seen in my life. She had a thin peaky face, cropped hair, a gold pince-nez on a chain, and a dress apparently made from an old schoolmasters gown.

'Oh, er, good evening. You're Mrs Digby?'

'Yes.'

'Good. Well, you see, I wanted a room.'

'Yes?'

'You have a room?'

'Yes.'

I was now plainly nervous, for we had reached the point in our adventure that I had rehearsed the most in the secrecy of my room. It all seemed so easy in novels and the Sunday papers: once the initial difficulty of persuading the girl was overcome, the rest of the trip was sheer enjoyment. I had hoped at least for a genial boniface at the reception desk, but now I felt more confident of seducing a hundred women than convincing this sharp-eyed shrew that we were married.

'What name?' she demanded, opening a ledger like the Domesday Book.

'Phillimore,' I said. I had decided that was the most natural-sounding alias I could imagine.

'Sign here.'

She handed me a pen, and spattering ink freely over the page I anxiously filled in the name, address, and nationality. I noticed that the last column left a space for 'Remarks.'

The manageress blotted the book. 'Which of you's Framleigh?' she asked, frowning.

'Eh? Oh, yes, of course, I am. I'm Framleigh. Mr Framleigh. The young lady's Phillimore. Miss Phillimore.'

I cursed myself. Framleigh had been my second choice of *nom d'amour*, and in my agitation I had scrawled it over the visitors' book. Mrs Digby was now looking at me like Hamlet sizing up his uncle.

I tried to smile. 'We want two rooms,' I said.

'And I should think so, too!'

I put my hands in my pockets, took them out, and scratched the back of my head.

'The young lady must register.'

Mrs Digby handed the pen to Nurse Macpherson, who coolly wrote across the page 'Hortense Phillimore. Park Lane, London. Manx.' Feeling I should offer some innocent explanation of a young unmarried couple arriving for a single night in an unfrequented hotel in mid-winter, I said, 'We happened to be travelling north. We're cousins, you see. We're going to our uncle's funeral. Charming old gentleman, in the brass business. You may have heard of him. We both work in London, and to save the expense we decided to come up together by car, and we asked a man on the road for a good hotel—'

'Er-nest!' Mrs Digby poked her head out of the hatch like a cuckoo-clock. 'Er-nest! Where are you, Er-nest?'

The head reappeared from the coffee-room. 'Yes?'

'Ernest take up the baggage.'

Ernest, who looked unfit to carry anything heavier than a letter, creaked arthritically across the floor.

'The lady's in number three,' said Mrs Digby, taking from the rack behind her a key secured to a steel flag nine inches long. 'And the gentleman–' She carefully went to the far end of the rack. 'Is in number ninety-four.'

'Right,' said Ernest, picking up our cases. 'Foller me.'

'We happen to be cousins,' I told him as he stumbled up the stairs. 'We're going north for our uncle's funeral. He used to be in the brass business, poor fellow. We happen to work in London, so Miss Phillimore and I decided to come up together. On the road we met a man, and I asked him to recommend a good hotel, He said, "You can't beat The Judge's Arms—"'

'Number three!' Ernest interrupted, as though announcing the winner of a raffle. He threw open the door and switched on the light. We found ourselves in an apartment the size of a billiard-room, lined with dark-brown wallpaper and containing a pair of marble-topped tables, a bowl of waxed fruit, a dressing-table ornamented with cherubs, a wash-stand with a mauve jug and basin, and sufficient solid wardrobes to lock up a gang of burglars. In the centre of the room was a large knob-garnished brass bedstead.

Nurse Macpherson, who had said nothing since signing the register, drew in her breath.

'I don't believe it,' she muttered.

'Foller me,' Ernest repeated.

'I'll see you downstairs in five minutes for a drink,' I said. 'Hope you'll be comfortable.'

'Oh, I'll be comfortable all right. I'm used to sleeping in the middle of St Paul's.'

'Foller me!' Ernest insisted.

Number three was on the first floor, but my room appeared to be at the far end of the latest extension to the building, several of which had been added with floors at different levels.

'Don't know why she put you up here,' Ernest grumbled, pausing for breath half-way up a narrow staircase. 'There ain't been no one in ninety-four since the Farmers' Union.'

Number ninety-four was immediately under the roof, a narrow, cold, low, damp room, with a bed, a commode, and a wash-stand topped with a marble slab that reminded me of the post-mortem room. I gave Ernest a shilling, which he looked at carefully before saying, 'Good night!' and disappearing. I sat heavily on the bed. If this was romance, I could understand why Casanovas flourished only in warm climates.

Chapter Twenty

I reached the ground floor before Nurse Macpherson. As the hotel had resumed the sullen silence with which it had greeted us, I decided to explore the door marked 'Lounge'. This led to a small room with some furniture arranged haphazardly, like the bodies of mountaineers frozen to death where they stood. There were three or four more palms, and in the corner was an iron grate, bare of fire irons, in which a tiny fire blushed with shame.

I was now feeling really ill and I needed a drink desperately. There was a bell by the fireplace labelled 'Service', but knowing the hotel I supplemented a ring on this by opening the door and shouting, 'Hoy!' several times loudly.

From the coffee-room, which was now lighted as a preparation for dinner, came a thin, dark, short young man in a tail-suit that stretched almost to his heels. 'What'll you be wanting?' he asked, with the amiability of citizens of the Irish Republic.

'I want a drink.'

'Sure, you can have a drink if you want to.'

'What have you got?'

'Oh, anything at all,' he told me expansively. 'There's gin, whisky, rum, Guinness, crème de menthe, port, egg nogg—'

'I'll have a whisky. Two doubles, in one glass. And have you any aspirin?'

'Wouldn't you be feeling well?'

'I'd be feeling bloody awful. And please hurry up.'

By the time Nurse Macpherson appeared I had downed my quadruple whisky and twenty grains of aspirin, while the waiter found some coal and brought the poker from the office. 'We have to be careful over the fires,' he explained to me. 'Some of them commercial gentlemen pile it up as though they were stoking the *Queen Mary*.'

'Nan, my dear,' I greeted her more cheerfully. You're looking very beautiful.'

'My God, I could do with a drink, too. That room up there's absolutely freezing.'

'That would be number three?' asked the waiter sympathetically. 'Oh, that's a terrible room that is. It's a wonder they put humans in it at all. I'd rather sleep in the tent of a circus, that I would.'

'We want some more drinks.'

'Would the lady like a cocktail, now? I could do her a good cocktail, and very reasonable.'

'Two large whiskies will do.'

As he left and we sat down on each side of the fire I began to feel better.

'It's a pity about the single rooms,' I said, looking shiftily to see if the door was shut. 'That old buzzard in the office quite put me off my stride.'

'It doesn't matter,' she said, lighting a cigarette. 'You can creep down as soon as everyone goes to bed. It saves a lot of bother in the long run.'

'You've had some experience of this–this sort of thing?' I asked.

'Really, darling, I wasn't born yesterday.' She glance round her. 'What a bloody hole you've taken me to, if you don't mind me saying so. This place looks like a waiting-room got up for the wake of a dead station-master.'

'I'm sorry. Really I am.' I reached for her hand. 'But I've never done anything like this before. And–and I did so much want to do it with you, Nan.'

She smiled, and squeezed my fingers. 'You're really very, very sweet.'

The waiter then returned with the drinks.

'I was looking you up in the visitors' book, and I see you're from London,' he said. 'What sort of line of business would you be in, now?'

'I'm a doctor.'

I bit my lip; it was my second idiotic slip. Apart from the danger of discovery by confessing my profession, I was now the target for everyone's intimacies.

'Are you now? And that's very interesting.' The waiter settled himself, leaning on his up-ended tray. 'I've a great admiration for the medical profession myself, Doctor. It must be a great work, a great work. I had a brother, now, and he started off to be a doctor, but he had some sort of trouble with the authorities. Now he's an oyster-opener in one of the big hotels in O'Connell Street. Oh, he would have been a fine doctor, he would, a lovely pair of hands he had on him. And the lady wouldn't be a nurse, would she?'

'It happens that we are cousins,' I told him firmly. 'Our uncle, who was in the brass business, has unfortunately died suddenly. We are attending his funeral. The reason we are travelling together is that we both work in London, and it is obviously more convenient for us to share the same car. The reason we are in this hotel is that we met a man on the road—'

'Now it's a very convenient thing that you should have come tonight, Doctor, because I was having a lot of trouble with my feet, you see, and I was meaning to go to a doctor tomorrow. But now you're here, it'll save me the journey. I think that the arches must be dropped, or something, but I get a sort of burning pain along here which sort of moves round and round—'

'I'll hear about your feet later, if you really want me to. Will you please get us two more drinks.'

'But you've only just started those.'

'I know. But we shall have finished them before you can turn round.'

'I've had some trouble with my kidneys, too, I'd like to talk to you about, Doctor.'

'Yes, yes! Later if you like. But drinks now.'

'Just as you please, Doctor. I don't mind at all.'

We had several more drinks, after which Nurse Macpherson became more romantic. The waiter fortunately had to go and serve dinner.

'How about some food,' I suggested.

'Ummm! I'm ravenous. And there's a good three hours to kill before we can decently disappear.' I kissed her, and she began to laugh. 'I wonder how old Plumtree is?' she asked. Both laughing, we entered the coffee-room.

I later decided that the decline of the evening really started with dinner. The coffee-room itself instantly damped our spirits. It was a long, cold place, decorated only with pictures of horses in heavy gilt frames. Most of the tables were bare, those laid for dinner being huddled round a small fire in a large grate at one end. Our fellow diners were a pair of old ladies at a table thickly covered with patent-medicine bottles, an elderly couple, a red-faced, fat man with a ginger moustache, and a thin, white-haired man who was drinking soup and reading the paper propped against a bottle of beer. Everyone was silent and eating steadily, as though they were anxious to get back to the unknown corners of the hotel where they lurked.

'If you please, Doctor, over here, Doctor,' said the waiter loudly, interrupting his service and clattering a vegetable dish on the table. 'I've put you nice and near the fire, Doctor.' He crossed to a small table almost in the hearth and began beating the seat of a chair violently with his napkin. 'There you are, Doctor. And the young lady, too, now, Doctor. Nice and cosy, would it be?'

Coming from a land where only the church and the medical profession are venerated, the waiter had automatically made us his favourites. This was good for the service, but it immediately made everyone in the room fix us with their fiercest attention.

'And what would you be having, Doctor?' he continued as we sat down.

I looked at the menu. 'I'll have some of the Potage Dubarry,' I said, trying to appear unaware of the spectators.

'Oh, I wouldn't have any of that, Doctor.'

'Very well,' I glanced at Nurse Macpherson. 'We'll try the steamed plaice with pommes vapeur and cabbage.'

The waiter, who had his order-pad in one hand, scratched his head with the butt of his pencil. 'I wouldn't touch the fish if I was you, Doctor. Mind, it's not a thing I'd tell anybody but even the cats downstairs are refusing the fish.'

'How about the casserole de mouton? And we'll have some wine.' He looked blank, so I added. 'You have some wine?'

'Sure, we've got wine. I'll bring you a bottle.'

'Red wine,' I insisted. 'I'd like to choose a Burgundy, if you've got one ready at room temperature.'

'You just leave it to me, Doctor.'

'Did I understand, sir,' said the man with the ginger moustache, 'that you are a medical man?'

I nodded.

'My name is Major Porter,' he continued. 'If I may effect an introduction to your good self and your lady wife—'

'I'm a lady, but no wife,' Nurse Macpherson said tartly.

'We're cousins, as it happens,' I explained. 'We have an uncle in the lead business in Scotland, who died, and we've been to his funeral. So we came together because we both work in London. I mean, we're going to his funeral. Poor fellow.' I felt that my whisky before dinner had made the story mildly confused, so to clarify it I added, 'He wasn't in the lead business, I mean the brass business.'

I noticed Nurse Macpherson's mouth harden.

'I hope you don't mind my saying so,' Major Porter continued, 'but I don't believe in doctors. I've nothing against doctors individually, mind–not a thing. Some of my best friends are doctors. I've no faith in the medical profession as a whole.'

'Neither have I,' said Nurse Macpherson, with the frankness of the slightly tipsy.

'Really, madam? I'm interested to hear it. Are you–forgive me if I ask–at all connected with medical work?'

'Yes, I'm a member of a Sisterhood of Druids. We use a good deal of mistletoe, and aren't past sacrifice at sunrise. Can I do anything for your warts?'

Major Porter seemed surprised, but continued, 'I'm sure you'll be interested in my case, Doctor. In fact, I'd like your opinion on it. Not that I expect you to approve of my treatment.' He looked at me shyly. 'You fellows stick together, eh? There's no closed shop like the doctors' shop, I often say. I mean no offence, of course. Now would you believe it, Doctor,' he said, drawing back his coat and protruding his abdomen proudly, 'at the age of five I was given only six months to live?'

I recognized wearily the doctor's second social blight: worse than the men who insist on telling you about their orthodox illnesses are the people cured by faith, herbs, and osteopathy. Major Porter addressed the coffee-room about his miraculous lease of life while we ate our mutton stew and drank our wine, boiling hot from under the stillroom tap. By the time the waiter reverently bore us the porcelain slab with the remains of the cheese, the Major was tugging up his trousers and pointing to the scar of his old tibial osteomyelitis. The white-haired man, who like the Major was a commercial traveller, joined in with the story of the remarkable cure effected by a man in Catford on his sister-in-law who came out all over when she ate strawberries. Then the waiter made himself comfortable leaning against the fireplace and began talking about his kidneys.

'What you need for your kidneys', declared Nurse Macpherson, with slight slurring, 'is pure water. Flush them. Drink water–several gallons a day.'

'That's a damn silly remark,' I said. I was beginning to have a hangover, my throat was raw, and I was starting to shiver. 'That treatment went out with pneumonia-jackets and ice-bags. You restrict fluids and give 'em a high protein intake.'

She looked at me steadily. 'Have you ever nursed a case of nephritis?' she demanded.

'You don't have to know any medicine to be a nurse, my dear. Any more than you have to know dietetics to be a good cook.'

She was about to reply, when the old gentleman said, 'Doctor and nurse, eh? What brings you to this part of the world?'

'We met a man on the road who recommended the hotel. You see, we're cousins. We're going to the funeral of our uncle in the brass business—'

'For God's sake!' shouted Nurse Macpherson. 'Not again!' She stood up. 'I'm going to bed.'

Bed! I suddenly remembered what we were there for.

'I'm going in a minute, too,' I said, as she stalked from the room.

'It isn't ten yet,' said the Major. 'Let's have a drink.'

'No thanks.' I turned to the waiter, who was rubbing his loins thoughtfully under his coat. 'Bring me what's left in the whisky bottle. I'll take it to my room.'

I sat on the edge of my bed feeling miserable. I wished I were tucked up in a ward at St Swithin's, with someone bringing me throat lozenges every half-hour. But I would have to go through with it. Nurse Macpherson, the unruffled heroine of a dozen such adventures, would roast me in her contempt if I didn't. After waiting for the hotel to become silent I slowly undressed and put on my dressing-gown. Carefully I opened the door. I began to creep down the stairs towards the first floor.

The effect of fever, excitement, and alcohol raised my pulse rate alarmingly as I felt my way along the darkened corridor towards room number three. I had carefully memorized my landmarks before dinner, and I remembered that you turned left by the fire-extinguisher, went down three steep stairs, and reached the first-floor landing. I was checking my position by feeling for a marble statuette of Britannia when the light went on.

'Yes?'

Mrs Digby, in hair-net and dressing-gown, stood at her bedroom door.

I tried to smile again. 'Good evening.'

She said nothing.

'I was looking for the bathroom.'

'There's a bathroom on your floor.'

'Oh, really? Is there? I didn't notice it.'

'It is opposite your room. There is "Bath" written on the door in large white letters.'

'Thank you. Thank you very much. Stupid of me, coming all this way. Should have seen it. All conveniences, what? Good hotel. Capital!'

She made no reply, so I made my way back along the passage. She waited at her open door until I had disappeared, then put the light out. I tried to creep back after shivering on the upper landing for ten minutes, but she opened her door again before I had reached the foot of the stairs.

'Did you say opposite my room?' I asked. 'With "Bath" on it?'

'Yes.'

'Well. Thanks. Good night to you. A very good night to you.'

I went back to my bedroom and drank the rest of the whisky. It was then eleven-thirty. Clearly I should have to wait another hour, or even two, before operating my risky sortie. I lay down on top of my bed and picked up the *Lancet*, which I had somehow included in my packing.

When I woke up it was eight-thirty in the morning.

'God Almighty!' I said. I already saw myself the laughing-stock of St Swithin's. I dressed quickly, dashed downstairs, and threw open the door of Nurse Macpherson's room. It was empty, with her pink nightie rumpled on the bed. So was the hall below, and the coffee-room.

'If you're looking for the lady,' said the waiter, 'she's gone out for a walk with the Major.'

Nurse Macpherson and I said little on the journey home. When we were nearing the Zoo again she began to laugh.

'I don't really see there's anything very funny in it,' I told her sourly. 'I've been extremely unwell all the time, I've got a roaring temperature, and how did I know what the bloody place was like?'

'I'm not blaming you about the hotel I was just thinking what a laugh the girls will get in the Nurses' Home.'

'You wouldn't tell them?' I asked anxiously.

'Why not? A nurse's life is a dull one. It can always do with brightening up.'

'If you breathe a word about this to your friends,' I said savagely, 'I'll spill it all round the Residency.'

She laughed again. 'You wouldn't dare.'

'I damn well would.'

But I knew she was right.

Nurse Plumtree never spoke to me again. Two weeks later Nurse Macpherson became engaged to Bingham.

Chapter Twenty-one

'It was hard luck, old lad,' Grimsdyke said sympathetically. 'Still, it might have been worse. There was one fellow I knew who took a girl away for a week-end to Torquay. Best hotel, no expense spared and so on. They'd just got to their room and he'd opened the windows to have a breath of sea air, when what do you think he saw? Her whole bloody family arriving for their summer holidays at the front door, ma, pa, and several small sisters and brothers. Phew!'

We were sitting in his room some time later. I stared gloomily at my drink in his toothglass; my throat was better, but my pride would wear its scars for a lifetime.

'My trouble', I said solemnly, 'is women.'

'Come, come, Richard! A less flighty citizen than you would be hard to discover. Disregarding the pocket harem you were running until this disaster, I've never thought of you as one of nature's bottom-pinchers.'

'I don't go chasing women right and left, I admit. But ever since I qualified I seem to keep getting involved with them just the same. First it was the shocking female married to Hockett. Then there was that smooth piece of goods in Park Lane. Next Plumtree. Then that frightful nympho Macpherson.'

'Personally, I'm all for getting in the clutches of unscrupulous women now and then,' Grimsdyke said cheerfully. 'Rather fun.'

'But it was never like this when we were students!'

'You underestimate the fatal allure of a medical qualification, old lad. In a quiet way, it's about ten times as powerful as any uniform.'

'You think so?'

'Sure of it. Look at all these chaps that get hauled in front of the G.M.C. Why do you suppose every textbook starts by telling you to have a nurse handy when examining any female from nine to ninety? Then look at the medical profession as a whole. A more pug-ugly collection of badly-dressed social misfits would be difficult to find.'

'True,' I admitted.

'Allure, old lad. Remember it. Have another drink.'

'The unpleasant truth', I said, 'is that I've shirked the responsibility of my ambitions. I'm not saying I've been a good-time Charlie, but now it's a year since I qualified and I haven't gone far towards becoming a surgeon.'

'You've learnt a lot about men and women, as opposed to male and female patients, though.'

'Unfortunately that cuts no ice with the Fellowship examiners. There's no easy way out. I'll have to buckle down to the books again.'

'How about a job?'

I sighed. My appointment at St Swithin's had only another week to run. 'I'll have to start on those beastly interviews again, I suppose. This time, I'll address the committee "Dear Sir or Madam".'

The next few days were sad ones. I would be sorry to lose the companionship of the Residency, and to leave at last the hospital that had been the centre of my life for seven years. But there was no alternative: under the hospital rules I had to make way for the junior men just qualified, and I could never gain promotion to become a registrar like Hatrick without my Fellowship. I could only say good-bye to St Swithin's as cheerfully as possible, turn again to the back pages of the *B.M.J.*, and mark the date to the next reunion dinner in my diary.

Then hope appeared, outlandishly embodied in the Professor of Surgery.

I had gone to his laboratory behind the surgical block to fetch the notes of one of our patients, when he unexpectedly appeared from his office.

'Gordon!'

'Sir?'

'Will you step inside a minute?'

Licking my lips nervously, I followed him into his tiny room, which was filled with ungainly physiological apparatus, pickled things in pots, piles of text-books, journals in several languages, and the forbidding photographs of his predecessors in the Chair.

'Sit down,' he commanded.

I gingerly took the edge of a packing-case marked RADIOACTIVE MATERIAL, while he sat in his swivel chair and pulled his white coat tightly round him. I wondered what was coming. I had carefully avoided the Professor since my return, but every time I caught his eye I had felt him mentally signing my Certificate of Lunacy.

'I had lunch with my friend Mr Justice Hopcroft today,' he began.

I said nothing.

'We recalled that incident when you were my Casualty H.S.'

'I had hoped, sir, he might have forgotten it.'

'On the contrary, we laughed about it heartily. Most amusing in retrospect. Hopcroft has a lively sense of humour, you know. Some of his remarks when passing sentence have caused many a chuckle in the Bar.'

'I'm sure they have, sir.'

There was silence, while the Professor stared hard at a pair of kidneys mounted in a glass jar.

'I was perhaps rather hasty with you, Gordon,' he confessed.

'It's kind of you to say so, sir.'

'Unfair, even.'

'Not at all, sir.' The interview was developing more comfortably than I had imagined, 'I deserved it,' I added indulgently.

'I might say it has worried me somewhat since. If one's judgement once becomes clouded by one's emotions, there's no telling where it will end.'

There was another silence.

'Bingham,' said the Professor.

'Yes, sir?'

A friend of yours?'

'Hardly a close one, sir.'

'I will confess, Gordon–in confidence–that Bingham has been something of a disappointment to me. The young man has ability, I'm not denying it, but I sometimes have a little difficulty in the operating theatre deciding which of us is the Professor of Surgery.'

'Quite so, sir,' I said.

'I gather he is not one of the most popular members of the Residency?'

'Not the most popular, sir.'

'A job on the Unit here has come up unexpectedly,' the Professor went on. 'The resident pathologist–Shiradee–has had to return to Bombay. It's a fairly leisurely job, which would give a man plenty of time to work for his Fellowship. Some minor research would be expected, of course. The appointment will be made with the others at the Committee on Wednesday evening–naturally it's my duty to support Bingham for the job. But I can't answer for the rest of the Committee. And in the present state of my relations with Bingham I assure you it would not take a great deal to make me change my mind. In short, Gordon, if you agree, I'd like to make up for my somewhat high-handed treatment of you earlier in your career by at least offering you a chance of the job. Will you apply on the usual form?'

I was so excited that I was almost unable to sleep for the rest of the week. In the operating theatre, where I now approached the table with the confidence of Robert Liston in his prime, I began fumbling so badly that Hatrick declared wearily that I was again in love.

Every time I saw Bingham approaching I avoided him: indeed, I had hardly spoken to him at all since his engagement, apart from stumbling out my congratulations with the rest. But on the evening before the meeting I was forced to seek his company. I was sitting in my room after dinner writing up my case notes, when I became aware of an unpleasant smell. As I sniffed, it grew stronger. From a whiff of the Southend mudflats it rapidly turned into the odour of a faulty sewage farm, and within a few minutes it appeared that some large animal was decomposing in the room next door. Holding my handkerchief over my nose, I banged on Bingham's door.

'Come in!'

Bingham was in his shirt-sleeves, boiling something in a glass beaker over a spirit-lamp.

'Good God, man!' I exclaimed. 'What the devil are you cooking?'

'What, this? Oh, it's manure, old chap,' he said calmly.

'Manure!'

'Yes, old chap. Ordinary horse manure. You see, the Prof.'s very interested in the enzymes present in the manure of different animals. Pure research, you know. I've studied it a bit, and it might easily throw a good bit of light on the old human guts. Interesting, eh?' He blew out the lamp. 'I've collected specimens of all sorts of animal manure,' he continued proudly, picking up a row of small test-tubes. 'This one's dog, that's cat, that's pigeon, and the end one's ferret. I just caught the horse when I saw a carter's van stop outside casualty.'

'And what, may I ask, is all this in aid of, Bingham?'

'If you can keep a secret, old chap. I'll tell you. Fact is, I've put in for the path. job on the Unit. Knowing the Prof.'s interested in this line of research, I had a go at it. I've had one or two interesting ideas which I've put to him already, as a matter of fact.'

'And you think you'll get this job do you?'

'Don't want to boast, old chap,' said Bingham, rubbing his hands, 'but I fancy my chances a bit. It happens that the Prof. of Bacteriology and a few of the consultant surgeons have heard of this research I'm doing off my own bat, and it seems to have impressed them. As for the Prof., he's tickled pink. For some reason he particularly wanted to study the elephant's manure, and was talking about cabling to Africa, when I said, "What's wrong with the Zoo?" I've asked them to send a specimen round to him.' He sat down on his bed, and pulled out his pipe. 'By the way, old chap,' he continued, with a sheepish grin. 'Best man win, and all that?'

'Eh?'

He nudged me. 'Know what I mean, old chap, don't you? Don't worry, I'm as broadminded as the next. About Nan. You were a bit sweet on her yourself, eh? When she went on nights, I mean. You couldn't blind me to it. Still, no hard feelings. Only one of us could be chosen, couldn't he, old chap? I hope the fact that you didn't make any headway doesn't prevent our shaking hands?'

'It certainly doesn't,' I said shaking.

'She tells me you tried to kiss her once,' he added, nudging me again. 'But no ill will, old chap.'

'One of us, Bingham, is a very, very lucky man,' I told him, laying a hand on his shoulder.

'Very decent of you, old chap.'

'Not a bit,' I said. 'Old chap.'

The next twenty-four hours were worrying. Knowing Bingham's ability to worm his way into the estimation of his seniors, I was increasingly despondent about my chances of stealing the pathology job from under his nose. As the morning of Wednesday passed I felt that I was again waiting for the result of an examination, with the recollection of having made one certain boner in the middle of the fourth question.

'It's no good worrying,' Grimsdyke said, as we sat in my room before supper. 'The old boys will gather for the meeting in about an hour's time, and you'll either be in or you won't. And anyone with half an eye can tell that Bingham's a first-class tapeworm.'

'But he's a damn clever tapeworm,' I insisted. 'Look how he bamboozled the Prof. in the first place. Now he's playing mother's little helpmeet over this research business. Oh, blast Bingham!' I said with sudden bad temper. 'He did me out of the first job, and now he'll dish me with this one. I wouldn't mind if he was a decent human being, but of all the nasty, grovelling, slimy–' The telephone began ringing in the room next door. As it continued, i yelled, 'And now I have to answer his bloody phone for him!'

When I came back I was grinning.

'I think I'm going to get that job,' I told Grimsdyke.

'You do? And why?'

'That was the Prof. The Zoo have sent him his specimen of elephant's manure all right. Seven tons of it. They've unloaded it in his front garden.'

I was appointed Resident Pathologist to the Surgical Professional Unit, and at the same meeting Grimsdyke was promoted to Senior Resident Anaesthetist.

'Very gratifying,' he said, as we strolled contentedly into the Residency after the pubs had shut that night. 'Very, very gratifying. Virtue triumphant, vice confounded and all that.'

'I can't believe it,' I said. 'I just can't believe it! It means we've got another whole year to enjoy the hospitality of dear old St Swithin's. We will grow old together, old lad. But I didn't know you were putting in for the anaesthetics job. You never told me.'

'Didn't I?' He screwed in his monocle. 'Must have forgotten to mention it. The fact is–and far be it from a Grimsdyke to express any liking for the toil that earns his daily bread–but I'm getting quite interested in doing dopes. Also–I fancy myself–I'm getting the hang of it right and left. Did you notice that endotracheal tube I passed this morning? Very pretty.'

'You're as bad as Bingham,' I said laughing.

'Ah, Bingham! I might add that, in case my sterling qualities as an anaesthetist were overlooked at tonight's meeting, yesterday I handed that old trout's cheque for ten thousand quid to the senior anaesthetist to buy himself some research. I fancied that might strengthen the old boy's determination if voices were raised against me.'

'You're *worse* than Bingham!'

I found Bingham in his room, starting to pack.

'Well, old chap,' he said, trying to look pleasant, 'you got the better of me this time, eh?'

'I'm afraid so, Bingham. No ill will, I hope?'

'Oh, no. Not a bit, old chap. We've always been chums, haven't we? Besides, I have something which you can never have.'

Deciding that he was referring to Nurse Macpherson, I said, 'Too true.'

'I think I'll have a go at general practice,' Bingham went on. 'Just for a spell, of course, before I get my Fellowship. Does a chap good.'

'Have you anywhere in mind?'

'Not exactly,' he continued, folding his trousers. 'But there's a jolly smart agency I'm going to tomorrow called Wilson, Willowick, and Wellbeloved. They'll fix me up.'

'Yes, they'll fix you up, all right.'

'There's just one thing,' he continued. He grinned sheepishly. 'Fact is, not getting this job's a blessing in disguise. In G.P. I can afford to get married a bit earlier, and–well, Nan and I will probably be man and wife by the end of next week. It's jolly good, and I'm jolly pleased, of course, but it's a bit of a rush. Hasn't given me time to arrange anything. Thing is, old chap, where's a good and fairly inexpensive place to spend the–ah, honeymoon? Do you know of anywhere?'

'The Judge's Arms,' I said immediately. 'It's a hotel on the way north. Very romantic.'

'Thanks, old chap. I'll remember that.'

'There's just one thing. I'd make a surprise of it–keep it quiet where you're going until you actually arrive. A chum of mine did, and claims it gives you something to talk about in the painful journey from the reception.'

'By jove, old chap, what a terrif. idea! I'll certainly do that. Well, thanks a lot, old chap.'

'Don't mench, old chap,' I said. My happiness was complete.

Richard Gordon

Doctor in Love

Doctor in Love

To Anthony and Simon, naturally

All characters are fictitious

Chapter One

It is a fact well known to the medical profession that doctors marry either nurses, other doctors, or barmaids. During the most marriageable years these are the only women they meet. Indeed, at the age when other young men's fancies first lightly turn to thoughts of matrimony they are unable to marry at all, being still supported by an allowance from home. It is a small consolation to reflect that the further you ascend the evolutionary scale the longer you find the young depend on the parent, which makes medical students the highest form of animal life known to science.

Although my classmates at St Swithin's Hospital included a couple of harassed young men who arrived at lectures with notebooks dutifully sharing string bags with sprouts and soap-flakes, a married medical student is almost as much an impossibility as a married Boy Scout. Then the magic touch of a diploma changes his emotional life as violently as his economic one. As an unqualified scallywag he has the alternative of dishonourable intentions or no intentions at all; but after the examination results engagement rings sparkle round the nurses' home as gaily as summer stars, and if the Royal Colleges of Physicians and Surgeons knew how many unions were first solemnized by their examiners they would be much alarmed.

The first of my companions to wed was Tony Benskin, who married a night nurse. This was reasonable, as he had once offered matrimony to all of them on duty one night to invalidate an over-enthusiastic proposal to one earlier in the evening. It was almost two years until I saw him again, for medical students at the end of their course, like ships' passengers at the end of their voyage, exchange addresses with more enthusiasm than earnestness. I ran into him one summer evening in the corridors of St Swithin's, where I was still working on the junior resident staff.

'Tony!' I cried. I stared at him in alarm. His face was pale and unshaven, his eyes wild and bloodshot, his hair and his tie awry. 'Tony! What on earth's the matter?'

'Hello, Richard,' he said absently. 'I brought Molly into the hospital last night.'

'Oh, my dear fellow! Was it an accident?'

'Of course it wasn't an accident! We planned it.'

'You mean . . . Oh, I see. She's having a baby?'

'What, you mean you didn't know?' His tone indicated an affair of universal importance.

'No, I'm afraid the news didn't reach me. So she's in the tender care of the midder department? There's nothing to worry about.'

'Nothing to worry about! What do you understand about it? You've never had a baby.'

'But it was a normal pregnancy, I hope?'

'Oh, yes, her pregnancy was normal enough, down to the last molecule of haemoglobin. But just think of the things which might go wrong now! Why, at the best it may be a breech. It could be a persistent occipito-posterior or a transverse lie, or a placenta praevia or a prolapsed cord. She might have a P.P.H. or a Caesar or anything. . . . Do you remember all those frightful pictures in the midder books?' He thrust his hands disconsolately into his trouser pockets. 'It's alarming, isn't it?'

Seeing that his clinical detachment was as disarranged as his appearance, I laid a hand consolingly on his shoulder.

'Remember all the women who're having babies every minute of the day. Why, at this very moment Molly will be lying there pleasantly doped with pethidine, listening to old Sister Studholme telling her to bear down nicely, dear, and try and save your pains.'

'But that's the ruddy trouble!' Tony looked more anxious than ever. 'I rushed her in all the way from Hampstead in the middle of the night, and not a thing's happened since.'

'She's just gone off the boil, as they say in the midwifery trade.'

'But think what it *might* be! She could have uterine inertia, deep transverse arrest, contracted pelvis . . .'

'Look,' I decided. 'What you need is a drink.'

He paused. 'You know, Richard, I believe you're absolutely right.'

He calmed a little under the effect of three large whiskies in the King George opposite the Hospital.

'I'm afraid I'm not quite myself,' he apologized.

'But that's understandable in the circumstances. Traditional in fact.'

'I'm sorry, Richard. I ought to have slapped you on the back and asked you how you were and talked about the good old days, and so on. But it's upsetting all this–bringing new life into the world, and so on.'

I laughed. 'I'm not sure they shouldn't have stuck you in the labour ward instead of Molly.'

'It may look funny to you, but it's a shattering prospect for the first time. Just wait till it's your turn.'

'Not me! I'm going to stay a bachelor. Changing imperceptibly from gay young to dirty old.'

'Bet you fifty quid you don't!'

I considered the proposition. 'I'll take you on. It's a good bet, because I'm determined to get my F.R.C.S. before I even think of marrying.' I still wanted to specialize in surgery, and the Fellowship of the Royal College was as essential as a flying licence to a prospective pilot. 'And at the present rate I can't see much chance of passing the exam before I get prostatic hypertrophy and the male menopause.'

'But you'll *have* to get married, old man. Take it from me, a doctor's got to. The patients don't like you messing about with their wives unless they know you've got one of your own at home. Then you must have someone to answer the telephone and open the door and keep all the N.H.S. cards straight and cook the dinner and do the laundry.'

'I could get a housekeeper.'

'The only housekeeper you could possibly employ would have to be so ugly and respectable she wouldn't bear living with. No, Richard. You'll have to settle for the pipe and armchair and the slippers and taking the dog for a walk at closing time.'

I took a mouthful of beer thoughtfully.

'But even allowing you're right, Tony–where do I find the right girl? Supposing I picked the wrong one?'

'Sheer defeatism! Anyway, what's the matter with one of the matron's little charges? They're all healthy girls, they know how to cook and make the beds, and they're trained to put up with any amount of irritation from crotchety old men. You couldn't ask for more. It has long been my contention that the most useful function of any nursing school in the country is turning out a supply of fully trained doctors' wives. Though,' he added reflectively, 'they tend to worry a lot about the regularity of your bowels.' Suddenly I noticed his jaw drop. 'It's just occurred to me,' he muttered. 'Supposing the poor little thing's got mixed-up guts or no feet or two heads, or any of those hundreds of congenital defects we had to learn about in embryology?'

'Don't be ridiculous, Tony! Despite the fact that it has you for a father, it will turn out a perfectly healthy and normal baby. The very worst you can worry about is twins.'

He shook his head. 'At least it can't be that–I sent Molly down to the X-ray department long ago. Do you want to see baby's first photo? I've got it in the back of the car.'

The next afternoon I was surprised to see Molly Benskin sitting in the sunshine that pierced the dusty plane trees in the hospital courtyard, still looking like an over-ripe poppy-head.

'Hello!' I said. 'I thought you'd be otherwise engaged.'

She wrinkled her snub nose. 'It's all Tony's fault. Instead of acting in a perfectly calm and professional manner as he would if I was his patient instead of his wife—'

'He's been behaving like any other expectant father?'

'Oh, much worse! Do you know, for the last month he's been trying to take my blood pressure pretty well hourly? And every time I had a backache he got the car out. In the end I couldn't stop him rushing me here at four in the morning as though I was on fire. I think he was scared stiff he'd have to deliver it himself.'

'As far as I remember, Tony was never very accurate at midder,' I told her sympathetically. 'When I was a student with him we always seemed to arrive either three hours too early or five minutes too late.'

'Now I've got to stay in the ward, I haven't got any of my things, my hair's terrible, I look most unglamorous, the food's uneatable, sister's a bitch, and I'm fed up.' She pouted. 'On top of that, I feel that I'm never going to have the poor little thing at all.'

'Don't you worry, Molly. So do all expectant mothers. It's never been known to fail yet.'

Two days afterwards she was delivered of an eight-pound baby boy, which Tony Benskin later carried through the main gate of the hospital with the expression of one who had discovered and patented the process himself. Helping them into the car, I was surprised to find that even I experienced strong avuncular feelings. Marriage, I had always felt, was some sort of disease which creeps up on everyone with age, like hardening of the arteries. For the first time I began to wonder how long my immunity would last.

Chapter Two

The following morning I woke in my bare room in the St Swithin's resident staff quarters feeling like Sisera, who I remembered learning in Divinity had a tent-peg driven through his temple while he slept. The old diagnosis would have been *hangover vulgaris*; but now that my former classmates were scattering both geographically and professionally I rarely had anyone to go drinking with, and I had gone to bed at eleven after a cup of coffee with the night nurse down in casualty.

In the gloomy residents' dining-room, sitting beneath the chiding eyes of Hippocrates, Lord Lister, and Sir William Osler, I found that I couldn't eat my breakfast. This was unusual, because after even our most shameful student debauches I was always ready for my porridge and kippers as usual the next morning. I managed to swallow a cup of tea, then put on my white coat and crossed the hospital courtyard to my laboratory.

At the time I was coming to the end of my appointment as the junior resident pathologist. I spent my days in the pathology block, sitting at a bench richly engrained with the brilliant blues, greens, and reds used for staining bacteria, doing calculations and tests on 'specimens'. These were of various sorts, and either sent across daily from the wards by the trayful or borne to us proudly by out-patients in a selection of jam-jars and beer bottles produced from inside the jacket or shopping basket.

'Do you mind if we have the window closed?' I asked the junior pathology demonstrator, my overseer. I pulled a high wooden laboratory stool to my usual place. 'It's a bit nippy this morning.'

'Nippy? It's a lovely hot summer's day!'

I drew my microscope towards me and shivered.

'Be a good lad and get on with this pile of blood counts,' he continued. 'There's been a rush of them over from the wards. Then there's some urines over there I'd like you to tackle when you're free. They're beginning to niff a bit.'

When the demonstrator went off to lecture I shut all the windows. Then I was surprised to find that the weather had suddenly turned warmer and I was sweating. The climate was particularly irritating, because that morning my work was twice as troublesome as usual. I had difficulty in focusing the microscope, I kept shaking drops of blood from the little glass slides, and I couldn't add up. By lunch time I slunk back to my room and laid down, wondering why I felt so tired.

It didn't occur to me that I was ill. It never does to doctors, who are as shocked to find themselves sick as a policeman to discover that his home has been burgled or a fireman to see his own roof on fire. It was almost through curiosity that I rummaged for a clinical thermometer I kept somewhere in my sock drawer, and slipped it under my tongue.

'Good God!' I said. I had a temperature of a hundred and three.

I sat down on the edge of my bed, faced with the unnerving problem of self-diagnosis.

I gingerly felt my pulse. Ninety-six. Crossing to the mirror I stuck out my tongue, which looked like the inside of an old kettle. I stared down my throat, but found I couldn't see very far. Opening my shirt, I ran a stethoscope over as much of my chest as possible, and discovered that listening to your own breath-sounds for the first time is as alarming as hearing a record of your own voice. After thinking for a few minutes I decided that it must be typhoid fever.

Another characteristic of doctors is never allowing themselves to be ill by half-measures. In the process of self-diagnosis they think first of all the fatal diseases, next of the most outlandish, thirdly of the most uncomfortable, and finally reach a decision which would have had them thrown out of any qualifying examination in the country. Failing typhoid, I suspected glanders, psittacosis, or incipient cholera, and remembering the light-hearted way in which we manipulated dangerous bacteria in the laboratory I threw in rabies and plague as well.

After diagnosis comes treatment, and fumbling in my shaving locker for some white tablets which I thought were aspirins I swallowed a few. A further peculiarity of the physician healing himself is a wild disregard for labels and dosage: men who terrify patients by repeating sternly 'Not more than two teaspoonsful after food' treat their own complaints largely with the pharmaceutical samples sent from drug manufacturers, in doses of either a moderate handful or a large swig. Feeling afterwards that I should call for professional advice, I picked up my bedside telephone and rang my friend Grimsdyke, who was working as a resident anaesthetist in the operating theatre.

'I'm ill,' I told him, describing my symptoms. 'What do you think I should do?'

'Go and see a doctor.'

'Look here, this isn't a laughing matter. I feel terrible.'

'Seriously, old lad. Get one of the house physicians. I don't know much more about pure medicine than I do about pure mathematics. We live in an age of specialization, don't we? Must get back to the theatre now–patient looks a bit blue.'

I then rang Hinxman, houseman to Dr Pennyworth, the St Swithin's senior physician.

'You've probably got the measles,' he said cheerfully on the other end of the line. 'There's a lot of it about at the moment.'

'I've had it. A most nasty attack when I was six.'

'It's quite possible to get it twice, of course. And it's usually much worse the second time. Or it might be mumps. You know what that leads to, don't you?' He roared with laughter: fellow-doctors show as little sympathy for each other in trouble as fellow-golfers. 'It's a bit of a nuisance, because we've hardly got a spare bed in the ward. But I'll pop along and see you when I've got a moment.'

Hinxman appeared an hour or so later. He was a red-faced, curly-headed young man much given to tweeds and pipes, who always entered a room as though coming from a brisk tramp across open moors on a gusty day. I found his aggressive healthiness deeply depressing as I nervously watched his broad pink hands pummel my abdomen.

'Deep breath, old man,' he commanded. He frowned. 'M'm.'

For the first time I realized how alarming a doctor sounds when he goes 'M'm'.

'Think I can get a touch of the spleen there,' he added.

'Good Lord!' I jumped up. 'It might be one of those horrible leukaemias.'

'Yes, and it may be the chlorotic anaemia of young virgins. Don't get excited about it. I haven't felt a spleen for weeks, anyway, and I'm probably wrong. I'll get old Pennyboy along when he looks into the hospital at six. Meanwhile, go to bed?'

'Bed?' I protested. 'But I don't really want to go to bed. I hate lying down doing nothing.'

'My dear chap, you must. The first thing any physician does is to put his victim to bed and tell him to keep quiet. It doesn't do the patient the slightest harm, and it gives everyone time to think. Why, we've had some of our patients in bed for weeks upstairs while we've been thinking. We're not like surgeons, you know–never happy unless they're doing something violent.'

Dr Pennyworth himself came to my room that evening, followed by Hinxman and his medical registrar. The hospital's senior physician was a small, thin, pale man with two tufts of grey hair jutting over his ears, dressed in a black jacket and pin-striped trousers. He was so quiet and so modest that he seemed to enter the room like a ghost, without using the door. He stood by my bedside, softly wished me good evening, perched a pair of rimless pince-nez on his nose, and inspected me through them in silence.

'Ever been in India?' he asked mysteriously.

'No, sir.'

'H'm.'

After some moments' thought he gently took my hand and stood staring at my nails. This I recognized as the manner of a true physician: a surgeon would have burst into the room, pummelled me briskly, exclaimed 'Does it hurt? Where? There? Don't worry, old fellow, we'll have it out!' and telephoned the operating theatre. Dr Pennyworth silently listened to my chest, scratched the soles of my feet, pulled down an eyelid, shook me by the hand, and after a whispered discussion with his assistants disappeared as softly as he came.

As no one had told me what was wrong, I lay staring at the ceiling and speculating on the further possibility of malaria, cerebral abscess, and *spirochaetosis icterohaemorrhagica.* I had almost given myself up for lost by the time Hinxman reappeared.

'You're to be warded, old man,' he announced cheerfully. 'I've fixed everything up. Just slip on a dressing-gown and wander up to Honesty when you feel like it. Try not to breathe on too many people on the way, won't you?'

'But what have I got?'

'Oh, didn't we tell you? Look at your eyeballs.'

'Good Lord!' I exclaimed, turning to the mirror. 'Jaundice.'

'Yes, you'd pass for a good-looking Chinaman anywhere. I'll come and see you later. By the way, we'll be needing a contribution for your own laboratory.'

Collecting my toothbrush, I obediently left the residency for the main hospital block and made my way upstairs to Honesty Ward. I had rarely been ill before, and I had never been in a ward in a subjective capacity at all. I now approached the experience with the feeling of a judge mounting the steps to his own dock.

'Well, well, fancy seeing you,' said the staff nurse, a motherly blonde I had once met at a hospital dance. 'Sister's off, so I've put you in the corner. You're not terribly infectious, and we'll have you on barrier nursing.'

I got into the white iron bed, which was ready with hot-water bottle in knitted cover, red rubber sheet next to the mattress, back-rest, air-ring, and a small enamel bowl on the locker in case I wanted to put my teeth in it.

'Sorry we can't have you in a side-room,' she apologized. 'But they're both in use. One might be free in a few days,' she added significantly, 'and you can move in then.'

My first few days as a patient were delightful. My disease wasn't serious–though I kept remembering the nasty phrase in one of my textbooks, 'a small percentage of cases are fatal'–and it had the advantage that no treatment whatever was known to medical science. This left my days and nights undisturbed by having to swallow oversized pills or having to tolerate over-used needles. All I had to do was lie on my back and get better.

But I soon realized that being ill in a modern hospital is far from a passive process. A few years ago it dawned on physicians that patients shouldn't be allowed simply to rot in bed, but should be provided with daily exercise for both body and mind. This idea is now applied so enthusiastically and ward routine has become so strenuous that only people of a basically sound constitution can stand it.

Our day, like the Army's, started at six-thirty with a wash in tepid water, and continued almost without a break until lights-out at nine. Apart from the regular upheavals caused by bedmaking, meals, hot drinks, blanket baths, temperature-taking, visits by the doctors, and the distribution of 'bottles', there always seemed to be some hospital functionary waiting to see you. Each morning there appeared a blonde girl looking like a Wimbledon champion in a white overall, who came from the Physiotherapy Department to conduct a horizontal P.T. class. When we had flexed our knees and twiddled our toes in unison under the bedclothes, another girl arrived from the Occupational Therapy Unit with a basket of felt scraps for making pink bunnies. Afterwards came the hospital librarian to see if you felt like reading, the hospital dietitian to see if you felt like eating, and the hospital chaplain to see if you felt like death. Next appeared the man who brought the post, the boy who sold the newspapers, and several women with brooms who swept under the beds and carried on a loud conversation between themselves about everyone's illnesses. If you still had time, you could explore the arid stretches of the morning and afternoon radio programmes through the headphones, or swap symptoms with your neighbour. There was a welcome period of enforced sleep after lunch, but this was generally disturbed by fifty students clattering in for a ward-round or one of the medical staff appearing to examine you to test some private theory. Later, those of us allowed up sat round the empty fireplace stroking the ward cat, smoking our pipes, and exchanging opinions in a tranquilly companionable atmosphere reminiscent of an old men's home.

It was in these circumstances that I first fell seriously in love.

Chapter Three

She was the new night nurse on Honesty Ward. She was a pretty, pale girl, with large dark eyes and thick curly hair on which her official cap perched ridiculously, like the top of a *vol-au-vent*. She had a playful way of looking at you when she spoke, and the first words she addressed to me–'Would you like Horlicks or Ovaltine?'–sent odd sensations running up my spinal cord.

I had then been in the ward five days, the time I later learned from other nurses at which young men confined to bed start becoming amorous. Physicians perhaps overlook that patients' feeling towards sex, like their feelings towards beer and tobacco, are not automatically held in abeyance while enjoying the benefit of medical care in hospital. Seeing the same half a dozen young women regularly all day naturally concentrates the invalid's thoughts on any one of them, which has led many a convalescence to run concurrently with a honeymoon. The patient's state is probably exacerbated by the nursing tradition of twice daily 'doing the backs'–that is, massaging the lower spine with surgical spirit as a precaution against bedsores, which I understand is the method used to encourage recalcitrant bulls in the Argentine.

It was clearly worth making the night nurse's closer acquaintance. As soon as the ward was dark, the flowers had been removed, the day nurses had gratefully reached for their corridor capes, and sister had left for the modest evening pleasures of the sisters' home, I felt for the dressing-gown in my locker and crept out of bed.

She was in the small kitchen just outside the ward, starting to butter a large pile of bread for the patients' breakfast.

'Hello,' I said.

She looked up. 'Hello. But shouldn't you be in bed?'

'I just thought I'd like to establish social contact as well as our professional relationship.'

Stretching her apron, she gave me a curtsy. 'I am indeed honoured, kind sir, that a second-year houseman should take such trouble with a second-year nurse. Aren't you terribly infectious?'

'Not much at this stage. Anyway, I'll be frightfully careful not to touch anything. I'm afraid that I've just forgotten your name, Nurse—?'

'Florence Nightingale.'

I laughed, but catching her eye apologized quickly. 'I'm terribly sorry. Of course, there *could* be a nurse called Florence Nightingale . . . I mean, really it's quite a common name, though I suppose unusual . . .'

'Oh, don't worry. I'm quite used to it. My mother was desperately keen on the Red Cross. Hence the name. Hence the career. My friends call me Sally, by the way. But oughtn't you really to stay in the ward?'

'You're not worried about the night sisters, are you? They won't be on the prowl for hours yet.'

'Ah, the night sisters! "How now, you secret, black, and midnight hags! What is't you do? A deed without a name?"'

'You must be the first nurse I've ever heard quote Shakespeare on duty,' I said in surprise.

She went on buttering a piece of bread with a faintly aggressive air. 'You housemen! You seem to think we confine our reading to Evelyn Pearce's textbooks and the Engagement column in the *Telegraph*. Didn't you see me when the Dramatic Society did *As You Like It*?'

'No, I'm afraid I missed that one,' I confessed. But seeing a common interest in sight I continued warmly, 'I was terribly keen on the Dramatic Society myself. When I was a student and had more time.'

'I know. I saw your last appearance. It was the week I arrived as a new probationer, and I'll never forget it.'

This was perhaps unfortunate. My dramatic career at St Swithin's had reached its climax with the hospital production of *The Middle Watch*, in which I was cast as the Commander. At the start of the second scene the Captain, played by Grimsdyke, was to be discovered alone in his cabin turning over the pages of *The Field*, until interrupted by a knock and the appearance of Tony Benskin as Ah Fong the Chinese servant. Unfortunately I had mistimed the length of the interval, and Tony and I were still drinking pints of beer in the King George when the curtain rose. There being no knock, Grimsdyke anxiously scanned the entire *Field*, throwing imploring glances into the wings. He then thumbed his way through the *Illustrated London News*, the *Tatler*, and the *Sphere*, and finished the *Sketch* and *Punch* before striding off the stage in a fury and bringing down the curtain, leaving the audience mystified for the rest of the evening at the significance of this short but powerful scene.

'Are you sure you're feeling quite well?' Sally Nightingale continued, interrupting her slicing and laying a hand softly on my cheek. 'You certainly *do* seem a little warm.'

I was just reflecting how much pleasanter this was than having a glass-and-mercury icicle tasting of Dettol rammed under your tongue, when the door opened and Hinxman walked in.

'What are you doing here?' he said immediately.

'Oh, hello, old man. Yes, I know I should be in bed by rights. But being in the trade I thought I could take a few liberties with ward routine.'

'Routine? It's nothing whatever to do with routine. It's a matter of your treatment.'

'Have you met our new night nurse?' I asked.

'I know Nurse Nightingale very well. She was on day duty here until last week. Good evening, Sally.'

'Good evening, Roger.'

'Oh, I'm sorry,' I apologized. 'I didn't realize you'd met.'

There was a silence, in which I felt that my professional adviser and colleague was behaving oddly. Hinxman was one of those enviably uncomplicated men who sing in their baths and never have hangovers or catch colds or feel draughts, and he had the most amiable personality in the whole resident staff quarters. We had previously enjoyed a friendship which ran to mutual loans of razor-blades and textbooks, but now he was breathing heavily and staring at me as though I were some particularly striking specimen in a bottle in the pathology museum.

'Well, you're the doctor.' I shrugged my shoulders, remembering that many young housemen appear weighty when first testing the delicate balance of the doctor-patient relationship. I decided to obey graciously, and said lightly to Sally Nightingale: 'Good night, Nurse. I'll get back to my little waterproofed cot. If I'm still awake, come and talk to me when Dr Hinxman's gone.'

The next morning the motherly staff nurse hooked my treatment board to the foot of my bed. 'You're on complete bed rest,' she announced.

'Oh no!'

'Yes, Mr Hinxman's written you up for it.'

'But what on earth for? I'm getting better. Why, I ought to be out of hospital completely in a few days.'

'I really don't know, I'm afraid. Ours is not to reason why, but to do what the houseman tells us.'

My annoyance came less from the prospect of immobility than the threat it held–bedpans. These traditional features of the hospital scene, which defy the laws of geometry by possessing length and breadth but no depth, have never had, nor deserved, a word written in their favour. So far I had escaped them, but from now on I should have to catch the eye of the junior probationer like everyone else. I decided angrily to tackle Hinxman on his line of treatment as soon as he appeared.

'Look here,' I complained. 'I must say, this bed-rest business is about the limit. Why, I'm pretty well convalescent! Or have you just got me muddled up with someone else?'

Hinxman stared at me in silence. His face was pinker than ever; his eyes were heavy and bloodshot; his hands were thrust deep into the pockets of his white coat, among the percussion hammers, tuning-forks, and other little diagnostic toys beloved by physicians.

'You are at liberty to complain to the Chief about my treatment if you want to.'

'Oh, I wouldn't want to go as far as that. After all, we're both in the trade. I know doctors make rotten patients, but I'm prepared to do as I'm told. I just can't see the point of it, that's all.'

Expression for a second played on his face like the top of a milk saucepan caught at the boil. Then he turned and strode down the ward, with the step of a man finding things too much for him.

Chapter Four

Romances in hospital, like romances at sea, progress rapidly. This is probably because both patients and passengers have little else to occupy their thoughts between meals. I spent the following days lying strictly in bed trying to read Boswell's *Life of Johnson* and thinking about Sally Nightingale, and the nights staying awake trying to snatch brief chats as she passed in the romantic twilight of the sleeping ward. Like the addict waiting for his daily dose of morphine, I found myself fretting as the evening dragged through its routine of supper, bedpans, and thermometers towards eight o'clock, when the tousled day staff went off duty and Sally reappeared in her fresh starched wrappings.

'Would you care for a little barley water?' she asked as she came to my corner a few nights later. 'I've just made some.'

'Barley water? I'd love it, thanks.'

It would have been all the same if she'd offered hemlock.

'And how are you tonight, Richard?'

'Immeasurably better for seeing you.'

'Now, now!' She gave me a playful look. 'Don't you realize you should think of me purely as your nurse?'

'But that's impossible! Do you know, when I got this beastly disease I thought it was about the unluckiest thing that had happened to me for a long time. But the moment you walked into the ward, Sally . . . Well, I began to feel that it was the brightest event of my life.'

She laughed as she gave my pillow a professional smoothing. 'Pure delirium, doctor.'

'I'm not at all febrile. Just you feel.'

I had often heard the expression about laying cool hands on fevered brows but I had never until then experienced it. It was most satisfying.

'Perhaps for the sake of us both I'd better fetch you an ice-bag.'

Just at this moment I became aware that Hinxman, too, was standing at my bedside.

'Hello,' I said in surprise. 'Rather early with your night round this evening, aren't you?'

He made no reply. Instead, he stared hard and said, 'Nurse Nightingale, I should like the night report, if you please.'

'Of course, Dr Hinxman. If you wish.'

Hinxman listened to the report sitting under the green-shaded lamp at Sister's desk a few feet from my bed, and afterwards he settled there to write up his notes. He was still working when at last I fell asleep. The next morning I found myself prescribed three-hourly injections of Vitamin C and a diet of soya flour soup.

This rivalry naturally acted as a supercharger to my increasingly powerful feelings about Sally Nightingale. To lose her to such a passionless pachyderm as Hinxman struck me as not only a personal tragedy but a shocking waste. But I was miserably conscious of my present disadvantages in wooing her. I was static, and Hinxman was menacingly mobile; and though I was entitled to enjoy her company all night, Hinxman now stood sentry at Sister's desk until I joined in the snores of the rest of the ward.

My one advantage came on Thursday nights, when Dr Pennyworth's firm was on emergency duty and his house physician liable to be called at any time to the casualty room by the main gate. The next Thursday I was delighted to see Hinxman's combination of lights flash on the indicator above the ward telephone, and he had to pay the penalty of choosing a self-sacrificing profession by taking himself downstairs to see a suspected coronary thrombosis.

'What *are* you doing to poor Roger Hinxman?' asked Sally, appearing almost at once from the sluice room.

I felt a little disappointed that she seemed to find such a serious affair amusing.

'What's he doing to *me*?' I replied warmly. 'Why, the fellow's breaking his Hippocratic oath every time he picks up my treatment board–that bit about not administering any noxious thing, and so on.'

She laughed. 'I suppose I should be gratified. But it's a rather unusual way for a girl to be fought over.'

'Is he in love with you?' I asked anxiously.

'Oh, of course. Roger's been in love with me since my first day in hospital. I broke a thermometer and he told Sister he did it. He's really awfully sweet, you know. But he *does* make me feel like a piece of china in a bull shop sometimes.'

This sounded encouraging. Feeling that the coronary in casualty might easily turn out to be a simple case of indigestion, I immediately asked if she'd like to come out to dinner when I was better.

'That's a terribly bad principle,' she replied.

'What is?'

'Going out with your convalescent patients. When you see me in a world full of other women you'll think I'm just like any other banana in the bunch.'

'Not a bit,' I said stoutly. 'I'm absolutely certain you're more beautiful than ever out of uniform.'

'You'll think I look about four feet tall and sixteen years old. It's wonderful how this get-up puts years on you, isn't it? I suppose it's designed to give girls authority to tell men old enough to be their fathers to get back into bed.'

'But uniform suits you wonderfully, too. It makes you look like a sort of clinical Joan of Arc.'

She tucked in my bedclothes. 'I'm afraid the only resemblance is that a lot of people would like to see me burnt alive. I've got to watch my step with matron's office just now. I'm due for my second-year report, and I don't really want to be thrown out.'

I saw Hinxman's silhouette appear beyond the double glass doors of the ward.

'Will you come, Sally?' I whispered. 'I know an awfully cosy little place in Soho.'

'All right,' she whispered back. 'Slip a note into the nurses' home when you're in circulation.'

Then she laughed and disappeared, to pretend she was fixing an intravenous drip.

Hinxman did nothing to my treatment board that night. But the crisis came three nights later, when he arrived to find Sally carrying out standing instructions for patients on full bed-rest by giving me a blanket bath. The next morning I found myself written up for a turpentine enema.

'It certainly *is* strange treatment,' said Sister, when I complained angrily. 'it's possible Dr Hinxman made a mistake.'

'I'm quite certain he didn't make any mistake at all. And I absolutely and completely refuse to have it, Sister. I'll discharge myself from hospital first.'

'Perhaps you'd better have a word with him yourself,' she suggested tactfully. Like all St Swithin's sisters, she knew much more that went on in the ward than her nurses gave her credit for. 'I'll get him to come over from the residency.'

My interview with Hinxman was fortunately held behind screens, which had been put round my bed in anticipation of his sentence being carried out.

'What's all this damn nonsense about enemas?' I demanded.

In reply, he clenched and unclenched his fists. 'You rotter,' he said.

'That's a fine way to speak to a colleague, I must say.'

'I love Sally more than anything else in the world.'

'Oh, do you? And so, it happens, do I.'

'I intend to marry her.'

'And so do I.'

It was the first time I had decided on the fact, and I think the answer surprised me as much as him.

He stood breathing heavily. 'I've known her for more than two years.'

'I've known her for less than two weeks. And I've made more progress.'

'Look here, Gordon! I'm not up to all these fancy tricks. I'm no . . . blasted Casanova. I'm an ordinary simple chap, and I love her. If you try to . . . to . . .' But words were beyond him. He crashed one fist into another, then silently pushed his way through the screens and disappeared.

'I'm not having the enema,' I called after him. 'I'll complain to Pennyworth tomorrow.'

When Dr Pennyworth reached my bedside on his ward-round the following afternoon Hinxman seemed strangely composed. I supposed that was because he had already countermanded the enema, and thought that I had nothing to complain about.

'How are you getting on?' whispered Dr Pennyworth, peering at me through his pince-nez.

'He's sleeping very badly,' cut in Hinxman, before I could say anything. 'We've tried him on all the usual narcotics of course, sir. But he seems to be one of these resistant cases.'

'Very interesting.'

'So I thought, sir, as he's desperate, you could prescribe him an effective dosage.'

'Sleep,' murmured Dr Pennyworth as I tried to protest, 'is the physician's greatest friend. "Oh Sleep! It is a gentle thing. Beloved from pole to pole?" Eh?' He then prescribed with his own pen a dose of barbiturate that would have kept a woodful of owls quiet.

'You'll have to swallow them all,' said Sister, handing me the scarlet capsules that evening. 'It's Doctor Pennyworth's own orders, you know.'

I slept twelve hours a night solidly for a week, when to the relief of both Hinxman and myself, Dr Pennyworth officially discharged me for convalescence at home.

Chapter Five

My father, Dr Gregory Gordon, M.B., B.Chir., had a general practice in a popular South Coast town, where we had lived as long as I could remember in an over-large Edwardian villa looking across the roofs of innumerable boarding-houses towards the sea. He too was a St Swithin's man, having qualified there about thirty years before I did. Since then he had been occupied in building a prosperous practice, and was now beginning to suffer success. The hourly ringing of doorbell and telephone were as natural a part of my childhood as the chiming of the grandfather clock below the stairs; but in those days my father still had time to read textbooks and occasionally take me to the County ground, while now that his patients included not only the Mayor but most of the Corporation and the Chamber of Commerce as well, he had barely a moment to sit down with the *Lancet* or glance at the cricket scores. Even as I arrived home the next afternoon I met him dashing from the front door with his bag.

'Hello, Richard my boy! Good to see you. Better?'

'Very much better, thanks.'

'What was it you had? Catarrhal jaundice?'

'Yes, except that nowadays they call it infective hepatitis.'

'You're a bit on the thin side. Sorry I couldn't get up with your mother to see you. They looked after you all right in St Swithin's, I hope? Who was your doctor?'

'Old Pennyworth.'

'Good Lord, is he still going? I thought he'd be dead long ago. How are you feeling in yourself?'

'A bit tottery still.'

'You'll soon get over it. As a matter of fact, I was rather hoping you could help me out with a few surgeries a little later on. Must rush off now–I've got a perforation miles away on the other side of the housing estate. Ask Miss Jamieson to make you some tea.'

'Isn't mother in?'

'Mother? I can't remember whether it's her afternoon to help with the Young Conservatives or the Old Contemptibles.' As my mother honoured all the obligations of a successful doctor's wife, she rarely seemed to meet my father at all between his being called away from breakfast to see a suspected appendix to his coming in at midnight from seeing a suspected drunk-in-charge. 'By the way, if any phone calls come in be a good lad and see what you can make of the symptoms. Such a help to Miss Jamieson at this time of the year.'

He then jumped into his car and drove off.

I had hoped during my convalescence gracefully to introduce the subject of Sally Nightingale. Although I had seen little more of her before leaving hospital–and I was conscious that she had seen me only lying on my back with my mouth wide open–the prospect of perhaps one day marrying her now lay on my mind much more excitingly than the prospect of perhaps one day passing my F.R.C.S. examination. It would be equally stimulating to my self-esteem, just as useful to my career, possibly easier, and much more fun.

With other nurses I had fancied at St Swithin's my plans never went further than our next outing to the cinema, but with Sally Nightingale I already saw myself looking like an advertisement for an insurance company. My knowledge of marriage, like my knowledge of medicine, was still dangerously theoretical, and I had taken advantage of Tony Benskin's calling to see me in hospital to ask frankly what it was like. His reply had been, 'Magnificent, old man, simply magnificent!', which I felt was as unreliable as the cry of midwinter bathers, 'Come on in, the water's fine!' This was confirmed immediately by his producing two dozen photographs of John Tristram Benskin, all of which looked to me exactly the same, though the father seemed to find subtle differences in each.

I now wanted to discuss the whole problem of matrimony with my parents, but it is as awkward a subject for a sensitive young man to work into the conversation as a plea for more cash. Another difficulty was never finding my parents together, or even one of them alone for more than a couple of minutes on end. The days slipped past with walks on the pier and rounds on the golf course, until it was the night before I was to return to St Swithin's. Then at last I managed to catch my father alone in his consulting room, where he was telling an anxious mother on the telephone that green nappies in the first month were nothing to be alarmed about.

'Father,' I began, as he put the instrument down, 'I wonder if I could have a word with you?'

My solemnity surprised him. 'Why, of course, Richard. What's the trouble? Do you want to buy another car?'

'No, it isn't that–though of course I'd love one of the new Austin Healeys if you felt you could raise the wind. But as a matter of fact,' I said sheepishly, 'I've recently been thinking rather seriously about marriage.'

'Have you really, now? Good Lord! I never saw this note Miss Jamieson left on my desk–there's a gallstone colic at the Grand Hotel. So you're thinking of getting married, are you, Richard? What's her name?'

'Florence Nightingale.'

'Come, come, Richard, surely you've got beyond childish jokes—'

'That really is her name, Father. Though everyone calls her Sally.'

'Is she nice?'

'Terribly nice! Wonderful, in fact. Of course, I only got to know her in bed.'

'Good gracious! I know you young people go the pace a bit, but I didn't think you'd be as brazen about it as that.'

'I mean while I was having jaundice.'

'Oh, I see. A nurse, eh? Well, you could do far worse than that. Most of my friends married nurses. I didn't. I met your mother when she had a Pott's fracture on my doorstep. However . . .' He fiddled with the blood-pressure machine on his desk. 'Don't think I'm interfering in your affairs, Richard–damn it all, you're a registered medical practitioner, and therefore one of the few people legally credited with more sense than the average population–but don't you feel you ought to get to know this girl a little better before you decide to spend the next half-century in her company? You mean you've proposed to her?'

'Not properly, Father. Nothing as dramatic as that. I was only thinking of matrimony in a . . . well, a general sort of way. I don't think Sally even knows that I really want to marry her yet.'

He raised his eyebrows. 'Well, I can only hope it comes as a nice surprise.'

'But I really think I *will* marry her one day,' I continued earnestly. 'Of course, I've had plenty of girl friends before–we all had at St Swithin's–but never have I met anyone in which so many delightful feminine qualities have been collected together. You see she's so—'

The telephone rang.

'One second, Richard. Yes? Speaking. Yes. Right, I'll be along in five minutes. Fits somewhere behind the station,' he explained. 'It's an old G.P.I. I've been nursing along for years. Delighted to hear your plans, Richard. We must have a long chat about them. What's her name again?'

'Sally.'

'Sally. Look here, we'll split a bottle over it when I get back from this case. Then you can tell me all about her.'

But after the fits behind the station and the gallstones in the Grand there was an acute retention down the road and a Colles's fracture at the bus depot, so that my father didn't arrive home until one-thirty. As the next morning I had to catch an early train, I left home without discussing my theoretical wife with anyone.

The date of my return to work was fixed less by my physical condition than Sally's impending official three nights off duty, two of which she was dutifully spending with her mother at home in Barnet. As soon as I reached St Swithin's I sent her a note suggesting a meeting the following evening. Taking advantage of my involuntary saving through lying in bed, I had picked a fashionable restaurant in Soho in which a pair of Sicilian brothers carried on their family tradition of banditry. It was a small place, with tables, waiters, and diners so crowded together that it was difficult to eat the establishment's famous spaghetti without it becoming entwined with a neighbour's asparagus. But it had an orchestra of Charing Cross Road gypsies with a fiddler who breathed encouragingly down girls' necks, and I thought it an excellent place to pursue my suit.

I was sitting in the laboratory that morning thinking excitedly of the hours slipping past, when I was surprised to see Hinxman appear. He had not only refused to talk to me since my return to the hospital, but had pointedly got up and left rooms as I entered them. Now he seemed desperate to start a conversation. After making some distracted comments about glucose tolerance curves until the other pathologists were out of earshot, he exclaimed 'She's gone.'

'Gone? Who's gone?'

'Sally Nightingale, of course.'

I stared at him.

'But gone where?'

'For good.'

'No!'

'She has. She simply packed up this morning and left the hospital. She dropped her resignation in matron's letter-box as she went past.' He sat down heavily on to a laboratory stool. 'I've just this minute heard it from the staff nurse on Honesty.'

My first feeling was of bewilderment. 'But what on earth did she want to do that for? She seemed so terribly keen on nursing.'

He made a despairing gesture over some samples of stomach contents. 'It must have been Godfrey, I suppose.'

'Godfrey? Godfrey who?'

'John Godfrey. That air pilot she specialled when he was in Honesty with virus pneumonia. She's gone off with him–that's obvious. What other reason could there be for a girl to disappear? They're probably half-way to South American by now. It's either him or that fellow from the B.B.C. who had asthma, or the stockbroker chap in Private Block with the ulcer.'

'But I didn't know anything about these men!'

'Huh! You didn't know anything about Sally. Fine monkeys she made of us, I must say.' He rested his elbows wearily among a batch of throat swabs. 'There are far too many girls in this hospital who imagine a nurse's uniform isn't complete without a couple of housemen's scalps dangling from the belt. And to think,' he added painfully, 'that I actually wanted to marry her.'

I said nothing.

Suddenly Hinxman held out his pink hand. 'Richard, we've been complete and utter fools. I want to give you my apologies about everything. Particularly the enema.'

'Roger, I accept them with humility.'

We clasped hands across a pile of agar plates growing streptococci.

'You're a gentleman,' he said. 'It's been a lesson to me, let me tell you. Never again.'

'And I thought she was such a nice girl.'

'The nicer they seem, the deeper they bite.'

But it was only when I left the laboratory after a busy morning's work that the numbness of my psychological wound wore off and I felt how painful it really was. I found a letter in my room from my mother saying how delighted she was, and asking when I was bringing Sally down to see them.

Chapter Six

'Woman,' sighed Grimsdyke reflectively. 'A creature I once saw described in an American gynaecology book as "A constipated biped with pain in the back."'

'Well, there's one thing,' I told him firmly. 'It's going to be many a long day before I get involved with another one.'

'I only wish I could agree with you, old lad. I really do. But unfortunately it's a striking psychological fact that once a man has made a fool of himself over one woman, he can hardly wait to repeat the performance with another.'

The conversation then lapsed. It was our last night at the hospital we had first entered as students over eight years before, and we were sitting together in a corner of the empty bar of the King George, looking dejected. My final weeks in St Swithin's had not been particularly happy ones. Gossip spreads in a hospital like sand at a picnic, and my companions in the residency had enjoyed chaffing me heartily, while all the nurses bit their lips and giggled every time I went past. Our jobs had come to their inevitable end, and now my old friend Grimsdyke and myself were to part and make our separate professional ways.

'Haven't you any idea at all what you want to do next?' I had asked him a few days previously in the surgeons' room, as he took off his sterile gown after the day's operating list.

'Not in the slightest,' he had replied cheerfully. 'I shall again throw myself on the medical labour market. The happiest times in my life have always been when I was out of work.'

I was concerned, because I felt that Grimsdyke's unusual talents needed careful organization. But I had overlooked his most enviable quality, which generally saw him out of his scrapes and difficulties–a knack of meeting chaps in pubs. A few days after our conversation in the surgeons' room he had run into a doctor called Paddy O'Dooley in Mooney's Irish House off Piccadilly Circus, who discovered that Grimsdyke was a graduate of the Society of Apothecaries of Cork and immediately offered him a locum in his practice in County Wexford. This my friend accepted, and he was leaving from Paddington the morning after our farewell drink in the King George. His only worry was discovering the exact whereabouts of his new post, the letter of appointment being scrawled on the back of a packet of Player's cigarettes which his new employer had pressed into his hand before disappearing into the seductive glare of Piccadilly.

'I'm a bit vague about the whole set-up,' Grimsdyke confessed, ordering another beer and a tonic water. The gloom of our evening was deepened through Dr Pennyworth's forbidding me to taste alcohol for three months. 'I gather it's really Paddy's old man's practice, which is at the moment being run by a Polish chum of doubtful morals and doubtful qualifications. Still, it'll be a change of scenery. There's a lot of money round there, so I hear–estates and so on. *And no N.H.S.*'

'You're sure you don't want to go on with anaesthetics? You might have a big future there, Grim. You didn't kill anybody and you kept the operating team amused when things were going badly. Those are the only attributes a successful anaesthetist needs.'

'Ah, a professional stuffist! I really wouldn't have minded specializing in it, I must confess. I rather like messing about with the knobs, and it brings out the artist in me. A good anaesthetist's like a French chef, you know–take some pure oxygen, flavour with a touch of ether, add a *soupçon* of pentothal, mix with pethidine, and serve garnished with gas. But you realize the trouble with anaesthesia as a life work?'

'Surgeons?'

He nodded. 'Charming and erudite chaps most of them, but as soon as they get into their operating theatres their characters change. It's just like other people getting into their cars. And their stories! Even such an amiable bird as old Cambridge insists on telling his five funny ones to each new batch of students. When you're one of the permanent fixtures in the theatre, the laughter comes less blithely to the lips after the eighth or ninth repetition. Has he told you the one about him and old Sir Lancelot Spratt chasing a duke in his pyjamas down Devonshire Place?'

I nodded.

'Well, imagine hearing it regularly once a month for the rest of your life. Not that it's much of a tale to start with. No, I'm afraid anaesthesia is going to lose me.'

'But haven't you thought of trying some other speciality before burying yourself in Ireland? E.N.T., for instance? Obstetrics? Or psychiatry, now? That ought to be in your line.'

'I've thought of it all right. But contrary to popular belief, psychiatry doesn't consist of listening to beautiful blondes lying on couches telling you all about their sex life. Before you get to that you have to sweat it out for years with ordinary common-or-garden lunatics. I don't think I'd last long working in a mental institution–they say the medical staff soon get dottier than the patients. No, old lad. Not Uncle Grimsdyke's cup of tea. In fact, the whole ruddy National Health Service isn't. Some chaps may like being able to look up the book and see exactly how much cash they'll be getting at the age of sixty, but not me. I've got the pioneering spirit. The only trouble is, these days there's nowhere left to pioneer to.'

'Well . . . County Wexford might be the start of a distinguished and prosperous career, then?' I suggested hopefully.

'As well it might, Richard. I feel I've got sympathetic vibrations with the Irish.'

'Steer clear of the poteen.'

'And you steer clear of the girls.'

The following morning I packed my books and belongings at St Swithin's, and saying good-bye to my friends went into lodgings in that indistinct part of London known as 'South Ken'. I had chosen for economy a seedy Victorian house which seemed to have every Underground train on the Inner Circle passing immediately under its foundations. As each of the rooms had a ring attached to its gas fire they were called 'flatlets', and were occupied by young women who dashed in at six and dashed out again at six-thirty, students from the hotter parts of the Commonwealth, and several fat fair-haired women who puffed up and down stairs with cigarettes between their lips, carrying cats. Like many similar houses I had occupied as a student in London, it was a place where people seemed to arrive from nowhere, talk to no one, and leave suddenly. Rent was always payable in advance, and the green-baize letter-board next to the bamboo hatstand in the hall was heavy with official-looking envelopes to former tenants who had gone to the happy lands of no address.

Without the distraction of gainful work, I now settled down to study for the next Primary Fellowship Examination. As the National Health Service pays it junior hospital doctors about the same as its junior hospital porters, my savings were so small that I had to live frugally. I fed mostly on fried eggs and kippers, cooked on the gas-ring in defiance of the grease-spattered notice demanding 'No Frying'. I spent my time reading *Gray's Anatomy* and Samson Wright's *Physiology* and staring out of the window at the forbidding outlines of the Natural Science Museum opposite, until after a few days it became clear that either the Museum would have to move or I should. Perhaps I was still looking at the world through jaundiced eyes, but I soon became unable to concentrate, to feel enthusiastic about the exam, or to see any future in the medical profession at all. Even if I passed my Primary I should have to find a house surgeon's job before taking the Fellowship Final, and the only ones advertised in the *British Medical Journal* seemed to be in large industrial towns, which, however useful their population for aspiring young surgeons, didn't strike me as places to spend the summer. After a spell as house surgeon I might be promoted to a surgical registrar, but the step between that and full consultant was as uncertain as the naval one between commander and captain. I remembered so many registrars fretting into middle age looking hopefully for signs of arteriosclerosis in their seniors that I even began to wonder if I should have taken up medicine at all. But it was far too late for such reflections. An unemployed doctor, unlike an unemployed barrister, is fitted for nothing else whatever. I supposed that a knack of analysing confusing noises at a distance in people's chests would make me a reasonable garage mechanic, and an ability to feel hidden lumps coupled with a smattering of practical psychology might be of use in the Customs, but otherwise I was a national economic loss. Then as the Natural Science Museum showed no signs of shifting, I decided to take my books across London each day for a change of scenery by exercising my rights as a member and working in the British Medical Association building.

B.M.A. House in Bloomsbury is a large, red-brick place standing about midway between the Royal Free Hospital and the National Union of Railwaymen, originally designed as a temple for the Theosophists. Its doorway, barely large enough to take a consultant's Rolls, leads into a pleasant courtyard in which the medical intellectuals responsible for the *British Medical Journal* and the medical politicians responsible for keeping up the doctor's pay can be seen coversing thoughtfully in the sunlight. There is a club room as satisfyingly gloomy as any in St James's, which is decorated with animal heads sent by sporting African doctors and provides desks and writing-paper. As it seems to be used only by provincial practitioners waiting for trains at nearby St Pancras, or surgeons sleeping off official luncheons, I found it an excellent spot for concentration.

I was sitting at my writing-desk one morning about a week later trying to master the perplexing arrangement of tendons and nerves round the ankle, when a voice behind me said, 'Timothy doth vex all very nervous housemaids.'

I spun round in my chair.

'Dr Farquarson!'

Dr Farquarson was Grimsdyke's uncle, with whom I had spent the most pleasant, and probably the most instructive, fortnight of my medical life as assistant in his general practice in the country. He was a tall, lean Scot who wore a stiff wing collar which he considered as much a professional mark as a clergyman's, and for London a dark suit replaced the tweed one that he used impartially for shooting and surgeries. On the whole, he resembled one of Low's old caricatures of Ramsay MacDonald.

'A very useful mnemonic I always found that for the ankle,' Dr Farquarson said. He had the knack of starting conversations with acquaintances as though he had left them only a moment before. 'Not so good as the one giving you the advanced signs of Casanova's infection of course–

There was a young man of Bombay
Who thought lues just went away
Now he's got rabies
And bandy-legged babies
And thinks he's the Queen of the May.

Did you know it?'

I laughed, and admitted I did.

'And how's that idiotic nephew of mine?'

'Very well, I gather. You know he's gone to Ireland? He sent me a postcard the other day.' This had shown the main street of a village which seemed to consist of alternate public houses and betting shops. On the back Grimsdyke had scribbled, 'Note Irish town planning. Natives friendly, though much addicted to funerals.'

'Ireland, eh? It's about time he decided to settle down and place whatever brains he has got at the service of some unfortunate community. And this anatomical effort,' he added, indicating my open books, 'would be in aid of the Primary Fellowship examination, I take it?'

'Yes, I'm afraid so.'

'Of course, since my day they've gone and anglicized the whole anatomical nomenclature,' he went on. 'Which is a pity because it gives the medical profession at least the appearance of being educated like gentlemen if they can mouth a few Latin words occasionally. I remember the time I found myself asked to say grace at some luncheon or other. I bowed my head and intoned: "*Levator labii superioris alaeque nasi*, Amen." A small muscle in the front of the face, you will recall. No one was any the wiser.' Producing a large gold watch from his waistcoat he added, 'Talking of lunch, could you tear yourself away from your studies to listen to me rambling over a meal?' Dr Farquarson enjoyed giving the impression of extreme age, though he could not have been much older than my father. 'I might even be able to give you some tips on how to bamboozle the examiners.'

'Why, I'd be delighted. If we go now we'll still find a table in the members' dining-room.'

'Members' dining-room, rubbish! We'll go to a place I know in Holborn. The last thing I want to do is eat looking at a lot of doctors.'

Dr Farquarson led me to a restaurant in a cellar at the end of a dark alley, in which steaks were cooked on an open fire and customers from the City sat in high-backed chairs like choir-stalls with their bowler hats clustered like bunches of huge black grapes above them.

'So you're still going in for surgery?' he asked in the middle of his mutton chops.

I nodded.

'These days it's no good just doing surgery, y'know. The hairs of specialization are split finer than that. In America, so they tell me, they have a man for the right kidney and another man for the left kidney. I always believe a specialist is a fellow who charges more and more for knowing less and less, and if I had my own time over again I'd become an omphologist.'

I looked puzzled.

'From the Greek *omphos*. A specialist in the umbilicus.' Dr Farquarson rarely smiled, but his sandy eyebrows quivered violently whenever he was struck by something amusing. 'There can't be many people smitten by diseases of that particular organ, but on the other hand there can't be many people who've made it their lifelong study. Folk would flock from all over the world. That fellow James Bridie once wrote something about it.' He took another sip from his tankard. 'Which brings me to my point. Would you consider going into general practice?'

'You mean as a temporary measure?'

'I mean as a permanent measure.' As I said nothing, he went on, 'I've just changed my pitch. I've done a swap with a fellow called McBurney I knew up at the University–he's had bad luck, poor fellow, going down with the tubercule. So I'm in Hampden Cross now.'

'You mean north of London?'

'That's right. Do you know it? It's in the so-called green belt, which consists largely of a forest of traffic-signs and petrol pumps. But there's pleasant enough country nearby, and there's an old Abbey and a cricket ground to satisfy a man's spiritual needs. They're building one of these new town affairs on top of it, so I'll soon be wanting an assistant–with a view, as they say in the advertisements.'

I hesitated.

'I apologize for asking,' he said quickly. 'You'll be through your Primary this shot, and you'll have your Fellowship in your pocket by Christmas. You'll be in Harley Street soon enough. Then you can be sure of getting some cases from an old has-been like me.'

He spent the rest of the meal talking about Test Matches.

I took the Primary Fellowship a fortnight later. In the days before the National Health Service the examination was conducted for a handful of candidates in the quietly academic atmosphere of a dissertation in a medieval university. But as young doctors now enter for it in the same spirit as they back horses in the Grand National, the contest has to be run on sharper lines. The written papers had for once left me reasonably hopeful, and a few days later I was back again in that bleak little upstairs room which is decorated with the particular blend of green and yellow paint so heavily favoured in Britain for mental hospitals, station waiting-rooms, and the surroundings of police courts. Waiting for my oral, I suddenly felt sick of all examinations. I calculated that since childhood I must have sat for a dozen of them, including my School Certificate and driving test. As a medical student I had taken them in company with my friends, which gave the ordeal something of the sporting air of a chancy rugger fixture; but now I not only had to face the examiners alone, but I was aware that my next year's salary depended on it.

These depressing thoughts seemed to be occurring to the other occupant of the waiting-room, a sad-looking young man with mauve socks who sat staring out of the window in silence until he said suddenly, 'If you get old Professor Surridge, you'll know if you've failed.'

'Will I?' I asked in surprise. 'How?'

'He always asks people he's decided to plough what the dose of morphine is.'

'A tough examiner, is he?'

'On the contrary, he's very jolly. He's too kind-hearted to keep chaps in suspense until the results come out. My registrar got through last time–sixth attempt–and was so amazed to find himself outside without being asked the fatal question he put his head back and said, 'It's an eighth to a third of a grain, sir.'

We sat without speaking for a while, pondering what the kindly Professor and his less considerate colleagues were at that moment asking the candidates across the green-baize tables.

'You from Bart's?' asked my companion.

'Swithin's.'

'I'm Guy's. First shot?'

'Second.'

'I had a go at the Membership last time.' He was referring to the corresponding examination for prospective physicians. 'Damn near passed, too. I thought my long case had a collapsed lung, and I even decided to perform the coin test for good measure.'

'The coin test? That's a bit old-fashioned, isn't it?'

'Oh, yes, it went out with leeches and gold-headed canes. But some of the examiners are pretty old-fashioned, too. Anyway, in this case it proved a most valuable investigation. I had just produced two half-crowns from my pocket to bang together on the chest–as directed in the textbooks–when the patient stuck out his hand and pocketed them whispering, "Thanks, Guv, it's a gastric ulcer, actual."'

I managed to overcome my surroundings with a laugh. 'Didn't that see you through?'

'No, worse luck. The next case–the short one–was a heart. Damn it, I diagnosed it perfectly! The patient was sitting up in bed, and I had plenty of time to listen all over his chest, "Patent ductus, sir," I told the examiner. "Quite correct," he said. "Anything else?" And I said, "No."'

This seemed unreasonably unfair. 'But why on earth didn't they pass you?'

'I hadn't noticed that some blighter had cut both his bloody legs off as well.' A bell tinkled, and we made for the examination-room door. 'I hear they've got a bottle with an orange-pip impacted in a parotid duct,' he whispered helpfully as we went in.

I was directed to Professor Surridge, who turned out to be a little pink fat bald man, giving the impression of just having been lifted from a pan of boiling water.

'Well, Doctor?' he said genially, passing me a large bottle. 'What's that?'

'It could be an orange-pip impacted in a parotid duct, sir.'

'Indeed it could,' he agreed. 'But it *is* a cherry-stone impacted in an appendix. Both rare conditions, eh?' He handed me an odd-looking syringe. 'What would you use that for?'

'Syringing ears, sir?' I suggested.

'Better than the last candidate, at least, Doctor. He wanted to inject piles with it. Actually it's from Clover's chloroform apparatus. Historical interest, of course. Now let us discuss the anatomy of the appendix and its various aberrant positions.'

I soon felt I was doing well. I fumbled an answer about the course of the appendicular artery, and I made a slight error over the muscular structure of the intestinal wall, but if my own critical standards equalled those of the Royal College of Surgeons I thought that this time I should be through.

'You are familiar with Poupart's ligament?' asked the Professor, as we got on to hernias.

'Of course, sir.'

'Ah! But where is Poupart's junction?'

For a second I felt panic. This was an anatomical feature I'd never heard of.

'It's the next station to Clapham Junction,' he said with a chuckle. 'Truly, Doctor. Have a look at the signal box the next time you go to Brighton. And which hospital do you come from, Doctor?' He leaned back in his chair, looking at me benignly.

'St Swithin's, sir,' I said, smiling back.

'Of course, you know how to tell the difference between a Guy's man and a St Swithin's man, don't you, Doctor?'

'No, sir?' I realized with added excitement that the oral period must be almost over; at last I seemed to have got a toe on the surgical ladder.

'They say a Guy's man always examines his patients with a hand in his pocket,' the Professor continued, laughing.

I laughed, too.

'And they say a St Swithin's man always examines his patients with *both* hands in his pockets,' he went on, laughing heartily.

I threw back my head and roared.

A bell tinkled in the distance. 'By the way,' said the Professor. 'What's the dose of morphine?'

Chapter Seven

'It was a pity about your Primary,' said Dr Farquarson.

We were sitting together in his consulting-room, which like those of all best British doctors had the air of a Victorian gentleman's study and exhibited nothing much more clinical than a bust of Edward Jenner. I had just arrived at Hampden Cross, a pleasant place on the edge of London's saucer, which had once flourished as the last stop for stage coaches but had long ago been overtaken by their destination. Away from the new by-pass it had the cheerfully inconvenient air of any other busy little English town, with the pedestrians and the traffic struggling for possession of the High Street. But there was fortunately an area of quiet grass and gardens near the Abbey, where Dr Farquarson's surgery was contained in a narrow Georgian house. I was relieved to find such agreeable surroundings, as I was likely to spend the rest of my life in them.

'All these higher examinations are a bit of a gamble, I'd say, if that's any consolation,' Dr Farquarson went on. 'I remember when I took the Edinburgh Membership the clinical hinged on whether you could just feel the tip of the patient's spleen or not. Even the examiners disagreed over it. One failed all the candidates who said they could, and the other failed all the ones who said they couldn't. I happened to be in the unlucky bunch.' He scraped out his pipe with the old scalpel he kept on his desk for the purpose. 'Still, it's better to have studied and lost than never to have learnt anything at all. There's a lot to be said for the old Indian habit of putting "F.R.C.S. (Failed)" after your name. And now I suppose you're waiting for me to give you weighty advice on the ways and means of general practice?'

I looked at him expectantly. I was now reconciled to making my career as a G.P. rather than a consultant surgeon, and I was determined to be a good one. The modern doctor unfortunately comes from his medical school with haughty views on general practice. For six years he is taught by specialists, who maintain at hospital lectures and hospital dinners that the G.P. is the backbone of British medicine, but never hesitate to dissect the backbone whenever given the chance. The residents of both Harley Street and the house surgeons' quarters are understandably tempted to show their superiority over cases sent singlehanded into hospital with the wrong diagnosis, and we thus came to look upon our teachers as infallible and general practice, like the Church, as fit for the fools of the medical family.

'Looking back over my long years of experience,' Dr Farquarson went on, 'I would say . . . What would I say? That I can't think of anything in the slightest way useful to a young man with reasonably active intelligence. You'll know most of the ropes from your father. Patients are much the same all the world over, whether you see 'em being ill at the Government's expense in hospital or being ill in their bedrooms at their own.'

'I hope you'll be forbearing for my first few weeks,' I said.

'That's when you'll get most of your work, of course. They'll all want to have a look at you. Even now they're gossiping over their teacups wondering what you're like.' He stretched his long thin legs under the desk. 'I'm converting the little room next door as a surgery for you. I'm sorry I can't put you up in the house,' he apologized. 'My flat upstairs is hardly big enough for all the junk I've accumulated over the years. And anyway you wouldn't want to room with such a senile specimen as me, would you? The other flat is of course occupied by our estimable Miss Wildewinde.' This was the receptionist who had admitted me, a middle-aged woman of the type seen so often in England in charge of dogs, horses, or other people's children. 'Miss Wildewinde is a lady of intimidating efficiency, as you will shortly find out. She also dwells lengthily on McBurney's professional and personal attributes, which occasionally makes life like marriage to an overfresh widow. Anyway, living away from the shop means you'll escape a lot of night calls. And this Crypt Hotel place will probably look after you all right.'

My illusions about general practice were lost within a week. My first discovery was that diseases affecting the population of Hampden Cross seemed to have no connexion with the ones we were taught in St Swithin's. Many of my patients suffered from easily identifiable troubles of those overstrained systems The Tubes, The Nerves and The Wind, but many others seemed only to exemplify mankind's fruitless struggle against Nature. There were old women who complained of being too fat and young women who complained of being too thin, people who found they couldn't sleep and people who found they couldn't stay awake, girls who wanted less hair on their legs and men who wanted more on their heads, couples anxious for children who couldn't have any and couples who had too many and didn't know how to stop. The rest simply wanted a certificate. I signed several dozen every day, entitling the holders to anything from more milk to less work, and from getting the youngest off an afternoon's school to getting the eldest off his National Service.

'The poor doctor's signature,' observed Dr Farquarson when I mentioned this to him, 'is the Open Sesame to the Welfare State. Folk can't exist these days in a civilized community without it. Did you know there's a dozen separate Acts of Parliament that call for it? I've counted 'em myself.'

'Well, I hope I'm not doing down the national Exchequer,' I said anxiously. I knew the penalties for careless certification from a chilly little notice issued by the General Medical Council. Mistakenly entitling an applicant for a bottle of orange juice to a free pair of surgical boots might land me in the local Assizes. 'I also seem to be prescribing about twice as many bottles of medicine as are therapeutically necessary.'

'Don't worry, lad. A citizen's bodily contentment for half a pint of coloured water is cheap at the price for any Government. Anyway, once the public's got the idea in their heads that something does them good you'll never get it out–whether it's medicine, milk drinks, or meat extracts, which as you know consist of eighty per cent flavouring with no food value whatever and twenty per cent salt to save them from the putrefaction they so richly deserve.'

Dr Farquarson started filling his insanitary-looking pipe.

'The trouble with this generation is that its environment's outstripping its intelligence. Look at the village idiot–a hundred years ago he sat contentedly on his bench outside the village inn. Someone occasionally gave him a little beer, and someone occasionally gave him a little hoeing. He never got in his own way or anyone else's. But what happens today? He's got to cope with pedestrian crossings, income-tax, football pools, national insurance, welfare workers, and God knows what. As he can't, he either plagues his doctor as a neurotic or they put him inside. Another fifty years and anyone without a working knowledge of nuclear physics will be certified as mentally defective. Oh, it'll be a happy day when there's more of us inside than out. But at the moment the job of general practice is separating the idiots from the ill.'

'I hope I've done so today,' I told him, noticing his eyebrows quivering. 'I think I spotted an early tubercule and an early schizophrenia. I packed them off with notes to the appropriate hospitals.'

'You were right, of course. The tuberculous one would sooner or later infect the family, and the mad one would sooner or later smash up the china.

Though I try to keep people out of hospitals as long as possible, myself. They're abnormal institutions. It's often better for both sides if patients are nursed by their own relatives. A man ought to be given a chance to be born at home, and he certainly ought to have a chance to die there. The family gathers round, you know, and it's only right he should feel the event is something of an occasion.'

'Sterility . . .' I murmured.

'Ah, sterility! In the old days there were plenty of prostatic old gentlemen going about with their catheters tucked in their hat-brims. If you're going to be infected, it might as well be your own bugs. In hospital you'll get someone else's, and penicillin-resistant ones they'll be, too. Still, I'm boring you. Remarkable how senility makes a man ramble, isn't it?'

I thought practice with Dr Farquarson looked like being stimulating.

My enthusiasm for my new life was dimmed only by crossing the peeling portals of the Crypt Hotel. The hotel stood on the other side of the Abbey, and was a typical English boarding-house of the type I had slept in so many nights since first becoming a medical student. There were yellowing net curtains sagging across the front windows, an austere card askew in the transom announcing VACANCIES, a hall containing chessboard lino worn red down the middle, and a picture of shaggy cattle standing uncomfortably with their feet in a Highland pool. There were notices desiring punctuality over meals and settling accounts, and a landlady whose manner suggested that she was summing up the chances of your murdering the lot of them in their beds. But the place had seemed clean enough and the customary smell of cooking rising up the staircase smelt savoury, so I had decided to stay.

I had been given a room the shape of a cheese-dish tucked under the roof, which was filled with a polished brass bedstead and was as awkward to undress in as a telephone box. There was a bathroom next door with plumbing apparently designed by Emmett, and a threadbare sitting-room downstairs containing a curly marble fireplace, a set of *The British Campaign in France and Flanders*, and a picture of a fat female albino peeping through a waterfall entitled 'Psyche In Her Bath Glen Gurrick Distilleries Ltd'. This room was filled nightly with the 'commercials', red-faced men in blue suits who I felt were welcome for ensuring both variety of company and maintenance of the catering standards. The hotel's regulars were composed of faded old ladies and retired school-teachers. Then there was Mr Tuppy.

Mr Tuppy was the hotel's funny man. I first met him at dinner the day of my arrival, when he entered the dining-room with the self-assurance of Danny Kaye taking the stage at the Palladium and demanded in general 'Is there a doctor in the house?' This simple remark sent everyone into roars of laughter. Sitting at the table next to mine, he tucked his napkin under his chin and continued to make funny remarks about doctors while I tried to concentrate solemnly on the *Lancet*. When he shortly struck up a conversation he expressed overwhelming surprise that I happened to be of the medical profession, but by this time I was clearly established as his straight man.

'Knew a feller who went to the doctor's once,' he told everyone over his steak pie. 'Had a throat complaint. Couldn't talk above a whisper. Our professional friend here will know all about it, eh, won't you, Doctor? Anyway, this feller–went to the doctor, see. Door opened by a beautiful blonde–all right, Mrs Knottage, you won't have to leave the room–where was I? Oh, yes. Door opened by a smashing blonde. Feller says in a hoarse whisper, "Is the doctor home?" Blonde whispers back, "No, he isn't–come on in."'

The old ladies roared loud enough to shake the medicine bottles on their tables, while I tried to raise as good-natured a grin as possible.

'Reminds me of another one,' Mr Tuppy breezed along, helping himself to more potatoes. 'Chap goes to a psychiatrist–our professional friend here knows what a psychiatrist is, eh? Feller who goes to the Windmill and looks at the audience. Well, chap goes to psychiatrist, see. Says, "Nothing's wrong with me, doctor–only these red beetles and blue lizards crawling all over me." "All right," says the psychiatrist. "But don't keep brushing them all over me."'

Collapse of everyone, including Mrs Knottage. I later unwisely tried to combat Mr Tuppy by telling a joke about doctors myself, but no one seemed to think it at all funny. I made an even bigger mistake in offering some mild chaff to Joan, our anaemic waitress. She accepted from Mr Tuppy a run of innuendo which would have had the proprietors of any teashop telephone the police, but to me she said frozenly she was not that sort at all, thank you, which lowered me even further in the estimation of my fellow-guests. Mr Tuppy also had an annoying habit of appearing for breakfast rubbing his hands and declaring 'Hail shining morn, don't say it's kippers again', and of raising the special glass of brown ale to his lips every lunch and supper with the expression 'Lovely grub–you can feel it doing you good!' I shortly developed the habit of sitting with clenched fists waiting for these remarks, and it became clear that I should suffer permanent psychological damage unless I shortly made a change of accommodation.

Chapter Eight

When I began to look for other lodgings seriously I had been in Hampden Cross almost three months. By then the shadow of the Abbey was falling noticeably earlier across our doorstep, the draughts in the surgery were finding their old corners, the mornings had the evasive chill prodromal of autumn, and the evenings stepped softly up the streets in mist. My resignation to an existence spent handling the small change of medicine had already turned into enthusiasm, and our partnership began to stride along successfully. To the patients, Dr Farquarson was the wise, conservative physician, though possibly rather outdated; I was the young, dashing doctor, though possibly rather dangerous. Life was busy, but it seemed uncomplicated. Until the morning I was called to see Mrs Tadwich.

The address given by Miss Wildewinde turned out to be a flat over a sweetshop near the main street. I now always followed Dr Farquarson's advice of trying to make the diagnosis before ringing the doorbell, and I stood on the mat deciding from the careless hang of the curtains and the grubby air of the paintwork that I was about to be confronted with an ageing widow with progressive myosis and rheumatoid arthritis. I felt an involuntary spasm of pity and prepared to do my best for her. Then the door was opened by a plump blonde in a pink néglige.

'Er–Mrs Tadwich?'

'That's right.'

'I'm the doctor.'

She gave a bright smile. 'Come on in, do. I wasn't expecting you so early in the morning,' she explained, deftly flicking a pair of drying nylons from a string in the untidy sitting-room.

'I usually see my new patients first.'

I followed her through the door beyond, and found myself in the bedroom.

'Do you live here alone?' I asked.

'Oh, yes. Mr Tadwich left,' she explained amiably. 'There's a divorce pending. Would you like me on the bed?'

I began to feel alarmed. This was a situation never experienced in the ordered routine of hospital. At St Swithin's we were strictly forbidden to examine any female patient lower than the clavicles without a nurse as a bedside chaperone, and I saw my career ending prematurely in the bleak chambers of the General Medical Council in London. But I decided that it would look foolish if I simply grabbed my bag and hurried out. Besides, I was under an equal moral obligation to examine her, and if I didn't I might land just as ignominiously before the local Executive Committee to have my pay stopped like a naughty schoolboy's pocket-money.

'What's the trouble?' I asked, hoping that it was some complaint wholly free of ethical dangers, like sinusitis or nits.

'It's my heart, Doctor.'

My spirits fell lower. But there is fortunately one refuge for the nervous young practitioner – the cold professional manner. This is a psychological defence mechanism, which explains why so many newly qualified men appear brusque and unintelligible to their equally terrified patients. Assuming an air that went out with broughams and Gladstone bags in Harley Street, I gripped my lapels and declared, 'The heart, madam? And what are the symptoms?'

'Oh, no symptoms.' She lay back on the pillow, more at home in the situation than I was. 'Just the palpitations sometimes, you know. I've got a problem heart.'

'Indeed?'

'Leastways, that's what the specialist said. There's a funny quiver you can feel in the middle of my chest, just here.'

'No other manifestations of the condition, I presume?'

'Oh, no. They said in hospital it doesn't mean any harm. Don't you want to examine me?' She slipped off her nightdress down to the waist.

'An idiopathic condition, eh?' I said steadily. 'Umm. Nothing to cause any alarm, then. And now,' I announced with dignity, 'let me palpate this vibration in the cardiac area.' I laid the flat of my hand sharply between her breasts, as though swatting a mosquito. Sticking strictly to clinical terms, I admitted loftily 'I certainly feel a distinct thrill.'

'Go on with you, Doctor,' she said, giving me a wink and a poke in the ribs. 'We're all human, aren't we? How about coming round one evening for a drink?'

'You'd better treat her here in the surgery in future,' said Dr Farquarson, his eyebrows quivering violently. 'Or else send me along. That would finish her.'

'But the whole thing was all my fault,' I said bitterly, tossing my stethoscope on to the examination couch. 'I should have had more control of the situation.'

'It's an occupational risk we've got to run. A woman gets bored in the afternoons, whether she lives in Canterbury or in Canonbury. And the doctor's the easiest one she can run after.'

'But it might have led to all sorts of complications with the G.M.C.! I didn't realize how I had to watch my step.'

'You know the working rule, of course? "It's all right to make your mistress into one of your patients, but it certainly isn't all right to make your patient into one of your mistresses." ' He scratched his cheek with the tip of a pair of forceps. 'If I had my way, that would be engraved in stone over medical school doorways. It's much more useful than "The Art Is Long", not to say much less depressing. But speaking as a comfortable widower, Richard my lad, the best deterrent is a wife of your own in the background.'

I considered this. 'But don't you think that marriage isn't to be tackled as an emergency operation?'

'That's true,' Dr Farquarson agreed. 'Take your time. But not for ever.'

I sat down in the patient's chair. 'Anyway, who could I marry? I don't know any girls.'

'Come, Richard! Even to my old eyes the streets of Hampden Cross seem full of them.'

'But they're all on other men's arms or the backs of other men's motor-bikes. I don't seem to know any girls these days. Besides, how do I know I'd choose the right one?'

'I'd say pick the one with the nicest legs. It's as reasonable a way of choosing a wife as any.'

I persuaded Mrs Tadwich to let me continue her cardiac investigation in the surgery, where she appeared in a tight black dress, three-inch heels, and two-inch nails. Hitching up her skirt, she started every consultation by discussing her absconded husband in tones suggesting that an intimate bond now existed between us.

'We didn't see *that* type of patient in Dr McBurney's day,' declared Miss Wildewinde, pointedly opening the surgery windows afterwards.

It was only a day or two after meeting Mrs Tadwich that I first made acquaintance with the family at 'Capri'. This was one of the houses known as 'Tudor style semi-det.', for which British builders developed such a distressing addiction between the wars. I had been called to examine a Miss Porson, and as I approached through a garden of crushing neatness I diagnosed either a middle-aged housewife with an obsessional neurosis, or an under-occupied elderly spinster putting on weight through idleness, chocolates, and gin. But the door was opened by a classical gall-bladder case, a fair, fat, fertile female of fifty, who was wearing a tweed skirt and a pink blouse.

'Miss Porson?' I asked, speculating when she last had her attack of gallstone colic.

'Why, you're Dr Gordon!'

'That's right.'

'I'd have known it the moment I set eyes on you.' I looked surprised, and she added, 'You're so like your father. He looked after my little girl when we were down with the Rotarians only this year.'

'Really? That's most interesting.'

'My husband knew your father from the days when he was studying engineering in London, you know. They had lots and lots of mutual friends among the students.' Knowing the company my father had kept at St Swithin's, this didn't seem much of a recommendation. 'It's my little Cynthia you've come to see,' Mrs Porson went on. 'The poor child's so *very* delicate.'

I followed her upstairs anxiously. My family's clinical honour was clearly at stake, and I wasn't at all well up in children's medicine. 'Cynthia's a very highly strung child,' Mrs Porson whispered outside the bedroom door. 'You will make allowances, Dr Gordon, won't you? Here's the doctor, dear,' she announced, entering. 'Let Mummy do your pillows and make you comfy, now.'

Cynthia turned out to be a pale, dark, subdued, but pretty girl, sitting up in bed in a flowered nightie, and aged about twenty.

'Good morning,' I said, trying not to look surprised. 'And what's the trouble?'

'She's got one of her feverish bouts, doctor,' said Mother, behind me. 'I took her temperature this morning and it was ninety-nine point six. So I said "Off to bed you go, my girl, and we'll get the doctor." '

'Quite. Well, Miss Porson. Have you any particular symptoms?'

'She had a headache just above her eyes and buzzing in her ears,' said Mother.

'And do you often get such attacks?' I asked the patient.

'Yes, doctor,' replied Mother immediately. 'About every six weeks. She's *very* delicate, aren't you, dear?'

'I'm not,' murmured Cynthia, her lower lip protruding almost imperceptibly.

'Yes you are, dear.' Mother wagged her finger, with fairly playful reproach. 'Mother knows, dear.'

'There's nothing physically wrong with Cynthia,' I said to Mrs Porson, accepting a cup of coffee downstairs afterwards. 'Her temperature's quite normal by the thermometer.'

'But I know how careful one has to be. Cynthia's so delicate, particularly now the nights are turning chilly.'

'Quite. Has she any job?'

'Oh, no, Doctor! She's such a help to me in the house.'

'I see.' The diagnosis was now becoming clear. As Dr Farquarson sometimes put it, it isn't only the obstetricians who have the privilege of cutting the umbilical cord.

'You know, I think you'd find her general health would benefit from some outside interests.'

'But she's such a shy girl, the poor dear.'

'Has she any boy friends?'

Her mother looked surprised. 'Why . . . no, Doctor. No, none at all.' She added quickly, 'It's not that she isn't interested in the opposite sex, of course.'

'I wasn't suggesting that for a moment,' I said with a smile. 'I'll come and see her tomorrow, if I may.'

'You really must have supper with us one evening, Dr Gordon,' Mrs Porson invited from the front door. 'How about next week?'

I wasn't anxious to be involved in the private lives of my patients, but I accepted–partly because of the family connexion, and partly because it would be an evening away from the Crypt and Mr Tuppy. I hoped meanwhile that Cynthia would find some presentable youth to take her to the pictures, because girls who have regular dates with young men don't develop regular headaches.

The supper was a dismal meal. Mr Porson, who seemed to be some sort of iron merchant, talked only about business. Mrs Porson talked only about her daughter's health. Cynthia talked about nothing at all.

After the meal I suddenly found myself alone with her in the sitting-room. She seemed a pleasant girl, though she appeared to lack all the things mentioned in the advertisements. She hadn't anything to chat about except her symptoms, until she sighed and said, 'I often wish I could go away. For a long, long sea voyage, for instance. I'm sure it would do me ever so much good.'

'Well–why don't you have a try? You might get a job as a stewardess?'

'I've thought of that. But I couldn't really leave Mummy.'

'Perhaps one day the time will come when you'll have to,' I said, as she looked so miserable. 'You know–starting a home of your own.'

She gave one of her rare smiles and began talking about the garden.

'You've done absolute wonders for Cynthia,' whispered Mrs Porson as I left. 'She's *quite* a different girl since you've taken her in hand.'

'I'll tell my father next time I see him,' I smiled back.

'Oh, Dr Gordon,' she breathed. 'Do you really mean it?' I thought this an odd remark, but returned to the Crypt satisfied with my evening's treatment.

'There's another call for Miss Porson,' said Miss Wildewinde the next day. 'We never had anything like so much trouble from that family when Dr McBurney was here.'

This time Cynthia had vague stomachache. A couple of days later it was vague headache, and three days after that vague earache. Every time Mother took her temperature, packed her off to bed, and picked up the telephone. My work in the New Town was now increasing daily, the influenza virus was jubilantly starting the open season for human beings, and I decided that I must take a firm line. Besides, far from benefiting from my advice, the poor girl was becoming a flourishing neurotic.

After I had examined Cynthia a few days later for a vague backache, I called Mother into the sitting-room and announced as weightily as possible, 'Mrs Porson–I want to have a serious talk with you.'

'Yes, Doctor?'

'About your daughter.'

'But of course, Doctor.' She gave me a smile.

'Mrs Porson, you may think me perhaps rather young and inexperienced—?'

'No, no, not at all!' she interrupted. 'Not a *bit* too young. Why, these days young people make up their minds ever so much earlier, don't they?'

'I mean, you may think me rather young to speak to you like this.'

'Say *exactly* what's on your mind, Doctor. I know *just* how you feel.'

'Thank you. Naturally I wanted to mention it to you before saying anything to Cynthia herself.'

'But how terribly, terribly sweet of you! And they say the younger generation are so inconsiderate.'

'To be blunt, Cynthia needs marriage.'

She threw her arms round me and burst into tears. 'Oh, Doctor! Now *you* can call me mother, too!'

My departure was a blur of Mrs Porson's face, the chintz curtains in the hall, the gnomes in the garden, the white wicket gate . . . The rest of my rounds passed in a daze.

'But how can the beastly woman possibly have got hold of the idea that I personally wanted to save her blasted daughter from the psychological scrap-heap?' I complained angrily to Dr Farquarson as soon as I got in.

'A doctor's a bit of a catch for any fond mother,' he said, trying to keep his eyebrows under control. 'Though I must admit it's an awkward situation for a young man.'

'But what on earth can I do? And what a fool I've been! I thought even the Porsons couldn't expect me to swallow the medicine as well as prescribe it.'

Dr Farquarson twisted the bell of his stethoscope thoughtfully. 'I'll take over the Porson household from now on. Though I'm prepared to wager they'll ask for their cards after a couple of visits.'

But even this relief was denied me. The next night Dr Farquarson himself went sick. For several days he had been complaining of 'the screws in the back', and when I returned a syringe to the surgery after a late call I found him stuck in his chair.

'It's only the lumbago,' he explained, rubbing himself painfully. 'Don't you fash yourself, Richard–I'll be as right as rain in the morning.'

'Oughtn't you to see someone?' I asked anxiously. 'I could call up old Rogers. I saw him go into his surgery as I passed.'

'No, no,' he said, with unusual weariness. 'Don't bother him at this hour. He's as overworked as we are. Besides, I haven't much faith in the medical profession, anyway.'

'Will you let *me* have a look at you, then?' He hesitated, so I added, 'You know you complain yourself about the pig-headed idiots who only go to the doctor feet first.'

'I'm afraid this looks like a slipped disk to me,' I announced a little later.

He sighed and admitted 'Well, now you've said it, that's what I suspected all along.'

'Don't you think you ought to see a specialist?' I asked with concern. 'I could get you into the private wing at the local hospital. After all, we send them enough patients.'

'Heaven forbid! That place?'

'Look here,' I decided, seeing that I must be firm. 'I'll lay on a car tomorrow and have you run down to London to see Sir Robert Cufford. He knows more about disks than anyone else in the country. Won't you agree to that? Especially as you knew him as a student.'

'And a bumptious stubborn little blighter he was, too.'

'And that's just the type you want, to make you do as you're told. He'll take you into the Royal Neurological and investigate you. I insist on it. It's doctor's orders.'

'But it's impossible, Richard! Who'll run the practice?'

'I will.'

'With the best will in the world, it's too much for one pair of hands.'

'Then I'll get a locum.'

'You won't at this time of the year.'

'I'll try the newly qualified men at St Swithin's.'

'They'll all have got jobs.'

'I'll write to an agency.'

'You never know who they might send.'

We were still considering this problem when the front doorbell rang.

'Damn it!' I said, tired, irritated, and worried. 'That's bound to be some small child with a note saying please send more cotton-wool and some ear cleaners because father's run out.'

On the mat stood Grimsdyke.

Chapter Nine

'Irish medicine's quite unlike medicine anywhere else,' Grimsdyke reflected. 'The chaps don't actually use leprechaun poultices, but there's a cheerful element of witchcraft about it.'

We were in the saloon bar of the Hat and Feathers behind the Deanery the following evening. I no longer visited public houses myself, because a doctor in general practice spotted refreshing himself with half a pint of mild ale is stamped as an incurable drunkard for life. But Grimsdyke had less inhibitions than me about everything, and insisted that our reunion must be celebrated.

Grimsdyke was now our *locum tenens*. That morning I had seen Dr Farquarson off to the Royal Neurological Hospital in London, where Sir Robert Cufford had arranged to take him into the private wing. He had disappeared protesting that he was really much better and warning me of the dangers of having Grimsdyke anywhere near the practice. But Grimsdyke himself, who suffered the chronic delusion that he was the apple of his uncle's eye, seemed delighted to have arrived at such a critical moment.

'You know,' he said warmly, 'I may be flattering myself, but I think I can contribute a lot to the old uncle's practice. On the business and social side, you know. Uncle's a dear old stick, but terribly old-fashioned in his ways. I expect you've found that out? Anyway, until the old chap recovers his health and strength–which I sincerely hope won't be long–you and I, Richard, are going to form one of the brightest partnerships in medicine since Stokes and Adams.'

'Or Burke and Hare,' I suggested. 'Tell me more about Ireland. How did you find Dublin?'

'Just like Cheltenham, except the pillar boxes are painted green. But full of the most amiable coves drinking whisky and water and talking their heads off about nothing very much and telling you how beastly the British were to their aunt's grandmother.'

'But come, now, Grim! Surely that's a stage Irishman?'

'My dear fellow,' he said authoritatively, '*all* Irishmen are stage Irishmen.'

'But what about Irish doctors? After all, they're one of the most popular exports, next to racehorses. How did you find your professional colleagues down in the country?'

'Ah, my professional colleagues! Outside Dublin things were a bit quainter. I hired a car and went down to Enniscorthy in County Wexford, and put up at Bennett's Hotel while I searched round for my practice. I finally ran his to earth in a pub in that village on the postcard.'

'Doctor O'Dooley, you mean?'

'No, the practice. There was only one patient. He was an old chum called Major McGuinness, though what the devil he'd ever been a Major in except the Peninsular War, I can't imagine.'

'A bit of a waste of medical manpower, wasn't it?' I asked in surprise. 'What became of O'Dooley's father and that Polish fellow you talked about?'

'One was dead and the other had gone off with the pub's chambermaid and started an ice-cream business in Wicklow. Young Paddy himself draws his cash from a brewery or something, and hadn't been seen for months. The Major was the only patient left. He was as fat as a football, and as he'd been pickling himself in whisky since puberty he had bronchitis, arthritis, prostatic hypertrophy, and I think a touch of the tabes as well. He was pretty pleased to see me.'

'I bet he was.'

'Yes,' said Grimsdyke ruefully. 'He couldn't eat his dinner. He'd got toothache.'

I ordered some more drinks, and Grimsdyke went on. 'My first operation was a resounding success. Under the reassuring influence of Power's Gold Label for both of us, I removed the offending molar. Damn neatly, too, I thought.'

'What with? A corkscrew?'

'No, the whole of Paddy's kit, such as it was, was in the Major's house–a great rambling place, like living in the Albert Hall–where Paddy had been lodging for some years. So I moved in too. It was quite simple. You just found some blankets and cooked your own food if you could collect anything to start a fire, and there you were. There seemed to be about a dozen other people doing the same thing, and very odd characters some of them were, too. You kept running into new ones round corners. They didn't seem to know each other very well, but there was usually some whisky knocking about which made for conviviality. The Major was a genial old soul, although the British had apparently been beastly to his aunt's grandmother, too. I settled down quite comfortably.'

As it seemed unlike Grimsdyke to refuse a job offering no work and free drinks, I asked why he left.

'The practice died,' he explained simply. 'One night the old boy got more bottled than usual, and passed out under the delusion he was riding in the Grand National and the upstairs bannisters were Becher's Brook. Caused quite a sensation, even in that household. Soon the whole village were in. Then we got down to the serious business of the funeral. You've heard about Irish funerals?'

I nodded.

'There hadn't been so much fun in the place since the night the postmistress went potty and took her clothes off in the High Street. I became a figure of great importance, because the old Major, like a good many people, always worried that he'd be good and cold before he was put in his grave. Thought he might wake up again under six feet of earth. all rather morbid. I had to open veins and things, which worried me a bit, because the last doctor I knew who did the same thing jumped the gun and ten minutes later the blood was running down the stairs. Questions were asked at the inquest.'

He took another drink, ruffled even by the recollection.

'Anyway, the old boy was clearly no longer with us. But he'd also been worried about being eaten by worms and so on, and had asked me to fix up some sort of container that would keep him looking in good shape. Until unearthed by archaeologists, I suppose. Fortunately, the local joiner-cum-undertaker was a jovial bird called Seamus, and although he was out of stock in lead coffins we worked out an ingenious method of wrapping the Major in rolls and rolls of lead sheeting, like you put on the roof. Damned expensive, of course, but the Major was paying. Eventually, we boxed him in, there was a good deal of whisky-drinking, and Seamus went round telling one and all that he was going to screw him down. Tears were shed and speeches were made and at last we were ready to move off for the churchyard.'

'I hope,' I said, 'that after such extensive preparations the ceremony proceeded smoothly?'

'It didn't proceed at all. When the moment finally came to leave, we couldn't get the bloody Major off the floor. Absolutely impossible. We couldn't budge him an inch, all lifting. We had a long discussion about it, and decided the only thing was to send for Jim O'Flynn's breakdown van with the crane on it, or to unwrap him again. The guests became divided on this point, and as you know, when Irishmen are divided they become heated. After a while I gathered that I was thought the cause of the trouble, so I slipped away and gathered my few possessions and caught the afternoon bus. And here I am. There wasn't any more point in staying anyway.'

I laughed. 'I don't believe half of that story.'

'It's true. Even I don't have to exaggerate about Ireland. Still, my emerald phase has now passed, Richard. I am to restart as a respectable English G.P. And I might say how delighted I am to find myself in practice with an old chum like you.'

'And so am I, indeed!' I clapped him on the shoulder. 'It was always one of my more sentimental hopes at St Swithin's.'

'I'm mugging up my medicine, too. I opened Conybeare's textbook this afternoon at the section on Diseases of The Alimentary Canal. I started with Oral Sepsis and got as far as Disorders of the Salivary Glands by teatime. I should be down to the caecum and appendix by Saturday.'

Grimsdyke's gay demeanour and gay waistcoats certainly came refreshingly to the practice. His manner was perhaps more suited for the bookies' enclosure than the bedside, but he had the superb gift of being able to draw smiles from anyone between nine and ninety. He was obviously popular with the patients–except the Porsons, where he sportingly went in my stead when Cynthia developed her next vague pains, and was received 'very much like the third-rate understudy appearing at short notice on a Saturday night'. Otherwise, only Miss Wildewinde seemed to take a dislike to my friend.

'A cheeky young man,' she described him to me one morning after he had been with us a week.

'Oh, I don't know, Miss Wildewinde. Dr Grimsdyke has a rather cheerful manner, but he's a serious soul at heart.'

'I'm quite sure that Dr McBurney wouldn't have taken to him for a moment, if I may say so.'

'Come, now,' I said charitably. 'He may attract lots of rich old ladies to us as private patients. Who knows?'

'It seems as if he's started,' she said tartly. 'There's a car outside that doesn't look at all National Health.'

I had just finished my surgery, and opening the front door was surprised to find at the kerb a long, new, black Bentley, with a smart young man with curly hair and a six-inch moustache lightly polishing the windscreen with a

Paisley handkerchief.

'Dr Gordon?' he asked, a row of teeth appearing beneath the moustache.

'That's right.'

'How do you do, Doctor?' He shook hands with great affability.

'How do you do?'

'Well,' he continued, a slight pause occurring in the conversation. 'Here's a very great motor-car.'

'Of course,' I agreed. 'There's none better.'

'Not in the whole world. It's got everything, plus.' He gave the bonnet a reverent pat. 'Automatic gearbox, variable suspension, built-in lubrication, sunshine roof, three tone radio–the lot. A wonderful motor-car. A cigar, Doctor,' he insisted, producing a box of Havanas from the glove locker as I offered my cigarette case. 'Take a few for afterwards. That's right. A drink, Doctor? The fittings include a cocktail cabinet.'

'I'm afraid I can't touch a drop during the day.'

'I'm Frisby,' he said, producing a card. He was the sort of man you often find yourself next to in saloon bars, drinking light ales and talking about tappets. 'Buckingham Palace Motors, of course.'

I nodded. Car salesmen share with insurance agents and medical equipment manufacturers a quaint belief in the solvency of junior members of the medical profession. I had as much chance of buying the Bentley as the *Queen Mary*, but as I had a few minutes free I agreed when he suggested 'I expect you'd like a spin in the motor-car?'

'That was a delightful experience,' I said gratefully, as we drew up after a run round the Abbey. During this, Mr Frisby had pointed out the detailed mechanical advantages of his charge in terms I understood as little as he would have followed an anatomy demonstration.

'Doctor,' he said, 'you going to be very, very happy indeed with this motor-car.'

'I'm sure I would be,' I agreed. 'Except that I'm afraid there's not the slightest prospect of my being able to buy it.'

He stared at me in amazement.

'It was kind of you to demonstrate it, Mr Frisby,' I said, starting to get out. 'But I don't really want it. Or rather, I can't possibly afford it.'

'But you've bought it!' he exclaimed.

'Bought it?' I began to feel annoyed. 'But how could I? I've never seen the car or you before in my life.'

For a second I thought he was going to take back his cigars.

'Now look here,' he went on, much less affably. 'Is this your signature or isn't it?'

He produced a printed order form from his pocket. It was signed 'G. S. F. Grimsdyke, L.S.Apoth. (Cork)'.

'This is nothing whatever to do with me,' I protested. 'I can't imagine how my partner found the money to buy a Bentley, but that's his affair. If you want him, he'll be back in half an hour.'

'Now look here–you're Dr Gordon, aren't you?'

I agreed.

'Well you *have* bought the car. We were instructed to charge it up to your practice.'

'What! But . . . but . . . damn it! Dr Grimsdyke had no authority whatever—'

'See here, Doctor,' said Mr Frisby, now sounding menacing. 'You can't muck about with Buckingham Palace Motors, you know. I've brought this motor-car all the way from London. I'm a busy man. Not to mention that there's a lot more customers interested—'

'Well, you'll just have to take it back again,' I said sharply. 'There's been a mistake.'

'Mistake, eh? I don't think I like the smell of this, Doctor. You can't pull any wool over the eyes of Buckingham Palace Motors.'

'You can leave the bloody thing here, if you like,' I said. 'But you'll never get paid for it before it qualifies for the Old Crocks' Race.'

By this time our conversation had drawn a small crowd staring through the open windows. I jumped out and ran inside the house. Shortly afterwards I saw Mr Frisby drive his merchandise away, possibly to apply for a writ.

'What the devil's this business about the Bentley?' I demanded, as soon as I saw Grimsdyke.

'Oh, it's come, has it? That's quick service. I only posted the order yesterday.'

'Do you mean you were so insane as actually to try and buy one?'

'Of course, old lad,' he replied calmly. 'Just what the practice wants. Window-dressing. You know what they say–a successful doctor needs a bald head to give an air of wisdom, a paunch to give an air of prosperity, and piles to give an air of anxiety. A posh car continues the process. Why, that's the only way people judge their doctor. You must have heard dozens of times, "That feller must be good–he's got a Rolls." Ever tried to park in Harley Street?'

'But it's ridiculous!' I exploded. 'The thing costs thousands and thousands of pounds.'

'But it's perfectly all right, my dear old lad,' he explained condescendingly. 'We'll get it off the income-tax.'

'Income-tax! Income-tax! Do you know how little we really make in this practice? We couldn't pay for it with our income, income-tax, and post-war credits combined.'

'I must say, you're being a bit of a reactionary,' he said, sounding annoyed as well. 'I think you've been with the old uncle too long already.'

Relations between Grimsdyke and myself remained cool for the rest of the day.

The next morning he unexpectedly wandered into my consulting-room as I was about to start the morning surgery. 'Hello, old lad,' he asked. 'Seen the *Medical Observer* anywhere yet? It's out this morning, isn't it?'

'It usually comes second post,' I explained. I was surprised at this eagerness to get his hands on the weekly press.

'Oh, does it? Be a good lad and put it aside for me, will you?'

The *Medical Observer* happened to arrive just as I was starting my rounds. I tore open the wrapper wondering what item was likely to have interested Grimsdyke so keenly. I found it in the correspondence columns.

> To the Editor, Dear Sir, (*it said*). We feel we should bring to your notice our remarkable success treating osteoarthritis with massive weekly injections of Vitamin B. In a series of two thousand cases seen in our practice we have obtained lasting relief with this treatment in no less than ninety-eight per cent of patients. The effectiveness of this therapy in our hands leads us to bring it to the notice of your readers, and we should be interested if others have achieved comparable results. Yours, etc.

The letter was signed:

Richard Gordon,
C. S. F. Grimsdyke,
4, Monks Walk,
Hampden Cross, Herts.

'My dear fellow, don't work up so much steam about it,' Grimsdyke said, when I waved the *Medical Observer* in his face. 'Of course I wrote it.'

'But it's advertising!' I said in horror.

'And damn good advertising, too.'

'But what the hell! It's unethical.'

'Oh, come off it, Richard. Surely you don't believe the old idea that doctors never beat the drum? Why, that's how half Harley Street keeps going. I admit they don't put cards in their windows like the Eygptians saying, "Dr Bloggings Good For Everything Especially Diarrhoea." They write to the medical journals pointing out such things in a helpful way. It soon get to the ears of the general public.' He sat down in the surgery chair and put his feet on the desk. 'Why, the world will be hobbling a path to our door in a week's time. Just think of it! We're made, old man.'

'I'm damn well going to write to the Editor and tell him it's a forgery.'

'Steady on, old lad! No need to get excited.'

'I've never come across such a piece of flagrant dishonesty.'

'Dishonesty? That's not dishonesty, that's good business.'

'In your mind they seem to be one and the same thing.'

He rose to his feet. 'Are you making reflections on my morals, old man?'

'Yes, I am. You're nothing but a dyed-in-the-wool inconsiderate rogue.'

'Oh, I am, am I? Well you're nothing but a stick-in-the-mud old maid.'

On this note the two doctors separated to attend their patients.

Chapter Ten

Grimsdyke and I did not speak for some days after that. We communicated only by notes passed between our consulting-rooms by Miss Wildewinde:

'Dr Grimsdyke presents his compliments to Dr Gordon, and will he refresh Dr Grimsdyke's memory as to the dose of *Tinct. Belladonnae*?'

'Dr Gordon presents his compliments to Dr Grimsdyke. It's five to thirty minims, and what have you done with the auroscope?'

'Dr Grimsdyke hasn't got the bloody auroscope.'

'Dr Gordon also wants the multivite tablets back, if you please.'

'Dr Grimsdyke has finished the bottle.'

'My God, what are you treating in there? A horse?'

My worries were increased through the commotion of changing digs. It had seemed reasonable for Grimsdyke to move into his uncle's flat, and as two new regulars had arrived at the Crypt and Mr Tuppy had started to tell his stories about doctors all over again I had to go.

Feeling that I could not face another boarding-house, I looked down the Personal column of the local newspaper until I saw an advertisment saying:

'Lady of Refinement shares her lovely home with a few similar as donating guests. Write Miss Ashworth, "The Lodge", Alderman's Lane.' I decided that 'The Lodge' would at least offer a fresh experience. Although my years at St Swithin's had brought me across all types of landlady from the frankly hypochondriacal to the frankly sexy, medical students don't usually get within sniffing distance of Ladies of Refinement.

'The Lodge' turned out to be a neat villa with a faint air of antiseptic discipline about it, like a military convalescent home. The hall had a polished parquet floor on which a footstep would have stood out as startlingly as Man Friday's, there was a hat-stand starkly bare of hats, a brass gong between a pair of brass bowls, pink-and-green leaded windows, and a fleet of galleons sailing boisterously across the wall paper. There were also two pokerwork notices saying 'Good Doggies Wipe Their Paws' and 'Who Left The Lights On? Naughty!'

Miss Ashworth turned out to be a small thin middle-aged woman in glasses, who wore sandals and a dress like those issued to the inmates of mental hospitals.

'You'll be *so* comfortable here, I'm sure,' she said, fussing me into a small room overlooking the back garden. 'But you *will* be careful of the ornaments, won't you?' She indicated the pieces of glossy china which covered almost every horizontal surface above floor-level. 'They all have such *very* deep sentimental attachments for me.'

I assured her that I would be most careful.

Looking me full in the face she said, 'You remind me *so* much of a dear, *dear* departed friend. Supper is at six-thirty.' She then softly closed the door and disappeared.

The other refined people turned out to be a disgruntled bank manager called Walters, a thin woman in a sweater who spent all her meals intently reading the *Manchester Guardian*, a serious-looking young man with dirty collars and furnunculosis, and more old ladies. We all wished each other good morning or good evening, then sat through our meals in an atmosphere of depressed silence, as thought waiting for something nasty to happen.

'Sorry to see you've ended up here,' said Mr Walters morosely when we were left alone after supper, which had consisted of sloppy things in thick china bowls.

'Oh, it doesn't seem too bad,' I said, to cheer myself up. Digs are the curse of higher education. I had been living in one sort or another since I was eighteen and I was now so sick of other people's houses that even rooms in St James's Palace wouldn't have excited me. 'Been here long?'

'Three years. And I'd move tomorrow if I could raise the energy. Not that there'd be much point. I'm a bachelor, you know, and I've lived in pretty well every lodgings in Hampden Cross by now. I suppose I shall just go on here until I drop dead. Then I'll be able to join one of Miss Ashworth's parties.' I looked puzzled, so he continued. 'Didn't you know that Miss A. communicates with her dead guests nightly? It's sometimes quite difficult in this house to tell who are the living inhabitants and who the defunct ones. No, no, my lad,' he said shaking his head gloomily. 'You take my advice. Don't unpack.'

It was perhaps these disturbing remarks which led to my absently knocking over a small group of china cats in my bedroom. Hoping that one ornament the less wouldn't be noticed, I carefully collected the fragments and hid them in my suitcase. I was just getting into bed when I carelessly pushed a china seal off the edge of the mantelpiece, and this too I gathered guiltily and hid in my case. Three days later I wondered if my subconscious antagonism to lodgings was being transferred to the ornaments, because I had disposed of a china rooster, a little girl holding out her pinafore, and a dog with big eyes and its lead in its mouth. Miss Ashworth's maid didn't seem to notice, but I was aware that my luggage was steadily being filled with pieces of jagged porcelain.

The hostility between Grimsdyke and myself naturally softened as the days passed. I think that we were both looking for a chance to put out our hands and admit we'd been bloody fools. I had in fact decided to seek him out and suggest we sank our quarrel in a pint of bitter, when I arrived back in surgery one evening and found our narrow hall filled with steel and red plastic furniture.

'What the devil's all this?' I demanded of the man waiting with the invoice. 'It looks as though we were going to start a cocktail bar.'

'I wouldn't know about that, sir. The other doctor gave instructions to deliver today?'

'Oh, he did, did he? Well, my instructions are to take the lot away again. And what are *you* doing, may I ask?' I demanded of a solemn-looking man in dungarees screwing something on the broom cupboard door. 'PATHOLOGICAL LABORATORY? What on earth's the meaning of this?'

Beside him were two other notices, saying ELECTROCARDIOGRAPH ROOM and PSYCHOLOGICAL CLINIC. One reading X-RAY DEPARTMENT was already fixed to the door of our downstairs lavatory. 'Take them off immediately,' I ordered.

'Can't do that.'

'Can't? Why not?'

'I've got my orders from the other doctor.'

Before the argument could blossom, we were interrupted by the appearance of Dr Rogers through the open front door. Dr Rogers was a fat man who always seemed to be breathless and perspiring, summer or winter, sitting or running. He was the senior practitioner in Hampden Cross, and though growing into the pomposity almost unavoidable from a lifetime of telling people to eat less and go to bed earlier, he was a friendly professional neighbour. He now seemed in a more heated state than usual.

'Ah, Doctor!' he began, wiping his bald head with his handkerchief. 'Just a word . . . if you'll permit . . . awkward time, I'm sure.'

'Well, I *was* going to take surgery, Dr Rogers.'

'Matter of some importance.'

I showed him into the empty consulting-room and closed the door.

After looking at me with rising embarrassment for some seconds he announced, 'Went to the cinema last night.'

This seemed a thin excuse for interrupting my evening's work, but I said politely, 'A good film I hope?'

'Oh, passable, passable. Can't remember what it was about now. Never can these days. Generally go to sleep. My daughter tells me about them afterwards.'

There was another silence.

'Well, Dr Rogers,' I said. 'I'm certainly glad to hear you had a pleasant evening. Now I'm afraid that I have to get on with the surgery—'

'A medical man's got to be on call,' he announced. 'Any hour of the day or night. It's only right.'

I agreed.

'Wouldn't be doing his duty to his patients otherwise.'

I agreed with this too.

'But . . . well . . . Professional dignity, and so on. Eh? Quite inadvertent really, I'm sure. *I'm* not saying anything. Very pleased to see you in Hampden Cross. But obviously gossip starts among the others. Advertising, you know. Grave charge.'

'I'm afraid I don't quite follow—'

'Trying to make myself clear. In the pictures. "Dr Gordon Urgently Wanted" flashed on the screen.'

'What! But that's impossible!'

'Afraid so, Doctor. Right in the middle of the big picture. Ah! Remember now–about an American fellow and another American fellow and some sort of girl.'

'But it must have been a mistake,' I said. 'I wasn't even on duty last night.'

'Mistake, Doctor? Couldn't be. Was on *every* cinema in the district. Not only that, Doctor, it's been appearing every night of the week. And, so I am to believe, at every separate performance.'

I managed to show him out without seizing a scalpel from the suture tray and searching for Grimsdyke. I ran into Miss Wildewinde coming downstairs, carrying a suitcase.

'Miss Wildewinde! Where are you going?'

'Well may you ask!' she said furiously.

'You don't mean–you're leaving us?'

'That's natural enough, surely? As I have been discharged.'

'But . . . but you can't! Miss Wildewinde, you can't possibly,' I implored, gripping her arm on the doorstep. 'It was Grimsdyke, wasn't it? Yes, of course it was! He's gone mad, Miss Wildewinde. Mad as a hatter. Insane. Certifiable. He's got no right to, whatever—'

'Take your hands off me, Dr Gordon, if you please. I don't know anything about Dr Grimsdyke's mental state. All I know is that he gave me a month's notice this morning. And to think! All the years I'd been here with Dr McBurney.'

'But Miss Wildewinde! I withdraw it, absolutely and immediately—'

'I wouldn't stay in this practice another second!'

'I'll double your salary,' I said desperately.

'I wouldn't even stay in the same district as Dr Grimsdyke, sane or insane, if you paid me a king's ransom. Good-bye, Dr Gordon. A man will be calling for my trunks.'

'Oh, she's gone already, has she?' asked Grimsdyke calmly, as soon as I tackled him. 'All the better.'

'What the devil do you mean by it?' I demanded, banging the consulting-room desk. 'I've never heard of such mean and miserable behaviour.'

He looked offended. 'Don't get so shirty, old man. It's all for our own good. Why do you think people travel by airlines?'

'I can't see what that's got to do in the slightest—'

'Because all the airline advertisements show a blonde hotsie welcoming them up their gangway. Simple psychology. And that's what we want,' he went on lightly. 'Get a smasher for a receptionist, and trade'll double overnight. As a matter of fact, I was rather looking forward to interviewing a few tomorrow afternoon. And how do you like the new furniture? It's the American idea. In the States a doctor's surgery really looks like one–all white paint and white trousers and you could do a gastrectomy on the floor. Impresses the patients no end. And of course the patients like to think you've got all the latest gadgets. Hence the door labels. Good idea, don't you think? *Excreta tauri cerebrum vincit*–Bull Baffles Brains.'

'If I'd had the slightest idea you'd be behaving in this criminally irresponsible manner—'

'You don't appreciate what I'm doing for you, old lad,' he said in a hurt tone. 'Why, for the last couple of weeks I've had your name on the screen twice nightly in every flick house in town. Not my idea, of course,' he added modestly. 'Remember Ben Allen and Bob Sawyer in *Pickwick*? They did it by being called out of church. I just brought the technique up to date.'

I sat down heavily on the consulting-room desk. There didn't seem to be anything to say to Grimsdyke. I still faintly believed that he had the best intentions; but his ideas on the legal limitations of salesmanship, if applied to merchandise instead of medicine, would long ago have landed him at the Old Bailey.

'Wouldn't you like a holiday?' I suggested quietly.

'That's very decent of you, old lad, but I've only just come. Anyway, uncle will be back as soon as they've whipped his disk out.'

'Couldn't you just clear off? I'd willingly stand your fare back to Ireland.'

'That's hardly the way to talk to a friend, if I may say so, old lad.'

'I was not aware that you were one.'

'Oh, I see. That's your attitude, is it?'

'It certainly is. And all I can say, Grimsdyke, is that the sooner you realize it the better.'

'A fine expression of gratitude!' he said indignantly. 'If you're trying to tell me I'm not wanted—'

'I can assure you that you're not.'

'I shan't bother you with the trouble of my company any longer. I might tell you, Gordon, that my uncle shall hear of this as soon as I get to Town. If you want to ruin his practice, it's not entirely your affair.'

Half an hour later Grimsdyke had followed Miss Wildewinde to London.

He left a difficult life behind him. Apart from repairing his ethical sabotage and soothing down Buckingham Palace Motors and the furniture shop, I had to run the practice single-handed without anyone to sort out the National Health cards, the telephone calls, or the patients from the waiting-room. I also had a disturbing note from my father saying, 'Got an extraordinary letter from a fellow called Bill Porson I've hardly seen for years. Are you going to marry his daughter Cynthia? Is she the same one as last time? Are you behaving like a gentleman?' In 'The Lodge' I started hiding a bottle of gin in my wardrobe, and I broke a china pixie, two shepherdesses, and an idiotic-looking horse. I felt that I was going rapidly downhill, psychologically and professionally.

Chapter Eleven

'It is still beyond me to suggest a locum off-hand,' wrote Dr Farquarson from the Royal Neurological. 'But I think you should really try to get an assistant of some sort or another, otherwise you'll be joining me here. I suspect I shall be another couple of months out of things yet. Bobbie Cufford and his retinue seem unaware of any measurement of time more delicate than the calendar. I saw him again this morning–I regret to say that he has developed a most prosperous-looking stomach, and the bedside manner of a dead halibut–and he seems intent on keeping me out of circulation until the time comes for me to retire for good. They still haven't got their diagnosis. Whether Bobbie cuts or not seems to depend on whether my right ankle jerk can raise a flicker. At least with general surgeons you're in, cut, and out before you've time to draw a breath.

'I was visited yesterday by my nephew, who very thoughtfully brought me a bunch of grapes and borrowed ten pounds. I am sorry that you had your differences. After hearing his story I can only express my heartfelt gratitude for your keeping both of us on the *Medical Register* and out of the *London Gazette*. I have long classified my nephew as a high-grade mental defective, but I am beginning to feel this too generous a diagnosis. He has gone I know not whither.'

Finding a new receptionist was easier than finding a new locum. A couple of days after Grimsdyke's departure, as I struggled to hold two surgeries single-handed and see fair play in the waiting-room at the same time, a small cheerful-looking redhead of about nineteen pushed her way forward explaining that she had a 'special appointment with the doctor'.

'Well, I'm the doctor,' I said, starting to shut the consulting-room door. 'And I'm sorry, but you'll have to wait your turn with everyone else.'

'No, not you. The other doctor. The one with the bow tie.'

'Dr Grimsdyke has been called away on a long case and isn't likely to return,' I explained.

Seeing her face drop in childlike disappointment, I added, 'I'm Dr Gordon. Is there anything I can do for you?'

'Dr Grimsdyke promised he'd make me his receptionist.'

'Did he?' I said, brightening immediately. 'That's different. There's no reason why I shouldn't keep a promise for him, is there?' She gave a glance which I felt compared me unfavourably with my late colleague. 'If you'd like to join the practice, I assure you it's a most interesting job. Plenty of time to yourself, too. Not to mention being part of the great army struggling against the forces of disease, and so on. Have you tried it before?'

'I can type a bit,' she said. 'I was with Jennifer Modes.'

'How about a change? There's nothing like variety.'

She hesitated. 'The other doctor told me there was a free flat as well. He said it would be nice for him to have me in easy reach for emergencies.'

I had hoped to move into Miss Wildewinde's apartment myself, but I was prepared to put up with my present lodgings in exchange for the chance of occasionally being able to get back to them before midnight.

'Of course there's a flat.'

'O.K. I'll take the job,' she agreed. 'I'm proper sorry the other doctor isn't here, though.'

I found her one of Miss Wildewinde's overalls and she started on the spot. Her name was Miss Strudwick, and she was as out of place in the surgery as a fan-dancer in church. But she was a willing helper. She had a chronic sinusitus which made her sniff a good deal, and an irritating habit of saying 'Aren't I a silly?' when she'd done something like spilling a carefully-gathered twenty-four-hour specimen over the lino, or sending a patient to a psychiatrist for a post-mortem report and a request to the coroner about the mental condition of his subject. She had no idea of professional sterility or professional secrecy, but she seemed to like the patients and gossiped affably with them all in the waiting-room. After a few days she even began to mellow towards me.

'Mind, all the girls at the Palais thought Dr Grimsdyke was ever so nice,' she confessed one night after surgery, while I was trying to teach her how to sterilize a syringe.

'That's where you met him, was it?' I always wondered how Grimsdyke had spent his evenings in Hampden Cross. 'Now you make sure the sterilizer is on, so, and wait until the water has come to the boil.'

'Oh, yes. There every night he was, almost. He did the mamba something delirious.'

'You first of all dismantle the syringe into its component parts, thus.'

'Mind he wouldn't let on he was a doctor to begin with,' she said, giving a giggle. 'But of course I ought to have known from the start. He had such lovely soft hands to touch you with.'

'Then you wrap the barrel of the syringe in lint, like this.'

'Don't *you* ever go to the Palais, Doctor?'

'I'm afraid I never seem to get the time, Miss Strudwick.'

'Go on–don't call me Miss Strudwick.' She came a little nearer round the sterilizer. 'Everyone calls me Kitten.'

'Er–the plunger is always boiled separately to avoid breakage—'

'You're one of the shy sort, aren't you?' She looked up at me. 'You couldn't say that about Dr Grimsdyke, I must say.'

'And the needles of course are sterilized as quickly as possible to avoid blunting—'

'But you've got ever such nice kind eyes.'

'Threading them through a square of lint for convenient recovery—'

'Wouldn't you like to get a bit more friendly, seeing as Fate has brought us together?'

'Er–Miss Strudwick. The–er–temperature of the sterilizer has to be maintained at one hundred degrees Centigrade for two minutes—'

Our conversation was fortunately broken by the telephone calling me out to a confinement, and when I got back I was relieved to find that Miss Strudwick's emotions had cooled wit the sterilizer.

In the next few days it became clear that Grimsdyke must have been a highly popular partner at the local Palais. Girls looking almost the same as Kitten Strudwick appeared hopefully in the waiting-room every morning, and I could have taken my choice of half a dozen receptionists. But finding a locum seemed impossible. I wrote to the Secretary of St Swithin's Medical School and to a medical employment agency in Holborn, as well as drafting a mildly misleading advertisement for the *British Medical Journal*. I interviewed one doctor, but he was so old that he seemed likely only to add to the number of my patients; another, with a red face and tweeds, not only arrived drunk but seemed to find nothing unusual in it. There was one excellent young man from India who politely told me that I was too young to be his professional senior, and another excellent young man from Inverness who politely told me that he suffered from schizophrenia. I seemed to have struck the hard core of medical unemployment. Whenever I had been out of work and wanted a locum's job myself every practice in the country seemed fully manned, but now that I was in the usual position of employer I couldn't find any takers. I even began to hope that Grimsdyke would appear again at the front door–as indeed he might have done, with no embarrassment whatever–when I had a letter from the City General Hospital, in the East End of London.

Dear Dr Gordon (*it said*),

I should be glad if you would consider me for the post of your locum tenens, of which I heard today from Messrs Pilcher and Perritt in Holborn. I am twenty-three years of age and qualified from the City General last December, subsequently holding the appointment of house surgeon to Mr Ernest Duff. I am now anxious to have some experience in general practice before continuing with surgery, in which I intend to specialize. Perhaps you would kindly let me know your decision as soon as you conveniently can? I would add that I possess a car.

Yours sincerely,

Nicholas Barrington,

B.M., B.Ch (Oxon).

I don't think I had read a letter more gratefully since I opened the official envelope after my final examinations. The writer seemed sane, and wasn't young enough to be a glorified student nor old enough to be a chronic drunkard. He sounded a little prim and precise, but that was only to be expected of an Oxford man. He had worked under Duff, who was so surgically eminent as to have two operations named after him. And even at St Swithin's we recognized the City General students as a genially beery crowd like ourselves. Apart from this, the poor fellow's following the will-o'-the-wisp of surgical specialization struck sympathy from my bosom: I felt that it would be nice to work with someone else who had probably failed the Primary too. Wasting no time, I took a risk and telegraphed Dr Barrington saying

APPOINTED FORTHWITH COME IMMEDIATELY IF POSSIBLE ACCOMMODATION RATHER SHORT BUT CAN MUCK IN WITH ME UNTIL SETTLED STOP WORK HARD BUT FUN HOPE YOU DRINK BEER

GORDON

To which I had the reply

ARRIVING NOON TOMORROW STOP YES I DRINK BEER

BARRINGTON

'Our troubles are over,' I told Kitten Strudwick happily that evening. 'A Dr Barrington is arriving tomorrow to help us.'

'Oh, really? I wonder what *he*'ll be like?'

'Soft hands and a kind heart like Dr Grimsdyke, I expect. So put on your best pair of nylons.'

'Go on with you! I didn't think you noticed my nylons.'

'Doctors are trained to be observant, Miss Strudwick. Yes,' I reflected, relaxing in the surgery chair comfortably for the first time since Dr Farquarson's departure. 'It's going to be a bit of fun to have someone three years junior of me to kick about. I shall be able to hold my lapels and say "Come come, my lad–can't you spot a simple case of craniocleidodysostosis? What on earth did they teach you at the General?" Oh, yes, I'll make the poor chap work all right.'

'I really don't know, I'm sure,' she confessed. 'You doctors, ain't a bit like what I thought you was. Do you want these prong things put back in the hot water?'

I was unable to meet my new colleague on his arrival the next day, as I expected to be out on my morning rounds until well past one o'clock.

'Tell him to stick his car round the back,' I told Miss Strudwick. 'And I'll be home as soon as I can. Make him a cup of tea, if he looks the tea type. Anyway, I'm sure you can entertain him.'

I struck a difficult hour trying to persuade a house physician to take a pneumonia into the local hospital, and it was almost two o'clock when I returned. I was at once both annoyed and worried to find that Barrington hadn't arrived. It suddenly occurred to me that he'd found a better job and let me down, and I should have to start the dreary advertising and interviewing all over again. At that hour of the day the hall and waiting-room were empty, and Miss Strudwick had disappeared for lunch. The only person in sight was another of Grimsdyke's clinical camp followers.

'I'm very sorry,' I said as I came in. 'But you're wasting your time. The job's filled. Good morning.'

She looked disappointed. I felt rather sorry myself, because she was a small pretty blonde in a black suit, who looked much cleaner than Kitten Strudwick.

'Filled?' She frowned slightly.

'I'm afraid this is really not my responsibility at all. I'm Dr Gordon. If you were led to think there was a job here it's my partner's doing, and he's left for good. It's too bad, but I can't do anything about it now. Good day.'

She gave a quick sigh. 'Well, I'll have to go home again, I suppose?'

'Yes, I'm afraid you will.'

'I must say, Dr Gordon, mistake or not, it's been a good deal of inconvenience coming all this way from the middle of London.'

'The middle of London? Good God! Is he offering jobs in all the Palais in London now?'

'I don't think I quite understand?'

'Perhaps you didn't meet Dr Grimsdyke in a dance hall?'

'I have been to a dance hall, certainly. I went to one in Tottenham Court Road last year. And, if you are at all interested, I enjoyed myself very much. But I haven't been with or met a Dr Grimsdyke in those or any less interesting surroundings.'

'But then how on earth did you know that . . . ?'

In my days as a student at St Swithin's I had established a modestly flattering reputation among my companions for imitation of members of the hospital staff. I would often entertain the class with these impressions between theatre cases or while waiting for unpunctual physicians to arrive for ward rounds. Although I could mimic most of the mannerisms of many of the consultants, both my audience and myself agreed that my masterpiece was the hospital's senior surgeon, Sir Lancelot Spratt. Using some cotton-wool for his beard, my impression of his lecture on chronic retention in old men brought laughter from even our most earnest students. I never gave this performance so well as the afternoon I delivered it from the lecturer's rostrum itself, ten minutes before Sir Lancelot was due to occupy it. The laughter of my waiting classmates swelled almost to hysteria as I reached his description of the patient's social difficulties on a picnic. It was at that point that I suspected even my own brilliance, and nervously turning round saw Sir Lancelot observing me with folded arms from the lecturer's entrance in the corner. My feelings of that moment were exactly paralleled in Dr Farquarson's surgery.

'You . . .' I said, staring at her. 'You . . . you're here instead of Dr Barrington?'

'I am Dr Barrington.'

'Dr Nicholas Barrington?' I snatched the letter from my desk.

'*Nichola* Barrington. And it would be rather a coincidence if there were two of us applying, wouldn't it?'

'I'm most terribly sorry,' I gasped. 'I thought you were one of my late partner's popsies. I mean, I thought you were someone else. Oh, God!' I collapsed into the chair. 'What a frightful business! Won't you sit down? Will you have a cup of tea? Have you had lunch?'

'I had some at the local hotel, thank you. I thought I'd better install myself there. Though I'm very grateful for your kind offer of accommodation in the telegram.'

I covered my face.

'You must think me an absolute horror,' I said miserably. 'You see, I hadn't the slightest idea you'd be a woman. I know it's ridiculous, but somehow you always think of a doctor as a man–at least, I do. Oh, God! Why can't they have some term like a doctorix, or something? This is quite the worst thing that's happened to me for years,' I groaned. It seemed the climax of all my troubles. 'How can I ask you to forgive me? Or do you want to walk straight out again?'

But Dr Barrington now seemed to find the situation comfortably amusing.

'Don't worry, Dr Gordon. It's a mistake that's always happening. When I first went to the General I was put down for a rugger trial and a Lodge meeting.'

'I shall never really be able to look you in the face again.'

'I hope you will. Otherwise it's going to make the practice rather difficult isn't it? I've never done any G.P. before, and I'm hoping to learn a lot.'

'I don't know yet if I can teach you much. Have you failed the Primary yet? Or haven't you taken it?'

'Oh, I got my Primary when I finished my pre-clinical work at Oxford.' This ripped another fragment from my tattered self-esteem.

'When would you like to start work?' I asked humbly.

'Any time you like.'

'This afternoon? We're rather pressed.'

'Just give me time to change. I only put this on to impress you–I thought you might be a rather overwhelming old man.'

'You know,' I said apologetically, 'I shall never forget this meeting until my dying day.'

I was right.

Chapter Twelve

Living professionally with a woman is an unusual relationship. There were women students, women housemen, and even women registrars at St Swithin's, but like most of the big London teaching hospitals it was a traditionally anti-feminist institution. It had refused to take females at all until obliged to by the grant-paying Government at the onset of the National Health Service, and the novelty was greeted with gloom from all section of the staff. The consultants objected because they felt it was another expression of the general degeneration of things (particularly when some well-intentioned official from the Ministry pointed out that the bulk of the medical profession is feminine in Soviet Russia). The medical school objected, because such frivolous objects as women would be as out of place in our leathery tobacco-drenched common room as in the Athenaeum. The patients objected because they didn't like the idea of being 'mucked about by young girls'. The housemen objected because they would have to behave in the Residency. And the nurses objected because their noses would be put out of joint.

Obstacles were strewn thickly in the new students' path. Would they need chaperones to examine patients in the male wards? (No.) Where would they have their lavatories? (In the old fives court.) Could they join the students' clubs? (They soon ran most of them.) Wouldn't they all get married and have babies before they'd finished the course? (They didn't at R.A.D.A.) The first batch arrived, without ceremony, at the start of the new session, and were watched with eager indifference by their established classmates. These were divided into the gloomy ones expecting thick tweeds and thick spectacles, and the even more unbalanced hopeful ones looking for a bunch of smashers. In the end the new students turned out like any other collection of middle-class young women, and within a week no one took particular notice of them. Meanwhile, we had at least the compensation of knowing that the School of Medicine for Women in Gray's Inn Road was now obliged to admit men.

When I left St Swithin's for good there were still occasional arguments whether women make as good doctors as men. There were certainly no doubts about Nichola Barrington, whose usual name appeared to be Nikki. She was academically sound and clinically practical; she had the knack of managing patients old enough to be her grandfather or young enough to be her boy-friend; and she had a flair for sick children, which pleased me particularly because I have long held that this branch of medicine is the equivalent of veterinary science, and could never join in the mother's delight when the little patient tries to eat the doctor's tie and pukes down his shirt front. My pediatric consultations generally ended in struggles and screams, doubtless laying the foundations of several awkward neuroses in later life, and I was delighted to hand all patients arriving in prams over to my new assistant.

'You seem to be making quite a hit in Hampden Cross,' I told Nikki a few days after her arrival. 'Why, twice today I've been met with disappointed looks and a demand to "see the other doctor".'

'It'll wear off,' she said modestly. 'At the moment they just want to see the freak.'

'I'd hardly call you a freak, Nikki. But I must say I'm delighted you're getting on so well. Some of the patients can be pretty difficult at first, especially in the New Town. They think it's asserting the rights of citizenship to be rude to the doctor.'

'Well, I might tell you I was as nervous as a kitten when I started.'

'Of the patients?'

'No. Of you.'

'Of me! Whatever for?'

'In my long clinical career–now stretching over the best part of twelve whole months–I've found that whatever they say about it, men really think they're rather superior to women at medicine and driving cars. But you've been absolutely sweet.'

I laughed. 'By the way, talking of driving. . . .' I started playing with a syringe on the surgery desk. 'I wondered if you'd like to run out to the country tonight for a spot of dinner? We could try the Bull–it's the local beauty-spot, you know, horse-brasses round the fire, draughts under the doors, and waiters with arthritis. You don't get a bad meal there. We could ask old Rogers to be on for us both.'

She looked doubtful.

'I thought it would give me a chance to put you wise about the practice,' I continued. 'You know, over the relaxed atmosphere of the dinner-table. difficult to think of everything in the rush-and-tumble of the surgery.'

'All right,' she agreed. 'Though I must say, when I left the General I didn't expect to be out to dinner again for months.'

Under the mellowing influence of the Bull's roast beef and Yorkshire we talked a good deal. Over the soup I had started by describing the local arrangements for disposing of people going mad in the middle of the night, but we soon started chatting generally about hospitals and housemen, students and sisters, patients and parties.

'What's it like being a woman doctor?' I asked, when the old waiter had gone puffing away over the cheese board.

'My heavens! That's a big question.'

'Or is it a question at all? It's just like being any other doctor, I suppose.'

'Well, it leads to complications sometimes.'

'Please spare me the memory,' I said blushing.

She laughed. 'I'd quite forgotten about my arrival. But I think everyone usually falls over backwards to be fair to female doctors. Sometimes you find examiners who are a bit fierce with you, but that's only because they're so worried they're being prejudiced in the opposite direction. People make life too easy for us, really. Which is gratifying when you consider what our prototypes were like.'

'You mean Sophia Jex-Blake and her friends, who made such nuisances of themselves in Edinburgh?'

'That's right. Isn't it a pity that there's nothing quite so unfeminine as a feminist?'

'I've certainly known a few qualified battle-axes,' I admitted. 'But you don't look the chained-to-the-railings type yourself.'

'Well, I'm going to stand up for women's rights now. I'm paying for half the dinner.'

'What? Nonsense!'

'There you are–wounded masculine pride. Now you can see what women are up against all the time.'

'It's not masculine pride,' I insisted. 'It's good manners.'

'Which is often an excuse for the same thing. Women doctors enjoy equal pay, so it serves them right to suffer equal expenses. After all, we only had dinner to discuss the practice.'

I admitted this.

'Then there's another thing, Richard we want to keep our relationship on a strictly professional basis, don't we?'

I admitted this too.

'I mean, it wouldn't do at all if we didn't?'

'No, not for a minute. Bad for the patients and all that.'

'Good,' she said, reaching for her handbag. 'But if you like I'll let you pay for the tip.'

I realized that Nikki was instinctively right in setting an austerely businesslike stamp on our relationship from the start. Anyway, I asked myself the next morning, what right had I to force my company on such a delightful girl just through the accident of her coming to work in the same place? It occurred to me as I started on my rounds that Nikki had been mixing on equal terms with men since she tore up her gym tunics for dusters, and must by now have collected the cream of the country's manhood in her train. I was no more than a passer-by in the road of life, and in future it was only fair to approach her exclusively on clinical matters.

I happened that evening to get a set of electrocardiograms from the hospital that I particularly wanted to interpret. I always had as much difficulty over the squiggles of the P-Q-R-S-T waves set up by the heartbeat as over the evasive shadows on X-rays, and all I could remember about them from my teaching was the old cardiologists' joke about 'Always getting a premature P after T'. I sat puzzling over the spiky lines in the deserted surgery until it occurred to me that Nikki might know more about the subject than I did. It was clearly my duty to the patient to call in a second opinion.

'I do hope I'm not disturbing you,' I said as I rang at the door of Farquarson's flat, where I had insisted she lived.

'Not a bit, Richard. I was only working through some old surgery notes. Do come in.'

I was surprised to see the change. Dr Farquarson's tastes in interior decoration ran largely to framed photographs of his old class groups with stamp-paper over the ones who had died, dingy native carvings picked up in his travels, sets of indestructibly-bound classics, and neat piles of the *B.M.J.* and the *Lancet*. Nikki had put flowers in his pair of presentation tankards and a couple of bright cushions on the sofa, while Ian Aird's *Companion in Surgical Studies* and *Gray's Anatomy* lay among scattered sheets of lecture notes on a new coloured table-cloth.

'I'm terribly sorry to interrupt your work,' I apologized, 'but I've a set of E.C.G.s I'd very much like your opinion on, Nikki.'

'Of course, Richard. Though I can't think my opinion's any better than yours.'

'I must say,' I added admiringly, 'you've brightened up old Farquy's room somewhat. I always thought before it looked like Sherlock Holmes's study in Baker Street.'

'I haven't really done much,' she said modestly. 'But won't you sit down?'

'Do you mind a pipe?'

'Heavens, no! I've been kippered in tobacco since I first went up to Oxford.'

'I think Farquy's impregnated the place pretty thoroughly already, anyway. He has some horrible black mixture made up specially in Dundee. It would do excellently for fumigating mattresses.'

'I must say I sometimes itch to redecorate the place.' She looked round her temporary home. 'It *could* be absolutely lovely. I'd have all that herbaceous wallpaper off for a start.'

'Yes, and I think that mahogany affair with the mirror in the corner's a bit of a mistake, don't you?'

We talked about redecoration for a while, then about flats in general, and about digs and landladies (which we disliked), and living in London (which we enjoyed), and the Festival Hall and the riverside pubs and the Boat Race and the places you could get a good meal in Soho and Espresso coffee bars and Hyde Park in springtime. Then I was startled to hear the Abbey clock chime eleven.

'Good Lord!' I said, jumping up. 'I've wasted your whole evening, Nikki.'

'Of course you haven't, Richard. I wasn't really concentrating on surgery. Besides,' she smiled, 'wouldn't it be terrible to start work if you didn't feel there was a sporting chance of being interrupted?'

I agreed warmly with this, but I felt that I ought to wish her good night.

'By the way,' she said, as I opened the door. 'You forgot these.'

'Oh, the electrocardiograms! But how on earth did they slip my memory? I'll look them up in the book tomorrow, anyway. Good night, Nikki.'

The next evening I had a difficult X-ray which I thought she could help me interpret, and the one after there happened to be a worrying case of diabetes I felt I ought to discuss. The following night I had to ask her opinion about a child I'd seen in the afternoon with suspected mumps, and the next I thought she could advise me about a couple of septic fingers I was treating. Nikki always made some coffee and put some records on her gramophone, and on the whole we were pretty cosy.

It was about this time that I became aware of some peculiar symptoms. I didn't feel ill–on the contrary, I was in a state known clinically as 'euphoria', in which the subject goes about in an unshakable condition of hearty benevolence. But I was beginning to suffer from anorexia and insomnia–I couldn't eat or sleep–and I kept finding myself undergoing mild uncinate fits, in which the patient lapses into a brief state of dreaminess instead of attending to the business in front of him. Then there were my bursts of paroxysmal tachycardia. My pulse rate would suddenly shoot up alarmingly, whenever–for instance–I had to find Nikki to discuss some clinical problem. I put this down to nervousness springing from my naturally shy character. But the whole symptom-complex was highly disturbing to a mildly introspective young man.

'You've got it bad,' said Kitten Strudwick one morning, between patients.

'I beg your pardon?' I said in surprise. 'I've got what bad?'

'Go on with you!' She gave me a playful dig with the percussion hammer. 'I thought Dr Grimsdyke was fast enough. But as they always say, it's the quiet ones what a girl has to watch.'

'I'm afraid I haven't the slightest idea what you're talking about, Miss Strudwick.'

'Well, whatever next? I never thought I'd have to tell a doctor all about the birds and the bees. Who do you want in now? The old duck with the arthritis or the Colonel with the hammer-toes?'

Chapter Thirteen

The next morning I arrived in the surgery to find an alarming letter from Grimsdyke. The envelope was post-marked FOULNESS, but the official-looking writing-paper bore no address.

> Dear old boy, (*it said*)
> Shame forbids me to tell you where I am. Little did I think, in those happy days at St Swithin's that the Grimsdykes would be reduced to such shifts. But there are compensations. I always thought 'Sweet are the uses of adversity' was a damn silly remark, but languishing in my present chastening surroundings I have had time to reflect. I made an absolute idiot of myself at Hampden Cross, old lad. You should have kicked me out into the street much sooner than you did. I can only ask you to believe that I was full of good intentions and hope that the friendship of our youth will be preserved. Could you possibly manage to fix me up with twenty-five quid? I shall be released from here at dawn on Saturday, and I could meet you in St Swithin's for a beer at lunch. Please bring the cash with you.
>
> Yours,
>
> Grim

'Good Lord!' I said to Nikki, handing her the letter. 'The poor fellow's been sent to jail, or something.'

'Foulness?' She picked up the envelope. 'I don't know if there's a prison there or not.'

'It's either that, or he's in some sort of mental institution. Poor old Grim! His career's absolutely up a gum tree now.'

Remorse struck me like the taste of some unpleasant drug. I sat at the consulting-room desk and stared gloomily at the prescription pad.

'Don't worry,' said Nikki kindly. 'It may not be as bad as it looks.'

'With Grimsdyke it generally is,' I said. 'And the whole thing's entirely my fault. He's a wonderful chap really, old Grim. We've known each other since my first day at St Swithin's. I remember it well–he taught me how to slip out of lecture-rooms without being spotted from the front. Why, we shared each other's books and beer for years. And now the unfortunate fellow's in jail because I was a bit hasty with him and kicked him out of the first regular job he ever held.'

'If you hadn't,' said Nikki, 'you'd have been spared the trouble of taking me in.'

'Oh, Lord! Sorry, Nikki. I didn't mean for one moment—'

'I'm sure you didn't.'

'It's just that I can't help feeling sorry for poor Grim. I'll have to go down and see him on Saturday. It's the least I can do. Would you mind staying on duty? And I must pop out to the bank now to collect twenty-five pounds. The chap's probably got nothing between him and starvation except the Prisoners' Aid Society, or whatever it is.'

I drove anxiously into London the next Saturday morning wishing that I had allowed more generously for my friend's enterprising spirit. I was also worrying what to say when I called at the Royal Neurological to see Dr Farquarson, who a few days before had finally fallen under the knife of his old classmate.

An Englishman's hospital is his club, and former graduates of St Swithin's often met in the musty students' common room, with its sofas looking as uncomfortable to sit in as horse-troughs and its caricatures of surgeons who had long ago pursued their patients across the Styx. I was early, and sat alone in the corner with *The Times*, reflecting how young the students were getting these days and wondering what Grimsdyke would look like when he appeared. When he did arrive he seemed in sparkling health and as cheerful as ever.

'I thought you'd been run in,' I said immediately.

'Run in? Good God, old lad! The Grimsdykes may have come close to the wind pretty often, but none of them have suffered the disgrace of ever getting caught. What on earth gave you the idea?'

'Your letter, of course. It sounded as if it had been posted from the condemned cell.'

'Ah, my letter. By the way, are you able to oblige with the small loan? Thanks a lot,' he said, pocketing the notes. 'It'll only be till I've found my feet.'

'Now I've lent you the cash you might at least tell me where you've been,' I insisted.

'In view of your opening remarks, perhaps I'd better. Possibly I overdid the pathos a bit. But my dear chap, the surroundings were really getting me down. I've had a fortnight at the Foulness Hospital.'

'What, as a locum?'

'No, as a resident guinea-pig. It's a research place–you know, where they make you catch measles to see why.'

'Oh, of course, I've heard of it–the unit that Professor MacRitchie runs?'

'That's it. If you want to find out how well you really feel, just go down there for a bit. They're always screaming for volunteers, so it's just as easy to sign on as letting yourself in for seven years in the Army. And a damned sight more uncomfortable, I should think.'

I was puzzled. 'But why on earth did you want to go there? I didn't know you were all that keen on the progress of medical science.'

'I was reduced to it, old lad. A bit *infra dig*, I thought, a doctor becoming a mere bit of research material, but I had no choice. The exchequer was pretty low when I left Hampden Cross, you know. Also, various coves in London were after my blood–hence the twenty-five quid. And I wanted time to think over a little scheme, of which I'll tell you later. I knew Foulness hospitality ran to free board and lodging and five bob a day for cigarettes, and as you're kept in complete clinical isolation even the bailiffs can't get their hands on you for a fortnight. Above all, of course, no work. You sit on your fanny and wait to sneeze. It seemed just the job at the time, and I wondered why more people didn't do it.'

'I nearly had a go at the place myself once. Quite a few of the chaps went when we were students.'

'Yes, but wait till you've seen the dump. They used it during the war as a survival school, and they haven't had to alter it much. It looks like a concentration camp up for sale as a going concern. There were about a dozen of us, and we were greeted at the gate by old MacRitchie himself. He's a tall gloomy chap with a long nose and a handshake like a wet sock full of cold porridge. He told us that we had to split into pairs and each pair could take one of the huts. I had the idea of coupling up with a nice little piece of goods from Bedford College for Women, but that apparently wasn't the idea at all. So I decided to chum with the fellow standing next to me, who was a quiet sort called Erskine who said he was a schoolmaster.

'We got on all right at first. We were put in a sort of packing-case-bungalow with all mod. cons. The food and the daily beer issue were left at the doorstep, just like the plague of London, and MacRitchie appeared every morning to drop measles virus down our noses. There were a few books, of course, but these ran largely to the *Stock Exchange Yearbook* and novels about chaps doing other chaps in by various means. There was also a draughts board. I never realized,' Grimsdyke said with sudden heat, 'what a damn silly game draughts was. After the first three days, when I was leading in the series by a hundred and six to a hundred and five, we had an argument. Old Erskine said I'd shifted a draught with the edge of my sleeve. I said I hadn't. The discussion widened. Questions of cheating at draughts, whether chaps are gentlemen or not, and the general state of family morals were brought up. With some force, I might add. We didn't actually come to blows, but we spent the rest of the day staring out of opposite windows.'

'I must say, it seems a silly thing to argue about–a game of draughts.'

'Ah, but you don't understand, Richard. The draughts squabble was only a symptom. This fellow Erskine–admirable chap that he was, no doubt, and kind and thoughtful to his little pupils–had the most irritating habit of saying "Doncherknow?" The blasted phrase used to explode in his conversation, like land mines. You wondered when the next one was going off. Damned hard on the nerves, you understand. Also he had the most irritating way of holding his teacup with his fingers right round the bottom. If he'd only done it every *other* time, it would have been all right. It was the inevitability of the thing which got you down. Hence the sober reflections expressed in my letter.'

I sympathized with him, remembering the table habits of Mr Tuppy. 'At least, I'm relieved you suffered nothing worse. And I expect he found just as many objectionable habits in you.'

'Good Lord,' said Grimsdyke in surprise. 'That didn't occur to me.'

'But couldn't you have gone out for a walk by yourself? Even in the condemned cell you get regular exercise.'

'Oh, yes, they rather encouraged healthy walks, as long as you steered clear of other people. But the weather, old man! Pouring rain and gales for the whole fortnight. And like a fool I forgot my raincoat. I couldn't possibly have gone out. Why, I might have caught a most fearful infection.'

I laughed, and told him, 'May I say how glad I am that this unfortunate experience has anyway led to the re-establishment of diplomatic relations between us?'

'My dear Richard, and so am I. I behaved like a moron, and I'm sorry.'

'No, no, Grim! I was a bit edgy having the responsibility for Farquy's practice on my plate.'

We shook hands.

'Let us cement our reconciliation in the usual way,' he suggested.

'Capital idea!'

We went across the road to the King George.

After the first pint Grimsdyke remarked, 'You're looking full of beans, Richard. Hard work must agree with you, or something. Have you got anyone else to help you?'

I nodded as I slowly filled my pipe. 'I've got a woman doctor, actually.'

He whistled. 'Good God, old man! How simply ghastly for you. I can just see her now–some frightful piece with legs like a billiard-table, who walks like a haycart turning a corner. I suppose she's got spectacles and dandruff and knows everything?'

'As a matter of fact, she isn't at all like that. She's one of the best-looking girls I've come across.'

'Really? Then she's ruddy hopeless as a doctor.'

'On the contrary, she's very good. She gets on well with the patients, works hard, doesn't miss a thing, knows all the latest stuff, manages all the sick kids and midder—'

'Look here, old lad.' Grimsdyke suddenly stared at me narrowly. 'Have you got any social life in common with this–this piece?'

'Well–I must admit I've taken her out to dinner.'

'Oh yes? You mean you think she's a case of malnutrition, or are you getting soft on her?'

I suddenly decided that there was no point in self-deception over the diagnosis any longer. I had to talk to someone. I drew a deep breath.

'I'm terribly in love with her,' I said.

Grimsdyke spilt his beer.

'Think! Think, old lad!' he implored. 'You can't mean it? You can't! Or can you?'

'But it's wonderful,' I continued, as the idea crept through my consciousness like sunshine on a spring morning. 'Nikki's absolutely a girl in a million.'

'But you can't go about the country falling in love with girls at your age!'

'Why ever not? My endocrine system isn't past it.'

'I mean,' Grimsdyke protested hotly, 'you're not an impoverished medical student any more. She'll expect you to marry her.'

'I only wish she did,' I sighed.

Grimsdyke seemed to find words difficult.

'But think what it *means*, old lad! Staring at her every morning over the top of the *Daily Telegraph* for the rest of your life. Listening to the funny noise she makes when she cleans her teeth. Waking up every night and hearing her snore. There's nothing romantic about marriage. Oh, I know all about it. I've lived with a few hotsies in my time. Once you get the sex stuff worked out of your system it's just like the measles place. Think of it, Richard! She probably says "Doncherknow" and holds her teacup all wrong.'

'Nikki does *not* say "Doncherknow". She happens to be a remarkably good conversationalist.'

'This is terrible,' Grimsdyke went on, wiping his forehead with his silk handkerchief. 'You don't want to get married, I assure you, old man. Not till you're too old to go out in the evenings anyway. Think of the fun and games you can have yet. Look here–just to restore you to your senses, let's ring up a couple of nice bits of crumpet and all go out together and have a hell of a good party? I don't even mind going back to Foulness to pay for the treat. It would be a useful social service.'

I shook my head. 'I'm afraid I've got to get back to Hampden Cross. I promised Nikki I'd look in tonight.'

'There you are! You might as well be married already. Just because she lets you get into bed with her—'

'She does *not* let me get into bed with her! I mean, I haven't even tried to find out.'

'Then what the hell's the use of rushing back then?'

It was clear that Grimsdyke had given me up for lost. He shortly had to hurry away, throwing more warnings over his shoulder, to meet a chap in a pub in Fleet Street. I went to visit Dr Farquarson in the Royal Neurological in Bayswater.

It was a wonderful day. It had been one of those rare sunlit autumn mornings when the English countryside looks as if it had been specially designed by Mr Rowland Hilder, and now even Oxford Street seemed as carefree as a fairground as I pulled up benevolently at pedestrian crossings and smiled chivalrously to jostling taxi-drivers at traffic lights. I had been in love before–I shivered to remember that a few months ago I was in love with Florence Nightingale–but those were just transient attacks compared with the real, florid, full-blown disease I was now suffering. Why, I asked myself as I light-heartedly weaved my way round Marble Arch, should it be Nikki? Was it simply the accident of work throwing us together? I decided there was clearly more to it than that, or I'd long ago have married one of the pretty hand-maidens of medicine at St Swithin's. Perhaps it could all be explained biologically. Something in Nikki's arrangement of hereditary genes appealed to something in the arrangement of my hereditary genes, with the eventual object of producing something else with an arrangement of genes suitable for the continuance of the human race. Meanwhile, all the chemicals with impossible formulae that I had tried to learn in biochemistry were pouring out of my endocrine glands like juice from over-ripe oranges, and giving me this delightful outlook on life. Having confessed my condition to Grimsdyke I wanted to tell everyone in sight, even the policeman holding me up at the bottom of Edgware Road. The only person I felt I should keep in the dark was Dr Farquarson, who might lie in bed developing doubts on the efficient running of his practice.

'Wonderful thing, modern surgery,' Dr Farquarson told me, as I found him sitting up in excellent shape, cleaning his pipe with one of the hospital's throat-swabs. 'When they took my appendix out somewhere in the Highlands they stifled me with chloroform and handed me a bucket automatically when I came round. Here a charming young feller came in and pricked me with a needle, and the next thing I knew I was back in bed asking the lass where my teeth were. Now they say I can think about starting work again in a couple of weeks.'

'A couple of weeks!' I said, aghast.

'Yes, and that's not soon enough for me. They don't take long to get you on your feet after surgery these days. It's all the vogue, I hear, to get the patient to push his own trolley back to the ward.'

'But a fortnight!' I exclaimed. 'That's hardly any time at all. After a serious operation—'

'Oh, in Bobbie Cufford's hands it isn't at all serious.'

'I mean . . . well, you never know what complications might ensue

–fractured vertebra, meningitis, all kinds of things. I really think you ought to have a rest, Farquy. How about a long sea voyage in the sunshine?'

I became aware that he, too, was looking at me strangely.

'Well, we'll see,' he said. 'How's this young lady locum getting on?'

'Oh, her? Very well, I think. I don't see much of her outside surgery hours, of course. She seems very competent.'

'Well, Richard my lad, I'll stay an invalid as long as possible. Though even for you I'm not going to stand more than a couple of weeks with my married sister in Swanage.'

Until then I had somehow overlooked that Dr Farquarson was coming back to the practice at all. Perhaps it was the prospect of his return that made me propose to Nikki that evening. Or perhaps it just happened spontaneously. Few amorous young men sit down and think out a speech and look round for a likely spot to lay their bended knee. Most of them happen to be sitting with a girl in the back of a cinema or the top of a bus, and in a couple of seconds somehow find themselves bound to her for life.

I found Nikki alone in the surgery, repacking our midwifery bag from the sterilizer. She was surprised to see me.

'You *are* back early, Richard. But everything's very quiet. Mrs Horrocks popped at lunch-time, without any trouble. Another boy, but she doesn't seem to mind.'

'Nikki,' I said. 'Nikki, I . . . that is, you see, I . . .'

'Are you all right, Richard?' She suddenly looked concerned. 'You seem rather flushed. Are you sure you haven't got a temperature?'

'I'm in wonderful shape, Nikki. Never felt better in my life. Absolutely terrific form. Nikki, you see, I—'

'Ah, I know.' She smiled. 'I'd forgotten you were meeting your old friend. I should have spotted the symptoms.'

'Honestly, Nikki, I've hardly touched a drop,' I protested. 'I may be drunk, but not with alcohol. You see, Nikki, I really must—'

'Oh, these X-rays arrived from the hospital this morning. They're Mrs Tadwich's oesophagus.'

'Nikki!' I said firmly, grabbing the brown-paper packet.

She looked startled. My nerve failed me.

'Yes, Richard?'

'I love you,' I said, as though mentioning that it was raining outside.

There was silence. Nikki suddenly looked very solemn. We both dropped our eyes and stared at the floor.

'Do you . . . do you mind?' I asked timidly.

She shook her head. 'I'm terribly, terribly touched,' she whispered.

'Would you . . . would you think of marrying me?'

For a few seconds there was another silence, broken only by the sound of the surgery refrigerator going through one of its periodical attacks of ague.

She looked up. 'That's really a very serious question, Richard.'

'I know it's serious, Nikki. Terribly serious. But . . . well . . .'

I began to have the same unpleasant feelings I experienced at the end of my viva in the Primary: things weren't going quite as swimmingly as I expected.

'You see, there's a lot of things,' she went on.

'What sort of things?'

'Well . . . there's my Fellowship, for instance.'

'Your Fellowship?'

'You may think me stupid, Richard, or heartless, or both. But I swore I'd never marry . . . or even fall in love . . . until I'd passed it. I'm a bit obsessional, I suppose. But you know what you hear–women wasting everyone's time, going in for medicine and then going off and getting married. I was determined no one could say that about me. But I'm terribly, terribly fond of you, Richard. Do you think me an ungrateful fool? I expect you do. I suppose I'm just a pig-headed little girl underneath.'

'No, not at all,' I said. There was nothing for it but to be as brave as possible. 'I think you're perfectly right. Absolutely, Nikki. I had exactly the same feelings about the Fellowship myself once. I'm sorry. I shouldn't have had the nerve to raise the subject at all.'

We talked a good deal after that. Then I kissed her good night and drove slowly back to my digs. I played cribbage with Mr Walters till midnight and I knocked over two more china ornaments.

'Had a row?' asked Kitten Strudwick a few days later.

'I beg your pardon?'

'You two. Lovers' tiff, I suppose?'

'Miss Strudwick, I am at a loss to know what you're talking about.'

'Go on with you! Why, the way you've been avoiding each other since Monday anyone would think you was both incubating the measles.'

'My relationship with Dr Barrington, if that is what you're referring to, Miss Strudwick, is strictly and completely professional. I do wish you wouldn't try and invent romance where it doesn't exist. I'm afraid you've been reading too many of the waiting-room magazines.'

'Don't worry, dearie,' she said cheerfully. 'It'll all come right in the end.'

The week had been a miserable one. I didn't visit Nikki in her flat. I didn't take her out to dinner. I saw her only briefly in the surgery, and I spoke to her only formally about medicine. I was short with Miss Strudwick, morose with the patients, forgetful with myself, and I developed a tendency to stare out of the window for long spells at a time. I suppose failure doesn't cross the mind of a young man starting a proposal any more than it occurs to a young man starting a fight, or he wouldn't embark on either. Now I realized in my periods of painful introspection gazing into the street how absurd it was for such a Caliban as myself to ask Nikki, or even any other girl, to marry him. I was simply the unmarriageable type, condemned to spend the rest of my life in digs, probably playing cribbage with Mr Walters until both of us joined Miss Ashworth's floating band of non-paying guests.

'I dunno,' said Kitten Strudwick, interrupting one of my bouts of window-staring a few days later. 'Why don't you give her a whopping great kiss and be done with it?'

'Miss Strudwick,' I said resignedly. 'I cannot try and hide the situation from you any longer. I appreciate sincerely the kind motives behind your advice, but I have to remind you that we're not all playing in the pictures. In real life that sort of thing isn't done. Besides,' I added, 'it wouldn't work.'

'It would work all right with me, I can tell you.'

'Possibly. But not with . . . other people.'

'Oh, don't you be so sure. All girls are the same underneath. Look at all them kings and queens you read about in *Everybody's*.'

'You would spare my feelings, Miss Strudwick, if you began to realize–as I do–that Dr Barrington wishes to have nothing whatever to do with me outside our mutual professional interests.'

'Go on with you! Why the poor girl's eating her heart out. I've just been talking to her.'

'What?' I asked in horror. 'You mean you've actually been discussing me with her?'

''Course I have, dear. In a roundabout sort of way, mind you. But a girl's got to get it off her chest to someone, hasn't she? Even if it's only to yours truly.'

'I think perhaps you'd better get the next patient in, Miss Strudwick.'

'Okeydoke. Don't forget what I said, though.'

It happened that that evening Nikki and I found ourselves together for the first time in several days, through Miss Strudwick abruptly leaving us alone in the surgery.

'How's the work going?' I asked as breezily as possible.

'Work?' She looked up from an intense search through the filing cabinet.

'For the Fellowship.'

'Oh, quite well. Quite well, thank you.'

'Difficult exam, of course, the Fellowship.'

'Yes, it is. Very.'

'Only ten per cent pass, so they say.'

'So they say.'

I fiddled with an ampoule of pencillin.

'I expect we'll see each other before you go next week,' I said. 'To say good-bye, I mean.'

'Yes. Yes, of course. I expect we will.'

At the door she hesitated. 'Richard—'

'Yes?'

'I–er, talking of the Fellowship, I'm having a bit of trouble trying to learn up my pathology. You used to be a pathologist at St Swithin's, didn't you?'

I nodded.

'Could you possibly spare a moment some time before I go–just to come up and run through some blood slides?'

I felt the least I could do after forcing my attentions on the girl was to teach her a little pathology.

'Of course. I'll do anything to help, Nikki. I'll bring up my microscope tonight.'

There are few situations leading to such intimacy between a man and a woman as sharing the same microscope. You have to sit close together, with your heads touching as you take turns to look down the eyepiece, and your fingers keep getting mixed altering the focusing screws. It happened as unexpectedly as a sneeze. We were calmly discussing the pathology of pernicious anaemia and I was pointing out the large number of megaloblasts at the other end of the instrument, when I looked up and said, 'Oh, Nikki!' and she said, 'Oh, Richard!' and she was suddenly in my arms and I was kissing her wildly and we were going to be married.

Chapter Fourteen

Nikki and I, like several million others, decided on a 'quiet' wedding. But there is as little chance of planning a quiet wedding as planning a quiet battle: too many people are involved, all with conflicting interests. To the bride, the event seems mainly an excuse for the uninhibited buying of clothes; to the groom, the most complicated way of starting a holiday yet devised. The bride's friends see it as a social outing with attractive emotional trimmings, and the bridegroom's as the chance of a free booze-up. The relatives are delighted at the opportunity to put on their best hats and see how old all the others are looking, and to the parents it comes as a hurricane in the placid waters of middle-age.

It is a shock to any young man when he realizes that his fiancée has parents. I had always seen Nikki as a single star outglittering the firmament, and it was strange to think that she belonged to a family like everyone else. But my first duty as a betrothed man was to meet them, and this was arranged for teatime the following Saturday on the polite excuse of my coming to ask her father's permission to propose.

'I'm terribly sorry to shoot off so soon after you're back at work,' I apologized to Dr Farquarson before I left Hampden Cross. He had taken my original breathless news with disappointing calmness. But he was the sort of man who on hearing the Last Trump will only demand who's making that horrible din.

'So you're off to be inspected, then?' He gave a quiver of the eyebrows. 'Well, I can think of pleasanter ways to spend a Saturday afternoon, to be sure. I remember when I first faced the parents of my own poor dear wife. She was the daughter of a Presbyterian minister with views. I'd only one suit at the time and I'd just got in from a midwifery case, so I reeked to high heaven of chloroform. Her father had hardly opened the door before he accused me of being at the bottle. I told him that if a man couldn't distinguish the smell of whisky he wasn't fit to preach to Scots parishioners. After that we got along excellently.'

I laughed. 'I expect I shall drop my tea on the best carpet and trip over the cat and give all the wrong opinions on her father's pet subjects.'

'Och, it'll be no worse than your surgery finals. Don't fash yourself.'

Nikki had now left the practice, and I was meeting her for lunch in the West End before driving out to her parents' home at Richmond. Once I saw her again all thoughts of my coming teatime ordeal flashed away. We drove over Kew Bridge in tremendous spirits, our conversation running largely to 'Is my little bunny-wunny quite comfy-wumfy?' 'Of course your little bunny-wunny's quite comfy-wumfy if my big bunny-wunny is', which proves that everyone becomes slightly unhinged at such times in their lives.

The Barringtons lived in a pleasant white house by the River, and as I stopped in the short drive the door was flung open by a pink-faced young man of about eighteen with whipcord trousers, a check sports jacket, and a pipe the size of some small wind instrument.

'Richard, this is Robin, my young brother,' Nikki said as we got out of the car.

He gave me the look of deep suspicion reserved by men for chaps likely to go off with their sisters.

'Fancy anyone wanting to marry Nikki.'

'Robin, don't be a beast!'

'I thought you'd marry Bill Wharton.'

'Robin!'

Noticing that I looked surprised, he added, 'Oh, Bill Wharton was an old friend of Nikki's. Didn't you know?'

'Robin! Really!'

'Anyway, how do you do,' he said, shaking hands powerfully. 'I say,' he went on, indicating my modest saloon car. 'That isn't this year's model, is it?'

'Yes, it is, as a matter of fact.'

He whistled. 'But didn't you know? On that model the back axle always goes after ten thou. You ought to have got one of last year's.'

'Good Lord, does it?'

'I think we'd better go and face the family,' said Nikki, taking my arm.

Bracing myself, I followed her into the house.

The Barringtons' sitting-room looked like the third act of a domestic comedy when the curtain had just gone up. To the right, a slim dark woman who might have passed as Nikki's elder sister was sitting behind a tea-tray. Centre, his back to the fireplace and hands deep in his jacket pockets, stood Commander Barrington. He was a tall, grey-haired man in a blue suit, who I gathered from Nikki had now given up sailing ships for insuring them. Symmetrically on the left was an older woman in a yellow dress that seemed to be composed mainly of fringes, whom I took to be Aunt Jane. Aunt Jane, Nikki had explained, lived with them and had a secret of amazing complexity. All three were now looking at me with the strained but polite interest shown by parents when their young children appear during cocktail parties with some strange object found in the garden.

'Mummy, this is Richard.'

'So you're *really* going to marry Nikki!' exclaimed Mrs Barrington at once.

'Shush, shush, Connie!' whispered the Commander loudly. 'We're not supposed to know about it yet.'

'Oh! Of course.'

I was introduced all round. Then there was silence, broken only by Robin blowing loudly through his pipe. But the Commander, clearly the man for any crisis, said heartily, 'How about a spot of tea?'

'Milk or lemon?' said Mrs Barrington with great relief.

The British nation is fortunately at its best when overpowering some awkward social situation, whether caused by mutual embarrassment or water suddenly appearing through the dining-saloon deck. The brilliant national ruse of discussing the weather allowed us all to exchange stereotyped phrases while wondering what the devil to talk about next, then the Commander and I maintained a thoughful conversation on fishing before realizing that neither knew anything whatever about the subject. Aunt Jane started to say something about her tragic life but was silenced by an abrasive glance from Nikki's mother, and Robin found time to tell me that my particular make of watch and fountain-pen were unfortunately those known to collapse inexplicably during use. I made an unfortunate noise drinking my tea and I dropped a cake plate on the poodle, but the occasion wasn't nearly as bad as I had feared. I felt that the Barringtons were relieved to find that at least I didn't lick the jam spoon or suffer from multiple tics.

'I expect,' said Nikki with a meaning look as the cups were being stacked, 'that you and Daddy want to have a word together?'

'A word?' The Commander sounded as if nothing had been farther from his mind. 'Yes, of course. By all means. Anything you like. Perhaps you'd like to step into my cubby-hole, Richard?'

I followed him to a small room on the other side of the house, which was filled with books and decorated with pictures and models of ships. The terrifying moment had come at last. The scene was so familiar from comic drawings that now I didn't know how to perform it. Did I stand to attention and ask for the honour of the hand of his daughter? Or did I just make some sort of joke about adding Nikki to my income-tax? Either approach would not only make me look foolish but–as I hadn't taken the measure of the Commander yet–might land me in the Thames.

I caught his eye. I suddenly realized that he was as nervous as I was.

'How about a gin?' he suggested.

'What a good idea, sir.'

'I was afraid you were a teetotaller.'

'Teetotaller? But what on earth gave you that impression?'

'Nikki said you were sober in your habits.'

'Good lord! I hope she isn't too blinded by love.'

'Wasn't that meal absolutely ghastly?' he said, taking a bottle and two glasses from a cupboard. 'Talk about torture by teacups.'

I made some polite remark about the nice cakes.

'The trouble is, women will insist on doing things that way. I hate tea usually. Never eat it. I generally have a cup alone in the potting-shed. Water?'

'Thank you.'

'And didn't you think we were about the dreariest family in creation?'

This remark was not what I had expected. 'But I thought that was what you were thinking about me.'

'You! You looked frightfully composed and superior.'

'If I may say so, sir that's just what struck me about you.'

'Good God! I've been sweating blood at the thought of this afternoon for a week.'

We both laughed.

'Besides which, you blighter,' the Commander continued, handing me my drink, 'you've done me out of a perfectly good afternoon's golf. Do you play?'

'Yes, I do a bit, as it happens.'

We discussed golf for twenty minutes over a couple more gins, then the Commander stood up and said, 'I suppose we'd better go back to the ladies.'

I re-entered the sitting-room feeling much better than when I had left it.

'Sorry we've been so long, Connie,' Nikki's father said jovially. 'But we seemed to find a lot of things to discuss. Richard here's coming down one Sunday, and Robin and I'll make up a foursome with old Doc Clark. You'll like Clark, Richard–a good scout, though he does putt like a one-armed fiddler. We'll give you a run for your money all right.'

'It's really very kind of you to invite me.'

'Not a bit. Delighted to see you. Can't tell you what a strain it is, playing against the same old crowd week after week. It might do my game a power of good. Couldn't do it much worse, eh, Connie?'

'What did Father say?' whispered Nikki, beside me on the sofa.

'Say? What about?'

'About *us*, of course.'

'Good Lord, Nikki! As a matter of fact I completely forgot to ask him.'

None of the family raised the subject again, and in a few minutes we were all discussing where Nikki and I were going for our honeymoon.

'This is my father,' I said, introducing Nikki.

'My dear Sally! How delighted I am to see you at last.'

'Not Sally, Father. I think you've—'

'But how perfectly stupid of me. How are you, Cynthia?'

'Nikki, Father, Nikki. And here comes my mother. Mother, this is Nikki.'

It was the return fixture the following week. Nikki went through it more comfortably than I did. Within ten minutes she was sitting close to my mother by the fire, cosily discussing the technical details of wedding-dresses.

'But I *must* show you these, Nikki.' My mother suddenly produced a large leather-bound scrap-book from her bureau. I viewed this with intense alarm. I had for years suspected its existence in the house, like some unpleasant family ghost, but I had hoped that it would never be materialized in my presence.

'Not that, Mother!' I cried.

'Why ever not, Richard? Nikki will be terribly interested. The first ones aren't very good,' she explained, opening the pages. 'That was taken when he was three months. Wasn't he sweet, with his little frilly nightie?' Nikki gave a delighted gurgle. 'And this one was when he was two, down on the beach with nothing on at all. And this one—'

'Mother, I'm sure Nikki really isn't at all interested. . . .'

'But I am, Richard, tremendously. And I don't think you've changed a bit. Especially when you've forgotten to get your hair cut.'

'*Didn't* he have lovely curls? Here's the one of him down at Frinton in his little sailor suit. . . .'

I had to sit for twenty minutes while my future wife followed me from infant nudity to my academic gown and rabbit's fur hood, holding my qualifying diploma and sharing a corner of a Greek temple with a palm in a brass pot. I felt this gave her a bitterly unfair advantage in our marriage before it had started.

'If we have any children,' I said, as we started to drive back towards London, 'I'm going to take dozens and dozens of photographs of them and put them in the bank. It's a better way of keeping them in their place than a slipper or a child psychiatrist.'

'But I thought they were lovely, darling. Particularly when you were an oyster in the *Walrus and the Carpenter*.'

I groaned.

'Nikki,' I said. 'If you still want to marry me after that, shall we have the wedding on February the first?'

'In two months' time? But why particularly the first?'

'It'll be a nice easy date for me to remember for anniversaries.'

'Of course, darling.'

'We'll put it in *The Times* on Monday,' I said.

Chapter Fifteen

'Whom *The Times* hath joined together let no man put asunder,' said Dr Farquarson, as I proudly showed him the page.

'We'd have been top of the column, too,' I said, 'if some blasted Honourable hadn't been allowed to jump the queue as usual. Son of a Socialist peer into the bargain, I shouldn't be surprised.'

'Well, it looks very fine. You know, it's an odd thing, but I hardly glance at the Engagements column myself now. I did when I was a young fellow like you. Then my attention shifted to the Births, and now I suppose I look at the Deaths for my morning's satisfaction. Surprising how you can tell a man's age from the way he opens his newspaper, isn't it? But it'll make your friends sit up over their breakfast all right.'

He had hardly finished speaking when the telephone rang. It was Grimsdyke.

'My dear fellow!' he said in alarm. 'You'll have a hell of a job getting out of it now.'

'But I don't want to get out of it.'

'What? You mean–you actually want to go through with it and marry the girl?'

'Of course I do. I'd do so tomorrow if it was considered decent.'

'But what on earth for?'

'Well, for one thing I'll be able to get out of my digs. Also, I love her.'

'But are you crazy, old lad? You must be! Marriage is a much too serious business to be decided by the emotions. And have you ever actually been to a wedding? Just think of yourself in some beastly reception-rooms off the Brompton Road, with not enough to drink and all the aunts in their best mink tippets and everyone making frightful speeches about going down life's path together and all your troubles being little ones. There'll probably be beastly little boys in pink silk suits, too,' he said with added horror. 'No, no, old lad. Think again. Get a job on a ship and stay out of the country for a couple of years. Remember there's always that useful little escape paragraph underneath saying the fixture will not now take place.'

'I hope the reception won't be too terrible,' I told him. 'Because you're going to have a leading part in it.'

'Me?'

'I want you to be best man, Grim, if you will.'

'My dear chap, I'd lose the ring and get the telegrams all mixed up.'

'Look,' I suggested. 'Nikki's coming out here tonight. If you're free, drive up from town and we'll all have dinner together.'

After some persuasion he agreed, adding, 'As a matter of fact, old lad, there's a certain little scheme I've started that I'd like to tell you about. I'll come down about seven. It'll be a bit of a treat for uncle. I know the poor old chap's dying to set eyes on me again.'

'My friend Grimsdyke,' I warned Nikki, as the 1930 sports car pulled up noisily outside the surgery, 'is a rather unconventional character. He also has a fertile imagination. I mean, if he should start telling tales of things that used to happen when we were students together, they'll be pure fabrications. A great chap for making up embarrassing stories about people, old Grimsdyke.' I gave a little laugh. 'Not a word of truth in them from beginning to end.'

The doorbell rang loudly.

'Nikki,' I said, 'this is Gaston Grimsdyke, known to one and all as Grim. Grim, this in Nikki.'

I had never seen Grimsdyke put out before. His was such a self-assured character that not even the shock of passing his final examinations had upset him. But Nikki seemed to throw him off his psychological balance. I believe that he really thought I had shackled myself to someone looking like a Russian long-distance runner, and he was flummoxed to find a neat little blonde beside me on the doorstep.

'But, my dear Richard . . .' he said, rapidly recovering his poise. 'My dear Richard, my heartiest congratulations. Lots of long life and happiness to you both, and so on.' Taking Nikki's hand he bowed low and kissed her knuckles loudly. 'My dear fellow, I *do* congratulate you.'

'Well, Grim,' I said proudly, as nothing flatters a man more than impressing his philandering friends with his fiancée. 'I hope you approve of the bride?'

'Approve? Good heavens, yes, my dear fellow! If I may say so, Nikki, I consider old Richard's taste has improved immeasurably in his old age. When I think of some of those bits you used to go about with at St Swithin's, Richard–I mean, damn it, when I think of . . . of . . .'

'Shall we go straight out to dinner?' suggested Nikki helpfully.

'Delighted.'

Grimsdyke bowed and kissed her hand again.

'If I may use the phrase,' said Grimsdyke, when the three of us were swallowing the Bull's staunchly English coffee, 'you're a very lucky man, Richard.' He reached for Nikki's hand on the tablecloth and patted it in a fatherly manner. 'Nikki, may I say that you are quite the most beautiful and charming girl I've met since I once asked Vivien Leigh for her autograph.'

'Now isn't that sweet of him, Richard?'

'And the thought that old Richard can send you out and make you work as well almost makes me wish I wasn't a confirmed bachelor.'

'I'm really the lucky one,' Nikki told him. 'Don't forget Richard's a confirmed bachelor, too.'

'Ah, yes,' he said, giving her hand another fond pat. 'He won't be able to go round looking at girls' legs any more.'

'Oh, I don't know,' I interrupted. I felt that Grimsdyke was turning the meal into a *tête-à-tête*. 'He who has plucked the fairest rose in the garden can still admire the stalks of some of the others.'

But Grimsdkye took no notice, and continued staring into Nikki's eyes. 'I want you always to think of me as an old, old friend of the family,' he said.

'What's this scheme of yours, Grim?' I said forcefully. I was now definitely uneasy. I remembered the time Grimsdyke had neatly charmed away from me a chorus girl from the Windmill, in whom I had already invested most of my quarter's allowance. 'The one you mentioned on the phone.'

'Ah, the scheme, old lad. Yes, of course. I'm a bit of a rolling stone down the avenues of medicine,' he explained to Nikki, still absent-mindedly holding her fingers. 'Never will you see Grimsdyke as the dear old G.P. who's brought half the district into the world and pushed the other half out of it. I'm an individualist, which is a dead loss these days when everyone gets pushed steadily up the N.H.S. ladder, unless you fall off with a coronary on the way. Making a private ladder of your own is somewhat frowned on. Some outside job, like personal physician to an old millionaire with a fondness for travel and no relatives, would suit me down to the ground. Or doctor to some posh hotel–private suite, of course, and use of cellar. But those rackets have been buttoned up long ago. Now at last I've really found something that gives me freedom of action and limitless opportunity.'

'You're going on an Antarctic expedition?' suggested Nikki.

'Good Lord, nothing *uncomfortable*. Do you remember, Richard, when I was Editor of the *St Swithin's Hospital Gazette*?'

I nodded. This was a slim magazine which appeared in the hospital with the irregularity of fine days in April. The editorial duties were not trying, because its pages contained mostly rugger reports and lectures by the senior staff to dull too be published elsewhere. Grimsdyke took the job not through literary ambition, but because he had heard that the medical publishers trustingly sent a steady supply of free textbooks for review. These Grimsdyke appraised personally, before taking them to the second-hand medical bookseller's round the corner and getting half-price . I remember that I once left my own new copy of Bailey and Love's *Surgery* on the editorial desk while I went to a lecture, and returned to find the book already sold and the review on its way to the printers.

'And a very efficient Editor I was too, if I may say so,' Grimsdyke told Nikki, giving more fatherly pats to her forearm. 'Do you remember my account of old Professor Worthington's funeral, Richard? Real good stuff it was. Bags of dignity. It wasn't my fault the damn fool printer put it under "Sports News". Anyway, on the strength of such experience,' he went on proudly, 'plus a bit of salesmanship, I managed to persuade the cove I met in the Fleet Street pub the other day actually to publish some of my stuff in his paper.'

'What about? If it's racing tips you won't last long.'

'No, no, old lad. I became forthwith "Our Harley Street Specialist", ready to write about anything at the drop of a guinea from scabies to rabies and cardiology to calf's foot jelly.'

'That sounds terribly grand,' said Nikki.

'But aren't you going to find it a bit stiff? Writing like the combined Professors of Medicine, Surgery, and Obstetrics?'

'My dear old lad, don't be silly. Do you suppose those characters in Fleet Street know the slightest thing of what they're writing about? I just go down to the St Swithin's library, take the librarian out for a beer, and curl up with the *British Encyclopaedia of Medical Practice*. You pick a nice good morbid subject like hanging or hermaphrodites, and write it out as though you were describing the Cup Final. There you are. The public love it. My first article, as a matter of fact, appears tomorrow morning–a jolly piece about how to commit suicide, and apparently it's just the sort of stuff they want to buck their readers up over breakfast.' He looked at the clock. 'Good God, I must be going! The paper will be on sale round the Fleet Street coffee-stalls in about an hour's time, and professional though I now am, I'm still bursting to see what it looks like in print.'

'You'll be my best man, then?' I asked, as we stood by our two cars outside the pub.

'My dear old lad, how could I refuse with such a charming girl as Nikki coming to the wedding?' He slipped his arm round her waist and squeezed her tightly. 'Now in view of my official position in the proceedings, may I kiss the bride?' He did so, making quite a noise over it. 'And you *are* charming, Nikki, my dear,' he told her, patting her cheek. 'Much too good for old Richard. As an old friend of the family I shall now also claim the privilege of kissing you good night.'

'Here, steady on!' I said. I now wished that I'd asked Nikki's brother to do the job instead.

Grimsdyke looked round in surprise. 'But it's all right, old man. The best man's allowed to kiss the bride before the wedding.'

'But not too long before. Or too long after,' I added firmly.

We exchanged glances, and for a second we might have had another of our Hampden Cross rows. But Grimsdyke suddenly realized that he was not behaving like a doctor and a gentleman, and Nikki said tactfully, 'Perhaps we'd all better be getting along.'

'Of course.' Grimsdyke put out his hand. 'Sorry, old lad. Understandable enthusiasm. Anyway, Lords Beaverbrook and Rothermere have probably been charging up and down Fleet Street looking for me with cheque books for the last half-hour. I'll just bid the happy couple good night and push off.'

'Your friend Grimsdyke may be a charming young man,' said Nikki, as we drove away. 'But he's as fresh as a new-laid egg.'

'He had me a bit worried,' I confessed. 'I've seen him in action too many times in the past. He'd just got to the end of his opening manoeuvres.'

'Is that so? Well, I could hardly have slapped his face over the Welsh rarebit. But I will next time if you like, darling.'

'Oh, don't slap my dear old friend Grimsdyke's face,' I told her. 'Just kick him hard on the kneecap instead.'

'I don't really think he means it,' said Nikki charitably. 'It's just that he looks on life like an excited small boy climbing a big tree.'

'You know, I've often tried to analyse old Grim. And I think you've put your finger exactly on it.'

We drove in silence for a while, agreeably breaking the Highway Code by holding hands on the steering-wheel.

'That's the best man fixed, anyway,' I said. 'We've told the parents, bought the ring, put it in *The Times*, and fixed my holiday for the honeymoon. What else is there to do until they call the banns?'

'To start with,' said Nikki, 'we must really look for somewhere to live.'

Chapter Sixteen

'I'm not going to *sell* you a house,' said Mr Slivers of Slivers and Sons, estate agents at Hampden Cross. He was a fat, red-faced, tweedy man with the cosy manner of a good G.P. 'Oh, no, Doctor. That's not our policy at all. We're going to let you *buy one from us*. There's no salesmanship about this firm,

Doctor. No pressure. We show you the residence and you make up your mind. If you don't like it we won't worry in the least, even though it means showing you every property in Hampden Cross. Cigarette?'

'Thank you.'

'What sort of residence did you have in mind?' he asked.

'A two-roomed flat with central heating,' I said.

'Something detached with at least two bedrooms and a garden for the washing,' said Nikki.

We looked at each other.

'Well, now,' said Mr Slivers paternally. 'I'm sure we can find a residence that will satisfy you both. Here are particulars of some most attractive properties, Doctor.' He handed me a sheaf of duplicated sheets. 'Just ask for the keys. Our junior will be pleased to show you round at your convenience.'

There is nothing that brings home to a young man the full seriousness of marriage more than buying a house. I had begun that morning by paying a call on my family's solicitors, Doubleday, Westmoreland, Berridge, and Horsepath in Chancery Lane. These names seemed now to be only window-dressing, the firm being run by a Mr Robbinson, whom I had known since I sat on his knee and listened to his gold watch while he patted me on the head and called me 'the little legatee'. I therefore felt entitled to bounce into his office exclaiming, 'Good morning, Mr Robbinson. I've got magnificent news–I'm going to be married.'

The natural boisterousness of a young man in love was augmented by a crisp January morning and the expectation of meeting Nikki for lunch, and tossing my hat on to a pile of pink-taped papers I continued, 'Absolutely terrific, isn't it? Such a wonderful feeling! The whole of life seems to be going past in Technicolor.'

Mr Robbinson sniffed. The solicitor was a skilled sniffer. When you said anything he doubted, he sniffed with his right nostril; if he disbelieved you, he sniffed with his left; if he thoroughly disapproved as well, he gave you both barrels. He was a tall, thin, white-haired, stooping man with a long nose, who wouldn't have looked out of place standing on one leg in a pond in the zoo. His office, like that of all the best London solicitors, looked like an illustration from *Bleak House*, and he himself sat in a legal mortuary of black tin boxes marked with clients' names and 'Deceased' after them in lighter paint.

'A marriage, eh?' Mr Robbinson always addressed clients in a gloomy undertone directed towards his top waistcoat button.

'That's the idea,' I continued brightly. 'Saturday, February the first, two-thirty at the church. Of course, I've told Nikki–that's my fiancée–all about you, and we'd both be tickled pink if you'd come along. But first of all we're buying a house, and I'd like you to fiddle all the legal stuff for us.'

'You wish me to act for you?' asked Mr Robbinson, sniffing with both nostrils.

A cold draught seemed to rattle the parchment bones of his dead litigation.

'Yes, please,' I said.

Mr Robbinson drew a blank sheet of paper carefully towards him. 'I think you are wise. House purchase has many pitfalls. If the original deeds are not in order you might easily find yourself evicted from the messuage without compensation.'

'Oh, really?'

'Then there is the inevitable heavy expenditure. You will, I take it, need a mortgage? And I trust you understand that after marriage the income of your wife is added to your own for tax purposes?'

'Yes,' I replied brightly. 'I know that these days the Government are making it so much cheaper for people to live in sin.'

He gave me his three sniffs in succession. 'I will attend to the alteration of your P.A.Y.E. coding. When did you say was the date of your change in tax status?'

'February the first,' I said, in a subdued voice.

'Have you made a will?' he asked.

'Good Lord! Is it as bad as that? I mean, ought I to?'

'It would be wise. I will draw you a draft will this afternoon. You may have one drawn specifically in anticipation of your marriage, if you wish. Then it can be signed immediately after the ceremony.'

'I think it might be more agreeable all round if I just had an ordinary one to sign here, Mr Robbinson.'

'Very well. It would, of course, be more prudent to make provision in the will for your wife's death as well as your own. Supposing that you were involved in a motor accident on your way back from the church? I will insert a clause stating that she must survive a month longer than you to inherit. Thus we would avoid double estate duty.' Mr Robbinson found little to amuse him in life, but he now gave a laryngitic laugh at the expense of the Inland Revenue. 'Then there is the possibility of issue.'

'Issue? Oh, you mean . . .'

I saw myself telling Nikki that I was going to pin the nappies on the issue.

'And you will naturally have to make adequate arrangements for the death of the issue, too,' continued Mr Robbinson, warming to his work. 'I would also advise you to take out a life policy for your wife's widowhood. Then there will be the questions of house insurance and sickness benefit. The pitfalls,' he repeated, shaking his head, 'are very, very many. And now as an old friend of the family, may I wish you every happiness?'

'The house agent was better than old Robbinson,' I told Nikki, as we left Mr Slivers' office with the Junior, a lad of sixteen who seemed to have slipped through the fingers of the Lunacy Commissioners. 'This morning I felt like a patient coming in for an operation and being told he'd make a jolly fine post mortem.'

'Poor Richard! You did rather look as though you'd seen your own ghost. I'm sure marriage can't be quite as bad as that.'

'Well, we'll soon find out, won't we? Anyway, we can always cheer ourselves up reading our wills to each other across the fireplace.'

'If we have a fireplace.'

'That's the point. Good Lord,' I said, as the Junior stopped outside a large, gloomy, overgrown, mildewy Victorian villa. 'Is this the desirable period residence with many interesting features? It looks more like Borley Rectory in its heyday.'

In the next fortnight we saw a large number of residences, none of which, in disagreement with Mr Slivers, gave us any desire to live in them at all. All we gained was a campaigner's knowledge of house agents' tactics. We soon found that 'A spacious residence' described something big enough to lodge a boarding-school, and 'a compact dwelling' meant that the front door opened directly into the parlour. 'An easily run modern apartment' indicated that the owners had left behind their old refrigerator, and 'property capable of improvement' was another way of saying the place was ready for the demolition squad. Anything described as 'suitable for a gentleman' meant that it was criminally expensive, 'very convenient for station' showed that it backed on to the railway lines, and 'an unusual house of character' meant the local eyesore. We began to develop sore feet, frayed tempers, and an envy of the nomadic life.

'If we don't find anything we like this afternoon,' I said, as we rested our tired legs with a pub lunch, 'I'm going to give up the whole idea of a house. We'll try for a furnished flat in some beastly block somewhere in London, and I'll sleep on the surgery couch when I'm on duty.'

Nikki disagreed. 'I want to start with a place of my own. I've lived among other people's furniture far too long as it is.'

I caught her eye. Fortunately, perhaps, I was not so dazzled by love to see that Nikki could sometimes be a highly determined young woman. But knowing my own habits, I felt that this might not be a bad thing.

'All right, darling,' I said. 'We'll carry on the search for Shangri-Là. My metatarsal arches are at your disposal until they collapse.'

'I know exactly what I really want,' Nikki went on. 'A small whitewashed cottage tucked out of sight in a country lane with a garden and a thatched roof and a twisted chimney.'

'And I expect at best we'll end up in a tasteful bijou residence convenient for shops and buses.' I sighed. 'Come along, Nikki. The idiot boy will be waiting.'

The three of us drove in my car between the depressing brick rows on the main road leading away from London. After a mile or so, the Junior stopped staring vacantly through the window and indicated a side turning. Through one of the heartening paradoxes of the English countryside we suddenly found ourselves in a quiet lane winding between tall hedges, looking much the same as when Henry Ford was still playing with his bricks.

'This is it,' said the Junior.

We stopped at a gate in the hedge. Behind the gate was a garden. In the garden was a whitewashed cottage. The roof was tiled, admittedly, but there was a tall twisting chimney.

'I don't *sell* houses,' Mr Slivers repeated, smiling benevolently. 'I only want to help you to buy one.'

'The price *is* rather on the high side—'

He made a sympathetic gesture. 'Alas, Doctor. We have to take our instructions from the vendor.'

'It needs several things doing to it,' said Nikki.

'There is scope for personal touches certainly,' Mr Slivers agreed.

'Would you mind if we thought it over?' I asked.

'But of course, Doctor. Think it over at your leisure. As long as you like. Never let it be said that we rushed a client into purchasing a property he didn't want.'

There was a knock on the door, and the Junior's head appeared.

'Mr Slivers, the other people wants to know if they can see Floral Cottage at three?'

Nikki and I sat up.

'Other people?'

'Oh, yes,' said Mr Slivers. 'And it's only been on the market since yesterday. Surprising, perhaps, but not with such a desirable rustic retreat.

Yes, Herbert, three o'clock will do. Tell them to hurry, because Major Marston will be viewing it at four.'

'Major Marston!' I jumped to my feet. 'You mean that terribly rich chap who owns the brewery?'

'That's quite right, Doctor. I think he is intending to demolish the property and build a large garage. Yes, Herbert, tell the people—'

'One moment!' I felt myself shaking a little. 'Do you think . . . is there any possibility . . . could you take just a hundred pounds less . . . ?'

'I'm *sure* that can be arranged, Doctor,' said Mr Slivers at once, producing his pen. 'Perhaps you'll let me have a cheque for the deposit? Then you can look upon the property as your own.'

Chapter Seventeen

Our first reaction to having a home of our own, or at least a ten per cent deposit on it, was to go back and dance in the garden. Then we went through every room, striking matches in the gathering twilight while Nikki delightedly planned the arrangement of our wholly hypothetical furniture. I insisted that I had my old camping kit sent from home and moved in at once, at last saying good-bye to Mr Walters and my digs. Nikki maintained that all men remain as incapable of keeping themselves fed and clean as at six months, but she agreed and later left for London to organize an expedition of her parents.

'Good heavens, you didn't pay all that for *this*?' said her brother Robin, as he smoked his way through our four small rooms next day.

I nodded.

'But didn't you get to know of the Hampden Cross housing estate? The Council are putting one up all the way round here. Heard about it from a chap in the City yesterday. Knock the value of the property for six, of course.'

I felt hot and cold sensations travel up and down my spine.

'I hadn't thought of that,' I muttered.

'Then, of course, the value of property's going to drop like a stone next Easter, anyway. All the chaps in the City could tell you that.' He jumped up and down on the bare floor-boards. 'I suppose these joists are all right. Did you have the place surveyed?'

'Ought I to have done?'

'Gosh, yes! Why, you don't know what might be the matter underneath.' He gave a deep sniff. 'I shouldn't be at all surprised if that wasn't dry rot.'

It was about this time that I started to sleep badly. My exuberance at joining the landed gentry soon turned into a bleak pessimism that our home was becoming as valueless as an igloo on a hot day. This was particularly serious, because it had now been mortgaged by Mr Robbinson to something called the Spa and Pier Employees' Retirement and Benefit Society. I knew nothing about mortgages except that they were always foreclosed on Christmas Eve in the middle of the third Act, and I had a vision of Nikki and myself barricading the place against hordes of angry pier attendants in peaked caps demanding their money back. Apart from this, the cottage seemed to attract bills as naturally as a herbaceous border attracts bees. I shortly felt that I had staked my savings and my future in something as risky as a string of racehorses, and a little while afterwards I began to wish that I had.

'We'll have to get some builders to do a few things,' said Nikki, as I drove her from the surgery to the cottage a couple of days later. 'Do you happen to know of any?'

I frowned. 'I don't think there's one among the patients, worse luck. It's always a help if you've got some sort of hold on these people.'

'How about those on the corner?'

We stopped the car by a small builders' yard with the notice:

CONTRACTORS
DOGGETT & BUZZARD

'I expect they're as good as any,' I said, as we went inside.

Mr Doggett was a tall, grey, bony man in a shiny blue suit, behind the lapels of which a pair of serviceable braces peeped coyly. He also seemed to be one of the interesting cases of hat-addiction. Although he removed his bowler in respect for Nikki as we entered, he kept it near him on the desk as we talked and was clearly itching to resume its comforting embrace as soon as we shut the door.

'You leave it all to me,' he said.

'There isn't really much that needs doing,' said Nikki. 'It's mainly a matter of stopping the water coming through the sitting-room ceiling and starting it coming out of the bathroom taps.'

I remembered the magic word. 'Can we have an estimate?' I asked.

'Estimate? By all means, Doctor. Just as soon as you like. I'll bring it round tomorrow afternoon.'

'This estimate thing doesn't look too bad,' I told Nikki over the telephone the following evening.

'What do they want to do to the place, darling?'

'Well, the estimate says "To well cut out and make good all cracks to ceiling properly prepare line and distemper same bring forward all woodwork the sum of twenty-five pounds." There's also another ten quid for something I can't understand that has to be done to the cistern. But I don't think it's going to break us.'

'That's wonderful, dearest! When are they going to start?'

'Tomorrow, if we like. Old Doggett says he's putting his three best men on the job. It's a great advantage, this estimate system, isn't it? It lets you know exactly where you are. It's a wonder surgeons don't do it. You know–"To making six-inch abdominal incision, properly securing haemostasis, clamping, dividing, and ligaturing gastric arteries, removing stomach, fully washing down, making good and suturing firmly with best-quality absorbable catgut, the sum of one hundred guineas."'

Nikki laughed on the other end of the line. 'They'd have to put "Errors and Omissions Excepted", of course. There go the pips again. Ring me tomorrow, darling one.'

Mr Doggett's three best men arrived at the cottage the morning after I had gone into residence myself with a camp bed, a primus, and the surgery oil stove, after burying several pounds' worth of broken chinaware in the garden. There was a tall thin man with a sharp bald head, a long pale face, and the expression of painful despair with mankind seen in paintings of martyred saints; there was a fat jolly man in a striped sweater and an American baseball cap; and there was an old, bent man with long moustaches and bloodhound's eyes, who shuffled slowly about the rooms and was clearly recognized by his companions as being far too senile for work of any sort.

The men greeted me kindly, putting me at ease, then started their day's work. With a private supply of sticks and coal they lit a fire in the bare sitting-room grate, put on a kettle, and settled round reading bits of the *Daily Mirror*.

'Like a cup, Guv?' called the fat man, as I finished dressing. 'We're just brewing up.'

I had to hurry away to the surgery, where Dr Farquarson was sportingly giving me breakfast, but the temptation to sneak back at lunch-time to see what they had done was irresistible. I found the three still sitting round the fire, now eating sandwiches. I wondered if they had been there all morning, but as the room was littered with paint-pots and buckets I supposed that one of them must have stirred some time.

'We're waiting for the ladders, Guv,' explained the fat man cheerfully, his mouth full of bread and beetroot. 'They've got to send 'em on the other lorry.'

I apologized for disturbing them, and retired to tidy up my own quarters. Through the open sitting-room door I heard the thin one announce, 'Surprisin' what people will buy for 'ouses these days, ain't it?'

'Yes,' agreed the fat one. 'I can't say I think much of this job. Cor! It's as draughty as a chicken run.'

'Them windows is all wrong as well. Warped.'

'And look at them floors.'

'Well, *I* wouldn't live in it, that's straight.'

'We don't 'ave to, thank Gawd. Still, I suppose the people knows what they're about. He's a doctor, ain't he?'

'Doctors is made of money,' said the old man. 'You've only got to look at the stamps on your 'ealth card.'

They then started a brisk argument on football pools, which I hoped would occupy them until it was time to knock off work.

'They've established a bridgehead,' I told Nikki on the telephone in the evening. 'They spent today consolidating their positions, and tomorrow they might begin active operations. There's one thing, thank God–even though we have to live with this trio for the first five years of our married life, Mr Doggett can't charge a penny more for it.'

I put down the instrument and was surprised to find the builder himself in the hall, looking worried and clutching his hat as though it were some sort of moral life-belt.

'Might I have a word with you, Doctor?' he asked anxiously.

'Well . . . is it urgent, Mr Doggett? I'm just starting my surgery.'

He said it was, so I suggested 'Perhaps you'd like to slip into the consulting-room for a minute?'

He sat down with his hat on his knees and announced, 'I've been looking at them there soffits of yours, Doctor.'

'Soffits?' It sounded like some sort of French confectionery.

He nodded. 'They're a bit of a joke, you know,' he continued solemnly.

'They'll all have to come off.'

'Oh, really? Would it be a big job?'

'Few shillings only, Doctor. But I thought you ought to know.'

'That's perfectly all right, Mr Doggett,' I said with relief. 'Just add it to the bill. Is that all there is?'

'Yes, that's all, Doctor. Thank you very much.' He replaced his hat and left me with the prospect of a life free of soffits, whatever they were.

When I looked into Floral Cottage during my rounds the next morning, I was glad to see that the trio had at last started work. You could tell that because they were singing. I doubted if they sang purely from the joy of artistic creation as they slapped distemper on the ceiling but rather to occupy their nervous system, because they each seemed to know only one tune. The fat man repeated *You Made Me Love You*, the thin one alternated with the first four lines of *Underneath The Arches*, and the old man whistled a bit of *William Tell* as he discharged his duty of watching the kettle boil.

'I hear you're getting married, Guv,' said the fat one as I opened the front door. They now accorded me the privilege of accepting me as an equal.

'That's right.'

'I've been married eighteen years,' remarked the thin one, between strokes of his brush, 'I wouldn't if I was you.'

'Go on with you,' said the fat one. 'There's nothing like marriage. Buttons on your shirt and hot dinners every Sunday.'

'And that's about all,' said his companion.

'I only hope,' I told them, 'that you'll be finished here before you see me carrying the bride over the threshold.'

'Don't you worry, Guv. There ain't all that much more to do.'

But that evening I was surprised to find Mr Doggett again in the hall. He was still clutching his hat and looking anxious.

'It's that there plumbing of yours, Doctor,' he said, when he had sat down.

'Plumbing? What about it?'

'Well . . . it's a bit of a joke, you know. It'll all have to come out.'

'Good God! Won't that be terribly expensive?'

'Not so much in your job, Doctor. Just a few quid, that's all.'

'If it must be done it must, I suppose. Put it on the bill.'

'Thank you, Doctor. Then there's them there fylfots of yours.'

'Fylfots!'

'They're a bit of a joke, you know. They'll all have to come out.'

'But isn't that a tremendous operation?' Fylfots sounded like something fundamental in the foundations.

'Only a few shillings, Doctor.'

'Oh, well, take them out, then.'

'Thank you, Doctor. It's a pleasure to do business with a straightforward man like yourself, if I may say so.'

The next day he appeared to tell me that the lavatory was a bit of a joke, and the one after it was the front door and something called the architraves. The following morning I was horrified to get a letter from Messrs Doggett and Buzzard respectfully requesting advance payment of seventy-five pounds in respect of work carried out at above site.

'Seventy-five pounds!' I exclaimed to Nikki on the telephone. 'Think of it! Why, the whole estimate was quids less than that. That rogue and swindler Doggett! He's been sticking it on right and left. I've a damned good mind to get Mr Robbinson to issue a writ.'

'But darling, does it matter so long as we get a nice little home of our own?'

'We'll never get a nice little home of our own. We'll get a nice little home of the Pier Attendants' Benefit Society, or whatever it is. And at this rate we won't even have enough left to buy a frying-pan and a tin opener as well. You wait.' I added, banging the phone book with my fist. 'Just wait till I see that Doggett fellow again.'

'Don't be too angry with him, dear. He seemed such a nice man.'

'Angry with him? I'll shake the blighter to his very soffits!'

I summoned Mr Doggett to see me at the surgery that evening. He sat in the patient's chair looking more miserable than usual.

'Of course, all them items mount up,' he admitted, gripping his hat.

'Mount up! I'll say they do! Why, at this rate we don't need a house at all–we can spend our entire married life at the Savoy for about half the price.'

He hung his head. 'I'm sorry, Doctor.'

'If you think I'm going to hand over seventy-five pounds just like that, Mr Doggett, you're damned well mistaken. I'm going into this matter. I'm going over your work with a magnifying glass. I'm going to get my solicitor in London—'

To my alarm, two large tears spilled from Mr Doggett's eyes down his cheeks.

'Don't be too hard on me, Doctor,' he sobbed.

'But my dear Mr Doggett, I'm so sorry. I'd no idea I'd—'

'Times are very bad with me.' He wiped his eyes lavishly on his sleeve. 'I dunno, Doctor. Once I was full of vim and go, and now I feel that miserable I don't know where to turn. I can't sleep and I can't eat proper. Sometimes I wish I wasn't here at all. I can't even have a pint to cheer myself up because of this here pain in my stomach.'

'Pain?' I looked interested. 'How long have you had it?'

'A year, on and off. I'm not signed on with any doctor, you see.'

I looked at him earnestly. 'As you're here, perhaps you'd better lie down on the couch and slip off your things,' I suggested. 'Do you get the pain before or after food? And is there any sickness?'

'Of all the builders in Hampden Cross we had to pick the neurotic one,' I told Nikki when she came up the next day. 'Why, the poor chap's a melancholic. And he's got a functional dyspepsia, or even a duodenal ulcer, into the bargain. Damn it! I ought to have spotted it when I first set eyes on him.'

'What did you do, dear?'

'What could I do? I couldn't just say, "It's a bit of a joke you know, it'll all have to come out." I took him on as a patient.'

'And you paid his bill?'

'Good Lord, yes. Remember the first object of treatment is to remove the source of the patient's anxiety.' I looked down at the sheet of paper I held. 'Though I must say, Nikki, it's rather knocked my careful budgeting for six. Can't we cut down a bit on the furniture? Do we *really* need three chairs in the house?'

'Darling, do be sensible. Supposing somebody calls?'

'We could borrow old Farquy's shooting-stick, or something.'

'Richard, you really must take this seriously. And don't forget you're coming round the furniture shops with me on Thursday.'

'Oh, dear! Must I?'

'Richard! Remember, you promised.'

'Oh, all right, Nikki.'

'After all, darling, it's only a fortnight till the wedding. And we must have some furniture of some sort.'

'I see your point,' I said. 'Though I must admit, there's a hell of a lot to be said for the Arabian idea of sitting on the floor and eating with your fingers.'

Chapter Eighteen

It was either the stimulating effect of my treatment or the stimulating effect of my seventy-five pounds, but Mr Doggett managed to finish at Floral Cottage in another couple of days. The three men retreated from room to room, taking their fire and teapot with them, until they made their final brew out in the back garden. As I paid the bill I reflected that the laughter of beautiful women was cheaper to enjoy these days than the honest ring of hammer on chisel. Nikki meanwhile seemed to be insisting that all manner of utensils and oddments were essential to our married life. I started having dreams in which I found myself chased by furious ironmongers or struggling with gangs of builders in bowler hats trying to brick me into the ramparts of the Tower of London. I assumed that this was a manifestation of the normal psychological disturbance before marriage.

Then there was another complication.

'I've got a proper surprise for you,' said Kitten Strudwick after surgery one evening.

She opened the waiting-room door and led in a pale young man with spectacles and a blue suit, whom I recognized as a gas-fitting salesman I had just treated for varicose veins.

'This is Harold,' she explained. 'We're going to get married.'

'Good Lord, are you!' I exclaimed. The idea of Kitten's emotional life extending much further than the Palais and the Odeon came as a shock. 'I mean, how wonderful. It certainly seems a catching complaint, doesn't it? My heartiest congratulations,' I said, shaking hands with Harold. 'And long life and happiness to you both.'

'Thank you, Doctor,' replied Harold solemnly. 'I might add, had it not been for your good self Catherine and I would not thus have been blissfully brought together.'

'We met in the waiting-room,' Kitten explained. 'The day you were such a long time over Mrs Derridge's sinuses.'

'Might I now intrude further on your valuable time, Doctor?' Harold continued, as I motioned them to seats. 'I have long believed, Doctor, that all persons about to be joined in the state of holy matrimony should first undergo an extensive physical examination.'

'Well . . . perhaps that's putting it a bit seriously. As far as I'm concerned, I think doctors should be kept out of it as much as possible. I'd say if you feel strong enough to walk up the aisle you're all right.'

'I also believe that the happy couple should have a frank talk with their doctor before the ceremony.'

I put my finger-tips together as I caught Kitten's eye.

'Er . . . yes, I suppose you're right.'

'Sex,' Harold continued, as though describing some particularly attractive form of gas-fitting, 'is, as they say, an important factor in marriage.'

I agreed, though I felt at the moment that it took second place to Doggett & Buzzard in ours.

'I should like now, Doctor,' Harold went on warming a little, 'for you to give my future wife and myself a frank talk.'

He folded his arms expectantly. I noticed Kitten was grinning broadly over his shoulder, and I shifted in the surgery chair. I had many times since qualification been asked to give patients several years my senior frank talks on their sex lives. I always felt that I discharged this professional duty inadequately, because the St Swithin's teaching staff had a sound British attitude to such things and any patient mentioning sex was immediately packed off to the psychiatrists. I felt that Kitten knew far more about the subject than I did, and I was sure she was anxious to hear my views on her future sex life only for the light it would throw on my own.

'Well, you see,' I said, starting at the beginning, 'in marriage there's a man . . . and a woman . . . and possibly children.'

'I am naturally concerned about our relations, Doctor.'

'Oh, I shouldn't think they'd mind if you had children a bit.'

'I mean our sexual relations.'

'Quite, of course. Well now. There are several excellent books on the subject, you know.' Grimsdyke had once recommended one to a married couple, and the man had angrily reappeared the next day having fallen out of bed and fractured his ankle. 'But most people worry too much about the whole business.' I continued. 'That's how you get a neurosis. After all, sex is nothing to get excited about. I mean, it doesn't do to . . . When are you getting married?' I asked Kitten abruptly, feeling that the consultation was being held under too many difficulties to be effective.

'Next May. But I want to leave next week, please.'

'So soon?'

'Harold has to go back to Hartlepool.'

'Of course you may leave when you wish, Miss Strudwick. Though we shall all be sorry to lose you.'

'I've quite liked it here. Life's interesting.'

'And I am sure you'll find life with Harold here even more so. I suppose I'd better advertise for a new receptionist in this week's paper. Good evening, now, to you both. I hope you'll be very happy. If you want to know any more, why not go and see the Vicar?'

I hoped that had set them up physiologically for life.

'It's a nuisance about the lass leaving,' said Dr Farquarson when I told him. 'Particularly when you're so preoccupied with impending matrimony yourself.'

'I could stay here and work all next Thursday,' I said eagerly. 'Nikki only wants me to meet her to do some shopping in Town.'

'Och, I wouldn't hear of it for a moment, Richard. Anyway, the work's slackening off a bit. There's nothing like a few fine days in midwinter for making folk forget how ill they are. And anyway, getting married's a much tougher job than running a practice.'

I agreed with him. At that stage the preparations for our marriage seemed to be as complicated as Noah's preparations for the Flood.

I left Floral Cottage early on the Thursday and met Nikki outside a large furniture store in Oxford Street.

'We'll choose the curtains first, darling,' said Nikki. 'I won't get anything you don't like every bit as much as I do.'

'Fine! You won't forget our little budget, though, will you dear?'

'We only want some cheap contemporary designs. Just something to keep us out of sight of the neighbours.'

We were approached inside the door by a tall, silver-haired man with the lofty bearing and formal outfit of a nineteenth-century Harley Street physician.

'We want curtains,' Nikki told him, instinctively taking charge. 'Then kitchen equipment and tableware, and after that inexpensive suites and beds and bedding.'

For a second I caught in his eye the expression of the wolf welcoming Little Red Riding Hood. Then he bowed low, and we followed him through thickets of Chippendale into the shop.

'This is *absolutely* contemporary,' said the young man with the high voice and the loud vowel sounds in the curtain department, 'but rather *busy*, wouldn't you say?'

'Yes,' Nikki admitted. 'Rather busy.'

'This,' he continued, holding up another length, 'is less busy, but of course more pricey.'

'I *do* rather like that one.'

'How about that?' I interrupted, pointing to some material in the corner. 'The one with the beer-mug pattern. Rather jolly, I think. I expect you sell a lot of that?'

'Only to public houses, sir.'

'Oh.'

'And now perhaps madam would like to see an amusing little damask?'

Shortly after we had bought the pricey curtains I realized that the shopping expedition was really nothing but a conspiracy between Nikki and the salesmen. We left the curtain department ten pounds above our budget, in the kitchen department we overspent forty with ease, and there was a difference of fifty guineas between the store's notion of inexpensive suites and ours.

'I suppose we'll *have* to take this one,' I told Nikki, as we self-consciously bounced together on a double bed. 'Even though it does cost twice as much as I allowed. I really don't know how we'll ever pay the deposits, let alone the instalments. Do you really need as many pots and pans as that? When I lived in a flatlet I found a frying-pan and an old mess-tin quite enough for anything.'

'But darling, do be reasonable! You'd soon complain if your bacon and eggs tasted of Irish stew. Assuming, of course,' she added, 'that I learn how to cook Irish stew.'

'Anyway, thank God this is the last port of call. Now we can go and have a drink. I've been dreaming about a beer for the last half-hour.'

'But Richard, you can't just go wandering into pubs. We've got to go to glass and china and linen and blankets yet. Then we must simply rush back to Richmond. I promised we'd be there at lunch-time to settle the invitations.'

'Invitations? But they all went out weeks ago.' I remembered the bitter evening when aunts and uncles were sacrificed ruthlessly as we tried to cut the list to a realistic length.

'Yes, but a lot can't come and there's lots of people we really *must* ask that we'd forgotten, and there are people who've sent presents who haven't been asked, and so we must do something about it. Then we've got to settle about the reception and fix the photographer and you'll have to meet the bridesmaids. By the way, what presents will you be buying them?'

'A packet of Player's apiece, at this rate.'

'I think they'd like ear-rings, Richard, and that's the traditional gift. Right, we'll have this,' Nikki told the salesman. 'Now how about hanging cupboards?'

In Nikki's home, the table in the sitting-room where I had first been received looked like a shoplifter's den after an energetic but erratic day. All round, the chairs were draped with dresses and the floor was deep in hat-boxes, and a number of young women were chattering excitedly amid the disorder like birds after a hurricane.

'This is Jane,' said Nikki. 'And this is Cissy, and this is Helen, and this is Carmen, and this is Greta.'

She introduced five girls, all of whom looked to me the same. They stared at me for some seconds with uninhibited curiosity before returning to trying on hats.

'Now,' said Nikki, 'we must decide whether the invitation that Mummy's old nanny refused can go to Lady Horridge, because a title would look good in the account in the local paper, or to Mrs Grisewood who was so nice to Mummy and Daddy when they were in Madeira. By the way, it's only sandwiches for lunch, I'm afraid. And I'd kept a bottle of beer for you, but Robin seems to have drunk it.'

Thenceforward no one seemed to take much notice of me, though Aunt Jane got me in a corner and said she thought we were very, very brave getting married at all in such difficult times. I agreed with her. Later, Robin arrived with his father from the City, and after pointing out that several presents were well known to fall to pieces immediately on use, asked 'Where are you going for the honeymoon?'

'South of France.'

'What, at this time of the year? Didn't you know the rainfall comes in February? And it's the worst season they've had for years down there, too. I met a chap today in the City who's only just come back.'

'Thank you,' I said. 'On the strength of your kind advice I shall cancel the bookings, and Nikki and I will go to Manchester instead.'

'Manchester? That's rather an odd place for a honeymoon, isn't it?'

Fortunately the Commander spotted me, and carried me off to his cubby-hole for a gin.

I had been invited to stay the night, but as two of the bridesmaids were also in the house I had to share a room with Robin, who not only snored but got up at six and did exercises. I left alone early the next morning, because I had my own shopping to do. First I went to the travel agent for the tickets, then to the jewellers to collect the wedding-ring, then to fix the flowers and confirm the cars, afterwards to buy the bridesmaids' ear-rings, and finally to try on my own clothes. It is a curious reflection on the psychology of the British middle-classes that their inhibitions about appearing unsuitably dressed for any occasion overcome their inhibitions about getting into a pair of trousers already favoured by half a dozen unknown occupants. As I was expected to be married in the costume of a Young Man About Town at the start of the century, like every other male on the invitation list I went to a large clothes shop near Regent Street where they could fit you out by the day for anything from a hunt to the House of Lords.

'Yes, sir?' said one of the aristocratic-looking figures inside the door as I nervously approached.

'I wanted to . . . er, that is . . .' I felt like the first time I took my microscope to the pawnbroker's. 'I wondered if it would be possible to see someone about . . . actually, the loan of some morning clothes?'

'Our hiring department would be delighted to be at your disposal, sir. Small door off the street, just round the corner.'

As I was greeted by another man inside the discreet door, the performance suddenly brought a sense of *déjà vu*, as though I had somehow observed it all before. The first nervous and shameful enquiry, the cheerfully broad-minded tone of the directions, the sheltered door, the tactful segregation, the air of silent comradeship among the other customers. . . . Of course! I had it. The V.D. Department at St Swithin's.

'Would you take the end one, sir?' asked the attendant, my morale rising rapidly as I walked down the line of cubicles overhearing 'Yes, My Lord . . . of course, General . . . not at all, Professor . . . the trousers are perhaps a shade too tight, Your Grace?'

'We'll fix you up in a jiffy, Doctor,' he continued, looking at me with the glance of an experienced undertaker. 'How about a lilac waistcoat? Just the thing for a wedding.'

I took the lilac waistcoat, and also a grey top hat specially cased in a black tin box resembling those used by pathologists for taking interesting organs back to their laboratories. As I stowed my trousseau in the back of the car before driving off for a week-end's duty in Hampden Cross, it suddenly occurred to me that in eight days' time Nikki and I would be man and wife.

Chapter Nineteen

'My heavens, darling! You can't possibly wear that!' said Nikki in horror. After another week of fevered preparation we had reached the day before the wedding. I had just shown her the lilac waistcoat.

'But why ever not?' I felt hurt. 'I rather like it. And the man said it would give a festive air to what I always thought was a festive occasion.'

'But I positively refuse to be seen in church or anywhere else with you wearing *that*.'

'It's a jolly nice waistcoat,' I said more warmly. 'And after all, I don't make nasty comments about your wedding-dress.'

'I didn't make a nasty comment, Richard. I merely expressed a reasonable opinion.'

'Oh, all right, all right! I'll take it back and change it when we get to Town this afternoon.'

'You can't this afternoon–the Vicar might want us for a rehearsal.'

'Must we really have one? We've only got a couple of lines of dialogue in the whole performance.'

'We've got to choose the music. I told the Vicar I wanted to make my entry to the *Trumpet Voluntary*.'

'What's wrong with old Mendelssohn's *Wedding March*? Everyone else has it.'

'That's the point, Richard. Everyone does.'

'Oh, have anything you like,' I grumbled. 'Have *The Entry of the Gladiators* if you want to.'

'Richard! You don't seem at all interested in your own wedding.'

'I hardly look on it as *my* wedding. It seems to be only yours.'

'*Richard!*'

Suddenly she came close to me.

'We mustn't have a row, darling,' she whispered. 'Not just before we're married.'

'Of course not, my sweet. Let's keep them all until just after.'

We laughed, and I kissed her until I heard Dr Farquarson's footsteps outside the surgery.

'I've got to go away and see two or three cases before we can get to London,' I told her. 'I'll meet you back here for a cup of tea, then we'll be off.'

'I'll go down to the cottage, darling. Just to see if everything's all right.'

It is understandable that I didn't give my patients my most powerful attention that afternoon. I made flashing diagnoses and scribbled my prescriptions, and I was back in the surgery within half an hour.

'There's a lady wot's waiting for you inside,' announced the old woman who cleaned our front steps and our brass plate.

'Damn it! A patient?'

'No, she says she's come for that there receptionist's job.'

'I'd clean forgotten I'd got to fix that.' The advertisement had appeared in that week's paper, but was apparently less inviting than Grimsdyke's charm. 'As she's the only applicant, I might as well let her have the job on the spot if she's respectable.'

Waiting in the surgery was Sally Nightingale from St Swithin's.

'Good God!' I cried. 'You!'

'Surprised?' she said, with a laugh.

'Surprised? Demoralized!' I took a good look at her. 'But what on earth are you doing here?'

'I only live in Barnet.'

'I mean in this surgery.'

'I have come in answer to your advertisement, as the expression is.'

'You mean, you really want the job?'

She nodded. 'My nursing career having been brought to an abrupt end, I tried the stage. Repertory, you know, up north. *Othello* sandwiched between *Charley's Aunt* and *Where the Rainbow Ends*. But alas! Despite an enviable self-confidence, I soon found I wasn't as good at acting as I was at nursing. And it was harder on the feet. Then there was a horrible stage-manager who tried to seduce me one night in the interval. When I was playing Hamlet's mother, too. I used that as an excuse to walk out and abandon the profession for good. So here I am, looking for gainful employment.' She sat herself on the desk and swung her legs.

'But what about Godfrey?' I exclaimed.

'Godfrey?'

'John Godfrey. That pilot fellow you ran off with from St Swithin's.'

'Richard, dear, what in heaven's name are you talking about?'

'Roger Hinxman told me you'd eloped with him to South America. Hence your abrupt departure.'

She laughed. 'Roger *is* an old fool, really. I'm sorry I walked out on you both. But it was due to circumstances beyond my control.' Seeing my expression, she explained, 'I was chucked out.'

'Chucked out?'

'My second-year report came up, and within ten minutes I was summoned to matron's office and told politely that continuing my training would be a waste of time all round. To spare my feelings I was allowed to slip away and nothing official was said about it. Hence the mystery, I suppose.'

'But what on earth did they chuck you out for, Sally? You were such a good nurse.'

'It was silly, really. But you know what matrons are. They said I got too friendly with the patients.'

'But how stupid! Why . . .' Suddenly I paused. 'You mean, that ridiculous business with Hinxman and myself had something to do with it?'

'I suppose it did, in a way,' she admitted. 'It had got to Matron's ears, anyway. But it was all my fault. Now,' she said, with determined cheerfulness. 'How about the job?'

This put me in as delicate a position as any man since Solomon. There was no doubt, I felt remorsefully, that my behaviour in Sally's ward had ended her nursing career. But can a bridegroom start employing his old flames the night before his wedding, however well they are extinguished? I realized now the sense of Sally's remark that convalescent patients should never meet their nurses over the dinner-table. She was a pleasant enough person, certainly, but seen without uniform and from levels above the horizontal she looked like a jolly schoolgirl out for the half-hols.

'Well,' I said guardedly, deciding to say nothing about my own status for the moment. 'You may find this sort of job rather difficult.'

'But it's just my cup of tea! It's absolutely made for an unfrocked nurse.'

'Yes, but . . .'

'Seriously, Richard, I *should* like it, if you'll have me. It's near home and it'll give me the evenings free to go and help look after mother. It'll be wonderful dealing with patients again, and you can't imagine what it means to work with someone you know after being in that beastly rep.'

What could I say?

'All right,' I told her. 'You can start on Monday.'

'Richard! You dear. I feel I want to kiss you.'

'No, no, please! I mean–not . . . not . . . You see, Sally, I must explain that many things have happened—'

'Oh, don't worry, Richard,' she laughed. 'But just six months ago you *did* love me to distraction and told poor Roger you wanted to marry me, didn't you?'

'I suppose I did,' I confessed.

'I was really quite fond of you, too. But from painful experience I knew it wouldn't last once your temperature was down.'

'Perhaps,' I said anxiously, 'you might develop amnesia about the little affair?'

'I promise. But it's really quite fascinating in retrospect. Your partner thought so, anyway. I said I knew you personally when I arrived, and before I knew where I was I'd told the whole story, proposals and all.'

'To Dr Farquarson, you mean?'

'Is that her name? The nice young lady doctor who was here when I came.'

'I believe you met the girl who came to apply for the receptionist's job?' I asked Nikki.

It was half an hour later. I had loaded my cases into the car, and for the last time we were starting off to London. Nikki's manner since returning from the cottage was as remote as the far side of the moon, and just as cold.

'Yes. I did.'

I pressed the starter. 'She's Florence Nightingale.'

'Really, Richard! I—'

'That actually is her name. Didn't I tell you I knew her at St Swithin's?'

'You overlooked it.'

'Did I? Funny how I forgot.'

'It also slipped your memory that you proposed to her about a month before you did to me.'

'Nikki, as it happens, I can easily explain that.'

'Please do.'

'You see, I was slightly unbalanced at the time. I was having jaundice, remember. You know you get mental changes, don't you?'

'I'm wondering whether they're permanent.'

I edged my way into the London Road traffic.

'I suppose you've given her the job?' Nikki asked.

'As a matter of fact,' I said, staring intently at the tail-board of the lorry in front, 'I have.'

Nikki said nothing.

'You see, darling,' I went on quickly, 'everything was over and done with long ago between Sally Nightingale and me. Well, six months ago, anyway. But I *did* feel I had a sort of debt to her, because it was through me that she got chucked out of the hospital. I mean,' I added, feeling that I was not putting my case at its strongest, 'it will be so nice for her to be able to get home to her old mother in the evenings.'

Nikki still said nothing.

'You *do* understand, darling, don't you?'

'Oh, perfectly, Richard. As you say, it'll be nice for her mother.'

'Good,' I said, most uneasily.

We crawled along the road for about half a mile without exchanging a word. Thinking I had better restart the conversation as we drew up at the traffic lights, I said 'I suppose we'd better make up our minds about the music we want at the wedding.'

In a pointedly normal voice Nikki said, 'I suppose we must.'

'Do you still want the *Trumpet Voluntary*?'

'I can't really see anything wrong with it.'

'It's a very nice piece of music,' I agreed. 'But so is Mendelssohn's *Wedding March*.'

'The *Wedding March* is about the most hackneyed tune in the world. It booms from practically every organ in Britain on a Saturday afternoon.'

'But so does the *Trumpet Voluntary*. It's what they use at Harringay to get the boxers into the ring.'

'Richard! There's no need to be insulting.'

'I'm *not* being insulting. I'm being perfectly reasonable about the serious question of church music.'

'You're not. You're being damned annoying and pig-headed. You haven't been a bit helpful in getting ready for the wedding—'

'A bit helpful! I like that! First of all you've ruined me with your outrageous extravagance—'

'Extravagance! Do you know what it's like to furnish a house on the never-never?'

'I haven't been able to do any work because I'm always being dragged round some shop or other in London—'

'I suppose you expect me to get a home together entirely by myself?'

'No, but I think we could have done with a flat instead.'

'You do, do you? If you'd married your other girl friend—'

'She's not my girl friend!'

'Whom you are now installing comfortably in your surgery—'

'I tell you I was sorry for her mother!'

'If you're so idiotic as to expect me to take that as an excuse for playing fast and loose—'

'I am *not* playing fast and loose! The girl means nothing to me whatever. Anyway, what about you and Grimsdyke?'

'Me and Grimsdyke? What on earth do you mean?'

'The way you were carrying on with him that night in the Bull.'

'Richard! I've never heard such beastly rubbish in all my—'

We were interrupted by a fanfare of car horns as the lights changed to green.

'Oh!' cried Nikki. 'You're impossible!' She pulled her glove off. 'There's your ring back. Good-bye!'

She leapt out of the car and slammed the door. I drove steadfastly on to London.

Chapter Twenty

Grimsdyke had taken a small flat in a large block in Chelsea. I left the car outside, stamped into the lift, and banged on his door.

'Here comes the bride,' he greeted me brightly. 'All ready for the big day, old boy? Which side are you going to hold your orange blossom?'

'There's not going to be any wedding,' I told him. I flung Nikki's ring on the table. 'It's off.'

'Off? But whatever for?'

'We had a row.'

'Good Lord! What about?'

'The music we were going to have in church.'

'The . . . the what, old lad?'

'I told you–the music. She wanted the *Trumpet Voluntary*. I wanted the *Wedding March*. We had a disagreement about it, and now the wedding's off.'

'Richard, old man,' he said anxiously. 'I always thought you were a bit barmy, but I didn't know you were quite so cracked as that.'

'Well, you know how these things are. It was like your blasted draughts game at Foulness. One thing led to another. Old scores were raked up. Before I knew where I was, I'd got a spare ring on my hands.'

'You need a drink,' said Grimsdyke.

'I do,' I said.

'But you can't put the wedding off now, old lad,' he complained, pouring me half a tumbler of whisky. 'I've laid on a tremendous bachelor party for you tonight. Tony Benskin and all the boys are coming. Even old uncle Farquarson's appearing, determined to add his Edinburgh repertoire to our usual songs, God help us.'

'You'll just have to ring up and put them all off. I'll have to wire all the wedding guests, anyway.'

'But Richard, you chump! Can't you be sensible?'

'I *am* being sensible! Perfectly cool, calm, and sensible. It's perfectly obvious that Nikki and I—'

'But you can't behave like this!'

'Now at last I can behave as I damn well like.'

The doorbell rang.

'Oh, damn!' said Grimsdyke. He admitted Tony Benskin, who was looking much the same as when suffering incipient fatherhood in St Swithin's.

'You're a bit soon for the party, Tony,' said Grimsdyke shortly. 'Did Molly let you off the chain early or something?'

'Is that a drink?' demanded Benskin. He grabbed my glass, murmured 'Hello, Richard,' and took a long swig. 'There isn't a chain any more, Grim,' he announced. 'Molly and I have separated.'

'What!' we cried together.

'Irrevocably and completely separated,' said Benskin, swallowing the rest of the whisky. 'Molly's gone back to mother. She went this afternoon, taking young Tristram.'

'But why on earth?' exclaimed Grimsdyke.

'Why? Hah! I've never known a woman to behave in such a ridiculous, unappreciative, and generally dangerous manner.'

'But what did she do, Tony?' he asked. 'Pull a gun on you, or something?'

'Oh, it's not me. It's what she's been doing to poor little Tristram. Do you know, I've bought pretty well every book on infant feeding and child welfare there is, and Molly absolutely and completely refuses to do what I tell her. Do you realize, when every single authority says you've got to start a baby on a cup at six months, she insists on keeping him on the bottle? Think what she's doing to the poor little thing's psychology! He might develop all sorts of frightful unpleasant habits when he grows up. She says the bottle's easier and he likes it, so there.' Benskin poured himself another drink. 'Then there's the matter of putting him out in his pram. Of course you put children out in their prams, even if it's bloody well freezing. Stimulates the metabolism no end. But Molly says his feet get cold. Oh, and lots of things besides. Vitamins and immunization and conditioned potting and God knows what. She accuses me of interfering. I accused her of ignorance. We had a hell of a row over lunch, and she walked out.'

'You're not the only one,' Grimsdyke told him morosely. 'Richard's nuptials are off, too.'

'And a jolly good thing,' said Benskin warmly. 'Never, never, never get married, old boy! Stick to the single life while you've got a chance.'

'What rubbish,' said Grimsdyke. 'Now look here, you idiots. I know you've always regarded me as the licensed lady-killer of our little band, but I don't mind telling you that you're both damned lucky because you've got yourselves attached to a couple of wonderful girls who are about fifty times too good for your miserable characters anyway. Richard, you can get into your car and go crawling back to Nikki and crave forgiveness and ask her to wipe her feet on your neck.'

'Never!'

'That's right, old boy,' Benskin told me. 'You stick up for yourself. Let the ruddy woman go and stew in her own juice.'

'If you do, Richard,' said Grimsdyke, 'you'll end up a repulsive old bachelor with tender memories. And a fat lot of good tender memories are for keeping your feet warm in bed.'

'What the hell can you know about it, anyway?' I said angrily. 'You've never been married.'

'The spectator sees more of the game, doesn't he?'

For a second we stared each other in the eye, then I collapsed on Grimsdyke's divan and said, 'This is absolutely ridiculous. Six months ago Tony was telling me how wonderful it was to get married, and you were telling me not to touch a wedding-ring with a barge-pole. And now here's Tony congratulating me on my lucky escape and you're telling me I'm committing moral suicide.'

'Well, damn it,' said Grimsdyke. 'I've got more sense than either of you fellows. *I*'ve never got myself in a mess like this to start with.'

The argument continued. Tony refused to go back to Molly. I refused to grovel to Nikki. Grimsdyke finally refused to have anything to do with either of us. We were interrupted only by another ring on the doorbell and the appearance of Dr Farquarson.

'I thought I'd arrived rather early for the party,' he said to Grimsdyke, putting down his hat among the glasses. 'But I see it's already begun.'

The three of us said nothing. We were all staring in different directions, trying to look as though we'd been having a jolly time.

'But still, now I'm here I'll take a dram.' We stood in silence, while Grimsdyke hastily poured his uncle a drink. 'I don't think I've had the pleasure of meeting your other friend?'

'That is Tony Benskin, uncle,' Grimsdyke muttered. 'Tony, Dr Farquarson.'

Tony Benskin nodded absently.

'Well now, you young fellows. I'm a bit of an old fogy, but I still flatter myself I can rise to the occasion when required. We should have a high old time tonight and no mistake, eh? After all, it's the happiest of occasions. A young man getting married. Who could argue with that?'

'Oh, quite.' I stuffed my hands into my trouser pockets.

'Your very good health, Richard my boy.' Dr Farquarson raised his glass. 'On this most joyful occasion.' He looked round at us. 'Aren't you young fellows drinking at all?'

We hastily found glasses and gave the toast, with the enthusiasm and the expressions of men honouring a suicide pact.

'On the whole,' said Dr Farquarson, filling his pipe, 'I'm in favour of weddings. If a couple can survive the emotional strain, hard work, and demands for tact and self-discipline they involve, they can overcome pretty well anything else in their married life to come.'

I said nothing.

'Marriage,' Dr Faquarson continued, 'is a strange psychological cat's-cradle. And as you know, it's generally easier to make a cat's-cradle if you don't worry yourself stiff whether it's going to collapse before you've started. Och, I'm not saying that every main road in the country should be signposted to Gretna Green. But it's a good idea to take the complications of modern marriage in your stride, like you take the complications of modern motoring. Try and reduce it to its simplest essentials. It's just another example of my favourite theory about civilization being too much for us. Any of you fellows got a match?'

The three of us offered him matchboxes.

'Hello,' he said, picking up Nikki's ring from the table. 'Haven't I seen this somewhere before?'

'Yes,' I said quickly. 'But it wasn't fitting very well, so Nikki gave it to me to take down to the jewellers and get it altered.'

'I see. What was I rambling on about now? I remember. But fortunately, marriage is about the only thing left in our lives that can be reduced to its essentials by the thought of a moment. You just have to ask, Do I love the girl? Then you have to ask, Does she love me? Page one, chapter one, any biology textbook. If the answer's "yes" in both cases, you needn't worry about incompatibility of temperament and whether you like your eggs boiled or scrambled.'

I wished heartily that Dr Farquarson would finish his drink and get out.

'Or even,' he continued, 'who you give the job of receptionist to.'

For the first time I noticed his eyebrows quivering.

'Dr Farquarson—!'

'The young lady of yours is in my car,' he said. 'I met her in the surgery and dried her tears and exercised an old man's privilege of talking the hind leg off a donkey.' As the bell rang, he added, 'That'll be her now. I just wanted time to say my piece, that's all.'

'Nikki darling!' I exclaimed, throwing open the door. I nearly embraced Molly Benskin and her baby.

'Tony angel!' she cried, pushing past me into the room.

'Molly, my sweet!'

'How can you forgive me, Tony? You were absolutely right about the cup and the potty and putting him out in the cold.'

'No, no, no, darling! How can you possibly forgive *me*? I was absolutely wrong about everything.'

'Tony, no!' she said, bursting into tears. 'It was all my fault. Every bit.'

As I started to rush downstairs, I heard Grimsdyke exclaim, 'I knew women made chaps a bit soft in the head, but I never quite thought I'd run into benefit night at Bedlam like this.'

'Nikki, my dearest, sweetest, little lovely one!' I said, embracing her wildly on the pavement, to the alarm of a man delivering the milk.

'Richard darling! My beautifullest loveliest little bunny-wunny!'

'How can I ask you to forgive me? How can I cringe enough? Won't you please wipe your shoes on my neck?'

'But darling, the whole thing's been my own silly stupid fault.'

'Yours? Nonsense, Nikki! I'm to blame all along. I was a ridiculous silly idiot.'

'Sweet Richard.' She ran her fingers through my hair. 'How can you want to marry such a shrew as me?'

'If you're a shrew, may you never be tamed.'

'I love you so much, darling one.'

'So do I. To distraction.'

'Do you two mind if I have my car back?'

We jumped apart at Dr Farquarson's voice behind us.

'I'll be seeing you later this evening, Richard my lad,' he added, opening the door. 'I'm off to Mappin and Webb's to buy a wedding present.'

'But you've already given us one, Farquy.'

'But didn't I tell you? Our Miss Wildewinde went back to old Dr McBurney, and would you believe it they're getting married next week. It'll do them both a power of good. Yes, there's a lot of it about at this season, as we say to the patients when there's nothing we can do to stop it.'

Chapter Twenty-one

'Arise and shine!' called Grimsdyke heartily. '*For I'm to be married today–today. Yes, I'm to be married today!*'

I sat bolt upright.

'What time is it?'

'Eleven-thirty.'

'Good God! Only another three hours and we've got to be at the church!'

'Steady on, old lad! You don't take three hours to get dressed on an ordinary day, do you?'

'But this isn't an ordinary day. God!' I tried to stand up, but stopped abruptly. 'My head! What on earth did you give me to drink last night?'

'Oh, just beer and whisky and gin and brandy and port and vodka and so on.'

I became aware of my surroundings. Grimsdyke's flat resembled a ship's cabin after a heavy gale, and I had been sleeping on the floor with my head on Dr Farquarson's hat and wearing Tony Benskin's jacket and a grass skirt.

'Where the devil did I get this grass thing from?'

'What, the skirt? From the girl in that night-club, of course.'

'What girl in what night-club?'

'Come off it, Richard! You couldn't have been as blotto as that.'

'The last thing I can remember is when we were all thrown out of that pub. With Nikki's brother slapping me on the back and telling me I wasn't such a bad fellow after all.'

'The skirt came much later. It was the girl old Farquy kept wanting to dance with. Believe me, I've never seen the old uncle in such form since Scotland won in the last minute at Twickenham. Don't worry,' he added, 'she only gave you her spare one. You insisted it would go well in church with your lilac waistcoat.'

I groaned and laid down again. 'Have you got any codeine?'

'Better than codeine. I've got a bottle of champagne in the oven.'

'In the where?'

'As Grimsdyke doesn't indulge in home cooking, the oven's useful for hiding such stuff from a crowd of determined dypsomaniacs, such as I entertained last night. Keeps it nice and cool, too.'

I shortly afterwards had the pleasant experience of drinking champagne in the bath.

'We've bags of time,' Grimsdyke told me. 'There's no need to worry, because you really haven't got anything more to do. It's in the enemy camp that confusion will be reigning unbounded until the Daimler with the white ribbons rolls up at the door.'

'We aren't having white ribbons,' I said firmly. 'We agreed on that long ago.'

'By the way, what music did you decide to have in the end?'

'Oh, the music,' I said lightly, as I started to shave with Grimsdyke's razor, 'I just left it to Nikki. It doesn't matter a damn.'

'I'd say it was dashed important myself, old lad,' Grimsdyke said thoughtfully. 'As she's finally decided to marry you, I should be very interested to see whether she sticks to her own *Trumpet Voluntary* or whether she bows to the wishes of her future lord and master and orders the *Wedding March*.'

'Blast!' I exclaimed. 'I've cut myself again. I'll arrive at the altar looking like Banquo's ghost.'

'If you feel anything like you look, Richard, I should think you'd be glad to find you bleed at all.'

That morning I began to realize what it was like to indulge in mescalin or suffer one of the odd psychological diseases which derange your time-appreciation. At one moment time would seem to drag by like an old horse on its way to the knackers, at another it flashed past like a space-ship, and at others I felt certain it was going backwards.

'I suppose you'll think me bloody silly if I tell you not to look so worried,' Grimsdyke said to cheer me up, as I sat about in his spare dressing-gown. 'But don't forget you've only got to do it once. If Nikki discovers your true character after a couple of years and unloads you, you can marry the next one in a registry office.'

'Never again,' I said firmly. 'Never, never, never again. Do you suppose everyone feels like this?'

'Ever since Adam had his thoracotomy.'

'I wish I hadn't got this horrible vacuum sensation in my upper abdomen. I feel as if old Sir Lancelot Spratt had been at me on one of his demonstration days.'

'Have some more champers. Nothing like it for restoring the roses to the cheeks.' He looked at his watch. 'Or perhaps we'd better be getting into our finery. Then I'll pop down and get the car out.'

'Supposing it breaks down on the way?' I asked in alarm.

'Oh, it probably will. Then we'll take it in turns to push. I say, this waistcoat's pretty snappy. Did you hire it with the rest?'

'I'm glad you like it, Grim. Nikki and I had a difference of opinion about it. Do you think I ought to leave it off?'

'Leave it off? Not a bit, old lad. If you like it, wear it.'

'I'm not so sure, Grim. I really ought to do what Nikki wants.'

'Now see here, old lad. There's nothing like starting off the way you mean to go on. You wear the thing. And keep your coat open, too.'

Twenty minutes later Grimsdyke and myself stood in front of the mirror, admiring the two elegant English gentlemen before us.

'What do I do with the hat?' I asked.

'Carry it.'

'In church, I mean. They don't have cloakrooms, do they?'

'Shove it under the pew.'

'Supposing I sit on it?'

'My dear chap, don't go on making difficulties! It doesn't matter a damn what you do, anyway. Everyone will be looking at Nikki.'

'True,' I admitted.

'Well, old lad. Off to the gallows.'

'You've got the ring?' I demanded hoarsely.

'Cosy in the waistcoat pocket.'

'And you won't forget to pick up Nikki's new passport in the vestry?'

'Not on your life.'

'Oh, and the telegrams. Reading them out afterwards, I mean.'

'I shall sound like the town crier announcing tax concessions.'

'What I'm getting at is . . . I mean, some of the chaps from St Swithin's think themselves pretty funny at times, you know. They forget there's all sorts of sticky relatives there to hear. You'll censor them a bit, won't you, if necessary?'

'Leave it to me, Richard. I shall let no shade of embarrassment cross your rosy path today. I remember I once sent one to a girl I knew on the stage, and like a fool I tried to be topical and wrote, "All the best for your first night." Husband wouldn't speak to me for months afterwards.'

'Well, that's about all, then?'

'Yes, old lad. That's about all.'

For a second we looked at each other. Grimsdyke and I had been the closest of friends since the day we had first met outside the lecture-hall at St Swithin's, when we both faced life from the laughably low status of first-year medical students. Together we had cheerfully struggled or schemed our way through the course, and together we had made our first exciting forays into the world beyond the protective walls of St Swithin's itself. Each of us knew enough comfortably to blackmail the other for life, and we would have readily shared our last crusts–provided there was absolutely no possibility of being able to swop them for half a pint of bitter. And now I was getting married, and it could never be quite the same again.

'Good-bye, Grim old man,' I said instinctively. We shook hands. 'And thanks a lot.'

'Good-bye, Richard. And all the luck. You'll need it more than me.'

'I don't know if . . . I mean, you're always a lot more cynical about these things than I am. I suppose you can't understand how much I really love Nikki and how wonderful all this really is to me.'

'Of course I do, old lad. All my fooling about's just to keep your knees from knocking.'

We stood clasping hands for a second, then Grimsdyke said, 'The tumbril awaits' and stuck my top-hat on my head.

We were soon in the car, through the streets, at the church. I had a blurred impression of the congregation, which seemed large enough to fill the Albert Hall. There was my mother and father, there was Dr Farquarson, there was Robin stalking the aisle to ask if you were friends of the bride or bridegroom. There was the Vicar, waiting in the wings. There was the organist, twiddling idly away and glancing into his mirror like a nervous driver in a police trap.

'Don't worry, old lad,' Grimsdyke whispered in the front pew. 'Twenty minutes and it'll all be over.'

'But it ought to have started five minutes ago!' I hissed back.

'Haven't you heard the bride's always late, you idiot?'

'Perhaps she's changed her mind.'

He shook his head. 'Nikki's a sensible girl, but not as sensible as that.'

Suddenly everyone stood up.

'Here you are, Richard. On your feet.'

Glancing down the aisle I had a vision of Nikki, white and radiant at the other end. The organist stopped twiddling and struck a chord. Then he broke into Mendelssohn's *Wedding March*.

'Whacko!' said Grimsdyke delightedly, digging me in the ribs. 'She gave in in the end, old lad! From now on, you're the boss for life.'

And so we were married.

I'm sure that we shall live happily ever after. But I'm not so sure that Grimsdyke was right.

Richard Gordon

Doctor in Clover

Chapter One

'You may be surprised to hear,' I announced to my cousin, Mr Miles Grimsdyke, F.R.C.S., 'that I've decided to do the decent thing and settle down in general practice.'

'Do I attribute this decision to a severer sense of professional duty or to a severer hangover than usual?'

'Neither. But all my chums from St Swithin's seem to be installing wives and families and washing machines, and it seems high time I did the same. Take my old friend Simon Sparrow, for instance. Why, in the days of our youth we got chucked out of pubs together, and now his idea of whooping it up on a Saturday night is taking the lawn-mower to pieces. Believe me, I'm going to become dear old Dr Grimsdyke, the chap who's brought half the district into the world and pushed the other half out of it, beloved by all until it's time to collect old-age pension and chiming clock from grateful patients.'

'I suppose you realize, Gaston, how difficult it is these days to get into general practice?'

'Of course. Quite as bad as getting into the Test Matches. But not for fellows like me who know the ropes. You've heard of Palethorpe and Wedderburn, the medical employment agents?'

Miles frowned. 'The people in Drury Lane? I have never had recourse to them myself.'

'I happen to know old Palethorpe personally. We met last summer, on an occasion when I was able to offer him valuable professional advice.'

I didn't mention to my cousin we'd run into each other at Sandown Park races, where I put Palethorpe on such a good thing he'd kept my medical career close at heart ever since. Unfortunately, Miles has no sense of humour. It's the tragedy of modern life that so many people–dictators, tax-collectors, tennis champions, teddy boys, and so on–seem to have no sense of humour either.

'If you really intend to settle down,' my cousin continued, 'I might say I am delighted that you have chosen this particular moment to do so. In fact, I will confess that is exactly why I invited you for lunch today. More greens? One should keep up one's vitamin C this time of the year.'

'Enough is enough, thank you.'

It was one of those beastly days in midwinter when dusk chases dawn briskly across the London roof-tops, and fog was hazing even the chilly halls of the Parthenon Club where we sat. The Parthenon in St James's struck me as about as comfortable for lunching in as the main booking-hall at Euston Station, but Miles was one of the newest members and as proud of the place as if it were the House of Lords. I supposed it fitted into his self-portrait of the up-and-coming young surgeon. He was a small, bristly chap, generally regarded as embodying the brains of the family, who had just reached that delicate stage in a surgical career when your car is large enough to excite the confidence of your patients but not the envy of your colleagues.

'And how exactly are you earning your living at this moment?' Miles went on.

'I have many irons in the fire,' I told him. 'Though I must confess the fire isn't too hot. There's my medical articles for the popular press, to start with.'

Miles frowned again. 'I can't say I've noticed any.'

'They're all signed "By A Harley Street Specialist". Of course, it would be gross professional misconduct to put my own name.'

'You certainly show a remarkable ingenuity for practising without actually doing any medicine.'

'Which just proves what I've always held–medicine's a jolly good general education. It teaches you the working of everything from human nature to sewage farms. Not to mention all those little bits of Latin and Greek which are so useful in the crosswords.'

'But you must realize, Gaston, the time has come to put this free-and-easy existence behind you for good. You're not a mountebank of an undergraduate any more. You must now maintain the dignity of a qualified practitioner.

'Oh, I agree with you. Being a medical student is really the worst possible training for becoming a doctor.'

Miles dropped his voice below the hushed whisper permissible for conversation in the Parthenon.

'I am now going to tell you something in the strictest confidence.'

'Oh, yes?'

'Mr Sharper at St Swithin's is to become Professor of Surgery at Calgary University.'

'Really? I hope he enjoys crawling about in the snow potting all those bears.'

'That isn't the point. There will therefore be an unexpected vacancy on the surgical consultant staff. I shall in due course be applying for it. As Mr Sharper's own senior registrar, I do not flatter myself in believing that my chances are excellent.' He then helped himself to another boiled potato. 'Though as you know, considerations other than the strictly surgical will sometimes weigh strongly with the selection committee.'

I nodded. 'I remember one chap was turned down because he wore knickerbockers and arrived for the interview on a motor-bike.'

'Quite so. To be perfectly frank, Gaston, it might embarrass me if you simply continued to flit about the medical scene—'

'My dear old lad!' I hadn't realized this worried him sufficiently to stand me a lunch. 'I may be a poor risk for a five-bob loan, but you can always rely on me to help a kinsman. A couple of weeks to say farewell to the haunts of my misspent youth, and I'll have made myself scarce from London for good.'

Miles still looked doubtful.

'I hope the permanency of your new position is more durable than some of your others.'

'They were mere flirtations with work. This is the real thing. And everyone will say, "See how that steady chap Miles has put even old Gaston Grimsdyke on his feet."'

'If that is indeed so, I'm much indebted to you. We may not always have seen eye to eye, Gaston—'

'Oh, come. Every family has its little misunderstandings.'

'But I assure you I have always acted entirely for your own good. And what precisely is this position you have in mind?'

'G.P. up north,' I explained.

I had been in Palethorpe's office that morning, when he'd greeted me with the news:

'I have exactly the right opening for you, Dr Grimsdyke. General practice in the Midlands–the backbone of England, you know. Assistant wanted, with a view, as we say. Start end of January. Dr Wattle of Porterhampton. A very fine man.'

'It doesn't matter what the doctor's like,' I told him. 'How about his wife?'

Palethorpe chuckled. 'How I wish our other clients were half as perspicacious! Fortunately, Mrs Wattle accompanied the doctor when he called, and I can assure you that she is a highly respectable and motherly middle-aged lady.'

'Nubile daughters?'

'It is their sorrow to be a childless couple, alas. I believe that is why they particularly asked me to find some decent, honest, upright, well-mannered, single young practitioner to share their home with them.'

'I can only hope you come as a nice surprise,' muttered my cousin when I told him.

'At last I feel set for a peaceful and prosperous career,' I went on, enlarging on my prospects a little. 'Who knows what the future holds? The dear old Wattles might take me to their bosoms. They might look upon me as a son to enlighten their declining years. They might send for their solicitors and start altering their wills. There should be plenty of lolly about in Porterhampton, too. They make turbines or something equally expensive up there.'

'My dear Gaston! You know, you really must grow out of this habit of counting your chickens before the hen's even ovulated.'

'What's wrong with a little imagination?' I protested. 'Lord Lister and Alexander Fleming wouldn't have got far without it. Anyway, at the moment roots are fairly sprouting from my feet like spring carrots.'

Chapter Two

Until then Porterhampton was just another entry in my football pools, but a fortnight later I found myself driving past the Town Hall on a morning as crisp as an icicle, and pretty solemn I felt about it, too.

While lunching with Miles, I'd been putting an optimistic face on a pretty desperate situation, which is another of the useful things you learn from studying medicine. I didn't really like the prospect of being a respectable provincial doctor. In fact I didn't really like the prospect of being a doctor at all.

I was a *médecin malgré lui*. I'd taken up the profession because nobody in the family ever had the originality to think of anything else, and anyway all my uncles and cousins seemed to have a pleasant time of it, with large cars and everyone listening to their opinions at cocktail parties. But with medicine and marriage, the earlier you go in for either the riskier the project becomes. Quite a different chap emerges at the end of the course from the apple-cheeked lad with big ideas who went in. It's great fun at first, of course, being casualty houseman in a clean white coat with all the nurses saying 'Good morning, doctor,' even if the job does consist mostly of inspecting unpleasant things brought along in little white enamel bowls. It's a bit of a shock finding afterwards that you've got to make a living at it, though I suspect a good many housemen feel the same and keep pretty quiet. The public doesn't much care for entrusting their lives to doctors who don't love their profession, even though they entrust them every day to bus drivers and no one expects a bus driver to love his bus.

But as I couldn't go exploring like Dr Livingstone, become a Prime Minister of France like Dr Clemenceau, or play cricket like Dr W. G. Grace, I had to find a steady job like everyone else. And what of these Wattles? I wondered, as I drove past the Porterhampton fish market. They might at that moment be hopping about like a small boy waiting for the postman on his birthday. Or they might be plotting to kick me about like a medical tweeny. Fortunately for my low psychological state, I was soon reassured over my conditions of work.

I found the Wattles' house somewhere on the far outskirts, in a road of roomy Victorian villas apparently reserved for prosperous turbine-makers. As I drew up in the 1930 Bentley, the motherly Mrs Wattle herself appeared at the gate.

'Dear Dr Grimsdyke!' she greeted me. 'We're so delighted you've decided to bury yourself in our rather sleepy little town.'

'Charming place, I'm sure.'

'Mr Palethorpe spoke so highly of you, you know. I'm awfully glad he persuaded you to come. But you must be tired after your long drive. I'll show you to your room, and there's a nice lunch ready as soon as my husband gets in from his rounds.'

I slipped off my overcoat.

'Dear, dear! No buttons on your shirt, Doctor! You must let me have it tonight. And any socks and things that need darning, just leave them on the kitchen table.'

My room ran a bit to chintz and water-colours of St Ives, but seemed very cosy. There was a bookcase full of detective stories, a desk, and a large double bed already airing with a hot-water bottle like an old-fashioned ginger-beer jar. Going downstairs after tidying up, I found roast beef and Yorkshire on the table, with apple pie and Stilton waiting on the sideboard.

'I'm sure you'd care for a bottle of beer today,' cooed Mrs Wattle. 'Mr Palethorpe said you took the occasional glass.'

I'd met Dr Wattle himself only for a brief interview in London, and he was a little pink, perspiring chap with a bald head, resembling a freshly-boiled egg.

'Delighted to see you, my dear doctor.' He shook hands warmly. 'We may call you Gaston, may we? I hope you'll be very happy with us. Is that your car outside? Very dashing of you to drive an old open tourer. But do take my wife's Morris when it's raining, won't you? Would you care for an advance of salary? We'll sort out your duties later. If you ever want time off for anything, don't hesitate to ask.'

'Your chair's over here, Gaston. Sure you're not in a draught?'

'I hope you'll find my wife's cooking to your taste.'

'The roast beef's not overdone?'

'Anything special you fancy to eat, do please let us know.'

'Horseradish?' asked Mrs Wattle.

Later we had crumpets for tea and finnan haddock for supper, and in the evening we all three sat round the fire making light conversation.

'Mr Palethorpe revealed you had quite a roguish wit,' said Mrs Wattle, playfully shaking her finger.

So I told them the story about the bishop and the parrot, though of course altering the anatomical details a bit.

'How pleasant to hear a young voice in the house,' murmured her husband.

'We've *so* missed company in the evenings!'

'Ever since the dog died,' agreed Dr Wattle.

After years of living on tins of baked beans and packets of potato crisps, and mending my own socks by pulling a purse-string suture round the hiatus, it did my physiology no end of good to have regular meals and all the buttons on my shirts. There wasn't even much work to do, old Wattle himself handling all the posher patients and leaving me with a succession of kids in the usual epidemic of mumps. After surgery and supper we all three gathered for the evening in the sitting-room. Sometimes we watched the telly. Sometimes we played three-handed whist. Sometimes they asked me to tell the story of the bishop and the parrot all over again. I was glad to see the Wattles had quite a sense of humour.

But even the Prodigal Son, once they'd used up all the fatted calf, must have hankered to waste just a bit more of his substance on riotous living. As the local amenities ran largely to municipal parks and museums, and so on, and as I couldn't go to any of the pubs because I was a respectable G.P., or to any of the pictures because I'd seen them all months ago in the West End, I longed for one final glimpse of the lively lights of London.

'Dr Wattle,' I announced one morning, when I'd been enjoying three square meals a day for several weeks. 'I wonder whether you'd mind if I popped down to Town this Saturday? I've just remembered I've got some laundry to collect.'

'My dear boy! Go whenever and wherever you wish.'

'That's jolly civil of you. Awfully annoying, and all that, but I'd better make the trip.'

The following Saturday evening found me once again in the genial glow of Piccadilly Circus, breathing the carcinogenic hydrocarbons and watching the neon sunrise as the lights came on.

I don't think there's any sensation to compare with arriving in London after a spell of exile, even if it's only your summer holidays. I felt I'd never seen anything so beautiful as the submarine glow of the misty street-lamps, heard anything as cheerful as the nightly torrent ebbing towards the suburbs, nor smelt any perfume so sweet as the reek of a London Transport omnibus. But I couldn't waste time admiring the scenery, and went to a telephone box, looked through my little black book, then rang up Petunia Bancroft.

Petunia was a little brunette and an actress. I've had a weakness for the stage ever since I was a medical student and nearly eloped with a young woman who was sawn in two twice nightly by a Palladium conjurer, until I discovered that she was in fact a pair of young women, and I'd picked the half with the shocking varicose veins. Petunia had been a chum of mine for many years, though unfortunately her ideas of entertainment rather exceeded her theatrical standing–usually she just walked on the stage and announced dinner was ready, but after the show she knocked back champagne like the great leading ladies when the stuff was five bob a bottle. Also, she had a rather hysterical personality, and was likely to throw the dessert about and bite the head waiter. But after a month in Porterhampton, Petunia seemed just what I needed.

'Darling, I'd love to meet you', she agreed. 'Don't come to the show, it's lousy and closing any minute, anyway. See you at the stage door after ten.'

The London streets were as deserted as Porterhampton on a Sunday afternoon by the time I took Petunia home to Balham–like most glamorous hotsies these days, she lived quietly with Mum and did the washing-up before catching the bus to the theatre. We'd had a pleasant little evening, what with supper and a night-club, and even if it did demolish Dr Wattle's advance of salary I was feeling like a sailor after ninety days at sea.

'Lovely time, darling,' said Petunia at the garden gate. 'When are you coming to live in London again?'

'One day, perhaps. When I retire.'

'When you retire! But darling, I won't ever recognize you then.'

'I'll have a chiming clock under my arm,' I told her. 'Night-night.'

The next morning I made my way back to the provinces for good, having wrapped all the Sunday newspapers in a large brown-paper parcel which I labelled THE EVERCLEEN LAUNDRY WASHES WHITER.

This little jaunt of mine was a mistake.

One taste of Metropolitan delights had ruined my appetite for Porterhampton for good. I'd tried really hard to fool myself I could merge with the local landscape. Now I realized I couldn't be comfortable anywhere in the world outside Harrods' free delivery area. I faced endless evenings watching the television and talking to the Wattles, and that night the prospect of both made me feel rather sickly over supper. But I had to stay in the place until the St Swithin's committee had shaken my cousin by the hand and told him where to hang his umbrella, and anyway the dear old couple were so terribly decent I'd never have forgiven myself for hurting their feelings over it.

'Dr Wattle,' I began, when we were alone after the meal. 'I don't know if I've told you before, but I've decided to work for a higher medical degree. I hope you'll not think me rude if I go to my room in the evenings and open the books?'

He laid a hand on my arm.

'I am delighted, dear boy. Delighted that–unlike so many young men these days, inside and out of our profession–you should take a serious view of your work.'

There was a catch in his voice.

'We are all mortal, Gaston,' he went on. 'In another few years I may no longer be here—'

'Oh, come, come! The prime of life—'

'And I should like you to be well qualified when you eventually take over this practice. My wife and I have become very attached to you these few short weeks. As you know, we have no children of our own. As a young man I suffered a severe attack of mumps—'

'Jolly hard luck,' I sympathized.

The mump virus, of course, can wreck your endocrine glands if you're unlucky enough to get the full-blown complications.

'If all goes well,' he ended, 'I hope you will inherit more from me than merely my work. I will detain you no longer from your studies.'

The rest of the week I sat in my room reading detective stories, and pretty beastly I felt about it, too.

Then one morning Mrs Wattle stopped me outside the surgery door.

'Gaston, my husband and I had a little chat about you last night.'

'Oh, yes?'

'We fear that you must find it rather dull in Porterhampton.'

'Not at all,' I replied, wondering if some revelling turbine-maker had spotted me in that night-club. 'There's always something happening,' I told her. 'The Assizes last week, the anti-litter campaign this.'

'I mean socially. Why, you never met any young people at all.'

It hadn't occurred to me that in Porterhampton there were any.

'So next Saturday evening I've arranged a little party for you. I do hope you can spare the time from your studies?'

Naturally, I said I should be delighted, though spending the rest of the week steeling myself for the sort of celebration to make a curate's birthday look like a night out in Tangier. When Saturday came I put on my best suit and waited for the guests among the claret cup and sandwiches, determined to make the evening a success for the dear old couple's sake. I would be heartily chummy all round, and ask the local lads intelligent questions about how you made turbines.

'Here's the first arrival,' announced Mrs Wattle. 'Miss Carmichael.'

She introduced a short girl in a pink dress.

'And here come Miss Symes and Miss Patcham.'

I shook hands politely.

'With Miss Hodder and Miss Atkinson walking up the drive. That's everyone,' she explained. 'Gaston, do tell us your terribly amusing story about the clergyman and the parrot.'

It struck me as an odd gathering. But old Wattle handed out the drinks while I sat on the sofa and entertained the girls, and after a bit I quite warmed to it. I told them the other one about the old lady and the bus driver, and a few more that I hadn't picked up from the boys at St Swithin's, and they all laughed very prettily and asked me what it was like being a doctor. I was quite sorry when eventually midnight struck, and everyone seemed to think it time to close down.

'I'm sure Gaston would drop you at your homes in his remarkable car,' suggested Mrs Wattle.

With a good deal of giggling, I discarded girls at various respectable front doors in the district, until I was finally left with only one in the seat beside me.

'I'm afraid I live right on the other side of the town, Gaston.'

'The farther it is, the more I'm delighted,' I replied politely.

She was the Miss Atkinson, a little blonde who'd given the parrot story an encore.

'Quite an enchanting evening,' I murmured.

'But you were so terribly amusing! I always thought medicos such stodgy old things, even the young ones.'

I gave a little laugh.

'We doctors are only human, you know.'

'I'm so glad,' she said.

After leaving her at another respectable door, I hurried home for some sleep. Nothing takes it out of you quite so much as telling a lot of funny stories.

Chapter Three

'I know you'll be pleased,' announced Mrs Wattle a few mornings later. 'I've asked little Avril Atkinson to supper.'

'Very pleased indeed,' I told her courteously.

The fact is, I'd have been pleased whoever they'd asked, even my cousin. By then I'd discovered the dear old Wattles were incapable of conversation about anything except happenings in Porterhampton, which if you hadn't lived in the place for thirty years was like trying to enjoy a play after arriving in the second interval. It did me no end of good to hear another voice at table, even if they did make me tell the story of the ruddy parrot from the beginning.

After the meal I announced that my studies could slide for another evening, and politely joined the company in the sitting-room. Then Dr Wattle suddenly remembered he had a patient to see, and Ma Wattle had the washing-up to do, leaving Avril and me on the sofa alone.

'How about the television?' I suggested, Avril's conversation being almost as strait-jacketed as the Wattles'.

'Oh, let's. It's my favourite programme tonight.'

I switched on the set, turned down the lights, and when we'd watched a few parlour games and chaps pretending to get fierce with each other over the political situation, I very civilly drove her home.

'Do you like classical music, Gaston?' asked Mrs Wattle a few mornings later.

'I'm not adverse to a basinful of Beethoven from time to time,' I admitted.

'I'm so pleased. I've got a ticket for our little amateur orchestra next Friday in the Town Hall. Would you care to go?'

I was glad of an excuse to go out in the evening, now being rather bored with all those stories about chaps killing other chaps by highly complicated means. As I sat down among the potted municipal palms, I found Avril in the next seat.

'Quite a coincidence,' I remarked.

She smiled.

'You have such a sense of humour, Gaston. Wasn't it nice of Mrs Wattle to give us the tickets?'

'Oh, yes, quite.'

The dear old thing seemed to be getting forgetful, which I put down to the normal hormonal changes in a woman of her age.

The next few days were brightened by excitement over the great event in professional circles at Porterhampton, the annual medical dinner. As the Wattles seemed to find this a combination of the Chelsea Arts Ball and the Lord Mayor's Banquet, to please the dear old couple I agreed to put on a dinner jacket and accompany them, though personally nothing depresses me quite so much as a lot of other doctors. I had just eased into my chair in the ballroom of the Commercial Hotel, when I realized that I was once more sitting next to Avril Atkinson.

'So nice of Dr Wattle to have invited me,' she began. 'Are you going to make a speech with your terribly funny stories?'

'Not for me, I'm afraid. Though the fat chap with the microphone has a wad of papers in his pocket the size of an auctioneer's catalogue. Remarkable, isn't it, how men find so much to say after dinner when their wives haven't had a word out of them for years over breakfast?'

She giggled. 'Gaston, you're terribly witty.'

'Just wait till you've heard the fat chap.'

The guest on my other side having nothing to talk about except the progress of his patients and his putting, I passed the meal chatting lightly to Avril and when the floods of oratory had subsided took her home in my car.

'You simply must come in and meet daddy,' she invited.

Her father was a decent old boy, who gave me a whisky and soda and seemed intelligently interested in the National Health Service–rates of pay, prospects of promotion for young practitioners, and so on. I put him right on a few points, and went home with the pleasant feeling that I'd done my social duty by the dear old Wattles pretty thoroughly.

I suppose I'm a trusting sort of soul. Strangers at race meetings sell me useless tips at a quid a go. Motorists miss me by inches on zebra crossings. I cash dud cheques for fellows I meet in pubs. Small boys have me in knots on April the first. But it was probably the soporific effect of life in Porterhampton which delayed tumbling to my plight until the morning I was called to treat the girl with the pink dress from my party for mumps.

'When's it to be announced?' asked this Miss Carmichael, as I removed the thermometer from her mouth.

'What announced?'

'Don't play the innocent, Doctor. Everyone in Porterhampton has known about it for weeks. Your engagement to Avril Atkinson, of course.'

'Avril Atkinson!'

I picked up the bits of shattered thermometer from the floor.

'But dash it, it's ridiculous! I hardly know the girl.'

'Now, now! You're always being seen together, at concerts and dinners and things. As for the time she went to the Wattles' for supper–phew! She told me all about it. Sitting alone all evening on the sofa in the dark.'

I drove straight home and confronted Ma Wattle.

'So Dame Rumour hath been at work,' she said coyly. 'I am delighted, Gaston, for your sake. You see, my husband and I felt we were selfish monopolizing your cheery company. Now you're settling down here, it's only right and proper you should take unto yourself a wife. Unlike us, your later years will be comforted with sons and daughters, whom we shall look upon almost as our own grandchildren. I'm afraid I've rather been playing the matchmaker. But I'm so glad you chose Avril. Such a jolly girl! The pair of you are ideally suited.'

I had nothing to say. I went to my room. I paced up and down and glared at St Ives. I sat on the double bed and bit my nails. I wished I'd taken the advice of the Dean at St Swithin's and made my career in the Prison Medical Service.

I certainly didn't want to pass the rest of my life in Porterhampton, even if old Wattle bequeathed me the Town Hall as well. I certainly didn't want to marry Avril Atkinson, who'd probably make me tell the story of the parrot every morning over breakfast. Now I couldn't see how to avoid either. I've often read in psychology books about the acute anxiety state, but I never really understood it until then. Then I had one of those masterly ideas that sometimes come before the bell rings at the end of examinations.

'Mrs Wattle–Dr Wattle.' I appeared downstairs to find both of them in the sitting-room. 'I have something very painful to confess.'

They looked alarmed.

'I am already married.'

I felt this was the simplest way out. It was beyond me to tell the dear old couple that their own idea of my spouse was as ridiculous as picking the Matron of St Swithin's. With a bit of luck they'd kick me out on the spot, and possibly use up Avril on my replacement.

'My wife works in London. She is a nurse. A night nurse. I couldn't reveal her before, because . . . because the position which I have the honour to hold was advertised for a single man. I needed the work.'

I sounded so pathetic, I felt quite sorry for myself.

'If you will give me a few minutes to pack,' I ended solemnly, 'I shall remove my unworthy self from your lives for ever.'

'How unreasonable I've been!' cried Mrs Wattle, and burst into tears.

'We've deliberately set asunder two who have been joined together,' added Dr Wattle, beating his bald head.

'You must ask your wife to come at once, Gaston.'

'I'll double your salary.'

'We'll give you the run of the house till you find a place of your own.'

'All this might be rather inconvenient,' I interjected quickly. 'My wife's working every night. Important private case.'

'Then bring her for the day,' insisted Mrs Wattle. 'How about lunch on Saturday?'

'Yes,' agreed Dr Wattle. 'We shall be terribly upset if you don't.'

I felt the script had somehow got out of hand. Perhaps it might have been easier simply to have married Avril.

Chapter Four

The following Saturday morning the Wattles' house was twittering with expectation.

'I'd better be off,' I announced, as the roast pork and stuffing sizzled in the oven. 'Her train's due in twenty minutes.'

'Do greet her with these chrysanthemums, Gaston.' Mrs Wattle pushed a bunch the size of a sheaf of corn into my arms. 'They're fresh out of the greenhouse, and I'm sure she'll love them. And I'm quite sure we're both simply going to *adore* her.'

I parked the car in the station yard, bought a platform ticket, and thoughtfully munched a bar of chocolate from a machine. I sat on a bench and read the paper until the train arrived. Peering through the passengers, I soon spotted the familiar red hat.

'Hello!' I called. 'Hope you didn't have a beastly journey.'

'It was stinking.'

'Welcome to Porterhampton.'

'And what a dump, too!'

'The city has several charming features, I assure you. Though I shan't be able to provide much of a conducted tour, as your train home's at nine-ten.'

'Thank God for that. What on earth have you got in your arms?'

'They're chrysanthemums, from the greenhouse.'

'You look as though you've lost your street barrow.'

'I think we'd better get off the platform. I might be spotted by one of my patients.'

I led Petunia Bancroft to the car.

'I've had some pretty funny parts in my time,' Petunia complained as we drove away. 'But this one makes the Crazy Gang look like the Old Vic.'

'It's perfectly simple,' I reassured her. 'You've only to play The Doctor's Wife, straight. To an accomplished actress like you, Pet my dear, it's as easy as selling theatre programmes.'

'If I hadn't been out of work I wouldn't have sniffed twice at the idea, believe you me.'

'Regard it as a professional challenge.'

'Costume all right?'

'Perfect for the part.'

'I thought I'd better leave off my ankle bracelet.'

'Can't say I've seen a nurse wearing one.'

'Supposing this old fellow–what's his name?–asks a lot of questions with long medical words and that? What the hell am I supposed to say?'

'Leave it to me. Anyway, all he's likely to talk about is our epidemic of mumps. Just remember the time you had it yourself.'

'I haven't.'

'Neither have I. Good job, in your case,' I smiled. 'Might possibly have mucked up your hormones.'

She asked how, so I gave a brief dissertation on the pathology and virology of mumps until we arrived at the Wattles' front gate.

'Petunia,' I announced. 'Your cue.'

I was pretty worried about the performance, though I didn't let on to Petunia. Another of the useful things you learn from studying medicine is radiating cheerful confidence all round while wondering what the devil's going to happen next. But I must say, she created the part of Mrs Grimsdyke magnificently. In half an hour the old couple were all over her.

'Where did you train, my dear?' asked Dr Wattle, as we sat down to lunch.

'Oh, at R.A.D.A.' said Petunia.

He looked puzzled. 'That seems a hospital I haven't heard of.'

'An affectionate name for the Royal Diabetic,' I told him.

'Is it really? Dear me, I never knew. One learns something every day. And what is the trouble with this important case your husband tells us you're nursing?'

'Er–foot and mouth disease.'

'Attacking a human? Good gracious me! How extraordinary. I've never heard of such a thing before in my life.'

'Petunia means the poor fellow is down in the mouth because he's got one foot in the grave. Quite a common nurses' expression.'

'Is it indeed? Of course, you've had more recent contact with such things than I, Gaston. How one hates to be thought behind the times! I must try it out at the next B.M.A. meeting. I expect, my dear, you've had wide experience nursing cases of mumps?'

But I neatly managed to steer the conversation away from shop, and as the afternoon wore on I felt my troubles were sorting themselves out splendidly. The old couple's feelings were saved, I was out of the matrimonial target area, and I could make a leisurely exit from Porterhampton as soon as Miles was safely on the St Swithin's staff. Besides, I now had a handy excuse for nipping down to London any weekend I felt like it.

'My train goes in about an hour,' Petunia reminded me, when we'd reached the cold ham supper stage.

'What a shame you can't stay longer,' sighed Mrs Wattle.

'Petunia has to be on duty at midnight,' I explained. 'As a matter of fact, I might as well be getting the car out.'

I opened the front door, and a nasty complication to my little plan rolled all over me.

I suppose this country wouldn't be the same if it weren't dosed regularly through the winter with fog. Can you imagine such national heroes as Sherlock Holmes or Jack the Ripper prowling about on nice mild summer evenings? How would Dickens' characters have looked in the Neapolitan sunlight? Or the dear old Houses of Parliament shining like the Taj Mahal? Our national character gets regularly tested by the frightful complications of fogs, particularly the great big grey thing that rose like a wall of dirty muslin from the front doorstep.

'I'd better telephone British Railways,' I muttered.

The word 'trains' evoked only a mystified silence on the wire.

'The midday hasn't turned up yet from Manchester,' said the fellow at the station. 'And where the morning express from Glasgow's got to, nobody knows. If you want your prospects of getting to London tonight, sir, they're nil. It's the biggest and thickest we've had this century, according to the wireless.'

'So now Petunia will have to stay till morning,' said Ma Wattle, smiling benevolently.

'But that's impossible!' she cried.

'Has to be back to her case,' I explained quickly.

'Surely under such circumstances a replacement could be found in London?' insisted Dr Wattle.

Petunia stamped her foot. 'Gaston can drive me.'

'Only into the first ditch, I'm afraid.'

'I absolutely and positively—'

I managed to shut Petunia up, the Wattles clearly thinking this rather odd behaviour for a pair of lovebirds.

'Don't worry, my dearest,' I pretended to give her a tender kiss. 'Leave it to me,' I hissed in her ear. 'I'll get you out of it.'

'I'm not worrying at all, my sweet. You'd blasted well better,' she hissed back.

We all sat down and looked at the television.

I spent the rest of the evening trying to concoct some fog-proof excuse. Should I pretend to perforate a duodenal ulcer? Or set light to the house? Or simply make a clean breast of it on the hearth-rug? I rejected each one. They would all upset the Wattles too much.

In short, nothing I could evolve by ten-thirty prevented the pair of us being ushered by Ma Wattle into my room, with two hot-water bottles in the double bed.

'You dirty little stinker!' started Petunia, as soon as the door was shut. 'This is the meanest and nastiest trick—!'

'For Lord's sake don't make so much noise! We're supposed to be a devoted couple.'

'I'd like you to understand, Dr Grimsdyke, that I am most definitely not that sort of a girl—'

'I know, I know! But if you'll only give me a moment's peace I can sort the whole thing out. No one is sorrier than I—'

'Nobody will be, by the time my brothers hear about this.'

'I can't help the ruddy fog, can I? Anyone would think I'd put it there myself.'

Petunia threw herself on the bed and started pounding the eiderdown.

'You've got to get me out of here! At once, I tell you. In five minutes. Otherwise I'll smash the window and scream for the police.'

'Pet, I'm doing my best! There must be some way of—'

'I'll scream. I will. I'll wake all the neighbours. You just listen—'

She drew a deep breath.

'For God's sake, Pet—!'

The telephone rang in the hall.

'Hold off the sound effects till I've answered it,' I hissed.

'Dr Grimsdyke?' said a woman's voice on the line.

'Speaking.'

'You swine! You cad! You beast! You bigamist!'

'Now just a second. If you'll tell me who's speaking—?'

'You know perfectly well who's speaking. Avril, of course. I'm only ringing to inform you that tomorrow morning I'm starting a breach of promise suit, that'll blow you out of Porterhampton so hard you won't stop till you reach the white cliffs of Dover, which I hope you'll drop over and break your filthy neck. Let me tell you—'

'But I can explain absolutely everything,' I insisted. 'Can't I come round in the morning and see you?'

'You most certainly can't come anywhere near me. Apart from everything else I'm in bed with mumps, which I caught at your beastly party. *And* I've changed my cards to another doctor. You just wait till my brother comes on leave from the Commandos. Good night!'

In the space of five minutes I'd been abused by two women and threatened with assault from their relatives, which I felt was a record even for chaps like Bluebeard. But the telephone had given me an idea.

I tapped on the Wattles' door.

'I've been called to a case,' I explained. 'I don't expect I'll be long.'

Wrapping a scarf round my neck and pocketing a tin of cough lozenges from the surgery, I set out to spend the night in the fog while Petunia tucked herself cosily into the double bed.

Chapter Five

The fog was lifting as I tramped back to the Wattles' home. I'd coughed my way into the darkness, with no particular object except keeping alive till morning. About a hundred yards from the house I'd wandered into the main road to London, where I met a chap who'd lost his lorry. He remembered a place in the area called Clem's Caff, which we found by walking an hour or so along the white line. The Caff sported a coke stove, and was full of lorry drivers in steaming overcoats, resembling overworked horses. I bought a cup of tea, which seemed to entitle me to sleep on the table like everyone else. About five-thirty I woke up, feeling as if I'd just been released from the rack in the Tower.

I crept inside the house, tapped softly at the bedroom door, and Petunia let me in.

'You look as if you've just come off Everest,' she said.

'I hope you passed a good night yourself,' I replied shortly.

'Absolutely adorable. I haven't been so warm for months.'

She was already up and dressed, and seemed more amenable than the evening before.

'Poor Gaston! Are you sure you won't catch your death?'

'I wouldn't really care at the moment if I did.'

'I'm sorry–but it wasn't really my fault, was it? Perhaps you could have slept on the floor behind the wardrobe, or something.'

'I think it was a far, far better thing that I did.'

'You know, there really is something of the Sidney Carton about you, dear. No other man I know would have been half so noble.'

'Anyway, it's all over now. The fog's thinning rapidly, and as far as I remember there's a good train about five on Sunday afternoons. If you can stick it out till then.'

'I'm sure I can,' said Petunia. 'It's really awfully cosy here.'

'You *do* look pale this morning,' giggled Mrs Wattle when I appeared at breakfast. 'I hope you got plenty of sleep.'

The day passed without mishap. Petunia seemed quite to enjoy herself sitting about the house reading magazines, and in the afternoon I drove her to see the Town Hall, the water-works, the bus depot, and the new abattoir.

'Quite a pretty little place after all,' she remarked, as I pulled up outside the municipal baths. 'It's a wonder I've never been here on tour.'

'Would you like to see the statue of the first Mayor?'

'Yes, please,' said Petunia.

After tea and Dundee cake I looked at my watch and announced to the Wattles, 'Perhaps my wife ought to be getting ready. We're due at the station in half an hour.'

'But isn't there a later train, darling?' asked Petunia. 'I could always catch that.'

'There's the eight forty-two,' I told her, looking surprised. 'And the ten six.'

'I'll take the ten six.'

'A far better idea,' agreed Ma Wattle. 'A few more hours together mean so much at your age, don't they?'

Shortly afterwards we were left alone. As a matter of fact, we were always being left alone, and Dr Wattle must have got awfully tired of sitting in his cold consulting-room.

'What's the idea, Petunia?' I demanded at once. 'I thought you couldn't get out of the place quick enough.'

She helped herself to a cigarette from the silver box.
ston,' she said, 'I've been thinking.'

I flicked the Wattles' table lighter.

'Thinking what?'

'That this is the nicest part I've ever played.'

'You were a great success at it, thank you very much. And now for the final curtain.'

'But do you know *why* I was a success? I've just realized it myself. It was because I *felt* the part–here.'

She indicated her mid-sternal region.

'That's essential for all high-class acting, so they tell me.'

Petunia sat on the sofa.

'Do you remember, Gaston, what you told me in that night-club, the last time we were out together?'

Remembering what chaps tell them in night-clubs is another illustration of how women are congenitally defective in sportsmanship.

'That I was the dearest and sweetest girl you'd ever met, and how you wished you could live in my arms for ever?'

'Ah, yes.'

'Perhaps, Gaston, dear, you didn't think I took your remarks seriously?'

'Of course I did.'

As far as I remembered, she was hitting someone on the head with a balloon at the time.

'It's terrible how I have to disguise my feelings, my sweet. We actresses must always put our career first. We can never enjoy the simple home life of other women. It's awfully tragic.'

'I think you're perfectly right,' I told her briskly. 'Wonderful thing, devotion to one's vocation. You'll never regret it once you're a famous star with half London at your feet.'

'I'd never be a famous star. Not someone like Monica Fairchild, with every manager in London fighting over her. It's no good fooling myself. I'd just continue with walking-on parts, and live with Mum year in and year out, except for a few weeks on tour in miserable theatrical boarding-houses.'

'Oh, come! You're just a bit depressive for the moment. I bet Sarah Bernhardt felt exactly the same dozens of times.'

'But seeing you here,' Petunia went on, flicking her ash over the bearskin rug, 'in your dear little home in this sweet little town, has opened my eyes. My racket isn't worth the candle. I want to settle down.'

'But this *isn't* my dear little home,' I argued. 'It's Dr Wattle's dear little home. As for the town, I came here intending to settle for life and now I wouldn't even touch it for bed and breakfast. It would send a girl like you crackers in less than—'

She got up and stood so near me I could see the arteries in her conjunctivae.

'This last twenty-four hours I've realized how wonderful it is being your wife—'

'But dash it! You're *not* my—'

'You're so sweet, so modest. So honourable, so upright. So tender, so considerate. Gaston, darling, I've decided to accept you. We can get married secretly in some registry office—'

'Sorry to disturb the nest of lovebirds,' Ma Wattle chuckled, entering at that moment. 'I just wondered if your wife would like some nice hot soup for supper, to brace her for her journey.'

'Mrs Wattle.' Petunia turned to face her. 'I'm not going. I must stay with my husband. I'll send a telegram to London and resign my job. My mother can send on my things tomorrow.'

'I'm absolutely delighted!' exclaimed the old dear, embracing us. 'As I always say, a woman's place is at her husband's side, come what may. Of course, my children, you may stay with us as long as you wish. I'll just put the kettle on for your hot-water bottles. I expect after such excitements you'll both be wanting to go early to bed.'

If I wasn't keen on marrying Avril, I'd rather have swallowed the entire poisons cupboard before marrying Petunia. An agreeable companion for a gay night out, certainly. But you can't make a life partner of a woman who keeps trying to conduct the band with sticks of celery.

'You haven't eaten your nice soup, Gaston,' said Ma Wattle at supper.

'Not very hungry, I'm afraid.'

'What a wonderful thing love is!'

I was nearly sick over the sliced brawn.

I was edgy and jumpy the rest of the evening, which, of course, the idiotic Wattles put down to passion, or the expectation thereof. Worst of all, the mental trauma kof the past two days seemed to have beaten my brain into paralysis. Nothing I could contrive by ten o'clock prevented Petunia and myself again being shown into my bedroom.

'Alone at last!' breathed Petunia.

'Yes, but only for a couple of shakes,' I told her smartly. 'As soon as the Wattles have bedded down, I'm going to skip it into the night again.'

'But Gaston! Surely you're not going to leave your wife?'

'Pet, you chump! You're not my wife–only on the programme. Let me make it perfectly clear I'm not going to stay with you up here.'

'How honourable you are!' she breathed. 'How fine! How different!'

The Grimsdykes, of course, have their honour. But I must admit I wouldn't have objected to the same arrangement if we'd been in a hotel at Brighton instead of the Wattles' spare bedroom. Under prevailing circumstances the only place for me was Clem's Caff.

'We'll be married tomorrow if you like,' she said, starting to unzip her dress. 'A girl friend of mine once got a special licence terribly easily.'

'Petunia! You don't understand—'

'I understand everything, darling. You're a wonderfully honest man, and I shall love you more and more as the years go by.'

About twenty minutes later I was sitting again over one of Clem's cups of tea. I woke at five-thirty the next morning, so ill from the effects of prolonged exposure that I would almost have married Petunia on the spot for a comfortable night's rest in my own bed. I got back to the house shivering and with a shocking headache, and found Dr Wattle in the hall.

'Just come in from seeing the Mayor's gout,' he greeted me. 'I didn't know you'd been called out too. I never heard the phone.'

'It was someone with fits. Difficult diagnosis. Took a lot of time.'

'You don't look very perky, my boy. Are you sure you're all right?'

'Bit chilly, this night air.'

'Perhaps I'd better take your temperature?'

As he removed the thermometer from my mouth he asked, 'Ever had mumps? Well, I'm afraid you have now.'

'Mumps!' I cried. 'But–but that means isolation.'

'I'm afraid so. You'll have to stay in your room. Your wife hasn't had it either? Then you'd better be strictly alone. I'll go up and break the sad news. It's best for you not to breathe over the poor child.'

'Petunia's rather alarmed about it,' explained Dr Wattle, returning with some surprise. 'She seemed remarkably upset over those hormonal complications. I told her how terribly rare they are, but she's still awfully agitated. Keeps saying it would ruin her career. I shouldn't have thought it would have mattered much one way or another to a nurse. However, it's none of my business. We'll make you up a bed in the attic.'

I slept for twenty-four hours, which Dr Wattle later wrote a letter about to the *B.M.J.* entitled 'Unusual Stupor in Epidemic Parotitis'. Petunia spent the morning gargling, then disappeared for London. As soon as my lumps were down I announced I must go to the sea-side for convalescence, and sent a wire from London explaining I'd been summoned to a dying uncle in South Africa.

I felt pretty sorry for myself. I'd broken a couple of girlish hearts, had a nasty illness, and expected hourly to be assaulted by Commandos, and so on, in the street. Porterhampton had thenceforward to be blotted from my atlas. And now I had to explain it all to my cousin.

But at least I never hurt the dear old Wattles' feelings.

Chapter Six

'From your appearance,' started Miles, 'you would seem to have finished some protracted party.'

'If you must know,' I replied, rather hurt, 'I've had a nasty attack of epidemic parotitis. I've hardly got over it yet.'

'I'm sorry.'

It being one of my principles always to confess my short-comings promptly, particularly if they're likely to be discovered pretty quickly anyway, I'd telephoned Miles on arrival and invited myself to dinner. I now sat in his South Kensington drawing-room wondering how best to explain the retreat from Porterhampton.

'And when are you returning to your practice?' asked Miles.

I shifted on the sofa.

'As a matter of fact, old lad, I'm not.'

'What? Damn it! You've not been thrown out already?'

'Thrown out?' I looked offended. 'I resigned, with the dignity of a high-principled Cabinet Minister.'

Miles fell silent. To fill the gap I reached for a magazine–one of the shiny ones which report the activities of all our best-bred young women and horses.

'That's what I need,' I said, indicating a photograph of people with long drinks on a yacht at Cannes. 'A few weeks in the sunshine to buck me up.'

Miles made a noise like a tearing sheet of canvas.

'Damnation, Gaston! Are you mad? Are you fit for some institution? Here you are–out of work, penniless, a walking disgrace to your family if not to your entire profession, and you ramble about weeks in the sunshine. Really!'

I tossed the magazine aside with a sigh.

'The trouble is, you're perfectly right,' I admitted. 'I'm not the shining figure of the eager young doctor.'

'You're the shining figure of the shiftless young wastrel, and I don't mind telling you. I seriously advise you to see a psychiatrist. He might at least be able to explain your highly unstable occupational history.'

'The fact is, old lad, I don't need a psychiatrist to tell me that I don't like medicine very much.'

Miles stared as though I were Cinderella telling the Fairy Godmother she didn't care greatly for dancing.

'At Porterhampton the dear old couple handed me every chance to settle down as a respectable family man and family doctor. But do I want to be the modern G.P., signing certificates for all the uninteresting patients and hospital letters for all the interesting ones? No, I jolly well don't. And neither do a lot of other chaps, judging by the correspondence in the *B.M.J.* As I'll never be a specialist in anything, and I couldn't possibly sit in the Town Hall with a map of the local sewers doing public health, there isn't much left. The trouble is, I'm temperamentally unsuited to my work.'

'But think of all those years of study–wasted!'

'They're not wasted a bit,' I argued. 'Look at all the famous chaps who've benefited from a medical education–Leonardo da Vinci, John Keats, Chekhov, and so on. Not to mention Crippen.'

'You must quite definitely see a psychiatrist. And meanwhile, how precisely are you going to earn your bread?'

'Ah, yes. I agree, that's the problem.'

Further discussion about my professional future was prevented by the appearance of Miles's wife.

'How charming you're back so soon, Gaston,' she greeted me. 'We quite thought you'd gone to seek your fortune up North.'

'I decided that opportunity taps less faintly in London, Connie.'

'I'm so glad. Now we'll see much more of you. What did you say, Miles, dear?'

'Nothing, nothing,' muttered Miles.

I knew Connie pretty well. In fact, once I was in love with her.

This happened when I was a student and Miles had just qualified as Mr Sharper's junior casualty house-surgeon, and pretty pleased with himself he felt about it, too. As I reflected during dinner that evening, Miles and I had never really hit it off at St Swithin's, or even as kids. Miles was the one who didn't get his boots dirty, always had his sums right, wasn't sick at all the parties, and didn't make a fuss about his tonsilectomy. At school he used to make me blow up his football and toast his crumpets. Then I followed him to St Swithin's, and like everyone else started medicine by dissecting the dogfish, which has put me off fish suppers ever since. Miles was already well into the course, and by the time I got as far as the anatomy rooms kept buttonholing me in the corridors with fatherly advice.

'If you spent a little more time dissecting and a little less writing all those stupid jokes for the students' magazine,' was his usual line, 'you might show you were taking your career seriously.'

'I thought the last one was rather funny. About the girl who said she suffered from claustrophobia because she had a terrible fear of confinement.'

'Take it from me, Gaston, you'll regret this frivolity one day. You stick to your anatomy. It's the grammar of medicine.'

'Personally,' I disagreed, 'I think they only fill medical students with anatomy like they used to fill kids with brimstone and treacle. The experience is obviously so unpleasant, everybody agrees it must be doing them good.'

'I'm not at all certain it isn't my duty to write to my father,' he generally ended.

My own father having unfortunately perished in the R.A.M.C., I was brought up under a Victorian system of guardians, with Dr Rudolph Grimsdyke as chief paymaster. Uncle Rudolph practising at the time out East, Miles was his nark on the spot, and I suppose he sneaked in the end because half-way through the course the old boy cut my allowance by half. I know that ever since *La Bohème* it's been thought rather romantic for students to starve in garrets holding the tiny frozen hands of their girl-friends, but that sort of existence didn't appeal to me at all. Particularly as all the girls I knew seemed to complain shockingly of the draughts even in comfortable cocktail bars.

Shortly after the onset of this financial anaemia Miles qualified, glittering with scholarships and prizes.

'Gaston,' he said, getting me into a corner of the St Swithin's Casualty Department one winter afternoon, 'I want a serious word with you.'

'Oh, yes?'

'I'd be much obliged if you'd try to embarrass me a little less now that I'm on the St Swithin's junior staff. You must realize that I, at least, don't wish the entire family to be made ridiculous throughout the hospital. It's bad enough your always disappearing to the dog-races, but this habit of taking menial employment—'

'My dear old lad, I assure you I don't do it for fun. Anyway, it's all your old man's fault, being so tight-fisted. Surely you know by now I dislike work in any form whatever?'

I was at the time restoring my enfeebled exchequer with such casual jobs as dish-washing in West End restaurants and bar-keeping in East End pubs, and had just finished a profitable though strictly limited run as Father Christmas in an Oxford Street store.

'That's not the point at all. Mr Sharper was certain he saw you the other day. He was extremely blunt to me about it this morning.'

'Oh, really? I thought his keen surgical eye had pierced the whiskers. But I bet he only made a fuss because I told his beastly kids to ask for a complete set of electric trains and a couple of motor-cars.'

'I do wish you'd take this seriously, Gaston!

'Let's talk about it another time. I must be off now, I'm afraid. Otherwise I'll be late for work.'

A few days after this argument I met Connie, by accident.

All medical students dream of witnessing some really satisfactory road smash, then appearing on the scene to calm the panic-stricken bystanders with the magic words, 'I am a doctor.' I've done it myself three times. The first, the policeman told me to run home to mother. The second, I grabbed a tourniquet from some fumbling old boy and discovered he was the Professor of Surgery at St Asaph's. Now, of course, I walk rapidly in the opposite direction and leave it to the ambulance boys, remembering Sir Lancelot Spratt's resuscitation lecture–'When I chuck myself into the Thames in despair, ladies and gentlemen, I hope I'll be given artificial respiration by a fit Boy Scout, and not some middle-aged medical practitioner who's soon more out of breath than I am.' But when one is young, one doesn't consider such things. On this third occasion, as soon as I heard the scream of brakes and tinkling of glass, I leapt into the middle of Sloane Square and took sole charge.

In the next part of the dream, the injured party isn't a poor young child or a dear old lady, but a beautiful girl having hysterics. And that's exactly what I found. So I popped her in a taxi and drove her round to the casualty entrance at St Swithin's, where Miles organized X-rays, diagnosed a Colles' fracture, and signed an admission form for his ward.

'Charming girl, too,' I observed, as Connie was wheeled away.

'Thank you, Gaston, for holding the X-rays.'

'Always glad to help. I might pop up and see her later. Terribly important to follow-up cases, so they keep telling us.'

'Mr Sharper allows only his own students in his wards, I'm afraid.'

'Oh, come. Can't you stretch a point?'

'A point being defined as possessing position but not magnitude, is incapable of being stretched,' said Miles.

All the same, I went up the next morning with a bunch of roses.

'How terribly sweet!' exclaimed Connie, looking beautiful despite the plaster and bandages. 'And your assistant's just called too, with the mimosa.'

'Assistant?'

'The doctor who helped you with the X-rays.'

'Ah, yes. Useful chap.'

The staff in modern hospitals outnumbering the patients by about five to one, the inmates can be excused for confusing the ranks. I remembered there was once a frightful row when Sir Lancelot Spratt in a white coat was mistaken for the ward barber.

'You'll be out of here this afternoon,' I went on, not bothering to start long explanations. 'When time has healed all your wounds, would you care to come out for a bite of dinner?'

'But I'd love to, Doctor!'

'Jolly good. I'll get your telephone number from the ward notes.'

Unfortunately, Connie turned out to be the daughter of a shockingly rich fellow from Lloyd's, so I couldn't buy her a pint of beer and show her the ducks in St James's Park and pretend I'd given her an exciting evening. Also, I knew a determined chap like Miles wouldn't easily give up. While I was sitting with her a few weeks later in the Savoy, hoping she wouldn't feel like another drink, I remarked casually, 'Seeing much of my cousin these days?'

'As a matter of fact, yes, I'm going to the theatre with him tomorrow.'

'It may be rather cheeky of me to ask this, Connie, but I'd rather you didn't mention me to him, if you wouldn't mind.'

She looked surprised. 'Why ever not?'

'Just to save the poor chap's feelings. These little family jealousies, you know. He feels it rather, being my underling at the hospital.'

'How awfully considerate of you, Gaston. Naturally, I won't say a word. But supposing he talks about *you*?'

'He never does,' I assured her. 'Another Martini?'

'Yes, please,' said Connie.

I passed a couple of enjoyable months escorting Connie to all the more fashionable plays and restaurants, particularly as she still seemed to imagine that I was some wealthy young specialist, and I never seemed to find the chance to put her right. Then one afternoon Miles cornered me in the surgeons' room.

'I believe you've still been seeing Connie?' he demanded.

I tossed my sterile gown into the students' linen bin.

'On and off, yes.'

'I'd like you to know that I–I'm perfectly serious about her.'

This didn't disturb me. Miles was perfectly serious about everything.

'May the best man win, and all that, eh?'

'Damn it, Gaston! I wish you wouldn't regard this as some sort of sporting contest. I happen to love Connie deeply. I wish to make her my wife.'

'Good Lord! Do you really?'

The notion of Miles making anyone his wife seemed as odd as palm trees growing on an iceberg.

'And I'll thank you not to trifle with her affections,' he added.

'You will, will you?' I returned, feeling annoyed at his tone. 'And how do you know I don't want to make her Mrs Grimsdyke, too?'

'You? You're in no more position to marry than a fourth-form schoolboy.'

I felt the conversation was becoming embarrassing, and edged away. Besides, I had to be off to work again.

Entertaining Connie was making such inroads into my finances that I'd been obliged to find more regular employment. Fortunately, I'd met a chap called Pedro in a Shaftesbury Avenue pub, and after giving him some free advice about his duodenal ulcer and a good thing for Kempton Park, I was offered five evenings a week as a waiter in his Soho restaurant. Pedro was a fierce task-master, most of his relatives still chasing each other over Sicilian mountains with shotguns, and I had to clean all the soup off my best set of tails every night before going to bed, but the tips were good enough compensation for both.

Or they were until that particular evening, when Miles walked in with Connie.

'Shall we sit over here?' she said, advancing towards my corner. 'I hate a table too near the door.'

I ducked quickly into the kitchen.

'What the 'ell are you up to?' demanded Pedro.

'I–er, just wanted to adjust my sock suspenders.'

'I don't pay you to adjust your socks, mister. You get back in there. There's customers just come in.'

I passed a hand across my forehead.

'You know, Pedro, I don't think I'm feeling very well tonight. A bit faint.

I might be sick over the fish or something. If you don't mind, I'll just totter through the staff entrance and make home to bed.'

''Ow the 'ell you think I run my business one man short?' Pedro picked up a carving knife. 'You leave this restaurant only over your dead body, see mister? If you want to be sick, come out and be sick in the kitchen, like everybody else. You go to work.'

I edged back through the swing doors. I slipped my menu and table-napkin behind a bread basket, and prepared to dash for the pavement. I'd almost made the main entrance, when Connie glanced idly round and spotted me.

'Why, it's Gaston! Hellow, there! You dining here, too?'

Miles turned round and scowled.

'Oh, hello, Connie. Yes, I am, as a matter of fact. Expecting an old school chum. Chap called Honeybank. Doesn't seem to have turned up.'

'Charming little restaurant, isn't it?'

'Oh, very.'

'You seem very dressed up,' muttered Miles.

'Going on, you know. A ball, and all that.'

'I think men look their best in tails,' remarked Connie. 'Don't you Miles? What on earth's dear Pedro doing?'

I thought dear Pedro was probably putting that knife on the grinding machine, but only murmured something about having to be off.

'But if you haven't eaten you must stay for a bite with us,' Connie insisted. 'I'm sure Miles wouldn't mind.'

'Not a bit,' growled Miles.

'It might be a little awkward, actually—'

'But definitely, Gaston. Tell the waiter to bring another chair. Ah, there you are, Pedro. How is your lovely *canneloni* tonight?'

'Delicious, Madame.'

Pedro came over rubbing his hands. I stood on one foot, leaning against the table. Dashed difficult, striking an attitude simultaneously suggestive of helpful servility and long-standing chumminess.

'And the *osso buco*, it is excellent,' Pedro added.

'Then shall we all have *canneloni* followed by *osso buco*?' Connie looked inquiringly at Miles and myself. 'I'm terribly hungry.'

'Two *canneloni* two *osso buco*,' snapped Pedro in my ear. 'Didn't you 'ear what madame says?'

'How extraordinary repeating the order like that,' exclaimed Miles.

'Just a little joke,' I explained, as Pedro backed away. 'I know him very well.'

Connie sighed. 'How lucky you are! I can't imagine anything more useful in London than being friends with all the head waiters. But Gaston, *do* sit down. You make me feel uncomfortable, standing about like that.'

'Just a second, if you'll excuse me. Phone call–the school chum, you know.'

I slipped back to the kitchen.

'What the 'ell's the matter with you tonight?' demanded Pedro. 'You stick around with a silly grin on your face like a drunk monkey. How you expect me to run my restaurant if you don't listen to the customers?'

'Look, Pedro, I really think I ought to be at home tucked up in bed—'

'Take that in, and don't talk so much.'

He handed me two dishes of *canneloni*.

'Good Lord!' exclaimed Miles. 'You've brought the food yourself.'

'Ha ha! Just another little joke. Dear old Pedro, you know. I keep threatening a public health inspection of his kitchen, and just nipped in to take him by surprise. The *canneloni* was ready, so I brought it along.'

Connie found this terribly amusing.

'But Gaston, you haven't a plate. And do *please* sit down.'

'I'll just prop on the back of this chair.' I edged myself into a position where I might be mistaken for serving the spinach. 'They get so terribly crowded, I'm sure Pedro hasn't got a spare seat. I don't think I'll try any *canneloni* myself, thanks. But let me help you.'

'You serve quite professionally,' exclaimed Connie.

'Jack of all trades, you know . . .'

'Are you sure you're quite all right tonight?' demanded Miles.

'Oh, fine, thank you.'

I felt that the situation was reasonably hopeful, as long as they crammed down their blasted *canneloni* before Pedro came back.

'What were we talking about? I suppose you've heard the story of the bishop and the parrot—'

Just then a voice behind me called, 'Waiter!'

'Well, you see, this bishop had a parrot—'

'Waiter!'

'And this parrot used to belong to an old lady who bought it from a sailor—'

'Say, Waiter!'

'There isn't a waiter in sight,' interrupted Connie.

'Never is when you want one,' grumbled Miles.

'I think he's an American who keeps shouting,' said Connie.

'And the old lady always used to keep it under a green baize cloth in the front parlour. Every morning she'd take the cloth off the cage, and every morning the parrot said–'

'Hey, Waiter, for chrissakes!'

A fat man I'd just served with cigars and brandy appeared at my elbow.

'Excuse me, folks. I just wanted to tell the waiter here I've had a darned fine meal and darned fine service. I reckon it's the best I've struck since I've been in Europe. I was just getting on my way when I thought, shucks, I gotta give credit where credit is due. Thanks a lot, son. This is for you.'

The beastly chap stuffed a pound note into my top pocket.

'But how extraordinary,' exclaimed Miles.

'He thought you were the waiter!' laughed Connie.

'People never notice the fellows who serve them with food,' I mumbled. 'Conan Doyle or Edgar Wallace or someone wrote a story about it.'

'But he did seem pretty definite.' Miles gave me a nasty look.

'Oh, Miles, you know what Americans are,' said Connie.

At that moment, Pedro appeared again. I pretended to be arranging the flower vase.

'Everything all ri'?'

'No,' said Miles. 'The waiter hasn't brought any grated parmesan with my *canneloni*.'

Pedro glared across the table.

'Zere is no grated cheese with the *canneloni*.'

I glanced round for the cheese thing. I might reach across for it with a little laugh.

'That's exactly what I said,' Miles returned. 'It happens that I'm particularly fond of grated cheese with my *canneloni*.'

'So am I,' said Connie.

'There is no grated cheese with the *canneloni*!' shouted Pedro in my direction.

'Good gracious, man!' exclaimed Miles. 'Don't yell at me like that.'

'I am *not* yelling at you like that, monsieur. I am yelling at *'im* like that. *There is no grated cheese on the canneloni!*'

Connie jumped up.

'How dare you address my guests in that manner! I am going to leave this restaurant this very instant.'

Pedro looked as if he'd been hit in the neck with one of his own *canneloni*. 'Guests, madame? What guests? You're fired,' he added to me.

'I shall never eat here again, and I shall tell all my friends not to eat here either. Come along, Miles. Treating our guest here as one of your waiters—'

'But, damn it, madame! 'E *is* one of my waiters. 'E come every night, part time—'

'Only five days a week,' I insisted.

'Gaston!' Connie gave a little gasp. 'Is this really true?'

I nodded. The Grimsdyke ingenuity had been beaten back to its own goal-line. I reached for my napkin and automatically flicked the tablecloth.

'I'm not a doctor, really,' I murmured. 'I'm a student. I take this on for a little extra dibs.'

There was a silence. Connie started to laugh. In fact, she laughed so long she almost asphyxiated herself with a stick of Italian bread. In the end we all four thought it a tremendous joke, even Pedro.

But Connie never looked at me the same way again. And a fortnight later got engaged to Miles. I was pretty cut up about it at the time, I suppose. I often wonder how life would have turned out if Miles had been more of a gentleman and taken her somewhere like the Ritz.

The only compensation was that, according to the American chap, if I had to be a waiter I was a damn good one.

Chapter Seven

'I'm afraid I was somewhat over-optimistic at the way things would go at St Swithin's,' announced Miles.

Connie had left us after providing a charming little dinner, and I was guessing my chances of getting a cigar.

'The appointment of Sharper's successor has as usual got mixed up with hospital politics.'

He stared gloomily into the fruit bowl.

'Sir Lancelot Spratt is making an infernal nuisance of himself on the committee. He is opposing my candidature, purely because Mr Cambridge is supporting it. Sir Lancelot has quarrelled with him, you know. Cambridge refuses to knock down his old clinical laboratory, and Sir Lancelot wants to park his car there. To think! My future decided by a car park.'

'There's nothing like a mahogany table and a square of pink blotting-paper to bring out the worst in a chap's character,' I sympathized. 'How about the other runners?'

'There are thirty other prospective candidates for the post, all as well qualified as I. But we are mere pawns, mere cyphers. Perhaps I should apologize for being short with you earlier, Gaston. The strain, you know. The uncertainty . . .'

He miserably cracked a nut.

I felt sorry for the chap. Personally, there was nothing I'd have liked less than being a consultant at St Swithin's, having to wear a stiff collar every day and never being able to date up the nurses, but it had been Miles's ambition ever since he was cutting up that dogfish. And I rather felt that Connie, too, fancied herself in a new hat running the hoopla with other consultants' wives at the annual hospital fête. Besides, Miles was the brightest young surgeon St Swithin's had seen for years, and I should have felt a bit of a cad not helping so worthy a practitioner along the professional path.

'If you didn't get on at St Swithin's,' I tried to console him, 'you'd find a consultant job easily enough in the provinces.'

'But it wouldn't be the same thing. And, of course, Connie and I would have to leave our home.'

I nodded. Since the waiter episode girls had been in and out of my life like people viewing an unsatisfactory flat, but I'd always retained a soft spot for Connie. The thought of her confined for life to a place like Porterhampton upset me so much I'd almost have had another go at living there myself to prevent it.

'In such delicate circumstances,' I suggested, 'I take it you'd more than ever like me tucked away in some respectable job?'

'Exactly.'

'Find me one, old lad, and I will. I can't possibly face Palethorpe for months, of course.'

'I have some influence with the Free Teetotal Hospital at Tooting. They'll be needing a new house-surgeon next week.'

'And the week after, I'm afraid, as far as I'm concerned.'

Miles stroked his pale moustache.

'A pity you didn't keep your position on the *Medical Observer*. At least it utilized your talent for the pen respectably.'

'That was a congenial job,' I agreed, 'until the old editor banished me to the obituaries.'

The *Medical Observer* was the trade press, which lands on doctors' doormats every Friday morning and is widely appreciated in the profession for lighting the Saturday fires. It has an upstairs office near the British Museum in imminent danger of condemnation by the health, fire, and town planning authorities, where I'd been assistant to the editor, a thin bird with a wing collar and severe views on the split infinitive.

'You can't imagine how depressing it was, writing up dead doctors from nine to five,' I told Miles. 'Though I composed my own for the files while I was there, and a jolly good one it will be, too. Yours isn't bad, either.'

'I am gratified to hear it. Perhaps you should go abroad? An oil company for which I do insurance examinations are prospecting up the River Amazon in Brazil. They have a vacancy for a medical officer on a five-year contract. The salary would certainly appeal to you. And you just said you could do with some sunshine.'

'But not five years of it, all at once.'

Miles began to look irritable again. 'I must say, Gaston, for a man in your position you're being extremely difficult to please.'

'Oh, I don't know. If I'm going to sell my soul I might as well get a decent price for it.'

'I do wish you'd discuss the subject of your livelihood seriously.'

'I was just about to, old lad. I don't suppose you could advance me ten quid, could you? Resigning abruptly from Porterhampton left me a month's salary short.'

'You know I am against loans among relatives. But I will agree if you accede to my suggestion about the psychiatrist. I am certain that's what you need. I can easily arrange for you to see Dr Punce, who manages the aptitude tests for the oil company. He rather specializes in whittling down square pegs.'

I don't share the modern reverence for psychiatrists, mostly because all the ones I know are as cracked as a load of old flower-pots. But the financial blood was running so thinly I accepted.

'I suppose you have no serious plans at all for maintaining yourself?' Miles asked, putting away his cheque book.

'I've a few more medical articles on the stocks. I'd also thought of trying my hand at a bit of copywriting–you know, "Don't let your girdle be a hurdle, we make a snazzier brassière," and so on.'

Miles winced.

'Gaston looking for another job?' asked Connie, appearing with the coffee. 'That's no problem anyway. A bright young man like him should be in demand anywhere.'

A bit *infra dig*, I thought, a doctor going to a psychiatrist. Like a fireman ringing the station to say his house was alight. I didn't remember much of the psychiatry course at St Swithin's myself, except the afternoon Tony Benskin was left to hypnotize a young woman with headaches, and once he'd got her in the responsible state suggested she took her blouse off. Apparently Tony's hypnotic powers are low voltage, because the girl clocked him one against the corner of the instrument cupboard. Quite some confusion it caused when the chief psychiatrist came in, to find the patient stamping about shouting and the doctor unconscious.

But I dutifully appeared at Dr Punce's rooms in Wimpole Street the following afternoon, and found him a tall, thin fellow in striped trousers, a pince-nez on a black ribbon, and side-whiskers. I was shown in by a blonde nurse, which put me in a awkward position at the start–if I gave her the usual once-over the psychiatrist might decide something pretty sinister, and on the other hand, if I didn't, he might decide something even worse. I hit on a compromise, and asked her what the time was.

I took a seat and prepared for him to dig into my subconscious, shaking the psychopathic worms out of every spadeful.

'I don't suppose you treat many doctors?' I began.

'I assure you that all professions are fully represented in my case-books.'

'Psychiatry is the spice of life, and all that?' I laughed.

But he had no sense of humour, either.

'The note I have from your cousin mentions your difficulty in finding congenial employment,' he went on, offering me a cigarette, as psychiatrists always do.

I nodded. 'Miles seems to think I should find a job with security. Though frankly I rather prefer insecurity. But I suppose that's a bit of a luxury these welfare days.'

'H'm. I am now going to recite a succession of words. I wish you to say the first word that comes into your head in reply. Light?'

'No, it's going very well, thank you. I've got some matches of my own.'

'That is the first word.'

'Oh, I see. Sorry. Yes, of course. Er–sun.'

'Night?'

'Club.'

'H'm. Sex?'

'Psychiatrists.'

'Line?'

'Sinker.'

'Straight?'

'Finishing.'

'Crooked?'

'Psychiatrists. I say, I'm terribly sorry. I didn't mean to say that at all.'

Dr Punce sat for a while with his eyes closed. I was wondering if he'd had a large lunch and dozed off, when he went on, 'Dr Grimsdyke, I have had a particularly heavy month with my practice. I fear that I am sometimes tempted to be rude to my more difficult patients.'

'If it's any consolation,' I sympathized with him, 'I'm tempted quite often too. But don't worry–the feeling will pass. I recommend a few days in the open air.'

'Have you heard the story of the donkey and the salt?' he asked bleakly.

'No, I don't think I have.' I settled down to listen, knowing that psychiatrists pick up quite a few good ones in the run of their work.

'I'd like you to follow it carefully. There was once a donkey who fell into the water, crossing a stream on a very hot day with a load of salt. Eventually he got to his feet, feeling greatly relieved because the water had dissolved his burden. The next day he was crossing the stream loaded with sponges. This time he deliberately fell, but the sponges soaked up so much water the donkey was unable to rise at all. The animal succumbed. What do you think of that?'

'Ha ha!' I said. 'Jolly funny.'

In fact, I thought it a pretty stupid story, but one has to be polite.

'You think that the story is *funny*?'

'Oh, yes. Best I've heard for weeks. I suppose you know the one about the bishop and the parrot?'

'Dear me, dear me,' said the psychiatrist, and started writing notes.

After a good many questions about the Grimsdyke childhood, which was just the same as any other beastly little boy's, he asked, 'Any sexual difficulties?'

'By Jove, yes.'

I told him the story of Avril Atkinson, but he didn't seem impressed.

'Your trouble, Dr Grimsdyke,' he finally decided, wiping his pince-nez, 'is that you find yourself in uncongenial employment.'

I asked him what I was supposed to do about it, but he only said something about it being a consulting-room and not the Labour Exchange.

'I mean, being a doctor doesn't train you for anything else much, does it? Not like some of those barristers, who get fed up standing on their feet drivelling away to judges and collect fat salaries running insurance companies.'

'There have been medical bishops and ambassadors. Rhodesia had a medical Prime Minister. Goethe and Schiller were, of course, once both medical students.'

'Yes, and Dr Gatling invented the machine gun, Dr Guillotin invented the guillotine and Dr Dover became a pirate. I don't think I've much qualification for any of those professions, I'm afraid.'

'I suggest some non-clinical branch. How about entomology? Are you fond of insects?'

I thought deeply. 'Well, if I'm really no good as a doctor I suppose I could always end up as a psychiatrist. I say, I'm terribly sorry,' I added. 'Just for the moment I was forgetting—'

'Good afternoon, Dr Grimsdyke.'

'Right-ho. Do you want to see me again?'

'No. I don't want to see you at all. The nurse will show you out.'

I left him shaking his head and fumbling nervously with his pince-nez. The poor chap looked as though he really ought to have seen a psychiatrist.

'How did you get on?' asked Connie, answering the door when I called to report.

'Well, I think I won.'

'I hope he recommended shock treatment. Your Uncle Rudolph's in the sitting-room.'

'Good Lord, is he really? Where's Miles?'

'Out on a case. But don't worry–Uncle only wants to offer you a job. One of those rich patients who've been buying up the local country houses has asked him to Jamaica for a holiday. As he's got twenty-four hours to find a locum for the next three months, I suggested you.'

'That's really very decent of you, Connie.'

Since returning from the East, the old uncle had settled at Long Wotton, a pleasant niche in the Cotswolds with thatched roofs and draught cider and cows in the High Street. My session with the psychiatrist not producing much alternative to a lifetime of G.P., and Miles's ten quid already having undergone severe amputation, I felt glad of a decent job anywhere. I consoled myself that half rural practice is veterinary medicine anyway, and I'm rather fond of animals.

'My daughter-in-law talked to me for thirty minutes before persuading me to take you as my locum,' Uncle Rudolph greeted me. He was smaller and bristlier than Miles, with hair and eyebrows like steel wool under the influence of powerful magnets, and an equally prickly ginger tweed suit.

'That's very civil of you, uncle,' I told him, 'but as a matter of fact, you're not putting me to any trouble, as I'm quite free at the moment.'

'If you come to Long Wotton on Thursday, I can hand over. My Mrs Wilson will look after you adequately. Though she is attuned to the habits of an elderly widower, so don't expect champagne and caviar for breakfast.'

'Good Lord, no. I couldn't possibly manage anything heavier than cornflakes in the morning, anyway.'

'Kindly remember, Gaston, that there are a large number of important people in the neighbourhood. Most of them are my patients, and I wish them to remain so. Now listen to me. I understand from Miles that you are short of cash?'

'I am rather undernourished in the pocket at the moment,' I admitted.

'You know I have certain funds under my control which I saved you dissipating as a medical student. If you behave sensibly and efficiently at Long Wotton I am prepared to release them. If not, you will have to wait until my demise. And I can assure you that my blood-pressure is excellent.'

'All that matters, uncle,' I told him, 'is giving you satisfaction. In fact, you might just as well advance me the cash now.'

But he didn't seem to grasp the point, and hurriedly asked Connie to fetch him another whisky and soda. Shortly afterwards Miles came in, and nobody took much notice of me any more.

Chapter Eight

I arrived in the country on one of those April days when all the flowers look freshly painted and all the girls look beautiful. The English spring had arrived, as described in the poems and travel advertisements instead of the grey slushy thing we usually get.

I'd already spent a few week-ends at Long Wotton, and found it a friendly place where the inhabitants are all acquainted, if not, as I later suspected from the general feeble-mindedness, all actually related. Although I'm not much of a one for country pursuits–guns make such a frightful noise, fishing gives me a bad cold for weeks, and I regard horses as highly unroadworthy vehicles–it was pleasant to find myself respected locally as a learned chap, and not just the fellow who dishes out the chits for false teeth. Also, there was a very amiable young sub-postmistress, and I was looking forward to a few months quietly letting life go by and Avril Atkinson and Porterhampton fade into my subconscious.

After a week or so I was even becoming a little bored, with existence presenting no problems more complicated than keeping the uncle's housekeeper happy, and she seemed very satisfied with the story of the bishop and the parrot. Then I returned one evening from repairing the effects of a pitchfork on some bumpkin's left foot–a very pleasant consultation, with everyone touching their forelocks and asking if I could use a side of bacon–and found the old dear herself standing at the garden gate, looking distraught.

'Doctor, Doctor!' she called. 'Something terrible's happened.'

I was a bit alarmed the cream might have gone off. I was looking forward to my evening meal of fresh salmon followed by early strawberries, particularly as the old uncle had overlooked handing over the cellar keys in his hurry to be off, and I'd just found them–buried under the coal in the outhouse, of all places.

'Doctor, you're to go at once,' she went on. 'It's very urgent. To Nutbeam Hall,' she explained, when I asked where. 'It's his Lordship, there's been a terrible accident.'

A bit of a tragedy, I felt. Fancy missing a dinner like that. But the Grimsdykes never shirk their professional duty, and pausing only to load the Bentley with sufficient splints and morphine to tackle a train crash, I sped up the road to Nutbeam Hall.

Everyone in Long Wotton knew Lord Nutbeam, of course, though I don't mean they played darts with him every night in the local. In fact, most of the inhabitants had never seen him. The old boy was a bachelor, who lived in a rambling house apparently designed by Charles Addams, his younger brother's missus doing such things as ordering the coal and paying the milkman. He appeared only occasionally when they gave him an airing in an old Daimler like a mechanized glasshouse, always with brother or wife as bodyguard.

This was the pair who received me in the hall, a long, dim place crammed with furniture and as stuffy as the inside of the family vault.

'I'm the doctor,' I announced.

'But Dr Grimsdyke—?'

'Dr Rudolph Grimsdyke is enjoying a little well-earned holiday. I'm his locum and nephew, Dr Gaston Grimsdyke.'

I saw them exchange glances. The Hon. Percy Nutbeam was a fat chap with a complexion like an old whisky-vat, which I suppose he'd acquired at his brother's expense. His wife was one of those sharp-faced little women with incisors like fangs, to whom I took an instant dislike.

'Of course, I'm perfectly well qualified,' I added, sensing they might not take kindly to anyone but the accredited family practitioner.

'Naturally, naturally,' agreed Percy Nutbeam, very sociably. 'We don't question that for a moment.'

'I am sure you've had very extensive experience, Doctor,' put in the wife.

'Well, very varied, anyway. Look here,' I told them, feeling rather awkward, 'unless it's a matter of saving life on the spot, if you'd rather call another practitioner—'

'Not at all,' said Mrs Nutbeam briskly. 'My husband and I have the utmost confidence in your handling his Lordship's case. Haven't we, Percy?'

'Of course, Amanda.'

I must admit this made me feel pretty pleased. The old uncle's full of homely advice about wool next to the skin and so on, but after all those years among the hookworm and beriberi he's as out of date in medical practice as a Gladstone bag. I could see they were delighted at an up-to-date chap like myself with all the latest from hospital.

'Then what's the trouble?' I asked.

'We fear a broken hip, doctor,' announced Amanda Nutbeam. 'That's serious, I believe?'

'Could be. Very.'

'Our aunt died after a broken hip,' murmured Percy.

'It all depends on the constitution of the patient,' I told them, remembering my orthopaedic lectures.

'Please let me impress upon you, Doctor,' said Amanda, 'that his Lordship is very delicate.'

'Very delicate indeed,' added her husband. 'This way, Doctor, if you please.'

I went upstairs feeling pretty curious. I'd already decided it was the old story–poor old Lord Nutbeam was potty, and the family were making themselves thoroughly miserable keeping it quiet, instead of getting him decently certified and sending him baskets of fruit every Friday. I was therefore a bit startled when my clinical examination provided a couple of eye-openers.

In the first place, far from being dotty, Lord Nutbeam had an I.Q. in the professorial class.

'I fell from the library ladder, Doctor,' he explained from his bed. 'Appropriately enough, as I was reaching for my first edition of *Religio Medici*. You are familiar with the work? Perhaps you have also read Dr William Harvey's *De Motu Cordis* in the original Latin? I should much like to discuss it with a medical man.'

Not wishing to chat about all those books I'm going to read whenever I get a spare moment, I put my stethoscope in my ears. Then I got my second surprise. From the conversation downstairs I'd gathered Lord Nutbeam's grip on life was as secure as on a wet conger eel, but I quickly discovered–fractures apart–he was as hale and hearty as I was.

'I am very delicate, Doctor,' he kept on insisting, though he looked a spry old boy with his little white moustache. 'I neither smoke nor drink and live on soft foods. Ever since I had the fever at the age of twenty-one my dear brother and his wife have been devoted to my welfare.'

'Don't worry,' I told him. 'We'll soon have this little matter cleared up, and you'll be able to go on reading just where you left off.'

A few minutes later I again faced the ambulant members of the Nutbeam family in the hall, and announced in suitably sepulchral tones that his Lordship had indeed fractured the neck of the right femur.

'Ha!' muttered Percy Nutbeam. 'Auntie!'

'Then it *is* serious, Doctor?'

'But please let me reassure you.' I possibly gripped my lapels. 'Once we get anyone as chirpy as Lord Nutbeam into hospital and the hands of a decent orthopaedic surgeon, we'll have him on his feet again in no time. Meanwhile, I have administered a sedative and the fracture isn't very painful. I guarantee he'll stand up to everything wonderfully.'

I was then rather jolted to hear Amanda Nutbeam ask, 'Doctor, don't you think it would be far, far kinder just to do nothing?'

'A very eminent specialist left our aunt to pass peacefully away,' added Percy.

'But dash it!' I exclaimed. 'How old was your aunt?'

'Ninety-two.'

Lord Nutbeam was fifty, the age when most men are telling their secretaries they're in the prime of life.

'Look here, this is quite a different case—'

'His Lordship is so delicate, life is merely a burden to him,' persisted Amanda.

'Been delicate for years, Doctor. Even in the nursery he was always being sick.'

'Surely, Doctor, it would be a happy release?'

'He will have no more troubles among the angels,' ended Percy Nutbeam, looking at the chandelier.

Now, I may not be the most erudite of medical practitioners, but many years' patronage of the sport of kings has left me pretty sharp at spotting something fishy. So I eyed this couple pretty sternly and said, 'If I don't get Lord Nutbeam into hospital this very night, it'll be–why, gross professional misconduct, to say the least.'

'You can hardly get him there without his consent,' replied Amanda sharply.

She gave me a smile as unfriendly as one of Sir Lancelot Spratt's laparotomy incisions.

'And Lord Nutbeam would never consent to anything whatever without consulting us first,' said Percy.

'Now just a minute—'

'You are very young, Doctor,' Amanda continued. 'I can assure you his Lordship would be much happier passing away peacefully in his own home, rather than being mutilated among strangers.'

'Our aunt,' added Percy, 'was very contented right to the end.'

'Here, I say—'

'I think your consultation is over, Doctor. The butler will show you to the door.'

Chapter Nine

I was so furious I couldn't enjoy my salmon. But I managed to cram down the strawberries and a bottle of the uncle's *Liebfraumilch*, then I paced the room and smoked a couple of his cigars. I looked up Watson-Jones' *Fractures and Joint Injuries*, and I found a copy of Hadfield's *Law and Ethics for Doctors*, but though this is pretty hot on such things as Relations with the Clergy and Opening a Vein after Death, it's a bit short on handling murderous relatives. I wondered what the devil to do. I thought of telephoning another doctor, but felt this would produce only an action for slander. Finally I decided (a) if old Nutbeam continued to lie flat on his back he would undoubtedly perish; (b) you can't press-gang people into hospital; and (c) some pretty nasty questions were going to be asked at the inquest.

Apart from medical ethics, the thought of the beastly brother and wife itching to get their fingers on Lord Nutbeam's cash and title fairly made my blood boil. Particularly as I now realized my welcome to Nutbeam Hall didn't come from heartfelt appreciation of my clinical abilities, but because they thought I had more chance of knocking his Lordship off than my uncle had. After sitting down with a drop of the uncle's special liqueur brandy, I made my decision. My only course, as a doctor and gentleman, was to return to Nutbeam Hall forthwith and give all concerned a jolly good piece of my mind.

Five minutes later I arrived again at the front gates, turning a few choice phrases over in my thoughts, when I noticed a ruddy great Rolls parked outside. I was wondering if the Nutbeams had simply preferred to by-pass me and summon a specialist off their own bat, when the front door opened to admit a severe-looking bird of consultoid aspect, wearing striped trousers and carrying a brief-case.

'Good evening, sir,' I said.

'Good evening,' he replied, got into his Rolls, and drove off.

I'd hardly time to sort this out when the door flew open again and Mrs Nutbeam fell on me like her long-lost baby.

'Doctor, Doctor! Thank God you've come back! You must get his Lordship into hospital at once.'

'This very instant,' cried Percy, panting up behind.

'With the very best specialist available.'

'Regardless of expense.'

'Everything humanly possible must be done for him.'

'The telephone is just inside the hall, Doctor.'

'Now just a minute.' I found this rather confusing. 'A couple of hours ago you told me—'

'Please disregard whatever I said a couple of hours ago,' returned Amanda Nutbeam, 'I was too upset by my dear brother-in-law's accident to think properly.'

'We both were, Doctor. We were quite beside ourselves.'

Deciding there was no point in asking a lot of silly questions, I telephoned an eminent bone-basher in Gloucester who'd done a neat job on a patient who went through a threshing machine. Shortly afterwards I was gratified to see Lord Nutbeam departing tucked-up in an ambulance, particularly as the original Grimsdyke diagnosis had been confirmed.

Like any G.P. pushing his patient into hospital these days, I didn't see his Lordship again for a fortnight. I was meanwhile kept agreeably busy remedying the rustics, and though the uncle didn't even send a postcard, Miles telephoned a couple of times, but he was too concerned over Sir Lancelot's car park to ask how I was getting on. Then one Saturday I decided to drive over to Gloucester to watch an afternoon's cricket, and looked into the Jenner Memorial Hospital to see Lord Nutbeam during the tea interval.

I found his Lordship very perky in a private room with a Smith-Petersen pin holding his hip together, though we hadn't much time for a quiet chat–modern orthopaedic wards are pretty active places, with all those nice girls from the physiotherapy department laying cool hands on fevered joints and making you kick your legs in the air as though you were about to turn out for the Arsenal. But the old boy seemed to be enjoying it all, and while a little red-headed staff nurse brushed his hair he started asking my views on the original works of Hippocrates.

'You'll soon be back among your books again,' I said, not wishing to pursue the subject.

'Indeed, Doctor, I believe my library is the only pleasure in my life. Except on Saturday nights, when I sometimes play the piano.'

I was reflecting that this sort of existence would have me stone dead in a fortnight when we were interrupted by the surgeon himself, a big, red-faced, jolly Irishman. Most orthopods are, when you come to think of it, just as ophthalmologists look like dyspeptic watchmakers and bladder surgeons resemble prosperous commercial travellers.

'He's all yours now, m'boy,' said the surgeon, as we left the room together after examining the patient. 'His rehabilitation will go much smoother at home, and this sister-in-law seems agreeable enough to nurse him. Anyway, I'm off on Monday for a month's fishing in County Mayo. How is he for cash, by the bye?'

'According to village gossip, crammed with it.'

'Is he now?' The orthopod seemed to brighten at the prospect of having his fishing on Lord Nutbeam's hip. 'Odd sort of feller, don't you think? I couldn't see him saying "Boo" to a newly hatched gosling. I'll be sending you the usual letter about treatment. Meanwhile, tell him to confine his reading to the bottom shelf.'

When a few mornings later they unloaded his Lordship at Nutbeam Hall and I pushed his new wheel-chair into the library, I felt pretty contented with myself. The whole episode had already increased my professional standing in Long Wotton no end. I'm far from saying the natives were hostile, but in the country they regard anyone who hasn't lived among them for thirty years as a day tripper, and now there was plenty of glowing gossip to warm the ears of the old uncle on his return. If I could present him with a Lord Nutbeam skipping about the front lawn, he'd not only give fewer of those old-fashioned looks whenever I suggested enterprising lines of treatment, but painlessly disgorge my cash on the spot.

'I am certainly glad my brother-in-law is back in his own home, Doctor,' remarked Amanda Nutbeam. 'It is only here, I think, that we really understand his best interests.'

'So I've noticed,' I told her. 'And now for a few weeks of rest and quiet and nourishing food,' I added confidently, 'and his Lordship will be dancing the Highland Fling if he wants to.'

But I should have learned long ago that in the turf and therapeutics it's disastrous to back a dead certainty.

For some reason, Lord Nutbeam didn't want to get better. I'd imagined that once he was home he'd settle down to a nice long read, but instead he sat staring out of the window with cups of beef-tea getting cold at his elbow. Sometimes he picked up *The Anatomy of Melancholy*, but it didn't seem to hold him. Sometimes he pushed himself to the piano, but he could manage only a few bars of *Valse Triste*. To cheer him up, I wheeled him round the garden telling funny stories, but he never seemed to see the point. 'Alas, poor Yorick!' was the most I could get out of him.

His Lordship grew steadily feebler and feebler, while everything else in sight was burgeoning wildly in the sunshine. It wasn't long before I began to grow alarmed about his condition. Modern medicine's all very well, with antibiotics and heart-lung machines and so on, but once a chap's decided he doesn't want to live any more we're not much better off than the witch-doctors in Central Africa. And my professional problems weren't made easier by the other Nutbeams, who now the excitement had died down treated me like the man come to mend the drains. Far from his Lordship, they were terrible snobs–particularly the missus, whom everyone knew in the village was only a road-house remnant from Percy Nutbeam's youth, anyway.

'It would be much more convenient if you could make your daily visit earlier,' she said, as I limped into Nutbeam Hall one evening after a heavy day's practice among the pigsties. 'We are expecting Lord and Lady Farnborough for dinner any minute, and I should naturally prefer my guests not to be greeted in the hall by the doctor. Perhaps you would also have the goodness to change your shoes before coming to us, Dr Grimsdyke. I realize that you cannot avoid walking through the farmyards during the day, but–'

I must say, her attitude made me pretty annoyed. Particularly as I felt she wouldn't have tried it with the old uncle, not with those old-fashioned looks of his. Then, a couple of days later, Lord Nutbeam went off his food and started looking like Socrates eyeing the hemlock.

'We're all bursting to see you back to normal again,' I told him, hopefully writing a prescription for another tonic. 'Here's something which will have you chirping with the birds in no time.'

'Thank you, Doctor. You are very kind. Indeed, everyone is very, very kind. Especially, of course, my dear brother and his wife.' He listlessly turned a few pages of Gibbon's *Decline and Fall*. 'But I fear my accident had more effect than I imagined. I've hardly been out of Nutbeam Hall for many years, you know, on account of my delicate health. Meeting so many people in the hospital was something of a disturbance. You are doubtless familiar with the lines in Gray's *Elegy in a Country Churchyard*—'

Feeling that churchyards were definitely out, I interrupted with the story about the parrot. But I don't think he got that one either.

I left him in the library, wondering whether to assemble the family again and confess the old boy wasn't living up to my prognosis. But I was stopped by Percy Nutbeam himself in the hall.

'Could you spare time for a whisky and soda, doctor?'

My professional duties being over for the day, I accepted.

'I'm very worried about my brother's condition,' he declared, after a bit of chat about the weather and the crops.

'And so am I,' I told him.

'I remember the case of our aunt so well. The collapse seemed to set in all at once. Like a pricked balloon. I suppose there's not any danger of–er, is there?'

I nodded. 'I'm afraid I've got to say there is.'

The poor chap looked so concerned I felt I must have misjudged him all along.

'Then how long, Doctor, would you give him–?'

'Might be a matter of only a week or two,' I said gloomily.

'Good God! Not before May the twenty-eighth?'

I looked puzzled, wondering if they'd arranged a picnic or something.

'This is a very delicate business, Doctor.' He poured himself another whisky. 'But I must be frank with you. You remember Sir Kenneth Cowberry?'

'I don't think I've had the pleasure—'

'He was leaving as you returned, the night of the accident. He's the head of Hoskins, Harrison, Cowberry, and Blackthorn. My brother's accountants, you know. I thought we'd better send for him at once, in case there were any arrangements my brother might have wished—'

'Quite,' I said.

'Lord Nutbeam naturally desires to leave my wife and myself his entire fortune. After all, we have devoted our lives to his welfare.'

'Quite, quite.'

'But it was only that evening we learned–my brother is oddly secretive about money matters–that he had in fact already made over his estate to me. In order to–er, escape death duties. You may have heard of other cases, Doctor? But under the rules of the Inland Revenue Department my brother must stay alive for five years after signing the document, or it doesn't hold water. And those five years are up at midnight, May the twenty-eighth. So, Doctor, if you can keep him alive till then–I mean, I hope and trust he will have many happy years among us yet–you understand the position . . .?'

I didn't think highly before of this pint-sized Lord and Lady Macbeth. Now I felt it would serve them damn well right if the Government carted off the lot, to pay, among other things, my National Health salary.

'I understand the position very well,' I replied, wishing I could produce one of the uncle's looks.

I'd very much taken to old Nutbeam, and I was determined to keep him alive for the full three score and ten. But the situation was getting beyond a chap of my modest experience, and out in the country I hadn't any of my chums to ask for advice. I wished the uncle would get fed up sitting on the beach at Montego Bay and come home. I even wished Miles would turn up for the week-end. I was wondering what to say next when I had another of those profitable inspirations of mine.

'I think it would be wise,' I announced, 'to have another opinion. There might be some other condition I've overlooked. After all, doctors can make mistakes. Just like accountants.'

'As many opinions as you wish, Dr Grimsdyke.'

'There's a man in Harley Street just right for this type of case. Though his private fees are rather high.'

'That's of no concern at all, I assure you.'

'And, of course, he'll charge a guinea a mile for the visit.'

Percy Nutbeam looked a bit concerned doing the mental arithmetic, but he agreed, 'Nothing is too expensive with my brother's life at stake.'

'Plus his first-class fare and meals, naturally. He's a general surgeon, but I guarantee he's got the sharpest diagnostic nose in London. His name's Sir Lancelot Spratt.'

Chapter Ten

'Delightful air,' declared Sir Lancelot.

I'd driven over to Greater Wotton Junction to meet him, and pretty nervous I felt about it, too. In my days as a student at St Swithin's, Sir Lancelot and myself disagreed about everything from the way I tried to treat appendicitis to the way I tried to treat the nurses, and his last remark the day I proudly told him I'd qualified was that the Archbishop of Canterbury would presumably now have to make an addition to the Litany.

I bowed him from his carriage like royalty come to open the local fat stock show.

'I hope you've no objection to travelling all this way, sir?' I began, feeling that I'd sent for Rembrandt to paint the attic.

'Objections? Why, boy? It is the duty of consultant surgeons and the fire brigade to give their services whenever and wherever they are needed. It is, moreover, extremely pleasant to escape from London on a summer morning, and I'm being handsomely paid for it. Don't be so damned humble, Grimsdyke!' He poked me in the epigastrium with his walking-stick. 'A doctor must feel humble only towards his own abilities. Excellent roses, these, Apricot Queens, I believe? What sort of mulch d'you use?'

This remark was directed to the stationmaster, Greater Wotton being one of those junctions regarded as an exercise in landscape gardening interrupted by the occasional arrival of trains. Sir Lancelot then ignored me for ten minutes' erudite discussion on the merits of horse and cow manure. Come to think of it, that sort of ability represents his genius. Most surgeons can talk only about the inside of their patients or the inside of their cars, but Sir Lancelot has informed views on everything from nuclear physics to newts.

'I am presumably obliged to travel in that,' he said, indicating my car. 'Am I permitted a bite to eat before seeing the patient?'

'I've arranged a modest meal, sir.'

Remembering that a high blood-sugar is conducive to mental tranquillity,

I'd decided to give the old boy a jolly good lunch before getting down to business.

'I rarely take wine at midday,' Sir Lancelot observed later, mellowing over the roast lamb and a glass of the uncle's Château Lafite, 'but I must say Dr Rudolph Grimsdyke has excellent taste in it.'

I agreed, though I'd been a bit alarmed to notice the cellar had somehow got down to only a couple of bottles.

'The only locums I did were in the East End of London, where in those days the doctors were as half-starved as the patients.' Sir Lancelot gazed through the window, where the cuckoos were tuning up among the blossoms. 'He seems to have found himself a very agreeable spot–botanically, ornithologically, and even meteorologically.'

'But not anthropologically, sir,' I said brightly, feeling it time to mention the Nutbeams.

'According to the essayist Hazlitt,' Sir Lancelot observed with a nod, 'all country people hate each other. You will now kindly recapitulate the family history of your patient. You were not particularly explicit on the telephone.'

An hour later the pair of us were marching into Nutbeam Hall.

I think the Hon. Percy and his repulsive missus were staggered to find themselves faced with a chap in a frock coat and a wing collar, who glanced round as though he'd been sent to condemn the place by the local Medical Officer of Health.

'We are delighted, Sir Lancelot,' simpered Amanda Nutbeam, who of course thought doctors were all right as long as they had titles. 'I am so pleased you accepted our invitation to take over his Lordship's case.'

Sir Lancelot looked as though she were a junior probationer who'd dropped a bedpan in the middle of his weekly ward round.

'Madam, I have *not* assumed clinical responsibility for Lord Nutbeam. His medical adviser remains Dr Gaston Grimsdyke, at whose invitation I stand here now.'

'Oh! Of course, Sir Lancelot—'

'That is normal professional procedure.'

These remarks put my morale up no end. Despite our difference in the past, Sir Lancelot wasn't so much offering the olive branch as proffering ruddy great groves. But I should have realized that a chap like him would back me to the scalpel hilt, now that I was qualified and one of the boys.

'We shall see the patient, if you please.' The Nutbeams looked rather flustered. 'And I should be glad if you would kindly provide me with a clean hand towel.'

I remembered Sir Lancelot always demanded a clean towel in uppish households, and in a tone inferring that it was a pretty stiff request.

'Dr Grimsdyke will lead the way,' he went on, as I stepped respectfully aside. 'The patient's doctor precedes the consultant into the sickroom. That is etiquette, and I should be the last to alter it.'

Our consultation was a great success. Sir Lancelot started by discussing ancient Chinese medicine for twenty minutes, then he examined the patient, had a chat about Byzantine architecture, and left his Lordship looking his brightest for weeks.

'And you discovered the original fracture solely from the physical signs, Grimsdyke?' he asked, as we left the room.

'Yes, sir.'

'Congratulations. The difficulty in making such a diagnosis is matched only by the disaster of missing it.'

'That's–that's very kind of you, sir.'

'I believe in giving credit where credit is due. In your case it happens to be remarkably easy.'

I felt jolly pleased with myself, all the same. Though I've always maintained that orthopaedic surgery is only a branch of carpentry, and now I come to think of it I was rather hot stuff in the woodwork class at school.

The other two Nutbeams were waiting expectantly in the hall, but at the foot of the stairs Sir Lancelot simply picked up his hat.

'Sir Lancelot–?'

Percy looked as though this wasn't much of a run for their money.

'Yes, Mr Nutbeam?'

'Have you–er, anything to say about my brother?'

'I shall have a consultation with my colleague here, who will inform you later. That is the normal procedure.'

'But if you could hold out even a word of hope–' exclaimed Amanda, I fancy glancing stealthily at the calendar.

'I think my colleague will allow me to say that you will shortly see an improvement in his Lordship's condition.'

'Thank God for that,' they cried together.

'Now, if you please. Dr Grimsdyke, we shall return to your surgery.' He pulled out that great gold watch of his. 'We have really little time for discussion before the four o'clock train.'

Sir Lancelot didn't mention the patient on our way back to the uncle's cottage, being more interested in describing all the different methods of thatching. I had to wait till he was enjoying a cup of tea in the parlour, when he declared:

'Apart from an uncomplicated healing fracture, there's nothing whatever wrong with Lord Nutbeam. But there's one thing he needs desperately–an interest in life. Believe me it's perfectly easy to be bored to death. What do you suggest?'

'More books, sir?'

Sir Lancelot seemed to find this amusing.

'From you, Grimsdyke, a remarkable answer. The advice about never judging others by yourself is one of the stupider of proverbs. If humanity didn't show an astounding sameness, the practice of medicine would come to a dead stop.'

He spread a scone with clotted cream and strawberry jam.

'I agree that after a lifetime playing the recluse, Lord Nutbeam's expedition to hospital was something of a shock. With the appalling advance of specialization, hospitals have become quite overcrowded with staff–it is, of course, completely impossible to get any rest in them. Did you notice his nurses?'

'As a matter of fact I did, sir. There was a staff nurse and—'

Sir Lancelot raised his hand. 'It is quite enough answer, Grimsdyke, that you noticed them. No doubt Lord Nutbeam finds the amateur administrations of his sister-in-law less agreeable. I shall send down a qualified nurse from a London bureau tomorrow. You will see to it that she isn't overruled by the family.'

'That might be a bit difficult, sir.'

'Rubbish!' he helped himself to a slice of fruit cake. 'There's only one way to handle difficult patients, difficult relatives, and difficult horses, and that's by keeping on top. I hope my visit has clothed you with a little added authority. That's often the only value of the consultant appearing on the scene at all.'

'How about tonics, sir?'

'To my mind there is only one effective tonic. I shall arrange for that to be sent from London also. I think I have time for another cup of tea, if you please. By the by,' he went on, as I put down the pot. 'You knew your cousin Miles was putting up for the consultant staff at St Swithin's?'

'He did mention it to me, sir.'

'How's he fancy his chances?'

'I think he's modest by nature, sir,' I replied cagily.

'H'm. I am only betraying an open secret by saying that Cambridge is being remarkably difficult in the selection committee. Obstinacy is such an extremely unpleasing characteristic.' Sir Lancelot stroked his beard. 'How are your relations with your cousin?'

'We do rather move in different worlds, sir.'

'I don't know if you are sufficiently familiar to drop a hint that his chances at St Swithin's would be considerably bettered if he were a little more disgustingly human. Otherwise he's an exemplary candidate. His work has ability, his manner has confidence, and, what is more important, his wife has money. But whoever the committee elects, you have to live with the feller for the rest of your professional lifetime. And nothing is more trying than being yoked to a pillar of virtue, as you can find from the divorce courts any afternoon.'

'I'm sure Miles is dedicated to his profession, sir,' I remarked, taking the chance to slip in a good word for the chap.

'Nothing,' declared Sir Lancelot, 'is quite so dangerous as the dedicated man.' Shortly afterwards I drove him to the station. I no longer had any qualms about tackling the Nutbeams, even over the nurse.

'A nurse? That will be rather tedious, Doctor,' Amanda objected at once. 'We had one in the house before, the time my husband had pneumonia. It really was most difficult. They feel quite entitled to have their meals at the same table, and even attempt to sit with one in the evenings.'

This annoyed me more, because I'm a great admirer of the nursing profession, or at least some of it. Remembering Sir Lancelot's advice, I said pretty stuffily, 'If you don't obey your doctor's orders, there really isn't much point in having one.'

'I assure you I can put up with any inconvenience for the sake of my brother-in-law's health,' she returned. 'I will instruct the housekeeper to prepare a room immediately.'

I myself wasn't much looking forward to sharing the clinical management of Lord Nutbeam with a nurse, knowing how Sir Lancelot's taste in them lay. His ward sisters at St Swithin's were a couple of women who could have kept Attila the Hun in bed for a month on bread-and-milk, and I expected someone about six feet tall with a chin like a football boot, old enough to have spanked Lord Nutbeam as a baby and tough enough to try it now. It was therefore with some astonishment that I arrived at Nutbeam Hall the next evening to discover the most beautiful girl I'd seen in my life.

'Good evening, Doctor,' she greeted me. 'I am Nurse Jones. I have given the patient his bath, and he is ready for you to see him now.'

I couldn't do anything except stare and bless my luck. She was a dainty, demure creature, with a little bow thing under her chin. She looked like

Snow-White, just growing out of her dwarfs. I was hopeful that our professional relationship would quickly ripen into something more promising, the sub-postmistress being all very well for country rambles but having the annoying habit of continually explaining how you counted postal orders.

'Oh, jolly good,' I said. 'Hope you like it here in the country? Perhaps you'd care to see the local beauty spots one afternoon when you're off duty?'

She gave a smile as gentle as the ripples on the village pond.

'That is really most kind of you, Doctor, but I'm afraid I shan't find much time to spare with such an important case.'

'We'll see, eh?' Nothing brings a man and woman together like treating someone else's illnesses. 'Let's go and inspect his Lordship.'

I found Lord Nutbeam sitting in bed sipping a glass of champagne.

'Where on earth did that come from?' I exclaimed.

'But the note from Fortnum and Mason's said you'd ordered it for me, Doctor.'

'Oh, did I? Yes, of course I did. Bollinger, eh? Sir Lancelot's favourite tipple. Jolly good tonic, don't you find?'

'I would never take alcohol except on doctor's orders, of course. But I must say, it does make me feel extremely well. How much do you want me to drink of it, Doctor? I believe six dozen bottles arrived downstairs.'

I murmured something about a bottle a day keeping the doctor away, and invited myself to a drop.

'How do you like your new nurse?' I asked, as she disappeared to find a glass.

Lord Nutbeam thought for some moments.

'She reminds me of a little Crabbe.'

'She doesn't walk sideways,' I said, feeling this rather uncomplimentary.

'"Courteous though coy, and gentle though retired,"' he quoted. '"The joy of youth and health her eyes display'd, And ease of heart her every look convey'd."'

I felt that the case had taken a turn for the better

Chapter Eleven

Nurse Jones was a great success all round. In a couple of days she had old Nutbeam out of his wheel-chair tottering round sniffing the flowers. The next week she'd taken to driving him about the countryside of an afternoon in the Daimler. And, calling one lunch-time, I was surprised to see he'd gone off his usual diet of poached egg on pulverized spinach and was tucking into a steak the size of a bath-mat.

Even the Percy Nutbeams didn't object to the new régime, partly because his Lordship was every day in every way getting better and better, and partly because of the way Nurse Jones handled the missus. Nurses are charming girls, though unfortunately inclined to be bossy, doubtless the effect of spending their formative years telling old men to get back into bed. But Nurse Jones was as sweet and gentle as Gee's Linctus, and always took care to address Mrs Nutbeam like an Edwardian housemaid straight out of the orphanage.

'The nurse at least knows her place,' Amanda admitted to me one afternoon. 'Which is a very welcome discovery in anyone these days. Though, of course, she could hardly expect to mix with people of our class. Not only was she trained at some extremely obscure hospital, but her father, I believe, is an engine driver.'

'You mean *in loco parentis*?' I suggested. But Amanda Nutbeam definitely had no sense of humour, either.

'All the same, I'm glad Sir Lancelot Spratt recommended her. She seems to be doing his Lordship the world of good.'

She was doing me the world of good, too. After passing the day sticking penicillin into rural posteriors, you can't imagine how you look forward to half an hour with a civilized popsie in the evening.

'Good evening, Nurse Jones,' I would greet her at the bedroom door. 'And how is his Lordship this evening?'

'Very well, thank you, Doctor. He has taken his vitaminized milk and played *Clair de Lune* twice on the piano.'

'And how are *you*, Nurse Jones?'

'Very well, thank you, Doctor.'

'Perhaps one afternoon you would like a spot of fresh air and a view of the beauty spots, Nurse Jones?'

'Perhaps one afternoon, Doctor.'

After a week or two, I felt the time had come to put our acquaintance on a rather jollier footing.

Old Nutbeam had hobbled out of the room somewhere, and Nurse Jones had been listening very respectfully while I held forth on the osteopathology of uniting fractures, so I put my arm round her waist and kissed her.

The result was rather unexpected. I'd imagined that she'd drop her eyes and dissolve into grateful sobs on my waistcoat. Instead, she caught me a neat uppercut on the left ramus of the mandible.

I don't know if many people have been clocked by nurses, but quite a lot of power they pack, after all those years shifting patients about with their bare hands. She hit me clean off my balance, right into the remains of his Lordship's dinner. But I was even more startled at the appearance of little Nurse Jones herself. She looked as though she'd been charged with a powerful current of electricity. She was all eyes and teeth and finger-nails.

'You despicable young man!' she hissed. 'Do you take me for one of your hospital pick-ups? Keep your hands to yourself, and your manners to the saloon bar.'

'I say, I'm most terribly sorry.' I brushed off the remains of a fruit salad. 'It was all meant in a perfectly friendly spirit. Like at Christmas.'

'Oh, I know you young doctors!' She looked as though she wanted to spit out something nasty. 'Do you imagine I put up with five years' hard labour in a hospital like a workhouse just for people like you to maul me about? Huh! I want more out of life than that. It's bad enough drudging away night and day, without having to defend yourself against ham-fisted Romeos as soon as you're left alone in the same room. You make me absolutely nauseated.'

Strong words, of course. But the Grimsdykes, I trust, are ever gentlemen, and sensitive to the first hint that their attentions might be unwelcome.

'A thousand apologies,' I told her, rather stiffly. 'It's all this hot weather we're having. I can assure you, Nurse Jones, that the incident will not occur again.'

'I can assure you, too,' she said.

At that moment old Nutbeam pottered back, and she became her usual demure self once more.

For the next few days I didn't know whether I was more confused than disappointed. After all, every houseman's tried a bit of slap-and-tickle in the sluice-room, and the worst response is usually a few remarks about not being that sort of a girl and Sister might come back in a minute, anyway. But Nurse Jones could look as if butter wouldn't melt in her mouth while comfortably able to digest red-hot nails. It was puzzling, and rather a shame. I'd been particularly looking forward to those beauty spots.

Arriving at Nutbeam Hall a few evenings later, I thought at first that Nurse Jones was in form again. Then I recognized the voices behind the drawing-room door.

'For a man in your position behaving like that with one of the servants,' Mrs Nutbeam was declaring, 'is absolutely disgusting.'

'My dear!' bleated Percy. 'She's hardly a servant—'

'Of course she's a servant. I've had lady's maids in the past who were twice as good as she is.'

'But my dear—'

'And in our own home, with your own brother lying ill in the next room. Really, Percy!'

'My dear—'

'You've always treated me atrociously, but this is too much. Far too much. Haven't I enough on my mind at this moment?'

'But, my dear, how was I to know she'd make such a fuss? I was only trying to hold her hand.'

'And you have the affrontery to offer that as an excuse! If I had my way I'd bundle the little baggage out of the house in the next five minutes. It's only that she's kept your brother out of his grave that I tolerate her at all.'

'Let me tell you, my dear, the scene won't be repeated.'

'And let me tell you, my dear, that if it is, I'll break your neck.'

It was quite a consolation to find that Nurse Jones dished it out impartially to all comers.

Thereafter I paid fewer visits to Nutbeam Hall, his Lordship no longer needing my constant attentions, anyway. There wasn't even much excitement for the Percy Nutbeams watching L.S.D.-day approaching, as he quietly became haler and heartier every moment. Under the mellowing influence of the coming largesse the ghastly couple grew quite friendly towards me, and even asked me to a cocktail party with a lot of their friends, who looked as though they'd been delivered in horse-boxes.

At last the twenty-eighth of May dawned, another jolly Elysian summer day. In the afternoon I drove to Nutbeam Hall for my final visit.

I found Percy and his wife standing in the hall, looking as if they'd just checked off the winning line in their penny points.

'Dr Grimsdyke,' Percy said at once, 'we both want to thank you for restoring my dear brother to us.'

'It is a great comfort, Doctor, to have him with us today. And, of course, for many more years to come.'

'If God spares him,' added Percy, looking at the chandelier again.

'To mark our appreciation,' Amanda went on, 'my husband and I would like you to accept this little gift. I hope it will remind you of one of your earliest successful cases.'

Whereupon Percy handed me a gold cigarette case, still in its box from Cartiers.

I stumbled out a few words of thanks, wondering how much it had set them back. Then I suggested I'd better make my *adieus* to the patient himself.

'My brother's out for his afternoon drive at the moment,' Percy told me, 'but of course he's due home any minute.'

'He never likes to be far from Nutbeam Hall,' said Amanda.

'Do wait, Doctor. Perhaps a cup of tea?'

At that moment we heard the Daimler in the drive, and as we opened the front door Lord Nutbeam got out with Nurse Jones. It was then I noticed something about him–possibly the look in his eye, like a chap reaching for his first pint at the end of a tough game of rugger–which made me slip the cigarette case into my pocket and prepare for trouble.

'Percy . . . Amanda,' began Lord Nutbeam, 'allow me to introduce Lady Nutbeam.'

The two Honourables looked as though they'd been run through the middle by a red-hot cautery.

'That's impossible!' cried Mrs Nutbeam.

'Not impossible at all, my dear Amanda. Ethel and I were married half an hour ago in Gloucester Registry Office. Two very pleasant young men from the Waterworks Department were our witnesses.'

Percy Nutbeam gasped. 'But the money!'

'I'm afraid there isn't any, Percy. Not for you, anyway. The deed is, of course, annulled by my marrying before the five years are up. You will inherit the title when I eventually perish, unless Ethel and I happen to have children . . .'

Mrs Nutbeam burst into tears.

'But I doubt whether there will be much money left, because I intend to spend it. I realize now how I have wasted my life, because you two cleverly insisted on keeping me under your noses. I'm not at all delicate. Ethel tells me I'm as vigorous as any man of twenty. I knew I'd been missing something, ever since I was among all those nice young people in hospital.'

Lord Nutbeam smiled benignly all round.

'Dear Doctor, do you recall I once mentioned Gray's *Elegy in a Country Churchyard*? I was about to quote–"Full many a flower is born to blush unseen, And waste its sweetness on the desert air." Charming poem. Well, I'm going to blush all over the place from now on. Ethel and I are off tomorrow for our honeymoon at Monte Carlo. You must come, Doctor, and visit us then when we've settled down. You probably prefer to stay here, Percy. And so you may, if you wish. Until we get back.'

'Don't forget the present, darling,' said Lady Nutbeam, looking as unruffled as when she changed his Lordship's pyjamas.

'Ah, the present. It was you, Doctor, who brought dear Ethel and I together. So perhaps you will accept this little token of our lasting gratitude and affection?'

And he handed me a gold cigarette case, still in its box from Cartiers.

Chapter Twelve

'I don't believe a word of it,' said Miles.

'Don't you indeed?' I replied, and produced a couple of identical gold cigarette cases from my pockets.

'The only snag is knowing what to do with the things, my life never being organized to meet such a situation. I think I'll reserve one for the hock shop, and have the other engraved "With Gratitude From a Successful Patient." Then I can offer people cigarettes from it, and do my professional standing no end of good. Though I suppose I might as well have "With Gratitude from Her Royal Highness" while I'm about it, don't you think?'

I'd left Long Wotton that morning to the touching distress of everybody, particularly the sub-postmistress, who burst into tears and gummed up all the threepenny stamps. Even the old uncle had congratulated me on handling the Nutbeams, and not only written a comfortable cheque as promised but given me a straw hat from Jamaica. Percy Nutbeam himself had smartly disappeared from the district, it was rumoured to sell cars in a Piccadilly showroom, and I'd half a mind to go along later and make faces through the plate-glass window.

It was a beautiful afternoon in the middle of Ascot week as I arrived in London, when even the chaps with placards announcing Doom is Nigh at the bottom of the Edgware Road looked as though the world wasn't such a bad old place after all. I was sorry to find the only drab patch on the whole cheerful canvas of life was poor old Miles himself.

'They've postponed the appointment at St Swithin's for six months,' he announced, not seeming really interested in cigarette cases. 'The committee have invited Professor Kaiser from Kentucky to fill the gap with a clinical visit.'

'Gloved hands across the sea, and all that?'

He snorted. 'Not a bit of it! It's nothing but a transparent ruse for everyone to organize their forces. My only encouragement is that Mr Longfellow from the Neurosurgical Department is now supporting me. Though, of course, he always opposes Sir Lancelot in everything.'

'Because Sir Lancelot gave him out, umpiring the last Staff and Students cricket match.'

'I shouldn't be at all surprised at that.' Miles stared gloomily at the print of Luke Fildes' *The Doctor*. 'If only the patients knew what went on behind their backs!'

'Why don't you and Connie get away from it all and take a holiday?' I suggested. 'The yearly change of scene is essential for mental and bodily health–lesson one, social medicine.'

'Nothing depresses me quite so much as packing.'

'But the sunny shores of the Mediterranean—'

'Only seem to give me the gut-rot.'

I'd thought of passing on Sir Lancelot's advice, but the poor fellow looked so hopelessly miserable I said instead, 'Don't worry about me, old lad. I'll do my bit by staying out of sight and out of trouble. At least for the next six months.'

'You know, Gaston, you're . . . you're being rather decent about all this.'

'Not at all. One of the family, good cause, and all that.'

'I'm sincerely grateful to you. If I can be any help in finding a new position—'

'Not necessary, old lad. I have a scheme which will take me right out of everybody's hair for a bit.'

'You're not emigrating?' I thought his voice sounded a little too hopeful. 'Apart from the oil company, I know the Secretary of the Commonwealth Resettlement Board pretty well at the club. He could easily fix you up somewhere like Australia or Canada.'

I shook my head. 'Worthy places all, but I shall remain based on this blessed plot. What was it old Sir Lancelot used to tell us? "I know one-half of this country thinks it's under-paid and the other half that it's over-taxed, but believe me, gentlemen, it's cheap at the price." Anyway, my immediate future is taken care of in the homeland.'

'Respectably, I trust?'

'Very. But I must maintain strict professional secrecy about it at the moment.'

Miles looked surprised, but asked no more questions. We parted on such excellent terms I wished afterwards I'd thought of asking him for another ten quid.

I didn't enlighten Miles that I was planning to write a book, because he would have told me it was a stupid notion, and I should have agreed with him. Though a good many other doctors seem to have had the same idea–Oliver Goldsmith, Smollett, Rabelais, Conan Doyle, Somerset Maugham, and so on. The thought had come to me in the uncle's study at Long Wotton, where I'd been browsing to keep up with Lord Nutbeam's conversation. Half-way through *The World's Ten Great Novels* it struck me that a chap who could write the obituaries for the *Medical Observer* ought to be pretty good at producing convincing fiction.

The only snag was paying the rent while writing it, and I suppose the same problem worried Goldsmith and Smollett as well. But now I had the uncle's cheque I could afford to take a small houseboat in Chelsea, if I managed to live largely on baked beans and benzedrine.

The next afternoon I'd an appointment with some publishers called Carboy and Plover in Bloomsbury, a district with high-class literary associations but now consisting of small hotels for drunk Scotsmen missing the night trains from King's Cross.

'A hospital story, eh? They're generally sellers, at any rate,' said Mr Carboy.

He was a fat chap in a tweed suit, whom I'd found sitting among photographs of his best-selling authors and prize-winning cattle reading the *Farmer and Stockbreeder*. But he was very civil, and gave me a cup of tea.

'The drama of the operating theatre,' murmured Plover, a thin, pale fellow on whom nothing seemed to grow very well–hair, moustache, bow-tie, all drooped like a sensitive plant after a thunderstorm.

'I'll have a go, then,' I said. I felt the interview was more encouraging than the one you got on entering St Swithin's, when they just told you the number of chaps they chucked out for slacking.

'Have a go by all means, Doctor,' agreed Carboy. 'Just send us the manuscript when it's finished. Can't promise anything definite, of course. But we'll certainly read it.'

'Er–one small point–'

I didn't want to raise sordid questions among such literary gents, but I went on, 'I met an author chap once, who said publishers often made a small advance—'

'We should be delighted, Doctor,' said Carboy.

'Absolutely delighted,' agreed Plover.

'Nothing gives a publisher greater pleasure than encouraging the young artist. Eh, Plover? But alas! The state of the book trade.'

'Simply terrible just now,' affirmed Plover, drooping further.

'Quite indescribable.'

'Bankruptcies weekly.'

'Poor Hargreaves. Shot himself only yesterday.'

'I'm not at all certain,' ended Plover, 'that I didn't hear the crack of a pistol shot on my way to lunch.'

I left, wondering whether I should offer to pay for the tea.

In the absence of patronage from Carboy and Plover, I put one cigarette case up the spout, bought a second-hand typewriter and Roget's *Thesaurus*, and settled down to work.

Being a medical student is jolly good training for becoming an author. In both occupations you have to sit at a desk for hours on end when you'd rather be out in the pubs, and to live on practically nothing. Though I must admit it was only late in the course that I developed this knack for the studious life. The old uncle had become even stickier with the money after a surprise visit to my new digs one evening, when the landlady answered his question, 'Is this where Mr Grimsdyke lives?' with, 'That's right, sir, bring 'im in and mind 'is poor 'ead on the doorstep.'

I also found that writing a book, like taking out an appendix, looks rather easier from the appearance of the finished product than it is. The snag in writing a book about hospitals is that everyone imagines the atmosphere inside resembles the closing stages of a six-day bicycle race, while the operating theatre is really a relaxed and friendly place, like a well-run garage. Also, the public thinks all surgeons are high-principled and handsome, though most of them are little fat men with old pyjamas under their operating gowns, mainly worried about getting the next hernia done in time to have a decent lunch. My hero, one Clifford Standforth, F.R.C.S., was a brilliant, upright, serious young surgeon, and somehow he didn't seem the sort of chap who'd last half an hour at St Swithin's without getting his leg pulled by everyone down to the first-year students.

After a few weeks, with foolscap on the floor as thick as the snow on a Christmas card, I found myself like any other hermit in pressing need of a decent meal and some conversation, and I invited myself round to Miles's flat for dinner. I thought I could finally pass on Sir Lancelot's remarks about slapping chaps on the back a bit more, but I found the fellow in an even deeper condition of acute melancholia.

'What's up now?' I asked. 'Sir Lancelot still creating about that car park?'

'Barefoot,' Miles replied.

'Oh,' I said.

'He's putting up for the job, too.'

'Unfortunate,' I agreed.

'Everything's against me,' muttered Miles. 'I thought the fellow had settled down for life as Reader in Surgery at West Riding.'

'He's your only serious rival, I suppose?'

'As ever,' agreed Miles bitterly. 'You've never said a word, I suppose, Gaston? Not about the true story?'

I shook my head. 'Not even to Connie.'

'Thank you, Gaston. I appreciate that deeply.'

I felt so unhappy for him, I had to help myself to some of his whisky and soda. The Barefoot incident was the only shady part of old Miles's rather sad salad days. Everyone at St Swithin's thought it pretty mysterious at the time, the general rumour being that the poor chap had suffered a nervous breakdown following years of chronic overwork, which was highly gratifying to students like myself who believed in long periods of recuperation between exams.

It all happened just before Miles went up for his finals, before either of us had yet run into Connie. Charlie Barefoot was a small, untidy, pink chap who resembled a cherub in glasses, and the pair of them had met their first week in St Swithin's, over that beastly dogfish.

'I say, isn't that Hume's *Treatise on Human Nature* you have there?' asked Miles, waiting for the class to start one morning.

Barefoot nodded. 'I like to keep my mind occupied while I'm hanging about for anything–trains, haircuts, scholarship exams, and so on. But isn't that Darwin's *Origin of Species*?'

Miles said it was. 'I thought it a useful start to one's medical education.'

'But I've been waiting for months to discuss Darwin's views on natural selection!'

'And I've been waiting for months to discuss Hume's views on subjective idealism!'

After that they were great pals.

Medical students in the first year have hardly shaken the schoolroom chalk from their shoulders, but they soon learn to crowd the rear benches of the lecture-room so that unobtrusive exits might be made should the subject start to pall. Miles and Barefoot were always left with the front row to themselves, where they answered all the questions, took notes by the armful, and generally gave the impression intellectually of a pair of young Mozarts. At the end of the first year Miles won the Dean's Prize in Biology, with Charlie Barefoot *proxime accessit*.

That got rid of the dogfish, by promotion from the medical kindergarten to the anatomy rooms. They shared the same leg.

'Miles, I've got some capital news,' Barefoot announced, as my cousin arrived one morning. 'There's a vacancy in my digs. Tony Benskin doesn't want to stay any longer. I don't know why, but he got quite shirty the other day, just because I wanted to discuss the popliteal fossa over breakfast. If you were thinking of making a change—'

'I'll give my landlady notice tonight,' Miles replied at once. 'My lodgings are really very difficult for studying in the evenings. Quite apart from the noise of Paddington Station, there are a couple of ladies on my landing who seem to have a tremendous succession of visitors.'

'You'll find it much more agreeable at Muswell Hill. Mrs Capper provides use of the parlour and lets us make cocoa as late as we like in the evening.'

Miles moved his books and bones across London, and from Monday to Friday every night afterwards the pair of them swotted at Mrs Capper's parlour table. On Saturdays they went for a long walk in the country and took supper at Lyons'. In time, Miles won the Gold Medal in Anatomy, with Barefoot again runner-up.

By the time I'd shaken off the blasted dogfish myself, Miles and Barefoot were already at work in the St Swithin's wards. Despite the standing impression of hospital inmates, medical students are let loose on live patients only after a couple of years of cutting up dead ones, and a pretty testing transition it is, too. A good many bright young anatomists I've seen floundering about among the dirty dressings and vomit bowls, and they say all the best surgeons were as hopeless at anatomy as all the best judges were at law. But even Sir Lancelot Spratt agreed it was simply a matter of time before Miles won the University Prize in Surgery, with Barefoot as usual panting a few marks behind.

Then a most unusual dislocation nobbled this pair of academic steeplechasers.

When I started in the hospital myself, I found that once you'd sorted out the odd sounds that come rumbling up a stethoscope the greatest difficulty in a medical ward is not making a diagnosis but making a bed. Hospital sisters regard the students as farmers regard their own unavoidable pests, and insist on all blankets being replaced complete with official hospital corners, which was totally beyond old Miles. He couldn't examine a patient without leaving him like a finisher in a sack-race.

After inspecting a particularly tricky case of splenomegaly one evening, Miles was struggling to tuck back the foot of the bed without repeatedly folding his tie into it, when a voice behind him said softly, 'If you let me do it, perhaps it would be easiest for both of us in the end?'

My cousin found a small, blonde junior nurse smiling at him.

'Awfully decent of you,' he stammered.

'You're working terribly late, arent you?'

She gave the bed-cover a professional flick.

'Oh, I don't know. I rather like work. You new on the ward?'

'I came down from E.N.T. yesterday. My name's Nurse Crimpole.'

'Mine's Miles Grimsdyke.'

'Of course I knew that.'

'You did?'

'Surely everyone in the hospital has heard of the clever Miles Grimsdyke. Quite unlike the other one.'

She gave him another smile. Miles's stomach felt as though he'd swallowed a nest of glow-worms.

'What would you enumerate as the differential diagnosis of acute nephritis?' asked Charlie Barefoot across Mrs Capper's red-plush tablecloth later that evening.

Miles switched his eyes from Mr Capper's Buffalo Group over the fireplace.

'Eh?'

'You all right?' Barefoot looked concerned. 'You haven't touched your cocoa.'

'Yes, I'm fine, thanks. Fit as a flea. Though perhaps I'm overdoing the

Saturday tramps a little. Sorry, old man.'

'It wasn't important. Anything interesting happen in the ward this evening?'

'No. Nothing worth mentioning at all,' said Miles.

Chapter Thirteen

The next Saturday Miles told Barefoot he was visiting his aunt in Sydenham, and took Nurse Crimpole to the pictures.

'You really mustn't work so hard,' she murmured, as he held her hand afterwards outside the mortuary gate. 'I shouldn't like anything to happen to you.'

'Perhaps I'll cut down in the evenings a bit, Dulcie. The finals aren't for a couple of years yet, anyway.'

'And I'm sure you're not getting nearly enough to eat.'

'Mrs Capper's a bit mean with the first-class protein, I must say.'

'Do look after yourself, Miles–won't you?' She looked into his eyes and stroked his lapel. 'For my sake.'

Next week Miles told Barefoot he was visiting his uncle in Beckenham, and took Nurse Crimpole to the Palladium.

For once in his life old Miles found he couldn't concentrate. Unlike myself, whose thoughts tend to wander from the books in the direction of Lord's or Epsom, Miles could control his brain like a prizefighter his muscles. But now Nurse Crimpole's smile kept coming between him and such things as the electrocardiographic diagnosis of Fallot's tetrology. No nurse had wasted her time on the poor chap before, with such grand people as housemen and registrars about in the ward. Come to think of it, no woman had wasted her time on him at all. I wish I'd known what was going on. I might have buttonholed the chap and offered some fatherly advice.

Miles decided the next Saturday to tell Barefoot he was visiting his nephew in Croydon, and take Nurse Crimpole to the Corner House. When he slipped into the ward sluice-room to issue the invitation, he was surprised to discover her chatting to his room-mate.

'Just looking for my diabetic specimens,' Miles said quickly.

'They've been taken down to the path. lab., old man,' Charlie Barefoot told him. 'If you're going that way, I'll come along and collect my own. Bye-bye, Dulcie,' he added to Nurse Crimpole. 'See you on Saturday.'

'Two o'clock outside the Nurses' Home,' she replied, and went on polishing her bedpans.

Miles felt he'd been given the electroconvulsive treatment he'd seen in the psychiatric department. It had never occurred to the idiot that Dulcie Crimpole could have eyes for anyone else–particularly, he felt angrily, a stodgy old bookworm like Charlie Barefoot.

'Known Nurse Crimpole long?' he asked in the pathology laboratory, his hand trembling as he unstoppered a bottle of Benedict's reagent.

'I've seen her about the ward, you know.'

Miles paused.

'I didn't go to my relatives those last weekends,' he scowled.

'So she tells me.'

'I think Dulcie's a very nice girl.'

'So do I,' said Charlie Barefoot.

That evening, Miles glanced up sharply from his Muir's *Pathology* and said, 'Perhaps, Barefoot, you would have the kindness to return my pencil, when you've finished chewing it.'

'This happens to be my own pencil, Grimsdyke. And I am *not* chewing it.'

'I distinctly saw you chew it just now. Apart from ruining the pencil–my pencil–you ought to know that chewing pencils is a thoroughly unhygienic habit, leading to the transfer of *Streptococcus viridans* and large numbers of other oral pathogens.'

'Oh, take the bloody pencil!' said Barefoot, and went up and sat in his bedroom.

It was the old business of sex. Cut-throat rivalry in class had never ruffled the two chaps' friendship. Now they glared at each other all night across the top of their textbooks. The following Saturday evening, Miles sat alone miserably drinking cups of cocoa and wondering blackly how to do Charlie Barefoot down. The Saturday afterwards he told his chum he was taking Dulcie to the Festival Hall, and visited her parents in Guildford. On the Monday morning the whole hospital discovered that he and Nurse Crimpole were engaged.

Barefoot was very decent about it.

'I won't say I am not disappointed,' he confessed in Mrs Capper's parlour. 'Dulcie's a wonderful girl, and I was getting rather fond of her. But . . . well, there's no one I'd rather lose her to than you, Miles.'

'It's really extremely generous of you, Charlie.'

'And when's the wedding?'

'Not till I've qualified, of course. I've cabled my father out East that my new status certainly won't interfere with my work. You'll be my best man, I hope?'

'That will be my only consolation for the whole affair.'

'You're a brick, Charlie.'

'And you're a real sport, Miles.'

They shook hands across Eden & Holland's *Obstetrics*.

'Now,' began Charlie Barefoot. 'What would you consider the leading features in the management of a case of puerperal paranoia?'

The years which stretch pretty chillingly ahead of you as a junior medical student soon start to melt away. As far as I remember, after that Miles took Dulcie out regularly every Saturday, while Barefoot went by himself for tramps in the country. The rest of the week the pair of them studied as steadily as before.

'You'll collar the Medical and Surgical Prizes in the finals all right,' conceded Barefoot, when the exams were only a few weeks ahead.

Miles smiled across the plush tablecloth, now a little faded.

'It could easily be your turn, Charlie.'

Barefoot shook his head. 'No, Miles. You're streets ahead of me on the practical. But I suppose we'd both better get on with some work. There's really so much revision to get through. What are the ninety-four causes of haematuria?'

When Miles next met Dulcie, he explained he couldn't spare his Saturday afternoons from studying any longer.

'But you really must get some fresh air,' she insisted. 'After all, now I'm a staff nurse and know all about these things. Lack of sunlight can reduce your vitamin D right down to danger-level.'

'Damn vitamin D!' exclaimed Miles. 'And A, B and C as well.'

'Miles!' she said, horrified at such blasphemy.

'I'm sorry, dear. I'm a bit irritable these days. It's only the pressure of work.'

'Are you sure that's all? You're looking terribly peaky.'

'Yes, of course that's all.'

Old Miles is fundamentally honest, which has nearly wrecked more careers than his own. He disliked telling Dulcie a lie. But how could he explain that he wished the ruddy woman were dead? A couple of years in the rough-and-tumble of the hospital wards has changed far worldlier young fellows than my cousin. As a junior student he'd been surprised at any girl smiling at him. Now he was almost a doctor and got smiles all round, some of them very pretty ones. And he could no longer dissuade himself that the woman was a shocking bore.

'Are you sure you're getting enough sleep?' Dulcie went on. 'The Professor says seven hours is the normal minimum. And what about your diet? I'm certain you're not taking nearly enough calories. Dr Parsons gave us a smashing lecture about them yesterday.'

'Very interesting, dear. How would you like to pass the afternoon? Shall we go round an art gallery?'

'If you don't think it would tire you too much. From the way you walk about, Miles, I'm not at all sure you haven't got flat feet.'

The wedding was planned for a fortnight after the examinations, and I was already wondering how to raise the rent of a Moss Bros. suit. I hadn't seen anything of Miles for weeks, and supposed he was swotting steadily for the exam. In fact, he was mostly sitting in Mrs Capper's parlour trying to find some honourable escape from his obligations short of suicide. After my own later experiences in Porterhampton, I could sympathize with the chap. He told me afterwards he'd almost reached for Murrell's *Poisons* before the answer appeared, with the clarity of all great inspirations.

Miles decided deliberately to fail his exam.

Even I could appreciate the simplicity of the scheme. Miles couldn't sit again for another six months, and by then Dulcie Crimpole might have got tired of waiting. She might have got a sister's job miles away in the North. She might have got run over by an ambulance. At least he wouldn't be walking up the aisle with her in exactly six weeks' time.

'Hello!' exclaimed Barefoot, arriving home from his tramp in the Chilterns. 'You're looking much happier with life tonight.'

Personally, I always find the day of the examinations as unattractive as the Day of Judgement, but Miles and Barefoot strode into the examination hall a few weeks later without flinching.

'Good luck, Miles,' whispered Barefoot, as they separated among the schoolroom desks just far enough apart to make cribbing rather tantalizing.

My cousin smiled. 'This time you don't need any, Charlie.'

Miles told me he did well in the written paper–bottling up that knowledge from Mrs Capper's parlour would have been almost as heartbreaking for him as marrying Nurse Crimpole. Besides, the clinical session presents more opportunities for spectacular failure under the eye of the examiner himself. When a few mornings later Miles approached the bedside of his allotted examination case, he felt both determined and serene.

'Well, my boy,' began the examiner, appearing after the interval they give you for diagnosis, 'what do you find wrong with your patient?'

'I am afraid, sir,' said Miles, 'that I can't make a diagnosis of anything at all.'

The examiner seized him by the hand.

'Congratulations! We've put in a perfectly normal man, and you'd be horrified at the peculiar diagnoses I've had to put up with all morning. Mr Miles Grimsdyke, isn't it? I thought so. Only a student of your outstanding ability could have seen through our little deception. Excellent, my dear sir! Good morning.'

Poor old Miles staggered into the street, gripped by an alarming thought–after all those years of being an academic athlete it was impossible for him to fail an examination at all. He made his way from the hall in a daze, wondering what the devil to do. There was still the oral examination that afternoon. He'd half a mind simply to clear off to the cinema instead, but they'd only give him another appointment like a candidate taken ill.The vision of Nurse Crimpole rose before him, wearing a wedding dress.

When he finally focused on his surroundings, he found himself facing a sign announcing THE RED LION–Ales and Spirits.

I don't believe Miles had ever swallowed a drink in his life, but he felt so miserable he decided to experiment with the treatment he'd seen me administering to myself for years.

'Good morning, sir,' said the chap behind the bar. 'What can I get you?'

'I want a drink.'

'Of course, sir. What sort of drink?'

It had never occurred to Miles that there were different ones.

He noticed an advertisement showing bottles glistening on blocks of ice, which looked very refreshing.

'A drink of that.'

'Vodka, sir? Large or small?'

'Oh, large, please. I didn't have time for my second cup of tea at breakfast.'

The story of Mile's oral examination never got out. No one likes a bit of gossip better than me, but even I should have felt a cad so much as hinting about it. His answers to Sir Lancelot Spratt at first flew across the green-baize table, even though he was grasping it for support as he wiped away the perspiration with his handkerchief.

'Now, Mr Grimsdyke,' went on Sir Lancelot, perfectly used to the oddities of nervous candidates, 'let us discuss the subject of gastric pain.'

'No,' said Miles.

'I beg your pardon?'

'I said no. You're always discussing gastric pain. And do you know why? I'll tell you. It's because you know all about gastric pain. You might know sweet Fanny Adams about anything else, as far as your students are concerned. You've bored me stiff with gastric pain for three years, and I'm not going to talk about it now.'

'You're perfectly correct, Mr Grimsdyke,' agreed Sir Lancelot after a thoughtful pause. 'Of all dead horses to flog, dead hobby horses are the worst. I'm glad that a gentleman of your courage had the decency to stop me becoming a tyrannical bore on the subject. Thank you. We shall discuss nausea and vomiting instead.'

'Oh, God!' said Miles, and gripped his waistcoat.

He still might have passed if he hadn't been sick into Sir Lancelot's Homburg.

The next evening the pass-list was read from the examination hall steps, with the announcement that Charles Barefoot (St Swithin's) had won the University Prizes in Medicine and Surgery. Miles wasn't mentioned at all.

He'd arranged to meet Dulcie Crimpole outside Swan and Edgar's, and hurried to detonate his news. But before he could speak she held out her hand and said:

'Goodbye, Miles.'

'Goodbye?'

'Yes.' She felt for her handkerchief. 'I–I'm afraid I've been a bad girl. I'm very fond of you, Miles, but–I'm really in love with Charlie Barefoot after all. Now we want to get married.'

Miles gasped. 'But–but–how long has this been going on?'

'Just a few weeks. I've been out with him every Saturday, while you studied at home. But I didn't want to tell you before. I thought it might upset you for your examination.'

Chapter Fourteen

'Even Sir Lancelot himself doesn't know the full story about Dulcie Crimpole,' Miles whispered on the doorstep, as I left for the houseboat after dinner. 'I believe I read in an advertisement somewhere that vodka leaves no smell on the breath . . .'

I nodded. 'A wise choice at the time.'

'Having such a formidable rival for the job as Barefoot is bad enough as it is. But if the tale got out just at this particular moment—'

'Rely on Gaston, old lad. Compared with me an oyster is garrulous. Besides, I have problems enough of my own.'

'Not serious, I hope?'

'Purely professional, and happily resolving every moment.'

He frowned slightly. 'What exactly *are* you up to, Gaston?'

'One day I hope you'll find out. Meanwhile, don't worry. I'll take any odds you end up with a permanent stable at St Swithin's.'

'It's certainly kind of you to give me some encouragement. I'm afraid I don't seem to get much of it these days.'

Dinner had been pretty gloomy that evening, with Miles brooding on Barefoot and even Connie hardly able to raise a laugh when I told a few funny stories to cheer them up. Falling into the prevailing mood, I started pondering on my own troubles with the book. Then I suddenly had another of those brilliant inspirations of mine. Here I was, stuck over portraying to the public the brilliant and dedicated young surgeon. And sitting opposite glaring into his raspberries was the prototype, known intimately from childhood. Whenever my Clifford Standforth was faced with a tricky situation I had only to ask myself, 'How would that chump Miles have tackled it?' and that should be good for another twenty pages. I was so taken with the idea I could hardly finish my coffee before hurrying back and trying it out on the typewriter.

I felt I could have the manuscript on Carboy and Plover's doormat in a fortnight, which I might have done if a telegram hadn't arrived a few days later from my forwarding address saying:

COME IMMEDIATELY MONTE CARLO ALL EXPENSES PAID

LADY NUTBEAM

The summons wasn't a particular surprise. I'd been following-up my former patient closely, this being easy from the newspaper placards, which generally said something like LORD NUTBEAM AGAIN. The old boy was whooping it up on the Riviera at a rate which made Champagne Charlie look very small beer, and people read so much about him on the bus going home he'd become one of the things the British public wondered how on earth they existed without, like penicillin and television.

I'm not one to refuse a free trip even to Margate, and anyway the houseboat had sprung a leak which I'd calculated in another ten days would put me completely under water. But I hesitated, wondering if Lord Nutbeam should have summoned a more high-powered doctor than myself. Finally, I decided that if he really wanted my own humble ministrations I couldn't let the old boy down, and stuffing my manuscript and stethoscope into a suitcase I rapidly switched professions and booked on the next plane south.

The following afternoon found me driving in his Lordship's new Rolls among the palm trees.

'It was Aubrey who insisted on sending for you,' said Lady Nutbeam, greeting me at her hotel. She looked just the same, except for the diamonds. 'He doesn't trust foreign doctors.'

'Are you sure he shouldn't have got the President of the Royal College of Physicians instead?'

'Not at all, Doctor. After all, you've saved his life once already, haven't you?'

I found old Nutbeam lying in a darkened room, suffering from nothing worse than a chronic hangover. Fortunately, I have wide clinical experience of this condition, and prescribed a diet of dry biscuits with some French spa water that tasted like bottled gasworks.

'That's a relief,' Lady Nutbeam agreed, as we left him suffering in peace. 'Though I didn't think it was anything serious. But I hope the poor dear will soon be himself again. He's so enjoying life at the moment.'

'He was rather out of training for it, that's all.'

'Perhaps you could stay on a few days, Doctor?' She paused on the terrace, gazing at the millionaires' yachts parked in the harbour as thickly as the cars on Brighton front. 'As a matter of fact, I *am* a little worried about my husband.'

'You mean,' I suggested, 'that party I read about in the papers? Pouring champagne over the Maharajah?'

She nodded. 'And setting off fireworks under the Greek millionaire. Not to mention the ice cream down the French ballet dancer's dress. I'm afraid, Doctor, Aubrey might sometimes strike one as a little childish.'

'Pure boyish high spirits, I'm sure.'

'I should like to think so. I'd be much obliged if you'd keep an eye on him for a while. You might be able to control him a little. You know he thinks the world of your advice. You would be our guest, of course.'

I gathered the Nutbeams, and a good many other people in Monte Carlo, had cash in lands where you didn't have to fill in beastly little forms to get it out.

'I could possibly spare a day or two,' I admitted, 'if you're still sure I'm the right chap?'

'But you've learned the penalty of boyish high spirits already, Doctor, haven't you?' Lady Nutbeam smiled. 'I noticed in Long Wotton you took the lesson to heart.'

As the days went by and nobody asked me to leave, I found myself a regular member of Lord Nutbeam's household, along with the chauffeur and the valet. Come to think of it, I'd always wanted the job of private physician to a travelling millionaire, though these days there's as much chance of finding anybody travelling with their private executioner.

His Lordship being an easy patient, I passed the time sitting in the sun, finishing my book, and brushing up my French–I flatter myself I'm rather hot stuff at this *défense de crâcher* and *crêpes Suzette* business.

'*Garçon*,' I was saying fluently after a week or so, '*apportez-moi une verre du bon vieux bière anglaise, s'il vous plaît*. And if that's the luncheon menu you have there, I'll try the *gratin de langoustines Georgette*. That's sort of mucked-up shrimps, isn't it?'

'*Monsieur* has the true English sense of humour.'

'Remind me sometime to tell you the story of *l'évêque et le perroquet*. Were the roses sent to the young lady I met in the Sporting Club last night?'

'*Mais certainement, monsieur*.'

'*Jolli bon spectacle*. And waiter–inform the chauffeur I'll be taking the car this afternoon. I might do a little shopping in Nice.'

'*Entendu, monsieur*.'

I felt that life for Grimsdyke was looking up.

The waiter had hardly left the terrace to collect my mid-morning refreshment, when my patient himself appeared. Lord Nutbeam seemed in excellent spirits, and was smoking a cigar.

'My dear Doctor, when on earth are you going to let me have a drink?' he started as usual. 'I was passing such a delightful time going through the barman's cocktails. I'd just reached that most interesting concoction of tomato juice and vodka. There is so much to catch up on in life!'

'Next Monday you might run to a glass of *vin blanc*,' I told him sternly.

'But Doctor, the Film Festival! It starts tomorrow, and I do so want to give a little party for those bright young people. I've never met a real film star, you know. Indeed, the only one I remember is a dog called Rin-tin-tin. I don't expect he'll be coming, of course.'

He offered me a cigar.

'They say *this* young lady is arriving at the hotel from London this afternoon,' he added, picking up a magazine with Melody Madder on the cover.

It was difficult at the time to pick up any magazine that hadn't. She was a red-head in a tight dress, who–struck me as suffering from pronounced mammary hyperplasia. But it seems a condition in which people are widely interested, and in the past few months she'd become better known to the British public than the Britannia on the back of a penny.

'Fascinating creature,' mused Lord Nutbeam. 'Remarkable how the point of interest changes, isn't it? Forty years ago it was all legs, and forty years before that the girls wore bustles. I do so hope I shall live to see what it is next.'

'The odd thing is,' I remarked, 'I've a feeling I've met her somewhere. I suppose I saw her in a picture.'

'I only wish you had met her, Doctor. I should so much like the pleasure of doing so myself, though Ethel seems most unenthusiastic at the idea. If you could ask her to my party I should certainly express my appreciation tangibly. You haven't a Rolls, have you?'

I promised to do my best.

'And how is the book coming along? Alas! For some reason I seem to be getting so behind with my reading these days.'

For the past couple of days the hotel had been steadily filling up for the Festival, mostly with actresses who were more or less overdressed or more or less undressed and all anatomically impossible, actors holding their breath while photographed in bathing-trunks, and film stars' husbands discussing their wives' income tax. The rest I supposed were the financial wizards, who could be spotted through their habit of approaching closed doors with their hands in their pockets, with about fifteen people fighting to grab the handle first.

It didn't seem easy to make the acquaintance of such a high-powered hotsie as Melody Madder, even if we were staying in the same hotel. I didn't even see more of her arrival than the top of her famous red hair, what with all the chaps trying to take her photograph. I found a quiet corner of the lobby and searched for a plan to present her with his Lordship's invitation. There wasn't much point in simply going along with a bunch of flowers, even Lord Nutbeam's name not cutting much ice with the woman who'd become as much a national institution as the the lions in Trafalgar Square. I supposed I could send up an elegant little note, which at least might produce her autograph in return. As the first step seemed finding her room number, I was approaching the reception desk trying to remember the French for 'suite' when I was elbowed aside by a fat woman in a hat with cherries dangling from it.

'It's an utter disgrace,' the fat woman started on the unfortunate chap behind the counter. 'Our room's that stuffy I daren't draw a breath. Hasn't been aired for years, if you ask me. And as for the beds, I don't even like to think about them.'

'But if *madame* will open the shutters—'

'Open them? You try and open them. You'll have to use dynamite.'

I was a bit annoyed at the elbowing, though I saw her point–fresh air is provided free in English hotels, all round the windows and under the doors, but in France they get some inside a bedroom and like to keep it for years.

'And another thing. The light won't go on and I got stuck in the lift.'

'The hotel engineer will attend to it at once, *madame*.'

'As for the plumbing, it's disgraceful. What's the idea of that ridiculous wash-basin six inches off the ground? Sir Theodore Theobald shall hear about this, believe you me. Furthermore, my daughter is still airsick, and I must have a doctor at once.'

'A doctor, Mrs Madder? We shall send for the best available.'

I pushed myself forward.

'Forgive my butting in,' I said quickly, 'but if you want a doctor, I happen to be the chap.'

She looked as if I were another of the local inconveniences.

'The gentleman, *madame*, is personal physician to Lord Nutbeam.'

'Oh, are you? Well, I suppose you'll do. But I don't mind telling you here and now that you can't expect any fancy fees.'

'In an emergency, Mrs Madder, it would be quite unethical for me to make a charge.'

This seemed to tip the scales, and I felt pretty pleased with myself as I followed her into the lift and up to a bedroom stuffed with flowers. Not only could I issue old Nutbeam's invitation as I felt Melody Madder's pulse, but I might be able to go over her chest as well.

'Get yourself ready, my girl,' said Mrs Madder, advancing to the bed. 'I've brought the doctor.'

'Good Lord!' I exclaimed. 'Why hello, Petunia.'

Chapter Fifteen

Petunia gave a little shriek and sat up in bed.

'Gaston! What on earth are you doing here?'

'But what are *you* doing here? In that hair, too.'

'What's all this?' demanded Mother.

'Mum, it's Dr Grimsdyke–you know, the one who used to bring me home in the rattly old car.'

'Oh, it is, is it? Yes, I remember now. I've often seen him from the bedroom window.'

'You seem to have come up a bit in the world, Pet,' I observed warmly. 'Jolly good job you didn't get the mumps after all.'

I kicked myself for not recognizing all those photographs. Though I must say, she'd been heavily camouflaged since the days when we shared the same bedroom. In her natural state old Pet would never strike you as particularly short on the hormones, but the way the film chaps had got her up she looked like an endocrinologist's benefit night.

'She's still feeling sick,' said Mother.

'Mum, I'm not. I told you I'm not.'

'Yes, you are. It was just the same when we went on the coach to Hastings. You're always sick for hours afterwards.'

'Perhaps you will permit me to prescribe, Mrs Madder–or Mrs Bancroft, rather.' I took charge of the situation. 'If you'll run down to the chemist's with this, they'll concoct it on the spot.'

'What's wrong with the hall porter, may I ask?'

'Better go yourself to see they make it up properly. These French pharmacists, you know.'

Mum hesitated a moment, but seeming to think it safe because I was the doctor, left the pair of us alone.

'Gaston, it's divine to see you again.' Petunia held out her arms. 'But what on earth are you giving me to take?'

'Bicarbonate of soda, which you could get from the chef. I just wanted a moment to find how the transformation had taken place.'

She laughed. 'Of course, I haven't seen you since that place up north–what's it called? Mother was furious. She'd no idea I'd met you, though. Wanted to hear what I'd been up to, fog or no fog. You know what she's like.'

'I'm beginning to find out.'

'She almost threw me out of the house. I was terribly hurt. After all, nothing in the slightest immoral happened there at all.'

'Quite,' I said.

'She told me to get a respectable job–usherette, nursemaid, secretary, or something. I was awfully upset, because I never really wanted to leave the stage. Not even if I hadn't half a chance of reaching the top.'

'You seem to have disproved that one, anyway.'

'Oh, being an actress isn't much to do with all this." Pet picked at the bed-cover. 'It's the other things that count. I wanted a mink coat.'

'And what girl doesn't?'

'I mean, to get a start you have to wear the right clothes. Appear in the right places. Meet the right people. The only people I met were as broke as I was, which I knew for a fact because I tried to borrow money from all of them.'

'I know the feeling.'

Petunia smoothed back her new red hair.

'The very day after the fog I went to Shaftesbury Avenue to see my agent, and as usual he said, "Sorry, darling, nothing at the moment. Unless you happen to be a distressed gentlewoman."'

'I asked why, and he told me Monica Fairchild had just been in. You know who *she* is, Gaston?'

'I certainly do. I was her doctor for a bit. Before she had the baby.'

'Whoever her doctor is now told her to get away from it all and have a rest. She was leaving the baby with her husband and taking a Mediterranean cruise, and wanted this distressed gentlewoman as her secretary–expenses paid, no other dibs, of course.'

I remembered Miss Fairchild was as open-handed as a dyspeptic tax-collector.

'When I got out into Shaftesbury Avenue again,' Petunia continued, as I took her hand in a professional sort of clasp, 'it struck me–wham! If I could play a doctor's wife in a fog, why couldn't I play a distressed gentlewoman on a cruise? And if I got friendly with Fairchild, there's no knowing how she'd help me along. Anyway, I'd have four square meals a day, and perhaps a bit of fun. Also, I could get away from Mum for a bit. So I put on my old tweed skirt and went round to her flat in Mount Street and got the job. She didn't know me from Eve, of course.'

'You then developed one of these famous shipboard friendships with the Fairchild,' I suggested, 'and that's how you got on all the magazine covers?'

'Not on your life. In fact, when I see her again, she'll probably tear my hair out to stuff her pillow with.'

I looked surprised.

'We went down to the ship with enough luggage for a circus,' Petunia went on. 'You can't imagine the fuss, with the photographers, flowers, and all the sailors trying to get her autograph. Nobody took any notice of me, of course, especially in my old tweed skirt.

'If I didn't know I was dogsbody there and then, I soon found out. It was "Miss Bancroft, tell the Captain I must have my special diet," and "Miss Bancroft, complain the water's too hard for my complexion," and "Miss Bancroft, if they don't stop that awful siren thing this very minute, I shall positively have hysterics." I should have gone crackers if the old hag hadn't been sea-sick. You know she usually looks like a combined operation by Dior and Elizabeth Arden? Lying on her bunk groaning under an ice-bag, she reminded me of one of my touring landladies when the rent was overdue. I think if gave me a bit of confidence.'

'Great leveller, the nausea,' I agreed.

'In fact, it gave me enough confidence to put on my new dress. I'd bought it with all the money I had left in the world. It was the one I wore on the cover of last month's *Gentlemen's Relish.*'

I remembered it was a thing fitting Petunia as closely as her epidermis, to which it gave way for a large areas about the upper thorax.

'It was the first night we had dinner at the Captain's table. He was ever so nice. Kept leaning over to pass me the butter and things with his own hands. He didn't take half as much notice of Fairchild, sitting there in her best mink. She was furious, of course. Developed a headache and disappeared to her cabin, and next morning the steward told me I'd been shifted to another table. It was behind a pillar thing in the corner, with five commercial travellers from Birmingham.'

'A bit of a come-down,' I sympathized. 'Eating below the old salt's salt.'

'Can't blame Fairchild, I suppose. Even off-stage a star has to keep in the limelight. And don't I know it now.'

'But I don't quite follow how this made you into Melody Madder.' I felt puzzled. 'All Fairchild did was chase you about enough to have made all Cleopatra's slaves give notice.'

'*That* all started when we got to Naples. When Count Longrandesi came aboard.'

'What, the terribly rich chap, who takes horses all round the world to jump on them over bits of wood?'

Petunia nodded. 'By then Fairchild had found I was in the profession. She wasn't so easy to fool as that little fat man up north. I had to read scripts to her in the afternoons, and one day she turned on me and said, "You've been on the stage, Miss Bancroft." I said yes. "You came to me under false pretences," she said. I told her an actress could still be a gentlewoman, and I happened to be a distressed one. That turned her nasty, and she made me do all her laundry. Pretty grubby, some of it was, too.

'Anyway, the Count appeared with his horses for London. He was all big eyes and kiss your hand, and, of course, Fairchild was after him.'

'Out for the Count, in fact,' I laughed.

'He saw me first,' Petunia continued, not seeming to see the joke. 'I had that dress on. Ever so sweet he was, what with buying me a Green Chartreuse in the Veranda Café. Though I suppose I should have known better than putting Fairchild's nose out of joint all over again. The next morning she told me I wasn't to wear my dress any more.'

'What a bitch in the manger!'

'After that the Count didn't take much notice of me, not in my old tweed skirt. But at least he kept Fairchild quiet for the rest of the cruise. She hardly spoke to me until we were nearly home again. Then, just before we got in she said, "Miss Bancroft, I'm sorry if I've been overwrought during the cruise. My nerves, you know. Do tell me if there's anything I can do in London to help you, though, of course, I'm going to Hollywood in a couple of weeks for the next two years. Just look at this lovely blue mink the Count's given me," she said. "He was bringing it to London for his sister, but he'll buy her another one at Bradley's. Isn't he sweet?" she said.

'"Do be a darling," she said, "and slip it over your shoulders when we go through Customs. They'd charge me the absolute earth if I tried to bring two minks through the barrier. And I can't possibly afford to throw my money away on stupid things like duty. Why, it quite suits you," she said.'

'And you agreed, Pet?'

'Didn't have much choice. Actually, the Customs' man was an absolute darling, though I suppose he rather liked the idea of running his hands through Monica Fairchild's underwear. As soon as he'd done that little squiggle with his chalk and left us, Fairchild said, "Thank you, Miss Bancroft."

'So I said, "Thank you for what?"

'And she said, "For wearing my mink, of course."

'So I said, "Your mink? But my dear, this is *my* mink."

'"Don't be an idiot, Miss Bancroft!" she said. "You know perfectly well I only asked you to wear it through Customs."

'"Did you?" I said. "I can't remember. Perhaps we'd better call back that nice Customs' man and see if he does?"

'"Miss Bancroft! Petunia! You wouldn't—!"

'"As you know yourself, Monica dear," I told her, "the road to success is strewn with unfortunate accidents. Good-bye, and thank you for a lovely trip. By the way, I noticed on that little card thing that the penalties for even suspected smuggling include long periods in the clink."

'So there I was, Gaston–loose in London with a blue mink cape and an old tweed skirt. I suppose I wasn't very honest, really, but I promise I'll send it back once she's home from Hollywood.'

'Jolly quick thinking, if you ask me,' I said admiringly. I suddenly felt that Pet had a bit more power under the bonnet than I'd imagined. 'It's about the most innocent way I've heard of a girl getting a mink coat, anyway.'

'After that, all the breaks seemed to come at once. My agent took me to lunch–in the mink, of course. We met Adam Stringfellow. He's a director, who was casting some models for a picture. He gave me a few days at the studio, and since then everything sort of built up.'

'And what's it like?' I asked.

'Bloody hard work,' said Petunia.

I looked surprised, having gathered from the newspapers that all she did was drive about in big fat cars with big fat chaps and draw a big fat salary.

'Do you know what time I get up in the morning? Before my milkman. I have to be at the studio by six, if you please, for hair-do and make-up. You can't imagine how ghastly it is playing a passionate love scene before breakfast, lying on a bed and remembering to keep one foot on the ground to make it all right for the censor.'

'Like billiards,' I observed.

'And I'm not myself any more.'

'Oh, come. Perfect health, I assure you.'

'I mean I'm Melody Madder Limited. With a board of directors, and things. Everyone does it because of the tax. And, of course, there's Mum.'

'Ah, yes, Mum.'

'Then there's another thing . . .' She looked up at me, fluttering her brand-new eyelashes. 'Gaston, my sweet–do you remember how once you loved me?'

'Only too well, Pet my dear.'

I was still getting a bit of rheumatism in the shoulder, the long-term after-effects of Clem's Caff.

'Do you know, I believe you're the only friend I've left in the world? And I need help, darling.'

'Good Lord, do you?'

'Desperately. I'm in terrible trouble.'

'Oh, yes?'

I looked cagey, knowing the sort of trouble girls specially reserve the doctors among their old friends for. But Petunia went on:

'It's all Mum's fault, really. Promise cross your heart you won't say a word?'

'Of course not. We doctors, you know. Professional secrecy.'

'Well, I'll tell you. It's simply that–'

But at that moment Mum arrived back with the medicine.

'This will have your daughter spry in no time,' I told her, shaking the bottle. 'I particularly hope she's in form again tomorrow night, because I've been asked to invite her to Lord Nutbeam's little party.'

'She'll have to get permission from Sir Theodore first,' said Mother. 'And from Mr Stringfellow, of course.'

'I have to ask their permission for everything,' Petunia apologized from the bed.

'And my permission, I might say,' added Mrs Bancroft. 'I'm still your mother, you know.'

'Yes, Mum,' said Petunia.

Chapter Sixteen

'I do so hope the young lady is free,' agreed Lord Nutbeam, when I arrived at his suite to explain the snags. 'I'd planned such a splendid little evening. There will be champagne, of course, and a band to play South American dances. Have you heard of the rumba, Doctor? It does my hip tremendous good. I wanted fireworks as well, but Ethel seems most disinclined.'

I made a consoling remark about Guy Fawkes coming but once a year, and he gave a sigh and went on, 'Don't you think, Doctor, that people are becoming such spoilsports these days? Not Ethel, of course. The dear girl is most understanding. I wanted to buy a tank of those tiny fishes in the Aquarium and serve them frozen in the water-ice tomorrow night. It would have been such a capital lark. But the hotel management wouldn't hear of it.'

I shot the old boy a glance. I'd wondered more than once since arriving at Monte Carlo whether his wife's diagnosis of pre-senile dementia wasn't correct. I supposed it was all right to make your medical adviser an apple-pie bed, and to stick a champagne bucket on his bedroom door to dowse him with ice-cold water on retiring. Or even to bust in with shouts of 'Fire!' when he's enjoying an early night, and have him looking pretty stupid running into the hall in his pyjamas with everyone else in tails and tiaras moving off to the opera. All right when your adviser's a chap like me, perhaps, but if Lord Nutbeam really had summoned the President of the Royal College of Physicians the little episodes might not have ended with such hearty laughter all round.

'But we shall have a lot of fun,' his Lordship went on. 'I'm arranging for a life-size statue of Miss Madder in ice-cream, and we can eat her. Also, the delightful gentleman from South America has promised to let me conduct the band all evening if I want. I'm sure everything will be very jolly.'

By then I was as keen as old Nutbeam for Petunia to get clearance all round and come to the party. As Pet Bancroft she'd always been a very decent sort, whom you didn't mind introducing to your friends when she wasn't in her waiter-biting mood, but dancing round the room with Melody Madder I felt could make you seem no end of a chap. The odd thing was, though I hadn't been keen on marrying Petunia Bancroft I wouldn't at all have minded Melody Madder. I supposed Freud was right–if adult happiness comes from fulfilling the longings of childhood I'd always wanted to marry a film star, along with opening for England at Lord's and beating the school record of twenty-four strawberry ices at a sitting. The only snag was not much liking the idea of getting into bed every night with a limited company.

I idled away the following day seeing some of the films, which were all about peasants and chaps in factories who took a gloomy view of life, then I put on my white dinner jacket and wandered into Lord Nutbeam's party. Sure enough, there was Petunia, bursting at the gussets with bewitchery.

'Miss Madder.' I bowed. 'May I have the pleasure of this dance?'

'Gaston, darling! But I must introduce you to Sir Theodore first.'

I'd heard of the chief financial wizard of Union Jack Films, of course, generally making speeches after eight-course banquets saying how broke he was.

'What's he like?' I asked.

'Oh, perfectly easy and affable. As long as you're used to dealing with the commissars in charge of Siberian salt-mines.'

I found him sitting over a glass of orange juice, with the expression of an orang-outang suffering from some irritating skin disease.

'Of course you know Quinny Finn?'

Of course, everyone knew Quintin Finn. You keep seeing him on the pictures, dressed in a duffel coat saying such things as Up Periscope, Bombs Gone, or Come On Chaps, Let's Dodge It Through The Minefield. Actually, he was a weedy little fellow, who smelt of perfume.

'And this is Adam Stringfellow.'

I'd always imagined film directors were noisy chaps with large cigars, but this was a tall, gloomy bird with a beard, resembling those portraits of Thomas Carlyle.

Everyone shook hands very civilly and I felt pretty pleased with myself, particularly with my old weakness for the theatre. I was wondering if Pet perhaps retained the passions of Porterhampton, when she interrupted my thoughts with:

'I'd particularly like you to meet Mr Hosegood.'

Petunia indicated the fattest little man I'd seen outside the obesity clinic. He had a bald head, a moustache like a squashed beetle, and a waist which, like the Equator, was a purely imaginary line equidistant from the two poles.

'My future husband,' ended Petunia. 'Shall we dance, Gaston?'

I almost staggered on to the floor. It was shock enough finding Petunia already engaged. But the prospect of such a decent girl becoming shackled for life to this metabolic monstrosity struck me as not only tragic but outrageously wasteful.

'Congratulations,' I said.

'Congratulations? What about?'

'Your engagement.'

'Oh, yes. Thanks. It's supposed to be a secret. Studio publicity want to link me with Quinny Finn.'

'I hope you'll be very happy.'

'Thanks.'

'I'll send a set of coffee-spoons for the wedding.'

'Thanks.'

We avoided Lord Nutbeam, chasing some Italian actress with a squeaker.

'Gaston–' began Petunia.

'Yes?'

'That's exactly what I wanted to talk to you about yesterday. Jimmy Hosegood, I mean. I don't want to marry him at all.'

'You don't?' I looked relieved. 'That's simple, then. Just tell the chap.'

'But Sir Theodore and Mum want me to.'

'Well, tell them, then.'

'You try telling them.'

I could see her point.

'Gaston, I need your help. Terribly. Don't you see, I've simply no one else in the world to turn to? How on earth can I get rid of Jimmy?'

I danced round in silence. It seemed a case of Good Old Grimsdyke again, always tackling other people's troubles, helping them to get out of engagements or into St Swithin's.

'This chap Hosegood's in the film business?'

She shook her head. 'He's in gowns. He's got lots of factories in Manchester or somewhere. But he puts up the money for the films. You follow?'

'But I don't even know the fellow,' I protested. 'And you simply can't go up to a perfect stranger and tell him his fiancée hates the sight of his face.'

'Come down to our tent on the beach and have a get-together. I'm sure you'll think of something absolutely brilliant, darling. You always do. Promise?'

But before I could make a reply, Mrs Bancroft was elbowing through the crowd.

'Petunia–time for bed.'

'Yes, Mum.'

'Here, I say!' I exclaimed. 'Dash it! it's barely midnight.'

'The only advice I require from you is on medical matters, young man. Up you go, Petunia. Don't forget your skin-food on the dressing-table.'

'No, Mum.'

'Or to say good night to Sir Theodore.'

'Yes, Mum.'

'And Adam Stringfellow.'

'Yes, Mum. Good night, Gaston.'

They left me in the middle of the dance floor, feeling pretty cross. I'd been looking forward to a jolly little party with Britain's biggest sex symbol, and here she was pushed off to bed like a schoolgirl on holiday. I stared round, wondering what to do with the rest of the evening. As I didn't seem to know anybody, and Lord Nutbeam was starting to throw Charlotte Russe into the chandeliers, I thought I might as well go up to bed, too.

'Excuse me,' said a voice behind me.

I turned to find a tall blonde with a long cigarette-holder and one of those charm bracelets which make women sound like passing goods trains whenever they reach for a drink.

'You're Dr Grimsdyke, aren't you?'

'Quite correct.'

'Known Melody Madder long?'

'Years and years,' I returned pretty shortly. 'Almost at school together, in fact.'

'Really? How very interesting. Don't you think it's stuffy in here? Shall we go outside for a drink?' She took my arm. 'You can tell me the story of your life in the moonlight.'

'I don't really think you'd be very interested.'

'But I'm sure I'll be very interested indeed, Doctor.' She made for the terrace. 'Let's sit in the orangery, where we'll not be disturbed.'

I didn't see Petunia for the next twenty-four hours, Lord Nutbeam being in such a state after the party we had to spend a quiet day motoring in the mountains. In the end, I'd passed a pleasant little evening with the blonde, who's name turned out to be Dawn something and was one of those sympathetic listeners who make such good hospital almoners and barmaids. After a few glasses of champagne she'd got me telling her all my troubles, including Miles and trying to write a book, though I kept pretty quiet about Petunia and Jimmy Hosegood.

I'd already decided it was as dangerous to go mucking about gaily in people's love affairs as to go mucking about gaily in their abdomens, and to let poor old Pet manage this amorous Tweedledum herself. I supposed I could have told him she was married already with a couple of kids in Dr Barnado's. I could have said she ground her teeth all night in bed. I could have challenged him to a duel, when at least I'd have stood the best chance of scoring a hit. But these ideas all struck me as leading to unwanted complications.

It was a couple of mornings later when I wandered down to the beach to find Petunia, and discovered Hosegood in the tent alone, on a deck-chair that looked as unsafe as a birdcage under a steam-roller.

'Nice day,' he said, as I appeared. 'Great stuff for toning up the system, a bit of sunshine.'

As he was fully dressed except for his boots and socks, I supposed he was drawing up the beneficial ultra-violet rays through his feet.

'Mind if I sit down? I was looking for Miss Madder.'

'Make yourself comfortable, lad. She was called on some photographing lark somewhere.'

He seemed very civil, so I took the next chair.

'Enjoying all the fun of the Festival?' I asked.

Hosegood sighed.

'I'd be happier on the sands at Morecambe, I would, straight. I don't hold with all this flummery-flannery myself, though there's plenty as does. Not that I'm one to interfere with anybody's enjoyment, as long as it's decent.'

'I expect you're a pretty knowledgeable chap about films?' I went on, trying to work up some sort of conversation.

'Me? Don't be daft, lad. I never go to the pictures, unless I can't help it.'

He sat for some time staring at his bunions. There didn't seem much else to talk about.

'What's your line of country?' he asked.

'I'm a doctor.'

'You are, by gum?' He almost rolled off the deck-chair. 'Just the feller I'm looking for.'

'Delighted to be of assistance,' I said politely.

'Tell me, Doctor–how can I get some of this blessed weight off?'

'Losing weight is perfectly simple,' I replied.

'Is it?' He brightened up a bit. 'Then what do I do, Doctor?'

'Eat less.'

'But I don't eat enough to keep a bird alive! Not fattening foods, at any rate. Nothing like–well, oysters, for instance.'

'One dozen oysters,' I disillusioned him, 'have only the food value of a lightly-boiled egg.'

'Go on? But I thought . . . I can be frank with you, of course, Doctor? Now that I'm getting married–Melody and me, y'know–and none of us are getting any younger, perhaps a few oysters . . .'

I disillusioned him about that one, too.

'How about massage?' he asked hopefully. 'Isn't that good for taking off weight?'

'Excellent,' I told him. 'For the masseuse.'

Hosegood looked gloomily at the agreeable combination of blue sea and girls in bikinis frolicking in the sunshine. I recalled a dietetic lecture at St Swithin's, when a professor resembling an articulated meat-skewer explained how he lived on a diet of crushed soya beans, while Sir Lancelot Spratt, who held that no gentleman ever dined off less than four courses, suffered violent trembling attacks and had to be taken out.

'They say in the papers it's dangerous to be fat,' Hosegood added sombrely.

'The commonest instruments of suicide,' I agreed, 'have rightly been described as a knife and fork.'

'But I've led a good, clean life. There's some I've seen in the club eating like steam shovels, and never putting on an ounce. I've only to look twice at the menu myself, and I'm letting out all my trousers again.'

'One of the nastier jokes of Nature,' I sympathized. 'it's all a matter of the appetite-regulating centre, nuzzling in the cranium between your pituitary gland and your subconscious fixations about Mother.'

'Then perhaps you can suggest some sort of diet, Doctor?'

'As a matter of fact, I can.'

Usually I prefer professional incognito in social surroundings, what with people keeping coming up and telling you all about their ruddy prolapsed kidneys, but old Hosegood struck me as a very decent sort, and even a good bridegroom for a girl prepared to risk getting stuck in the door of the church.

'The St Swithin's Hospital Diet,' I explained, producing the card from my wallet. 'All perfectly simple, as long as you remember to treat potatoes and puddings like deadly nightshade.'

'No fish and chips?'

'Nor alcohol.'

'I'm rather fond of a drop of beer.'

'So am I. That's the bitter pill.'

But he didn't seem in the mood for joking and pocketed the card in silence.

'Thank you, Doctor. I'll give it a go at lunch-time. I'm having a bite with Stringfellow in the Café de Paris. I suppose he wants to talk me into more brass for Melody's picture.'

'Talking of Miss Madder,' I went on, 'I certainly wouldn't contemplate marriage until you've lost a couple of stone.'

He looked alarmed. 'You really think so?'

'Without a doubt. Most dangerous.'

This wasn't strictly correct professionally, though I remembered a fat chap brought into St Swithin's orthopaedic department on his honeymoon with a dislocated shoulder when the bed broke.

'Besides,' I went on, 'there's always the risk of–'

I was aware of Lady Nutbeam standing in front of us, looking flustered.

'Doctor! There you are. I've been looking simply everywhere. We have to go back to England at once. This very afternoon.'

'Good Lord, really? Nothing serious, I hope?'

'My husband—'

'He hasn't fractured his other hip?'

'No, no! It's the hotel management. The white mice he let loose at breakfast.'

'Oh, I see.'

'I'd like you to come in the car with us, Doctor. I'm afraid Aubrey . . . sometimes a little trying, even for me.'

'Of course,' I said, though I'd counted on another fortnight of free drinks in the sunshine. 'If Mr Hosegood will excuse me, I'll pack at once.'

'And this telegram just arrived for you.'

'For me? I didn't think anyone knew my address.'

I opened it. It said:

RETURN ENGLAND INSTANTLY WHOLE COUNTRY DISGUSTED BY YOUR BEHAVIOUR.
MILES

Chapter Seventeen

'And how, pray,' started Miles, 'do you account for *that*?'

It was a few days later, and I'd gone round early to his flat to see what the fuss was about.

'Account for what? It seems like the morning paper to me. Not even today's, either.'

'You fool! Read what's on the middle page.'

'Good Lord!' I exclaimed. 'There's a photo of me.'

There was a headline saying MELODY'S MEN, also pictures of Quintin Finn commanding a battleship and Jimmy Hosegood lying on the beach like a jettisoned beer barrel.

I gave a laugh. 'It says, "Dr Gaston Grimsdyke, the fashionable young London physician is also tipped at the Festival as the future Mr Madder." I wonder what gave them that idea? Lots more about me, too.'

'Good God, man! You actually seem proud of it.'

'Well, I've never had my photograph in the papers before.'

Miles got rather excited.

'The disgrace and scandal of your being mixed up with this–this—'

'Melody Madder's a very decent type, and I won't have anyone being beastly about her.' I helped myself to a cup of his coffee. 'Anyway, you've been advising me to marry and settle down for years.'

'Not to the woman with the most advertised thorax in Britain.'

'But Miles!' interrupted Connie, dusting somewhere in the background, 'nobody believes what they read in the papers.'

'Kindly leave this discussion to us. Far from people forgetting it. I had a most uncomfortable evening of ribald jests last night at the club. As you have deliberately bruited my name abroad—'

'Me? I haven't bruited anyone's name anywhere.' I glanced again at the paper, and noticed something about my cousin, the brilliant Harley Street Surgeon. 'Oh, well, you know what reporters are for getting up a story. I suppose it was that blonde in the hotel. I should have spotted she was a journalist, but I just thought she was nosey and sporting about paying for the drinks. Mind if I have this piece of toast?'

'This happens to be my breakfast.'

'Oh, sorry.'

'And what's all this rubbish about you writing a book?' Miles began again.

'Put that in too, did she? As a matter of fact, I've just sent off the manuscript to Carboy and Plover. Jolly good advance publicity.'

'You've really written a book?' exclaimed Connie. 'How terribly clever of you.'

'May I remind you that you were not trained to waste your time scribbling penny dreadfuls? It's high time you made some contribution to the progress of medicine.'

'My best contribution to the progress of medicine, old lad, would be giving it up.'

'Not to mention your obligation to suffering humanity.'

'Suffering humanity's so overstocked with doctors there's always a few of the poor chaps on the dole,' I told him. 'And all of them probably better than me. Now look here.' I started to feel annoyed with my idiotic cousin. 'I may not have written *War and Peace*, but I'm jolly proud of my modest literary efforts. And I'm not going to have them sneered at by chaps who've never written anything except the footer reports for the school mag., and pretty terrible they were, too, if my memory serves me right.'

'You have utterly ruined my chances at St Swithin's, of course,' Miles went on, staring at me icily. 'It happens that the committee is in an extremely delicate state at the moment. Barefoot has obtained a large grant from the McKerrow Foundation, which he will use for surgical research at St Swithin's if appointed. As you know, Sir Lancelot is combing London to find funds for exactly that purpose. Now the possibility of my becoming related by marriage to a woman with–with her bosom brazened on every billboard in the country, is a stick for Sir Lancelot and every other opponent to batter my chances into nothingness.'

I reached for one of his cigarettes.

'Miles,' I said, 'I'm getting a bit fed up with all your beastly little backstairs bickering at St Swithin's. As a matter of fact, you're a selfish and self-opinionated chump, who thinks everyone in sight's got to drop what they're doing and rally round to help you get exactly whatever you want. You were just the same at school, over the jam cupboard.'

'How dare you!' exclaimed Miles. 'Damnation,' he added, as the telephone rang in the hall.

'Sorry, old girl,' I said to Connie, as he disappeared to answer it. 'Afraid I got a bit out of hand with your old man.'

'But I think you're right.' She put down the duster. 'Absolutely right. I'd hate to think of Miles getting anything except on his own merits.'

'And pretty good merits they are, I'm the first to admit.' I took another look at the newspaper. 'I suppose he rather got my dander up about the novel,' I apologized. 'Though I expect he's right. It's a bit stupid of me giving up a nice safe profession like medicine. Safe for the doctors, at any rate.'

'Do you know what I think?' Connie sat on the chair beside me. 'Listen to me, Gaston–I've known a lot of writers and artists. Particularly before I met Miles. I suppose I've run across most of the ones who've since made a name for themselves in London. I've darned their socks and stood them meals, as often as not. And I can assure you of one thing. If you really want to write books or paint pictures, a little matter like starvation isn't going to stop you.'

'That's jolly decent of you, Connie.'

This was the first really cheering word I'd had, even from Carboy and Plover.

'Anyway,' she added. 'If you're not suited for being a doctor, you're not. And it strikes me as better to face it now instead of killing a couple of dozen people to find out.'

Miles returned.

'It was Sir Lancelot Spratt,' he announced. 'He wishes to see you in his theatre at St Swithin's as soon as you can possibly get over there.'

I was glad to leave, both Miles and myself becoming a little exhausted by the conversation. But I edged through the traffic across London feeling pretty worried about whatever Sir Lancelot had in store for me. I supposed he took the same view as Miles, and was going to choke me off for disgracing the hospital by appearing in the same newspaper column as poor Petunia. It had been great fun telling my cousin what a pompous little pustule he really was, which I'd been meaning to ever since he confiscated my private bag of doughnuts, but it seemed a bit hard if the old boys at St Swithin's could use my chumminess with Petunia to wreck his hopes of promotion. I decided it was only fair to repair what damage I could. His remarks about my literary efforts had been pretty galling, I admitted, but in this country authors are thought a pretty unproductive class, anyway.

I hadn't been back to St Swithin's for months, and it was pleasant to stroll again through the old gateway and have a word with Harry the porter about the prospects for Goodwood. I took the lift up to Sir Lancelot's theatre, thinking how frightfully young the students were getting, and waited rather nervously in the surgeons' room while he finished off a gastrectomy.

'Right, Mr Hatrick, you sew him up and be careful of that tatty bit of peritoneum,' I heard him booming. 'Nurse! My morning tea and two digestive bisuits, if you please. Ah, there you are, Grimsdyke.'

He appeared in the pair of bright-blue pyjamas he used for expressing his personality under sterile operating gowns.

'Our patient from Long Wotton seems to be making a satisfactory, if not spectacular recovery,' Sir Lancelot began.

'So it would seem, sir.'

'But I want a word with you about another matter.'

'Ah, yes, sir.'

I braced myself. At least he couldn't throw anything handy and messy at me, like he used to inside the theatre.

Sir Lancelot untied his mask.

'I believe you are acquainted with this young Miss Melody Madder?'

'You mean Miss Melody Madder the actress, sir?'

'Naturally. Your cousin buttonholed me in the Parthenon yesterday with some garbled and apologetic story on the matter. I understand there has been something in the newspapers. I only read *The Times*, of course.'

'I–er, don't really know her, sir. Merely on nodding terms.'

'Oh.'

'Just happened to pass her in a crowd, sir.'

'I see.'

'Not my type at all, sir. I don't much like mixing with those sort of people. Always avoid them, sir.'

'Indeed.'

'In fact, sir, I can confidently assure you that she wouldn't know me from Adam.'

'Then I am extremely disappointed to hear it. It happens that I particularly wish for an introduction to this young woman myself.'

'Good Lord, do you really, sir?'

Sir Lancelot started munching a digestive biscuit.

'I had hoped to prevail upon your kindness to effect it, Grimsdyke. Under the circumstances there is no reason for my detaining you any longer. I am much obliged to you for calling. Good morning.'

'One . . . one moment, sir. I mean to say. I know her pretty well, sir. That is, I could easily get to know her, sir.'

'What the devil *do* you mean? You are being insultingly evasive.'

'Fact is,' I confessed, 'I didn't think you'd approve of her, sir.'

'And why not, pray? I am as appreciative of success on the stage as in surgery. I have attended sufficient theatrical people to know that it comes in both professions only from exceptional talent and exceptional hard work.'

He took another swallow of his tea.

'Now listen to me. You may be aware that I'm launching an appeal for funds to carry on surgical research at St Swithin's. The National Health Service, of course, doesn't run to such luxuries.'

'Miles mentioned it, sir.'

'I am arranging a meeting in the Founder's Hall at the beginning of the next academic year to initiate the campaign. You are familiar with the words of Horace, "*Si possis recte, si non, quocumque modo rem.*" No, of course you're not. It means, "Money by right means if you can, if not, by any means, money." I should much like Miss Madder to be present. She is, after all, of considerable more interest to the public than the appearance of merely the Prime Minister or Archbishop of Canterbury. And in this case beggars fortunately can be choosers. You think you can persuade her? Good. Then I leave it entirely to you.'

He brushed away the digestive crumbs.

It was perhaps the odd sensation of doing Sir Lancelot a favour which suddenly gave me another of my brilliant ideas. I felt I could now put poor old Miles right back in the running for St Swithin's.

'How much does the fund need to get it off to a good start, sir?' I asked.

'Some ten thousand pounds, I should say. You are surely not going to write a cheque, Grimsdyke?'

'No, sir, but Lord Nutbeam might.'

'Indeed?'

'It was Miles who suggested it, sir. He felt sure Lord Nutbeam would cough up for medical research in view of his clinical history.'

Sir Lancelot stroked his beard.

'H'm. Well, if either of you can persuade him, I need hardly say that I should be delighted. Keep me informed. Now I must get on with the next case. Good day.'

'Good day, sir.'

'By the way, Grimsdyke.' Sir Lancelot paused in the doorway. 'Miss Madder.'

'Sir?'

He made vague movements in front of his thorax.

'It's all done with wires and whalebones, isn't it?'

'Oh, no, sir! it's all living tissue.'

'Is it, by George! You must be a more enterprising young man than I imagined.'

'She was one of my patients, sir,' I explained.

Though I thought it best not to tell the old boy I'd only been treating Petunia for nausea.

Chapter Eighteen

'A fund for surgical research? I should be delighted to contribute,' said Lord Nutbeam.

'That's really terribly decent of you. You see, I was talking to Sir Lancelot the other day, and he felt that–shall we say–ten thousand pounds would make a nice shot from the starting gun.'

'My dear Doctor, I assure you I shall give the utmost that I can possibly afford. I'm so glad you drew my attention to it. And what are you doing this lovely morning? Ethel and I are continuing to explore London. Such fun, you know. We are going to the Zoo again, where I find the monkeys absolutely intriguing. Would you care to accompany us?'

'Jolly kind of you, but I've got to drive out to the Union Jack film studios.'

'Have you, indeed? I should love to visit a film studio myself. If you have a moment before you go, would you be kind enough to slip round the corner and buy me a large bag of monkey nuts?'

It was a few days later, and one of those mornings which make you think of flannels on the village green, punts dozing on the river, strawberries and cream in the garden, and all the other gentle English summer delights which compensate for the place being uninhabitable most of the winter. I was still staying with the Nutbeams in their house in Belgravia, and the previous evening I'd telephoned Petunia about Sir Lancelot's meeting.

'Come and see me at the studio tomorrow,' she'd invited. 'And, darling, what *are* you doing about Jimmy Hosegood?'

I didn't mention I intended to do nothing about Jimmy Hosegood, though feeling a bit of a cad, like St George pretending the fiery dragon was only something to do with the roadworks.

'And he's got so peculiar lately,' Petunia went on. 'Ever since you put him on that diet thing.'

'Peculiar how?'

'Like a centipede with corns. Ever so gloomy and grumpy and biting everyone's head off, even Sir Theodore's.'

'The sudden drop in blood-sugar is inclined to make people touchy. St Francis must have been absolutely intolerable until he got into his stride.'

'He's even being sticky about putting up the money for my picture. Adam Stringfellow's awfully upset. Not to mention Mum.'

'Perhaps I might be able to prescribe some counter-therapy,' I suggested. 'See you for lunch.'

I was as curious as old Nutbeam to explore a film studio, though rather disappointed to find the buildings stuck in the middle of the Sussex countryside resembled a municipal sanitorium. There were even the same long concrete corridors inside where you could fancy you smelt the antiseptic, the only difference being the place hadn't any windows and everyone was walking about dressed up as Roman soldiers and Hawaiian dancing girls. As nobody took any notice of me and all the doors had NO ENTRY on them, I stood wondering where to go. Then Petunia appeared, in an evening gown nicely displaying her gynaecoid pelvis.

'Gaston, darling! Have you been waiting long? I've been in the rushes. Let's go down to the canteen, I've only twenty minutes before I'm due on the floor again.'

'All right for this St Swithin's lark?' I asked, after greeting her warmly.

'Oh, that. Yes, studio publicity have passed it. But what about Jimmy, Gaston? I'm absolutely at my wits' end. Honestly.'

'How's he looking?' I asked.

'You can see for yourself. He's in the canteen with Mum.'

The studio canteen looked like any other work's eating-place, except that being full of actors it suggested supper at a fancy-dress dance. In the corner were Petunia's Mum and Hosegood. He brightened a little as I appeared and exclaimed, 'Doctor! Don't you notice the change in me?'

'I was just wondering who the thin chap was,' I told him, though he looked exactly the same, except for an expression like Mother Hubbard's dog.

'Rolls, sir?' asked the waitress.

'Take it away!'

Hosegood recoiled as though offered a basket of live snakes, and asked for lean meat, poultry, game, rabbit, cooked by any method without the addition of flour, breadcrumbs, or thick sauces.

'See, Doctor–I'm sticking to that diet like glue.'

'I didn't come all the way out here today to talk about your diet,' Mum interrupted, giving me a chilly look. 'Nor did I expect to discuss my business before strangers. I simply want to know why you refuse to put up the end money for Melody's film.'

'I've got to think about it,' mumbled Hosegood gloomily. 'Money's a serious business, y'know.'

'As managing director of Melody Madder Limited I demand a better explanation.'

'Look, Mrs Bancroft–once Melody and me's spliced—'

'Mum, I really—'

'Be quiet. This is nothing to do with you. I can't understand this change of attitude at all, Mr Hosegood.'

This started an argument which made a pretty miserable lunch of it, especially with Hosegood ordering cabbage, broccoli, spinach, root vegetables, not parsnips, boiled or steamed without the addition of fat. Then a thin chap with long hair appeared to tell Melody she was wanted on the set, and Mum, of course, went too, leaving me to finish off with her fiancé.

'Very difficult, Mrs Bancroft, sometimes,' he remarked.

'Why not tuck into a whacking four-course meal tonight for a treat?' I suggested. 'Things will look much rosier afterwards.'

But he only shook his head and asked for lettuce, radishes, watercress, parsley, with dressing not containing vegetable or mineral oils.

'And I,' I announced, jolly hungry from the country air, 'am going to have a slice of that nice ginger flan.'

Hosegood's jaw dropped. 'My favourite dish!'

The poor fellow salivated so much as I cut myself a large wedge and covered it with cream, I fancied he'd ruined his tie for good.

I'd just stuck my fork into the sticky ginger bit, when the waitress said I was wanted on the telephone. It was Petunia, from her dressing-room.

'Gaston, you must do *something*.' She seemed almost in tears. 'It's Mum. Now she tells me I've got to marry Jimmy next month, and Sir Theodore's to give it out to the papers tonight. What on earth am I going to do?'

'I'm terribly sorry about it, Pet,' I apologized weakly, 'but I really don't see how I can possibly—'

'But, Gaston, you *must*. Oh, God, here's Mum again. See you on the set.'

I went back to my place with the nasty feeling that I'd let down poor old Petunia. But she was an idiotic little girl to imagine I could ruffle the amorous intentions of a high-powered financial wizard like Hosegood. Besides, no scheme had occurred to me except eloping with her myself, and Miles would be chasing us all the way to Gretna. Then I noticed my plate was empty, with Jimmy Hosegood looking like a cat climbing out of an aviary.

'Good Lord!' I exclaimed. 'You didn't—?'

'The ginger tart,' mumbled Jimmy, 'Five hundred calories. What a fool!'

'Cheer up,' I told him, after he'd repeated this continually for several minutes. 'To err is not only human, but rather fun. Anyway, we'll get some of it off with a brisk walk down the corridor to Petunia's studio.'

'Studio?' He laid a hand on his waistcoat. 'I don't know if I'm well enough to get on my feet.'

It must have been a shock to his gastric mucosa, having a dish like that slung at it after weeks of fish and soda-water. But I was more interested at what went on inside the studio than what went on inside old Hosegood, and insisted he showed me the way.

'All right, Doctor,' he said, lumbering up. 'But by gum! I do feel queer.'

I'd often wondered how they set about making a film, the only one I'd seen being on the diagnosis of skin diseases in St Swithin's out-patients', which wasn't quite the same thing. We arrived at a door marked STAGE D, and went into a dim place the size of a cathedral filled with chaps sawing up bits of wood. The studio seemed to be lined with old sacks, was decorated only with notices telling people not to smoke or drop hammers on each other's head, neither of which anyone was paying any attention to. The floor was covered with an undergrowth of cables and copses of arc-lamps, there were chaps running about girders in the roof like Hornblower's sailors in the rigging, and there were other chaps pushing trolleys from one end to the other and back again with shouts of 'Mindcherbacspliz!' On the whole, I was rather disappointed. It reminded me of the St Swithin's operating theatre–the object of attention was illuminated with bright lights, it all seemed highly disorganized to the onlooker, there was nowhere to sit and rest your feet, and everyone not working was drinking cups of tea.

In the far corner was a typical night-club, except that it had no roof and all the guests in evening dress were reading the morning paper or knitting. In the middle stood Petunia talking to Quintin Finn, and pretty smashing she looked too, with her red hair glittering in the lights. Hosegood was meanwhile complaining he wanted to sit down, and noticing a canvas chair next to the camera with MELODY MADDER stencilled on the back I eased him into it.

'Right, children,' said Adam Stringfellow, who seemed to be a sort of referee, 'we're going now. Quiet, please.'

'Quiet!' yelled the two assistant directors, more young chaps with long hair who acted as linesmen.

Someone in the background went on hammering, sounding like a machine gun at a funeral.

'Quiet!' Yelled all three directors. 'Ready, Melody?' asked Stringfellow. 'Take one. Action.'

Just at that moment I sneezed.

'Quiet!'

'Terribly sorry,' I apologized. 'Purely reflex action.'

'Quiet!'

'Speck of dust, I'm afraid.'

'Quiet!'

'Rather dusty places, these Studios.'

'For God's sake!' shouted Stringfellow. 'Can't you control yourself at your age? We'll go again. Stand by, everyone. Take two. Action.'

Hosegood hiccupped.

'Would you have the kindness to hiccup just a little more softly, Mr Hosegood?' asked Stringfellow. 'I fear it may inconvenience us by getting on the sound-track. Once again. Take three. Action.'

But Quintin Finn had some dandruff on his collar, and a chap with a whisk came to brush it off.

'Take four,' continued Stringfellow, now looking like Thomas Carlyle in the middle of one of his famous attacks of the sulks. 'This is only costing us a hundred and fifty quid a minute. All right, Melody? Action.'

'One second,' said Petunia's mum.

'Oh, God,' said Stringfellow.

'My daughter's hair's not right at the back.'

I began to feel sorry for the Stringfellow chap, even though he didn't understand the elements of nasal physiology.

'Make-up! Please fix Miss Madder's hair. At the back.'

They got ready to start again, and I was feeling pretty excited at seeing a real film being shot, when there was a shout from the back of 'Tea break!' and everyone knocked off for a cup and a bun.

I didn't have the chance for a word with Melody, because she was kept talking in a corner by Adam Stringfellow. And anyway my attention was divided between Hosegood, who'd gone green, and Quintin Finn, who was asking my opinion of all his pictures.

'Do go and see my next one, dear,' said Quintin. 'I'm a commando major, and it's ever so exciting. There goes the shooting bell again. I *do* so hope this won't make us late this evening. My chauffeur Roland gets ever so cross if I keep him waiting, the naughty thing.'

'With the permission of Mrs Madder and the man with the chronic hay-fever,' Stringfellow announced, as the bell stopped, 'we will now go again. Quiet everyone, for God's sake. At your marks, Melody? Right. Take five. Action.'

That time they started, but Melody got her lines mixed up.

'Again,' said Stringfellow, with the expression of Sir Lancelot Spratt when the gastroscope bulb went out. 'No wonder people watch television. Take six. Action.'

Poor Melody, possibly rattled by the sight of Hosegood undoing his waistcoat, made a mess of it again.

'In Heaven's name, Miss Madder! You've only to say, "Thank you for a wonderful evening." *Do* try and concentrate, darling, *please*.'

'Don't you talk to my daughter in that tone,' said Mum.

'If you interrupt any more, Mrs Madder, I shall ask you to leave the set.'

She got up. 'You will, will you? And where would any of you be without my daughter, I'd like to know?'

'I'm sorry, Mrs Madder. Deeply sorry. But I am suffering from bad nerves and an inadequate budget and I cannot stand any more nonsense from you or anyone—'

There was a howl beside me, as Hosegood staggered to his feet gripping his epigastrium.

'Damn it!' he gasped. 'It's all the fault of that bloody ginger tart!'

'*What* did you call my daughter, you swine?' Mum shouted. 'Marry her? Over my dead body!'

And she hit him on the head with a convenient carpenter's hammer.

Chapter Nineteen

'What am I supposed to do at this performance, anyway?' asked Petunia.

'Nothing, except read Sir Lancelot's little speech. I've sub-edited it a bit, by the way. I didn't think there was much point in your quoting in Latin.'

'Won't I have to talk to a lot of doctors?'

'Only my cousin Miles, and he's been incapable of speech for days. The posh job he's after at St Swithin's is decided next Thursday week.'

Petunia lit a cigarette.

'One thing, I'm not half so scared of doctors and hospitals as I used to be. Not after visiting poor dear Jimmy after his accident?'

'How is the patient, by the way?'

'Oh fine. The doctors have let him out for convalescence. He's gone to Morecambe.'

It was the middle of September and autumn had come to London, with the news-vendors' placards changing from CLOSE OF PLAY to CLASSIFIED RESULTS and the first fierce winds starting to tear the summer dresses off the trees. I'd just picked up Petunia at her Chelsea flat and was driving her across to Sir Lancelot's meeting in St Swithin's.

'I'll nip in and collect his Lordship and his lolly,' I said, drawing up in Belgrave Square. 'Once you've said your little piece he's only got to hand Sir Lancelot his ten thousand quid, then we can all go off and have a drink. It's as simple as that.'

I found Lord Nutbeam sitting by the fire, sealing the envelope.

'Hello,' I greeted him. 'And how are we feeling this morning?'

I'd become a little worried about my patient in the past few weeks. He'd been oddly subdued and gloomy, and inclined to sit staring out of the window, like in his worst Long Wotton days. But I supposed this was reasonable in a chap who'd just finished a couple of months trying out all the night-clubs in London.

'I am still a little low, thank you, Doctor. A little low. Indeed, I fear I'm hardly up to the strain of presenting my modest donation in person.'

I nodded. 'I certainly wouldn't recommend a stuffy meeting if you don't feel equal to it. Though everyone will be frightfully disappointed, of course.'

'Besides, I have a visitor calling at noon, and I shouldn't like to keep him waiting.'

'I'll give it to the Lord Mayor to hand over, then,' I suggested.

'The Lord Mayor? I'd prefer it if you'd just quickly present it yourself, Doctor.'

'Me? But dash it! I'm not nearly important enough.'

'Oh, come, my dear Doctor. I assure you that you are, in my eyes, at any rate. I shall stay here, I think, and read a book. Or perhaps I shall play a few pieces on the piano.'

'Right ho,' I agreed, anxious to be off. 'I'll tell you all the nice things they say in the vote of thanks.'

The meeting itself, like any other of Sir Lancelot's special performances inside or out of his operating theatre, was organized on a grand scale. The old Founders' Hall at St Swithin's could look pretty impressive, with all those portraits of dead surgeons glaring down at you from the walls, not to mention the scarlet robes and bunches of flowers and chaps popping about taking photographs and the television cameras. I'd been a bit worried how the consultants at St Swithin's would react to Petunia as she appeared in a dress cut down to her xiphisternum, but they seemed delighted to meet her and all bowed over her politely as they shook hands. Sir Lancelot himself greeted us very civilly, ushering us to a couple of gilt chairs in the middle of the dais, where he'd arranged the Lord Mayor and some of the most expensive blood-pressures in the City.

'I am indeed sorry to hear Lord Nutbeam is indisposed,' he remarked, 'but I need hardly say your appearance here today, Miss Madder, will attract considerable interest to our cause. May I introduce one of my junior colleagues, Mr Miles Grimsdyke? He is taking the chair.'

Sir Lancelot banged on the table.

'Your Grace, My lord Marquis, My Lords, My Lord Mayor, ladies and gentlemen,' he began, 'may I invite silence for our Chairman?'

My cousin made an efficient little speech, and if he did dwell rather on the dear old hospital and his unswerving affection and loyalty towards it, I suppose a chap has to advertise. Then the flash-bulbs went off like Brock's benefit night as Petunia got to her feet. She made an efficient little speech too, though I don't think anyone was paying much attention to what she said. Next it was my cue.

'In the regrettable absence of Lord Nutbeam,' I announced, 'I have great pleasure, as his friend as well as his doctor, in presenting this cheque for ten thousand pounds to start so worthy a fund.'

There was applause. I wondered for a second whether to give them the story of the bishop and the parrot as well, but decided against it.

'This is a very proud moment for me,' declared Sir Lancelot, taking the envelope. 'As many of you know, it is well over forty years since I first came to this hospital as a student. In that not so distant age appendicitis was still a desperate operation, tuberculosis was indeed the scourge of our civilization, and pneumonia as often as not a death warrant. It was also an age when any political gentleman trying to interfere with the affairs of our great hospital would get his fingers burnt very smartly indeed.

'With the passing years, these walls which St Swithin's men grow to venerate so deeply have remained much as for the previous two centuries. But inside them has occurred a revolution in therapy as great as during those exciting times when Lister was introducing asepsis, Pasteur founding the science of bacteriology, and John Snow first alleviating the ordeal of the patient and the frustration of the surgeon with ether anaesthesia. Much, of course, remains to be done. Many of our old hospital buildings, for example, cry for demolition to ease our lives with a little space to park our cars. But surgical research is the cause nearest the heart of many assembled in this Hall today. It is certainly nearest to my own. I am sure we all have in mind the words of the immortal Martial–"*Non est vivere, sed valere vita est*"–as I gratefully accept this gift–this most generous gift–from Lord Nutbeam to relieve our cares in that direction.'

Everybody clapped again.

I must say, I felt pretty pleased with myself, as it hardly seemed yesterday sinceSir Lancelot was kicking me out of the theatre for stamping on his left foot instead of the diathermy pedal under the operating table. Particularly as he went on:

'I feel I must express in public my appreciation–the whole hospital's appreciation–of these young men, Dr Gaston Grimsdyke and his cousin Mr Miles Grimsdyke. It is through their agency that we are honoured this afternoon with the presence of such a charming and distinguished lady of the stage as Miss Melody Madder.'

There was further applause, this time more enthusiastic.

'Indeed,' continued Sir Lancelot, tearing open the envelope, 'it is to these gentlemen that we are indebted for the suggestion of Lord Nutbeam's most munificent–'

He went pink all over. I glanced at him anxiously. I wondered if the poor chap was going to have some sort of fit.

'Grimsdyke!' he hissed. 'What's the devil's the meaning of this?'

'Meaning of what, sir?'

'Look at that, you fool!'

Feeling a bit embarrassed, what with everyone watching and the television cameras, I took the cheque.

'Seems all right to me, sir,' I said, shifting rather from foot to foot. 'Payable to you and signed "Nutbeam". I hope you are not suggesting it can't be met?' I added, a bit dignified.

'I do not doubt that for one moment, considering that it is made out for one pound four and eightpence.'

'Good Lord, sir, so it is! But–but–dash it! I mean to say there must be some mistake—'

'Get out of this hall this instant! You rogue! You vagabond! You unspeakable idiot! Never let me look again upon your unbearable—'

'I'm sure there's some explanation–' I was aware that an odd sort of silence had fallen on everybody.

'Get out!' roared Sir Lancelot.

'Oh, yes, sir. Right-ho, sir.'

I left the meeting in some confusion. I think it was the Lord Mayor who had enough presence of mind to jump up and start singing *God Save The Queen*.

Twenty minutes later I was throwing open Lord Nutbeam's front door, and bumped into the severe bird in striped trousers I'd last seen emerging from Nutbeam Hall. But I didn't intend to pass the time of day with him and burst into the drawing-room, where I was a bit startled to find Lady Nutbeam next to his Lordship on the sofa wearing her old nurse's uniform.

'Look here!' I began at once. 'If this is another of your stupid jokes—'

'My dear Doctor! What on earth's the matter? You look quite beside yourself.'

'I jolly well am beside myself.' I chucked the cheque at him. 'You've made an absolutely booby of myself, Sir Lancelot, and the entire staff of St Swithin's, not to mention all sorts of City nobs. I go along to this jamboree, thinking I'd got the ten thousand quid you'd promised—'

'But my dear Doctor! I feel I never promised any such sum at all.'

'But damn it! You did. I told you ten thousand was wanted to start this blasted fund, and you agreed on the nod. Don't tell me you've simply forgotten. Or perhaps you've just omitted to add the noughts?' I added a bit hopefully.

'I indeed remember perfectly well your mentioning the sum,' Lord Nutbeam continued calmly. 'But I fear I never said I would present Sir Lancelot with it all.'

'But hell! Why on earth one pound four shillings and eightpence?'

'Because, my dear Doctor,' replied Lord Nutbeam simply, 'it is all I have left.'

There was a silence.

'Oh,' I said. 'I see.'

'We wondered why everyone was making such a fuss over the presentation,' added Lady Nutbeam.

'Though I assure you, Doctor, it gives me great pleasure to present my all to such a deserving cause as surgical research.' He took his wife's hand. 'I fear I have been overspending rather of late. But Ethel and I have had a lovely summer, haven't we, my dear?'

'And now I'm going out to get a job and we can start all over again,' said Lady Nutbeam.

'The men will be coming for the cars and the furniture this afternoon. Fortunately, I still have a cottage near Nutbeam Hall, and with my books and my piano no doubt we shall be just as happy. Though I fear, Doctor, I can no longer offer you employment in my household, as much as I should like to.'

There didn't seem anything to say.

'Goodbye, my dear Doctor. And my warmest thanks.'

I put my hand in my pocket.

'I–I don't use this very much,' I said. 'I'd rather like you to have it. It might be able to help you out a little.'

I gave him back his gold cigarette case.

Miles was already in his flat when I arrived.

'Oh, Gaston!' said Connie, opening the door.

He didn't look up as I entered.

'You'd better emigrate,' he remarked quietly.

'Yes, I'd better,' I said.

Chapter Twenty

It had been raining heavily all day. It had been raining heavily all the day before. In fact, it had been raining heavily as long as I could remember, and I was beginning to get the feeling of living under water.

I looked through the window of the clinic, which was constructed largely of old petrol tins. There was the River Amazon, very muddy and full of crocodiles. Beyond were some trees. Behind were some trees, and all round were more trees. It struck me what a damn silly song it was they used to sing about the beastly things.

I wondered whenever I'd see London again. I'd had a pretty miserable week while Miles fixed me up with the oil company, mooching round saying goodbye to things I'd hardly thought twice about before, such as Nelson's Column and the swans on the Serpentine. I'd already forgotten how long I'd been in Brazil, the only newspapers coming with the weekly launch, but I supposed it was only a couple of months. That meant another four years or so before I would ever again taste a mouthful of good old London fog. I wondered if Miles had got his job. I wondered if Sir Lancelot had got his cash. I wondered who had won the November Handicap. I wondered if I were going steadily potty, and would see my old chums again only between a couple of those chaps in neat blue suits you sometimes saw lurking round St Swithin's.

My reflections were interrupted by a cry behind me of, 'Hello, Grimalkin, old thing! How'd you like another little game of rummy?'

I turned to face Dr Janet Pebbley, my professional colleague.

'I suppose so. There doesn't seem anything else much to do for the next five years.'

'Gosh, you're funny! But I always say, there's nothing like a game of cards for passing the time. When my friend Hilda and I were doing our midder at the Femina, I always said to her, "Hilda," I said, "let's have another little game of rummy, and I bet they'll be popping like corks again all over the place before we've even had time to notice it."'

Janet Pebbley and I had arrived together to share the job of looking after the locals' bad feet and yellow fever inoculations, and she was the only Englishwoman I had to talk to. In fact, she was the only person in the whole of Brazil I had to talk to except myself, and I'd tried that a few times already. Personally, I'm generally in favour of female doctors, who these days all wear nice hair-dos and nice nylons, but Janet was one of the standard type whose psychological development became arrested somewhere about the hockey stage. She was a tall, pink-faced girl, qualified a few years before from the London Femina, who looked as if she could rearrange Stonehenge single-handed.

The trouble was, I was falling in love with her.

I suppose that psychiatrist in Wimpole Street would have explained it as a conflict between my id and my super-ego, but as far as I was concerned I knew it was a damn silly thing to do. But seeing Janet every day, I somehow had no alternative. It's like when they stick a pair of rats in a cage in the physiology laboratory. When she emerged from her tiny bungalow for breakfast every morning with a hearty cry of, 'Hello, there, Grimalkin! How's the old liver today?' I knew perfectly well I should lock myself in and tell her to call me in five years' time. But I didn't. I sat at the table, eyeing her like a hungry cat in a cheesemonger's.

'What are you going to do, Grimalkin?' she asked, when we'd finished our meal of pork and beans that evening. 'When your contract's up and you go home, I mean.'

I looked past the oil-lamp through the clinic window, where insects nobody had ever heard of before were jostling in the darkness. It was still raining, of course.

'I don't think I can see quite as far ahead as that.'

'I can. This five years will pass in a flash. An absolute flash. As I said to my friend Hilda the very day we were starting together at the Femina, time always does flash by if you will it to. You know what I'm going to do?'

'No?'

'I'll have a bit of money saved up then. We'll both have, won't we? Nothing to spend it on here except fags. First I'm going to have a jolly good tramp all over Scotland. Then I'm going to settle down in practice somewhere in the Midlands. My friend Hilda's up there, and strictly between *entre nous* she could fix an opening.' She made a little squiggle with her finger on the tablecloth. 'Two openings, if she wanted to.'

I realized I'd taken her other hand.

'Janet—'

'Yes?'

'You're jolly nice, you know.'

'Go on with you, Grimalkin.'

'But you are. Honestly. The nicest girl I can remember. Janet, I—'

But luckily the old super-ego fell like a trip-hammer.

'Yes, Grimalkin?'

'Nothing,' I said.

'You're not looking very bright tonight.'

'The heat, you know. The rain. Bit worked up.'

'How'd you like a nice game of rummy? It will help you to unwind.'

'I suppose so,' I said, though I felt the spring had bust long ago.

The next night I kissed her.

'Grimalkin!' she shrieked. 'You shouldn't?'

'But Janet, I–I love you.'

There was silence, except for the rain on the roof.

'I do. Really and truly. Cross my heart, you're the only girl in my life.'

'Oh, Grimalkin! I knew it. As soon as I set eyes on you at London Airport, I could tell you'd taken to me. I don't know what it was. Perhaps it was the sad sort of look you had. I knew you'd want someone like me to cheer you up.'

Being cheered up by Janet Pebbley was like having your back scratched with a horse-rake, and perhaps the memory of it brought down the super-ego again.

'Haven't you anything else to say?' she asked.

But I shook my head, and we had another game of rummy.

The next day she left in the launch for a week at the company's headquarters in Manaus. As I'd read all the books and damp had got into the gramophone and you can't play rummy by yourself, I spent the evenings contemplating life somewhere like Porterhampton with Janet. There would be her friend Hilda, of course. And that tramp round Scotland. But I was so ruddy lonely looking at the rain, I started counting the days till she'd come back as carefully as the months till we'd both be released. After all, she wasn't a bad sort of girl. A bit jolly at breakfast, admittedly, but I could get used to that. Her friend Hilda might be quite witty and delightful. Come to think of it, I'd always wanted to have a good look at Scotland. The British Consul in Manaus could marry us, and that would leave a whole bungalow free for playing rummy in. I started to prepare little speeches, and wonder if it would possibly be a fine day for the wedding.

Janet came back to the camp with more pork and beans and a couple of new packs of playing cards. I waited until we finished our evening meal, and when the Brazilian cook chap had cleared away the dishes said:

'Janet—'

'Yes, Grimalkin.'

'I have something I want to ask you.'

'Really, Grimalkin?'

The super-ego quivered on its bearings. The mechanism had rusted like everything else in the ruddy climate.

'Janet, we've got on pretty well these last few weeks or months or whatever they've been, haven't we?'

'Like houses on fire, Grimalkin.'

'I mean, we've managed to hit it off pretty well together.'

'You've certainly kept me entertained with all your jokes. Especially that one about the bishop and the—'

'What I mean is, I thought, in the light of experience and under the circumstances, that is, you wouldn't mind if I asked you—'

'Go on, Grimalkin.'

There was a shocking crash, indicating somebody knocking on the corrugated iron door.

'Just one moment.'

I unlatched the door. Outside was Mr Carboy, in a Homburg and holding an umbrella.

'At last!' he cried. 'I am in the presence of the master. Allow me to shake you by the hand.'

He did, scattering drops of water all over the place.

'But–but what on earth are you doing in Brazil?' I stared at him. 'I thought you were busy correcting proofs in Bloomsbury.'

'My dear fellow! Luckily I was half-way here on holiday in Nassau when the news came.'

'News? What news?'

'But haven't you heard? About your book, of course. Tremendous success, my dear chap! We've reprinted it six times already and burnt out two rotary machines. Magnificent notices–look, I've got some of them here. Union Jack have been cabling me every day for the film rights. I might tell you that Melody Madder herself is absolutely desperate for the part of the girl. Why, you've got the whole country laughing its head off with your portrait of that pompous and pig-headed little surgeon.'

This was all very confusing.

'But–but–dash it! When you gave me that contract thing to sign in London, you said the book trade was in such a state nobody read any new novels any more.'

'Ah, well, you're a doctor. You know it's sometimes better to say the patient's going to die and collect the credit, eh? Ha ha! Talking of contracts, a fellow from Potter and Webley hasn't been prowling round, has he? Nasty little man with a moustache and a dirty brief-case. Good! Well, perhaps you'd like to sign this here and now for your next six books. Substantially increased royalties, of course. How d'you do, madam.' He noticed Janet. 'So sorry to disturb your evening. But we won't be long, as we can't keep the launch waiting.'

'Launch waiting?' I felt a touch of the vertigo. '"We,"' did you say? But I've got a job here. For the next five years, at any rate.'

'My dear fellow, I soon fixed that with the oil people. Your replacement's arriving tomorrow. Why, you've got receptions, television, personal appearances, and no end of work to face. Better hurry up, the plane leaves at midnight. Another few hours and you'll be facing the photographers in London.'

I wondered whether this was all hallucinations, due to the collapse of my psychological mechanisms.

'Well,' I said, 'I suppose I'd better pack.'

'Grimalkin—'

'Ah, yes?' I'd forgotten Janet.

'What was it you . . . you were going to ask me?'

'I was just going to ask if you'd care for another game of rummy,' I said.

Ten minutes later I was in the launch. I noticed that the rain had stopped.

Chapter Twenty-one

The literary lunch at Porterhampton was a great success. I'd spent the morning autographing copies of the novel in the local bookshop, and even if most people did come up and ask if I sold postcards it had been fun signing something different from prescriptions for cough mixture. The old Wattles were all over me, and Ma Wattle even made a speech.

'We look upon Gaston Grimsdyke as one of Porterhampton's own sons,' she asserted. 'It will be a great consolation to Dr Wattle and myself, now that we have reached the later years of our lives, to remember that he once lived beneath our humble roof. But I must not keep you from our honoured guest, whom I am sure will treat us to that delightful wit which we in Porterhampton are already privileged to know so well. Meanwhile, it is my great pleasure to present him, on behalf of his former patients, with this splendid chiming clock.'

After that I told them the story of the parrot, which everyone now seemed to think funnier than ever. Though I was a bit put off half-way through noticing little Avril Atkinson eyeing me from the end of the table.

'Sorry I was so cross that foggy night,' she smiled, catching me as I dashed for my train. 'It was only the mumps, you know. Doesn't it make you feel wretched?'

'All healed, I trust?'

'Everything is healed now, Gaston. But there's just one little favour I'd like to ask you. Could you possibly get me Melody Madder's autograph? I suppose these days you actually know her, don't you?'

I reached London in time to decide comfortably which West End restaurant to try for dinner, and felt it would be rather pleasant to drop into my club for whisky and soda. The first person I met in the morning-room was old Miles.

'My dear chap,' I said, offering him a cigar. 'How's the new job going at Swithin's?'

'Congratulations.'

'That's jolly kind of you. But I believe you very kindly gave me them shortly after the book came out.'

'Not that. I mean on becoming a member of this club.'

He seemed to have some difficulty in talking, what with grinding his teeth.

'Oh, that. Thanks. Actually, old Carboy put me up. He says an author needs a bit of standing. Care for a drink?'

'No. No thank you. I must get off to a meeting at St Swithin's.'

He turned to go.

'Gaston—'

'Yes, Miles?'

'I admit I'm finally on the consultant staff at St. Swithin's. I admit I've struggled and schemed all my life to get there. I admit it is my major ambition achieved even before my middle age. But damnation! When I think of all the work, the years, the worry . . . and . . . and . . . you, just scribbling away on bits of paper . . .'

The poor chap seemed about to burst into tears, which I'm sure would never have done in the Parthenon.

'Here, steady on, old lad.'

'All right. I'll steady on. I won't say any more. Except one thing. Do you happen to know, Gaston, that you have made me the laughing-stock not only of St Swithin's but of the entire medical profession? Do you? I am aware of it. I am aware of it perfectly well. People don't come out with it, of course. Oh, no. Not now I'm a consultant. But the students . . . only the other day I heard one shout, "Three cheers for Clifford Standforth" as I walked in to lecture. Everyone knows as well as I do that you made the character a ghastly caricature of myself. Your own cousin, too!'

'If I may refer you to that little bit inside the fly-leaf, all characters are entirely imaginary and any resemblance—'

'Bah!' said Miles, and walked out.

'Give my love to Connie,' I called after him.

I ordered my drink and wondered if I could nip down to Cartier's before they shut and buy a wedding present for Petunia. I'd been rather startled when she'd told me at the studio the day before she was marrying Jimmy Hosegood after all.

'It was Mum, I suppose,' she explained. 'She wanted me to marry Jimmy, so I didn't. Then she didn't want me to, so I did. But I'm terribly in love with him, darling. Even Mum's becoming reconciled. Now he's got a seat on my board.'

I didn't say anything. I supposed all women are a bit potty, and actresses especially so.

'Besides,' Petunia went on, 'look at the difference in him now he's got back from Morecambe. He's even skinnier than Quinny Finn.'

The odd thing was, after Hosegood's blow on the head he could eat as much as he liked without putting on an ounce. A jolly interesting piece of clinical research, I thought, which I'd have written up for the *British Medical Journal* if they hadn't been after my address all these years over those arrears of subscription. As for Petunia, she was just the same, though I noticed she'd turned into a blonde.

I lit another cigar, and was making for the front door feeling pretty pleased with myself, when I heard a roar behind me.

'You, boy!'

I turned round.

'You, Grimsdyke. I want a word with you.'

'Ah, yes, sir.'

'Come here. And shut the door after you. I can't tolerate draughts.'

'No, sir.'

'Sit down there. Not like that, boy. You haven't got a spinal curvature, have you, from leaning all your life on the counters of four-ale bars?'

'No, sir. Sorry, sir.'

'Now just you listen to me, young feller me lad.'

Sir Lancelot sat back and placed his fingers together.

'I recall you once tried to make a fool of me as a student. Some nonsense about distributing invitations for my non-existent birthday party. I could easily forgive that, knowing your pathetically infantile sense of humour. But I cannot forgive your making a much bigger fool of me in front of a duke, a marquis, and a couple of earls, not to mention a mixed bag of civil dignitaries. And please chuck that cigar away. If you haven't the taste to choose something better, my advice is to give up smoking.'

'Yes, sir. Terribly sorry, sir. But I did explain in my letter of apology how I'd sort of put the *carte blanche* before the horse.'

'An explanation is not an excuse. Fortunately for St Swithin's, nobody quite understood what passed between us on the platform. I suppose they were all too intent looking at the young woman you brought. Equally fortunately, Sir James McKerrow was singularly sympathetic when I confided the story–not to mention singularly amused–and donated an additional ten thousand pounds from the funds of his Foundation. None of this prevents my telling you, Grimsdyke, that you are a young man of extremely limited intelligence, mediocre ability, flabby moral fibre, and more bright ideas than are good for you. The fact that you, a grown adult, let everyone push you about as they wish is a perfect disgrace, particularly when it's your own cousin. You understand me?'

'Yes, sir. Exactly, sir.'

'You agree with me?'

'I suppose I do, sir.'

'You will kindly take pains to mend your ways in future. Please remember however much your name appears in the papers, as far as I am concerned you're still the miserable little moronic worm I remember when you first stuck your beastly acne-infected face into my operating theatre.'

'Yes, sir.'

'Good,' said Sir Lancelot, suddenly very affable. 'I thought I'd get that over to prevent yer getting a swelled head. Now let's have a drink, and I'll buy you a decent cigar.'

It was midnight when Sir Lancelot and I left the club together.

'Can I give you a lift?' he asked. 'Though I suppose you've got a Rolls of your own now.'

'I'm sticking to the old 1930 Bentley, thank you, sir.'

'And what are you going to do now?'

'Write another book for Mr Carboy, I suppose.'

'No more medicine?'

'I'm afraid not, sir.'

'It's nothing to be ashamed of. Medical truants have played as much of a part in helping our world forward as a good many doctors. And personally I find nothing so stimulating as the smell of burning boats. But you'll miss it.'

'I think perhaps I shall, really, sir.'

'However, as you will remain on the Medical Council's *Register* till death or striking off do you part, you are perfectly at liberty to open an abcess or deliver a baby whenever the occasion arises and you happen to feel like it. And you probably will. Medicine, like murder, will out.'

'Unless I send my cases to Miles at St Swithin's,' I smiled.

'If you see him, by the way, say I'm sorry I made him sweat a bit over his appointment. Of course, it was a foregone conclusion. I just wanted to cut him down to size. That, Grimsdyke, is one of the most valuable operations in the whole repertoire of surgery. Good night, my boy.'

'Good night, sir.'

'And you might also tell your cousin I knew perfectly well he didn't have a nervous breakdown at that examination. But I don't really think a fellow ought to get bottled just before he comes up for his finals.'

Sir Lancelot drove off, leaving me with plenty of food for thought. I realized more than ever what a really great chap he was. But the most important thing about him was having such a jolly good sense of humour.

Richard Gordon

The Facemaker

The Facemaker

This is the first of three stories about the Trevose family.

They were no more immoral nor noble than most human beings, including those who are both the servants and the gods of the others–the doctors.

They were simply worse at concealing their vices, that is all.

The youth who became Sir Graham Trevose, K.B.E., D.Sc., F.R.C.S., Consultant in Plastic Surgery to Blackfriars Hospital and the Royal Air Force, never even bothered to try.

Chapter One

He had been in the sanatorium three months and was glad to find everyone apologetically giving up the idea that he really ought to die. He knew perfectly well he had the fatal *habitus phthisicus* described by Hippocrates. His skin was soft, pale and veined. The whites of his eyes were tinged blue. His shoulder-blades stood out like wings, and they could almost count the ribs of his flat chest across the room. It was not at all the sort of chest the sanatorium liked to see. It was a chest which gave in to tuberculosis without the flicker of a fight. A cowardly chest. He ought to be ashamed of it.

They put him to bed in the cold January air, with a mackintosh sheet as a counterpane to catch the rain dripping monotonously under the verandah. They gave him a spittoon with a cap like a German beer-mug, fed him like a fighting-cock, submitted him to the indignity of bedpans and bottles, measured his weight once a week, his spit once a day, and his temperature four-hourly. His doctors and nurses were solicitous to the point of tenderness, which depressed him, as he soon found this attitude reserved for the most desperate cases. They forbade him to wash and shave himself, to sit up or even to read. He had nothing to do but chase his thoughts round his head, and no news of the world except sometimes carried by the rumble of the guns across the Channel.

The sanatorium's medical superintendent was a sad-faced Scot, whose scrawny frame and club-like finger-nails told knowing eyes that he was seeking revenge on his own disease, by spending what it had left of his life in treating it. He had the habit of declaring at the bedside, 'Only *Mother Nature* can cure tuberculosis, not the physician. We provide fresh air, rest, a suitable diet, a carefully balanced regimen–we are but Mother Nature's handmaidens, standing at her elbow while she performs her healing work.'

His patient thought this had at least the advantage of justifying the sanatorium's shortcomings in advance.

It was impatience to get out of the place rather than desperation to get better which made him ask the superintendent for remedies more specific than Mother Nature, dragging from his own half-forgotten lectures such nostrums as gold by injection, creosote by inhalation, or iodine mysteriously liberated internally to disinfect the body by the drinking of chlorine (which struck him as likely to taste very nasty). But the superintendent looked sadder than ever and said, 'Placebos, placebos! I should prefer to insult neither your body nor your intelligence, Dr Trevose. More important than any drug in the world is your will-power, your determination to recover, your *strength of character*.'

Young Graham Trevose found this Presbyterian bleakness more depressing, having suspected for years that the strength of his character was even more fragile than that of his chest.

Graham's misfortunes had started at two in the morning, an hour when our resistance is supposed to reach some mysterious lower ebb, a favourite one in the mythology of hospital sisters for birth or death to shake the human frame. He had woken coughing a salty taste from his mouth, and hastily lighting the bedside candle found an alarming red stain staring at him from the sheet. When John Keats, another young doctor, underwent the same unsettling experience he cried with poetic quick-wittedness that he saw the seal on his death-warrant. There occurred to Graham only a less spectacular idea–now he'd get out of military service.

It was over three years since most of his fellow-students at Blackfriars Hospital had gone off to join Kitchener's army, in the same spirit as they went off to play football matches. But Graham's puny frame clearly being no use to a drill-sergeant he had stuck to his books, braving such inconveniences as Zeppelins and white feathers, until graduating before Christmas in 1917. Then he found King and country wanted his new qualifications however insecurely they were embodied, and conscription threatened to scoop him up with the other scrapings of the barrel.

The First World War being a more informal one than the Second, his Aunt Doris could persuade her brother, a captain in the Royal Navy whom Graham had disliked since birth, to pull a few strings for the lad. It was settled that he should be commissioned as a surgeon-lieutenant and posted to his uncle's own command, the *Inviolable*, a brand-new battleship bristling with guns, her sides the thickness of a medieval castle, advertised by the Admiralty to friend and foe as unsinkable. Aunt Doris thought the sea air would do him good.

But a haemoptysis in the middle of a cold January night of 1918 seemed likely to change this and many less immediate plans. The household was roused, the gas-mantles lit, hot-water bottles filled, a fire kindled in his bedroom despite the dissuasive level of coal in the cellar. A chest physician was summoned later from his breakfast–Dr James Wedderburn, F.R.C.P., of Blackfriars Hospital, plump, side-whiskered and prosperous, with an air of such smug good health as deeply distressed his more self-pitying patients. He arrived, radiating confidence like a lighthouse, in a magnificent Rolls-Royce Silver Ghost chauffeured by a man so pointedly past military age as in seeming danger of dropping dead over the wheel. Graham's father, Professor Trevose, waiting to receive him in the hall of his tall and gloomy Hampstead house, knew the physician well. The professor was in charge of the anatomy department at Blackfriars, and frequently pressed his company on Dr Wedderburn, who found it tedious to the extent of sometimes forgoing his lunch to avoid it.

The consultant's examination was more impressive than conclusive. He fancied the right upper chest might move a little less freely than the left, the note on percussion with his pudgy fingers could be a little impaired, the breath sounds rustling up his expensive stethoscope a shade diminished. There might be an area of tubercular consolidation at the apex of the right lung–though on the other hand there might not. But fever conspiring with blood-spitting in such a fragile body was a deadly alliance. Experience alone told him the disease would gallop through the poor young man and bear him off to Heaven in the year. This view he put privately to Graham's father downstairs, suggesting the course of events should more fittingly occur in a sanatorium.

'This damnable Koch's bacillus,' cried Professor Trevose. He tugged his heavy moustache irritably, wondering why God was so unkind to him. If the calamity had put him in a doubly bad temper, it was his normal reaction to any emotional stress. 'Hasn't it done us enough damage already? It's the curse of our family.'

'Ah, it was so sad about your poor wife.' Remembering she had expired from tuberculosis in his care, the physician added even more devoutly, 'I did all that was humanly possible, of course.'

'Of that I have no doubt, Wedderburn.' They stood in the dark-panelled hall, with its elaborate hatstand and pair of prints from Leonardo da Vinci's anatomical sketches. 'But of course, the boy's been foolish. He was overworking badly for his finals, that must surely have made him run down generally? It was his own fault. Entirely his own. He lived in bone idleness till a month before the examination, however severely I chivvied him.'

'We can hardly expect our students to spend their lives with such unpleasant experiences as examinations hanging perpetually over them, can we?' Dr Wedderburn took a cosy view of everything, even illness and death. The young flat-chested maid with acne handed his top hat and grey gloves. 'Have you noticed Graham off-colour for long?'

'No. Not at all. It's a bolt from the blue.'

'No night sweats?'

'None that I have been informed of.'

'The weight has been pretty constant, I take it?'

'Certainly in my observation. Of course, it may not be as serious as we fear,' Graham's father hazarded. 'A burst vein in the throat, something like that?'

'Possibly, possibly,' said Dr Wedderburn. Both knew well enough this was the first of many straws grasped by the tubercular sufferer. 'We shall need a specimen of the sputum to stain for acid-fast bacilli. Perhaps you would have the kindness to leave the bottle at the bacteriology lab in Blackfriars? Naturally, we would revise our ideas of the diagnosis should it prove negative.'

The professor suggested an X-ray. Dr Wedderburn was shocked. Such dodges were not for the responsible physician. He spread out his gloved hands. The good Lord has blessed the doctor with his five senses. The hallowed tetrad of the bedside–inspection, palpation, percussion, and ausculation–was powerful enough to evoke the most evasive diagnosis, and ever would be. Those gentlemen with their crackling and dangerous machines produced only time-wasting photographic plates of November fogs. The professor apologized. The physician then left, scattering a few more grains of comfort to be pecked at leisure.

The professor went into his study and sat at his roll-topped desk, struggling with the new situation. Graham ill in bed upstairs would be an enormous complication to the single-handed running of a wartime household. Life was worrying enough already, with one son in France, a medical officer at the front. It would be better, as Wedderburn suggested, to tidy Graham away in a sanatorium where they specialized in such tragedies. He could visit the poor boy regularly, though wartime train journeys were becoming unbearable and the fares deserved thinking about. He wished crossly that Graham's mother were alive to halve the burden. It was a grave distraction for the professorial mind, which should have been freed from domestic responsibilities both trivial and weighty to soar like an academic eagle over the bleak and mountainous problems of human anatomy. He pulled the bell-handle for the young maid with the acne spots. It was only ten in the morning, but he asked her to bring him a glass of port.

The sanatorium recommended by Dr Wedderburn was on the Kent coast near Pegwell Bay, surrounded by scummy-looking sea, mud, scrubby sand-dunes and fields full of cabbages, which gave off a smell setting Graham's heart against the vegetable for the rest of his life. Three months passed before its authorities even let him see a newspaper, from which he learned that the *Inviolable* on her first foray to sea had sunk, guns, armour-plate, crew, uncle, and all. From that moment he got steadily better.

'*Spes phthisica*,' muttered the medical superintendent, using a mildly contemptuous technical term for the hope which was keeping so many of his patients alive when clearly nothing else was. But the angry spikes on Graham's temperature chart subsided to gentle ripples as the disease blew itself out. Perhaps the substitution of the chance of dying for the certainty had stimulated the will-power prescribed by the superintendent. Perhaps Graham was tougher than he looked. Perhaps–an almost unthinkable possibility–Dr Wedderburn had made a mistake in diagnosis. By the spring of 1918 even the superintendent had to agree the young doctor might live, and allowed him the luxury of sitting up.

With nothing to fill the time between having his temperature taken, Graham started to draw. He drew everything in his world, the cherry tree flowering charmingly a yard from the foot of his red-blanketed bed, the neighbouring patients, Harry the boot-faced orderly, even Sister Constable. She was square-faced, red-cloaked, and medal-ribboned, disliked in the sanatorium far more than the Kaiser who, Graham decided with a few strokes of the pencil, she would closely resemble if she let her moustaches grow. He was surprised at his skill. He supposed he had inherited it from his mother, along with his chest.

Chapter Two

Dr Olaf Sarasen–he disclaimed the English surgeon's self-assumed title of 'Mister'–had plunged impatiently into the war long before it submerged his own country. In the summer of 1915 he arrived at Liverpool from New York unannounced, unknown, and unowned by any authority, with several crates of operating equipment, a pair of gorgeously-fitted ambulances, and apparently unlimited money. He wore a uniform of double-breasted leather-buttoned khaki jacket, twill breeches, cavalry boots, and spurs, each shoulder decorated with the Stars and Stripes and an announcement in gold thread, 'U.S. Medical Volunteers'. This body, like the costume, he had invented entirely himself.

Once in London, Dr Sarasen trumpeted a single-minded doctrine of plastic surgery across the tranquil though arid plains of medical thought, by exploiting indiscriminately lectures both professional and public, influential dinner-tables, the pages of any publication prepared to print his views, and the ears of any doctor trapped into hearing them. His motives were taken by English surgeons as either charming native enthusiasm or some sort of complicated swindle, his manners regarded somewhat as the old aristocracy regarded those of the new war profiteers. Such advertising was thought as all very well among those Yankee fellows, but not for the discreet doctors of Harley Street, who anyway had more soft-footed ways of advancing themselves. The plastic surgeon was laughingly dismissed as 'The Wild Saracen', a bounder, probably a quack, and worse still terribly vulgar.

But with men of power rather than men of physic 'The Saracen' got on splendidly. He talked their language, especially about money. The quicksilver tongue which raised funds in New York persuaded a junior minister of Asquith's to suggest that the War Office should loose him on the troops, and surprisingly the War Office agreed. Though the idea of reconstructing battle-damaged features was pretty footling–the duty of medical people in wartime was returning casualties to the front as quickly as possible to be shot at all over again–the generals felt it good for morale. A man would know that should his face get blown off, someone was employed to put it back on again. And with the Saracen providing his own pay and equipment the scheme was attractively cheap. They commandeered half a sanatorium on the Kent coast and packed him off.

The skill which the Saracen applied to New York noses was almost defeated by the ravages of battle. He raised pedicles of skin from chests and shoulders to plug holes in cheeks, so at least a man's tongue no longer worked in full view of his comrades. He took grafts from hip-bones and ribs to remake shattered jaws in patients fed on fluids by an enema syringe stuck down their throats four-hourly. He covered raw areas of flesh with paper-thin grafts of skin cut by a Thiersch knife like an oversized barber's razor. Everywhere he tidied up busily, under-cut tissue, and tried to join it up again without tension or scarring. About half his repairs survived and half sloughed away through sepsis. Some of his patients left hospital unblemished, most looked peculiar, one or two died. 'Maybe we're not making Greek gods,' he would claim proudly, 'but at least we're turning out something their mothers won't scream at.' Every afternoon, under King's Regulations, the convalescents were put on parade, ordered to form fours, and were marched round the countryside by a sergeant-major.

To the nearby villagers the 'Face Hospital' was a place to be mentioned in whispers, the haunt of freakish monsters beyond the imagination even of H. G. Wells. Old ladies shuddered and sometimes screamed at the patients' approach, mothers locked up their children, and pregnant women feared (or welcomed, as may be) the possibility of sudden abortion. A deputation hurried to the sanatorium, puffing righteous indignation like an overtaxed railway engine. They demanded the village be put out of bounds. The Army obliged. With nowhere else to go, the men started wandering along the beach.

Graham first noticed the Saracen's patients from an isolated summer-house where–a doctor mysteriously remaining a doctor even when a patient–he alone was privileged to sit that summer and inhale, though without undue exertion, the reputedly therapeutic Channel breezes. At a distance he imagined they were curious congenital monstrosities, like the London Hospital 'Elephant Man' befriended by Edward the Seventh's appendicectomist, Sir Frederick Treves. But with their approach, hospital blues proclaimed the deformities man-made rather than born. There were three of them, holding back as they caught sight of his deck-chair, but he struck up an acquaintance easily enough through the reassurance of his medical title and the cigarettes bought in the village by Harry the orderly (on a commission basis). He was smoking them with a two-inch bandage bound with professional neatness round his fingers, to baffle Sister Constable's witch's eye for tobacco stains.

'Sit down and let's swap grouses,' he invited. 'Life's a bore down here, isn't it? Do you get anything but Tickler's plum and apple jam on your side? We tubercules are fed to the teeth with it.'

They were soon getting on splendidly. The patients were glad of anyone taking an interest in them–and they weren't even officers, either–with the village barred any diversion was welcome, and a man could always do with a few extra fags. Besides, the poor young bastard had T.B. Nothing cheers the afflicted like discovering someone to be sorry for.

They were relieved that Graham showed neither horror nor pity towards them. He felt neither. No doctor seems so heartless as a newly-qualified one, his brain bristling aggressively with cures for cut-and-dried clinical conditions, his experience rich in demonstration cases if not yet in human beings. He was simply interested in them as specimens. Particularly the corporal with no nose, but a bump instead, like the beak of a hen, in the middle of his forehead.

'Next month it'll be my new nose, Doctor.' The man fondled the lump with a mixture of amusement and pride. 'Last month it was a bit of my rib, down here. Oh, he's very clever, Dr Sarasen.' He spoke with the reverence of any man for another who has cut him about sufficiently often and extensively. 'Mind, we looks a bunch of bogeymen, I suppose. Can hardly blame them in the village, can you? But it's not very handy if you're wanting to buy a pint or some smokes.'

'Where did you get wounded?'

'Wipers. That there big push last summer.'

'Would you object if I drew you?' Graham asked suddenly.

The man looked alarmed. 'Draw me? I ain't no oil-painting, am I?'

'You're more interesting to me than anything in the National Gallery, I assure you. Do you know what you are? You're a medical pioneer. Yes, I'm not joking. The whole elaborate paraphernalia depends on a few guinea-pigs and brave fellows like you. You're like Jupille, the shepherd lad Pasteur tried his anti-rabies serum on. Or Eben Frost, who risked his life sniffing an unknown anaesthetic to lose a tooth. Or little Jimmy Phipps, the boy Jenner first vaccinated.' Graham was well up in medical history, which he found by and large more interesting than medicine itself. 'They put up a statue to Jupille in Paris. Maybe they ought to raise one in the village to you. Think of yourself as a benefactor to humanity.'

The corporal's grin disclaimed such hollow honours. 'What worries me, Doctor, is which bit I blow if I gets a nasty cold in the nose.'

In a world which shutters its windows and hides its children at your approach, you have to develop a highly specialized sense of humour.

The more Graham drew, the more the patchwork faces fascinated him. He had heard nothing of reconstructive operations in the tuition condescendingly bestowed on him at Blackfriars Hospital. Their great surgeon Sir Horace Barrow, though acclaimed in amputating a limb to have no equal in speed, dexterity, or relish, ran his practice strictly on the principle that if thine eye offend thee, pluck it out. Graham drew half a dozen of the wounded men from a score of angles, sometimes pencilling slight improvements of his own. He thought the sketches rather good, almost worthy of a textbook. Then one morning his interest in the subject was brought abruptly to a halt.

It was after breakfast, when the sanatorium verandah was busy with nurses and orderlies tidying away the bedpans, bowls, trays and other domestic trappings of illness, presenting the patients in a neat clean row for stately inspection by their medical attendants. A stranger came down the line of beds, a pink-cheeked, red-eared tall young man rather older than Graham, in a well-valeted khaki uniform with lieutenant's pips on the cuffs, a Sam Browne, breeches, and shining boots, his intensely military appearance hardly softened by the twined-serpent R.A.M.C. badges on his lapels.

He saluted. 'Dr Trevose, isn't it?'

Graham nodded.

'My name's Haileybury. I'm attached to the plastic unit in the other block.'

It was clearly no social call. The visitor looked as unfriendly as a barbed-wire entanglement. 'It's my duty to speak to you on an important matter.'

It suddenly struck Graham how much in an argument a man flat on his back is at a disadvantage to one standing on his feet. 'In that case it's my duty to listen.'

The officer seemed to seek words. Then the colt frisked through the trappings of a war-horse. 'Look here, you're jolly well infecting my patients,' Haileybury burst out boyishly. 'We take tremendous trouble keeping our chaps separated from you T.B. people. Surely you appreciate that? And there you are, hobnobbing with them every afternoon. It's not playing the game at all, you know.'

Graham's reply was a laugh. Haileybury looked quickly up and down the verandah. He had started out aware that a row between two medical practitioners must always be a delicate affair, and he hoped there was no possibility of being made to look at all foolish. 'It doesn't strike *me* as the slightest amusing,' he said bleakly.

'But I'm not infective. Honestly. There's no Koch's bacilli in my sputum. None at all. They only found them twice, and I think they were cheating because I didn't fit the classical pattern of the disease. If you don't believe me you can always look at my notes.'

'Oh, I wouldn't doubt your word.' Haileybury's tone underlined the hideousness of one medical man's lying to another. 'Then perhaps you'll oblige me by giving up drawing the poor fellows? You must know how they feel about their appearance. It's bad enough with the village shying away as though they were in the last stages of leprosy. If those pictures got into the wrong hands–or into a newspaper . . .' His almost colourless blue eyes expressed horror. 'Why, it would be terrible. Our work here might become wellnigh impossible.'

As a civilian, even a sick one, Graham was faintly alarmed at any clash with the military. But the man was clearly a bore. He must not be misled that the drawings, the patients, nor especially himself, had in Graham's eyes the slightest importance.

'They won't get into anybody's hands. I only did them for my own amusement.' Graham handed a sheaf of papers from his bedside locker. 'You can take them if you want to–tear them up, do what you like with them. I'll go back to drawing the seagulls, if it makes everyone happier.'

The young medical officer hesitated but took the sketches. He had not allowed for this. He was piqued. He was as touchy as the fuse on a shell over his position as the only Army officer on the Saracen's staff, or over association with such an inglorious unit at all, and felt the mysterious doctor in the summerhouse was somehow straying on to the parade-ground of his authority. But as he ruffled through the drawings he had to admit the interloper's knack for art, and that sort of thing. It occurred to him they might possibly tickle the fancy of the Saracen. And any such stimulation would make life easier in the other half of the sanatorium.

'Well . . . if you really don't want them, I'll take them.'

'Do.'

'We've got an artist chappie on the unit, of course, but he's not much good.' Haileybury's tone set such occupations in their place. 'Thank you,' he added.

'Please don't mention it.'

'By the way, I've put that summerhouse out of bounds.' He saluted. 'Good day, Dr Trevose.'

An amusing idea struck Graham. 'Dr Haileybury–'

He turned. 'Yes?'

'Fetch me a bedpan, old man, will you? They're in the cupboard by the door. I'm absolutely bursting.'

Haileybury went pinker. 'I'll send a nurse,' he snapped.

He disappeared down the verandah, with the dignity of the Guards in retreat.

'*What* a bore!' thought Graham. 'Thank God I won't see him again. What a frightful, crashing, A-one bore.'

It was a term he used freely at the time, to embrace any unpleasantness from the lack of a cigarette to the loss of an uncle.

Chapter Three

Graham didn't notice the girl until she was almost on top of his deck-chair. He was concentrating on sketching the rotting black timbers of a breakwater, stretching forlornly after its departed tide. His reaction to any rebuff being immediate loss of interest in the subject, the man (or more often the woman) who offered it, the faces which had fascinated him one day dropped from their slot in his mind the next. He had turned his talents to the seagulls, as promised.

Three weeks had gone since the row, and he was becoming as bored and dispirited as a prisoner of war. He tried reading, but the sanatorium's stock of books was as tattered as they were old and uninteresting, new ones were beyond his pocket, and no circulating library could possibly allow their volumes into such an infective midden. He had only the newspaper, the *Strand Magazine*, copies of *Tit-Bits* fingered by the whole ward, and his elder brother Robin's letters from 'Somewhere in France', as the address went. These were inclined to be ponderous, filled with sound advice, and impregnated with vinegary morality, like Robin himself. Even the excitement of his father's monthly visit was denied him, the professor writing that weighty matters of academic anatomy unhappily tethered him to London, though Graham suspected his own returning health made the sooty carriages of the South Eastern and Chatham railway less endurable. He had even stopped smuggling cigarettes. His only aim was to exchange the sanatorium beach for the wider shores of life as soon as possible.

But now a girl. He caught her in the corner of his eye. Quite a flapper.

'I hope you're keeping your distance only because you're afraid I'll infect you,' he asked, without looking up.

'Oh, no!'

She was pretty, unmarried, and very young–about eighteen, he calculated. She wore a blue-and-white striped civilian dress, her long fair hair loosely drawn into a bun below her wide-brimmed hat. A refreshing change from the drab-uniformed, middle-aged, war-cropped V.A.D.s in the sanatorium.

'I was just watching you drawing.' Overcoming scruples about tuberculosis or moral contamination she advanced a pace or two. 'I hope you don't mind the liberty?'

Her voice is a disappointment, he told himself.

'I don't mind a bit. Any artist is flattered by an audience, even a man painting a pillar-box.' He was anyway a natural exhibitionist, a trait which furrowed so many lofty professional brows later on. 'May I introduce myself? Dr Trevose. Though at present locked up here serving a sentence.'

'I work on the other side,' she volunteered. 'Helping with the letters and records for Dr Sarasen.'

'*That*'s very brave.' He was being honest. 'Putting your head in a nightmare factory.'

'Oh, it's not that bad.' Now her smile's quite nice, Graham decided. 'You soon get used to the boys. And it's awfully good work, isn't it?'

'Oh, very praiseworthy,' he said off-handedly. Anything connected with Lieutenant Haileybury deserved scant respect. 'How about letting me draw *you*?'

She blushed, such a suggestion striking her as much too intimate for a few moments' acquaintance.

'Yes, come on! If you don't like it I'll set fire to it. I promise. Perch yourself on that flat stone. It won't take a minute.'

'No, *honest*,' she protested. 'I'm not worth a picture.'

'Nonsense! You'll make a very pretty one.' She blushed more deeply, but sat as directed. 'May I ask your name?'

'Miss Pollock.'

'I mean the name people call you.'

No reply. Under the rules of courtship in a more leisurely age the exchange of christian names was a milestone far down the primrose path.

'Forgive me,' apologized Graham gallantly.

'It's Edith,' she decided to impart.

'Isn't that a nice name?'

He sketched until she started to fidget, then abruptly tore the paper up. 'It was far too unflattering,' he told her, as she gave a charming little cry of disappointment. 'You'll have to come back tomorrow.'

Wooing Edith without the usual accompaniments of theatres, chocolates, flowers, and even nightfall struck Graham as an uphill task. But after six months of feverish chastity woo her he must. He felt it unfortunate that the raised bodily metabolism in tuberculosis should increase the desire, while the treatment precluded the performance. Rumours regularly ran round the sanatorium of unexpected bursts of co-operation by the nurses, or irregular shapes in the female beds at night, even of attempts on Sister Constable herself. They were good for the patients' morale, and if they came to the ears of the medical superintendent he dismissed them. He had long ago stopped believing that people in the care of himself and Mother Nature dared indulge themselves in the feelings of ordinary men and women.

A few afternoons later, sitting with their backs against the summerhouse in the sun, the pretence of sketching wordlessly abandoned, Graham judged the moment had arrived to kiss her.

'No, no!' she protested, automatically.

'But I'm not in the slightest infective,' he assured her considerately.

In her attempts to explain this was not the point, the first step to Edith's downfall was mounted.

'Do you actually live somewhere in the san?' asked Graham, resuming the conversation.

She collected herself. 'Oh, no. I cycle over every day from Ramsgate. My father's in business there.'

'Really? What sort of business?'

Edith picked a blade from a tuft of grass, and fixing it between her thumbs blew into her cupped hands, producing what struck him as a very unpleasant noise.

'He's a butcher.' She blew at the grass again, but this time it didn't work. 'I used to help in the shop, behind the cash-desk. Then I learned the typewriter. I wanted to better myself, you see.' He was struck by the power of this motive force, as expressed by the solemnity of her tone. She extruded a piece of grass with the tip of her tongue and added more cheerfully, 'Anyway, we've all got to do *some* sort of war work, haven't we?'

'My father's a butcher, too. Well, a professor of anatomy.' Seeing this meant as little as announcing his father was a troglodyte, he added, 'He cuts people up. Dead ones.'

'*Dead* ones!'

'Yes, he finds it very interesting.'

'Where's he get them from?' she asked, aghast.

'Oh, they don't have to dig them up any more. From poorhouses, infirmaries, jails. People with no relatives, no friends, nothing at all but the flesh and bones they stand up in.'

It thrilled him to feel her shiver against him. He had won over a few girls with this Bob Sawyer approach, easy familiarity with the unmentionable, and even the unspeakable, giving any young man an undeserved fascination.

'I shouldn't like it to happen to me.'

'That's not very likely. You know, my father always smells of formaldehyde, even on holiday. That's what they pickle the corpses in. They hang them up in racks by their ears till wanted, like suits of clothes–'

Edith decided to change the subject. 'He must be dreadfully clever, your father. Being a professor, and that.' She had a natural reverence for intelligence. 'Tell me about your mother.'

'She died when I was a child. T.B., same as me.' Graham switched to a tone of tragedy, adding with enthusiastic pessimism, 'I suppose it'll carry me off too, in the end.'

This on top of the clothes-racks of corpses melted Edith. She started to cry. 'Don't say that, Graham! Oh, don't say that!'

She was torn from the misty contemplation of his distant death to grappling with his immediate vitality by feeling his hand groping up her skirt.

A week later Graham faced a complication spared other young men with similar plans in cornfields or punts. He knew he had the choice between copulation and convalescence. His regimen was such a finely balanced one of rest and carefully graduated activity, he had taken pencil and paper and tried to express his much-desired expenditure of energy with Edith in terms of his daily exercise allowance. How far would the pulse rate rise? And the respiration? What about the muscular movement? He finally equated it with a mile, walked on the level at an even pace.

He prepared himself by cutting a mile from the prescribed three of his morning walk, and getting Harry to buy the necessary apparatus in Ramsgate (also on a commission basis). But Edith seemed horrified by his suggestion of a 'bit of fun'. The eager young fellow was rushing her down the primrose path with the speed of launching the Ramsgate lifeboat. But she agreed to go inside the summerhouse. After all, it had just started to rain.

The admittedly misleadingly simple occurrence had so many terrors for the girl Graham almost despaired. He explained pressingly his medical knowledge put the better-publicized sequelae out of the question. After all, he reflected a shade impatiently, not every young woman had the privilege of being deflowered by a dissector of the entire female pelvis. But there were sighs and tears, regrets and recriminations. He grazed his knee badly, and in the confined space there was a great deal of dust. He felt he had won a hollow victory. And he worried dreadfully that night it would put his temperature up.

Graham's experience of the female pelvis being unfortunately greater than his experience of the female as a whole, he was unprepared for the adoration Edith now beamed on him. In the hot pursuit of love she became the hare and he the tortoise. It made him worry about his temperature more than ever. She brought him gifts–chocolate, strawberry jam, calf's foot jelly, which everyone knew was good for tuberculosis. She also brought him a tenderness which he had never experienced from girls picked up in the hospital or shops, in his motherless home, nor anywhere else, except in the sanatorium during the strictly limited period when everyone imagined they would be transferring him any day to the mortuary. They enjoyed the intimate exploration of each other's personalities almost as much as of each other's bodies. For the first time in his life Graham felt someone cared that he was living. When the summerhouse started becoming too cold in the afternoons he found himself taking a solemn step. He asked Edith to become his wife.

She burst into tears, but agreed, quite quickly. They decided nothing could be announced until his discharge from the sanatorium with a clean bill of health, or the medical superintendent would find too many awkward questions. If he were faintly surprised at himself, he supposed it a feeling shared by all young men proposing marriage. Every night in his red-blanketed bed he felt obliged to find a hundred reasons for asking her. All of them were really irrelevant. With nobody else nubile in sight they were joined together as compulsively as Adam and Eve in that tubercular Garden of Eden.

Chapter Four

Four generations of the Trevose family had been doctors of one sort or another. Like many other Cornishmen they had once reaped a living from the sea, by fishing, the service of their sovereign, or smuggling. Then about the time of Queen Victoria's accession, the same bacilli lodging briefly in Graham's chest settled permanently in the spine of young Enoch Trevose and he suffered Pott's disease, in sad ignorance of the splendid eighteenth-century London surgeon who had dignified it with his name. The tuberculous process turned Enoch's vertebral bone into a cheesy mass, which in time solidified as a wedge of misshapen chalk and plainly closed the family livelihood to him. Like many sufferers from chronic illness he developed a lively interest in medical matters generally, and decided to set up as a quack. He felt his sinister hunchback would be a valuable asset.

Enoch started by peddling among Cornish villagers cures for over-indulgence in the pleasures of board and bed. Then he flirted with phrenology, assessing underlying mental aptitudes from bumps on the scalp, but found it too sophisticated for his patients. He tried instead mesmerism, which scared them from their wits. He finally prospered by reviving the medieval craft of uroscopy. From inspection of the urine in a crystal flask Enoch could advise not only on his patient's disease but on his problems in affairs of commerce, agriculture, or the heart as well. A shrewd judge of human nature, he died with a practice extending from Truro to Bath and a gold-headed cane as grand as any sported by a fashionable London surgeon, his only failures occurring once or twice a year when some joker substituted for the vital fluid the offering of his mare or cow.

Money blurring even the worst deformity, Enoch married the pretty daughter of a Camborne innkeeper, and produced a son who was put to looking after the ledgers and leeches of a local apothecary. The young man found in himself a skill at setting the bones of men injured down the tin mines, or of their masters dropping drunk from their horses above, and grew to bask in the respect of learning rather than of witchcraft. Then the Medical Act of 1858 blew a blast through the profession which stripped like beggars' rags the gorgeous privileges in which he had clothed himself. In official eyes he was unexamined, unregistered, probably unlettered, unfit to practise and unallowed to use the title of 'Doctor'. Bitterness almost killed him. He prized the title more than the shameful fortune of his father. He determined his own children should learn proper medicine at a proper hospital, much of it in Latin. A daughter travelled to Edinburgh behind the bustling skirts of Miss Jex-Blake. His sons went to Blackfriars Hospital in London. One of these rewarded him–admittedly less through brilliance than availability, being handy when the former occupant of the chair cut his finger dissecting a carelessly-pickled corpse and died of blood-poisoning in a week–by flowering into the professor of anatomy who stood in his study one grey morning in January 1919 contemplating the psychological ruins of his household.

It was a disturbing time not only for the professor but for everyone. As Boccaccio described an earlier visitation, many valiant men and many fair ladies breakfasted with their kinsfolk and that same night supped with their ancestors in the other world. A fearsome influenza virus had leapt on a populace congratulating itself on escaping death in the hands of one another, to make short work showing how Nature could outdo her creatures in the matter of mass-destruction.

The week of the Armistice had left Britain two thousand citizens the less from 'Spanish flu'. Families crawled helplessly round their houses or died together behind locked doors, as in the Great Plague. Jails and nunneries suffered impartially. The Army which had conquered a too apparent enemy dropped in thousands to an invisible one. Telegrams warned next-of-kin of men dangerously ill, who were already blue-faced and dead in the mortuary. Lloyd George caught it. Pneumonia, the 'old man's friend', instead of releasing him from the pains of senility marched in the epidemic's footsteps and asphyxiated his grandson. Undertakers were reduced to papiermâché coffins. The doctors' only treatment was a poultice to deaden the pain in the chest, and straw to deaden the traffic in the street.

Professor Trevose had sneezed that morning, five times–he had counted them. A nervous, edgy man, he worried if the ultramicroscopic thunderbolt was now descending on himself. His bodily resistance was surely lowered by overwork, channelling the flood of post-war students into his anatomy department at Blackfriars. (The corpse situation was extremely tight.) His precious professorial thought had still to be dissipated on a home sadly short of coal, food, and the woman's touch. His younger son Graham, sent to a sanatorium to die, had not died at all, but returned engaged to a girl ridiculously below his social station. His elder son Robin, in the professor's opinion mistaking a natural smugness for piety, had announced that on release from the Army he was disappearing as a medical missionary to the remote Straits Settlements–he certainly wouldn't get very fat on *that*. The cistern was leaking into the professor's bedroom and the butcher's boy had been rude. All were unbearable distractions, he reflected bad-temperedly, from the essential tranquillity of academic life.

There was a noise from the breakfast-room next door. His two sons were quarrelling as usual.

Graham and Robin had quarrelled about many things since their fights over rocking-horses and bicycles, but now Graham refused to take his brother's new vocation seriously their disputes took on a loftier air.

'Mind you, I bear God no ill-will,' Graham told him amiably over the remains of his breakfast. 'No more than any other distinguished gentleman I've heard a lot about but don't see much prospect of meeting.'

Robin glared. He was still in his R.A.M.C. uniform, with broad shoulders, sleek black hair, and glowing complexion–the family genes, shaken in the professor's reproductive process, had landed heavily in his favour. He found much to disapprove of in Graham–his unstarched collars, his atheism, his laziness, this girl in the sanatorium (even before submitting to the pain of meeting her), above all his general underestimation of the earnestness of life. 'I'm sorry you should deny the existence of the human soul. Genuinely sorry. It grieves rather than angers me you should deny yourself the comfort of a life hereafter. Perhaps if you'd served in France you'd have come back with different ideas.'

'Oh, come, Robin, that's below the belt,' Graham told him cheerfully. 'I ended up C-three, totally rejected. I'm not a conchie. No one was more eager to do his bit. I couldn't help getting T.B., could I?'

'There you go, deliberately misunderstanding me as usual. Of course I didn't say you were a shirker.'

'I'd like to believe it all. I really would. It would be great fun existing for ever, playing the harp and sitting on a cloud. Though that would be rather dampish, and likely to give you piles. But why flatter only we top dogs in the evolutionary scale with souls? It strikes me a bit hard on the runners-up, like the apes.'

Robin banged on the tablecloth with his coffee spoon. He was a flamboyant breakfast-eater, always getting down first and surrounding himself with a nest of letters, torn envelopes, and pages of newspaper, attracting all the jugs and bowls to his own end of the table as if by magnetism. He was a man who saw each new day as a challenge, and liked to fortify himself to meet it. It all irritated Graham very much. 'I agree that man is, zoologically speaking, an animal. But you must concede that we are the only animals God created with an awareness of our own inevitable death. Surely that suggests some difference?'

'Then I only hope there's some mechanism for opting out of immortality. There're plenty of people I want to avoid in London, let alone in Heaven. But what on earth are we discussing things like this for at breakfast time? It's far too early for serious thought.' He was becoming bored with teasing his brother. He had long ago decided his own intelligence bettered Robin's, and was coming amiably to suspect it exceeded that of his father the professor. He took out a cigarette. 'Let's change the subject.'

'Yes, you're smoking too much.'

'Nicotine hasn't been shown to do people any harm. Only cats.'

'That statement applies only to *normal* people.'

'I do wish you'd stop treating me as one of the chronic sick.' It was Graham's turn to be annoyed. 'I've no sputum, no cough, no temperature, nothing. I'm cured. My lesion's calcified. If it wasn't by now I'd be dead.'

'I don't believe you're even taking your temperature, are you?'

'Of course I am. Well, when I remember. Anyway, I'm not going to be bewitched by a damn thermometer. It ruled the sanatorium like a rod of iron.'

Graham got up and started wandering round the shabby breakfast-room looking for a match. Like everywhere else in the Hampstead house it had a medical air as inescapable as the stench of iodoform in hospital. On one side was a mahogany case with rows of old anatomy books imprisoned behind lattice-work for life. On the other stood a sideboard with copies of the *Lancet* scattered round an old brass microscope under a glass dome like wax fruit. One wall exhibited a black-and-white reproduction of Rembrandt's *Anatomy Lesson*, the other an equally harrowing photograph of the newly-qualified professor, in academic robes brandishing his rolled diploma at the world like a truncheon. Over the fireplace hung a water-colour of a highly eventful storm at sea. It had been executed by the professor's wife when sent to Cornwall to convalesce and paint, during their weird triangular courtship with the tubercle bacillus always in the third corner.

Graham struck a vesta. 'I'm feeling fit enough to start work, you know.'

Robin looked up from the *Morning Post*. 'What as? Demonstrator in the anatomy rooms, I suppose, as Father suggested. That's a fairly light occupation for an invalid.'

'No, I'm taking a surgical job, I fancy.'

'But I didn't think you were much interested in surgery.'

'Well, yes and no. At best, I've thought it mutilation as a fine art. At worst, a generally losing battle against sepsis and haemorrhage–all chloroform, pus, and slipping tourniquets. Most depressing. But this is reconstructive surgery.'

Robin laid down his paper in horror. 'Not *plastic* surgery?'

'Plastic surgery, reconstructive surgery, cosmetic surgery, facio-maxillary surgery, call it what you like. In the san I did some drawings of Olaf Sarasen's patients. He must have been impressed, because now he's moved to Town he's written offering me the job of clinical assistant. I'm seeing him this afternoon.'

'"The Saracen"! You can't work for that mountebank.' Robin sounded more shocked at his brother's attitude to his profession than his attitude to God.

'I don't believe he is a mountebank. No one at Blackfriars could take more care over his patients.'

'Of course he's a mountebank! Everyone in London says so,' Robin corrected him flatly. 'Take up throats, eyes, orthopaedics, anything you like. But not this trivial face-lifting business.'

'Listen.' Graham leant on the table. 'Do you know what the Saracen can do? He can take a cartilage from a man's rib, transplant it to the middle of his forehead, wait till it's developed a new blood-supply, then draw it down to remake a shot-away nose. Isn't that fascinating? Just think–soon we'll be able to replace precious fingers with toes, make rosy cheeks from the broad unseen acres of the abdomen–even transplant whole organs from one patient to another–if they're prepared to put up with the inconvenience of being Siamese twins, which will anyway be comparatively trifling and strictly temporary. Once the new blood-supply's taken, we'll just snip them apart, like a pair of paper dolls.'

Graham Trevose had imagination. It was a quality in medical men uncommon, and probably downright dangerous.

'We shan't have people dying from Bright's disease with shrivelled kidneys any more,' he went on enthusiastically. 'We'll simply graft in a new kidney from a condemned criminal, or some other co-operative donor. Plastic surgery's going to take the whole subject by the ears, shake it up, and revolutionize it. You mark my words. It's like Morton's ether, or Lister's carbolic spray.'

'Poppycock,' said Robin.

Graham shrugged his shoulders. 'Well, if I don't like it, in six months' time I can always get a job doing something else.'

'Not after working for an adventurer like Olaf Sarasen you won't.'

'Oh, rats!' said Graham, losing his temper, throwing his cigarette into the fire, and abruptly leaving the room.

The professor heard the door slam and pulled his moustache irritably. There was no peace in the house since the boys had come home. Academic contemplation had been so much easier with one in the trenches and the other on his death-bed. And another thunderous disturbance was rising above the horizon. He had better weather it as soon as possible. He pulled the study bell-handle again for the little maid with the acne.

Chapter Five

Graham made his way to the Saracen by his favourite form of transport, well wrapped up in the frontmost seat on top of an open General omnibus. The capital was settling down from the flag-waving of the Armistice, but there were plenty of khaki vehicles on the roads and khaki uniforms on the pavements. Apart from Tommies there were Canadians, Australians, and Americans kicking their heels and occasionally authority while waiting for ships home, and women were still to be seen in khaki caps and baggy service jackets. But the flu virus had replaced the excitement in the air. People hurried about with scarves drawn protectively over mouth and nostrils, and anyone sneezing was regarded with the outraged suspicion recently reserved for possible spies and traitors.

Graham found the Saracen himself bald and amazingly fat, smoking a cigar which he flicked into a large ashtray shaped like an American eagle. The surgeon had so enmeshed himself in the British military machine he proved impossible to detach when the sanatorium pleaded for its wards back with peace. Having nowhere else to put him, the Army transferred him to Princess Alexandra's Hospital for Officers in Kensington, one of several peculiar London institutions never certain if they were really hospitals or nursing-homes, where the Saracen was undaunted to find himself restricted to six beds and use of the operating theatre only on Saturdays. He had a talent for expansion in the teeth of competition which would have brought admiration from his many friends on Wall Street. He had already achieved eviction of the hospital secretary from a downstairs office, where he received Graham behind a large desk with a signed photograph of Mr Woodrow Wilson and the American flag on one side, and a signed photograph of Mr Lloyd George and the Union Jack on the other.

'Tell me, Doctor,' he asked at once. 'Why did you choose our profession?'

Graham always found this embarrassing. His family had expected him to 'go in for' medicine, and he had been too young to resist such unoriginality. As he searched for a fittingly solemn reply the Saracen saved a lie by adding genially, 'It's the family business, isn't it? Well, medicine owes a lot to it's dynasties.' He picked up the sketches Graham had given Haileybury. 'You've got quite a talent for drawing, Dr Trevose. Maybe it isn't great, but you don't find it much among medical people at all. I guess the Renaissance has to answer for divorcing science from art.' He waved the cigar in his other hand. 'I don't need to tell you what we do here–or what we try to do, which is more to the point. Do you think you could become interested in this branch of surgery?'

'In my present state of inexperience I'm in the happy position to become interested in anything, sir.'

The Saracen grunted. 'No "Sir", if you please. We're civilians.' He spread out his well-polished cavalry boots under the desk. '"Doc" is my title on the unit. Now we're reorganizing I'm looking for another pair of hands in the operating-room. I could take a young fellow out of the Army or some place, but I'm after a man with feeling for the job.' He assessed Graham through the cigar-smoke. 'Are you ambitious?'

Graham had never asked himself. 'Averagely, I suppose.'

The Saracen chuckled. 'Are you interested in money?'

This struck Graham as frankly indelicate. The consultants who trained him at Blackfriars would no sooner have discussed in public their financial dreams than their sexual ones. Besides, he was still in the charming stage of any professional career when the rewards seem as irrelevant as they are insubstantial.

'I won't believe any man who tells me otherwise,' the Saracen continued cheerfully. 'Not outside a madhouse or a monastery.' He leaned back in his chair, cigar aimed at the ceiling. 'Do you know what I'm going to do with this hospital? I'm going to make it the greatest centre for plastic surgery in Europe. In the world! People from the four corners of the earth will come to see our work, as pilgrims.' He leant abruptly forward, chins wobbling earnestly. 'Oh, I know the war's over and the wounds are healing and there's some Jeremiah telling me every week we plastic surgeons have nothing left to do. Out of a job, they say. We'll have only warts, club feet, girls scalping themselves in machines. By God, they're wrong! "For the children of men, they are but vanity."' Graham thought he had a good voice for Biblical quotation. 'Vanity, Doctor! That's going to bring us more casualties than the Germans did. I'm a man of vision. I see the day when we'll provide mankind with new noses, new ears, new chins, as easy as drawing a tooth. We'll change the contours of its breasts and its buttocks. We'll wipe away the ravages of age. The features you're born with won't signify any more. We'll usurp the functions of the Almighty! And if you dedicate yourself,' he explained, coming down easily from lofty generalities to commercial particulars, 'I can guarantee you an income in five years' time— Come in!'

This itinerary of the road to Eldorado was interrupted by a knock on the office door and the appearance of Lieutenant Haileybury. The two young men stared at each other. Haileybury silently inclined his head. With the population of the world shifting like sand at the end of the war, both thought a second encounter terribly bad luck.

'Think it over, Dr Trevose.' The Saracen started busying himself with some paperwork. 'I'll give you two days. Don't write. Use the telephone. Time is money. Eric, show the doctor out, will you?'

Haileybury nodded again, without speaking. The pair crossed the over-polished parquet of the small hall, which like everything else at Princess Alexandra's had an air of decorous homeliness, broken only by an elderly V.A.D. arguing crossly with someone down a brass voice-pipe in the corner.

'Do I gather the Saracen's invited you to join the circus?' he asked at last. 'I'm just back from leave.'

Graham nodded.

'Of course, the man's no end of a card.' Haileybury's tone indicated that offers of any sort from this source were suspicious, if not sinister.

'Then how come you're working with him yourself?'

'Oh, the Army posted me. To keep an eye on him, I imagine. He's an impossible spendthrift, and no idea of discipline among the men.' They reached the glass-panelled street door. 'I wouldn't accept, if I were in your shoes.'

'Why!'

'There's no future in it.'

'I don't know if I agree.'

A wintry smile relieved Haileybury's features, which had frosted over at the sight of Graham. 'But you've just been subjected to the sales patter.'

'Well, he certainly did most of the talking,' Graham agreed.

'Oh, that's typical. He'd be wanting to see your reactions. He's got a full enough dossier on you somewhere, don't you worry. Anyway, the Saracen's completely impossible to get on with.'

'I don't know if I agree with that, either.'

Haileybury smiled again. 'I see you're an enthusiast, Trevose. Take my tip. Don't make up your mind till you're clear of his magnetic field. You wouldn't be the first it's lured in the wrong direction.'

Graham was puzzled. Was Haileybury's cocky attitude merely showing off, or a genuine attempt to scare him away? And why? Because he had asked the man to fetch a bedpan? Some people take life immensely seriously.

'Thank you, Haileybury. I'm much obliged for your advice.'

'I'm only trying to be helpful. Plastics is a very new specialty–if it's a specialty at all. Nobody knows where they are yet. Have you got transport?'

'I'll walk, thanks. It's a fine afternoon.'

As the glass door swung shut behind him Graham made the second biggest decision of his life. As impulsively as he had decided to marry Edith he decided on the Saracen. Throughout his life, inside the operating theatre or out, no path beckoned him so invitingly as one the angels feared to tread. It was his natural luck that so often the angels were standing about afterwards looking foolish. It struck him that for the first time in his life he had entered upon gainful employment. He started to whistle like an errand-boy.

Inside the hospital, Haileybury made straight back to the office. The Saracen looked up impatiently. He was calculating how to buy some speculative shares with money he didn't have, an exercise giving him as much pleasure as reconstructing a nose.

'Eric, it'll wait, won't it?' he asked shortly.

'I think I should have a word with you, Doc.' The young medical officer looked awkward. The subtleties of the game of life were beyond him, he felt demeaned even by having to play it at all. 'About Trevose.'

The Saracen flicked ash from his cigar. 'What's the matter with him? I checked at Blackfriars. He's got a good brain, when he's pushed to use it. A bit lackadaisical and over-concerned with number one, but we can straighten that out. He looks a fragile specimen, but his lesion's healed. Do you know anything else?'

Haileybury went pinker. 'He isn't exactly out of the top drawer.'

The Saracen grunted. He disliked the British idea of society as some sort of tallboy. 'His father's a distinguished professor.'

'You know he's engaged to marry Miss Pollock?'

The surgeon raised his eyebrows. 'No?' He grinned. 'Pretty girl.'

'He was carrying on with her in a most distasteful way,' Haileybury went on. He disliked discussing such things, but he disliked Graham more. The man was encroaching on his little kingdom. He wished ardently he'd torn up the drawings. 'Yes, in that beach hut. I wondered where she was going in the afternoons. I made it my business to find out.'

The Saracen laughed. 'Well, well! So you were Miss Pollock's chaperon? Or was he putting your nose out of joint?'

'There was no question of that,' said Haileybury hotly.

'As long as it doesn't interfere with his surgery, I don't care what the hell the boy does with his spare time,' the Saracen told him amiably. 'Now let's have a little peace, eh, Eric?'

Haileybury retired, baffled. The game of life, played against the Saracen, always seemed to be a losing battle.

Graham reached home to find the psychological dilapidation of the household completed by Sally, the flat-chested seventeen-year-old maid with the spots, having been found pregnant. The professor's diagnostic suspicions had been aroused that morning over his breakfast by noticing her acne had vanished, pregnancy being an infallible if drastic cure for this skin condition. She was summoned to his study, an intimidating room with curtains of Nottingham lace excluding the light from the window, and another of red velvet over the door excluding the world in general from his rarefied anatomical thoughts. Tall, stooping, heavily moustached, the distinguished academic towered before the marble fireplace as the embodiment of Divine wrath on her miserable failings. She burst into tears, confessed, and so forgot herself as to sit in his presence.

But the veins in the hand which grasped her little rough one seemed that morning to run not with blood but the milk of human kindness. The man of science perched on her chair, encircled her with his arms, and let her sob into his austerely-trousered lap. He removed her little starched cap, the more soothingly to stroke her dark hair. The culprit, it emerged, was an assistant at the greengrocer's. For a moment he had even suspected Graham, with his new penchant for the lower classes. The professor promised to shoulder the massive diplomacy not only of interviewing the youth, but of Sally's return home to Edmonton and her eventual admission to the maternity wards at Blackfriars. Afterwards he dried her tears on his handkerchief and kissed her tenderly, not once but several times.

When Aunt Doris, up from Brixton for the afternoon, nosed out the news she had to lie down and be brought tea with chocolate biscuits. She blamed the professor roundly for employing such wretches, as she had blamed him for bullying Graham over his books and ruining his health, indulging Robin's religious mania and catapulting him from the family bosom across the face of the earth, even for marrying her poor delicate sister in the first place and killing her by exposure to housework, childbirth, and the London fogs.

This emotional explosion made the professor rude to Miss Timworth, who came two days a week to do his typing. Though he was often rude to Miss Timworth, that afternoon she was feeling unwell and pinning on her hat left for ever, embarrassingly eloquently. She was typing his monograph on the synovial membranes lining the joints of the body, a topic of deeply-argued interest to his brother anatomists, if its fascination escaped a wider public. Like the flower on the cactus the book represented fifteen years of quiet unseen effort, and there it was in useless bundles of illegible longhand all over the floor. This was the bitterest dose to swallow of all.

With everyone is such straits it was remarkable that among the rare jollifications of the professor's home the supper-party that evening should count an outstanding success.

Chapter Six

'We are such a masculine household you mustn't expect anything elaborate,' the professor apologized to Edith, inspecting her for the first time as though she were some interesting anatomical specimen in a bottle.

'I'm sure it'll be ever so comfy,' she said. 'Oh! what a lot of books!'

It suited the professor's ideas of economy to hold the feast in the shabby breakfast-room, pleading the continued scarcity of coal as an excuse for not broaching the big front dining-parlour. And with the country's convalescence from the war insufficiently advanced for meat to be freed from its coupon, he felt the fare could be blamelessly–indeed, patriotically–unsumptuous.

'What a lovely house!' Edith exclaimed. 'It must have looked a treat decorated for Christmas.'

'We celebrate such occasions very quietly,' said the professor.

'Perhaps you would like the chair nearest the fire, Miss Pollock?' invited Robin.

'Oh, thanks,' invited Edith. She fluttered a smile. 'Ever so much.'

They made a peculiar quartet in the gaslight, sitting on well-repaired plush-seated chairs round a table decked with a shining linen cloth and the family silver, eating cold ham and pickles. The professor himself, dark-suited and heavily watch-chained, smelt of his corpse-preservative as usual. Robin was anatomizing Edith with his eyes as closely as his father, though the pain he feared on meeting his prospective sister-in-law seemed somewhat anaesthetized by her transparent desire to please. Besides, he was fidgeting to talk interestingly about kala-azar, yaws, trypanosomiasis, latah, chappa, chiufa, kubisagari, and other complaints unknown in the world of sanitation, street lighting, and taxi-cabs. Edith herself wore the blue-and-white dress Graham had first seen her in, though she had taken it up a daring six inches above the ankle, and her fair hair had been submitted to a fashionable crop. She was perfectly at ease. Professional gentlemen were becoming to her very ordinary creatures indeed. As for Graham, he sat in unusual silence, feeling like the author of some passionate, secret correspondence seeing it produced as a red-taped bundle in open court.

Graham's first uncomfortable adjustment on coming home from the sanatorium was to the distance Edith lay beyond the outermost ripples of his social circle. His father made plain that the dissectors of humanity and the dividers of Sunday joints simply did not mix, though seeming less concerned over the alliance than with scotching any hopes it might have of financial assistance. Aunt Doris burst into tears, finding consolation in Graham's mother no longer being alive to witness the disgrace. The young man began to wonder if he had perhaps been a trifle over-enthusiastic.

He tried blowing cold on Edith's passions by post, but this only made them blaze the brighter. At the first Christmas of peace his escape-hatch closed with a crash. Now the Face Hospital was shut and air-raids were over for ever, she was coming to London to live.

In the new year they made a rendezvous at Charing Cross station, where he watched her appear through the steam of the suburban platform wondering nervously if she would cling to him outside W.H. Smith's bookstall as passionately as outside the sanatorium summerhouse. That would never do, under the eyes of the railway employees. But she kissed him politely, asked after his health and his father, and said she wanted a cup of tea.

Across the marble-topped table at a Lyons' teashop Graham discovered with some disappointment that the attraction of London lay less in himself than in the previously declared and still pressing idea of self-betterment. Edith was living in a suburb with the refreshingly pastoral name of Hither Green, with a sister who had already undergone the betterment process by marrying a barrister's clerk in the Temple. The clerk had found Edith a typist's job in the chambers of a neighbouring silk, Mr Wellingford–*K.C.*, she emphasized, this tenuous connection with Buckingham Palace apparently being gratifying. Her affection for her new job seemed so much warmer than for Graham, and in the less bracing air their relationship seemed no more wonderful than any joining the other office-girls and boys around them. He suddenly panicked at losing her, particularly as he had forgotten how pretty she looked. He told her hastily that his intended wife must come home to meet the family. So there she was, with the professor holding her hand.

'The anatomist's snuff-box.' The professor filled the hollow below Edith's thumb with salt. 'You see that little triangle? It is formed by the tendons of the muscles *extensor pollicis longus* and *extensor pollicis brevis*.' The edge of his false teeth appeared under his moustache as he smiled. His idea of small-talk was a string of anatomical jokes, unintelligible outside a dissecting-room. 'Should you wish to indulge in snuff, you would find it a convenient repository for each dose.'

'Why, fancy that!' Edith sounded quite breathless.

'*I*'m going to need all the anatomical knowledge I can muster,' Robin interrupted. 'I'm off overseas shortly to a missionary settlement. I shall be completely single-handed. For medicine, surgery, obstetrics–everything. It's quite a challenge.'

Edith's eyes widened. 'Won't you be eaten by cannibals?'

They all laughed. Only Graham knew she really meant it.

'I shall be much more likely eaten by mosquitoes.' Robin's tone nevertheless implied that any cannibals straying on the scene would get short shrift from *him*. He was about to give a lecture on yaws, but the professor forestalled him by tickling Edith behind the ear.

'There!' he exclaimed. She looked startled. 'I have stimulated your *alderman's nerve*. Through its connection with the vagus nerve, which descends from the brain into the abdomen, you know, it stimulates that much-abused organ the stomach to empty. Very useful after a Lord Mayor's banquet.' He laughed heartily. 'That's the legend, at all events.'

'Well!' Edith was amazed at the scientific wonders unfolded for her. 'Who'd have guessed it?'

'It seems rather optimistic invoking the reflex tonight,' remarked Graham morosely.

'This rationing,' sighed the professor. 'Will it ever end?'

He took a sip of the wine, which had as its main virtue value for money. He was enjoying himself. With no female patients, and the nurses at Blackfriars as far beyond his department as its lady students were in the future, he had no opportunity of talking to young women at all. But a chance word from a girl on a bus could set him aglow, he warmed to the touch of young ladies serving in shops, a waitress leaning across with his teacake inflamed him with thoughts far from academically anatomical. Well, it was lucky to be attracted more by girls as the years advanced rather than less, he told himself. There was no fun withering into a dry old stick. And, of course, no one could possibly notice.

Frustrated over yaws, Robin started a dissertation on faith in healing. Graham looked up. 'Oh, you mean like Monsieur Coué? "Every day in every way I am getting better and better"? If you run your practice on those principles, Robin, you'd better make jolly good friends with the coroner. That's if they run to such inconveniences out where you're going.'

Robin looked angry. 'You're misunderstanding me again. Quite deliberately.' In respect for Edith, he decided not to pursue the argument. He started talking about the flu epidemic instead, holding it as an illustration of Divine wrath on the wrongs of warring mankind.

'My dear fellow!' Graham didn't like the way his brother was taking the stage in front of his girl. 'Now you're confusing theology with bacteriology.'

'I do wish you wouldn't make sweeping remarks,' said Robin.

'But be reasonable. If faith in God can save us from our ills, what's He want to send the epidemic for in the first place?'

'It's all due to the low state of nutrition,' the professor declared, dabbing his mouth with his napkin. To strangle the row he suggested playing his violin.

The breakfast-room was cramped for Mozart, with airs from *Chu Chin Chow* and *H.M.S. Pinafore* as light relief, but all three listened attentively. Particularly Edith. She thought his music less of a strain than his conversation. As he finally packed his instrument away the professor brought up the topic of typewriting.

Edith blushed. She suspected such modest achievements unworthy of the company. 'I only learned so as to do my war work,' she explained hastily. 'I'm helping Mr Wellingford as a personal favour, you know. Strictly temp.'

'I am writing a book,' the professor revealed. 'It is a labour of love, but nonetheless a labour. My last typist left, somewhat unexpectedly, and I am hard put to find a suitable replacement. I don't know if I could poach a little of your time—'

'I'd be very glad to help, I'm sure.' Edith smiled round. 'I mean, it's all in the family now, isn't it?'

'But Father will pay for your trouble, of course,' said Graham.

The professor looked irritably at his son. 'The fee must perforce be small. Academic life, I'm sure you understand, is totally unmotivated by financial considerations.'

'Oh, yes,' said Edith.

The professor mellowed into a smile. 'Which may or may not be a disadvantage.'

'I expect I could come on Saturdays.'

'That would be a great help.'

'When I can manage, of course.'

'I think you will find the material very interesting. It is on the subject of the synovial membranes.'

'Is it really?' said Edith eagerly. 'Yes, I expect I shall.'

The professor bowed low over her hand. Then, exhausted with sociability, he made straight for bed.

Returning from leaving Edith at the Tube station, Graham found Robin standing thoughtfully before the dying fire.

'Well? What do you think of her?'

'She's certainly very gay and very agreeable. *And* very pretty.' Robin paused, and added, 'I congratulate you, Graham.'

'Thank you.' Graham sprawled in a chair.

'You wouldn't know she was common at all.'

'Thank you,' Graham repeated.

To be 'common' was such a hideous social disfigurement during the meal they had tactfully not mentioned Edith's parents. It was like avoiding the topic of noses if entertaining the Saracen's patients. She certainly hadn't brought the subject up herself. To sup with a professor and a doctor son you were about to marry was such a shining milestone up the hard road of self-betterment father and mother could be temporarily ditched.

'You mean her table manners weren't too bad?' Graham lit a cigarette. 'Or too good, which would have been worse?'

'When are you getting married?'

'Oh, some time this summer.' Graham flicked the match into the grate. 'It depends what we can screw out of the old man. She made quite a hit with him, didn't she? And I'll make a bit on the side assisting the Saracen in private. It all helps. I expect he's pretty generous.'

'So you've really made up your mind over the job? You realize plastic surgery is not thought even respectable in the right circles?'

Graham blew a chain of smoke-rings. 'Neither was chloroform.'

'You know that isn't the answer, Graham.' Robin shook his head sadly. 'You seem to forget our family has a certain position to uphold in the profession.'

'Yes, our grandfather was a quack bone-setter and our great-grandfather was a piss-prophet,' said Graham, getting up and going to bed.

Chapter Seven

She was the most beautiful, or anyway the smartest, woman to come within range of Graham's handshake. Her hair was as fashionably short as her jade-green dress. Her hands rested on a matching silk parasol. A fox fur hung over her shoulder. She got more effect than displaying a load of jewellery by wearing one enormous pearl on a golden chain. He fancied she was older than himself, but such elegance baffled his calculations. As she turned to smile he saw on her right cheek a hairy mole an inch across, as ugly as a stain on a bridal gown.

'I'd like have you meet Dr Trevose, one of my staff,' the Saracen introduced Graham grandly from behind his desk. 'Dr Trevose will be assisting me with your operation.'

This was news to Graham, who had been planning to leave early that hot Saturday afternoon.

'Miss Cazalay is giving us the privilege of creating perfection where there is yet only beauty.' The Saracen flourished his cigar. He had abandoned his uniform, but not his smoking habits. 'As I shall be performing the procedure under local, I should like you to administer a sedative.'

'Oh, no!' objected Miss Cazalay at once. 'I utterly refuse to be doped.'

The surgeon looked doubtful. 'We've got some pretty frightening-looking toys up there.'

'Now you're trying to make my flesh creep.'

That's the voice of a woman who knows what she wants, thought Graham.

'You're just as bad as all the other doctors,' Miss Cazalay smiled. 'They say you're harbouring the most *awful* things, just to make you more grateful when they find they've made a mistake and you aren't. I want to keep my mind *perfectly* clear. I'm not going to miss the chance of telling absolutely everybody about my operation. Particularly in the hands of the famous Dr Sarasen.'

Possibly mollified by the praise, the surgeon surrendered.

The events of the hot, arid and consequential summer of 1919 included the peace treaty signed at Versailles and the German fleet scuttled at Scapa Flow, but not so far the marriage of Edith to Graham, who was beginning to feel the snowflakes would be descending on his shoulders before the confetti. For the Saracen's dreams had been roughly ended, and Graham's prospects had faded with the rest of the highly insubstantial pageant.

At first Graham had revelled in assisting at operations performed in flesh and blood rather than confined to his pencil and paper. He even struck a workable relationship with Haileybury for the good of the patients, though careful to disagree with him about everything from the quality of the postwar surgical catgut to the wave of postwar strikes, Ireland, the gold standard, and the collapse of morals generally. It all induced in him mildly socialistic views, which Edith's father on their single meeting over Sunday lunch in Ramsgate found so distressing.

Professionally, the two young surgeons' ideas drew further apart daily. Haileybury was the son of an engineer officer in the Indian Army, who on retirement had dabbled in jute and found to his alarm this unexciting commodity caused his swift impoverishment. Afterwards he sang praises of the simple, trustworthy Service virtues in the ears of his son, who struggled on short commons to finish his education and was rewarded almost at once with a chance to cut the figure he envied–a uniformed surgeon. When the casualties of war were regrettably supplanted by the more trivial ones of peace, Haileybury still brought to his work the mind of the military doctor. Graham thought he brought also the mind of the sempstress and municipal architect–though admitting this a valuable corrective to the Michelangelo approach of the Saracen, to which he inclined himself. To Graham, plastic surgery was artistry in flesh, creation in the most exciting of all media. To Haileybury, it was the prosaic repair of injury and deformity. The acorn of discontent sown between them in the sanatorium ward so flourished in this disputed ground, its sturdy branches overshadowed the pair of them all their lives.

Though for now, Haileybury simply dismissed Graham as too clever by half.

'Why don't you sew the two free edges of the pedicle together?' Graham asked him one afternoon in the operating theatre.

The pedicle was a thick two-inch-wide six-inch-long strip of skin raised from the patient's shoulder, to which one end was still anchored. The free end plugged a crater in the man's cheek, a Canadian officer whose misfortunes had begun two years before at Vimy and, bedevilled by sepsis, were at last coming to an end.

'Join these?' Haileybury ran his needle-holder up and down the raw edges. 'Why?'

'Because it would help preserve the blood-supply of the pedicle, cut down the risk of sepsis, and what's as important be less painful for the patient.'

Haileybury considered this for some moments. 'No,' he decided. 'You'd end up with a sort of septic sausage. The whole pedicle would slough away in a week.'

'But can't you see how the two edges are curling together, like a scroll of parchment?' Graham insisted. 'Why, they're simply asking to be joined up.'

'Put the dressings on please, Trevose,' said Haileybury, closing both the operation and the discussion.

'Won't you let me put three or four stitches in?' Graham pleaded. 'We can take them out if there's any sign of infection. Just as a favour.'

'I remember the last time you asked me a favour.' Haileybury stripped off his gloves. 'You wanted a bedpan.'

By June 1919 Graham could sew up the pedicles as much as he liked. Some movement in the mystic machinery of the War Office demobilized Haileybury, as much to his own surprise as the Saracen's. With Haileybury out of the way the Saracen let Graham work alone at operations which, though comparatively minor, were intensely flattering to his junior status. He realized excitedly that he had a flair for the handicraft of surgery, the cutting, stitching, snipping, and remodelling. This gave him a satisfaction which for long periods of the day put all else from his mind, including Edith. Now he stood on his own feet any doubts about his marching to the head of the specialty were dispelled. He had self-confidence, as essential in a young surgeon as in a young politician or young pugilist. But Graham's thanks for relief from his vinegary overseer were brief. A month later the Saracen announced with extravagant regret that he must go himself.

The Saracen had underestimated the toughness of the charming London consultants, lurking to slip their own cases into his profitable beds at Princess Alexandra's. Like many other gay upstarts tolerated during the war, he found himself shunned in the more formal society of peacetime. Though nobody could send him home because nobody had dispatched him, and he showed no inclination to repatriate himself (it was said through the imminence of prohibition), his cases simply trickled away until the once lusty unit became too enfeebled to support even a single assistant. His right to practise at all on New York qualifications was publicly doubted, facing Graham with perilous questions of assisting an unlicensed practitioner, which the young man recognized as a professional crime as grave as committing adultery with your patients, if less enjoyable. The Saracen was sad. He had expected a gift of ready-made British qualifications in gratitude for his work during the war, but the serious-minded surgeons who decided such things read rather too much in their newspapers about his fondness for large motor-cars, race-horses, champagne parties, and any attractive woman he could lay hands on.

Graham's next discomfiture was an admission that his brother was right.

His impulsive foray into plastic surgery had not only ended in defeat, but a testimonial from the Saracen was an invalid passport to the most respected hospitals. He felt he should have some sort of employment before marriage, even though he had arranged to live with Edith on the top floor at Hampstead, over the professor's bedroom. The ceremony must perforce be delayed. Meanwhile, his bride-to-be came every Saturday afternoon and typed about synovial membranes.

Chapter Eight

'I forgot to ask how your try at that throat job in Islington went,' the Saracen said to Graham as they creaked and wobbled towards the top floor in the lift, having left Miss Cazalay to prepare for her unsedated ordeal in charge of the Princess Alexandra's matron.

'It didn't go at all.'

'That's tough. A throat job would be useful. It's next-of-kin to plastics, and maybe you could have tried your hand reshaping a few noses on the quiet. But don't lose faith in yourself, son.' The Saracen opened the lift gate. 'You've got the mind and the hand for this sort of surgery. Your idea of stitching up the pedicles–it's a great advance.' Chuckling at his own wiliness, he went on, 'You've got quite an attraction for the ladies, too. It all helps in our line. I've noticed it with the nurses, the stenographers, the other girls around.'

Graham looked surprised. 'I've never flattered myself at cutting a particularly romantic figure,' he objected modestly.

'Looks don't count all that much.' The Saracen was sensitive over his own waistline. 'Maybe it's because you keep them amused. There's not much amusing in a woman's life. It's all menstruation, constipation and backache.'

'But Doc!' Graham grinned. 'You seem to forget I'm shortly to be a married man.'

'Maybe I did. Your little girl must be getting mighty impatient.' The surgeon threw his cigar into a fire-bucket outside the anaesthetic room in respect less for professional convention than the explodability of ether vapour. As they brushed past the new Boyle's anaesthetic apparatus like a display of water-filled jampots, he added over his shoulder, 'I guess our patient won't faint. Miss Cazalay's a tough baby.'

'She's an actress?' If Graham had never heard of her, actresses the Saracen associated with had never been heard of by anybody.

'Christ, no! You know Lord Cazalay?'

Graham raised his eyebrows. Everyone had heard of Lord Cazalay during the war. He was always cajoling or coercing the population from posters, newspapers, or flag-hung platforms, honoured by the Germans with the threat of postwar hanging. Graham felt the quantity of the Saracen's practice might be dropping, but the quality seemed to be keeping up.

'She wanted the operation back in her place, but I wouldn't have it. Risk of sepsis, any number of things. It'll be a simple job. I took the same sort of thing off the tit of a girl last week. It seemed her boy-friend kept confusing it with her nipple.' The Saracen laughed. His patient had put him in a splendid temper. 'Don't use the brush on your skin, son,' he warned as they started scrubbing up. 'It'll give you a dermatitis and maybe in thirty years a cancer.'

The operating theatre was a small, plain room with a long window down one side admitting the afternoon sunshine. It was sketchily furnished with a spindly-legged operating table under a wide-shaded electric lamp, a couple of enamelled slop-buckets on the lino floor, and a tier of hand-bowls opening like a teatime cakestand. Along one wall a white-painted Welsh dresser bore flat dishes of suturing materials submerged in carbolic, shiny metal drums and sterilized dressings, flasks of brightly-coloured antiseptics, and bundles of swabs in jars like those in sweetshops. Graham looked around as the patient appeared, lying on a trolley. Without her hat she looked older–thirty at least, he thought. Her dress was stripped to her waist, and she was wearing what they called a brassière.

'This *is* very elaborate,' complained Miss Cazalay. 'For a minor operation.'

'My dear, no operations are minor.' The Saracen deftly covered her shoulders, neck, and eyes with white sterile towels. Taking a syringe of local anaesthetic from Graham and announcing cheerfully, 'Just a little flea-bite!' he ran the needle through her skin.

'Ouch!' she complained through the towels. 'That hurt.'

'Sorry, my dear.'

'Now remember–you're to tell me absolutely *everything* that's going on.'

'Sure, my dear, sure.'

Miss Cazalay found doctors trying. She had been brought up to assume as much without vanity as without question that no one could occupy a better position on the stage of life than herself. Her acquaintances were no bother because they recognized it too, but parsons and doctors demanded a tiresome readjustment of the personality. Even parsons weren't too wearisome, any she met being accustomed to treat such personages as herself and the Almighty with equally well-bred respect, but she felt you *surrendered* so to doctors. Your frame might be your housemaid's, if rather cleaner. In their power you become a nobody. And Miss Cazalay could never allow herself to be a nobody. She therefore made up her mind to impress her personality on her operation.

But operations like battles unhappily do not always run as smoothly as in the minds of their planners. For a start, there was too much bleeding. The Saracen decided crossly that the adrenalin mixed with his local anaesthetic to constrict the cut blood-vessels had deteriorated in the sunlight. Trickles began to evade Graham's swab and run across Miss Cazalay's shapely but unanaesthetized chin. Her demands for a running commentary became steadily less enthusiastic. The Saracen impatiently pulled the half-detached mole with his forceps, and she cried out.

'Not long now, my dear,' he muttered. 'Not long.'

No reply.

At last the mole was detached. The Saracen picked it with forceps from its bloody bed and dropped it into a waiting kidney-dish on the operating table. Unfortunately he had overlooked the towels being pulled awry in the struggle, and the scrap of pigmented oozing flesh lay squarely in its owner's view. Miss Cazalay screamed.

'Get some water!' he commanded, slapping a swab on the open wound.

Graham hastily found a feeding-cup like a small teapot. He dashed in some water and held it between Miss Cazalay's lips. She remembered somehow to say, 'Thanks most awfully.' She had been extremely well brought up.

The Saracen then ordered Graham to hold her hand for the rest of the operation.

It occurred to the surgeon after such a performance he really should escort the patient home in her car, particularly as the sight of his bill would be as severe a shock as the sight of her mole. But in half an hour he had an appointment with a man he was hoping would lend him money. For a moment he struggled between duty and solvency. Then he told Graham to accompany her instead.

With a rug round her knees in the back of the Daimler Miss Cazalay apologized torrentially for her stupid behaviour. Graham made most sympathetic remarks. The woman was clearly as sensitive to the terrors of surgery as to the blemish it had removed.

'I don't know why I bothered to have it done,' she told him distractedly. 'Except that Dr Sarasen kept persuading me. And he *is* terribly persuasive, isn't he? I was really awfully fond of that little mole thing. I shall feel quite lost without it. Anyway, it was awfully sweet of you to hold my hand, Dr Trevose. I do hope it wasn't a bore, when you'd so much rather be cutting me up. And now I shan't be fit to be seen for a month. Thank heavens it's the end of the season! I shall be able to vegetate in total solitude. For weeks I've been working like an absolute slave.'

The idea of Miss Cazalay slaving so startled Graham he exclaimed, 'What sort of work?'

'Oh, all sorts. The Red Cross, the Cazalay Mission in Canning Town, the Belgian Children's Charity, the Sunshine Fund, the Free Medicine Club . . . I never have a moment.'

'Oh, I see. Well, I suppose it's best not letting yourself be bored.'

'Bored?' She looked irritated. 'I could never possibly get bored.' He might have suggested it were some disgraceful illness. 'Here we are,' she said abruptly.

They had arrived at a house in Half Moon Street, off Piccadilly. It was not a part of London Graham frequented, or even knew. As the chaffeur opened the door and he helped Miss Cazalay from the car he noticed with alarm that she was pale and starting to tremble.

'Are you sure you're all right?' he asked anxiously. 'It might be a delayed reaction from the local.'

'Of course I'm all right!'

The front door was opened by a tall figure in dress clothes. The hall was high and dark and seemed full of marble and paintings. As Graham helped Miss Cazalay inside she said, 'Now I'm being silly again,' and he caught her as her knees gave way.

The figure in dress clothes, whom Graham took to be a butler or footman, stared at them in horror. Lord Cazalay's only daughter was a person of such assertive importance in the household, round whom his own life distantly spun its humble daily revolutions, to see her suddenly insensible was as though the sun had gone out.

'Shall I get a doctor, sir?' he gasped.

'I am a doctor,' Graham told him briefly. 'Fetch some brandy.' The butler still stared. 'Hurry up! Can't you see it's urgent?'

Graham sat Miss Cazalay on a chair and pushed her head between her knees. Her hat fell off. He wondered whether to lay her on the floor and rip open her dress to free her breathing, but perhaps the intense decorum of the surroundings inhibited him. He looked round hopefully for some relative or other female help. Two girls in maids' uniforms were leaning over the banisters, more alarmed than the butler. It was unbelievable to find Miss Cazalay in such an undignified posture. Fainting in front of the servants was really not done at all. As his patient showed no signs of recovery, Graham panicked for a second that she were dead. He felt her pulse, beating away threadily. The butler reappeared with a decanter and glass on a silver tray, his hands shaking. He had been so paralysed by the irregularity he automatically served the stimulant as if ordered from the dining-room after luncheon.

After the brandy Miss Cazalay gave a gasp.

'Where's the lady's bedroom?' Graham demanded.

The butler hesitated. Even in such a crisis he doubted the propriety of directing a strange and rather unkempt young man to the shrine. Graham picked her up. 'Come on! She's got to lie down somewhere.'

The butler led the way upstairs. Graham was not strong and Miss Cazalay was rather heavy. He smiled as he suddenly pictured the pair of them tumbling down the dignified staircase and ending as not one but a couple of insensible patients in the hall. Miss Cazalay's room seemed all mirrors and orange silk hangings. He laid her on the bed and covered her with the eiderdown. One of the maids, who had recovered from the shock sufficiently to think action expected of her, appeared helpfully at his elbow with a large bottle.

'What's that?' Graham demanded.

'Jeyes' fluid, sir.'

'Good God!' he muttered. 'It's a disinfectant for drains.'

Miss Cazalay opened her eyes. 'I've got an awful headache.'

'Haven't you any aspirin?' he asked the maid irritably.

'There's some in my dressing-table,' murmured Miss Cazalay, colour hesitatingly taking repossession of her cheeks. 'What a performance! I *am* stupid,' she apologized again as the maid returned with tablets and water. Miss Cazalay had been brought up to see all illness as a form of weakness. 'How did I get up from the hall?'

'I carried you.'

She managed to smile. 'How romantic.'

The door burst open, and a woman in street clothes threw herself upon Miss Cazalay in a torrent of Italian. Lady Cazalay came from a noble family in Venice, and when overcome by her emotions found only her own language adequate to express them. Her only recognition of Graham's presence was repeating loudly to him that Dr Whitehead be summoned at once.

'But, madam! Miss Cazalay will be right as rain if she lies down for a while.'

'No, no! We must have Dr Whitehead. He always attends my daughter. Since she was a little girl.'

Graham thought this doubtful, Dr Whitehead not being a practitioner of advanced years. But he dutifully sought the butler to summon the royal physician. After all, they could call who they liked, as long as they could afford to pay. He watched the butler reluctantly make for the telephone room off the hall, to pick the instrument from the Louis XIV table on which it was displayed with the pride of all the Cazalays' privileged possessions. The poor fellow felt after the upheaval of the afternoon this was the final blow. He was never comfortable with the telephone, someone having told him it could attract dangerous atmospheric electricity from miles around.

It seemed Graham had no more to do. The patient was recovering, and Dr Whitehead might be displeased to find him on the scene in his shabby suit. He opened the door and quietly let himself out. He walked along Piccadilly in the sunshine, to the corner of Bond Street opposite the Ritz Hotel, and sat reliving his experiences on the foremost seat on the top deck of an open Hampstead bus.

Chapter Nine

Graham reached home to be greeted in the hall by a pair of black metal trunks, securely roped, sealed in lead, and stencilled neatly in white, DR ROBIN TREVOSE NOT WANTED ON VOYAGE. Having a natural fussiness which he mistook for conscientiousness, Robin had started packing weeks ago. His books were carefully crated, his tent, mosquito-net, hip-bath and hot-water bottle (it was liable to become quite chilly at night, he told Graham severely) all boxed and garlanded with pretty steamship labels. A passage being difficult to extract from the tangle of postwar shipping, he had spent the entire summer amassing a mountain of kit and presumably an equally large knowledge of tropical medicine. But at last he was due to sail, by White Funnel to Singapore in a fortnight. He seemed to his family to have been on the point of leaving home all his life.

Graham heard the rattle of a typewriter from his father's study.

He had found London a cruel place for lovers. He had taken Edith hopefully into the country now and then, but her terror of discovery by passers-by proved so totally inhibiting he even sighed for the quarantined seclusion of the sanatorium summerhouse. Now he recalled that his father was delivering some ceremonial lecture at Blackfriars, Robin was buying a compass from a particular shop in Greenwich, the maid was absent through family illness, and the cook as usual was visting her mother and leaving a cold supper.

It was worth a try.

Edith looked up from rolling a clean sheet of paper into the ungainly machine. 'Oh! It's you, dear.' He seldom got home on a Saturday afternoon. 'I didn't hear the front door. Anything exciting happen at the hospital?'

'Yes, I had to take some woman home after we excised a mole from her face, and she fainted in her own front hall.' He did not elaborate on these facts, Edith sometimes asked unending questions once her interest was aroused. He slipped his hands over her shoulders and felt her breasts under her white blouse. 'How about a bit a fun?' he suggested.

'Fun?' Suddenly understanding he meant the serious sort of fun she looked startled and asked, 'What? Here at home?'

'Why not?' he grinned. He noticed the erectile reflex of her nipples.'

Edith's mouth opened. 'Where?'

'In my room.'

She looked even more doubtful. 'Something might happen.'

'But we're absolutely alone.'

'I mean babies and that.'

'What of it?' He laughed. 'We're getting married anyway, so it wouldn't matter.'

'Oh, it would be awful! Everyone would notice. Just think.'

'Nothing happened before, did it? Science is truly wonderful.'

She laid her hands on his. 'When are we going to get married, dearest?'

He had been afraid of this question. 'As soon as I get a job. The very next day if you like.'

'You're sure you *want* to, Graham?'

'Of course I am!' He sounded deeply offended. 'Why on earth should you ask?'

'Oh, I don't know. You've been a bit down in the mouth recently.'

'Things haven't been particularly cheerful at Princess Alexandra's. The physician St Luke himself would have been a bit down in the mouth. How about coming dancing tonight?'

As he expected, she brightened up at once. Edith loved dancing. She was particularly good at the bunny-hug. 'Then come and have a bit of fun first,' he persisted.

She giggled. 'Oh, all right, then.'

He took her by the hand upstairs. His own bed looked rather cramping for fun. An idea struck him which could bring a lifetime of amusing memories. 'In here,' he directed.

The professor's room had mauve patterned wallpaper, brown paintwork, and heavy crimson curtains. In the middle his big brass bedstead stood under its purple coverlet as impressively as a catafalque. Underneath, brilliantly tinted and embossed, was a chamber-pot of the highest quality.

'Not on the professor's bed!' Edith gasped. She had a strong sense of propriety.

'Why not? It'll be so much more comfortable.'

'Supposing he comes in?'

'He's addressing a lot more anatomists. About synovial membranes. Though we'd better look sharp.'

She started to giggle again, and began taking off her silk stockings.

The broad soft bed played genial host, though the springs creaked like arthritic ligaments with the unaccustomed exercise and in the middle one of the big brass knobs fell off, bounced like a cricket ball, and rolled noisily across the lino. Edith lay afterwards with a reverent expression she felt fitting to the moment. Graham couldn't help himself thinking it gave her a half-stunned look. He inspected her nose, an inch or two away. It really did turn up too much at the end. If you made an incision through the mucous membrane inside, thus avoiding a scar, then with a pair of curved scissors snipped away the tips of the little alar cartilages–

She leapt up. 'Listen! There's someone downstairs.'

'Probably the boy with the joint for tomorrow.'

'No, no! It's in the house. Honest.'

She looked so frightened Graham said, 'I'll go and see.' They both hastily began pulling on their clothes. In the hall Graham found his brother, looking disagreeable.

'Where have you been?' Robin asked shortly.

'Getting some cigarettes.'

'Where's Edith?'

Graham raised his eyebrows. 'I wouldn't know. In the old man's room, I think. Fetching some notes.'

'From his *room*?' Robin frowned. 'Everything's kept in the study.'

'Oh, he probably took them to read in bed.'

'I've never heard of him doing such a thing.'

'What are you so worried about?' Graham demanded crossly. 'Do you suppose my future wife is going through his pockets, or something?'

Robin looked flustered and replied more civilly, 'I just wondered why she wasn't at her work, that's all.'

The brothers stood staring at each other. Graham wondered anxiously if Edith had remembered to screw the knob back.

'Did you get your compass?' he asked.

'Compass?' Robin seemed puzzled. 'Oh, the compass. Not in the end. I decided to try somewhere nearer on Monday.'

Graham glanced at his wristwatch. Somehow he had to shift Robin from the hall. Edith might appear in the most suspicious physical and mental disarray. 'How about a cup of tea?' he suggested. 'As everyone's off we'll have to brew up ourselves.'

'Yes, go ahead.' Robin nodded. 'I'll be in the drawing-room. I've got another bundle of those Customs forms to fill in.'

Graham watched him close the drawing-room door before making through a green-baize one leading to the kitchen. He suddenly noticed how hot and stuffy it was inside the house. No wonder they had been sweating so much, their bodies slapping together like a pair of fresh Dover soles. He hoped it hadn't shown. Robin's eye was trained for physical abnormalities like his own. Feeling for a match, he put the black iron kettle on the gas and started to whistle 'Alexander's Ragtime Band'.

Robin waited. He was close against the drawing-room door, peering through the crack. Edith appeared on the stairs. No notes, no other documents. And what of Graham's cigarettes? He certainly wasn't smoking, and a man doesn't traipse up to his bedroom for a packet unless in pressing need of a gasper. But before he could say anything Edith smiled and remarked blandly, 'Hello, Robin! Well, *I*'ve got work to do, if no one else has,' and made serenely for the study.

'What were you doing upstairs with Graham?' he asked angrily, following her.

She placed her hands on the typewriter keyboard. 'Nothing.'

'You swear it?'

'Go on with you! Don't be daft.'

Robin fell on his knees, grasping both her legs, and in his enthusiasm those of the chair. 'My darling, my darling! You won't go back on me?'

'Of *course* I won't.'

He looked up anxiously. 'You haven't said anything to him?' She shook her head. 'My angel, I could stoop and kiss your little feet,' he continued, though contenting himself by lifting her skirt and caressing her knees with his nose.

'You'd better go, my sweet.' She smiled. Robin was such a hot-headed, vigorous man. Like a bull. Very exciting, really. She softly stroked his head and he groaned loudly. 'He might come in, mightn't he?'

'He's got to know some time.'

'But not just now, dear. Not just now.'

Robin got to his feet. 'It's not easy for me–having to face him morning to night.'

'Yes, we're ever so naughty, really,' said Edith. 'Aren't we?'

As the door shut, she turned back to her work. Graham had interrupted her while transcribing, 'In the knee-joint the *meniscus medialis* and the *meniscus lateralis* are devoid of synovial membrane: now it becomes necessary to turn our attention to the interesting fact that the surfaces of these cartilages are fully and normally clothed with synovial membrane–' She looked for her place and added, 'in the foetus'.

She often wondered what that funny-looking word meant.

Chapter Ten

A letter, delivered by hand, was waiting for Graham at Princess Alexandra's the following Monday morning. It depicted a Miss Cazalay as apologetic over her failure to have him shown out properly as over her unforgivable lapse of fainting at all. Then she explained that a branch of the Red Cross (Graham never discovered what it was or did) met at her house once a month for a talk by some medical man. Unfortunately, the Dutch doctor with the completely impossible name, invited the next Saturday to unravel the mysteries of psychology, had been obliged to excuse himself through illness (she fancied the poor man had been forced to enter some sort of mental home, she added with a gay little exclamation mark). Could Dr Trevose step into the breach? The audience would be small but appreciative. Tea would be served. She *so* hoped he found the date convenient.

Graham did.

To demur that he was hardly an authority on plastic surgery after a few months' practice, most of them under Haileybury's irritatingly close supervision, never occurred to him. If he were given the stage he was confident of providing the show. It was again his natural exhibitionism. Later he lectured in countries still unborn, to peoples then dismissable as savages, about surgery at the time undreamable, but none had the importance of his little talk before tea in Miss Cazalay's upstairs drawing-room.

As armour against the treacherous shafts of stage-fright he simply reduced his hearers to a collection of hats–the lampshade, all fringes, shimmering in front of his nose, the shoe-bag drooping to his right, an affair like the frill on a mutton-chop very upright to the left, something right out of *Alice in Wonderland* nodding at the back, probably asleep. The group were all women, middle-aged to elderly, he supposed rich, mostly titled, and dreadfully arrogant. The flattery of the crush in the drawing-room was unmarred by his ignorance that Miss Cazalay had drummed up the audience by telephone, through feelings of obligation, even of guilt, towards her involuntary physician.

Graham spoke without notes, rustling the ladies with a little laughter, shaking them with a mild shudder, explaining with great gentility the principle of moving skin and bone from one part of the body to another. His feeling for an audience was as natural as Gerald du Maurier's. They found themselves quite taking to this pale, slight, soft-spoken young doctor with such magical powers at his finger-tips. Particularly as Graham had gone to the trouble of sprucing himself up, even stealing some of the fragrant lotion which Robin bought (as he carefully explained) to nourish the roots of his hair. He ended by passing round a few of the most undisturbing photographs he could find in the Saracen's office, which were eyed by about half the audience, shivering dutifully. He invited questions.

Could you move skin from one person to another? asked a hat. He regretted not, though it might be possible with identical twins. Another enquired in more theoretical tones if the shape of one's nose could *really* be changed by an operation. Certainly! You had the choice of Greek, Roman, retroussé . . . More theoretically still, what exactly was this 'face-lifting' one heard so much about? Quite simple! An incision was made at the temple, buried behind the hairline, the skin was drawn upwards and the excess snipped off. It was 'putting a tuck in' the face, if they cared to see it that way. He fancied they stole looks at one another. Quite a few quids' worth of work for the Saracen in the room, he told himself cheerfully. The lecture was ended only by the butler whom Graham had psychologically dismembered in the hall appearing to serve tea. There were cucumber sandwiches, for which he shared the passion of Wilde's Algernon Moncrieff.

'You were awfully good,' smiled Miss Cazalay, a square of plaster on her cheek. She was relieved that the risk of inviting him instead of the Saracen had been justified. He thanked her, reaching for a second sandwich. 'Have you always been a face doctor?'

'I haven't been a doctor of any sort very long. For most of my first year I was in a sanatorium–as a patient.'

'*Were* you? How awful!' Contracting tuberculosis was perhaps the most shameful weakness of all. 'Then what made you *become* a face doctor?'

He took another sandwich. 'More or less accident. I suppose it's the same with everything of fundamental importance in life.'

She pouted. 'What a pity. I thought you might be some Pygmalion hankering to create your Galatea.' This was lost on Graham, who had a strictly scientific upbringing, but it sounded pleasant. 'Well, there's time yet, Dr Trevose. Perhaps half London will be at your door one day.'

'That depends on whether I get another job or not, I'm afraid.'

She looked amazed. 'Do doctors have *jobs*? How peculiar! Fancy thinking of Dr Whitehead having a job.'

This reflection was inspired by Dr Whitehead himself, who had promised to look in. He was a skilful looker-in at fashionable gatherings, finding it a convenient way of impressing himself on prospective patients without overstraining the liver or stomach. A tall, spare, pink-and-white man, he wore the frock-coat many of his colleagues in the Harley Street area had abandoned during the war (as many of them had abandoned their practices as well for the Forces, he had started doing handsomely). He was a specialist who specialized in nothing, much sought after by people making money enough to afford distrusting the homely ministrations of their family practitioners. He had a delicacy of manner in not only the drawing-room but in the most unpromising clinical circumstances, which had endeared him to greater personages even than Miss Cazalay. His name always appeared on bulletins hung from the Palace railings, varying its company according to the occasion.

'This is Dr Trevose, and he wants a job,' Miss Cazalay said at once.

Dr Whitehead regarded Graham loftily. 'You're with the Saracen, aren't you?'

In his confusion at finding himself facing the royal physician, Graham had taken another sandwich. He told himself sharply such gross functions as appetite must never be displayed in the salons of Half Moon Street. Reference to the Saracen disarrayed the young man even more, but Dr Whitehead smiled and said, 'We should be grateful for his livening the London scene for us. Is it true he has one Rolls-Royce for himself and another for his instruments?' He could appreciate the noble qualities of the successful as sensitively as his colleagues in the East End appreciated the noble qualities of the poor. 'So you're after a job, eh? I heard the Saracen was having to cut down.' He took a cup from a footman. 'What sort of a job? In plastic surgery I should say they were non-existent.'

'I was hoping for something in E.N.T., sir. At least it would keep me going while working for the Fellowship.'

'There's a throat job coming up at the Sloane, I believe.' He implied a kingly disinterest in minor promotions. 'I'm on there, of course. Grafton wants a junior–you've heard of him doubtless?'

Graham nodded eagerly. The Sloane was a small hospital tucked behind Oxford Street, its consultant appointments bitterly fought over through its liberality with private beds. To land a junior job there would be a most valuable by-product of the afternoon.

'I fancy a word from me would settle the matter.' Dr Whitehead broke a biscuit. 'Though you'd have your visiting to do. At the Sloane we're rather a club, you know. We like applicants to call on the consultants beforehand. With their wives. It's a practice which used to be common in London hospitals before the war. I'm sorry to see it dropping out.'

'I haven't a wife,' said Graham hastily.

'Ah, you are at the fortunate age when the chase is more satisfying than the choice.' He smiled. 'Well, take your time. I've seen more promising careers wrecked by the wrong wife than by the wrong diagnosis. I'll mention it to Grafton, if you like.' Abruptly turning his back, he started talking to someone else.

Graham noticed through the window it was going to rain, and he had brought no overcoat.

'*Must* you go?' asked Miss Cazalay, as they descended the marble staircase. 'But perhaps you're right. You'd only be badgered with a lot more silly questions. Did you know I drove an ambulance during the war? Though I probably endangered far more lives than I saved. I'm a terrible driver.' She laughed. 'But it was the only way to go on living in my own home. Biddenden was turned into a convalescent hospital, you know.'

Graham remembered pictures of this Kentish mansion in the *Bystander*. Very grand. Officers only, he supposed. They reached the hall. A door opened and a short, fat, black-jowled man in morning clothes hurried across, followed by a younger one carrying a red dispatch-box. 'Daddy! This is Dr Trevose. You remember–he was talking to my Red Cross people. He's a *plastic* surgeon.'

Lord Cazalay registered a look of intense interest. He extended his hand and shook Graham's earnestly, holding his elbow. 'Very pleased to meet you, Dr Trevose. You people did tremendous work during the war. The country owes you a debt of gratitude.'

'Thank you,' said Graham, remembering to add, 'My lord', just like he'd read in novels.

Lord Cazalay switched off the look, withdrew the hand, and disappeared through the front door. It was his principle that a politician must butter up his public like a shopkeeper his customers, however neatly he manages to short-change them. He was so adept at this little scene, performed without interruption to his buzzing inner thoughts, he could have played it in his sleep–indeed he often did, awaking muttering earnest platitudes to all manner of well-deserving citizens flying away in his dreams.

'But we must see you in Biddenden one week-end this summer,' Miss Cazalay invited vaguely. 'Perhaps when the Whiteheads are there, then my mother can talk about all her complaints at once.' A footman opened the door. 'Are you interested in plants? We're supposed to have one of the most splendid collections of exotic vegetation in the country. In the greenhouses are Chinese rhododendrons, Himalayan bamboos, Singapore forest orchids . . .' She ticked them on her fingers. 'No, I expect you'd be bored with them. I am, terribly. The footman will get you a taxi.'

'It's all right, I'll walk.' Graham had been brought up to number taxicabs among dissipations.

'But it's teeming!'

'I've got to visit a shop–just round the corner.'

'Oh, well, good-bye, Dr Trevose. Thank you *so* much for all your trouble.' She smiled and held out her hand. By then Graham had touched a good deal of Miss Cazalay. But innocently taking her invitation as a suggestion she thirsted after his company, it gave him an excitement almost impossible to keep unnoticed. The door shut. He walked down Half Moon Street in the rain.

As he reached the corner of Bond Street the downpour started to take itself seriously. The buses were full, the top-deck passengers huddling miserably with their laps under the tarpaulins. He started making for Dover Street Tube station, but impulsively decided to walk home. Walking, a man was self-contained and alone, and he had something to think about.

Chapter Eleven

Edith.

My God, Edith! He didn't want to marry her at all.

It had been worrying him all summer.

He had just enjoyed a day excursion into a delightful world which contained marble staircases, plentiful servants, glasshouses full of idiotic plants, 'work' that disguised bone idleness, ornamental hats, beautifully cut cucumber sandwiches, and Dr Whitehead. Why shouldn't he, Dr Trevose, take up permanent residence in it? Miss Cazalay's drawing-room fired him with more ambition than the Saracen's operating theatre. He had brains. As good as Dr Whitehead's, at any rate. He had energy–he'd work twenty hours a day. But of course pure intelligence wasn't enough, no more than pure gallantry in war.

For success in modern medicine you needed social position, money, connection, airs and graces. Dr Whitehead, Graham seemed to remember, married the daughter of a duchess. He wondered gloomily what she would make of Edith. Or for that matter, what would the wife of any ill-qualified g.p. struggling with a large panel and a larger mortgage? She'd turn up her nose and probably make it twice as plain. His family were right. Graham Trevose, the great plastic surgeon, couldn't start married to a girl from a butcher's shop. He had not only magical skill but charm with the ladies–the Saracen had told him as much, and he was a sound judge of both. His depression was fleetingly lightened by recalling his taming the roomful of overbearing rich harridans. But charm, like artillery, was useless, wasteful, and downright dangerous if directed on the wrong target.

Besides, he didn't love Edith.

Or did he? He wished the condition had clearly recognizable signs and symptoms, like typhoid fever. His life with Edith was happy enough, but surely the great passion was different, running like a fever in your blood? It looked like it on the moving pictures, anyway. Would he *ever* really know if he loved her? Would he ever really know if he loved anyone? It was a wretched disability. Or perhaps he was incapable of love? He began to feel even more sorry for himself.

But he was engaged. It was a solemn bond, he had given his word, only a scoundrel would break it. He must go ahead like a gentleman. Besides, he totally lacked the cruelty to make the final break with her. Well, the courage, anyway. He supposed everything came down to that lack of character so lamented by the Scots medical superintendent. He reached Oxford Street, and it started to thunder. He turned up his jacket collar, aware of becoming remarkably wet.

The storm had stopped when he reached Hampstead, but the afternoon was still dark and the gas in the house ablaze. It was a Saturday, and Edith would be still here, tapping out wisdom on the synovial membranes. He couldn't face her. He would plead a chill, go to his room, and smoke cigarettes. He opened the front door, and found Robin standing in the hall amid his luggage.

'Graham—'

'Oh, hello.' He stripped off his jacket. 'I'm damned soaked. Couldn't get a bus.'

'Graham, I've got to talk to you.'

'What, here and now? Can't you see I'm drenched to the bone? Do you want me to get pneumonia?'

Robin jerked his head. 'There's a fire lit in the study.'

His expression was so funereally grave Graham followed him. He wondered with alarm what was up. Their father? Perhaps he had met the same anatomical accident as his predecessor. He was surprised to find Edith away from the typewriter, sitting beside the grate with her hands crossed in her lap. As he ripped off his wet tie, Robin announced, 'Edith and I are going to be married.'

Graham paused in the motion of undoing his front stud. 'You're *what*?'

'Going to be married. Edith and I. Next Friday.'

Graham's first thought was that Robin would no longer need to take his hot-water bottle.

'Yes, I should have told you everything before.' Robin stuck his hands into the pockets of his clerical-grey suit and started pacing the carpet with much agitation. 'I admit freely I've been deceiving you the past few weeks.

Deceiving you–my own brother! It's a terrible thing. But I did it only for your peace of mind. Honestly, Graham. For the peace of mind of all of us. It would have been impossible, wouldn't it, for you and I to have shared the same roof?'

Graham said nothing. He's quite frightened of me, he thought. A refreshing change.

'I suppose I could have gone somewhere else,' Robin admitted with a shrug. 'But it would have been terribly awkward with all my preparations for the journey. Now that I'm off next week–we're off next week,' he corrected himself, 'it can wait no longer.'

Graham decided to play his part in the scene. 'You bloody hypocrite,' he said impressively.

'Yes, revile me. Revile me as much as you like. I deserve it.' Robin stood looking his brother nervously in the face, his ruddy cheeks starting to tremble. 'But you'll understand, Graham–you *must* understand–out East a man needs a companion. Particularly for the sort of task I've undertaken. It's absolutely essential. I need a companion to look after the women and children. A companion to look after *me*. I'd go mad, otherwise. There're no other women out there, you know. Only natives. Yes, I'd go mad. Quite mad. And Edith's so suitable. She knows a lot about medicine. Working in that plastic surgery place prepared her for the horrors—'

'You and your claptrap about faith and the beautiful life hereafter! Setting yourself up as the personal friend of God—'

'I'm still a sincere Christian, Graham,' Robin protested lamely. 'This has made no difference.'

'I don't know how you've the face to appear as a medical missionary. You've just driven a coach and pair through the Ten Commandments.' Graham was uncertain which ones applied, but felt it a telling phrase. 'You're disgustingly selfish. You're dragging Edith away just to suit your own damn convenience.'

'No, no, that's wrong! I love her.' Robin was too self-centred to allow Graham's possibly sharing this attitude. 'Unless I loved Edith with all my heart and soul how do you imagine I could endure this present agony–'

To Graham's alarm, his brother fell on his knees at his feet. 'We must pray, pray,' he started muttering. 'O God forgive thy humble and weak servant, O God forgive me! I am wretched, weak, I cannot support the turbulent passions in a man—'

'This is really getting us nowhere,' said Graham.

'Graham, you must forgive me. Please forgive me, Graham. I beg you! Scourge me, flay me, but in the end forgive me.'

Robin broke into sobs.

It occurred to Graham this was exactly the situation he had longed for all his life. Here was Robin the paragon, Robin the handsome, Robin the righteous, Robin with the chest impenetrable to tubercle bacilli, Robin who always got down first to breakfast, grovelling round the dripping ends of his trousers. He was wondering how to make the most of it when the door opened. The professor was bad-temperedly complaining about the commotion.

'What's this? What's going on? Robin, what's the matter? Has there been an accident?'

Graham slung his wet jacket over his shoulder. 'Robin's going to marry Edith instead of me.' He looked at his wife-to-be of that morning. She was sitting by the fire with exactly the same placid expression. He thought he should say something to her, but no remark particularly fitting or self-flattering coming to mind he decided to leave the room in dignified silence instead.

The professor twitched his moustache nervously. The scene was so beyond the experience of an academic gentleman he simply withdrew, in great haste. He sat in the cold and dark breakfast-room rocking backwards and forwards on the edge of an overstuffed chair muttering, 'My God, what has come upon us now?' It was an emotional tangle far too complex for a mind attuned to the solid mysteries of anatomical thought. Even an attempt to unravel the mess would be an impossible distraction from professorial life. Had his ears heard aright? Surely not! Was *Robin* to marry Edith? To carry her off to the Straits Settlements? He leapt up with an angry cry. The synovial membranes! Now they would *never* be finished.

In the study, Robin groped his way to Edith, laying his head on her lap and muttering, 'O God, what have I done? What have I done? Edith, my darling, you must punish me. You must *punish* me, severely, severely . . .'

His voice soaked away, into the shifting dark sands of his psychology. Edith thought he became rather fanciful sometimes. She put her hand gently on his. She had been afraid of rather a scene, but everything had really gone quite well. 'Don't worry, my love. We'll soon be far away over the sea.' A thought struck her. 'Oh!' she exclaimed. 'Did you remember to tell the shipping line about the double cabin?'

Her severely practical mind would be a great help to them out East.

Upstairs, Graham threw himself on his bed and laughed. He laughed so much he began to choke. He had to jump up and vomit into the slop-bucket under his washstand, where he had rinsed the streaks of blood from his mouth after his haemoptysis eighteen months before. Floating round in the brownish froth he could see dozens of little pieces of cucumber.

Chapter Twelve

For the newly-engaged couple's last week in Hampstead Graham maintained an attitude of dignified sulkiness. As Robin took care never to leave him alone with Edith, their only exchange was by chance on the stairs.

'I hope you will be very happy with my brother,' he said.

'That's ever so nice of you, Graham.' She sounded as though they had just been formally introduced rather than ripped asunder. Going down a step she turned and added, 'You didn't want to marry me, not really, did you?'

Graham affected a look of such pained surprise she remounted the stair, bringing herself close to him. 'No, you didn't. You're going up in the world, aren't you?'

'What's that got to do with it?'

'You've got the power to make something of yourself.' She tapped her forehead. 'Up there. You'd resent me. I'd be just a millstone round your neck,' she told him charmingly. 'You're going to be famous some day. Like Dr Sarasen. You're not afraid to strike out, you see.' She glanced round the dark, ill-decorated, untidily masculine hall. 'You want something better in life than this. Don't you?'

Graham smiled. 'That all sounds very clever, Edith.'

'I'm not clever. Not a bit. Only about the way I get people to think of me. And then not all the time. Anyway, Graham–good luck.'

Her smile flooded him with regret that his mind had been made up for him. 'Come on!' he exclaimed. 'Let's just run off together, the pair of us. To Gretna Green. We don't need any luggage, only a wedding-ring.'

She laughed and waved her finger. 'Don't be daft,' she said.

She ran downstairs, still laughing, her dress flying up and showing her calves.

Robin quickly lost his remorse in a cloud of fussiness over steamship tickets, special marriage licences, medical supplies, flowers, letters of introduction, Keating's anti-bug powder, hymn books, and contraceptives. He even expressed surprise at Graham's refusal to attend the wedding, which was performed quietly in the missionaries' chapel at Woolwich by one of his brethren. There was a reception afterwards with a large cake and a little champagne. Robin made a speech which would not have disgraced a groom taking a more straightforward path to the altar. The barrister's clerk from Hither Green made a speech which would not have disgraced Marshall Hall. The butcher and his wife looked stunned, but they supposed if their daughter found one doctor as good as another they were hardly in a position to challenge her experience. Aunt Doris provided the tears, and the Professor provided a smallish cheque. The couple spent the night at the Euston Station Hotel, early the next morning leaving for Liverpool and a high-minded if impecunious future.

Edith felt the greatest adventure of her life had begun. It was even more exciting than working in the Face Hospital. There was no one on the dockside to bid them good-bye, but they stood and waved wildly from the rails just the same, Robin observing heartily, 'That's the last we'll see of the old country for a bit, my darling,' to which she replied breathlessly, 'Isn't it such *fun*!'

Everything fascinated her–the docks with their gawky cranes, warehouses the size of cathedrals filled with strange-smelling sacks, her new husband flashing their new blue-and-gold passport, the ship's ventilators drooping like unwatered plants, the fascinating gusts from the hatchways of burning oil or roasting pork, Englishmen in gold braid and Chinamen in starched jackets. She even giggled excitedly over the printed instructions for donning lifejackets, with their hint of the stirring perils of the sea, which Robin made her read carefully before leaving harbour. The prospect of sleeping in a bunk tickled her more than of watching some eight thousand miles of blue water pass under their porthole.

They were quickly picked out as newly-weds, though Robin being such a poor sailor was obliged to let several nights pass before putting this circumstance into action. He approached his duties with great enthusiasm, having in the back of his mind notions of embellishing the plain fare of human intercourse with such piquancies as embracing Edith's feet and submitting himself to some indignity, or even violence, in her hands. But she only said, 'Robin, don't be daft,' and he realized such plans had to be left, however regrettably, theoretical. He had suspected that women took a different view of such ideas. He would have liked to discuss the topic with Graham, with his wider experience of the sex, but recognized that might have been somewhat difficult.

The other passengers were civil servants, officers, planters, and businessmen making for the East to restore or start their fortunes after the war. Once the ship passed Suez the sun shone hotter than Edith believed possible, awnings were rigged on the decks, and metal scoops fitted to direct the clammy atmosphere of the Red Sea into the portholes. A change overtook the commonplace middle-class people who had filed aboard in Liverpool. In their white ducks the men strode the decks like lords, talked more loudly, laughed more heartily, and clapped their hands for drinks not only more resoundingly but more often. Their wives showed even better the strange aggrandizement kindled in the British by strong sunlight. Edith was too happy to appreciate at first the little condescensions by which they made plain their relief at being spared the embarrassment of her company after Singapore, and too eager to chatter to notice that the few seeds of conversation she carried in her head were increasingly nipped by social frost.

'That woman at our table–she's a real cat,' she complained to Robin when the ship turned east round the foot of Ceylon. 'When I said I'd never learnt to play bridge, she just sniffed and said, "Mrs Trevose"'–she imitated the astringent voice–'"I'm sure you were much better advised putting your hands to *work*."'

Robin frowned. Though he generally described Edith as a nurse, he knew it was stupid to delude himself that without the eye of love she struck the world as most definitely and distressingly 'common'. 'I don't see anything particularly offensive in that, dear.'

'You should have *heard* her,' Edith told him spiritedly. 'Oh! I'd like to scratch her eyes out.'

Robin sat on the bunk and reached for his Bible. He read a passage every day, and found it a handy way, in the tiny cabin, of quashing conversation. 'We must draw strength from God to overcome such maliciousness, and ask Him to forgive them.'

Edith pouted. She had accepted God as something that came along with Robin, and genuinely did her best to please both. But she didn't want the woman at their table forgiven by anyone.

'I'm afraid there is an awful lot of petty snobbery out East,' Robin went on sorrowfully. 'Or so I hear.'

'Snobbery?' She had been gazing from the porthole and turned with such fury she startled him. 'Then what have we got to worry about? We're the snobs now. Aren't we?' The road to self-betterment, stretching behind her all the way to Ramsgate, had been triumphantly marched. To find the destination much the same as the start was heartbreaking. 'Aren't we?' she repeated.

But Robin was deep in the Scriptures.

Edith quickly forgot her rebuffs in renewed excitement over Singapore. She revelled in such strange sights as girls in cheong-sams split to the thigh (which she thought would be fun to wear), the vertical writing outside the cupboard-like shops, women squatting with babies slung from their backs eating rice with chopsticks in the street, toddy shops, and even death houses, where ailing relatives might be conveniently stacked away in rows of bunks until extracted for a joyous and extremely noisy Chinese funeral. They stayed a week or so with an old Scottish doctor and his wife, who had lived out East so long as to have Chinese complexions but talked with the undiluted accents of Inverness. Their final journey was to Province Wellesley, the northernmost of the Straits Settlements opposite the island of

Penang, a three-day voyage by steamer up the coast broken at Port Swettenham. A motor-lorry brought them and their possessions at last to the mission settlement at Kapala Batas, which consisted of three buildings the size of a village hall, the one with the bell the church, another housing the school, and the most dilapidated the hospital with its dispensary. There were three bungalows, one for the doctor, one for the schoolmaster, and one for the reverend missionary, who they found had taken the chance of moving into his medical brother's larger and more comfortable and temporarily vacated premises.

Even when the novelty of four servants to order about became simply a matter of domestic routine, Edith never felt bored. Her placid nature was as incapable of boredom as of malice. She found something of interest every day, a new plant or a new bird, or the surge of battle in their war against the ants. Besides, isolation saved her from the daggers of social ambushes. Their only companions were the schoolmaster and his wife, a dried-up couple who had come to Province Wellesley before the war, and the missionary, who was old and talkative and inclined to dribble down his beard. These three thought the newcomers agreeable enough, though from experience were reserving judgment for a reasonable spell, say a year or two.

Robin quickly became very bored indeed. He arrived seeing himself as a crusader, simultaneously bringing health and enlightenment to people well advertised as lacking both. He found neither offering particularly welcome. He was regarded with suspicion and fear, not as the adversary of illness and death but their closest associate, into whose view it was unwise to stray. He was so clumsy over the finer adjustments of human relationships he regarded his ungrateful and reluctant patients with short-tempered puzzlement. He stubbornly avoided advice from his missionary colleague, partly through pride and partly through the danger of finding himself deluged with saliva and conversation. Most frustrating of all, instead of presenting him with interesting tropical diseases to be cured by white man's magic, his patients mostly had ordinary European complaints and a shocking number suffered from syphilis. He began to worry if he really wanted to practise such strenuous medicine, though as he had committed Edith and himself for five years, not only morally but on paper, this was a theoretical doubt. They would just have to put up with it.

Meanwhile, the professor in Hampstead was still wondering bad-temperedly why one of the knobs on his bed kept falling off.

Chapter Thirteen

The tide of life, once it had borne Robin and Edith away to Asia, turned in Graham's favour.

Dr Whitehead was as good as his word, though more out of respect for Miss Cazalay's guineas than Graham's talents. Graham anxiously called on Mr Grafton at the Sloane Hospital, finding him a large prosperous surgeon so goodhearted he welcomed a nominee to spare him the pain of disappointing unsuccessful applicants.

'You'll find life here quite a holiday after all that pioneering stuff,' he told

Graham amiably. Unlike most throat surgeons he was an admirer of plastic work.

'I'd better tell you, sir, I've had no experience of E.N.T. work at all.'

'You'll soon pick it up,' said Mr Grafton. 'Mostly I do tonsils.'

Tonsillectomy was as much a feature of conventional English education as confirmation, both procedures doing the candidates as little observable good. Graham certainly got the hang of Mr Grafton's technique quickly enough. The little patient was dumped on the operating table by a nurse, then John Bickley, the sharp-featured young anaesthetist, muzzled him with a wire-and-lint mask and hurtled him into unconsciousness with a jet of sweet-smelling ethyl chloride from a miniature soda-syphon. At some precise point between wakefulness and death John whipped away his machinery and retired to watch the proceedings, wearing the cheerful Sam Weller expression of a perceptive servant common to all anaesthetists. A twist and snip of Mr Grafton's long tonsil guillotine produced the offending organs, a deft scrape with a curette removed the adenoids as an encore, then Graham held the victim upside down by his heels, to prevent drowning in his own blood while coughing and retching his way back to the world.

After the operating list, when the hot little theatre resembled the Place de Grève at the end of a busy day during the Terror, Graham had to collect the tonsils and adenoids to present in a jar to his chief. He imagined this was for some deep otorhinolaryngological research until he discovered the surgeon put them on his strawberry beds, for which they apparently had no rival as fertilizer in the seedsmen's catalogues. As all the patients were private ones–not losing your tonsils being one of the few contemporary blessings of poverty–as Graham got a guinea or two a case, and as Mr Grafton achieved the turnover of a skilled Chicago slaughterman, he began doing quite well.

During the winter of 1919, when the world abolished war for ever by creating the League of Nations, Mr Grafton promoted Graham his registrar. Then the Saracen suddenly became eager to stuff guineas into his pockets. Leaving Princess Alexandra's after a complicated row (with the Saracen's fading glamour the secretary had demanded his office back for a start) the American had rented with borrowed money a suite of rooms in Wimpole Street, which he fitted out magnificently as an operating unit. Graham hesitated to accept the invitation to assist him. In the eyes of the General Medical Council the Saracen did not exist. But John Bickley, who gave the Saracen's anaesthetics, reassured Graham that legal proceedings were afoot against the G.M.C., in which the Saracen had put his own money and was therefore plainly expecting to win. And reshaping a nose, Graham found, could be worth several jarfuls of tonsils.

Even the professor added to Graham's affluence. Possibly feeling his younger son had suffered a little roughly in the hands of his brother, his fiancée, and the tubercle bacillus, he unexpectedly offered a small allowance. As he had no longer Robin to house he calculated the overall outlay would not be large. Besides, he was in a good mood because the synovial membranes had started up again. They were typed by a girl of eighteen called Sybil, who wore the closest crop in London and smelt like a hothouse of violets.

Of more value than money was Graham's Fellowship of the Royal College of Surgeons. He was allowed to sit the examination on turning twenty-five in the winter of 1919, having already kicked aside the stumbling-block of the

Primary examination in anatomy and physiology at his father's insistence while still a student. Passing at the first try, he could revert from the still novel title of Doctor to the grander one of plain Mister, a complicated exercise in surgical snobbery he was never able to fathom. With a Fellowship he had a future. He began to dress more smartly. He bought a small Jowett car. He was in the position to think again of taking a wife.

This time, he had already decided, I know what I'm after.

His uncoupling from Edith had left him free to forgo the simple pleasures of marriage for love in favour of a woman with money and position, but the difficulty lay in finding one. Now, Miss Cazalay, he calculated, must have friends, and a man had to start somewhere. He wrote to Half Moon Street on the pretext of thanks for his new job, suggesting pointedly he hadn't forgotten the invitation to Biddenden. Miss Cazalay was irritated. If everyone insisted on taking her at her word, she could have filled Windsor Castle every week-end. But she asked him for the following Saturday. Graham bought a new set of plus-fours and was so on his best behaviour he bored everyone.

But Maria Cazalay's mother took to him. He listened patiently to all her ailments, many of which were unknown to medical science. During the autumn of 1919 she asked him regularly to Half Moon Street for tea. She thought him more *simpatico* than Dr Whitehead, who was inclined to be vain, and anyway treated tea as a consultation and sent in a bill for a guinea. Maria was often there, between dashing to meetings of the Cazalay Mission, the Belgian Children's Charity, the Sunshine Fund, and the Free Medicine Club. Graham began to see a good deal of her. She began to think he wasn't so boring after all.

One afternoon the pair of them were talking about free medicine, when Maria burst out impatiently, 'The poor really have no sense of responsibility. Some of these lower-class families produce enormous broods of children–eight, nine, ten or more sometimes. And they haven't a penny to bless themselves with. No wonder they all get rickets and scurvy and nits and such things.'

'The world suffers an unhappy division–into couples who want to have children and can't, and couples who have too many and don't know how to stop.'

Graham was sitting in an easy chair, swinging his leg over the arm. He was now perfectly at home in the drawing-room. Maria's mother had gone to lie down with a headache, induced by a surfeit of clinical recollections.

'Yes, of course.' Maria looked awkward. 'I've heard there are ways in which one can stop . . . well, breeding.'

'Oh, birth control,' said Graham lightly.

Maria blushed. It was not at all the sort of subject one mentioned to young gentlemen. Only a year or two previously, she seemed to remember, people were sent to prison for advocating the use of such apparatus, whatever it happened to be.

'You must have heard of Marie Stopes?' Graham suggested.

'The name, certainly.'

'She's planning to open a clinic next year. That'll let off a splendid fuss. Questions in Parliament, thunderings, from the pulpit, that sort of thing. It'll be just as bad as Mr Willett's Daylight Saving Time.'

'I can't say I altogether agree that *clinics* are necessary,' said Maria primly. 'It's such a very private matter between husbands and wives.'

'There'll have to be some sort of clinics for those new diaphragms. They don't go in by instinct, I'm afraid. It's amazing the average women's lack of knowledge of her own anatomy.'

He saw Maria bite her lip. But they were talking about 'women', a detached and philosophic subject, she told herself, like the poor. 'I don't think even I know how these things operate.'

'The diaphragm sits snugly under the neck of the uterus–the womb.'

'The womb . . . that's different from the other . . . the other passage, is it?'

'I'll draw you a diagram,' Graham offered.

She brought him a sheet of writing paper, which had a coronet on it.

It amused him to see the flushed discomfiture of the leading light in the Sunshine League and Free Medicine Club. It was his Bob Sawyer approach again. He never shook off the grinning ghost of this Dickensian roustabout all his life. With Edith he used racks of corpses, but a lady of Maria's intelligence and sensibility he confronted with the womb.

At their next meeting the subject of contraception somehow brought itself up again.

'But the *poor*, what method do they use?' Maria asked. She had beaten down her embarrassment. After all, it was perfectly permissible to discuss such intimate generalities with a young man if he happened also to be a young doctor. And it was also rather exciting. 'These implements cost money.'

'*Coitus interruptus*. As free as the air we breathe.'

'I don't think I understand.'

'It's a ceremonial salute to the goddess of love rather than firing in deadly earnest.'

'I still don't understand.'

'I'll draw you another diagram.'

He began to wonder if she were really quite innocent. He could tell from the *Tatler* she floated through life on a cloud of 'admirers', well-born and well-tailored young men who could buy half Bond Street for her presents, but perhaps she was not the generous bestower of gay favours he imagined. Perhaps, it struck him suddenly, there was even a chance for a serious-minded professional young gentleman like himself. An exciting thought. At least she seemed to find him more interesting than the committee of the Sunshine League.

And Maria began to wonder how much of his knowledge he had got from books.

During that winter Graham occupied her thoughts quite as much as her committees. She was touched by his simplest attentions. After all, he was kindly, he was amusing, he was sensitive, he had perfectly passable manners, and he knew all about the female pelvis. She fancied he was falling in love with her. Graham fancied he was, too–if she encouraged his advances, he was ready enough to supply the passion. At Christmas she let him take her to the Sloane Hospital Ball, a sumptuous annual affair in Park Lane when the rich dutifully fed and frolicked to raise funds for the undernourished poor. She decided afterwards she was really becoming quite fond of him, and he danced wonderfully. He had enjoyed plenty of practice with Edith.

Maria finally made up her mind to marry the little doctor as clear-headedly as she decided anything on an agenda. Many men had confessed themselves tortured with love for her, but none in the end seemed inclined to make his agonies exclusive–she knew the reason well enough, though at the moment preferred not mentioning it. And she had to marry *someone*. At Easter 1920 she asked him with three other admirers down to Biddenden, but one developed mumps, another was suddenly dispatched by the Foreign Office to make peace with the Turks at Sèvres, the third, a gay fellow in journalism, wired last-minute excuses in expensive profusion. She suddenly saw herself an old maid, banished from the stage of life altogether to the wings, a cheerless prospect. She was already thirty-four. She told Graham twenty-nine, but she knew he didn't believe it. He was an admirably shrewd young man as well.

After tea on the Easter Monday she invited him into the hot-houses. She knew she would leave a betrothed woman. Once she had firmly made up her mind on a subject, she couldn't envisage anything whatever standing in her way.

That evening found Graham opposite Maria's father at the dinner-table, waiting a chance to ask his formal blessing. He felt not only overwhelmed by the events of the afternoon but most uncomfortable. The points of his dress collar were sticking into his neck. The coming interview had blunted his appetite for the food while sharpening it for the drink, leaving him flushed and muzzy. Not that he needed Dutch courage, he told himself. After all, he had been through the experience once already. But the Ramsgate butcher had been a simple hurdle to mount. Lord Cazalay was more in the nature of a portcullis.

Graham watched the man across the table. He was talking animatedly, banging the cloth, his face scarlet, his starched shirt-front crackling as if unable to contain the passion surging in his bosom. Graham had given up following the trail of the argument, an elaborate diatribe balanced on some delicate point of party politics. People who knew, or who said they did, awarded Lord Cazalay a mastership of intrigue bettering Lloyd George's, who, they hinted, became Prime Minister only through some refined shaft of Cazalay's treachery towards Asquith. They whispered that Cazalay had not only ruthlessly engineered the sinking of the Dardanelles expedition through hostility to Churchill, but equally ruthlessly engineered the sinking of the *Hampshire* through hostility to Kitchener. Graham found it simple to imagine such ferocity behind his exterior, which at the moment resembled an ape sitting unexpectedly on a wasps' nest. On the intelligence which had carried him to command the country's affairs in the Cabinet he was unable to form an opinion, any remarks by Lord Cazalay to himself on their few meetings being polite, formal, brief, and wholly automatic.

Lord Cazalay disposed of his port and his point, extinguished both his cigar and his outraged expression and rose from the table. The dinner-party was as informal as anything could be in his company, and to Graham's alarm his host would not for once be rightly joining the ladies. Instead, he made for a panelled door leading to his study, with a call of, 'Here, Arthur!' indicating a desire for words with a fellow Cabinet minister. Graham stood gripping his chair. He had only that evening to settle his business, and hadn't counted on forcing precedence over the Home Secretary. His resolve stiffened by wine, he pushed forward and asked, 'May I have a word with you, sir?'

Lord Cazalay looked startled, but gave a quick smile. 'Let's leave it till the morning, young man. You're staying overnight, I hope?'

'It's about Maria.'

Lord Cazalay resumed his ape-like expression. 'What about Maria?' As Graham found himself incapable of reply the politician's brain busily swept up a pile of suspicions. 'Would you mind biding a moment, Arthur?' he muttered.

'Our young friend seems possessed of information of some importance,' smiled the other politician. 'If we leave him to boil, it may well vaporize away.'

'Charles! Henry!' Lord Cazalay snapped his fingers to summon his two sons, neither of whom Graham knew very well through their having addressed him hardly a remark between them. 'And you, George,' he added to the secretary Graham had seen with the red dispatch-box. They all went into the study. Lord Cazalay took up battle-positions in front of the grate. 'Now–what's all this about Maria?' he repeated, scowling.

This was not the scene Graham had pictured. For a start, he hardly expected to find himself so heavily outnumbered. Unfortunately he had overlooked the total lack of communication in the Cazalay family. Lord Cazalay was far too deep in politics to pay attention to the others, Maria had for years stepped her own way, and if Lady Cazalay had been terrified of her husband before her marriage the event had done nothing to relieve it. When Lord Cazalay snapped at Graham, 'I know of nothing you need discuss with me about Maria,' it was one of the few times in his life that he meant what he said.

'We want to become married,' Graham told him, simply.

'Did you hear that, Charles?'

'Yes, I did,' agreed one of Maria's brothers, grinning.

Graham suddenly felt angry. After all, he was a registered medical practitioner, a surgeon, a healer. He was a man entitled to respect in the world. 'I have a very good position in the Sloane Hospital,' he said defiantly. 'In the throat department,' he added. 'And now I have my Fellowship.'

'What Fellowship?'

'The Fellowship of the Royal College of Surgeons.'

'Never heard of it,' said Lord Cazalay.

Graham was stunned. Ignorance of such precious honours was unbelievable. Then it struck him sickeningly that the lives of Lord Cazalay and himself were calibrated on widely different scales.

'I agree there's a gap socially between Maria and myself,' he retreated. 'But she and I have discussed it—'

'Maria and *you* have discussed it? What's it got to do with Maria and *you*? It's Maria and *me* who'll discuss such matters, if they are to be discussed at all. Who are you? I don't know anything about you. Does anyone know anything about you?' Lord Cazalay implored in general. 'What are you doing in my house anyway?'

This seemed a crashingly discouraging turn in the conversation. Graham was about to defend both himself and the Royal College of Surgeons, but suddenly losing heart made abruptly for the door.

'Don't run away, you fellow. I haven't finished with you yet. I know the type of people about these days—'

Graham slammed the door behind him, catching Maria's brother exclaiming, 'Throat hospital!' and roaring with laughter.

He ran from the house, ripping off his collar. The alcohol had evaporated from his blood. He fancied he was going to vomit. He knew perfectly well he would for years have cut a petty figure at Maria's side, but having his nose rubbed so vigorously in the malodorous fact took away his breath. He wanted to get away, to escape to the academic security of Hampstead. He didn't want to see anyone in the place again. He started wandering round the grounds, getting lost, somewhere or other dropping his collar.

Lord Cazalay had no need to summon Maria. Hearing the door bang she sensed something amiss and hurriedly excused herself from the drawing-room. She found her father haranguing the other three about the dangers of fortune-hunters, quite as fiercely as he had harangued gatherings in Trafalgar Square about the dangers of the Germans.

'Don't be stupid,' she said angrily. 'Do you imagine I'm fool enough to give myself to a gigolo?'

This subdued Lord Cazalay. He had respect for his daughter's mind, which he felt shared something of his own. 'But surely, Maria! You can't be fond of him?'

'Of course I am! It is unworthy and wounding to suggest otherwise.'

She also shared something of his ear for a phrase.

'But what of all the other men you've been mixed up with?' Lord Cazalay continued briskly. 'I've lost count of them. There isn't a woman in London who's had your opportunities. Why do you want to pick on this throat doctor, or whatever he is?'

'Do you wish me to die before I marry?' She clapped her hand to her cheek. 'Why do you think I had this thing cut out? Every affair in the past has come to nothing. I'm going through with this one, whatever anybody says. There're things about me you don't understand–couldn't understand. I know what I want, and I'm going to get it.' She sat down abruptly in an armchair.

Everyone fell silent. They saw Lord Cazalay was thinking. The lightning mind which flashed clarity on so many obscure political situations was trying to decide the inevitable first question, 'Where is the advantage to me?' An unmarried daughter was somehow a reflection on himself, particularly when the misfortune was so clearly not through want of trying. He had never understood Maria's failure in that department. He supposed she was clear-headed enough not to be duped by an out-and-out rogue. Perhaps it would be best to give in. Anyway, she generally got her own way in the end. The door opened, and Lady Cazalay appeared, erupting Italian.

'Oh, shut up, for God's sake!' said Lord Cazalay. 'Charles–fetch that doctor fellow back.'

They found Graham sitting beside the lake, smoking cigarettes. It occurred to Maria he might have been contemplating throwing himself in, which though the water was only three feet deep would have made a pleasant gesture. In the study Lord Cazalay shook him warmly by the hand, explaining his petulance as the result of the shock–which Graham, as a medical man, would easily understand. The house burst into uproar. Everyone congratulated him heartily, even Maria's brothers, who followed their father's opinion in everything, and the Home Secretary, who followed the novels of Elinor Glyn. The servants were summoned with champagne. The emotional see-saw left Graham stunned, until at last he escaped to bed, when he discovered he still had no collar on.

They were to be married in September, as fashionably, socially and spiritually, as possible. Graham was stopped in the street by reporters, his photograph appeared in the *Illustrated London News*, *Punch* made a heavy-handed joke. The professor was delighted, particularly as financially the flow of current had been repolarized. Aunt Doris was rapturous. Dr Whitehead promised to look in at the wedding reception. They were to honeymoon on the Riviera, spending the first night at Dover. It had never crossed Graham's mind to suggest any fun with Maria beforehand. When she undressed in the Dover hotel he found she was covered with really rather a lot of moles, from one end of her thin trunk to the other.

Chapter Fourteen

The most thrilling event of Graham's honeymoon was his discovery that the tides of the Mediterranean really did not come in and go out at all. He had never believed this distinction from less sophisticated waters. But there were the waves, beating as regularly as a pulse all day long on the same filthy strip of shingle. He felt a Galileo, making some original observation in astronomy.

It was a wonderful holiday, the best of his life, his first abroad. It fascinated him to hear people chattering in French, to handle the fragile-looking coins with holes in the middle, to post letters with gay, complicated stamps rather than the solemn monochrome features of the British king. He took an appropriate scientific interest in the aquarium tucked below Prince Albert's castle, and in the plants of the *Jardin Exotique* up the hillside. He was struck by the spotless artificiality of the Casino square, crammed with flowers as thickly as a London coster's barrow, where even the excreta dropping from the cabhorses seemed made of some synthetic and totally inoffensive material. He easily adapted himself to the food and attention lavished on them by the Hôtel de Paris, and there was no other 'high life' to test him. After the excitement of the wedding, his wife declared she wanted a quiet time of it. And anyway, gambling bored her. Graham sketched her on the Casino terrace every morning and organized picnics in the mountains every afternoon. She was always gay, smart, and a creditable companion. The sea stayed blue and the weather was charming.

It was soon clear why Maria had ripened so long on the topmost branches of the nuptial tree. Her promiscuity in London had been virginal. She was frigid.

Every night the fortress lay defenceless and eager for surrender, but the gates defied the battering-ram. It was most exhausting for both of them. When she demanded why she was cursed with such a disability Graham explained patiently it was a sort of spasm, like the cramp when swimming. A form of hysteria, he added–most unwisely, because, she told him quite severely through the darkness she was not hysterical in the slightest.

'I didn't mean it in that sense, my darling,' he apologized. 'But you mustn't *worry*. That only makes it worse. You worry that you can't do it, then you worry that you worry that you can't. You understand?'

She understood very well. It had worried her for years, more than her moles. So many men had started making love to her but retired hurt and baffled, she had begun automatically expelling them from her life once she sensed their taking range for an attempt. But Graham she expected would be different, with his knowledge of the female pelvis. Though she had rather feared a fuss, remembering a novel where a similar honeymoon terminated with the husband short-temperedly strangling the wife.

Graham was not over-upset. An exchange of intimate confidences was hardly to be expected *before* a marriage. After all, he hadn't told her anything about Edith.

'But what can we *do*?' she demanded.

'We can but persist.'

He persisted there and then, but it still didn't work. He persisted the following night, several times. He persisted when the waiter took away the bedside trays after their *petit déjeuner*. He persisted suddenly in the middle of the afternoon, remembering from some gynaecological textbook that success might occur when there wasn't time enough to worry about achieving it. But they stayed out of luck. He began to wonder if persisting in a relaxing warm bath might do the trick.

Then suddenly it happened. It may have been the reward of Graham's considerate handling of the situation, or simply of his physical endurance. It may have been two bottles of champagne at dinner dissolving Maria's inhibitions, or it may simply have been the rest and fresh air doing her good. But everything clicked as precisely and excitingly as the little ivory ball on the roulette table dropping into its slot. She was terribly grateful. And terribly proud. She had been perfectly right in her choice. He really was a clever little doctor after all.

They went home. Mentally, she rolled up her sleeves. The honeymoon was over, and Graham had to be fitted into place with the rest of the household.

The ambition of her womanhood achieved, Maria slipped almost immediately into middle-age. She dressed more drably and drew back her long black hair into an intimidating bun. She abandoned with relief the gay calendar of flirtatious parties for the more substantial and less tiring joys of domesticity. She had rented a house in Great Ormond Street, not far from the children's hospital, where she intended they should live in fairly modest style with only half a dozen servants. The district would be convenient for her work with the Red Cross, the Cazalay Mission in Canning Town, the Belgian Children's Charity, the Sunshine Fund, and the Free Medicine Club, to which had been added the Garden City Housing Trust, the Libraries for the Poor Scheme, the Keep Fit Society, and the general feeding and care of Graham. She entertained only at home, conscientiously rather than lavishly, and Dr Whitehead looked in repeatedly, remaining under the dictates of professional ethics Maria's personal doctor (he charged a guinea for tea, but appeared for dinner gratis).

Graham never saw Lord Cazalay, who seemed to be fully occupied persuading the miners to take lower wages. He occasionally met Maria's brothers, who still had nothing to say to him. He first came across the man who would in time mean more to him than any of them–Valentine Arlott, a young Australian who had founded the London *Daily Press* on Lord Cazalay's money before the war, and during it had praised both Australia and Lord Cazalay so handsomely his readers might be forgiven for imagining the pair could have beaten the Kaiser without outside assistance. He was starting a newspaper insurance scheme, and questioned Graham closely about the cash value of various items of anatomy. Short, pudgy, ginger-haired, and bouncy, he asked across the dinner-table if an arm was worth more than a leg. How much more? What about an eye? What were the chances of losing both in an accident? Not very high, Graham assured him. Splendid! He'd make a big feature about eyes. It would set the public shivering. It amused Graham to see his casual remarks inspiring the next morning's headline. Even his father the professor couldn't have managed that.

A month after the honeymoon the black vulture of gloom settled on his shoulder. It was not an unknown visitant. He knew he had a manic-depressive personality, his mood swinging from bright sunlight to black night, never lingering in the comfortable greyness of more stolid minds. Even as a child, a casual rebuke from the professor, or refusal of cake for tea, could throw him into the sulks for a day. Now he was more miserable than he could remember in his days of impecunious irresponsibility. He hadn't entered a new world with Maria–the struggle of putting himself on terms with her friends told him that. He had simply excluded himself from his old one. At the Sloane he was no longer the up-and-coming young Mr Trevose. He was Maria Cazalay's husband. The clash between his social and lowly professional status seemed resented by everyone, even the goodnatured Mr Grafton, perhaps because Graham arrived to work in a better car than he did. He felt he was becoming a social waif and began feeling terribly sorry for himself. Particularly when Maria started discussing his career, a project in which she took even keener interest than in the Garden City Housing Trust.

There was no plastic surgery post at Blackfriars, nor any of the grand London hospitals–Harold Gillies himself had got back to Bart's only as an assistant in the throat department. Graham wanted some small hospital as a springboard, somewhere he could, like Gillies, start doing throat work and later teach himself plastics without the world seeing too much of his failures. But where? The Sloane was no use. When Maria insisted he leave it to her he raised no objection. After all, she was far better versed in the ways of the world than he was. Also, she was about nine years older.

The day after they buried the Unknown Warrior in Westminster Abbey the Saracen invited Graham to assist with a case. He drove to Wimpole Street with John Bickley in the anaesthetist's Wolseley (the chauffeur-driven Lanchester Forty went back from the Sloane for Maria's use), the dickey crammed with cylinders of nitrous oxide gas and oxygen, lengths of rubber piping, and pieces of anaesthetic apparatus. They found the Saracen in a good mood, for four reasons.

First, his patient was female, young, and wealthy, the daughter of a City man who had sought his assistance without even a breath of canvassing.

Secondly, his lawsuit was snowballing to a climax. If the General Medical Council refused to recognize the Saracen's qualifications there was nothing he could do, the Council being as much above the bother of appeals against its wisdom as the Star Chamber. But he had cunningly started a libel action against a member of the body, a worthy general practitioner elected by his medical peers, who had unwisely strayed outside the stockade of privileged speech to comment severely on the Saracen at some otherwise unexciting medical meeting.

The lawyers found his case interesting, which should have been warning enough. When doctors find a case interesting the patient is generally doomed. A judge and jury of the King's Bench also found his case interesting, but rejected it. Then three judges in the Court of Appeal, equally interested, threw it out as well. But agreeing the case of interest to the country in general they allowed a final plea to the House of Lords which the Saracen was convinced would award him damages, restore his costs, and gloriously settle his professional status. He could simply have gone home to New York instead, but like many Americans of nobly expensive tastes he enjoyed the life of decadent old Europe. And he was so shouldered with debt even his appearance in the Cunard offices would have produced writs like a snowstorm.

The third reason for the Saracen's good mood was meeting Graham for the first time since his marriage. He felt the young man could now start being useful to him, particularly as he had brought the happy pair together. The fourth was having a proposition to discuss. A proposition always made the Saracen happy.

The patient was so pretty her hare-lip was doubly disfiguring, making Graham think of some vandal daubing the smile of the Mona Lisa. The Saracen set to work excising its edges and undercutting the skin, taking care not to shorten the lip and leave it worse than before, gathering up the superfluous red tissue in a fetching Cupid's bow. He operated as usual in silence, only when inserting his final stitches asking Graham abruptly, 'Are you a Catholic?'

Graham wondered if they were in for some ethical discussion about tampering with girls' features, but the Saracen went on, 'You know St Sebastian's, out Uxbridge way? It's a small Catholic hospital. I've been working on Sir John Blazey, their chairman of governors. They're starting a plastic unit out there. Nothing colossal, mind, just a few beds, less than we had at Princess Alexandra's. I'm to be made surgeon-in-charge.' The Saracen took another needle-holder trailing fine catgut from his theatre nurse. 'How'd you like to be first assistant?'

'But I'm *not* a Catholic,' Graham objected.

The Saracen chuckled. 'What's wrong with a sudden conversion? I guess the good Lord would have to look mighty sharp to find I was still one of the Faith. It doesn't signify much with the hospital, though it helps, maybe. Think it over.' He dropped his voice as though passing confidential information of momentary value. 'It's the chance of a lifetime. You'd be crazy not taking it.'

'But first assistant–' The offer was so unexpected Graham felt confused. 'I'm too young, surely?'

'This is a young man's specialty!' The Saracen cut out a stitch which displeased him and inserted another. 'Ours is a stern discipline,' he reflected as an aside. 'Other surgeons' scars are but lights under a bushel. Ours shine on the world for life. I guess you wouldn't mind making a small investment in these rooms–to join me in partnership,' he added as casually. 'They cost a mint to run.'

'When's your case reach the House of Lords?' asked John Bickley sharply from the head of the table.

'Oh, pretty soon,' the Saracen replied vaguely. 'Pretty soon.'

This had a dampening effect on the conversation. The Saracen was always having to tell himself his anaesthetist was smarter than he looked.

Graham decided to discuss the idea with Maria, because he discussed everything with Maria. She was working at her desk alone in the drawing-room when he came in.

'St Sebastian's–yes,' she decided. 'Partnership with the Saracen definitely *no*. You mustn't give the man a penny piece. I don't trust him.'

Graham shrugged his shoulders. 'You trusted him to remove your mole.'

'Really, Graham! That's hardly the same thing. Anyway, I was prepared to put up with him to get rid of it. No, you must go and see Sir John Blazey yourself, my dear. I can easily arrange an introduction.'

'I couldn't possibly see Blazey without asking the Saracen's permission.'

'Why?'

'That would be going behind his back.' She made a contemptous pout. 'It's the Saracen who's offering me the chance of first assistant, not the hospital. Don't you see? The partnership in Wimpole Street is part of the bargain.'

'Now you're talking rubbish.'

Graham's resentment awoke. 'I don't need any advice about the Saracen's morals or character. I've seen him working among patients long enough to form my own opinions, thank you very much.'

'Well! I'm only trying to help with your career.'

'Are you? Or is it an excuse for running my life for me? I can't call my soul my own these days. The house is filled with people I don't know or I don't care for. I can't even eat what I like or dress as I like. You don't seem to want a husband at all. You want a puppet.'

'Now you're being stupid.' She sat with her lips tight, wondering if she were angry or simply afraid she might cry–an unthinkable weakness. 'You ought to be grateful for meeting so many useful people.'

'Do you imagine I enjoy everyone pointing a finger at me?' It was the first row he'd had with her. In fact, it was the first row he'd had with any woman. He and Edith had parted with never a cross word. Like many outraged spouses, he seized the chance for amateur dramatics. 'People everywhere say I only married you for your money. What do you think *that* does for my self-respect?'

'Who say that? Who? I haven't heard of anyone.'

'Everyone at the Sloane. I can't endure working in the place much longer.'

'Oh, the Sloane! They're envious, that's all. Surely you've sense enough to see that? *Why* should they think such things?'

'You're nine years older than I am, for a start.'

It was the first time this weapon had been drawn from its sheath of tact. 'Why do you accuse me of that?' Maria demanded furiously.

'It isn't an accusation. It's a statement of fact.'

'God! You're being horrible to me.' Graham folded his arms and stared at her nobly, an effect badly upset by her adding in a low voice, 'I'm pregnant.'

His mouth fell open. 'What?'

'Yes, I'm certain of it. I haven't seen anything for two months. My breasts are getting bigger.' She clasped them. 'That's a sign, isn't it?'

He recalled she had recently been emitting a new radiance, remarked upon by her friends and taken as a compliment by himself. Now he realized this was enjoyed by all newly-pregnant women, and due to an upsurge of hormones rather than cohabitation with himself. He told himself crossly he should have spotted the diagnosis weeks ago.

'Aren't you pleased?' she asked, looking at him timidly.

'But, my darling . . . of course I am!' He sat on the edge of her chair and put his arm round her. He supposed all men were pleased when their wives became pregnant. 'Of course I'm pleased! As pleased as anyone in the world.'

He smothered her in a blanket of solicitude, and arranged for her to see Mr Harold Berkeley from Blackfriars. Mr Berkeley smilingly confirmed her suspicions. The baby would be born the following June. He put it tactfully that a primiparous lady of thirty-four should take her state seriously, reduce her activities, avoid riding horses or the possibility of falling downstairs, and leave all theatres and cinematographs the instant the plot threatened to become too exciting. Maria wrote jubilantly seeking leave of absence from the Red Cross, the Cazalay Mission in Canning Town, the Belgian Children's Charity, the Sunshine Fund, the Free Medicine Club, the Garden City Housing Trust, the Libraries for the Poor, and the Keep Fit Society. All the freed energy was concentrated on her pregnancy. With every mouthful she ate, every breath she drew, every movement of her swelling body, she thought of the foetus inside her. No mother could have lavished on her child greater intrauterine devotion.

Lady Cazalay came into residence at Great Ormond Street at once. Lord Cazalay, after briefly and earnestly congratulating Graham, put the matter from his mind in favour of more important affairs. The dinner-parties stopped. As a doctor-father, Graham found himself pulled into the limelight of their marriage. He arranged the consultations, collected the specimens, and explained in detail to both wife and mother-in-law the anatomical, physiological, obstetrical, embryological, and psychological facts. He became almost as favoured a figure in his own home as he had been in Half Moon Street before the wedding. Even Maria's brothers took him aside and asked in confidence if the going was likely to be heavy. He felt the pregnancy was doing him a deal of good.

Every afternoon at four, Dr Whitehead looked in for tea, and charged a guinea.

Chapter Fifteen

Perhaps deciding that Maria's delicate condition called for all consideration possible, Graham fell in with her views and visited Sir John Blazey at St Sebastian's. He found the little hospital charming, with its atmosphere of graciously bestowed charity, its nursing nuns in billowing coifs (which he feared were terribly unsterile), and its crucifixes on the walls of the operating theatres. He saw he would have to overcome a puritanical disapproval of religious trappings in medical surroundings. He failed to see the connection between medicine, which was a science, a business of cutting and curing, and religion, which was a highly unscientific matter altogether. Though he supposed it was a comfort, believing you passed from the care of your physician not simply to that of your pathologist but to the more enlightened solicitude of St Peter. As he had once told Robin, he wished he could believe it himself. But doubtless the priests who made so free with the wards kept the patients' peckers up wonderfully, and at very moderate cost, for he understood the poor fellows' stipends were pitiful.

Sir John Blazey was a thin, colourless man, fussing to explain the new unit was certainly not for such questionable practices as face-lifting and nose-making, but for the crop of accidents from the factories sprouting all round the hospital. He showed Graham the wards with such fussy diffidence the young man left for home in the Lanchester feeling more depressed than ever – Sir John would have awarded some unknown registrar from a throat department a more dusty reception. And he still had to explain the visit away to the Saracen.

He was spared this awkwardness. From that evening's paper Graham learned the world the poor man was struggling to balance on his shoulders had finally flattened him.

Five judges of the House of Lords, unmatched for experience, wisdom, and senility, had considered his case. Two thought he was right, three thought he was wrong, though all five found it most interesting.

The decision came at a bad time. In the winter of 1920 the goods which were to flood from Britain into a threadbare post-war world were somehow left silting up the factories, and unemployment grew as credit diminished. The *Daily Press*'s front page announced the Saracen's bankruptcy, hinting the more exciting whiff of a criminal charge was in the air–even the surgeon himself recognized his creditors had been treated to more enthusiasm than frankness. The rooms in Wimpole Street were locked, his instruments and his racehorses were impartially impounded.

'Always knew he'd come to a bad end,' Dr Whitehead told Graham, taking his hat after looking in for tea. 'Commercial motives have no place in our profession.' He paused at the front door. 'I was most interested in the news of your father.'

Graham looked blank. Had the longed-for Fellowship been awarded by the Royal Society temporarily out of its collective mind?

'You don't know?' Dr Whitehead gave a smile. 'Then perhaps you'd best hear it from the professor himself. It's anyway hardly more than a rumour.'

'Nothing discreditable, I hope?' asked Graham quickly. He had in his time overheard plenty of students' gossip in the dissecting-room, where his father was known as 'The Rubber', not through any erasive qualities.

'Far from it! Highly creditable.'

'Then tell me. Surely you can tell me what it is?'

But whatever the pearl of information, Graham failed to prise it from the oyster. In Dr Whitehead's practice he learned to take professional discretion to extremes.

With St Sebastian's and Maria's pregnancy Graham had too much on his mind to seek his father out. He was also expecting the Saracen to appear any day at Great Ormond Street, but the American delayed his visit till the week before Christmas. He was perhaps hopeful of the seasonal atmosphere, having his eye on a loan.

'Things haven't been going too well,' he admitted, sitting by the drawing-room fire with a cigar. It was the first understatement Graham had heard from him. 'Though I still know I'm right. What man before God could say otherwise? It needed only one of those law lords to think just a little differently. Judges are like horses, I guess,' he sighed. 'You can never tell which way they're going to jump all the time.'

Graham expressed sympathy.

The Saracen explained that matters were not so black as printed in the newspapers. His powerful friends in New York would straddle the Atlantic with a financial lifebuoy before seeing him go under. But rescue operations took time. He hated asking–because he regarded Graham as a personal friend rather than a professional colleague–but he would much appreciate two or three thousand pounds for a while. When Graham shook his head he generously reduced his demand to a single thousand. Graham shook his head again. The Saracen began to lose his temper.

'Don't you feel you owe me anything? Aren't you going to make your life's work in plastic surgery?'

'Yes, that's what I hope, certainly.'

'And who gave you your chance?' Graham made no reply. He would gladly have handed the man the money, but Maria was against it for more than economic reasons. If he were seen siding with the Saracen his own professional status might be called to question. Besides, the purse-strings were in her hands as firmly as if they had remained in Lord Cazalay's own. Suspecting the true frustrator of his hopes, the Saracen added sourly, 'Would you have the courtesy to tell Mrs Trevose I called to ask after the health of my grateful patient?' He then left with dignity, wondering if he'd the chance of a less ambitious sum from John Bickley.

Sir John Blazey came fussing into the house on Christmas Eve. He apologized for calling on business at such a time, but the situation at St Sebastian's had to be resolved as a matter of urgency. Now that Dr Sarasen was so painfully out of the question–Sir John made agitated little bounces on his heels–the committee had met and decided more care must be expended on his replacement. They had carefully considered Graham's application for the post of first assistant–thank you, he must decline a glass of sherry, he was sorely pressed for time–and notwithstanding Graham's age felt his experience and obvious talents, in the strictly circumscribed specialty of plastic surgery, merited their appointing him as deputy to the surgeon-in-chief. He could start the good work of the new unit until a suitable senior could be found. Would he accept such heavy responsibility?

Graham would.

He found himself in full charge of his own plastic surgery beds around his twenty-sixth birthday. Whether his work was so brilliant or the committee shirked the risk of appointing another trickster like the Saracen he never discovered, because the appearance of the threatened overlord was never mentioned from the day he joined the hospital staff to the day he retired from it at the age of sixty-five.

Chapter Sixteen

In the new year Graham's father called at Great Ormond Street to congratulate his son on his new appointment. Their meetings were becoming fewer and increasingly embarrassing, the professor being so overwhelmed by his son's marrying riches he treated the young man with a grotesque respect. He wore his usual dark suit and emitted his usual smell of corpse antiseptic, but something struck Graham as different–his eye had a sparkle, and even his drooping moustache seemed to wear a sheen. First they discussed Maria's pregnancy. Everyone coming to the house first discussed Maria's pregnancy. Then the professor brushed his moustache and announced coyly, 'Well, Graham, my boy, I have some news which will surprise you. Though I fancy your autonomic nervous system will survive the shock.' He paused. 'I am to be married again.'

Graham looked aghast.

'Well, Graham? Aren't you pleased? Eh?'

He sounded painfully impatient for a reply, but Graham could only stare and ask, 'Marry? Marry who, Father?'

'Mrs Fanshaw,' said the professor.

It had been a sad little episode for the academic gentleman.

At first during that summer, he had come into his study only to help Sibyl with the difficult words about synovial membranes, which she'd misspelt for months.

'"Epiphysis",' he explained smilingly over her shoulder. 'With the "i" first, then the "y". If I may explain, that is the portion of bone separated in early life from the main shaft by a ring of cartilage. But as we grow the cartilage disappears, the bone becomes one entity. Now–' He ran his long fingers up the sleeve of her cotton dress to grasp her elbow. 'Here we have the lower *epiphyses* of your humerus–"es" in the plural, you understand. How old are you, Sibyl?'

'Nineteen, sir,' she told him in a crushed voice.

'At such a delightful age the lower *epiphyses* are as yet ununited with the shaft. That occurs only with the onset of senility, at twenty.' He laughed. 'The humerus at its *upper* end ossifies in the same way, from centres at the head and at the greater and lesser tubercles. They are eight in number.'

He felt her shoulder through her dress. He considered making the demonstration more accurate by slipping his hand in her neckline, but decided against it.

'Just here,' he said.

'Thank you, sir.'

Sibyl found such difficulty with anatomical nomenclature that the professor often felt obliged to sit with her, painting her wrist, and sometimes her thigh, to emphasize the quaint classical words. But the girl's attempts were hopeless. He had to correct whole pages beside her, so close he could feel the hard line of her femur through her skirt. Reaching for a book or a pencil his hand might accidentally brush her breasts or sometimes lie in her lap, quite forgotten, often for minutes on end. Recognizing young Sibyl was doing her best, even his severest reprimands were delivered with his arm round her. He knew that she would interpret such attentions as kindly and fatherly.

But Sibyl was more experienced than he imagined. In her last post at a tea merchant's in Mincing Lane the merchant had done exactly the same.

Arriving home one summer afternoon from Blackfriars the professor advanced with jaunty step into the study to find with his typist an overweight high-coloured woman in a flowered hat, knitting.

'Oh! Good afternoon.' He pulled his moustache irritably.

'This is my mum,' said Sibyl, looking guilty.

'Very pleased to meet you, Mrs Fanshaw,' said the professor, leaving little doubt that he wasn't.

'I hope my Sibyl is giving satisfaction, Professor Trevose?'

'Perfectly. She is having a little trouble grasping the nomenclature, but that will doubtless be overcome in time.'

'My Sibyl's an intelligent girl and a good worker, I've always said.'

'Most intelligent. For her age. It is of course not given to all of us to comprehend the embryology of the synovial membranes at first blush.'

'That's why I was glad of her working for a professor. "You take the post, my girl," I said. "It will improve your mind."'

'I expect she has found me merely dull,' said the professor, a shade hopefully.

'Though it's a sacrifice for me, and that's a fact. I'm a widow, you know.

Without Sibyl it's lonely in the afternoons at Cricklewood. If it's all right with you, I'll come over to sit with her.'

The professor said he would be delighted, backed out hurriedly, and sat in the breakfast-room next door in a bad temper.

Sibyl remaining in strict quarantine all summer, the professor could hardly avoid paying attention to Mrs Fanshaw, whom he discovered to be the widow of some official on the Great Western Railway. By September he started inviting her to join him for tea in the breakfast-room, leaving Sibyl floundering among synovial membranes alone.

'It must be wonderful your son marrying the daughter of Lord Cazalay,' she told him. 'I read all about it in the papers.'

'A satisfactory match,' the professor admitted modestly. He handed her the wedding photograph of Robin and Edith, next to the silver-framed one of his late wife on the mantlepiece. 'I have another son, you know. He is, alas, far away in the Straits Settlements, engaged in missionary work. He has a most praiseworthy sense of vocation.'

Mrs Fanshaw took a bite of madeira cake. 'Pretty girl.'

'Edith will be a great help to him out East, I fancy.' The professor added with unthinking accuracy, 'She is very adaptable.'

'So you're quite alone, then?'

'I suppose it comes to us all.' The professor replaced the photograph. 'It is a bitter discovery–realizing how much we rely on our children's companionship. We only make it when they are grown up and gone.'

'It's a shame,' agreed Mrs Fanshaw. As he fell silent she added, 'It's a wonder to me how you manage. A man by himself. Things aren't back to normal even yet, not after the war.'

The professor sighed. 'Sometimes it *is* a struggle. Responsibility for the household is such a distraction, when really I should be concentrating on my work. Academic life is extremely trying, you know. There is no holiday, no escape. One's brain can never be unfettered from its problems. I have servants, of course, but sometimes I feel them more trouble than they're worth.'

'They don't know their places these days, none of them.'

He nodded. 'Now all the girls are working in factories you have to pay them the earth.'

'It's a scandal,' said Mrs Fanshaw, taking another mouthful of cake. 'Money's changing hands.'

The professor agreed with all these sentiments. The shared pains of the postwar middle-class so distracted him he finished his tea without mentioning anatomy once.

By November the book was finished. The last word on synovial membranes stood in two three-inch piles of typescript, presenting no problem but the pleasant one of transferring it to the medical publishers. If the professor's great task was over, so was Sibyl's. He asked Mrs Fanshaw to marry him.

After all, the house *was* a terrible burden. He was becoming dreadfully lonely, and would be more so as the years galloped by. Besides, she hinted at a little money of her own. She agreed readily, her sharp mind having outwitted the organ of academic contemplation by assessing his income and total assets with far keener accuracy than he imagined.

'Yes, the ceremony is to be in February,' the professor told Graham in Great Ormond Street. 'Very quietly, of course. I think a registry office would be more suitable.' As Graham tried to stumble out appropriate congratulations, his father gave a weak smile and added, 'How strange that in such little time Robin, you, and myself should all find brides? We're quite gay dogs, aren't we?'

But he suspected any such frolicsomeness was for him at an end. Mrs Fanshaw was beyond the desirable age in his eyes by some forty years, but the man who wants the moon must philosophically content himself with a candle.

Chapter Seventeen

The professor felt crossly that becoming a grandfather twice within three months was unfair on a comparatively newly-married man.

It had seemed to Graham the whole of London stood still and waited breathlessly for Maria's confinement. She had given up the exertion of everything except reading the untaxing works of Mr Wodehouse and Mr Maugham. He had bought her a crystal set as a diverting toy–Northcliffe and the *Daily Mail* had produced Melba singing through the earphones, while Val Arlott and the *Daily Press* were hoping to produce Chaliapin–but she was spared the danger of such excitements because however much Graham fiddled with the catswhisker the receiver never seemed to work. A room upstairs was stripped for obstetrical action, a nurse was engaged, Dr Whitehead looked in twice daily. But the mother-to-be continued to pass her days on a sofa in the drawing-room, every twinge of backache sending a ripple of agitated expectancy through the whole household.

It happened on Midsummer Day. Maria was scrupulously punctual, as usual.

'The first stage has definitely begun,' Mr Berkeley smiled to Graham while coming downstairs with Dr Whitehead. 'As you know, with a primiparous subject, it may be anything up to eighteen hours before we have full dilatation. Whitehead will telephone when I am needed.'

It was at two in the morning when they judged it time to resummon Mr Berkeley. He announced the child to be born in a couple of hours. Graham sat downstairs with Dr Whitehead, who had apparently looked in for the night, at unthinkable expense. The royal physician entertained him with stories of royal personages, but Graham wasn't listening. Despite his knowledge of the female pelvis he was worried. Everything to do with Maria's reproductive system seemed so inefficient. When Mr Berkeley reappeared, still smiling but regretting matters not as smooth as he had hoped, Graham leapt from his chair with a cry.

The obstetrician explained calmly the lie was a breech with extended legs, even drawing a little diagram of the balloon-like uterus with the baby trying to kick its way out instead of butting head-first. In the case of an elderly primigravida–he hastily excused himself, he used the word 'elderly' in the purely relative and technical sense–extraction under anaesthesia was indicated.

Graham was shattered. His wife, whom he felt he had come to love deeply amid the tenderness bestowed on her in general, was running into unthinkable dangers.

A nursing-home overlooking Regent's Park was hastily telephoned, an ambulance ordered. Lord Cazalay was called from Half Moon Street, and arrived with his secretary as though his daughter were already on her death-bed, scowling thunderously at Graham as the author of her misfortune. Lady Cazalay had gone into Italian at the onset of labour, required sal volatile with the return of Mr Berkeley, and now had to be laid down and attended by the nurse. Then Graham suddenly felt irrelevant again. When one of the Cazalay line was to be born, and in dangerous circumstances, he was merely someone else to get in the way.

He drew Mr Berkeley aside and asked the risk.

'I'll tell you,' the obstetrician said frankly, still smiling. 'For a manual extraction after version under anaesthesia, the accepted figure of maternal mortality is thirty per cent.' Graham flinched. 'In my hands, I would say fifteen.'

'Couldn't you perform Caesarean section?'

'I'm afraid the chances would be no better, Graham.' He paused. '*Even* in my hands. It's a desperate operation once labour's started, even in these days.'

Graham's lips trembled as he went on, 'How about puerperal sepsis? After all these complications?'

He remembered too many cases in the maternity wards at Blackfriars, seeing the first horrifying swing of the new mother's temperature chart, watching it mount until the fever burnt her life out under the helpless eyes of her doctors.

'I shouldn't worry overmuch. Admittedly there's a chance of puerperal infection, but it's very much a danger of the public wards, you know. Private patients in single rooms largely escape such things. And we've the new antistreptococcal serum up our sleeves, which is a comfort.'

'If it works,' said Graham.

'Well, yes,' said Mr Berkeley.

As Mr Berkeley left for the nursing-home Graham realized he hadn't even asked the chances of the baby. The unborn child had become so much a possession of Maria's no one seemed able to imagine its independent existence at all.

The obstetrician was as good as his word. Before daybreak Desmond George Arthur Graham Trevose was scrambled out of his mother's exhausted uterus, battered, blue, but ready to breathe. Lord Cazalay ordered champagne, and congratulated Graham handsomely. If his daughter were going to live, he took it as a compliment to the Cazalay constitution. She certainly made splendid progress, after a week becoming physically almost herself again. After a month, even Lady Cazalay had started to recover.

On the other side of the earth, Edith's pregnancy was a welcome diversion for the entire mission settlement.

Her married life had been placid. The couple grew fonder of one another, much because it was her nature to scuttle away from quarrels like a rabbit from a gun, and Robin fussed more over the pregnancy than she did herself. Edith declared the child would be born in October, and their year's local leave being due Robin arranged for them to travel a month beforehand to Singapore, where his wife could enjoy the best obstetrical attention in south-east Asia. Edith was so excited about the trip that she had the trunks brought out to start packing a good fortnight before sailing. It was trying work in the heat and her back began to ache, but she was never given to complaining and told herself cheerfully a pregnant woman must tolerate a discomfort or two in the good cause. She suddenly felt exhausted, sent the cook-boy to make her a cup of tea, and collapsed in a wicker chair in the bare living-room. She felt something warm between her legs. Only when the flood of amniotic fluid drenched her dress did she realize things were seriously amiss. As badly befitted a girl once behind the cash-desk of a butcher's shop, Edith had made a mistake in her dates.

Robin was brought hurriedly from the dispensary. He had a sketchy experience of midwifery–his patients neither tolerated nor needed the interference of a stranger–but everyone else for hundreds of miles had even less. He gathered Edith up and moved her to the bedroom, issuing orders for boiling water, clean towels, and bottles of antiseptic. He left her on the bed with hasty expressions of reassurance, and hurried back to look up *Practical Obstetrics*. The schoolmaster couple were away on some expedition. The missionary's assistance he quickly ruled out. He wondered if he should pray for Divine guidance, but he decided there wasn't time, and anyway he hoped supernatural intervention wouldn't be necessary.

The labour was as uncomplicated as Edith herself. A few hours later, the professor was turning in his fingers at Hampstead a cable bringing the name of Alec Quentin Trevose into the family. Well, it was splendid enough, he thought sadly, but the grandsons underlined that his active life was nearing its end. He feared less his years pressing on him than his days, once he retired from Blackfriars and had nothing to call him daily from the house. His marriage had brought some wearisome complications. His wife, though companionable, was not intellectually stimulating. His new stepdaughter had refused to move in, found another job, and sought the roof of an aunt in Southsea. Aunt Doris simply refused to speak to him. And the second Mrs Trevose was alarmingly extravagant. She had already redecorated the house and herself out of recognition. She also insisted on doubling the servants, on one of whom she discovered the professor demonstrating the bony origin and insertion of the *gastrocnemius* muscle in the calf.

'But, my dear,' he complained pathetically, 'the girl had hurt her ankle. I was only trying to calm her by explaining exactly what went wrong.'

'You keep your hands off young women,' snapped Mrs Trevose.

The professor looked shocked. 'You must please remember that I am a medical man. The human body is my rightful province.'

'Don't give me that! You're always pawing and fondling girls, rubbing yourself up against them when you get half a chance. Why, the way you interfered with my Sybil! Disgusting, it was.'

'How can you say such a thing?' cried the professor, though with more pathos than conviction.

'It's as plain as a barn door. You should see some of the looks behind your back when we're out, in shops and that. You'll get run in one day if you don't mend your ways, you just mark my words.'

The professor was saddened. He really didn't think anyone ever noticed at all.

Chapter Eighteen

Graham found the burden of fatherhood lay lightly on him. Maria took control of his son as she took control of everything else. His longest contact with the lad lasted for half an hour each evening, when Desmond was presented in a state of abnormal cleanliness by the crisp-aproned nurse. But the dramatic birth of the child had a dramatic effect on the mother. Desmond left Maria feeling the fragility of her own life. For the first time she realized that death must be allowed into the scheme of things. She pondered over it deeply and morosely, confiding in no one, not even Graham, any more than she had over her sexual shortcomings. She turned for comfort to works of philosophy (religion she dismissed as too frivolous). She entertained little, and withdrew from half her committees. Some days she became totally introverted, sitting for hours on the drawing-room sofa as she did when pregnant, staring before her. Graham asked himself if some subtle change had occurred in her endocrine system, possibly some minute thrombosis in her pituitary gland. Whatever it was, a shade had been drawn over her personality and life in Great Ormond Street became chillier. He began to wonder how Edith was these days.

The London season Maria now preferred to spend by the sea in isolation–apart from four maids, the cook from London with a couple of girls in the kitchen, nurse and nursery-maid, and a few gardeners. Seeing no reason why her own child shouldn't enjoy the same fresh air provided for the beneficiaries of the Sunshine Fund (who were dispatched once a year in relays to take a day's ration of it at Southend), she bought a house in Cornwall overlooking Falmouth Bay where she took Desmond from June to September. Graham joined them for a week or two, killing the long days painting the view and tracing his ancestors, delighting to find in the nearby churchyard sloping so prettily towards the setting sun that many of the headstones where the fat gulls dozed belonged to his kin. It amused him to discover that other adventurous Cornishmen were recorded as meeting their end through drowning, gunfire, or fever in distant lands, while his family always seemed to die in their beds. He supposed they were naturally lucky, the one quality essential for the successful doctor if never for the good one. The rest of the year he busied himself at St Sebastian's, writing papers for the medical journals, lecturing whenever he had a chance, and generally making a name for himself. Maria read every word before it was printed or uttered.

In 1924 Maria took Desmond to Cornwall early, declaring that the crowds jostling for the British Empire Exhibition at Wembley made London doubly impossible. Graham doubted if he could travel down before August. His father was doing as well as expected after prostatectomy in the hands of Sir Horace Barrow, but the cells in the histologist's section had shown large dark nucleae, the malignant eyes of cancer. If a crisis occurred, diplomacy might be needed as much as surgery–he doubted if Aunt Doris and his stepmother would speak even if adrift in the same lifeboat. Anyway, his presence in London during July was essential. He seemed likely to achieve so youthfully the ambition of his life, a consultancy in plastic surgery at Blackfriars.

He admitted freely it was Maria's doing. If Graham wanted a department of plastic surgery at Blackfriars, she would create one. She sought the aid of Val Arlott, whose *Daily Press* then struck its readers as less of a newspaper than a Santa Claus insisting on Christmas every day of the year. Any of them wishing to insure against their deaths or against the loss of bits of themselves meanwhile, to refurnish their houses with six-piece suites of fumed oak, to own the new Austin Seven, to read Dickens and Shakespeare from beginning to end, or to holiday in the millionaires' playground of Biarritz, had simply to register as a regular subscriber and try one of the paper's amusing and untaxing competitions. If the prizes were less often fumed oak and the company of millionaires than the works of Dickens, Val Arlott bought literature in bulk and showed a profit on the transaction.

Maria's idea tickled him. Therefore, it would tickle his public. He would start a campaign for this wonderful new science to be established in a great hospital in London–it was a public disgrace no such unit existed–he would raise funds, get important people interested. And what better institution to house the centre of healing than Blackfriars, hardly a newsboy's shout from the *Press*'s own offices?

But Blackfriars was not a stable for everyone's gift horses. Though younger than St Bartholomew's at Smithfield, whose walls were already ancient when darkened by the fires of Bloody Mary's martyrs, it was a City institution like the Old Bailey. It was backed by the shrines of the nation's liberties in Fleet Street, flanked by the repository of its legal wisdom in the Temple, fronted by the soft-running if no longer sweet Thames, and had the Church of England embodied in the bold redoubtable dome of St Paul's looking over its shoulder. It was controlled jealously by its board of governors, the State not presuming to meddle with the health of its citizens, beyond seeing their water was clean and they didn't catch smallpox too often. As the governors were City worthies knowing nothing of medical technicalities, their power had as usual in great and lazy institutions fallen into the hands of the four most pushful professionals. These were Dr Wedderburn, who had consigned Graham to his grave, Sir Horace Barrow, who resembled a retired prize-fighter with a good tailor, Maria's obstetrician Mr Harold Berkeley, who resembled an actor with an even better tailor, and Mr Cramphorn, a clipped-moustached, pipe-smoking, short-statured surgeon, given to pepper-and-salt suits, half-moon glasses, elastic-sided brown boots, and enigmatic grunts.

The *Daily Press* was not the sort of newspaper these four enjoyed reading, or at least enjoyed being seen reading. They feared a 'stunt'–a horrible ravishment of the hospital's dignity.

'I suppose we could preclude any distasteful advertising at our expense,' Sir Horace decided. 'The lawyers might draw up something to that effect. I don't think we should reject the offer out of hand. After all, money's money.'

The other three agreed. But they feared even more a plastic unit would upset the delicate balance of surgical power in the hospital. Sir Horace, backed by Dr Wedderburn, felt strongly that the cause of many chronic diseases which irritated the human frame–things like headache and rheumatism–though admittedly totally unknown, lay somewhere among the churning coils of the patient's gut. It was perfectly logical. Such problems were traditionally ascribed to intractable constipation, and Sir Horace had cut the Gordian knot by slicing out the colon. But relief unfortunately evading both him and the sufferer, he now chased higher and higher up the alimentary canal in pursuit of this elusive mischief, removing more and more of the intestines until he seemed in danger of being the first surgeon to perform tonsillectomy from below.

Mr Cramphorn was a 'pexy' man. He believed these baffling complaints, in which he included dysmenorrhea and migraine for Mr Berkeley's benefit, sprang from undisciplined organs straying from the sites ordained by God and anatomy and careering round the belly like sailors on a Saturday night. Every morning he performed splenopexy by tacking the errant spleen sternly into place with strong catgut, or nephropexy by suspending floating kidneys from the last rib like monkeys on a stick. The hospital was finely divided over the merits of these two panaceas, and the new plastic surgeon would swell one camp or another.

But Mr Berkeley depicted the problem as more complicated still.

'If we *don't* accept a plastic unit,' he said, lighting another of his Turkish cigarettes, 'we shall be under irresistible pressure to start one in neurosurgery, or thoracic surgery, or some such. These specialized departments are springing up everywhere nowadays like asparagus.'

It was a telling point. A nerve surgeon or a chest surgeon would steal everyone's glory by inventing his own operations for rheumatism and headaches. But the interference of a plastic surgeon could never be more than skin deep.

'If we do have a plastic unit, then who will be our plastic surgeon?' asked Sir Horace.

'Trevose's boy, of course,' grunted Mr Cramphorn. 'He's going great guns at St Sebastian's.'

'He's very well off,' murmured Mr Berkeley.

This was another consideration. Graham wouldn't take more than his fair share of the precious beds in the private block. The doctors had to live as well as the patients.

'The post must be properly advertised, naturally,' declared Sir Horace sternly. 'It would be most irregular otherwise. There must be no suspicion of favouritism.'

'No, none at all,' the others agreed.

As the surgeon was to be installed before the building, the post was advertised by early summer in the medical journals and *The Times*. All aspirants had to provide each of the hundred or so established consultants with a *curriculum vitae*, printed at their own expense. It was Blackfriars' practice, impressing candidates with the solemnity of trying to join such a majestic institution at all and, like an election deposit, scaring off the more faint-hearted or eccentric ones. The short-list interviews were fixed for the last week in July, and Graham was requested to attend.

Three days beforehand Maria sent a telegram announcing she was coming home. Graham was alarmed. He met her at Paddington to find her pale and agitated, trembling beside him in the car. He thought she was ill, his mind automatically searching for a diagnosis.

'No, I'm perfectly well,' she said firmly. 'And so is Desmond.' The child had been left in Cornwall. 'It's my father. He wishes to see me. He's coming to the house in half an hour.'

It was beyond Graham why the rendezvous should be so shattering–he never presumed to pry into the Cazalay family affairs. Lord Cazalay arrived punctually, hurrying into the house alone. It was the first time Graham had seen him unaccompanied, his habit being to plough through life like a battleship, screened by escorts. He was scowling as usual, and hardly noticed his son-in-law. He took Maria into the study and locked the door.

'Something's gone wrong,' Maria told Graham when her father left an hour later.

He frowned. 'Is he ill?'

'No, no!' she cried impatiently. 'All the disasters of life aren't bodily ones.' She paused, biting her lip. 'We're ruined. Penniless.' Graham looked at her blankly. 'Oh, it's a long story. I don't understand half of it. It goes back to the war. Everything seems to have crashed all of a sudden.'

'When will this get out?' he asked impulsively. 'In the newspapers? It would never do, not before I go up for the interview at Blackfriars.'

'My God!' she shouted angrily. 'Is *that* all you worry about?'

She left the room, slamming the door. Graham couldn't believe her. For Lord Cazalay to come down in the world was like Lord Nelson crashing into Trafalgar Square. She had been running through bouts of depression recently, and brooding alone in Cornwall had done her no good. He should have made the effort of travelling down for a week. But he fancied she had left the room crying, for the first time since he had known her.

The next three days were crammed with confusion. Men Graham had never seen before kept appearing at the house with heavily-sealed envelopes for Maria. Whatever they contained she kept to herself, hardly sparing a word for him at all, refusing all soothing by drugs or words. The afternoon of his interview at Blackfriars she hardly noticed he had quit the house.

The candidates had to wait on hard chairs outside the hospital committee-room, in an anteroom where the staff left their hats and coats. It was a bare apartment, decorated only with a board showing the day's operations and post-mortems, penned in elaborately handwritten lists like the menus outside French restaurants. Graham hated the room. He had waited there often enough as a student, and it always meant something unpleasant was going to happen, even if it was only meeting his father, who always left committees in a bad temper. He found one candidate waiting already.

'Hello,' Graham greeted Eric Haileybury. 'I heard you were putting in for the job.'

Haileybury was wearing a severe blue serge suit and holding a grey trilby hat on his knees with bony red hands. His fair hair was thinning, and Graham thought he showed the five years since their last meeting. But he remembered the man always affected a seniority beyond his age. He wondered absently why he always imagined the fellow shaved with cold water, a blunt razor, and carbolic soap.

Haileybury inclined his head. 'I think I owe you belated congratulations, Trevose. On your marriage.'

'Oh, thank you.' Graham gave a nervous laugh. He felt it hardly the best time to receive them. 'I hope they are congratulations I can reciprocate?'

But it appeared that wedded bliss had evaded his fellow-surgeon.

Graham sat down. There was a silence. 'You're at the Radcliffe Infirmary, aren't you?'

'Yes. Officially I'm doing orthopaedics. There're no plastic beds, of course. It's very much a little country town hospital. The ancient university, I fear, turns up its distinguished nose at anything more vulgarly useful than Latin and Greek. But I'm managing to apply a good deal I learnt during the war. Thiersch grafts to heal up old osteomyelitis, bone grafts in general, pedicles for burns, or for any sort of tissue-loss after injury. It's really remarkable the number of casualties being caused by motor-cars.'

The warmth they felt for their common subject began to melt the ice. 'I'm doing work on wrist pedicles.' Graham demonstrated, moving his wrist from his stomach to his forehead. 'You raise a pedicle of skin from the abdominal wall, like we did in the old days. You attach it to the wrist till it takes. Then up goes the wrist and you fix the free end to the face, or wherever you want it.'

'What happened to the Saracen?'

'He escaped to France. Beyond that I've heard nothing.'

Haileybury gave his thin smile. 'He's probably making a fortune lifting the faces of these fast-living Frenchwomen.' He fiddled with the brim of his hat, and went on, 'This is all a formality, isn't it, Trevose? The job's booked for you.'

'Of course it isn't.' Graham sounded indignant. 'The committee will pick who they fancy.'

'Oh, come, Trevose! Everyone knows your wife got that newspaper to drum up the money. If you *don't* get it, I can only say it will be a gross miscarriage of justice.'

Graham's irritated denial was scotched by the arrival of the other candidates–two assistants of Gillies and Pomfret Kilner and a sallow, moustached, middle-aged surgeon from Manchester no one had heard of. Graham folded his arms and stared straight ahead in silence. Life was too short, he told himself, to bother with its Haileyburys. Of course the job was his. He deserved it. Quite simply, because he was the better surgeon. Nobody spoke. The man from Manchester produced a penknife and nervously cleaned his nails. Haileybury blew his nose. The clock on the wall ticked away like a trip-hammer, irritating everyone.

Unhappily for Graham the selection committee's deliberations were more open-minded than they deserved. His life's ambition was in danger of frustration by the caecum. This inoffensive bulge of bowel near the appendix was the venue of a furious new battle between Sir Horace and Mr Cramphorn. Sir Horace fell upon the caecum with his scalpel like a tramp handed a hot dinner. Mr Cramphorn tacked it the firmer into place. The two men were hardly on speaking terms.

'The caecum,' Sir Horace had thundered over his lunch that very morning, 'lying at the extreme blind end of the colon, is a sump, a sewer for every intoxicant in the patient's faeces.'

'Nonsense,' disagreed Mr Cramphorn shortly. 'The caecum is to the colon as a breech-block to a gun. Without a breech-block both won't fire properly.'

'Balderdash,' said Sir Horace.

Meanwhile, patients with such disabilities as headaches and rheumatism had their caecums either totally extracted or embedded like foundation-stones, depending on which morning they happened to present themselves at Blackfriars for a consultation.

Haileybury was surprised after the usual questions to be invited to express views on the caecum. Should it be excised? asked Sir Horace. Or immobilized? demanded Mr Cramphorn. Haileybury said guardedly it depended on the experience of the surgeon. But Graham declared flatly the caecum should be left utterly alone, even delivering something of a lecture on interference with Nature by her surgical handmaidens. His departure was followed by a hostile silence. The half-dozen other doctors round the table were against him already, purely because he had money and influence. It is always sweet on committees to adopt high principles at someone else's expense.

After an hour's wrangling the only choice seemed the man from Manchester, a throat surgeon who had done no plastic surgery at all. Dr Wedderburn, the chairman, wisely adjourned for tea. Graham found himself alone in a teashop round the corner, his cup and sandwich untouched. This was serious. Supposing he was rejected? The job suddenly meant more than ever. He could hardly set up in Harley Street and keep a newly-impoverished Maria from his foothold at St Sebastian's. If they *were* impoverished. But the unthinkable to both himself and Lord Cazalay was with every moment becoming the feasible.

Luckily Dr Wedderburn unveiled after tea his monolithic argument–Trevose was a Blackfriars' man. This sobered the committee up. Moreover, his ailing father was a Blackfriars' professor, his brother and two uncles had walked their cherished wards. The hospital staff must stick together. Even Mr Cramphorn and Sir Horace agreed. Both had sons and nephews with ambitions along the same lines as Graham. They sent the secretary to summon him from the anteroom, where the clock had become deafening.

Graham reached home elated. In the hall he found a detective and two policemen, looking for Lord Cazalay. Maria was unashamedly in tears. When he tried to comfort her, he might have been a stranger. She never asked about Blackfriars. He suddenly felt disgusted with the whole Cazalay apparatus. What of them anyway? He had made use of them, he had got what he wanted. Now he was his own master, a consultant at Blackfriars, irremovable, irrefutable, irreproachable except in his own eyes. The detective left after furious writing in his notebook and Maria locked herself in the bedroom. Graham took his hat and quit the house.

He hailed a taxi in Southampton Row and gave an address in Pimlico. Brenda was at home, in her short skirts, her shocking nude-looking beige artificial silk stockings, her cigarettes of black tobacco and yellow paper, her holder eighteen inches long. Since Desmond's birth Maria had shut up sexual shop, and Graham had no urge to play the monk. He supposed Brenda was a 'bright young thing', while Maria was increasingly plainly neither. In many ways the girl reminded him of Edith. And Maria? She reminded him of his mother's photograph on the professor's mantelpiece. One day he really must settle down to a serious study of this fellow Freud.

Chapter Nineteen

The professor had come to smell worse than ever.

He had spent his second honeymoon in Brighton, at a hotel away from the sea-front chosen through the modesty in its accommodation, menus, and bills. It was the middle of February and bitterly cold, the sea leaping angrily to drench unseasonable intruders on the promenade. He thought the change would do him good. His wife felt even the provision of two separate piers poor compensation for the midwinter bleakness, which was liable to trigger off her rheumatism. And she was sleeping badly, through her new husband's habit of rising once or twice a night to make noises in the bedside chamber-pot. Mr Fanshaw certainly hadn't submitted her to such interruptions, but she supposed such things were normal in men, of whom he had exclusively provided her virtuous experience.

The professor's disability grew gradually worse. After a year or so he had trouble on cold mornings getting through his lectures, despite a hurried though often ineffective dash to the basement beforehand. Usually a wordy expounder of anatomical mysteries he began boiling down his wisdom, to the relief of both himself and his students. He hesitated submitting himself to professional advice. After all, the process was entirely natural. The book he opened on the subject gave him the philosophical balm of Sir Benjamin Brodie, the nineteenth-century surgeon at St George's–

'When hair becomes grey and thin, when atheromatous deposits invade the arterial walls, when there has formed a white zone about the cornea, at the same time, ordinarily–I dare say invariably–the prostate increases in volume.'

It was inescapable, the professor accepted. Though it was sad. Life was becoming gloomier, and his marriage instead of brightening it with forgotten joys made it even blacker with unremembered pains. It was poor comfort to learn that the affliction worried elderly retrievers just as badly.

His clinical crisis occurred almost six years to the day after Graham's in the bedroom next door. The flow had abruptly stopped and no effort, mental or physical, could restart it. The professor lay with a hot-water bottle clutched hopefully to his bursting abdomen, and Sir Horace Barrow was summoned from a City banquet. He was not surprised. His views on prostatic hypertrophy were summarized less elegantly than Sir Benjamin Brodie's with the dictum, 'By their boots ye shall know them', and for months he had noticed evidence of uriniferous dribbles on the professor's. He even felt relief the enlargement might account for the man's conduct, the unuttered scandal of the hospital. Only a week before the professor had come into Sir Horace's own wards on some anatomical pretext, and the nurse he had called behind a screen to assist his examination complained red-cheeked to the ward sister. The ward sister told her briskly she was imagining things. Such conduct was by definition impossible in a Blackfriars' man.

After the operation the professor fell as totally into the power of his wife as a baby. Catheterization had often to be performed, and he instructed her in the art. She was not a cheerful nurse, having certainly not bargained for this sort of complication to her marital duties. The professor began to remember bitterly the old London surgeon's nightly prayer, 'Lord, when Thou takest me do not take me through my bladder', and became more bad-tempered than ever.

'There's one or two matters we've got to go into,' his wife told him firmly one afternoon. 'The will, and that. After all, you never know, do you?'

The professor thought this in most questionable taste. He knew well enough from Sir Horace's guarded reassurance the cancer might recur, but prying into his private financial affairs on any pretext struck him as indelicate.

'Everything's in order,' he told her crossly. 'In apple-pie order. The relevant documents are safe with my solicitors.'

'That may well be. But I want to know how I stand, don't I? It's only right.'

'You stand very well indeed. Surely you can take my word for it?'

'Well! I don't know, really I don't. What are you keeping everything so secret for? Anyone would think I wasn't your wife but your woman.'

'The details are extremely complicated,' he told her hopefully. 'Only solicitors and such people can understand them.'

'I'm no fool, you know.' She patted the curls ringing the base of her neck. 'Fanshaw told me everything, every single thing. Like a gentleman.'

She dropped the subject, until the next occasion when the professor had to be catheterized. The following morning they went to his solicitor.

'I think it's scandalous!' she declared, once told the details. The estate was to be split three ways between Graham, Robin, and herself. 'What's Graham want the money for? He's rolling in riches. I come first, don't I? I'm your lawful wedded wife.'

The professor's brain was not the sharp organ of anatomical thought it once was. With the failing of his excretory apparatus the level of urea in his blood began to rise, leaving him fuddled, listless, and prone to headaches. He finally changed his bequests, mainly to get peace from her nagging, particularly during the catheterizations. His new will stood unaltered a week after Lord Cazalay's flight filled the newspapers, when the professor died in his brass bedstead, and in a bad temper. A lifetime of economy and shrewd investment had left no less than thirty thousand pounds. Graham and Robin were awarded a thousand apiece, the residue passing to his widow.

She set about the Hampstead house, where she was determined to live in a style compensatory to the victim of a double widowhood. The place was decorated over again, and all the medical books and medical furnishings thrown out for what they could fetch at an auction. She summoned Sibyl back from Southsea. Both mother and daughter agreed that the house during the professor's lifetime, with all those gruesome reminders of mortality scattered about, was enough to give any healthy woman the creeps.

Chapter Twenty

In 1930 Graham's new unit at Blackfriars was producing the goods with enough confidence to put some in the shop-window. A conference was arranged of plastic and throat surgeons from all over the country, with demonstrations of patients and operations. It was to be the finest moment of Graham's career.

It had taken him six years to find his feet at Blackfriars, which he decided was no better nor worse than any other big hospital. Its specialists gave the London poor the same care as the London rich–often better, any hospital at all outdoing the fashionable West End nursing homes with their small resources and large bills. The patients came mostly from Islington and Shoreditch in their shawls and their corduroys, burdened with their symptoms, their specimens, their strings of children, and often their unseen companions, against which the doctors ostentatiously buttoned themselves up in long white coats. The specialists treated the patients kindly, as Tolstoy's enlightened Dmitrich Levin treated his serfs. But their worlds could only possibly touch at the point of disease, and even this was thought more the doctor's possession than the patient's, few being considered intelligent or refined enough to be let into the secret of their maladies. Neither could the beneficiaries of free care expect the comforts of private patients, Blackfriars adding to the enfeeblement of illness the austerity of a workhouse and the discipline of a barracks. Apart from several hours' sitting on long hard benches in the reek of strong disinfectant before anything happened at all, the patients' inferiority was underlined by bullying porters and brusque sisters, insensitive after years of handling bemused humanity. They accepted it all with the stoicism of everything else in life. When half your street was on the dole, you had to.

The consultants ruled their little empires, rubbing shoulders as uneasily as the states of the prewar Balkans. As Sir Horace had foreseen, a plastic surgeon would be the odd man out, even something of a freak. Graham's self-centredness anyway made him a neutral in hospital politics. Even physically he was isolated in the new Arlott Wing, which had displaced the old hospital bakehouse, obliging its cockroaches and mice to seek alternative accommodation. He was unbothered by students, who saw no reason to waste time on plastic surgery, which was never asked in examinations. He shared a houseman with orthopaedics, but had a full-time registrar, Tom Raleigh, a short, dark, plump young man with tiny hands and feet, his mole-like appearance matched by the blind earnestness with which he followed Graham in everything. There was a sister in charge of the dozen beds, another in the theatre, and a mechanic with a lathe for turning out facial splints and prostheses. Graham did most of the sketching himself, but had called in a commercial photographer.

Graham's private practice was disappointing, most of the cases finding their way to established men like Gillies. This was awkward, because bank-managers shied away as though he were contaminated with the same financial leprosy as his father-in-law, who had disappeared with Lady Cazalay to Venezuela, a well-chosen destination from which it proved impossible to get them back. Graham had first mooted a loan to Dr Whitehead, but that experienced skater on thin ice skilfully cut a few delicate figures before dropping him into very cold water indeed. Then he found that impoverishment, like everything else in human experience apart from virginity, pregnancy, and death, was strictly comparative. True, they exchanged the Great Ormond Street house for a flat in Ladbroke Grove, the one in Cornwall was sold, the Crossley was replaced by a Morris Cowley, and the army of servants was demobilized, but his first impression that they would have to call on the Salvation Army for coal and hot soup proved exaggerated. There was an enormous 'scandal', of course, the tongues of London wagging like ears of wheat in a storm. But under darkening skies the shadow of the Cazalay family no longer fell on him, and he found it on the whole rather stimulating.

Maria herself was badly hurt in the crash. She rarely left the flat at all, except for taking Desmond every afternoon round the streets–Kensington Gardens, where she might cross paths with the nannies of former friends, was forbidden territory. She developed insomnia, and vague aches in the joints and abdomen, disastrous had they come to the attention of Sir Horace or Mr Cramphorn. Graham wisely treated her with small doses of aspirin and larger ones of sympathy. After all, she was now nearing forty-five and such symptoms might be expected.

The plastic surgery conference over which Graham had worked so hard and worried so much was to start on a Monday morning early in September. It was to be different from anything seen before. No one was to be bored, no one would miss a point. Graham would stage-manage the show with the panache of C.B. Cochran at the Palace Theatre. It was to be held in the eighteenth-century hall of Blackfriars, a stately apartment brought to life by the sweetest breath of English architecture, pillared, vaulted, and lined with the delicate tones of tight-packed leather-bound books. He arranged photographs and sketches with typed case-histories connected to their relevant points by coloured ribbons, everything as clear and as enjoyable to follow as the cutaway battleships and motor-cars in the *Illustrated London News*. At one end slides of interesting cases were displayed in stereoscopic viewing boxes, like those inviting seaside holidaymakers to share the butler's voyeurism. At the other was a screen for lantern slides and a lectern on the dais, which Graham mounted with some excitement to open the proceedings.

'My first case,' he explained, as the curtains were drawn and the lights lowered, 'is an unfortunate girl whose mammary appendages I can only describe as resembling in size and shape a pair of vegetable marrows.' He indicated with his pointer the lantern slide. 'If her physical discomfort was considerable, her mental discomfort was immeasurable. She was denied the sports for which the "modern girl" we hear so much about in the news-papers regularly half-undresses herself–swimming, tennis, sunbathing, and so on. And, far more sadly, courtship too. Can you imagine even Romeo bringing himself to fondle a Juliet equipped with monstrosities like these? Though admittedly, gentlemen, we must beware of accepting *any* plea for a reduction mammoplasty. A girl's fashions change. So do her young men. She may come back wishing to restore the *status quo*.'

There was a murmur of embarrassed laughter. From the start, Graham's exhibitionism struck a false note. The audience felt it hardly right referring to such things as breasts light-heartedly. After all, theirs was a stripling specialty, badly needing clothing in an outfit of dignity. General surgeons never spoke of the stomach except with the greatest solemnity.

Graham described an operation he had invented himself, the cutting out a wedge of fatty breast tissue like slicing an overripe orange. It was simple, surgically crude, and sometimes a failure, but it was a forerunner of more elaborate manipulations some fifteen years later when the female breast threatened to turn from a decoration to an obsession.

'May I end by impressing upon you, gentlemen,' declared Graham, 'the most important step of the operation occurs in the ward beforehand. It is then the site of the new nipple is measured and marked out with Bonney's blue. It must stand at the apex of a triangle, formed by a perpendicular running through the centre of the clavicle'–he demonstrated on his jacket–'and another line seven-and-a-half inches long, drawn from the suprasternal notch. Symmetry is everything, gentlemen. A lop-sided Venus de Milo would be more amusing than admirable.'

The lights went up. A door concealed in the bookcase opened behind him. His ward sister appeared with a brown-haired girl in a dressing-gown, which she silently slipped from her shoulders with the air of a prospective purchase in an ancient Oriental slave market.

'You see the transformation?' Graham exchanged a smile with his patient. 'I hope you will agree that these neater organs are as today favoured by dress-designers, emperors of the cinema, and other less drastic creators of the female shape than ourselves.'

The patient withdrew. Haileybury rose from his seat at the front.

Graham tightened his jaw. It was their first encounter since his rival had been appointed plastic surgeon to King Alfred's Hospital, an institution equally splendid as Blackfriars across the river. Doubtless he was anxious to make an impression.

'I think we would all congratulate you on an admirable result, Mr Trevose.' Learned heads nodded. 'But might I enquire precisely your indications for performing this type of operation at all?'

'Certainly, Mr Haileybury. You ask my indications. For the physiological enlargement of puberty–never. For a patient under twenty or over fifty–never. For chronic mastitis–I would advise total amputation. For any other healthy woman sufficiently deformed to demand it–always.'

Haileybury folded his large hands in front of him. He was still wearing his blue serge suit. Graham found himself wondering if it were the only one he owned, or if he bought them in job lots. 'Then it is always in your opinion a purely cosmetic procedure?'

Graham was ready for this. 'I think I would be unfair if I suggested you equated "cosmetic" with "trivial". You yourself must agree the mental and social benefits of the operation are tremendous.'

'The knife seems rather a drastic innovation in psychological treatment,' returned Haileybury dryly. 'Freud, Jung, Adler and such gentlemen are hardly renowned for their surgical skill.'

This caused a laugh. Mention of psychologists in gatherings of more practical doctors always had the effect of Mr Leslie Henson's appearance on the stage. Graham began to feel annoyed. The man seemed set on ruining his effects.

'As for social reasons,' Haileybury persisted, 'might I question the correctness of surgery straying into the province of the beauty-parlour?'

'The benefit of this operation is quite as great as that of gastroenterostomy to kill the pain of duodenal ulcer,' Graham told him shortly.

That was unwise. Gastroenterostomy, the by-passing of a troublesome duodenum, was less of a surgical procedure than a sacred rite. The operation was starting to busy the abdominal surgeons of the thirties, as much as the abdominal surgeons of the forties were busied dismantling it. Dissent broke from the audience. Graham bit his lip, but controlling himself announced, 'Gentlemen, we have hardly begun the day's proceedings. I think we can discuss such general questions more pleasantly over lunch. May I pass to the next case?'

The body of his lecture was less sensational. As he showed them his surgery of burns–a new branch, in which he had become intrigued–of fractures of the jaws, of injuries to the fingers, of Dupuytren's contracture closing up the palm, even Haileybury was denied ammunition for criticism. Finally Graham came to Miss Constantine.

She appeared through the bookcase door, tall, heavily boned, in a short frock, artificial silk stockings, cropped hair, and a hat with an enormous feather.

'Please inspect the patient, gentlemen.'

She posed a minute in silence, then disappeared.

'Perhaps you were struck by Miss Constantine's gait?' Graham suggested. 'She strode into my consulting-room like some huntswoman of the shires, though she had never mounted a horse in her life. I discovered she worked at a famous emporium in Oxford Street, behind the sports goods counter, where her athletic appearance was doubtless thought an asset. Now, gentlemen, I must reveal to you there is a disgraceful amount of flirting behind the scenes in such places. But Miss Constantine was not at all amused. She complained that even the most polished advances of the gentlemen floorwalkers simply embarrassed her. As for accepting their invitations to cinemas or dance-halls, the very idea was repulsive. She became worried, understandably enough. But worse was to follow. She found herself developing a strong romantic attachment to a girl in the millinery department.'

Graham called for a lantern slide.

'Observe, gentlemen, these genitalia. They are at a careless glance feminine, and the nameless practitioner who brought Miss Constantine into the world must have been very careless indeed. Look more carefully. This clitoris is in fact a penis, these *labia majora* an ill-developed scrotum. There are no *labia minora*, no hymen, no vagina.' He rapped for another slide. 'I operated on this deceptive state of affairs. You will see the organs are now undeniably male. I was glad to rectify an error of a somewhat fundamental nature.'

The lights went up. Through the door appeared a smiling, dark-haired youth in a double-breasted grey suit. 'Miss Constantine,' Graham added smugly, 'has become Mr Constantine. A fine figure of a man.'

As the patient left Haileybury was on his feet.

'I fear I cannot share your equanimity at changing a fellow human being's gender.'

'I did *not* change the sex,' Graham told him irritably. The man was a fool, thick-headed and thick-skinned. 'The patient has been male since conception.'

'But she had been brought up as a girl. You talked about the mental aspects of your surgery. I should imagine the psychological effects of the abrupt change highly detrimental.'

Mr McMannus rose beside him. He was short and fat with a squeaky voice, a throat surgeon who hated Graham with an intensity in the profession restricted to close colleagues at the same hospital. He was outraged at Graham's filching the broken noses, cleft palates, and hare-lips he thought his personal property. Worse still, Graham refused to recognize the new doctrine of 'septic foci'. The cause of the headaches and rheumatics had been transferred from lazy guts and errant kidneys to malevolent pockets of pus lurking all round the body, for which Mr Cramphorn rummaged the abdomen like an earnest Customs official and Mr McMannus cracked open sinuses with his hammer and chisel, or extracted teeth like shelling peas, particularly if the patient that morning came in with smelly breath.

'I feel it my duty,' the throat surgeon squeaked, 'to express my distaste at the manner the case was presented.'

'I found nothing in the slightest distasteful,' Graham told him shortly. 'The patient gave her willing consent. *His* willing consent,' he stumbled.

To relieve tension over the exchanges the audience laughed. It made Graham lose his temper.

'I may be somewhat old-fashioned,' continued Mr McMannus, drunk with the heady wine of righteous indignation, 'but I find such theatricality sadly out of place at Blackfriars.'

'If you cannot distinguish knowledge from dullness, then I'm sorry for your students.'

Mr McMannus glared. 'If we are here for an exchange of insults rather than an exchange of views, I withdraw.'

He sat down, to some applause. Graham saw he'd been a fool. 'I apologize,' he said hastily. 'I'm sure, with your great experience in the pathology of the tongue, you will agree that running away with itself is one of that organ's more desperate conditions.'

There was a sympathetic murmur, but the damage was done. Graham's authority was broken. Most of the assembly agreed with McMannus. The lecture was 'flashy', an insult to the austere intelligence of a medical audience. Besides, this young fellow Trevose was already getting himself a bad name for pushfulness. They nodded their heads. At what age was he appointed to Blackfriars? Less than thirty. Disgraceful! They all seemed to remember at once he had been linked with the infamous Saracen.

Graham decided to end the lecture. He left the hall without a word. He went straight to his room in the Arlott Wing, sitting alone in a mood of unbearable gloom. He had worked hard for originality, and the dunderheaded audience were blind to it. He compared himself tragically to Manet presenting the world with *Le Déjeuner sur l'Herbe*. It was all Haileybury's fault. He'd started them off. Graham felt the hospital was unbearable. Tom Raleigh could handle the afternoon demonstrations. He hurried out to his Alvis and drove to Queen Anne Street, where he had taken consulting rooms.

He wondered afterwards how he managed to drive through the London traffic without hitting anyone. He was preoccupied with the sickening realization that a fundamental belief in his life was wrong–the charm, humour, and fairly cynical flattery which had carried him so handsomely right from Maria's drawing-room lecture through countless awkward committees at Blackfriars was not enough. His skill as a surgeon was as genuine as his flair as a lecturer, and both had been sneered upon by a bunch of pompous, self-satisfied, haughty men encased in their own sense of importance like a limb immobilized in plaster of Paris. At least, Graham told himself bitterly, I'm not a hypocrite. I'm pushful, I suppose I'm selfish, I like the limelight, but I make no bones about it. Right! If they're going to look down on me as a flash Harry, an upstart, a moneymaker, I'll live up to their little expectations. I'll make a fortune out of face-lifting, let my burns and repair work go hang, and the lot will die painfully of ingrowing jealousy.

He arrived at his consulting rooms. His desperation for originality had led him to decorate them in Japanese style, so he greeted his patients alarmingly before a painted screen like some medical mikado.

'I didn't expect you,' exclaimed Kitty Rivers. She was a slight, fair girl in a white overall, his secretary. She studied his face and asked, 'What's wrong?'

'Oh, everything's wrong!' He fell into the chair behind his consulting desk. 'The meeting's a flop, a fiasco, even before it's started.'

'But how? You were so confident about everything.'

'I overestimated the intelligence of my audience.'

She put her arm round his shoulder. 'Oh, darling! I'm sorry.'

He took her hand eagerly. This was why he had hurried from the hospital, he supposed, to attract some sympathy. He sat in silence for a moment, then seeing no point in doing things by halves asked, 'Can't we go round to the flat?'

She shrugged her sharp shoulders. 'But, darling . . . I mean, it's broad daylight, with patients buzzing about everywhere. Someone you know might easily see us. Someone from Blackfriars.'

'I don't give a damn who sees us. Not today, anyway.'

As he fell silent again, she added in her meek voice, 'I loathe this hole-and-corner business as much as you do.'

'Now please! Don't start that all over again.'

Kitty bit her lip. She never dared argue with him about anything, from a slip in the appointments book to the relationship which had grown in the little garden of her life to over-shadow everything else. 'I wasn't really starting anything *again.*'

'Weren't you? Well, there's no point anyway. You know the situation perfectly well. I'll leave Maria as soon as I can. I've told you dozens of times, haven't I? I'd leave her today if I could. I can't, and that's all there is to it. Surely you don't imagine I *want* to go on living with her?'

'But *can't* you get a divorce?' She looked down at him imploringly. 'It wouldn't hurt your practice. I'm sure it wouldn't, darling. Everyone's getting divorces these days.'

'Oh, it's more complicated than that. Maria's a sick woman. And there's the boy.'

'Of course, I appreciate the difficulties.'

It irritated him when she made herself pathetic–it was the only effective weapon in the pasteboard armoury of her personality. 'We've got to be patient. You can't switch one marriage off and another on, you know, like the electric light.'

She brought herself to put something terrible into words. 'I suppose there isn't anyone else, Graham? I mean apart from Maria?'

'Don't be stupid.'

'You really went to Paris alone?'

Graham lost his temper for the second time. 'Why do you keep on about it? I went to Paris alone to sell some pictures. I didn't. I came back again. Still alone.'

'I just wondered, that's all.'

Her capacity to sound totally crushed enraged him more. 'Well, don't wonder. I don't like people wondering about my activities. Now leave me in peace, for God's sake. I want to think.'

It really was being a most trying morning.

Chapter Twenty-one

Graham had taken Jean Dixon to Paris, and it had been a dreadful failure.

Jean was a red-headed, green-eyed cockney, who had been proudly started at art school one year and sadly withdrawn the next, when her father, in the building trade, was crushed into bankruptcy by the depression. She thought herself lucky to find a job with a West End photographer, a young man Graham had once treated for some minor blemish, which led to her appearing at Blackfriars to take pictures of the patients. Graham soon asked her to dinner at the Savoy, and noticed she ate like a horse.

After a few weeks he supposed she was a tart, more or less. She seemed to have plenty of men friends and plenty of presents. He felt a trip to Paris a reasonable *quid pro quo*, for it seemed not only risky but indelicate inviting her to the little flat near his consulting rooms in the engineered absence of the mistress-in-residence. Besides, Paris was romantic, as everyone knew. And he had been overseas only once since his honeymoon, the Cazalay family not being keen on 'abroad'. He had accompanied Maria and her mother to Venice, a dreadful crawl by railway across the roasting face of Europe, with Lady Cazalay devastated by everything from palpitations to the incomprehensibility of ticket-collectors, both of which she expected Graham instantly to rectify. Venice itself had been hot and smelly, his painting things had been lost on the way, and Lady Cazalay's family were exquisitely impolite to him.

First he'd had to break the news about Paris to Maria.

'It's a bore going all alone,' he complained, 'but I don't suppose you feel up to the trip.'

'Paris? I must have been hardly a girl when I was last there.' Maria sighed. She was spending another day in bed. Her headaches and pains now conspired with fits of depression to poison her with feelings of inadequacy for life, so she simply retired from it between the sheets. Graham's modestly rising affluence ran to a cook and a maid, who between them looked after Desmond and shuttled him to day-school round the corner. They had moved from Ladbroke Grove to a terrace house in Primrose Hill, a tall, poky place with steep stairs, a narrow hall floored with cracked tiles, and a front-door which borrowed gay patterns from the sun through a panel of gaudy stained glass. He recalled this afterwards as his 'suburban phase', and had even equipped himself with suburban trappings–a dog, a cabinet radiogram, and a lawn mower, which he pushed on one or two occasions.

'I remember the underground railway stations in Paris,' Maria reminisced. 'All curly green ironwork, like some strange sort of plants growing out of the pavements. There was a ball at the British Embassy, and several of the girls fainted. It was a terribly hot night. I suppose we all dressed so unsuitably in those days. I met Clemenceau, a kind-looking old man, nothing tigerish about him at all.'

'Clemenceau–another qualified doctor,' Graham told her. He was wondering if Jean had a passport.

'Was he? Didn't he die last year? These days I can't remember who's alive and who's dead. Where shall you be staying?'

He mentioned a small hotel out at the Porte Maillot–'After all, I'm on my own.' She was shocked he had overlooked the Crillon. He had noticed for some time how the focus of her mind was falling more and more sharply on the past.

Jean Dixon was at first girlishly excited by French sounds and smells, the racing taxis, the musical-comedy policemen, the tables on the pavements, the stuttering advertisements for Dubo . . . Dubon . . . Dubonnet, the poster of the lugubrious Nicolas man with his fists sprouting dozens of bottles–the sudden, breathtaking, dirty Paris of the Gare du Nord, memorable for ever. The trouble really began with the cockroach in the bidet. The whole hotel frightened her. It was tall, gloomy and airless, with ill-painted shutters, smelling like a museum, its windows apparently incapable of opening without a set of joinery tools. Graham telephoned down about the cockroach, but nobody understood the French he had been painfully learning from the Berlitz booklets. Then he developed gastroenteritis.

It must have been something he had eaten on the boat–he suspected the ham had definitely turned. It necessitated an urgent and colicky search for a *pharmacie* stocking the only trustworthy remedy known to British travellers, the intestinal equivalent of Keating's Powder, the famous Dr Collis Browne's Chlorodyne. The shop produced only the mockery of a bottle of Eno's Fruit Salts, until Graham finally found it stocked by a smart chemist's in the Rue du Faubourg St Honoré, rather as the smart bars in the neighbourhood stocked Scotch whisky. He swallowed the opiate mixture with glasses of neat brandy, feeling the alcohol might sterilize the interior of his gut, or at least make him appear more cheerful. But it was a sadly unromantic disability.

Still, Jean tackled the Louvre with the same youthful enthusiasm as she tackled the *marrons glacés*, and they both agreed the Mona Lisa was ridiculously overrated. His excuse for being in Paris at all was selling a few of his paintings, but art-dealers on the banks of the Seine seemed as insensitive to his talents as their counterparts beside the Thames. One blunt fellow, an Englishman Graham met long ago in the sanatorium, even described his work as 'distinctly amateurish'. He was hurt. He was as proud of his canvases as of his operations, which could hardly be shown off to impress his friends.

The essential part of the excursion was even more devastating. On the first occasion he threw himself at young Jean so eagerly he suffered *ejaculatio praecox*, which was quite a social embarrassment, as he really knew her only very slightly. On the next he had taken either too much cognac or too much chlorodyne, for the opposite occurred. He had never suffered before the dreaded students' condition of 'whisky prick'. He lay wondering if he were already too old for such adventures. He pictured his endocrine glands, the cherry-like pituitary below the brain, the bilobed thyroid embracing the windpipe, the neat adrenals capping his kidneys, the twin plums of the testes themselves–was the whole constellation cooling down from blazing suns to sterile planets? But he was only thirty-five, dammit! he consoled himself. And it always seemed to work with Kitty Rivers.

Most depressing of all, he met the Saracen. Graham never discovered how the surgeon knew he was in Paris. He simply appeared at the hotel, his fat cheeks sagging, his clothes untidy, his cigar replaced by pungent Gitanes. The three of them went to a café and drank Pernod, the American seeming to accept the redhead as too natural to require comment. It appeared the French were no more eager than the British to recognize his qualifications and he had given up surgery for finance, for which he felt an equal flair, until the Wall Street crash had put an end to that career as well.

'I guess you'd call me a retired man.' He opened and closed his pudgy fist. 'Though I still feel the itch to use the knife, almost every day. Maybe they'll let me give them a hand at the American Hospital at Neuilly, if I ask nicely enough. I've something left to offer humanity, even now.' He stared at the milky liquid in his glass. 'But I've been misunderstood too often to care much any more.'

He cheered up as they explored with rose-tinted lamps the caverns of the past, remarking in a low voice only as they broke up, 'And Maria?'

'She's in rather poor health these days, I'm afraid.'

'I'm sorry. Please convey my regards. It was too bad about her father.' He paused. 'The lady must think herself very fortunate, having married a gentleman with a profession.'

'That man!' said Graham bitterly, undressing for bed. 'He has brains, skill, imagination–the same imagination that brought Morton to use ether or Harvey to discover the circulation of the blood. And what happened to him? He was beaten. By snobbishness, small-mindedness, envy, greed, and arrogance. Instead of enriching the stream of human happiness, his talents were deliberately thrown out like dirty water. My God! They might as well have chopped Rembrandt's arms off.'

Jean was lying naked on the bed, eating Swiss liqueur chocolates and reading the *Continental Daily Mail*. She made no reply. She never understood half that Graham said to her. Of course, as she told her friends, he was terribly brainy, by which they understood she meant he was terribly dull. She often wondered if he behaved as oddly with his wife.

Chapter Twenty-two

'I'm in a mess,' Graham told John Bickley.

The anaesthetist looked up from the menu. 'Oh, there you are. I was just going to order. I thought you'd been trapped by that jamboree of yours at Blackfriars.'

Graham smoothed the black tie against the points of his dress-collar. 'The governors are giving a reception, but I got away on some excuse or other.' It was the evening of the first disastrous day of the plastic surgery conference, but after his rebuff of the morning Graham was already losing interest in the cherished project. 'It's good of you to come along at a couple of minutes' notice, old man. I simply had to talk to someone.'

John put another Abdulla in his cigarette-holder. 'What about?'

'Women.'

'Oh, dear.'

'It's serious.'

'In that case, you need a drink first. The sidecars they make here are excellent.'

They were in a small, underground, smoke-filled restaurant in Soho, as yet 'undiscovered', but where, John explained, on a clear day you could often see as far as Tallulah Bankhead. He was doing pretty well. Since the war anaesthetists had transformed themselves from seedy practitioners creeping in their surgeons' shadows, a bottle of chloroform in one tail pocket of their coat and a scrap of lint in the other, frequenters of coroners' courts and merchants of death rather than passing oblivion. With the growing complexity of both surgery and their own apparatus they were becoming respectable specialists entitled to ten per cent of the operation fee, which allowed John Bickley to lead a life of bachelor ease with a Green Label Bentley, chambers rather than rooms, and even a manservant. As he administered most of Graham's anaesthetics they had become close friends. They saw too much of each other's mistakes to be otherwise.

After the cocktails they ordered the six-shilling dinner. They had decided to be extravagant.

'Do you know about Kitty Rivers?' asked Graham, coming to the point. 'I never confessed I'd installed her in a flat near my rooms, round the corner in Marylebone High Street.'

'I'd be the only qualified man in London who didn't know about it.'

Graham shrugged his shoulders. He always hoped his misdeeds would be somehow overlooked by the world, like his father.

'Well, it was better than her own place, over a sweet-shop in Shepherd's Bush. You could only get upstairs through the shop, which was always full of the most horrible-looking and extremely inquisitive children, buying humbugs.'

John summoned the wine waiter.

'Do you know, Kitty was my secretary for an entire year before anything in the slightest shaming happened,' Graham went on. 'I remember selecting her for that fair, well-scrubbed look. I thought it would lend an appropriately hygienic air to the waiting-room.' He tipped a glass of sherry into his turtle soup. 'She also struck me as having an amenable, undominating personality. That's her strongest weapon. She keeps imploring me pathetically to kick out Maria and marry herself.'

John Bickley smiled. 'There's a tendency for this complication to set in, Doctor.'

'But how can I?' exclaimed Graham. 'Apart from anything else, it would play hell with my practice. Far too many people know Maria's more or less bedridden. You can't keep these things quiet. Though I try. I'm rather ashamed of Maria, I think. What do you imagine our nose-in-the-air brethren would say if I abandoned her? And I can't afford to drop a guinea. I'm living beyond my income as it is. I got used to having money, before the Cazalay business. It's always been damn difficult doing without it.'

John nodded. Anaesthetists, who serve many masters, are the profession's gossipmongers like Shakespeare's servants. He had a fine sense of the monetary value of scandal.

'Besides, there's Desmond,' Graham added, as an afterthought. He swallowed his glassful of burgundy in three gulps. 'I've a clear conscience over Kitty, mind you. I deserve some fun. You can't live without love, can you? No more than you can cook without salt. God knows, I don't get much of a ration of it at home.' As the waiter refilled his glass he promptly emptied it. John's idea about a drink was a good one. 'That's how it all started, you know–Kitty being beautifully sympathetic to me about Maria's disabilities. Peculiar.'

'How long's Kitty been going on about marriage?'

'Oh, months. Why do people keep talking so airily about divorce these days? It's the cinema, I suppose. They aren't easy, not at all. I went to a solicitor once, just to keep her quiet. Maria would have to divorce *me*. And she doesn't even know of Kitty's existence. Just imagine how I'd introduce *that* topic into the conversation.'

'And are you in love with Kitty?'

Graham shrugged his shoulders. 'I don't know. I don't know if I'm in love with Maria, either. I've never known if I've been in love with anyone. Perhaps I've an inborn immunity to the condition, as some people have for tuberculosis. I can't give love, and, what's worse, I can't receive it. That's what makes me so cold and callous in the eyes of a lot of people. Perhaps I'm a bit schizophrenic–emotional blunting, you know the thing. Anyway, it's all come to a head. I took a girl I met in a photographer's studio over to Paris. I suppose Kitty's found out. It's terribly worrying. Yes, I suppose I must love Kitty. I wouldn't care otherwise, surely?'

John laughed. 'Really, Graham! Look yourself in the face. One woman's much the same as another to you, isn't she? As long as she's got a vagina in working order, you're happy.'

'Perhaps so. We're a terribly randy family.' He sounded self-pitying, as if describing some sad congenital affliction. At least, he told himself, he had insight into his faults. He couldn't help what Nature had made of him. If only people would *understand*. 'But what's the odds? I've got to stay and look after Maria. Though she doesn't want a solicitous husband. Rather a solicitous doctor. Do you know why I picked Maria in the first place? It wasn't the money, or the kudos, or all that. I wanted a mother-substitute.'

'Oh, steady! Let's keep Freud out of it. You've enough on your hands as it is.'

'But it's true,' Graham told him seriously. 'Now she's my poor sick mother, I'm giving her all due devotion and running after girls my own age. How can I sort the mess out? I've my brother and his wife coming home on leave this month, too. That's another story I won't go into,' he ended despondently.

'We must do a lot more drinking. Then the answer will come to us,' John decided cheerfully. 'Brandy's a wonderful cerebral stimulant.'

After the meal and the brandy he suggested to Graham, 'Would you like to go on to a bottle party?'

'What's that?'

'They're all the thing just now. People can't afford to give parties because of the depression. You bring your own bottle and in you go.'

'All right. I'm game.'

The bottle party was in a top-floor room in Pont Street, with sloping ceilings and cuboid furniture. As most of the men and girls were wearing pyjamas it was apparently a pyjama party as well, which Graham supposed too was all the thing. He also supposed he was rather drunk. He had no idea who the hostess was, nor any of the guests either. He found himself on a divan covered with a leopard-skin rug, talking to a pyjamaed girl wearing not only the newly fashionable long, pink-painted finger-nails but–he observed with intense fascination–painted toenails as well. She asked him what he did for a living, and he said he was a bank manager.

There was a gramophone on the divan, which he wound up to play Bobbie Howes and Binnie Hale singing 'Spread a Little Happiness'. Everyone was making too much noise to notice. He took the record off, and somehow broke it in two. The girl with the toenails giggled and handed him another. He joined in the vocal himself, shouting very loudly and tunelessly, 'I lift up my finger and I say, "Tweet tweet, shush shush, now now, come come!"' As he tried to change the needle he was surprised to find the manoeuvre beyond him, spilling the little tin of bright metal spicules all over the floor. He began to feel terribly ill. He never drank much, but they had bought a bottle of whisky and another of Gimlet, and they felt they might as well enjoy their entrance-fee.

He lay back on the leopard-skin with his eyes shut. When the girl with the toenails asked if he was all right he felt disinclined to reply. Somebody got John Bickley, who like all anaesthetists–possibly through daily contact with gusts of powerful narcotics–had an inhuman resistance to alcohol. John got him down the stairs. Graham insisted he wanted to go to a night club. John found a taxi and took him instead to his own front door, where Graham remembered to ask, 'What about Kitty? What do we do about Kitty?'

'Give her a nice diamond bracelet and tell her to go to hell.'

'And what about Jean?' Graham asked soulfully. 'I can't leave little Jean.'

'Little girls who work in photographers' studios aren't lonely for long.'

Graham burst into tears.

The next he knew it was the morning. He woke aware of three unfortunate facts.

He was lying on the bed in his own room wearing his dress-clothes and patent-leather shoes. He remembered being sick on the stairs. And the maid was disclaiming a Mr Haileybury wished to see him in the hall. He groaned.

'I'm sorry I'm not shaved,' Graham greeted Haileybury bad-temperedly, appearing in a dressing-gown after hastily splashing his face with cold water from the washing-jug. 'I don't usually expect visitors at this hour.'

Haileybury was standing holding his grey trilby, in a trench-coat wet about the shoulders. From somewhere inside he silently drew a copy of the *Daily Press*.

'I get this newspaper myself, you know,' said Graham shortly. He took the copy, noticing on the front page,

WOMAN INTO MAN
LONDON DOCTOR'S FEAT

'Then possibly you have already enjoyed reading the middle pages?'

Graham ripped open the paper. There were two photographs, one of Miss Constantine holding a bouquet of flowers, another of Mr Constantine holding a golf club. The columns of type in between seemed to cover her confusing past, her eventful present, and her hopeful future as a husband and father.

'You must forgive me for thinking such self-advertisement quite disgraceful, Trevose. Though I don't think I shall be the only one.'

'My God, man! Surely you don't suppose I had any inkling the rubbish was to appear? The newspapers are always getting their hands on these titillating little stories. They paid Constantine handsomely, I have no doubt.'

'Your name is mentioned.'

'What of it? *I* can't help it. The *Press* must have thought it of public interest.'

'I should be more inclined to believe you were you not a close friend of the paper's proprietor.'

This was too much, especially on such a morning. Graham's head hurt terribly. 'If you want to call me a liar, please do it in as many words, then leave me in peace, for God's sake.'

'A liar is not something I would lightly call any man. It just strikes me as an unhappy coincidence that you should owe your position at Blackfriars to Arlott.'

'You've got the wrong end of the stick. Quite the wrong end. Barrow and the others insisted from the start that Arlott renounced any right to interfere with the unit or the appointment of its staff. *Or* to use it for any sort of advertising. There's a document to that effect. If you still think I'm lying, I'll have the governors' clerk bring it to you by lunchtime.'

Haileybury said nothing. Then his humourless smile appeared. 'That won't be necessary. I only wish I had known of this document's existence when we faced the appointment committee together. It would have given me more heart.' He turned towards the front door. 'I shall not be attending the conference any further, Trevose. I did not wish my absence to go unexplained. I will bid you good morning.'

What a fool the man is! Graham told himself, hurrying upstairs to shave. What a priggish, sanctimonious ass! But a dangerous fool, always lurking to do a mischief. He must himself that very morning write to the medical journals, plainly disclaiming foreknowledge of the article in the *Daily Press* and seeking protection for the profession from such abhorred publicity. Val Arlott had strongly advised such a course when they had discussed the case of Miss Constantine together the week before.

Chapter Twenty-three

On the third Sunday morning of September Robin's family arrived at Primrose Hill via Tilbury and Fenchurch Street Station, with the same white-stencilled tin trunks strapped to the roof of the cab. Robin had assumed as a matter of course Graham would be putting them up.

Robin hadn't taken home leave until 1930 because he couldn't afford it. Their spell on the mission station had been five years of ill-paid boredom, broken only by the schoolmaster's bungalow burning down one night and the talkative missionary's spectacularly falling silent for ever in the middle of one of his sermons. They decided to settle in Singapore but somehow it hadn't worked, then Robin took a job in Kuala Lumpar as medical officer to a Scottish engineering company with a thrifty view of salaries. These adventures he had painstakingly spelt out in many-paged monthly letters to his brother, some of which Graham had read all the way through. But now the time had come to install his son Alec in an English boarding-school, the child having already defied the principles of contemporary paediatrics by showing a young white skin in the tropics at all–particularly as the poor little boy had turned out so depressingly delicate.

Edith left the cab first. She wore a plain blue cotton dress, her skin was as brown as boot polish, the hair under her tight-fitting hat was bleached by the sun as savagely as any London girl's by hydrogen peroxide. Like many English-women in the tropics she had grown thin to the point of scrawniness, but Robin lumbered out behind her as fat as the Saracen, pale-faced and puffing, his hair grey, his gait shuffling, his suit as though he had slept in it all the voyage, his voice so husky Graham wondered with alarm that his brother might have succumbed to the tropical hazard of drink. Though few words passed between them. All three were overcome by the meeting more than they liked to show. As for the circumstances of their parting, Robin and Edith seemed to have buried them in forgetfulness with the equanimity of a pair of municipal gravediggers.

'Here's Alec,' announced Edith proudly. 'Alec, darling, this really *is* your uncle Graham.'

Graham became aware of a pasty, large-headed, spindly-legged boy of nine, looking at him in terror. He felt the lad hardly looked strong enough to survive an outing to the Zoo, let alone the rigours of English residential education.

'I expect you've noticed a lot of difference in London,' said Graham, leading him into the house.

'Haven't had much chance to look,' mumbled Robin.

'Yes, the buses have got tops on,' Edith declared brightly.

Robin stopped to appraise the hall. Graham seemed to be doing quite well.

'It was a pity about father.'

Graham needed to remind himself the professor had died after Robin's departure. He had reached the age when memory starts to shuffle the years. 'Yes, it was sad.'

'The sordid details–the will, and that? They stood, I suppose? One can't do anything now?'

Graham shook his head.

'What's she like?' Robin asked. 'The woman?'

'Well . . . perhaps you'd better go up to Hampstead and see. After all, I suppose we've a perfect right to call on our stepmother.'

'And how's your wife?' smiled Edith. 'We're dying to meet her.'

'Maria will be down by and by,' said Graham.

Maria didn't appear until immediately before lunch.

'I must apologize for not greeting you,' she began stiffly, coming downstairs in a black dress. 'But I have been rather poorly. I hope you will be comfortable with us.'

The newcomers were shocked. They had suspected Graham sold his manhood for a mess of pottage–which was anyway soon dashed from his lips–but they imagined him married to the smart, active woman whom they remembered from the papers strode through postwar society. Certainly not to the thin, bent, greying invalid shaking hands so unsmilingly. It had taken all Maria's old courage to force herself down that Sunday morning. She had become terrified of strangers. But she felt she owed it to Graham–his brother must not fancy anything amiss. After all her husband deserved it. He was very good to her.

'I'm sure we'll be comfy,' Edith said quickly. 'Ever so.'

'I have so long admired you from my husband's description,' Maria told Robin. 'One seldom meets an Empire-builder these days. Well! We are to have a family lunch. That will be very pleasant. Two generations at the same table. Graham–it's cooler than I expected.'

Graham fetched a shawl and draped her shoulders. Maria led them into the small green-papered dining-room, almost filled with an oval table, the relic of more spacious days. 'I'm afraid you have come back to a sad country,' she went on, taking her seat. 'We have two million unemployed, we shall be abandoning the gold standard at any moment, and we have a government of red revolutionaries.' She rang a little handbell and added to Edith, 'You must be hungry after your long journey,' as though they had accomplished it by open boat.

Robin noticed Graham busy at the sideboard, half-filling one graduated medicine glass with red liquid and another with green, placing two white pills on a spoon laid neatly across a tumbler of water. Maria swallowed the medicaments, apparently unaware of Alec's fascinated gaze. He thought she might be some sort of witch.

'I take it you're doing pretty handsomely?' Robin eyed his brother's establishment more critically. 'Well, we should have plenty to talk about.'

'Oh, I stored up thousands and thousands of grains of gossip,' smiled Graham, starting to carve the joint with the calm authority of any less distracted suburban paterfamilias. He had thoughtfully ordered roast beef and Yorkshire pudding, the edible counterpart of the white cliffs of Dover. 'But it's a peculiar thing, now you're actually here I seem to have mislaid the cache. Tell us about Malaya instead.'

'Didn't you keep my letters?'

'Should I?'

Robin looked annoyed. 'They might have made an interesting book.'

'Not too much meat for Alec,' Edith interrupted hastily. 'He has such a small appetite.'

'*I* haven't got a small appetite,' growled Desmond. He had been sizing up his little cousin across the table with the intense suspicion of one small boy for another.

'I myself eat nothing, nothing,' muttered Maria, who like all chronic invalids could not imagine her symptoms less interesting to her hearers than to herself. 'It is all something to do with my low blood-pressure, so Graham says.'

Graham thought she was conducting herself rather well.

'I've one piece of news,' he added casually. 'I'm going overseas myself next week. To Egypt.'

Robin looked up. 'Oh?' He felt he had a proprietorial interest in the world beyond the Mediterranean.

'I'm flying,' Graham went on more sensationally. 'In the new airship. Do you know Val Arlott–the man who owns the *Daily Press*? He fixed it for me at short notice. It seems he persuaded the powers-that-be a doctor aboard would be a good thing. For the first leg of the flight, anyway. The rest are going on to India. Cairo takes only thirty-six hours, you know. *Thirty-six hours.* Imagine that!'

Edith gasped. 'Graham! Do you suppose it's quite safe?'

He grinned. 'You can hardly expect me to funk a comfortable ride in a sky-borne hotel when Amy Johnson went all the way to Australia in a tiny little aeroplane by herself. Besides, the Air Minister's coming with us. I can't imagine a better guarantee of safety.'

'It can do over sixty miles an hour, and there're five power-cars,' Desmond interrupted eagerly. Since the news of his father's adventure he had become an expert on airships. 'If it crashes, they press a button and cut open all the fuel tanks with special knives. I saw it at the air pageant over Hendon,' he continued proudly in Alec's direction. 'It's as long as the *Mauretania*.'

'I sailed in the *Mauretania* once,' observed Maria, more to herself. 'When my father took me to America before the war. It was all very gay, but of course everyone made a fuss of us in those days.' She shivered. 'Graham, the window's open.'

The conversation was then stopped by Alec's going white in the face and fighting for breath.

'Oh dear! It's one of his attacks,' said Edith apologetically.

'Bronchial asthma,' explained Robin.

Graham looked alarmed. Like all surgeons his knowledge of pure medicine had atrophied like a disused limb, but he recalled the disease came from spasm of the tiniest tubes in the lung under the influence of something baneful, in either the air or the psychology, which had so far evaded the wisdom of the doctors. Only the week before a young girl had died at Blackfriars in *status asthmaticus*, despite oxygen, camphor injections, and two professors.

'Do you want some adrenalin?' he asked anxiously, though from the calmness of Alec's parents to the attack the poor child seemed to come under fire pretty frequently. 'I've some in my bag, for mixing with locals.'

'A tablet of ephedrine will have him right.' Robin took from his breast pocket a grubby envelope, handing the wheezing boy a small white tablet with the air of distributing sweets. Without a word or even a sip of water, Alec dutifully swallowed it. Desmond looked fascinated. He hadn't witnessed such excitement since the maid fell in the kitchen underneath a scalding kettle.

'An asthmatic attack is always more frightening for the onlookers,' Robin pointed out.

'How unfortunate to be ill at his age,' said Graham sympathetically. It suddenly struck him how sturdy young Desmond resembled Robin, and puny little Alec himself. His head buzzed with figures in a fundamental calculation. No, it was quite impossible, he and Edith couldn't have managed it even had they been a pair of elephants. Oh well, he told himself, heredity is as full of surprises as any other game performed in the dark, and if the human race is so earnest about its reproduction Nature must get a laugh from the antics now and then. Maria, who had taken no notice of the disturbance, rang her handbell for the maid and said, 'Illness is unfortunate at any age.' Robin then started on tropical medicine, though sticking to the clinical side. It seemed to Graham that since the days in Hampstead his brother and God had somehow fallen out.'

After lunch, Maria retired immediately to bed and Desmond insisted that Alec and Robin admired his model railway, displayed in full complexity in a back room recently upgraded from his nursery to his 'den'. Graham took Edith into his small study beside the front door. It was almost the first time they had been alone together since the afternoon the professor's bed-knob fell off.

'All those books!' exclaimed Edith. 'Just like the old house at Hampstead.'

'In which I should, by rights, now be living.' Graham smiled. 'In which *you* should, by rights, now be living. With me.'

'Yes, I might have.' She seemed not put out by this reminder. 'It was a rum do, wasn't it? I mean about your father marrying that woman. I'd never have thought it, not of the professor. He was always so learned.'

'In my job you come to expect anything of anybody. Even your own father.'

'Whatever happened to the professor's book?' Her face lit up. 'All about . . . oh, what was it? Something funny to do with bones.'

'It came out! Didn't he send you a copy? Perhaps he thought it would be rather extravagant, with the overseas postage. Do you know, in the eyes of a lot of people, I'm only the son of the greatest authority in the world on synovial membranes?' He paused. 'It's very touching.'

'Go on, Graham–you're standing well enough on your own feet. I said you'd be a success, didn't I?'

'But I'm not a success. Not yet. It's still a struggle. There's an awful lot of prejudice against plastic surgery. There's an awful lot of prejudice against *me*. I'm ambitious, I suppose, which is thought most ungentlemanly in our bigoted and back-scratching profession. Not that it worries me. Only my dear colleagues. Are you happy with Robin?' he asked abruptly.

'Oh, yes,' she told him cheerfully. 'We're happy together, all three of us. It's lovely really. I never thought I'd deserve it, back in the old days.'

'But is he all right?' Graham added with concern. His brother's leaden complexion had been as much of a warning in his eyes as a leaden sky in a sailor's. 'Physically, I mean. He's changed terribly.'

'Yes, he's been rather poorly,' Edith admitted. 'Headaches, and that. He tries to keep it from me.'

'Any vomiting?'

She looked surprised at the question. 'Now and then. In the mornings, when he gets up. How did you guess?'

Graham frowned. 'What's his blood-pressure doing?'

'I don't know.' She suddenly sounded helpless. 'He's fainted once or twice, and we had the other doctor in. But he's an Irishman who drinks a lot. I don't think he's much good.'

'He really ought to see someone in London. Wedderburn's gone, of course, but there're plenty of bright new sparks about. And you ought to think pretty carefully before going back out East.'

'He wants to go back all right.' She smiled again. 'He's already fussing about the journey–you know Robin. His life's there.' She turned to stare out of the window at the small, dusty London garden. 'He's always trying to . . . well, debase himself. It's funny. When we left the mission station he wanted to work in a leper colony. I told him he was daft. That partnership he had with the doctors in Singapore–it didn't come to anything, because he said he didn't like making money out of ill people. Mind, there was a row as well, over the terms of the agreement. I don't know what, but they were all very angry. It's a pity. We could have had a nice house in Singapore, near Farrer Park up on the hill with the nobs. After twenty years we could have come back to England forever, living like lords. In 1944–it isn't that far away. But he's happier in Kuala Lumpur, though it's rough. Perhaps it's because he feels more important.'

'He always put the practice of his profession before its rewards,' Graham told her charitably. 'Unlike me, I suppose.'

'Then there's other things.'

'Oh?'

Edith still stared through the window. 'Funny things he does sometimes. With the natives. I've found him kissing their feet, and that. He always seems to like treating their sores, the nastier the better. Once something happened when . . .' She swallowed. 'Well, he was all naked and tied up. I shut my eyes to it.' She turned towards Graham and smiled once more. 'It's peculiar, isn't it? I've never breathed a word of this to a soul before.'

Graham wondered how to comment on this arresting spectacle. 'I think we're realizing these days that the sexual urge, like other blessings, comes in some strange disguises.'

'I expect it does. Well, Graham–if I *hadn't* married him you'd have left me on the shelf, wouldn't you?'

'Nonsense!' he said stoutly. Emboldened by her confidences, he tried to kiss her. He was startled at her force pushing him away.

'Don't be daft,' she said.

The phrase was her fire-extinguisher on the blazing insanities of the world.

Chapter Twenty-four

Robin brushed aside questions on his health, seeming more concerned in fussing over Graham's preparations for his adventure in the air. Graham had already been vaccinated at Blackfriars against smallpox (which went septic) and inoculated against typhoid fever (which he felt as unpleasant as having the disease), but Robin insisted he also bought a spirit stove to boil every mouthful of water as protection against the deadly *vibrio* of cholera. Robin spent his most enjoyable afternoon for months in the Army and Navy Stores fitting his brother with tropical kit, while delivering a running lecture on the perils of the direct sun falling upon the head, of mosquitoes, of bedbugs, and the rapid sapping of even an Englishman's moral fibre in tropical climes. He counselled a *sola topi*, ample supplies of quinine, a small Bible, and that powerful agent of British colonialism, Keating's Powder.

The airship herself was seven hundred and seventy feet long, at once the queen of the air and the nursling of British engineering. She had rows of double-bunked passenger cabins, reassuringly lit through artificial nautical portholes. Her saloon provided not only hot meals for sixty, but hot music through the wireless loudspeaker. She had a promenade deck with a ship's rail and deck-chairs for enjoying the view. The lounge was the size of a tennis-court, decorated as tastefully as any transatlantic liner's with little pots of ferns and palms. The furniture was lightweight wicker, to be arranged in the evenings for dancing.

The airship was to flash past Paris, Tours, Toulouse, and Narbonne, skirting the Pyrenees (the Alps were considered inadvisable), to Ismailia on the Suez Canal, where a mooring mast had been built for her like a desert-bound Eiffel Tower. There was to be a ceremonial dinner while attached to it, with the High Commissioner of Egypt taken aboard–though no fuel, the stench of diesel oil being thought too nauseating for high official nostrils. Then she was off to Karachi in India, awaited by another Eiffel Tower and the R.A.F. with gas cylinders, the whole journey finished in an incredible seventy-two hours. The passengers for this maiden flight were restricted to a distinguished six, whom Graham would treat presumably for sickness, nervousness, or other unknown hazards of the air.

Graham was to disembark at Ismailia, a convenient P. and O. was leaving Port Said for Genoa, then he would take train and Channel steamer home. He would be away from Blackfriars a bare month. He was looking forward to the trip excitedly, having discovered in himself a taste for travel. Besides, it would give him a breathing-space with Kitty Rivers. And it was always rather pleasant for a while to get away from Maria.

Graham's coming absence had brought a flurry of work at Blackfriars and St Sebastian's, but he found time to give Robin and Edith a treat or two. He took them to *Bitter Sweet* at His Majesty's, and even Robin, whose puritanical views of the stage saved him the expense and effort of theatre-going, admitted this man Noël Coward had a deal of charm with a scene or a tune. Graham even made an impulsive offer, immediately regretted, to drive them to Alec's school at the seaside resort of Birchington-on-Sea, on the tip of Kent not far from the sanatorium where he was sent to end his days. He supposed he'd made the suggestion through pride in both his new Alvis and his skill as a motorist, though it was an enormous distance–almost eighty miles. Robin and Edith would be returning later by train for the thrill of seeing him leave for Egypt, staying meanwhile with Edith's mother in Ramsgate. The butcher himself had some time before gone the way of all flesh, edible or otherwise.

Little Alec's school had been chosen through its connection with Robin's old missionary society and its modest scale of fees, but above all for its air. The air circulating round the Isle of Thanet, Robin declared, had no equal in the whole therapeutic armamentarium for a chesty child. Graham hoped so. Alec had thrown an attack of asthma regularly twice a night, which was extremely noisy in the house and becoming a shade boring. Graham wondered if they were caused by the dust or by the emotional effect of Desmond, who awarded his cousin sly punches and kicks whenever he had half a chance without detection.

They were to leave for Birchington early on September the twenty-fifth, which was a Thursday. The weather had turned so bad Graham telephoned the Air Ministry to see if the airship's flight the following week might be postponed. An official tetchily assured him only the most tempestuous skies could delay such a monster, and anyway the Air Minister must be home in London to make a gloriously prompt entrance at the Imperial Conference in mid-October. Besides, it was a matter of British prestige getting her off on time, and British prestige, with Gandhi and the depression, was having a thin time of it. They set off for Kent, Alec as pale as his new wooden iron-bound tuck-box. Graham feared the child might be sick continually on the way, and he was.

That afternoon Graham's housemaid, still in her brown morning uniform, was asleep in the kitchen, when the front-door bell jangled in the rack above her. Desmond was at school, her mistress as usual upstairs in bed, and they expected no visitors. Rubbing her eyes and smoothing her apron, she clicked across the tiles of the hall and found outside a slight, fair-haired young woman in a plain brown coat and small round black hat, which had, in fact, been bought specially for the occasion.

'Could I see Mrs Trevose, please?'

'Which Mrs Trevose?' asked the maid, half-asleep. 'There's two living here, madam.'

'Mrs Maria Trevose.'

'Is she expecting you?'

'No. I don't suppose she's even heard of me. But I must see her at once. It's vitally important.'

The maid looked alarmed. Such announcements, though commonplace on the talkies, were rarely uttered by human tongue. 'Not an accident?' she gasped, alive to the untrustworthiness of such contraptions as motor-cars.

'No, it's nothing like that. But I *must* see her. Please.'

Maria faced her visitor sitting up in bed, a shawl round her shoulders, a book from Boot's library on her bed-rest, her medicine bottles and pills neatly at her elbow. She carefully inserted a leather bookmark, closed the page, indicated a chintz-covered upright chair, and apologized. 'You must forgive me for receiving you in my bedroom. My poor health I hope is excuse enough. Do please sit down. I'm afraid I didn't catch your name properly. That silly girl was almost incoherent. Reliable servants are unfortunately things of the past.'

'It's Miss Kitty Rivers. I'm your husband's secretary.'

'Strange,' mused Maria. 'He had often spoken about his secretary, but I can't recall his once mentioning your name. Well? She lay back on her pillows, as though already weary of the interview. 'What have you to tell me?'

For a girl of such meekness as Kitty Rivers the confrontation had been almost unthinkable. But when desperation failed her revenge urged her on. Now she wondered what to say. Words came only because there lies in every woman an actress, waiting in the wings for the cue which comes too rarely in the humdrum performance of life. 'I am your husband's mistress,' she declared startingly.

Maria said nothing. She stared at her visitor with dark eyes, as though some remark had been made about the weather.

'I've been living with him. He got me a flat near his consulting room, in Marylebone High Street. He used to come round, often. It's been going on almost two years now.' As Maria still looked blank she said more nervously, 'Don't you understand? We were lovers. We were *intimate*,' she added, falling back on the more comfortable sexless language of the newspapers.

Maria continued to stare.

'It's true!' Kitty insisted. 'I swear it. I thought I loved him, you see.'

'I don't believe you,' said Maria.

'But why should I make it up? Why on earth? I could prove it, if you like. I could tell you all sorts of things about Graham. Yes, I could. Some things I don't expect you know yourself. You've *got* to believe me.'

Maria still stared. 'I don't believe you.'

'I'm sorry.' Kitty began to sound miserable. 'I didn't really want to hurt you. But it is true–every word.'

'You're a liar, Miss Rivers.'

'I'm not!' she exclaimed. 'For two whole years—'

'I have been expecting your visit, Miss Rivers.' Maria slowly smoothed the sheet with her thin hand. 'It would be you, or somebody else. I know my husband is an attractive man. There must be any number of young girls at his work or among his patients likely to lose their heads over him. Since my health started to fail I have prepared myself for one to come out of spite and jealousy to poison my mind against him. You don't know my husband, Miss Rivers. You don't know him at all. You could never have spoken about him in such a manner if you did. He is devoted to me. Devoted! And I to him. How do you imagine he could bring himself to give me such tenderness, such sympathy, and such love, if he were diverting his affections to another woman?'

'But, Mrs Trevose!' Kitty jumped up. 'I ask God as my witness, *it's true*!'

'I don't see any necessity for calling the Almighty to your rescue,' said Maria shortly. 'I must ask you to leave me. I tire very easily these days. You will find the maid to show you out.'

'You *horrible* woman!' Kitty started to cry. The staircase, the stairs, the hall, the maid–who had dutifully changed into her afternoon black frock–were a blur. Graham was an utterly damnable man. For two years he had used her body, regularly, twice a week, on Tuesday and Thursday afternoon, after private consultations. Now he had not only humiliated her over some girl in Paris. He had denied her the gratification of infuriating his wife.

As Maria heard the front door slam downstairs she reached calmly for her novel. She removed the bookmark and stared at the page. She was still staring at it four hours later when the maid, worried at no summons from her bell, came to draw the curtains and switch on the light against the gathering dusk.

It was eleven that night before Graham reached home. It had been a trying drive, particularly in the dark. He noticed a light under Maria's door at the back of the house–unusual, because she always took her hypnotic mixture of chloral at ten. He found her sitting up in her shawl, with her book.

'Oh, Graham, dear! I'm so glad. It was getting terribly late and I was worrying. You had a safe journey?'

He smiled. 'Haven't you taken your medicine?'

'I stayed awake because I have some news for you. About Miss Rivers.'

Graham felt as though his stomach had turned to ice.

'I'm afraid you will have to find yourself another secretary, my dear. Miss Rivers had tendered her resignation. Or so I take it. She came here specifically this afternoon to blacken your character.'

'Oh?' Graham's trembling hand reached for the bottle of colourless sedative medicine. It seemed a good idea getting Maria off to sleep as soon as possible. 'What did she say, for God's sake?'

'She was accusing you of making advances to her. It was a very silly attempt. I wouldn't bother repeating all she said, even if I could remember it. I was alone in the house with Bridget, and half-asleep anyway. It was too ridiculous even to be embarrassing. I know you too well, my darling.' She smiled at him. 'And she is, after all, only a working woman.'

'But it's unbelievable!' Graham hastily covered his moral nakedness with a fiery cloak of indignation. 'I just can't understand it. I suppose it's because

I've been meaning to sack her–she's got terribly inefficient lately. Always making mistakes of one sort or another. A stupid girl, really.'

Maria swallowed her dose. She turned up her mouth to be kissed. He could taste the sickly chloral hydrate on her lips. 'Graham, you really know very little about women.'

He escaped. He paced up and down his own room. He wanted to dash to Marylebone High Street at once, but even with Maria drugged leaving the house was too risky. Early the next morning he made straight for Queen Anne Street, to find the trivial belongings Kitty kept on her desk in the hall–a flower vase, a travelling clock, a photograph–were ominously absent. In his Japanese consulting room one of the desk-drawers was half-open and the contents of all of them awry. She had been having a good rummage round before leaving. He went to Marylebone High Street to find the flat deserted, her clothes gone. He stood in the tiny bedroom, cursing. Where did her family come from? Norfolk or somewhere. She'd probably bolted back there. But there wasn't time to start chasing her now. He had an operating list at Blackfriars in half an hour. He drove to the hospital, thanking God Maria hadn't taken the little bitch seriously. The dulling of her senses with the years had a few advantages.

Graham's last week in London was too full of worries at Blackfriars and complications over his journey for him to suffer as Kitty intended. She didn't even send him a letter. He thought of trying to trace her, even of employing a detective agency, but decided against it. It might leak out among his colleagues at the hospital. Then he began to tell himself it was perhaps all for the best. Now he could hold his head up, behave decently in future, act as a good husband, father, and Blackfriars consultant. As for the girl in the photographer's, John Bickley was right–she didn't merit a second thought. He was well rid of both. His life henceforward was to be virtuously uncomplicated. The long-standing anxiety of deception had evaporated overnight. The feeling was quite exhilarating. Though he had to admit he rather missed Kitty, particularly on Tuesday and Thursday afternoon.

Saturday arrived. The airship was at last to leave. Graham was going to Bedford by train with Robin, Edith, and Desmond, where an official car would be waiting. He was to rise from the airfield at six in the evening, and the weather that morning was horrible. It had turned bitterly cold and the wind ripped the trees half-naked in the sedate avenues of Primrose Hill. At breakfast-time Graham rang the *Daily Press* to be told everything proceeded smoothly, with Mr Arlott already in Bedfordshire to observe the departure on behalf of his readers and the nation. Graham had hardly hooked up the earpiece when the bell rang again. It was Tom Raleigh from Blackfriars. One of his cases was badly infected, and perhaps he should look in before leaving.

Graham hastily arranged to meet the others at St Pancras Station, and hurried upstairs to say farewell to Maria. It suddenly struck him how old she looked. How old *was* she? he asked himself. Mid-forties. Good God! That morning she seemed at least sixty. Perhaps it was the greyness of the light.

'I'm off now,' he told her cheerfully. 'I've got to call into Blackfriars.' She looked alarmed at the unexpectedly sudden parting. 'Don't worry, darling, such are the miracles of the modern world I'll be back in a month. Robin will look after your medicines and things, he promised that. He's a very good doctor, you know.'

As Graham kissed her, she said, 'Perhaps your absence will be relieved by another visit from some hysterical woman?'

Graham gave a laugh. Even to him it sounded as hollow as Mr MacDonald's promises of prosperity just round the corner.

At the door he heard a cry. He found her staring after him, her hand at her throat. 'Desmond–you're not taking Desmond? Not on the airship?'

'No, of course I'm not.' He was desperately impatient to get to Blackfriars. 'Why on earth do you ask?'

'Oh, I don't know. I get so confused sometimes. I didn't think it was this morning you went at all.'

He came back and stroked her cheek. 'You mustn't worry about yourself,' he said as tenderly as he did a dozen times a day to his patients, and as automatically. He sometimes worried that his feelings for his fellow-humans, like his work on them, went no deeper than the skin. 'Desmond will be right here, with Robin and Edith. You won't be alone.'

She clasped his hand. 'Without you I am always alone.'

Holding his bag with his *sola topi* tied to the handle, Graham hurried into the blustery cold, wearing the lightweight suit Robin advised for the autumn sun of Egypt. The airship, Graham had been repeatedly assured, enjoyed even central heating.

The patient at Blackfriars was a twenty-year-old girl who had nearly amputated her thumb with a guillotine machine in a cardboard-box factory. Graham had made her a new one, on the same principle as the Saracen made his corporal another nose. He had first chipped away a strip from the crest of her hip, leaving it still attached to the main bone and sticking out like a little pyramid under the skin of her groin. A few weeks later, he brought down her injured hand and stitched it to the lump. Later still, once the chip of bone was newly nourished by the arteries of the girl's arm, he freed it from her hip completely. 'It may not look very elegant,' he told Tom Raleigh at the time, 'but at least she's got a grasp–it's something to pick up a knife and fork or a bar of soap, to feed and wash herself in a civilized manner. You can use the rest of your fingers for wearing rings, but your thumb's essential. It's what keeps us ahead of the animals, isn't it?'

Tom Raleigh had objected mildly, 'Some of the new artificial limbs are very good, sir.'

'I will not have my patients going about with hooks like pantomine sailors,' Graham told him curtly.

But something had gone wrong. As Tom Raleigh gently removed the dressings from the girl's hand that morning Graham saw too clearly the classical tetrad of Celsus, *calor*, *rubor*, *tumor*, *dolor*–heat, redness, swelling, and pain, the danger signals of inflammation. The girl was shivering. A new four-hourly temperature chart had been started, an ominous sign in itself, recording a hundred and three. Graham carefully raised her arm. Two long red fingers of infection were reaching past her elbow for the lymph-glands in her armpit.

'When did this all begin?' he asked Tom Raleigh quietly.

'Sister noticed the temperature was up last night, sir.'

'When was it normal? Where's the ordinary ward chart?' Graham saw from this a sudden and violent infection had taken hold. 'You'd better get a swab across to the lab.'

'I did last night, sir.'

Tom Raleigh handed over a pink slip of paper, the bacteriologist's report. The girl's attacker was, as Graham suspected, a virulent streptococcus.

Such cases were common enough among pathologists, slaughtermen, and others whose occupations drew their fingers into unhealthy nooks and crannies. Too often a gruesome leap-frog ensued, the surgeon amputating the hand with infection already on its way to the elbow, then a second amputation at the shoulder was performed too late to prevent generalized blood-poisoning which snuffed out the flames of fever for good. If only, Graham thought bitterly, we had some chemical, something like Ehrlich's arsenicals against the spirochaete of syphilis, some other 'magic bullet' to kill the everyday bacteria marauding as dangerously as tigers all round us. He returned his attention to the patient. 'My dear, you are very ill.' He stroked her burning cheek. 'You have an infection in your hand which can spread up your arm and reach your heart. You understand? We are going to make you better–and quickly, too. Though I am afraid you are going to lose your arm.'

The girl stared at him. Graham knew nobody could grasp the significance of his sentence at once. He moved away from the bedside. 'I'll send Sister to speak to you.'

'Wouldn't incision and drainage be adequate, sir?' asked Tom, as they walked down the ward.

'Either I amputate today with the chance of saving her life, or someone amputates tomorrow and she's dead on Monday. Tell the theatre to prepare for a forequarter. You'd better call Cramphorn if you're worried about her afterwards. I've got to leave London on the afternoon train whatever happens.'

'Yes, sir.'

'And I want her isolated, or we'll have the whole ward infected. How did she get it in the first place?' he demanded brusquely. 'I'm careful enough about asepsis in the theatre. Are you?'

Tom said nothing. His chief's temper seemed to be worsening these days. He sometimes threw instruments in the theatre, blamed the nurses for blunt knives and broken stitches, and himself for everything else from the unit's mortality-rate to the patients' food arriving cold. He was becoming a shade tired of it. 'We'll have to get her parents' permission, sir,' he remembered, 'she's under twenty-one.'

'Damn her parents,' said Graham.

He wished Tom didn't sound so bloody meek. He reminded him of Kitty. Perhaps that was why he had chosen both of them.

Chapter Twenty-five

The operation was barely completed when the telephone rang in the tiny surgeons' room behind the theatre. Graham impatiently laid aside the board on which he was finishing his notes. It was Robin.

'Graham? You've got to come home. At once.'

'That's out of the question. I've just done an emergency forequarter, and the patient isn't even back in the ward.'

'It's Maria.'

His tone was enough. An idea which for years had been dissolved almost invisibly in the fluid of Graham's mind abruptly precipitated in spiky crystals.

'What is it?' he asked nervously.

'I can't tell you on the phone. It's a matter of life and death.'

'Do what you can. Don't call in anyone else,' Graham ordered hastily. 'I'll be there straight away.'

He left the patient in the care of Tom Raleigh, grabbed his bag with his *sola topi*, and took another taxi back to Primrose Hill. The house was in confusion. Edith was trying to quieten Desmond, who was insisting loudly on seeing his mummy. The maid in the brown dress was crying hysterically. The dog was barking. The cook was sitting in the hall staring straight ahead of her, and from the kitchen came an alarmingly strong smell of burning. Only Robin seemed as stolid as usual.

'Is she dead?' asked Graham at once.

'No, she's still got a fair pulse.' The two brothers started upstairs. 'Her breathing's shallow, but there's no cyanosis.'

Maria was lying on her back, snoring loudly. Graham saw Robin was wrong, she was tinged with blue. On the bedside table, beside a glass in which her teeth had been left with customary precision, were two empty medicine bottles. Graham had prescribed a double supply to cover his absence, and as he was giving a small nightly dose of fifteen grains of chloral hydrate in solution he calculated that she must now have some fifteen doses inside her–two hundred and twenty-five grains, enough to be fatal.

'How on earth did she swallow it?' he asked distractedly. 'They usually vomit on half as much.'

He tugged up her chin, easing her noisy breathing by drawing her flaccid tongue from the back of her throat. He felt her pulse and raised her eyelid. The pupil was not widely dilated, which was hopeful. He touched the eyeball with his finger-tip, but the lid failed to flicker in response.

'When did she do it?'

Robin shrugged his shoulders. 'I don't know. She gave orders not to be disturbed and we thought she was just upset at your going. Then Edith came in about something or other.'

Graham grabbed his wife. He tipped head and shoulders over the edge of the bed and rammed his fingers into her throat. Nothing happened.

'I thought of an emetic–mustard, or something.' Robin sounded plaintive. 'But she was already unconscious—'

'Damn it! If only I had some apomorphine to inject! That would bring it up.'

'Hadn't we better get her to Blackfriars?'

'No, no, not Blackfriars! I don't want her seen there. We'll take her to the Sloane.' He replaced Maria on the bed, tugging away the pillows so she lay flat. 'Saturday's John Bickley's day at the Sloane–he'll know how to handle this. If it isn't too late for anyone to handle it.'

'I'll ring up for an ambulance.'

'No ambulance,' Graham insisted. 'I don't want ambulances outside the house. People talk. We'll take her in the car. Tell Edith to get Desmond out of the way.'

They carried Maria downstairs wrapped in a blanket, her mouth sagging open, her head lolling on her shoulder, one naked foot sticking out of the bundle. Graham dumped her in the back of the Alvis with Robin. John Bickley had been warned by telephone and was waiting in the downstairs casualty room. He laid Maria on the leather-covered couch and tipped one end until her head touched the floor. He pumped oxygen into her from his anaesthetic machine, squeezing a bag like a red rubber football bladder. Then he ran a thick tube down her gullet and into her stomach, washing it through with salt solution. Graham had lost Robin, who decided to stay in the corridor either through delicacy or because he found with a pair of nurses the little room was most uncomfortably crowded.

'I'll give an injection of strychnine.' John Bickley drew up the dose in a syringe. 'With luck it'll get her breathing going. I only wish I'd one of those new German analeptics. They'd wake the dead.'

Graham muttered, 'What are her chances?'

'Oh, we'll pull your wife through.' John had an anaesthetist's professional optimism. 'But it's a pretty awful penalty for such a simple mistake.'

'Mistake?'

'Yes. The mistake of dosing herself from the wrong bottle.'

Graham looked at him silently. Both saw how the lie could be established if they lied to each other. 'Yes, a most unfortunate mistake,' he said.

Maria groaned and moved her head.

'You really must read her a lecture on studying the labels, you know,' said John. 'Like we give the nurses.'

Graham sat on a short wooden bench, suddenly exhausted. His heart glowed towards the anaesthetist. Maria's essay in self-destruction must somehow be kept quiet. It was disgraceful, a reflection on himself. No one must suspect at Blackfriars. As she moved an arm John Bickley shifted her to a less drastic slope, reached for a sphygmomanometer, bound on the cuff, and listened with a stethoscope at her elbow.

'The diastolic pressure's not too bad,' he announced, 'which shows we're getting on. Though she's having a few extrasystoles.'

Graham looked round as the door of the casualty room opened. To his consternation Mr Cramphorn appeared, with pepper-and-salt suit, half-moon glasses, brown boots, and puffing pipe. Damn! Graham thought. He had overlooked Saturday was Cramphorn's day at the Sloane as well.

'Halloa! Trevose, what's this? Your wife, isn't it? Not serious, I hope?'

'Yes, it's Maria. She took an overdose of chloral hydrate. By mistake.'

'I say, I'm sorry. That's bad luck. I hope she makes a speedy recovery. Anything I can do? I fancy she's in good hands. Please accept my sympathy.'

Graham cursed. The man could see perfectly well what was up. On Monday all Blackfriars would know of the suicide attempt–if they got away with merely an attempt. The valley of the shadow of death from which John had rescued Maria led only to further shades, of heart-failure, bronchopneumonia, or delayed collapse. If there was the publicity of an inquest . . .

'I think we can put her to bed,' said John Bickley.

The two nurses laid Maria on a trolley, moving her upstairs to a private ward. Outside the casualty room Robin was still waiting. 'You know, it's very late,' he told Graham. 'The train for Bedford's left already.'

'I'm not going.'

'But surely you don't want to miss the trip? Not after all the preparations?' Robin sounded cross. His valuable advice about Graham's kit and health might all be wasted. 'She'll be all right now, won't she? Edith and I can stay here to keep an eye on things. We can get a car to take you to the airship.

You'll still be in good time.'

'It's out of the question. Completely out of the question. I've got to stay with her. Get on to Val Arlott–he's at Cardington, waiting for me. Tell him my wife's seriously ill. He'll have to make my excuses to Sir Sefton Brancker and the rest.'

'Oh, very well, I suppose it's up to you,' Robin agreed morosely. 'Though it's going to be no end of a job getting through to this Cardington place. Where on earth can I find the telephone number?'

They put Maria to bed with her feet still tipped up, to prevent her own secretions filling her lungs and drowning her. They laid a row of rubber hot-water bottles down each flank like sucking pigs and left Graham alone with her. The day grew prematurely dark and rain started dashing against the window. Nurses came and went, but he hardly noticed them. He smoked cigarettes until his packet ran out. He sat staring across the small room at his wife, white-faced and with her mouth open, illuminated by the dim light of a bedside lamp.

The moment seemed to have arrived when he really ought to decide if he loved her or not. She was admittedly hardly a decorative consort at the best of times. He often thanked God her withdrawal from the world saved him the trouble of hiding her from his friends. But his work was leaving him progressively disillusioned over the value of beauty. How many wives had come to him with wrinkles, baggy eyelids, or misshapen noses for the magical transformation of their marriages with a wave of his scalpel? And how often did surgery on the wife have the slightest effect on the husband? Not once that he knew. Well, only once, he reflected. The operation was such a success the woman went off with another man, leaving the husband furious and threatening litigation.

He took a sheet of blank paper from Maria's folder of notes. He wrote at the top, 'History of Present Condition'. Underneath he put, 'Ten years ago, I married Maria through a combination of impulsiveness, ambition, self-flattery, disappointment, and lack of maternal influence during formative years. Plus need for regular sexual outlet, of course.' He suddenly wondered what had happened to Brenda of the foot-long cigarette-holder. He seemed to have lost her somehow during the General Strike. 'A few hours ago, I was overwhelmed at the tragic possibility of my wife's death. Compare: her labour, in 1921.' He paused, and added, 'Or at my own responsibility for both?' He screwed up the paper and stuffed it in his pocket. It really was a difficult diagnosis. 'Why aren't I a nicer person?' he asked himself. 'My God, why aren't I a nicer person?'

It was a frequent plea, and the inner voice always sounded most pathetic.

Some time during the night Maria regained consciousness.

'Graham . . . !' She held out her hand.

He went over to her. 'My darling . . . you're all right.'

Without moving her head from the pillowless bed she looked round the white cubicle. 'What happened? Where am I?'

'You're in hospital. You've been ill. You're getting better.'

'Oh, I remember . . .' She gave a faint smile. 'I was silly, wasn't I?' It reminded him of the afternoon she fainted in Half Moon Street. 'You hurt my pride, Graham.'

He nodded guiltily. Somewhere in the doped blood circulating in her prematurely wizened body lingered the spirit of the old Maria Cazalay.

'How did they find me? I thought you were already gone on the airship?

I've been confused lately.'

'Edith discovered you. I was still at Blackfriars.' He held her hand tighter. 'I promise there'll be no more of this–no other women. I was foolish, selfish, heartless. It'll never happen again. Never!'

'Graham, don't leave me–don't leave me alone. Not in the hands of strangers. Everyone's a stranger to me now. Except you.'

'I won't leave you. I'll never leave you.'

The flicker of a smile lit her white face again. 'You were always so considerate to me. Even on our honeymoon.'

She relapsed shortly afterwards into normal sleep. Graham sat beside her, taking her pulse every half-hour. At six in the morning it occurred to him he had eaten nothing since breakfast the previous day. Maria was out of danger. He could go home. It was still dark, a terrible morning, cold and wet. There were no taxis, and he'd told Robin to take the Alvis. He turned up his jacket collar and walked north from Oxford Street in the rain, as he had walked years before from Maria's house in Half Moon Street. He felt equally gloomy, and what was worse, shameful. From now on, he decided solemnly, he was to be Maria's alone. He would turn for satisfaction to his work, give more time to patients like the factory girl he had been obliged to mutilate less than a day ago. He would be Maria's lawful wedded husband, in sickness and in health. Well, she always got her way in the end, somehow or other.

The house in Primrose Hill was dark, the newspapers sprawled on the front step next to the milk. Graham absently gathered them, feeling for his key. On top was the *Sunday Times*, with its unexciting front page of advertisements. Underneath, as their usual *Daily Press* ran no Sunday edition, lay the *Sunday Express*. The headline caught his eye.

R 101 DISASTER: 45 DEAD

His hand started to shake. He read down the column.

AIRSHIP CRASHES IN FLAMES
FAMOUS AIR ACES PERISH
Lord Thomson and Sir S. Brancker Dead
ONLY EIGHT SAVED: 45 TRAPPED IN AN INFERNO

He found Edith in the kitchen, in her dressing-gown boiling a kettle. Seeing his expression she gasped, 'Maria!' but he told her quickly, 'Maria's all right,' and laid the newspaper silently on the table. Edith read it, her eyes growing wider. 'Oh, Graham!' She threw her arms round him, hugging and kissing him. 'Oh, Graham! You're alive, you're alive!'

'I'm very much alive! Thank God I didn't go.'

'Oh Graham, darling Graham!' Edith started to cry. 'I don't know what I'd do, in a world without you in it somewhere. Honest, I don't. I always think of you, wherever I am, however far away.'

He took her head gently in his hands. The shock of his reprieve was starting to wear off. 'Why, you're still in love with me,' he accused her smilingly.

'Oh! Don't be daft,' Edith told him faintly. She blew her nose. The news was too much for her vocabulary. They just stared at each other in silence. 'I expect you could do with a cup of tea?' she said.

She was as practical as ever.

During the day, as the telephone woke him with enquiries and even condolences, a strange feeling came over Graham of living through it all before. Suddenly he remembered. It was the *Inviolable*, all over again. He wondered wryly if his luck could turn as handsomely twice.

On the Monday the *Daily Press*, piqued by young Arthur Christiansen's scoop in the *Express*, ran a front-page story of Graham's escape. He later learned with amusement that even Haileybury had seemed quite sorry to learn of his supposed incineration in a wood outside Beauvais. The *Daily Press* continued its discreet puffs in the sails of his career, speeding him on his course. He was amazed at the effect of Miss Constantine's story in its pages. Patients who had never heard of him, or even of plastic surgery, besieged his door in Queen Anne Street with all manner of structural complaints. His notion of revenging himself on his sneerers with the terrible weapon of their own jealousy became a reality. Miss Constantine was the hinge to the lid which opened suddenly on the riches of his career.

Maria left the Sloane after a week. The girl Graham had operated on in Blackfriars died the same day from streptococcal septicaemia. She suffered one of the bitterest human misfortunes, contracting a fatal disease while its fangs were already being drawn by a man in a white coat busy among his test-tubes, unknown in a foreign land. It was five years before the bacteria-killing properties of a red dye called prontosil were described in a German medical journal, inaugurating as some compensation for the age of Hitler the age of antibiotics.

After all the fuss Graham intended to give up the Marylebone High Street flat, but decided at the last moment against it. The rent was modest, and you never knew.

Chapter Twenty-six

Alec Trevose reflected afterwards that his school on the Kent coast was arranged architecturally like the ocean liners of the time, steaming thrustfully across the Atlantic after the profitable Blue Riband. It was divided strictly into three classes. The headmaster with his scrawny wife and pair of small daughters went First, in the manor house of Kentish ragstone which looked so well on the cover of the prospectus and emitted sadistic whiffs of savoury cooking. The masters were Tourist, in a brick lodge converted from servants' quarters and stables, which smelt of cheap tobacco and linseed oil or dubbin according to the cricketing or football season. The hundred and fifty-odd boys went steerage. Behind the manor house spread a wake of remarkable buildings, all different, their only common factor being economy in construction. The predominant materials were asbestos boarding, corrugated-iron roofing, concrete flooring, reluctant and pungent plumbing, broken windows, and dim electric bulbs. Throughout the year they always smelt the same, of freshly-sharpened pencils, spilt ink, sweaty shirts, and urine.

Still, the famous air was there. It was provided liberally, whistling across the North Sea unhindered from Scandinavia all winter, through the ill-fitting doors, window-panes and floorboards, chilling the boys' raw and scarred bare knees, piercing their bedclothes, and freezing over the washing-jugs in the dormitories. It all took Alec's mind off his asthma, if it didn't improve it.

The headmaster, known for some forgotten but undoubtedly entertaining accident with his trousers as 'Old Flybuttons', was a pinched, gloomy fellow with dark clothes and a wing collar, a frustrated–or, Alec wondered afterwards, unfrocked?–clergyman, wearing a mixed expression of piety and dyspepsia. He appeared in the school mainly to supervise prayers and to teach divinity, though regrettably not holiness. But he seemed a jovial enough man underneath. Even the solemnity of Alec's deposit there by his parents was broken by Old Flybuttons' short and unexpected bursts of laughter like nutmeg on a grater.

'Of course, he's very highly strung,' Edith explained, after Robin had given the bronchial case-history.

Alec wondered again what 'highly strung' meant. He imagined himself as a wooden marionette, the sort you found in your Christmas stocking, which you suddenly jerked rigid by a thick string running through its head. In maturity, he felt this self-assessment of his nature fairly correct.

'Highly strung, eh?' said Old Flybuttons gloomily. 'I expect the good air and regular life will do him the world of good. Eh? Ha, ha! It's done wonders for more delicate boys. Eh? Eh? What? Ha, ha, ha!'

Old Flybuttons was always laughing. Sometimes the noise rang from his own quarters through the silenced dormitories after nightfall. At others it burst from him while elucidating obscure Biblical points on the blackboard, or announcing the next hymn from his *Ancient and Modern*. As all the boys could imitate it sometimes it ran like hysteria round an unsupervised classroom, everyone crowing like startled cockatoos until suppressed by the arrival of a master and desperate punishment. Alec felt it all livened the place up.

In his second week at the school Alec stole a carrot.

The appetizing qualities of the famous air failed to affect him, largely through the school food, though adequate, not always being edible. It was mostly carbohydrate in the form of bread brushed with margarine, potatoes roasted in their jackets and occasionally much of their soil, rice pudding as a matter of course, and dried butter beans providing an unexpected dash of protein with a dead maggot or two. There was the treat of fish on Fridays, and a boiled egg on Sunday morning before church, though if a boy got a bad one it was just his luck, for they were never provided with spares.

Alec noticed the sturdy red shoulders of a row of carrots in the headmaster's garden on his way to football. He was alone. He uprooted one, wiped it on his jersey, and ate it. Nothing ever tasted so wonderful to him again.

As he cunningly replaced the feathery top he was observed by the headmaster's scrawny wife washing her hair in the bathroom. After tea he found himself summoned to the study. It was his first entry to the manor house since the day of his arrival. With its pretty flint-walled garden, which Robin and Edith agreed provided the correct English background to Alec's maturing, it was as inaccessible to the boys as Buckingham Palace.

'Trevose, you stole a carrot.' Old Flybuttons swivelled his chair from his roll-topped desk the better to eye the sinner. Even without the headmaster in it Alec felt the study an intimidating enough place, full of forbidding shelves of religious books and photographs of disagreeable-looking religious gentlemen. This brilliant detection left him speechless. 'Eh? What?' asked Flybuttons. 'Ha, ha!'

Alec joined the merriment with a timid smile.

'What's funny about it, young man? Are you making mock of me? You broke the eighth commandment,' the headmaster declared, raising the offence from a matter of mere carrots. 'Get over the arm of that chair. Ha, ha, ha, ha, ha!'

From a corner cupboard, of whose terrible contents Alec had been advised with relish by his schoolfellows, Old Flybuttons selected a stout bamboo cane and beat him six times. That evening Alec discovered the headmaster's laugh was a nervous affliction striking him in moments of tension, like stammering. It was his first disillusionment with human nature.

The establishment had long ago abandoned trying to convince the outside world it resembled a public school and, possibly aware of being as doomed to extinction as Dotheboys Hall, was wearying of trying to convince itself. The masters changed often and in mysterious circumstances, the big boys bullied the smaller boys, and the smaller boys dismembered live bluebottles. Alec suffered immediately from the bullying, through innocence about those terror-striking gatherings of the whole school after some untraceable offence like carving the desks or silently passing flatus during prayers, when 'owning up' was demanded, in default of which justice would be spread impartially over everybody. Failing to see why all should lose a half-holiday through a few rude words on the wall, Alec piped up the name of the culprit. He discovered painfully 'sneaking' was a hideous crime, even worse than 'swotting', and like all under-sized people having to be quick on the uptake he avoided both for the rest of his life.

Of the two elderly masters who stood rocklike amid the ebb and flow of staff, one was badly addicted to beer, which was never overlooked by the heartlessly keen perception of small boys when it showed in his breath or behaviour. The other was badly addicted to washing the smaller boys on their weekly bath-night with the school's rough yellow soap, all over. Alec's asthma brought him into continual contact with the school matron, who was also the school cook, and some relative of the headmaster's wife. She was thought by the boys incredibly ancient, though he reflected afterwards the poor woman could hardly have been past thirty. He also reflected on the terrible frustrations and neuroses which must have raged within her. She dosed Alec with his cough mixture in her room behind the kitchen which always smelt of hot ironing, often keeping him for a chat, sitting untidily in her chair and fascinating him with glimpses of thick worsted stockings and now and then even green bloomers and hefty pink suspenders. She once asked laughingly if he thought she had nice legs, and rewarded his confusion with a pat on the cheek and a toffee. He had a mysterious attraction for women right from the start.

The school had its sex-scandals, though as Old Flybuttons' daughters grew with adolescence into objects of ridicule rather than distant desire these were of a homosexual or autosexual nature. Discovery led to a ceremonial beating, presided over by the headmaster before the highly appreciative eyes of the whole school. As the years passed these became Flybuttons' only appearances, along with prayers on Sunday night. He had a taste for hymns penned by Victorian divines dwelling heavily on Those Who Have Gone Before, Little Mounds in the Churchyard, and similar reminders of the extreme unreliability of the human frame and medical science. He gave long sermons on sin, which seemed to cover everything, and was an enthusiastic prayer for people, not only such standing targets as the leaders of Church and State, but boys incapacitated with quite minor ailments whom he brought undeservedly to the attention of the Almighty. An epidemic would put him in such a good mood he might even distribute afterwards from a tin of chocolate biscuits. With all this religion and caning, Alec supposed the place formed his character as well as anywhere else.

He occupied the most underprivileged social class in the school, of boys left 'in sole charge', their parents having sailed away in P. and O.s to rule, police, or defend the British Empire. Even the holidays were spent at school–poor compensation for letters with excitingly coloured stamps. Either through prolonged lack of contact with their kin or prolonged over-contact with each other these boys became the awkward squad, stealing freely and using quite horrible language, though one boy usually brightened things up with some highly diverting fits. To keep them out of mischief, Old Flybuttons held classes three mornings a week, right through the summer. When Alec finally qualified in medicine he told himself that he might not have had a particularly good education, but he had had an awful lot of it.

Alec was lucky in escaping occasionally to his grandmother in Ramsgate, or to his uncle the barrister's clerk, who with increasing prosperity had moved two stops down the Southern Railway to a jerry-built villa in the even more bosky-sounding suburb of Elmstead Woods. The barrister's clerk didn't care for Alec much. There was some financial arrangement with Robin over his upkeep, and like all Robin's financial arrangements it was on the mean side. Now and then he had a few days with his uncle Graham, spells of long-awaited and unbelievable luxury, though his cousin Desmond still punched him. But at least he was spared the pressing anxieties of the world in the early thirties. Of Hitler, Mussolini, or even Don Bradman he was privileged to know little, Old Flybuttons refusing his boys newspapers on the grounds that everything they reported was sinful. In this Alec afterwards agreed he was probably right.

One summer day in 1933 Old Flybuttons summoned Alec to his study.

'Er, Trevose–' He gave a short laugh. 'Trevose, I have some news for you.'

He laughed again. Alec decided at least it couldn't be a beating.

'Trevose–ha, ha! I have some news of an extremely serious nature. Bad news, in fact. Ha, ha, ha! Eh? Eh? What? Trevose, your father has died. Ha, ha, ha, ha, ha, ha!'

Chapter Twenty-seven

Graham was startled by his brother's death, however, half-expected. The two men had never enjoyed anything in common–if they excluded Edith–but Robin dead like Robin alive preached a moral lesson. Graham realized that time was no longer grains of sand under youthful flying feet, but rather dangerous grains of gunpowder to be used in blasting your path and liable to blow up in your face any minute. He got the news by telegram in a cottage he had bought to replace the Marylebone flat, overlooking the sea at Swanage in Dorset, which gave him the excuse to get away at week-ends and paint.

He was there with a girl called Jeannine, who embodied his first adventure since Maria's attempted suicide. The shame of that, or anyway the fright, had condemned him to three years' chastity. His relationship with Jeannine was admirably workmanlike. He never saw her from one week-end to the other, each Monday morning giving her the means to 'buy something nice', an arrangement which struck her as perfectly genteel through the transactions being completed by cheque rather than hard cash. And now, Graham told himself, as they drove back to London with the depressing telegram in his pocket, Edith would be coming home as an attractive widow of thirty-three. She had already been his fiancée, his mistress, and his sister-in-law, and this further relationship filled him with some disquiet.

She appeared early in 1934 from Elmstead Woods with young Alec, the sunburn above her black dress grotesque in the London weather. Graham was then earning and spending a good deal of money. He had a new Bentley, and had moved from the leafy avenues of Primrose Hill to a house in fashionable Queen Street, Mayfair. He had a cook, two maids, a housekeeper, and a pointedly ugly governess for Desmond, who had grown as tall as himself and in a year was leaving for a public school of enormous expense, antiquity, and incomprehensible traditions.

'Yes, it was ever so sudden,' said Edith. They were taking tea in Graham's upstairs drawing-room, Alec in his best grey flannel suit and highly-polished black boots, which he was idly kicking against the expensive furniture. 'He'd been having these headaches, but I don't think he ever let on how bad they were, not really. Then one evening he had the stroke. And that was that.'

She folded her hands in her lap. She had the same expression she wore beside the grate that stormy afternoon in Hampstead.

'I should have stopped him going out East again,' Graham reproached himself.

'It wasn't for you to tell him, Graham. Besides, you had worries enough yourself at the time, didn't you? Maria, and that. It was me who should have put my foot down, I suppose. But he wanted to go back. He was only happy out East. In a funny sort of way it made him glad, thinking he was giving up his health like he'd given up everything else.'

Graham shrugged his shoulders. He supposed malignant hypertension would have been equally fatal in London.

'Here are a few of his things. I think he wanted you to have them.'

She produced from her black handbag a crumpled manilla envelope containing some cuff-links, a set of pearl dress-studs, and a gold pocket watch. Graham slowly wound it up. He remembered Robin buying it, as a fittingly dignified instrument for taking pulses the day he qualified.

'Well!' Edith straightened herself. Graham saw Robin as a harrowing subject was to be dropped. 'How's Maria getting along?'

He laid the envelope aside. 'She has her ups and downs, you know. She's rather on the sick side at the moment.'

'Poor soul.' Edith reached for her teacup, which was of the best china, from Harrods. 'Would she like me to go up and see her?'

'Of course! She'd love it. But what about yourself?' Graham enquired pressingly. 'What are you going to do, back in England alone like this?'

'Oh, I'll manage,' she replied gaily. 'I shall find a position. Perhaps companion to some lady. I can nurse, remember, and Robin taught me lots of medical things. And I haven't forgotten my typewriting.'

Graham found this declaration of independence encouraging. He had feared Edith would impose herself for board and lodging, and there was no telling where that might lead to. Besides, he was living above his income as it was, and tax still stood at Snowden's crisis level of five shillings in the pound. But he was always amazed at the concrete robustness of her personality, weathering stormy tides which would have washed his own away in rubble. As he inclined his head enquiringly in the direction of her son she declared, 'I want Alec to be a doctor, you know. Like you and his father. He's terribly brainy and awfully sweet, honest,' she assured him.

'Yes, I'm sure he is,' said Graham. He surveyed this prospective entrant to the profession, the embodiment of Edith's transferred self-betterment, who had abandoned kicking his chair for playing with his yo-yo. She abruptly put down her teacup. 'Alec, darling, go outside a minute. I want to talk to your Uncle Graham.'

The boy obediently made for the door leading to the hall. Graham wondered uneasily what she wanted to talk to Uncle Graham about.

'I'm sure Alec would make a wonderful doctor,' Edith started. 'It's in the blood, isn't it? I'd love him to take it up. But I couldn't do it myself, of course. Not the expense. Robin left so little, and the pension's pitiful. I thought you might help, you see. Only a loan. He'd pay it back once he grew up and started earning. Lots of the students do, don't they? That's what Robin told me. It's a terrible liberty, I know. I hope you don't mind me even asking. It would have been different, of course, if only the professor hadn't met that woman.'

Graham felt this something of a tall order. A medical education would cost hundreds of pounds.

'I'm only sponging on you for old times' sake,' Edith added in a subdued voice.

Old times! Graham thought. The span of my early idiocies. He saw the professor's bed-knob again, rolling over the lino. But of course he was genuinely fond of Edith–much more than had he actually married her. The ideal lifetime's relationship with a woman, perhaps.

'Of course, I'm not expecting you to make up your mind here and now, Graham.'

'But I have. I'll do it,' Graham decided impulsively. Despite his selfishness, he was generous to the point of stupidity. He had been kind to less worthy women over necklaces and bracelets, and you couldn't heartlessly pawn a medical degree afterwards. 'I've set up a settlement affair for Desmond, and I expect Alec can be tacked on somehow. We'll go to my solicitors and get a document signed, sealed and delivered. As soon as you like.'

'Oh, Graham!' She got up and came near to him. 'It's my only hope left in the world–suddenly come true.'

'Let's not mention it again. It's all cut and dried.' Emotional thanks always embarrassed him, whether for the gift of money or a new face. 'I only ask you to keep it a secret from the lad. I'd hate have him treat me like Father Christmas.'

It occurred to him that Desmond might not be entirely pleased at sharing his inheritance. But his son was anyway well provided for–which was about the limit of Graham's interest in him at the time. He was too busy, and anyway what were schools and governesses so handsomely paid for?

'Graham, you're a darling.' He saw she was near to crying and about to kiss him, both of which he found gratifying, but they were interrupted by the maid throwing the door open even without knocking and exclaiming that 'the doctor' must see madam at once. His wife had been in the bathroom for hours washing herself, and the water was starting to come down the stairs.

For a year after her suicide attempt Maria had been quite gay. She was getting up, going out, even speaking of rejoining her committees. The dose of chloral hydrate seemed to have acted as a mental aperient. Then the assassin of depression started stalking again in the shadows of her life. This time Graham invoked a psychiatrist. He had felt earlier that he knew Maria's mind better than anybody, but events had plainly proved him wrong. Besides, now he had nothing to hide. After Cramphorn's gossiping, everyone in Blackfriars knew he had a half-mad wife.

Maria had been against the idea. She detested sharing her troubles with an outsider, it seemed yet another manifestation of weakness. But the psychiatrist himself–Dr Dency, youngish, fair-haired, thin, long-fingered and effeminate, a delicate watch-chain of little gold rods spread across his double-breasted dove-grey waistcoat–won her confidence with professional expertness. Another argument which influenced Graham was of such practitioners becoming not only fashionable but almost respectable. Dr Dency had recently been installed in a brand-new department at Blackfriars itself, to the outraged annoyance of Mr Cramphorn, who believed that all mental conditions from the feminine vapours to frank schizophrenia were curable by the removal of a sufficient number of abdominal organs.

Maria's washing was a recent affliction. She had started repeatedly washing her hands, but now her whole body after the slightest contact with other humans or even the chairs and tables they touched. A spill from her meals or even a speck of dust falling in the sunlight sent her in anguish to the wash-basin, where she muttered and followed a strange ritual inexplicable even to Graham's eyes. When, after Edith's visit, the water started coming downstairs quite regularly he felt it time to summon Dr Dency again. The psychiatrist diagnosed an obsessional state and prescribed one of the powerful new sedatives derived from barbituric acid. He told Graham solemnly to keep the tablets locked up in his study, and to issue them one at a time.

Maria became more depressed. She lay in bed all day staring blankly ahead of her, constantly smoothing the turned-over strip of sheet with her skinny hands. One evening Graham knocked over the flower-vase on her bedside table, uncovering a cache of misshapen veronal tablets under its hollow base. For a week she had been holding every dose under her tongue until he had quit the bedroom.

'You mustn't!' he said angrily. 'You *mustn't* try again. This time you might pull it off.'

Maria dumbly eyed her uncovered secret.

'I don't think I'd be silly again,' she said faintly.

'Then what did you collect them for, damn it?'

'I don't know. I don't know, Graham.' She stared round in confusion. 'I wanted to leave a door open. In case.'

'In case of what? Of what? Tell me!'

'In case I was left alone.'

'Of course you won't be left alone.' He scooped up the half-sucked tablets.

'I promised you, didn't I?'

'Oh, yes, you promised.' Her voice became even fainter. 'That's how I know you still love me, don't I? Even if I am . . . even if I am silly sometimes.'

Afterwards Graham inspected her mouth following every dose, like a child. But her fears of being abandoned became intolerable whenever he left the house. It was interfering with his practice. The servants were threatening to leave. Desmond was becoming frightened. He summoned the psychiatrist again. Almost casually Dr Dency mentioned, 'Have you thought about a home?'

'I couldn't possibly do that to her,' Graham objected at once.

'It would be justified by the suicide risk alone, you know, Graham. You can't be your wife's policeman for ever.'

'No, no, it's out of the question.'

After a week, he began to wonder if it might not be such a bad idea after all. She would be well looked after. It would stop wrecking his home and his work. It would be better for Desmond. It would be an enormous responsibility off his shoulders. But to be left among strangers was something she dreaded, and deliberately submitting her to it would be quite inhuman. On the other hand, it would be terribly convenient. He supposed it all came down to the old question–did he love Maria or not?

He thought about it for another week. Then he asked the psychiatrist. Dr Dency's long fingers played with the gold bars of his watchchain. 'I don't think love for your wife really has anything to do with the decision, Graham,' he advised in his soft voice. 'You're suffering feelings of guilt towards Maria, that's all. You've something of the same anxiety neurosis, you know. Luckily, you're able to compensate extremely well.'

'But I *do* love her. Well, I suppose so. Anyway, I must surely have loved her once? When I married her?'

'If I may say so, you have difficulty distinguishing your moods from your emotions. But none of us must be the slave of either.'

'What are you trying to tell me? That I'm hoping to convince myself I still love Maria simply to expunge the guilt I feel over various things I've done against her?'

'Yes,' said Dr Dency.

'Well, where shall we put her?' asked Graham.

Modern psychiatry could really be most helpful.

The psychiatrist recommended a discreet institution amid charming scenery in Sussex, where mildly deranged gentlefolk were housed in the comfort to which they were accustomed. Graham went down with Desmond to see her one week-end a month. The others he generally spent at the cottage with Jeannine. He left a standing order with a local greengrocer to send his wife a large basket of fresh fruit, regularly every Saturday morning.

Chapter Twenty-eight

It had been an exhausting three months, and Graham was glad to throw himself into the arms of the transatlantic liner stewards for five days' spoon-feeding to Southampton. He was travelling far too much. He had brought plastic surgery to the colonies with lectures in Kenya and Tanganyika, he had been received warmly in Prague if less so in Berlin, to Swedes and Danes his name was as familiar from the newspapers as Mr Eden's, his enlightenment of Madrid was frustrated only by the Civil War. The Dominions had done him proud, but the United States had outshone the world in enthusiasm and hospitality. In San Francisco he had driven ceremoniously across the amazing new Golden Gate bridge, in New Orleans he had lived in Edwardian luxury amid a regiment of negro servants, New York he had so enjoyed he promised to return for the World's Fair the following year. In Washington he had been introduced to the President, smiling in his wheel-chair, and in Los Angeles he had been introduced to Ginger Rogers. His only regrets were missing a return passage on the brand-new *Queen Mary*, and disappointing the many who asked, after a few moments' conversation, if he personally knew Mrs Simpson.

In August 1938 the sea promised to be calm, he would sit wrapped in a rug on a steamer-chair, smoking Camel cigarettes and reflecting on life in general. There was plenty to reflect about, with Hitler and Mussolini on the rampage. Graham felt the world was starting to move too quickly for him, Perhaps at forty-three he was already like members of his club–he had joined one of the best in St James's–despairing old gentlemen with minds shaped by the more elegant moulds of the past. But at least his private life was undemandingly simple.

Jeannine had been swallowed up by marriage years ago. Then came Annie, a lively young spark, neither well-off nor intelligent, who had half-starved herself to see him as a private patient for a scar on her chin, overgrown with an ugly growth of keloid tissue after a burn from her bathroom geyser. She was what Maria would have called 'a working woman', a shop-girl selling art books in Charing Cross Road. This common interest led Graham to the shop and her later to the cottage in Dorset. He found she had a profound curiosity in copulation, questioning him lengthily about such technicalities as erections and emissions, orgasms and ovulations, and even impregnations and insufflations. He felt she never mastered his explanations, but that hardly mattered. Annie may have been weak on the theory, but he awarded her top marks in the practical. It occurred to him sometimes his conduct with Annie, strictly speaking, was professionally infamous. He had admittedly operated on the girl, but he felt this could hardly be construed as a doctor-patient relationship, as though he were her family physician in charge of her health from one year to another. And anyway, he told himself, the scar had been an extremely small one.

When Annie drifted away, Graham found his booming private practice left him hardly time or energy to find her replacement. To be free of any entanglement was in a way refreshing, like relief from some chronic itch. He had nothing to love but his work, and his work was rewarding him more kindly than any woman. As for Edith, she had returned to square one and was typing for a Gray's Inn solicitor. Maria was well, even putting on weight, and got her basket of fruit every Saturday.

Graham tucked in the rug of his steamer-chair and opened Margaret Mitchell's *Gone With the Wind*, which he felt would outlast a voyage even to China. No more entanglements, no more excitements, just work and the riskless relaxation of painting.

He had no idea Stella Garrod was aboard the liner until the cocktail party in the captain's cabin. He hadn't intended to go, hearing from more seasoned passengers it would be a tedious affair, but he always had difficulty refusing invitations to go anywhere. The captain received him in gold braid and stiff shirt, an amazingly small man, Graham thought, to command so large a ship. The other guests, he presumed business people, were at first soberly dull and then drunkenly duller. He was trying to leave when Stella Garrod arrived–or exploded into the cabin like a shell from some passing battle-cruiser.

She was late. She was always late. To a star of stage and films, time is something to be calculated by others from her own celestial movements.

'My God, I'm sorry, it's really awful of me, I'd no idea of the hour.' She set the little captain awash with gushing apologies. 'The day flies like a dream when you've absolutely nothing to do from morning to night. *Je regrette mille fois, mon cher capitaine, je suis désolée.* Yes, gin, champagne makes me violently ill.' She shuddered as a second steward approached with a tray, caviar apparently inducing similar pathology. 'This weather! So hot and stuffy. My God, I wish I was a seagull! How wonderful to spread your wings and soar all the way across the ocean. Haven't you got Camels? I only smoke Camels. *Merci.*'

The thanks were directed to Graham's cigarette-case. She didn't even look at him, though he inspected her closely enough. She was almost as beautiful as her photographs, which you came across everywhere, even in gentlemen's lavatories. She seemed shorter off the screen. She wore a black chiffon-and-lace dress with a design of pink and gold flowers in sprays, seeming to clasp the gentle contours of her bosom and pelvis as eagerly as half the world apparently wished to. Her blonde hair fell in a jumble of curls over each ear, her lower lip was full, the eyes under geometrically precise arches of mascara she kept half-shut. Graham wondered if she thought it more alluring, or if she possibly suffered from some form of facial palsy.

As the little captain introduced his guests Stella Garrod greeted them all warmly–indeed, affectionately–though Graham saw she never bothered to notice their names or even their faces. She seemed to hear neither what anyone said to her nor what she was saying herself. She was totally self-centred. After a few puffs she crushed out her cigarette, immediately demanding another. She hardly touched her cocktail. As she chattered, her little hand, brilliant with diamonds and nail-polish, flicked out to illustrate the points of stories about Ivor Novello, C.B.Cochran, Clark Gable, Alexander Korda and others who crowded round her to exclude the daylight of the normal world. She's really amazingly nervous, thought Graham. He supposed her self-possession on the stage had the same professional quality of his own self-possession in the operating theatre. Actresses were interesting people. He wished he knew more of them. But quite damnably they all seemed to take their faces to Archie McIndoe.

After twenty minutes the performance was over. As the captain and the businessmen swept aside for the star's exit, Graham mentioned on an impulse, 'I believe I know a friend of yours–Lady Pocock.'

'Oh, God! Pat Pocock.' She paused, patting her blonde curls. 'But nobody recognizes her these days, my dear. She got herself a new nose for the Coronation.'

Graham smiled. 'I know. I made it.'

'*You* did? Then you're a beauty doctor? How terribly exciting.' Recognition dawned in the pale green eyes under her lazy lids. 'This week in

Life–it was you, wasn't it? Pages and pages, quite sensational publicity. I was livid with envy.'

She disappeared, leaving behind a pungent perfume, like the exhaust from some beautiful racing-car.

Stella Garrod ate alone in her stateroom with her secretary, which she told herself was *triste, mais très nécessaire*. If she lost her remoteness she was on her way to losing her all. Besides, people on ships were unbearable, and anyway she had decided to spend the voyage in a bad temper. Her play had expired in the heat of a New York summer, unmourned, its obituaries written at its birth. She had missed the chance of a part in the new Bridie show opening at home in London. The film industry was in a state of jitters because it feared a war, which she felt crossly was really no concern of hers. The script her agent had sent from London was hopeless–the man was impossible, for all he cared she would end up that Christmas playing in pantomime. Her new secretary, an English girl she had hired in New York, was impossible too, and would be fired promptly on arrival. Her mood was not lightened by remembering the shipping company, in reverence of her publicity value, was carrying the pair of them half-fare.

But even the remotest of film stars needs exercise. The next evening Graham found her on deck, trailing a flimsy scarf and wearing sunglasses, leaning in sulky contemplation over the rail.

'Aren't ships ghastly?' she began before he could reintroduce himself. He leant beside her, resting a brown-and-white buckskin shoe on the metalwork. 'They feed you like animals to keep you quiet, the decks resemble the Broad Walk at Atlantic City, and the people are just as horrible. It's my twentieth crossing–I think so. I've lost count. Five days gone from my life. A hundred days altogether. Just think! Couldn't you give me a drug or something, Doctor? To keep me insensible till we landed? So you made Pat Pocock her new nose?' she went on without pausing. 'Well, there was plenty of room for improvement.' She wrinkled her own. 'You've got to be a doctor, have you? Just for that sort of business?'

'It's a rather more drastic procedure than a shampoo and set, you know.'

'Everyone seems to be having their noses bobbed these days. Or their faces lifted. I suppose that's your line of country, too?'

He nodded. 'A more desperate operation. To revive past glories rather than embellish present ones.'

'Where do you operate, Doctor? In London or New York?'

'In London. Mainly at the Cavendish Clinic. And at hospital, of course. Blackfriars. On the charity patients.'

'Tell me some other operations you do,' she invited. 'I can take it. I'm tough, you know. You've got to be in this business.'

Resting his arms on the teak rail, Graham gave her a brief and undisturbing, if self-flattering, sketch of his work. He had the valuable quality of lecturing interestingly and acceptably to the lay public, which he had discovered in himself that afternoon at Half Moon Street. She listened in silence, and he ventured to end with, 'At least you, Miss Garrod, are spared the necessity of my attentions.'

She gave a laugh. She seemed to be mocking him. Then she fell silent, looking towards the stern, watching the evening sun dowse itself with amazing swiftness in the sea. 'Come with me,' she said abruptly.

Graham followed her. It was rather peculiar, but she was a peculiar woman. They took the lift down four decks and made their way along the main alleyway, fringed with its ferns in little pots, towards her stateroom. As she still said nothing Graham speculated on the reasons for the sudden invitation, all of which seemed flattering or even exciting. The door of the suite was opened by the English girl, red in the face and hot, having discovered her secretarial duties included washing and ironing Miss Garrod's underwear. She was curtly dismissed to the bedroom. The actress turned to face Graham, pulling up the curls from her right ear. 'Well, Doctor?' Her expression was laughingly mischievous. 'What do you think of that?'

The ear was twisted and deformed, hardly more than a few blebs of scarlet flesh.

'That surprises you, Doctor? The studio can give me a false one.' She let the hair drop into place. 'Marvellous the movies, nothing is beyond them. But now they say hair's going up. Perhaps it'll be the ruin of me, like the talkies were the ruin of half Hollywood.'

She reached for a cigarette.

'But that must have been a tremendous handicap,' Graham burst out. He was moved to pity. A dying man or a crippled child left him unaffected, but marred beauty always touched him.

'Yes, I suppose it was a hindrance,' she agreed offhandedly.

'Wouldn't you like me to do something about it? I could, you know. I could give you an ear just like the healthy one.'

She exhaled smoke from her open mouth. 'How?'

'May I have another look?' She acquiesced. 'Gillies has an operation–you must have heard of him? He uses cartilage from the ear of the patient's mother.'

'My mother's dead.'

'Well, I'm dubious about moving tissue from one person to another, anyway.' He inspected the deformity. 'I'd take a slip from one of your rib cartilages as a basic strut. Skin-grafting and moulding would complete the job. I'd make a sandwich of tissue, skin on the outside, cartilage in the middle, you understand. The lobe and a lot of the outer rim are intact. It would be done in stages, the whole business spread over six or nine months—'

'Impossible! Six months away from the limelight and I'd be forgotten.'

'But you wouldn't be out of action longer than a week at a time. If you were filming it would be quite easy to fit in, surely? I could get you into the Cavendish the day we docked.'

'How much would it cost?'

'Three hundred guineas.'

'My God! I could buy a car for that.' She had a sharp grasp of the value of money.

'But you *must* let me do it,' he pleaded. 'I shall never be able to see your picture again without thinking of it, aching to do something about it. You shouldn't have let me into the secret,' he added reproachfully.

'Oh, life's too complicated. Particularly just now. Everyone has to replan their whole existence after another of Hitler's speeches.' She stubbed out her partly smoked cigarette. She wondered if there was something in the idea. The operation could hardly be more fuss and trouble than an abortion. She supposed the doctor was clever enough–after all, he had been in *Life*. 'Maybe it's an investment for the future? Any man's flattered now to be seen with the famous, fantastic Stella Garrod. Who'd make love to a one-eared old hag?'

Graham nodded understandingly.

She lit another cigarette. 'I'll think about it.'

'Will you promise? Let me know before we dock. You could leave absolutely all the arrangements to me.' He smiled. 'I'd even make sure you didn't back out.'

'I never back out. Once my mind is made up *les jeux sont faits*.'

Leaving the stateroom, Graham remembered something John Bickley had once said–'Never trust a woman who quotes French', though adding over his drink, 'Unless, of course, the dear girl happens to be a Frenchwoman.'

Chapter Twenty-nine

Graham's first distraction in London was a flaming row with Tom Raleigh.

'What have you been doing all these cases for?' he demanded. 'Look at this . . . four rhinoplasties, reconstruction of eyelids, face-lift . . . two face-lifts . . . three face-lifts. You now perfectly well what the arrangement is. I do the cosmetic operations and you can have your pick of the reconstructive work. It's not particularly loyal of you to take advantage once my back's turned.'

Graham scattered the pile of folders angrily over his desk. He had moved from his Japanese surroundings in Queen Anne Street to a consulting room at the new clinic at Cavendish Square, in which he had made a shrewd investment while it was still a tangle of girders in the sky–a tangle inducing many doubtful shakes of heads behind Harley Street windows. It wasn't the sort of clinic illuminating the earnest dreams of the socialists, with their far-fetched ideas of lighting beacons of free healing throughout the land and pinning patients' bills on the taxpayer. It was as luxurious as the Dorchester Hotel, though naturally the service was more expensive. The operating theatres on the top floor had the most modern American stainless-steel fittings, and coffee was served to the surgeons in silver pots. The consulting rooms on the lower one were decorated in the latest style, the furniture shinily tubular, the lights in severe glass globes with their dregs of parboiled flies, the clocks dispensing with strict accuracy in favour of strict angularity. Graham had one of the largest rooms, and the rent was enormous.

Tom Raleigh opened and closed his small fists behind his back. He had become a partner in the practice when the flood of private cases rose too high for Graham to stem by himself. Graham had picked Tom because he was easy to get along with–he never argued, never complained, and took the blame for everything. He allowed the young man twenty per cent of the profits, though, like the Saracen, had demanded a sweetener to start with. Graham often wondered how the poor little devil raised the money. The poor little devil had forsworn smoking, drinking, and holidays, sacked the housemaid, and mortgaged the modest roof under which his wife and three children lived in permanent hope and temporary forbearance.

'I didn't think you'd mind, Graham,' he said timidly. 'The private waiting-list was getting enormous.'

'Of course I mind! Breaking the spirit of our partnership is far more repugnant than breaking the letter. That's how I see it, if you don't.'

Tom started obediently gathering up the scattered folders. 'I'll tell you why I really did those cases. Because I don't think I'm getting enough experience.'

'My God, you're getting the best experience in the world! I've given you a free enough hand at St Sebastian's and Blackfriars, haven't I? I could have picked up fifty young fellows in America to fill the job instead of you. Think of that next time you're feeling so cocky. Of course I must handle all the cosmetic work, in private, at any rate. There's a perfectly good reason. I'm much better at it than you are.'

Graham lay back in his tubular desk chair, folding his arms across his smart double-breasted chalk-stripe grey suit. Tom went on, sounding casual, 'I've been thinking everything over while you were away, Graham, and I want to leave you.'

'Oh?' Graham sat up. 'So *that's* why you've really been doing all these cosmetic operations? Getting yourself a nice little reputation among the patients' friends and doctors while I was out of the way. I understand.'

'No, no, it wasn't like that at all.' Tom twisted his little hands. He looked more like a mole than ever, a mole dragged at last into the highly uncomfortable daylight.

'All right, if you want to set up shop on your own go ahead,' said Graham impulsively. 'We'll split asunder. Get the lawyers to scribble something on a piece of paper.'

'Of course, I realize I shall lose my investment—'

'I wouldn't load my conscience with a pound of *your* flesh,' Graham told him airily. 'God knows what you're going to live on, anyway. This is the toughest specialty in the world. I cracked my way into the ring, but I'm damned if I'm going to help you to. That's your affair. I'm just upset by your gross ingratitude, that's all.'

'Listen, Graham–' Tom leant over the desk, his teeth showing and his eyes blazing. Graham looked startled. An angry mole is an unusual sight. 'Do you remember that paper you published on mandibular fractures? Who did the work?' He tapped his tubby chest. 'I did. Whose name appeared on it? Yours. Do you remember those hare-lips you talked about to the Paediatric Society? Whose cases were they? Who did the operations? And who got the credit? Why, you won't even let me give a lecture on my own! I can't understand why you're jealous of me. I've never done anything to harm you, never got in your way.'

'Jealous of *you*?' Graham was outraged. 'Don't be so bloody stupid. You might as well say Carnera was jealous of a fly-weight.'

Tom's anger sputtered out like a match, leaving him with black remorse. 'I'm sorry, Graham. I shouldn't have lost my temper like that. You've been very good to me, and I recognize it–I hope you'll believe that.' Graham said nothing. 'After all, I've been working with you now one way or another the best part of ten years. The last thing I wish is to let you down. I'll certainly stay in the practice until you want to see the back of me.'

Graham looked at his watch. 'It is now eleven fifteen a.m. Shall we say twelve noon?'

Tom Raleigh pursed his lips. Slowly he gathered up five or six files of notes. Without saying anything else he left the consulting room.

Graham sat at the desk in a temper, worsened by the suspicion that Tom had been perfectly right. Of course he'd been jealous of him. He couldn't help it, he had to be the cock of the walk. He had even been quite jealous of his son Desmond one afternoon before leaving for America, when the housemaid came complaining of seduction attempted with an enthusiasm bordering on rape. He swept the files from his desk into a heap on the floor. He would start from scratch, train up somebody else. Spiritless little Tom had been mentally enervating, anyway. He remembered he wanted a bed that night in the Clinic for Stella Garrod. Now he would have to arrange it himself, which would be a dreadful bore. Anyway, he had to hurry to Blackfriars. He had a long-standing assignation with Lilly.

He arrived at the hospital to find everyone talking about the coming war. Fresh from the secure remoteness of America he was astounded by this mental attitude–people seemed not only to expect the fighting to start, but to have little conversation for anything else.

'Scaremongering,' he dismissed it to John Bickley in the anaesthetic room of the Arlott Wing. 'The Americans don't think anything will come of it. Over there you can take a properly balanced view.'

'So you reckon Hitler's bluffing?' asked John cheerfully. He slowly opened the ether valve of the anaesthetic machine as his patient slid into unconsciousness with nitrous oxide gas.

'Of course he is,' Graham assured him. 'He couldn't possibly start a war over Czechoslovakia. He's no money, no supplies, and all his doctors are in Hampstead.'

He was gratified to find everyone excited to see him back–his new registrar, the houseman he still shared with orthopaedics, his theatre sister, even the pair of nurses scurrying in the background with long-handled Cheadle's forceps plucking sterile instruments from steaming water. Graham could be infuriating while operating, his usual charm ousted by concentration on his work. But he always apologized afterwards, and anyway he was their 'Chief'–a light-fingered wizard to be proud of, a possession and honoured commander. As John Bickley trundled the patient in he said, 'Let's hope this is our final go at Lilly. We'll be glad to see the last of each other.'

'The last pedicle certainly took like a dream.'

'I suppose she's still drinking?'

'Judging by the amount of ether I've had to push into her, yes.'

Graham inspected the face, shoulders, and chest in front of him. There seemed nothing of the original left. Lilly was a drunk–middle-aged, fat, and ugly to start with–and like many drunks destined at some time or other to fall into her sitting-room fire. When she appeared in Blackfriars three years earlier, charred black from the waist upwards, the general surgeons so despaired of her they simply put her in a side room to die. Graham heard about her casually over lunch and asked if he might see her, a request which Mr Doxy, her surgeon in charge, thought typically pushful. But he agreed. After all, she was beyond reclaim by any practitioner on earth and in a matter of hours would have the choice of any in Heaven.

Graham moved Lilly to his own wards and set to work. Since Maria's hospitalization Graham had interested himself in the reparative side of plastic surgery with the enthusiasm of Haileybury, if not his exclusiveness. He was still too fond of the easy fees of vanity. He somehow kept Lilly alive with transfusions and oxygen, then started grafting skin from her plump legs to her raw burns. The more times he operated the more he became obsessed with her case. It was a severe technical exercise, and only he was capable of it. He was proud of the healing body, as he was proud of the burnt children he repaired at Blackfriars and St Sebastian's for no money and scant professional renown. As for the woman herself, he thought little about her. The surgery of burns interested him a great deal and burnt patients very little.

He cut a paper-thin oblong of skin from Lilly's thigh and stitched it to a still untreated area under her chin. The final result he thought spectacular. His pieces had grown into place, his scars were beautifully faint, at least she had a recognizable face and was alive and drinking. 'I'll quite miss her,' he told John Bickley as he put the dressings on. 'She's become to me a regular mental exercise, like the stockbroker's daily crossword puzzle.'

'Don't speak too soon, Graham. She can still fall in the fire again.'

'Human nature,' murmured Graham. 'The more I see of people the more I sense in them the seeds of their own destruction. We bring half the miseries of this world on ourselves, whether we're obsessed at escaping from the shape of our nose or from life in general.'

As he was walking with the anaesthetist from the Arlott Wing for a late lunch in the hospital refectory, Graham said, 'I've come back from America with a new ambition.'

'Let me guess. No, I can't. You're the man who has everything. To buy a string of racehorses and win the Derby?'

'To become President of the Royal College of Surgeons.' John raised his eyebrows. 'That's the one thing I *haven't* got–recognition in the profession. Mention me to any woman over a dinner-table in London or New York and she'd say, "You mean the face doctor?" But how do I stand in the eyes of the general surgeons, toiling away among their ribbons of gut and cobbling up whatever they decide in their majesty to yank out? Nowhere. Plastic surgeons are trivial men, comic-cuts characters.'

'So are anaesthetists.'

'To my modest mind the work I do here on cleft palates, allowing children to grow up without a terrible deformity in their speech, is just as worthy as theirs, allowing them to grow up without a deformity in their guts. What girl can face adolescence sanely with a cleft lip? How about those burns? I've taught myself more about burns than anyone in London. I've saved limbs and lives. If I have to perform an amputation I'm depressed for a week. The general boys do one without thinking twice. And they all dismiss me as a sort of beauty specialist, Elizabeth Arden with a knife.'

'They envy your glamour with the public, Graham. *Life* magazine, and all that. They're all exhibitionists themselves–they wouldn't become surgeons otherwise. Though I agree, they don't waste any chance to get nasty behind your back.'

'"And what is fame? A gilded butt, for ever pierced with the arrows of malignancy",' sighed Graham. 'Do you know who said that?'

'No?'

'Edward Jenner. He also invented vaccination. But I've made up my mind I'm standing for the committee of the College next year. That'll shake the boys up a bit. I even think I can pull it off. I've got friends enough to push me. I've grasped the technique of electioneering. I'm going to rely on you to accomplish some subtle canvassing for me.'

'I'll do anything I can, and willingly. But it's a tough proposition. The competition's terrible.'

'Nonsense.' Graham laughed. 'If I can turn the bulbous-nosed daughter of a stockbroker into a classical beauty under the hour, I can do anything.' They reached the stairs to the refectory in the basement of the main hospital building. 'By the way, I'd like you to dope a case for me in the Cavendish tomorrow morning at eight. Female by the name of Stella Garrod.' John stared at him. 'I crossed on the boat with her. It's a first-stage reconstruction of the auricle. Yes, you may well look surprised. Keep it under your hat, there's a good lad. She's coming into the Cavendish this evening, if you want to have a look at her.'

'I most certainly *do* want to have a look at her!'

Graham laughed. 'I don't think she'll destroy even your illusions.'

At eight the next morning the mouth the world yearned to kiss was blocked with a stout red-rubber tube, through which John Bickley was delivering his anaesthetic. Graham was encouraged to find he had more tissue to play with than he expected. The lobe was normal, the shrivelled upper part of the ear lying more or less in its right position. He could do the first two stages in one. He cut a strip of cartilage from a rib, and on a small sterile block of wood in the corner of the operating theatre fashioned it into a flat plate the size and shape of her normal ear. Then he cut a semi-circle of skin behind the malformed one, slipped the plate of cartilage inside and sewed up the incision with his usual fine, close stitches. Once the wound had healed and the transplanted cartilage was living healthy in its new site, like the corporal's nose of long ago, the plate with its covering of skin could be raised away from the side of her head. Unless, of course, the lot went septic... Graham's hands sweated inside his gloves at the thought.

'This is enough to put me off the pictures for good,' said John Bickley.

Chapter Thirty

The Cavendish Clinic was as understanding in providing its distinguished patients with secrecy as with publicity. Three days later Stella Garrod was smuggled back to her flat in Brook Street, near Grosvenor Square. Graham called to remove the stitches after ten days more, the dressings were abandoned a week later. At the end of September her new secretary telephoned him. Yes, Miss Garrod was perfectly fit, and delighted with the operation. She was taking a party to the first night of a new musical the following Thursday. She would be thrilled if Mr Trevose could join them.

They met in Stella's flat for cocktails. There were about a dozen guests, including Lady Pocock, accompanied not by Lord Pocock but an exquisitely brilliantined young man whom Graham supposed his handiwork had attracted. It was a bad evening for a party. The Prime Minister was in Munich and the peace of Europe, for so long as fragile as the Crystal Palace, now looked like following that structure in rapid conflagration. There were actually trenches in Hyde Park–it was serious. Everyone had a gas-mask, even Miss Stella Garrod. The forty-four anti-aircraft guns possessed by the country were bared in public, to influence the will of their protégés if not their prospective enemies. The eagles' wings of the German Air Force shadowed streets and minds everywhere across the face of Europe.

If the musical comedy was to be a distraction from such alarming times, it failed sadly. Even Graham found the show dull, and he had the advantage of no ear for music. Stella Garrod was in a bad mood from the start. A playwright, an old bed-companion of hers, was supposed to be with them and had failed not only to appear but to apologize. Only the cascade of boos descending on the cast with the curtain put her in a better temper. She insisted on taking them to one of the most expensive restaurants in London for supper, which Graham found more exciting. It was splendid to sit among stage people, to hear their chatter, even to impress such worldly creatures with his own calling. He wondered vaguely if the party might get in the newspapers, and what Haileybury would say. About one o'clock the guests started drifting away, and Graham found himself presented with the bill. It was enormous. He looked round hopefully, but no one seemed inclined to dispossess him. He took out his cheque-book and fountain-pen, feeling it rather a blatant imposition. Why, it ran away with the profits of his hostess's operation.

In the lobby of the restaurant he found her in a sable coat, and on an impulse offered her a lift home. He explained he lived more or less round the corner.

'But of course, you're very kind,' she told him. 'And I detest taxis, you never know who's been in them.'

He drove his Bentley to Brook Street. She yawned and said casually, 'Come in.'

The flat was empty, the sitting-room as they had left it, full of ash and empty glasses. She yawned again. 'Wasn't it a putrid show?'

'I've seen better, certainly.'

'Do you want a drink?'

'No, thank you. Not so late. I'm operating at nine.'

She yawned a third time. Graham stood in the middle of the carpet, his hands clasped behind his back, feeling foolish.

'Alors? Nous nous amuserons en faisant l'amour?'

'I beg your pardon?' asked Graham, whose French was not very good.

She gave a laugh and, starting to sing a tune from the show, made her way to the bedroom, throwing the sable wrap on the floor. The playwright had failed her, and she thought no evening complete without a sexual finale.

Graham found her at the dressing-table, taking off her jewellery.

'Didn't you say you had a wife?' She was looking at herself in the mirror. 'Or is she dead?'

'Virtually. She's in a home for chronic invalids.'

'Oh, I'm sorry,' she consoled him offhandedly. 'Yes, I imagined you weren't attached to a woman.'

'Why do you say that?'

'Oh, I don't know . . . ' She kicked off her shoes and started to strip her silk stockings. 'You're too polite, too considerate. A man who lives with one woman soon takes all women for granted. Did you have any children?'

'Yes, a son.' Graham slipped off his dinner-jacket. The calmness of the scene startled him. The pair of them might have been married for years. 'He's seventeen.'

She let her dress drop on the floor, and kicked it aside with her bare foot. 'Is *he* interested in women?'

He started undoing his dress-studs. 'I'm afraid rather too much for a boy of his age,' he smiled. 'Now he's left school I suppose he's nothing else to think about. That's one reason why I'm sending him away for a year in Switzerland.'

'Much better! On the Continent they bring up young men to see girls as a necessity instead of an occasional treat.' She pulled the hair from her ear. 'Well, Doctor–you can admire your handiwork.'

The wound was healing beautifully.

When Graham woke up it was pitch dark. Where was he? Ah, yes . . . He looked at his wrist-watch.

My God!

Five past nine.

He leapt up. Light seeped round the edges of the heavy curtains. He snatched one aside. Brook Street was busy with the traffic of an autumn morning. Under the canopy of the four-poster bed Stella Garrod stirred lazily.

'What's the matter, darling?' She focused her sleepy eyes, trying hard to remember who he was.

'I should be at the hospital,' he said frantically.

It came back to her. He looked quite different without his clothes on.

'Darling, do forgive me,' he apologized briskly. He leant across the bed to kiss her. 'I'll ring you later in the day.'

She smiled, and apparently went to sleep again. He looked round for his clothes.

My God!

A dress suit.

There was no escape. He could hardly telephone his house and have Desmond bring across his day things. If he turned up the collar, perhaps no one would notice. He scrambled into the black trousers. Stella Garrod started to snore, quite loudly.

He tiptoed from the bedroom. The sitting-room was harsh with light. The mess had been cleared away. At a desk in the corner sat a mannish-looking short-haired woman of about thirty, in tweeds and thick horn-rimmed glasses, smoking a cigarette in a holder and snipping cuttings from the morning papers.

'We're saved,' said the woman. She held up the front page of the *Express*, decorated with the five enormous letters PEACE and an exclamation mark. 'He's flying home today, it says. Umbrella and all.'

Graham stared at her blankly, clutching the jacket round his throat.

'Like some coffee?' she asked.

'No . . . no, thank you.' He felt he should give some explanation of himself. 'Miss Garrod's still asleep', was all that came to mind.

'She likes her lie-in when she can get it.' The secretary tipped ash from her holder. 'She deserves it, poor dear, and that's a fact.'

'I've got to get going,' mumbled Graham.

'See you again sometime.'

'Yes . . . yes, of course.' He sincerely hoped not.

His car was outside. He would explain at home he'd been caught in some revels to do with this peace business in Munich. He'd explain at Blackfriars that . . . oh, God, what *would* he explain? He wished he had time for a bath. He must have a bite of breakfast somehow. Then he suddenly remembered the restaurant bill as well. A disastrous evening altogether.

Or was it?

That afternoon Graham stopped in Bond Street to buy a diamond and sapphire brooch. He sent it to Stella with a note saying he would die if he didn't see her. Even the secretary was softened towards him by the obvious cost.

He suddenly remembered he had been home over a month, and hadn't yet been down to Sussex to see Maria.

Chapter Thirty-one

Eric Haileybury led what he considered to be the life of a gentleman. He had a small, square, stone-built house off the Upper Richmond Road, amid a tidy garden where even the laurel bushes seemed to have been dusted daily against the London grime. He was forty-six, and still unmarried. There had been shadowy affairs, the most promising with a lady almoner at King Alfred's, whom he had taken once or twice to substantial and sober feasts at the Trocadero. But he forbore inviting her to browse with him on more settled pastures. Marriage meant sexual responsibility, which he was not prepared to shoulder. He didn't like the idea. He failed to see the attraction of submitting part of himself to a dark female tube surrounded by writhing muscles and other tubes of unpleasantly excretory function. It might not be the common view, but there it was. He settled for the housekeeping of his younger sister, who was devoted to him. She was eager for men normally enough, but was obliged sadly to restrict their advances to her dreams, through her close resemblance to his lanky, bony, big-handed self.

Haileybury drove a ten-horse-power Morris, never smoked, drank just a little wine, enjoyed a frugal board, and entertained himself three or four times a summer watching Henry Wood conduct the Proms at the Queen's Hall or Hendren and young Compton bat at Lord's. Where Graham expressed his creative urge in painting, Haileybury made model railway engines. Nothing soothed him like standing at his lathe in his shirtsleeves, breathing the sweet smell of warm lubricating oil and crunching underfoot metal shavings. He had scores of models, from Stephenson's 'Rocket' to the 'Coronation Scot', each executed with the same precision as his operations. They were all round the house, and his sister thought they took a lot of dusting.

As Graham observed, with the passage of years such abstemiousness was bound to set its mark on any man. Haileybury grew thinner, the tendons of his neck showing through the skin above his stiff white collars like hawsers under canvas. His outlook was becoming equally desiccated. His lectures suffocated his audiences with torrents of carefully graded facts to the points of occasional unconsciousness. His doctrine of plastic surgery remained as austere as ever, enshrined in the shining if profitless principles of reconstructive operations for congenital defects, burns, or accidents.

Cosmetic surgery he thought devilish handiwork. If we disliked the faces bestowed on us by Nature they were but trials to test us, to be borne with the cheerfulness summoned up by more horrible defects, not changed like an ill-fitting suit of clothes. He argued with Graham at every turn. 'So we may say, Trevose,' he remarked as Graham demonstrated a successful nasal reconstruction on a young Jewess with theatrical ambitions, 'you have turned the lady into not only a thing of beauty but a goy for ever.' It was the one joke of his life.

The only opinion he shared with Graham was on the impossibility of war. He had been to Germany for his holidays, walking across the Thüringer Wald from Weimar to Coburg, and the people were the most sensible, decent, hospitable, and clean you could meet anywhere. But when the olive branch planted with such ceremony at Munich bore only withered leaves of disillusionment, even Haileybury became troubled. He certainly didn't relish a war. He'd seen too much of its dregs with the Saracen. But to find himself again in uniform, with a rank unbelievable to the dapper young lieutenant of the Ramsgate face hospital . . . Anyway, his letter from the Army had to be kept secret, and so therefore had his excitement. Meanwhile, it led him into a good deal of self-questioning and self-doubt, tempered by some unusual self-deception.

One Saturday afternoon in May 1939, when a gentlemanly British mission was skirting the barren diplomatic pastures of Europe by leisurely taking ship to parley with the ruffianly leaders in Moscow, Haileybury sat in the living-room of his house with an unexpected visitor. When the man had written begging an appointment Haileybury felt the meeting might be a demanding one, and he was discovering that he had guessed right.

'Why precisely did you come to me?' he asked dryly.

Lord Cazalay nervously brushed the bar of black moustache on his fat, red face. He glanced evasively round the room, seeming to meet everywhere model railways engines. It must be like living in a workshop. People were becoming most peculiar in England these days.

Since his father made his trap-door exit from the political stage Maria's elder brother had lived on the fringe of the Pyrenees in Pau, but after succeeding to the title rumblings of wars and a vague call to clear his family name had brought him home. He was shocked to find how the crash of the Cazalays had been totally forgotten. People were far more interested in dog-racing and Mickey Mouse. He approached a publishing firm in Paternoster Row, seized such papers his father had felt prudent to leave behind in dozens of black tin boxes at his solicitors', and started work with desk, pen, and paper. He was starting to confess the vindication of his father might after all be a task beyond him, but the people in Paternoster Row were understanding. They felt it might be a task beyond anyone.

'I came to you because you are a medical man, Mr Haileybury,' Lord Cazalay replied carefully. 'I could have initiated action myself, I suppose–my solicitors say as much–but I should doubtless find myself tied in knots by you professional gentlemen. Anyway, to my mind, it's essentially a matter as between doctors.'

He sat back in his armchair, regarding Haileybury with his bulging cod's eyes.

'I see,' said Haileybury.

'The business is utterly tragic,' Lord Cazalay went on more fiercly. 'I wept when I first saw her. Wept! I don't mind admitting it. Why, she used to be one of the loveliest women in London. And not so long ago. Even twenty years isn't a lifetime. What is she now? A wreck of a human being, aged beyond her years, locked up like a madwoman. Of course she isn't mad! She's as sane as you or I. There's certainly no insanity in *our* family, believe you me.'

Haileybury said nothing. From his professional training he knew the lunatic of the family is always held as the victim of unhappy circumstances rather than of unhappy heredity.

'Everything's the fault of that swine Trevose, Mr Haileybury. He wrecked my sister's health. He's been damnably callous towards her. I knew the man was a rotter when I first set eyes on him.'

Haileybury turned over his Lordship's letter on the low brass-topped table before him. 'It's only fair to say I always heard Trevose was most attentive to his wife.'

Haileybury was the most dangerous sort of enemy, the righteous one.

'Quite frankly, I can't believe that.' Lord Cazalay brushed his moustache again. 'The trouble lay in his being attentive to a good many other ladies as well. I've made it my business to find out.'

'I believe there was some scandal with his secretary. However regrettable, hardly the first in Harley Street. I doubt if the affair was a burden on Trevose's conscience. You can hardly expect it to become a burden on mine.'

'What about this Stella Garrod woman?' Lord Cazalay demanded aggressively. 'You know, the actress. For months now he's been running after her like a little dog. It's disgusting. My sister might just as well be dead and buried, instead of shut away in her prime. And this is the point.' He tapped the brass table with his pudgy forefinger. 'He has operated on this woman Garrod. I don't know what for, some sort of face-lifting I should imagine. That's irregular, isn't it? Most irregular. It would get him in deep water with the authorities. He would be struck off. Struck off!'

Lord Cazalay's fat, high-coloured cheeks quivered. He wanted Graham's blood. But less from brotherly love of Maria than from the memory of past family glories embodied in her shrivelled and witless frame. He could not revenge himself upon the whole world, so one man must make do instead.

Haileybury placed his bony fingers together and blew softly on the nails. 'Why did you come to *me*?' he repeated, most irritatingly.

'Because the man's a damn scoundrel and a disgrace to your profession.' This not seeming to satisfy his host, Lord Cazalay added in a more subdued voice, 'And my solicitors tell me you have known him some years.'

'Your solicitors also told you that I disliked him intensely?'

The visitor shifted his fat buttocks uneasily in the chair.

'They imagined my standing in the profession would lend irresistible weight to a complaint before the General Medical Council? And doubtless perhaps that I would assist with the expense?'

'There would be no question of your being out of pocket,' said Lord Cazalay uncomfortably.

Haileybury rose. 'Very well, Lord Cazalay. I should like to give the matter some thought.'

'Certainly, certainly.' He was anxious to leave Haileybury's presence as soon as politely possible. 'Perhaps you would kindly telephone my London flat in due course?'

'I think I should prefer to communicate with your solicitors.'

Haileybury took time making up his mind. He did not want anything to misfire and make him look in the slightest foolish.

He would have to prepare the ground carefully. Professional misconduct must be uncovered and punished whoever the culprit, whether Trevose or some less flashy practitioner. It was the duty of any honest doctor. But he told himself duty must never be tainted by pleasure from personal antagonism. Besides, from ten minutes' acquaintance he had come to dislike Lord Cazalay even more.

In the middle of June he called at Tom Raleigh's new consulting room in Welbeck Street. He found the young man eager to receive him. Tom was wildly hoping the visit might bring the offer of superfluous cases, of a partnership even. In summer medical practice in fashionable London dropped like the country streams, but in the summer of 1939 it seemed likely to dry up completely. People simply weren't being ill any more. Where the doctors had failed to budge minds from the ailments of a lifetime the dictators had succeeded. Tom Raleigh had decided to spend even August in Town in hope of a good case or two dropping from some richer holidaymaking surgeon's table. He would take his family away in September, when the beaches were less crowded and anyway it was cheaper. He was assuredly revelling in the luxury of freedom from Graham, but he was finding it the most expensive one of his life.

Haileybury sat down and asked at once, 'May I be permitted to enquire the present nature of your relations with Trevose?'

Tom clenched and unclenched his little fists nervously. 'Why do you ask?'

'Would you permit me to explain that after I have heard your reply?'

'My relations with Graham don't exist. We might be two strangers. When we meet he simply ignores me.'

'Then would you be prepared to give me some information in confidence about his private affairs? Information which only you can know?'

Tom hesitated. 'I can't say I'm very keen. Whatever our differences, I worked with him for a good while. He was fair enough to me in many ways. I've got to admit it.'

'I accept that. But this is less a matter of concern to you and me than to the profession as a whole. I will tell you briefly what I wish to know. One, is he conducting an affair with the actress, Stella Garrod? Two, has he operated upon her?'

'It's common enough knowledge he did an auroplasty on her in the Clinic. I suppose it's also common knowledge he's going about with her. I think there's even been pictures in the papers. But . . . well, how do I know if there's any more intimate connection?'

'Contrary to widespread belief–' Haileybury smiled faintly. 'Possibly a dangerously widespread belief, the actual "misconduct" of a professional man need not be as the word is so euphemistically misused in our courts. Mere association can be enough. Anyway, we all know Trevose, don't we? I doubt if he lets grass grow under him. No more in his private life than in his professional one.'

Tom clasped his hands tightly in front of him. He had spent so much of his life kneeling at Graham's feet he was becoming ankylosed in that posture. Supposing the man *were* hauled before the G.M.C., to be executed as a doctor in full view of the public? It was all he deserved. Besides–another thought struck him. Some of the cases now flowing into Graham's hands would be diverted into his own. An attractive prospect. They could afford to engage the maid again.

'Yes, of course he's going to bed with this woman,' he told Haileybury quickly. 'I often pass her flat in Brook Street. It's on my way home. His car's parked there at all hours. Anyway, he's been boasting about it to John Bickley. It's all in keeping. First there was his secretary, then some girl who did our photographic work, and another with a French name . . . yes, and another he operated on, excision of a keloid scar on the chin, I remember it well.'

Haileybury nodded. 'Would you be prepared to give evidence to this effect?'

Tom hesitated again. 'Yes. I would.' He paused. 'Though have you considered the effect on his wife? She's a sick woman already. What if all this came out?'

'From other enquiries I must tell you with regret that his wife is no longer able to understand anything in the papers.'

'Oh. I see. I'm sorry she's worse.' Tom gave a wry smile. 'If it's of any interest, she too was one of his patients before Trevose married her.'

Haileybury fell silent. 'No,' he decided. 'I think in that case it would be permissible.'

He had been gone twenty minutes before Tom finally made up his mind the last remark wasn't a joke.

Chapter Thirty-two

Haileybury found himself so distracted by the prospect of new, alarming, but exciting responsibilities that all summer went before Graham's misdeeds were reduced to lawyers' language, typed on broad sheets of best quality paper and bundled with red tape, to be dispatched with his compliments to the Registrar of the General Medical Council in Hallam Street. The Registrar would doubtless pass the bundle to the Council's own lawyers for such action as they thought fit, about which Haileybury affected indifference. He was simply making his complaint in proper form, he was doing his duty. But before the torpedo could be fired to wreck Graham's career two matters had to be settled. The first was Lord Cazalay's contribution to the solicitors' costs, over which the son was showing the slipperiness of the father. The second was telling Graham frankly what the deadly red-taped bundle contained. To Haileybury's mind this was only fair.

He called one evening in August, unannounced. The door at Queen Street was opened by a maid. In the hall was a dark, good-looking young man in grey flannels and a Donegal jacket. Haileybury noticed with distaste the fellow was wearing suède shoes.

'My father will be down in a few moments, sir,' Desmond greeted him affably. 'He's just changing.'

In the drawing-room was another young man, short, peaky, spindly, and pale.

'Can I get you anything to drink?' asked Desmond. 'Cocktail, whisky and soda, that sort of thing?'

'No, thank you.' Haileybury felt shocked at being offered alcoholic refreshment by a youth, particularly with such familiarity–even condescension, damn it! But what could you expect of Trevose's son? He sat on the sofa with his hat on his knees. It was the same one he had worn for the selection committee fifteen years before.

'Well, sir, do you think there's going to be a war?' asked Desmond genially, spreading his legs before the fireplace and sticking his hands in his pockets.

'I fancy not. Mr Chamberlain is a more capable diplomatist than many give him credit for.'

'Everyone in Switzerland thinks there's going to be one. I'm just back, you know. They're pretty shrewd about things out there.' He rubbed thumb and forefinger together. 'Cash. The Swiss have a delicate sensibility for it, quite as touching as the Italians for art or the French for cooking and women. The bankers think war is inevitable.'

Haileybury did not look pleased with this correction.

'Did you know the Lufthansa plane still comes into Croydon regularly from Germany?' Desmond continued informatively. 'With a different pilot every trip. You understand? Familiarization with the route. Pretty significant, if you ask me.'

Haileybury's education in the knavish tricks of the Germans was interrupted by the other young man producing an apparatus with a rubber bulb from his pocket and noisily spraying his throat. 'My cousin Alec.' Desmond introduced him as an afterthought. 'He gets asthma.'

'A distressing complaint,' said Haileybury.

Graham hurried in, wearing his dinner-jacket. 'I'm sorry to leave you at the mercy of these two scamps. Desmond, can't you amuse yourself somewhere? Go to the pictures.'

'But I saw all the new pictures in Geneva.'

'Then go and have a meal, or something.' He took a pound note from his wallet. 'You can borrow the car.'

Desmond's eyes brightened. 'Gosh, Dad, can I? Come on, Alec. We'll have a spin in the country. Good evening, sir,' he added cheerfully to Haileybury.

He left the room whistling 'Jeepers Creepers'. Alec followed with mixed feelings. To drive a Bentley car was sophistication of undreamable brilliance, and he writhed in the painful dumb envy of adolescence. But he fell in as usual with Desmond's plans. Besides, a spin in the open air might possibly relieve his attack of asthma.

'What can I do for you?' Graham asked briefly as the door shut.

Haileybury shot the cuffs of his blue serge suit. 'I have something extremely disagreeable to say.'

Graham shrugged his shoulders. He was not discomfited. Haileybury nearly always seemed to have something disagreeable to say.

'I will come directly to the point, Trevose. It's about Miss Stella Garrod. I believe you know her personally?'

So that's it, thought Graham. 'I am extremely proud of my acquaintance with Miss Garrod. What of it? Perhaps you'd like me to get her autograph?'

'I'm afraid my mission doesn't lend itself to levity.' Haileybury drummed his fingers on the brim of his hat. 'I understand she is also one of your patients?'

'And why should I impart secrets about my practice to you?'

'I have it on good authority you *did* operate on the lady,' Haileybury persisted. 'And on equal authority that your relationship is somewhat deeper than ordinary friendship.'

'Oh, hell, man!' Graham lost his temper. 'What right have you got sticking your nose into my personal affairs? It's pure bloody cheek, that's all.'

'I have the right of a fellow practitioner, in affairs of this sort.'

'What do you think I am?' Graham started to shout. 'Some tuppenny-hapenny g.p. mixed up with an oversexed housewife? Some sordid little doctor snared in a surburban divorce suit? Be your age, man! Miss Garrod is an actress, famous, known throughout the world. You can take it from me she is perfectly capable of looking after herself. Without the assistance of the G.M.C., a body I doubt she's ever heard of.'

'The principle is precisely the same,' Haileybury told him calmly.

'Oh, rubbish! All right, I did operate on her. Well, then? I did my job and now it's finished. I'm not responsible for her welfare. I'm not her personal doctor. Good God, if you had your way I'd be debarred from talking to half the attractive women in London. Anyway, she's no husband, nothing. Nobody's objecting. Nobody except you.'

'You stood in professional relationship to this woman—'

'Will you please stop calling her "this woman"? You make her sound like a barmaid. You seem to overlook she's reached far higher in her own profession than you in yours.'

Haileybury rose. 'I wouldn't presume to know about such values. I merely called out of courtesy. I am making a complaint about your conduct to the G.M.C.'

'Oh, complain to whom you like. The Lord Chief Justice, the Bench of Bishops if you feel like it. But please leave me in peace.'

'I wish you would be fair both to yourself and to me, Trevose.' Haileybury was starting to sound irritated. 'You must take this seriously. It is not simply myself who is complaining. Others are prepared to come forward with evidence.'

'By others you mean Tom Raleigh, I suppose?' Haileybury's silence gave Graham the answer. 'All right, do your worst. I'll brief the best counsel in London, and have you looking a pack of fools.'

'I have no objection to looking foolish if I am doing something unpleasant through a sense of duty.'

'Duty? Jealousy, you mean. Yes, jealousy. You've always been jealous of me, Haileybury, jealous of my practice, jealous of my income, jealous of my social standing. And now you're jealous of Stella Garrod. If you can't catch up with me, you'll have me struck off. That's the plan, isn't it?'

For the first time in their relationship Haileybury lost his temper. 'How dare you say that to me! Of course I'm not jealous of you. I despise you. I've despised you since the day I met you. You'd do anything for money. You've neither morals, principles, nor charity. What have you done with this skill you're so proud of? Made a lot of old women look a couple of years younger. If you can't get anything for money you sell your self-respect for it. As easily as a whore sells her body.'

He fell silent. He wondered vaguely how he came to be talking of whores. It was not a word he recalled using before. 'If you will excuse me, Trevose,' he ended quietly, 'I shall leave.'

Graham said nothing. Haileybury bowed, half-turned to add a word, and left.

Haileybury's tactlessness seemed to operate even on the unconscious level. He could have chosen no worse evening for his visit. Graham had become infatuated with a woman, for the first time in his life, at the age of forty-four. She was admittedly a Titania, a sorceress enslaving men from one end of the earth to the other with the most potent weapon of all–their own dreams. She had enticed him easily into her own supernatural world, unreal in its careless extravagance over everything from material luxuries to human emotions.

At first it had rather tickled Stella Garrod to have a medical man in tow, particularly such a fashionable one. But she became bored with him, as she regularly became bored with her secretaries, her agents, her lovers, and herself. Then she took a fancy to a young Canadian actor with a small part in her film at Mr Rank's new studios at Pinewood. But Graham so infested her flat by then she was forced to make do with the Canadian's, and nothing embittered her against Graham so sharply as finding herself on a cheap bed amid cheap furniture, looking up at a sloping roof with a cracked and dirty skylight somewhere in Bayswater. She decided firmly to get rid of Graham. Thank God the ear business was finished! She wrote saying she never wanted to see him again in her life.

Aghast and disbelieving, Graham cascaded her with letters, flowers, and presents, delivered by the uniformed Corps of Commissionaires, an unlikely body of cupids. When the young Canadian's film part finished he made speedily back to Canada, convinced of the coming war and having no relish for being blown to bits in his bed, even with Stella Garrod in it. She relented, and admitted Graham once more. But an old friend appeared, a tall, rich Swede with colourless hair and eyes, engaged in the futile unofficial diplomacy scurrying that summer behind the skirting-boards of Europe's chancelleries. Graham was casually pushed out again. The night of Haileybury's confrontation he had managed to wear Stella down by self-pity and Commissionaires to agreeing he might take her to the theatre. He was so numbed with worry over her keeping her word he hardly felt the keenness of Haileybury's threat at all.

Immediately his visitor left, Graham took a taxi to Brook Street. He rang the bell of Stella's flat. As he already half-feared, nothing happened. He hammered on the door. He shouted through the letter-box. Hurrying back to the street, he saw all the flat windows were shut and dark. He stood on the pavement, cursing the woman. He found a telephone box and dialled her number. No reply. He banged down the telephone and stood outside with his hands in the pockets of his dress trousers.

He wondered what to do. He couldn't walk the streets–that would be undignified. It would be unbearable alone at home. He couldn't face his club, full of men talking blusteringly about the international crisis. He would look foolish trying to trace Stella through any of her friends, and it was futile, she would have tipped them off. He noticed a public-house in a mews across the street. He went into the saloon bar, and demanded a double whisky. He hadn't been in such a place for twenty years, since he was courting Edith.

He sat on a wooden stool in the corner of the bar, and drank several more whiskies. He supposed Stella was with some other man. After all, she was a diagnosable nymphomaniac. But he didn't care, as long as she favoured him once in a while. He had never bothered to consider his ethical position before that evening. There now crept upon him the worry that Haileybury might be right. To the General Medical Council one woman's body was the same as another's, whether she were a housewife, a hussy, or a harlot. And he had unquestionably stood in a 'professional relationship' to her. Supposing he were really struck off? An idea struck him like a second blow. He was going to be ruined.

Stella had been an appallingly expensive luxury. That summer his practice had dwindled alarmingly, like everyone else's. He was already in debt. There was his house, his income-tax, Desmond–and, oh God! Puny Alec. He could hardly go back on his word to Edith. And Maria! What would happen to Maria if Haileybury made him walk the plank into chilly liquidation? He supposed the municipal asylums were these days quite comfortable. He put his head in his hands and groaned loudly, disturbing the barmaid.

When the public-house shut Graham went unsteadily back to Brook Street. Stella's flat was still dark. He suffered the further humiliation of having to identify himself to a policeman. He went back to Queen Street and lay on his bed in his clothes. Why couldn't a doctor be like other men, he wondered restlessly, wearing one face for his work and another for his fun? A managing director could sleep with whomever he cared and still get knighted. He almost wanted to scream in the torture of exasperation. He wondered where Stella was at that moment. He pictured her as he knew her in bed, with a faceless man. Some twist of his visual imagery supplied the unknown copulator with the look of Haileybury. For a minute it made him quite cheerful again.

Then he wondered what Desmond and Alec were up to. His son's driving was getting dangerously fast.

Chapter Thirty-three

'Of course, I was delivered by my own father,' Alec remarked. 'That might make some difference.'

Desmond didn't seem to hear him. With a contented smile he was driving the Bentley saloon at eighty miles an hour along the Barnet by-pass. At eighteen he was a splendid driver. He was also highly intelligent, spoke fluent French and German, quoted Voltaire, knew how to order wine, whispered jokes which Alec had to pretend he understood, was a skilful cricketer, dressed well, and could dance the Continental.

'Difference to what?' Desmond asked, his eyes on the road.

'To this asthma business.'

'Oh, that. No, I shouldn't think so, Wheezy. Any hereditary influences, joyful or woeful, must have been exerted rather earlier in the proceedings.'

'I mean from the psychological point of view.'

'I don't think anyone's made a psychological study of children delivered by their fathers. I expect they're mostly the offspring of cranks and Esquimaux and people like that.'

It had been a miserable summer for Alec's chest. He wondered if it were the fault of his psychology or of the arid London air, but he fancied the basic trouble was girls.

His uncle Graham had engineered his release from the school in Kent, which Alec had grown into with the resigned docility of a long-term prisoner. Having agreed secretly to grub-stake the budding healer, Graham felt he must take some responsibility for the mechanics of his transformation into a doctor from a hopelessly undersized, painfully introverted, and noisily asthmatical fatherless schoolboy. The school horrified Graham as an educational monstrosity. The boy would never pass his First M.B., nor even his 'Little-Go' entrance examination–particularly in Latin, a subject beyond the preceptorial skill of Old Flybuttons' establishment but cherished by Cambridge as fondly as its other medieval relics. He decided to place Alec at Mr Turton's in Kensington, a 'crammer', highly regarded for preparing even the most feeble-minded sons of the aristocracy for Oxford and Cambridge, the Army and Navy, and the Church, so that in all five they did as little damage as possible.

At Alec's school girls were not conceded to exist, Old Flybuttons considering them to be sinful. All impure thoughts–and any boy's thoughts about girls were held by him to be impure, probably quite rightly–had on his strict orders to be wiped from the mind at once. He allowed that this psychological manoeuvre might at times present difficulties, when a sympathetic adult might be approached for guidance. Alec had once started confessing impure thoughts to Graham, but found his uncle baffled, alarmed, and uncooperative. In the free-and-easy atmosphere of the examination factory run by Mr Turton girls were everywhere, not schoolchildren but young ladies, some with quite considerable bosoms. Alec had no idea what to do with them. His shy confusion acted only as a stimulus to flirtation. One forward hussy lured him into the stationery cupboard and actually invited him to kiss her. He had rushed away in panic, knocking over a stone jar of Stephens' ink, which made a terrible mess and cost him five shillings. He felt ruefully that Desmond might have managed the encounter more successfully. He thought his cousin as sophisticated as an emerald bracelet, and envied him desperately.

'Let's go into this dump and have a drink,' said Desmond, pulling up.

The dump was a large modern building of Tudorish aspect, which Desmond explained was a roadhouse. They went into the long bright cocktail lounge, where Desmond ordered a pair of light ales and started teasing the pretty girl behind the bar. The school with the big bills and mysterious traditions had given him quite a number of manners and enormous self-assurance. The year he had just spent in Geneva, at a costly establishment of international outlook, had added such things as philosophy, languages, carpentry, Swedish exercises, a European polish, and a beguiling line in conversation. It was all most impressive, particularly to barmaids.

'This asthma really is tedious.' Alec climbed on to the red-leather and chromium stool beside him. 'I've tried everything by now. I even sent for some pills advertised "To stop an attack within five minutes". I sat down with my watch and swallowed one, but nothing happened. I was terribly disappointed. I've just taken to smoking medicinal herbs.'

'That's the ghastly stink in your bedroom, is it?' exclaimed Desmond. 'I thought you'd set your pillow on fire.'

Alec had been staying in Queen Street most of August since Desmond's return, Graham hoping the companionship would keep his son's mind, or anyway his hands, off the housemaids. Desmond himself had confessed bland neutrality to the invitation. His cousin might be a pathetic little wet, but he could luxuriate in showing off before him. Otherwise, he treated him with easygoing, polite, and total disdain, the heritage of the public-school Englishman.

'I'm sorry about the smell,' Alec apologized. 'I won't smoke them again. They contain stramonium, I think it says on the label.'

'Oh, you mustn't suffer for my sake. Smoke on. But can't we talk about something else? We always seem to be discussing your asthma. Let's talk about Cambridge.'

'I envy you going up in October. Look at me–almost the same age, and a whole year's beastly cramming to do at Turton's. Even if it gets me there in the end.'

'You'll get in all right, Wheezy. Anyone with a clean collar, the right accent, and enough money can get into Cambridge. They're not particular about brains.' Before the Second World War higher education, like motoring, was more free-and-easy, more the prerogative of the better-off and more fun. 'Anyway, they're not frightfully choosy at Latimer.'

'I suppose not,' Alec admitted.

Latimer College had been picked for Alec through its connection with his father's old missionary society. It awarded the sons of such dignitaries its lowest rates, as well as its most uninhabitable sets of rooms. Desmond had a whole year before passed all four parts of the Cambridge First M.B., in basic biology, physics, and chemistry of both sorts, inorganic and organic, to be accepted by Lady Clarice Hall. This was a small college lying between Clare and King's, with delightful gardens running down to the Backs, an expensive standard of living, and an air of self-sufficiency confusable with snobbishness.

Desmond lit a cigarette. 'I'll probably stay on at Cambridge to take a Part Two in the Natural Science Tripos, you know. Before going to hospital.'

'That's awfully difficult, isn't it?'

'Yes. I shan't even try unless I get a First in Part One.'

'You really think you will?' asked Alec admiringly.

'I don't see why not,' Desmond told him airily. He already had his career planned. 'It'll be useful for taking a scholarship to Blackfriars for the clinical work.'

Alec laughed. 'You don't need the money.'

'No, but the kudos is good. Everything helps. I'm going to get on the staff at Blackfriars one day, like the old man. You wait and see.'

Alec hesitated. 'You're pretty sure of yourself, aren't you?'

Desmond looked offended. He objected to Wheezy daring to be cocky while enjoying his own company. 'No, I've just got an idea of where I'm going, that's all.'

'But supposing you came unstuck? You might plough, or get sent down.'

'Now you're getting stupid,' said Desmond shortly.

'I'm glad enough just to be going to Cambridge. It must have been a terrible sacrifice for my father, saving up. They pay them hardly anything as missionaries.'

Desmond narrowed his eyes. Cocky Wheezy must be slapped down. 'You don't really believe that, do you?'

'Believe what?'

'Do you know *who's* paying for your education? I am.'

Alec stared at him. 'I don't understand?'

'It comes to the same thing. My settlement's being raided for the cash. Father fixed it all up. Oh, I don't mind. After all, you are my only cousin, and it wasn't your fault your old man died broke.'

The brightly-lit bar flickered in Alec's eyes. This was terribly confusing, even more than the girls at Mr Turton's. 'But Desmond, I . . . I can't believe you.'

'Ask my old man if you don't.'

'But what made your father do that? Why didn't he tell me?'

Desmond smirked. 'You don't know your own family history. I've smelt out a thing or two. Your ma was on the point of marrying my old man when your dad stepped in and whisked her off.'

'But I never knew!'

'Didn't you? Aunt Edith must be coy about it, I suppose. So you see, Wheezy, she might have been *my* mother. How do you think we'd have got on? I've hardly had the chance to find out with my real one. She's been ill so long.'

'You know, I . . . I *still* can't believe you, Desmond. I really can't.'

'Ask your ma about it some time.' Desmond gave another smirk. 'I gather my old man was an even gayer dog in his youth. She might have some interesting tales to tell.'

But it was all too much for young Alec. He developed another attack of asthma. It was the second of his disillusionments in life.

Chapter Thirty-four

Graham was in the bath when the war started.

In the last weeks of August the mighty gods sent their dreadful heralds to astonish the citizens of London, like the citizens of Rome before Caesar's assassination. Though no lioness whelped in the streets (those in the Zoo were proscribed to be shot if released by bombing), there were mountains of sandbags, sticky paper dazzlingly criss-crossing shop windows, trenches again in the parks, and the forty-four anti-aircraft guns on show, with perhaps a few more. Strange signs like ARP, HQ, AFS, or WD appeared as prodromal spots for the massive rash of initials to come. For three nights the country had been at its darkest since the Stone Age. Silver balloons, as cuddly as Walt Disney's cartoons, lay close-hauled to their lorries in open spaces, with, it said in the evening newspapers, a notice or two, 'The crew have orders to shoot the next person asking when the balloon goes up.'

The balloon did go up.

Graham had slept late, and felt Mr Chamberlain on the wireless too harrowing to face. During the past fortnight it had dawned upon him there really was going to be a war, as suddenly as it dawned upon him sometimes that a patient was going to die. He felt wearily irritated by the prospect. After all, it was quite soon after the termination of the one to end war. He supposed they'd be living again in the dour world of sickening casualty lists, hospital blues, the Defence of the Realm Act, rallies in Trafalgar Square, spy scares, U-boats, girls on munitions, and patriotic middle-aged ladies. There would be terrible air-raids, of course, like the ones in Spain, but otherwise it would be much the same. This view of the Second World War was shared by almost everyone who had lived through the First, including the Allied generals.

Graham's feeling of detachment was increased by his being alone in the house. Cook and maids had sped home for such a momentous and potentially dangerous week-end. The rising tide of events had swept a million and a half schoolchildren out of London, and he decided that Desmond too should go to the cottage in Dorset. Desmond had objected on the ground that this was funking. Unlike his father in 1914 he knew already that he had escaped the firing-line, medical students being classified among the 'reserved occupations' and forbidden to bear arms as strictly as aliens, miners and middle-aged ploughmen. Graham told him to take Alec for company, and pointed out the fun of looking after themselves. They could go swimming as much as they wished–or as much as Desmond wished, Alec's respiratory deficiencies having left him strictly a land animal. They could even amuse themselves with the local inns, if not with the local girls. Desmond decided evacuation might not be such a bad idea after all. And Alec would be someone to bait, though he really was a bit of a drip, and sharing a bedroom his wheezing at night would be dreadfully noisy.

But war took second place in Graham's mind to Stella and Haileybury. A man with severe enough toothache hardly heeds an earthquake. He had reported Haileybury's threat to his solicitors, and his solicitors were discouraging. If a complaint were made to the General Medical Council it seemed the Council must act, as surely as a steaming railway engine must puff at the shift of the requisite lever. They suggested briefing counsel specializing in doctors' misdemeanours and Graham agreed, though it irritated him calling a man who had saved from erasure back-street abortionists, drug-takers, drunks, canvassers, and the hapless foils of outraged husbands. He went home and counted up his material assets, which were laughable. He kept telephoning Stella, but without reply. He started waking at night with epigastric pain, and wondered if he were worrying himself into a duodenal ulcer.

He was still in his bath when the doorbell rang. That Sunday morning it might mean all manner of tremendous things–an Air Raid Warden to inspect his curtains, an armed party searching for spies, a dispatch rider with a summons to some mysterious headquarters. He briefly towelled himself and slipped on a crimson silk dressing-gown. The ringing had become supplemented by knocking. He remembered guiltily a shotgun and a pair of binoculars in his wardrobe, possession of either, he felt, making him liable to imprisonment for the duration.

He opened the door.

'Oh!' exclaimed Edith. 'You're up late. On a morning like this, too. I thought you'd be at the hospital standing by.'

'Sunday morning's Sunday morning, war or peace,' Graham smiled.

'Have the boys gone? Alec *never* gets anything right over the phone. I brought some of his things.'

Graham had seen little of Edith in the five years since her repatriation in weeds. He had grown rich (though extravagant) and famous (though professionally despised), while she had shrunk into the humble uniformity of the barrister's clerk's villa at Elmstead Woods. Her unchanging poverty kept them apart as effectively as Robin in her last days of spinsterhood at Hampstead. They met now and then to discuss Alec, and each Christmas she sent him a card with a tender inscription, generally in verse. She was now undisguisedly what Maria would have called a 'working woman', though dressed smartly enough in a new serge coat and skirt, with lace-up black shoes and a little round hat with frills round it. Her hair was still blonde, clearly with assistance, and in too thin curls round the back. She was holding a small fibre attaché case, the sort you got in Marks & Spencer's.

'Come in,' invited Graham eagerly. He was glad to see Edith, or anybody. He hated loneliness like pain. 'I must apologize for my—'

He stopped. They stared at each other across the doorstep. A new note sounded in their lives. The sirens started the first chorus of their five years' oratorio. For a second, Graham felt fear tug at his intestines. The moment with which the country had been obsessed for half a decade had finally come. Field-Marshal Goering had arrived, with expected German promptitude, to lay the place in ruins.

'Oh, dear!' said Edith. 'I've forgotten my gas-mask.'

'The cook left hers behind, and I expect it'll fit,' Graham reassured her hastily. As they went into the sitting-room the din growled away. 'What do you suppose we'd better do? Fill a bucket with water, or something like that?'

Graham looked into Queen Street. It was deserted, as it generally was on Sunday mornings. A fat policeman appeared and cycled the length of it, blowing his whistle. At his hip was a military gas-mask, on his head a steel helmet, tied front and back a cardboard notice saying in black letters TAKE COVER.

'What did we do in the last war?' Graham asked Edith.

'At Ramsgate we opened all the windows. My dad said it let the blast through.'

Graham acted on this suggestion. 'Shouldn't we lie on the floor?'

'Yes, perhaps we ought.'

'Under the table, I should think. In case the roof collapses.'

Together they lay solemnly under the small table, which was genuine Chippendale.

'I can't hear anything,' said Edith.

'I expect they fly higher now than they used to.'

'I don't think you ever used to hear the Zeppelins at all. You could see them sometimes if they caught them in the searchlights. Great big silver cigars in the sky. They looked so harmless, quite pretty really, I used to think.'

'Yes, I remember the one they shot down in Potters Bar. I saw it all from Hampstead.'

'They gave the pilot a V.C., didn't they? He must have been awfully brave.'

Graham became aware that nothing seemed to be happening. 'They may have turned them back at the coast.'

'It may be a false alarm.'

'Oh, I shouldn't think so. They say our defences are very efficient.'

They stayed under the table. Edith started to giggle. 'I never thought I'd find myself lying on the floor with you this morning, Graham.'

He grinned. 'Perhaps it's an ill war which blows no good?'

'Oh, go on with you! Don't be daft.'

The sirens sang again. Field-Marshal Goering had apparently got lost. Both stood up, looking foolish. 'I expect you'd like a drink after that,' he suggested.

He gave her a brandy and soda and shut the windows. Air-raid precautions were uncomfortably draughty.

'Well, Graham. War or no war, how's the world treating you?'

'By and large extremely badly.' He poured himself a small drink to keep her company. When she asked his troubles he refused at first to enlighten or entertain her with the details. But he found himself telling her about Stella Garrod, of meeting her on the boat, refashioning her ear, falling in love with her, then Haileybury's onslaught. 'I suppose I've been a fool,' he concluded self-pityingly. 'I've always been too eager, too impulsive, too unthinking where women come into it. Haven't I?' he asked her lamely.

'No, I wouldn't say that, Graham.' She put down her empty glass. 'You're fond of women, of course. So fond you let them do what they like with you.'

'Perhaps that's my only attraction to them?'

After a pause she said, 'I'm sorry, Graham. You *are* in a bit of a mess, aren't you?'

'I'm not beaten till the G.M.C.'s pronounced its verdict. I'm going to make a fight for it. It's all ridiculously old-fashioned, the whole conception of medical ethics. But it's the pillorying I can't stand.' He shuddered. 'Everything that happened between me and Stella will be trotted out and paraded in front of the public as though I were a criminal in the dock of the Old Bailey.'

'What happens if you *do* get struck off?'

'God knows! Join the Army as a private, I suppose.'

'If I can help, Graham . . . I've got a little bit of money, what Robin left mostly—'

'Let's not talk about such gloomy subjects.' He got up abruptly. 'Anyway, we'll probably all be blown to Heaven shortly, G.M.C. and all.' He was suddenly aware of being naked under his dressing-gown. Supposing the Air Raid Warden called? It would look terribly compromising. 'I must go and dress, but do stay for lunch,' he invited. 'I expect there's something in the fridge.'

When he came down in his week-end tweeds he found Edith in the cook's apron roasting a chicken. After all, she explained, even in a war you have to eat. He laid the dining-room table, a task he had not performed since his suburban days in Primrose Hill, finding it most enjoyable. The telephone rang.

'Mr Trevose speaking.'

'One moment. I have the Controller for you.'

The girl left him in baffled silence. The Controller of what? 'Controller'– wasn't that a piece of machinery? Perhaps the girl had the wrong number, and some essential ingredient of a tank or anti-aircraft battery–

'Mr Trevose? We were disappointed you weren't at the Ministry at noon.'

The voice was cultured, courteous, and plainly nettled. It was the voice of the Civil Service, frustrated in winning the war. Like the sirens', Graham was to hear more of it than he bargained for.

'Which Ministry?' he asked innocently.

'The Ministry of Health, of course. Surely you have all the documents?'

'My secretary's been rather overwhelmed of late.'

'It was priority.' The Controller sounded hurt. 'Perhaps it was not too serious. The meeting was cancelled at the last minute, and will be at noon tomorrow instead.'

Graham thanked him. He went to the cellar for a bottle of wine. Feeling hock out of place on such a day, he brought up a bottle of champagne. It was going to be a party.

They finished lunch at three in the afternoon, and had some more brandy. They had been talking so much about the old days in Hampstead, Graham suggested suddenly they go to look at the professor's house. Desmond had taken the car to Dorset, but they could go by Tube as they used to. Anyway, the Tube would be a useful place if the Germans came back again after their own lunch. Red in the face and giggling, Edith agreed. He gave her the cook's gas-mask, and they set out with the square cardboard boxes dangling from their shoulders. Edith said they could put you in prison otherwise.

Graham hadn't seen his old home for ten years. His stepmother had gone to seek the professor in Heaven, and Sibyl gone to seek a husband in Southsea. The place looked well enough kept, though the garden had been paved over and a shoddy garage set up. A row of bells beside the familiar front door told him the place had become flats, which he found depressing. It was like the ghost of Henry the Eighth returning to find the crowds swarming over Hampton Court. They stood inside the front gate, pointing out the windows, remembering the rooms and sometimes what happened in them. The professor's bedroom, Graham recalled, was round the back. After a few minutes the front door opened and a fat man in a check suit and horn-rimmed glasses said, 'Yes?'

'Are you the occupier?' asked Graham.

The man looked dubious. 'Of the ground-floor flat, certainly.'

'We're from the Ministry of Health. Didn't you get my documents? They were priority.'

The householder shifted his feet. The atmosphere was thick with such ominous requests, the most law-abiding citizen in danger of prosecution and social ignominy for impeding the march so bravely begun that morning towards eventual victory.

'We have to requisition some property in this area,' Graham told him. 'May we look round?'

So demoralized at the prospect of being turned homeless into the black-out, the man hastily threw open the door. Inside, the decorations had been brought up to date, which Graham felt on the whole an improvement. His father's study was hardly recognizable, with the afternoon sunlight flowing unimpeded through the windows. The grate before which he had found himself dispossessed of Edith was the same. The breakfast-room was still shabby, if in a different way, and still filled with books. Graham gathered their involuntary host was an academic like his father, with an interest in early English, which compensated him in some measure for the flats. 'Thank you,' said Graham curtly at the door. 'You'll be hearing from us.'

'I hope I shall have plenty of notice. If you're moving me, I mean.' The man looked agitated. 'I'm supposed to stay at my post. The rest of my university department has been evacuated to Bangor.'

'You shouldn't have said that,' Graham told him sternly. 'Walls have ears.'

'Oh, Graham!' Edith clasped his arm as they walked down the hill towards the Tube station. 'I could hardly keep a straight face! You *are* daft.'

He laughed, and said, 'Well, there isn't much to smile about at the moment, is there?'

There certainly wasn't. He blessed the unknown scholar of early English for taking his mind off Haileybury and the impending bankruptcy which made even the war a shade trivial.

Graham had put her in such a good mood Edith decided to stay to supper. They opened another bottle of champagne.

'You can't go home alone in the black-out,' he told her.

'Why not? I've got my torch. The trains are still running.'

'But supposing the sirens go again?'

'Perhaps they won't.'

'No, I won't allow it! You've got to stay here.'

She looked at him in alarm. 'But what about my sister?'

'You can ring them up to say you're safe and sound.'

'They're not on the phone.'

'Surely one of the neighbours is? They must get messages.'

'You can't go disturbing our neighbours, Graham. Everyone's got enough worry as it is.'

'Nonsense! Everyone's bursting with a sense of civic duty. The country's upside down, people must be passing messages right, left and centre. You've got to stay here.'

Edith became startingly aware that Graham was putting a most peculiar proposition to her. After all these years! And Robin, too. No, it was daft, really daft, quite unhealthy in fact. 'Oh, Graham!' she said reproachfully.

He sat on the edge of her chair and put his arm round her tightly. He had formed the idea over lunch. Spurned by Stella, hounded by Haileybury, his professional and financial ruin preventable only by his prior blowing to pieces by a German bomb, he desperately wanted consolation. Besides, it would be fun doing it again with Edith. He really was extremely fond of her. And he couldn't possibly sleep alone in the house, not on the first night of the war. It would be far too depressing.

'No, Graham,' she said. 'No, it's not right.'

'Edith, darling . . . why ever not? Don't you want to? It must have been awfully long since . . .'

She had to admit it had been. So long she had almost forgotten how nice it was.

'But we *couldn't*, Graham! Not you and me. I'd feel like . . . like my own ghost as a girl, looking at myself, shocked to death. It's unnatural.'

'I can't imagine anything more natural,' he said lightly. 'Do you remember the professor's bed-knob?'

She laughed. 'Oh, Graham, you're awful!'

'Come on!' he insisted, as eagerly as dragging her from her typewriter twenty years before.

'*No*, Graham!'

'But Edith, my angel. Just think. Tomorrow morning we might both of us be dead.'

In the end it was this argument which prevailed. During the next five and a half years a whole army of women surrendered to it.

'What about precautions?' she remembered as they got into bed, after carefully pulling the black-out curtains.

'Surely we don't have to worry?'

'Yes, we jolly well do!' She sounded offended. 'I'm not forty yet, if you please. I see something every month, as regular as the morning milk.'

He kissed her. 'When was the milkman's last delivery?'

'It finished yesterday.'

'Then we can take a risk on it.'

'Oh, Graham! You're sure it's going to be all right?'

'I'm the doctor,' he told her authoritatively.

She acquiesced. She always took doctor's orders, all her life.

Chapter Thirty-five

They both woke early. Graham had to visit Blackfriars and Edith had to go to the Temple, where her solicitor was busy moving shop to Ascot. Graham was putting on his jacket when the door-bell rang. Motioning Edith into the bedroom, he went down to the hall.

At first he didn't recognize the caller outside. He wore a military hat, with a red band round it. At his hip was the canvas case of a gas-mask. He had gloves, and some sort of cane. The trench-coat was possibly the same he had worn to call at Primrose Hill.

'Trevose, I must ask you to forgive my coming without warning,' Haileybury apologized. 'Like everyone else, I am severely put to it these days. I am just on my way to the War Office.'

The astonishing transformation left Graham dumb. He opened the door silently. Haileybury removed cap and trench-coat, revealing a Sam Browne, red tabs and assorted brassware on his shoulders which Graham interpreted as at least a brigadier's. The man Graham had despised for twenty years had with a change of clothes become one of his country's *élite*. Nothing brought home to him so keenly that Britain was truly at war.

'Come in.' Graham led his military visitor into the drawing-room. 'I must apologize for the mess. I let my staff go to the country.'

'So, Trevose, it has come to pass.'

Haileybury stood rigidly in the middle of the room. Even his face looked different. The outfit seemed to have taken over the man. His eyes blazed, his thin cheeks glowed above his khaki collar and tie, his expression suggested the martyr escaping from earthly torments into the congenial comfort of Heaven. Now he commanded more men and material than he had dared to dream, he saw the petty struggles and frustrations of his life as but preparations for this second call to arms. The past had become irrelevant, something to be inspected that morning with sad amusement, like one's passport. He was prepared to wipe the slate clean, to start again in the new framework of society–on which he perched at the top, as anyone could tell from his apparel.

'Will you have a cigarette?' asked Graham.

Haileybury slowly shook his head. 'Trevose, we both lost our tempers the other evening.'

'It wasn't a particularly pleasant encounter for me. I can't say if it was for you.'

'No, it wasn't pleasant at all. You know I wouldn't relish bringing down a man I have known so long? A colleague in the same specialty? Surely not! I hope you wouldn't think *that* of me. I was only doing my duty.'

'Yes, I'm sure you were,' Graham said briefly. He lit a cigarette himself.

'We are at war.' Haileybury stared glumly at his spledidly polished brown shoes. 'It is a stupid thing for the world to bring on itself. But I have never enjoyed a particularly high opinion of the intelligence of mankind in the mass. It is here, and we must do our best. We need every pair of skilled hands available.' He produced a red-taped bundle of papers which Graham had noticed bulging his immaculate jacket. Throwing it carelessly on the table, he added, 'That is the evidence I gathered of your doings, Trevose. You might like to look through it in your own interests. I shan't be sending it to the G.M.C. I should think the matter will end here.'

Graham took care not to change his expression. He picked up the bundle and looked at it idly. Haileybury fixed him with pale blue eyes.

'You were partly right in what you said the other night, Trevose. I don't envy your riches. I don't envy your practice among famous and smart people. I don't envy your ways in the world of fashion. But I do envy your skill. I've had to apply myself, to strain myself, stretch my own abilities to the limit, just to achieve half that you do so easily and so successfully. I've always envied that. Even when we worked for the Saracen. I've never been man enough to admit it to you. Or to myself for that matter.'

This dry confession made Graham feel highly uncomfortable. It was as though Haileybury had removed his splendid new uniform trousers in public. 'I've found plenty to admire in your work myself,' Graham told him.

Haileybury seemed to dismiss this as an unlikely platitude. Picking up his trench-coat, he said, 'I expect we shall be seeing a good deal of each other in the months to come, Trevose.'

'Yes, I expect we shall.' Why, in God's name? Graham asked himself.

'I take it you will be joining the Emergency Medical Service? The Ministry seem to have left your unit a little late.'

'I don't know what I'm going to do. As I'm told, like everyone else, I suppose.'

'An excellent precept.' Haileybury paused with one arm in his coat sleeve. 'By the way, you don't still want the services of Raleigh, do you?'

Graham looked up. 'No, the partnership was dissolved months ago.'

'I know that. But had you wanted him as your assistant in the E.M.S. I could get him left in civvy street. Otherwise the Central Medical War Committee will call him up.'

Graham flicked the ash off his cigarette. 'No. I don't want him at all. Call him up if you like. He'll probably make an excellent medical officer. He never questioned an order.'

'Very well, Trevose.' On the doorstep, Haileybury saluted. Graham saw outside a dun-coloured car with a uniformed girl at the wheel. 'If I can be of any help to you at all, please telephone me at the War Office. Room two-six-three.'

'Thank you.' Graham suspected the invitation was less a kindness than a temptation to demonstrate authority. The girl in A.T.S. uniform opened the car door with a salute. 'If I may give you a tip, I should avoid seeing more of Miss Garrod than strictly necessary. Things looked pretty black for you, believe me.'

'Who I see or who I do not see is entirely my affair.'

Haileybury gave a cold smile. 'Ah, Trevose, you don't change.'

He entered the car. The girl, who Graham noticed was remarkably ugly, released her salute and climbed behind the wheel. As the car drove down Queen Street he could see Haileybury in the back, as upright as a totem pole.

Graham went back into the house and slammed the door. His feelings were mixed. Relief–incredible relief, he wasn't to be ruined after all. Fury, gratitude, and black ingratitude to Haileybury. He could express them only by sitting on the sofa and laughing almost hysterically. He was still laughing minutes later when Edith appeared.

'Graham, love!' She looked alarmed. 'What's the joke?'

'Oh, nothing very much.' He wiped his eyes on his handkerchief. It would be too trying to tell her the details. They might show him as snivelling before an adversary. 'A stupid man called Haileybury whom I've known for donkey's years has just appeared all dressed up as a general.'

'Lieutenant Haileybury?' asked Edith. He stared at her in surprise. The connection had been thrown from his mind long ago. 'Yes, Lieutenant Haileybury, by God! The scourge of the face hospital and peeping-tom of the summerhouse.'

'Well, fancy!' exclaimed Edith. 'You, me, and Lieutenant Haileybury. Just like old times, isn't it?'

'Yes, just like old times,' he reflected. He paused. 'But I've had a lot of fun in between, haven't I?'

'Too much, Graham, if you ask me. That's your trouble, you naughty boy.'

He took both her hands. His worries had mostly driven off with Haileybury, but Stella could still be elusive. 'How about coming back here again tonight?'

'Definitely *not*!' She sounded firm. 'Graham, you are a fool, aren't you? You don't want to get tangled up with me all over again, surely?'

Of course, she was perfectly right, he told himself. He didn't want to in the slightest. It had caused enough bother the last time.

'I just didn't want you to think, Edith my dear, our bit of fun last night represented the limits of my feeling for you.'

'Oh, I'd never think that. After all, look what you're doing for Alec. Now where on earth's my hat? War or not, it's Monday morning and I've to get to work.'

'You'll be all right out at Ascot. A good spot to spend the war. I suppose you've somewhere to stay?'

'Yes, they're fixing up billets. I'll send you a postcard.'

'I'll come out and see you,' he suggested heartily. 'It'll be a change from London. They might even start up the races again one day.'

'If we haven't had to eat all the horses. Ta ta, love.'

She had hardly left the house before he picked up the telephone and dialled the number of Stella Garrod's flat. This time there was an answer. It was the secretary he had first encountered on leaving her bedroom, who explained that Miss Garrod had left unexpectedly three days previously on an American liner to New York. No, she didn't know when Miss Garrod might be back. But it would be quite soon. She had extensive plans for entertaining the troops. Mr Trevose could always contact her through her agent in New York.

So that seems that! Graham thought. He lit a cigarette. For a while, at any rate. He wondered suddenly if the woman was a bitch, anyway. At least Edith had offered to send him a postcard.

Miss Garrod stayed in the United States for the next six years. Her enthusiastic work in the Bundles for Britain campaign won warm commendation from the Embassy in Washington.

Chapter Thirty-six

Blackfriars Hospital had become a weird place. Its wards which had nursed the London sick since the Great Plague stood empty, its staff and students were evacuated to the country, its noble buildings muffled with sandbags and slabs of fresh concrete. Only the shored-up basement was alive. Down there, some more or less bombproof and gasproof emergency theatres and resuscitation wards were staffed by a handful of surgeons, to patch up as best they could the torrent of casualities expected in the first few days of the war from the air-raids. By the end of a month, they were worked off their feet patching up the torrent of totally unexpected ones from the black-out.

Towards the middle of October Graham wandered down the sandbagged entrance in the vague hope he might find something to do. He doubted it. Nobody seemed to want him at all. The 'pair of skilled hands' Haileybury had so condescendingly restored to professional life were idle. His private practice having disappeared with the other frivolities of peace, he felt totally useless, a failure, a man adrift beyond the currents of life. In Graham Trevose this unusual state produced some intensely painful thinking.

His sense of relief from professional death in Haileybury's hands had grown with reflection, until he could hardly bear to think of the episode at all. And Haileybury's motives for the reprieve began to obsess him. There was a war, and doctors were needed because men and women would be killed and maimed–men and women, not 'cases'. It occurred to him chillingly these casualties might include Desmond. Who knew how long the war would last, with his son swept up as a regimental medical officer and sent to the front like his brother? It struck him bitterly his relationship with Desmond was wrong. He had of course handsomely supplied the young man's material wants, and prided himself on being more an elder brother than a father. But that wasn't the point. Adolescents didn't want elder brothers, they needed fathers. What did Desmond think of him? A source of comfort without affection and amiability without authority. Feelings of inadequacy and failure drenched him as uncomfortably as after Maria's suicide attempt. It was all most humbling, and most of all there was no one to blame but himself–not even Haileybury.

But if only someone would order him to do *something*. He might be able to cut a more commanding figure not only in Desmond's eyes, but in his own. Haileybury proclaimed himself of enormous value to his country in the war simply by walking about in his new get-up. Graham Trevose the expert surgeon seemed as little use as Graham Trevose the sickly student in the last one. He had telephoned the Ministry of Health several times, but nobody now seemed to know who he was. He felt wearily his bad character left him totally unfitted for employment by His Majesty. He supposed he deserved it. He had even telephoned Haileybury, to be told the man was away at some secret destination, which filled him with envy. Graham was to be one of the first to rediscover the deadliness of war's shattering a man's fine opinion of himself, if Hitler was to be one of the last.

Among the timber props in a corner of the basement casualty reception room Graham noticed some screens. Idly he looked behind them. A form on a stretcher covered by a sheet. A corpse. The first casualty of the war? For some reason he drew the covering aside and found himself facing his own handiwork. Lilly was dead.

'Was she one of your patients, sir?' A young houseman in a short white jacket, whom Graham had never seen in his life, appeared at his elbow.

'More like an old friend,' he said morosely. He dropped the sheet into place. 'I worked on her for the best part of three years. What happened?'

'She's a B.I.D., sir. They found her in the fireplace at home. There was no sign of life when they brought her in.'

'Much burning?'

The young man shook his head. 'I put the cause of death as inhaled vomit. We'll see at the p.m.'

'I suppose she was drunk.' Graham sighed. 'If I had spent a little of my time trying to cure her drinking instead of trying to cure her burns I shouldn't see three whole years' work wasted. What's your name?' he asked abruptly.

'Fordyce, sir.'

'What do you think of me, Mr Fordyce?' The houseman looked uneasy. 'What does *my* name suggest to *you*? An exponent of surgery needing a high degree of skill, patience, and imagination? Or a quack? A man who makes new noses for ugly girls and lifts the faces of decrepit actresses? Am I a remoulder of scraggy bosoms, or the person who knows more about the treatment of third-degree burns than anyone in the country? Well? What do you say, Mr Fordyce?'

The houseman felt more uncomfortable. But the plastic boys were as mad as hatters, everyone knew that.

'I think you're a very skilful surgeon, sir.'

'Why do you say that?'

'Well . . . because you're on at Blackfriars, sir.'

Graham gave a loud laugh in the presence of the dead. 'Mr Fordyce, you have the right idea. Stick to it, and you'll find yourself on at Blackfriars as well. I'm alone, abandoned by my friends, my loves, my family, my patients, and my profession. Nobody wants me, Mr Fordyce. Because I'm really a charlatan, a quack, a moneymaker, a beautifier of human objects who don't deserve to look a wit less horrible than they do. True beauty is in the heart, Mr Fordyce. Here.' He struck his chest. 'Psychiatrists and priests might produce it. *I* can't. Not that I give a damn any longer about tarting up some hag who's willing to pay enough for the job. I was more interested in this old drunk under the sheet than in any of them.'

'Yes, sir,' said the houseman. They really were lunatics in the plastic unit, he decided. Worse than the psychiatrists.

'And all that's left of Lilly is a large number of beautifully healed scars. Hardly a trace, most of them. What the hell's the use of a skill like that in wartime? Sweet F.A.! They'll cobble up the soldiers' faces and give them a pension, like they did last time. Nobody's interested in getting wounds and burns looking perfect. Nobody's interested in re-creating the faces of young men who were bursting with sex-appeal one minute and burnt objects of horror the next. *I* could do it, but nobody's asked me. Nobody's going to.

This war will turn me into a total nonentity. I'm too good at my job to be any use to my country, that's all.'

He was never so wrong in his life, even when he asked Edith to marry him.

A nurse appeared behind the houseman's shoulder. 'Mr Trevose,' she said breathlessly, 'there's an urgent telephone call. It's from the Ministry of Health.'

'Tell them I've gone home,' he ordered. He couldn't speak to idiots in ministries just then. Lilly's death had quite upset him. He had overlooked for years there were persons attached to his beautiful workmanship. It was a frustrating moment to make the discovery. Graham Trevose at last wanted to help humanity, and nobody was going to let him.

He did make a call later that morning, to Maria's nursing home in Sussex. It was perfectly in order, they told him. Despite the war her basket of fruit would arrive as usual every Saturday.

Richard Gordon

The Medical Witness

The Medical Witness

Every man at the end of the rope knew exactly what he had done. There was little or no exception.

A FORMER CHAPLAIN AT WANDSWORTH PRISON

Chapter One

It was cold even for that particularly bleak April, the sun rising behind a mist like muslin over the London rooftops. In his bowler hat and his overcoat with the brown fur collar, carrying his bag as usual, Rumbelow made his way across the street from the Tube Station. He often travelled by Underground. He had never learned to drive a car, and though he could have found a taxi he was inclined to be mean, on the excuse that no career lasted for ever and it was prudent to care for the future.

It was still before seven, the other passengers in the lift all men scattering to their work. He had only a few hundred yards to walk. As he expected, a crowd of fifty or so had gathered on the pavement, many of them in black. He supposed they could hardly miss recognizing him. Ignoring their stares, he pressed the bell. The wicket gate opened at once. It was a morning they were expecting visitors.

In an office with a gas-fire roaring throatily in the corner, he uncapped his fountain-pen and with a gesture expressing familiarity signed the visitors' book on a steep desk like a lectern. The warder who had admitted him unlocked another gate in the screen of bars still separating them from the interior of the prison. The courtyard was empty, the men being kept in their cells, though Rumbelow recalled they could make an unholy racket banging on the bars with their spoons.

The sitting-room of the governor's house was invitingly comfortable, a leaping coal fire below a mantelpiece covered with framed photographs of austere-looking women, laughing children and the governor himself in Army uniform. He was scrawny and hollow-cheeked with a straggling yellow moustache, in a blue suit which looked brand-new. Rumbelow was amused to find him dressed in his best for the occasion.

'We renew our acquaintance, Doctor.'

'Yes, that's so, Major.' He offered his case. 'Cigar?'

'No, no, thank you. I don't feel like smoking this morning.'

Rumbelow cut one himself. They were among his few extravagances. Cigarettes made him cough, and a pipe he thought somewhat vulgar.

'I hate these affairs,' said the governor.

'I don't think any of us find them particularly agreeable.'

'Of course not . . . but frankly, I'm beginning to feel them quite unbearable.'

'You don't have to look you know.'

'I don't. Not when the man goes down. I turn to the chief warder and make some remark. I always keep an excuse in mind. I've one here for today.' He tapped his forehead. 'But the drop's only part of it. You see a perfectly fit human being come through the door, and you know in a second or two he'll be as dead as mutton. I shall never get used to that. It's an awesome business. It's like . . . well, like God coming into the room with you.'

He *is* rattled, thought Rumbelow. Probably been bottling it up to tell someone like me, who's in the habit of keeping secrets. 'But you must have seen men killed in the trenches?'

'There wasn't the inevitability about it. We all believed the next bullet wouldn't have our number on. God knows, that's what made the fighting possible at all.'

'You could send your deputy.'

'It's my duty.'

'Or take a stiff drink?'

'No, no, that wouldn't be right.'

Rumbelow smiled. 'Tilling gets one.'

'He refused. He said he didn't care to meet his Maker with alcohol on his lips.'

'He may change his mind.'

'I know. I've given instructions for the rum to be provided.'

The telephone rang. The governor apologized, and picking an instrument from the side-table became entangled in an argument which seemed to Rumbelow to be about a burst boiler in the prison laundry.

He leant back in the chintz-covered armchair, still in his unbuttoned overcoat. He was an impressive man. Women thought him handsome, being always touched by boyish looks. He was over six feet, in his early thirties, fresh-complexioned with pale blue eyes, though his chin was overlong and his soft fair hair was having to be arranged carefully to avoid showing patches of pink scalp. He wore a stylish brown suit with a faint crimson stripe, a canary waistcoat, a carnation in his buttonhole and spats. But he was fastidious rather than dandified. His vanity was of a more cerebral and complicated sort.

He glanced absently at a copy of the *Morning Post* lying folded on the low table of Benares brass. Herr von Ribbentrop was justifying Germany's denunciation of the Locarno Treaty. The Italians in Abyssinia were advancing on Addis Ababa. The *Queen Mary*'s maiden voyage was fixed for the end of May, and there was a photograph of Miss K. Stammers already being coached for Wimbledon by Mr Dan Maskell. It was 1936, a pause between two reigns in a truce between two wars, a waymark between two British states of mind, from God-given sovereignty to puzzled and resentful frustration.

'How's the prisoner bearing up?' he asked as the governor sat down.

'Until last night he didn't seem to realize it was actually going to happen.'

'That's often the case of course.'

'It's beyond his imagination. He's not very intelligent.'

'No murderer is. And their greatest stupidity is thinking how clever they are.'

'Doesn't that apply to all of us?' His distinguished visitor seeming to take this unkindly, the governor added, 'He might have got away with it, but for your evidence at the trial.'

'That's quite possible,' agreed Rumbelow, who never let modesty obscure plain fact. He drew from his waistcoat pocket the gold hunter watch which had belonged to his elder brother, killed on the Somme in the German push of 1918. 'My fellow from the hospital should have arrived by now. Have you done anything about the mortuary?'

'I've put in an electric fire.'

'Good. I'm always complaining about mortuaries. People seem to overlook some of the occupants still having warm blood in their veins.'

The mortuary was nothing but an outhouse at the back of the prison hospital, a grey light coming through glass in the sloping roof and a high-up window with bars across it, as though the authorities feared even the dead might commit the outrage of escaping. The whitewashed walls had broken into a cold sweat, the governor's fire being a feeble single red bar plugged to the only electric light. There was a deep square sink in the corner, with a brass tap which dripped. In the middle stood a narrow zinc-topped table, a slight slope on it from head to foot, its surface scored with a herringbone of gullies converging on a hole over a white enamelled bucket. Rumbelow thought it all horribly primitive.

Still in his overcoat, he finished his cigar while making some conversation with William, a squat, grizzled man, the head mortuary porter from Blackfriars Hospital. He suddenly found himself pausing. It was an instant before a clock somewhere with tinny strokes marked eight. A pair of three-inch-thick oak doors had fallen apart, caught neatly by two sprung hooks to stop the rebound. A white bag over his head, Tilling had dropped at the end of a thirteen-foot brand-new rope, three-and-a-quarter inches thick, made from five strands of fine Italian hemp, one end attached to a hook in an oak beam, the other twisted four times and threaded back on itself to form a non-slipping noose, the knot secured below his left ear. Now Tilling was rotating slowly in a narrow twelve-foot-deep brick-lined pit, always impeccably white-washed. Until the night before, he'd thought it really couldn't happen. But the perfection of the hangman's art–excercised at ten pounds a time–made it surer than anything since he had burst from his mother's womb.

'Will they wait the hour?' William's overcoat being of poorer quality, he was feeling the cold.

'They're supposed to. But they never do.'

Rumbelow knelt and unclasped his leather bag. The moment had stirred in him only an impulse to start work. Men died every day–in an imperfect world of murderers, accidents and wars, often enough before their time. The change from a living person to a dead one was of the highest scientific importance, but in his disciplined thinking there was no more to it than that. He began to arrange his instruments on another table of well-scrubbed wood like a butcher's block. To the right he set his long scalpel, with its black bone handle and nine-inch blade. Then smaller scalpels, forceps, a saw with a deep oblong blade, a smaller saw like one used for pruning rose-bushes, bone-cutters, scissors, a worn tape-measure, twine and needles with a cutting edge. There was room behind for two jars with screwcaps, the sort housewives bottled fruit in, with some blue-edged gummed labels. One end was free for the post-mortem report form, clipped to a board, on which he laid his fountain-pen with the cap off.

He took from his inside pocket a familiar square of paper–

> I, in pursuance of section twenty-one of the Coroners' (Amendment) Act, 1926, hereby direct you to make a post-mortem examination of the body of Thomas Tilling and to report the result thereof to me in writing.
>
> Norman Carlow, M.D., Barrister-at-Law,
> H. M. Coroner

Rumbelow slipped it behind the board. He liked to have everything exactly in place.

There was no need to roll up his sleeves. His shirts were all cut short and his suits had buttons for false cuffs complete with gold links, a time-saving invention of which he was extremely proud. He put on a bibbed apron of red rubber, tying the tapes round his waist. The pair of them waited, their breath coming in clouds.

There was a hurried noise outside. The door was thrown open. In came a green-painted new-looking handcart, of the kind costers pushed round the London streets. Tilling's body was under the canvas sheet. There were two warders pushing, both looking scared. Behind came the prison doctor–elderly, untidy, ill-paid and socially unalluring. His relations with Rumbelow in the past had not been good. It was among prison doctors' duties to cut up the executed, and he had resented the Home Office pushing in some outsider. But the brilliance and explosiveness of Rumbelow's fame had somewhat mollified him, until he could now take pride in the association and imply to everyone it was closer and more equilibrious than it was.

In the restricted space there was trouble getting the body from the handcart on to the zinc table. As the warders thankfully withdrew. Rumbelow asked the prison doctor, 'Have you the weight?'

'A hundred and thirty-six pounds. He was on the slight side.'

'And the drop?'

'Six feet eight inches.'

William had begun stripping the body of grey jacket and trousers, secured with tapes–there were no buttons, through fear the condemned man might somehow forestall with them his ordained end. The shoes were missing. They always were, Rumbelow noticed. The woollen vest and underdraws were a much-laundered yellow. He wondered how many people had been hanged in them already.

The body was warm, the colour of bluish wax, as limp as a jellyfish. One eye was shut, the other half open, giving a supercilious look. The lips were apart, a smear of blood at the left angle of the mouth. Rumbelow noticed a small fresh gash on the right wrist–pinioning with the executioner's leather body-belt had not been without a struggle. Round the base of the neck, where the cut end of the rope had been removed, was a weal an inch thick. Some urine had been voided, and Rumbelow noticed with interest semen at the tip of the man's penis. Quite often, the muscular spasm of death mocked that for the furtherance of life.

'There were some heart-sounds discernible at the apex for about ten minutes afterwards,' volunteered the prison doctor.

'That isn't exceptional.'

'It makes it a little difficult to give the exact time of death.'

'Not at all. He died when his neck was broken.' Rumbelow picked up a long scalpel. 'To all intents and purposes.'

'I'm wondering what might happen were the point actually raised during the inquest.'

'Raised by whom?'

'Some meddlesome juryman, for instance. You know what they can be like. Especially these days.'

'You say, "A very short interval elapsed, or some general expression of opinion of the same effect". It's in Home Office instructions to prison governors, 1926. I haven't heard they'd been changed in the last ten years.'

'That's very clever of you, remembering it.'

'Some things stick in the mind.' He turned to the body. 'Death was instantaneous. The heart may be alive. But the man is dead.'

'Oh, I'm not disagreeing with you. Nor suggesting Tilling knew anything once his neck was broken.'

'Perhaps he did?' asked Rumbelow contrarily. 'Dr Gaertner of Paris has given a most illuminating paper on the behaviour of decapitated heads–the eyes opening, the mouth trying to speak and so on. The man guillotined is very obviously dead, even though the head is capable of expressing unpleasant emotions.'

'Understandable in the circumstances,' observed the prison doctor. Rumbelow gave no reply.

With his long scalpel Rumbelow made a slit starting at the point of the man's chin and ending in the pubic hair at the narrow bone bridging the front of the pelvis. A few strokes flayed the front of the neck and chest. With the cutters he snipped apart the cartilages joining ribs to breastbone, and dividing the small joints connecting this to the clavicles pulled away the entire front of the chest. Natural dexterity reinforced by experience accomplished this in a minute or two. The man was split apart, his internal organs all neatly in place arrayed under Rumbelow's eye.

To mutilate so calculatedly the dead of his own species was a uniquely human experience. When the victim had somewhat ceremoniously been killed by his own kind, it became ecologically bizarre. Rumbelow could feel this, or had once done so, acutely and nauseously. But like much else in his life, he had shut it from his mind. Otherwise it would have been impossible to perform his duty to his profession, to the law, and to himself.

'I admire your thoroughness,' said the prison doctor. 'You could have left it at the neck.'

'To examine the whole patient is surely a fundamental principle of medicine?'

'Of course, of course.'

A dead man doesn't bleed. He leaks. Blood had started to run in the guttered top of the table, and drip with small distinct noises into the bucket. Rumbelow passed his knife round the inner surface of the lower jaw, separating the tongue. He pulled the whole tongue-muscle downwards with the larynx, out through the gaping neck. He severed the gullet just above the stomach, with a few more strokes of the knife freeing heart and lungs, holding them aloft by the wind-pipe like some weird freshly-plucked bird, then dropping them into an enamelled washing-bowl held out by William.

Rumbelow placed the bowl in the sink and turned the brass tap. As the water ran over the organs he examined them. He slit open the gullet and trachea for signs of vomit. He sliced into the tongue to seek internal bruising. He turned the contracted heart in his hands, opening its four chambers, washing out the blood, inspecting the valve-cusps which had opened and shut every second from Tilling's birth to some thirty minutes ago. Finally he took a pair of small pointed scissors from William and cut his way along the coronary arteries, the blood-vessels of the heart itself, twisting like worms across the shiny surface.

'All normal,' he said.

He turned back to the body. The abdominal viscera were removed and examined in the same way. As he opened the stomach the smell of rum met his nostrils. Tilling had decided to face God with a drink inside him after all.

'All normal,' he repeated.

The trunk was now eviscerated, its organs half-filling the sink. With a quick sweep of the scalpel Rumbelow cut the scalp through the hair across the top of the head, from ear to ear. Dissecting away the loose tissue beneath, he turned the scalp into a pair of flaps. The first he drew forward to cover, inside out, the man's face. The other he drew back on to the neck. With the oblong-bladed saw he cut round the skull just above the level of the ears, making a high-pitched noise and trailing pinkish-tinged bone-dust on to the stone floor. He gently wiggled the bony vault, eased it up and removed it like opening a child's chocolate Easter egg. The membranes surrounding the brain glistened in the poorish light. He slit these open, and inserting his fingers under the frontal lobes of the brain, severing the nerves below as he went along, raised it whole from the base of the skull. Dividing the medulla oblongata connecting the spinal cord, he put the brain into the enamelled bowl, rinsed it under the tap, and sliced it as if cutting a new loaf.

'All normal.'

William turned the body on to its face, still masked with its own scalp. With another scalpel, Rumbelow cut down to the vertebral bones of the neck.

'Fracture-dislocation of the cervical spine, at the level of the second and third vertebrae.'

'What's the spinal cord like?' The prison doctor was looking over Rumbelow's shoulder.

'Well and truly ruptured. Across about two-thirds of its thickness.'

'The hangman will be pleased.'

'I'll take this specimen.'

To study the mechanics of judicial hanging, Rumbelow had the largest collection of broken necks in the country. Pathologists attending executions in the provinces had proved co-operative, sending him additions through the post. He freed the two circular bones with the near-severed spinal cord running inside, and dropped them into a screw-topped jar. He went back to the sink, feeling among the organs lying in pink water like butcher's offal. Asking William for a magnifying-glass from his bag, he examined again the tissues round the larynx.

'No haemorrhage from the internal jugular. I should have expected it in a man of his feminine build. It's remarkable how often the vein is ruptured in executions. And how many pathologists miss it.'

The prison doctor nodded. Rumbelow held out his hand to William for a scalpel. 'I'll have the hyoid, too. There may be a fracture on microscopical examination.'

Pulling off his rubber gloves, he wrote on a blue-edged gummed label, *Tilling, T. Judicial hanging. Cervical vertebrae 2–3 and hyoid.* Like all medical men, he had an aversion to any receptacle standing about with its contents unmarked.

He began writing his report. Though London pathologists were starting to employ secretaries, Rumbelow thought it undignified for professional notes to be typewritten, and anyway a mortuary was no place for a young woman. He asked idly, 'Did he confess before the end?'

'No.' The prison doctor paused. He was feeling hurt. Rumbelow had been contemptuous and rude to him that morning, over his doubts about the continuing heart-beat. His resentment was only partly justified. Rumbelow seldom deliberately offensive. It was simply not in his nature to disguise facts, nor dress them in more agreeable garb. The prison doctor was frightened of crossing him, but he steeled himself and asked meaningfully. 'Why do you ask? Did you expect him to confirm your evidence at the trial?'

'No, but they often do confess in the last few minutes, you know.'

'You've no doubt about the correctness of the verdict, I hope?'

'Oh, no, no,' said Rumbelow hastily.

He finished writing without speaking.

Rumbelow washed his hands under the cold tap and put on his jacket. From his trouser pocket he handed William two half-crowns, the porter's cut of the post-mortem fee being traditionally paid promptly and in cash. William prepared to sew up the body with the needle and twine. The sliced-up organs in the sink would be stuffed back anyhow. So Tilling ended up like a haggis, shortly to be devoured by quicklime.

Everything that morning had to be performed with measured ceremony, from offering the condemned man his official tot of rum before eight to holding an inquest on his body at ten. Act of Parliament decreed that a coroner's jury must inquire into the deaths of all inmates of jails, and whether the event occurred at the end of a rope was immaterial. The inquest was held in the administrative block by the main gateway, in a largish, dark-panelled, ugly upstairs room, where the authorities had apparently through force of habit put more bars on the windows. There was the Royal Arms on one wall, an important-looking high-backed chair beneath, two long tables and a row of benches on which two reporters sat with notebooks staring into the middle distance. A police-constable appeared, the coroner's officer who Rumbelow knew well, and exclaimed, 'Be upstanding!' as though addressing troops across a windswept parade-ground. Dr Norman Carlow bustled in, wearing black jacket and striped trousers and polishing his monocle on a white silk handkerchief.

Carlow was a graduate of Trinity College, Dublin, a short fat Irishman with a shiny bald head ringed by small greying curls, a well-cared-for moustache, and a large pearl tie-pin. He had the appearance of a prosperous restaurateur or successful actor.

He was the only real medical friend Rumbelow had. He was an older man, but Rumbelow had a manner as well as a reputation befitting greater years, and was inclined to be impatient with his contemporaries. Unlike many coroners, who sat like little Lord Chancellors on the Woolsack of their dignity, Carlow was affable in court and breezy out of it, a mask for a shrewd and occasionally ruthless mind. They were both professionals, superb at their jobs. They both respected each other as such.

The proceedings were businesslike. The governor identified a document signed by the sheriff, an authorization to hang the prisoner. The prison doctor said death was instantaneous. Everything was put down in writing by the clerk and signed. When Rumbelow took the oath there was a stir among the jury, seven men dressed like the governor in their best and equally uneasy. He gave evidence with his usual brevity, lucidity, and authority, choosing his words as carefully as if addressing the Old Bailey. A coroner's court was still a court, whether held in a prison, a parish hall, or the upstairs parlour of a country inn, the coroner a powerful officer of the Crown begat by the Normans. Rumbelow had an awe of the law and its officers which his acquaintances put among his more ridiculous peculiarities. Besides, his evidence might always be thrown in his face by some astute counsel at later, unlooked-for and more stately proceedings. He was as cautious as a cat.

Carlow screwed his monocle into his eye and addressed the jury. 'You have been privileged–I don't think that's an inappropriate word–to hear evidence of the post-mortem examination from no less an authority than Dr Rumbelow. You will perhaps be satisfied in your own minds that the execution this morning was in every way conducted properly, and that death was occasioned instantaneously and without suffering.'

The jury was satisfied. They whispered a few seconds. The foreman announced a verdict of death by judicial hanging. The inquest was closed. The only difference from any other was the coroner failing to extend sympathy to the bereaved relatives.

Rumbelow, the governor and the coroner made their way down a back staircase to a small triangular courtyard. There was the handcart again, with a coffin on it.

'I'm afraid there's been something of a disturbance outside,' the governor said nervously. 'It started when the notice was put up on the gate. But I gather the police have everything well in hand.'

'I'm not worried,' said Rumbelow.

'I often wonder if they'll ever do away with all this business.'

'What, hanging?' asked Carlow. 'That would be hard on John Rumbelow. You'd do him out of his three-guinea fee, for p.m. plus inquest.'

'They've abolished the death penalty in twenty-one countries, you know. Denmark, Norway, Sweden. . . . I can't remember them all.'

'With the notable exception of Germany,' said Rumbelow.

'Even the Nazis are talking of abolishing it for civil crimes.'

'The Germans have a headsman in evening dress with a stiff shirt and tails, like an Englishman going to the opera,' said Carlow informatively. 'I suppose it fits with their Wagnerian concept of life and death. Do you think the fellow would have a top hat about him somewhere? Perhaps one of those collapsible ones. It's all part of the uniform.'

'I don't see what the fuss is about,' objected Rumbelow. 'There's only some dozen executions a year. In the reign of Henry the Eighth there were seventy-two thousand of them. I suppose it's all stirred up by those socialist highbrows.'

The governor looked offended. 'You could hardly call me one.'

'If they did abolish it, there'd soon be a clamour to bring it back,' Rumbelow told him. 'Hanging's as English as roast beef.'

Chapter Two

'I certainly shan't spill any tears over the little man,' said Lady Accrington. 'The whole affair was simply squalid. But the newspapers seemed determined to turn him into a national hero. They always do these days, with all sorts of unsavoury people, as long as they're flamboyant enough. Look at that awful Rector of Stiffkey!' She held up a thin wrinkled finger with a scarlet nail the size of an almond. 'Showing himself off at a fairground in a barrel, a disgrace to humanity. Perhaps they ought to have hung him, too. Well, Dr Rumbelow, you were there this morning?'

'I didn't attend the execution. I conducted the post-mortem.'

'There were some people making a fuss outside, I hear?' asked the Member of Parliament, a fat man in a wing collar with a fatter wife in a bright green silk dress.

'I shudder to think what might happen if they abolished the death sentence,' said Lady Odgers.

'*On a diablement peur de la corde*–that's what Queen Caroline of Brunswick said about England,' added Lord Odgers. 'We still need the rope, if only to keep the lower classes from killing one another on Saturday nights.'

'People are becoming far too sensitive,' decided Lady Accrington. 'Or too fond of making exhibitions of themselves.'

'Yours is a strange privilege, Doctor.' Evan Greensmith the author was sitting across the lunch-table, a thick-set man in a plain serge suit reminding Rumbelow disappointingly of a provincial shopkeeper. He made up Lady Accrington's party of eight with a thin, gingery-haired young man introduced as his secretary.

'What is?' asked Rumbelow.

'Yesterday you could refer to a living man and say with absolute certainty, "I shall be doing an autopsy on him tomorrow morning".'

'I can't see any privilege in it. It is only part of my work. I've performed four more post-mortems since, and I have at least another half-dozen before I'm free to go home tonight.'

'But you gave evidence against him at the trial. Surely that autopsy must have been a triumph? The end of a gladiatorial battle.'

This was too fanciful for Rumbelow. 'I'm afraid I don't follow. The word, by the way, is "necropsy" not "autopsy". "Autopsy" means an examination of oneself.'

The author looked annoyed at this correction of his grammar. Even Rumbelow saw he'd been tactless. But he found it impossible to turn his eyes from any inaccuracy.

'I was in Italy during the trial.' Greensmith's irritation was submerged by an eagerness for copy. 'Would you all be bored if I persuaded Dr Rumbelow to repeat his evidence?'

A murmur indicated that no-one would be bored in the slightest. Old Lady Accrington sat back, pleased with herself. The party was proving a success. An ambitious woman born into a world of barren fields for ambition, she had nothing in which to fulfil herself except the pursuit of social fame. Though her Mayfair house was delightful, her chef had come from the Ritz and her cellar specially chosen in Paris and Coblenz, she knew her prized consequence among the savagely competitive London hostesses depended only on her guests. She had invited Rumbelow for the day she calculated Tilling would hang, and a last-minute reprieve would have distressed her immeasurably. Had he been acquitted in the first place, she might well with admirable fairness have invited him instead.

'The two men, Hutchinson and Tilling, were homosexuals, of course.' Rumbelow was pleased to see them look faintly shocked. It was a condition thought dimly only to exist among artists, public schoolboys and sailors, never to be discussed in polite society. He always enjoyed impressing an audience. 'They'd had a quarrel. These people have quite heated rows, you know, even worse than ordinary couples.'

The M.P.'s fat wife laughed, but catching Rumbelow's glance stifled it.

'Hutchinson was found in bed in their Pimlico flat, shot through the chest. He died in hospital twelve hours later without recovering consciousness. Two shots had been fired. The first went through Hutchinson's chest-wall, chipping a rib. The second went into the left lung. Tilling said it was suicide, that he'd tried to wrench the gun away – which accounted for his fingerprints. But I could tell that both shots were in fact fired from some distance away, horizontally as Hutchinson was sitting in bed.'

'How could you?' said Evan Greensmith.

'I'll explain. At first I admit I believed Tilling. I'm an impartial medical expert, you know, not a prosecutor, however the defence sometimes cares to describe me. There were no powder-marks round the entry-wounds, as you'd expect from a gun fired close to the body. But the weapon was a ·25 automatic, and the cartridges of automatic pistols contain flake powder, which is smokeless. I went so far as firing the gun at close range into a square of fresh human skin, to prove as much.'

'Skin? Where from?' The M.P. looked startled.

'I should prefer not to say. But the angles of the bullets interested me. They couldn't possibly fit in with Tilling's story. The rib fractured by the first shot was of great significance–it could have been broken in the direction I found only had the gun been fired across the room. It was the same with the second shot. As this was perhaps a theoretical point to put to a jury, I fired the gun again–this time into an anatomist's skeleton. I drew diagrams and took photographs.' He paused. 'The jury was convinced.'

The author's secretary, who had said nothing throughout the meal, observed with great sadness, 'So Tilling was hanged through geometry?'

'But surely it wasn't cold-blooded murder, punishable as such?' asked Evan Greensmith. 'You admitted they'd had a bad row. Tilling was in a mental turmoil. Couldn't you regard it as a *crime passionnel*?'

'I don't recognize the term. Murder is the worst of crimes, as we all know perfectly well from childhood. Apart from those who are mentally deranged, such as schizophrenics,' Rumbelow added with his usual precision.

'But can't you distinguish between Crippen deliberately poisoning his wife, and a man who finds his wife in the arms of her lover and bludgeons her to death?'

'No.'

'I'm hardly likely to shake the great Dr Rumbelow with a cross-examination.' Everyone laughed.

'But taking your own life is a crime,' argued Lord Odgers. 'And the coroner invariably records that the balance of mind was disturbed.'

'That's a pious perjury. The Church won't afford a proper burial otherwise.'

'An improvement on the past,' said the M.P. 'They used to bury suicides in the public highway with a stake through their hearts, and confiscate all their worldly goods into the bargain.'

'I only wish I could enjoy your aloofness to the human tragedy, doctor,' said Greensmith.

Rumbelow had turned aside much bitterer sarcasm in court. He suspected the author enjoyed the same relationship with his secretary as that between the two dead men, which accounted for his trying to knock the wickedness out of the crime. 'That's a matter of training. Inwardly, I'm as sensitive as any man.'

'May I congratulate you on your aptitude? The training of a lifetime could never remotely bring me to perform those ghoulish duties.'

'Let me tell you something. Once I nearly gave up pathology–my life's work. I was a junior at Blackfriars Hospital. I'd been working in the mortuary only a few weeks. Then I felt I couldn't go on with it. I couldn't bring myself to enter the post-mortem room, to put on the rubber gloves, to make the incision. About that time a very great friend of mine went sick–he was one of the house-physicians, we'd been through medical school together, perhaps he was the only friend I had. As too often happens with doctors, no one seemed to know what was wrong. Of course, the grand physicians came in and made their grand diagnoses. But after considerable suffering, he died.'

'You didn't do the post-mortem?' cried Lady Accrington in horror.

'I attended it. I was curious, you see. I wanted to know all about the disease which had killed him. It's a matter of science. Medical science, any science, transcends human beings.'

'I agree the astronomer measures his stars, rather than writes poems on the glory of the heavens,' said Evan Greensmith graciously.

'A doctor's duty is to study and classify disease, so as to cure or prevent it in others. If he becomes emotionally involved with a dead body, exactly as with a sick man, he's finished. After I'd watched the corpse of my friend cut to bits, I knew that nothing again in the post-mortem room could ever unsettle me.'

There was a silence.

'You mean a doctor must possess a heart of stone?' asked the author.

'A good doctor, yes.'

'You showed a singular fortitude,' observed Lord Odgers admiringly.

'Not at all. I simply got my ideas clear. There's a prison governor I know who can hardly bring himself to witness an execution. But his duty is to observe an action of the law, which is created by man to preserve civilization. The human being involved must be shut from the mind. But he doesn't see that.'

A clock in the room chimed two. Rumbelow remembered the lecture he had to give at Blackfriars. He pulled himself together, forming apologies for leaving, feeling he had been talking too freely. Perhaps the wine he had drunk was aggrandized by his abstemious habits.

The others were still eating dessert. As they had enjoyed their fill of horrors, Rumbelow left to a babble of argument about Hitler's reoccupation of the Rhineland.

'Why shouldn't he walk into his own back garden?'

'It's only the French who want us to kick him out. They're too scared to lift a finger.'

'Well, they were our allies during the War.'

'We can forgive them for that.'

'*I* find it a most disturbing exhibition of feebleness on the part of the Empire.'

'Don't lose any sleep over Herr Hitler, I implore you. What's Germany to gain from re-starting the War? Absolutely nothing.'

'Some of his grievances are justified.'

'He's a man of peace. Like the Prime Minister. You can take my word for it.'

The door shut. Rumbelow was surprised that Lady Accrington had disregarded etiquette to abandon her guests and accompany him across the hall. A man of even greater self-control than himself would have relished the luxury of the house, the display of glass and silver, the practised discreet attentions of the footmen, the food and wine, the atmosphere of money having no more significance than the means of obtaining anything that for the moment happened to be desired. It would have been inhuman not responding to an environment beyond his imagination as a boy or a young doctor. But he took these invitations–which could come almost every week later, during the season–much as a matter of course. It was his right to move amid the rich, powerful and clever. He was a national figure. Any errand boy stopped in the street would know his name, which was more than could be claimed by Lady Accrington, or possibly even by Evan Greensmith.

'And how's your poor wife?' asked Lady Accrington, as an afterthought.

'Still very delicate, I'm afraid.'

'She's fortunate, having a doctor for a husband.'

He picked his famous bag from the black-and-white marble floor of the hall. It was of black leather, almost square, with stout silver locks. His hostess had taken pains to have it placed in immediate view of arrivals through the front door. It still contained the section of Tilling's broken neck.

Rumbelow turned, to find her face close to his, burning with eagerness. For a moment he wondered if she were going to pay him some glowing compliment, or more wildly that she was about to kiss him. 'That skin,' she whispered. 'The piece you shot at. Where did it come from?'

'Oh! a leg–amputated by the surgeons. Its owner was run over by a brewer's dray.'

'So that's it. Well, I'm disappointed. But I suppose flaying someone alive would be a little macabre. Even for you, Dr Rumbelow?'

The footman announced a taxi, and to Rumbelow's annoyance he had to take it.

Chapter Three

Blackfriars Hospital stood overlooking the Thames in the City of London, at the angle of Blackfriars Bridge and the Victoria Embankment. As Rumbelow took his unwanted taxi-ride, three consultants were talking in the ground-floor committee-room. This faced on to the Embankment itself, with its clanking, lumbering, red double-decker trams, then the chocolate-coloured river, and behind a row of cranes on the far bank some vast grime-encrusted warehouses, cathedrals of the Empire's commerce.

The room was like a hundred such others in the City–cheerless, dark-panelled, a long table down the middle, portraits of half-forgotten past luminaries on the walls, the sour smell of rooms which are used rather than lived in. A hospital crest hung over the broad stone fireplace, and down one side stood a couple of smaller tables with writing materials and reference-books. It had turned into the consultant staff's common room, gradually, unofficially, and more years ago than anyone cared to remember, like many usages both social and clinical in the ancient institution.

'But what a splendid photograph!' Sir George Smallpenny was looking at the lunch edition of an evening paper. 'Quite the Edgar Wallace touch.'

'It's all going a little far, surely?'

'"Dr Rumbelow leaving the prison this morning with his murder bag".' He laughed. 'I do wish he wouldn't wear that dreadful bowler. It makes him look like a vet, at the races.'

'I suppose there's nothing to stop the newspapers writing about him as they like–or as much as they like. But I don't see why he should encourage them.'

'They don't need encouragement. This nation is strongly addicted to ghouls.'

Sir George dropped the paper on the long table. He was in his usual pose, heels on the black iron fender, warming himself comfortably before the glowing coals in the basket-grate. He was a humorous, easy-going, good-looking man, grey-haired and clean-shaven, his dress of light-coloured lounge suit and spotted bow tie approaching informality. He was one of the consultant gynaecologists, believed to be the richest man on the hospital's staff. With his feet on the committee-table sat Dr Ian Bantrell. He was a physician, about the same age as Rumbelow, elected to a consultancy only some twelve months previously. Tubby, ruddy-faced, carroty-haired, he wore the professional uniform of black jacket and striped trousers, with wing collar and spats. The amiable Sir George–who eyed his colleagues more perceptively than the more inexperienced of them imagined–had decided that Bantrell's formal appearance, like his present aggressive posture, was the effect of his feeling unsure of himself.

'Rumbelow doesn't bring much credit to Blackfriars, does he? Putting himself on the level of Jack the Ripper and Sweeney Todd.'

'Isn't that a little unfair?' asked Sir George mildly. 'I don't think his ambition is ending up in the Chamber of Horrors at Tussaud's.'

'It's bad enough having one publicist on the staff already.'

'Who's that?'

'Graham Trevose.'

'Oh, Graham. But all plastic surgeons advertise themselves. They're prima donnas. It's all part of the performance.'

'Trevose is a lightweight, of course.'

'A very able lightweight.'

'I'm not denying for one moment he's clever. And he sticks to his noses and bosoms, which doesn't take private fees away from the other surgeons. I suppose that's why his antics are tolerated.'

Bantrell folded his arms pugnaciously. Sir George said nothing, reflecting what a prickly young man he was. Graham Trevose admittedly might hardly be more than a beauty specialist, but he was a colleague, and a good ten years senior to Bantrell. What might be deserved criticism delivered by a senior man in confidence became only insolence in the mouth of this new physician. But Sir George gave no rebuke. It was his way to soothe rather than ruffle, a valuable quality among the strong-minded, ambitious and often jealous men who composed the senior staff of any important hospital. He was popular, a sophisticated confessor and tolerant mediator, with great influence in the continual little discussions and arguments which eventually shaped the way their lives in the hospital were run. Because he grasped this, Bantrell was eager to talk that afternoon as they met by chance in the coming-and-going of their work.

'Trevose simply likes to get his name in the gossip-columns,' Bantrell continued. 'Well, all right. It's unethical, but I suppose it's healthy for his practice among the actresses and debutantes. But the public adulation of Rumbelow is different. He's known in every home from Land's End to John o' Groats, better than Mr Baldwin himself.'

'But not as a hangman's familiar. Rather as the infallible detective. That's another of our folk-heroes. Look at the fortunes to be made writing thrillers.'

'You're saying Rumbelow's infallible?'

'My dear Ian, all men are far from that. Though perhaps he thinks he is.'

'That is precisely my point. I don't mind him assuming an air of infallibility in court–as long as *I*'m not in the dock. But I cannot stand him adopting it towards the rest of us here. What do you think, Crampers?'

The third man in the room licked the envelope of a letter he had been finishing at one of the side-tables. The Blackfriars' consultants were as mixed a collection of individualists as might be found at the head of any large enterprise. Mr Cramphorn was the senior surgeon, short, broad-shouldered, grey-moustached, with half-moon glasses and a busily-puffing pipe, a brusque, buttoned-up man who was fond of pepper-and-salt suits, shot and fished, and operated beautifully. 'Think of Rumbelow? We've got to put up with the fellow, haven't we? We're like a club–take the rough with the smooth, or life's impossible. And it's always on the cards, *he* can't stand the rest of us.' He affixed a three-ha'penny stamp. 'No, I don't object to him. Mind, he's beastly dogmatic.'

'You may call it dogmatism. I'd call it vanity.'

'Same thing, often enough, isn't it? The Christian martyrs must have been as vain as peacocks. You have to be, if you believe in yourself to the point of going up in flames. He's certainly obstinate. Always was, even as one of my students. He'd stick to his diagnosis of a case, even if it was wrong as plain as the nose on your face. Funny thing, he sometimes turned out to be right and the rest of us had made a bloomer.'

'If he thinks rather a lot of himself,' suggested Sir George charitably, 'we're all sometimes guilty of that.'

'But I can't see what Rumbelow's done to merit such self-esteem.'

Mr Cramphorn puffed away, relighting his pipe. 'Strung up a dozen murderers.'

'Is that a lasting achievement?'

'Well, it was for the murderers.'

'But they'd have been convicted without Rumbelow so much as entering the witness-box. He cashed in because the trials were so sensational. Look at the Perryman case, the one he made his name with. You can't expect the newspapers to soft-pedal a situation where a man cuts up his mistress and sends her carriage-paid by rail to a dozen respectable and distinguished citizens.'

'Still, Rumbelow put the jig-saw together,' Sir George reminded him. 'At one time they thought the chap had carved up two mistresses, or even three.'

'I'm not denying his ability, no more than Trevose's. It's the public's fault if they imagine it's magic. Unfortunately, he gives them every opportunity to remain in that state of mind. Look at that next case, on the heels of the Perryman affair—'

'"The Brides at the Seaside",' smiled Sir George.

'Yes, the young fellow involved in those convenient boating accidents. What did Rumbelow do? Demonstrated the girl had been killed in a bath or a bucket or something, because there was fresh and not sea water in her lungs.

What's so clever about that? We all three know our pathology, our elementary chemistry. We could have shown exactly the same.'

'Not easy holding these things up in court.' Mr Cramphorn looked over his half-moons. 'I get roped in now and then, compensation cases and the like. Those legal johnnies could tie George Washington in knots.'

'But Rumbelow's an expert–as a witness. He sticks to his facts, avoids the pitfalls and talks so even the most dimwitted juryman can understand him. *That's* what his reputation's based on. No wonder the judges love him.'

They were interrupted by the subject of their conversation appearing through a door at the far end of the room. The three fell silent, suddenly feeling embarrassed, even Bantrell. There were always letters and rolled-up journals awaiting collection at one end of the committee-table, and without saying anything, or even seeming to notice the others, Rumbelow started looking through them. Sir George Smallpenny stared through the window at a tug with a string of deep-laden barges deferentially lowering its funnel to pass under the arches of Blackfriars Bridge. Bantrell had really become quite angry, he thought. He was uncertain if it distressed or amused him. He supposed Bantrell was simply jealous of Rumbelow. They were much the same age and seniority on the staff. They were exceptionally clever. Everyone knew Bantrell was fanatically ambitious to make his name in London medicine. And the more such people wanted from life, the greater they resented the success in it of others. To break the tension he asked humorously, 'Where's the murder bag?'

Rumbelow looked up. 'My bag? It's locked in the lab.'

'The hanging went off all right, I suppose?'

'Yes.'

'Anything interesting in the p.m.?'

'No.'

'We missed you at lunch,' said Bantrell, still with his feet up. 'We were hoping to hear all the grisly details.'

'I lunched with Lady Accrington.'

'*Did* you?'

Rumbelow looked at him blankly. 'A man must eat.'

'If the condemned man enjoys a hearty breakfast, the pathologist at least deserves a decent lunch,' said Sir George.

The four then split up. Bantrell felt satisfied he had sown his seeds. If he could persuade them to germinate, they lay where the roots would run deepest.

Chapter Four

It was almost midnight when Rumbelow reached home, by the last Southern Railway electric train from Charing Cross. Had he been later, he would have had to take a taxi all the way–a disaster.

Still carrying his bag, he trudged from Lower Sydenham station up a hill dominated by the twin towers and curved glass roofs of Prince Albert's Crystal Palace. His house was half-way along, square, brick and stucco, built fifty years previously when the railways were enticing prosperous City men to the unfashionable south-eastern suburbs. It had started to drizzle. He noticed each alternative gas-lamp wore a halo, the rest having been extinguished for the night. He felt for the latch of the wrought-iron gate leading to the constricted front garden, feeling very tired.

Despite popular notions, most of Rumbelow's work was like any medical man's–repetitive, mentally unexacting and even dull. At three that afternoon he had lectured in the steep-tiered theatre of the pathology block, its narrow much-carved benches crowded with students. They had little interest in forensic medicine, which seldom appeared in final examination papers and could therefore be safely skipped. They came to see Rumbelow. He was famous, he had his name in the papers, he was as much an object of pride as the hospital's sporting trophies. Besides, he was always likely to show with the epidiascope magnified photographs of murders, rapes, sexual aberrations and similar diversions. That afternoon he passed round the jar with the piece of Tilling's neck, and was gratified to see the impression on even such a notoriously hardened audience.

At the end of the hour he clattered down a short iron spiral staircase to the mortuary in the semi-basement. He was still annoyed at the three in the committee-room. That they were discussing him was clear from their expressions, their attitudes and their silence. He supposed Bantrell had started it. He knew how the young physician disliked him. That was something he had to tolerate, or ignore. But why should he become sarcastic over a lunch at Lady Accrington's? It was a perfectly reasonable engagement for a man in his position. Rumbelow was frankly puzzled.

He hurried into the small changing-room, already removing his jacket and false cuffs. 'How many today?' he asked Quinley, his assistant.

'Two, sir. A man with terminal bronchopneumonia following carcinimatosis—'

'Very well. Where's the primary?'

'In the left bronchus. And a woman with hepatic cirrhosis.'

'I don't want to waste time. I've six cases waiting for me at the Central Mortuary.'

He could hear the students shuffling through their own door. For some forgotten reason, the post-mortems at Blackfriars were always performed at four o'clock. Notices with the dead patients' names and particulars were posted round the medical school, all duplicated in violet copper-plate and resembling menus outside continental restaurants.

The dead man started his final journey already shrouded, a tag round his wrist with name and date like a newborn baby, on a trolley with a stiffened canvas cover to hide the load yet proclaiming it the more blatantly, Sister hurriedly rearranging screens to spare the still living the sight of a fallen comrade. He went to a new section of the mortuary, one of the many improvements Rumbelow had insisted upon in the three years since his appointment, his authority established even before by the Perryman and seaside cases. It contained a dozen drawers two foot square, refrigerated storage, in which he was left until the undertakers called or four o'clock brought him Rumbelow's attentions. Not every death meant a necropsy. Only if the doctors were interested or baffled were the bereaved relatives pressed to advance medical science, though before final examinations the dead were cut up less discriminately to give the students practice. The bereaved relatives generally agreed, in gratitude to Blackfriars, even though the patient would self-evidently have done just as well staying in his bed at home.

The post-mortem room itself was larger than the hospital's operating theatres. There were two porcelain tables with slightly raised edges, a pair of sinks, and a sloping surface like a kitchen draining-board with water trickling on to it continuously through a red rubber hose from the ceiling. At one end were half a dozen steps for the students, with metal frames to lean against, as on the terraces of football grounds.

A door led to the third room of the suite, with an abrupt change of atmosphere. The walls were of carved light oak, the lighting dim, and in the centre was a bier on which the coffin could lie beneath a cloth of tasselled velvet with a silver cross worked in it, the property of the hospital. It could be viewed by the relatives and other interested parties, strictly by appointment, though the lid could be open or shut according to preference. This transition from the impersonal to the emotional view of death, from science to sentiment, was one of the few things which always amused Rumbelow.

The row blew up suddenly.

Rumbelow did not like Quinley. He was inelegant, awkward, even clumsy, a man in his late twenties, prematurely bald with two tufts of fuzzy hair over his ears, his sallow complexion generally disfigured by an angry-looking spot or two. He had a troublesome liability to boils, for which he submitted to painful injections of staphylococcus vaccine with unnoticeable effect. Rumbelow conceded the boils were hardly Quinley's fault, but his appearance alone disturbed him. He had been more or less forced to appoint him on a memorable record of gold medals and scholarships. At least he was useful, being competent enough for the Blackfriars' post-mortems when Rumbelow was busy with the police or in court.

'I'll do the old man first,' said Rumbelow. He made the familiar sweep from point of chin to base of penis.

A house-physician stood beside him with a sheaf of the dead man's clinical notes, it being considered good form for the consultant, or at least his underling, to be faced with organs he had known only remotely and be either vindicated, puzzled, or shamed. The old man's diagnosis had been a fell one. He had come into the hospital already shot through with cancer, one side of his chest a barrel of fluid, secondary growths in the bones of his arm and his brain. Rumbelow sliced the organs on the porcelain slab under running water, announcing to the students, 'You see, gentlemen, the primary growth was a carcinoma of the left bronchus, infiltrating the lung and pleura and giving metastases in the brain.'

Quinley was in red apron and gloves as well. He looked up from the slit-open body. 'Isn't there something down here in the prostate, sir?'

Rumbelow turned sharply. He knew that for once his thoroughness had lapsed. He had opened the bladder, but left the prostate gland below unexamined. His hurry to be away had perhaps affected him, as it had seemed clear the lethal seeds spread from the growth in the chest. He crossed to the table, asking the house-physician, 'Was there any history of dysuria? You didn't mention it.'

The houseman ruffled through the notes. 'There's some difficulty in passing urine recorded sir. But we didn't think it significant.'

Rumbelow felt into the pelvis. The prostate was enlarged. It was a small growth compared with the others, but that was usual enough. Quinley was right.

He said nothing. He didn't want Quinley to be right. Particularly in front of an audience. He had second thoughts. It might simply be old man's enlargement of the prostate, not a malignant tumour at all. It was just possible. That could be definitely determined only by cutting sections and looking down a microscope–which could be done in the seclusion of a laboratory. 'You deceive yourself, Dr Quinley.'

The assistant shifted his body awkwardly, looking put out. 'It appeared the primary to me, sir.'

'Can't you see it's a benign enlargement? Commonplace in a man of that age.'

'No, I can't agree, sir. I think it's a malignant adenoma.'

It was tactless and graceless, but said without hostility–he had a genuine admiration for Rumbelow. But it forced Rumbelow into his second mistake. 'You doubt my opinion?' he demanded angrily. 'That's not very respectful of you, is it? If it's my word against yours, I don't think there's much doubt which would be accepted. In a court of law, at any rate.'

There was a gasp from the students, watching fascinated and amused. It was not at all done in Blackfriars to berate assistants in front of a class. Consultants generally affected a wry pride at being tripped by juniors whose cleverness had been instilled by themselves. Rumbelow was now angry with himself for losing his temper. For years he had trained himself to control it, a necessity in the witness-box with every K.C. in London on his mettle to confuse and discredit him. Perhaps his annoyance with Bantrell that afternoon had unsettled him.

'Very well, Quinley. Remove the prostate, and we'll section it. The microscope will say which one of us is right.' To lighten the scene he added, 'Would you care to wager a five-pound note on it?'

But it fell flat. Rumbelow saw he had demeaned himself before his students. He finished both post-mortems without addressing another word to Quinley at all.

He left Blackfriars shortly after five, still carrying his bag, taking the Tube to north London. The six cases in the Central Mortuary were deaths which never reached the newspapers. The first was a suicide, a man with his face still cherry-red from the carbon monoxide of his gas oven. A woman taken from the Thames. A fat man who had collapsed in the street, the jelly of his brain suffused with the blood of a burst artery. Two road accidents. Then a nineteen-year-old girl who had died during the night, the blood and discharge caked to the inside of her thighs already telling the cause. One more woman who should have given life to another but instead brought death on herself. He handled the body gingerly. She had died from streptococcal septicaemia following an abortion. There was no effective treatment in the world, and she still harboured the living germs. From inside he cut away uterus, ovaries and vagina with the connecting broad ligament. He slit the muscle of the enlarged septic womb on the porcelain slab, spreading the organ out in his gloved fingers. No foetus nor membranes. A professional job, no old woman with a knitting-needle in a back parlour. He wondered what doctor had performed the secret operation. It was the sixth he had seen in a year. He had his suspicions.

He wrote his reports, handed the mortuary porter a pound note and still with his bag took the Tube south to Piccadilly Circus. He always dined late, at his club in Pall Mall. This was a grotesque misplaced Venetian palace, a series of lofty, impersonal ill-heated rooms, its members less a fraternity than a collection of men with nowhere better to spend the evening. Everyone knew who he was, but through club convention avoided showing it–a consideration Rumbelow was not certain he appreciated. But he was new to clubland, put up by Norman Carlow, and he thought it all rather magnificent.

At his customary table in the corner he ordered a lamb chop and treated himself to his usual quarter-bottle of claret. He was half-way through when a porter called him to the telephone. It was Scotland Yard, with a message from Superintendent Sixsmith asking for him urgently at an address in Paddington. Rumbelow left his dinner unfinished, and took a taxi knowing he could claim it as expenses from the Home Office without any quibbling.

The house was in the grid of terraced streets south of Paddington Station, all small hotels, boarding-houses and bed-sitting rooms, where criminals and prostitutes drifted plentifully on the ever-flowing population. It was an area he had been called to more than once. Outside were cars, two uniformed policemen, the usual bunch of reporters giving him a cheerful greeting. If the superintendent was there himself, Rumbelow calculated, it was a major crime.

A policeman took him to a back room on the top floor. There was Sixsmith, another detective, and an inspector from the Yard's photographic department adjusting a bellows camera on a tripod. It was a cheap bed-sitting room with a sloping ceiling, a divan along one side, a washbasin half-hidden by a grubby curtain with pink flowers on it, an electric fire set in the wall, and a small oil-cooker in one corner with a saucepan, which Rumbelow noticed to contain congealed baked beans. There seemed to be blood everywhere. A middle-aged man with a thick black moustache was dead in a sitting position in the opposite corner, the length of clothes-line round his neck attached to a pipe in the roof. His throat and both wrists were cut, a bloodstained open razor lying in the middle of the worn carpet. On the divan Rumbelow saw a small revolver, the cylinder swung open and three bullets on the blood-spattered cover.

'Somebody seemed intent on making a proper job of it, Doctor,' remarked Sixsmith. He was a large red-faced man with the look of a prosperous farmer with sociable habits.

Rumbelow took off his bowler, his fur-collared overcoat and his jacket with the mock cuffs. The other detective considerately held on to them. 'Know anything about him?'

'Not much. He's German or Hungarian. Been here a couple of days.'

'Who found him?'

'The old lady below saw blood coming through the ceiling as she was making her supper.'

Rumbelow crouched over the body. He lifted an eyelid and felt the slack lower jaw. 'No rigor mortis. He's been dead about three hours. Certainly not more than six.'

'The case came up to me as murder.'

'It's suicide.'

'Oh. Well, in fact I thought as much, once I'd had a look at it. What's the cause of death, Doctor?'

'Asphyxia.'

'What about the wounds?'

'The ones on the neck are superficial. They've only gone through the skin and subcutaneous tissues and the platysma muscle just beneath. A few tentative cuts are common enough, if you've the idea of cutting your throat.

The ones on the wrists are deeper. The left has some of the tendons leading from the forearm muscles to the fingers severed. The right's more severe still. It's caught the radial artery, hence the blood as he staggered about after doing the deed. He was probably left-handed.' Rumbelow's eyes travelled to the oil-stove. 'The position of the saucepan handle seems to confirm that.'

'He didn't seem keen on leaving anything to chance, did he?'

Rumbelow stood up, carefully dusting his knees. 'That's often the case with suicide, isn't it? If you're going to kill yourself, I suppose you must be in an unusually determined frame of mind. Two methods combined are common enough. I did a p.m. last week on a girl who'd jumped from a window. She'd already swallowed enough aspirin to kill a heavyweight boxer. This chap probably meant to use the revolver as well, once he had his head in the noose.'

'He'd got the wrong ammunition.' Sixsmith nodded towards the body. 'He didn't give himself much drop.'

'Two inches are enough, if you stick out your legs. A murderer would hoist the body to the roof.' Sixsmith nodded. 'The p.m. will show death from suffocation by the tongue forced against the back wall of the throat. Plus pressure on the arteries bringing blood to the brain. That's a factor a lot of pathologists overlook. It killed a man last year. He'd got a tracheotomy opening in his windpipe below the rope, and everyone was very puzzled until I appeared on the scene.'

Rumbelow started to put on his jacket. As usual, there were endless notes to be made and photographs to be taken. Sixsmith finally offered him a lift to Charing Cross, on his way back to the Yard. In the car Rumbelow asked, 'is the Vickery case down for a hearing yet?'

'Soon after Easter, I gather.'

'As near as that?'

'Are you going away, Doctor?'

They had worked together, all over the country, during the past five years. They had become personal friends. Though Sixsmith perceived the relationship was improved–or only possible at all–if he steadfastly preserved the lay person's respect for the man of medicine.

'I've too much work.' They turned from Marble Arch down Park Lane, past the two newly opened luxury hotels. It prompted Rumbelow to ask, 'The Yard hasn't got any more on Dr Elgin, I suppose?'

'I could find out for you.'

'I fancy I encountered another specimen of his work today.'

'Young girl?'

'Nineteen.'

'It's difficult to trace these things. The women don't advertise who they're going to see. Often enough, they don't tell anyone about it at all. It may be all part of the bargain.'

'One day Elgin's going to make a slip, and we'll get him.'

'You're hard on your own black sheep, Doctor.'

'We are a privileged profession, but only because we are bound by a strict code of ethics. It is inexcusable to break it.'

Sixsmith grinned. 'It's a good job you're not a policeman.'

In the suburban train Rumbelow sat for the half-hour journey with his bag at his feet, reading the evening paper.

But he was not glad to be home.

Chapter Five

1936 was a good year for dance bands. He saw the light on downstairs, and the strong beat reached him even through the curtained window. As he unlocked the front door the music stopped abruptly. She knew it would only irritate him.

He set down his bag and removed his hat and coat. He took a brush from a shelf below the small oval mirror of the hall stand, and carefully removed the raindrops. Then he went into the sitting-room.

'You'd no need to stay up, you know.'

'I was listening to the wireless.'

'Anything good?'

'Some dance music. Sydney Lipton from the Grosvenor House.'

'Tune-in again, if you like.'

'It's almost twelve, anyway.' She held up the evening paper, the page folded so his photograph occupied the middle. 'Did you see it?'

'Yes. It's a little embarrassing, sometimes. I think they deliberately go out of their way to make me into some sort of monster.'

He wanted to go to bed, but felt some obligation to sit for a moment in his easy-chair beside the serenely dying fire. The room was comfortable, and furnished with neither expense nor imagination. The three-piece suite of chairs and sofa was a sort to be seen in the window of any large store in London. There were neither pictures nor photographs, and the small glass-fronted bookcase contained only textbooks and outdated copies of the *Medical Directory*. Under a standard lamp with a pinkfringed shade was a small table with the black-and-white bakelite case of their new wireless set. He saw his wife had been sewing. Her treadle-operated machine was without its cover, and on the maroon chenille tablecloth were his shirts with their cut sleeves, and a new jacket to which she had been attaching the secret buttons for his cuffs.

'I hope you weren't expecting me earlier. The Yard got hold of me at the club.'

'I only expect you when I see you, John. It's part of the job, isn't it?'

My job or her job? he wondered. She's no cause to complain about either. 'I haven't had an easy day. The inquest and so on this morning went very well, but people at Blackfriars were being extremely difficult.' He had no intention of telling her more.

'What did the Yard want?'

'Nothing very interesting.'

'What about your lunch? Did you enjoy yourself?'

'There were some quite important people there.'

She folded her hands on the library book lying in her lap. Her fingers were rough, and she never used nail-varnish. He had forgotten the times when they sat across the fire after he came home, eagerly sorting the small change of their day's activities, passing from one to another the small, familiar tokens valueless to anyone but themselves. She was the same age as himself. She was slim, almost to the dangerous point of scrawniness, with noticeable hollows at the neck of her plain green dress. She had good legs, quite arresting when she wore silk stockings. Her skin was pale, smooth and waxy, her mouth and chin small, giving her a waif-like look. Her fair hair was parted at the middle, and she curled it at home every Friday with a sixpenny Amami Wave Set from the chemist's.

'Were there any wives at the lunch?'

'Perhaps one or two. I honestly don't know. At such functions one is asked very much for oneself, you know. People in society have a different outlook from those in this part of the world.'

'Next time, say you must bring me.'

He decided she was being mischievous. 'You wouldn't be expected, Rosemary.'

'I'd like to meet Lady Accrington just once. I read about her in the *Bystander*.'

'She's rather formidable.' He got up and made abruptly for the kitchen.

There were two rooms at the back of the house. One he had fitted up as a laboratory, where he worked until midnight when he happened to find himself at home in the evenings. In the kitchen across the short corridor he started to prepare a milk drink, widely advertised to induce sleep of the finest quality and to overcome innumerable social and business problems. He hoped she wouldn't follow him, but she did.

'That new wireless, John. It's a wonderful tone. So much better than the last old thing.'

The feverishness of her voice put him more on his guard. 'Then I'm glad I bought it.'

'But you didn't want to, did you? How I had to talk you into it!'

'I've told you we can't be extravagant.'

'Oh, I know. We can't even have a maid.'

He turned the gas-tap. 'I thought this latest charwoman was satisfactory?'

'She's as good as any. As long as I work in the house myself. But everyone knows we haven't a maid. You can't blame them for wondering why.'

'I'm not interested in the slightest what the neighbours think of us. I've no time for such people.'

'But they don't understand. You can't deny you're famous, can you? They imagine you must be wealthy as well. The two go together in everyone's mind these days.'

'You know exactly what I earn. I've always been frank about it. Two guineas for a post-mortem, three if I give evidence at the inquest. As I'm entirely dependent on Norman Carlow for most of this, it's a good job I keep in with him. A day at the Old Bailey rewards me with the princely sum of one guinea. Plus sixpence a mile travelling expenses. For Assizes in the country I'm allowed my railway fare, third-class and at the reduced return rate. If I have to walk, I'm entitled to threepence a mile for refreshments. In both directions. A man can hardly grow rich on that. It's all in Home Office orders and the Coroner's Act. If you don't believe me, go to Dulwich public library and look it up.'

'The milk's boiling over.'

He turned off the gas.

'Couldn't you economize on your clothes?' she suggested.

'I've got to keep up a decent appearance. I can't go into the witness box in a shabby suit. It would look as if I didn't take the court seriously, or I was a second-rater. These things mean a lot. You seem to forget I've a lot of professional expenses.' He was becoming annoyed. 'I have to insure my life. I've no intention of leaving you destitute, you know. Mine's a risky trade. I could be dead in a week, if I pricked my finger tomorrow working on an infected corpse.'

'You could write articles for the newspapers. They always seem anxious enough to print your name.'

'That's a stupid idea. Apart from anything else, I'm governed by the Official Secrets Act.'

'Graham Trevose does.'

'Trevose is a slippery customer. He'll come a cropper one day.' He poured hot milk into a cup and added chocolate-coloured crystals from a tin. He was resentful of her again bringing up the business of a housemaid, when he was so tired. He supposed she had been tightly winding up the spring of her argument all evening.

'If you don't care what the local people think of you, what about Lady Accrington and that set?'

He sipped the hot drink. 'They're different. They're more intelligent. They understand the world. They're cultured.'

'Why do you keep me away from them?'

'Do I? What's this sudden enthusiasm? I thought you didn't care to mix with them.'

'You think that only because I don't create scenes and insist on going. I don't because it would only make things more difficult for you.'

'Don't I take you out often enough?'

'You're ashamed of me.'

'No, no, I'm not.' He felt he was doing badly in the argument. He was much more at home in the witness-box at the Old Bailey than in his own kitchen. Then suddenly he was sorry for her. It was an uncommon emotion. However much he saw of mankind's sad inadequacies, his soul was pitifully starved of compassion. She had been the only human to draw any tenderness from him, to pierce the isolation he felt in the world, to give him a precious sense of correlation with some other being. When they married he had recognized this as love–the very essence of love, as far as it could be distilled by the inaptly scientific apparatus of his mind. That was five years ago. Now he thought her dull, small-minded, obsessed with domestic trivia, lacking in social graces, a liability. In five years he had risen in the world, by his achievement alone. She had failed to keep up with him, and that was her failure. She was a disappointment to him. But somehow all women were a disappointment to Rumbelow.

'I know it's difficult for you, Rosemary,' he said more kindly, 'if only because my life hasn't turned out the way either of us expected. I hope you're glad I'm a success. It's easy enough to miss the boat in medicine. I'd no connexions, no money, no one in the family to help me at Blackfriars, nor even in the profession. I could have ended up running a shilling surgery in the East End, making up my own medicines, running my own errands, treating no one but the working classes. A drudge without prospects. It happens, you know. Even to men who were students with me.'

'I'm not decrying everything you've done. I'd never do that. I'm proud of you, John.' He stirred uneasily. He didn't want her to be proud of him. It only emphasized her attachment. 'I talk about you a lot, every day. Even to perfect strangers, who come up in the shops and ask if I'm really your wife. It's quite thrilling, you know.'

He drained the cup of flavoured milk. 'Things might have been better had you wanted a child.'

'Why must you bring that up?' She could grow angry about this, but now she sounded only helpless. 'Haven't we been over it often enough?'

'We've been over your excuses often enough. First you thought you'd go on with your job, teaching schoolchildren in London. Then you had the house to run. Then you didn't think you were strong enough—'

'They were reasonable excuses.'

'No excuse is reasonable for a woman to avoid having a child. It's a natural function. It's like making excuses to stop breathing.'

'Now you're making me sound inhuman.'

'I'm not. I only think you're rather pathetic. But it doesn't make your outlook any more agreeable.'

'Very well. I'll tell you the truth.' She hesitated. 'I'm scared.'

'Of childbirth! In this day and age?'

'Not of the birth itself. Of . . . of what I might produce. Some monster. A cretin, a mongol, an idiot?'

He stared at her, amazed. It was the first time she had even hinted to him of such fears. 'But that's ridiculous. They're remarkably uncommon.'

'I don't care. They can happen. I could see it happen to me.' He noticed her eyes fill with tears.

'But why *should* it happen to you? We're both healthy.'

'I don't know, I don't know. I just feel it, that's all. I've tried to conquer it, to hide it somewhere in my mind. But I can't. Won't you understand me? Won't you even try to?'

She was looking up at him imploringly, fumbling with a lace-edged handkerchief from the pocket of her dress. He was satisfied. He had dominated her, as he could dominate a jury at the Old Bailey or Lady Accrington's luncheon-table. After facing her for some seconds he said, 'I should much have liked a child, you know.'

He put out the light and made for the stairs. Partly through her aversion to motherhood and partly because there was no love left between them, they had enjoyed no sexual intercourse for some time. But they shared the same bed, Rumbelow thinking the expense of a new pair of twin ones somewhat unnecessary.

Chapter Six

When Sixsmith telephoned, Rumbelow imagined it was about the Vickery case. He knew by then the trial was to open at the Old Bailey after the Easter holiday, on the Wednesday, April the fifteenth.

'I've got a journey for you, I'm afraid, Doctor.'

'That's all right.' Rumbelow found himself out of London almost every month on police business.

'You said you weren't going away for Easter. I hope I was right taking you at your word?'

'Where's it to?'

'Mortlock. It's a hundred-odd miles west of London. Perhaps you know the place?' Rumbelow had been through it in the train. 'It's an exhumation. At a village just outside, to be exact. I'd like it done as soon as possible. You know how these affairs have the habit of leaking out.'

'Have you obtained the Home Office order?'

'It's in front of me.' The detective sounded a little offended. 'We could do it early tomorrow, as soon as the light's good enough. I'm going back there by the evening train. I'm now at the Yard, so I could come over to Blackfriars in a car and pick you up. Say about five o'clock?'

Rumbelow pulled out his dead brother's gold watch. 'Yes, that's convenient. I've time to get a bag with some clothes sent up from home.'

'I'll give you the background when we meet.'

'I'll be in my lab.'

Rumbelow put the receiver back on its hook. He had a telephone of the old-fashioned sort in his laboratory. The room was small, on the ground floor of the pathology department, just down the corridor from the committee room. The single window of frosted glass, looking inwards on to a small courtyard and the medical school library, Rumbelow had never been known to open. Under the window was a workbench with a pair of gas-taps for the Bunsen burners, a small, deep sink heavily stained with chemicals let into one end. Arranged on the bench were racks of test-tubes and a chemist's wash-bottle, his microscope with a hooded lamp, and beside it a wooden case the size of a cigar-box, notched inside to hold the glass microscope slides. One wall held racks of chemical reagents and a glass-fronted cupboard crammed with apparatus. The other was taken up with green metal filing cabinets. Everything looked as though it needed a good dusting. He always locked the door when he left, and there was only one other key, in the head-porter's lodge, in case of fire.

He had been sitting alone, on a high wooden stool, busy with the microscope. It was just after lunch on the Thursday before the Easter weekend. It suited him to be working over the next day or so. The coroners' courts wouldn't be sitting, and it was an unexpected chance to earn a fee. He picked up the telephone again and asked the hospital exchange for his home number. He told Rosemary to pack an attaché case and bring it up as soon as possible.

'How long will you be away?'

'It's impossible to say. I'm going down to the West Country. Perhaps a couple of days.'

'What about Brighton on Saturday?'

He had forgotten this promised excursion. 'We'll have to put it off. This bitterly cold weather wouldn't make it very pleasant, anyway.'

She did not seem disappointed, though he had felt she was in her small-minded way excited about the outing. Since the dispute in the kitchen they had mentioned neither maids, money nor progeny. They had continued the usual way between their fairly infrequent clashes, almost two strangers occupying the same house. What made life so difficult at home, Rumbelow thought as he replaced the telephone on the window-sill, was lack of the harmless little pretences and deceptions which made life outside it possible at all. He had no barrier of reputation or professional standing to dodge behind. There were not even any rules to control an argument, as in court. He was aware that *something* must happen to them, struggling with an unstable relationship. He seldom speculated what, because it was beyond his powers even to start formulating an answer, which upset him. But he wished she wasn't so damned proud of him.

He went back to the microscope slides. He was examining sections from the abdominal skin of a woman found with her head in a gas-oven in a Soho flat. She was a prostitute, new to the district, and nobody could identify her. She had the recent scar of a hysterectomy, which would be on the records of some hospital, and the police hoped for a lead if Rumbelow could tell them exactly when the operation had been done.

This sort of puzzle had interested him for a year. He had cut pieces of the scar from patients dying in Blackfriars at various times after operations, comparing them under the microscope. An operation incision was just like any other knife-wound, uninfected and healing 'by first intention', as the surgeons said. At first the slide would be full of macrophages, large round cells, the body's scavengers, eating up the debris. Then came young fibroblasts to form the connective tissue which permeated every organ in the body, mingled with minute blood-vessels, their walls only one cell thick, to make the richly vascular 'granulation tissue'. The fibroblasts were the key, Rumbelow thought. As the macrophages and blood-vessels shrivelled away, the fibroblasts turned into different-looking flattened cells, scattered sparsely amid the fibrous mass of the scar. If this process always went at the same speed, by counting the decreasing number of fibroblasts to the square millimetre, surely the pathologist could tell exactly the time since the wound was made? He recognized it might never be a matter of great importance. But no work for Rumbelow was too trivial to escape the full impact of his ability, concentration and diligence. His task was always to systematize the processes of the body and to describe them with exactitude, because that was the basis of medicine.

He was busy with his slides all afternoon. There was a knock on the laboratory door. Nobody was allowed in without knocking, not even his wife.

'Rosemary?'

But it was Quinley in his white coat.

Rumbelow was embarrassed. 'Yes? I'm rather busy.'

'I'm sorry, sir. But I wondered if you had a report on that prostate. From the p.m. last week.'

'Ah, yes, Quinley . . . come in, come in.' He reached to turn off the bulb directed at the reflector of his microscope. 'I must congratulate you. You were right.'

The news did not seem to give Quinley any particular gratification. Rumbelow had taken pains to be pleasant to him since their tiff, partly because he felt ashamed of himself and partly because he conceded the damage done to his reputation and he wanted to minimize it. There was no point in encouraging Quinley to spread the story more poisonously than necessary.

'The slides are in that box in the corner. Have a look at them in your own room. I sent the report to the ward, so the houseman could issue the death certificate without any more delay.' At least the painful admission was made privately, and a week was long enough for people to start forgetting. 'How many p.m.s today?'

'Only one.'

'You'd better do it. I've been called away, so I'm a bit pushed for time.'

Quinley stood inside the closed door, wearing his usual gloomy expression. 'Could I have a word with you, sir? It's rather important.'

Rumbelow wanted to be rid of him, but suddenly fearing it was something more to do with their disputed case he indicated a hard spoke-backed chair, the only other seating in the room.

'It's about the vacant readership.'

'You weren't thinking of putting in for it?'

'I was, in fact.'

'But you're too young. A readership is quite a senior post, you know.'

Quinley ran his tongue over his thick lips. '*You*'re young, sir.'

'Yes, but I'm exceptional. Anyway, there are no plans to fill the post. The whole department has to be reorganized. We're all at sixes and sevens, since the last reader upped and went to the Cape.'

Because he objected to the division of our work, Rumbelow recalled. The department was shared between Rumbelow, who was consultant pathologist, and Appledore, who was the professor of morbid anatomy. The distinction between the two titles was delicate, and had anyway become meaningless as Rumbelow now did nothing but post-mortems and forensic medicine.

'I gather it's in the professor's mind to appoint someone next autumn.'

'Is it? Well, possibly. I haven't seen him for some days. Did you mention your ambition?'

'He seemed rather encouraging.'

Rumbelow sat clasping his knee. Quinley's news was a shock. He had hoped to see the back of him within a year. To be faced with the man for the remainder of his career at Blackfriars was unthinkable. 'To anyone else?'

'Dr Bantrell.'

'Bantrell!' Rumbelow almost jumped from the stool. 'Why Bantrell? What have you to do with him?'

Quinley self-consciously indicated the red lump on his cheek. 'He's treating my boils with vaccine.'

'Put in for the job by all means, if you like. It's your decision.' Bantrell! thought Rumbelow. He won't get far trying to run me in the same harness. 'What do you wish me to do?'

'I know that appointments aren't always straightforward—'

'That merit alone isn't always rewarded? Well, that's a realistic way of facing things. Oh, I'll put in a good word for you where it matters, don't worry.'

The younger man's face filled with relief as suddenly as if caught by a spotlight. He had deliberately put himself at Rumbelow's mercy before even making up his mind to apply for the job. He didn't get on with Rumbelow–neither did many others at Blackfriars–but the bitterness of Rumbelow's dislike was beyond him. Despite his academic honours, he simply felt too humble to merit such hate. Now he decided that Rumbelow appreciated him, approved of his work, was prepared to be an ally, or at least not be a dangerous obstacle. He did not know that Rumbelow was for once deliberately telling a serious lie.

'I'm very grateful, sir. I know how valuable it is, having you behind me. I hope it wasn't cheek my asking?'

'Not cheek at all.' Rumbelow made an airy gesture. 'Are you still going to

Dr Bantrell? I suppose that vaccine's effective? He doesn't seem to be doing you much good.'

Even as Quinley left, Rumbelow knew he had been foolish. It would have been better to have informed the fellow straight out he wouldn't raise a finger to help. It didn't matter–he was hopelessly inexperienced for the job. But Quinley might have ascribed that to ill-natured resentment over the episode in the post-mortem room. He was a surly sort, who could spread a malicious story among the students and the junior staff. It would make Rumbelow seem petty and vindictive. He turned back to his microscope, satisfied with his excuse for his duplicity. A wound to a man's vanity can bleed away his reason.

Chapter Seven

The clock not yet having been put back, at half past five on Good Friday morning, the sun rising beyond the ridge of Salisbury Plain, Rumbelow in his bowler and fur-collared overcoat was walking down a country lane, smoking a cigar. Beside him was Sixsmith, behind a local policeman carrying his bag. It was cold, even with snow in the air. Rumbelow was in a buoyant mood. He always enjoyed official excursions to new places, and it was a relief freeing himself for a while from Blackfriars and from Rosemary. He was impressed with the tension he must have been suffering.

'That's surprising.' He paused, peering towards a hedge. 'The heckberry, or bird cherry. It's unusual so far south. It grows a bitter little black fruit, which the birds are very fond of.'

'I'm not much of a gardener,' said Sixsmith.

'I was brought up in the country.'

'This part of the world?'

'In Yorkshire. Perhaps that accounts for my obstinacy,' he added, an uncustomary self-admission. 'My father was a clergyman, a country rector. I nearly went into the Church myself.'

'You'd certainly have kept your flock on the path of righteousness,' said Sixsmith humorously.

'But I have one fundamental disadvantage. You see, I don't believe in God. Nor the life hereafter, which is a myth based on man's self-importance. He can't bear to think of himself extinct for ever. We are only bodies, and the only difference between a living and a dead one is between a machine which is running and another which is rusting to bits.'

'So you're not worried at anyone looking from Heaven when you're cutting up his remains?'

Rumbelow laughed. 'I have critics enough, without having to contend with ghosts.'

In the strengthening light they could see the square tower of Blayford church over the hedge. They had come to the village in a police-car from Mortlock, where they had spent the night. They were taking a short cut from the local constable's house, which served as a police-station. The lane led to a small road opposite the lych-gate, where a blue van was drawn up and a young policeman in a jersey, helmetless, without collar and tie and his sleeves pushed up, was taking a pair of sharp-pointed shovels from the back.

A yew hedge separated the churchyard from the road, where two policemen in overcoats were passing the time chatting to some twenty reporters, most of whom Rumbelow recognized. Sixsmith's fear of a leak was justified. Everyone in Mortlock the night before appeared to be gossiping about 'the case'. Rumbelow's manifestation with his black bag seemed to indicate that everything was over bar the hanging.

In the lych-gate stood the vicar in his cassock.

'The parson's in a state,' said Sixsmith. 'We're ruining his Easter services.'

'I suppose we should have postponed our resurrectionist activities till Sunday?' Rumbelow threw the butt of his cigar under the yew hedge.

A hearse drew up, blinds of grey cloth down behind the glass. Two men in dark overcoats climbed out. Behind stopped a black Triumph Gloria. 'The local doctor,' said Sixsmith. 'I'll introduce you.'

He was a fat middle-aged man with sagging jowls, in a brown tweed overcoat and a broad-brimmed weather-beaten trilby. He was called Halverston. They all entered the churchyard. Nobody took any notice of the vicar.

The canvas screens had been rigged to embrace half a dozen graves, giving everyone room to move about. Two policemen and a labourer in corduroy trousers stood waiting with shovels. There was a sallow young man in a black homburg who was introduced to Rumbelow as Copley, the solicitor representing the widow's interests. On the new marble headstone he noticed,

JAMES GERTHERIDGE JEAVONS
OF BLAYFORD AND SINGAPORE
WHO DEPARTED THIS LIFE
2.12.35 AGED 50.

'We can't start yet,' said Sixsmith. 'The Chief Constable hasn't turned up.'

He was a short man with a military moustache, who fussed into the churchyard from a police car a few minutes later. The labourer edged aside the headstone. The policemen started to dig.

'In popular imagination this is always done at midnight to the light of flickering oil-lamps,' Rumbelow observed to Sixsmith. 'And until quite recently it was. Quite ridiculous! You need all the light you can get. Particularly when you're liable to be closely cross-examined on the morning's activities.'

There was silence, except for the grating of the policemen's shovels against the frosty soil.

'You know we're almost in sight of his house?' said Sixsmith after some time, nodding past the church. 'You may have noticed that large red-brick place down the road.'

'The widow knows we're at work?'

'Oh, yes, I've got a man watching the house. You never know what might happen. All the blinds are drawn, like a funeral.'

'What's she like?'

'She seems a level-headed sort of woman. Scared, naturally. I've only had one interview.'

'Over twenty years younger than he was?'

Sixsmith nodded. 'She's not local, of course. She met him on the boat coming home.'

'And she gets all the money? She's been very stupid, playing fast and loose with that artist fellow.'

'It's all gossip, of course. We've still got to tread warily.' Sixsmith was in his fifties, approaching retirement, and there was nothing like the imminence of a pension to make a man cautious. 'But women *are* stupid, Doctor.'

'It should make your job easier.'

'It doesn't. They're so illogical it makes it twice as hard.'

A substantial pile of earth had grown to one side of the grave. Rumbelow noticed with dislike it was clayey and damp. A body could yield valuable evidence even after several years, but if it was badly putrefied too much might be left to medical detection to satisfy a jury. 'I'll have the first specimen of soil, please.'

With a wooden spoon, allowing no possibility of metallic contamination, he scooped a little and sealed it in a wide-mouthed jar from his bag. A blue-edged label affixed the night before said in his neat handwriting, *Grave Soil. Specimen 1.*

'I hate poisoners,' said Sixsmith unexpectedly.

'Why, particularly?'

'It's done at a distance. It's cowardly.'

'Murder's always murder. How it's performed is surely of interest but not of significance.' The superintendent made no reply. 'Perhaps she should have had him cremated. It's becoming sufficiently popular not to cause a stir, even in a place like this.'

Sixsmith gave a slight nod towards Dr Halverston, standing thoughtfully on the far side of the steadily deepening grave. 'Perhaps she wasn't too keen on the statutory requirement of an independent doctor to examine the body.'

'You may be right.' Rumbelow had a notorious contempt for provincial general practitioners.

'We're reaching the coffin, sir,' called out one of the policemen.

'Then I'll have another specimen,' said Rumbelow.

The policemen shovelled more carefully, until the still-polished wood with its brass plate came into view. Ropes were produced. Surprisingly easily, the coffin was pulled up and edged to one side of the grave. A plain-clothes man took photographs. When Sixsmith asked one of the undertakers from the hearse to identify it he exclaimed, 'I screwed it down myself,' clearly proud of his connection with such a notorious local affair.

'Before moving it,' said Rumbelow, 'I should like you to open the lid slightly, if Mrs Jeavons' solicitor agrees. That will be necessary to allow the escape of gases.'

Ten minutes later it was in the hearse on its way to Mortlock, a detective-inspector sitting in front.

By eight o'clock Rumbelow was in his shirt-sleeves and red rubber apron, starting work in the small whitewashed police mortuary behind the Shire Hall. He had with him a policeman who acted as mortuary attendant, Sixsmith and Dr Halverston. The pale-faced solictor had decided to wait just outside. As Rumbelow set out his instruments and specimen jars, Sixsmith passed across a copy of the death certificate. Rumbelow saw that his colleague in the tweed overcoat had given the cause of death as heart-failure secondary to high blood-pressure. He nodded. In sleepy areas like Blayford, such documents were often fictional.

Rumbelow unscrewed the lid of the coffin, which was standing on trestles. With his small bone-saw he took a specimen of the wood, and dropped it with forceps into a jar. There was a surprisingly heavy growth of white mould inside, much of it hanging like a curtain from the lid. 'The shroud's adherent to the body,' said Rumbelow, taking another specimen. 'Though it's not friable. So perhaps we shall find things better preserved than I expected.'

The body on a bed of sawdust was recognizable as a burly, thick-necked man with a snub nose. 'Very strange, meeting him again,' murmured Dr Halverston.

'How long was he ill?' Rumbelow and the police were moving the corpse to the post-mortem table.

'Terminally, only a few hours. I was called at eight in the morning. I remember I was having my lunch when they phoned to say he was dead.'

'And the symptoms?'

'Complete collapse. Poor pulse. Difficulty in breathing. I prescribed sedatives. There seemed no more I could do.'

'Any vomiting and diarrhoea?'

'A little.' He added defensively, 'As might be expected.'

'Indeed,' said Rumbelow, starting work with his long scalpel.

'He was a very nice man. Quite popular in the area, you know. So is Mrs Jeavons. I really can't imagine for one moment she'd have anything to do with . . . with this.'

'Then this is all for her own good, Doctor,' said Sixsmith shortly. 'It'll clear away all those unpleasant rumours.'

'I do so hope as much.'

'Did he complain of cramp in the calves before he died?' asked Rumbelow.

'Now, that's odd. It was about the only thing he was able to say to me.'

Rumbelow had changed from conventional post-mortem technique. For once, he examined the abdomen first. He wanted to avoid disturbing the stomach when removing organs from the chest. The stomach lining seemed normal, examined under running water. The duodenum had perhaps been inflamed, though that needed the eye of faith. There *could* be yellow streaks outside the stomach walls–if his vague guess was right, due to formation of the sulphide. Everything would need careful analysis in London. The intestines were normal. He cut specimens with his scissors from each section of the gut, sealing them in separate bottles.

He went back to the body, running his knife inside the man's jaw, drawing heart and lungs through the open cage of ribs. The lungs themselves still had fluid present, to be expected whether Halverston was right or wrong. The heart was enlarged. He snipped it open, and taking his magnifying-glass inspected closely the membrane covering the left ventricle. Perhaps a trace of petechial haemorrhages? he wondered. The microscope later would tell.

'Did he have a water-hammer pulse, Dr Halverston?'

'I never detected as much.'

'But he had aortic incompetence. Look–the ascending aorta is enlarged, you can still see longitudinal rugae on the intima. They shouldn't be there. The aortic valves are thickened, though the orifices of the coronary arteries seem to have escaped.'

'Yes, yes . . . all due to high blood-pressure.'

'Not at all. He had syphilis.'

'What! But . . . but I'd certainly no inkling he suffered from it. No inkling at all.'

'Well, he probably wanted to keep it to himself.'

'No, no, not a man like James Jeavons—'

'Or perhaps he didn't know he had it? This is a very late stage, perhaps thirty years after infection. A primary chancre as a young man out East–he may have thought it a tropical sore, something else.'

'But it's impossible! Surely he would have confided in his own doctor?'

'Not necessarily. You'd better put this to the widow.'

'Certainly not. I shall say nothing, absolutely nothing, until your post-mortem diagnosis is confirmed,' said Halverston crossly.

'By whom?' Halverston looked lost. 'Call in another pathologist, if you like. There's no urgency about re-burial. It will anyway be weeks before I can complete the analysis of these specimens. My hands are full with a big case at the Old Bailey next Wednesday.'

'But surely you don't expect to find anything more?'

'I don't know. If I do, you and Mrs Jeavons' solicitor will be informed.'

'But what? What *can* you expect to find?'

'I told you, I don't know.'

'The cause of death was heart-failure, following incompetence of the aortic valve.' Halverston was now angry, his face mottled and his jowls quivering. 'If that was due to syphilis and not high blood-pressure, then I made a clinical error in signing the death certificate. Very well. What's the point of recriminations? There was no possible treatment at that stage. A correct diagnosis would not have added a minute to the man's life.'

Rumbelow had disliked Halverston from the start. He was more irritated at his arguing as though they were professionally equals. 'Perhaps it's unfortunate the condition didn't suggest itself to you earlier, when something might have been done. If you look up the notes of his blood-pressure readings, which I admit might perfectly well be raised, you may see an abnormally large pulse-pressure as well.'

'I don't have notes on everything.' Halverston tapped his head. 'I prefer to keep things in here.'

No wonder people get away with murder, thought Rumbelow.

'Surely we can get all this settled and out of the way at the inquest tomorrow?' Halverston sounded more conciliatory.

'The proceedings will be only formal, without a jury. And adjourned, of course.'

'Why need it be? Why leave everyone in suspense? What of the strain on poor Mrs Jeavons? Nobody seems to have any consideration for her feelings at all. It can surely be established right away that death was due to the effects of syphilis. I certainly should not raise any objection,' he added with the air of a man striking a bargain.

'I'm sorry for everyone concerned in the case. But a coroner's jury cannot be asked to give a verdict until they have all the facts. And that will not be so until I have analysed these specimens. Even if the analysis turns out completely negative.'

'It sounds like a lot of official fussiness to me.'

'Yes,' said Rumbelow. 'It is.'

Rumbelow and Sixsmith were staying at the Red Lion, nearly opposite the Shire Hall. As they were crossing the almost deserted main street for a late breakfast, Sixsmith said about Halverston, 'He certainly seems to stand on his dignity.'

'He's precious little else to stand on.'

'Then Jeavons died of syphilis? Hardly worth an exhumation.'

'Wait till I've completed my analysis.'

'Do you suspect anything?'

'Yes. Arsenic. Which will make matters very complicated for the Crown indeed.'

Chapter Eight

Mrs Mavery's luncheon parties were gayer than those of Lady Accrington, who like many upper-class Englishwomen instinctively deplored immorality, social inferiors, bores and flippancy, but whose social ambitions increasingly obliged her to put up with all four. Mrs Mavery, like other sophisticated Americans in Europe, brought a freshness and energy to the local customs which outshone the natives. She was unimaginably wealthy–the asparagus that April Tuesday was casually ordered from the South of France by aeroplane. She preferred the respectable fringe of Chelsea to Mayfair. She was vivacious, amusing and open-hearted, always ready to take people as they were, providing they were rich and important enough. She asked Rumbelow regularly, partly because he was always in the news and partly because he was so often invited by Lady Accrington, of whom she was painfully jealous.

There were a dozen guests, including a pompous actor with a knighthood, about to play a murderer and hoping for a few hints from Rumbelow, in which he was hurtfully disappointed. The conversation was largely monopolized by Hugo Kirkham, the Washington journalist. Rumbelow's experience of the Press being restricted to crime reporters, he was surprised and at first resentful to find a newspaperman invited. They were hardly his social equals. But apparently journalists in America were grand people, deferred to even by the President.

'The trouble with your Empire,' Kirkham told them genially, 'is simply and fundamentally that it's a sham. Or would it be more complimentary to call it a brilliant confidence-trick? A magnificent one, the most audacious the world has ever known. All done by a huge fleet firing ceremonial salutes of blank ammunition over the heads of cleverly trained officials in plumed hats. There's no real force behind it.'

Rumbelow was shocked. To live in London was to be conscious of living in the hub of the Empire, an entity accepted as a matter of course by the newspapers and school-children's atlases, invoked continually by politicians, materialized by colourful visitors and showy exhibitions, the depository of countless younger sons, the wall of confidence at every Englishman's back, the last word to fall from the lips of the old King that blustery midnight the previous January at Sandringham.

'Surely, Hugo, all empires are only confidence-tricks?' said Mrs Mavery. 'Even Mussolini has to keep parading his soldiers all over the place to convince everyone how strong he is.'

'Or maybe to convince himself?'

'I happen to be proud of the British Empire,' said the actor.

'Well, there's *something* to be proud of. There may be no real force behind it, but there's no real oppression either.'

'I should think not! Why, the Empire exists with the deepest mutual respect between us and the Dominions. Look how we all stood together during the War.'

'Maybe the Empire didn't have much choice about that. Fifty million Africans and two hundred and fifty million Indians suddenly found themselves pitched into a war on a continent they'd never seen against an enemy they'd mostly never heard of. I don't remember their being asked nicely. King George simply signed a paper.'

'It was the responsibility of the Mother Country to organize their defence.'

Kirkham smiled. 'Isn't it perhaps time to unload the white man's burden? Those African colonies now–they're ready and waiting for self-rule.'

'I'm afraid I can't agree with you, Mr Kirkham. You must have been listening to the agitators. The African is definitely *not* ready for independence. And if we granted it, do you know what would happen in your own country? Why, your own black population would be stimulated to demand their rights. Oceans are no barrier to revolutionary ideas, as you well know. You'd have riots in your own streets, black against white, just as bad as anything that happened at Amritsar with General Dyer.'

'I'm prepared to take a chance on that.'

'Perhaps you would like us to cure our depression with your "New Deal" into the bargain?' asked the actor sarcastically.

'But Lloyd George suggested exactly that, back in 1929.' Kirkham sounded gleeful. 'It was all in something called *We Can Conquer Unemployment*. He'd almost exactly the same ideas as F.D.R. Perhaps you could do with your little Welshman back?'

The journalist was so frighteningly well-informed that Rumbelow had said nothing for fear of making a fool of himself. Now he was incited to speak up. 'There's a great feeling in the country the new King will mark a change for the better.'

'Why should he?'

'He's vigorous and comparatively young. Such things permeate the circles of government.'

'I could tell you something about your new King . . . but no, it is "bad form, old boy" to mention it. Or maybe the Empire couldn't stand the shock.'

Kirkham then said he wanted to watch British justice in action, and asked Rumbelow to get him into the Old Bailey for the Vickery trial next morning. Rumbelow said he'd see what was to be done, having made up his mind to do nothing.

By the design of both themselves and their hostess, Rumbelow left the house with Diana Flavell.

'Where's the famous bag?' smiled Diana.

'I'd no need for my instruments this morning.'

'Where are you off to?'

'Back to the hospital. I was intending to take the Tube. I've plenty of time.'

'Can I give you a lift to Hyde Park Corner Station?'

'That's awfully kind.'

'I hope you don't mind a sports car?'

Her red MG was parked outside. They sped towards Sloane Street, Rumbelow keeping a tight hold on his bowler. As they turned into Sloane Square she asked, 'I wonder if you'd mind doing something for me? I've got that book they published about the Perryman case–the one where the man cut up his girl-friend. We're almost going past my flat. Would you like to sign it?'

'I'd be delighted.'

They stopped outside a large red-brick block behind Harrods.

'It's only on the first floor.'

By then Rumbelow couldn't decide if he was excited or anxious. She was certainly giving him what people called 'the come hither'. They had been brought together several times at Mrs Mavery's–that winter, with the death of the King and the Court going into mourning, was not one of overfull guest-lists. He knew she had a reputation for being 'fast'. She was a blonde with large eyes and a turned-up nose, not strikingly good-looking. She must have been in her mid-twenties. She said she was divorced, though there were always people to tell you darkly she had a husband somewhere. The door was opened by a maid in a black dress and lace apron. Rumbelow felt relieved.

'Let's have some coffee. The Maverys' coffee was ghastly. Americans have just no taste for coffee, you know. Have you been over there?'

'I've never travelled abroad at all.'

The drawing-room had long windows giving on to a small balcony, a gaudy fireplace of steel and onyx, a sheepskin rug and a low marble table, an angular sofa, two vases crammed with daffodils.

'Smoke?' Diana held out a silver cigarette-box.

'Only cigars.'

'Do light one if you like.'

She lit her cigarette with a table-lighter fashioned like a mermaid. She sat on the sofa, Rumbelow taking the squarish armchair opposite, noticing how the slit in her tight-fitting black skirt extended to her knee.

'That's a nice picture.'

'It's a Picasso.' This meant nothing to Rumbelow. 'My dear Doctor, you look nervous.'

'I'm sorry. I don't often find myself alone with a pretty woman.'

'But how devastating! That *does* make me sound terrible.'

'I didn't mean anything discourteous, for one moment . . . I suppose I just wondered why you suddenly took it into your head to invite me up.'

'To be sociable.' She blew a jet of cigarette smoke. 'It's always interesting, talking to you.'

'More than to the others at lunch?'

She laughed. 'You sound as if I'm in the witness-box.' He apologized. 'Why do we never see your wife?'

'She has no interest in social life.'

'Then you must be unhappily married.'

'I wouldn't say that—'

'Yes, you must be. You go everywhere, and enjoy every moment of it. Your two outlooks are different. You're incompatible.'

'Well, possibly.' He disliked talking about Rosemary to anyone.

'Is she young? Is she pretty?'

'It would be fair to say "not particularly" to both questions.'

'A judicial pronouncement,' observed Diana.

The maid appeared for a moment with a tray containing two cups and a small, steaming brass pot. Rumbelow noticed the room had already been darkening, and now the wind threw a handful of rain against the windows.

'April is the cruellest month,' said Diana. 'Mixing memory and desire, stirring dull roots with spring rain.' He looked blank. 'That's T. S. Eliot.'

'I don't think I've heard of him. He sounds rather depressing.'

She handed him a coffee-cup. 'Don't you get depressed, spending your life cutting up dead bodies?'

'No more than a surgeon spending his cutting up live ones.' It was Turkish coffee, thick and too sweet for his taste.

'Doesn't death mean anything to you? Aren't you scared of it?'

'It's simply a nothingness, a negative factor. How can one be scared of something which doesn't exist?'

'But surely you must be sorry for the people who are hanged?'

'Why should I be? They have committed a crime, and they deserve their punishment. Anyway, they're complete strangers to me. The first time I set eyes on them is in the dock. The next on the post-mortem table.'

She sipped her coffee for a moment in silence. 'After the way you hold forth at the Old Bailey, I'd no idea you could be so shy.'

'Shy? I don't think so.'

'Of course you are. We've known each other–how long? Six months, on and off. You've told me absolutely nothing about yourself. What you feel, what goes on inside.' From his expression, she took him as disinclined to remedy this omission. 'Are you fond of women?'

'I'm only human. But I don't go chasing after them, if that's what you mean. It wouldn't be at all right for a man in my position.'

She laughed. 'It's the pastime of men in all sorts of positions, believe you me. You must have had girl-friends in the past?'

'Before I married, yes.'

'The wife who is neither particularly young nor particularly pretty seems to have a powerful hold over you.' She stubbed out her cigarette. 'Come and kiss me.'

The invitation was not one of unmixed delight for Rumbelow. He disliked finding himself in an unfamiliar situation which he could not see his way to master. But he told himself that among sophisticated people a kiss meant nothing–even intercourse little more. As he crossed the sheepskin rug she thrust out her hands, pulled him down, and he felt her tongue in his mouth. It was the first time he had experienced the 'French kiss' for some years. It was not an idea which appealed to Rosemary, who if she knew of it at all took it as a habit of only the lower classes and Continentals.

'What do you think of me?' Diana spoke more tenderly than he had known her.

Rumbelow was confused. What did one say? He searched for a word . . . fascinating, bewitching, glamorous, attractive. Expressions so uncustomary in his vocabulary they might have been another language. 'I find you very charming.'

'That means nothing . . . listen, you'll have to go now, darling. I'm expecting someone. But phone me. It's a Kensington number. I'm in the book. Promise?'

'All right.'

She drew him down and kissed him again. 'You don't seem particularly wild about the idea.'

'I . . . I'm sorry. I'm not a great ladies' man.'

She laughed again. 'Perhaps you'd feel more at home if I were a corpse?'

As he straightened up, he remembered, 'That book you wanted me to sign—'

She looked puzzled. 'Oh, that. No, I remember now, I only had it out of Harrods' library.'

Rumbelow walked down the stairs with a feeling which at least he could comfortably recognize. Relief mixed with elation. It was exactly like leaving the witness-box after a severe but triumphant cross-examination.

Chapter Nine

Rumbelow was at the Old Bailey early. He enjoyed being in court–of any sort, even some poky East End police-court with ink-stained desks and grimy windows, where the well-worn machinery of the law could rattle at a speed too fast for judicial purists. He relished the ceremonious courtesy of a trial, the theatricality of compressing the story into a few hours' telling within a few square feet, the contrast between a high-minded search for truth and the clever showmanship and trickery of counsel. He loved the Dickensian home of the law, the Temple itself between the Strand and the Thames. He often walked from nearby Blackfriars amid its warm brickwork and unexpected little courtyards, its twisting alleys and steep kerbs, so ill-lit at night appropriately to afford the unwary outsider an unexpected tumble. He liked barristers. They were so much more worldly than doctors.

'I say, John–that microscope we discussed last night at the conference. Could you do with one in court?'

In a grey chalk-striped suit with a red carnation in his button-hole, Rumbelow was sitting as usual on the solicitors' benches in the well of the court. Peter Ivors, K.C., who was leading for the Crown, had twisted round to speak. He was a tubby man, wigged and gowned, with large round glasses and an easy smile, wearing an air of faintly bewildered simplicity which had cost a good many wrongdoers their liberty and a few their necks. He and Rumbelow were in some half-dozen cases a year, and knew each other well.

'I don't think it necessary for me actually to produce one.'

'But it might be wise to have a microscope handy. Old Lynacre would love looking down it on the bench.'

'But if the jury did likewise, it would only confuse them.'

'Possibly.' Ivors gave a nod, turning again to a feverish study of his notes.

Rumbelow caught the eye of Sir Arthur Younghusband a couple of yards away. He was the defending K.C., a Member of Parliament, known in the Temple and the House to have ambitions in the direction of Attorney-General. A tall, hawk-nosed, bright-eyed, straight-backed man, Rumbelow knew him well also. As they exchanged smiles it warmed Rumbelow to feel the civilized lack of animosity between the two sides, the comradeship of cultured and intelligent gentlemen. They rose as Mr Justice Lynacre entered, florid-faced in short wig and red robe. Rumbelow had met him once or twice, was aware he had a large house in Northamptonshire and enjoyed fox-hunting, and felt approval of the reliability with which His Majesty chose the squirarchy to sit in judgement on his subjects. It was perhaps sad they should all be gathered that morning only to find if a young garage-mechanic from the lower middle classes had killed and burnt his bigamous wife or not.

There were three massive chairs of green-and-gold leather half-invisible behind panelling of light oak. The judge took that on the left. The grandest in the middle was reserved for the Lord Mayor of London or his Aldermen, who collectively held the Commission for the Assize, and if unrepresented about the building somewhere would invalidate the proceedings and presumably face all the prisoners with instant liberty. Everyone turned their heads. Vickery appeared with two policemen in the spacious dock, three sides screened by glass. He was thin and pale with a narrow black moustache and over-brilliantined hair, dressed in a white shirt and well-kept blue suit. Rumbelow had never set eyes on him before.

Rumbelow glanced at the crammed Press benches on his right, and the gallery sloping steeply under the huge skylight, full of inquisitive, or ghoulish, citizens who had queued all night. Vickery was being charged that on or about November the thirtieth last, in the County of Middlesex, he did murder Eileen Bertha Durban. He replied, '*Not* guilty', as though asked an entirely ridiculous question.

Twelve men in dark suits were ushered by a police-sergeant into the jury-box on Rumbelow's left. They don't look a particularly intelligent bunch, he thought as they were sworn. But perhaps that was for the best. Scientific truth could enlighten all the more powerfully the dim and unquestioning mind.

Unexpectedly, Sir Arthur Younghusband stood up. 'My Lord, I have an application to make.'

The judge glanced over half-moon glasses, pausing in making a note. 'Is it one which can properly be made in the presence of the jury?'

'No, my Lord.'

'Very well, Sir Arthur.'

The jury were led out again, looking disappointed.

'My application, my Lord, is that Dr Rumbelow should not be allowed to remain in court. Neither during the opening speeches of my learned friend and myself, nor during the examination and cross-examination of witnesses.'

Rumbelow was astounded. He always sat in court throughout, as a matter of right. It was as ridiculous as objecting to the presence of the judge.

'I haven't known this point to be raised before, Sir Arthur,' said the judge mildly. 'Expert witnesses–particularly medical witnesses–are customarily allowed to stay in court. The only object is to make them more valuable, through their hearing all the evidence.'

'Your Lordship may think I am within my rights?'

'You may be within your rights. But what are your reasons?'

Rumbelow noticed Ivors' shoulders moving slightly, a tic when he was worried.

'I would have no objection in a general way to any expert witness for the prosecution remaining throughout. It is perfectly proper for him to hear the defence put forward on behalf of the prisoner. It would be perfectly proper in this case for my learned friend to ask Dr Rumbelow in the witness-box whether he agreed, or not, with the defence suggested for my client. As the medical evidence is likely to assume great importance–indeed, the outcome may well turn on it–your Lordship will appreciate that the result of this exchange would have an effect of some weight on the jury.'

'Is this not all rather hypothetical, Sir Arthur?'

'If the prosecution has secured such a valuable witness as Dr Rumbelow, they will certainly use him to the full. There lies the point of my application. It is Dr Rumbelow's reputation. It is unnecessary for me to emphasize his outstanding skill, his wide experience in forensic medicine. Nor the lucidity and fairness of all he says in court. We must all be grateful that such a witness exists, to assist us in unravelling matters which can become highly technical. But, my Lord, Dr Rumbelow in the minds of the public–in the minds of the jury–has become an infallible expert on murder. He enjoys an affection which the British heart extends only to a few favoured detectives in fiction. In short, what Dr Rumbelow says goes. If in the present case he says that murder has been committed, the jury will be inclined to take his word for it.'

'But of course you would oblige him to give his reasons.'

'Such reasons coming from Dr Rumbelow might carry more conviction with the jury than they deserve.' Sir Arthur sat down.

Rumbelow was angry. He was no stranger to the insinuation that he was less than fair, that he put the weight of his reputation on one side rather than the other, that he was an instrument of the Crown rather than an impartial medical man. But for the first time it had been thrown in his face in open court. He could only console himself it was a trick of Sir Arthur's, who had his job to do and might be as cynical as he cared over a man's reputation.

'Well, Mr Ivors, what do you say to that?' invited the judge.

Ivors stood up. With an air of simplicity and sweet reasonableness he produced the result of some moments' anxious thought. 'My Lord, I can only leave you to decide whether the accepted practice of the court is altered or not.'

'Dr Rumbelow may stay,' said the judge. The jury returned. Rumbelow sat back on the uncomfortable bench, listening to Ivors outlining his case against Vickery, still ruffled.

Vickery had been a chauffeur, taught to drive in the Army before he was invalided out. The previous summer he had met Eileen Durban on holiday at Margate. She was then thirty, admitting twenty-eight. She had a tidy sum in a building society, almost a thousand pounds. She fell for him, and in September they got married. She did not reveal having spent a couple of years in a mental asylum. Nor he of a wife already somewhere or other.

A chauffeur's job being clearly unfitting for the husband of a lady of substance, they took the lease of a garage off the Bath road on the western edge of London. The motor business had promise, Vickery told her. Cars were getting cheaper every year, and once the slump was over almost every family in the country would possess one. Rumbelow had been called to this garage just before Christmas. He had found it not much of a place, an isolated cottage against a largish shed, and a single petrol-pump in front with a broken handle. Behind was a yard surrounded by a brick wall, in which Vickery kept tyres and spare parts. Here the police found Eileen Durban's body–burnt, but not beyond recognition.

Vickery's story was of her hanging herself from one of the metal crosspieces in the shed roof–he readily pointed out the spot. He had panicked, fearing his bigamous marriage would come to light, and that her family would make trouble, particularly as she had made her money over to him. He had burnt the body with petrol and buried it. He told the neighbours his wife had been poorly and had gone on holiday. But neighbours enjoy a gossip, and as at Blayford it travelled further than any of them expected.

Rumbelow listened to this story with no particular feelings. He had no thought for the victim, her excitement and happiness at finding a husband turning to anguish and terror, whether she lost her life by her own hands or his. The feverish scheming, the panic of Vickery never occurred to Rumbelow. He never speculated on the strange dark storms of the mind which moved a human to suicide or murder. Anyway, such behaviour occurred only among a different type of person. The people he mixed with himself never did such things, being ladies and gentlemen.

When the court rose for lunch, Ivors was still speaking. He observed to Rumbelow, 'Younghusband didn't get away with it.'

'I thought it rather cheek.'

'Were you annoyed?'

'Yes.'

'Oh, I shouldn't be piqued at all. It was really a tremendous compliment, in my mind.'

'Perhaps you're right,' said Rumbelow.

When appearing at the Old Bailey he generally lunched at Blackfriars, only a few hundred yards down Ludgate Hill. His mood was not improved by running into Bantrell in the gateway.

'Hello! Are you coming to lunch in the refectory? We're all agog to hear the sordid details.'

'I was intending to send across from my lab. for something. I've a deal of work to do on some books from the library.'

'How's the trial going?'

'It's early days. There are never many surprises in the opening speeches of counsel.'

'I understand Quinley's putting up for the readership?' said Bantrell without more ado.

'So he tells me.'

'And that you're supporting him?'

'I shall do what I can.'

'I heard you two had quite a scene in the p.m. room the other week,' Bantrell laughed. 'One of my students said it was like a Bateman cartoon–you know, "The Man Who Told His Chief He'd Made a Bloomer". I wish I'd been there.' Rumbelow made no comment. 'Are you serious about helping Quinley?'

'I shouldn't have given my word otherwise.'

'But there are degrees of support. We all know that. I shouldn't like the young fellow to be living in a fool's paradise, even though I suppose it's better than no paradise at all.'

'You seem to have taken his interests to heart.'

'He's a bright fellow. I'd like to see him get on. Particularly as he's handicapped by a rather unfortunate manner. Or perhaps it's just because I'm treating his furunculosis.' They started to walk towards the main courtyard of the hospital. The reason is simply that you hope somehow to get at me, Rumbelow thought. 'Of course, it's a staphylococcal infection, so even sulphanilamide would be useless. Not that I could possibly spare any for such a minor condition. Colebrook's doing the official trial in London, of course. My own supplies are painfully limited.'

'Do you think sulphanilamide has real possibilities?' Rumbelow did not object to the conversation heading away from Quinley.

'With streptococcal infections yes, I really think so. More strongly than Domagk himself, I fancy. I looked up his original paper over the week-end, in the *Deutsche Medizinische Wochenschrift*. It was rather lukewarm. And if Tréfouëls hadn't isolated sulphanilamide from the original protonsil at the Institut Pasteur, I doubt if anyone would have bothered with it at all. It seemed ludicrous to treat septicaemia with a vivid red dye.' Bantrell was fond of parading his learning.

'Of course, we've seen this sort of thing before. Intravenous thiosulphate of gold for tuberculosis, for example. The side-effects were so horrifying, most people have given it up.'

'No, I think we're on to a winner here. I just haven't met any side-effects to date, apart from some trouble with emboli.'

'If it works, your name will be linked with the new drug.'

'I suppose one must deserve some credit for pioneering.'

'It will be pioneering with a golden pick.'

'That's a little explicit, isn't it?' said Bantrell, but not unkindly.

Rumbelow left him as they reached the library. This was a showpiece amid the jumble of buildings dating from early Tudor to late Victorian, which met each other in awkward corners to make up the hospital. It was said to have been designed in the mid-eighteenth century by William Kent, and its elaborately moulded ceilings were certainly the same as Kent put into Kensington Palace. The walls of books were split into alcoves, there was a long table down the middle, a wide fireplace at once end and half a dozen comfortable armchairs in which there always seemed to be a student or two asleep.

The librarian was an old man with a long beard, immovable in a glass kiosk by the door–he was interested only in sixteenth-century herbals, and so resented being disturbed that everyone had long ago given up asking him for books. The library was run by three female assistants. Rumbelow had recently kept his own requests to the newest of these, a girl called Maria Osgood. She was about twenty, slim, pink-cheeked, brown-eyed, lively, pretty, though with a small mouth which gave her a prudish look. He saw her standing at the centre table over an open book, wearing a serge skirt and white blouse with blue dots on it. He noticed her dark hair had been newly Marcelled. She was talking to a young man in a rumpled suit, one of the students or housemen. Rumbelow suddenly felt a strong resentful feeling in his direction. He stopped, alarmed. Surely it couldn't be jealousy? That would be quite stupid. She turned and smiled. The young man seeing a consultant respectfully melted away.

'Could you get me McCarthy's *Histopathology of Skin Diseases*, please?'

'Of course, Dr Rumbelow.'

He waited as she hurried up the spiral staircase to the gallery. He wanted to refresh himself on the microscopical changes of familiar skin conditions–eczema, for instance, or even the chafing of tight clothing. The skin of the murdered woman's neck would take great importance in the case, and though he doubted Younghusband's drawing in the red herring of her suffering from a skin disease, he disliked leaving any loophole in his evidence. To quote an authority like McCarthy at him might be a useful shot in the locker.

'I thought you'd be at the Old Bailey today?'

'I am. It's the lunch adjournment.' He took the book. 'I expect it's quite improper to tell you this, but Vickery's neck is going to depend on a small piece of skin, just about six inches by three.'

She looked startled, which pleased him.

'And I wondered if you'd look out a couple of volumes of the *Lancet* for me? The second for the year 1921 and the first for 1922. There's two papers on the excretion of organic arsenical compounds I wanted to look up.' She pencilled the references on a scrap of paper. He added casually, 'Do you like working among books?'

'Yes, very much. I was going to the university, you see. To study English.'

'Oh? What went wrong?'

'The usual thing these days. Financial reasons. It isn't an easy time for my father.'

'I'm sorry . . .'

'I suppose there are other girls worse off. And at least I've got a job, haven't I?'

He would have liked to have asked more about the father and his financial straits. But it would not do to appear prying. 'If you can get those two books, I'll take them across to my lab. for half an hour.'

Rumbelow settled to work feeling more cheerful. Perhaps Ivors had been right. For an experienced counsel like Younghusband to object to his skill as a pathologist was praise indeed–and from a source he should appreciate, a sophisticated fellow-professional in the law. He shouldn't take it to heart. It was all part of the rough-and-tumble of the courts. Yes, seen in retrospect it was really a splendid compliment.

But it was the first cloud of the storm which was to drown him.

Chapter Ten

That evening Rumbelow took a taxi. He had locked his laboratory and was walking through the hospital gateway when one drew up, some patient's visitor jumping on to the glistening pavement with a bunch of daffodils. The weather was still bitter, with a freezing drizzle. Rumbelow grasped the open door, and asked for his club. It was an impulse, and he sat back surprised at something so uncharacteristic. He looked through the streaming window irritably as they made across Ludgate Circus and past the new black-glass-and-chromium *Daily Express* building in Fleet Street. These drivers always took you the longest way round.

He was dining with Norman Carlow. The cab had made him early, and he sat in the downstairs morning-room with the book he had bought when the court had risen for the day. As the coroner came bustling in, polishing his monocle, he greeted him, 'God, John, you look studious.'

Rumbelow held up the book. 'They're some poems.'

'Let me see . . . *The Waste Land*. Oh, T. S. Eliot. I can't understand this modern stuff. It doesn't even rhyme.'

'It certainly isn't easy going.'

'You've taken to culture in your old age, have you? Well, that's a splendid thing. A few apt quotations from your lips will impress a jury no end.'

Rumbelow was rather offended at this. 'I'm becoming aware that I'm somewhat ill-read. Not through choice, but there's never time for anything except technical literature in the struggle to keep up-to-date. It's worth an effort to remedy the deficiency. Will you have a drink?'

'As you are aware, I am the enemy of neither grape nor grain.'

Rumbelow rang the bell for a waiter. He ordered a sherry, Carlow a large whisky.

'How's it going at the Old Bailey?'

'Younghusband tried to kick me out of court.'

'*Did* he? If he's reduced to that, he can't have much of a case.'

'That's what I thought.'

'By the way, I've some news about your Dr Elgin, the fallen woman's friend, the king of the curette.' Rumbelow looked interested. 'I fancy the police have got something on him at last.'

'That's hardly before time. I've done p.m.s. on half a dozen cases of septic abortion in the past year. All obviously done by a doctor, or someone with specialized knowledge. I should imagine he's responsible for at least a few of them. That's not to mention girls from the provinces, perhaps going home to die in a week or ten days. Everyone in London knows what he's up to. It's quite a scandal.'

Carlow took his whisky and water. 'But there's a dozen abortionists flourishing under our feet. It's a thriving industry for the capital of the Empire.'

'That's not the point. If Elgin's responsible for even one death, it's our duty to prosecute him.'

'Sure, sure, I can hardly disagree with you, can I? As *Custos placitorum Coronae*, charged by His Majesty to look into the unexpected deaths of his subjects, not to mention treasure trove and fires in the City of London, if alas no longer shipwrecks and the health and welfare of his royal fish, the sturgeon. But I've every sympathy with the poor girl who has a lapse just at the wrong moment in her menstrual cycle. After all, a man doesn't ring the bell every time he gets into her. I'm half-inclined to think we should make abortion legal, as they say it is in Russia. Otherwise the world will be crawling like an ant-heap.'

'That's just your anti-papism.'

'No, it's my natural fondness for the fair sex.'

'I've met Elgin, you know. A couple of times. At cocktail parties, in perfectly respectable houses. He seems to enjoy some social standing. He struck me as the slippery sort.'

Carlow laughed. 'Like the slippery elm he probably uses to get his results?'

'How did the police nail him?'

'A dying declaration.'

'That's interesting.'

'Yes, it's a rare bird to fly into even my window. The girl's family must have known the ropes, or her doctor was wider awake than most. You'll be doing the p.m. on her tomorrow. I'll adjourn the inquest, of course. Elgin's bound to show up with some high-powered barrister only too anxious to tell me my job.'

Rumbelow noticed his companion's glass was empty, and rang the bell.

'I thank God every day for making me a Protestant,' added Carlow reflectively. 'Two kids are enough these hard times. If I put my wife in the family way again, I honestly wouldn't object to an abortion. Not if done properly, in sterile surroundings.'

'That's a purely theoretical problem for me.'

'Oh, come, now. You and Rosemary are young enough. You never know, you might find yourselves landed with a little surprise package.'

'Rosemary doesn't want a child.'

'What, for physical reasons?'

'No, mental ones.'

'Oh. I see. Well, of course, I don't know your lady well, her being something of a recluse—'

'She's got into her head a lot of old wives' tales. I suppose they've been preying on her. She's really quite deranged about it. Are such fears common in women? I don't know. It's out of my experience. I'm not a gynaecologist.'

Carlow picked up his second whisky and stared at it quizzically. It was strange, even a little shocking, to hear such things from John Rumbelow, whom he thought a typical Englishman–stuffy, clipped of speech, prim and proper, too inhibited to discuss his wife's cooking, let alone her performance in bed. 'At least, no one ever dies from them.'

'Perhaps she should see a psychologist? I've often thought of the idea. She's very . . . well, she's rather cold, you know.'

So she's frigid, thought Carlow, shutting her vagina like a trap-door with old John outside using his prick as a knocker. Or perhaps it's really his fault, not getting a proper stand on? It's a wonder these Englishmen in their bowler hats ever get an erection at all, it's all so frightfully vulgar, don't you know, perhaps they stuff their umbrellas up . . .

'What are you grinning at? It isn't amusing to me, I assure you.'

'I'm sorry. It was the idea of psychologists. I wouldn't touch them with a barge-pole.' Carlow knew more of sexual psychology than he was inclined to admit, having studied it in depth, for his own satisfaction, in books brought specially by friends from France and Germany. 'Now listen to me, John. I'll tell you what to do. Take Rosemary out for a nice dinner. Spread yourself, a bottle of champagne, all the trimmings. Talk to her like you did in your courting days. That'll put her in a better frame of mind. Women are terribly sentimental. If you play on it, you can do anything with them.'

Rumbelow looked doubtful. But before he could comment a voice behind him exclaimed, 'There's the great pundit himself!' The lean, bald figure of Dr Urrick leant over his armchair.

'Hello, Urrick. You're just down from Edinburgh?'

'This very moment.' The Scot had the habit of puckering his eyes and smiling over the most commonplace remarks, as though they were delicious specimens of wit. It always irritated Rumbelow greatly.

'You know Carlow, of course?'

'Oh, yes. A very good thing for men in our humble position to keep in with the coroners. Eh, Rumbelow?'

'Are you staying here during the trial?'

'I am. It's very convenient, the arrangement for reciprocal hospitality between your splendid club and mine in Edinburgh. You should take advantage of it yourself, in the other direction.'

'I seem very comfortable in that little hotel off Princes Street.' He did not relish anywhere likely to bring more of Urrick's company.

'Ah, I can't afford hotels. We're not all rolling in it like you, Rumbelow.' Urrick looked down with the same twinkling expression. He was a pathologist at Edinburgh, an expert in the Scottish courts, who had been called in to the Vickery case for the defence. He and Rumbelow had been on different sides of a courtroom before. 'I suppose I shouldn't be seen talking to you? You're great sticklers for convention in the legal world down here.'

'I couldn't tell you anything about the trial which isn't in the evening papers.'

Urrick clasped him firmly on the shoulder, another item of behaviour to which Rumbelow objected. 'I'll get a bite to eat. Perhaps we can meet for a social talk later? Though we'll be seeing quite enough of each other over the next few days.'

As his spindly figure disappeared, Rumbelow said, 'That was slack of him, travelling down today. He should have been in court from the start.'

'He can read the transcript of the opening speeches.'

'It's not the same thing. You miss how counsel looked, what he emphasized, any weak spot he hurried over. *I* always make a point of being there from the first.'

'You're not expecting Urrick to put a spoke in your wheel?'

'Not for one moment. I've a shrewd idea of the line he's going to take. It'll all come down to those two slides of the woman's neck-tissues. But I'm confident the jury's going to believe me rather than him.'

'Because you're Dr Rumbelow?'

'No, because I'm simply the better pathologist. Urrick is second-rate. He can hardly be otherwise, can he? In Scotland they simply don't get the volume of work we see down here. It's the cases which create the experts.'

'You don't care much for him, do you?'

'Frankly, no.' Rumbelow considered for a moment. 'He's far too much of a prima donna.'

'I think I'll have another whisky before dinner. It's your turn to foot the bill, I believe.'

'Is it? I'd forgotten.'

At dinner Carlow wanted oysters, but Rumbelow persuaded him they were poor at the end of the season. He was still remembering what he had paid for the taxi.

Chapter Eleven

'How would you define a pathologist?' asked Peter Ivors, in a tone suggesting such terms were beyond his own simple understanding.

It was the Friday morning, two days later, and Rumbelow had just started to give evidence.

'A pathologist is a person learned in that branch of medicine concerned with the essential nature of disease. And with all changes in the body caused by disease.'

'"Disease" would include injuries?'

'Yes.'

'And how would you define forensic medicine?'

'Medicine applied to such problems as might arise in the administration of justice.'

'Are all students of medicine instructed in both these subjects?'

'Yes. That is required by law.'

'So every doctor in the land possesses some knowledge of them?'

'Yes.'

'There is nothing mysterious or magical about either?'

'Nothing whatsoever. These subjects are exactly like any other specialized branch of medical practice.'

The tactic had been rehearsed at a conference in Ivors' chambers earlier that morning. Ivors now saw Sir Arthur Younghusband's objection to Rumbelow's remaining in court as a blunder–he had needlessly shown his hand. If the defence was going to rely on discrediting Rumbelow, presenting him as a witness who somehow mesmerized juries, then the Crown would have to show him as a perfectly ordinary medical man who happened to specialize in a perfectly ordinary branch of the profession. Rumbelow's skill at his job–particularly compared with that of the opposition's medical expert–could be hammered into the jury's heads far more effectively later in the trial. Rumbelow agreed. It was all part of an intellectual game, which he delighted in.

'In an average day's work, how many post-mortem examinations would you perform?'

'Twelve to fifteen.'

'Not all those cases would have met their end through criminal acts?'

'Very few of them.'

'Much the same proportion holds over Great Britain as a whole?'

'No. Statistics show criminality to be involved more often in the Greater London area.'

Peter Ivors then took Rumbelow through his main evidence.

Rumbelow described how he had arrived at Vickery's garage in the dark of a mid-December morning. Once it was light, he had examined Miss Durban's body in a shallow grave against the brick wall which surrounded the back-yard. It had been compressed into a fairly narrow hole, the legs bent, the head against the knees, its back towards him. There were signs of burning. It still wore the tatters of a pink winceyette vest. The wrists were tied behind the back with electrician's flex. He added that from examination of the skin this would have been done after death.

'How long had Miss Durban been dead?'

'Three weeks. Putrefaction was present. There was a generalized green discoloration, particularly where the surfaces were touching in the bundled-up position. The body as a whole was somewhat bloated, with blebs on the surface. The hair and nails were loose. There was a general softening of the tissues.'

'All this is consistent with death three weeks previously?'

'In the cold weather of the period. Had it been summer, I should have put it at two weeks.'

'How was the body affected by fire?'

'It had been badly burnt, but selectively. The back and left side were mainly intact. The right half of the trunk was severely charred, the skin and underlying tissues having been burnt away, and even parts of the right lung and abdominal organs.'

'Could these burns have been caused by petrol?'

'They could only have been caused by petrol.'

'Did they bring about Miss Durban's death?'

'No.'

'Then did they occur before or after her death?'

'They had the typical appearance of burns inflicted after death.'

'Would they be consistent with the prisoner having started to burn Miss Durban's body, perhaps with the idea of destroying it completely as evidence? And then having panicked, or appreciating the difficulty of his task, or even overcome by the sheer horror of it, abandoning the idea and burying what was left?'

'Yes.' Rumbelow was no spendthrift with words.

'Dr Rumbelow, you heard the evidence of the police. The accused in his first statement to Superintendent Sixsmith said he had discovered his "wife" hanging dead from the roof of his garage. In his concern over the repercussions to himself, the following night he buried the body after having set it alight with petrol. Well, you are agreed with the prisoner's statement as far as the burning and the burying go. Do you agree with the hanging?'

'No.'

'Why not?'

Rumbelow always knew the point to become more expansive. 'There were simply no signs of hanging. In my examination of the lungs, the left of which was completely intact, I found no evidence of death being due to suffocation. I found no small bruises on the thighs, as I would expect from breakages of the minor blood-vessels in a suspended body. The neck as a whole, particularly on the left side, was sufficiently unburnt for adequate examination. I found no bruising nor tearing nor any damage whatsoever to its structures. The skin, the underlying tissues, the muscles, the windpipe, the large arteries and veins passing from the chest to the head were all intact. There was no breakage of the small delicate bones round the voice-box. Above all there was no mark round the neck.'

'What sort of mark?'

'One circling the neck, showing the pattern of the ligature used. This would assume a brownish appearance after death–possibly some hours after death.'

'Does this mark always appear?'

'Invariably.'

'However smooth the ligature?'

'I would exclude only a silk or woollen scarf.'

'You have seen produced in court, as an exhibit, the rope of half an inch diameter with which the prisoner says Miss Durban killed herself?'

'Yes.'

'This would not fit with the medical facts?'

'No. The only marks to be seen on the neck were those of some burning.'

'To be seen by the naked eye?'

'By the naked eye and the microscope. I made sections of the skin and examined them. The slides are contained in the wooden box, Exhibit K.'

'Then what was death due to?'

'Shock, following blows to the head. There were probably three, of moderate severity. There was sufficient flesh intact for me to find evidence of bruising and splitting of the skin.'

'There was no other cause for you to attribute her death?'

'None whatever.'

'You think such injuries themselves sufficient?'

'In the case of Miss Durban. She was thin, small-boned, of poor physique–what is described as the "asthenic type".' He looked apologetic for introducing a technical term. 'Death is not uncommon in such persons from injuries which might leave a well-built man comparatively unscathed.'

'Had the whole of the surface of the neck been burnt away, you would then not have been able to exclude hanging?'

'Not to exclude it definitely.'

Peter Ivors sat down. The judge's half-moon glasses were still directed on his notebook, his hand still went steadily across the page. Rumbelow noticed two reporters slip away, he knew to catch the lunchtime editions. He stood as usual with the tips of his fingers resting on the witness-box, his shoulders a little back, in his brown suit with the stripe, a pink carnation in the buttonhole. He had often read in the papers of his 'fine presence in the witness-box'. It amused him, though he knew it was right.

Sir Arthur Younghusband rose for the cross-examination.

'Dr Rumbelow, did you undertake the post-mortem examination of Miss Durban's body with an open mind?'

'I undertake my examination in every case with an open mind.'

'You ascribed Miss Durban's death to shock following three blows to the head. Did you find any fractures of the skull bones in these regions?'

'No.'

'Would you not have expected them?'

'Not in a woman of Miss Durban's frailty,' Rumbelow repeated. 'She would succumb to a blow of less force than needed actually to break a bone.'

'But suppose she had been a woman of normal physique. You might have expected a fracture then?'

'It would have been more likely.'

'So there exists some ill-defined point between rude health and frailty, when it is no longer necessary to break a bone to kill someone with a blow to the head?'

'That would be the case,' Rumbelow admitted.

'But you never saw Miss Durban alive. You concluded she was frail only from her appearance when dead?'

'That is true.'

'Some small, apparently fragile, people may be surprisingly robust?'

'That is true.'

Sir Arthur picked up another sheet of foolscap. He's getting somewhere, Rumbelow thought.

'Let us turn to the question of the hanging. You say that a rope was never round Miss Durban's neck. You base this assertion on the absence of damage to the structures forming the neck, and in particular to the absence of a characteristic mark on the skin. You found no evidence of this, even on examination by the microscope?'

'No evidence at all.'

Did you cut the sections of skin for your microscope slides before or after the second post-mortem examination? I refer to the examination conducted after your own by Dr Urrick, before the remains were finally interred.'

'After.'

'You knew then that my client had made a full explanation to the police, of finding Miss Durban's body hanging in the garage?'

'Yes.'

'But you did not know this when you made your original examination of the body, Superintendent Sixsmith not then having interviewed my client?'

'That is right.'

'I suggest that you did not make your original examination of the neck with particular care?'

'That is incorrect. I took sections for the microscope later, purely as a confirmatory measure.'

'Why should your attention be directed to the neck, when you still had no notion this portion of the body would assume such importance in the case?'

'My attention is directed to all parts of the body in every case. That is a fundamental principle in medicine.' He was fond of repeating this.

'I suggest that once hanging was postulated as the cause of death–which would have exculpated my client–you returned to the body with the express intention of demonstrating somehow or other this could not be so?'

Rumbelow's expression stayed unchanged. In the witness-box he had the professional self-control of a champion boxer in the ring. 'Whatever is postulated as the cause of death, in whatever case, I set it from my mind in reaching my own conclusions.'

'Is this the practice of all pathologists?'

'I cannot answer for my colleagues.'

'It all comes down to a matter of bruises, does it not? You say there were no bruises on the skin of the neck. But that there were bruises and splitting of the skin of the head?'

'Yes.'

'I noticed you did not preface your replies to my learned friend with, "In my opinion", or some such formula. That is what it comes down to, yet again, does it not? All this is purely a matter of opinions. Yours against any other medical man's?'

'My opinion is correct.'

'Is that not overweening vanity, Dr Rumbelow?'

'No. It is assurance based on my professional ability and experience.'

The judge looked up. 'Sir Arthur, it is your client who is on trial, not Dr Rumbelow.'

'I apologize, my Lord, if I have given the contrary impression.' He reached for another sheet of paper. 'Well, Dr Rumbelow. You heard the evidence of Miss Durban's father. How she spent some time in a mental institution, undergoing treatment of neurasthenia and melancholia?'

Rumbelow wondered what questions the judge's interruption had obliged Sir Arthur to leave unasked. 'I did.'

'He described her as "neurotic". Would a neurotic person be more likely to commit suicide than a mentally robust one?'

'Yes.'

'And might not life in an isolated house, in the dark unpleasant days of winter, increase the tendency of a comparatively young woman towards suicide?'

'No. Suicide is committed most frequently in crowded cities. And among females at the age of fifty. The latest Registrar-General's report gives 243 cases of that age against 112 at thirty, which Miss Durban was. The commonest month for suicide is May. I quote from the same source.' This answer so satisfied Rumbelow, he became unusually expansive. 'Suicide has certainly some connexion with marriage, which Miss Durban at least believed she had contracted. Recent marriage is cited in point-three per cent of cases, as against six-point eight where the cause is given as mental conditions, and two-point-four per cent due to financial worry.'

I couldn't be fairer than that, he thought.

'But a person intending to commit suicide would hardly study the Registrar-General's tables beforehand, to find if the act were statistically feasible?'

Rumbelow did not condescend to answer.

'Thank you, Dr Rumbelow,' said Sir Arthur with great courtesy.

The court wanted its lunch.

'A bit below the belt, that, wasn't it?' Ivors observed mildly to Rumbelow as they pushed their way out. He had no reply.

Descending the front steps of the Old Bailey, Rumbelow's eye caught the newsvendor's placard opposite saying, RUMBELOW IN THE BOX. He crossed the street to get a paper. Sometimes he went to the expense of buying several, from different pitches all over the City. It always distressed him a little that the paper-sellers never seemed to recognize him.

Chapter Twelve

He was aware of being followed.

April of 1936 was one of the coldest in memory. Rumbelow turned up the fur collar of his overcoat as he walked down the Old Bailey southwards towards Ludgate Hill, with his usual intention of lunching in the refectory at Blackfriars. The case was making such a splash in the papers, the other consultants would be burning to quizz him about it, which would be agreeable. He stood on the pavement of Ludgate Hill itself, waiting for a gap in the traffic before crossing. Turning idly to his left, glancing towards the west front of St Paul's up the hill, he noticed someone standing in the doorway of a men's outfitters on the opposite corner. She was a slim woman with fair hair, eyeing him intently. She was smartly dressed in an overcoat of small black-and-white check, a fox-fur round her neck, on the top of her head a small hat with a large bow. She was quite young, under thirty. And pretty. He had already noticed her waiting to one side of the steps as he left the courts, the corner of his eye catching her following on the far side of the street after he had crossed for his paper. It was strange. Though perhaps only imagination, he told himself. Or she was from a newspaper office. They got up to all sorts of tricks these days.

He crossed the road, turning away from the cathedral towards Ludgate Circus. Stealing a glance behind, he saw her in his footsteps. He began to feel uneasy. He paused, while the policeman in his little wooden box changed the lights to stop the traffic. She crossed the Circus beside him, taking no notice of him but staring fixedly ahead. Rumbelow smiled to himself. He was really being unnecessarily anxious. Some men would have given a lot to be followed across the City of London by an attractive strange woman.

He turned towards the river. She kept close, just behind his right elbow. Really! thought Rumbelow. This is too much. In sight of Blackfriars Bridge, as he reached the walls of the hospital itself, he stopped. 'What is it? Why are you following me?'

She gave a gasp, a hand to her mouth.

'What do you want?'

He thought for a moment she was going to vanish in the lunchtime crowds, but she made an effort to speak. 'You're Dr Rumbelow, aren't you?'

She had a cultured voice, he noticed. 'What's your game?'

'I couldn't bring myself to stop you . . . I've got to speak to you.'

'Is it about the Vickery case? You know you may be committing an offence, approaching a witness like this? A serious offence.' She shook her head vigorously. 'You're from Fleet Street?'

'I'm nothing to do with the papers, nothing at all.' She looked round desperately. 'Can't we go somewhere to talk?'

'That's out of the question. I don't know who you are, or what your business is. But I must ask you to leave me alone.'

He turned away, though politely raising his bowler hat.

'Listen–' She hurried after him. 'Please, *please* listen to me. I'm Mrs Jeavons.' The name for a moment meant nothing to Rumbelow. Then he remembered it as the label on some of his specimens. 'You know. From Blayford. You were down with the police.'

'You mustn't talk to me about that. It is improper. This sort of behaviour won't do you any good at all, you know.'

She grabbed the sleeve of his coat. 'I saw in the papers you were at the Old Bailey. I had to come to London, just on the chance of meeting you. They think I murdered my husband. The police think so. They've taken away my passport. They've been searching my house. They've got a man opposite, nearly always, watching my movements—'

'Please take your hand off my coat.'

'But I'm innocent. I did nothing. Oh, it's a horrible notion, just put about by people because they're jealous of me, or they hate me, or they want to make trouble for me. It's wrong, it's ridiculous. I couldn't ever do a thing like that. Not in a million years. I couldn't take a human life. Particularly my husband's. It was impossible, impossible! We had rows, I'm not denying that. I've been foolish, I know I've been foolish, but I never knew where my stupidity would lead me. I could never do anything so terrible—'

'Stop it!'

'I know what you think. That I poisoned him. I know you're doing all sorts of tests, just to prove I did. I know you've only to say so, and they'll arrest me. But it's wrong, all quite wrong. Can't I appeal to you? Do I look like a murderess?'

'This is nothing whatever to do with me.' Rumbelow was angry. 'I'm not a police officer. If you've anything to say, go to Scotland Yard and tell them there.'

He noticed she was crying. 'Oh God, what a mess I'm in! Oh God. I know you'll say I killed him—'

'Go away. Go away at once. If you don't, I'll call a policeman and get him to take you off.'

'Haven't you got a heart?'

His anger suddenly turned to exasperation. 'This is really most unwise of you. Stopping me in the street like this. Do you understand that? I shall have to report it to Scotland Yard.'

'Why must you do that?'

'It's my duty, as an ordinary citizen. I advise you to make your position no worse.'

'Won't you listen to me? Won't you let me explain? About all the things that happened, about the circumstances of my husband and myself, even about my own weakness? It was bad enough with the shock of his death—'

Rumbelow abruptly walked on. She started to follow, but after a few steps she stopped, and as he turned the corner towards the hospital entrance on the Embankment he saw her standing still staring after him. What a stupid woman! he thought. Why on earth should she come up to London and attack *me*? If she wants to protest her innocence, she should go to Sixsmith. If she *is* innocent. He had seen how frightened she was, and supposed it was because she had something to hide–an innocent suspect would have stayed calmly at home. Well, we shall see better when I have completed my analysis, he decided. He intended to telephone Scotland Yard about the incident at once, and turned into the corridor towards his laboratory, feeling in his pocket for the key.

Standing outside the door was a fat grey-haired woman in a khaki overall, with a bucket and mop.

'This ain't good enough, sir. It ain't good enough at all.' She seemed deeply offended at something.

Rumbelow stared at her blankly. He could not recall setting eyes on her in his life. 'I beg your pardon?'

'It's your room, sir. How do you expect a body to clean it? I've got my job to do, you know.'

He still felt lost. 'It's . . . it's quite clean I think, thank you.'

'It *ain't*. It must be six whole weeks since I got in there. Always locked, it is.'

'Please don't bother yourself about it. I'm quite content as it is.'

'But I *must* bother myself, sir. I've had the House Governor after me. "When did you last clean Dr Rumbelow's room?" he said. "I was in there talking to him yesterday, and it was a proper disgrace," he said. I don't want to get myself into no trouble—'

'Very well, very well, I'll leave it open for you,' he said hastily. He wanted only to get rid of her. 'But please leave me in peace for now. Come back later.'

She stood with her hands clasping the top of her mop, not satisfied. 'I can't do my work properly, sir, if the door's always shut in my face—'

'Oh, just as you please. It'll be unlocked in the future, if that's what you want. But you must be very careful not to touch anything, or look into any drawers or cupboards.'

'I've been working in the medical school for ten years, sir. I don't need to be told—'

'Yes, yes, I'm sure you don't.'

He closed the door behind him, frowning. What amazing things people got up to in this day and age.

Chapter Thirteen

During the Monday morning, Dr Urrick was called to give evidence in Vickery's defence.

Rumbelow folded his arms on the uncomfortable seat he had occupied throughout the trial. He wore his light grey striped suit, not quite so smart as the brown one, spats, and his usual buttonhole. A carnation was kept for him every morning by an old lady with a basket outside the hospital gate, who did a fair trade selling flowers to visitors.

He listened while Sir Arthur Younghusband led Urrick through his qualifications and appointments–doctor of medicine in the University of Edinburgh, fellow of the Royal College of Physicians of Edinburgh, Pathologist to the McCurdy Institute in the same city.

'Taking the country as a whole,' suggested Sir Arthur, 'would you put your professional standing on the same par as Dr Rumbelow's?'

Urrick puckered his eyes. He had the habit of carrying his pawky manner into the witness-box, striking Rumbelow as a man telling diverting after-dinner anecdotes rather than giving evidence in a trial for murder. 'I should say that. Yes, definitely.'

Rumbelow grunted. Everyone knew–or they should–that the McCurdy Institute was mainly an institution which specialized in cramming hundreds of students through their examinations. And that Urrick was an uninspired, even a careless, pathologist. And that he owed his position largely to having failed at everything else. Still, Rumbelow thought hopefully, the man's evidence might shortly make all that apparent.

Most of Urrick's testimony was unexciting, uncontroversial, and long-winded. He described how he had been telephoned in Edinburgh by Vickery's solicitors. How he had left at once his urgent and weighty duties, had taken the very first express from Edinburgh, only to find that Rumbelow had already performed a post-mortem on Eileen Durban's remains. He recounted in intense detail his own examination of the body, made the next day in the Central Mortuary in the presence of a detective-inspector and the solicitor. He recited his post-mortem findings from a thick folder of notes on the edge of the witness-box, at which he peered through a pair of pince-nez. He was perfectly entitled to an *aide-mémoire*, Rumbelow knew, though he himself took pains to memorize everything thoroughly, having decided this looked more authoritative, and thus more impressive to the jury. He stared along the rows of reporters scribbling painstakingly in the Press benches, even for a few minutes allowing his attention to wander.

'To what opinion did your examination lead, Dr Urrick, on the cause of Miss Durban's death?' asked Sir Arthur.

Urrick tilted his head and screwed up his eyes. 'The young lady died by her own hand. From hanging.'

Having an ear for such things, Rumbelow caught a stirring among the pressmen. There could not have been a flatter contradiction to himself.

'Will you tell the court exactly why you reached that conclusion?'

'From examination of the deceased woman's neck. Even by the naked eye, there was undoubted evidence of a ligature.'

'What evidence, precisely?'

'A brownish mark circling the neck.'

'Will you indicate it on this photograph of the body, Exhibit G?'

Urrick adjusted the pince-nez on a black ribbon attached to his lapel. He took a propelling pencil from his pocket and carefully made a mark. The photograph was passed to the judge, who looked at it impassively, and then round the jury, who did their best to stare penetratingly.

'Did you take further steps to confirm that a ligature had been round the neck?'

'I did that.' Urrick swung the pince-nez on its cord. 'I made a dissection of the underlying neck-tissues. I was able to detect definite extravasation of blood, and certain trauma to the trachea.'

'You made this dissection, despite Dr Rumbelow having examined the same area previously?'

'Such interference is no hindrance to the trained pathologist,' said Urrick airily.

'Did you make any further investigations?'

'I took sections of the skin and subcutaneous tissues for microscopical examination. The black cardboard box you are holding up is that containing the relevant microscope slides, Exhibit M. My views were amply confirmed.'

'You have heard Dr Rumbelow. He put the cause of death as three blows to the head. Did you find any evidence which might support his theory?'

'Not a jot.' The pince-nez swung jauntily. 'I found contusions in the cephalic region. But from my examination of the neck, both macroscopical and microscopical, I have no doubt whatever the poor woman met her end through the agency of the rope produced in court.'

'Contusions?' The judge looked up.

'Bruises, my Lord.' Urrick sounded condescending. 'That is the lay term.'

'But you did find some bruising of the head,' the judge continued. 'You agree with Dr Rumbelow on that point?'

'I found some bruising.'

'Were these bruises trivial? Or were they severe?'

'I'd say . . . quite severe. Yes, quite severe.'

'Then how do you suppose they were caused?'

'They could have happened through the young woman striking some structure during the process of hanging herself.'

'While she was still living?'

'Oh, yes. They were not post-mortem bruises.'

The judge nodded towards Sir Arthur.

'I have no more questions, my Lord.'

Peter Ivors rose, immediately in front of Rumbelow. 'Dr Urrick, would you assist the court a little more about this mark on the neck? I should like to take you through it from the outside inwards, so to speak. Let us start with the photograph.' Ivors handed him the picture. 'The line you indicated with your pencil is somewhat faint, is it not?'

'But it is undoubtedly the mark of a ligature.'

'Might it not be one of the normal skin-creases of the neck? As one would expect to find in a woman of Miss Durban's age?'

Urrick screwed up his eyes. 'A skin-crease might be possible. Yes, just possible. But that is not at one with my dissection of the cervical tissues.'

'Let us move deeper, then. You say you found extravasation of blood and certain trauma to the trachea–that is the windpipe, is it not?'

'In the language of the laity.'

'You can see from the photograph the extent of burning on the body. Might not your findings be due to this?'

'They would not.'

'Or to Dr Rumbelow's already having dissected the region?'

'They would not.'

'Let us delve more. These microscope slides of yours, Exhibit M.' Ivors held up the small cardboard box. He opened it, and added in a tone of faint wonderment, 'But the glass slides have no labels on them. Unlike Dr Rumbelow's, they have no identifying mark at all. They might have come from anywhere, surely? From anyone? Is this your normal practice?'

Urrick looked offended. 'I can keep track of my own materials.'

'In a case with a man's life depending on it, would you not be more particular?'

'We are all open to criticism.'

'But not to a charge of gross carelessness?'

Urrick said nothing.

'Let us go deeper still, into the lungs. You agree with Dr Rumbelow there was no sign of suffocation? Or asphyxia, if you would prefer the medical term.'

'It is the only point on which I fully agree with him.'

'So what was the immediate cause of Miss Durban's death?'

'Shock.'

'Again, as Dr Rumbelow says.'

'Yes. But shock caused by suicidal hanging. Such an effect is far from uncommon.'

'Yet hanging itself is not common, among deaths due to criminal acts? You will appreciate, Dr Urrick, that suicide in England is a criminal act, though by one of our subtle differences of law not so in Scotland.'

'I will agree. Hanging is not so common.'

'You heard what Dr Rumbelow had to say. That among the cases a pathologist examines in his daily work, those meeting their ends through criminal acts are few? Do you agree with that?'

The pince-nez were now poked into a waistcoat pocket. 'I would agree with that, too.'

'Dr Urrick, how many post-mortems, on an average, do you conduct in a day?'

'One or two.'

'You also heard Dr Rumbelow say he conducts twelve to fifteen. Let us allow that criminal cases form a small proportion of these. Let us further allow that deaths from hanging form a smaller proportion still. Yet as a matter of simple arithmetic, Dr Rumbelow's experience of the signs of hanging–such as the presence or absence of ligature marks on the neck–must be very considerably greater than your own?'

'They see more of such things down in London,' said Urrick uncomfortably.

'The shock which killed Miss Durban could have resulted from blows to her head?'

'The blows were not very severe.'

'But allowing for her frailness, could they have killed her?'

'I suppose that would be possible.'

'You ascribe these blows to Miss Durban striking herself in some way while committing suicide. Have you seen such injuries in a case of hanging?'

Urrick hesitated. 'I cannot say.'

'Have you? Even in your limited experience of such cases?'

'No, I . . . no, I must say. I have not.'

'It never occurred to you that the blows might have been inflicted by the prisoner?'

Urrick made no reply. Peter Ivors sat down. He turned with a look Rumbelow had learnt to interpret. It meant, 'With a bit of luck, we've won.'

Chapter Fourteen

Towards the middle of that afternoon, Vickery himself went into the witness-box.

The prisoner's evidence was awaited by the Press even more eagerly than Rumbelow's had been. But Rumbelow himself was not in court. He had no more to contribute to the trial. He would certainly be there for the summing-up, to see how the judge treated his evidence–a valuable lesson for the future. But now he could release himself, having work to do.

In his laboratory at Blackfriars, he lit a Bunsen burner and placed a glass beaker on the tripod over the flame. The beaker contained a mixture, half of distilled water and half of concentrated hydrochloric acid. He then took a small piece of copper foil from a jar, burnished it with emery paper, and boiled it in the fluid for fifteen minutes. The copper strip remained bright. The chemicals and apparatus were free from any contamination with arsenic.

Rumbelow unlocked a cupboard under the workbench, and produced one of his wide-mouthed jars, the blue-edged label marked *Jeavons. Filtrate of Liver*. He added a few drops to the beaker, letting it all simmer for a further quarter of an hour. The copper foil was still bright. He picked it out with forceps, examining it through his magnifying-glass. No trace of any deposit. He turned off the Bunsen, making a note. *Reinsch Test–Negative, no arsenic present*.

He took more apparatus from the glass cupboard on the wall. He should already have completed the analysis, but the Vickery case was taking so much of his time, with the sessions in court and repeated conferences in Peter Ivors' chambers. The chemistry would be difficult, because he suspected only a small amount of arsenic had been given, and it would have to be thorough to stand up in court. But he supposed there was no particular urgency. Sixsmith still had a good many inquiries to make, with lines to follow in Singapore, and seemed confident that Mrs Jeavons wouldn't give him the slip. That the widow was frightened, ostracized, persecuted by malicious tongues, and living in horrible suspense was not a matter which occurred to Rumbelow at all.

He arranged on the bench a jar like the water-carafe on the platforms of public meetings. It had a glass stopper–a cork was a possible contaminant with arsenic. Through one hole in the stopper ran a funnel shaped like a thistle, with a glass tap. From another came a short bent glass tube. This tube entered a thicker one, running horizontally, filled with calcium chloride to dry out gases passing through it. At the end was a finer tube of the same length, made of transparent silica to withstand the Bunsen flame.

Rumbelow took the glass cover from a chemist's balance in the corner of the bench. He weighed out a few grams of zinc and tipped them into the flask. With a pipette, he added to the zinc some dilute sulphuric acid. He replaced the stopper with its funnel and tube, and watched the mixture bubbling as it evolved hydrogen gas. Then he poured through the thistle-funnel a little of the fluid from James Jeavons' liver. He lit the Bunsen burner under the fine end of the tube, watching the silica glow to redness. He would have half an hour to wait.

He sat on the wooden stool, writing up his notes of the case in a manilla folder. He placed on the bench the gold watch which had belonged to his brother. He waited the full thirty minutes before peering at the silica tube just beyond the edge of the flame. There was no deposit. He moved away the Bunsen burner. With a match, he ignited the gases escaping from the end of the tube. He took a small square of porcelain and held it in the jet. Now there was some discoloration, a greyish deposit.

'Very interesting,' murmured Rumbelow with satisfaction.

He added a drop of nitric acid to the stain, let it dry and touched it with silver nitrate. A brick-red colour formed at once. He reached for his fountain-pen, and wrote on his notes, *Marsh Test–Positive. Arsenic present in liver*.

He dismantled the apparatus, rinsed it out with distilled water, and reassembling it repeated the experiment. The same result.

'Good, good,' he said to himself. He wondered whether to telephone Sixsmith, but set the idea aside as too sensational. The proper method was to submit a written report. Anyway, time was getting on. At seven he would have to go. He wrote the report and carefully put everything away, locking the drawers and cupboards. He would leave the laboratory door unfastened, if it pleased the charwoman. He took his brown leather attaché case, the famous black bag staying behind on the floor. He supposed she would be curious about it, but it was securely locked.

He went by Tube to his club, where he asked the porter for the key of a changing room. He put on his dinner-jacket, and being a little early sat in the morning-room with a cigar, reading about the trial in the evening papers. He had left his book of poems at the club and considered dipping into them for a few moments. But he decided against it. Eliot's casual momentousness was rather beyond him.

In his coat and hat he walked across Trafalgar Square to Charing Cross Station. His wife was just coming through the barrier from a suburban electric train.

She smiled at him. 'You weren't late after all.'

'I was working in the lab. I had more time than I expected, as a matter of fact. Peter Ivors finished off Urrick pretty promptly this morning.'

'How's the trial going?'

'Very well for us, I think.'

'Yes, I thought so when I read about it in the train.'

'Urrick is a fool,' said Rumbelow, as though making a simple statement of fact.

They walked towards the station entrance. She was in a long gown of green shot-silk, tight to the knees and flaring over her feet. On top she had a grey cape of dyed squirrel, a wedding-present from her father. She clutched tightly a small handbag done in petit-point. Her lipstick was vivid red, her fair hair newly set–by a hairdresser–and drawn into a bunch of curls at the back of the head. He noticed she wore the pair of jade earrings he had given her on their first anniversary. She had met him from the train with an expression of admiration and tenderness heightened by excitement, which would have moved another man to take her into his arms.

'This is an unexpected treat, John.'

'I haven't been particularly attentive recently.'

'Let's just forget our worries and enjoy ourselves.' They reached the pavement. 'How are we getting to the theatre?'

'We'll take a taxi,' he told her impressively.

They had tickets for the Phoenix in Charing Cross Road to see Noel Coward's *Tonight at 8.30*. Rumbelow had half-decided on James Bridie's *Storm in a Teacup* at the Haymarket, solely because the author was also a doctor, but people at Blackfriars had told him the Coward show was awfully good. He knew nothing about such matters himself. He was careful over not hinting to Rosemary that the real begetter of her evening's entertainment was Norman Carlow.

They sat in the second row of the stalls. Rosemary put her fur in her lap, revealing her spiky shoulders. Rumbelow looked round, smoothing his bow against the points of his wing-collar, noticing people staring at him. He had figured in a good many newspaper photographs over the past few days. It was very pleasant. Though he was disconcerted to find the performance not one play, instead three short ones. But Coward himself was very clever, and he liked the red-headed girl who appeared in her brassière for the theatrical sketch. He looked at his programme, read 'Gertrude Lawrence', and felt he had heard the name before. He wished he could meet more actresses, but Lady Accrington thought stage people common and Mrs Mavery was jealous of them. He turned his head to glance at Rosemary. Her eyes were wide and her lips apart, like a child at the pantomime.

They went for supper afterwards at a nearby restaurant where, Rumbelow had gathered, actors and actresses themselves ate after their performances. This part of the evening had cost him the most thought. Unless the play finished remarkably early, they would not have time to catch their last train to Lower Sydenham. But he remembered some trains ran later from the station opposite Blackfriars Hospital for the convenience of late workers on Fleet Street. It would land them at Penge East, with a fair walk afterwards, but that was nothing compared to the expense of a taxi half across London, particularly as a meal for the pair of them could hardly cost less than thirty shillings, even if they had the carafe wine.

He asked the head-waiter for a table, glancing round for actors and actresses. A woman near him said loudly, 'But how devastating! Look–it's Dr Rumbelow,' and her companion added admiringly, 'I say, so it jolly well is.' It took him an effort not to turn and bow.

For much of the meal they talked harmlessly, mostly about the show.

'That scene where she takes the overdose of sleeping-pills,' Rosemary said. 'How would *you* have treated her?'

'Much less romantically, if more effectively. I'd have given her a mixture of mustard and water, and made her vomit.'

Rosemary laughed. 'That doesn't sound at all pleasant. I'd better not try it on myself, then?'

'Oh, you wouldn't.'

'Wouldn't I? Why are you so sure?'

He suddenly felt uneasy. He thought she was perhaps teasing him, one of her habits he found irritating. But he was unable to let the remark go by. 'You wouldn't contemplate suicide, would you? Not in any circumstances?'

'How you're looking at me! Have I frightened you?'

'No, of course not . . . but you *wouldn't* surely? You'd not even think of it.'

'How can I tell?' She still spoke lightly. 'Do you imagine some poor woman who has committed suicide today would even remotely have been able to answer the same question six months ago? Or six weeks, or six days? Perhaps even six hours before she put her head in a gas-oven.'

'I wish you wouldn't talk like this.'

'Why shouldn't I?'

'Because it's wrong. Suicide is against the law. Even attempted suicide is a crime. I hope you realize that.'

'That's how you see everything, isn't it, John? Legal or illegal. All inside the law shining pure, all outside wicked black.'

'You're speaking as though it was a lot of arbitrary rules. It isn't. The law is the essence of our civilization.'

'I'm not sure if I always agree with our civilization.'

'My brother was killed defending it.'

'A lot of things people do inside the law are horrible. Look at the way we treat the unemployed, for instance. We give them a few shillings a week, hardly enough to feed them decently, but it lets us all sleep with an easy conscience. Nothing constructive is done at all. Nothing to provide them with some sort of work. So that they'll feel useful, wanted in the community. Without that, a man might as well be dead.'

'I thought you'd grown out of your socialism?'

'It isn't socialism. It's simple compassion. And a lot of things which happen outside the law deserve that, not punishment.'

'What things?' he demanded.

'Well . . . look at some poor miserable unmarried girl, procuring herself an abortion. She's a criminal, because she doesn't want to give the world an unwanted life. But the law doesn't think twice about taking one, to justify itself.' He grunted. She took a sip from her wine-glass. 'Don't worry, John. I can assure you I've no immediate plans for doing away with myself.'

'Then I'm delighted to hear it.'

'It's only because you'd be afraid of the scandal, isn't it? How it would look in the newspapers. How you might be discredited in court. How a clever barrister might somehow use it—'

'Stop it!'

She fell silent, rebuking herself for going too far. She had told herself desperately she must do everything that evening to avoid upsetting him. But like every couple who strive hopefully to change old attitudes with fresh surroundings, they found the familiar shadow of their bitter home-life fallen across the restaurant table.

'You know I'm concerned only with your welfare, Rosemary.' She made no reply, carving the roast duck on her plate. 'I've been wondering lately if you should consult a psychologist.'

She looked up, startled. 'Why should I need that?'

'For those fears of yours. About giving birth to monsters, and so on. They're abnormal emotions in any woman.'

'Why must you bring all that up now?'

'It must be brought up sometime.'

'Forget it . . . just forget I said it.'

'I find that impossible.'

'I told you, it's stupid, all irrational. I'm ashamed of it.'

'Or is it an excuse?'

'An excuse for what?'

'To avoid me touching you. It must be ages since—'

'It's not always my fault. Often you're late, you're tired—'

'Excuses, excuses, more excuses. I don't believe you've these peculiar phobias at all. You're just using them as a convenience.'

'Very well. I don't like this sex business. The whole thing is repugnant to me. You must know that already, surely? Why do you force me to tell you in so many words?'

'Perhaps you *don't* care for it. But a wife has a duty towards her husband.'

She abruptly started to cry. Now it was Rumbelow telling himself he had been stupid, pushing her too far. But his main concern was their being in public. He wondered anxiously if people had noticed, perhaps even the woman who had spotted him at the entrance. 'Please control yourself. Get on with your dinner.'

She shook her head, groping for a handkerchief in the petit-point bag. 'I was so enjoying this evening—'

'Come along! Behave like an adult.'

She stood up. 'I want to go.'

Before he could stop her, she was making towards the door. He beckoned to a surprised-looking waiter for the bill. He glanced at the other diners in panic, but they were chattering away, apparently unaware of the 'scene'. He collected his overcoat and her fur. Outside the restaurant he took her elbow firmly, as they started to walk aimlessly along the pavement.

'That was very stupid of you, Rosemary.'

'Why are you so unkind to me?'

'I'm not unkind. Is it unkind to mention the very fault which is ruining our marriage?'

She turned to him angrily. 'All right. If you don't like me, if I don't give you the service you want, go off and leave me. Get it elsewhere.'

He gripped her the tighter. 'Why should I leave you? You're my wife. Your duty is to provide an outlet for my normal emotions. Why should I put myself out to look for another woman?'

'What a terrible way to talk!'

'How did you expect me to reply? To break into song about love?'

'You don't know anything about love.' He saw her lip trembling in the light of the street-lamps. 'Perhaps neither of us do.'

'What's it matter? A measure of affection, tolerance and habit–there's the average marriage for you. I nose into plenty of them in my work.'

'I'm not going home tonight.'

'Yes, you are.' She tore away her arm. He knew he would dominate her in the end, though sometimes it took longer than others. Then he was aware of a passer-by, a man of the lower classes in a cap, who had stopped and was staring at them with amusement. This so embarrassed Rumbelow, he said more gently, 'Perhaps we've had enough hysterics for one night.'

She hurried away from him, half tripping over her skirt. He caught up with her.

'If you're not coming home, where are you going instead? Back to your parents? You wouldn't be very welcome. Not at a poverty-stricken farm, with another mouth to feed these days. Or back to schoolmistressing? You wouldn't get a job. There are teachers on the dole already. You're stuck with me, you see. You'd better make the most of it.' She still said nothing, walking on, staring straight ahead. 'Or perhaps you've ideas of going off and finding another man to keep you? That certainly wouldn't work. You wouldn't be any use to him. Not all men are quite so patient in these matters as I am.'

She stopped. 'My God, I wish I'd never met you,' she said quietly.

'Are you coming home?'

She shrugged her shoulders. 'Where else can I go?'

'There you are. You're seeing reason.'

Rumbelow took her arm again. They started down the street. There would be just time if they stepped out, he calculated, to catch the last train from Charing Cross. She was now wholly subdued, and he even assumed a feverish jauntiness. In the train he remembered his attaché case with the grey suit which he had meant to collect from the club. He was most annoyed. His brown suit was at the cleaners, and he was anxious to appear particularly smart the following day for the verdict and sentence.

Chapter Fifteen

The next morning the British public had more on its mind than the outcome of the Vickery trial. It was Budget Day.

'How was Vickery in the box?' Rumbelow asked Peter Ivors, when they met in the Old Bailey during the lunch adjournment.

'Absolutely splendid. He gave the impression of a respectful and reliable chauffeur, whom anyone could entrust themselves to from London to Glasgow. You almost expected a blue peaked cap perched on the edge of the box. There's a wonderful bit I must tell you–when I took him up on the bigamy, he asserted he knew several people who'd done the same thing. I asked, "You're used to the company of men who commit crime?" and he said, "Such persons, sir, were among my employers and their friends, whose names I should prefer not to mention to save embarrassment". Of course I looked shocked, and said, 'Do you mean bigamy is rife in the motor-car-owning classes?" to which he answered, "Very rife, sir, you can tell that from the society papers".'

Ivors laughed heartily. 'But that's not the end of it. Old Lynacre looked down his nose and asked, "Aren't you confusing bigamy with divorce, Vickery?" He replied, "It always strikes me as the same thing, my lord, there's only technical legal matters in between." Not bad, eh? So I asked if his employers took him into their confidence over such matters. He replied that a chauffeur gets to know a lot, and I'd be surprised. Oh, he was very quick-witted. I really couldn't do much with him.'

'Do you think it'll make any difference to the result?'

'Not a scrap. It's all out of Vickery's hands. It's between you and Urrick.'

Counsel's closing speeches had occupied much of the morning. The judge's charge to the jury ran well into the afternoon. Rumbelow thought he summed-up well–he was becoming something of a connoisseur of judges. The medical evidence was, as expected, prominent in his address. He struck squarely the point already hammered by prosecution and defence alike–was Eileen Durban hanged, or was she not? Were the jury to take the opinion of Dr Urrick or Dr Rumbelow?

'Much has been made of the reputations of these two distinguished medical men, members of the jury,' the judge told them. 'Well, that is to some extent relevant. Dr Rumbelow is certainly not infallible. He would never claim to be, I am sure, no more than any other doctor, nor any member of the bar, nor of the bench. But his opinion is undoubtedly backed with great experience. You heard that he is in the habit of performing as many as fifteen post-mortems every day of his working life. Though only a few of these would be the result of hanging–either suicidal, or murderous, or judicial–that still leaves him with greater experience of such cases, and of their post-mortem appearances, than many other pathologists. At the same time you must, of course, take into account the qualifications and experience of Dr Urrick.'

An agreeably perfunctory reference to them, thought Rumbelow.

'These doctors were called solely to assist you, members of the jury, to decide some highly technical matters. You may feel their reputations outside this court are of less importance than what you saw and heard with your own eyes and ears. You have observed both in the witness-box. You have heard both give their opinions on the cause of death in this young woman. You have heard from both their reasons for these opinions. And you have heard the methods they employed to establish these reasons. You have all the facts. You must choose which set you prefer to believe, either Dr Rumbelow's or Dr Urrick's.'

The judge's pause emphasized this was the hub round which the whole case revolved. 'It is perhaps a strange position for you, as ordinary men. If you are attended by your own doctor, you accept his word on your illness without question. If he calls in a second opinion to assist him, and this is a contrary one, you rely on your doctor's view of that. You are not obliged to make up your mind which opinion is correct, or more nearly correct. Now you find yourselves, members of the jury, exactly in that position. It is your decision alone.'

The jury went out at ten past five.

'God!' said Peter Ivors in the corridor outside. He had tipped back his wig and lit a cigarette, and was holding an evening paper. On the front was a photograph of Mr Neville Chamberlain, Chancellor of the Exchequer, the traditional battered dispatch-box aloft, a smile on his droopy-moustached face, about to make his short trip from the Treasury across Parliament Square to dip ceremoniously into the electorate's pockets. 'Threepence on the income-tax! The Government's gone mad.'

Rumbelow was reading over his shoulder. 'Tuppence a pound more on tea, I see. And a pound a barrel on imported beer.'

'I don't touch either. I'm a coffee and scotch man. Thank heavens they haven't gone for those. Twelve-and-six a bottle is bad enough as it is.'

'How long do you suppose the jury will take?'

'About an hour.' He was a shrewd forecaster of such things.

'So short? With so much technical evidence?'

'The more technical the evidence the quicker they are. Everyone falls over backwards to make it simple. They can't look beyond what we tell them. They're too ignorant, anyway.'

'Do you still think he'll go down?'

'Yes. Though of course you can never be sure. It's like the races.' He looked back at his newspaper. 'Threepence in the pound! Really, this country is becoming far too expensive to live in.'

'Excuse me, sir.' A policeman was at Rumbelow's side. 'There's a telephone message just come for you, sir.'

Rumbelow took the scrap of paper. It asked him to telephone a Kensington number, which meant nothing to him. He wondered if it were Sixsmith, who would have had his report that morning on the Jeavons' specimens. He went to a public call-box, found two pennies, and dialled. 'Dr Rumbelow here.'

'You *do* sound official.'

'Who's that?'

'Diana. Diana Flavell. Where on earth have you been hiding?'

She should never have telephoned me at the Old Bailey, he thought irritably. 'I'm afraid I've been very busy.'

'I can see that. It's ever so thrilling reading about you every morning. And knowing you're not just some sort of figure invented by the reporters, but real flesh and blood.'

'The papers exaggerate everything, of course.'

'Why didn't you telephone me?'

The answer was simple–really, he was frightened of her.

'I was intending to.'

'I was utterly disappointed, not hearing a thing,' she added gaily. 'Listen, dear–I've got an invitation for you. To a party.' Rumbelow said nothing. 'Do tell me you'll come.'

'When is it?'

'Tomorrow night. Some friends of mine are throwing it.'

'It's rather short notice,' he said evasively.

'But you *must* come dear. I've promised to produce you. I'll be absolutely devastated if you let me down.'

'May I think it over?'

'Oh, come on! Be a sport. I promise you won't be bored.'

'I'll ring you in the morning.'

She laughed. 'You sound as if I was going to eat you. Do make the effort, dear. It's only in Chelsea. You could pick me up at the flat about nine-ish.'

Rumbelow left the telephone box both undecided on his actions and uncertain of himself. A party . . . that would be a more relaxed affair than even Mrs Mavery's luncheons. And after their last encounter, it was on the cards Diana would invite him into her flat afterwards. But would he really want her to? He stood with his hands in his pockets, in the middle of the hall of the Old Bailey, running his tongue over his lips trying to settle this delicate self-inquisition. Diana could bring unlooked-for and embarrassing complications. A man in his position must keep a sharp eye for spiders' webs. On the other hand. Rosemary herself had suggested he look elsewhere. It was all very difficult for a person of propriety.

At six-thirty they went back to court. The judge entered through his door under the Royal Arms. Behind came a chaplain. The prisoner reappeared in the dock. Everyone stared at him. Then the jury filed in, and they looked towards them instead.

The clerk of the court rose below the bench. 'Members of the jury, you are all agreed on your verdict?'

The foreman was a fat man in a brown tweed suit, with all three buttons done up. 'Yes.'

'Do you find the prisoner at the bar, Thomas Vickery, guilty or not guilty?'

'Guilty.'

'You find him guilty of murder, and that is the verdict of you all?'

'Yes.'

'Thomas Vickery, you stand convicted of murder. Have you anything to say why the court should not give you judgment of death according to law?'

Vickery said nothing. Now no one was looking at him.

They all stood. The judge's clerk fussed round the green-and-gold chair, placing a square of black flannel, point-forwards, on the judge's wig. The clerk wore a swallow-tailed coat, which Rumbelow knew to be specially bought for such occasions, and allowable from income-tax.

'Thomas Vickery, the sentence of the court upon you is that you be taken from hence to a lawful prison, and thence . . .' Even the fox-hunter faltered over his instrumentality in sending a man to oblivion. 'And thence to a place of execution and that you be hanged by the neck until you are dead, and that your body be buried within the precincts of the prison within which you shall last have been confined before your execution, and may the Lord have mercy upon your soul.'

'Amen,' said the chaplain.

Rumbelow turned. Vickery was being led out of sight like a sleepwalker. The judge departed very quickly. Everyone started to leave the court, suddenly making a lot of noise.

'That fellow was very foolish,' observed Peter Ivors, walking with Rumbelow down the corridor. 'He should never have made up the story that she hanged herself in the first place. I suppose he had to think of something on the spur of the moment. He should have said they'd had a fight, that he hit her and found he'd killed her. Then he'd have got off with fifteen years for manslaughter. Murderers should take counsel's opinion before talking to the police.'

'Or before doing the murder?' Rumbelow was in a good mood.

Ivors took off his large round glasses, rubbing his eyes with the back of his hand. Rumbelow noticed how exhausted he looked.

'Perhaps Vickery was right, sticking to his tale. It doesn't look too good to change it. Or perhaps he was just vain, and thought he could fool us all?' He put the glasses on again. 'Murderers are really very stupid. And murder is really such a simple crime. It takes much more in the way of brains to do a decent robbery.'

As Rumbelow left the court, several pressmen took his photograph. He was suddenly elated. The result of any trial was in his own mind never cut and dried. As Ivors had said, it was as uncertain as the races. But they had won. The judge had been fair, even complimentary in his summing-up. He had beaten Urrick–discredited him, crushed him completely. It all added up. It would be remembered by the jury at their next encounter. His own reputation stood higher than ever. Life was really very pleasant.

He strode rapidly towards the Embankment and into Blackfriars. As he came down the corridor he noticed with shock his laboratory door ajar. Then he remembered his concession to the charwoman. He pushed it open and found Quinley inside.

'What the devil are you doing here?'

The young man was leaning over the workbench. He spun round. 'Oh! I . . . I'm sorry, sir. I found the door open, so I came in.'

'What business have you to?'

Quinley held out a white foolscap envelope. 'I'd a letter for you, sir. It's a copy of my application for the new job. I was going to slip it under the door.'

'You know perfectly well how I dislike people nosing about.'

'I only looked in for a moment.' Quinley looked agonizedly apologetic. 'Perhaps I was prompted by curiosity.'

'Curiosity? You've been in here often enough.'

'I suppose I was fascinated to find myself in the holy of holies alone.' Rumbelow said nothing. 'Honestly, sir, I wasn't prying.'

'You wouldn't get far.' He produced a bunch of keys. 'Every drawer and cabinet is locked.'

'I'm awfully sorry, sir.'

Rumbelow took off his overcoat, and laid it carefully on the spoke-backed chair. 'Give me that letter.'

'Perhaps you'd rather not be troubled—'

'No, give it to me. I promised I'd help. Help I shall.'

'I'd be tremendously grateful if you'd look through it.' Quinley sounded a little encouraged. 'I don't know if I've said the right thing.' He handed over the envelope. 'I'm really most grateful.'

Rumbelow grunted. Quinley left, carefully closing the door behind him. Rumbelow unlocked a drawer under his workbench, threw in the letter, and locked it up again.

From his jacket he took his pocket diary. Vickery was officially given three weeks to compose his soul, but there would be an appeal, which would delay matters. It would certainly be dismissed–the man had been convicted on indisputable facts, there was no misdirection in law. The appeal would be heard towards the end of May. The most likely day after that was Tuesday, the second of June. Rumbelow made a note under the date: ?*Vickery, post-mortem.* Another addition to his superb collection of broken necks.

Chapter Sixteen

The attack started the next morning.

Rumbelow always kept his daily paper for the train from Lower Sydenham to Charing Cross. That day's leading article was expectedly a dissection of Mr Chamberlain's budget, but he was flattered to notice a shorter editorial headed *The Vickery Case*, his own name prominent in the first paragraph. It said,

'Vickery has been found guilty and condemned to death. His fate lay in the answer to a simple question–did his bigamous wife, Eileen Durban, hang herself or not? The jury obviously could not make up their own minds on the delicate points of forensic medicine by which this answer might be determined. They had to take the experts' word for it. Dr Rumbelow said she did not hang herself. Dr Urrick said she did.

'That Dr Rumbelow's word was accepted with little question–the jury were absent for barely an hour–is a disturbing inference from this distinguished expert's regular appearance in the courts. However little Dr Rumbelow would seek it, or desire it, the fact remains that he enjoys something of a reputation for infallibility. Jurymen read newspapers like everyone else. They remember Dr Rumbelow's evidence in former trials. They remember it is generally accepted as the truth. The remarks about Dr Rumbelow in the judge's summing-up, which stopped hardly short of the eulogistic, must have confirmed their belief that his version of the tragedy was to be preferred to that of the expert for the defence.

'This is surely a dangerous state of affairs. In important cases of this nature the Crown always has the big battalions. That Dr Rumbelow has a better-known name than Dr Urrick from Edinburgh is indisputable. That it should possibly cost a man his life is unthinkable. There may be a case for the establishment of a medical commission to decide on controversial evidence of this sort. Indeed, the Criminal Appeal Act gave the Appeal Court power to take this step. It will be of interest to see if such a plea is advanced on behalf of the condemned man when his appeal is heard.'

Rumbelow's immediate feeling was of amazement, of outrage at the ingratitude. His evidence had achieved the conviction of a murderer, and now he was being pilloried for it. It was ridiculous! The skill, the work, the experience he had brought to the case deserved instead the heartfelt appreciation of the public, who enjoyed unthinkingly the protection of the law. It was arrogant to question the opinion of judge and jury. He would never have expected it from such a responsible newspaper. Then he wondered if the anonymous journalist bore some grudge against him, was blackening his reputation to make one for himself. It was pompous, it was unnecessary, but of course everyone at Blackfriars would read it with relish, and he must prepare to have his leg pulled.

He walked into the hospital, carrying his attaché case with his dress clothes in it, deciding for once not to look into the committee-room for his letters. But as he was passing, the door opened and Bantrell came out.

'Well, John Rumbelow! You're hitting the headlines this morning.'

Rumbelow noticed a newspaper under his arm. 'They must have been very short of something to write about,' he said with exceptional modesty.

'You've seen it?' Bantrell opened the paper, which Rumbelow saw to his horror was not his own, but a cheap popular one he had hardly read in his life. 'Quite a spread they've given you. Almost a whole page.'

Rumbelow saw a photograph of himself. Next to it was one of Evan Greensmith. A headline above asked, IS HE DR GOD? He started to read the first paragraph, set in bold type.

'At the beginning of George Gissing's strangely neglected novel *New Grub Street*, a family are sitting down to breakfast in the country when the parish clock strikes eight. Someone says cheerfully over his boiled egg, 'There's a man being hanged in London at this moment . . .'

Rumbelow's eye ran more quickly down the columns. It was the same argument as the editorial's–was it right for a man's life to depend on

Rumbelow's reputation? But it was more pungent, more flamboyant in language. What irritated Rumbelow most was the author's sly impression of knowing him intimately, of their meeting constantly in the houses of fashionable London hostesses, of Rumbelow's relish for a social reputation gained from other men's necks. It even suggested he was something of an uncouth stranger in the elegant, civilized world decorated by Evan Greensmith himself. Rumbelow finished reading with a gasp, as though he had been struck. Bantrell was standing in silence, grinning at him.

'All this is . . . is most uncalled for,' said Rumbelow savagely.

'I didn't know you were a pal of Evan Greensmith's?'

'But I hardly know the man. I only met him once. God knows why he took it into his head to write this rubbish.'

'It's almost libellous, isn't it? Perhaps you can sue him, and get vast damages?'

'Oh, these newspapers have every word carefully read by a barrister,' replied Rumbelow seriously. 'I can only suppose Greensmith was paid for it handsomely.'

'With his name on the top, a lot of people will read it.'

'But it's all so puerile! It will amuse the students, at least. I can't believe anyone else would take it at its face value.'

He thrust the paper at Bantrell, and strode down the corridor to the security of his laboratory. Bantrell himself hurried out and across the main courtyard. It was just on ten o'clock, when he should catch Cramphorn going into the surgical block to start his ward-round. Sure enough, the surgeon was as usual stepping briskly towards the entrance, a white coat over his tweed suit, his houseman at his side. Bantrell caught them up.

'I say, Crampers, can you spare a second?' Cramphorn stopped, not looking particularly pleased. 'I thought you'd care to glance at this article in the morning's paper. It's about Rumbelow.'

'Eh? What?' Cramphorn inspected it through his half-moon glasses. The houseman moved away discreetly. He grunted as he finished reading, handing it back. 'A bit much, isn't it?'

'It's strong, admittedly. Though there's more than a germ of truth in it. I'm sure you'll agree with that?'

'No smoke without fire, I suppose,' Cramphorn admitted.

'I'm afraid Rumbelow imagines he's got some sort of Divine right in the witness-box,' Bantrell observed sorrowfully. 'We all know that. And I'm afraid he's a terrible snob. We all know that as well.'

'What do you expect me to do about it?'

'I don't see what any of us can do about it. I only thought I should bring it to your notice. It isn't very good for Blackfriars, these sort of things appearing in the papers. If the public's persuaded to lose faith in Rumbelow, they may lose faith in us all.'

'Shouldn't imagine so.'

'The hospital's mentioned by name. A lot of patients, and potential patients, will have read it.' Bantrell hesitated. 'I *did* wonder if you wanted to bring it officially to the notice of the committee? A letter might be written to the editor, deploring it.'

'What's the point? By then, people will have forgotten it.'

'But it's there in black and white—'

'It's only a newspaper, Bantrell. Tomorrow morning, everyone will have wiped their arses on it.' Cramphorn strode off.

Bantrell stood staring irritably after him. It really was frustrating. Rumbelow had clearly been responsible for the throwing of discredit and doubt on the hospital. But the senior surgeon himself couldn't see it. 'Crampers is an oaf,' murmured Bantrell. It was not the first time he had regretfully doubted his senior's intelligence.

Rumbelow meanwhile sat alone on the high stool in his laboratory, unable to start work. He kept telling himself it was childish to become angry over such personal attacks. He was still puzzled by both articles. His mind went back to Sir Arthur Younghusband's objections to his remaining in court on the first morning of the trial. Perhaps Younghusband was behind it, somehow trying to salvage political advantage from his defeat? Everyone knew his ambitions to join the Government. Bantrell was of course simply jealous of himself, Rumbelow decided. Yet he had not *sought* to become a public figure. He certainly made less money than Bantrell, much less than surgeons like Cramphorn or Graham Trevose. It was all so mysterious and so unfair.

He unhooked the receiver from his old-fashioned telephone and asked for Lady Accrington's number.

There was a long delay in reaching her. It occurred to him that she might well still be in bed. When she finally came on the line he realized he really had no idea what he intended to say.

'Did you see that article about me this morning? By Evan Greensmith.'

'In the newspapers? I hardly ever read them these days. They're so unreliable.'

'It wasn't very pleasant. It upset me very much.'

'How unfortunate.'

There was a pause. 'I wondered if you might possibly have some notion of what impelled him to write it.'

'I? But why should I?'

'Greensmith and I met only once. That was at luncheon in your house.'

'My dear Dr Rumbelow, I can't concern myself with all the little quarrels of my guests. I should never have a moment's peace if I did. Literary people can be quite savagely contentious, you know.'

'I'm sorry I troubled you, Lady Accrington.'

'Never upset yourself over what the newspapers say. They have to sell their copies, that's all. Sometimes they print the most awful things about *me*. But I assure you I never lose any sleep over it.'

He hung up the telephone. It had been an unsatisfactory conversation. Then he knew he had wanted reassurance, to learn they were all on his side–the right side–against Evan Greensmith. But he did not seem as important to Lady Accrington that morning as he had imagined. He picked up the telephone again.

'You're lucky to catch me,' said Diana Flavell. 'I was just going shopping.'

'I should very much like to accompany you this evening.'

'Oh, I'm thrilled. See you about nine.'

She made a noise which he interpreted as throwing him a kiss. He took off his jacket with the false cuffs, to begin work again on the Jeavons' entrails. He decided that perhaps Greensmith was only nettled by his saying 'autopsy' was bad English.

Chapter Seventeen

Rumbelow's deepest concern as he rang the bell of Diana's flat promptly at nine that evening was whether she had dined or not. Was he expected to take her to dinner before the party? He had no experience whatever in the social conventions of such occasions. He could hardly invite a woman of her tastes elsewhere than the Savoy or the Ritz Grill. The bill would be two pounds–perhaps three! She might want champagne, oysters, things out of season, though he would certainly order frugally for himself, even plead indigestion. As the maid showed him into the drawing-room, he was relieved at her greeting, 'I hope you haven't eaten? There'll be oodles there, I'm sure.'

He stood smoothing the black bow against his wing collar. It was warmer, and he had left his overcoat behind. 'I don't even know where the party is.'

'Didn't I tell you? It's at Archie Trexley-Blake's.' She seemed to imagine this a complete answer.

'Is that far?'

'Oh, no. Just off the King's Road. Hardly five minutes in a taxi.'

A taxi? Well, I must take such extravagances in my stride, he thought.

Diana stubbed out a half-smoked cigarette. She wore a plain black dress, tight-fitting, its shoulder-straps no thicker than shoe-laces showing off her shoulders and the tops of her breasts. The skirt was in overlaps of fringed material, and reached hardly below her knee. She wore heavier make-up than at their daytime meetings, Rumbelow noticed, and a perfume that made a new experience for his nostrils. He was most uneasy. He was starting an adventure so strange to him it was almost unbelievable. He had no idea exactly how it would end, which disturbed him with any new happening. He had the greatest difficulty picturing himself alone with Diana afterwards. The prospect of access to her willing body was less exciting than alarming. But he deserved a gay evening, he told himself. The day which should have warmed him with triumph had turned out sullen. He saw less clearly his need for the comfort of acceptance by society, the respect of people he himself respected, who would see those newspaper attacks for what they were, simply shafts of well-paid malevolence.

The maid appeared with a full-length mink coat.

'You were certainly all over the papers this morning, weren't you?'

'Was I? I never pay much attention to them.'

'*Don't* you? I thought you read avidly every word they printed about you?'

'What on earth gave you that impression?'

They left the flat, Rumbelow taking her arm. He hailed a taxi outside in Basil Street, and sat back holding her hand.

She laughed. 'Does your wife know you're out?'

He knew she was teasing, but it offended him. 'My wife never questions where I go.'

'She probably imagines you're digging up some corpse or other.'

'She might.'

'Well! *That's* not a very flattering alibi from my point of view.'

'I'm sorry, Diana. As a matter of fact, she thinks I'm at an official dinner,' he admitted with unusual frankness. 'I'm not going home tonight. I've taken a room at the club.' He wondered if she would make some encouraging comment on this. She said nothing. 'One can be quite comfortable there,' he went on. She was still looking through the window. He made to kiss her. After all, she was a woman of easygoing virtue who would think nothing of it. And he had to start somewhere. She pushed him away. 'You'll ruin my lipstick.' She added quietly, 'Later, later.'

The taxi turned off the King's Road and stopped in one of the dingy Chelsea streets which were being steadily eliminated by the huge newly rising blocks of service flats. It was a terrace house, narrow, of four storeys, the first-floor windows open and emitting a good deal of noise. The front door was ajar. He followed Diana up a steep boxed-in stairway with a tasselled rope for a handrail, his eyes on the level of her silk-covered ankles. The room upstairs ran the depth of the house, ending under a broad skylight suggesting a studio, though there was no sign of painting equipment. The furnishing was modern, the chairs scarlet leather across chromium-plated tubing. The place was crowded. There seemed to be opened bottles everywhere. He couldn't see anything to eat at all.

Diana threw her mink unconcernedly over one of the chairs, waving and calling out names and blowing kisses all round the room. A radiogram in the corner was playing a comic tune even Rumbelow could recognize, *The Music Goes Round and Round*. He noticed with a shock nobody else wore evening dress. The men were in their street clothes, one to his horror in a tweed sports-jacket. The women were dressed sloppily, mostly in brightly-coloured skirts and loose blouses, some with vivid chiffon scarves round their necks or festooned with beads and bangles. He supposed they were all the arty kind. Misgivings stirred in him. They were not at all the sort of people he cared to mix with. It was not at all the sort of place he wished to be. Then he saw on the far side of the room that a figure he'd taken for a small boy was in fact an adult, a dwarf, alone and looking unhappy.

'Why, there's an achondroplastic,' he couldn't prevent himself exclaiming. But Diana was tugging him by the sleeve towards a thin, fair, effeminate young man in a white tunic buttoned high round the neck like a Russian peasant's.

'John darling, you must meet Archie Trexley-Blake.'

The young man cringed in mock horror. 'The great Rumbelow! Where've you hidden the body?'

Rumbelow managed a faint smile. He supposed he had a duty to indulge his host. All of them anyway appeared pathetically childish, worse than the students at Blackfriars.

'And where's the murder bag?' asked the young man querulously. 'Don't say you haven't brought the murder bag? Oh, no. We were all hoping you'd show what's inside.'

'I hardly need my instruments on a social occasion. I hope not, at least.'

'But you *must* cut somebody up for me. I absolutely insist. There's lots of people I'm longing to know what's inside. I'm sure when my father died they found he was stuffed with cigar-butts and the ends from sticks of sealing-wax. Some of my friends must be nothing but masses of tiny compressed coiled springs, and would simply explode all over the floor once you slit them apart.' He caught a girl hurrying past with a glass of champagne in her hand. 'Or hundreds and hundreds of Coty's pink powder-puffs. Janet darling, this is Dr Rumbelow. He's come to cut you open.'

She gave a theatrical show of alarm.

'I hope there'll be no occasion for that for many years.' The chivalry sounded elephantine even to Rumbelow himself.

'Tell us all about a hanging,' she asked brightly. 'What happens?'

'Can you actually hear something when the neck breaks? Like a muffled pistol-shot?'

'I don't attend the execution.'

'Yes, but you must know what goes on,' she insisted. 'Do they have chaplains intoning the burial service as they all walk along?'

'With a bell tolling like mad in the background?'

'Is the condemned man really allowed to have exactly what he likes for breakfast?'

'And one last wish?'

'Do they always play draughts with the warders?'

'I do hope the warders let them win.'

'Do they actually have to walk up thirteen steps?'

'Or is the whole thing bogus? They simply fill the chap up with drugs, don't they, so he hasn't the slightest idea what's happening to him?'

'I'm afraid I'm not at liberty to disclose official secrets.'

'You *are* a fuss-pot,' said the girl.

'It's a serious matter, you know. If I did, I could face a criminal charge.'

'*We* won't tell on you. Will we, Janet?'

'Be a sport. Do give us the grisly details.'

'We're absolutely *aching* to hear.'

'I should prefer not to discuss my work at all,' said Rumbelow firmly.

The girl laughed. 'I think he's utterly bogus, don't you?'

'You've been invented by Sax Rohmer, like Dr Fu-Manchu,' said the young man. 'Come on, confess it.'

Two others came up and dragged the pair away, to Rumbelow's deep relief. What a ridiculous conversation! he thought. It was really most irritating, people having no idea how he deserved to be treated seriously. But he supposed such young things had little respect for anybody. Anyway, strangers often reacted oddly when he was introduced. He looked round for Diana, but she had disappeared. The radiogram had an automatic device for changing the records, and was now playing *Cheek to Cheek*. He wished she had suggested dinner *tête-à-tête* instead, and blow the expense. On a chromium-legged table beside him was a bottle of scotch and some glasses. He poured himself a whisky-and-soda, though usually he never touched spirits.

Another girl came up and asked if he knew Boris Karloff. He replied he had no acquaintances in the world of films. 'He was coming tonight, you know,' she told him. 'Though he's not a monster at all. He's just like a colonel from India who plays cricket.'

Rumbelow eased himself away from the noisy crowd, flattening himself against the wall, hoping no more of these peculiar persons would notice him. After some time another man and two girls came up to ask him about the

Vickery case, but drifted away apparently finding him dull. He discovered himself next to a small man with brilliantined hair and horn-rimmed glasses, in a badly-fitting blue suit and holding a glass of beer. Rumbelow would have put him down as a clerk. He was saying to Trexley-Blake in a flat, matter-of-fact voice, 'Yes, we use gas.'

'What, like in the cooker?'

'Same principle.'

'I suppose it is.'

'Mind, we don't do them all at once. The service takes twenty minutes, and it's the best part of a couple of hours to incinerate a human body. We've only one furnace, though they're talking of expanding.'

'I hope you haven't much backlog of work?'

'They're all done the same day. We've an unwritten rule about that.'

'What's left at the end?'

'Coffin ash. Handles, and that. Bones. The skull, often. We break it up with a hammer.'

'That's the official ashes?'

'Not quite. We grind it up. It ends the consistency of castor sugar.'

'Ah, but what about the gold teeth?'

'Sold off, and a cheque goes to charity.'

'I hope I shan't need your services for a while, but such shining honesty I find reassuring.'

'Have to be honest. Short-sighted policy otherwise, isn't it?'

'I thought you just bundled three or four stiffs in your crematorium together, and sold the coffins back to the undertakers?'

'You've been reading stories.'

Rumbelow felt himself nudged. It was the man in the green sports-jacket, fat and red-faced, in his hand a glass with some bright red liqueur. 'What's your line?'

'I am a doctor.' Rumbelow decided to let it go at that.

'Go on? I'm a slaughterman.'

'A slaughterman!'

'Yes, at the abattoir up in Islington. We do the killing for Smithfield Market.'

Rumbelow moved quickly away. An idea was forming in his mind, a suspicion so ridiculous, so terrible that he couldn't bring himself to delineate it with logical thought. He searched for Diana, but she was talking animatedly to someone and only waved at him. Some couples in the middle started to dance, he noticed, holding each other very close. Then he was comforted to see another man in evening dress. He was almost at his elbow, also abandoned by the others, pale, grey-eyed, with fair hair cut very short. Rumbelow struck up a conversation, to discover he was a foreigner.

'You speak very good English.'

'Thank you. All of us at the Embassy do our best with your formidable tongue.'

'Which Embassy?'

'Of the German Reich.'

'Oh.' Rumbelow could not remember having spoken before to one of the nation which had killed his brother. He added by the way of making conversation, 'Your ambassador has just died, hasn't he? I believe I saw it in the papers.'

'Yes, that was a sadness for us all. But perhaps it has opened the way for something important.' Rumbelow made no comment, but the diplomat was eager to be impressive. 'I can tell you that the Führer is shortly to appoint Herr von Ribbentrop to the Court of St James's.'

'What, your Foreign Minister?'

'It shows how valuable the Führer sees the links between our two countries. We shall never fight again. That is out of the question. Together, we can be the greatest force in the entire world.'

'Possibly.'

'Are you an artist?'

'No, I'm a pathologist. Dr Rumbelow.'

A smile lit the German's face. 'You are an important man. I know about you from the newspapers. I am most honoured to meet you.' He clicked his heels. 'I was talking of you only yesterday. To a Dr Bantrell. You know him?'

'Very well. He's a physician on the staff of my own hospital.' What's Bantrell up to with the Germans? Rumbelow wondered.

'It was at a reception in the Embassy. You know perhaps that he has a German mother?'

'I don't think I was aware of it.'

'She was the Countess of . . . the name is from my mind for the moment. I shall look it up the second I get back.' Rumbelow had the impression he meant that exactly. 'Of course, she is now as English as Queen Mary. Though she had something of a bad time during the War. In the days when the Battenburgs had to turn into the Mountbattens, you know, old chap.' He raised his glass. 'I give you a toast. To the amity of our two countries.'

Rumbelow matched his gesture hesitantly. 'I'm no apologist for the British Empire, please understand that.'

'Why should you be, Doctor? It is magnificent! The Führer has great respect for your Empire. He offers it only peace, as he does to all nations.' At least this fellow's more complimentary than the American journalist at Mrs Mavery's, Rumbelow thought. He saw the German looking at him appraisingly, and wondered for a moment if he were about to be entrusted with secret information, or even invited to perform some minor act of treason. 'If you would like to see the Olympics at Berlin in August, Doctor, I might be able to arrange something for you.'

'That is very kind,' said Rumbelow politely.

They drifted away. The room was becoming noisier. Now all the young people were dancing in the middle. Rumbelow found himself next to an old man with a pointed beard, gazing on the scene with an expression of bottomless sorrow. Then he saw it wasn't a man, but a bearded lady, the sort you paid to stare at in freak shows.

'Darling, you look terrifically bored.' Diana was at last beside him. 'Of course, you can't know a soul, can you?'

'I've certainly little in common with anyone.'

'Who's the other man in the stiff shirt?'

'A German. From their Embassy.'

She laughed. 'I suppose he's one of the horrors.' She put her arms round his neck and made kissing motions, her lips an inch from his. 'Are you cross that I asked you?'

'Why should I be?'

'Come on. Let's go home.'

'I'm not very good at parties, I'm afraid.'

'We'll see what you are good at.'

She took his hand, and snatching up her mink hurried down the steep staircase. It occurred to Rumbelow he had not taken leave of his hostess, nor was he aware who his hostess was, but he supposed it didn't matter.

Chapter Eighteen

They took another taxi. When Diana let herself into the flat there was no sign of the maid. Rumbelow wondered absently if the girl slept somewhere about the place. Diana went straight into the bedroom, throwing her coat over another chair. He followed automatically.

'Perhaps it was all a bore, that party.'

'Not entirely. Some of the people looked quite interesting.'

'No, they were all bores, crashing bores.'

She stuck a cigarette in her mouth. He saw a petrol-lighter on a dressing-table skirted with folds of pink satin. He flicked it and she leant towards the flame. 'Are you musical?'

'Why do you say that?'

'Your hands. You use them with such lightness, such precision, such economy of movement, like a concert pianist.'

'No, I'm not musical at all.'

She turned her back. 'Unzip me, darling.'

She slipped off the black dress, throwing it on top of her fur coat. Underneath she was wearing camiknickers. Rumbelow had noticed the thin pink shoulder-straps slipping from careful hiding under those of her dress. She sat on the bed and started detaching her silk stockings from their pink suspenders. She looked at him mockingly. 'Aren't you taking anything off?'

He removed his jacket and laid it carefully on a stool in front of the dressing-table. As he undid his dress-waistcoat she stepped out of her underclothes. 'No *soutien-gorge*.' She grasped her breasts with both hands and directed the nipples at him. 'Nice eh?'

Rumbelow was beginning to feel alarmed. This was not the woman he had met at Mrs Mavery's lunch-table. She was wearing only a pink suspender-belt, which she unhooked and threw on the rest of her clothes. He noticed her pubic hair was jet-black. That on her head must be bleached, which hadn't occurred to him. She picked up her cigarette again and lay on the bed. She started to sing *The Isle of Capri*, a tune which had always struck him as vulgar.

'What's the matter?' She laughed. 'You must have seen millions of bodies.'

'I'm not much of a ladies' man.'

'Of course you are. All men are.' She patted the bed reassuringly. 'Why are you so nervous?'

He would by then have liked to rush from the flat, but he decided that would in some way be cowardly. 'I'm just a little out of my depth, that's all.'

'Come and sit down. We must have a little chat.'

As she put her arm round him he saw the bristles where she had shaved her armpit, and thought it odd to notice such details.

'But must you be so shy?'

'I told you, I'm not used to women.'

'You can't be shy with your wife.' Rumbelow gave no reply.

'Tell me about her.'

'Is this quite the time and place?'

'Oh, yes. It seems to be for most men.'

'There's not much to say about her.'

'Is she good between the sheets?'

It was the casual intimacy of her questioning which snapped one of his strongest inhibitions. 'She's useless to me. Like a marble statue lying at my side. She isn't a wife. Only in name. She's my housekeeper, that's all.'

He had made this revelation to no other living soul, but Diana seemed unmoved by it. 'You picked a loser, darling.'

'It's hardly my fault. One can't tell these things beforehand.'

'Surely you slept together before you married?'

'I never touched her. My father was a clergyman. I was brought up strictly. Not that I regret that. The life any man builds for himself can be a rickety affair. It's best to have firm foundations.'

She leant over to stub out the cigarette. It struck him that she never seemed to smoke more than half of one.

'I didn't know much of the world when we married. Nothing of women at all. Only what I'd learnt in hospital. And that's all distorted. You're only handling people who are in trouble or in pain, sick or dying. You begin to imagine the whole world's the same. You get in the habit of keeping yourself aloof, detached from other people's problems. People imagine doctors are kindly. But we're not. In our hearts, we're utterly contemptuous of humanity, I think.'

'So it's a success story? Parson's son makes good? There's a joke somewhere in my mind. About "over my dead body".'

'I wish everyone wouldn't keep coming back to that,' Rumbelow said irritably.

But she was finding the conversation tedious, and started unbuttoning his flies. 'Well, darling, at least you're in the mood, I see.'

There are some things beyond any man's inhibitions, Rumbelow thought a little gloomily. He was averse to exposing himself before Diana. After all, she was a woman he really knew so little. As her fingers eased out his penis, he consoled himself that such directness was probably commonplace in her set. As he looked at her, his expression was of pathetic helplessness.

'Before we go on, darling, there's one little thing. What present had you in mind?'

'Present?'

'I'm a businesswoman. You have to be, these days.'

'I don't think I understand . . . of course, if there's anything you fancy in the shops—'

She took her hand away, and made a gesture rubbing thumb and forefinger. 'Cash.'

He was astounded. 'I . . . I thought you want . . . you wanted me.'

'I do, darling. I can assure you that you wouldn't be here otherwise. But I've got to live.'

It was almost too difficult for him to grasp. 'So you're . . . you're a prostitute?'

'That's putting it rather ungenerously, isn't it?' Her voice had an edge to it.

'But you quote poetry!'

'I don't exactly walk the pavements of Shaftesbury Avenue in high heels and an imitation fox-fur, you know. I choose my friends extremely carefully. You don't know how privileged you are.'

'I can't believe it! I just can't believe it. We met at Mrs Mavery's. I could never imagine for one moment she'd allow your sort of person under her roof.'

Diana sat up abruptly. 'Get out.'

He sat staring at her. To find himself with a prostitute–one of those whose worn-out bodies came so regularly under his knife in the mortuary–was an unbelievably sudden and terrifying degeneration. He had been thrown headlong amid the mass of human beings whom he handled dead, and despised. She grabbed a pink chiffon dressing-gown with a feathery collar. 'Go on. Get out.'

'You should have made your profession clear to me,' he said severely.

'God! What a stuck-up swine you are.'

'I have my name to think about. Which is more than you have.'

For a second she looked at him calmly. Then she spat in his face. 'Name? What name? Listen, you fool. Do you know why we ask you through our front doors? Because you're a clown. A ghoul or a clown. It's the same thing. You amuse us. You're a stupid and boring little piece of insignificance. But we listen to you because we like revelling in the gory details. It's a little more exciting than reading them in the Sunday papers, like the cook. You're a fad, that's all. Like a boxer or a crooner. And we kill ourselves laughing behind your back.'

He sat with his face set, wiping her spittle slowly with his handkerchief.

'Do you know why I took you to that party?' She was almost screaming at him. 'Do you know? Not for your blue eyes. But because I had to. It was a Chamber of Horrors party. But of course you were far too fond of yourself to notice it, weren't you? We wanted to get Pierpoint the executioner, warders from the condemned cell, maybe some Chicago gangster with his machine-gun. *That's* your place. You're a curiosity, a freak, a monster.'

He silently put on his waistcoat and dinner-jacket. She came and stood close to him–as close as an hour before at the party.

'You despise me, don't you? You damn well despise me. My God, that's funny! Because I think you're contemptible, utterly contemptible. You enjoy making people's flesh creep, don't you? You revel in all the flattery. You love us playing up to you, pretending you're something in society. You're a hypocrite. You're disgusting.'

Rumbelow strode from the room. He slammed the flat door and hurried down the stairs. There was a taxi passing with its flag up. He stopped it and asked for his club. He noticed the driver looking downwards, and realized his trousers were still unbuttoned.

The evening had been a crescendo of humiliation. He sat staring through the taxi window with the strange, almost unremembered sensation of tears coming to his eyes. He realized–he forced himself to realize–every word that woman had said was right. He only wondered how long he had really known as much, in his heart.

'I have not been true to myself,' he murmured. 'I have not been true . . . that is my evil, my one evil. It could be the end of me.'

For a man who had no pity for others, at least he kept none to lavish on himself.

Chapter Nineteen

The train had left Paddington just after seven in the morning, and was puffing with increasing briskness through the threadbare western fringes of London. Rumbelow sat facing the engine, in his striped grey flannel with a carnation in the buttonhole. Sixsmith opposite had his usual blue suit–Rumbelow seriously wondered if he possessed another. Scotland Yard had produced first-class tickets, so they had the compartment to themselves. It was almost a fortnight later, Tuesday May the fifth, and they were travelling to Mortlock for the adjourned inquest on James Jeavons.

'Vickery's garage must be somewhere in this area,' Sixsmith observed.

'When's his appeal?'

'It's not down for hearing yet.'

'It won't get him very far.'

'Mind, he might still end up with life instead.'

'Why should he?'

'There's quite a movement getting up to influence the Home Secretary.'

'Oh, I know that. Though I can't see why the Home Secretary should take the slightest notice. I can't even see the reason for it. Apart from misplaced sentiment, muddled thinking, or plain hysteria.'

'You know what people are, Doctor.'

'Only too well, I assure you.' Rumbelow opened his attaché case on the seat beside him and drew out a thick manilla folder. He was beginning to recover his enthusiasm for work and for life itself. His detractors in the Press had faded away. Even something of a counter-attack had been mounted by the intellectual weeklies, praising him as the world's first truly scientific forensic expert, a pathologist of international fame whom the country should cherish in an age of perilously rising crime. Rumbelow felt these writers were admirably clear-headed men, performing a duty in dispelling public prejudice, and probably paid only meagrely for it.

The wound he had suffered in Diana Flavell's bedroom was more reluctant to heal. He could only take comfort from his own unworldliness. There was no image in his mind of a prostitute who read T. S. Eliot and hung paintings by Picasso on her walls, much less one accepted by even the laxer fringe of London society. He supposed there were degrees of prostitution, like of most unsavoury activities. He remembered reading in some magazine about the grand courtesans of pre-Revolutionary France, who were most important ladies indeed. He even began to worry less about his moral contamination than at the horrific sum she certainly would have expected from him.

But the hurt ran far deeper. His self-esteem had been badly dented–in a man less sure of himself and his abilities it would have been shattered. He had enjoyed the self-delusion of moving in London society as a right, when he was only some kind of macabre entertainment. He would cut away that part of his life for good, however painful the stroke. When the next few days produced an invitation to lunch at Lady Accrington's, he wrote a courteous refusal, then tore the card into tiny pieces and burnt them in the flame of his Bunsen, an unusual act of symbolism. Henceforward he would lose himself in his work.

Rumbelow opened the manilla folder. 'Shall we run through the case now? It'll save us a last-minute rush before the inquest.' Sixsmith nodded. 'As you know, I've reached my opinion. I believe Jeavons died from the effect of arsenious oxide. That's white arsenic, the usual choice for the poisoner. You can buy it anywhere–in weed-killers, rat-poisons, even fly-papers. I extracted almost ten grains from one brand. Enough to kill five adults. And God knows how many flies.'

This was a broad joke for Rumbelow. Sixsmith was glad to find him in a good mood for the expedition. Over the past couple of weeks the doctor had been uncommonly snappish.

'Now for my reasons.' Rumbelow produced a silver propelling-pencil and started checking a foolscap page of numbered handwritten paragraphs. 'It's simply a matter of approaching the case systematically. Like every other in medicine, whether the subject is living or dead.' To Sixsmith, these were familiar footsteps in which he had often plodded. 'We start with the signs and symptoms of the man's last illness. I admit, here we're on weak ground. The weakest in the case. We have to take Halverston's word for everything. He said he found Jeavons collapsed, his pulse thready, his breathing bad. That was at eight in the morning, and he died about five hours later. Halverston put it down to heart-failure consequent to high blood-pressure. Some of these country doctors are the best accomplices any murderer could wish'

'The symptoms are typical of arsenic poisoning, aren't they?'

'Not entirely. In medicine, few things follow a rigid pattern–there'd be no need of our being particularly clever if they did. It's the small variations which mislead you so dangerously. In "typical" acute arsenic poisoning, one would expect severe gastroenteritis–uncontrollable vomiting and torrential diarrhoea. Plus burning of the eyes and mouth and cramp in the calves–Jeavons complained of cramps. I at least got that out of Halverston, you remember. Plus restlessness, sometimes even convulsions. And what's important to this case, the signs of heart failure. Now–in arsenic poisoning irritation of the gut with diarrhoea and vomiting may never happen at all. This is when the dose is so large the patient succumbs rapidly from heart failure. You follow, Sixsmith? The "typical" signs and symptoms may have *no time* to appear before death supervenes.'

'And a large dose was given in this case?'

'It was not in fact very large. But the man's heart was already severely damaged. It needed little more to push it into failure. It would have been exactly the same with other toxic drugs in quite moderate doses.'

Rumbelow moved his pencil down the paper. 'Point two. The post-mortem appearances. Here we can take a firmer stand. It's unfortunate I had to examine the body so long after burial. If that fool Halverston had reported the death to the coroner we should all have been spared a good deal of trouble. Though a fair amount of decomposition had occurred, there were two signs which immediately aroused my suspicion. One was the presence of tiny bleeding points under the lining of the left ventrical of the heart.

They're very common in arsenic poisoning, even with no irritation to be found in the stomach or intestines. Two, yellow streaking outside the duodenum, the highest part of the intestine, just below the stomach. These streaks were likely to be yellow arsenic. That's the sulphate form of the drug, to which white arsenic is converted by putrefaction.'

'But it still remains arsenic?'

'Yes. Arsenic can come in many forms. That's another matter of considerable importance in this particular case, as I shall explain in a minute. Now to our third step, chemical analysis. Here we are unassailable. Arsenic was definitely present in the body. I applied two tests, Reinsch's and Marsh's. They're both well established in toxicology. The results from the Reinsch test were inconclusive, but Marsh's was positive. Absolutely positive.'

'So we can at least take that as definite, Doctor? Death was caused by arsenic.'

Rumbelow leant back, his head against a white antimacassar embroidered G.W.R. 'This case has a very odd complication. One which affects it in two distinct ways. As I said at the p.m., Jeavons suffered from syphilis.'

'Dr Halverston disagreed with that.'

Rumbelow made a dismissive gesture. 'The aorta showed all the changes of syphilis, so did the valve leading to it from the heart. That is quite definite. The defence at the trial–if it comes to a trial– will anyway accept it. It could be their strongest card. You see, Jeavons might well have been undergoing injections of arsenic for this condition. In secret, either in the district or more likely up in London. You should be able to lay hands on the doctor who was giving them, if he exists.'

Sixsmith had his own note-book out. 'You mean, these injections killed him?'

'Not at all. *That* arsenic would be in an entirely different form. Organic arsenic, an arsphenamide, quite unlike the simple arsenical salts used to kill weeds, or rats–or humans. That organic sort of arsenic reacts to neither the Reinsch test nor the Marsh test. There is a special test for it, the Fresenius method, which of course I applied. It was negative. So if Jeavons were having injections containing arsenic, he certainly hadn't received one for several days. That's the time taken for an injection to be completely eliminated from the body. He might well not have had any for months, or even years, or even at all. The disease had done its damage and was quiescent. He was a 'burnt-out case', as the physicians say. But even had I found traces of organic arsenic, they would be totally irrelevant to the simple arsenic I found as well. So if the defence do decide to play that card, you see how easily I can trump it.'

Rumbelow closed the folder, looking pleased with himself.

'It seems an odd coincidence, Doctor?'

'A chance in several thousand. But far from an impossibility.'

'Have there been any other cases with this sort of complication?'

'I've combed the Blackfriars' library, but could find nothing. Of course, the possibility's been mooted often enough. But only as an exercise in theoretical toxicology.'

'Mrs Jeavons might have read something about it in a medical book. It would have given her the idea.'

'I fancy that's putting too fine a point on it. Though keep it in mind. You never know when counsel might find himself in need of more ammunition.'

'We've nothing yet to prove she gave the arsenic with her own hands. And I'm still not happy on a motive which will stand up in court. But she's an impulsive and foolish woman–she must be, coming up and tackling you in the street like that. I'll let her stew for a bit. There's a chance she'll give something away. That's why I don't want a coroner's verdict of murder against her this morning.'

'I shouldn't think that's likely. It's only a couple of months since the Wright report came down on "trial by inquest". How much do you want me to say, or not to say?'

'As little as possible. I'd prefer nothing definite to come out of the inquest. An adjournment *sine die* would suit me very well.'

Rumbelow locked his attaché case. The detective stared at the fleeting, neatly-edged fields of the Thames valley, coloured by spring late that year. The day had started bright but was turning thundery, with heavy drops of rain running almost horizontally across the carriage windows. Sixsmith remembered a joke someone had told him at Scotland Yard, about a man who wanted to kill his wife so 'took his razor and gave her arse a nick'. He wondered whether to tell Rumbelow, but decided the doctor would not be amused.

'I've finished with the newspaper, if you'd like it.'

Sixsmith took the *Morning Post*. 'What's happened about the Budget leak?'

'Parliament's setting up a tribunal.'

'That J.H. Thomas is a bit of a card, isn't he?' There was a photograph of the new King of Egypt, a slim youngster of seventeen called Farouk. Sixsmith wondered if the boy would be half as popular as the new King of England. Opposite was a map of the war in Abyssinia. 'You have to learn too many names of faraway places to keep up with things these days,' he complained.

'You soldiered out in Mesopotamia yourself, didn't you?'

'Yes. Perhaps I never really settled back into the world after the war. When I retire I'm getting right away from it all, I'm buying a bungalow in Jersey.'

'Jersey! That's certainly outlandish. When do you go?'

'I leave the force at the beginning of September, 1939. I'm looking forward to the peace.'

They steamed into Mortlock Station in good time for the inquest. It was held at ten-thirty in the Shire Hall, in a large, oblong, high-ceilinged room rather knocked about. Drawing out his chair, Rumbelow was startled to find several feet of red paper streamer twined round the legs. He supposed the place was hired for dances, and up on the dais with the coroner's desk the band played.

The coroner himself was thin and anxious-looking, in black with a wing collar, a local solicitor. This was the first point against him for Rumbelow, who believed all coroners should be medical men. The second was his opening the proceedings by warning the jury against ascribing to any doctor, however eminent, the gift of infallibility. Words which were galling enough from Sir Arthur Younghusband became in Rumbelow's ears plain insults from such a lowly functionary. He caught Dr Halverston's eye across the room, and fancied the fellow was grinning at him. His third objection was the widow's absence. It was Jeavons' solicitor who gave evidence of identifying the body. There seemed some agreement–or perhaps he should call it conspiracy–to save the woman the publicity of appearing in court. He supposed it was misplaced sympathy, or simply resentment of interfering people coming down from London. But there was nothing Rumbelow could do about it. A coroner alone had the right to call what witnesses he pleased, and in his own court was above correction by anyone.

Dr Halverston gave evidence that the cause of death was heart failure secondary to high blood-pressure. Rumbelow followed him into the witness-box, a portable structure like a low-church pulpit under a wooden umbrella. He said simply that the cause of death was poisoning by arsenic. He imagined almost everybody in court gave a gasp, and looked at each other as though they had just witnessed some horrific sight, like a child knocked down by a motor-car.

'Then you disagree completely with Dr Halverston's opinion of the cause of death?'

'Completely.'

'You found no evidence of heart disease?'

'I did. Of heart disease caused by syphilis.'

This brought another gasp. The coroner seemed unsure how to go on. He folded his hands on the desk, and Rumbelow noticed they were shaking. He's frightened of me! Rumbelow thought. Frightened of my reputation. Or frightened of seeming overawed by it. He felt less enmity towards the man.

'I see. But this–er, form of heart disease was not the cause of death, Dr Rumbelow?'

'No.'

'Not even a contributory cause?'

'That might be possible. Contributory to arsenic poisoning as the immediate cause.'

'Did you find any signs suggesting high blood-pressure?'

'No.'

The coroner asked no more. Perhaps through his agitated state of mind, perhaps prefering to guard his local reputation by appearing to know of syphilis only faintly by hearsay, Rumbelow thought. And Rumbelow was certainly not in the habit of volunteering evidence unasked. He signed his deposition. The coroner adjourned the inquest for three months, seeming glad to push everything from his hands into those of the police.

'More or less what we wanted,' said Sixsmith, as they left the court.

'Quite satisfactory. There's a train at twelve-fifty-five, I saw. I can get a sandwich in the station buffet and catch it.'

'I expect I'll be here for the rest of the week. Could you get down again if necessary, Doctor?'

'Yes, of course.'

Rumbelow made down the main corridor towards a lobby leading on to the front steps. It had a glass roof, the rain of a thunderstorm falling on it loudly. He became aware of someone walking close beside him, and turned to face Halverston.

'You were rather hard on me, weren't you?' The local doctor was plainly struggling to keep his temper. 'Disagreeing so flatly with my opinion. In open court, like that. It'll all get in the newspapers.'

'Aren't you being oversensitive?' Rumbelow stopped impatiently. 'Any clinician's liable to have his diagnosis upset by a pathologist. It happens often enough at Blackfriars. I don't remember any of the consultants objecting.'

'This isn't the same thing.'

'Isn't it? It strikes me as exactly the same principle.'

'Listen, Rumbelow. Jeavons was my patient at Blayford ever since he returned from the East. Now you're saying in public that I misdiagnosed him, that I treated him for the wrong condition. That I even got the cause of his death wrong. You're accusing me of professional negligence, in fact.'

'I'm not at all.'

'Yes you are. You're simply being insulting.'

'You take it as an insult, do you, anyone holding a different opinion from your own? No worthwhile general practitioner would feel insulted at being corrected by a consultant. That's what consultants are for.'

'I take a second opinion readily enough, I assure you. I know my own limitations. But I take them only from consultants I respect.'

The twin plate-glass doors leading to the street were suddenly illuminated by a lightning-flash. 'So you don't respect me?'

'Frankly, I don't. Not after what I've read recently in the newspapers.'

'If you believe all that, you're an even bigger fool than I took you for.'

'How dare you speak to me in that arrogant way! Have you no idea of the proper relationship between one doctor and another? Were you never taught the rudiments of medical etiquette? Or even of ordinary good manners?'

'You are a fool, Halverston, a fool. And I shall show you up.' Rumbelow abruptly opened the glass door, and turning up the collar of his trench-coat hurried down the steps. A policeman in a streaming cape asked if he wanted a taxi.

'No, no, it's only a few minutes, I'll walk.'

He was furious with Halverston. To do one's duty in court, and then to be attacked for it by the very man whose gross mistakes lay at the bottom of the whole case . . . oh, it was stupid, ridiculous, exasperating! If Halverston hadn't liked his evidence, that was Halverston's affair. But he had no right to come up afterwards and berate him for it. The man was an uncouth simpleton. So was the coroner. Perhaps they all were in that part of the country. He was eager to be back in the more civilized atmosphere of London. He paced the rainswept platform angrily. Then he saw a man put a fresh newsvendor's placard outside the bookstall saying RUMBELOW SENSATION and felt better.

Chapter Twenty

Rumbelow was back in London in time for the daily post-mortems at Blackfriars. Then he had his accumulated work in the Central Mortuary. He dined as usual at his club. It was after ten when he trudged up the hill towards his house, still carrying his bag. As there was no light downstairs, Rosemary had gone to bed. Perhaps she was growing tired of dance music.

He let himself in and switched on the hall lamp. He had a sudden feeling of uneasiness. Not being a man to let any irrational sensation pass unanalysed, he hung up his trench-coat and stood trying to account for it. The house was cold. Unusually cold, even for such a chilly evening. Rosemary must have let the kitchen stove go out.

He went to the kitchen and tipped some coke on the dull embers. Returning to the sitting-room, he found a few letters which had arrived after his departure for Mortlock that morning, and glanced through them quickly. There was also a new copy of the *British Medical Journal*, which he unwrapped and stuck under his arm before switching off the lights and making upstairs.

The bedroom was dark, though for once Rosemary had left the curtains undrawn, the yellow glow of the street-lamp outlining the familiar curves and angles. He switched on the reading-lamp and saw the bed was empty.

He stood frowning for a second. He threw open the bedroom door. 'Rosemary!'

He hurried through the house, opening more doors, switching on all the lights.

'Rosemary! Rosemary!'

He found a flashlight in the kitchen and searched the garden, peering under all the bushes and in the dark corners of the fencing. Nothing. He went back into the hall, carefully switched off the torch and laid it on the table. He stood still for almost a minute. He was frightened, an almost unknown sensation for him. Their quarrel in the restaurant came back. Had she killed herself? Was she already dead in the river, or beside some railway track? He had talked of suicide then in a detached, almost intellectual way, but to imagine the act really being accomplished was appalling. Then he wondered if she had been kidnapped, for ransom or out of revenge. There was no sign of a struggle, though he supposed she could easily have been tricked away. He reached for the telephone, about to dial Scotland Yard, but hesitated. She might have been taken ill. Or simply gone out for the evening. Though he felt either event was unlikely to have occurred without his knowledge.

He hurried from the house, leaving the front door wide open. Their neighbour was a middle-aged tea-broker, with a business in Mincing Lane. Rumbelow had exchanged barely a dozen snatches of conversation with him in his life. The house was exactly like his own. As he unlatched the front gate he saw a light behind the sitting-room curtains and heard the familiar rhythm of a dance band. He rang the bell. The tea-broker himself opened the door, immediately looking uneasy.

'May I come in?'

'Of course, of course, Doctor.' The broker was a little bald man with a thick grey moustache and large round glasses, in his shirtsleeves. He fussed Rumbelow into the sitting-room, quickly and stealthily putting on his jacket, as though trying to pretend he was wearing it all the time. Rumbelow noticed the room was much better furnished than his own, with brocade armchairs and deep matching pelmets over the curtains. The broker's wife, fat and in a flowered dress, hastily switched off the radiogram. They both stared as though he had called professionally to dig up the floorboards for bodies.

Rumbelow stood in the middle of the flowered carpet, rather at a loss. 'I called concerning my wife.'

'Not ill, I hope?' asked the broker quickly.

'Oh, no. At least, I sincerely hope not. You see, she's not at home.' This seemed to Rumbelow a scarcely adequate explanation of his presence. 'For various reasons, it's a little worrying. I wondered if you'd seen anything of her, that's all.'

The couple exchanged glances.

'We haven't set eyes on your good lady for some time, Doctor.' The tea-broker shifted from one foot to the other. 'Not for quite some time. Have we, my dear?'

The wife made no reply. Rumbelow stared hard at them in turn. Something made him suspect a conspiracy. 'I only ask your help because I'm concerned with my wife's safety. As you can imagine, I have plenty of enemies in the criminal classes.' Two red spots appeared on the woman's cheeks. 'Unless I've some positive idea where she's got to, I can assure you the police will be here in five minutes.'

This decided the woman to speak. 'Your wife's gone away, Doctor.'

'What do you mean, "gone away"?'

'She's left. Left her home. I saw her go this morning with her suitcase. She had a taxi.'

'But that's impossible!' They offered no comment. 'I think I'm entitled to ask why you didn't tell me as much in the first place?'

The woman stared at the carpet, slowly rubbing her hands.

'We don't care to meddle in other folk's private affairs.'

'But where's she gone? Didn't she say? Did she leave a message?'

The wife shook her head. The tea-broker cleared his throat loudly and began, 'You see, we were on something of the horns of a dilemma, Doctor. It being somebody famous like yourself—'

'Why should she do a thing like that? She never even hinted as much. Certainly never to me. Did she say anything to you?'

As the woman looked up, Rumbelow noticed her dull-looking features wore an expression of bitter reproach. She knows more about me than I imagined, he told himself. Rosemary must have been gossiping, in the hideously intimate way that women did. This tea-merchant's wife has decided I'm to blame for it all. For the second time that day he felt angry. These inconsequential people had no right to form judgments on him. They were nothing compared with him, nothing at all. They only knew him through the sheer accident of his living in the next house. He wanted them out of his sight. 'I wish you were more forthcoming. You might save me a good deal of trouble and anxiety.' He turned and strode from the house, the tea-broker following him to the door, looking aghast and still babbling about the horns of his dilemma.

In his own sitting-room, Rumbelow started searching in case she had left a letter. It was propped on the wireless-set, almost invisible with the pink-fringed standard-lamp unlit. It was written in her clear schoolmistress' hand, on stiff blue paper with a scalloped edge.

Dear John,

You may be surprised that I have left you. But perhaps only because you could not have thought me capable of such resolute action.

I have been near to doing as much several times. More recently, it has come into my head every time you've had to be away. Nothing in particular has made up my mind for me now.

I have always been unhappy with you. I was not happy even before we married, but I hoped that things would get better between us. I know what I am doing is wrong, because I know my responsibilities as a wife. God knows, they have been tested enough.

I am sorry for you, John. But at least you have your work, which is always your first interest. Please don't follow me. I'll be all right. When things become clearer to me, I shall get in touch with you through a third party.

Your wife,
Rosemary

He crumpled the letter and threw it savagely into a corner. He sat in his easy-chair, chin cupped in hand. It was humiliating. It was also genuinely puzzling. Their life together admittedly hadn't been blissful–not in the nonsensical way portrayed by advertisements for instalment-plan furniture and suchlike. But Rosemary had more reason for contentment than most women. In hard times he had given her security, a home–and a reflected glory to warm even her corner of the suburbs. It was most ungrateful of her to leave. Particularly so theatrically. He thought nervously of it getting into the newspapers, making him look ridiculous, drawing irritating sympathy from his friends in the hospital and the courts, and God knows what in the way of jokes behind his back. Then he wondered exactly where she had gone. He assumed back to her parents in Yorkshire. They wouldn't be overjoyed to see her. They might even throw her out again. Well, she was able to look after herself, he supposed. After all, she was basically a sensible woman. He began to calm down.

He returned to the kitchen to make his usual milk drink. It occurred to him she might be back the next morning. Even the most level-headed females did such hysterical things, as they so often ineffectively attempted suicide, simply to call attention on themselves. He decided he would leave matters for the night, that he would write the next day to the address of her parents' farm. He would be careful what he said, because in her absence they would certainly open it. A wire sent immediately might alarm them, and he knew they had no telephone. He went round the house again, locking the doors and carefully switching off the lights. He climbed upstairs and got into bed. He slept soundly, in the knowledge that if you intend to commit suicide you don't take your luggage with you.

Chapter Twenty-one

Whit Monday in 1936 was on June the first, cold and wet like most of the preceding month. Rumbelow rose early, leaving his bed unmade with the depressing knowledge it would be in exactly the same state on his return. He was managing his house with the charwoman–whom he suspected stole his groceries–and she enjoyed the bank holiday off.

He prepared himself two boiled eggs and a pot of tea, eating in the kitchen. In his attaché case he packed some medical journals and a sheaf of post-mortem reports on which he had work to do. Shortly before seven o'clock he made his way in bowler hat and trench-coat down the hill to Lower Sydenham Station. He took the Underground from his suburban train to King's Cross, which was already crowded with day-trippers. The bookstall was open, and he bought a copy of *The Strand Magazine* with a guilty feeling of extravagance. As he was travelling at his own expense, he went third-class.

He hoped for a compartment to himself, but at the last minute a young couple got in and started talking animatedly about King Edward's Coronation, officially proclaimed that Thursday for May the twelfth the following year. An experienced railway traveller, Rumbelow knew that once the excitement of the journey had dwindled they would lapse into tolerable silence. With the magazine on his knees, he stared through the window as the express jerked its way amid the tenements, the compressed terraces of houses and engrimed factories of Islington, then under the wall of the prison he would be visiting the following morning. Since his wife had gone away, he reflected, his professional career had certainly offered that satisfaction which her blue, scalloped-edged letter recommended as a substitute for herself.

Mrs Jeavons had been arrested by Superintendent Sixsmith a week after the adjourned inquest. While she was appearing briefly the next morning in the magistrates' court at Mortlock, a detective-inspector from Scotland Yard arrived at Blackfriars with an empty tin, rusty and unlabelled, found in the garden shed by the police. The detective told Rumbelow the tin was the kind used by a local manufacturer, to contain insecticide for spraying fruit-trees. There were traces of powder still inside, which simple analysis showed Rumbelow to be a mixture of white arsenic and barium carbonate. He supposed she had poured the rest of it down the lavatory, and either innocently imagined the traces too sparse to identify, or had been too frightened to throw the tin out or drop it into some river with a detective's eye always on the door. Anyway, that cooked *her* goose, Rumbelow thought. Though right from his own first appearance in Blayford, the public at large had imagined Mrs Jeavons already arrested, tried, convicted and hanged.

Vickery's appeal had been even more gratifying. A member of Parliament–a Labour man, Rumbelow noted–had several million signatures on a petition for the new King to exercise his prerogative of mercy, and was making speeches about it up and down the country. Attacks on Rumbelow were published again in the papers, with letters signed by collections of academics of impeccable conscience, the same bunch it seemed to him who protested regularly against everything from Italian atrocities in Abyssinia to the addiction of the working class to greyhound-racing. It all left him unmoved. He was even becoming used to such treatment by the public, if he could never be reconciled to it.

Rumbelow attended the appeal himself. It was held towards the end of May, as customary in the Law Courts in the Strand, before three judges in surroundings of elaborately carved light-oak, like the choir-stalls in a Victorian church of a prosperous parish. Vickery sat half-screened by the green curtain of the dock, between two warders and looking as dapper as ever. There were no witnesses. At that stage, his life was obliged to balance only on points of law.

Sir Arthur Younghusband had only one argument. That the judge in his charge had unduly influenced the jury to accept the evidence of Dr Rumbelow in preference to that of Dr Urrick. But he spoke at length, one of the appeal judges seeming to Rumbelow to show plain signs of boredom. As he finally sat down, the judges got into a huddle, whispering fiercely. Thus a man's fate was decided. Rumbelow wondered if they would want to hear from the Crown. But the senior judge in the middle said, 'We need not trouble you, Mr Ivors,' and Ivors rose to bow silently. The senior judge started to deliver the court's decision, painstakingly going over the medical evidence at the trial yet once again. Rumbelow saw the bored judge yawn widely, and felt confident.

'Counsel for the applicant has argued today that the learned judge during the trial was wrong in law–indeed, he put it more strongly than that, was quite improper–in praising the qualifications, experience and methods of Dr Rumbelow to the detriment of those of Dr Urrick. Sir Arthur maintained, in fact, that these two medical gentlemen were of equal worth in the witness-box, and should have been treated as such by the jury. And that it was quite outside the province of the judge to indicate which of them should be believed, or believed to a greater extent that the other.'

The appeal judge paused. 'The court does not accept that argument. Clearly, in any case both sides will call as experienced and skilful medical witnesses as are available to them. But there is nothing whatever to prevent either calling a doctor with little experience in matters of forensic medicine, or with no practical experience in the subject at all. It is not inconceivable that some medical man whose name is a household word–a surgeon, or a heart specialist–might be invited to give his opinion. That might well impress the jury. But the witness' knowledge of forensic evidence could be sketchy, or much like any other busy doctor's. Nothing said by the learned trial judge invaded the jury's province and right of deciding between the two medical experts. His observations about the relative weight of their evidence did not go beyond the limits of permissible comment. Both were distinguished medical men. They gave not only their opinions, but in some considerable detail their reasons for reaching those opinions. From a consideration of this, and from all he had learned in evidence of their comparative experience in similar cases, if the learned judge thought Dr Rumbelow was to be preferred to Dr Urrick, then it was only right he should say so.'

Rumbelow's movement, just easing up the sharp crease of his grey trousers, expressed an infinity of satisfaction.

'Sir Arthur made a further point. It is specific to a case of this nature, depending so largely on the medical evidence. He submitted that his evidence should be referred to arbitration by an independent medical commissioner, to be appointed by this court. Such a procedure is certainly authorized by the Criminal Appeal Act. But the Act makes clear that it is a special and exceptional power for the court to invoke. In this case, the court does not feel what it has heard today justifies such invocation. The medical evidence was correctly summed-up by the learned judge and acted upon by the jury. The court finds no ground to interfere. The appeal is dismissed.'

Vickery disappeared from the public view, for the last time.

As Rumbelow left the building he took out his diary. He had heard from Sixsmith on the telephone that the execution was fixed for June the first, but that must have been a slip of the tongue. He changed the date. It would not be at all proper to hang a man on a bank holiday.

As Rumbelow expected, the couple on the train soon fell silent, and sat staring across the compartment at each other rather sullenly. They got out at Grantham. He went on to Leeds, where he ate a sandwich and caught another train to Harrogate. There he knew he would be obliged to take a taxi. As they motored into the countryside, Rumbelow encountered an unusual sight. Not one aeroplane of the R.A.F. but two of them were making their separate ways across the rainy sky. An uneasy reminder of mankind's new power to destroy itself.

It was early afternoon when he reached the farm. He remembered it perfectly though he had hardly set eyes on the place since his marriage. It was neither large nor elegant, the outbuildings now appearing even more tumbledown and the ugly red-brick farmhouse even more in need of a coat of paint. He saw Rosemary in the front door as the taxi drew up. Rumbelow told the driver he had a train at six, and asked whether he cared to wait. But it was cheaper for the man to go and come back.

'You've had a long journey, John.' She didn't smile at him.

'It's a public holiday. I've not much else to do.'

There was no sign of her parents, to his relief. She took him into the small, neat, musty front room which he knew to be reserved for formal visitors. It was chilly, the well-blacked grate containing a fan of folded shiny white paper spattered with soot. The mantelpiece was covered with tasselled crimson cloth, and bore pictures of the family in silver frames. As he anticipated, his own had been removed. They sat opposite one another in a pair of high-backed chairs stuffed with horsehair, which were very uncomfortable.

'Why did you have to come?'

'I wanted to see you again.'

'I imagined you wouldn't be particularly sorry at getting rid of me.'

'You can't just switch a marriage off like the electric light, you know.'

He took out a cigar and cut it. He was surprised how at home he felt in the bleak little room, where he hadn't been alone with her since his days as a suitor.

'I'm only prepared to discuss strictly practical things, John.'

'So you said in your letter. I only wondered which ones.'

'Well . . . whether you wanted a divorce. Things like that.'

'A divorce is somewhat chillingly final.'

'You can't persuade me to come back to you. I hope you realize that?' She sounded a little hysterical.

'Oh, I shan't get down on my knees or throw myself at your feet, don't worry.' He lit the cigar. 'I thought you meant about money.'

She shook her head vigorously.

'You've got a job?'

'I'm helping on the farm.'

He suspected it was a superfluous assistance. 'You might find a teaching post if you searched hard enough in the newspapers, you know. People say times are beginning to look up. Though I'm quite prepared to make you a reasonable allowance. That's only right.'

'I don't want a penny.'

'Why did you leave?' She said nothing. 'And in that manner? It was most embarrassing.'

'I'm sorry.'

'Did it occur to you, the same end could have been achieved with considerably less drama had you told me of your intentions?'

'How could I speak to you about it? I never spoke to you about anything I really felt.'

'Whose fault was that?'

She rubbed the palms of her hands together uncomfortably. 'Mine, I suppose.'

'Yes, it was. I had the right to know at least something of what went on in your head.'

'The right!'

'Marriage has its duties. But you always took a rather selfish view of ours.' She refused to be drawn. 'It's not very pleasant, you know, living alone.'

For the first time in the room her eyes met his. 'I told you, there's no chance of my coming back.'

'That's your emotions speaking. As they spoke when they told you to leave home so suddenly. But listen, Rosemary. We're intelligent persons. We're mature. We've no need to behave like the children who get married today as soon as they're twenty-one. We can sit down and talk things over. All this . . .' He gave the room a depreciating glance. 'It's only an incident. We can forget about it. We need never mention it again. Hundreds of couples go through a similar sort of crisis every month of the year. I'm certain of that. No one gets to hear about it. They even begin to convince each other it never really happened. The most successful marriages are conspiracies of silence.'

'I know why you're asking this. Only because my absence might be an embarrassment to your career.'

'That's not the case at all.' He looked uncomfortable. She was only partly correct. He was genuinely lonely, and wondered how far he should go in admitting he missed her.

'You know it wouldn't work, John. It's not just my getting emotional, bottling it up till the cork blows off. There's that other business.'

'Your failure in the sexual department? I don't see that as a fundamental difficulty. In time we could overcome it. I'm sure there's some treatment.'

'I don't want any treatment.' She looked at him bitterly. 'You seem to imagine my body's yours, to do as you please with. But it isn't. It's mine, mine alone. It couldn't belong to you or to any man alive. I think all that part is loathsome–horrible, filthy, disgusting.' She turned her eyes away, and added in a helpless voice, 'I'm not made for marriage. That's all there is to it.'

He sat gently puffing his cigar. He perceived her feelings only dimly. He had learnt gynaecology at Blackfriars, but it was only a study of the machine for reproduction, with such airy peculiarities never mentioned. He decided he wouldn't press her, and for once wouldn't dominate her. Though that was the sensation he missed most from her absence. 'Very well. If that's final, I suppose a divorce can be obtained.'

'I don't want a divorce. Not if it will embarrass you.'

'It's a matter of law, isn't it? The law sees the attachment of man and wife as a singularly powerful bond. In many things they become simply one person. For them to live apart, never even to set eyes on one another, makes a nonsense of it.' He flicked his cigar-ash on to the sooty paper in the grate. 'I shall allow you to sue me. It's the gentlemanly thing to do, it appears. I shall go with some professional woman to Brighton. It will be in the papers, but some annoyances can't be helped. I'll get a firm of solicitors to write to you. One which specializes in the shadier side of practice. After all, I'm acquainted with plenty of them.' He took out his watch. 'I'm afraid I must continue to embarrass you with my presence. My train for Leeds isn't until six. Then I have a wait for the slow train at midnight. It'll be five in the morning before I reach London.'

'Poor John! You've had such a long trip, and all for nothing.' For the first time she looked tenderly at him. She felt guilty and ashamed, and sorry for him. But she dared to show it only over irrelevant details. 'Are you hungry?'

'I've no appetite today.'

'How about a cup of tea?'

He nodded. As she left him he stood up, and still smoking his cigar examined carefully the photographs, the china ornaments and other uninspiring objects in the room. When the door opened he did not for the moment look round, then he saw to his disconcertion it was not Rosemary but her father.

'Well! The famous Dr Rumbelow. I suppose we should feel ourselves honoured, having you here?'

He was a thick-set, grey-haired Yorkshireman in his fifties. Rumbelow had always despised him, even more than his neighbours in London. He wondered how pressingly Rosemary had tried to keep him out of the way. 'Feel how you wish. I only took the trouble of coming here to discuss a matter which concerns Rosemary and myself.'

'Aren't you ashamed? Of the way you've treated her?'

'I am not. And you have no reason to suggest as much. You don't know the full story.'

'Oh, yes, I do. Or as much as I need to. You married my daughter when you were an ordinary doctor, struggling to get on. There's half a dozen of them I could name in this area, killing themselves to keep up appearances without a couple of ha'pence to their name. Now you find yourself famous, you've no time for her. That's it, isn't it?'

'You can accuse me of what you like. Anyone can, if they're not particular about the truth.'

'You don't seem to care that you've ruined her life. All that money and effort it took for her to train as a teacher! It was a great achievement. A great achievement. And she gave it up. Gave up her job, everything. Just for you.'

Rumbelow regarded becoming a school-teacher as an achievement hardly worth mentioning, and as for the job he had seen himself as her saviour in releasing her from it. 'The facts speak for themselves, if only you'd open your eyes and look at them. Rosemary left our home of her own free will. She didn't even favour me with a warning, a hint. It was a great shock to me. I came here today inviting her to return. She refuses. You have no argument. You have nothing to reproach me with at all.'

Rumbelow staggered back in alarm as his father-in-law grabbed the lapels of his suit. 'If I were a few years younger, I'd thrash you.'

'Take your hands off me! This is completely uncivilized.' The farmer started shaking him. 'If you're not careful, you'll be facing a summons for assault.'

'You're not in bloody court now. Hiding behind the law, that's your game, isn't it? It's time you faced the world like a man.'

Rumbelow was afraid the man would lose his temper and hit him. But Rosemary appeared in the door with a tray of tea-things. He released his hold, giving a look of disgust. 'I've no time for you. Get out of my house, just as soon as you've done your business. Don't try to come back. Leave my daughter in peace. She's had enough of you.'

He gave Rosemary a sullen glance, but he left them alone together. They drank the tea almost in silence. The rain had stopped, so afterwards they went for a walk in the country. They talked about the Jeavons case and other impersonal things. When the time came for Rumbelow to leave, they were quite good friends.

Chapter Twenty-two

Rumbelow had left a clean collar and a razor in the laboratory at Blackfriars. By seven the next morning he was sprucing himself in the consultants' lavatory behind the committee-room, when Graham Trevose walked in.

'You're up early, John.' The slim, gnome-like plastic surgeon was as usual dressed even more stylishly than Rumbelow.

'I've just got off a train from the north.'

'Poor fellow. I hope you had a decent week-end. The weather's so miserable.'

'It was something of a duty call.'

'I got back last night from Paris.'

Trust Trevose, Rumbelow thought, to spend his holiday somewhere glamorous. 'Was it a rough crossing?'

'Oh, I went by plane.'

'By plane? That's very daring of you.'

'Safe as houses, Imperial Airways. So much more comfortable than the boat. And so much longer to enjoy yourself the other end.'

'I suppose you've been called in this morning for a case?'

'Not really. I rout my houseman out early, I'm afraid. I've so much private work piled up, I'd never see a hospital patient at all unless I missed my breakfast.'

Trevose did up his flies and strolled out. He hasn't expressed the slightest interest in my own activities this morning, Rumbelow thought. Irritating, but typical of Trevose. He moved in a self-centred little world of his own. As he knotted his tie, Rumbelow remembered rumours of Trevose's own wife, how she was neurotic, or even downright mad, locked away in an asylum. He wondered fleetingly if he dare approach the surgeon with his own problems. But he doubted if his advice would be more constructive than to find some pretty girl and sleep with her.

He still had good time to travel by Tube. He had expected a crowd outside the prison, but as he approached with his bag he was surprised to find it several times larger than on the last occasion. As he was about to cross the street someone shouted excitedly, 'That's him! That's Rumbelow!' The cry was taken up. There were jeers and boos, people started running across the roadway, one man even shook a fist in his face. The crowd was fortunately strongly laced with policemen, who under the orders of a flurried inspector hurried to form a bodyguard, pushing their way with Rumbelow in the middle to the prison gate. It was an unsettling incident, worse for being unexpected, but Rumbelow's only feelings were disgust at such unruly and hysterical behaviour in a London street. He had not been frightened. He represented the law, he was entering a citadel of the law, and the law was never attacked with impunity. But it left him in a bad temper.

The governor seemed jumpier than ever. The man really should pull himself together or find another job, Rumbelow thought impatiently. William was waiting in the mortuary. At least it was warmer there in June. Rumbelow remarked as he started laying out his instruments, 'The police will have to seal off the streets all round, if these disturbances go on much longer.'

'People have been getting over-excited, if you ask me, sir.'

'There'll always be trouble-makers. Insignificant men, eager to take up any cause, as long as it makes them seem more important than they really are. These people outside are blind to the protection they enjoy from the law. We'd be murdered in our beds if they had their way. Or perhaps it's just a fashionable thing to do. I wouldn't know.'

Eight o'clock struck. A noise rose outside, half a moan, half a shout of anger. Rumbelow waited silently. But instead of the body the governor appeared, white and shaking.

'Something went wrong. Oh, God! It was a terrible business.'

'Is he dead?'

'Yes, but it was bungled. Not the hangman's fault, not mine, not anyone's. Vickery seemed to know something of the procedure. I don't know where he got it from. You know the two chalk-lines? The ones the prisoner has to stand between.' Rumbelow gave a nod. 'At the last moment . . . when the hood was on and the hangman about to throw the lever, he managed to kick his feet away, trying to scramble on to the platform beside the trap.'

'Weren't there two warders supporting him?'

'They must have been taken by surprise. His legs were strapped below the knee, exactly as usual. Everything was in order. I took care to see as much myself.'

'It all sounds very unfortunate.'

'He went down, of course. But the base of his spine caught on the edge of the trap. There was a loud thump–perhaps not a violent one, but you can imagine how it affected us at the time. If he hadn't fallen cleanly, the result for the poor man could have been terrible.'

'The result for the Home Office wouldn't have been too pleasant, either.' Rumbelow was not in a mood to be sympathetic, particularly to the governor. 'Could the doctor pronounce him dead at once?'

'The pulse was still beating, but I understand that's not unusual. It's been one of the most awful experiences of my life.'

Rumbelow picked up his long scalpel, tapping it idly on the edge of the zinc-topped table with its fishbone of gullies. 'You might have expected a smart Alec like Vickery to discover such things. A pity he wasn't so cautious over his wife's death. He might still have been breathing at this moment.'

'He refused the rum, you know. I suppose he wanted to keep his head clear. I only hope your examination will show nothing untoward, Doctor.'

'We can only wait and see, can't we?'

'I really can't stand any more of these affairs. Next time I'll ask the deputy to take my place.'

'With desperate men you should always be prepared for anything,' Rumbelow told him primly.

Half an hour later the handcart appeared.

Rumbelow and the elderly prison doctor turned over the body on the post-mortem table. At the base of the spine the skin had been split horizontally, the top lip forced up as though by the blade of a large chisel. There was no bleeding. Rumbelow picked up the flap with forceps. 'Would that be a post-mortem wound or an ante-mortem wound? Perhaps the right term would be a "syn-mortem" wound. Though I shouldn't care to be accused of coining phrases.'

The neck bones were broken. The white spinal cord, running into the body from the base of the brain like the tail of a tadpole, was torn in two.

'The fellow's antics seem to have made the execution more efficient than usual,' Rumbelow observed. 'Perhaps it should be recommended practice on future occasions?'

The inquest went off commendably. The governor gave evidence the hanging was expeditious and efficient, and that death was instantaneous. Rumbelow gave evidence supporting him. They were in the same large upstairs room near the gate, and people were making a lot of noise outside.

'The police want us to slip away round the back somewhere,' said Norman Carlow to Rumbelow as they went down the staircase. 'It seems they've laid on a car. Would we appear like a couple of funks, do you suppose?'

'If the police recommend it for our safety, we have no alternative but to accept.'

'There's my conscience saved again. You're a useful fellow to know, John. Nothing like logic, when it agrees precisely with the unpleasant fluttering feeling in the pit of your stomach.'

As they drove away in the back of a police-car, unnoticed by anyone, Carlow said, 'John, you're looking dead beat. If I didn't know you, I'd have said you were out all last night on a jag.'

'It was less amusing, I'm afraid. I slept on a train. Or I tried to. I'd been up to see Rosemary.'

'Any luck?' Carlow was the only man in Rumbelow's circle to know of her disappearance.

'It depends which way you look at it. She certainly refused point-blank to come back. I'm beginning to think that's really for the best.'

'I see. So you're reconciled to your fate. Now you can make a fresh start. That's often a good thing, in the life of any man.'

'I'm not going to do exactly the same with a different person, if that's what you mean. I've learnt my lesson.'

'Oh, you're just down in the dumps for the moment.'

'I'm depressed, certainly. I could hardly avoid it. But I don't think it's prevented my mind from working clearly.'

'You need taking out of yourself. Listen, John. You know what day it is tomorrow?' Rumbelow looked lost. 'Derby Day. The greatest pagan festival in the land since they slaughtered virgins at Stonehenge, as I'm sure they did. The English in their full Hogarthian magnificence. The lower classes tight on beer and the upper on champagne, as ordained by Nature. We get up a party every year. Why don't you join us?'

'But it's a Wednesday. I've work to do.'

'My deputy sweats it out for me. You must have a registrar.'

'I don't think it's my style, Norman. I've never even been to a horse-race.'

'Come on, it'll do you good. A fellow like you needs to let his hair down now and then. Surely there's some pretty little thing you can take along, a secretary or something? You're a free man now, John, to all intents and purposes. I only wish to God I was.'

'That certainly isn't my style.'

'I'm counting you in for two seats. I'll be bitterly hurt if you let me down. Ah, here we are at my court. I wonder if that mob we left behind has brought down the prison walls? I hope the poor major doesn't suffer the same fate as the governor of the Bastille. I shouldn't much care to meet his head on a pikestaff when I'm walking along Pall Mall this evening.'

The police-car took Rumbelow on to Blackfriars. He sat thinking seriously about the invitation. It would be a day in the open air, and a spectacle a man deserved to see at least once in his life. It was quite respectable even for Carlow, his late Majesty had attended it often. He drummed his fingers on the leather of the seat. Perhaps he would accept. Quinley could do the work. Though of course he would avoid anything so foolish as betting on the horses.

Chapter Twenty-three

When he saw her his heart fluttered, an uncontrollable response which alarmed him greatly.

They had arranged to meet on the pavement outside Blackfriars. She was wearing a dress of yellow muslin in the latest fashion, short-sleeved, its square neckline edged with white lace, the hem to the middle of her calf. Her hat was wide-brimmed, decorated with a cluster of large imitation daisies. She wore white gloves reaching above the wrist, and though the day promised fine she carried an umbrella out of respect for the summer's poor weather–her usual one, in severe black.

'We'll take a taxi,' said Rumbelow.

'I'm ever so excited. I've never been to the Derby before, though I've listened to it on the wireless.'

'I hope you won't be disappointed.'

'I'm sure I won't. It's so kind to have asked me.'

'Not at all. It's a way of showing my appreciation. You've done an enormous amount of work for me. All that stuff I had to go through for the Jeavons case. You've been acting almost as my part-time assistant.'

'I was glad to help. Honestly.'

'Was there any trouble about the note I sent the librarian?'

'Oh, he looked a bit grumpy, but in the end he said I could have the day off.'

'I should think so, too! Though I hope you didn't say exactly where you were going.'

Maria Osgood laughed.

The taxi took them to an address Carlow had given Rumbelow in Soho Square. He hadn't thought how they would be travelling to Epsom, and was surprised to find an open-topped bus drawn up, the kind which had disappeared from the London streets but still plied between the Sussex coast resorts. About two dozen couples stood chattering animatedly on the pavement, the men in magenta jackets and waistcoats with silver buttons, some wearing old-fashioned straw hats with ribbons to match. Carlow greeted the pair effusively. It was apparently the outing of some dining club he belonged to, and to which the members looked forward throughout the year.

The rain kept off. They drove through the streets of London in high spirits, all on the top of the bus, passers-by grinning and waving good-humouredly. It was pleasant, Rumbelow thought, to steal a mid-week holiday which seemed to enjoy the traditional blessing of the entire country. He sat on the rearmost seat, Maria beside him. She kept her hands clasped tightly and smiled at everyone. Rumbelow was glad to see her so enjoying the reward for extra work.

The racecourse startled him. There were far more people than he imagined, a ragtaggle army encamped on the Downs as far as he could see. He had somehow expected horseboxes and stable-lads everywhere, but the middle was occupied by a fun-fair, the hurdy-gurdies grinding out music and emitting puffs of steam. Their bus joined a line of others in a roped-off field beyond the grandstand. Rumbelow stood with Maria on the grass, looking blankly while fat gypsy-women with shawl-wrapped babies offered him sprigs of white heather or a glimpse into the future, and a man with a greasy tweed cap and a handful of race-cards promised for trivial sums priceless information from the stables. Rumbelow looked at his watch, buttoning his jacket again securely, wondering how they could manage to pass the time till the races began. He noticed the coroner busily supervising the extraction of trestle tables from the lower deck of the bus. These were quickly set up under awnings in the club's colours, then two men in green-baize aprons appeared with a pair of new-looking galvanized dustbins, which puzzled Rumbelow until they disgorged bottles of champagne from among lumps of ice. The club certainly knew how to do themselves well, he thought. Carlow popped a cork with the expression of deep satisfaction, and approached with three glasses.

'A little early, isn't it?' Rumbelow protested.

'Oh, I just regard this stuff as a sort of mineral water. A nice astringent mouthwash for the mucous membranes. We'll have lunch by-and-by, and a drop of brandy to keep the cold out. John, you're a deep one. You never told me you were hiding such a pretty girl in the mortuary.'

'Not the mortuary. Miss Osgood's one of the Blackfriars' librarians.'

'Indeed? Brains as well as beauty?'

Maria continued to smile, but looked embarrassed. Rumbelow thought severely that Carlow's ebullience could make him somewhat brash. But he was glad to see he approved of her.

'Brains? She should by rights be a student at the university. That's so, isn't it?'

Maria made a wry face, and Rumbelow saw he had fumbled on a sore point. 'Perhaps I may still, one day. There's time enough yet.'

'You're not telling us you're a bluestocking? I just won't believe it. You're far too attractive. You're the right girl for handling John here. He's so clever he frightens me in court. I fancy he frightens the judges, too. I daren't think how scared stiff the prisoners must be.'

One of the men in baize aprons came up with a deep, square, leather-covered box. Rumbelow said humorously, 'Norman, you haven't brought a set of instruments? I'm not going to perform a post-mortem on a horse in any circumstances.'

'It's a portable wireless-set. Latest model,' he said proudly. 'We'll be able to hear the commentary as the race is actually going on. Providing of course I've remembered to get the accumulator charged. Now I must see the others aren't dying of thirst.' He poured a little more champagne into the glass in Maria's white-gloved hand. 'It's a fine hat you're wearing. This year all the hats seem to be either as big as umbrellas or as tiny as pillboxes. I much prefer that sort.'

'Do you really?' Maria sounded delighted, taking the compliment as heartfelt. She confessed, 'I put the flowers on myself.'

'You *are* a clever girl,' said Carlow.

Rumbelow had only a hazy idea of what would happen on the racecourse. The pair of them stood talking for some time. He saw she drank hardly any champagne. She was unused to it and perhaps frightened of it. Well, that suited him. He preferred people of sober tastes. But their conversation became stilted and difficult. It was inevitable when they had no idea what to say to please one another. Their relationship had seemed easygoing amid the leather bindings and mahogany shelves at Blackfriars, but it shrivelled in the noisy open-air crowds at Epsom Downs. Then she mentioned Carlow and said, 'Oh, I should *die* if I went into a mortuary,' an unconscious little joke at which they laughed uproariously. But it started them on an easier track.

'I don't even know where you live.'

'In Muswell Hill.' A good middle-class area of north London, Rumbelow thought with satisfaction. 'It's my parents' house.'

'Have you brothers and sisters?'

She shook her head. 'Have you?'

'I had a brother killed in the war. And a sister who died shortly afterwards of that terrible Spanish 'flu. I always think of her as a war-casualty, too. If it hadn't been for the privations we suffered, the epidemic would never have taken a grip. You can understand that I've no love left for the Germans.'

'Perhaps it's a good job I'm an only child. These days, my parents couldn't afford any more.'

'What's your father do?'

'He's an engineer. He had a business, but the Depression finished it off.'

'I'm sorry.'

'It's the times we live in.'

'It's nice to find someone being philosophical about their misfortunes. In my experience, nearly everyone makes the most of them.'

'This is hardly the day to be miserable, is it, Dr Rumbelow?'

'As we're so obviously off duty, why don't you call me John?' The invitation made her look flustered, whether through the suggestion of intimacy or his own enormous importance he was unable to decide. Before she could reply, Carlow appeared balancing two plates of cold salmon and cucumber. Rumbelow noticed Maria had used his Christian name deliberately three or four times before they finished eating.

It seemed to him the races were very short and the intervals between them very long. Carlow insisted Rumbelow put a shilling on the Derby, with advice on the right horse. Finding himself handing money to a bookmaker with chalked board and battered leather satchel, pressed all round by strangers holding out half-crowns and even ten-shilling notes, pocketing some strange gaudy ticket, Rumbelow had a feeling of unreality. Even the day before he couldn't have imagined himself in this setting. They all climbed to the top of the bus, which made a passable grandstand. Carlow lent Maria his binoculars and went back to manipulating his wireless-set, which emitted nothing but shrieks and whistles. Rumbelow pointed out the moving colours on the far side of the course, the horses assembling for the start. Maria was already jumping up and down with excitement. Suddenly he exclaimed, 'I say, this is fun!' He couldn't recall using the word 'fun' before in his life.

The crowd shouted, 'They're off!' Everything seemed to Rumbelow to be happening too quickly. In a few seconds the horses were thundering downhill towards Tattenham Corner. A few more, and they were slowing up past the winning-post. 'Who won?' he asked confusedly.

'Mahmoud. Smirke up.' Carlow had abandoned the wireless-set and was peering past Rumbelow, having lifted himself during the race on his shoulders. 'That's a double for the Aga Khan. He won it with Bahram last year.' He took the glasses from Maria. 'Gordon Richards on Taj Akbar second. Same stable, by God! Can't see who's third.'

'What about the horse you told me to back?'

'Didn't finish, I'm afraid.'

'Don't I get even part of my shilling back?'

'I'm afraid you don't, old bean.'

After the last race the bus started for London. The day seemed to Rumbelow to end suddenly and sombrely. As the club had some sort of ceremonial dinner, Rumbelow and Maria got off in Trafalgar Square. They stood looking at each other on the pavement, the protective wrapping of their companions' good fellowship disconcertingly torn away. It started to look like rain again.

'Well, that's that,' said Rumbelow.

'It was a lovely day. I'll always remember it.'

'Your parents don't mind your coming with me?'

'Why should they?'

'Some people think I'm a kind of Frankenstein, you know.'

'Oh, no! Those people couldn't know you.'

'It's what the newspapers say, I suppose.'

'I think you're very nice. And very kind.' She hesitated. 'And very misunderstood.'

'You mean all that criticism I had to stand? About the Vickery case.'

'I didn't believe that for one moment, John. I've seen you at work. I admire you.' She stopped again. 'I'm so glad you asked me today. I'd been . . . well, I suppose I'd been hoping something like this would happen.'

Rumbelow gave a grunt. 'You knew that I had a wife?'

'Yes, I did.'

'Though we're separated.'

'That's something I didn't know.'

'Perhaps it couldn't be helped. Our marriage was a mistake in the first place.'

'I'm sorry if it made you unhappy.'

'I don't think it did, really. It just brought me no happiness, which is a different thing.'

They fell silent. Rumbelow wondered if he should ask her somewhere, perhaps to a meal. He couldn't decide whether to feel relieved or disappointed when she announced, 'I'd better be getting along. My parents are expecting me. It was one of the nicest times I've had in my whole life.'

'I enjoyed it. I don't lead a very gay life, you know.'

Very delicately she held out a white-gloved hand. He took the tips of her fingers firmly. 'May I see you again?' She said nothing, but ran her tongue quickly over her lips. 'Nobody would know. Nobody in the hospital, I mean. I'd see to that.'

'Yes, I'd love that.'

She took her hand away, and she was gone down the Underground.

Chapter Twenty-four

Over the next six weeks Rumbelow saw Maria two or three evenings out of every seven. He took her to the pictures, or to a small French restaurant Norman Carlow had recommended in Soho, where you could get a tasty meal with wine thrown in at five shillings a head. His sexual advances ventured no further than holding her hand, kissing, and pressing her breasts through her dress in the back of cinema stalls and occasionally in taxis. He felt no obsession to be alone with her. He would hardly invite her to Sydenham, under the eyes of the tea-broker and his wife. He had anyway decided to shut up his house and instruct a local estate agent to sell it. A bedroom had unexpectedly become free at his club, through one of its few permanent residents dying suddenly over his soup, and Rumbelow appropriately enough was chosen to move in.

They were walking after dinner on one of those evenings in St James's Park, enjoying the long twilight of mid-June, when she asked, 'Have you any more news of your wife, John?'

She seldom mentioned Rosemary, he wondered whether through delicacy, through shyness, or to further the illusion that she did not really exist. 'Our solicitors are in correspondence. I'm perfectly glad to leave it at that.'

'Would you still have her back?'

'That's a very mature question for one of your age, isn't it?'

'I don't think so. Lots of girls my age are wives these days. I'm quite old enough to think sensibly about marriage.'

Even the distant implications of this remark disturbed him. 'I certainly can't think sensibly about it–not remarriage, that is. Even if I got a divorce from Rosemary, it could take a year, even two. I'm afraid speed is not among the law's virtues.'

'Oh, I know that.'

They stood on the edge of the lake watching the ducks, some of them already tucking their beaks under their wings for the night. Rumbelow wondered absently how they managed to get enough oxygen. 'Do your parents yet know I'm seeing you so regularly?'

'They don't know at all. They just think I've got a new boyfriend. I can make him sound wonderfully mysterious.'

'Don't you suppose the time's come for them to know?'

'Of course, I'd love to tell them, to tell everybody. But I haven't breathed a word, because I knew you didn't want me to.'

'There's so much malicious gossip in the hospital. It would be silly, going out of our way to attract a share of it.'

They started to move away. 'Why should you have picked on me? There're so many other girls in the world. In *your* world, John. Sometimes I don't think you realize how important and famous you are.'

He laughed. 'That's certainly an unfamiliar accusation.'

'But it's true. You talk about people–the other consultants at the hospital, for instance–just as a matter of course. To me, they're gods.'

'I'm really a very simple man.'

'What do you want of me?'

'I don't want anything of you. Just your company. No, that's inadequate, isn't it? And awfully unflattering. But there're some things in the world on which it's impossible to be specific.'

'Do you want to go on seeing me?'

'Of course I do. Very much.'

She looked up at him. 'Are you fond of me?'

'I hope that's a rhetorical question?'

'But why are you?'

'Perhaps because you don't frighten me.'

'*That* doesn't sound very flattering.'

'It is. It's perfectly true I've never felt so completely at ease with any other woman in the world. And that includes my wife.'

They parted as usual at the Underground. He walked towards his club in Pall Mall with an ill-defined feeling of something unpleasant behind their conversation. Of course he was fond of her. It was quite thrilling, as they said, to enjoy the company of a girl much younger than himself. That was a privilege he had believed confined to international financiers on the Riviera, though Norman Carlow had a succession of secretaries who Rumbelow imagined did more than type his letters. There was–there *must* be–no question of letting the affair go too far. But wherever was 'too far'? And what *did* he want of her? He didn't know.

Then something happened to him which was outlandish, even ludicrous, but in the end perhaps did more damage than all the outcry over the Vickery case.

It was a morning which had started badly. Quinley had come into his laboratory at Blackfriars, and announced with his usual expression of gloom and surliness, 'I've withdrawn my application for the readership.'

'You have? Well, quite honestly I think you're wise. You'd only have been courting disappointment, which is unpleasant for any of us. I don't truthfully believe you'd stand much chance for the job.'

'I was aware of that, sir, from the start. I saw you weren't keen on pushing me.'

Rumbelow took this as an affront. 'That's not a very pleasant accusation, is it? I told you I'd do all I could to help. Are you now trying to say I was deceitful?'

'I didn't mean it that way at all. I just thought you didn't consider my work good enough.'

'I'd let you know pretty soon if it wasn't.' Rumbelow noticed the boils on Quinley's cheeks were worse than ever. 'Have you been discussing my view–my possible view–of you and your work with anyone else on the staff?' Quinley remained silent. 'With Dr Bantrell, for instance?'

'I've talked about the job to him, yes.'

'You must take care that a man like Bantrell doesn't mislead you, Quinley. He's a busy grinder of axes. Let me tell you I was prepared to do everything I could to help. Had you got the job, I'd have been as delighted as anyone. Now you've withdrawn all this becomes irrelevant, doesn't it?'

Rumbelow turned on the high stool back to his workbench, but Quinley stayed in the room. 'Might I have my draft application back, please?'

Rumbelow had forgotten about it. He took out his keys, unlocked the drawer and handed over the envelope.

'You haven't looked at it, I see, sir.'

Rumbelow gave him a glance of annoyance. 'I intended to. There's time yet before the applications must be in, and I'm a busy man.'

'Had you looked at it, that would have at least afforded me some encouragement. You need it at my stage. Though perhaps you've forgotten that, sir.'

This was such a suprisingly insubordinate remark that Rumbelow was about to order Quinley angrily from the room. But he checked himself, and said only, 'You really must learn to develop a sense of tact. It's necessary even for a pathologist. Were you a physician, half your practice would depend on it.'

'Would you be happier if I resigned, sir?'

'What on earth put that idea in your head? Though of course you can leave tomorrow morning if you want to.'

'I don't want to at all, sir. I admire your work very much.'

Returning to his usual state of submission Quinley left the laboratory, carefully shutting the door behind him. Rumbelow went back to his microscope, still irritated. Quinley really was a strange young fellow, he thought. Still, he had only a few months left, thank God, in which to put up with him.

A few minutes later the laboratory telephone rang. It was the crime reporter on a popular daily, whom Rumbelow knew fairly well. He was never reluctant to chat with newspapermen, whom he knew to have a reliable professionalism over what to publish and what to suppress.

'I wondered if you'd any comment on this Gretna Green affair, Doctor?'

'What affair? I've been mixed with a variety of cases, but never yet called in to trace an eloping couple.'

The reporter laughed. 'It's enjoying some extra notoriety. There was a body found there this morning.'

'Oh? It's the first I've heard of it.'

'It was in a trunk, sent unaccompanied luggage by goods train from Euston to Glasgow. It got as far as Gretna Junction about two o'clock this morning, when the train stopped to unload some stuff. One of the railwaymen noticed a smell, and thought something had gone bad inside. Well, he was right. The railway police decided to open up. Our man up there says it was cut into little bits, and had been dead for a long, long while.'

'I expect the Yard will be on to me. Obviously, I can't comment when I still don't even know officially about the case.'

'Very well, Doctor. I'll ring you back later on.'

Rumbelow sat lightly drumming his fingers on the bench. That was strange. It was clearly a case of first-class importance, yet the newspapers had heard the news before himself. He picked up the receiver and asked for Scotland Yard. Sixsmith was on holiday–at that very moment on the boat from Weymouth to his bungalow on Jersey. Rumbelow got on to a detective inspector he knew well instead.

'Yes, we've had Glasgow on to us,' the detective told him cheerfully. 'Quite a jamboree they're having up there.'

'Do you want me to go to Gretna? Or are you bringing the body back here?'

'I'm afraid it's out of our hands, Doctor.'

'What do you mean?'

'It's the Scottish police's pigeon. The trunk was consigned to an address in Glasgow. Which they've checked and found not to exist.'

'What's that got to do with it? It was dispatched from London.'

'Oh, yes. But it was discovered north of the border. So it's not our headache.'

'I don't agree with that at all,' Rumbelow said sharply. 'It's quite immaterial where the body happened to be found. It was put on a train from London, so presumably in London the crime was committed. It's absolutely ridiculous to say the Scottish police have any jurisdiction in the matter. You might just as well maintain that a sailor knifing someone aboard a British ship should be tried in Valparaiso, or wherever it happened to be going to.'

'I wouldn't know about that, Doctor. But the powers-that-be seem quite happy.'

'Oh, very well, very well. It's one of those administrative muddles, I suppose. I'll have a word with the Home Office. I expect it can be easily sorted out.'

'I'm sorry if you're disappointed, Doctor. Not getting your hands on it.'

'I'm quite indifferent to whoever investigates the case, Inspector. I want to know where I stand, that's all.'

Rumbelow hooked up the telephone. The man to examine the remains would be Urrick. Urrick! Why, the murderer was as free as air already. Urrick would be useless at a case of such intricacy. And I made my name with exactly the same sort of murder, Rumbelow thought crossly. Putting together the bits of Perryman's mistress, and in the end bringing him to the gallows. But he did not telephone the Home Office. He feared in some way it might make him look ridiculous.

Bodies in trunks consigned by rail have a powerful attraction for the British people. The 'Gretna Green Murder' was for the next few days on the front of all the newspapers. The Scottish police seemed unable to say whether it was one body, or two, or even more, and whether they were male or female. So much for Urrick! Rumbelow thought. The investigation is pathetic. Such things are really perfectly straightforward to sort out, if only you approach them systematically. His fingers tingled almost physically to turn over the chopped-up human remains. One evening when he was not meeting Maria, he could stand it no longer. He made a trunk call from his laboratory to Urrick's home in Edinburgh. At least it would be charged at the cheaper rates.

'I hope this isn't an inconvenient time to telephone?'

'No, no, I've just finished my tea.'

Tea? Rumbelow reflected that the Scots did not dine, like civilized people. 'I've been reading about the Gretna Green case, naturally.'

'We're having some fun up here, Rumbelow, I don't mind telling you.' Urrick seemed to twinkle even over the telephone.

'I hope the newspapers are exaggerating your difficulties, like they exaggerate everything?'

'It's a tricky business, to be sure.'

'I wondered if I might offer my help?'

There was silence. 'Help?'

'You might care to draw on my experience of the Perryman murder?'

'That's very good of you, Rumbelow, very good of you indeed. But it won't be necessary.'

'I could catch the Flying Scotsman tomorrow morning, if you wish.'

'No, no, it won't be necessary. Not necessary at all. I am doing all that is possible up here, absolutely all that a man could do. And we're making progress. We're certainly making progress. We shall get there in the end. I was reminded of the line by Robbie Burns—'

'Three minutes,' cut in the operator. Rumbelow hung up the telephone.

If it hadn't rung again almost immediately, Rumbelow might have saved himself getting into deeper trouble. It was the reporter who had first telephoned with the news of the body's recovery.

'Any comments yet, Doctor?'

'Yes, I have a comment. Do you realize this case illustrates one of the most peculiar quirks in the administration of British justice? If that train had stopped just a mile up the line, Scotland Yard would have been in charge of the investigations and I myself would now be examining the body. The fact that the trunk was discovered a few hundred yards north of the Scottish border means all the forensic work's in the hands of Dr Urrick of Edinburgh.'

The reporter was interested. 'Dr Urrick, who was against you in the Vickery case?'

'Yes. And I don't need emphasize which of us came out best.'

'Oh, you trounced him, I remember. So you think you'd do a better job on this case, do you, Doctor?'

'Of course I would. Urrick's making a terrible hash of it. He doesn't seem to know if it's one body or an entire family. Today he announced there were two heads, yesterday there were three. He can't decide whether they were cut up by a surgeon or a slaughterman. He doesn't even say how long they've been dead. How he expects the police to identify them, I've no idea. He's a rotten pathologist, and that's all there is to it. They haven't a chance of catching the murderer.'

'Perhaps he sent the trunk to Scotland deliberately, Doctor? To get out of your clutches.'

'That's a flattering suggestion. But anyone who thought as intelligently as that would never commit a murder in the first place.'

Rumbelow did not usually read that popular newspaper. But the next day he idly looked into the morning-room before his club breakfast to see the result of his conversation. He picked it from the paper-rack in horror. Across the front page in heavy type was the headline, DOCTORS ROW OVER TRUNK TORSOS. He agitatedly read below. The reporter had clearly telephoned Urrick at once. It had all been turned into a laughable and undignified squabble between the pair of them, over who should get his hands on the remains. It made Rumbelow look ludicrous. It made Urrick look silly, too, but that was no consolation. He brought himself to open the paper and saw the political cartoon, Hitler and Mussolini with long aprons and scalpels, squabbling over a sheeted corpse marked AFRICAN COLONIES. Rumbelow stuck it back in the slot savagely. He had no doubt someone would draw his attention to it again as soon as he set foot in Blackfriars.

It was worse than that. The notion of two pathologists wrangling over a chopped-up body seemed to tickle popular fancy hugely. *Punch* next week had something to say in Charivari. A facetious fourth leader in *The Times* almost had Rumbelow making a bigger fool of himself by writing to the editor. Late one night he sat with a few men in the club waiting for the news on the wireless, when a variety performer broke into a comic song about it. Rumbelow rose and left, his face stony. He noticed the others laughing outrageously. It was a regrettable failing of the British public to take serious matters frivolously, he told himself bitterly.

Chapter Twenty-five

'I say, this is rich,' said Bantrell one morning about the middle of July. 'Look what one of my students presented me with.'

He handed Sir George Smallpenny a sheet of cartridge-paper. By luck, he found himself alone in the committee-room in the right company. Cramphorn was reading *The Times*. Sir George stood as usual with his heels on the fender before the empty grate.

'I thought you might be amused, George.'

It was a crayoned drawing showing a corpse on the post-mortem table, an open book propped against its feet. Reading it were Rumbelow and a girl, his arm round her. Underneath was written in large letters, DR RUMBELOW IS INFECTED WITH THE DEADLY BOOKWORM (ANKYLOSTOMA OSGOODII).

'It's rather well done,' observed Sir George. 'The fellow's quite an artist.'

'He's the firm's humorist. You always get one of them.'

'The corpse is extremely realistic. Rather more than Rumbelow. But it *is* somewhat libellous, don't you think?'

'Not at all. Unless you go on the dictum, "the greater the truth the greater the libel".'

Sir George looked startled. 'Not Rumbelow, surely?' He glanced again at the cartoon. 'Who's the lady?'

'Miss Osgood. She works in the library.'

'Oh, yes! I recognize her now. It really is a good resemblance. That young man might have quite a future, illustrating anatomical textbooks, or drawing Mickey Mouse cartoons, or something.'

Bantrell thrust the drawing towards Cramphorn, who studied it for some seconds, grunted, and went on with his newspaper.

'But surely you knew he'd been carrying on with this girl?' Bantrell asked Sir George.

'I certainly did not. It surprises me. Indeed, it frightens me. We shall have pigs flying at any moment.'

'I heard about it weeks ago, from one of the students. It's all round the medical school.'

'Well, she's very pretty. Perhaps we ought to congratulate him?'

Bantrell began to despair of piercing this air of good-humoured tolerance. 'It's hardly the thing for a consultant, is it?'

'But, surely, Ian you don't take students' gossip seriously? We'd be all struck off and in jail long ago if anyone did.'

'I'm *sure* there's something in this. The boys are pretty shrewd, you know. They're always about the hospital with time on their hands, far better placed to notice such things than we are.'

'But if Rumbelow's up to any tricks–which I really can't believe for one moment–it's his wife's job to put him back on the straight and narrow, not ours.'

'She's left him. Didn't you know? Some time ago now.'

'Really? Well, I suppose that's not an uncommon misfortune these days. If misfortune it is.'

'It's obvious she only did it because he's playing around with this girl.'

'I hardly knew her. Rumbelow never seemed to produce her in public. Perhaps he thought exposing her to the temptations of the world might involve him in more expense.'

'I don't know what you feel, George. But personally I think it's wrong on any count–completely wrong–for a Blackfriars' consultant to entangle himself with a working girl.'

'My dear Ian, aren't you being terribly old-fashioned? In this day and age social barriers are crashing down everywhere. I've a number of highly respectable friends with sons marrying girls who've never even been presented.'

'You don't believe the story, do you?' Bantrell asked bluntly.

'Frankly, I don't. Not with Rumbelow. He may have many faults, but he's as strait-laced as Queen Victoria.'

'What about you, Crampers? Do you think it's true?'

'No. I can't see any lass in her right mind taking up with Rumbelow. He's a typical pathologist–a fellow who sits all day on a stool examining other people's.'

Bantrell decided to illustrate another facet of his subject. 'We may not be perfectly sure he's making a fool of himself over a girl. But he was certainly a prize ass over that Gretna Green affair.'

'Oh, there's no love lost between Rumbelow and Urrick,' said Sir George.

'Like a couple of actresses, if you ask me.' Cramphorn looked over his half-moons. 'Get hysterics when the deadly rival lands the juicy part.'

'I think Urrick's a perfectly sound pathologist,' Bantrell said. 'He never gets a fair crack of the whip against someone so obstinate and plausible as Rumbelow.'

Sir George demurred. 'That's not the opinion of the general public.'

'I have the deepest suspicion of the opinion of the general public on anything, from household remedies to household names.'

'Well, perhaps the episode did Rumbelow some good.'

'It didn't do the hospital any good.'

'You're always on about that, Ian. But I doubt if the world at large connects him with Blackfriars. Or has even heard of us at all. The public doesn't *want* to hear of hospitals. They're only places where people do unpleasant things to you, and you have to go to die.'

'Be that as it may. But I'm growing a little tired of the amount of leg-pulling I have to stand from others inside the profession.'

'Aren't you being a little over-sensitive about Rumbelow?'

It was a mild rebuke, but Bantrell was discomfited to find the complaint recoil on him. He switched his line of attack. 'Crampers is right. He's a quite desperately jealous man. He did nothing to help Quinley towards the reader's job.'

'Quinley would never have got it.'

'That's beside the point. Rumbelow was outraged because Quinley dared to question his opinion about something in a p.m. The fact that Quinley was right makes it even worse.'

'Oh, come! You can't say Rumbelow's actually jealous of his own registrar. That simply doesn't make sense.'

'I think he's capable of being jealous of his own students.' Sir George was tiring of the conversation, and started to leave the room. 'And of course he's a snob,' Bantrell added, determined to make his final point.

Cramphorn folded his newspaper and rose. 'Snobbery? In this country, you're always liable to find that in anyone, even bishops. Like the pox.'

Bantrell was left alone, exasperated and disappointed. It seemed impossible to rouse a healthy feeling of hostility in the hospital. Another idea struck him. He went down the corridor and tapped on the door of Rumbelow's laboratory. There was no reply. He had intended confronting Rumbelow with the drawing, but instead propped it on the workbench. He walked away rubbing his hands and grinning. 'One must be allowed occasional indulgence in *schadenfreude*,' he told himself.

Rumbelow was in Norman Carlow's court, and appeared at Blackfriars about an hour later. He gave the picture one glance, tore it to shreds and threw it in the wastepaper basket. It was a terrible blow. The life which in his mind was separate and secret stood unexpectedly in the broad daylight of normal existence. This must be how a criminal feels, he thought distractedly, when he's confronted by the police. Or was it simply a typical student joke, a shot in the dark, because Maria did so much for him in the library? He panicked at a vision of the drawing in the hospital magazine, whose pages had seen worse lampoons of the staff. He started to pace the little room, asking himself who was behind it. Quinley, perhaps? But it was something you couldn't tax a man with. He took off his overcoat, sat on the high stool and wondered what to do. He decided he must not on any account approach the library. But after trying to work for half an hour he abruptly got up, went outside and crossed the small courtyard.

There was no sign of her. He opened a bound volume of the *British Medical Journal*, looking slyly round, wondering where she had got to. After a few minutes he shut the book impatiently, went to the librarian's cubicle, and tapped on the closed window through which he was supposed to dispense bibliographical information.

'Does Miss Osgood happen to be about?'

'Miss Osgood, sir?' The old man never seemed to have heard the name in his life. 'Oh, she's left.'

Rumbelow stared at him aghast. 'That's unexpected, isn't it?'

The librarian looked uneasy. Though Rumbelow had seen him almost every week since entering Blackfriars years ago as a student, it struck him they had exchanged hardly a dozen words before. 'I had to ask her to leave.'

'Why should you do that?'

The librarian fixed him with a hooded, bleary eye. Suddenly Rumbelow was a little scared of him. 'Her work was unsatisfactory, sir.'

'That's ridiculous. It always seemed perfectly satisfactory to me.'

The old man replied with a mutter. '*I* thought her unsatisfactory.'

'I suppose you know your own staff best,' Rumbelow told him shortly.

'She couldn't keep her mind on her work.' The librarian hesitated. 'It's not easy for me, sir, if I have to keep discipline among the students, when others take liberties . . .'

Rumbelow turned and strode from the building. He sat in his laboratory with a feeling of appalling disgrace. The librarian had noticed them. The students had noticed them. It would be all round his colleagues, all round London, that he was mixed up with a working girl–even one who should by rights have been at university, he thought in a faint attempt at consolation. He must never see her again. Never. He had been incredibly foolish. He had anyway no exact idea where she lived, and her parents would hardly rise to the telephone-book. Though of course she might pester him–that was very likely now she had a grievance to air. She might return to the hospital, make a nuisance of herself. He wished he could have vanished on a holiday, but that was impossible. He had too much work, he always had too much work. He blamed her for enticing him, quite mischievously in view of their different social standings. He blamed Norman Carlow for encouraging him to take her to the races. He blamed his wife for leaving him at a loose end. As usual, he blamed everyone but himself.

Chapter Twenty-six

Rex *v* Elgin opened at the Old Bailey on Wednesday, July the twenty-second.

The courtroom was the one which served Vickery and a good many others as an anteroom to the condemned cell. Peter Ivors led for the Crown. Dr Elgin had entrusted his defence to a K.C. named Brabner, a short square-faced Welshman with grey hair flowing in the style of Lloyd George, on whom he was reputed to model his oratory. On the bench sat the vinegary-voiced Mr Justice Easterbrook, who was as well known to the public as Rumbelow himself. The Press described him with unimaginative repetition as 'waspish', and with his sharp-chinned face, spiky eyebrows and puny body there was certainly some suggestion of a wasp about him.

Elgin himself was among the most elegant characters ever to be paraded in the glass-screened dock. Tall, handsome, in his sixties, with brilliantined white hair, superbly tailored, he sat with his hands folded in his lap, perfectly relaxed, his large dark eyes expressing faintly amused disbelief he could possibly be involved in such sordid proceedings at all. The public gallery was crowded with women in fashionable hats, causing Rumbelow to reflect that a woman's devotion to her gynaecologist was indeed a bond of poetic intensity. He wondered idly how many of them had sought Elgin's attentions, when suffering unlooked-for complications of Ascot week and the like.

The case made a welcome diversion for Rumbelow. For a week, he had hardly dared to show himself in the hospital outside his laboratory. To his relief, Maria had neither appeared nor even telephoned. No-one had mentioned the student's drawing–he preferred to imagine through ignorance rather than tact–though he fancied Bantrell had given some odd looks. Quinley plainly knew nothing of the episode whatever. He was beginning to hope that it would all die down, that he would remember Maria simply as some pretty girl who helped him in the library, and whom he had condescendingly taken to the races as a treat. When Norman Carlow asked after her Rumbelow tried to impress the coroner he barely remembered the girl's name, with no success whatever.

Elgin faced two charges. The first was manslaughter of Julia Mary Kendall, the twenty-one-year-old girl whose body Rumbelow had examined. On the second, of performing an illegal operation on her, Ivors intended to offer no evidence. A verdict of guilty on the other already exposed the prisoner to imprisonment for life. Rumbelow himself had suggested a charge of murder, pointing out this was possible for death after an abortion under the Offences Against the Person Act, 1861. But this struck Ivors as too much of a good thing, and likely to scare the jury away from a conviction at all.

Rumbelow already felt gratified by something which had *not* happened. It was his first appearance in an important trial since the Vickery case, and Brabner had made no application for his exclusion from the court. Of course, there was no reason why the Welshman should have taken Sir Arthur Younghusband's tactics. It might even have been foolish, trying a move which had already failed before a more easygoing judge. But Rumbelow had come into court with a nagging worry. That it was unfounded, he simply accepted as a further vindication of himself.

'The evidence I shall put before you concerns only the last fortnight of Miss Julia Kendall's life,' began Peter Ivors, with his usual air of an ordinary man thrust unexpectedly into complicated and important affairs and doing his best to explain things as simply as possible. 'Though it is necessary for me to go a little further back to make the actions of her final days, and of her final hours–those will assume great importance in this case–more readily understandable to you.'

He looked towards the two women jurors, sitting together in garden-party hats. 'You are going to hear of most unpleasant things. Of abortion–the taking of life from a human being yet unborn, indeed yet hardly formed, but still the taking of life. Of those parts of a woman's body we do not customarily mention in public, or across the barrier of the sexes. Of unmarried sexual relationships, which these days may hardly shock you, but may somewhat disgust you. Yet I must warn you now, as my duty, that in reaching your verdict you must not be influenced in the slightest by your feelings towards such things. Nor towards the prisoner, or any party in the case, but solely on facts proved to you beyond all reasonable doubt. This is not a court of morals.'

How unfailingly counsel say that, Rumbelow meditated, when they want to rouse the moral indignation of the jury on their behalf.

'Miss Kendall was what is known as a "bachelor girl". She worked in a flower shop in the West End of London, and shared a flat in the area of Earl's Court with a Miss Fuller, a secretary. She was an attractive girl, with the normal number of masculine admirers. But only one concerns this court, a Mr Edward Taylor, who hails from Cape Town in the Union of South Africa.

'Mr Taylor is a young man of substance, who made the acquaintance of Miss Kendall quite simply by walking into her flower shop. He invited her to various entertainments in London, and affection sprang up between the pair of them. We know that early this year intercourse occurred. That is not denied by Mr Taylor. And we know that some three or four weeks later Miss Kendall suspected she was pregnant. She confided her anxieties to Miss Fuller, then she confronted Mr Taylor with the situation. He responded that her condition was not his fault, that some other man must be responsible. This may strike you, members of the jury, as somewhat on the harsh side.

'Mr Taylor said it was merely a ruse on her part, to trap him into an immediate marriage. He claimed it was one used on him before in various parts of the world. This was a great shock to Miss Kendall. She was a young woman in love. As we shall hear from Miss Fuller, she looked on marriage to Mr Taylor as a serious possibility. Even he admits they discussed the prospect, if only in a distant way. Well, members of the jury, you may feel that marriage is not a topic which can be debated between two young persons at all distantly. She appealed to him for help. He gave her some money, a hundred pounds. Perhaps that was the instinctive gesture of a man wanting to get rid of her, and brought up to believe that anything could be achieved by the dissipation of banknotes. To a very tragic extent in the present case, achieved it was.'

Ivors paused for the judge's writing to catch him up. 'We do not know how Miss Kendall obtained the name of the prisoner. Mr Taylor says he had never heard of Dr Elgin in his life. Miss Kendall did not mention to anyone her intention of obtaining an abortion. She was perhaps deeply ashamed and frightened of what she was about to do. Miss Fuller will tell you that one day she returned from her employment to find her flat-mate in bed, looking unwell. Miss Kendall did not confess that she had been that day to Dr Elgin's consulting-room, where he had passed an instrument into her. Miss Fuller assumed the disability was the effect of her pregnancy, and the nervous strain of her treatment by Mr Taylor. For the next few days Miss Kendall stayed in the flat, most of the time alone. During this period, as you will hear from a medical expert, the abortion would have been proceeding.'

'Was she attended during that time by another medical man?' asked the judge.

'No, my Lord. In fact, she dissuaded Miss Fuller from calling one. Then she announced she felt better, and returned to work in the flower shop. But after the Easter weekend she suddenly decided to return to her parents' home.

'Miss Kendall's parents lived in Wimbledon. She appeared on the doorstep with the announcement that she was ill–very ill, those were her exact words. To her mother's inquiries about the exact nature of her illness she gave evasive replies. Her mother being naturally alarmed at this unexpected return put her daughter to bed and sent for their local practitioner, a Dr Carus.

'All this happened on the morning of April the fourteenth last. Unfortunately, there was some delay before Dr Carus appeared, and about eleven o'clock Miss Kendall announced that she must see Mr Taylor, giving her mother the telephone number of his flat in Mayfair. This was the first her mother had heard of the gentleman. He came to Wimbledon straight away in his motor-car, perhaps a commendable change in his attitude towards the unfortunate girl. Meanwhile, Miss Kendall's condition was causing her mother increasing concern.

'About three in the afternoon, she suddenly deteriorated. She suffered a profuse haemorrhage from the region of the womb–a haemorrhage which you will hear from medical experts had already been proceeding internally. It was the direct result of a secondary infection, itself occasioned by the surgical interference of Dr Elgin. The mother telephoned a second time for Dr Carus, who now realizing the extreme gravity of the case arrived within a few minutes. By then Miss Kendall was *in extremis*. And so we come to that part of the sad day's events on which the case against the prisoner stands.'

Peter Ivors picked up another sheaf of papers. Rumbelow was interested how he would illuminate for the jury the remote points of law now rising before them. 'Miss Kendall, in the presence of both Dr Carus and her mother, asked if she were going to die. Dr Carus at first made a soothing reply, but Miss Kendall, who despite her desperate state remained perfectly lucid, insisted she know the truth. Then she stated she had something to say concerning her plight. And Dr Carus realized that he was about to hear a dying declaration. I should explain that a "dying declaration" is to some extent a technical term of the law. It is a statement hedged by certain strict, well-defined conditions, which I have no doubt his Lordship will at the proper time make clear to you.'

'Do not let that inhibit your own explanations, Mr Ivors.'

'I am obliged to your Lordship for the encouragement,' said Ivors equally dryly. 'The statement itself, which will be read to you in due course, is only hearsay evidence–that is, evidence of what another person has said, not ordinarily accepted by a court. But the law admits such a declaration, subject to five conditions.

'The first is that the person must in fact die. If she recovers, the declaration is invalidated. Secondly, she must know she is dying, lost beyond hope of recovery. And she must be *compos mentis*, fully understanding what she is saying. On those two points Dr Carus was entirely satisfied. As a fourth condition, the statement must concern those circumstances causing the patient's death, and the trial must be for the infliction of that death–for murder or, as in this case, for manslaughter. Lastly, the declaration must be voluntary and unprompted. All these conditions, I submit, you will find completely fulfilled.

'Miss Kendall's declaration was taken down by Dr Carus in the presence of her mother, and her father who had been summoned from his office in the City. Mr Taylor remained outside the room. That all happened before four o'clock in the afternoon. Miss Kendall died just before eight that same evening.

'In her statement, Miss Kendall named Dr Elgin as the man who had performed her abortion, giving certain details of the event. When the next morning Dr Elgin was interviewed by a detective-inspector of the Metropolitan Police, he denied any knowledge of Miss Kendall. He denied he was in any way connected with the practice of abortion. But that is not a defence, members of the jury. A dying declaration, that solemn document, perhaps the most solemn ever to be admitted to a court of law, cannot be contradicted. The law assumes as a fact that a dying person tells the truth. You may perhaps have thought now and then that the law and commonsense sometimes part company. But how would you feel were you to know–to be fully assured–that you were about to meet your Maker? Would you not tell the truth? At such an awe-inspiring moment, would there be any room in your mind for duplicity? For animus, for wanting to get your own back? Or to damage someone you did not even know, except through ill-repute? Honestly, members of the jury! We have only to imagine ourselves in such terrible circumstances to realize that the petty animosities of the world would mean nothing to us, absolutely nothing at all.'

After this unusually florid peroration Peter Ivors announced he would call his first witness, but the judge looked at the clock and said they would have lunch instead.

Chapter Twenty-seven

That afternoon, during cross-examination of the dead girl's mother, Rumbelow was puzzled to notice Peter Ivors' shoulders twitching. The case seemed cast-iron. The only defence witness was Elgin himself, who would do nothing except stand in the box and deny the charges as plausibly as he could. Miss Kendall's dying declaration was an enormously powerful document in the hands of the Crown, the rest of the evidence simply painting the picture of her last days and hours in which to fit it. But if Ivors was worried, so was Rumbelow. He knew the barrister had a sixth sense for the way things were going in a courtroom.

They had already heard from Miss Fuller, a young lady whom Rumbelow marked in his mind as a 'dizzy blonde'. She was certain her flat-mate had never once mentioned the name of Dr Elgin. The mother was a forthright woman dressed unrelievedly in black, the sort Rumbelow occasionally encountered on committees concerned with prostitution, drunkenness, hooliganism and similar human frailties. When Ivors had finished the examination-in-chief, Brabner started by asking, 'Mrs Kendall, before your daughter arrived on your doorstep that ill-fated morning last April, when had you last set eyes on her?'

'Several months before. She wanted to lead an independent life. So many girls do these days.'

'She led her independent life remarkably close at hand, did she not? To see her parents was barely a five miles' journey across London?' There was no reply. 'Were you not concerned at the moral implications of a young woman setting up in her own flat, albeit with a young female companion?'

'I knew I could trust my daughter.'

'Mrs Kendall, do you know a Mr Thomas Hunter?'

There was another pause. 'Yes. He was a friend of my daughter's.'

'Was he the cause of her leaving your home?'

'You are not being very kind to my daughter's memory, dragging all this up.'

'I agree that I am not, but dragged up it must be. Did the relationship of your daughter to Mr Hunter result in her invoking the services of an abortionist?'

'No. That isn't right.'

'But did it result in an abortion?'

'Well . . . she took some drugs. Something a friend gave her.'

'Very well. When did you first meet the South African gentleman, Mr Taylor?'

'The day my daughter died.'

'Did you not suggest to him that he marry your daughter, were she to survive?'

'That would have been the right and proper thing for him to do.'

'Do you not think she bestowed her favours on him simply in return for the entertainment and the presents he bestowed upon her?'

'I certainly do not. She was in love with him.'

'As she was in love with Mr Hunter previously?'

'Girls fall in love many times.'

'Did you like Mr Taylor?'

'How can I say? I hardly knew him.'

'Your daughter was in something of the habit of procuring herself abortions?'

'Mr Brabner, will you kindly frame your questions in less extravagant language,' said the judge.

'I apologize to your Lordship. I shall in fact withdraw the question. Thank you, Mrs Kendall.'

Rumbelow was next. He felt satisfaction at being able to advance the case with evidence more solid than of vagaries of the female heart. He replied to Peter Ivors that he had examined the body of Julia Kendall in the Central Mortuary. That he found the cause of death to be shock associated with haemorrhage, which was both internal and external. That the haemorrhage, followed secondary infection of the uterus, Fallopian tubes, and related anatomical structures. And that the infection itself resulted from surgical interference to procure an abortion.

'How long before death, in your opinion, would the illegal operation have been performed?'

'About ten days.'

'And at that time, at what stage of pregnancy would Miss Kendall have been?'

'Not more than two months.'

'Will you tell the court, Dr Rumbelow, exactly how the operation would have been performed?'

He explained how a sharp instrument had passed through the girl's vagina and then the neck of her womb to damage and kill the embryo. And how the dead embryo with its nutritive attachments would be partly expelled by contractions of the womb muscles over the next few days, like the foreign body it had become.

'Did you in this case confirm your findings with examination of the relevant tissues under the microscope?'

'I do so in every case.'

Brabner rose to cross-examine. 'Dr Rumbelow, do you hold strong views on abortions and those who perform them?'

Rumbelow had expected something like this. The evidence of his post-mortem findings was unshakable, and defending counsel had to ask something to justify himself. 'I hold the views of every other citizen who respects the law.'

'Did you on Thursday, September the twenty-sixth, 1935, give an interview to several newspapers–I have a cutting from one here–in which you said, "The vile practice of abortion is performed not only by ignorant women using knitting-needles. I am ashamed that it is also done by members of my profession. This should be stamped out. Were I not so busy, I should be happy to hound these gentlemen down."'

'That is the gist of what I said.'

'Have you mentioned to your colleagues the name of Dr Elgin as one of the gentlemen to be hounded?'

'It was perfectly proper for me to do so among other medical men.'

'Have you any personal animosity towards Dr Elgin?'

'No more than to any doctor suspected of procuring abortions.'

'You would not be distressed at the prospect of his going to prison for a very long time?'

'Not if he were an abortionist.'

'Thank you, Dr Rumbelow.'

The court adjourned for the day. 'Brabner was on pretty thin ground with me, wasn't he?' Rumbelow said to Peter Ivors.

But the barrister had his mind elsewhere. 'So our snow-white chick had a few black feathers. It's disturbing. I wish the mother had been as frank when she first spoke to the police.'

'The colour of the girl's morals can't make any difference.'

'No, but you wonder what else the mother's kept locked in that ample bosom.'

'You and I together haven't lost a major case yet,' Rumbelow reminded him cheerfully.

'Possibly. But even Don Bradman will get bowled for a duck one day.'

The next morning was to start with the evidence of Taylor himself. But he was not to be found. The usher dispatched officially to proclaim his name three times in the corridors might have been calling to the wind. Peter Ivors looked angry. There were feverish conversations in whispers. Finally he apologized to the judge, 'I can only suggest my witness has been unexpectedly taken ill, your Lordship, or met with some mishap.'

'Or returned to South Africa?'

'I am reliably informed he is still in London.'

'Then you had better find him, hadn't you? If he does not appear by midday, I shall have him brought here.'

Dr Carus went into the box instead. He was short, bald, with large horn-rimmed glasses, agitated at finding himself in such painful surroundings. For over an hour Ivors questioned him about the desperate afternoon in Wimbledon. Then the essential document, the dying declaration, was officially produced for the doctor to read out. It was on sheets of thick, pinkish writing paper, as might bear the correspondence of any middle-class suburban home, in Dr Carus' barely legible handwriting. The dying girl had managed to sign at the bottom. Underneath was his own signature, and those of the mother and father as witnesses.

Brabner began his cross examination by asking, 'Dr Carus, what were your feelings that afternoon, when you realized you would have to write down a dying declaration?'

'I saw it as my duty.'

'You knew it would be a statement of solemn importance?'

'Of course I did.'

'Did you know that a magistrate should have been called? To undertake both the task of recording it, and the responsibility for seeing the strict conditions–already fully enumerated by my learned friend–were each and every one of them complied with?'

'I know as much now. I admit I didn't then. I believe I was perfectly competent to take such a statement, none the less.'

'Was there time to fetch a magistrate?' the judge interrupted. 'We know Miss Kendall had only another four hours to live. You may have thought, Dr

Carus, she was likely to die even sooner?'

'That was the case.' Dr Carus looked grateful.

'Though you may be perfectly competent in law to take a dying declaration,' Brabner continued, 'how much experience had you of so doing in your entire professional career?'

'This is the only one.'

'How did you come to learn of the procedure?'

'I learnt in medical school. All students have instruction in forensic medicine.'

'When did you leave medical school, Doctor?'

'I qualified in 1899.'

'Thank you.'

Dr Carus was released. By then, Edward Taylor had appeared. He was thin, ferret-faced, fair-haired, in his mid-twenties, stylishly dressed with a double-breasted waistcoat and a monocle. Rumbelow immediately put him down as 'a cad' or even 'a rotter'. He stood in the witness-box looking as if he expected to be dispatched forthwith to the gallows.

'Why were you not in court earlier?' the judge asked bleakly.

'Afraid my car broke down.'

'Have you not heard of a taxi? Or an omnibus?'

If he had, he was too frightened to say so. Rumbelow despised him more than ever. Peter Ivors' first questions were almost irrelevant, giving the young man a chance to collect himself. There was anyway not much he cared to ask. Taylor admitted giving the dead girl money. He denied having heard of Dr Elgin.

Again it was Brabner's turn.

'Mr Taylor, you are the only son of a family enjoying considerable social standing in the city of Cape Town, in the Union of South Africa, are you not?'

'I'd say that was right.'

'As this case has already received prominence in the Cape Town newspapers, you may think your position at this moment in the eyes of your family and friends somewhat unenviable?'

'I am not too happy about it, certainly.'

'You may also think the unfavourable way in which you have been presented not entirely fair?'

'No, I don't think it's fair at all.'

'You had real affection for Miss Kendall?'

'Yes.'

'But when she came and declared you were the father of her unborn child, you not only rebuffed her but added a grave insult?'

'I panicked. That's all it was. It was a situation I'd never been caught in before.'

'But when you went to her home in Wimbledon, when she was critically ill, you told her mother that you would marry Miss Kendall?'

'Yes. I meant it.'

'Your state of mind had changed?'

'Everything had changed.'

The man's trying to whitewash himself, thought Rumbelow. He can say what he likes, now there's no danger whatever of being obliged to keep his word.

'When did you last see Julia Kendall alive?'

'I was with her when she died.'

'That was after she had made the declaration to Dr Carus? Some four hours afterwards?'

'That's right. She seemed to rally.'

'During that late afternoon, in the period between her making the dying declaration and death itself, did you make a telephone call from the house in Wimbledon?'

'I may have done. I can't say.'

'About five o'clock did you telephone the passenger office of the Union Castle Steamship Company?'

'Yes. I remember now. I did. About a passage home to South Africa.'

'Two passages to South Africa?'

'That's right. I'd told Julie I wanted to marry her, that we'd go to South Africa as soon as she was better.'

Rumbelow noticed Peter Ivors tear a piece of paper with an angry gesture.

'She agreed to this course?' Brabner continued.

'Yes.'

'So you booked the passages there and then?'

'To cheer her up, mostly.'

'Doubtless it did. But the fact that Julia Kendall agreed to marry you, and to go to South Africa with you, plainly indicates that she really believed she was going to recover?'

The young man looked nonplussed. 'I suppose it does. I hadn't thought of that.'

Brabner turned towards the judge. 'With respect, my Lord, I submit that my client has no case to answer.'

'Well, Mr Ivors? What have you to say to this development?'

Peter Ivors was already on his feet.

'I do not accept, my Lord, that a subterfuge with the sole object of making the girl's dying moments more tolerable has any bearing whatever on the case.'

'But it may not have been a subterfuge, Mr Ivors. Mr Taylor might well have been perfectly sincere. The fact is, Miss Kendall did not believe that she was going to die. She had not resigned herself to enjoying no hope whatever of recovery. That must have been her state of mind when she made her declaration to Dr Carus. Even were it not–we heard from Mr Taylor she rallied before death overtook her–that would be immaterial. The belief of imminent dissolution is the foundation of a dying declaration, and the dying declaration was the foundation of your case. It need not have been, but it was, so there you are. If the first foundation is undermined the whole edifice collapses. You cannot make a valid declaration believing yourself to be dying one minute and not the next.' The judge squared up some papers before him. 'In short, Mr Ivors, if you really believe yourself to be on your deathbed, you do not make preparations to go on your honeymoon. The court rules the declaration inadmissable. There is plainly no case for the prisoner to answer.'

A few minutes later Elgin was free.

Rumbelow strode from the court without even glancing at Peter Ivors. He had been made to look a fool–and so soon after that ridiculous business of Gretna Green. He had been tricked, he thought angrily, out-smarted on a trifling point of law. He blamed Ivors for letting him down. It was intolerable, particularly after the difficulty in bringing Elgin to book. The barrister should have been more on his toes. The judge had said so, almost in as many words. As he strode across the hall of the Old Bailey to the main entrance, he suddenly found himself face-to-face with Elgin. The man who a few minutes before had stood in the dock greeted him with a pleasant smile.

'Well, Rumbelow, your little vendetta got nowhere.'

'I don't know what you're talking about.'

'You can't pull the wool over *my* eyes, you know, however skilfully you can festoon those of a British jury. I'm perfectly aware you've got your knife into me. Perhaps now you've been shown up in public as a self-righteous ass, you'll leave me in peace.'

'You've no right speaking to me like this.'

'I've a perfect right. I'm a free man, like yourself. Acquitted by a British court.'

'By a stroke of extreme good fortune.'

'That's a little carping of you, isn't it? Well, perhaps we were a trifle lucky. We only looked into those steamship bookings at the last moment, in case Mr Taylor had ideas of skipping the country. Listen, Rumbelow–' Elgin's manner changed. 'I have been acquitted, and so I can never again be charged with that dreadful business. I will tell you–and you alone–that I did perform an abortion on that girl. I suffer no qualms about it. I'm a realist, not a hypocrite like you. When she came to me in trouble, I saw it as my duty to help her.'

'Your duty as a doctor, I suppose?'

'I am far too humane to abide by our bigoted professional ethics.' Rumbelow tried to escape, but Elgin held his sleeve with a well-manicured hand. 'Where do you suppose such girls would go otherwise? To Sarah Gamp. You know how dangerous that is. Or they start messing about with themselves, which is often worse. You don't give me credit for the social service I perform, do you, Rumbelow?'

'You caused that girl's death. I'm sorry it doesn't trouble your conscience.'

'Some patients die. It's an inescapable fact of medicine.'

'Will you let me go at once?' Elgin released his hand. 'I don't wish to speak another word to you in my life.'

'And I hope that you will have no occasion to.'

Rumbelow strode from the court building. He walked halfway to Blackfriars Hospital, then changed his mind. He couldn't face any of his colleagues. He turned towards the Embankment and spent the next two or three hours walking aimlessly up and down, staring at the oily waters of the Thames, dreading the moment when the evening papers would start to appear on the streets.

Chapter Twenty-eight

August was the month when London, the flywheel of the Empire, dropped to idling speed. Rumbelow became miserable. The weather stayed bad–the July had been one of the wettest ever recorded. Norman Carlow and Peter Ivors were away, and he had no other friends in London. Most consultants at Blackfriars had chosen to holiday at the same time as their paying patients, often in the same places, but idleness did not appeal to him. He was in fact more heavily worked than usual, with so many other London pathologists away. People still met sudden death, holiday season or not, and he knew well enough the suicide rate always showed an August peak in its regular fall from May to November. He even had to give Quinley the post-mortem work at Blackfriars, the young man seeming to have settled into a taciturn respectfulness since the abandonment of his ambitions. Rumbelow's only cheer was public reaction to the Elgin case. He had expected another outburst from the Press, but there was no criticism of him at all. The acquittal had come by means too rarefied for the grasp of newspaper readers. Even at Blackfriars, the doctors were inclined only to gloat over the lawyers having made a hash of things. But the trial was undeniably another hit on the dreadnought of his self-confidence. As for Elgin himself, Rumbelow tried not to imagine his practice quadrupling overnight through the publicity.

It was the month when Rumbelow became homeless. His club in Pall Mall being shut annually, he took a room across Hyde Park in Bayswater, at a small private hotel where everyone stopped eating to stare whenever he entered the dining-room. He avoided his fellow-guests and became painfully lonely. He began to think more often of Rosemary. He had received through the post–anonymously, which disturbed him–a cutting from a Yorkshire paper reporting that the wife of the famous Dr Rumbelow had taken a teaching post in a Harrogate school. Thankfully, the London gossip columns seemed to have overlooked this titbit. He had heard no more from her solicitors. She seemed in no hurry for a divorce. As a matter of conscience he sent her a cheque for five pounds every month, which she never acknowledged.

One evening towards the end of the month the manageress appeared at his table in the dining-room, a little agitated. 'There's a gentleman to see you, sir. A Major Standring.'

For once Rumbelow's memory let him down. 'I don't know a Standring. What's he want?'

'He said it's official, sir. And very important and secret. I showed him into the office.'

'Oh, very well.' Rumbelow got up, under his arm the illustrated society paper he had been reading over his meal. It contained a picture of Lady Accrington in a tweed costume standing with a gun amid a carpet of dead grouse. In the manageress's tiny office beside the front door he found the prison governor, sucking his teeth and looking as jumpy as ever.

'Ah! Doctor.' He shook hands. 'Forgive my coming unannounced. But it's best to be discreet, as I'll explain. You heard I'd changed my job?'

'No, I don't think I did.' So the fellow's nerve has completely given way over the executions, Rumbelow thought.

'It's not been announced officially yet. In fact, it may never be actually announced at all. Very hush-hush, you know. But it's much more congenial than my last appointment. And I believe more important.' He looked round, as though spies might be crouching behind the roll-top desk. 'I'm still with the Home Office. But they've transferred me from the Prison Service to a team working with the Royal Air Force. We're studying the effect of blast from bomb explosions on civilians.'

'I hope it will turn out to be an unnecessary study.'

'So do I, with all my heart. But things in Europe look a little disturbing, and we can't close our eyes to it.'

'Aren't the Germans becoming more civilized? The Olympics were a great success.'

'I hope you're right. With von Ribbentrop himself in London, there might well be some understanding in sight. We'll see, when Hitler makes his speech next month at Nuremburg. And now there's the war in Spain, which could lead to more trouble. The Government is prepared for the worst, you can take my word for it. The Air Raid Precautions Department intends to see there's a gas-proof room in every house in London.'

'Gas! A lot of London houses are incapable of keeping out the rain, let alone phosgene.'

'We must protect our civilians as best we can. Though I must say, some of the local councils are being very difficult about it, putting up the rates. We've innumerable plans–the London streets might well be in complete darkness, you know, there'd be so much less warning than in the last dust-up, barely ten minutes perhaps. It's for one of these schemes we need your assistance, Doctor.'

'This is hardly my line, you know.'

'Let me explain. The Home Office is very anxious to find exactly the sort of injuries inflicted on human beings of various ages by aerial bombs. We're to conduct an experiment at one of the R.A.F. target areas on the East Coast, and we'd greatly value your assistance in performing the post-mortems. Indeed you are the only man in the country we can turn to with real confidence.'

'That presupposes a supply of particularly patriotic volunteers, doesn't it? Or are you offering it as an alternative for condemned prisoners?'

'Oh, the persons will be already dead. That's no worry. There're always plenty of people dying with no relatives or friends, paupers and the like. They're consigned regularly to the anatomy departments of medical schools, as you know.'

'I see.' Rumbelow thought the idea fantastic. 'And the R.A.F. are going to drop bombs on corpses? That indicates great confidence in their marksmanship.'

'They won't actually drop the bombs from aeroplanes. They will be detonated on the ground, the subjects occupying various structures considered by the Home Office to afford protection.'

'Well, I'm always ready to help my countrymen.' The proposed excursion could in its way be amusing, he supposed, and would give him some fresh air. There would anyway be a fee, perhaps a substantial one. Though he would have preferred a different companion on a bombing range to the jumpy major. 'And I've reason enough to detest the Germans and all their works.'

'Then you accept? Splendid! It will be within the next week or two. Of course transport will be provided. Though I must ask you, Doctor, to keep it a close secret.'

'You should know by now, Major, you can trust me in that respect!'

The major fussed on his way. Rumbelow finished his dinner, put the conversation from his mind and sat over post-mortem reports up in his bedroom. He had the habit before going to bed of walking as far as Piccadilly, to look at the lights in the Circus and watch the passers-by. It did something to lessen his sense of isolation. That evening he stood on the corner of Regent Street gazing across the traffic at the statue of Eros and thinking unpleasantly of bombs raining down on the Empire's capital. It seemed unreal, quite impossible, for high explosives to blast the plate-glass windows, to make craters among such everyday objects as pillar-boxes and telephone kiosks, to turn the familiar solid buildings into rubble, to kill the Londoners strolling peaceably all round him. But he had the fatalistic feeling that wars must come to all nations as death came to all men. Then the corner of his eye caught a figure, instantly recognizable, hurrying towards the steps of the Underground. Hardly knowing what he did, he ran after her, seizing her by the arm. She turned round, looking alarmed, only after some moments her startled stare melting into an uncertain smile. They stood looking at each other in silence. 'Maria, my darling, how I've missed you,' said Rumbelow.

Chapter Twenty-nine

There is a moment as a man wakes when he is filled with nothing but a pleasant sense of self-awareness, of rediscovery after sleep. Then there came to Rumbelow, before memory flooded the empty caverns of his mind, a feeling that something was wrong, that something strange had happened to him. He opened his eyes, for a second wondering where he was. He had never slept in such a room in his life. It was an Elizabethan bedchamber, walls and sloping ceiling of white plasterwork and oak beams. It looked an even bigger fake in the daylight. The door had a latch instead of a handle, the window through a gap in the flowered curtains was of blue- and green-tinted lozenges, on the walls hung a framed Victorian sampler depicting the alphabet and a coloured print of a grossly overloaded stagecoach. Rumbelow turned his head. Maria was still asleep, her dark hair spread over the pillow, her full lips apart. He noticed for the first time how long her eyelashes were.

He got carefully from the four-poster. Their window looked over a garden containing some bedraggled late-summer roses and an asphalt forecourt with a dozen cars–mostly open sports models and one new-looking Rolls-Royce limousine. Beyond was the main road and the amiable green slopes of the Sussex Downs. It was a sunny morning, a Sunday, almost a fortnight later. The establishment was a roadhouse, brand-new and fashionable, a place he had never contemplated visiting before.

He dropped back the curtain. His eye caught her underwear, thrown on a high-backed rush-bottomed chair in the corner. A pair of beige lisle stockings and a worn-looking pink suspender-belt with its dangling shiny buckles. A brassière, also not particularly new. A mauve petticoat on which he noticed a pair of careful darns in white cotton. How different from the stylish, immaculate undergarments of Diana Flavell, he reflected. How much more homely. How much less frightening.

Maria sat up suddenly, fully awake instantly, like a child. 'What's the time?'

'Almost eight.'

'You've got your pyjamas on.'

Rumbelow looked a little abashed. 'I prefer not to sleep without them.'

'Funny. I don't even remember you having any.' She smiled, pushing back her hair, her full breasts with their salmon-pink nipples the size of five-shilling pieces exposed above the bedclothes. He felt a return of the awkwardness which had afflicted him the night before.

'Wouldn't you like some breakfast, Maria? We can have it up here, if you want. Or we could go down to the dining-room.'

'I must look a mess. Do I?'

'No, of course you don't. You look lovely–so gay, so innocent.'

She gave a laugh. 'I've never been so happy. Honestly, John. Never in my life.'

'Last night–was it all right?'

'Why should you sound so worried?'

'It's such a paradoxical business. Receiving yet giving. Both of us, at the same time. I'd the feeling of taking more than I'd granted.'

'Don't be silly. Anyway, the giving is as nice as the having.'

'That's a womanly view.'

'Was *I* all right?'

'Oh yes.' He had no other words to express it.

She stretched, smiling and yawning together. 'Have you been to bed with lots of girls?'

'Not with any. Only my wife.'

'You fibber.'

'It's the truth. Quite honestly. I've had lady friends, of course I have. Before I was married, even afterwards. Even quite recently. I'd sometimes gone quite far, but never to the end. There's a whole world of difference between that and just kissing and cuddling, you know. It's the generative act. It has a purpose beyond itself, beyond the feelings, often beyond the intentions, of the couple concerned. People always seem to forget that.'

'But you were strictly brought up.'

'Well, I certainly didn't enjoy the bohemian existence the students have today. It wasn't so much my father being in the Church. He was extremely poor. And poverty forces a man to learn either self-control or the elements of crime.'

Another flowered curtain in the corner concealed the wash-basin. Pulling it back, he started to unbutton the jacket of his brown-and-white striped flannel pyjamas. 'I'm not complaining. In many ways it's an advantage to be brought up with few possessions and few pleasures. It gives you a correct sense of values. And that's the only object of any education.' He turned on the tap and started brushing his teeth.

'Are your parents still alive, John?'

He shook his head. 'My mother died only last winter.'

'What a shame.'

'It meant very little to me. She was a peculiar woman. She never got over my brother being killed. He was an infantry subaltern, so he hadn't really much of a chance, I suppose. But she hated the Germans for it, even more than I do.' He flicked the drops from his tooth-brush. 'She was even stricter than my father, you know. She brought me up to believe that sex–what we've been doing, you and I–was something nasty, unclean, horrible. It must have had its effect on me. I think it even led me to choose my own wife. *She* was sexless. Completely sexless. She'd no taste for it, though to give her credit she tried for a while. I knew all that well enough before marriage, though afterwards I did my best to pretend that I hadn't.' He filled a tooth-glass with water and rinsed his mouth.

'But why did you marry her at all?'

'I can tell you exactly. She gave me a sense of security. I felt she wouldn't make any sexual demands on me. I felt . . . not frightened of it, but that it was something of an unpleasant necessity. Something I didn't want the responsibility of providing night after night.'

Maria seemed amused. 'I hope you don't still think so?'

'With you it's all so different.' He said this solemnly. 'But with my wife . . . oh, I tried to pretend after we married that I hadn't thought all this, either. I still try to pretend it.'

'You poor darling. You poor darling.'

It occurred to him that he had told the girl more about himself than any person in the world. She had suddenly become in a way the most intimate of human beings to him–in a physical way, in a narrow mental way. Otherwise, they were almost strangers. And all divulged in the inappropriate surroundings of a roadhouse. He was amazed at himself. 'What about your own parents, Maria?'

'They're not very interesting.'

'They'll find out about this, won't they?'

She laughed. 'Why should they? They think I'm staying with my friend at Brighton. I often do at week-ends, you know. When I get home, my mother will say how much healthier I look.'

He had laid his shaving things out neatly the night before on the glass shelf over the basin. He let the hot tap run and started to lather the brush. 'Were they upset at your losing the library job?'

'A little.'

'It was my fault.'

'Let's not talk about it.'

'But it makes me feel so guilty. That a girl of your intelligence, a girl who should be at university, is now reduced to serving in a department store.'

'Jobs are difficult to get. Everyone has to take what they can these days, don't they? Anyway, it's enormous fun sometimes, with all the peculiar old ladies we get as customers. I'd hate to grow up like that.'

Half his face soaped, he turned and looked at her. 'Please don't grow up, Maria. I love you as you are.'

She was now sitting up in the four-poster, smoothing the edge of the sheet across her thighs. 'Shall we see each other again?' she asked timidly.

'Why shouldn't we? As often as we care to? Listen, I had an idea–I'm rootless. I'm selling my house, and living in a club is awfully depressing, seeing the same old faces day after day. Why shouldn't I rent a small flat? They seem to be building them everywhere these days. Then you could come whenever you liked, with no one any the wiser.'

'Perhaps you'd like to marry me?' She saw him look flustered, and added with a laugh, 'It's leap year, John. At least I'm entitled to ask.'

'I'm still married.'

'You won't be for ever.'

'No, that's true.' Their future was so complex, so fruitful with delights yet so spiked with dangers, so unpredictable and even uncontrollable, he found it painful to think of.

'If I thought I'd never see you again, John darling, I'd be wretched. Utterly wretched. I know I should, don't I? It happened before.'

'But you never tried to see me after that business of the librarian.'

'I was frightened, I think, of what I'd done. Just by going out with you.'

'Yet then we were miles distant from each other, compared with now.'

'Did you always want to make love to me?'

'Yes, I did.' He turned on more hot water. 'Did you always want me to?'

'I was awfully disappointed I wasn't making a hit.'

She said this lightly, but he took the teasing seriously. 'I had to hold myself in. To exercise self-control. I always have to. So's to keep myself worthy of . . . that part of me the public knows.'

'But that's a very small part of you.'

'The face is a very small part of the body, but it's what you're recognized by.'

'You *must* let yourself go now and then. Have a good time. Like other men.'

'Some other men have too good a time, I fancy. If a man murders his principles he murders his self-esteem, then life becomes pointless. And the principles which control his inner life–his secret life–are the important ones. He can betray them with absolutely nobody knowing except himself.'

Her response was to hold out her arms. 'John, darling–come to me now.'

He felt frightened. Making love to her he thought a highly inappropriate act in broad daylight, at breakfast-time, too. It was to his mind something done only at night, with the curtains drawn, in pitch darkness. 'Someone might come in.' His voice dropped to a guilty whisper.

'No, they won't. The door's locked.' He hesitated. 'Come on. Come on!'

He wiped the lather from his half-shaved face. She pulled the cord of his pyjama trousers as he lay against her, the skin of his body smooth, almost hairless, with a few clusters of caramel-coloured moles. The physical contact with her, as the night before, burst something in his mind. It was an immensely more powerful trigger than when he had first seen her naked. The steel bands of his inhibitions sprung apart, there was nothing left in his world but a simple desire for her. She kicked aside the bedclothes, falling on her back, drawing his penis avidly towards her. But he pulled away. 'We must be careful . . .

'I want to feel you . . . this time I want to feel you.'

Rumbelow's was a caution which could never abandon him, however strong the emotional tempest. He fumbled on the bedside table with the packet of condoms he had bought in an obscure chemist's off Shaftesbury Avenue. She leant on her elbow, pouting a little, watching as he drew one on. His fingers moved with the same controlled care as they manipulated the internal organs of the dead.

Afterwards, before he had left her, his inhibitions returned. That again had been exactly the same the night before. There was almost a physical sensation of something being tightened inside his skull. He was Rumbelow again.

They left shortly after breakfast. They would take the train to Brighton, they decided, and spend the day there, with a trip in the open bus along the coast. He paid the bill standing self-consciously next to a curly-haired young man with a ten-foot woollen scarf looped round his neck, his wife in a Maggy Rouff coat. He was surprised at the matter-of-fact way the manager took his money. He was almost prepared for a violent denunciation in the hall of his deceit and wickedness. He had intended immediately to tear up the receipted bill, to destroy the evidence. But instead he folded it and put it carefully in his pocket. If Rosemary still wanted a divorce, that bill would be first-class evidence. And it would save him a good deal of expense, undertaking a sham of the same expedition with a lady who charged for it as her profession.

Chapter Thirty

It was to be a long day.

At six-thirty Rumbelow stood on the pavement outside his club, in bowler and trench-coat though the September morning promised fine. It was still growing light, the grey-sided, broad gorge of Pall Mall almost empty. A taxi crawled past with its driver eyeing him hopefully, the milkman's pony-cart clattered from St James's Square, three official functionaries were at work–the policeman, the postman, and a man in a wide-awake hat sweeping the gutter. After a couple of minutes a black limousine appeared from the direction of Whitehall. 'I hope this isn't all dashed inconvenient?' said Major Standring through the window.

'I'm used to irregular hours.'

A chauffeur in peaked cap and leather leggings opened the car door and started strapping Rumbelow's black bag to the luggage-rack at the rear.

'Had any breakfast?' asked the Major, as Rumbelow settled beside him. 'Too bad. But I've brought a few things.' He indicated a wicker picnic basket at his feet. 'A Thermos of coffee, some hard-boiled eggs, chocolate biscuits and the like. We'll stop once we're in the country. One must always look after the inner man, don't you agree? They'll be giving us lunch out there, of course.'

Like many ageing military men, he had developed an old-maidish fussiness towards his personal comfort. He wore a heavy tweed coat with leather gauntlets, and obligingly shared a tartan rug over his knees with Rumbelow. He declined a cigar. 'At this unearthly hour I'd prefer a fag. These De Reszke Minors aren't bad at two bob for sixty. Quite enough to pay, these are hard times.' Rumbelow surmised that the major's transfer had brought a cut in salary. Well, he shouldn't have been so squeamish, he thought. 'We look like being in for an interesting day.'

'I hope so.'

'If the balloon *does* go up, at least this time we'll be ready for the Hun. Our Army may be small but it's damned efficient, you can take that from me. Mind, I'd like to see it attract more recruits. I'm a bit of a reformer, you know, I'm not against a few changes.'

'Such as?'

'Well . . . letting the Tommies get married before they're twenty-six, that sort of thing. At the same time, I'm not against conscription.'

'The country wouldn't stand for it.'

'I don't agree. Only the communists, socialists and persons of that ilk wouldn't stand for it. They're always ready to make nuisances of themselves. Take this Left Book Club thing. Have you come across any of its effusions?' Rumbelow shook his head. 'It's for those Bolshie school-teachers and journalists and the like, who make such an infernal clamour about arms for

Spain. To my mind, they're just as bad as Mosley's blackshirts.'

Rumbelow lit a cigar, leaning back and enjoying the luxury of the car. It must have cost the taxpayers at least four hundred pounds, he calculated. To the last minute he was prepared for the journey to be called off, the idea pigeon-holed like so many freakish products of official imagination. They drove eastwards through the awakening streets of London, filled with tradesmen's vans and early buses taking people to work. In the countryside north of the Thames at Tilbury they made a stop for their coffee, hard-boiled eggs and chocolate biscuits. The major produced also some slices of cold ham and tongue and a flask of brandy.

Beyond Southend they turned off the main road, and found themselves driving beside a fence of concrete posts and barbed wire which seemed to run across the flat scenery as far as the horizon. They stopped at a gate flanked by large notices. An R.A.F. sentry inspected some sort of pass the major thrust through the car window. Inside, they followed a straight narrow tarmac road towards a huddle of buildings, some brick, some wooden sheds, some the corrugated-iron half-cylinders of Nissen huts. The car stopped and the major got out. No one appeared. 'They don't seem to be expecting us,' said the major crossly. 'Just like the R.A.F.'

They sat in the car for ten minutes, the major increasingly impatient. Rumbelow lit another cigar, rather enjoying finding himself in some secret military establishment. Another car appeared down the narrow road. Two officers got out, one with pilot's wings and the rings of a wing commander, the other a squadron leader, twined gold snakes on his lapels denoting he was a doctor.

'Sorry to keep you waiting.' The wing commander was red-faced and in a bad temper. 'But I've a job to do, you know.'

Both cars drove beyond the buildings, until the road abruptly stopped. The ground was level and marshy, the mouth of the Thames estuary sparkling in the distance. They continued on foot beyond a board saying, FORBIDDEN TO PASS THIS NOTICE WHEN RED FLAG IS FLYING. A red flag fluttered from a pole beside it. Rumbelow supposed it was all right.

They halted at some concrete steps leading to a dugout, a sergeant and an airman outside vibrating at the salute. Rumbelow noticed wires running from it along the ground to a canvas screen in the distance. The wing commander disappeared briefly, then all four set off towards the screen, which was further away than it appeared. Behind it stood a military ambulance and two small structures, one of brick and one of concrete, recalling to Rumbelow photographs of Eskimoes' igloos. Upright between them on a metal tripod, connected to the wires from the dugout, was an aeroplane bomb about three feet high. It was one of the few things ever to induce a sickening feeling in him.

'I designed those two shelters myself.' The major's eyes were starting to glisten with excitement.

'That's very clever.'

'Right, Dr Rumbelow, now it's up to you,' said the wing commander.

The ambulance doors were already open. The stretchers were folded back, a pair of coffins occupying the floor. Rumbelow climbed in, glancing at the brass plates on the lids. One said,

JEREMIAH HACKTHORPE
BORN AUGUST 1, 1860. DIED SEPTEMBER 10, 1936.

The other.

MARY ALICE SMITH
BORN 1856. DIED SEPTEMBER 14, 1936.

'Anyone got a screwdriver?'

The R.A.F. doctor looked mystified.

'To take the lid off.'

'I rather thought we could leave the stiffs in the coffins.'

'Oh, no. That might invalidate the whole experiment. Besides, how do you imagine we'd squeeze them into those shelters? We'll have to get on all fours to crawl in ourselves.'

The ambulance driver produced a screwdriver from his tool-kit. Rumbelow got to work, noticing the wing commander and the major kept their distance. 'We'd better have the shrouds off, too.'

The R.A.F. doctor began to look uneasy. 'Is that really necessary?'

'I wouldn't suggest it otherwise. We'll have to get one of these stretchers out of the ambulance and lift the bodies on it in turn. There really should be a table of some sort. Your preparations are most inadequate.'

'We thought it would simply be a matter of popping the coffins back in the ambulance and sending them down to Blackfriars, as arranged.'

'The whole business is going to be much more difficult than that. Have none of you heard of rigor mortis?'

The body of the old man was so wizened he must have resembled a mummy during life, Rumbelow thought. They carried him on a stretcher to the brick shelter, then he took the shoulders, the R.A.F. doctor the feet. Rumbelow crawled inside. It was some eight feet square with a concrete floor and smelt damp. There was no lighting and no ventilation apart from the constricted entrance. He would not have cared to find himself inside during an air-raid. He pulled the body in, then crawled out carefully, dusting the knees of his trousers.

'This is becoming more trouble than it's worth,' complained the R.A.F. doctor. 'After all, we're only interested in the effects of blast. There may not be any. It's a subject nobody knows anything about.'

'I hope you're right.'

The body of the old lady was more difficult. She was extremely fat, and from her elephantine legs Rumbelow concluded she had died of congestive heart failure. 'At least they're helping to defend their country,' he remarked. 'Precious few can claim as much when they've been dead the best part of a week.'

The driver and an airman rolled up the canvas screen. They all got in with the empty coffins and drove over the bumpy ground back to the dug-out. The ambulance disappeared towards the safety of the main buildings. The four of them descended the concrete steps.

'We should be through in time for a drink before lunch.' The prospect seemed to put the wing commander in a better mood. 'I take it there's not much you'll want to do in the way of cutting up, Doctor?'

'I imagine that can be kept for my mortuary at Blackfriars.'

'I've great faith in those shelters,' said the major enthusiastically. 'I even volunteered to stay inside myself. But the Home Office wouldn't hear of it.'

Rumbelow was now enjoying his morning thoroughly. It was agreeable to watch the Armed Forces at work, to feel part of some military operation, to be doing something towards the country's security. The wing commander went up with a pair of field-glasses to satisfy himself nobody was left on the scene of the imminent explosion. In the dugout was a box with a handle, which Rumbelow had seen in countless illustrations for boys' adventure stories. They all put their fingers in their ears. The wing commander gave an order. The sergeant depressed the handle. The explosion seemed much nearer than Rumbelow expected, shaking the walls of the dugout. 'Well, let's have a look-see,' said the wing commander.

They walked over the ground again. There was a hole with smoke coming from it. There was no sign of the tripod holding the bomb, nor of the igloos.

The major fell silent.

They peered over the edge of the crater. Among crumbled bricks and concrete Rumbelow noticed the head of a human femur sticking up, glistening in the sunshine. His eyes ran round, identifying fragments of skin and muscle, the old man's head, an arm, a hand which could have belonged to either unknowing volunteer. Under a slab of concrete was the top of the fat woman's torso, torn across as though bitten by an enormous animal. 'Someone had better pick up the bits. If they can be put in a suitable container, you can send them down to me in London. I'll sort them out when they get there. I suppose there's arrangements to give them a decent burial?'

The major spent most of the journey back in silence. 'I was sure, so terribly sure, about those shelters. I had a lot of experience of that sort of thing in the Army, you know.'

'Many useful inventions have seemed unsuccessful at their first demonstration.'

'I just can't understand it. I just can't. It really is disheartening. I shall have to redesign them, going right back to basic principles.'

'Well, the war is hardly likely to break out tomorrow,' Rumbelow told him consolingly.

When Rumbelow got out in Pall Mall, the major thanked him effusively if sadly. 'We must keep in touch. I've reports to write, no end of details. I'm sure next time will go much better.'

Rumbelow scribbled on one of his visiting-cards. 'You'd better have my new address. I'm leaving here and moving to a service flat. I shall have to fend for myself, but I fancy I can manage that.'

'You're a bachelor?'

'In effect,' said Rumbelow.

Chapter Thirty-one

The next few weeks were the happiest of Rumbelow's life. The flat was new, still smelling of fresh paint, in a block the size of an ocean liner, risen on foundations of demolished workmen's cottages round the back of Chelsea Square. He had one smallish room with a divan bed in an alcove, a single armchair, a bathroom and a 'kitchenette' the size of a telephone kiosk. Everything was provided, down to the teaspoons. The tenants were assumed to work the week in London, or to come up for a few days' shopping and theatres, before returning to more socially acceptable accommodation in the country. But from the unfashionable look of most of them, Rumbelow suspected the rooms to be their only homes in the world. It was cramped but it was easy to keep himself tidy. And the rent was remarkably modest.

Maria came to him almost every evening. This caused severe reorganization of his work–he had to let some of it go to other pathologists, even to Quinley, and however delightful the reason this always caused him a pang. Maria insisted on cleaning the flat and cooking a meal. Often they just sat listening to the wireless, which was provided at the turn of a knob, like the bathwater. One weekend, she invoked the excuse which had served for the Sussex roadhouse and spent the Saturday night with him.

'Your people *must* be getting suspicious,' he decided. They were lying on top of the divan on the Sunday morning, the flats having excellent modern central heating. 'Either they're remarkably trusting–which would upset me. Or they know very well and don't let on. Perhaps not even to themselves. That's a convenient little human failing.'

'I don't think so. Honestly. They're terribly curious about you. They keep asking when I'm going to bring my young man home to tea.'

'I'll have to meet them *some* day.'

'You've never suggested that before. Never so positively.'

'Haven't I? Well, there's no point in keeping everything such a dead secret, is there? We've no longer the hospital to worry about.'

'They'll be thrilled meeting you.'

'They'll get an awful shock.'

'Why?'

'I'm hardly your "young man". I'm a good ten years older than you.'

'Does that worry you, darling?'

'It must be of some significance. Now and then I even think it's rather abnormal.'

'But I *love* older men,' she said playfully.

'That raises a terrible vision. Fat, heavy-jowled financiers with chorus-girls.'

'Oh, dear! Perhaps it's fairer to say I'm not mad about young ones? A lot of them just bore me. Do you suppose I should write to Dorothy Dix about it in the *Mirror*?'

'Have there been many others?'

'That's asking.'

He decided not to pursue it. 'Not that I set great store by a man's looks. Or a woman's, if it comes to that.'

'Now you're trying to tell me I'm plain, but you'll put up with it.'

As usual, he took her seriously. 'I didn't mean that for one moment. A man's intellect and character are what I see, not the set of his eyes or the shape of his chin. A philosopher can be as ugly as the devil, but the whole world admires him. I've met actresses who can hold an audience spellbound, but they're not pretty. Sometimes they're downright ugly under the paint. And I've seen criminals, even murderers, who've the looks of film stars. It's of no consequence, you see.'

'Oh, you're a good-looking chap.' She ran her fingers lightly down the ribs of his long chest, as though she were playing the piano.

'Why do I attract you, Maria? Why me particularly?'

'You're kind, sweet and gentle. And clever. I like clever people. That's why I enjoyed working in the library.'

'And I'm famous. I suppose that's a consideration? I'm hardly Ronald

Colman, but people have heard of me.'

'It *is* something. I can't deny it, can I?'

'I missed you awfully when you left Blackfriars.'

'So did I. Terribly.'

'Yet I didn't realize it. It's strange–I suppose I submerged it in my mind. It's easy enough, my days are so full. I've always relied on my work to help me forget anything that's jarring and unpleasant. Work's my drug. But I knew it at once, the moment I set eyes on you that night. I suppose the same thing happens to other people. Though it frightens me sometimes, how difficult it is to control our emotions.'

'Why should we try to?'

'They're dangerous things. I've seen too often the tragic results, when a man lets them dominate him.'

'Tell me you love me, John darling.'

He had no reply for the moment. She asked often, he supposed like any girl in love. She would only be after reassurance or harmless flattery. But whatever he said, he had been clear-sighted enough to know his was only an infatuation. He had heard of many men, responsible level-headed men like himself, who had thrown themselves overboard from society for the same reason. It accounted for his desperation to keep her a secret. He hadn't the sophistication and brazenness of Graham Trevose, who wore a scandalous life lightly, and even saw it add to his private patients and his popularity at Blackfriars as 'a card'. Any assumptions otherwise had been finally demolished by his fumbling humiliation in the hands of Diana Flavell.

But Rumbelow's mind was beginning to change. When he had made a stupid mistake in court and Norman Carlow accused him half-humorously afterwards of being in love, he had been terrified that the affair was slipping from his control. Now he wasn't so alarmed that the shrewd Carlow might be right. He was starting to ask himself–cautiously, being Rumbelow –exactly what his feelings were towards Maria. Over the past few weeks, the excitement of being alone with her in the flat–in his own home, where they could do exactly as they pleased–had turned to an acceptance of the situation as perfectly natural, which he found far more deeply satisfying. He was experiencing a domesticity quickened with love and tenderness which was never part of his marriage. The idea of making her his second wife had stolen upon him. After all, a man could not live alone for ever, it wasn't biologically normal. But he had not cared to put the feeling into words. He spent his life locked in a cell with himself his own jailer, only rarely the urge to escape becoming overpowering.

He asked abruptly, 'Maria, would you like to marry me?'

She looked solemn for a moment, still running her finger down his chest. 'You know how I would.'

'But you understand how it might take some time–the divorce, all that business?'

'I don't mind how long I wait.'

He smiled. 'There's the difference in our ages again. At yours, life is limitless. At mine, you're starting to see your days are numbered.'

She pressed closer to him. 'I wish you wouldn't keep thinking of that.'

'But it colours your thoughts, your actions. It's the young people who want to change everything–look at the Nazis, shouting youths with banners. When you get a little older you appreciate the world, you want nothing but to enjoy it. Do you suppose we could reconcile those two outlooks?'

'You think too much, John,' she told him gently. 'Why don't you trust your own nature?'

'Perhaps I should. A woman would, without question, wouldn't she?' He thought for a moment. 'If you'd like me to, I'll write to my wife.'

'I should like you to.'

'And see your parents.'

'I should love that, very much.'

'Then I shall.'

The rendezvous with the parents was left vague, but the following week he gave much thought to the letter. He finally composed it on the Friday afternoon, sitting in his laboratory. At the top, he put the address of his new flat.

> Dear Rosemary,
>
> I have not communicated before because there seemed no reason to. I understood that you had a job, and you seemed to wish nothing from me. For my part, my life and work continue in London more or less as usual.
>
> But now I have become involved in a relationship which you, who are still legally my wife, are entitled to know about. I have met a lady who was at first a solace for my loneliness, and has since become very dear to me. I will not say that we wish to marry in the immediate future, but obviously such an outcome must always be in the minds of us both. In the event, I should have to invite you to divorce me.
>
> You may not see your way to doing as much, of course. But I felt it only right to place the facts before you as early as possible.
>
> I hope that you are continuing to receive my monthly cheques safely.
>
> Yours sincerely,
>
> John

He read it through several times. An admirable letter, he thought, which might have been composed by an able solicitor. It was guarded, told her little and committed him to nothing. It threw at least some of the guilt on herself, for abandoning him to loneliness. Though he had to recognize that he was, if only technically, committing the sin of adultery. But after all, there was no law against that. He put the paper in an envelope and addressed it. It was a little before four o'clock. He posted it, and went down to the mortuary for the afternoon's post-mortems.

Chapter Thirty-two

There were three post-mortems that afternoon. The first was one of Mr Cramphorn's patients, a meat-porter from Smithfield Market, who had died a few hours after surgery for perforated duodenal ulcer. Rumbelow's sweeping incision contemptuously reopened the neatly-stitched operation wound, then he demonstrated to the students, craning over each other's shoulders from their football-stand steps, the internal stitches closing the hole in the gut. The pelvis was full of bad-smelling greenish-yellow pus, with fragments of carrot still identifiable in it, too much to drain through the stiff, red rubber tube hopefully stuck through a second incision above the bladder. Rumbelow slipped his gloved hand over the domed upper surface of the liver. 'There's a subprenic abscess as well,' he told Quinley, who was assisting him. 'That ulcer must have been leaking for some time. Anything about it in the clinical notes?'

'No, sir.'

'Then Crampers must have missed it.' He looked round for the house-surgeon, but supposed he was engaged in the operating theatre. 'What's the clinician's cause of death?'

'Peritonitis.'

'I suppose we can let it go at that. The abscess is all part of the same picture. Though I've a feeling that surgical shock had a good deal to do with it–they ought to warm these perforations up in bed, on morphine and rectal saline before they go into the abdomen. It would give them a chance to recover. Do you know, I once did a p.m. on a man who perforated in the street, right outside the hospital. They had him on the operating table in an hour, and killed him. Crampers is far too impatient. Though I suppose he wouldn't take very kindly to it, if I told him as much.'

'No, sir.'

They left William to sew up the body. On the other table was an old woman who had died after breaking her hip. Rumbelow sliced into lungs like wet sponges, demonstrating the pus and fluid which had filled the air-spaces to extinguish her life. 'Hypostatic bronchopneumonia. Nearly always fatal, at this age inevitably so. A disease which lives up to its reputation as "the old person's friend". There's no treatment.' He turned to Quinley. 'What's the next one?'

'A child, sir. Female. A patient of Dr Bantrell's. He particularly wants to see the p.m.'

'Why wasn't she in the pediatric ward?'

'It was a duty case, when his firm was on take-in.'

'I see. What's the diagnosis?'

'Epilepsy.'

'I suppose the immediate cause of death was asphyxia, or injury during a fit?'

'It's given as post-epileptic shock.'

'That's unusual. There won't be much for us to see, anyway. What was her age?'

'Six.'

William and his assistant busied themselves with a trolley. The meat-porter's body was replaced with that of the child. At the same moment the red-headed physician bustled in, in his long white coat and accompanied by his houseman. Rumbelow thought Bantrell greeted him with rather too emphatic cordiality.

'I see she died as long ago as last Monday.'

'Yes, we'd some difficulty getting permission for a p.m.,' Bantrell told him. 'The parents aren't very intelligent. I'm afraid. Do you mind if I have a word to the students? It's a case with some interesting features.'

'I don't mind in the least.'

'This girl was admitted early on Monday morning, with a story of fits during the night. She was in bed, apparently sleeping normally.' Bantrell enjoyed a first-rate reputation in the medical school as a teacher, of which he was fully aware. 'Her father works as a van-driver, and there are four older brothers and a sister, all alive and well. She had a history of fits and dizziness over the past two years, though it may have been longer–the mother was a somewhat unreliable witness. The fits lasted about half an hour, occurred about once a month, and were becoming more frequent. She had been seen by her local g.p., who prescribed bromides. Well, Doctor, have you already reached a diagnosis?' he asked a front-row student genially.

'I'd say epilepsy, sir.'

'Quite brilliant, Doctor. And the form? *Grand mal*, or *petit mal*?'

'*Grand mal*, sir.'

'Correct. She was unconscious when admitted, and in fact did not recover consciousness before she died. The blood pressure was low, so low that at first we couldn't get a reading. There was tachycardia. The pupil was dilated. The limbs were flaccid. There were no more convulsions. On examination, we found no further abnormality. There was nothing suggestive of congenital defects in the history, Mr Carten?' House-physicians at Blackfriars, like subalterns in the Army, were never awarded in speech their entitled rank.

'The mother described her as a normal healthy child, sir, though not very lively.'

'We will accept that for what it's worth. Dr Rumbelow may well demonstrate some congenital intracranial abnormality which could have caused these fits. In the absence of such evidence, we must of course put them down to idiopathic epilepsy.'

He turned aside, leaving the stage to Rumbelow.

'The body's very thin,' Rumbelow observed. 'At a glance, she might have died from starvation.'

'Some of the working class have odd ideas on diet for their young.'

Rumbelow pointed with the tip of his long scalpel. 'Note these scars, gentlemen. She had injured or burnt herself during previous attacks.'

'As we would expect.'

Rumbelow's incision split the front of the child's body in two. The knife cut cleanly through the soft breastbone, the ribs falling open like the carcass of a carved chicken. The heart, the lungs, the stomach and intestines, the kidneys, the minuscule uterus and ovaries, Rumbelow extracted together. He dropped them in a bowl, then crossed to the porcelain slab to dissect them under running water. Nothing abnormal, he thought. But behind the stomach, in the loop formed by the upper gut, lay the fish-shaped pancreas. As soon as Rumbelow felt it between his gloved fingers, he knew that something was wrong.

'This pancreas is rather thick.'

Bantrell frowned, looking over Rumbelow's shoulder. 'There's not much of it.'

'It's thicker than normal for a child of this size.'

'She may have suffered in the past from sub-acute pancreatitis. Any history of that, Mr Carten?' The houseman shook his head. 'It may be a minor congenital abnormality, as I suggested. Or it may be an artefact. Perhaps we can have a look inside the skull?'

'As you wish.' Rumbelow carefully put the scrap of pancreatic tissue to one side of the slab.

The child's hair was long and fair, matted from the refrigerator. Rumbelow made his usual incision from ear to ear across the dome of her head, pulling half the scalp forward over her face. Only a touch of his knife was needed to free the tissues from the bone. The other half he pulled back on the child's neck, which he supported on a wooden block before starting his circular saw-cut through the bone. He lifted the top half of the skull away. Bantrell and himself peered in together.

'No spurs or bony abnormalities. No injuries,' said Rumbelow. 'Quite normal.'

'Let's take a look under the membranes.'

Rumbelow dissected away the thicker dura mater, with its blood sinuses. Below was the fragile arachnoid mater, then the convoluted white surface of the brain crossed by wriggling blood-vessels. 'Normal,' said Rumbelow.

He lifted out the brain, cutting the nerves underneath, took it to the porcelain slab and sliced it. 'Normal.'

'Then the epilepsy was idiopathic, as we suspected.'

'Unusual to cause death, isn't it?'

'But not unknown.'

Rumbelow reached for the fragment of pancreas.

'There's no history of diabetes, you know.' Bantrell sounded a little sharp. 'We found no sugar or ketones in the urine.'

Rumbelow said nothing. He took his magnifying glass, turning the scrap of tissue over in his gloved fingers. The students started to yawn, mutter and shuffle their feet. Bored easily, they were wondering if there would be anything more worth seeing before they could escape for their tea.

Rumbelow handed the glass to Bantrell.

'Well, there's some thickening of the body of the organ,' Bantrell agreed. 'Any history of mumps, Mr Carten?'

'No, sir. Only the other childhood infections.'

Bantrell turned to the students again. 'As I suggested to Dr Rumbelow, this thickening might be the legacy of an attack on pancreatitis. That itself can be the somewhat rare complication of mumps. Can you offer any other cause?'

'Gallstones,' said the front-row student.

'Oh, very common in a child aged six, eh, Doctor?' The young man looked abashed. 'Trauma might be a cause, or duodenitis. But mumps is the most likely. The diagnosis must have been missed at the time. As I said, the mother was of poor intelligence.'

'This pancreas was never infected at all, at any time,' said Rumbelow.

Bantrell did not take to having his diagnosis questioned, certainly not before his houseman and the students. And most certainly not by Rumbelow. But to preserve his dignity he decided to swallow his resentment and treat the correction lightly. 'Perhaps Dr Rumbelow will enlighten us? We'll be privileged to observe his skill at nosing out clues.'

'The thickening is due to a tumour. A benign adenoma of the islets of Langerhans.'

Bantrell's ginger eyebrows shot up. 'That's a canary, isn't it? Don't you think it more useful to look for the common-or-garden sparrows?'

'I've seen two cases. Neither diagnosed during life.'

'It's an entertaining notion, at least. Gentlemen, you are aware that the pancreas has two functions, the production of digestive enzymes and—'

'Insulin,' several students interrupted at once.

'Malfunction of the islets of Langerhans cells usually causes diabetes. But Dr Rumbelow suggests we have here a growth of these same cells–a benign growth, one remaining *in situ*, not a carcinoma spreading through the body–causing an *overproduction* of insulin. We would have the unusual condition of natural hyperinsulinism, the exact replica of a diabetic patient inadvertently receiving an excess of insulin by injection.'

'Which I believe to be the cause of death,' said Rumbelow.

Bantrell gave a hostile glance. 'Surely you're not serious? My diagnosis was epilepsy.'

'In my opinion, that was incorrect.'

The students had fallen silent. The afternoon's diversion was, after all, far from over.

'The child's fits, her coma, were due to excess insulin in the blood,' Rumbelow went on steadily.

'I disagree.'

Rumbelow nodded towards the eviscerated body on the table. 'The emaciation confirms the condition.'

'I disagree.'

The ill-feeling which both had been suppressing burst to the surface. 'Had the diagnosis been made, had sugar been administered to the child, she would be alive today.'

Bantrell went white. 'As a man of your forensic experience should know, that's a slanderous statement.'

'I hardly think so. I am merely expressing an opinion. We all of us make mistakes.'

'There is *no* adenoma in that pancreas.'

'You cannot say that with any certainty until the organ has been sectioned. You are quite at liberty to inspect the microscope slides.'

'Slides! What do you expect them to show? Precious little! The pancreas degenerates extremely rapidly after death. I should have imagined you'd know that.'

'On the contrary, I should expect the slides to be conclusive.'

Bantrell thrust his hands into the pockets of his white coat, struggling to control himself. 'Very well. Make your slides. Tell my house-physician when they're ready. I'm perfectly confident they'll show nothing, nothing whatever.'

'If you like, a blood-sugar estimation would confirm it, one way or another.'

'Four days after death? Completely useless! Autolysis will have pushed the sugar-level in the blood right down. I should have imagined you'd know that, too.'

The pair of them suddenly looked self-conscious. They had forgotten the audience. It even occurred to Rumbelow that he could restore their dignity with some half-hearted apology, some sort of concession that he might not be completely right. He knew that Bantrell would have seized it, to save his face. But the depth of his obstinacy, and his dislike, were against it. He did manage a more matter-of-fact tone to say, 'Preparing the slides will be simple enough. You'd need a set anyway, before signing the death certificate.'

Bantrell said briefly. 'Thank you for performing the post-mortem, Dr Rumbelow,' and strode from the mortuary followed by his houseman. Rumbelow slowly stripped off his gloves. The students, always impressionable, were staring wide-eyed, embarrassed, fascinated, amused, but above all shocked at an explosion to them so incomprehensible.

'That will be all for today, gentlemen,' Rumbelow told them calmly.

Chapter Thirty-three

The trial of Mrs Jeavons was to open at Mortlock Assizes on Monday, October the eighteenth, 1936. Rumbelow went down on a train which left Paddington at seven-thirty on the Sunday evening. There was a dining-car, but he had some sandwiches and a glass of beer in the buffet beforehand–railway meals always struck him as ridiculously expensive. He travelled third-class, sharing the compartment with a fat, red-faced man with the air of a commercial traveller, silent and busy pencilling order books. Rumbelow sat watching the lights of western London flickering past with increasing speed, dimming and brightening in the steam from the engine, wondering exactly what to do about Bantrell.

On that Saturday morning, the day after the row, he had taken the pancreas of the dead child in a jar from a small refrigerator in the mortuary used for keeping specimens. In his laboratory he cut sections of it with a microtome, transferring the almost invisible wafers of tissue to half a dozen oblong glass microscope slides, spreading them out with a needle, then fixing them in pure alcohol. Three of the slides he stained with haematoxylin and eosin dye, the one employed for most specimens in his day's work. For the other three, he used a special stain which brought out the granular cells composing the islets of Langerhans, and even differentiated them into the alpha and beta types. He switched on the lamp and slipped one of these under his microscope.

'Ah,' he said at once, with great satisfaction.

There was undoubtedly an abnormal growth of the islet cells, the beta type predominating–as he would have expected, those being the producers of insulin. As he moved the slide his eye caught some clear patches–hyaline areas, which too might have been expected with an adenoma. Despite the time since death, despite the inevitable degeneration of enzyme-rich pancreatic tissue, his own diagnosis was confirmed. He was right. Bantrell was wrong. The question remained, exactly what should he do about it?

Rumbelow sat for a moment on the high stool, hands clasped on the bench. Well, the first move was to prepare a report. He took a tinted pathology form from the rack, uncapped his fountain-pen, and started to write:

Patient in the care of Dr Bantrell.
Monica Jane Evans. Aet 6. Died 12.10.36. Post-mortem 16.10.36.
Specimen: Pancreas.
Naked-eye appearance: Pancreas somewhat thickened with numerous discrete raised nodules occupying the body and tail of the organ. Head, pancreatic duct and ampulla normal.
Microscopical appearance: Nesidiocytoma. Adenoma of the islets of

Langerhans occupying the greater part of the body, largely arranged in trabeculae. Alpha and beta cells present, beta cells predominating. I would expect these latter cells to be insulin-producing, but estimation of the insulin-content would not be possible so long after death. Some hyalinization, no fibrosis, no calcification. No evidence of malignancy.

Opinion: This adenoma would have caused hyperinsulinism to a degree accounting for the patient's symptoms and death.

The adenoma was of the localized type, not a diffuse hypertrophy of islet tissue throughout the pancreas, and would in my opinion have been amenable to surgery.

Cause of death: Hyperinsulinism due to adenoma of the islets of Langerhans.

Signed,

John Rumbelow, M.D.

Just along the corridor, outside the door of the main clinical pathology laboratory, was a wire basket into which the report forms were dropped. They were distributed to the wards twice daily by one of the porters, who collected in return another batch of specimens in variously-shaped bottles. But the basket was empty, and looking at his watch Rumbelow realized there would be no further collection until the Monday. He set off with his slip of paper to find Bantrell's houseman.

The resident medical staff occupied an ugly six-storey red-brick building to the far side of the library, approached down a narrow alley from the main square. As Rumbelow turned into it he saw the young man himself approaching, in tweed jacket and grey flannels, a long scarf in hospital colours round his neck.

'Mr Carten, I have the report on that pancreas.' The house-man stopped, politeness and deference just managing to mask his impatience. Rumbelow supposed he was off to some football match or other. 'I was right, you know. It *was* an adenoma of the islet cells. You'd better take the report in your pocket. When you get back, you can sign the death certificate.'

'Oh, the death certificate, sir . . . as a matter of fact, I've already signed it. It's gone to the registrar's office.'

Rumbelow stared, the tinted paper still in his hand. 'That's rather irregular, isn't it? You knew I'd taken the specimen. You knew I hadn't completed the post-mortem report. The death certificate should have been held until you'd heard from me.'

The houseman looked at him miserably, cursing his ill-luck at not escaping a few minutes earlier. 'The chief told me to go ahead, sir.'

'Then what did you give as the cause of death?'

'Epilepsy–the original diagnosis.'

'That was Dr Bantrell, was it? He instructed you to do that?'

'I wouldn't have done it on my own responsibility, sir.'

'No, of course not.' Rumbelow put the form back in his pocket. 'Very well, Mr Carten. I'll take the matter up with Dr Bantrell.' The houseman looked relieved. 'Don't lose too much sleep over it. But it might pay you to reflect that any medical man's signature is a powerful instrument. If it's applied lightly, it can land you in trouble. It's not pleasant to be faced with something, perhaps in court, which you've signed without thinking.'

'I'm very sorry, sir.' He was edging away. 'Very sorry indeed.'

'I hope you have an enjoyable afternoon off.'

Rumbelow sat in the Mortlock train, still undecided what to do. The situation was as precise in his mind as a geometrical figure. Under the Births and Deaths Registration Act of 1926, the doctor attending a last illness was obliged to send the death certificate to the registrar forthwith (Rumbelow even remembered that in Scotland it was within seven days). The correct entry for the child should have been, 'Immediate cause of death coma, due to hyperinsulinism, due to nesidiocytoma'. The week's delay was of no significance, the certificates by custom being retained until the post-mortem was performed and the signed pathologist's report in the hands of the physician.

But young Dr Carten had given the cause of death as epilepsy. That was simply an untrue statement. The death certificate was fraudulent. Carten had committed a criminal offence–he was liable to be tried, convicted, punished, and struck from the *Register* into the bargain. That he had acted under instructions from Bantrell was no defence. He might claim it was a matter of convenience in hospital for the housemen to sign death certificates, but that wouldn't get him far with a judge.

Rumbelow had no wish to get the houseman into trouble. With Bantrell himself it was a different matter. He had deliberately caused the lie to be entered on the certificate–through pride, obstinacy and personal dislike of himself. It was he who deserved to be punished. But how could this be brought about?

Rumbelow continued staring from the window as the train steamed through the darkness of the Thames valley towards Reading. Once in Mortlock, he would be too preoccupied with the Jeavons trial to give Bantrell much thought. He must make his decision. He stood up, took his attaché case from the rack, extracted the *Sunday Times* and a sheet of Blackfriars writing-paper, and with newspaper and case as a desk on his knee started to write.

'Dear Cramphorn' (he began. It was unfortunate that the surgeon must be the recipient, but he was chairman of the hospital committee. The only thing Rumbelow and Bantrell had in common was an opinion of Cramphorn as a crass ignoramus).

> It is with much hesitation and distaste that I lay before you a complaint against one of our colleagues on the Blackfriars staff. But it is my duty to do so. In a recent case of Bantrell's I found the cause of death to be an excess of insulin in the blood, due to an adenoma of the islets of Langerhans. Nonetheless, his house-physician, on Bantrell's instructions, gave the cause on the death certificate as epilepsy, the erroneous diagnosis made during life.
>
> This is of course a criminal offence.
>
> I enclose my report on the pathology of the pancreas. The microscope slides are in my laboratory, clearly labelled. Should you wish to verify my statement during my absence from London on official business, Quinley will provide you with them.
>
> I leave it to the medical committee to decide on appropriate action.
>
> Yours,
>
> John Rumbelow

He posted the letter on arrival at Mortlock Station, though calculating it could hardly reach Blackfriars before first post on the Tuesday. With his attaché case, he walked the short distance to the Red Lion. He found a lively atmosphere inside. Peter Ivors had already arrived by road. He was pleased to be appearing for the Crown–it was said the Attorney-General had relinquished his traditional right in poisoning cases, through some complication involving the politically ambitious Sir Arthur Younghusband, retained by Mrs Jeavons for her defence. Ivors sat in one corner of the small, shabby lounge, which was decorated with the heads of stags and the masks of foxes, brass labels underneath giving the date and details of their extinction. He was with his junior counsel and a man from the public prosecutor's office, laughing over whisky-and-sodas. In another corner was Sixsmith, half-hidden by a spiky-fingered evergreen in a brass pot, enjoying himself with a dozen or so reporters. As Rumbelow appeared in the door, everyone shouted a hearty greeting. The man who had written up the Gretna Green case called out, 'They haven't found the trunk murderer yet, Doctor,' and Rumbelow replied, 'They never will,' for the moment almost forgiving him. He sat down with Ivors, ordering a glass of lager. The disagreeable business of Bantrell went from his mind. The familiar faces, the familiar task ahead, the comradely atmosphere, put him in excellent spirits. It was agreeable to find that for the Jeavons' trial Mortlock was *en fête*.

Chapter Thirty-four

The Shire Hall looked different. The high-ceilinged room which Rumbelow had last seen at the inquest had been repainted in cream picked out with gold, the wooden floor repolished, four new electric chandeliers suspended from the roof. He wondered whether the transformation was a compliment to the assizes, or prompted by the city council's awareness of national interest in the Jeavons case. The furnishing was more splendid than the shabby props afforded the coroner. The Royal Arms had been refurbished, hanging over the dais above a well-polished broadsword and vizored helmet, he supposed symbols from the local mythology. The dais itself was carpeted in red, dominated by an ancient high-backed chair like the coronation throne in Westminster Abbey, itself canopied with tasselled gold and scarlet, facing a massive desk with a green-shaded reading-light and the inevitable carafe of water.

Beside the judge's chair were two less magnificent places for the sheriff and his chaplain. Below to his right was the same witness-box with its wooden umbrella. To his left stood the jury-box. Tables piled with documents tied in pink tape were arranged between for counsel and solicitors. Here Rumbelow took his place as usual, behind Peter Ivors. At his back was the dock, still empty, a plain pen of light oak. Beyond were places for the Press, then three rows of backless uncomfortable benches, under the supervision of a trio of policemen, for the public.

The day was dry and gusty, the sun breaking dazzlingly for seconds at a time through high leaded windows emblazoned with arms in stained glass. Everyone started at a fanfare just outside the building. The judge had arrived, the wasplike Mr Justice Easterbrook. And there would be civic dignitaries in full regalia, Rumbelow thought–the Territorial Army, policemen in their best uniforms, notables of the entire county, all enjoying themselves. A stir in the room made him turn. Mrs Stella Jeavons had appeared in the dock, between two bulky and strikingly ugly wardresses. He saw she had lost weight since their encounter in the street, but she was still pretty and seemed composed. He supposed she had been brought up from the cells by a trap-door. He wondered if the couples who danced across it on Saturday nights gave such usage any thought.

'She's been waiting a long time for this moment, poor thing,' said Peter Ivors.

'That's hardly our fault. It was the defence who insisted on bringing witnesses from Singapore.'

'Did you know a crowd waited half the night to boo when she arrived in a black Maria? Nearly all women, too. That sort of thing sickens me. The whole county seems to have decided already she gave Jeavons the arsenic.'

'Well, someone did.'

They rose, as the judge entered. It was the first time Rumbelow had set eyes on him since the Elgin case. He recalled that Easterbrook was a bachelor, who had no country house and had never ridden a horse nor shot anything in his life. He felt he was not quite a gentleman.

The clerk read the indictment. The jury–eleven men, a solitary woman in a large pink hat–were empanelled and sworn. Peter Ivors rose to start the prosecution's case. Rumbelow leant back, carefully twitching up the creases of his grey striped trousers. He found it all immensely soothing.

He had sat late over his drink in the hotel lounge the night before, while Ivors and Sixsmith went over the case for him. It appeared that Jeavons came from a well-known family in the district–the name was to be seen on a shopfront or two and professional men's brass door-plates. His brother still farmed across the valley on the edge of the Mendip Hills, neither a popular nor likeable person, embittered by the struggle to keep going during the Depression. James Jeavons himself had been a ne'er-do-well, as they said, when he was a young man after the turn of the century. There had been a conviction against him at the same assizes where his widow now stood accused of his murder–for embezzlement, though the sum must have been small, or the judge unusually merciful, or his family influence powerful, because he escaped with a fine. Then he disappeared, to Australia everyone thought. He was renowned at the time as having 'an eye for the girls'.

The Colonial Office had found something of his wanderings. He had turned up in Singapore after the War, then in his thirties, apparently well-off. He took an expensive villa near the Government House Domain in the Cavenagh Road and started a business importing precious stones, buying gold from the mines up-country at Raub and selling to the local Chinese manufacturers of jewellery. He explained he had been in diamonds at Johannesburg, and turned down for war-service through ill-health. He was unmarried, but had a Malayan mistress in his early days. This was a common enough habit, but it helped his association with 'trade' to bar him from the higher levels of society.

Early in 1933, Jeavons decided to sell out. The Singapore police in fact had their eye on him for smuggling, but could prove nothing. The farmer had the first letter from his brother for twenty years. Sixsmith had read it, telling of a longing to end his life where he had begun it, describing the sort of country house he wanted and adding grandly that money was no object. After a shady life he was making a flight into respectability. Perhaps to strengthen this impression, he married the blonde lady some twenty years younger whom he met on the boat coming home.

The steamer had called in at Singapore *en route* from Shanghai and Hong Kong, where Stella Jeavons had been living with her sister, who was married to a Government official, supporting herself by teaching in a British girls' school. In Hong Kong she had the reputation of a bright young thing, flirting with the Naval officers but avoiding any serious entanglement. It was strange, Peter Ivors thought, for her to marry a comparatively elderly man after a shipboard romance. Rumbelow pointed out he had money, and perhaps she was fleeing into respectability as well.

At Blayford, they did not see much of the brother–as among many relatives, he seemed to find the pains of absence more bearable than the abrasions of their presence. Then appeared the man Rumbelow heard of fleetingly at the exhumation. A gardener called Terry Fitt, twenty-two and living alone in a cottage on the far side of the village. Gardening was not his métier. He had appeared from London some months previously giving out that he was a painter, and though the village had seen him occupied with palette and easel, no one had heard of his work and certainly not of anyone buying it.

Gossip about the young wife and the 'arty' gardener was inevitable, particularly as Jeavons travelled often to London leaving them alone with the maid, a local girl said to be weak in the head. Sixsmith had been sure of a liaison. The pair had been seen often enough inside the house. She had given him money–he said for his paintings. They searched the cottage, but found nothing. Terry Fitt was badly scared, and Sixsmith combined a warning that he might face a murder charge with the assurance that frankness would win the police's benevolence. Fitt admitted making love to Stella Jeavons twice in her bedroom, while her husband was away. He also said he had bought some insecticide to spray the fruit trees, at her urging. He had used only a little of it, as an experiment to test the spray-gun. This was the powder which Rumbelow had analysed as arsenic at Blackfriars.

Much of this story Peter Ivors told in the Shire Hall. He ended, 'It is the contention of the Crown, members of the jury, that on the morning of the second of December last year the prisoner administered a fatal dose of arsenic to her husband in a glass of medicine, a popular "tonic" he was accustomed to take. You are going to hear a great deal during this trial about the drug arsenic, particularly of the various chemical forms it can take. This substance, so lethal in one guise, in another becomes quite the opposite, a healing agent. You will hear that the dead man suffered from a disease for which this sort of arsenic might have been administered, by way of effecting a cure. But you will also hear that the man's death was caused through the other, quite different, form. I shall be calling the greatest forensic medicine expert in the land to guide you in this matter.'

'*One* of the greatest experts, Mr Ivors,' the judge corrected him.

That spitefulness in the newspapers, Rumbelow thought. No one's forgotten it.

The Crown's first witness was the farmer. He was not a success. He told Peter Ivors he was not at all surprised at his brother's reappearance, many businessmen out East coming home once their fortunes were made. He *had* been surprised at the marriage. Stella was unsuitable for him, too young, too flighty. He had his suspicions of Terry Fitt from the start, but kept silent for the sake of his brother's feelings. He had suspected at once that his brother's sudden death was not due to natural causes. His brother had never been seriously ill in his life. He had certainly never undergone treatment for syphilis.

Sir Arthur Younghusband made short work of this. The brother admitted he had disliked Stella from the start. When Sir Arthur suggested he had expectations under the will, and was angered and jealous at being cut out for the new wife, he made answers so ambiguous, so surly, so easily confutable to demolish himself in the eyes of the jury. He admitted his suspicions of Stella and Terry Fitt were based only on hearsay. He admitted he and his brother had met almost as strangers, and that his brother might well have been undergoing treatment for syphilis but kept such an embarrassing condition to himself.

The farmer was followed by the shopkeeper who had sold Terry Fitt the insecticide powder. Rumbelow noticed he managed to give the name and address of his establishment four times in five minutes. Afterwards came Sixsmith, whose evidence-in-chief filled the rest of the day. At four the court rose. There were more fanfares. The judge went back to official isolation in his lodgings, a castle five miles away. The sheriff prepared to chair the annual dinner of the local country gentlemen's association. The chaplain was dining with the bishop, in keen expectation of hearing his preferment to a richer living. Sir Arthur and his junior went back to one hotel, Ivor and Rumbelow to the other. Mrs Jeavons returned to prison in the next county, which had accommodation for women. Rumbelow calculated that during the trial she would cover a distance of some five hundred miles.

He had the local evening paper brought him in the hotel lounge. Since the preliminary hearings before the magistrates, no evening could pass in a Mortlock public-house without strong opinions being expressed on the case, and the school-children played gruesome games based on the exhumation. Everyone ascribed to Terry Fitt a sexual athleticism outstripping Casanova and everyone seemed to know a girl or two he had seduced. Rumbelow read the newspaper account carefully, pleased to see it held some flattery of himself. 'Today went pretty well, don't you think?'

Peter Ivors was sitting over a whisky-and-soda before dinner. The unusual state of inactivity, forced to spend days on end in small and generally uncomfortable county-town hotels, spasmodically made him irritable. 'On the contrary, it went badly. I made a mistake calling the brother, to start with. Younghusband scored all along the line.'

'It hadn't a great bearing on the case, surely?'

'Perhaps not. But once a jury see minor witnesses being rattled, they can get suspicious about the star turns.'

'You don't mean me, I hope?'

'No, of course I don't. But you must expect a rough ride from old Easterbrook. You know, he's a contrary old blighter. I've actually heard him with my own ears ask in court. "Who *is* Shirley Temple?" He gave us enough headaches over the Elgin business. Though I suppose that was largely through my own incompetence. Or your over-enthusiasm.'

'Why should you say that?'

'We should never have charged Elgin on a slippery thing like a dying declaration, with no corroboration at all. I know it's easy to look back, but we must have half-taken leave of our senses to start a prosecution like that against a defendant like him. We should have waited our chance. But you wanted to push on with it. You absolutely steamrollered us into it. Well, perhaps the chance will come again.'

Rumbelow thought this criticism unjust. He turned back to the newspaper. Someone had switched on the wireless, the flat voice of the B.B.C. announcer reading the six o'clock news declaring, 'The trial of Mrs

Jeavons, who is accused of murdering her husband, opened today at Mortlock Assizes, and is expected to last several days. Among the prosecution witnesses is Dr Rumbelow, the forensic medicine expert.'

'I see I've offended you,' said Ivors. 'I'm sorry, John. I'm in a mood this evening. Oh, we'll come through all right. Like most poisoning cases, this is perfectly simple. I've only to prove that Jeavons couldn't have taken the arsenic himself, and that Mrs Jeavons had one, the chance, two, the motive, and three, the means, to give it him. Convince a jury on all four points, and you get your conviction. Except there's the syphilis thing to mud the issue.'

'But there's no evidence whatever he was having arsenical treatment when he died. No doctor has been found, not even a quack. Even if the defence have something up their sleeve, I can counter it.'

Ivors gave an unexpected hoot of laughter. 'Good God! Something's just occurred to me. The syph's infective, of course? Do you suppose he gave it to the wife? And she passed it on to Fitt? There's an old joke about that, isn't there? Some husband wanting to get his own back on the milkman.'

'It would not be infective at that stage.' said Rumbelow soberly.

'What a pity.' Ivors finished his whisky and looked round hopefully. 'Never a damn waiter in sight. God knows how commercial travellers put up with such places.'

Terry Fitt entered the witness-box during the following morning. It was the middle of the afternoon when Sir Arthur Younghusband rose for his cross-examination.

'Mr Fitt, on the morning of December the second last, were you in love with Mrs Jeavons?'

The artist-gardener hesitated. He was a tall, sallow, skinny young man, Rumbelow wondering at any woman finding him prepossessing. He wore a suit of rough brown tweed and a woven tie. His dark hair was overlong, he had worn a beard but for his own reasons shaved it for the trial. 'I don't think so.'

'Were you in love with her on the afternoon of October the tenth last? And on the afternoon of September the twelfth?'

Another pause. 'No.'

'Yet at both these times you were in her bedroom enjoying sexual intercourse with her?'

'Yes.'

'Without being in love with her?'

'They're two different things.'

Well, thought Rumbelow, *that's* marked him down in the eyes of the jury as an outcast, unbound by the morals cherished by themselves–or at least purported to be.

'You are saying there was no affection between you? You simply took advantage of her husband's absence to persuade Mrs Jeavons to admit you to her bedroom?'

'It was more the other way round.'

'To use a popular phrase, she seduced you?'

'Yes. More or less. She was always after me.'

'Will you tell the jury on what you based that impression?'

'She was always coming out to me at my work. Inviting me in for tea, or a drink.'

Terry Fitt gave his answers in a low voice, staring at the floor of the court. He is really a simple young fellow, thought Rumbelow. He had seen him only once, at Mortlock for the magistrates' court hearings, when he had expected a dashing, raffish sort, a 'Bohemian', as the papers said. Perhaps he was telling the truth after all.

'Wouldn't you think that was the normal behaviour of a considerate employer?'

'No. It worried me. I knew what she wanted.'

'You could have left her employment?'

'Jobs aren't easy to find, sir.'

'But it was only a spare-time job?'

'I needed the money.'

'Will you be more explicit? Tell the jury exactly what Mrs Jeavons said on those two occasions when you claim she invited you to bed.'

'She told me her husband was away for the day. The coast was clear. She suggested I came and made love to her.'

There was a cry from the dock. Everyone jerked round. They had quite forgotten the presence of Mrs Jeavons. 'It's lies, lies! Nothing but lies. Terry, Terry, how could you?'

'Silence!' shouted several voices at once.

'It's not true, not a word of it's true—'

'Mrs Jeavons, I know it is a strain to hear such things,' said the judge quietly. 'But it is necessary for you to bear it in silence. You will have the opportunity in due course to make your reply from the same place. Meanwhile, you must compose yourself, so we may proceed in the proper manner. Please try to remember that others have found themselves in your position, and have similarly been obliged to exercise self-control.'

Her response was to start sobbing. One of the ugly wardresses leant forward with a whisper, but she started to cry louder, then to scream, each one ringing the more grotesquely, the more frighteningly, in that staid room with its pompous furnishings.

The judge rose. 'The court will adjourn for fifteen minutes.'

He was followed out by the sheriff and the chaplain. The wardresses hustled Mrs Jeavons out of sight, still screaming, until the noise suddenly stopped. They've closed the trap-door below the dock, Rumbelow thought. A foretoken of another she would in due course find herself standing upon.

Outside, Ivors lit a cigarette. Rumbelow said, 'That outburst won't help her.'

'It won't hurt her.'

'But the jury know the rules as well as we do. They don't care to see them broken.'

'This isn't a blasted game of cricket, you know.'

When they reassembled, Mrs Jeavons sat chalk-faced but composed between her two guardians. Sir Arthur's questions turned to the tin of powder for spraying the fruit-trees. Terry Fitt described how Mrs Jeavons had asked him to buy it. He agreed, it was the time of year for spraying apples. He had no idea the powder contained arsenic. The tin having already been produced as an exhibit, he was invited to look inside. 'How much powder was there left when you last saw it?'

'It was almost full.'

'How long ago was that?'

'Some time last November.'

'This is a common brand of insecticide in the district. Can you be sure now it's the same tin?'

'Yes.'

'Why?'

'It sort of . . . looks the same, I suppose.'

Sir Arthur switched his attack. 'What were your relations with Mr Jeavons himself?'

'I didn't see much of him, to tell the truth. He wasn't very interested in the garden.'

'Did you once say to Mabel Royce, the maidservant, that you wished him out of the way, preferably for good?'

'That was only a manner of speaking. He'd blown me up about something. Something to do with my work,' he added hastily.

'You said you were not in love with Mrs Jeavons. That did not however prevent your having sexual intercourse with her. Would it have prevented your marrying her after her husband's death?'

'I don't follow.'

'Then I must put it more bluntly. Despite your lack of affection, would you not have found it agreeable continuing to enjoy sexual intercourse with her, and to enjoy in addition the pleasures of her husband's money?'

For the first time he became animated. 'I'd never do a thing like that. I'd never marry someone I didn't love.'

'You would freely have intercourse with someone you didn't love. You don't seem very particular in such matters, do you?'

He gave no reply.

'Mr Fitt, you were not at the house on the day of Mr Jeavons' death?'

'No.'

'You avoided Mrs Jeavons afterwards?'

'Yes.'

'You were frightened?'

He again said nothing.

'You were cunning?'

'Frightened, perhaps.'

'Should you not be sitting in that dock with the prisoner?'

Again no reply.

'Or instead of the prisoner?'

'You should not have asked that, Sir Arthur,' said the judge.

'I apologize, my Lord. No more than anyone else, do I wish to put a witness in the position of incriminating himself. Thank you, Mr Fitt.'

'A sordid business,' murmured Rumbelow to Peter Ivors.

'Oh, it's six of one, half a dozen of the other. He and the wife both enjoying themselves, and now he's scared stiff. We can't blame him, I suppose. But it doesn't make his evidence look any better.' He pushed back his wig. 'There's something wrong with this case. I *know* there's something wrong with this bloody case.'

Chapter Thirty-five

Mr Cramphorn generally liked to leave Blackfriars about four in the afternoon, to make his living operating in the fashionable nursing-homes of the West End. He pulled off his gloves as he left the hospital theatre, which was hot and steamy, smelling strongly of ether and antiseptic. It was equipped with a brand-new American device called an air-conditioner, but he always had it switched off, because it made a noise and anyway he thought it only natural for a surgeon to work in such an atmosphere.

Sir George Smallpenny was waiting outside in the cubicle-like surgeons' room, a leather instrument-case in his hand, clearly anxious to be away. 'Sorry to get you up here,' Cramphorn apologized. 'Can you spare a minute?'

'I expect I can persuade my chauffeur to ignore this thirty-mile speed-limit business.'

The surgeon felt for his jacket in one of the narrow green metal lockers. 'Rumbelow.' He handed Sir George the letter. 'Gone potty, as far as I can make out.'

He sat down, filling his pipe, still in his operating vest and white trousers blood-spattered at the ends. Sir George read the letter and the enclosed report-form in silence.

'A bit strong, isn't it, Crampers?'

'Actionable, if you ask me.'

'I suppose Rumbelow feels put out.'

'I wish he hadn't sent it. I dislike all this unpleasantness.'

'Perhaps he's already thought better of it? We all send letters we wish we'd never written.'

Cramphorn struck a match. 'Bantrell will have to see it.'

'Must he?'

'If it were written about yourself, you'd expect me to come out with it.'

'What do you envisage? Pistols for two and coffee for one in the hospital square at dawn?'

'If Rumbelow wants to put it before the committee, to the committee it must go. He's perfectly within his rights.' Cramphorn was a man of flinty propriety.

'I do wish the damn fellow wouldn't make himself so awkward. But I suppose we've no alternative.' He knew as much as Cramphorn that a man with responsibility must often take unpopular or unpleasant action, for the sake of his own self-respect as much as the rights of others. Like most flippant people, it was only a mask for embarrassment at his own deep seriousness. 'Perhaps we'd better see the slides? After all, Rumbelow himself suggests it. We can get Bantrell along. I fancy he lectures this afternoon. Sister can telephone the nursing home to say I'll be late.'

Cramphorn took the coloured report-form, giving a chuckle. 'Nesidiocytoma! That's a very recherché word he's picked up. I certainly wouldn't meddle with one in anybody's belly. I wonder how long it is since Rumbelow examined a *live* patient?'

Cramphorn changed his clothes, and the three met some twenty minutes later in Rumbelow's laboratory. Cramphorn handed Bantrell Rumbelow's letter. They were both prepared for him to be angry, but were unprepared for the violence of his outburst.

'God in heaven, does he expect me to take that lying down? A crime! He's accused me of a crime. He might as well have said I'd been picking his pocket. Does he imagine that I have no honour?' He threw the letter furiously on the workbench. 'To my face he wouldn't say it, no. He's a coward. A contemptible coward. I despise him. He is a person of whom I no longer even wish to speak.'

'I'm sure he'll apologize.' Sir George was desperate to lower the temperature. 'He's not himself, you know. He's been grossly overworking, and his domestic life has gone to pot. One must make allowances.'

'The two of us cannot remain colleagues here. That's obvious, surely? He shall have to go.'

'One of you will have to go,' Cramphorn pointed out.

'Do I understand you're taking Rumbelow's side?'

'I'm taking nobody's side. If it comes to the committee, I'll be the chairman. I only want to get the facts straight, without everyone becoming excited.' Bantrell's tirade had upset Cramphorn badly. It was not the manner in which a gentleman behaved. 'Let's start at square one. Here are the slides. We'll shove them under a microscope and have a look.'

'Very well, I agree,' said Bantrell more calmly. He controlled himself, looking a little ashamed.

Cramphorn peered down the instrument first, merely grunting. Bantrell took his place on the high stool. For some minutes he looked through the eyepiece in silence, fiddling busily with the fine-adjustment knob. 'This is ridiculous,' he announced at last. 'It's impossible to make out anything particularly clearly. It was six days after death when these slides were sectioned. The pancreas would have degenerated badly by then. One of my students could tell you as much. *I* certainly can't make an adenoma out of it.'

'Rumbelow might,' said Cramphorn.

'All right, he's a pathologist and I'm not. But I'm no ignoramus with a microscope, you know. There's no adenoma, no trace of one, not in my opinion.'

'Can't say I was impressed myself,' Cramphorn agreed.

'Sir George took over the instrument. 'There might possibly be something, you know. Though it would need the eye of faith to see it.'

'Well? What's to be done?' asked Cramphorn.

'Couldn't the pair of you settle it over a cup of coffee?' asked Sir George hopefully. 'Once Rumbelow's back from this sensational murder trial in the West country.'

'I'm afraid that's out of the question. There's more than my personal feelings involved. Even if we dismissed that report as some sort of hysteria brought on by overwork–which I'm not for one moment prepared to do–it says plainly enough that had I treated the child differently she would still be alive. That could land me with a very nasty action for professional negligence. There's no reason why it shouldn't reach the child's parents. Rumbelow might make it his business to provide them with a copy. They're an unpleasant couple. And the working class these days are getting sensitive about their rights. There're plenty of trade unionists and Communists and so on, delighted to make trouble for people like us.'

'You'd be in court on one side, with Rumbelow on the other,' said Sir George.

'You can imagine what an uphill fight that would be. But isn't all this part of a wider issue?' He looked at both men. 'The idea of Rumbelow resigning from the staff is one I've had in my mind for some time, for quite different reasons.' He paused. Sir George, and Cramphorn after a moment, gave a short nod. Bantrell accepted that at some time or another the idea had entered their own heads. 'Does the hospital really want to be associated with all this publicity? With all that public criticism, after Rumbelow sent the poor little motor-mechanic to the gallows? And all the ridicule over that nonsense at Gretna Green?'

'I suppose some rubs off on Blackfriars,' conceded Sir George. Cramphorn said nothing.

Still sitting on the stool, Bantrell folded his arms in the formal black jacket. 'His chasing one of the girls from the library wasn't particularly becoming conduct.'

'Old whiskers sacked her,' said Cramphorn.

'Perhaps he was jealous?' suggested Sir George.

'But you must agree, it really was not to be expected from a colleague. He was behaving like one of the students. And it can well happen again, surely? But I won't labour the point. Much more important is one simple fact–that Rumbelow isn't doing his job here. How can he? Not when he's chasing guineas in mortuaries and coroners' courts all over London. Not when he's appearing in murder investigations all over the country. The trials alone take an enormous amount of his time. Where should he be today? Not giving evidence miles away in the country, but here working in the laboratory.'

'I'll agree to that,' said Cramphorn. 'It takes God knows how long to get a pathological report these days.'

'And then it's generally signed by young Quinley,' added Sir George.

'The routine pathology at Blackfriars is in a deplorable state,' continued Bantrell enthusiastically. For the first time he felt he was making progress with the pair. 'And there's a further matter. I've been going through the pathology pass-lists in the M.B. finals since Rumbelow was appointed. Did you know that only *half* the proportion of candidates from Blackfriars pass, compared with other teaching hospitals? That's quite disgraceful. But apart from his p.m. demonstrations, he takes no interest in teaching whatever. *Those* are the reasons I think his letter should go before the committee. Then his whole existence here can be thrashed out.'

Cramphorn relit his pipe. 'You'd put those views to the committee? With Rumbelow there?'

'Of course I should. Then I'd leave you to make up your own minds. If you ended by asking my own resignation, you would have it at once.' He looked at his wristwatch. 'Now I must go to my lecture, or the students will have cut it. If you want to speak about it further, Crampers, I'm always on the end of a telephone.'

He left quickly. Cramphorn started putting the microscope slides back in their wooden box. 'Can't understand why Bantrell and Rumbelow don't get on. I've put up with some frightful bounders myself.'

'They're two horses out of the same stable, that's why.'

'Pure jealousy, you mean? H'm. I suppose that can lead even to murder.'

'Good heavens, if they get to that stage, Rumbelow really will be in his element.'

Something that had been puzzling Sir George for most of the conversation clarified itself in his mind. Bantrell's angered sentences had a Teutonic ring to them. He remembered his mother, the countess. Perhaps the idea of a duel wasn't so outlandish after all. He understood the accepted way of settling such differences at Heidelburg was with rapiers. It would certainly save them all a good deal of trouble, particularly if they succeeded in cutting each other's throats.

Chapter Thirty-six

At Mortlock, Rumbelow thought Peter Ivors to be growing more and unnecessarily pessimistic.

'It's all starting to look rather tenuous. It was a mistake to call that maidservant girl this morning, for a start. She was far too frightened or too dim-witted to be the slightest use.'

'Her evidence was somewhat contradictory, certainly.'

'God, it was incoherent!' Ivors took a sip of beer. They were lunching off overdone chops in the dining-room of the Red Lion, which contained more palms in pots and large sepia prints of defiant stags and lank-haired Highland cattle. It was the Wednesday, the third day of the trial. 'I've been through this experience before. You have a case which seems absolutely cast-iron, then you come into court and it melts like ice. I don't know why it happens. I suppose you get into a certain frame of mind when you read the witnesses' proofs. Once they stand up in the box, nothing seems to mean quite the same.'

'I hope I pitched my own voice at the right level?' asked Rumbelow, taking this as a personal slight. He had succeeded the maid, Ivors completing his examination-in-chief before a delayed lunch adjournment. As the jury consisted of three fruit-farmers, two housekeepers, an accountant, a local government official, the housewife, and four describing themselves with serene baldness as 'gentlemen', Rumbelow had assumed them reasonably intelligent.

'Don't worry, you sounded like a lecture to a Rotarian luncheon. But I do wish you'd get out of your head, John, that every murder trial is decided solely on the medical evidence.'

'This one will be.'

'Will it? Well, in another couple of days perhaps we'll find out.'

'Surely you're not really worried the jury's going to acquit her?'

'Frankly, I think there's a perfectly good chance.'

Rumbelow made no comment. Perhaps Ivors had passed his best, he thought, was 'losing his grip', as the Americans said. If they lost the case, it would certainly be Ivors' fault, not his own. He turned the conversation to the quality of the local apples, a topic they self-consciously stuck to until the end of the meal.

When the court reassembled, Rumbelow resumed his place under the wooden umbrella of the witness-box. It was Sir Arthur Younghusband's time to attack.

'Dr Rumbelow, what is the normal content of arsenic in the human body?'

'Nil.'

'You are aware, are you not, that other forensic medicine authorities believe arsenic to be a normal constituent of us all?'

'They are incorrect. They are not responsible authorities.' *That's* a hare shot long ago, Rumbelow thought. But his surprise at Younghusband's trying it on was mingled with wariness of some motive behind the question.

'Would you agree that these authorities maintain that an exhumed body can be contaminated by arsenic? From the soil of the grave, the burial garments, even from the coffin?'

'Yes. But those are other, recognized authorities. I examined the articles you refer to, and found no arsenic. Nor in Mr Jeavon's medicine glass, his tonic medicine, nor in various household articles passed to me by Superintendent Sixsmith.'

'You put the fatal dose of arsenic as two grains. Is that not low?'

'It is low. But Mr Jeavons suffered from a weak heart. Two grains would be fatal.'

'Were you surprised that before death he did not show the classical signs of acute arsenic poisoning?'

'He *did* show the classical signs of acute arsenic poisoning. These are of two main forms. Jeavons exhibited the form marked by sudden collapse. I would expect as much from the diseased condition of the heart. And from a highly soluble type of arsenic being absorbed rapidly and completely from the stomach.'

'Surely you would not expect it to be absorbed elsewhere than from the stomach?'

Rumbelow decided to counter this sarcasm. 'Fatalities have occurred from its absorption by the rectum, the female vagina, and the lungs–out East there exist "death lamps", their wicks impregnated with arsenic.'

'We are in Mortlock, not Baghdad,' said the judge.

'Yet you found no arsenic whatever in the stomach, only in the liver and kidneys?'

'Yes.'

'In equal or differing amounts?'

'Equal.'

'And none in the "keratin" tissues, the hair and nails?'

'I would expect to only in a person living at least five days after absorbing the poison. Arsenic is stored in these tissues only because they have no blood-supply to remove it, and grow slowly–point-four of a millimetre a day in the case of hair, point-one for the nails.'

Which shows I know what I'm talking about, Rumbelow thought.

'You say you tested chemically for arsenic by the Marsh and Reinsch processes. Will you please describe these to the jury?'

Rumbelow took some time, simplifying the technicalities for the fruit-growers and the gentlemen. Sir Arthur tried to make a point. After five months' burial the organs had so degenerated that the Marsh test–the positive one–was of doubtful value.

'Arsenic is well known to preserve the liver and kidney,' Rumbelow told him.

'You say that Mr Jeavons suffered from syphilis. At the post-mortem did you examine the meningeal membranes surrounding the brain?'

'I did.'

'Were they normal? Not thickened, with adhesions?'

'They were normal.'

'Did the brain itself show atrophy of the convolutions?'

'No.'

'There was not, then, any sign of syphilis affecting the brain and its membranes, as you might expect to accompany its affecting the heart? Had there been, might he have suffered from mental symptoms–depression, a tendency to suicide?'

'Had there been,' Rumbelow repeated.

'Dr Rumbelow, did you examine the brain under the microscope?'

'No.'

'So that syphilis of the brain, with the tendency to suicide I mentioned, might after all have been present?'

'It might.'

That's unfortunate, Rumbelow thought. He's raised the possibility of suicide and dented my reputation in the same breath. I should have sectioned that brain. He searched his mind for someone to blame, and decided it was Dr Halverston's distracting him with quarrelsomeness.

'Mr Jeavons might have been receiving treatment by arsenic for syphilis, might he not?'

Rumbelow was ready for this. The defence must try to get their kite in the air somehow. 'There was no evidence of any medical man treating him. It would in any case be a different sort of arsenic.'

'Let us leave aside your negative assumption about treatment. The drug injected would have been of the "salvarsan" or "606" type, would it not?'

'Yes.'

'Would you explain the difference between "salvarsan" and poisonous arsenic?'

'Therapeutic arsenic is a combination of arsenious acid and aniline. The correct name for salvarsan is dioxydiaminoarsenobenzole dihydrochloride. It is perhaps enough to say that it contains thirty per cent of arsenic, and must be stored in sealed ampoules with an inert gas, to prevent its becoming poisonous under the influence of atmospheric oxygen.'

'Is it completely free of danger?' asked the judge.

'No, my Lord. Even normal doses can have a toxic effect on the heart and liver.'

Sir Arthur resumed. 'Would the "safe" arsenic give the same results in the tests you described as the poisonous sort?'

'No. The safe arsenic is a far more complicated substance.' This had been his object in reciting the long chemical name. 'The tests would react anomalously.'

'Did you perform the Fresenius test, a specific one for this safe arsenic?'

'I did. It was negative.'

'Are you aware that other authorities–other, recognized authorities –regard this test as inconclusive?'

'I am.' He studied Sir Arthur's face. Then he added, 'I also did the Vitali test, on an extract of acidified, dried, minced tissue. Though complicated to perform, it is accepted as reliable. It was negative.'

'What happens to this safe arsenic in the body?'

'It is stored for some days in the same way as ordinary poisonous arsenic. It is excreted in the urine, bile, and faeces.'

'Let us return to the Marsh and Reinsch tests. You say the safe arsenic would give an anomalous result. Could that expression include a positive result–as for poisonous arsenic–with the safe arsenic?'

'That is a possibility.'

'A possibility you had in mind while performing the tests?'

'Yes.'

'So that, while the Marsh and Reinsch tests might not definitely tell you there was safe arsenic present, a positive reaction might *not* indicate the certain presence of poisonous arsenic?'

'Only if the patient had in fact been receiving arsenical treatment.'

'We will continue to leave that question aside. Would you expect to find traces of the safe arsenic in the kidney and the liver?'

'Yes.'

'In which of the two organs would it predominate?'

'In neither.'

'In which organ would you expect poisonous arsenic to predominate?'

'In the liver.'

'Yet in this particular case you found arsenic in kidney and liver in equal amounts?'

'That is so,' Rumbelow admitted.

'Thank you, Dr Rumbelow.'

He made to leave the witness-box, but the judge stopped him. 'One moment, Doctor. Had Mr Jeavons been undergoing treatment with these arsenical preparations, for how long afterwards would arsenic be detectable in his body?'

'Two weeks.'

'You told us a good deal about your analysis. This confirmed a suspicion–you put it to Mr Ivors as no stronger than a suspicion–which came to your mind at the post-mortem examination. But what made you think of arsenic at all?'

'I always think of arsenic, my Lord.'

'Why do you?'

'Despite the Arsenic Act of 1851, it is easy to obtain. It is easy to administer. And it mimics everyday illness. It is the poisoner's friend.'

'So you are telling the court that many poisoners with arsenic go undetected?'

'Yes. But not if I am performing the post-mortem.'

With a small gesture of a skinny hand, the judge dismissed him.

'I wish you hadn't made that last remark,' whispered Peter Ivors as Rumbelow resumed his seat.

Ivors is quite rattled, Rumbelow thought. Yes, he is definitely losing his grip.

Chapter Thirty-seven

After Sir Arthur Younghusband's opening speech for the defence the following morning, the first witness was that brought with much trouble and cost from Singapore. Dr McInch was thin, bent and birdlike, with a white cropped moustache; his tanned skin, his not quite correctly cut suit and his air of self-justification marking him as a colonial newly returned 'home'.

'When did you first meet Mr Jeavons?' Sir Arthur asked.

'After the War, sir.' He still had a Scottish accent, and reminded Rumbelow of Urrick. 'When he came to live in the Colony.'

'Your relationship to him was simply that of doctor and patient?'

'Not at all. We enjoyed a considerable intimacy.'

'What was your opinion of him?'

'He was a fine man, sir. In every sense. That's all I need say, isn't it?'

'It is more customary for counsel to ask the questions, not his witness,' murmured the judge.

'Did you ever treat him for a syphilitic infection?'

'I did. It was in 1919. He suffered a primary chancre on the genitals. It was contracted from a native.' His air suggested that in such circumstances the disease was a matter to be expected, and hardly counted against anyone. 'I treated it by injections of salvarsan. With complete success. Syphilis is one of the few diseases we can cure, you know. It is very remarkable. Nobody thinks of that.'

'When was the last injection?'

'Before he sailed for home in 1933. I had thought it wise to continue treatment, an injection every six weeks, as a precaution.' That's ridiculous, thought Rumbelow. Quite unnecessary. Though I suppose he wanted to keep up the fees.

'Did you then give Mr Jeavons advice of a personal rather than medical nature?'

Dr McInch hesitated. 'Do you want me to start at the beginning? I've forgotten what I'm supposed to tell you.'

'Perhaps you might help the witness by rephrasing your question,' suggested the judge.

'Did you discuss his relations with the other sex?'

The doctor looked relieved, picking up the thread. 'After his infection, he swore he would never go again with a native. Or any woman at all. I was very familiar with such a reaction. But with a man like James Jeavons, I felt he meant it. Well, perhaps he did not keep to it–we are human. But before he left for home he said to me, "Jim, you tell me I'm completely cured." I remember it exactly like yesterday, we were sitting on the verandah of my house at sundown. "That is correct," I said. "I'm no danger to anybody?" he asked. Then he asked me outright if it were allowable for him to take a wife. I reassured him, though I was surprised, sir, very surprised. He was not in the first flush of youth, and was regarded in the Colony as a confirmed bachelor.'

'Did he ask your advice specifically on whether he should reveal his medical history to the woman of his eventual choice?'

'He did. I recommended silence. Least said soonest mended.'

'Wasn't that somewhat irresponsible advice?' asked the judge. The doctor looked startled at such wisdom being questioned.

'Of the arsenic you injected, every six weeks until 1933,' Sir Arthur went on, 'would any trace remain in Mr Jeavons' body on the morning of December the second last?'

'It would. That is how the cure is effected, by arsenic remaining in the body. It could remain for several years.'

Rumbelow had been listening with rising irritation. He scribbled a note to Peter Ivors, *This man is an ass. His treatment is wrong. His pharmacology is wrong. He knows nothing.*

With this paper in his hand, Ivors rose for cross-examination. 'Dr McInch, how old are you?'

'Seventy-six.'

'When did you qualify?'

'The date was 1883.'

'When did you go to Singapore?'

'In 1885.'

'Have you returned to your university, or to any medical centre since then?'

'I have never left the Straits Settlements. I am happy there, sir. I shall die there. I didn't want to come home on this occasion, but I had to.'

'How have you kept yourself abreast of medical progress since 1885?'

'I read books,' said the doctor vaguely.

He was followed by Dr Halverston, who gave most of his evidence to Sir Arthur while glaring at Rumbelow. He stuck tightly to a slightly adapted theory–that Jeavons died from heart-failure, caused by high blood-pressure and an old, ill-treated syphilitic infection. When it was Peter Ivors' turn, he asked, 'What is your opinion of the accused, Dr Halverston?'

'I have the greatest admiration for her.'

'Would you do everything in your power to help her in her present predicament?'

'I wouldn't commit perjury, if that's what you mean.'

Ivors sat down. Dr Halverston looked round, staying in the witness-box, unable to believe his contribution to the drama already over. He was replaced by an analytical chemist from Cardiff, the nearest university, to whom Rumbelow had sent specimens of Jeavons' organs. He told Sir Arthur that he found no arsenic at all. Peter Ivors pressed him strongly on his lack of medical qualifications and of experience in investigating cases of suspected arsenic poisoning. The chemist agreed he was more at home analysing water supplies and the atmosphere of Welsh coal-mines than fragments of the human body. The defence were prepared to see their witness discredited. But they had no one better to call. There was only one expert in such things, and that was Rumbelow. There was always Urrick north of the border, of course, but the suggestion had only caused Sir Arthur to shiver.

Then came Stella Jeavons.

She disappeared from the dock, re-entered through a side-door, and took her place under the wooden umbrella. The wardresses had seats almost out of sight. She stood with her hands folded on the edge of the witness-box, looking composed.

'Mrs Jeavons,' began Sir Arthur, 'did you kill your husband?'

'No, no. I did not. It's inconceivable.'

'Will you indicate to us the general early-morning routine of your husband and yourself?'

She seemed relieved to find herself facing familiar innocuous domestic things. 'I would get up about seven. The maid wouldn't have arrived from the village then, so I made the tea in the kitchen and poured out his medicine. He liked to have it every morning, first thing. I would take it up on the tea-tray to our bedroom.'

'You shared the same bed?'

'Yes.'

'What differences were there on the morning of your husband's death?'

'He was asleep when I went downstairs. I knew he wasn't well. He'd been terribly restless during the night, and had got up to be sick. I thought it was something which had upset him at dinner. When I came back with the tray he was awake, and complained he felt very unwell. I could see he wasn't breathing properly, and he was a bad colour. I was very worried.'

'He took the medicine?'

'Yes. He didn't want any tea.'

'What did you do then?'

'I telephoned Dr Halverston.'

'What did you do with the medicine glass?'

'I rinsed it out and put it back in the kitchen cupboard.'

'You always did that?'

'Yes.'

'Mrs Jeavons, you heard Mr Fitt say that on two occasions in that bedroom, during your husband's absence, you had sexual intercourse with him. Is this correct?'

'It is correct.'

Sir Arthur spent some while trying to establish it was at Terry Fitt's urging, that he forced himself upon her. But it was an unconvincing effort. Six of one, half a dozen of the other, as Ivors had said, Rumbelow decided.

'Were you happy with your husband?'

'That's a difficult question to answer.'

'Please do your best.'

'Perhaps I should say it's a complicated question to answer.'

'Would you like to present your witness with specific points?' remarked the judge. 'We all know that human happiness is really a highly complicated affair.'

'What were your sexual relations with your husband?'

'Almost non-existent.'

'Did you forsee the risk of this, when agreeing to marry a man so much older?'

'I didn't think about it. I suppose I assumed everything would be all right.'

'Apart from this, were you normally fond of your husband?'

'Yes, I was.'

'You met on an ocean liner, and married after what I suppose we could term a "shipboard romance". Did these conditions influence your choice?'

'Not in the slightest.' Her voice sounded firmer. 'I was attracted to him because he was older and more experienced. Ready to settle down. That's what I wanted. I'd had plenty of the other.'

'What other?' asked the judge.

'Well . . . gadding about.'

'You asked Mr Fitt to buy some insecticide for the fruit-trees in your garden. What decided you to do this?'

'I met someone in a shop in the village. She said the trees had been neglected for years. She was a farmer's wife, so I supposed she knew what she was talking about.'

Sir Arthur picked up the insecticide tin. He started a delicate line of questioning about the fate of its contents. She had seen it only once before her husband's death, she told him, the morning Terry Fitt bought it. She saw from the label it was poisonous, but she did not know it contained arsenic. After her husband's funeral, when the village was humming with gossip, she remembered it. She found it in the garden shed and threw the powder away, sprinkling it on some garbage in a corner of the garden. She had done it on an impulse, because she was badly frightened. If everyone was saying she'd murdered her husband, it would never do to have poison about the house. She was already terrified the police might call. And when shortly afterwards they did, she could hardly tell of her action without seeming to damn herself. Sir Arthur brought out the story as a chain of perfectly natural acts, prompted by worry and alarm from the wholly undeserved maliciousness of her neighbours, and calling only for the jury's sympathy.

'You didn't even bother to dispose of the tin?'

'I put it back among all the other odds and ends you collect in garden sheds.'

'Why did your husband go regularly to London?'

'On business.'

'What sort of business?'

'He never said exactly. I supposed it was to do with his old business in Singapore.'

'How often did he go?'

'It varied, but I suppose about once every six weeks.'

'How long before his death was his last visit?'

She thought for a moment. 'I'd say about ten days.'

So they're trying to establish he went on with his injections, and arsenic from the last one would still be in his dead body, Rumbelow thought. But who gave him them? The case has had publicity enough, and no doctor's come forward. No, it won't wash, not with Easterbrook.

Stella Jeavons replied to Peter Ivors' opening question, 'Did you not, last December, feel you had made a grave mistake in marrying James Jeavons?' with a spirited, 'Certainly not!'

'We have heard from your paramour, Terry Fitt, that he was never in love with you. What is your opinion of that?'

'He *was* in love with me. He was absolutely infatuated.'

'You liked the idea of that?'

She gave a small shrug. 'It was flattering, I suppose.'

'It was all part of the "gadding about" you mentioned in reply to his Lordship?'

'No. That was something in my past.'

'Then you were in love with Terry Fitt?'

'I definitely was not.'

'You let him come to bed with you although you were not in love with him? That is "gadding about", surely?' She said nothing. 'From what you have both said under oath, you enjoyed sexual intercourse though neither of you cared tuppence about the other. That is a little unusual, is it not?'

Ivors waited patiently. 'I *was* in love with him.'

That's good, thought Rumbelow. There's her motive cut and dried. Perhaps Ivors isn't losing his grip, after all.

'On the morning of your husband's death, you could count on being alone in the kitchen until the maid arrived at eight o'clock?'

'It was the same every morning.'

'Why was your husband's medicine kept in the kitchen cupboard?'

'It was more convenient, because I brought it up with the tea.'

'What time did you telephone Dr Halverston?'

'It must have been shortly after seven o'clock.'

'Dr Halverston told my learned friend it was after eight. The maid said she heard you telephoning as she walked into the house.' It was the only concrete evidence Ivors had been able to extract from the girl. 'She was not early that particular day?'

'It was a very confusing morning.'

'I'm sure it was one of great strain. But you waited a good hour until you telephoned? Until the dose had been absorbed? Until you had washed out the medicine glass?'

'I . . . I don't know exactly when I telephoned.'

'When did you first learn your husband had syphilis?'

'Before the inquest. Dr Halverston told me.'

'You mean, in the intimacy of marriage, in the intimacy of the marriage bed, your husband never confessed it to you?'

'Never.'

'Did you ever notice after his visits to London marks on his arms indicating that he had been given an injection?'

'I never looked. Why should I?'

'In the intimacy of marriage, it is unnecessary deliberately to look for such things, surely?'

'I couldn't go over him with a magnifying glass.'

'May I put it to you that you were perfectly aware of your husband's medical history, you were perfectly aware he was having arsenic injections, and you thought it a splendid chance to outwit the doctors who might have to examine his body?'

She shook her head, and abruptly started to sob. *That* scheme wouldn't be past the deviousness of poisoners, Rumbelow thought, particularly female ones. When she recovered, Ivors continued, 'Do you recall accosting Dr Rumbelow outside Blackfriars Hospital in London?'

'That was very stupid of me.'

'Were you afraid that Dr Rumbelow would find arsenic in your husband's body?'

No, no. . . .'

'Then if you had nothing to fear, why did you take the trouble of travelling to London and bearding him in the street?'

Rumbelow noticed how tightly she was grasping a tiny handkerchief between the fingers of both hands. 'I was afraid that Dr Rumbelow might find something, even if nothing was there.'

'That is rather strange, is it not?' You knew that Dr Rumbelow was the leading–one of the leading —' he corrected himself, glancing at the judge, '—forensic medical experts in the country. Would you expect him, of all people, to find something which wasn't there?'

'He always seems to find something.'

'But only if there is something to find?'

The judge intervened. 'Mrs Jeavons, did you wish to protest your innocence to Dr Rumbelow in the same way as to Superintendent Sixsmith? Did you regard him as part of the police force, intent on securing your arrest and conviction?'

'That's what he is, isn't he?'

The judge gave a nod. Ivors went on, 'You would seem to be a little confused over Dr Rumbelow's official position. But could you possibly believe that any man–particularly a medical man of high reputation, bound by a strict ethical code–would lie under oath simply to see you convicted of a crime you did not commit?'

'I don't know.' Now she sounded helpless.

'Did your husband ever talk of suicide?'

'He got depressed sometimes.'

'But did he talk of suicide?'

'I can't remember.'

Ivors sat down. The judge looked at the clock. 'The court will adjourn. I expect to complete my summing-up, after the closing speeches of counsel, by tomorrow afternoon.'

So early tomorrow evening we shall know, Rumbelow thought. A jury with four gentlemen on it will not go overlong without its dinner.

Chapter Thirty-eight

Rumbelow arrived at the Shire Hall the following morning to be greeted by Hugo Kirkpatrick, the American journalist he remembered meeting at Mrs Mavery's the previous spring. 'Hello there, Doctor! I'm taking bets. Would you like some money on the verdict?'

'I don't think that would be at all proper.'

'I'm offering six to four on an acquittal.'

'That's favourable to Mrs Jeavons, isn't it?' Rumbelow's knowledge of such things had not widened since the Derby.

'Very favourable.'

'You've come to cover the trial?' He was flattered at the international interest.

'I'm taking in the last day of it. It's great value. Any number of overtones. This Terry Fitt–it's straight out of *Lady Chatterley's Lover*, very fundamental in understanding the British psychology. I hope you've read the book?' Rumbelow had never heard of it. 'But there's another big story breaking. About your King.'

'About the King? What about him? I've certainly heard nothing.'

The journalist laughed. 'You will! You know Wallis Simpson's divorce comes up at Ipswich Assizes next Tuesday?'

'I'm afraid the name means nothing to me.'

'She's going to marry the King.'

Rumbelow looked indignant. 'Surely you must be exaggerating? I haven't seen a word in the papers.'

'Of course you haven't. Your Press is muzzled.'

'I can hardly believe that. We're a free country.'

'Oh, sure. So's the United States. Every newspaper publisher's free–to write a headline or put a story on the spike and forget it.'

'I'm very much afraid you're simply wasting your time on a wild goose chase.'

'Would you like to bet on that, too?'

'How do you find Mortlock?'

'It's charming.'

'The local apples are very good.' Rumbelow moved away.

As the court resumed, Ivors rose to apply that Rumbelow might be recalled. The judge agreed, with testy reluctance.

'Dr Rumbelow–' They had rehearsed the exchange the evening before in the Red Lion. 'You heard Dr McInch say that arsenic used for medical treatment might still be found in the body several years afterwards. Do you agree or disagree with this?'

'I emphatically disagree.'

'Are you familiar with this paper by Chalmers Watson, published in the *Lancet* in April, 1922?' With foresight, Rumbelow had brought it among his documents for the trial.

'I am.'

'It says that arsenic may be found in the body fifteen months after such treatment. Do you agree or disagree with that?'

'I disagree. It is an overestimation. The findings have been confirmed neither by myself nor by any other scientific worker.'

Sir Arthur Younghusband offered no cross-examination. His closing speech for Mrs Jeavons relied mainly on the arsenic being injected as a drug, either on Jeavon's last visit to London or lingering from his treatment in Singapore. The alternative defence was of no arsenic being in the body at all. Peter Ivors felt that his opponent should have made more of this. But when Rumbelow said one thing, and another scientist–not even a qualified doctor–said the opposite, the jury knew who to believe.

The judge summed-up half the morning and all afternoon. As Rumbelow had come to expect, he warned the jury to choose impartially between the expert witnesses, not to be influenced over any opinion by its utterer's performance in other murder trials. They must decide if the dead man was secretly having injections of arsenic. 'From what hand?' the judge asked. 'The police, the Press, have all appealed for the doctor, if he exists, to come forward. You may think that a medical man, with a high sense of responsibility towards the community, would most certainly have responded and given evidence in this court.' They must decide, in any case, if there would still be traces of such arsenic in the body. They must rule out poisonous arsenic taken by accident, or for suicide. They must be sure beyond all reasonable doubt that Mrs Jeavons had access to arsenic, had the chance to administer it, and reason enough for doing so. They must think carefully about the timing of her telephone call to Dr Halverston, and about her disposing of the insecticide in the tin. If doubt remained in their minds, they must acquit.

'Pretty fair, I suppose,' said Ivors. He and Rumbelow left the court together as the jury filed out.

'What's the chances?' For the first time, Rumbelow sounded anxious.

'Were we in Scotland, I'd say she'd get away with "Not Proven". Like Madeleine Smith, you know, who gave arsenic to her lover.'

He nodded. 'Yes, she got it from fly-papers.'

'The result's pretty balanced, but . . . yes, I think she'll get off.'

'*Why* should she?' Rumbelow sounded annoyed. Ivors' pessimism had irritated him all week.

'She's pretty.'

'What's that got to do with it in the slightest?'

'Juries don't like hanging pretty girls.'

'They've their duty, haven't they? They've taken their oath.'

'It's just like you, thinking of it that way.'

'Why not? It's the right way. Our whole system of justice would break up if juries went by the prisoners' looks, or manners.'

'I'm sure you're quite right,' said Ivors.

Rumbelow felt a grasp on his shoulder. It was the American journalist again. 'Now I'm offering ten to one against a conviction.'

'I prefer not to bet on human life.'

'Well, you make a pretty steady living out of it,' the journalist told him amiably.

Rumbelow turned and strode down the steps into the street. It was chilly, and almost dark. He paced rapidly along the pavements, not knowing where he was going, taking no notice of his surroundings. The verdict was of enormous importance to him. Every verdict was. His reputation was at stake each time he stepped into a witness-box. Once juries started to disbelieve him, to accept the testimony of lesser men, he saw himself as finished. It was partly by chance, but mainly by desperate effort, he had created the Rumbelow known to the world, and that Rumbelow must not be destroyed. It was good to serve his country, to further the cause of justice. It was magnificent to be above ordinary men, to be the arbiter of their life and death. Only that gave his work, his whole existence, any point.

He found himself walking down a narrow street with blank-faced warehouses on one side, on the other railings enclosing some sort of park, which closer inspection through the darkness revealed as a cemetery. He was lost. He took out his brother's watch. As usual, he had noted precisely when the jury retired. He was surprised that half an hour had passed already. He was alarmed they would return in his absence. In the Armstrong case at Hereford in 1922, another of arsenic poisoning, the jury had been out for only fifty minutes. There was no one to help, only some children squabbling in the lamplit gutter. He tried to retrace his steps, after a while recognizing a landmark or two, hurrying at last, breathless, up the Shire Hall steps. The jury were still deliberating. There was no sign of Peter Ivors, who had probably calmly gone for a drink. Rumbelow stood in front of a board covered with municipal notices, pretending to read them, stuffing his hands in his pockets lest anyone noticed them trembling.

After the best part of half an hour there was a stir in the lobby. Someone said, 'They're coming back.' Another, 'They haven't been long–she's got off.' Rumbelow looked at his watch. Eighty-four minutes. It had no significance, except they had already made up their minds before entering the jury-room. The court reassembled. Mrs Jeavons reappeared in the dock. The jury found her guilty. Everyone stood up. The judge pronounced the death sentence, one corner of the black cap slipping over his right eye, making him look a shade ridiculous. The sheriff's chaplain said 'Amen' very loudly. Rumbelow hurried from the court-room with hardly a word to Peter Ivors. He collected his bag from the hotel, caught the London express, and was at Paddington before ten. For once he took a taxi. He knew Maria would be at the flat. He hardly greeted her before fumbling with her clothes, pushing her back on the divan, pulling on his contraceptive, driving himself into her. It was a delicious break from tension, a celebration of unexpected triumph, a reward for his labours, for his skilled application of cold scientific knowledge, which had put the strained, blonde widow of Blayford into the condemned cell.

'John, darling,' Maria whispered. 'You were never so wonderful as tonight.'

Chapter Thirty-nine

On the Monday morning, Rumbelow went to Blackfriars. He made first for the committee-room to collect his accumulated letters. He was surprised to find Sir George Smallpenny there, heels on the fender as usual before the glowing coals. It was ten o'clock, when Rumbelow knew the gynaecologist took a ward-round.

'You seem to have cooked that lady's goose in Mortlock,' said Sir George by way of congratulations.

'It was a simple case really. My task was to demolish a lot of unnecessary complications raised by the defence. She should never have got away with it at the time. But the local doctor was incredibly incompetent.'

'I gather you imagined a good many of his patients had been murdered successfully.'

'Doctors never think of poison. Particularly arsenic.'

'Once the news got round, that village might have become a favourite spot to retire with your unwanted wife or rich uncle.' Sir George stared down at his spatted, highly-polished shoes. 'Crampers showed me your letter.'

In his elation over the Jeavons verdict, Rumbelow had almost forgotten it. 'Has he put it to the committee?'

'Not yet. We thought it only right that Bantrell should see it too. Bantrell was very upset, you know.'

'I'm not responsible for his feelings.'

'No, of course you're not.'

'You've seen the slides?'

Sir George nodded. 'So has Bantrell. May I be frank? I must say that we–all three of us–were not terribly convinced.'

Rumbelow put down his handful of letters. 'I'll go over the slides with you, if you like. They struck me as perfectly straightforward sections of adenoma. Surely you noticed the hyalinization? It's remarkably significant.'

'That might be an artefact.'

'It isn't.'

There was a silence. 'Very well, John. Let's leave the slides as an open question. We had a chat about the whole business last night in Crampers' house. The week-end gave us time to reflect, you know, and for Bantrell to calm down. We thought the best course all round would be for you to withdraw the letter. Then we can forget the whole unfortunate episode.'

'And you were deputed to waylay me this morning, to pass on the decision?' Sir George nodded. 'No, I shan't withdraw the letter. Bantrell has committed an offence.'

'Isn't that taking a somewhat legalistic view?'

'And isn't that the only possible one to take, when a man commits a crime of any sort?'

'True, true . . . but John! Aren't you being overzealous? Do try to see things in proportion. The child's dead. She would have died anyway, Crampers is perfectly certain that neither he nor any surgeon living could have excised that pancreatic tumour. If it existed,' Sir George added. 'The parents have dried their tears. To lose a young daughter is sad, but illness is no respecter of human feelings. So what's the odds, whatever diagnosis goes on the death certificate? It might make a minute dent in the Registrar-General's annual returns. But I for one am not particularly reverent about their statistical accuracy. And you must admit that Bantrell's diagnosis from the clinical signs is as admissable as your own from the post-mortem appearances.'

'That's something I won't admit.'

'John, you're being difficult.'

'Anyway, Bantrell should have signed the certificate himself. He's trying to hide behind his house-physician.'

'Now that's downright rubbish.' Sir George for once sounded bad-tempered. 'And you know it.'

'He was the physician in charge of the case.'

'If we all signed our bits of paper, work in the hospital would come to a stop.'

'I always sign mine.'

'I'm not going to argue on such equivocal points. Instead, let me give you a plain warning. Don't let that letter go to the committee. You'd only stir up a hornets' nest for yourself.'

Rumbelow was astounded. 'Why?' I've nothing to fear. Nothing but Bantrell's tongue. That's not worth a second thought.'

'Then let me tell you something else. I'm sure you are quite unaware of it–you're always so terribly busy with so many different things outside–but you are not performing the duties for which you were appointed to this hospital.'

'Who has complained of that?' Rumbelow demanded angrily. 'Please tell me, here and now.'

'*I* am complaining, for one. You are supposed to be our medical school pathologist, but you teach no pathology. Our students' record in their exams is unimpressive, to say the least. You *do* little pathology, in the wider sense. You delegate or skimp the routine work from the wards. You do only the p.m.s, which interest you.'

'I should have imagined my work outside–which hardly escapes public notice–and my contribution to forensic medicine in general amply justify my appointment.'

'Your colleagues don't think so.'

'That's pure mean-mindedness.'

It was among the worst few minutes Sir George could remember in his life. And his seat was becoming uncomfortably hot. He moved away towards the window.

'Very well, I shall resign,' said Rumbelow.

'Oh, John! Please don't make the grand gesture. It's so unlike you.'

Rumbelow picked up his letters again. 'I shall resign. I don't need to bother with Blackfriars, if Blackfriars doesn't want me. I could get a consultant post tomorrow at any hospital I cared in London.'

'Why not meet Bantrell half-way? I've seen this sort of thing happen a dozen times. Men have the bitterest squabbles, but in a few years they're forgotten, the pair are the closest of colleagues. Look at old Crampers. He's crossed everyone at Blackfriars in his time, and today no one sits more firmly in our affections. And if you went elsewhere, would you be any the happier?'

'I could hardly be more wretched than you've made me feel this morning.'

'I do wish you would let me help you, rather than turning me into an enemy. Sleep on your decision, at least.'

'That's not necessary. My mind's made up. My resignation will be effective as from the end of this year.'

'It will take us much longer to appoint a successor, you know.'

'Quinley can be my successor. Everyone in the hospital wanted him to have that reader's job–everyone except me, it seems.'

I wonder, thought Sir George, if the fellow is really quite right in the head?

Rumbelow went immediately to his laboratory, to write a letter of resignation to Cramphorn as chairman of the committee. He had been neither impulsive nor dramatic, as Sir George had suspected. The letter was a deliberate act, the only one open to him–that wound from Sir George had been mortal to his self-esteem. Then he began to see it as a stroke of good fortune, a chance to break free of Bantrell and all the unappreciative men at Blackfriars with a few justified and righteous sentences. With his reputation high from the Jeavons case he would easily find another consultancy, to shine even more dazzlingly elsewhere. He left the letter on the committee-room table and walked out of the hospital. He had a word for no-one. He was determined never to set foot there again.

Chapter Forty

November was a misty month. On the sixth, the King drove in State to open Parliament, and promised from the throne that his Government would do all in its power to further the appeasement of Europe.

Rumbelow kept his intention of not entering Blackfriars. He had a handwritten letter of great charm and ingenuity from Sir George, imploring him to reconsider a sudden decision, but he ignored it. He made himself busier than ever in the public mortuaries and coroners' courts. And with his usual energy, he started angling for another post at once.

He found it a discouraging pastime. Two London hospitals turned him down flat, if politely. Others were puzzlingly non-committal. He supposed indignantly that gossip from Blackfriars had spread, that established pathologists had no relish for an extra colleague who would reward a share of their duties and laboratories only by eclipsing them. Well, he would bide his time, Rumbelow decided. He knew two or three London pathologists nearing retirement, and he would be accepted more gratefully as a replacement than a supernumerary. He would be settled all right in the end. The great Rumbelow on the dole was unthinkable.

His irritations were sharpened by a resounding public outburst over the verdict at Mortlock. He had expected a good deal of sentimental journalism, but it was galling to see the facts so twisted almost to make him appear the murderer rather than Mrs Jeavons. Another petition was organized. Public meetings were held, one in Trafalgar Square, where he was disgusted to hear the despised Dr Halverston had made a fiery speech against him, hardly short of slander. He supposed the doctor was a pawn, moved by Labour politicians and similar agitators, the whole possibly a dark plot to upset the civilized running of the country. He became short-tempered with Maria. She didn't seem to understand what he was enduring, the troubles which had struck so suddenly and mysteriously after the greatest success of his career. She only wanted to go to bed, and to cook his dinner.

One morning while Rumbelow was dressing, a post-office boy knocked at his flat with a telegram saying Rosemary would arrive at St Pancras at noon the following day.

He spent the day in some confusion. He would have to see her. He didn't want her at the flat, that was Maria's territory. For the pair to mix even tangentially was distasteful to him. He had an inquest at twelve, but Carlow could be persuaded to change his cases round. He wondered why Rosemary had decided on the journey. It was plainly a sudden decision, or she would have written rather than telegraphed. It would be a painful meeting. Her presence alone would make him shameful about Maria. But it would have to be faced. He decided against a telegram confirming his meeting the train, as an unnecessary expense.

As Rosemary appeared walking towards the barrier, he was relieved that she carried no suitcase. They greeted each other civilly. He suggested lunch in the station buffet. They sat at a marble-topped table talking about the Jeavons case, which she had followed closely in the newspapers. He thought she was livelier than he remembered. She had put on a little weight, she was less peaky, quite good-looking in fact.

'I'm afraid I've an inquest at two-thirty,' he apologized. 'That had to be rearranged, as it is. I'd have made more time, but it was rather short notice.'

'I'm going back on the four-ten.'

'It's a long way for a short meeting.'

'I'm glad to get out of the house.'

'I suppose it's not very agreeable, living at home?'

'It never was, even before we were married. Perhaps it's worse now. My affairs are the main topic of conversation. My father alternates between the I-told-you-so and the if-I-were-in-your-shoes approach. Both are unbearably irritating. but I'm only a stranger in the family. I always was to some extent, I think.'

Rumbelow was relieved to find her neither hostile nor plaintive. 'I heard you'd got a job.'

'Only temporary. A girl was in the san with TB. Now I'm one of the unemployed again.' He ordered some food. 'How is your flat?' she asked.

'It's convenient. I can look after myself.'

'But you have someone.'

'She doesn't stay all the time.' It sounds as though we're discussing the charwoman, he thought.

'Is she nice?'

'Yes.'

'What is she? Does she have to work?'

'She's an educated woman. She was a librarian at Blackfriars.'

'Well, I could hardly expect you to play the monk. In fairness, I couldn't have expected as much when we were still together. I wasn't any use in that respect. Though I tried. Honestly, I tried.' She might be excusing deficiencies in her cooking, he reflected. 'I always supposed you went with a lot of society women.'

'Only one.' Her expression didn't change. 'Are you annoyed, now you know?'

'Oh, no. Nor had I known at the time. If I didn't know about it, I wouldn't care. I often told myself as much. It's strange how your mind works.' The waitress put two plates of vivid green soup before them. 'I wouldn't mind again, you know. It's done us a lot of good, being apart this six months. There's nothing like distance to reveal the proper landscape of a marriage. If you had someone else, John–just for sexual purposes–I shouldn't be jealous, you know, not in the least. As long as I didn't actually see her.'

So she wants to come back. Rumbelow drank two mouthfuls of soup. He didn't know if he felt frightened, uncertain or quite pleased at the idea. 'I've sold the house.'

'We could find another.'

'That takes money.'

'We don't need anything pretentious.'

'But it would be a very . . . well, peculiar arrangement.'

'On the contrary, in my particular circumstances it would be a very natural one.'

'You haven't thought much about Maria–that's the lady's name. What about her feelings?'

'She could see as much of you as ever. Keep on your flat, if you can afford it. Why should I concern myself with her feelings more than that?'

'It's not the thing for a man in my position.'

'But it's going on all the time in society, isn't it?'

'I just don't think it would work.'

'You want to live with the girl?'

'No, not exactly. . . .' He didn't know what he did want. 'You've rather sprung this on me, Rosemary.'

'I certainly wasn't expecting an answer on the spot. Why don't we meet after a pause for reflection?' She took a small diary from her handbag. 'Today's the twelfth. How about December the twelfth? It's a Saturday.'

'All right. Though I may have to change it. I'm very occupied just now. I'm leaving Blackfriars for another hospital.'

She looked surprised. 'Which one?'

'One of two or three. Everything's a bit in the air at the moment.'

Rosemary replaced the diary, with a gesture so familiar to him, pushing back her fair hair. She smiled. It was pleasant being with her, he thought. 'Now we've completed our business, John, we've nothing else to talk about.'

'Talk about anything you like, I don't often enjoy an intelligent conversation with a woman.'

She laughed. 'Well! That's not very gallant towards your girl-friend.'

'Let's say you know me better than anyone else.'

'I do. Far better. But I wonder if that is really very much?'

'Perhaps not. Sometimes I fancy I don't know myself very perfectly.'

Suddenly the world looked brighter to Rumbelow. Yes, Rosemary would come back. They would find a house. He would enjoy her company, her cooking and sewing, her intellect. Maria would occupy the same position as at present. If Maria objected, if she ran away . . . well, that would be too bad, but it would save the expense of the flat. He would certainly be invited soon to join the staff of another hospital. A new post, perhaps a professorship, would justify himself in the eyes of the profession. And despite Dr Halverston, despite the speeches and signatures, he would justify himself in the eyes of the public the morning that they hanged Mrs Jeavons.

Chapter Forty-one

'Why do you tell me now? Why not before? Long before?'

Rumbelow paced angrily the confined space of his flat.

'I don't know . . . I didn't know . . . oh, I'm so muddled about everything.' In the solitary armchair Maria sat crying.

'Are you sure?' He grabbed her by the shoulders, making her gasp with fright. 'How long is it?'

'I can't remember exactly . . . two months.'

'Two months! Come on, pull yourself together. You must answer my questions. When did you last see anything? Two months ago, was it? About the middle of September? Nothing since? No bleeding at all?'

'No . . . nothing.'

'Have you been sick in the morning?'

'Yes. This last two weeks. I thought it was something I'd eaten.'

'God!' He released his grip, pushing her away from him. Perhaps it's only a trick, he thought, a trick to hold me. She had accused him of being cold and surly often enough since the morning he walked out of Blackfriars. But she sounded damnably genuine about the vomiting.

'I thought you'd taken precautions,' Maria reproached him, still crying.

'Precautions sometimes don't work. It's science, not magic. You should have taken some notice of that side of it, tried to understand the mechanism better. Then perhaps you wouldn't be in this state. It's your fault as much as mine.'

'How can I understand such things?'

'You ought to. You were supposed to be a university student.'

She screwed the handkerchief in her hand. 'I'm not. I never was going to a university. I couldn't have done it. I'm not all that brainy.'

'Then why did you say so?' he asked furiously.

'Oh, I don't know . . . working in the library, I suppose, I wanted to make out I was a bit cleverer.' She looked at him pitifully. 'We all like to do that, John, don't we?'

He turned away in disgust. She was nothing but a common little shopgirl. And she had trapped him. 'I'm not your first lover by a long way, am I?'

'How can you say that? You make me sound awful.'

'If you lied about the university, you probably lied about a hundred things.'

'John, John, why are you so angry with me? I've never done anything to hurt you.'

He stuck his hands in his pockets, staring down at her. 'Anyone else know of this?'

'My mum and dad. I told them this morning. I had to.'

'What did they say?'

'Mum said you must come and see her.'

'That's out of the question.'

'Others will get to know.'

'You're threatening me, are you? Public exposure, the shame of Dr Rumbelow? It's a good line. You'll get some money out of the newspapers.'

'I didn't say that. I didn't say it at all. I meant when I began to swell.'

This vision turned his mind towards the practical side of his troubles. 'Well, we don't even know it's happened. Not definitely. Women miss their periods for all sorts of reasons. Sometimes for no reason at all. You'll have to be examined by a doctor, one who specializes in these things.'

'Will you see my mum?'

He hesitated. 'Very well. Yes, it's only correct. Can she come here?'

'I'd rather you went to our house.'

'Oh, all right, all right. Anything you want.' He decided it would be less painful to get the interview over at once, before the pregnancy was confirmed by a gynaecologist. Then he wouldn't appear fully laden with guilt.

'Am I to have an abortion?'

'What put that idea in your head?'

'Well, what else? Do you want me to have the baby?'

'I told you, I'm not sure that you're having one.'

'*I*'m sure.'

When he took her to the Tube Station, holding her arm tightly, he said as they parted, 'Don't do anything stupid.'

'What do you mean?' She looked at him wide-eyed. 'Suicide, and that?'

'I said, don't do anything stupid.'

He walked away, sick at the idea of her killing herself, leaving a note, then an inquest with everything in the papers. As soon as he reached his flat, he rummaged in a drawer for the roadhouse bill and tore it to pieces.

He had agreed to call on her mother at four the following afternoon. The house was one of the semi-detached villas which had spread over London in the past five years – one gable, pebble-dash front, pocket-handkerchief garden, well-clipped privet hedge. Rumbelow pushed open the gate and strode resolutely up the front path. Maria herself answered the front door. She seemed delighted to see him.

He took off his overcoat. Maria led him into the front room. It had a beige carpet, pink wallpaper with white swans on it, an upright piano with a wireless-set on top, a pair of magenta armchairs and two wooden ones imported for the occasion. Mrs Osgood was fat with glasses, in a red woollen dress. Mr Osgood was small, moustached, nervous, in a blue suit that looked just out of the shop. There was bread-and-butter, a dish of raspberry jam, and an iced cake with walnuts on it. That they were turning it into a social occasion filled Rumbelow with nausea.

The mother beamed at him. 'I'm sure you'd care for a cup of tea while you're here, Dr Rumbelow.'

'I'd prefer not, thank you. But please take tea yourselves.'

'Where did you leave your car?'

'I came by Underground. I have no car.'

She looked disappointed. She's entertaining the most eminent visitor of her life, Rumbelow thought, and hoping for a Rolls-Royce outside the front door for an hour or so. As she went with Maria to fetch the tea-pot, the father said, 'I've read a lot about you in the papers.'

'Thank you.'

'That case you were in last month – that Mrs Jessop. Mind, I don't think she did it.'

'Don't you?'

'Everyone thinks the same, don't they?'

'I would have no idea.'

'I think the other fellow did it. The boy-friend.'

'Do you?'

'You must lead a very interesting life.'

'Not particularly.'

Mr Osgood looked lost, then taking a black briar from his jacket pocket began scraping it noisily with a penknife.

Only when the teacups were full and the first sips swallowed was the subject broached. 'I hear that my daughter's in trouble, Dr Rumbelow,' said the mother.

'She tells me she suspects she is pregnant. Though of course this may not be the case. The symptoms can occur from other causes, or for no physical cause at all. She will have to be examined by a specialist before we can be sure one way or another.'

The mother did not seem to hear this. 'And you're the father,' she said, in a complimentary tone.

Rumbelow winced. For the first time he saw Maria with a bouncy baby, the product not of himself but of them both. A horrible prospect.

'So what do you intend to do about it? As her mother, I'm entitled to ask.'

'You are perfectly entitled to.'

'Well . . . what, then?'

'What would you expect me to do?'

'I should expect you to marry Maria.'

'But I have a wife already. You've known that, haven't you, Maria, all along?'

Maria had been sitting in silence, but eating the walnut cake. 'You said you were getting a divorce, John.'

'That takes time.'

'With money you can do anything,' said the father, but nobody took any notice.

'My wife may not wish to divorce me. As the law stands, I could go no further.'

'If you love Maria, I'm sure you'll do everything to persuade her,' said the mother.

'I might add that I've already made my wife aware of Maria's existence.'

'Then we shall have a doctor in the family.' The mother's eyes twinkled. 'The famous Dr Rumbelow! Never did I think of it, when I read about you in the papers. Mind, there's a discrepancy in ages. But the older man often makes the more satisfactory husband, don't you think?'

Rumbelow could endure no more. He stood up. 'I'm afraid this must be a short visit. As you know, I'm an extremely busy man. Can Maria be at my flat by ten tomorrow morning? I'm arranging for the specialist to see her. She will have to make some excuse at her work.'

'She's had to give her job up, of course. Before the other girls could begin to notice.' Something else to lay at my door, Rumbelow thought. 'I know I can rely on you to do the right thing by her. Don't forget, Maria's our only child.'

Rumbelow was already moving towards the door. The father came quickly across the room to cut him off. He halted, for the second alarmed of being kept prisoner, or even of outright assault. He saw a slip of blank paper in the man's hand. 'What's this for?'

'Your autograph.' Rumbelow obliged by scribbling. 'They won't half sit up tonight, when I pass it round the local.'

Chapter Forty-two

Rumbelow was waiting in his flat for Maria the following morning when the telephone rang.

'Hello? What's happened?'

The shock of the last two days had upset the precise mechanism of Rumbelow's mind. The enmeshed cogs of fact and logic which drove him were so loosened that he had already embarked on a plan inconceivable in his normal state, horridly repellent. And he had begun to imagine things. The call might have been telling of Maria's suicide, or that her mother forbade her to come–or more happily that she had aborted spontaneously.

'Dr Rumbelow? It's Major Standring here.'

With an effort, Rumbelow made some civil acknowledgement.

'I've persuaded the R.A.F. to lay on another show for us, Doctor. I've completely redesigned those shelters. It was quite wrong having them circular. Lozenge-shaped would be more blast-resistant. There'd be no difficulty over getting our hands on another couple of bodies. I wondered if you'd a day free at the beginning of next month?'

'I'm afraid that's impossible. I'm very busy. I should need at least three months' notice.'

The major sounded sadly disappointed. 'Sorry about that. Of course, the days are short this time of the year, but we could get the job done if we started early enough. I was rather keen to see the structures tested.'

'The war isn't going to start before Christmas.'

'One can't be sure of anything these days.'

Rumbelow promised to telephone in three weeks and rang off.

Maria arrived promptly at ten. He was ready in his fur-collared overcoat and bowler hat. Without inviting her in, he took her elbow and hurried her back towards the lift.

'Where are we going?' She looked at him anxiously as they went down.

'You know. To a specialist.'

'Will I be hurt?'

'Of course you won't.'

She said nothing more until they were walking out of the block. 'You're not going to marry me, are you?'

'That's out of the question. Be reasonable about it, please. It would be a complete failure, right from the start. I don't want to spend the rest of my life in misery, even if you do.'

'What will my mum think?'

'I choose to leave her out of my calculations. It's you and I in this mess, not her.'

'Then if you don't want to stay with me, what about the baby?'

'I'll make all provision for it, all that's right and proper. It's not impossible to have it adopted.'

'You don't think about me, do you? I don't want it. No more than you do.'

'If you're still thinking of an abortion, that's against the law.'

She made a slight expression of contempt. 'Perhaps it is. But lots of girls have them. A girl in the shop had one, while I was there.'

He stopped, giving her a hard look. 'If in some way that could be arranged . . . you'd agree to it?'

'Yes. I always thought it would come to that.'

'Do you know what it involves? There are risks.'

'It's better than having a baby.'

'And risks for me, as well. It would be my ruin, were anything to come out.'

'You thought it would come to that, too, didn't you?'

'In this situation, one must think of everything. I'm still worried lest you'd refuse to go through with it, when you were actually faced with the prospect.,

'I'd go through with it. You can rely on that.'

He felt a little easier. He had dominated her. His resolve even to break the law to rid them of this problem had steeled her. He did not see that only her own resolution, her own screwed-up courage, carried along the pair of them.

'What doctor am I seeing?'

'I told you. A specialist.'

'That's only to find if I'm pregnant?'

'Oh, I don't think there's any doubt about that.' He hailed a taxi. It was a desperate morning.

The consulting rooms were as Rumbelow expected, smartly furnished with bowls of flowers everywhere. A woman in a starched white overall opened the door. He said, 'I made an appointment with Dr Elgin over the telephone last night.'

'Oh, yes, Dr Rumbelow.'

Elgin had shown no surprise at his requesting a consultation 'for a friend'. He only implied that Rumbelow was favoured in being granted his appointment at such short notice. Rumbelow had first thought of telephoning Sir George Smallpenny, throwing himself on the gynaecologist's mercy. But he knew that Sir George would never perform an abortion, however much he cared to help Rumbelow out, and it would have ended merely as an embarrassing encounter for both of them. After his call to Elgin, Rumbelow had to make for the bathroom of his flat to be sick.

In the consulting-room, Elgin rose to shake his hand affably. They might have met before only at some social occasion. All three sat down. 'This young lady believes herself to be pregnant,' Rumbelow began.

'How long?'

'Two months.'

'That should be simple to discover clinically. We've no need to resort to this new-fangled business of frogs and toads.' Elgin pressed a button on the desk. 'Perhaps she would step behind the screen in the corner with my nurse.'

Rumbelow returned to the waiting-room. He sat impassively, still in his overcoat, bowler hat on his knee. Three other patients arrived, one an elderly woman, two young, all smartly dressed. He wondered if any of them recognized him. He became suddenly overwhelmed at what he was doing, and sweat sprung abruptly from his palms. He was about to break the law. But unthinkable misfortune can push a man into unthinkable acts. It was twenty minutes before the nurse opened the consulting-room door to call his name. Elgin was behind the desk, smiling. Maria sat again in her chair, her back straight.

'Well?'

'Two months gravid, as you suggested.'

'Beyond doubt?'

'I can certainly seek a second opinion, if you wish.'

'I see.' Rumbelow remained standing, clutching his bowler. 'I needn't go into the circumstances. They must be obvious to a man of your experience.' Elgin inclined his head, graciously accepting the compliment. 'My next question must be equally well expected.'

'I don't think so.'

Rumbelow made an impatient gesture. 'We're after an abortion.'

'Really?' Still smiling, Elgin raised his thick eyebrows. 'Well, you're frank about it. I suppose between a pair of medical men that's quite reasonable.'

'Will you do it?'

'My dear fellow! You're inviting me to perform a criminal act.'

'I'm no *agent provocateur*, you know. This is a genuine misfortune. I need your help.'

'Oh, your official position is far too elevated to be turned into such a menial capacity. I've had them here, you know. Policewomen with heart-rending stories. Some of them genuinely pregnant. I don't know if Scotland Yard arranged for the condition deliberately, with its customary zeal.'

'Please stop playing with me, Elgin. You don't imagine, surely, I came here today imagining you'd simply overlook that case at the Old Bailey? In fact, I doubted if you'd even see me. But you must realize–you *do* realize–that prosecution had no connexion with myself personally. I was merely the expert witness for the Crown. I had to perform my duty, just as any other citizen must do his duty to his country. Anyway, you can have few complaints, as you got off.'

'I will ignore that surprising last sentence. It is perhaps understandable from your long association with the mentality of the law. But I don't think you're being very frank, Rumbelow. I know perfectly well you've been after my blood for years. "Gunning for me", as the gangsters say in Chicago. That's the case, isn't it?' Rumbelow saw he was getting nowhere. 'In the first place, I can't understand how you had it in your head that I performed illegal operations.'

'The whole of London knows it.'

'A very imprecise accusation for one so trained in the rules of evidence.'

'Let's not beat about the bush. Listen, Elgin. I'm not rich, but everything I own is at the disposal of this present emergency. I know your fees are high. I'm prepared to offer double.'

'You do seem to think I'm a mercenary sort of chap.'

'Well, if you won't do it, who will?' Rumbelow asked angrily.

'I have no idea. I know no abortionists. I don't move in shady circles. I should have imagined you yourself would have compiled quite a list. But perhaps you don't regard them as at all reliable.' Elgin stood up. 'Rumbelow, long before we faced one another in court I regarded you as conceited, self-centred, ruthless, pushful and unfeeling. Now I know that I was wrong. You are simply an enormous fool. To have come to me like this, with this unfortunate young lady, indicates that quite plainly. Or you have the hide of a rhinoceros, and you're so wrapped up in yourself you don't trouble what other people might think of you. Or you've just gone out of your mind. No, I think it more likely you're a fool.' Rumbelow pulled Maria to her feet. 'My receptionist will show you out. The fee for the consultation will be two guineas. It is customary to pay her before leaving.'

'What are we going to do now?' asked Maria on the pavement.

'I haven't the first idea,' Rumbelow told her.

Chapter Forty-three

Before they started their dinner, Rumbelow had confessed the whole story to Norman Carlow. The coroner listened in silence, his usual jollity leaving him. From the urgency of Rumbelow's voice on the telephone, he had supposed his trouble something to do with Rosemary. A meeting would be inconvenient, he had another appointment, but Rumbelow persuaded him to put this off. Well, he would sting old John for a good meal at the club, at any rate, Carlow decided. No halves of indifferent claret, but something chateau-bottled with liqueur brandy to follow.

'This is a serious matter, John.'

'There's no need to tell me, of all people.'

'When did you see this Elgin fellow?'

'This morning. About ten o'clock.'

'That must have been a terrible experience for you, in itself.'

'It wasn't pleasant. I was prepared for some humiliation. I was not prepared for its having such an agonizing effect on me.'

'No, you'd be something of a stranger to such feelings.' The waiter set a dish of a dozen Whitstable oysters in front of them both. 'But you've no business whatever to be in that *galère*.'

'What option had I? The whole episode–every aspect of it–simply fills me with horror. The thought of that common girl, with her common parents, having a child by *me*. Besides, there's Rosemary.'

'I thought you and she had parted brass-rags for good?'

'I want her back again.' Carlow was unable to stop himself looking half-exasperated and half-resigned. He turned to his oysters. 'Rosemary's willing to come you know. She suggested it herself. We could set up house again whenever we felt like it. We'd almost fixed a date, when this terrible thing happened. Oh, it's a nasty business. I hate talking about it, I hate even thinking about it. But it's happened to better men than me, hasn't it?' he added, trying to excuse himself.

'True, true. . . .'

'I know it's unfair of me, involving you in it. But who else could I turn to? Honestly, I'm badly rattled.'

'Anyone can see that.' Carlow swallowed two oysters in quick gulps of enjoyment. 'But you can't go breaking the law. Apart from anything else–apart from your own feelings–if it came out, that would be the finish of you.'

'I'm perfectly aware of it. But need anything come out? Hundreds and hundreds of such cases are performed in London every year, and the police never get to hear of them.'

'They'd hear of yours. You're not exactly the criminals' friend.' Rumbelow sat staring at the table. 'You're not eating your oysters.'

'I don't want any. You eat them.'

Carlow reached to remove a shell from Rumbelow's plate. 'You know, the law we live by is an odd instrument. A lot of it's world-wide–kill a man in Lucknow or in London, and you get the same desserts. A lot more is quite parochial. When it's legal to buy a drink or open a draper's shop, that sort of thing. Which includes your little trouble.' Rumbelow looked at him closely. 'Surely, John, you read the society papers? How the Honourable Flossie this-and-that has been over to Switzerland to have her appendix out, or some such twaddle. She always comes home with a great big smile on her face. They take a more tolerant view of a poor girl's plight out there.'

Rumbelow needed some moments adjusting himself to the idea. 'But how do you imagine I'm to get to Switzerland?' he asked shortly.

'It's not you needing the operation. Maria can go herself.'

'No, that's impossible.'

'Is it? She seemed a self-reliant young thing when I met her at the Derby.'

'But it's an enormous journey.'

'Not at all. You can go by the aeroplane now. I knew a fellow who did as much only last week.'

'That's terribly dangerous.'

'Not these days. No more than crossing Piccadilly Circus.'

Rumbelow remembered Graham Trevose, hopping in and out of aeroplanes without a second thought. 'It's enormously expensive.'

'You've got to decide if you think it worth the money or not, haven't you?' Carlow took another of Rumbelow's oysters.

'Who would she go to? I'd have to fix it all from London. I've not even the name of a gynaecologist in a remote place like that.'

'I think I might help you.' For the first time, a watery ray of hope shone on Rumbelow. 'I happen to have an address in Lausanne. One gets to know things, you understand. It's a clinic. Lausanne's only a short train ride from Geneva, where the aeroplane lands.'

There was a silence. Carlow went on eating the oysters.

'Should I do it?'

'I can't see you've any alternative.'

'Very well. Very well, I shall. Give me that address. I'll write straight away.'

'Why not telephone?'

'Someone official might be listening-in.'

'My dear John! Sometimes you're beyond me. This is London, not Rome or Berlin.'

'She may refuse to fly.'

'That's your look-out,' said Carlow, a little wearily.

The next week was one of feverish and alarming activity for Rumbelow. Maria agreed to go, surprisingly readily. She seemed simply excited at the prospect of a trip abroad, particularly by an aeroplane. A week's absence had somehow to be explained to her mother. She had pressed him to perform the duty himself, but he refused point-blank. Maria agreed to lie that they were going away together into the country. Rumbelow didn't imagine the mother would swallow it, but he heard nothing more. Perhaps she had a shrewd idea of what was up, he thought, as she'd had a shrewd idea about the fictitious weekends in Brighton. She might be glad enough to see her daughter's condition righted, abandoning dreams of a famous son-in-law. If she had ever seriously entertained them, Rumbelow wondered. He could never understand how the minds of others worked. He envisaged human thought as the logical cause of human action, which was ridiculous. He still did not appreciate how Maria had nerved herself to lose the child at all costs. And how his sudden hate of her had engendered a hate against that part of him which was also part of herself. A hate no less revengeful for being beyond her power of expression, even in her own mind.

She was to leave on Friday, November the twenty-seventh. There were tickets to be bought from a bureau in Regent Street. She needed a passport. He signed the declaration of good character himself, as permitted to a medical practitioner, saying he had known her since childhood. He wondered about inoculations and vaccination, but apparently they were not demanded by the cleanly Swiss. The aeroplane was to leave at ten in the morning. It started a clear day. He hired a car to drive the pair of them to Croydon Aerodrome. The expense of the expedition was already staggering, a little more would make no difference.

At the door of the Customs shed, he said, 'Be brave.'

'I'll be glad when it's all over.'

'I'll be waiting with the car when you get back.'

'It's only a week. It hardly seems worth going.'

'Swiss doctors are very good. Everyone knows that. They've a splendid reputation throughout the world.'

She looked through the window pointing excitedly. 'Is that my air liner?'

'I'd presume so.'

'You sit *inside*. I thought I'd have my head in the open, with goggles on, like you see in the pictures.'

'It's quite comfortable. You'll have something to eat. They carry a stewardess, you know, who serves a picnic lunch. You can even have hot coffee.'

'*Hot* coffee!' This amazed her most of all.

'There's no sign of yesterday's fog coming back. You should take off all right.'

'Perhaps I should be getting along?'

He glanced at a clock on the wall. 'Perhaps so.' He kissed her.

'Thank you, John. Thank you for everything.'

All the way back in the hired car he wondered why she had said that.

Chapter Forty-four

For the next week, every day seemed to dawn in hope and end in black anxiety. Rumbelow heard nothing of Maria whatever. From Croydon Aerodrome he might have dispatched her not to Geneva but to the moon. He had half-expected a card, a letter, even a telephone call. But he kept telling himself she would be kept in bed, in no position to communicate with her distant homeland. He worried that everything had gone well. Death on the table during a therapeutic abortion, for tuberculosis and the like, was far from unknown. And what about her family? They would have expected at least a picture-postcard from the country. They might worry, even talk to the newspapers, or report the pair of them to Scotland Yard. When she got back, she would have to rest in bed for a day or two after the exhaustion of the flight. Then everything would come out. But once the deed was done, he didn't give a damn.

He could console himself only with the internationally acclaimed excellence of Swiss doctors. His work meanwhile went to bits. He had still not been back to Blackfriars. He started turning down coroners' cases, not caring if they were snapped up by others. He spent much of the time in his flat, or idly watching the streets in the fog which seemed to have settled on London permanently. He started marking off days on a calendar, something he had never done before.

While Maria was still away, on Thursday, December the third, he was summoned to the Law Courts in the Strand as expert witness in a long-drawn-out compensation case finally come to trial. As often happened, the unsolvable dispute was settled between opposing counsel with the judge's encouragement after an hour or two. Rumbelow was not called to give evidence. As he walked out through the cathedral-like hall of the courts, filled with hurrying barristers, litigants, blue-uniformed porters, and inevitable hangers-on, he ran into Peter Ivors.

'It's a bad business, isn't it?' Ivors said at once. He was in wig and gown, smoking a cigarette. Rumbelow stared, wondering how he had learnt of Maria. 'About the King. All over this morning's papers. It came as a terrible shock to me. I hadn't heard a word about it.'

'It's been brewing for months, I believe. I met an American reporter down at Mortlock, who hinted something was in the air. I still can't understand why our own Press never breathed a word.'

'I suppose they were entitled to exercise discretion. We can't print anything distasteful about our Monarch, you know.'

'Nor the Germans about Hitler.'

'That's not at all the same thing.'

'Isn't it?'

'Ah, your usual severe view of life, John. Though I admit, all this is bad for the Empire.'

'If it comes to an abdication, we may find ourselves without one.'

'I sometimes think of you as our prime minister of pessimism. I suppose that's unavoidable, with your job. The Empire will stick together, don't worry. It always does. And Baldwin's no fool.'

'By the way, when's the Jeavons appeal coming up?'

'It's down for hearing on the fourteenth. That's Monday week. Their Lordships have a rather severe backlog.'

'How will it go?'

'I can't see how they'll upset Easterbrook. I suppose Younghusband will make something of that Welsh chemist's finding no arsenic in the body. He could claim the trial judge misdirected the jury, by not emphasizing this sufficiently. But it's pretty thin. No, she'll go down, all right.'

'What about the fuss–all those petitions?'

'That's a different kettle of fish.'

'Do you suppose the Home Secretary will order a reprieve?'

'I honestly don't know what Simon will do. Though I doubt it. This country doesn't like poisoners.'

'You also said it didn't like hanging pretty women.'

'She's out of sight now. She's no longer human, only an abstract quantity. Nobody loses their appetite through killing off an idea. I suppose you'll be at the execution?'

'When's it to be?'

'Before Christmas, I suppose. They can hardly expect her to spend a particular festive time in the condemned cell.'

'At Holloway?'

'I don't fancy the authorities would think that at all right. She'll have to be executed where she is, down near Mortlock. As they'll have her in Holloway during the appeal, it seems a pity they can't save her a journey.' They had reached the plate-glass doors giving on to the Strand. 'John, I heard you were in some sort of personal trouble. I do hope it isn't true?'

Rumbelow felt a sinking inside. 'What kind of trouble?'

Ivors gave a short laugh. 'That you'd committed some crime or other.'

'But how ridiculous! Who told you that?'

'I can't be sure. There's a rumour going round. You know how it is. I think my clerk told me. Yes, that's it, my clerk. They tell you everything.'

'I have done nothing illegal in my life. Nor shall I.'

'Oh, I'm sure you haven't. We're all doing too well out of the law to bite the hand that feeds us, aren't we? But I must say–I didn't want to mention this, John, after all you're the doctor, not me– but you're looking pretty run down. In my eyes, at any rate. I noticed you were overstrung down in Mortlock. Why don't you ease up for a bit, take a holiday?'

'I am having something of a rest at the moment.'

'I'm delighted to hear it. Look–why not come to us in the country. Say the week-end after next? We could get some golf.'

'I can't play golf. I can't play any games. They've never interested me.'

'I'll teach you. It's terribly simple. Think it over. Give me a ring at my chambers.'

'Very well. I'll see if I can fit it in.'

Ivors made towards the barristers' robing-room. Rumbelow stepped into the street. Tomorrow Maria would be home and his anxieties over. He might even think seriously of taking up Ivor's invitation. For the moment, he couldn't see beyond the following afternoon.

He drove in another hired car to Croydon. As soon as he saw her, he was shocked. She was pale, drawn, miserable, shivering, ill. He helped her into the car, the chauffeur tucking the rug round her knees. He noticed her skin was hot.

'What's the matter? Did something go wrong? Wasn't the operation a success?'

'I don't know. I just feel queer.'

'When did all this start? It's important. Try to remember.'

'Only this morning. Perhaps last night.'

'You should have stayed in the clinic. They should never have let you go.'

'I wanted to come home. Anyway, I wasn't too bad till I got on the aeroplane. It was very bumpy.'

'Perhaps it's only airsickness.'

'Yes, perhaps it is.'

'The operation–it achieved its object, did it?'

'Oh, that was all right.'

She fell silent. In a few minutes, he noticed that she was sleeping heavily. He rapped on the glass partition of the Daimler. They were bound for her parents' home in Muswell Hill, but he redirected the man to his block of flats. He had to rouse her as they drew up. When she asked, 'Where am I?' he reassured her it was only a break in the journey.

In the flat, she slumped into the armchair and started to shiver. Rumbelow ransacked the drawers of his desk for a clinical thermometer. He shook down the mercury, and she neither objected nor even seemed surprised when he thrust it under her tongue. For three agonized minutes he waited. She had a temperature of a hundred and four. He was terrified.

'Your temperature–was it up in the clinic?'

'I don't know.' She lay back listlessly, her eyes shut. 'They use different numbers. They didn't seem to worry.'

'Which day did you have the operation? Which day exactly?' He shook her. 'Try to remember. It's essential.'

'It would be . . . Saturday. The day after I arrived. In the afternoon. I had to see a lot of doctors first.'

Rumbelow picked up the telephone, looking at his watch. Sir George Smallpenny would still be at his consulting-rooms in Wimpole Street.

Their conversation was brief. Rumbelow turned back to Maria. 'I've just been speaking to another doctor. A gynaecologist.'

'I know. The one we went to see.' She still had her eyes closed.

'No, you don't know him, though I do myself, very well. He thinks you should go into hospital. Just for a few days, you understand.'

'Aren't I going home?'

'Later, later. We must get you well first.'

'What about Mum? She's expecting me.'

'I'll get in touch with her. Come along. The car's still waiting.'

He pulled her from the chair and bundled her through the door, as if every second counted.

'Which hospital?'

'Blackfriars.'

'Oh . . . that'll be nice.'

They put her in a small side-room off the ward, to keep her in isolation–with the added, slim hope of avoiding gossip. Sir George drove back from Wimpole Street. After examining her, he walked with Rumbelow slowly down the corridor.

'There's a secondary infection of the uterus and the Fallopian tubes, I'm afraid, John. It's damned bad luck on the poor girl.'

Rumbelow was unable to say anything. He noticed that Sir George hadn't questioned him about an abortion, nor about his part in the affair at all. He seemed considerately to forget hearing of any connexion between the pair of them.

'I gathered from the patient it was one of the Swiss jobs,' said Sir George.

'Yes, in Lausanne. It's perfectly legal there.'

'Oh, of course. Has she parents, relatives, or anyone else in London?'

'Yes, her mother and father live in the suburbs.'

'Do they know of her plight?'

'I was about to tell them. I've hardly had a chance. It's barely three hours since I collected her from the aeroplane.'

'Yes, I think they should know pretty soon. You might ask them to come and see her.'

Rumbelow's terror increased. 'Is she in danger?'

'I can't disguise that, can I?'

'But is there septicaemia?'

'We won't know until we get a blood-culture back from the lab. My house-surgeon's taking a specimen now.'

'You know, don't you? On clinical signs?'

'Well, she's having rigors, and her temperature's pretty high. And there's albumen in a catheter specimen.'

'What're her chances?'

'Some of them recover.'

'Damn few.'

'It depends a lot on the nursing. She can't be better off than here.'

They had reached the end of the corridor. 'I thought that in Switzerland . . . where everything was done properly and above board . . .'

'Infection's always difficult to keep out. The tissues are abnormally vascular, of course, at the time of operation. I'm afraid the fact that the procedure is perfectly legal doesn't automatically exclude bacterial contamination.'

'So we can only wait?'

Sir George nodded. It's sad, but there just isn't any remotely effective treatment. I'm sorry, John, but there it is. It's no good my trying to sugar the facts for *you*. I've told my houseman to telephone my home if there's any change. He's a sensible chap, and I can rely on him. I'll be in like a shot, of course.'

He gave Rumbelow a reassuring grip on the arm, and made his way downstairs. Rumbelow wished the gynaecologist had stayed with him–or that someone had, someone friendly in a world which had so suddenly and resolutely turned hostile. He wondered if he should go back to see Maria. Then he remembered her parents. They had no telephone, so he would have to wire. Appearing in person was impossible. He stood in the empty corridor, staring at the floor of polished marble, hands clasped tightly in front of him. 'I'm broken, broken, broken. . . .' He stood repeating it, twenty or thirty times, until someone walked past and stared at him.

He went slowly down to his laboratory. It was exactly as he had left it. He picked up the old-fashioned telephone and dictated a wire. He supposed her parents would be after him, but whatever they said or did was now only a minor irritation. He put the telephone back in its usual place on the windowsill, looking round the familiar little room, unable to believe how disastrously everything outside had changed and how he had changed himself.

Then he remembered Bantrell.

Chapter Forty-five

Rumbelow knew that Bantrell lived in a large Edwardian block of mansion-flats in the Marylebone Road, not far from Regent's Park. At that hour, he would be at home eating his dinner. Or if he were out, someone would know how to reach him. The heavy, highly-polished oak door on the fifth floor was opened by a girl wearing a black satin dress with lace apron and cap.

'Can I see Dr Bantrell, please?'

'Was the doctor expecting you, sir?'

He heard the noise of cheerful voices inside. The Bantrells were holding a dinner-party. He supposed that a rising fashionable physician had to give a good many. 'I'm not a guest. It's a professional matter.'

'Are you a patient, sir?'

'I've come about a patient. My name's Dr Rumbelow. It's a matter of some urgency.'

'Just a minute, sir.' The maid seemed used to dramatic interruptions of the Bantrell's home-life.

Rumbelow stood in the small hall-way. He shivered. It was a cold night, and until on his way had forgotten that both overcoat and bowler-hat were up at Sir George's ward. He had asked the Blackfriars' gate-porter to find him a taxi. Rumbelow's foibles being better-known than he imagined, the man had looked as amazed as if asked for a sedan chair.

Bantrell appeared almost at once, in a dinner-jacket.

'I'm afraid this is very inconvenient,' Rumbelow apologized.

'No, no, we've almost finished eating.'

'You must be surprised–my bearding you in your den.'

'It's about our lamentable affair at Blackfriars, is it?' Bantrell was perfectly courteous, even affable.

'No, it's not about that at all.'

'Isn't it? I couldn't imagine anything else which would bring you here. You'd better come into my room.'

Bantrell opened the door of a small study. It had shelves of books, a desk with a tidy arrangement of papers and a pile of white-covered *Lancets*, two photographs of a Teutonic-looking castle on the wall. The Countess' family *schloss*, Rumbelow supposed.

'That affair at Blackfriars between us,' said Rumbelow. 'It was trivial, nothing at all, compared with my reason for coming tonight.'

Bantrell glanced at him with concern. 'I say, you don't look too good. Have you had an accident, or something?' Rumbelow shook his head. 'Will you take a scotch? No? Well, sit down, anyway, while I have one myself. I'll have missed the brandy stage in there.'

Bantrell took a heavy cut-glass decanter from the cabinet at his elbow. Rumbelow said, 'I want some sulphanilamide.'

Bantrell raised his ginger eyebrows. 'What, have you cut yourself doing a p.m.?'

'It's not for me. It's for a young woman. You know her. Maria Osgood. She used to be in the library.'

'Yes, I remember.' Bantrell paused. From his expression, Rumbelow knew he had seen that hurtful student's drawing. 'I'm sorry to hear she's ill.'

'She's very ill. She's in Smallpenny's ward with streptococcal septicaemia. It's the result of a septic abortion, performed last week at a clinic in Switzerland. Performed quite legally, you understand.'

'I see.'

'I will save you the embarrassment of asking my interest in the affair. If an embarrassment it would be. I am the man responsible.'

'It *would* have been an embarrassment.' Bantrell looked serious. 'Quite apart from the unfortunate girl, I don't care to see a colleague in such straits.'

'*Former* colleague.'

Bantrell made a small accommodating gesture. 'What's the temperature?'

'A hundred and four. More by now. Oh, all the physical signs are there.'

'Does Smallpenny give much hope?'

'There isn't any to give.'

Bantrell reached for a silver box, heavy and ornate–like everything else in the flat, Rumbelow noticed. As Rumbelow refused a cigar, Bantrell cut one and lit it in silence. 'Look, old man, you've put me in a bit of a fix.'

'You've got some sulphanilamide. You're using it in a trial on septicaemic cases at Blackfriars. I'm only asking you to add Maria Osgood to your series.'

'It couldn't be an addition. It would be a replacement. There's hardly any of the drug in the country, you know. I'm able to use it only with very few patients. Each carefully selected on his clinical merits.'

'You mean, this girl is going to die instead of somebody else?'

'I wish you hadn't put it like that.'

They sat for a moment in silence, Rumbelow looking at the glowing end of Bantrell's cigar.

'Some people are more likely to benefit from sulphanilamide than others, Rumbelow. It's exactly the same with any drug, new or old, isn't it? The condition of each patient needs the most careful study before a decision is made to use it. I'm conducting an investigation, remember. I'm not using sulphanilamide primarily for therapy. Not at all. And I know nothing of this girl's case whatever, apart from what you've just told me.'

'You could go to the hospital and examine her.'

'Quite frankly, it seems already too late. There's a deal of work to be done first–typing organisms, and so on. Anyway, there's another complication. Unless I receive fresh supplies in the next twenty-four hours, I can't even continue treating the patients I have. I'll just have to withdraw it, and they'll possibly die. So I can't risk diverting my precious store to a new case.'

'You're just making excuses.'

'No, I'm not ,' Bantrell said calmly.

'You're denying the girl this drug because you don't like me. That's right, isn't it? Because you were angry with me, over that business of the death certificate. Very well, I give in, I concede your point. You were right and I was wrong. Is that good enough for you?'

'That has nothing to do with my present decision whatever.'

'I've resigned from the staff. You've got me out of Blackfriars. Isn't that good enough for you, too?'

Bantrell raised his voice. 'I told you, that quarrel not so much as crossed my mind in deciding whether or not to put the girl on sulphanilamide. It was a decision dictated purely by clinical necessities.'

'You're lying. Ever since you've been on the staff at Blackfriars you've been against me, stirring up trouble for me, spreading gossip like poison, running down my work, trying to break me. I don't know why. I've never troubled myself to find your reasons. I can only suppose it's something in your character.'

Bantrell stood up. 'God! I've never known anyone so stiff-necked. You're right, the rest of the world's wrong. That's your view, isn't it?'

'I've been proved right often enough.'

'Proved right in court. What's that mean, one way or another? That's all artificial, rules, tricks, mumbo-jumbo. It's not the world.'

'So there's no place in your world, is there, for truth and justice?'

'Truth and justice! It's a game, chess, bridge, poker. The cleverest player wins. I'm a realist. I respect those ideals as much as you do, Rumbelow, but I don't let myself become anaesthetized with them.'

Rumbelow stood up too. 'Very well. You will not release any of the drug?'

'No.'

'Then I'll go over your head. To Professor Colebrook at the Middlesex.'

'I'm nothing to do with Colebrook.'

'That's not the truth. He's doing the only official trial in the country. The M.R.C. sends all available supplies to him.'

'I get my supplies direct. Through the Leopoldpalast in Berlin.' Bantrell looked away slightly. 'As you may know, that's the Ministry for Propaganda and Public Enlightenment. Luckily, I have an uncle there. He has eased the way. The Reich Foreign Office quite favours the idea. Oh, it's a great privilege.'

'I see. You're establishing your reputation, by being one of the first to use sulphanilamide in the country. You get it for this purpose from the Nazis.'

'I will ignore your remark about making a name for myself.' Bantrell was speaking calmly again. 'I certainly look to Germany for my supplies. Why not? Why do you blame me? After all, it's a German drug. You know it was invented by Domagk, in Elberfeld last year. As for the Nazis . . . there's a lot of hot air talked in London, of course. But I for one have yet to meet someone unable to admit they've a lot of good ideas.'

'And you talked just now of justice and truth,' said Rumbelow quietly. Then he did something which was never in his mind, and a second later he couldn't explain to himself. He hit Bantrell's cheek with his palm.

Bantrell stood impassively, cigar trailing smoke between his fingers. With his other hand he took a white silk handkerchief from the top pocket of his dinner jacket and slowly wiped the red mark, as though cleansing himself from Rumbelow's contamination. 'You'd better go,' he said quietly.

Rumbelow turned, left the flat, hurried down the stairs and walked into the darkness. Only when the cold of the December night brought him to a stop was he forced again to think. Maria was certainly going to die. Just as certainly as Mrs Jeavons.

Chapter Forty-six

Maria lingered for six more days. Perhaps the excellence of the Blackfriars nursing kept her alive, or perhaps it was her own toughness. Rumbelow never retained any doubt that her finger-tips would slip eventually from the rim of the world. He knew the 'will to live', some force of the mind influencing the diseased body, was only hopeful nonsense. She became anaemic, wore an ugly purplish rash, and developed abscesses in her knee-joint, below her right lung, finally in the sac round her heart. She died just before six in the evening, on Thursday, December the tenth. Rumbelow was in a small room outside the ward, part laboratory and part waiting-room. Her parents came in. The mother was already dressed in black, and weeping. The father wore the same blue suit. During Maria's illness they had acquired a dignity Rumbelow could never have imagined. He no longer thought them laughable. He was frightened of them.

'She's gone,' said the father.

Rumbelow stood, hands folded, staring at the floor. 'I'm sorry.' That was all it seemed possible to say.

'You used her for your pleasure, and you killed her.'

A few days before, the sentence would have struck him as quaint and amusing. Now he accepted it as a simple statement of fact. 'I'm sorry,' he repeated.

'This isn't the end of the matter.'

'I shouldn't wish it to be. There will be an inquest on your daughter. It will be in two or three days' time. I shall be attending as a witness–as an ordinary witness.'

'I hope they send you to jail.'

'I shall suffer disgrace. That's a worse punishment.'

'Perhaps it is. For someone who's always had it soft.'

He took his wife, and led her away. Rumbelow stood in the little room, waiting for them to be well out of sight. Maria's death had not moved him. He had suffered the shock of it when he first took her temperature in his flat, knowing the mercury pronounced the sentence. He felt no grief, and it was not in him to pretend he did. He had never loved her. The father was perfectly right. He had used her and killed her. He felt only guilt and debasement, emotions the more agonizing for being strange, loathed and frightening.

He took out his watch. He started along the corridor and down the stairs to the main courtyard. He wondered which London coroner would conduct the inquest, as he knew them all. He preferred not to speculate on the newspapers afterwards. There was at least no criminal charge they could lay against him. Nothing in the slightest illegal had been done. But he was finished. He tried to see a future not black to eternity, but it was difficult. After all, he was a first-rate pathologist. Even his enemies, even Bantrell, must give him that. There was always need of pathologists while civilized man kept himself alive through studying the death of his fellows–that was the very basis of scientific medicine, ever since the first anatomists broke the thralldom of the Church. Perhaps he could get some minor official post. Perhaps with Major Standring and his Air Raid Precautions. Being Rumbelow, he tried to comfort himself with logic. But he was learning at last that the world continues at all only by remaining perversely irrational.

His steps led automatically to his laboratory. He went inside, sitting again on the familiar high stool, his microscope tilted in position as he had left it. Now Maria was dead, he told himself, he must recover his balance, turn to the everyday business of life. Before his resignation became effective at the end of the month he must clear out the lab, taking away his filing-cabinets. He had started to open a drawer of files, when there was a knock on the door.

He was surprised. No one knew he was in the lab, or even in Blackfriars. 'Come in.'

The visitor was Quinley. It was the first time Rumbelow had set eyes on him since leaving for the Jeavons trial at Mortlock. He noticed the young man's boils looked rather better.

'Might I have a word with you, sir?'

'How did you find I was here?'

'I knew you were up at Sir George's ward. I waited till you came down and I saw you cross the courtyard.'

Rumbelow drew out a pile of files in manilla folders, laying them neatly on the workbench. 'Anything important?'

Quinley stood in his white coat, arms dangling, looking lost. 'Yes. It is.'

'Well? Can you be brief? I've had a very unhappy day.'

'I've been using this lab in your absence, sir. I've been checking your findings.'

'What do you mean?'

'In the Jeavons case. That zinc you used . . . for the Marsh test. It's contaminated. With arsenic. That's not uncommon, is it? You must have forgotten to test your materials before starting the analysis.'

'How the devil dare you accuse me of something like that?'

'I tested it,' said Quinley simply.

'Why? Why did you go behind my back? I'm still a consultant here, you know. You'd better get that into your head. I can still cause trouble for you, before I finally walk out of the place.'

'I tested it because I suspected there was something wrong with the case. I don't know why, exactly. It just seemed fishy.'

'If you entertained those suspicions you should have told me, to my face. How long have you been sneaking about in my footsteps?'

'Only after you'd left it came into my mind to confirm anything. I admired your work, sir. Quite honestly, I did. I learnt an enormous lot from you.'

'Well, you're wrong about the zinc.' Rumbelow paused. 'You think I dished your chances for the readership job, don't you?'

'I don't think that at all.'

'Yes, you do. You're against me, you and all the others. You're always trying to find a new stick to beat me with.'

'That just isn't true, sir.'

'Well, none of you need bother any more. I've done your job myself. I'm disgraced, finished, broken. You know the story. Nobody will have wasted time putting it round the hospital. Now get out and leave me in peace.'

Quinley went on, 'It isn't only the Jeavons case. Once I could look round this lab without being stopped like a thief. . . .' He stared at Rumbelow, frightened by what he was saying. But Rumbelow was leaning against the workbench, arms folded, his face now expressionless.

'Then there was that homosexual who shot his friend. The Tilling case. Tilling said it was suicide, didn't he? I've been through your case notes, in the cabinet there. I found a key which would open it, don't ask me how. You got Tilling hanged on the direction the bullet took. You got your facts from firing at a skeleton. One strung up for the anatomists, the ribs held together by wire. In the living human it's not the same at all. The muscles pull the ribs into different positions entirely. I tested it in the p.m. room, running wires into the bodies then compressing the chests. I got one of the house-surgeons to put a long spinal needle into the wall of my own chest, and had it X-rayed. The bullet may have come from the angle you said it did, across the room. But . . . well, there could be doubt, sir, you must admit. I've the X-ray picture up in my room, if you want to see it—'

'I'm indebted to you for your observations,' said Rumbelow quietly. Quinley seemed to have exhausted himself. 'It's a pity you didn't make them earlier. Then we could have checked my own work and your experiments on it together. The needle in your own chest-wall was an extremely bright idea.'

Quinley slowly stroked his cheek, disfigured by the puckered skin of past boils. 'Have you nothing else to say to me, sir?'

'No.'

'I'm afraid you must be very angry.'

'No scientist is angry at another contradicting his results. On the contrary, he welcomes it. That is the only way to approach perfection.'

'You don't take me seriously?'

'I do. In this context, at least.'

'Then what's to be done about the Jeavons case?'

'You've no more to add? No more than that the zinc was contaminated with arsenic in the first place?'

'Nothing more, sir.'

Rumbelow remained silent, arms still folded. Slowly, looking more miserable than ever, Quinley left the laboratory. As the door shut, Rumbelow opened the glass-fronted cupboard where he kept his chemical apparatus. His movements again precise and quick, he set up the flask with its thistle-shaped funnel and long, angled tube for the Marsh test. Into the flask he tipped a little metallic zinc, from the same bottle used when testing organs from Jeavons' exhumed body. He ran in the dilute sulphuric acid, watching as the mixture bubbled with hydrogen. He lit a Bunsen burner, placing it in the middle of the angled tube. He took out his watch. There was half an hour to wait.

He sat on the high stool, hands clasped in his lap, staring blankly at the frosted glass of the window. He did not turn his eyes until the full thirty minutes were up. Then he looked at the tube beyond the flame. A faint deposit, brownish-coloured against the flame, then passing through steely grey to jet black. Arsenic.

Rumbelow turned off the Bunsen.

'I didn't test this zinc.' He spoke aloud. 'I didn't forget. I didn't want to test it. I wanted to find arsenic. That's what it is. I wanted to.'

Suddenly a load rolled from his brain and the whole of life became brilliantly crystal-clear.

Chapter Forty-seven

Rumbelow had three letters to write on the 'Flying Scotsman' from King's Cross to Edinburgh the following morning. The first was to Peter Ivors.

> Dear Peter,
>
> You will have heard by now of the letter I left at the Home Office last night. I thought that the correct manner in which to make my move. Whether it will simply be admitted as fresh evidence at Mrs Jeavons' appeal, or whether she is released immediately, strikes me as a matter for the Home Secretary.
>
> Mrs Jeavons would seem to have a case for compensation by the Crown. It will be of interest whether her claim is limited from the moment of her conviction, or from her arrest. There will doubtless be not only considerable legal but political repercussions. But I think Sir John Simon will ride the storm. Anyway, Mrs Jeavons will certainly do handsomely selling her life-story to the newspapers.
>
> I made a mistake. I am sorry, when you yourself put so much work into the case. I may have made mistakes in the past. That is more than possible. But at least this one can be rectified.
>
> I am also sorry that I'm not able to play golf with you.
>
> Yours,
>
> John.

The second was to Major Strandring, at the Air Raid Precautions Department of the Home Office.

> Dear Major Standring,
> The air-raid shelters should be of metal, preferably of corrugated steel, which can be assembled from sections and sunk in people's gardens. They would be cheap, and most valuable if war comes. Please put this idea up to your people.
> You might also mention in the proper quarters that I have decided from a study of my notes the drop should be increased by one inch in all cases. This will make hanging more humane.
>
> Yours sincerely,
> John Rumbelow.

He started the third one to his wife.

> Dearest Rosemary,
> I have always loved you. . . .

He stopped. It was so difficult, conveying such concepts on paper with any exactitude. The words meant different things to different people, and at different times. If they had any meaning at all. Would she expect him to write that? Did it really matter or not, her knowing he loved her? Did he know himself? Once he believed he knew what love meant. But like much else in his life, that was an expression of his own over-confidence. He crumpled the paper, let down the leather strap, and threw it out of the window.

Rumbelow settled back with the morning's paper. King Edward was abdicating. He would be broadcasting that night to the Empire as a private individual, Mr Edward Windsor, and was expected to leave the country afterwards for an unknown destination. He was succeeded by his brother, who nobody seemed to know much about but had a lovely wife and two pretty little daughters, pictured playing in the garden. Were Mrs Jeavons immediately released, Rumbelow wondered if she would get much space after all. A dining-car attendant put his head in the compartment to announce lunch. Rumbelow was going first-class, even if he wasn't on official business.

In Edinburgh that evening, he carried his attaché case from Waverley station to the small hotel where he had reserved a room by telegram. It was the one he had stayed at before, and the staff remembered him. He was shown to a pleasant single room on the first floor. 'We're still serving tea, sir,' said the porter.

'I've a good deal of work to do. I'll step out and find a meal somewhere later.'

'Very good, sir. Sad about the King, sir, isn't it?'

'Yes. Very sad.'

It was chilly. Rumbelow lit the gas-fire. He left his case unopened, sitting with arms folded on the bed, still in his overcoat. It was all part of a process, he thought, perfectly logical when looked at sensibly. It had started that night in Diana Flavell's flat and ended with Maria's death and the contaminated zinc. Things which had seem unrelated, or even passing irritations–his wife's leaving, her brief return to London, Dr Halverston's tantrums, Evan Greensmith's pen–they were all meaningful parts of it. It was like the manifestation in various organs of a single, generalized disease.

Like the abscesses and the fever which killed Maria.

After some fifteen minutes Rumbelow stood up abruptly and took his overcoat off. He started to undress, removing jacket, shoes, collar and tie. He stopped, collar in hand, wondering exactly why. He picked up the eiderdown and laid it along the bottom of the door. He lifted the curtain and turned the catch on the closed window. He switched off the gas-fire, waited a minute for the mantles to cool so that would not re-light, then turned on the gas again and lay on the bed. He laid his brother's watch on the table beside him. Ten minutes would be enough. Well, he would never have to admit publicly he was wrong. And through a legal quirk, in Scotland suicide was not a crime. When there was ringing in his ears and his head was bursting, his last thought was that he had never in his life broken the law.

Chapter Forty-eight

Dr Urrick had a different system than followed at Blackfriars. At noon he came into his post-mortem room, brisk as usual, bibbed red rubber apron tied round his waist, pulling on yellow rubber gloves. He was accompanied only by one young assistant in a white coat, report-form clipped to a board, fountain-pen in hand, ready to take notes as Urrick went along.

'Oh, the fellow was really a bit of a fool. The public's right, in its heart. It always is. The greatest experts are the crassest blunderers in life. Never trust an expert. Though he did the right thing in the end for the Jeavons woman, we must allow him that much.' Urrick started arranging his instruments. 'Do you know what his real trouble was? He never understood people. He never saw they were human entities, who ate and drank and frolicked with their girls, and had passion running in their veins. He thought we were all the theoretical concepts of a lot of lawyers. That's a depressing idea, isn't it?'

He picked up his long scalpel.

'But God knows how many poor folk went to the gallows because of his ignorance and pig-headedness. Maybe he's been introduced to a few of them up there by now?' Urrick gave the laugh which had always so irritated Rumbelow. 'Though mind you, it wasn't all *his* fault. The law let him get away with it. Well, if there can be worse, prejudiced, blind fools in the world than some of us doctors, it's the whole lot of the lawyers.'

Urrick adjusted the tip of one glove-finger. 'Do you know his greatest virtue? He was an enormous snob. That was his only human frailty, and alone it raised him to what he became. It's a powerful thing, snobbery. More than love or money any day of the week.'

Urrick made the sweep from chin to pubis, through skin bright pink from the coal-gas, exposing the organs which God distributes with impartial exactitude among the two fundamental divisions of His creatures, the judges and the judged.

TITLES IN THIS SERIES:

Eric Ambler
The Mask of Dimitrios Passage of Arms The Schirmer Inheritance Journey into Fear The Light of Day

John le Carré
The Spy Who Came in From the Cold Call for the Dead A Murder of Quality The Looking-Glass War A Small Town in Germany

Raymond Chandler*
Farewell My Lovely The Lady in the Lake Playback The Long Goodbye The High Window The Big Sleep

Catherine Cookson
The Round Tower The Fifteen Streets Feathers in the Fire A Grand Man The Blind Miller

Monica Dickens
One Pair of Hands The Happy Prisoner Mariana Kate and Emma One Pair of Feet

F. Scott Fitzgerald*
The Great Gatsby Tender is the Night This Side of Paradise The Beautiful and the Damned The Last Tycoon

Ian Fleming
Dr. No Thunderball Goldfinger On Her Majesty's Secret Service Moonraker From Russia With Love

C. S. Forester
The Ship Mr. Midshipman Hornblower The Captain from Connecticut The General The Earthly Paradise The African Queen

E. M. Forster
Where Angels Fear to Tread The Longest Journey A Room with a View Howards End A Passage to India

John Galsworthy
The Forsyte Saga: The Man of Property In Chancery To Let
A Modern Comedy: The White Monkey The Silver Spoon Swan Song

Erle Stanley Gardner
Perry Mason in the Case of the Gilded Lily The Daring Decoy The Fiery Fingers The Lucky Loser The Calendar Girl The Deadly Toy The Mischievous Doll The Amorous Aunt

Richard Gordon
Doctor in the House Doctor at Sea Doctor at Large Doctor in Love Doctor in Clover The Facemaker The Medical Witness

Graham Greene
The Heart of the Matter Stamboul Train A Burnt-Out Case The Third Man Loser Takes All The Quiet American The Power and the Glory

Ernest Hemingway*
For Whom the Bell Tolls Fiesta The Snows of Kilimanjaro The Short Happy Life of Francis Macomber Across the River and into the Trees The Old Man and the Sea

Georgette Heyer
These Old Shades Sprig Muslin Sylvester The Corinthian The Convenient Marriage

Franz Kafka*
The Trial America In the Penal Settlement Metamorphosis The Castle The Great Wall of China Investigations of a Dog Letter to His Father The Diaries 1910–1923

Rudyard Kipling
The Just So Stories Stalky and Co. Puck of Pook's Hill The Jungle Book The Second Jungle Book

D. H. Lawrence
Sons and Lovers St. Mawr The Fox The White Peacock Love Among the Haystacks The Virgin and the Gipsy Lady Chatterley's Lover

Norah Lofts
Jassy Bless This House Scent of Cloves How Far to Bethlehem?

Robert Ludlum★
The Scarlatti Inheritance The Matlock Paper The Osterman Weekend The Gemini Contenders

Thomas Mann★
Death in Venice Tristan Tonio Kröger Doctor Faustus Mario and the Magician A Man and His Dog The Black Swan Confessions of Felix Krull, Confidence Man

W. Somerset Maugham
Cakes and Ale The Painted Veil Liza of Lambeth The Razor's Edge Theatre The Moon and Sixpence

W. Somerset Maugham
Sixty-five Short Stories

Ed McBain★
Cop Hater Give the Boys a Great Big Hand Doll Eighty Million Eyes Hail, Hail, the Gang's All Here! Sadie When She Died Let's Hear it for the Deaf Man

James A. Michener★
The Source The Bridges at Toko-Ri Caravans Sayonara

George Orwell
Animal Farm Burmese Days A Clergyman's Daughter Coming up for Air Keep the Aspidistra Flying Nineteen Eighty-four

Jean Plaidy
St. Thomas's Eve Royal Road to Fotheringay The Goldsmith's Wife Perdita's Prince

Nevil Shute
A Town Like Alice Pied Piper The Far Country The Chequer Board No Highway

George Simenon
Ten Maigret Stories

Wilbur Smith
When the Lion Feeds The Diamond Hunters Eagle in the Sky Gold Mine Shout at the Devil

John Steinbeck★
The Grapes of Wrath The Moon is Down Cannery Row East of Eden Of Mice and Men

Mary Stewart
The Crystal Cave The Hollow Hills Wildfire at Midnight Airs Above the Ground

Evelyn Waugh
Decline and Fall Black Mischief A Handful of Dust Scoop Put Out More Flags Brideshead Revisited

H. G. Wells
The Time Machine The Island of Dr. Moreau The Invisible Man The First Men in the Moon The Food of the Gods In The Days of the Comet The War of the Worlds

Morris West
The Shoes of the Fisherman The Second Victory Daughter of Silence The Salamander The Devil's Advocate

Dennis Wheatley
The Devil Rides Out The Haunting of Toby Jugg Gateway to Hell To the Devil—A Daughter

Fourteen Great Plays★

★ Not currently available in Canada for copyright reasons

IARD GORDON RICHARD GORDON RICHARD GORI
ICHARD GORDON RICHARD GORDON RICHARD G
IARD GORDON RICHARD GORDON RICHARD GORI
ICHARD GORDON RICHARD GORDON RICHARD G
IARD GORDON RICHARD GORDON RICHARD GORI
ICHARD GORDON RICHARD GORDON RICHARD G
IARD GORDON RICHARD GORDON RICHARD GORI
ICHARD GORDON RICHARD GORDON RICHARD G
IARD GORDON RICHARD GORDON RICHARD GORI
ICHARD GORDON RICHARD GORDON RICHARD G
IARD GORDON RICHARD GORDON RICHARD GORI
ICHARD GORDON RICHARD GORDON RICHARD G
IARD GORDON RICHARD GORDON RICHARD GORI
ICHARD GORDON RICHARD GORDON RICHARD G
IARD GORDON RICHARD GORDON RICHARD GORI
ICHARD GORDON RICHARD GORDON RICHARD G
IARD GORDON RICHARD GORDON RICHARD GORI
ICHARD GORDON RICHARD GORDON RICHARD G
IARD GORDON RICHARD GORDON RICHARD GORI
ICHARD GORDON RICHARD GORDON RICHARD G
IARD GORDON RICHARD GORDON RICHARD GORI
ICHARD GORDON RICHARD GORDON RICHARD G
IARD GORDON RICHARD GORDON RICHARD GORI
ICHARD GORDON RICHARD GORDON RICHARD G
IARD GORDON RICHARD GORDON RICHARD GORI
ICHARD GORDON RICHARD GORDON RICHARD G
IARD GORDON RICHARD GORDON RICHARD GORI
ICHARD GORDON RICHARD GORDON RICHARD G
IARD GORDON RICHARD GORDON RICHARD GORI
ICHARD GORDON RICHARD GORDON RICHARD G
IARD GORDON RICHARD GORDON RICHARD GORI
ICHARD GORDON RICHARD GORDON RICHARD G
IARD GORDON RICHARD GORDON RICHARD GORI
ICHARD GORDON RICHARD GORDON RICHARD G
IARD GORDON RICHARD GORDON RICHARD GORI
ICHARD GORDON RICHARD GORDON RICHARD G
IARD GORDON RICHARD GORDON RICHARD GORI
ICHARD GORDON RICHARD GORDON RICHARD G
IARD GORDON RICHARD GORDON RICHARD GORI
ICHARD GORDON RICHARD GORDON RICHARD G